1 MONTH OF
FREE
READING

at

www.ForgottenBooks.com

By purchasing this book you are eligible for one month membership to ForgottenBooks.com, giving you unlimited access to our entire collection of over 1,000,000 titles via our web site and mobile apps.

To claim your free month visit:

www.forgottenbooks.com/free1000562

ISBN 978-0-331-00116-7
PIBN 11000562

RECONCILED.
A Study in Black and White by Thos. Davidson.

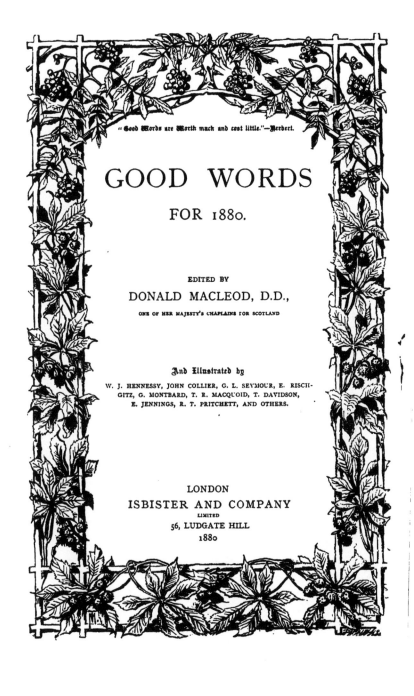

"Good Words are Worth much and cost little."—Herbert.

GOOD WORDS

FOR 1880.

EDITED BY

DONALD MACLEOD, D.D.,

ONE OF HER MAJESTY'S CHAPLAINS FOR SCOTLAND

And Illustrated by

W. J. HENNESSY, JOHN COLLIER, G. L. SEYMOUR, E. RISCH-
GITZ, G. MONTBARD, T. R. MACQUOID, T. DAVIDSON,
E. JENNINGS, R. T. PRITCHETT, AND OTHERS.

LONDON
ISBISTER AND COMPANY
LIMITED
56, LUDGATE HILL
1880

GOOD WORDS FOR 1880

THE TRUMPET-MAJOR.

By THOMAS HARDY, Author of "Far from the Madding Crowd," etc.

CHAPTER I.—WHAT WAS SEEN FROM THE WINDOW OVERLOOKING THE DOWN.

IN the days of high-waisted and muslin-gowned women, when the vast amount of soldiering going on in the country was a cause of much trembling to the sex, there lived in a village near the Wessex coast two ladies of good report, though unfortunately of limited means. The elder was a Mrs. Martha Garland, a landscape-painter's widow, and the other was her only daughter Anne.

Anne was fair, very fair, in a poet's sense of the word; but in complexion she was of that particular tint between blonde and brunette which is inconveniently left without a name. Her eyes were honest and inquiring, her mouth cleanly cut and yet not classical, the middle point of her upper lip scarcely descending so far as it should have done by rights, so that at the merest pleasant thought, not to mention a smile, portions of two or three white teeth were uncovered whether she would or not. Some people said that this was very attractive. She was graceful and slender, and though but little above five feet in height could draw herself up to look tall. In her manner, in her comings and goings, in her "I'll do this," or "I'll do that," she combined dignity with sweetness as no other girl could do; and any impressionable stranger youths who passed by were led to yearn for a windfall of speech from her, and to see at the same time that they would not get it. In short, beneath all that was charming and simple in this young woman there lurked a real firmness, unperceived at first,

XXI—1

as the speck of colour lurks unperceived in the heart of a milk-white parsley flower.

She wore a white handkerchief to cover her white neck, and a cap on her head with a pink ribbon round it, tied in a bow at the front. She had a great variety of these cap-ribbons, the young men being fond of sending them to her as presents until they fell definitely in love with a special sweetheart elsewhere, when they left off doing so. Between the border of her cap and her forehead were ranged a row of round brown curls, like swallows' nests under eaves.

She lived with her widowed mother in a portion of an ancient building formerly a manor-house, but now a mill, which, being too large for his own requirements, the miller had found it convenient to divide and appropriate in part to these highly respectable tenants. In this dwelling Mrs. Garland's and Anne's ears were soothed morning, noon, and night by the music of the mill, the wheels and cogs of which, being of wood, produced notes that might have borne in their minds a remote resemblance to the tones of the stopped diapason, the organ-pipes of that stop being of the same material. Occasionally, when the miller was bolting, there was added to these continuous sounds the cheerful clicking of the hopper, which did not deprive them of rest except when it was kept going all night; and over and above all this they had the pleasure of knowing that there crept in through every crevice, door, and window of their dwelling, however tightly closed, a subtle mist of superfine flour from the grinding-room, quite invisible, but making its presence known in the course of time by giving a pallid and ghostly look to the best furniture. The miller frequently apologised to his tenants for the intrusion of this insidious dry fog; but the widow was of a friendly and thankful nature, and she said that she did not mind it at all, being as it was, not nasty dirt, but the blessed staff of life.

By good-humour of this sort, and in other ways, Mrs. Garland acknowledged her friendship for her neighbour, with whom Anne and herself associated to an extent which she never could have anticipated when, tempted by the lowness of the rent, they first removed thither after her husband's death from a larger house at the other end of the village. Those who have lived in remote places where there is what is called no society will comprehend the gradual levelling of distinctions that went on in this case at some sacrifice of gentility on the part of one household. The widow was sometimes sorry to find with what readiness Anne caught up some dialect word or accent from the miller and his friends; but he was so good and true-hearted a man, and she so easy-minded, unambitious a woman, that she would not make life a solitude for superfine reasons. More than all, she had good ground for thinking that the miller secretly admired her, and this added a piquancy to the situation.

On a fine summer morning, when the leaves were warm under the sun, and the more industrious bees abroad, diving into every blue and red cup that could possibly be considered a flower, Anne was sitting at the back window of her mother's portion of the house, measuring out lengths of worsted for a fringed rug that she was making, which lay, about three-quarters finished, beside her. The work, though chromatically brilliant, was tedious: a hearth-rug was a thing which nobody worked at from morning to night; it was taken up and put down; it was in the chair, on the floor, across the handrail, under the bed, kicked here, kicked there, rolled away in the closet, brought out again, and so on, more capriciously perhaps than any other home-made article. Nobody was expected to finish a rug within a calculable period, and the wools of the beginning became faded and historical before the end was reached. A sense of this inherent nature of worsted work rather than idleness led Anne to look rather frequently from the open casement.

Immediately before her was the large smooth mill-pond, overfull, and intruding into the hedge and into the road. The water, with its floating leaves and spots of froth, was stealing away, like Time, under the dark arch, to tumble over the great slimy wheel within. On the other side of the mill-pond was an open place called the Cross, because it was three-quarters of one, two lanes and a cattle-drive meeting there. It was the general rendezvous and arena of the surrounding village. Behind this a steep slope rose high into the sky, merging in a wide and open down, now littered with sheep newly shorn. The upland by its height completely sheltered the mill and village from north winds, making summers of springs, reducing winters to autumn temperatures, and permitting myrtles to flourish in the open air.

The heaviness of noon pervaded the scene, and under its influence the sheep had ceased to feed. Nobody was standing at the village Cross, the few inhabitants being indoors at their dinner. No human being was on the down, and no human eye or interest but Anne's seemed to be concerned with it. The bees still worked on, and the butterflies did not rest from roving, their smallness seeming to shield them from the stagnating effect that this turning moment of day had on larger creatures. Otherwise all was still.

The girl glanced at the down and the sheep for no particular reason; simply that the steep margin of turf and daisies rising above the roofs, chimneys, apple-trees, and church tower of the hamlet around her, bounded the view from her position, and it was necessary to look somewhere when she raised her head. While thus engaged in working and stopping her attention was attracted by the sudden rising and running away of the sheep squatted on the down; and there succeeded sounds of a heavy tramping over the hard sod which the sheep had quitted, the tramp being accompanied by a metallic clanking. Turning her eyes farther she beheld two cavalry soldiers on bulky grey chargers, armed and accoutred throughout, ascending the down at a point to the left where the incline was comparatively easy. The burnished chains, buckles, and plates of their trappings shone like little looking-glasses, and the blue, red, and white about them was unsubdued by weather or wear.

The two troopers rode proudly on, as if nothing less than crowns and empires ever concerned their magnificent minds. They reached that part of the down which lay just in front of her, where they came to a halt. In another minute there appeared behind them a group containing some half-dozen more of the same sort. These came on, halted, and dismounted likewise.

Two of the soldiers then walked some distance onward together, when one stood still, the other advancing farther, and stretching a white line or tape between them. Two more of the men marched to another outlying point, where they made marks in the ground. Thus they walked about and took distances, obviously according to some preconcerted scheme:

At the end of this systematic proceeding one solitary trooper—a commissioned officer, if his uniform could be judged rightly at that distance—rode up the down, went over the ground, looked at what the others had done, and seemed to think that it was good. And then the girl heard yet louder tramps and clankings, and she beheld rising from where the others had risen a whole column of cavalry in marching order. At a distance behind there came a cloud of dust enveloping more and more troops, their arms and accoutrements reflecting the sun through the haze in faint flashes, stars, and streaks of light. The whole body approached slowly towards the plateau at the top of the down.

Anne threw down her work, and letting her eyes remain on the nearing masses of cavalry, the worsteds getting entangled as they would, said, "Mother, mother; come here! Here's such a fine sight. What does it mean? What can they be going to do up there?"

The mother thus invoked ran up-stairs, entered the room, and came forward to the window. She was a woman with a sanguine mouth and eye, unheroic manner, and pleasant general appearance; a little more tarnished as to surface, but not much worse in contour than the girl herself.

Widow Garland's thoughts were those of the period. "Can it be the French?" she said, arranging herself for the extremest form of consternation. "Can that arch-enemy of mankind have landed at last?" It should be stated that at this time there were two arch-enemies of mankind, Satan as usual, and Bonaparte, who had sprung up and eclipsed his elder rival altogether. Mrs. Garland alluded, of course, to the junior gentleman.

"It cannot be he," said Anne. "Ah! there's Simon Burden, the man who watches at the beacon. He'll know!"

She waved her hand to an aged form of the same colour as the road, who had just appeared beyond the mill-pond, and who, though active, was bowed to that degree which almost reproaches a feeling observer for standing upright. The arrival of the soldiery had drawn him out from his drop of drink at the Three Mariners as it had attracted Anne. At her call he crossed the mill bridge, and came towards the window that framed in the two women.

Anne inquired of him what it all meant, but Simon Burden, without answering, continued to move on with parted gums, staring at the cavalry on his own private account with a concern that people often show about temporal phenomena when such matters can affect them but a short time longer. "You'll walk into the mill-pond!" said Anne. "What are they doing? You were a soldier many years ago, and ought to know."

"Don't ask me, Mis'ess Anne," said the military relic, depositing his body against the wall one limb at a time. "I were only in the foot, ye know, and never had a clear understanding of horses. Ay, I be a old man, and of no judgment now." Some additional pressure, however, caused him to search further in his worm-eaten magazine of ideas, and he found that he did know in a dim irresponsible way. The soldiers must have come there to camp: those men they had seen first were the markers; they had come on before the rest to measure out the ground. He who had accompanied them was the quarter-master. "And so you see they have got all the lines marked out by the time the regiment have come up," he added. "And then they will—well-a-deary! who'd ha' supposed that Overcombe would see such a day as this!"

"And then they will——"

"Then——. Ah, it's gone from me again!" said Simon. "Oh, and then they will raise their tents, you know, and picket their horses. That was it; so it was."

By this time the column of horse had ascended into full view, and they formed a lively spectacle as they rode along the high ground in marching order, backed by the pale blue sky, and lit by the southerly sun. Their uniform was bright and attractive; they wore white buckskin pantaloons, three-quarter boots, scarlet shakos set off with lace, mustachios waxed to a needle point; and above all, those richly ornamented blue jackets mantled with the historic pelisse—that fascination to women, and encumbrance to the wearers themselves.

"'Tis the York Hussars," said Simon Burden, brightening like a dying ember fanned. "Foreigners to a man, and enrolled long since my time. But as good hearty comrades, they say, as you'll find in the King's service."

"Here are more and different ones," said Mrs. Garland.

Other troops had, during the last few minutes, been ascending the down at a remoter point, and now drew near. These were of different weight and build from the others; lighter men, in helmet hats with white plumes.

"I don't know which I like best," said Anne. "These, I think, after all."

Simon, who had been looking hard at the latter, now said that they were the ——th Dragoons.

"All Englishmen they," said the old man. "They lay at Weymouth Barracks a few years ago."

"They did. I remember it," said Mrs. Garland.

"And lots of the chaps about here listed at the time," said Simon. "I can call to mind that there was—ah, 'tis gone from me again! However, all that's of little account now."

The dragoons passed in front of the lookers-on as the others had done, and their gay plumes, which had hung lazily during the ascent, swung to northward as they reached the top, showing that on the summit a fresh breeze blew. "But look across there," said Anne. There had entered upon the down from another direction several battalions of foot, in white kerseymere breeches and cloth gaiters. They seemed to be weary from a long march, the original black of their gaiters and boots being whitey-brown with dust. Presently came regimental waggons, and the private canteen carts which followed at the end of a convoy.

The space in front of the mill-pond was now occupied by nearly all the inhabitants of the village, who had turned out in alarm, and remained for pleasure, their eyes lighted up with interest in what they saw; for trappings and regimentals, war-horses and men, in towns an attraction, were here almost a sublimity.

The troops filed to their lines, dismounted, and in quick time took off their accoutrements, rolled up their sheep-skins, picketed and unbitted their horses, and made ready to erect the tents as soon as they could be taken from the waggons and brought forward. When this was done, at a given signal the canvases flew up from the sod; and thenceforth every man had a place in which to lay his head.

Though nobody seemed to be looking on but the few at the window and in the village street, there were, as a matter of fact, many eyes converging upon that military arrival in its high and conspicuous position, not to mention the glances of birds and other wild creatures. Men in distant gardens, women in orchards and at cottage doors, shepherds on remote hills, turnip-hoers in blue-green enclosures miles away, captains with spy-glasses out at sea, were regarding the picture keenly. Those three or four thousand men of one machine-like movement, some of them swashbucklers by nature, others, doubtless, of a quiet shop-keeping disposition who had inadvertently got into uniform—all of them had arrived from nobody knew where, and hence were matter of great curiosity. They seemed to the mere eye to belong to a different order of beings from those who inhabited the valleys below. Apparently unconscious and careless of what all the world was doing elsewhere, they remained picturesquely engrossed in the business of making themselves a habitation on the isolated spot which they had chosen.

Mrs. Garland was of a festive and sanguine turn of mind, a woman soon set up and soon set down, and the coming of the regiments quite excited her. She thought there was reason for putting on her best cap, thought that perhaps there was not; that she would hurry on the dinner and go out in the afternoon; then that she would, after all, do nothing unusual, nor show any silly excitements whatever, since they were unbecoming in a mother and a widow. Thus circumscribing her intentions till she was toned down to an ordinary person of forty, Mrs. Garland accompanied her daughter down-stairs to dine, saying, "Presently we will call on Miller Loveday, and hear what he thinks of it all."

CHAPTER II.—IN WHICH SOMEBODY KNOCKS AND COMES IN.

MILLER LOVEDAY was the representative of an ancient family of corn-grinders whose history is lost in the mists of antiquity. His ancestral line was contemporaneous with that of De Ros, Howard, and De La Zouche; but owing to some trifling deficiency in the possessions of the house of Loveday the individual names and intermarriages of its members were not recorded during the Middle Ages, and thus their private lives in any given century were uncertain. But it was known that the family had formed matrimonial alliances with farmers not so very small, and once with a gentleman-tanner, who had for many years purchased after their death the horses of the most aristocratic persons in the county—fiery steeds that earlier in their career had been valued at many hundred guineas. It was also ascertained that Mr. Loveday's great-grandparents had been eight in number, and his great-great-grandparents sixteen, every one of whom reached to years of discretion : at every stage backwards his sires and gammers thus doubled and doubled till they became a vast body of Gothic ladies and gentlemen of the rank known as ceorls or villeins, full of importance to the country at large, and ramifying throughout the unwritten history of England. His immediate father had greatly improved the value of their residence by building a new chimney and setting up an additional pair of millstones.

Overcombe Mill presented at one end the appearance of a hard-worked house slipping into the river, and at the other of an idle, genteel place, half-cloaked with creepers at

this time of the year, and having no visible connection with flour. It had hips instead of gables, giving it a round-shouldered look, four chimneys with no smoke coming out of them, two zigzag cracks in the wall, several open windows, with a looking-glass here and there inside showing its warped back to the passer-by, snowy dimity curtains waving in the draught; two mill doors, one above the other, the upper enabling a person to step out upon nothing at a height of ten feet from the ground ; a gaping arch vomiting the river, and a lean, long-nosed fellow looking out from the mill doorway, who was the hired grinder, except when a bulging fifteen-stone man occupied the same place, namely, the miller himself.

Behind the mill door, and invisible to the mere wayfarer who did not visit the family, were chalked addition and subtraction sums, many of them originally done wrong, and the figures half rubbed out and corrected, noughts being turned into nines, and ones into twos. These were the miller's private calculations. There were also chalked in the same place rows and rows of strokes like open palings, representing the calculations of the grinder, who in his youthful ciphering studies had not gone so far as Arabic figures.

In the court in front were two worn-out mill-stones, made useful again by being let in level with the ground. Here people stood to smoke and consider things in muddy weather; and cats slept on the clean surfaces when it was hot. In the large stubbard-tree at the corner of the garden was erected a pole of larch fir, which the miller had bought with others at a sale of small timber in Lammer's Wood one Christmas week. It rose from the upper boughs of the tree to about the height of a fisherman's mast, and on the top was a vane in the form of a sailor with his arm stretched out. When the sun shone upon this figure it could be seen that the greater part of his countenance was gone, and the paint washed from his body so far as to reveal that he had been a soldier in red before he became a sailor in blue. The image had, in fact, been John, one of our coming characters, and was then turned into Robert, another of them. This revolving piece of statuary could not, however, be relied on as a vane, owing to the neighbouring hill, which formed variable currents in the wind.

The leafy and quieter wing of the mill-house was the part occupied by Mrs. Garland and her daughter, who made up in summer time for the narrowness of their quarters by overflowing considerably into the garden on stools and chairs. The parlour or dining-room had a stone floor, a fact which the widow sought to disguise by double carpeting, lest the standing of Anne and herself should be lowered in the public eye by the use of the room in its primitive state. Here now the mid-day meal went lightly and mincingly on, as it does where there is no greedy carnivorous man to keep the dishes about, and was hanging on the close when somebody entered the passage as far as the chink of the parlour door, and tapped. This proceeding was probably adopted to kindly avoid giving trouble to Susan, the neighbour's pink daughter, who helped at Mrs. Garland's in the mornings, but was at that moment particularly occupied in standing on the water-butt and gazing at the soldiers, with an inhaling position of the jawbone and circular eyes.

There was a flutter in the little dining-room—the sensitiveness of habitual solitude makes hearts beat for preternaturally small reasons—and a guessing as to who the visitor might be was hurriedly made. It was some military gentleman from the camp, perhaps? No, that was impossible. It was the parson? No, he would not come at dinner-time. It was the well-informed man who travelled with drapery and the best Birmingham earrings? Not at all; his time was not till Thursday at three. Before they could think further the visitor moved forward another step, and the diners got a glimpse of him through the same

friendly chink that had afforded him a view of the Garland dinner-table.

"Oh! it is only Loveday."

This approximation to nobody was the miller above mentioned, a hale man of fifty-five or sixty—hale all through, as many were in those days, and not merely veneered with purple by exhilarating victuals and drinks, though the latter were not at all despised by him. His face was indeed rather pale than otherwise, for he had just come from the mill. It was capable of immense changes of expression: mobility was its essence, a roll of flesh forming a buttress to his nose on each side, and a deep ravine lying between his lower lip and the tumulus represented by his chin. These fleshy lumps moved stealthily, as if of their own accord, whenever his fancy was tickled.

His eyes having lighted on the table-cloth, plates, and viands, he found himself in a position which had a sensible awkwardness for a modest man who always liked to enter only at seasonable times the presence of a girl of such pleasantly soft ways as Anne Garland, she who could make apples seem like peaches, and throw over her shillings the glamour of guineas when she paid him for flour.

"Dinner is over, neighbour Loveday; please come in," said the widow, seeing his case, and wondering why he called at that unusual hour. The miller said something about coming in presently, but Anne, who always liked his news, pressed him to stay, with a tender motion of her lip as it played on the verge of a solicitous smile without quite lapsing into one—her habitual manner when speaking.

Loveday took off his low-crowned hat and advanced as if he had thought that this might be the end of it. He had not come about pigs or fowls this time, he said. Seeing their door open as he passed he determined to step in and tell them some news. "You have been looking out, like the rest o' us, no doubt, Mrs. Garland, at the mampus of soldiers that have come upon the down?"

She said pleasantly that they had both been doing so.

"Well," said Loveday, "one of the horse regiments is the ——th Dragoons, my son John's regiment, you know."

The announcement, though it interested them, did not create such an effect as the father of John had seemed to anticipate; but Anne, who liked to say pleasant things, replied, "The dragoons looked nicer than the foot or the German cavalry either."

"They are a handsome body of men," said

the miller in a disinterested voice. "Faith! I didn't know they were coming, though it may be in the newspaper all the time. But old Derriman keeps it so long that we never know things till they be in everybody's mouth."

This Derriman was a squireen living near, who was chiefly distinguished in the present warlike time by having a nephew in the yeomanry.

"We were told that the yeomanry went along the turnpike road yesterday," said Anne, following out this track of thought; "and they say that they were a pretty sight, and quite soldierly."

"Ah! well—they be not regulars," said miller Loveday, keeping back harsher criticism as uncalled for. But inflamed by the arrival of the dragoons, which had been the exciting cause of his call, his mind would not go to the yeomanry. "John has not been home these five years," he said.

"And what rank does he hold now?" said the widow.

"He's trumpet-major, ma'am; and a good musician." The miller, who was a good father, went on to explain that John had seen some service, too. He had enlisted when the regiment was lying at Weymouth, more than eleven years before, which put his father out of temper with him, as he had wished him to follow on at the mill. But as the lad had enlisted seriously, and without a drop of drink in him, and as he had often said that he would be a soldier, the miller had thought that he would let Jack take his chance in the profession of his choice.

Loveday had two sons, and the second was now brought into the conversation by a remark of Anne's that neither of them seemed to care for the miller's business.

"No," said Loveday in a less buoyant tone. "Robert, you see, must needs go to sea." Loveday was more hopeful, however, in expressing his belief that Bob would not stick to a sailor's life as John had stuck to soldiering. Bob was of an easier nature and more his mother's child than John; and being the youngest they used to call him the "nestleripe,"—meaning the last in the nest. All which information, and more, Loveday gave with the greatest readiness, as he had given it several times before.

"He is much younger than his brother?" said Mrs. Garland.

About four years, the miller told her. His soldier son was two-and-thirty, and Bob was twenty-eight. When Bob returned from his present voyage, he was to be persuaded to stay and assist as grinder in the mill, and go to sea no more.

"A sailor-miller!" said Anne.

"Oh, he knows as much about mill business as I do," said Loveday; "he was intended for it, you know, like John. But, bless me!" he continued, "I am before my story. I'm come more particularly to ask you, ma'am, and you, Anne my honey, if you will join me and a few friends at a leetle homely supper that I shall gi'e to please the chap now he's come? I can do no less than have a bit of a randy, as the saying is, now that he's here safe and sound."

Mrs. Garland wanted to catch her daughter's eye; she was in some doubt about her answer. But Anne's eye was not to be caught, for she hated hints, nods, and calculations of any kind in matters which should be regulated by impulse; and the matron replied, "If so be 'tis possible, we'll be there. You will tell us the day?"

He would, as soon as he had seen son John. "'Twill be rather untidy, you know, owing to my having no womenfolks in the house; and my man David is a poor dunderheaded feller for getting up a feast. Poor chap! his sight is bad, that's true, and he's very good at making the beds, and oiling the legs of the chairs and other furniture, or I should have got rid of him years ago."

"You should have a woman to attend to the house, Loveday," said the widow.

"Yes, I should, but—— Well, 'tis a fine day, neighbours. Hark! I fancy I hear the noise of pots and pans up at the camp, or my ears deceive me. Poor fellows, they must be hungry! Good day t'ye, ma'am." And the miller went away.

All that afternoon Overcombe continued in a ferment of interest in the military investment, which brought the excitement of an invasion without the strife. There were great discussions on the merits and appearance of the soldiery. The event opened up to the girls unbounded possibilities of adoring and being adored, and to the young men an embarrassment of dashing acquaintances which quite superseded falling in love. Thirteen of these lads incontinently stated within the space of a quarter of an hour that there was nothing in the world like going for a soldier. The young women stated little, but perhaps thought the more; though, in justice, they glanced round towards the encampment from the corners of their blue and brown eyes in the most demure and modest manner that could be desired.

In the evening the village was lively with

"On a fine summer morning . . . . Anne looked rather frequently from the open casement."

soldiers' wives; a tree full of starlings would not have rivalled the chatter that was going on. These ladies were very brilliantly dressed, with more regard for colour than for material. Purple, red, and blue bonnets were numerous, with bunches of cock's feathers; and one had on an Arcadian hat of green sarcenet, turned up in front to show her cap underneath. It had once belonged to an officer's lady, and was not so very much stained, except where the occasional storms of rain, incidental to a military life, had caused the green to run and stagnate in curious watermarks like peninsulas and islands. Some of the prettiest of these butterfly wives had been fortunate enough to get lodgings in the cottages, and were thus spared the necessity of living in huts and tents on the down. Those who had not been so fortunate were not rendered more amiable by the success of their sisters in arms, and called them other names than those they had been christened, to which the latter pleasantly retorted, bringing forth rejoinders of the knock-me-down class of speech; till the end of these alternative remarks seemed dependent upon the close of the day.

One of these new arrivals, who had a rosy nose and a slight thickness of voice, which, as Anne said, she couldn't help, poor thing, seemed to have seen so much of the world, and to have been in so many campaigns, that Anne would have liked to take her into their own house, so as to acquire some of that practical knowledge of the history of England which the lady possessed, and which could not be got from books. But the narrowness of Mrs. Garland's rooms absolutely forbade this, and the houseless treasury of experience was obliged to look for quarters elsewhere.

That night Anne retired early to bed. The events of the day, cheerful as they were in themselves, had been unusual enough to give her a slight headache. Before getting into bed she went to the window, and drew aside the white curtains that hung across it. The moon was shining, though not as yet into the valley, but just peeping above the ridge of the down, where the white cones of the encampment were softly touched by its light. The quarter-guard and foremost tents showed themselves prominently; but the body of the camp, the officers' tents, kitchens, canteen, and appurtenances in the rear were blotted out by the ground, because of its height above her. She could discern the forms of one or two sentries moving to and fro across the disc of the moon at intervals. She could hear the frequent shuffling and tossing of the horses tied to the pickets; and in the other direction the miles-long voice of the sea, whispering a louder note at those points of its length where hampered in its ebb and flow by some jutting promontory or group of boulders. Louder sounds suddenly broke this approach to silence; they came from the camp of dragoons, were taken up farther to the right by the camp of the Hanoverians, and farther on still by the body of infantry. It was tattoo. Feeling no desire to sleep she listened yet longer, looked at Charles's Wain swinging over the church' tower, and the moon ascending higher and higher over the right-hand streets of tents, where, instead of parade and bustle, there was nothing going on but snores and dreams, the tired soldiers lying by this time under their proper canvases, radiating like spokes from the pole of each tent.

At last Anne gave up thinking, and retired like the rest. The night wore on, and, except the occasional "All's well" of the sentries, no voice was heard in the camp or in the village below.

CHAPTER III.—IN WHICH THE MILL BECOMES AN IMPORTANT CENTRE OF OPERATIONS.

THE next morning Miss Garland awoke with an impression that something more than usual was going on, and she recognised as soon as she could clearly reason that the proceedings, whatever they might be, lay not far away from her bedroom window. The sounds were chiefly those of pickaxes and shovels. Anne got up, and, lifting the corner of the curtain about an inch, peeped out.

A number of soldiers were busily engaged in making a zigzag path down the incline from the camp to the river head at the back of the house, and, judging from the quantity of work already got through, they must have begun very early. Squads of men were working at several equidistant points in the proposed pathway, and by the time that Anne had dressed herself each section of the length had been connected with those above and below it, so that a continuous and easy track was formed from the crest of the down to the bottom of the steep. The down rested on a bed of solid chalk, and the surface exposed by the roadmakers formed a white ribbon, serpentining from top to bottom.

Then the relays of working soldiers all disappeared; and, not long after, a troop of dragoons in watering order rode forward at the top and began to wind down the new path. They came lower and closer, and at last were immediately beneath her window, gathering themselves up on the space by the mill-pond. A number of the horses entered it at the shallow part, drinking, and splashing and tossing about. Perhaps as many as thirty, half of them with riders on their backs, were in the water at one time; the thirsty animals drank, stamped, flounced, and drank again, letting the clear, cool water dribble luxuriously from their mouths. Miller Loveday was looking on from over his garden hedge, and many admiring villagers were gathered around.

Gazing up higher, Anne saw other troops descending by the new road from the camp, those which had already been to the pond making room for these by withdrawing along the village lane and returning to the top by a circuitous route.

Suddenly the miller exclaimed, as in fulfilment of expectation, "Ah, John, my boy; good morning!" And the reply of "Morning, father," came from a well-mounted soldier near him, who did not, however, form one of the watering party. Anne could not see his face very clearly, but she had no doubt that this was John Loveday. There were tones in the voice which reminded her of old times, those of her very infancy, when Johnny Loveday had been top boy in the village school, and had wanted to learn painting of her father. The deeps and shallows of the mill-pond being better known to him than to any other man in the camp, he had apparently come down on that account, and was cautioning some of the horsemen against riding too far in towards the mill-head.

Since her childhood and his enlistment Anne had seen him only once, and then but casually, when he was home on a short furlough. His figure was not much changed from what it had been; but the many sunrises and sunsets which had passed since that day, developing her from a comparative child to womanhood, had abstracted some of his angularities, reddened his skin, and given him a foreign look. It was interesting to see what years of training and service had done for this man. Few would have supposed that the white and the blue coats of miller and soldier covered the forms of father and son.

Before the last troop of dragoons rode off they were welcomed in a body by Miller Loveday, who still stood in his outer garden, this being a plot lying below the mill-tail, and stretching to the water-side. It was just the time of year when cherries are ripe, and hang in clusters under their dark leaves. While the troopers loitered on their horses, and chatted to the miller across the stream, he gathered bunches of the fruit, and held them up over the garden hedge for the acceptance of anybody who would have them; whereupon the soldiers rode into the water to where it had washed holes in the garden bank, and, reining their horses there, caught the cherries in their forage-caps, or received bunches of them on the ends of their switches, with the dignified laugh that became martial men when stooping to slightly boyish amusement. It was a cheerful, careless, unpremeditated half-hour, which returned like the scent of a flower to the memories of some of those who enjoyed it, even at a distance of many years after, when they lay wounded and weak in foreign lands.

Then dragoons and horses wheeled off as the others had done; and troops of the German Legion next came down and entered in panoramic procession the space below Anne's eyes, as if on purpose to gratify her. These were notable by their mustachios, and queues wound tightly with brown ribbon to the level of their broad shoulder blades. They were charmed as the others had been by the head and neck of Miss Garland in the little square window overlooking the scene of operations, and saluted her with devoted foreign civility, and in such overwhelming numbers that the modest girl suddenly withdrew herself into the room, and had a private blush between the chest of drawers and the washing-stand.

When she came down-stairs her mother said, "I have been thinking what I ought to wear to Miller Loveday's to-night."

"To Miller Loveday's?" said Anne.

"Yes. The party is to-night. He has been in here this morning to tell me that he has seen his son, and they have fixed this evening."

"Do you think we ought to go, mother?" said Anne slowly, and looking at the smaller features of the window-flowers.

"Why not?" said Mrs. Garland.

"He will only have men there except ourselves, will he? And shall we be right to go alone among 'em?"

Anne had not recovered from the ardent gaze of the gallant York Hussars, whose voices reached her even now in converse with Loveday as the others had been.

"La, Anne, how proud you are!" said Widow Garland. "Why, isn't he our nearest neighbour and our landlord? and don't he always fetch our faggots from wood, and keep us in vegetables for next to nothing?"

"That's true," said Anne.

"Well, we can't be distant with the man. And if the enemy land next autumn, as everybody says they will, we shall have quite to depend upon the miller's waggon and horses. He's our only friend."

"Yes, so he is," said Anne. "And you had better go, mother; and I'll stay at home. They will be all men; and I don't like going."

Mrs. Garland reflected. "Well, if you don't want to go, I don't," she said. "Perhaps as you are grown up it would be better to stay at home this time. Your father was a professional man, certainly." Having spoken as a mother, she sighed as a woman.

"Why do you sigh, mother?"

"You are so prim and stiff about everything."

"Very well—we'll go."

"Oh no—I am not so sure that we ought. I did not promise, and there will be no trouble in keeping away."

Anne apparently did not feel certain of her own opinion, and, instead of supporting or contradicting, looked thoughtfully down, and abstractedly brought her hands together on her bosom, till her fingers met tip to tip.

As the day advanced the young woman and her mother became aware that great preparations were in progress in the miller's wing of the house. The partitioning between the Lovedays and the Garlands was not very thorough, consisting in many cases of a simple screwing up of the doors in the dividing walls; and thus when the mill began any new performances they proclaimed themselves at once in the more private dwelling. The smell of Miller Loveday's pipe came down Mrs. Garland's chimney of an evening with the greatest regularity. Every time that he poked his fire they knew from the vehemence or deliberateness of the blows the precise state of his mind; and when he wound his clock on Sunday nights the whirr of that monitor reminded the widow to wind hers. This transit of noises was most perfect where Loveday's lobby adjoined Mrs. Garland's pantry; and Anne, who was occupied for some time in the latter apartment, enjoyed the privilege of hearing the visitors arrive, and of catching stray sounds and words without the connecting phrases that made them entertaining, to judge from the laughter they evoked. The arrivals passed through the house and went into the garden, where they had tea in a large summer house, an occasional blink of bright colour through the foliage being all that was visible of the assembly from Mrs. Garland's windows. When it grew dusk they all could be heard coming indoors, to finish the evening in the parlour.

Then there was an intensified continuation of the above-mentioned signs of enjoyment, talkings and haw-haws, runnings up-stairs and runnings down, a slamming of doors and a clinking of cups and glasses; till the proudest adjoining tenant without friends on his own side of the partition might have been tempted to wish for entrance to that merry dwelling, if only to know the cause of these fluctuations of hilarity, and to see if the guests were really so very numerous, and the observations so amusing as they seemed.

The stagnation of life on the Garland side of the party-wall began to have a very gloomy effect by the contrast. When, about half-past nine o'clock, one of these tantalizing bursts of gaiety had resounded for a longer time than usual, Anne said, "I believe, mother, that you are wishing you had gone."

"I own to feeling that it would have been very cheerful if we had joined in," said Mrs. Garland, in a hankering tone. "I was rather too nice in listening to you and not going. The parson never calls upon us except in his spiritual capacity. Old Derriman is hardly genteel; and there's nobody left to speak to. Lonely people must accept what company they can get."

"Or do without it altogether."

"That's not natural, Anne; and I am surprised to hear a young woman like you say such a thing. Nature will not be stifled in that way . . ." (Song and powerful chorus heard through partition.) "I declare the room on the other side of the wall seems quite a paradise compared with this."

"Mother, you are quite a girl," said Anne in slightly superior accents. "Go in and join them by all means."

"O no—not now," said her mother, resignedly shaking her head. "It is too late now. We ought to have taken advantage of the invitation. They would look hard at me as a poor mortal who had no real business there, and the miller would say, with his broad smile, 'Ah, you be obliged to come round.'"

While the sociable and unaspiring Mrs. Garland continued thus to pass the evening in two places, her body in her own house and her mind in the miller's, somebody knocked at the door, and directly after the elder Loveday himself was admitted to the room. He was dressed in an intervening suit between sober and gay, which he used for such occasions as the present, and his blue coat, yellow and red waistcoat with the three lower buttons unfastened, steel-buckled shoes and speckled stockings, became him very well in Mrs. Martha Garland's eyes.

"Your servant, ma'am," said the miller, adopting as a matter of propriety the raised standard of politeness required by his higher costume. "Now, begging your pardon, I can't hae this. 'Tis unnatural that you two ladies should be biding here and we under the same roof making merry without ye. Your husband, poor man—lovely picters that 'a would make to be sure!—would have been in wi' us long ago if he had been in your place. I can take no nay from ye, upon my honour. You and maidy Anne must come in, if it be on'y for half an hour. John and his friends have got passes till twelve o'clock to-night, and, saving a few of our own village folk, the lowest visitor present is a very genteel German corporal. If you should hae any misgivings on the score of respectability, ma'am, we'll pack off the underbred ones into the back kitchen."

Widow Garland and Anne looked yes at each other after this appeal.

"We'll follow you in a few minutes," said the elder, smiling; and she rose with Anne to go up-stairs.

"No, I'll wait for ye," said the miller doggedly; "or perhaps you'll alter your mind again."

While the mother and daughter were up-stairs dressing, and saying laughingly to each other, "Well, we *must* go now," as if they hadn't wished to go five minutes before, other steps were heard in the passage; and the miller cried from below, "Your pardon, Mrs. Widow Garland; but my son John has come to help fetch ye. Shall I ask him in till ye be ready?"

"Certainly; I shall be down in a minute," screamed Anne's mother in a slanting voice towards the staircase.

When she descended, the outline of the trumpet-major appeared half-way down the passage. "This is John," said the miller simply. "John, you can mind Mrs. Martha Garland very well?"

"Very well indeed," said the dragoon, coming in a little farther. "I should have called to see her last time, but I was only home a week. How is your little girl, ma'am?"

Mrs. Garland said Anne was quite well. "She is grown up now. She will be down in a moment."

There was a slight noise of military heels without the door, at which the trumpet-major went and put his head outside, and said "All right—coming in a minute," when a voice in the darkness replied, "No hurry."

"More friends?" said Mrs. Garland.

"Oh, it is only Buck and Jones come to fetch me," said the soldier. "Shall I ask 'em in a minute, Mrs. Garland, ma'am?"

"Oh, yes," said the lady; and the two interesting forms of Trumpeter Buck and Saddler-sergeant Jones then came forward in the most friendly manner, whereupon other steps were heard without, and it was discovered that Sergeant-master-tailor Brett and Farrier-extraordinary Johnson were outside, having come to fetch Messrs. Buck and Jones, as Buck and Jones had come to fetch the trumpet-major.

As there seemed a possibility of Mrs. Garland's small passage being choked up with human figures personally unknown to her, she was relieved to hear Anne coming down-stairs.

"Here's my little girl," said Mrs. Garland, and the trumpet-major looked with a sort of awe upon the muslin apparition who came forward, and stood quite dumb before her. Anne recognised him as the trooper she had seen from her window, and welcomed him kindly. There was something in his honest face which made her feel instantly at home with him.

At this frankness of manner Loveday—who was not a ladies' man—blushed, and made some alteration in his bodily posture, began a sentence which had no end, and showed quite a boy's embarrassment. Recovering himself he politely offered his arm, which Anne took with a very pretty grace. He conducted her through his comrades, who glued themselves perpendicularly to the wall to let her pass, and then they went out of the door, her mother following with the miller, and supported by the body of troopers, the latter walking with the usual cavalry gait, as if their thighs were rather too long for them. Thus they crossed the threshold of the mill-house and up the passage, the paving of which was worn into a gutter by the ebb and flow of feet that had been going on there ever since Tudor times.

CHAPTER IV.—WHO WERE PRESENT AT THE MILLER'S LITTLE ENTERTAINMENT.

WHEN the group entered the presence of the company a lull in the conversation was caused by the sight of new visitors, and (of course) by the charm of Anne's appearance; until the old men, who had daughters of their own, perceiving that she was only a half-formed girl, resumed their tales and toss-potting with unconcern.

Miller Loveday had fraternised with half

the soldiers in the camp since their arrival, and the effect of this upon his party was striking—both chromatically and otherwise. Those among the guests who first attracted the eye were the sergeants and sergeant-majors of Loveday's regiment, fine hearty men who sat facing the candles, entirely resigned to physical comfort. Then there were other non-commissioned officers, a German, two Hungarians, and a Swede, from the Foreign Hussars—young men with a look of sadness on their faces, as if they did not much like serving so far from home. All of them spoke English fairly well. Old age was represented by Simon Burden the pensioner, and the shady side of fifty by Corporal Tullidge, his friend and neighbour, who was hard of hearing, and sat with his hat on over a red cotton handkerchief that was wound several times round his head. These two veterans were employed as watchers at the neighbouring beacon, which had lately been erected by the Lord-Lieutenant for firing whenever the descent on the coast should be made. They lived in a little hut on the hill close by the heap of faggots; but to-night they had found deputies to watch in their stead.

On a lower plane of experience and qualifications came neighbour James Comfort, of the Volunteers, a soldier by courtesy, but a blacksmith by rights; William Tremlett of the Local Militia, and Anthony Cripplestraw of the Fencibles. The two latter men of war were dressed merely as villagers, and looked upon the regulars from an humble position in the background. The remainder of the party was made up of a neighbouring dairyman or two, and their wives, invited by the miller, as Anne was glad to see, that she and her mother should not be the only women there.

The elder Loveday apologised in a whisper to Mrs. Garland for the presence of the inferior villagers. " But as they are learning to be brave defenders of their home and country, ma'am, as fast as they can master the drill, and have worked for me off and on these many years, I've asked 'em in, and thought you'd excuse it ? "

" Certainly, Miller Loveday," said the widow.

" And the same of old Burden and Tullidge. They have served well and long in the foot, and even now have a hard time of it up at the beacon in wet weather. So after giving them a meal in the kitchen I just asked 'em in to hear the singing. They faithfully promise that as soon as ever the gun-boats appear in view, and they have fired the

beacon, to run down here first, in case we shouldn't see it. 'Tis worth while to be friendly with 'em, you see, though their tempers be queer."

" Quite worth while, miller," said she.

Anne was rather embarrassed by the presence of the regular military in such force, and at first confined her words to the dairymen's wives she was acquainted with, and to the two old soldiers of the parish.

" Why didn't ye speak to me afore, chiel ? " said one of these, Corporal Tullidge, the elderly man with the hat, while she was talking to old Simon Burden. " I met ye in the lane yesterday," he added reproachfully, " but ye didn't notice me at all."

" I am very sorry for it," she said ; but, being afraid to shout in such a company, the effect of her remark upon the corporal was as if she had not spoken at all.

" You were coming along with yer head full of some high notions or other, no doubt," continued the uncompromising corporal in the same loud voice. " Ah, 'tis the young bucks that get all the notice nowadays, and old folks are quite forgot. I can mind well enough how young Bob Loveday used to lie in wait for ye."

Anne blushed deeply, and stopped his too excursive discourse by hastily saying that she always respected old folks like him. The corporal thought she inquired why he always kept his hat on, and answered that it was because his head was injured at Valenciennes, in July, Ninety-three. " We were trying to bomb down the tower, and a piece of the shell struck me. I was no more nor less than a dead man for two days. If it hadn't a been for that and my smashed arm I should have come home none the worse for my five-and-twenty years' service."

" You have got a silver plate let into yer head, haven't ye, corpel," said Anthony Cripplesttraw, who had drawn near. " I have heard that the way they morticed yer skull was a beautiful piece of workmanship. Perhaps the young woman would like to see the place. 'Tis a curious sight, Mis'ess Anne ; you don't see such a wownd every day."

" No, thank you," said Anne hurriedly, dreading, as did all the young people of Overcombe, the spectacle of the corporal uncovered. He had never been seen in public without the hat and the handkerchief, since his return in Ninety-four ; and strange stories were told of the ghastliness of his appearance bare-headed, a little boy who had accidentally beheld him going to bed in that state having been nearly frightened into fits.

"Well, if the young woman don't want to see yer head, maybe she'd like to hear yer arm?" continued Cripplestraw, earnest to please her.

"Hey?" said the corporal.

"Your arm hurt too?" cried Anne.

"Knocked to a pummy at the same time as my head," said Tullidge dispassionately.

"Rattle yer arm, corpel, and show her," said Cripplestraw.

"Yes, sure," said the corporal, raising the limb slowly, as if the glory of exhibition had lost some of its novelty, though he was willing to oblige. Twisting it mercilessly about with his right hand he produced a crunching among the bones at every motion, Cripplestraw seeming to derive great satisfaction from the ghastly sound.

"How very shocking!" said Anne, painfully anxious for him to leave off.

"Oh, it don't hurt him, bless ye. Do it, corpel?" said Cripplestraw.

"Not a bit," said the corporal, still working his arm with great energy.

"There's no life in the bones at all. No life in 'em, I tell her, corpel!"

"None at all."

"They be as loose as a bag of ninepins," explained Cripplestraw in continuation. "You can feel 'em quite plain, Mis'ess Anne. If ye would like to, he'll undo his sleeve in a minute, to oblige ye?"

"Oh, no, no, please not! I quite understand," said the young woman.

"Do she want to hear or see any more, or don't she?" the corporal inquired, with a sense that his time was getting wasted.

Anne explained that she did not on any account; and managed to escape from the corner.

REDUCED CIRCUMSTANCES.

MRS. MACPHERSON lived, after she became a widow, in a small house in the new town of Edinburgh—a house of one parlour and two bedrooms, and up three stairs. Once in, all was tidy and even elegant. The view of the Castle and St. Giles's and Arthur's Seat was such as only Edinburgh, among British cities, can furnish; and "5, Argyll Terrace" was an address that sounded well in the ears of those who did not know the big, factory-looking "lands" of houses lately erected on the side of the Meadows.

Her married life of twelve bright years had closed suddenly. Andrew, her husband, a good, earnest man, was working his way hopefully into a considerable practice, when a fever cut him off at the age of thirty-eight. Of a good Highland family, but an orphan and poor before their marriage, Mrs. Macpherson found that only rigid economy could enable her to live and educate her two children. Her strong, quiet character came out in the quickness and thoroughness of her new arrangements. Within a month after Dr. Macpherson's funeral, the distance of the Bridges and the Meadows had been put between her and the desolate home in Great King Street, and the new life began. One faithful servant, old Flora, a Highland woman who might be any age between forty and sixty, and so much of the furniture as the three little rooms required, went with her; the remainder of the furniture and the horse and the carriage (not two years old) were turned into money, not without a pang, but resolutely and promptly.

Isabel was eleven years old, a thoughtful child, making fair progress with her education, and winsome. But Andrew had been blind from within a few weeks of his birth. All his father's skill could not find a remedy for the effects of some slight exposure. His education, too, was far advanced for eight years, but it had taken unusual direction. The raised alphabet had been his toy, and he had rapidly acquired a knowledge of letters, but the only literature he had in character was the Gospel of St. Luke; for the rest, he listened with quiet eagerness to all that his mother and Isabel read to him, asked questions sometimes too deep for either to answer, and discussed all manner of subjects with his father at meals. The worthy doctor's one amusement was a small violin, treasured from his lonely student days, and brought out whenever he had a quiet evening to spend in his own drawing-room. Almost before he could walk the blind boy had evinced the keenest delight in listening to the old Scottish airs, sometimes tearful, sometimes gay, which his father rendered with so much skill and feeling.

When the crash and the change came, you may be sure the violin was among the few household treasures carried to Argyll Terrace; even the children and the staid Flora knew it as "the wee sinfu' fiddle," and understood the humour of the story about the doctor's father, a country minister, to whom the instrument had belonged. It had got rumoured in his parish that the good man was too much attached to vain, worldly music, and a deputation of elders had come to the manse to present a faithful remonstrance. They did not declare their errand at once, but the shrewd old minister suspected it, and entertained his visitors with one psalm tune after another, Coleshill, Old Hundred, Montrose, York—played on a larger and graver instrument. At length one of the elders ventured quietly to broach their errand.

" But didn't you like these tunes I've been giving you ?" asked the minister.

" Ou, aye," said one of the deputation, "we likit them grandly; but it wasna that fiddle we were complainin' o', it was the wee sinfu' ane."

After they were fairly settled in their little home and Isabel's lessons were resumed, Andrew sorely missed his father's music. Even when his mother could bring herself to play some of the same airs on her piano, he was not satisfied. Isabel had no great taste for music, but if ever there was a child in whom was exemplified the Christian idea of love, the serving of others, it was she. Untold, unasked, her love taught her how she might help and comfort her mother in a hundred ways ; and now she began to make persistent efforts to master the difficult manipulation of the violin. Her success was by no means rapid. The learner had a stern master in Andrew's keen ear. He screamed, he stamped at every false note ; but when, after many a week, Isabel had become able to play the air of " Bonnie Bessie Lee" to her blind brother's satisfaction, she had love's reward. He stroked her cheeks and hair, he kissed her again and again, tears fell through the eyelids that were never lifted.

Thus five years went by. Isabel had become a woman ; but the change was chiefly in stature, so douce had the girl been for many a day : not that she was prudish and affected—as far as possible from that—but the stern nursing of adversity had ripened her pure, loving nature into a sweet wisdom rarely met at any age. During the long winter of 1863 Mrs. Macpherson was rarely out, except to attend a neighbouring church now and then, and Isabel was her right hand. She shopped ; she marketed ; she took full share in the household work and in sewing, relieving her mother's busy hands in many an hour which another girl might have spent in amusement. All the while her attendance at the Normal School continued, and it was a very happy day for her when she carried home her first little earnings as a pupil teacher. But a dark hour was at hand.

When February, 1864, came, the good, patient mother went out for the last time. The cold which had begun the previous autumn was now a settled thing. Mrs. Macpherson had never known illness, and treated it lightly at first; but now the persistent cough, the thinness, the failing strength awakened her to a terrible alarm. Might it be that she was not to watch over Andrew till he was a man, and to accomplish her purpose of having his musical faculty trained so that he might support himself by teaching the art he loved? Saying nothing to Flora, and leaving Andrew happy at the piano, Mrs. Macpherson went out one Monday morning early in February, soon after Isabel had gone off to school. There was a little deceitful sunshine, but a shrewd wind met her before she had got into Nicholson Street. For five years the widow had not crossed the Bridges, keeping herself away from the associations of her earlier life, not with any bitterness, but making the self-denial as complete as possible by which alone she could carry out her plan of economy ; and 'for many a day the wish to walk in Prince's Street or shop in George Street had quite disappeared from her heart. The new life was, notwithstanding reduced circumstances, a cheerful one, as every faithful life is ; and till now it was lighted up with hope. But the lonely woman's face had a sad, weary, anxious look as she lingered at the corner of Adam Square till the Newington omnibus came up. In it she sat with her veil down till the Scott Monument was passed : then the wind, sharper than ever, struck her as she went up Castle Street and made her way to the door of an eminent physician who had been the friend of her husband.

After Mrs. Macpherson's return, going slowly, and with frequent stops for breath up the long stairs to her house, she was never out again. Flora said nothing, but brought her milk unbidden, and wheeled the little couch nearer the parlour fire. Andrew talked pleasantly of something that interested him, happily not seeing his mother's face ; but when Isabel came in, half an hour later, she could not restrain herself from crying, " Oh, mamma, are you worse ?" and the gentle answer, " No, darling ; only tired,", could not deceive her. There were, indeed, no worse symptoms : the cough was less frequent even, but from that hour Isabel saw an undefined change on her mother's face—not sorrow nor anxiety so much as a shade of solemn awe overshadowing without displacing the familiar smile.

Isabel shared her mother's bedroom, and sometimes her bed. About a week after that sad day the girl was gently called.

"Are you sleeping, Bella?"

"No, mamma," she answered, quickly moving to get what the invalid might wish.

"Then come in beside me."

The gas was turned low. The little table, with the medicine she had lately begun to use, and the milk that was now her only food, stood under it. Though there was but imperfect light, Isabel saw more of the strange heavenly solemnity on the tenderly loved face as she lay down in her mother's arms. But there was scarcely any change in her voice as she talked a little while about household matters, and then gently glided from these to graver things. I cannot repeat the words in which the heroic woman fulfilled her last duty of love with a triumphant courage such as martyrs at the stake have not excelled. She told her child that the half of their income—fifty pounds—was an annuity, and made her understand that it would cease with her life. She explained that the other half had been taken from the sum produced by the sale of the furniture in Great King Street, and named the bank in which the little remainder of that sum was lying. She talked of Isabel's prospect of passing her examinations, getting a certificate, and becoming mistress of a school in two or three years. Then she said that Dr. Burton had been very kind when she went to consult him the other day, had spoken like a Christian as well as a man of skill, and had told her quite plainly she could not recover. (The noble mother did not tell that he had said she would not see the summer;—why should she? It was not by him that her days were numbered.) Then she dried Isabel's tears, speaking of the great peace which the Lord Jesus had given her in all her trials; of the last words of her husband, which Isabel and Andrew knew by heart, for they were those of the hundred and forty-sixth Psalm; of the comfort she had had in the love and goodness of both her children; and of the joy it was to think they knew and loved her Saviour. There was nothing excited in her words, or manner; and after reminding Isabel of something that should be done in the house to-morrow, and of a message to be given to Flora, the mother kissed her daughter and said they should both try to sleep.

Isabel was wearied, and before long had fallen into the sound sleep of healthy youth, with her arm under her mother's neck and her mother's arm under hers.

* * * *

Grey light was coming faintly in at the window when Isabel awoke. A strange, fearful chill ran through her; the arm which was under her mother's head was gently drawn out; she rose and moved about the room, hoping to wake the sleeper; then she called Flora, and too soon found that the sleep was that from which there is no awaking till the Redeemer shall come again.

* * * *

Dr. Burton came, being called by Flora without any knowledge of the interview her mistress so recently had with him, and took charge of the simple funeral. He talked kindly with the orphans, and, hearing of "a little money in the Bank of Scotland," made Isabel's way easy for drawing it. But he had been rather deceived as to the amount by the air of comfort which Flora, cunning as Caleb Balderston, contrived to put on the little house. Isabel knew the way to the grave in the Grange Cemetery, where both father and mother now lay, and took Andrew there the next Saturday. He tried to comfort her like a man with hopeful words about what he would do for her when he was a little older. Was he not thirteen already? But Isabel, and he, too, got their best consolation when he sang beside the grave the old Scottish version of the divine words they had loved so long to the tune York, which Andrew knew had been composed by the father of the great blind poet Milton:—

> "The Lord doth give the blind their sight,
>   The bowed down doth raise:
> The Lord doth dearly love all those
>   That walk in upright ways.
>
> "The stranger's shield, the widow's stay,
>   The orphan's help is He:
> But yet by Him the wicked's way
>   Turned upside down shall be."

The lives of the orphans returned into their old groove, with the sad, sad blank felt every day—Isabel's lessons, Andrew's music, the reading and talking, and sometimes a walk in the dusk. To Andrew the dusk did not matter, and Isabel preferred it. But when autumn came round the brave little woman found she had a serious difficulty to face. Her own small earning of £15 would not be due till Christmas, and there was less than £10 remaining in her hands. Where was daily bread to come from, not to say fuel and rent? Isabel could only fall back on

"REDUCED CIRCUMSTANCES."

Page 27.

her mother's motto, "Do ye next thynge," and go on working and praying, keeping her trouble to herself. The length that Flora made a pound go in these days surprised her ; but the little lady said nothing.

Early in November she took eagerly to the old violin and practised "The flowers of the forest" till Andrew was entirely satisfied with her execution ; then she whispered to him her plan. Not just at once did he apprehend that they were poor, so carefully had he been shielded from the wind ; but when the idea took hold of him that he could do something to help her and himself, he embraced it eagerly without a thought of humiliation. They kept this secret from Flora, Isabel instinctively fearing opposition in that quarter. It was not an unusual thing for the two to be out for a couple of hours in the early part of the evening, so the trusty servant suspected nothing. With the violin under her cloak, and Andrew's arm in hers, Isabel and he walked briskly across the Meadows and George IV. Bridge, down the Mound, along Prince's Street, and stopped under the garden railings in Ainslie Place. There the first effort was made. Andrew sang with all his heart : Isabel played without a fault. Then came the trial. How were they to seek or take money ? Isabel kept her eyes on the pavement, and controlled her excitement, putting the violin safely into its case. Then slipping her hand into her brother's arm she turned toward Melville Crescent. The little crowd of listeners, errand-boys, tradespeople, visitors, with one or two gentlemen getting home for dinner, were taken by surprise. This was not a usual performance. The music had been finer than was ever heard on the streets, and the customary appeal for money was wanting. First, a little boy, with a basket on his arm, who had stopped his whistling as he heard the better music, ventured to put a penny into Isabel's hand, and started off with a louder whistle than ever to divert attention. Then as the two slowly moved along several hands were pushed out to them, and coins passed to one or the other. Isabel was glad to stop when they had turned the corner, not to count her gains certainly, but to recover her composure. The song was repeated in Melville Crescent with similar results ; and the pair slipped home, walking on the unbuilt side of Prince's Street till they got to the Mound.

Two or three times a week the money-making undertaking was repeated on nearly the same ground. The excitement did good

to Andrew, waking him up ; and it did his sister no harm. Ten or fifteen shillings a week Isabel was able to store up against the day when the last coin taken from the bank should be spent.

That day had come about the first week in December. Dr. Burton was returning to his house in Ainslie Place about six o'clock when his ear was arrested by the pathetic rendering of the most pathetic of Scotch songs. He was in the shade for the moment, and kept there till he had satisfied himself who the singer and player were. Then he turned slowly back : if he had gone forward he must have passed in front of them, and Isabel might have recognised him. He lingered on the pavement and played the spy till he saw them pass along Maitland Street into Prince's Street, and cross to the pavement beside St. John's Church, walking smartly homeward down Lothian Road.

It was a singular circumstance, and one which Isabel could never trace farther than to the God who filled the widow's cruse, that the next day there came to Miss Macpherson, of No. 5, Argyll Terrace, a formal letter on blue paper from the bank, informing her that £200 had been placed at her credit by "a friend of her father."

And the next week the doctor called. He talked about Isabel's work at school, and answered Andrew's eager questions about men and things, ending by asking if they would not come to spend Christmas time with him and cheer his lonely house.

The visit went off delightfully, and other visits followed. The old man was alone now till his only son returned from completing his studies in Paris, and was glad whenever he could induce Isabel and Andrew to be with him. She was nothing loath, but would not suffer the new-found pleasure to interfere with her daily work. The certificate was still the point of her ambition.

But somehow the young doctor when he came home reasoned her out of that ; and now Dr. Burton's house is full of the beauty and love of fresh life.

Andrew is a busy, happy man, who may be seen threading his way along George Street to the music shops, and to the Asylum for the Blind ; or in the front seats at all manner of literary and musical assemblies. Sometimes there is a fair girl with him, about ten years of age, whom he affects to guide, and who conceals in the most delightful way that she is guiding her uncle.

R. D. N.

FOOD FOR THE ECONOMICAL.

By J. MILNER FOTHERGILL, M.D.

"BUT then you English will not try to live economically even when you are told how to." Such was the remark made to me one day by an American in Messrs. Thurbers' wholesale store in Cannon Street. I was looking round their large variety of tinned foods—hominy, flour, both wheat and maize, fruits, meats, &c., &c. The conversation turned on economy in food, and the above remark was made by a stalwart western American, who was "raised on hog and hominy" he told me ; and certainly his appearance did credit to, indeed, spoke volumes for, his dietary. This remark of a foreigner is sadly too true, and our living has become extravagant in the first cost of our food material ; in the waste in our ordinary methods of cooking ; and the unnecessarily large quantity of butcher's meat which is consumed. This indulgence in butcher's meat has spread through all ranks of society, from the affluent to the labouring classes. But with this universal taste for meat there has not been an equivalent development in cookery ; and this meat which is dear to buy is not made the most of in the kitchen. The English housewife must not feel offended and wrathful if I preface my remarks by saying that a joint roasted the first day, eaten cold the second, and the remains reappearing the third day as a hash, is neither the most economical nor the most appetising method of using meat. A delicate stomach cannot tolerate that British abomination—a hash made with meat which has been already cooked. No matter how pleasing to the palate it may be made ; it is never acceptable to the stomach and digestive organs. To make the most of meat it should be so prepared that one cooking alone is practicable, even when "hotted," a hash or stew is not so digestible as when fresh. This should be made a primary law in every household.

As the different readers of GOOD WORDS comprise all classes, including those who are all but absolutely ignorant of food and cooking, my remarks must be made so as to bring them within the comprehension of these readers ; and the better-informed readers must excuse me if, in doing so, I appear to insult their intelligence and knowledge ; I have no intention of doing anything of the kind.

My aim here is to point out what combinations of the various constituents of our food are required to supply our body-needs ; to describe how these constituents can be procured in their most economical form, giving the cost price in the West-end of London ; to construct typical dishes, which may be varied in preparation, the main constituents remaining the same ; contrasting their actual "food-value" with their money cost. Such a plan of handling the subject will make it clearer to the reader, and enable him, or rather her, to approach the subject scientifically ; and also to pave the way for medical men and earnest ladies, treating of the subjects of Food, and How to Cook it, at the different local penny readings throughout the country. For further information as to the food value of the different articles, these persons may profitably consult the well-known work of Dr. Pavy, F.R.S., "A Treatise on Food and Dietetics," where they will find the subject treated exhaustively. Dr. Pavy's book is followed in the remarks made here. As to what cookery book they should use to guide them, these books are all much on a par ; when cooks take the pen in hand, they always appear to me to have a quiet dinner party in their eye, rather than the daily demands of an ordinary household.

For the needs of the body a variety of foods is necessary : (1) the albuminoids ; (2) the hydro-carbons ; and (3) the anti-scorbutics. The first are requisite for tissue building and repair ; the second, for body-heat and force ; the third, to prevent disease, especially scurvy.

Albumen is found in a variety of forms, and consists of a complex arrangement of the four main elements, with some sulphur and some salts. Its chemical composition is about as follows :—

C.	H.	N.	O.	S.*
52	7	15·5	21	0·8
to 54	7·3	16·5	23·5	2·0

It is found in the white of egg, in the lean of meat, as caseine in cheese and in legumes, to a less extent in the various cereals, and in other seeds, as nuts. It is required for the formation of the tissues ; but in much less quantity than is usually supposed. It gives what is called "the strength" in food, and many men insist that it is requisite in considerable quantities, in order that they may

* C., carbon ; H., hydrogen ; N., nitrogen ; O., oxygen ; S., sulphur.

be equal to the demands made by toil. There is a certain amount of truth in this; but there is also a large factor of error. Meat does give a sense of energy which is agreeable, especially to the Anglo-Saxon; but the mistake is made of supposing meat alone can furnish this. The Sikhs of North-western Hindostan are forbidden by their religion to eat meat, yet stouter warriors we never met on the battle-field. The Zulus, whose physique has been the admiration of our soldiers in the recent war, live on Indian corn and milk. Can our meat-eating artisans and mill-hands in Lancashire and York-shire compare with either of those races in physique? The pulse food of the Sikh, and the albumen in the milk and in the maize, are quite sufficient for the needs of the body; but it is not likely that our working classes will adopt either dietary.

The hydro-carbons are furnished from the starch of cereals, the potato, and of pulses, having a formula as follows :—

	C.	H.	O
	12	10	10
or sugar—			
	12	11	11

or fat, having the formula of—

	C.	H.	O.
	10	9	

Thus we see that fat contains little or no oxygen, and is a purer hydro-carbon than starch or sugar, and has a higher heat-pro-ducing value. Sugar is made in the body from starch, and is found in the sugar-cane, beet-root, mangolds, turnips, carrots, the banana, &c., and as honey. Fat is formed as animal fat, oil, butter, and is largely con-tained in seeds, as rape-seed, linseed, olives, almonds, cocoa-nuts, &c. They are required for the production of body-heat, muscular energy, and are also essential to healthy tissue formation. Starch and saccharine matters are stored up from each meal in the liver; when taken in excess of the body-needs, the superfluous amount is stored in a permanent form in the body as fat. We make animals do this fat-storing for us on a large scale; which is convenient for us, and constitutes a large factor in our commerce. Our manufacturing hordes draw their food supplies now from all corners of the earth.

Then the third class, or anti-scorbutics, is very essential to health. The older navigators, as Anson and Cook, used to have their crews suffer dreadfully from scurvy in consequence of their dietary not containing vegetables.

Their salt beef and biscuits provided a suffi-ciency of albumen and of hydro-carbons; but did not furnish anti-scorbutics. As soon as vegetables of any kind could be procured, the men soon got well. As anti-scorbutics stand the potato, cabbage, and its congeners, onions, fruits of all kinds, especially limes and lemons, fresh meat, and milk. Ships now all carry lime juice, where they have not unlimited supplies of fresh food. For proper dietaries the anti-scorbutic articles must not be forgotten; though their food value otherwise may be very low.

With such preliminary remarks the reader will understand the different combinations of foods shortly to be given. What constitutes the anti-scorbutic property is not known; it is not the potash salts, nor yet the free acids, for these given alone will not prevent scurvy. The anti-scorbutic property cannot be put in a formula and therefore stands outside the term "food value," which will be applied to albuminoids and hydro-carbons, which have a formula. Most of our dishes contain these elements, as boiled beef, fat and lean, and potatoes, with carrots and turnips. The lean furnishes albuminoids; the fat, the starch of the potato, and the sugar of the carrot and turnip, the hydro-carbons; while the anti-scorbutics are present in the vegetables. But a piece of fat bacon boiled with peas-pud-ding, though possessing a high food value, lacks the anti-scorbutic, and so it is custo-mary to boil a cabbage in the pot with the bacon and the peas. Now at the head of this article stands the word "Economical;" and it is my intention to present to the reader a series of economical dishes, which shall contain all the three requisite ingredients. The food value will be given with each dish; the actual cost to myself of each; and my personal experience as to the attractiveness of each dish. They will be given in the cheapest form for the poorest readers; but they can all be made a little better by those whose purses are somewhat bulkier.

The compounds having the highest "food value" will be found in vegetable albuminoids, and the cheap animal fats of the sheep and pig; anti-scorbutics can be added, which also possess a flavouring value. The cheapest albuminoids are furnished by the legumes, the haricot - bean, the pea, and the lentil. As to the pea it is found as the split-pea, or ground into powder, the "brose meal" of Scotland, and in the form of dried green peas—"the blue boiler." Now let us see how the combination can be made. The dishes will be made for one; of course their relative cost is not increased when more are to be provided for. Haricot-beans cost 6d. a quart; a third of a quart should be put in water the evening before they are to be eaten. The bacon with which these dishes have been tested consisted of part of a Wilt-shire prize pig, price 6½d. a pound. Spanish onions cost from 1½d. to 2d. a pound. Of course in this combination the beans take the place of lean meat, at a higher food value and at less cost. That vegetable albuminoids are more digestible than meat albuminoids is not only my own individual experience—my expe-rience as a physician—but is the experience of others. Sir Henry Thompson, in his excellent and well-known article on "Food and Feed-ing," in the *Nineteenth Century*, last year, said, "By most stomachs, too, haricots are more easily digested than meat is ; and consuming weight for weight, the eater feels lighter and less oppressed as a rule after the leguminous dish, while the comparative cost is very greatly in favour of the former." This is good news for that unfortunate class, "the dyspeptics." To proceed : about half a pound of bacon, cut in strips, and a Spanish onion a pound weight, shredded and added, should be put into a basin. The haricots are put on to boil, and are allowed to boil half an hour, when they are drained and put over the bacon and onions ; then the whole is put into the oven and baked an hour and a half. The mess should be stirred up from time to time, to prevent the beans at the top from becoming dry and hard. When served up, the mess has a most appetising flavour, both to smell and taste. The pepper, salt, and bread amount to 1d. more. Thus we have beans (2d.), bacon (3d.), onions (2d.), and the rest 1d., altogether 8d. ; with enough for two good meals for any workman. This may be considered a typical dish for a very hard working man. For those who dislike onions, a large carrot, shredded or grated, may take the place of the onion. To add a teaspoon-ful of brown sugar to the dish is an im-provement, though the onion is itself sweet.

Another like combination, which is very palatable, is achieved as follows : Put half a pint of dried green peas into water containing a little carbonate of soda, and let them stand over-night, then boil them for half an hour; put half a pound of bacon in slices in a small pie-dish, pour over this the peas, and cook the whole in the oven for three-quarters of an hour, at least. This is a very nice dish, but does not contain anti-scorbutic. In the same way lentils may be used; but to my own individual taste, lentils are not so

good as either the haricot-bean or the dried peas.

A very appetising family dish may be made as follows, where the vegetable albuminoids are used to eke out the meat : half a pint of dried peas at 6d. a quart will furnish as much albuminoids as two pounds of lean meat at 8d. a pound. Put half a pint of peas to soak over-night ; then cut up half a pound of fat mutton from the brisket at 7d. a pound, or even less ; then cut up a large carrot (1d.), and a large turnip (1d.), and a large Spanish onion (1½d.) into pieces the size of dice ; put the whole into a pie-dish in the oven, and cook for an hour and a half. When served up, the dish is excellent, and may be eaten with or without potatoes ; and no housewife need fear a friend taking pot-luck with her when this dish is to come on the table. The "food value" of this dish is also high ; it would scarcely do for very hard work so well as those just given, but it is amply sufficient for ordinary persons. Such, then, are a few typical dishes which can be cooked in the humblest household.

Another dish of high food value can be made as follows. Buy a pound of pork sausage meat, at 10d. a pound, or a piece of pork, pretty fat, and mince it fine at home ; put this in a stewpan with one pound and a half of Spanish onions, chopped small, and a flavour of sage, with some pepper and salt. Stew all thoroughly for an hour and a half, and serve up with potatoes or boiled rice. This is a most appetising dish in cold weather. For those who are fond of pork, the following dish will be found to be agreeable. Take a large cabbage, and remove all the outer green leaves—the green leaves of the cabbage are not suited for the food of man—cut it in four, and put it into a pan and boil for five minutes; then pour the water down the sink at once, for cabbage water is an objectionable thing, which grows more ob-jectionable as it cools. Put the cabbage in a colander to drain, then shred it fine, and with a large Spanish onion, also shredded, put the whole into a stewpan, together with three-quarters of a pound of fat pork, chopped fine, and stew for an hour. This is also a capital cold-weather dish. Vegetarians are fond of this dish, substituting two ounces of butter for the pork. So cooked, cabbage forms an agreeable vegetable to cold meat. Cabbages cost about twopence apiece ; and none but good large cabbages, with a heart the size of a large cocoa-nut, should be used. The cabbage, as ordinarily cooked, is far from an attractive article of food ; plain boiled it is simply loathsome ; but it can be prepared in a manner that renders it very palatable. Cut a large Savoy cabbage in four, boil it ten minutes, then let it drain on a colander, after which it should be chopped up into pieces the size of the thumb-nail, two ounces of butter (2d.), and some salt, and a generous allowance of pepper should be added ; and the whole put back into the stewpan, or into a pie-dish in the oven, and cooked fifteen minutes. So prepared, cabbage is eatable. But cabbages, cauliflowers, Brussels sprouts, spinach, broccoli, endive, leeks, onions, sea-kale, and asparagus possess but a low food value, and are eaten with meat, either to help to fill the stomach, or to make the meal more agreeable. The same holds true of the materials of our summer salads ; salad dressing, however, having a high food value. Eaten with fat meat—by this I mean not fat solely, but fat and lean from a fat animal—these vegetables are useful for their anti-scorbutic qualities.

Another economical preparation of high-food value is made as follows. Put a pound of bacon in a pot with two quarts of water, and a pint and a half of split peas (4½d.), and boil for an hour ; eat the bacon and the peas-pudding together the first day ; next day take the water, add to it the remains of the peas-pudding, and chop up a Spanish onion, or break up two boiled potatoes, and boil up for soup. Then to the cold bacon add a dish of haricots, cooked as follows. Put half a pint of haricots, previously soaked, into a stewpan, chop up an onion, some salt, and boil gently for three hours, as much water only as · is sufficient to cover them. Serve up with the liquor.

As to an economical way of cooking mutton or beef, either is excellent in the form of that good old dish, an Irish stew. But it is better, from the standpoint at present taken up, that the mutton be not taken from the lean neck, but from the fat ribs in front of the loin. If beef be used, the fat brisket is to be preferred. Done with peas, onion, carrot, and turnip, as given above, either mutton or beef can be made into an excellent appetising dish of fair good value, at a very reasonable cost. This seems to leave but a very limited number of dishes at the reader's disposal ; but then it is not the writer's intention (nor the editor's either) to write a complete cookery book ; but rather to point out what are the necessary constituents of a proper meal for the needs of the body, leaving the readers to make such variations as to methods of cooking and serving as seems best unto them. The palate and the stomach both must be consulted, and the latter especially in the case of the dyspeptic. Dyspeptics are apt to meet with derision rather than sympathy ; but it is a serious thing to be a dyspeptic. The dyspeptic is seriously handicapped ; he or she can earn less, and must pay more for food than do those who can digest anything. And if there is one thing more than another —unless it be roast pork and greens—at which a dyspeptic's gastric apparatus rebels, it is a hash made with cold meat.

In a succeeding article, the writer will deal with some other forms of food—combinations which will include a rational mode of cooking cheese, a matter of much importance ; as cheese is cheap, and likely to remain so, and has a high food value.

BLUE GENTIAN: A THOUGHT.

By THE AUTHOR OF "JOHN HALIFAX, GENTLEMAN."

I SHALL never be a child,
　With its dancing footsteps wild,
　　Nor a free-footed maiden any more ,
Yet my heart leaps up to see
The new leaf upon the tree,
And to hear the light winds pass
O'er the flowers in the grass,
　And for very joy brims o'er,
　As I kneel and pluck this store
　　Of blue gentian.

I shall never climb thy peak,
Great white Alp, that cannot speak
　Of the centuries that float over thee like dreams,
Dumb of all God's secret things
Sealed to beggars and to kings—

Yet I sit in a world of sight,
Colour, beauty, sound, and light,
　While at every step, meseems,
　Small sweet joys spring up, like gleams
　　Of blue gentian.

I shall not live o'er again
This strange life, half bliss, half pain ;
　I shall sleep till THOU call'st me to arise,
Body and soul, with new-born powers.
If Thou wakenest these poor flowers,
Wilt Thou not awaken me,
Who am thirsting after Thee ?
　Ah ! when faith grows dim and dies,
　Let me think of Alpine skies
　　And blue gentian.

SPLUGEN, *June*, 1879.

The Dyke Ferry.

HOLLAND.

PART I.

Flushing Stadthaus.

GREAT is the respect due, and most
deservedly so, to the man who by
steady perseverance and self-denial raises
himself from the humblest position, till he
finally benefits all around him, and leaves a
name behind him which stands forth in
history as a beacon to guide those who
come after him, and encourages them to
follow his noble example. Such, in a
national sense, may be said of Holland.
How humble her origin—a mere swamp;
the delta of the Rhine, buffeted by the
German Ocean on the west, deluged by the
Rhine and Scheldt on the east—and yet how
grand a result shines forth in the seventeenth
century, when William the Silent had completed his great work, and De Ruyter and
Van Tromp swept over the sea with a broom
at the mast-head! Holland is full of interest,
and especially to Englishmen, although the
description of it occupies but a small space
in Murray's Handbook. Even in the present
day it remains a mine of wealth to the historian, the archæologist, the painter, and the
true lover of the picturesque. We are indebted to Julius Cæsar for the earliest
mention of this remarkable country, frequently called "Verdronkenland," or the
drowned land. Never was there a more
characteristic motto than that of "Luctor et
Emergo," under a lion swimming. Tacitus
did not consider the persevering and drenched
people beneath his notice.

Shakespeare mentions the Nervii, and Virgil
brings in the two-horned Rhine, which we
shall have to describe later on. Inundated
by ocean and river, the vast swamp seems
hardly the birthplace of a powerful nation.
The first foothold was to raise *Zerpen*, or
mounds—a few still remain, and one is

shown in the tailpiece of this article ; their object being for the inhabitants to rush to in case of sudden deluge. Next comes the dyke process, which has gradually developed into a vast national system and education, culminating in the Water Staat, or Corporation or College of Water Engineers : this had made the country, and sustains its existence.

The whole Dutch life has been one of continuous and well-sustained struggle : first against the elements, for existence ; secondly, against the furious despotism of religious oppression. Both of these Holland has survived and overcome, and, by God's blessing, she now rests in peace. We must not be carried away by our admiration of her, and rest too long on a subject which Motley, in his admirable book, "The Rise of the Dutch Republic," has done such justice to. Let us now visit her as she is, peaceful and plodding. First to the Island of Walcheren, the southern extremity of Holland ; the scene of the Anglo-Saxon Willibrod's efforts to introduce Christianity in 800, *circum*, when he destroyed the images of Woden and abolished his worship.

We first land at Flushing, or Vlissengen, which is the seaport of Walcheren, or Zealand, and famous for the first flame of liberty that burst out in connection with Brill on the opposite bank, situated on the north bank, at the entrance to the Scheldt, a town suggesting melancholy association to the Englishman, as during the unfortunate Walcheren expedition in 1808, 7,000 of his countrymen were victimised in a few months to fever. No wonder that fever was one of the earliest subjects mentioned on our arrival. The Dutch name for it is *koorts*. Having letters to the Consul, we immediately waited upon him, and found him at home. When ushered into his presence, we found an old gentleman seated in a high-backed chair, with black velvet cap, dressing-gown, both arms leaning on the table, both hands wrapped in cotton wool ; a painful expression pervaded his features. Behind his chair, over the mantelpiece, was the coat-of-arms of Holland, with the English and Dutch flags pendant behind them. " Good morning, gentlemen ; have you yet had the fever ? " Having arrived at 6 A.M., and it being then nine, the answer was, " Not as yet." " Then you must have the fever, sir, before leaving the island. Do you know what the fever is? I will tell you. First you shall be for three days so hot that you never can get cold ; and then, sir, for three days you shall be so cold that you shall never be hot. I am now in the cold state." A little cheerful conversation

seemed, however, not only to warm but melt the Consul. He told of much that was to be seen in Flushing, and was full of De Ruyter, who was born there, and served his time in a rope-yard, the machine he worked at being still preserved. Then the Consul held forth on the

Young Smokers.

daring spirit of the future Dutch admiral, how he climbed up to the top of the spire of the church in the town, and could not get down again for a long time, and naturally reminded us of the successful close of his career—referring, of course, to his visit to England.

The first thing that struck us was the prevailing smell of peat smoke ; walking along the quays, the delicious perfume came up from the vessels, and constantly we met people selling their turf in the street, and singing in a kind of Gregorian chant, " Wat sen mooye turreven zestien vooreen dubbeltje," " What beautiful turfs, sixteen for twopence."

The Consul's instructions were carefully carried out. The pilot-boats were visited ; the De Ruyter relics also ; the carillons interested us greatly, as the chimes were very good, and manufactured at Delft in 1683 A.D. The hours and quarters are played by clock-work, and the bells can be free handled when required and played by levers, which are struck down by the clenched fist, much power being required ; and the performer can hear how the bells are going by placing his ear near the pipe on the right hand. Besides the carillonneur there is another important man in the steeple, the tower " Watcher," who blows a horn at 10, 11, and 12 o'clock, and gives alarm in case of fire, and sounds his horn when there are signs of thunderstorms. The Dutch are great in all kinds of "Wachter," or watch-men; below, in the streets, are "klapper-men," with wooden "klappers," to frighten thieves, and call out the weather and hour of the night; their general cry is, "Ten of the clock, still, still, still." The Germans were considered smokers, but the Dutch boys are incorrigible; the illustration is matter-of-fact, and true.

The Consul was anxious that we should go down to see the pilots go off at the entrance of the Scheldt. The north side is Flushing, and by some amiable treaty the Belgian pilots are allowed to start from Flush-ing to take up vessels going to Antwerp. The result of this is, that directly a vessel comes

Shooting at the Gaal.

inside the bar off start two pilot boats, the Dutch with a red flag and the Belgian with a blue flag, and the races which ensue—espe-cially in bad weather—are most interesting.

We next started to see the town, under the guidance of a young naval cadet, nephew of Mr. Enkhuysen. Before starting we found that in Holland juniors are kept well in their place, although they may be in the navy. The Consul has sent for his nephew to escort us. The nephew, in the presence of his uncle, was very taciturn. When the Madeira was passed round, the kindly old gentleman said, in a stentorian voice, "Wilhelm, you may have a glass of wine." Wilhelm received it modestly and with considerable satisfaction; and when he had received his final instructions, carried away by his uncle's unusual kindness, said, "And I will show the gentlemen the Roman Catholic Church."

"No, sir, you will not," was the immediate and official reply. "Do you suppose these gentlemen would condescend to look at a Roman Catholic Church? No, sir, never."

But we did afterwards, and were well rewarded, particularly by seeing the flood marks :—

Mark in Oude Kirke.

Vaterfloed 4 feet from floor, Jan. 15, 1808.
    ,,   2 feet   ,,   Jan. 26, 1689.

Wilhelm was an agreeable and instructive cicerone. He took us to see the old dockyard, sad and deserted, empty and forlorn ; the hopes of the town, which once belonged to Queen Elizabeth, and had been the great naval arsenal of Holland in the south, seemed now to live on the hope that it would be used as a point of debarkation for a line of steamers from England; and there seemed a rumour that the Americans had made an offer for the dockyard as a naval station in Europe. The line of steamers have been successfully started. The idea of Flushing as an American naval station has not been matured. The city has some of those trade signs for which Holland is well known ; one particularly struck us, that of a timber merchant—a piece of carving painted in vivid colours, representing Joseph as a Carpenter, with the words, "Jozeph was een Timmerman, 1623," and one of the shells thrown by the English fleet still remains sticking in a wall, with a Dutch inscription underneath. Our naval cadet told us of a very interesting custom held once a year in the neighbourhood, and hoped we would go and visit the chief man in the village, who was farmer, landed proprietor, butter-merchant, and magistrate, in fact, quite a character ; especially as a letter of introduction would elicit much information which was sure to interest us. We started at once armed with a letter of introduction. Sourburg is the name of the village, Ritthem the name of the parish, Abele the name of the farmer. The farmers are addressed here by the name of "Baas," their wives "Bazena." The word "Baas" is most likely the derivation of the word "Bos," used in America for the chief man or leading character; at the Cape it is used in that sense also.

We found him at home dressed in Zeeland costume, which consists of black suit, short jacket, large gold buttons for the neck of the

The Drummer.

shirt, tall hat almost rimless, knee-breeches, with two large buttons of silver holding the waistband together, smaller buttons to secure the flap; a silver knife is carried in a special pocket by the side of the seam ; silver watch-chain, flat, about an inch wide, and pendant from the fob, silver knee and shoe buckles, a clean-shaven face, the hair cut square across the forehead.

On our arrival he was going to look after his churning, which is carried on by the unusual process of dog-power. A large mastiff runs round inside a vertical wheel ten feet wide, and this power is sufficient for butter-making. It was with much pride that our host described how he had sent butter to the King, and when we asked him to favour us with his autograph, the solemnity with which he wrote it, after great preparation and many precautions, was truly amusing. He lit up brilliantly at the mention of the Kermesse, or fête, in the spring about the end of April, and gave a long description of riding at the ring with lances on horseback, also running on foot with lances for the same object ; and his good wife, the "Bazena," joined heartily in the invitation to be sure and come in the following spring, accompanying it with renewed tumblers of *melk en persico*—milk with

Old House, Flushing.

such old guns, the marvel is they ever hit anything they really aim at—still more surprising that they never burst; old flint-guns, some obsolete military pattern, some shot-guns, used for ball, with little powder, from a conviction of their weakness. One altered to percussion was evidently considered an innovation and foppish. Having seen the implements, let us inspect the little crowd. Close by is, of course, a booth erected, where Schnapps, Schiedam, Persico, or aniseed and milk, can be obtained. The farmers' wives are all in costume, so neat and clean, with old silver ornaments; no second-hand worn-out finery, everything real, solid, and good, intended to wear well and long; no shoddy or transient gloss that will fly at the first shower. The most important man seemed to be the drummer, whose duty it is to beat directly the bird is struck, and then he gives way heartily, and vents his feelings and pent-up energy in a prolonged roll. The peasants were very kindly, and seemed gratified that we took so much interest in their festivities. After the shooting I sent for the drummer to make a sketch of him. He sent the drum with a boy, but it was the drummer himself that I wanted, and his earnest gaze. At last he came, and the gaze was elicited thus. I had noticed that he smoked. I therefore got him into position and gave him a cigar; pointing to another cigar nailed up to the ceiling, I explained to him that if he would keep his eye fixed on that he should have it when he had smoked the one then in his mouth. To this he replied "Mooje," or beautiful, and stood like a statue whilst I endeavoured to sketch him. The whole thing seemed as if we had woke up in the seventeenth century.   R. T. PRITCHETT.

aniseed in it. Good people they were, and sorry we were to say adieu.

What a novelty to rise in the morning and think that after breakfast we are going to see an old Dutch fête, shooting at the "Popin-jay," or, as they call it, "Shooting op de Gaai," or "La Perche"! A tall pole is raised with an iron top to prevent its being shot away. This top is branched for stuffed birds to be placed on at fêtes; a second pole is erected for shooting at the man with the nose or "Neus." And now what a scene awaits us! First let us mention that the competitors fire with ball lying on their backs; but the variety of implements used is astonishing—

The *Zerp*, or Mound, near Oost Kapelle.

SUNDAYS IN MANY LANDS.

By JAMES CAMERON LEES, D.D.

I.—IN "HOLY RUSSIA."

WE had spent some days in Moscow—days of hard work, for sight-seeing is very hard work; we had wandered from morning to night through the city—had explored its wonders, examined its bazaars, drank tea to the music of the usual barrel-organ in its most famous *traktirs*, gone to the top of its highest towers, visited the Foundling Hospital, ascended the Sparrow Hills where the French got their first view of Moscow—the "golden clasp," as Napoleon called it, "between east and west"—and stood under the grand triumphal arch which spans the road by which they commenced their famous retreat. All these things and many more had we seen, and very tired and weary men were we, when the first day of the week, with all its blessed associations, dawned upon us.

Sunday morning was warm and full of sunshine, and when we looked out of our window shortly after daylight, we saw the streets crowded with a gaily dressed throng, clearly bent on church. Innumerable bells were ringing from the domes of church and monastery—sweet-toned, silvery bells. The Russian Church is famous for its bells, none in the world are greater in size, and none purer in tone. "Let us," said my companion in travel, a Celt of the best quality and my comrade in many wanderings, "go to the Kremlin," and to the Kremlin we went, moving slowly along in the mighty human stream flowing in the same direction with ourselves.

The Kremlin is the heart of Moscow, as Moscow is the heart of Russia, and is looked upon by every Russian as one of the great wonders of the world. It is the Jerusalem of the Muscovite. It forms a quarter of the city, and is built upon one of the seven hills on which Moscow, like Rome, stands. The summit of this hill is of triangular shape, and round its base on two sides flows the sluggish river Mosqua. The buildings of the Kremlin, which literally means fortress, cover two square miles of ground, and comprise many cathedrals, churches, and monasteries. The palace, the arsenal, the senate-house, the office of the Holy Synod, and various other buildings are also situated within the walls by which the Kremlin is surrounded, and over them all rises the great octagonal tower of Ivan Veliki, 269 feet high, surmounted by a large golden cross, which flashes brilliantly in the sunlight. We entered the Kremlin by one of the most conspicuous of its portals—the Spaski Vorota, or Gate of the Redeemer. It is so called from having placed upon it a picture of Christ, called the *Redeemer of Smolensk*, which was borne at the head of Bojarski's army in his Polish campaign. This picture is regarded by the Russians as specially sacred. Artistically speaking it does not inspire reverence, but no one is allowed to pass under it without taking off his hat, and a soldier watches by, bayonet in hand, to see that this mark of respect is paid. Rigid Presbyterians though we were, children of the Covenant and the Westminster Confession and other respectable ancestry, the sight of this sharp instrument made us quickly uncover, and we passed bareheaded as the most orthodox member of the Greek Church into the inclosure of the Kremlin. We trust this frank confession of our conformity may induce the authorities at home to let us off with a mild censure. Had the Moderator of the General Assembly of the Church of Scotland, or even the Primate of All England, been in our place, we are fully persuaded he would have uncovered as quickly as we did when he looked upon the swarthy face of the watchful Cossack, and felt in imagination the point of his cold steel in the region of the spine. It was a fine chance of martyrdom, however, which we, perhaps, should not have lost.

We had come to church, and here in our view were three famous cathedrals, each of them thronged with worshippers, who went in and out like a swarm of bees round a hive on a summer day—three notable temples, those of the Assumption, of the Archangel, and of the Annunciation. We stood in the great square deliberating to which of them we should go. We had explored them pretty thoroughly during the week, and had got up from our guide books all their wonderful associations. Yes,—they are suggestive enough. In one of them the Czars are buried, at least the earlier Czars are; in another they are baptized; and in the third they are crowned, or rather they crown themselves, first reading aloud on their knees the orthodox creed, and then taking the crown with their own hands from off the altar, and putting it on their heads. Our indecision as to where we should bend our steps was broken by the voice of a Yankee friend. We had met him everywhere. We had heard him again and again repeat the same speech to every Russian who could understand him : " My country and yours are to be the countries of the future." How often he told us that he was "a lineal descendant" of the celebrated theologian Timothy Dwight ! It was like a patent of nobility apparently to him. Probably some of my readers may never have even heard of this theological Timothy. "I've been," said this youth, pointing to the Cathedral of the Archangel with his " Harper's Guidebook," " to see Old Ivan, and now I'm going in here," with a patronising nod to the Cathedral of the Assumption, " where I'm told there's a great fandango going on." This "old Ivan" of whom he spoke was no less a person than the famous " Ivan the Terrible " of Russian history, the most cruel of a cruel race— certainly not a loveable personage in any way.

We had seen the iron-shod walking-stick with which in his rage he would pin to the ground any messenger who brought him evil tidings. We had stood in the box, like a summer-house in the Kremlin wall, from which he viewed the constant executions that took place in the square below, and from which, infuriated by the sight of blood, he would rush down, hatchet in hand, and hew and hack the bodies of his victims ; we had explored the Church of St. Blagennoi, built by him to the memory of a hermit, who used to come naked into the monarch's feasts and reprove him for his crimes, and whom in a passion he had put to death. This terrific potentate lies in the Archangel Cathedral, with a pall over his tomb to show that he died a. monk ; and here we have a flippant Yankee poking fun at him and calling him " Old Ivan." Truly death is a great leveller.

We followed this flippant youth into the Cathedral of the Assumption. He screwed a glass tight into his eye, and looked around with the *nonchalance* of a citizen of the world. The church was full. All classes were there. Rough-bearded drosky drivers, meek-looking tea-sellers, gentlemen of high rank, corpulent merchants, people in rags, people in broad-cloth, people in sheepskins, officers, soldiers, peasants, water-carriers, neatly dressed ladies, women in rough homespun—all on the same level, for the Greek Church knows no dis-

tinctions. There was no pew for the man with the gold ring ; indeed, there was no pew at all, beggar and noble stood there side by side, looking towards the altar, bowing lowly and crossing themselves mightily. There was a fine smell of incense—much needed, I should say, in the inodorous, packed crowd, and a blaze of lights, and many pictures covered with jewels, that sparkled brightly in the semi-darkness. The Russian Church makes as to the latter a fine distinction, she allows no images into her temples, but places no restriction on pictures. Sacred pictures or *icons* are everywhere. They are in the corner of every room, no pious Russian travels without one among his belongings. The making of them is a great trade, and in a restaurant the waiter, as he glides along with his pile of dishes, always stops before the icon to cross himself. Many famous and even wonder-working pictures are in this church. Every pillar is covered with them, and the fine spacious domes are magnificently frescoed. Here also is the celebrated Virgin of Vladimir, painted, so says the Church, by Luke the Evangelist. This must be worth seeing, so we edge ourselves into its neighbourhood, and in the process I am afraid nudge some devout persons. We saw a figure with a black face, literally covered with precious stones, rubies, emeralds, pearls, diamonds. The whole of these precious stones are valued at 200,000 roubles.

What a haul for an unorthodox thief ! Great, truly, are the riches of this church. Here is a tabernacle representing Moses receiving the Tables of the Law ; it contains nineteen pounds weight of gold and twenty of silver. One silver lustre alone weighs about eight hundred pounds ! The lineal descendant of Timothy Dwight, as he fixes his eye-glass on these splendours, allows that there is nothing like them even in his own country, and my matter-of-fact companion whispers that one of these precious stones would be sufficient to build and endow a church, a notion which at that time exercised him greatly.

But let us leave these vanities and look about us. Here round the church are the tombs of the Patriarchs of Moscow. There, where the woman with the shawl over her head is devoutly praying, is the resting-place of the Patriarch Jonas, a good man, and to be held in reverence. Napoleon ordered his coffin to be opened, to see whether the body of the saint was really uncorrupted, but the old patriarch shook his forefinger at him, and the warrior retreated in dismay! And here in this chapel is the sarcophagus of the great Philip, the Metropolitan, murdered by Ivan the Terrible; you can see his skull through a glass window in his coffin, but his body, like that of Jonas, is as fresh as the day it was buried, so say the faithful. There is a good deal of strain put on faith in this as in some other countries.

What sweet singing this is that comes from a divided choir of men, who stand on each side of the altar-screen and alternately chant the responses! Wonderful are some of the voices of these monastic-looking young persons in black cassocks and with long tangled locks, that seem sadly in need of a barber. There is no organ allowed in the Greek Church. The great Emperor Nicholas sought to introduce one into this very cathedral, but the Metropolitan, the devout and blessed Philaret, resisted the innovation with all the energy shown by some Scotch divines. The mighty Czar had to submit. The Scotch divines have had to give in gracefully, but no "kist of whistles" has found its way into the Russian temples. Let us, therefore, give all due respect to the bold Philaret.

A Greek church, as my readers probably know, is divided into two parts, or rather a screen called the iconostasis cuts off a portion of it at the eastern end. In this screen are three doors. Behind one is the sacristy, or robing chamber. Behind another the credence table, where the sacramental elements are prepared. Behind the centre door stands the high altar. This screen is generally profusely decorated, and behind it a great part of the service is performed, the priest being out of sight of the people.

There are times in the service when the centre or golden door opens and the priest comes forth from the Holy of Holies, as this hidden portion of the church is called. He comes out to read the Gospel, and to give the Sacrament to the people. The service is conducted not in Russian but in the old Sclavonic. The people do not understand it, but have a general idea what the different parts signify, and so follow as best they can.

There are no pulpits in the Greek church, and consequently no sleepers; no worshipper seems to be under the impression that he is in a public dormitory. All the congregation appeared very devout. Whether they were so in reality it is not for me to say. Just look at this poor old broken-down Mujik, with his long hair and matted beard, and ragged clothes girt about by a greasy red girdle. I try to count how often within a certain space of time he cries "Gospodi, pomlimsa! Gospodi, pomlui!" "Lord, we pray thee! Lord, have mercy on us!" but have to give up the attempt. Poor old Mujik! it is a prayer that very much resembles one said in the temple at Jerusalem long ago, and which was commended by One whom you and I both, I trust, love and revere in our own way. I don't know much about your worship, and I dare say if you were in my church you would make but very little of mine, but I can at least join in this prayer of yours. "Gospodi, pomlui!" sings forth the choir, and "Gospodi, pomlui!" croaks the old Mujik, and "Gospodi, pomlui!" say two sturdy Protestants from Scotland who happened to be by at the time, and who have not yet become ashamed of their conduct.

The whole service had a certain wild barbaric air about it. The priest's vestments were resplendent beyond description. No Anglican ritualist could ever hope to rival him as he stood there at the golden gate with his deacon, also richly clad, beside him, wearing his stocharion, and his epinanikia, epitrachelion, and phaelonion, each of which pieces of vestment symbolizes some great mystery. In one hand he carried a large jewelled copy of the Gospels, and raised the other to bless the congregation. He was a fine benevolent-looking white-bearded old man. We thought he sent his blessing specially in our direction, but happening to look behind us we saw the abominable American coolly taking a sketch of him, which artistic effort probably attracted the attention of the good man.

Let me say here that my companion and myself received every courtesy from the Russian clergy and people, when we visited their churches. They welcome any Protestant, and will even give him the "kiss of peace," should he care to take it, which it is more than probable he will not. Roman Catholics they treat with theological hatred, a species of aversion which neither in the Greek, or the Anglican, or the Scotch, or in any other Church, is apparently regarded as particularly sinful.

To most strangers there seems very little difference between Orthodox Greek and Roman Catholic, but they do not think so themselves. The Greek gives the Sacrament in both kinds to the people, uses no instrumental music, forbids images, and allows only pictures in the churches. These are the principal points of difference between the two communions. In Russia the Church allows the circulation of the Bible, and this may yet have results of a beneficial character; indeed, I have been told that in many peasants' houses the Bible is regularly read with the approbation of the clergy, but if I may judge from what I saw of the peasantry, no literature, sacred or secular, can be much in their way, and a bottle of gin comes more handy to them than àny book. No Church has a greater hold outwardly of its people than the Russian. Its blessing is asked on every circumstance of life. If a man builds a house, changes his dwelling, launches a ship, starts on a journey, opens a shop, or does anything of a special character, the priest has to be sent for to read a particular service, and receive a particular fee.

What the spiritual result of all the organization of this great Church is I am unable to estimate; but I fear, from what was told me by people well able to form an opinion, that the religious life of the Russian Church is at a very low ebb. I hope they are wrong. The clergy are of two descriptions. The black clergy or monks, and the white clergy or parish priests. All the highest offices in the Church are filled from the ranks of the black clergy, and many of the dignitaries are eminent both for learning and piety. The common parish priest is little above the rank of a peasant, and is generally as fond of strong drink as any of his parishioners, which is saying a great deal.

But the priest and his deacon have gone into the sacristy, and the long service is over. The crowd go out to amuse themselves for the rest of the day, and with a curious feeling we pass from the candle-lit church out into the bright sunshine; very sweet and fresh seemed the pure air after the incense-laden atmosphere. Ere we leave the Kremlin we sit on the battlements, and silently look down upon the wonderful view. None that we have seen in our roaming to and fro is more striking, not that from the Prophet's Seat at Damascus, nor that from the Mount of Olives, nor that from the Pincian at Rome, nor even that from the Alhambra at Granada. Below us lay the great oriental-looking city, with its thousand domes, its coloured roofs, and green gardens, winding river, and the great flat plain stretching away as far as the eye could reach. . It was a grand view, one we were never tired of going to gaze upon. But our thoughts as we sat there that Sunday morning were very full of the strange scene we had just witnessed in the great cathedral. How different from what was going on in our far-away homes! What a mighty Church this Greek Church is, numbering one hundred million souls, "extending," as an admirer has said, "from the sea of Okhosk to the palaces of Venice, from the ice fields that grind against the Slovetsky monastery to the burning jungles ot Malabar, embracing a thousand languages, and nations, and tongues." * We speak at home of the greatness of the Church of Rome, but here is a greater still; if the one be anti-Christ, as many at home call it, what of the other? "The wind," sayeth One, "bloweth as it listeth, thou hearest the sound thereof, and canst not tell whence it cometh or whither it goeth." It blows a thousand ways. "There are diversities of gifts, but the same spirit. There are differences of administrations, but the same Lord." These good old texts seem to apply here; at least I think I see an application. They strike at the root of a good many bigotries both of home and foreign growth. . . . "That was a good prayer that they had in there whatever," said my Highland friend, breaking our silence with his honest Celtic voice. "It sounds very like the Gaelic, 'Gospodi, pomlui! Gospodi, pomlui!'" "Amen," said I.

---

* Neale's "Holy Eastern Church."

THE RABBIT AND THE TEAL.

(From the French.)

IN Friendship close and fair
   Once lived a happy pair:
A Rabbit and a Teal,
   Who sought each other's weal.
On the border of a park, with a streamlet by its side,
The Rabbit had its burrow, and at morn and eventide
The friends full often met, choosing now the water's edge,
Or finding sheltered corner 'mid the rustling foliage.

There, taking their repose they would talk of many things,
Repeating what they loved the most. which deepest pleasure brings.
All things they held in common : loss and sorrow, joy and pain ,
They shared, and by the sharing each a double joy did gain.
Such the life they lived, till one day—Oh, day of sorrow dire !
When the Rabbit came to dinner at the Teal's express desire,
He found the chamber empty, and in agony he cried :
But to his dolorous callings all answer was denied.
      Completely stunned with fright,
      He was a piteous sight,
Running here and there, and turning oft times amid the reeds ;
It might have seemed he wholly lacked a method in his deeds ;
And when he came to water's edge, he would have plunged in,
If with strength and life he could have hoped the other shore to win,
And find his friend, but suddenly with impulse sharp he ran
Along the marshy water's edge, each wonted nook to scan.
"O dear companion, sister," he fervently appealed,
" I would that I might see thee, though then my eyes were sealed ;
Far rather I would die than know that thou art suffering now.
I tremble sadly for thy fate : a pain is in my brow."
      At last, in all its grace,
      Rose the Château of the place,
      Before him as he stood
      In melancholy mood,
Not knowing how to turn, or what pathway to prefer,
As he found himself in midst of a beautiful parterre.
      Looking round him very wary,
      He espied an aviary,
Where a thousand birds disported o'er a basin bright and gay,
And, Love imparting courage, to the grating he made way.
      He looked and recognised—
      Oh, the friendship that he prized—
His sister Teal, and suddenly he raised a cry of joy.
But better methods also he was ready to employ :
His four feet setting vigorously to earth without delay,
To join his friend by hollowing out a subterranean way.
Soon by this path he entered without a scratch or scar,
Like to some skilful miner taking armed place of war.
      The birds, all frightened, pressed and flew
      To see a face so strange and new !
But soon the Teal was led to the entrance of the way,
And by help of careful feeling was quickly led to day,
      And to share all freedom's treasure :
      He was like to die for pleasure !
      What a moment for the friends !
Who, deeming all was safe, to themselves would make amends
      For the grief that both had known
      In a confab all alone.
But angry was the master when he became aware
Of the sad destruction wrought upon his aviary fair.
He cried, "My guns and ferrets, have them ready quick, and come ! "
And dogs and keepers marchèd out, as if to tuck of drum ;
The terriers following after through the brushwood filled the train,
And all the rabbits that appeared did die in throes of pain.
That day the banks of Styx by their manes was bordered thick :
But the master of his massacre was very far from sick,
      And fixed to-morrow morning afresh the war to wage
      Against the wretched rabbits, and to finish the carnage !
Our Rabbit trembling waited, all through this dreary while
Cowering 'mid the thick-set reeds, close by his friend, the Teal ;
Imploring that his sister should fly to the other shore
Should he be stricken mortally or wounded her before.

"I will not leave thee ever," said the faithful sister Teal;
"Death only shall divide us, my words with life I'll seal!
Ah, if thou wert but able to cross the stream; but stay!
I think that I am equal to find for thee a way!"
She quickly left. The Rabbit stood, more wildly beat his breast;
The Teal returnèd shortly, dragging after her a nest;
With the stems of reeds made stronger for the work it was to do,
Pressed and pierced by feet and beak, rough woven through and through:
      A little boat in state
        To support a heavy weight:
And to the tiny vessel a rope of rush she bound
For a cable thus to drag her through the water safe and sound.
      And when the little boat
        By the Teal was set afloat,
The Rabbit entered gently and sat him down with ease,
Whilst before him swam the Teal, drawing on by slow degrees,
And directing very skilfully the skiff to him so dear.
At last they cross and, landing, throw off all thoughts of fear,
And they found at little distance a much-desired retreat;
Where happily they dwelt for years alike in cold and heat,
And the joys of life were doubled thro' the sorrows undergone,
For in the deepest heart and soul the friends were truly one.
                        A. H. J.

SARAH DE BERENGER.

By JEAN INGELOW.

CHAPTER I.

"THEN where is that woman now, Mrs. Snep?" asked the curate.

"Well, sir, half-way to the town by this time, I should judge."

Mrs. Snep had a very large wash-tub before her, and was using it with energy in the very small kitchen of a whitewashed cottage. Such a pretty little one-storied abode; so rural, so smothered in greenery. Too much so, indeed, for it stood with its back to a great hop-garden, and the long lines of hop poles terminating against its wall rose as high as the thatch of the roof, so that all the view obtained out of the kitchen casement was down one long overarched lane of hop-bines, under which the softened light appeared to be endowed with both colour and quietness, it was so strangely green and still.

The curate glanced rather helplessly into that shadowy lane. He wished he was a good way down it.

There was something trenchant, capable, and rather defiant about the words and fashions of the cottager's wife. The curate was afraid of her.

Young curates often are afraid, and blush under the eyes of such women. We do not half enough consider their difficulties and their fears, specially that fear of making themselves ridiculous, which, perhaps, under the circumstances, this particular young curate felt just then with all the reason in the world.

However, he made up his mind to do his duty. To that end he said, "Considering how weak she was when I saw her yesterday, poor thing, and how very young her infant is" ("Eleven days old come nine o'clock this evening," Mrs. Snep put in as a parenthesis), "I think her getting as far as the town to-day," he went on, "must be quite impossible."

Mrs. Snep, as he spoke, moved towards the fire. "You'll excuse me, sir"—meaning, "You'll please to get up."

"Oh, certainly," he exclaimed, rising, for the place was so small that unless he made way she could not pass; and she took a large iron pot of boiling water from the fire and emptied it over her cooling suds, before she addressed herself to the task of making him any direct answer.

Then, having set the iron pot on her stone

XXI—3.

threshold, as if on purpose that in his exit he might knock it over, she ensconced herself behind the mounting clouds of steam, and while energetically rubbing and wringing, said with an air of calm superiority—

"It ain't to be expected, sir, as you should know much about these here things. Not at present. But if you was to ask your ma, she would tell you that poor folks can no ways afford to cocker themselves up as lying-in ladies do. When my oldest was eleven days old I took him on one arm and his father's basket of dinner on t'other, and off to the field with 'em, thinking it no hardship neither. But your knowing the ways of poor folk, let alone the ways of tramps such as she, is not, as I said, at all to be expected."

The curate felt annihilated. She had got the better of him not so much by pointing out his inexperience, as by the use of those words "your ma."

He was young enough to feel keenly ashamed of his youth. She made him feel ignominiously young just then. He actually envied her superior age; and the fulness of her knowledge raised in his mind something like a wholesome fear.

She had, however, intended to express civility. That a man so young should have been placed over her head as a spiritual guide, when he knew no more about sickness than he did about washing, or, indeed, about many of the other most important and familiar experiences of her life, was a thing at once ridiculous and aggravating; but not the less would she acknowledge that he was a gentleman. Common men had mothers, and were thankful for them, but the delicate-handed woman who had brought him up was worthy of a finer name, so she gave it (as she thought), and politely called her "your ma."

"She's a tramp, sir," proceeded Mrs. Snep; "and in my opinion no better than she should be, though some folks (kind-hearted, if I say it) took pity on her in her trouble, and brought her in."

"And were paid for it, I suppose," observed the curate; for the trodden worm will turn; and she had made him smart, and knew it.

"Yes, sir," she answered, with a solemnity most impressive. "I should hope I know better than to throw money into the dirt, away from my own poor husband and children. She paid me, but little enough it were; and glad I were to see the back of her when she went away of her own free will—of her own free will—at ten o'clock this blessed morning."

"Did you show her the path to the road, the road to G——?" inquired the young man.

Mrs. Snep gave an energetic wrench to a much-twisted swathe of linen, then shook a snowy drift of foam from her hand with a contemptuous action, as if she was thinking of her late lodger, and made answer—

"No, we'd had words, and I took not to say any particular notice on her when she walked herself off. But she did say, 'Mrs. Snep, you've been a good friend to me, and I ask your pardon if I've offended you, for,' she says, 'I didn't ought to have said it. I've counted over my things now, and I'll allow you're as honest as the day.'"

"As honest as the day," she presently repeated, for she saw that this speech, which was entirely of her own invention, had impressed the curate very much.

But not as she had intended. "I always thought you were robbing that poor thing," was his mental comment on it, "and now I am sure."

"Well, good morning, Mrs. Snep," he exclaimed, forming a sudden resolution. Between his zeal and his discomfiture, he failed to notice the iron pot, which, dashing through the door, he overturned upon a fresh clump of white pinks, blacking them and his own legs, and being obliged to submit to the loan of a duster to wipe them. "I always have to leave that woman with an apology," he exclaimed, as he began to stride along the path towards the town.

He did not find the woman—naturally he did not—though he walked all the way to the town, for he had been right in his belief, and Mrs. Snep wilfully wrong. The woman could only walk a very little way. It was a sultry morning. She was very weak; a little child not two years old dragged upon her gown; she had her infant on her arm, and from it depended a bundle. She had been excited and angry, so that she trembled, and her little strength soon giving way, she turned off the dusty road to court the shade of the hop-garden, skirting it till she reached the end, and intending to enter the road again.

And so it came about that when the curate passed, this woman was still in the hop-garden, within fifty yards of him. Instead of turning to the left and regaining the road, she had taken the path to the right, and after wistfully gazing up some of the narrow bowers of fragrant bines, had crept into the shelter of one of them, all cool and shaded and still; there, propped up by the hop-poles, she wept, at first with a sick heart, but presently she found admittance to the enchanted valley of slumber; and if, instead of that, it had been the lost Eden, secret since our first mother's fault, she could hardly have shown a face of more supreme content.

"Oh, how common, but oh, how sweet is sleep!"

She was tall, dark-haired, and thin. One hand, which was rather pale than white, touched with protective care the head of her little two-years-old girl, who, curled up on the skirts of her gown, slept more soundly than herself; the other was spread over her young infant, whose meaningless blue eyes stared up from its mother's lap into the space of sky overhead.

Her possessions were but the clothes she wore—a cotton gown, a flimsy shawl, her small bundle, a little paper parcel of bacon and bread, an almost empty purse, these two infants over whom her heart yearned with unutterable love and despair, and nothing else at all except the wedding-ring—that was conspicuous enough on her honest, labour-hardened hand, and was the symbol of as bad a bargain as ever was made.

She had not lost a good husband by death, but had to mourn a bad one yet in life—a mean and cruel fellow, who from the moment she married him had let her see his contempt for the foolish passion that, spite of warnings, had dared to waste itself on him. She was free of him now for awhile, free from this object of her once impassioned love, and now of her fear and shame. He had been arrested for a robbery with violence, convicted, and sentenced to penal servitude for fourteen years. She had been very foolish, but to know that was no element of consolation.

Her story in brief was this. She had in her early days been employed by a young invalid lady as reader, and when old enough had entered her service. The lady had taken some pains to improve her; the books, also, that she read had enriched her mind; insensibly she had become different, softened. She had a natural love of beauty and harmony; her light tasks and delicate surroundings fostered it.

The rough children she had played with, and her vulgar relatives, became daily more unlike her; their ways, not themselves, distasteful to her. She envied not so much the rich as the refined.

"SARAH DE BERENGER."

Oh, to be a lady !

Her old mother in the tripe shop was still dear to her, though she shrank from her petty dishonesties and sordid aims—still more from the boast she made of these things in the bosom of her family. She hated the meanness, the meagreness, the smallness of life in the lanes, and the "smoots "and the "wynds." She had an ardent, yearning nature, always looking out for something more, something higher; she wanted expansion—bright, soft air, decent living, truth and honesty, and also clean and becoming clothes.

She did not care for the footman's jokes, or even for the butler's gracious smile ; courtship from those of her own class did not move her; she had left her world behind, and cared for nothing in it—with one sad, one fatal exception.

Among her better surroundings this one exception had fast hold of her still: a lad with a beautiful face, very pathetic and fair. He was extremely lame of one foot, but contrived to do more mischief than most can though they be swift runners. He could sing, oh, so sweetly; and sometimes when he would pass, while in the dark, with blinds drawn up and the street lamps shining in, she sat watching her sick lady, she could hear him—two or three soft, wild notes as he went by—and hear the tread of his weighted shoe, and her whole heart would cry after him. She longed to be walking beside him, in the soft night air, on that wet pavement, walking by him and weeping, asking—could he care for her if she gave him herself and all she had ? praying him to be a better lad for her sake.

But it was only her heart that went out to him ; she never spoke. He did not love her, nor know how she loved him.

She saw his possibilities, but of course he was not on the way to attain, he never would attain, them ; they had being only in her thought. For this woman was a poet in her degree, which means that she was a partaker of nature's boundless hope. She was made welcome to a hint of nature's wishes.

She was not one of those poets who write verses—very few are ; none but such as are poets through and through should ever do that. Verse is only words, the garment that makes the spirit of poetry visible to others ; and poets who have but little of the spirit often fritter that little away in the effort to have it seen. But she was a poet in this, that the elemental passions of our nature were strong in her, and she bowed to them with childlike singleness of soul.

Her love was so fresh, it might no more be withstood than the moss can withstand the dew that drenches it, and makes it sparkle in the morning. Her wonder was more unsated for ever, her hope was more nearly possession than ours. If sorrow came up, it was a dark amazement. Would it not soon be over ? There are many days of sunshine for one thunderstorm.

The youth, by name Uzziah Dill, was a journeyman shoemaker; might have done well enough but for his love of drink and bad companions, and for occasional fits of idleness, during which he would sit and brood. Sometimes she would pass him then, and wonder at him—was he in pain ? was he wishing to do better ? Once, as he sat under a little bridge, hidden to the waist in tall rushes, she went by, and their eyes met ; for she had not been able to forbear stopping to say a few civil words to him. His beautiful face was clouded and dissatisfied, but a gleam of surprise lighted it up when he looked at hers. Her fate was sealed. She passed on, her cheek hot with blushes ; but he came to see her. She had saved forty pounds, and was then three-and-twenty. She was easily persuaded that he meant to be a different man. She married him, and in spite of his evil ways her love died hard, and almost broke her heart. It was not till he had spent all her money, and brought her and their little child into the deepest poverty, that he cured her of it. He had always neglected her—he now went off with another woman ; and jealousy did in one day what coldness and evil living of all other sorts could not have worn out in years.

It was almost noon. The curate had not found her ; none had come to help. She slept on, and the least little movement in the air lifted a corner of the old newspaper in which was wrapped her food. It was shaken loose and rustled, showing its name—*The Suffolk Chronicle*, a provincial newspaper. What was it doing there ? The woman, sitting on the slope of a long hill, had her back toward the Worcestershire beacon, and was looking to the south, over a lovely expanse of country. A small red-roofed city, with its cathedral peaks, folded into the hollow of a hill ; a shining reach of river, with a bridge over it ; walnut woods, hop-gardens, and remote points of rocky blue cliffs ; and then another town, with spires piercing through the haze-like smoke in which it slept, and to which the sun had given a golden show of glory, that made it seem to hang low, roofing the place like yellow thatch, or a suspended crown.

The *Suffolk Chronicle* had come a long way—had been sent, in fact, to the vicar's wife, who was a Suffolk woman; from her the curate had begged some tea and sugar for his poor protégée, and she had given them wrapped in it. It was now doing duty again as a wrapper, but though the air had in part loosened it, there were creases and folds so that the news (if any had been awake to read it) was only visible here and there. A certain fishmonger, whose name was hidden, advertised his ware. The parishioners of St. Matthew's had presented their vicar with—what did not appear.

After that came a notice—

"If this should meet the eye of Hannah Dill——"

As these words were set free, a little portion of the bread became visible also, and a robin, emboldened by long silence, sprang upon the paper and weighed it down. He only stole one crumb and flew off, when up floated the paper again. "If this should meet the eye"—then a fuller waft of air shook the crumpled lines, and if any one had looked, it would have been at this—"If this should meet the eye of Hannah Dill . . . . hear of something to her advantage. This is the fourth time of advertising."

It did not meet the eye of any one. But just then, with a sudden start and tremor, the baby turned and cried, and the exhausted mother woke, ravenous with hunger and cramped with the long restraint of her attitude.

It was high noon, and very hot. While she suckled her infant, she began with hollow eyes to open her parcel, and divide its contents with her elder child, who, rosy and smiling, now sat up, and held out dimpled hands, expectant of a share.

The child had never felt the gnawings of hunger; the mother had been familiar with them of late. She took as much for herself as she dared, then folded up the small remainder, and thrust it under some dockleaves out of sight, lest she should be tempted to eat more, and leave nothing for the supper that she knew not where to procure.

She did not feel rested; a sense of her position seemed to fall upon her like a blow. Where should she go? what should she do? She had been on her way down to Plymouth when her trouble had come upon her. There had been some wild fancy in her mind that she and the other poor mothers and wives of convicts would stand on the shore as they embarked, and take leave of them and see them sail.

She was not so free, in truth, of this wretched husband as she seemed; she had indulged strange notions as to her duty towards him. He would think it hard if she did not come, and bring him such comforts as she could beg or buy for him. Some despairing questions asked of such women as knew of these matters had let her know that the police would not suffer this, that the government would not hear of that. Yet what he might be thinking of her was frequently in her thoughts. He had deserted her and not let her know of his whereabouts for some time, but no sooner had he got himself into serious trouble, than he had contrived to have her informed of it. It must have hurt him, surely, never to have seen her anxious face in the court during his trial. Did he think she would not appear because she was ashamed of him?

A step coming on, and presently the curate standing before her.

She had her baby at her breast, and as she gently drew the flimsy shawl over its little head, he lifted his hat and made her a bow. It was not the sort of greeting a very poor mother, a probable tramp, might have expected, but she understood it; she knew it as the instinctive reverence of his young manhood for her occupation. There was something in the gentlemanhood and sympathy of this curate that was inexpressively comforting to her, but now the contrast between him and her wretched husband forced itself on her with miserable force, and the tears fell fast over her thin hands.

She could not speak or at first think, but shortly she recovered herself and dried her eyes, and saw the curate seated on the grass before the opening of the tent-like bower. He was perfectly silent, not looking towards her, and he showed no wish to speak.

Oh, what a sigh! She herself could not have sighed more deeply. Then, but not without hesitation, he began to talk—to tell her, with all gentleness, that since she had so little in this world, he was the more fain to see her endowed with a sacred hope; and shortly, to her great surprise, though he spoke with such consideration—it might almost be said with such respect—she perceived that he took for granted she was not a married woman.

"Yes, sir; I know we're all sinners," she exclaimed a little proudly; "we none of us have anything to boast of."

"No."

"And as you said, sir, 'our sins do find us out.' But, sir——"

"Yes, my poor friend."

"I do thank my God for His divine gift of a Saviour (you put it beautiful). I've often thought of it, since I sank so low. But, sir"—spreading forth her left hand to his view—"a true church parson like you put on that ring. I have a husband, and if I didn't fear God I should say, worse luck."

"My poor friend, I earnestly beg your pardon."

"For I can never get free. I was warned—oh, I was warned. It's not a sin, sir, that weighs me down ; it's a mistake I made—my great mistake."

"Indeed," he answered, in a tone of the deepest sympathy.

"Oh, my poor husband ! My mistake ! I must bear it; there's nothing can rid me of it—nothing."

"No," answered the curate ; and he sighed again. "Divine Love came down to take on itself our sins, but there is no Saviour to do the like for our mistakes."

She looked up. It must have been a sharp pang of pity that could have imparted such a tone to his voice. It could not be all pity, she thought. No, he too must have made a mistake.

So seldom is true fellow-feeling found, that when it is really present, it almost always deceives. It had done so then. Her first thought was never forgotten, and it influenced her so long as that conversation remained engraven in her mind.

Perhaps in her fine, though homely face, he saw the sudden change of expression which answered to this thought; he may have even perceived what it meant. But what need to explain himself to this stranger, this almost beggar ! He turned away his face instead, and she noticed again what she had seen before, that, young as he was, he had one lock of perfectly white hair among the brown.

He stood a moment silent, then he took occasion to bring the conversation round to a point from whence he could draw his moral. Experts in teaching easily do this sort of thing, and the poor commonly expect it of them.

"If our sins were forgiven, our mistakes need not break our hearts. Nature was hard upon us, for their sake. She did not forgive them, and she could not forget. God did not interfere with her. But to us He would give a heart that should be the better for her discipline ; even they should be among the 'all things' that shall work together for our good."

CHAPTER II.

"IF this should meet the eye of Hannah Dill, whose maiden name was Goodrich, and who was born in the parish of St. Peter, Ipswich, she is desired to apply (by letter only) to H. G., Blank Court, High Holborn (she knows the number), and she will hear of something to her advantage. This advertisement appears to-day for the fourth time."

The curate gone ; the woman silent in her bower, with wide-open eyes full of amazement and fear.

The *Suffolk Chronicle* had done its work at last.

She had sunk very low; that, alas ! is common enough. The uncommon thing is the rising again.

"I fare to feel as if I must eat another piece," the poor nursing mother had said, for she was hungry again ; and she looked wistfully at her parcel under the roofing dock-leaves.

The curate had left her with the gift of a shilling ; moreover, he had promised to arrange with a carrier, who was to pass by the hop-garden about three o'clock, to take her and her babes as far as the town, in his cart. For in that scattered hamlet, as he explained, he knew of no one who could lodge her.

What a slender hold she had on the care and thought of the world ! None at all on its heart. She heard what little kindness it held for her only from the mouth of this one man. The pledge of it with which his hand had met hers was that one bit of silver, and the sigh with which he had murmured that he wished it was more.

She could not thank him, for little as he was to her, he was all ; and he was sending her away.

She meant to go : what else could she do ? She could not walk far ; she could not stay all night in the hop-garden. She possessed little more than the cost of two nights' lodging. When should she be strong enough to earn a maintenance for herself and her infants ?

"I fare so hungry," she repeated. She drew her parcel from under the leaves, and there was her own name staring her in the face. *If this should meet the eye of Hannah Dill.*

She had been so long unused to good fortune, that at first she could see no promise in this. Suspicions had been cast upon her. The magistrates had said her husband must have had accomplices. Could this be a trap ? But why, if so, should they advertise for her in Ipswich? No, this advertisement was put in by her uncle the pawnbroker, the great man of the family, known to be "well to do," said to be rich. He had long cast off her mother, and all his relations, because they plagued him so for money. He had been fond of her in her childhood, but when she married had gone out of his way to let her know that he meant to have no more to do with her. It was only when she heard this that she supposed he might have hitherto intended some kindness to her.

She had not been to Ipswich for several years. Her uncle did not know it; and the date of the newspaper was earlier than that of her husband's trial.

This was no trap, this was real. She read again and again—took courage; but still wary, still unused to joy, weighed it and weighed it, between hope and fear, till hope suddenly got the upper hand, and she acted upon it at once. She opened wide her parcel, and with a little help from her baby-girl, ate up all that remained in it, then and there.

A daring venture! but when she began to waver again and doubt, the sight of that empty paper was an evidence to her of how sure she had felt when she made it.

It helped the joy of certainty to recur, and she felt so much the better for this and for the good meal, that when the carrier saw her seated on the step of the stile, and her little one playing by her with some flowers, he could hardly believe she was the poor creature whom he had been told to look out for.

Oh! the bliss of lying in a golden shade, under the tawny tilt of that waggon, as it slowly moved along; of hearing the carrier's whistle while he trudged beside it; of conning the leaf of the newspaper, with oft-repeated scrutiny; then looking out over the long blue hills, while they melted softly into air, and feeling as if all the world, with herself, was conscious of some great reprieve.

Soon they halted at a little wayside inn, half smothered in walnut trees, and while the carrier's horse leaned over a long water-trough, she bought some milk, and the hostess came out to look at her baby, and compare its age and weight with her own. "It thrives," she observed.

"Yes, thank God," answered the Ipswich mother, "that do."

"And so you're going on to the town?"

"And farther! I am going to a relation that have written for me from London."

"My way lies toward London," observed the old carrier, when they had started again.

Hannah Dill found that she should be twelve miles nearer to London if she went with the carrier to his destination, than if she stopped at the town. She agreed to pay the small sum he asked, in addition to what her kind friend the curate had already given him, and, after stopping at a little hostelry outside the town to have her tea, set off again in the cool of the evening, and went on with the old man and a market woman.

Up and down the long hills they moved till the crescent moon rose, and then till it grew dark and the great horn-lantern was lighted, and the old man carried it, sometimes flashing its light on his horse, sometimes on the green hedges, and into fields, whose crops they could guess only by the smell of clover, or fresh-cut hay, or beans that loaded the warm night-air; anon, on whitewashed cottages, whose inhabitants had long been asleep, and again upon the faces of great cliff-like rocks, where cuttings had been made for the road into the steep hills, and where strange curly ammonites and peaked shells and ancient bones high up showed themselves for an instant in the moving disk of light that rose and sank as the lantern swayed in the carrier's hand. Strange sights these; and curious now and then to see it flash on the bronzed face of some wayfaring man, passing from the dark into the dark, with the customary "Good night."

It was eleven o'clock when they reached the hostelry, and Mrs. Dill got down with her two sleeping infants. She felt that this had been a strangely long day, but that she was refreshed by food and hope and rest.

In the meantime the old man who had advertised for her had long given her up. He had soon taken to a sick bed, and for awhile had asked if Hannah had written—if Hannah was come. Then he ceased to ask, but sometimes bemoaned her absence; and then he forgot her, and all the concerns of this life, and asked no more.

The morning after her arrival at the hostelry, Mrs. Dill wrote to her uncle, and as soon as possible afterwards received the money needful for her journey. The letter was not in her handwriting, and said nothing about him. It was curt, and, without any kind words, desired her to be as quick as she could.

Between twenty and thirty years ago there were not so many railways in the west of England that one could count on getting to London in one day. Mrs. Dill was thirty miles from the nearest railway station. She reached it by the aid of another carrier's cart, and stood at her uncle's door about five o'clock the following afternoon.

She had never been in London before. The glaring white pavements and close heat oppressed her, while the swarms of people and of vehicles, the noise and hurry, made her tremble with a sense of danger for herself and her children. But she had not a shilling left, find her uncle she must; and she still asked her way and pressed on, till at last she reached a shabby house in a dusky court, and, overcome with fatigue and excitement, rang the bell. A woman, dressed in new mourning, presently came to the door, and seeing her shabby, woe-begone appearance, and her two children, took her for a beggar, and made this remarkable announcement, "No, we never give anything away in charity," and was proceeding to shut the door in her face, when she exclaimed, "Wait a minute; I am come to see Mr. Goodrich. I'm his niece; you'll show me in, if you please."

"Bless my heart!" exclaimed the woman, with an irrepressible smile, "if here ain't another on 'em;" and then she became suddenly grave again, and answered coldly, "You're too late, young woman. You may come in, if you choose, and see *all the others*, but you will not see Mr. Goodrich; he was buried yesterday."

A sharp sense of misery and disaster, a sudden cry to the woman, "Oh, my babe! don't let that fall," then an eddy of blackness swirling over all things, and Hannah Dill fainted away.

After that, her first sensation was that her little girl was crying, and next that several other voices made a din about her—voices that long ago she seemed to have known, voices that made her think of Ipswich. In the midst of it all, and while still she could not move or open her eyes, a commanding voice quelled the others. "Either be silent and stand back, or at once leave the room."

With a sharp sigh she presently got her eyes open, and saw dimly several people, but before them stood a gentleman, who spoke at once. "You are better. No need to raise your head. Your name?"

"Mrs. Dill."

The assembly received this announcement with an audible groan.

"There was an advertisement," she proceeded faintly, "in the *Suffolk Chronicle;*" and she tried to fumble for the paper.

"Thank you. We know all about that. There are several copies of the *Suffolk Chronicle* here."

Something scornful in the voice helped her

to rouse herself; and at the same time a murmur of congratulation floated round the room. Somebody ventured to congratulate *Mr. Bartlett.* "You're not the gentleman, sir, to be so easy taken in. Hannah Dill, indeed? Is it likely?"

"Not at all likely," answered the commanding voice; "but let her alone for the present."

"Where's my babe? where's my child?" she exclaimed, trying again to raise herself, and failing.

"Close at hand," answered the same voice, and a glass of wine was held to her lips; after drinking which she sat up, and observed that she was in a small wainscoted parlour, accommodated on a horsehair sofa. Several people were in the room; for the moment they seemed to float before her; but presently she gathered strength, and then, as they settled down into their places, her attention was attracted almost at once by a little stout old woman, with eyes like black beads, a long nose, and a curled "front" of brown hair. She was dressed in neat mourning, and no sooner met the full gaze of the tall, gaunt young woman, than she slipped into the background; whereupon the gentleman whom they had called Mr. Bartlett looked surprised, and requested her to come forward, which she did, looking both irate and abashed.

Still Mrs. Dill looked at her. "You'll excuse me, ma'am. It's many years since I saw my aunt Maria—Mrs. Storer; and folks alter strangely. I don't wonder, either, that any one should forget me, not expecting to see me dressed so as I am. You are the very moral of what my dear mother was before she died. Why, dear me, ma'am, you *are* my aunt Maria! I'm your sister Susan's daughter, aunt. I'm Hannah Goodrich."

"Tcha!" said the old lady, "it's no such thing; you're not a bit like her. What did you expect you were going to do here, deceiving of us?"

"It don't much signify what I expected," she answered, bursting into tears; but she had looked round the room first, and was quick to perceive at once how unwelcome she was there. "It don't much signify what I expected; I shall not have it now. He's gone that meant to be a good friend to me! You have no call to be so envious. He's past doing me any kindness; and I was more in need of it than you are."

Here followed a scene which the one silent spectator looked on at with equal surprise, interest, and attention; a scene of excitement, rage, and recrimination, during which all the old heart-burnings and delinquencies of the Goodrich family were raked up and argued over again.   Two aunts and two uncles were challenged by Hannah Dill, in whose teeth it was forthwith flung that her husband was a convict, and that this was already known all over Ipswich, and that if the dear departed had only known it too, he never would have suffered her to enter his door ; and who, in a passion of tears, replied by upbraidings of their unkindness in suffer-ing their own sister, in spite of her humble en-treaties for help, to die in receipt of parish pay, and be buried with a pauper's funeral ; and then, after this short outbreak of indignation and outraged feeling, partly at their refusal to recognise her, and then, when they did, at their cruel mention of her wretched husband, being completely quelled by numbers, and cured of her faintness by passionate excite-ment, snatched up her baby in her trembling

Page 35.

arms, and seizing her other child by the hand, turned her back on them all, and, without any words of farewell, moved hastily towards the door.

But that gentleman, still looking on, was standing before it, leaning against the lintel. "Where are you going, Mrs. Dill ? " he now asked, with slow composure.

"I don't know," she answerèd, with a choking sob. "I have nowhere to go to. I've come to-day and yesterday all the way from beyond Glastonbury, to see my poor uncle. But I'm not wanted ; it's no use my stopping now."

" Oh ! the person I wrote to, then ? I think you are rather in a hurry," he answered, with his calm, slow smile.

Here the two aunts said it was a shame, and they had never been used to convicts' wives in the family. She quivered all over, and, with entreating eyes, appealed to him to let her be gone. But he, taking no notice, proceeded calmly—

" Your uncle, you know, might have left

you something; you don't seem to think of that, Mrs. Dill."

To this speech, still trembling with excitement and passion, she made a remarkable answer.

"It's no use at all what. he might have said I was to have; they would divide it amongst themselves just the same—I know they would! They are that grasping and contemptuous, that they would never let me touch a thing!"

In the meantime, the aunts and uncles

Page 35.

were all appealing to Mr. Bartlett, and saying it was a shame.

"So it may be," he answered coldly, "for anything I care. There is no doubt, then, that this is Hannah Dill. You had better sit down, Mrs. Dill."

Mrs. Dill, having received this command,

wept, but obeyed; and, observing the silence that had fallen on the company, felt her excitement suddenly give way to shame at the passionate language into which she had been betrayed. Here she was obliged to face everybody, and all eyes were upon her.

"I'm sure I humbly beg your pardon,

uncles and aunts," she cried, drying her eyes with another sob.

"Mrs. Dill," continued the lawyer, "have I your attention?"

"Sir?"

"I am the lawyer who made your uncle's will. This being the day succeeding his funeral, I have just been reading it here, according to his directions."

"Indeed, sir."

"There it lies upon the table. You will please to make yourself at home. Everything is yours."

"Mine?" with a sharp cry of amazement.

"Yours."

To say that on the instant Mrs. Dill was pleased or proud, would be quite a mistake. Compunction and confusion strove in her mind, with doubt as to whether the family would let her take what had been given her, and utter abasement at her position as a convict's wife tied her tongue. She gazed helplessly at the lawyer, who, having taken a pair of new gloves from his pocket and deliberately put them on, was now buttoning them one after the other, as if they were of more consequence than her inheritance.

So they were to him.

It may have been, perhaps, that he saw her bewilderment as she gazed at them, that he put his hands behind him and said, with slow composure, "Mrs. Dill, I have some advice to give you, in the presence of these good people."

Having said this, he presently took up the will and put it in his pocket.

"Yes, sir," she answered, the sense of his words reaching her at last; and she gathered her first feelings of possession from the deep silence around her, and from his speaking to her only.

"I advise you to make no promises whatever, and, in fact, utterly to decline any sort of discussion on business matters, till after you have seen me to-morrow morning."

Hannah Dill gazed at him, and the room seemed to be full of sighs; there was not a person present that had not heaved one.

When they reached the lawyer's ears he said, with rather more sharpness in his tone than he had used before, "I may hope, I suppose, that I have your attention, Mrs. Dill?"

"Yes, sir," she replied.

"And that you will attend to my advice, and make no promises till after you have seen me to-morrow morning."

The room was full of sighs again.

"You promise?"

"Yes, sir," she repeated, "I do."

Thereupon, having done his duty, he promptly retired, but, as if struck by an after-thought, had scarcely closed the door when he opened it again, and beckoned her out with his finger.

"Have you any money?" he whispered kindly.

"Only a few half-pence, sir."

"You would like to borrow this, then," he said, and he put two sovereigns in her hand; whereupon, feeling more relieved every instant, she returned, and, as is often the case on a great occasion, her first words were very simple and commonplace.

She looked round; no eyes met hers. It was evident that she was mistress of the situation. "Aunts and uncles," she said, in a deprecating tone, and after an awkward pause, "if you're agreeable to it, let's have our tea."

By this time the aunt who had not hitherto spoken had got the baby in her arms. The other, seeing that the matter was inevitable, constituted herself spokeswoman for the party, and said, in a way half grumbling, half ashamed—

"Well, Hannah, I for one am willing to forgive and forget; and there's a gel downstairs you might send out for anything you wanted—muffins, a relish, or what not."

"Or spirits," put in one of the uncles; "or, in short, anything as you might think well to hev."

Mrs. Dill sent out for new bread, fresh butter, plenty of muffins, green tea, loaf sugar, sausages, ham to fry, a bottle of gin, and a quart of milk.

When the meal was ready, the "gel" was trusted with the baby, and took it downstairs, while they all sat down and did it full justice; but to nobody were the steaming sausages and delightful cups of hot strong tea so welcome as to Hannah Dill herself, for she had eaten nothing that day but a dry crust of bread, which her little girl, after a sufficient meal, had daintily declined, so short had she been of money till those two sovereigns, the first pledges of prosperity, touched her honest hand.

She did not preside, would not have presumed to do so. One aunt served the ham and sausages, another poured out the tea, her uncles kept the bottle of gin under their special superintendence, and all was silent satisfaction, if not harmony, till the company could eat and drink no more.

CHAPTER III.

TIME, ten o'clock in the morning after this tea-drinking.

Scene, the parlour before mentioned, and Mrs. Dill seated in it quite alone.

Her baby, once more in charge of the "gel," was down in the kitchen, staring just as contentedly at its dingy ceiling as she had done some days before at the celestial azure that showed between the leaves of the hop-bines. Her little girl, having found a dead black-beetle, was putting it to bed in a duster, with just as much pleasure as she had received beforetime from the flowers.

Mrs. Dill had borrowed a black gown, and a very large flat black brooch, from the taller of her two aunts, and was awaiting the lawyer's visit.

A lanky sunbeam, having got down between two opposite chimneys, seemed to be pointing out to her country eyes how dirty London was, what nests of dust there were in the corners of the window-panes, and how, wherever there was a crack in the plaster or the wainscot, blacks were attracted towards it, and marked its course by a winding line, that reminded her, as it has done so many other people, of a river traced upon a map. There was a garniture of pipes round the small looking-glass; ill-matched tumblers, standing on a card-table, flanked the now almost empty bottle of gin. But yet this was a parlour, and her sensations towards it, though made restless by suspense, were, on the whole, pleasure and pride.

And now Mr. Bartlett appeared, and took the will from his pocket, which he read to her with all gravity, while she sat in state opposite.

It treated of certain shares in the Brighton Railway, of a particular messuage or tenement, of two fields bought of Richard Prosper, the butcher of Stoke, near Ipswich, and then, in the midst of a good deal of jargon concerning property real and personal, came the name of Hannah Dill whose maiden name was Goodrich, and who was to have and to hold this same messuage or tenement, with other his said property real and personal, during the term of her natural life, and if she survived her husband, to have power to will it away.

Here followed a codicil.

When Mr. Bartlett had read the will and the codicil from beginning to end, he got up and stood on the rug. She then rose also. How could she think of sitting unless he did?

He perceived this, and also that she was very little the wiser for what she had heard.

"The name of the executor, you perceive, is Gordon. He is a very respectable trades-man, but he is ill just now—not able to appear."

Still silence.

"I dare say the codicil puzzles you. Mr. Goodrich added that himself. His real property having proved troublesome and a losing concern to him, the executor is at liberty to sell it, provided it is forthwith rein-vested, or laid out prudently. He also ex-pressly permits that a portion be laid out in buying a business, or in stocking a shop."

Then he sat down again, and so did she, and gathered courage to ask a question. "Might she take the liberty to inquire how much a week the things he had been good enough to read about would bring in?"

"How much a week—how much—a—week?" he repeated slowly, as he took out a pencil. "The income you should derive from this property," he said, adding the various items together, "is as near as may be one hundred and eighty pounds a year; that is about three pounds a week, you know."

Though she had been in such poverty, and this was riches to her, she betrayed no vulgar elation.

"Indeed, sir. Thank you. Is that money mine, to do as I like with?"

"Well, yes; for though you are a married woman, your husband cannot interfere with you at present."

"No, sir," she answered faintly. "He was sentenced, poor fellow, for fourteen years, and I know now that he is in the convict prison at Dartmoor. He is most likely not to leave the country, as I had thought; he is to work there at his trade."

"You know, of course, that if he behaves well, he will be allowed to come out in eleven or twelve years with a ticket-of-leave."

"Yes, sir; and that he will be allowed to write to me, and I to him, twice a year. I heard so from his brother, Jacob Dill, who felt sure that, in time, I should hear of that advertisement, and come. So he wrote here accordingly. They gave me the letter last night. I suppose, sir, that, when my poor husband comes out, he will have just as much right to the money, and to his children and to me, as if he had never got himself into trouble?"

"Certainly he will; nothing but a sentence for life can dissolve the marriage contract. You took him for worse as well as for better."

"I know, sir. Am I responsible to him, then, do you think, for what I do with the money while he is under his sentence?"

"No, Mrs. Dill; it cannot be said that you are."

Here, being a restless man, Mr. Bartlett forgot himself, rose, and stood on the rug again. Mrs. Dill took occasion to rise also.

"About those relations of yours? I suppose you took my advice?"

"I did as well as I could," she answered, with apologetic respect.

Here he gravely seated himself, and she followed suit.

"As well as you could?" he repeated.

"Sir, they made the remark so many times, that it seemed very hard and very unnatural —in short, they were that low about the will——"

"Well, Mrs. Dill?"

"That at last I said, if you were quite agreeable, I would endeavour to come to some sort of agreement with them. If you were quite agreeable, sir," she repeated, seeing him knit his brow. "On consideration of which," she went on, "they all promised faithfully that they would go away. And they thought it would be as well that they should be out of the house till dinner-time, that I might be wholly free to talk it over with you."

"Your object in coming to an agreement, as you call it, would simply be in order to get rid of them."

"Well—yes, sir."

"Mrs. Dill, if once you begin to pay your relations to go, they will return and return, to be paid again. I should send them all to the rightabout, if I were you. They have enough. They all get a decent living."

"Oh, you simpleton!" was his thought; "you will be fleeced of every shilling before you are a year older."

"You must think of your young children," he remarked, "and their almost worse than fatherless state. They have no one but yourself to look to."

"Yes, I feel that, sir."

"And, then, something surely is due to your uncle's wish, the old man's wish who earned this property, and has deliberately chosen to leave it to you."

"And I thought of that too. But it's mine now, and I fare to feel hurt by their reproaches. If it was only a trifle, my eldest uncle said; and so did his son, my cousin. I said perhaps Mr. Bartlett would not allow me to——"

"To give any of the income away?" he asked, when she hesitated. "I could not prevent it, nor Mr. Gordon either."

"So they said, sir," she replied, with an ingenuous sigh of regret. "They said, 'Hannah, if you choose to take and chuck it all in the Thames, they could not prevent it.'"

"Quite true."

Then she tried to explain to him her distress at having to do anything mean. She thought the old man had left his property to her more to spite his brothers and sisters than out of any love to herself. She could not bear to hear those nearer to him speak so hardly of the dead; she would buy his memory into better repute by making some sacrifice of his goods.

She had, as he observed, notions of honour and right not common in her class, but also she was simple in some other matters to a degree not common in any class. She had that temperament which, with one touch more of the Divine in it than others, has also one touch more of the child. The child in her nature was destined never to grow up, as the yearning idea was too high ever to be satisfied.

"You seem very much afraid of your aunts and uncles," he said. "But let me tell you one thing for your comfort: the law will not permit you to make away with any of the principal; you can only deal with the income."

"That was what they made me promise to ask; they seemed to be afraid it was the case."

"As long as your husband is living you can only touch the income."

"Still for the next ten or eleven years I could give them what I pleased out of the income."

"What *they* pleased, I think you mean! You could. Did they name any particular sum that would satisfy them?"

"Why, sir, there are five of them. If I kept half for myself till such time as poor Dill came home, the other half wouldn't be much divided among them; but I reckoned, by what they let fall, it would satisfy them if it was paid regular."

Here Mr. Bartlett got up once more, and stood cogitating by the window. She was a fool; but he did not despise, for he understood her.

He remained a few minutes turning over in his mind, between pity and amusement, what to do for her. It was no business of his, as he assured himself, but yet he meant to take it in hand. A sudden thought seemed to strike him just as a cab passed the window. He tapped and stopped it.

"These *harpies* are gone out, you say. Where are your children?"

"Down-stairs, sir."

"I have a note to write. Suppose you fetch them up, and come back to me with your bonnet on."

Her bonnet was so shabby! She knew not whether to think most of it, or of Mr. Samuel Weller, who went to Doctors' Commons to prove a will. Was Mr. Bartlett going to take her there?

Mr. Bartlett was in the passage when she appeared with her children. He had a note in his hand, the ink of which was not dry. He had already opened the street door; he moved to her to enter the cab, and straightway shut her in. "I have told the man where to drive," he said. "The direction is on the note, also;" and before she had recovered from her astonishment, she had left her late uncle's house, never to enter it again.

It may be as well to draw a veil over the scene that ensued, when her aunts and uncles having returned, and waited dinner for her a reasonable time, began to suspect that she had escaped them. To obtain the half of everything was the very least they had counted on. Some of them remained within, in case she should return; others went to Mr. Bartlett's office. Mr. Bartlett, they were informed, was engaged, and could not possibly see them, but they learned from his clerk that no person resembling Hannah Dill had called there that day.

The note that Mr. Bartlett had put into Mrs. Dill's hand was addressed, "Mrs. George Bartlett." Its contents may as well be given here.

"DEAR LOVE,—

"You remember the scene I was describing to you last night? This is the heroine of it!

"Her relations have arranged a plan for chousing her out of her money; and she is so *chousable*, that if left with them another day, she will be committed to it irretrievably. So, unknown to herself, I have caused her to run away from them. Tell her so, and tell her I say, that in justice to herself and her children, she must not decide to give anything to these people while under the constant pressure of their importunity.

"I suppose, love, she can dine in the nursery? And then I want you, as soon as possible after, to let nurse take her in the omnibus up the New Road to old Mrs. Prentice, who can lodge her, or recommend her to somebody who can. Tell her to keep herself perfectly quiet till she hears from us.

"Thine,
"G. B."

Mrs. Dill had been driven to Mr. Bartlett's house, and, in a high state of astonishment and perplexity, was waiting in a handsome dining-room, and keeping her children quiet with some difficulty, when a plump, pleasant-looking young woman came in, with the note open in her hand, and a face full of amusement and curiosity.

Mrs. Dill exclaimed that she hoped there was no mistake. And the lady answered cordially, "No mistake at all. I am Mrs. George Bartlett. I could not come down sooner; I was nursing my baby. Yours looks very young."

"Only sixteen days, ma'am; and I believe that's hungry."

"Poor little lamb!" said the other mother, and paused an instant, as if she hardly knew how to go on; then glancing at the note again, and catching an idea from it, she said, with a smile of amusement, "Well, suppose you come up to the nursery, and nurse it there, and see my baby. But he is a great big fellow, eight months old. Come, I will lead your little girl."

The baby by this time was so *fractious*, that Mrs. Dill, in spite of her surprise, was very glad of any proposal which promised to allow of her satisfying its little requirements.

"The children are gone out for their walk," observed Mrs. Bartlett, as they entered a light, roomy nursery. "Take the rocking-chair, and make yourself at home."

Then, as soon as the baby was quiet and happy, and little Miss Dill had been propitiated with a sponge rusk and a rag doll, Mrs. Bartlett said, "And so my husband has made you run away from your relations?"

"Ma'am!" exclaimed Mrs. Dill, "I do assure you I shouldn't think of such a thing."

"He says so," repeated Mrs. Bartlett, much enjoying her task.

"I never thought of such a thing!" the other exclaimed again.

"What did you think you were doing, then, when you got into the cab? Why did you do it?"

"Why, ma'am, because Mr. Bartlett told me."

Mrs. Bartlett now, at some length, explained the true state of the case, and soon observed that to know she was freed from these relations, and had got her future in her own hands, was a most welcome thought to Mrs. Dill. Her gratitude was fervent, but she could not help smiling while she answered the questions of her hostess as to what had passed.

"I wonder you did not at least ask Mr. Bartlett where you were going."

"Oh, ma'am, Mr. Bartlett is such a commanding gentleman! I couldn't take the liberty."

Mrs. Bartlett laughed. On reflection she laughed again. "Well, I suppose George has rather a commanding manner with strangers," was her thought. "But, dear me! who would expect him to be obeyed and no questions asked!"

Mr. Bartlett was his wife's humble servant. He was what is sometimes called an "outsized man," large-handed, heavy-footed, imposing in appearance, commanding in voice and gesture; a great dark, plain, downright, upright, kind-hearted personage.

It is said that in a thoroughly strong and good government the weight of the governing hand is least felt. Mr. Bartlett was ruled with such utter ease and skill that he thought he was free.

In two hours' time Mrs. Dill had entered her lodgings at Pentonville, and was divesting herself of her aunt's gown and brooch, which, to prevent discovery, were to be returned by the Parcels Delivery Company.

Having no gown, she was obliged to stay indoors till a dress-maker could finish one for her. The shop-windows were not then, as now, full of "costumes" ready-made. Mrs. Dill and the nurse did some shopping on their way, and then, left alone with her babes, after the latter had withdrawn, she sat down to think over the astonishing events of the last twenty-four hours.

Now the long journey, and the excitement she had since gone through, began to tell upon her, and for several days she was glad to lie quietly on her bed, finding it enough to wonder at and be thankful for that she could procure whatever she wanted, and civility too. For, as the landlady would sometimes remark to her, "A fat trouble, ma'am, is much better than a lean trouble; and however bad you feel, you know you've only to put your hand in your pocket, and send me out to buy the dinner."

Mrs. Dill soon constituted herself Mr. Bartlett's client, and taking, by his advice, or rather by his orders, several days to think

the matter over, conveyed to him her deliberate wish that he would keep for her one hundred and fifty pounds a year, and divide the remainder of the income, with the furniture and clothes left by her deceased uncle, equally among his brothers and sisters.

Mr. Bartlett and the executor grumbled over this decision, but they carried it out; and of their own accord obtained from each of the recipients a written promise, never again to molest Hannah Dill in the possession of her property, and never at any future time to apply to the said Hannah Dill for money, on any pretence whatever.

They were all satisfied, especially Hannah Dill, who read the signed paper, and heard that her relations were gone back to Suffolk, with almost incredulous joy.

Poor woman, she was now safe for awhile from the unkindness of her husband. She began to try hard to forgive him, being helped by the consciousness that he could not now be offending against her. Her natural jealousy as a wife was appeased; she pitied him. He would surely now become a better man. In about five months he would have leave to communicate by letter with her. He should hear of her good fortune, and for the sake of this promise of secured future comfort, if not for her sake, surely he would reform.

She dreaded him sorely; but what hope was there for her, excepting in thus hoping the best for him? This crime had been hateful to her, for the house he had robbed was that of her own dear lady, and there could be no doubt that he had obtained the knowledge which made this easy during the time when he had come courting there to her.

She had been somewhat of a wanderer. Born at Ipswich, she had moved with the family of her lady to Bristol; but Uzziah Dill belonged to Chester, and soon after her marriage with him, he had returned there on a promise of work, and there they had lived till he went off with the woman for whose sake he had for some time neglected her.

She was very weak and ill all that winter: she had gone through so much misery, that she could not soon recover. But she had the solace of her children, and having plenty of money and time, she employed herself mainly in making an abundant supply of comfortable and handsome clothing for them.

She went now and then to see Mrs. Bartlett, and observed how her children were dressed. "Mine have a right to the best," was her thought; "and, bless them, they shall have it, and the best of wholesome eating too."

Hannah Dill was a tall young woman, with a large frame, and dark hair and eyes. Her children were two delicate little fairies, flaxen-haired and blue-eyed, with all the pensive beauty of their father, but with little promise of strength and vigour.

When she knew that it was almost time for her husband to write to her, she wrote to his brother, Jacob Dill, and gave him her address.

She little thought this would bring the whole tribe of the Dills upon her; she knew that they had not money enough to come, and they had been so unfriendly to her, that she supposed they would be ashamed to apply to her for money, even by letter.

She was quite mistaken, and soon found herself worse off with them than she had been with the Goodriches.

On the evening of the third day old Mrs. Dill appeared and established herself in Hannah Dill's lodgings, having borrowed the money for her journey, and expecting her daughter-in-law to return it forthwith. She brought her youngest girl with her, and said she would be very handy for taking care of the children.

Hannah Dill was at that time so restless with expectation, that she was even less able than usual to cope with these encroaching spirits. Everything seemed to depend on her husband's first letter. Was he penitent? was he hardened? How would he write, and what should she reply?

It is probable that she would have succumbed, and perhaps have even agreed to receive Uzziah's drunken old father, but for a blow that she was not prepared for, and which hurt her more sorely than all that had gone before.

Jacob Dill wrote, for he said he was ashamed to show her his face. He was the only one of the Dills that had a spark of spirit or good feeling. It was better she should know it, he wrote. Uzziah had written, had written the first day that he was allowed. Of course he had not heard, when he did it, of his wife's having got the money. "You see, Hannah, they are only allowed to write to their wives, or their families if they have no wife. He told the governor he had a wife; and I am sorry to let it out to you, for I know you'll be hurt, but he wrote to *her*. Why, she was with him at his trial, and called Mrs. Dill and all; and he told her how he wanted to hear on her, and asked if her baby was born, and she were to write back as though she was his wife. It was not at all sure as he should be long at Dartmoor; he might get sent over the sea. And, oh! would she write off directly? It was a shame, but he never mentioned you at all."

What people have been taught how to do, they should be able to do. Hannah Dill ran away again.

Old Mrs. Dill had, now she had come to London, two ambitions. She wanted to see the Crystal Palace, and also to see Smithfield.

She accomplished the last while her daughter-in-law, cold as a stone after this blow, sat shivering in silence by the fire. She accomplished the second a few days after, and took her daughter. When the poor wife heard the door shut after her, and knew that she would be away for hours, she lifted up her face, that was full of moody and brooding thought, asked the landlady to watch her children, and went out.

She came back in a cab, with three large boxes; and, some hours after that, left the house again with those same boxes and her children, and a hearty hug from the landlady, whose claims she more than satisfied.

When old Mrs. Dill came back, she found, instead of her daughter-in-law, certain articles of clothing laid out for her acceptance — a brown paper parcel, containing money enough to take her and her daughter home; and a letter, setting forth that her daughter-in-law had left London for good, and she would hear from her and see her no more.

EL MARHUM SA'ID ABU 'OMAR ERNEB.

ONE of the first men I knew in Syria, one of the last to whom I bade farewell on leaving the country, one whom I ever regarded as a true friend and a good man, was the man whose name stands at the head of this paper. He was one for whom many besides myself had a great regard, and, if I am not mistaken, many readers of GOOD WORDS will be glad to know something of him.

A word in regard to his name, before speaking of the man. Beginning at the end, "Erneb," or *Hare*, is the family name—whence derived I know not; I knew no one else called by that name in Syria. "Abu 'Omar," *Father of Omar*, was his name of honour; for, according to a well-known Eastern custom, a father assumes the name of his eldest son, by which he is always by preference addressed, and when he has no son it is quite common for a fictitious name to be bestowed on him, which ranks him in the honoured class. "Sa'íd" was the name properly speaking. The prefixed "El Marhûm" can only apply to one departed, for I am sorry to say my friend died not long after I left the country. The phrase is, literally, "the compassionated," "the man who has found mercy," and has originated in the Eastern custom of avoiding the use of the word "dead," and of speaking of one departed as having gone to the mercy of God. It may be compared with the German word *selig*, or "blessed," applied to the departed.

In one of the narrowest of the streets of the old part of the city of Beyrout, at a corner where four ways meet, Abu 'Omar had his place of business. It was a small shop of the old Oriental type. The front was composed of a pair of shutters opening outwards. One of these, when turned upwards and fixed to the wall, formed a shelter from the rain ; the other, turned downwards, formed a counter. The owner, in order to enter, had to swing himself inwards by the assistance of two ropes hanging from the roof, and when once inside made room for himself by disposing on the counter sundry baskets and boxes containing his goods. Little shelves around the wall, and a dark recess behind, were stored with other items of the stock-in-trade. The customers, of course, never actually entered the shop. From the neighbouring streets muffled female figures or little children would, from time to time, emerge, and, standing in front of the place, make their purchases of soap, oil, rice, lentils, matches, or whatever else the establishment contained ; and should a friend stop for a moment to have a chat with the owner, he had to be accommodated with a stool in the street and guard himself as he best could from being squeezed by the loads of water-carriers or muleteers, of whom many passed to and fro, as one of the city gates and one of the public fountains lay near by.

The owner of this little shop had nothing in his outward appearance that would have struck a stranger. His dress consisted of a thick round turban of white with yellowish spots, an indigo-blue cotton blouse faced with white braid, and confined at the waist by a girdle of simple leather, cotton trousers reaching to the knees, and the common red-leather shoes. He was neither tall nor corpulent, and had not the dignified slow step which Orientals who are in office, or are otherwise of importance, so naturally assume. But there was an expression of great dignity in his finely-cut features, and a depth of good sense and good nature in his calm grey eyes ; and from intercourse with him I came to learn that among the natives of the East whom one passes unheeded in the mass there is many an individual who, beneath a very simple exterior, and underneath the coating of ideas and associations very different from our own, possesses a great deal of what is best in human nature.

He was introduced to me on my arrival in Beyrout, a stranger to the place and the language. He was to assist me in house-hunting, and in all the arrangements necessary for settling in a new place ; and one of his recommendations was that he knew a little Turkish, a smattering of which I had picked up in Constantinople—his native language, of course, being Arabic, the common language of Syria. We both made, I remember well, very little progress with our Turkish, and our house-hunting was a tedious business ; but before many days had passed we had become fast friends, as we remained to the last.

At the time of which I speak Abu 'Omar was about fifty years of age, though he looked older. He was, in fact, at the period of life which has well been described as *anecdotage* —a stage reached sooner, and by more people, in the East than in the West ; and from this circumstance I am able to give a

brief outline of his life as I heard it in snatches now and again from his own lips.

It should be known, then, that in the year 1832 there were great commotion and alarm among the young Muslims of Syria. Ibrahim Pasha of Egypt had taken the country from the Turks, and was recruiting his army by conscription of all the young Mohammedans he could lay hands on. I do not vouch for the truth of all that is told of the expedients resorted to in order to escape from military service. It is said that so many cut off their right thumbs and put out their right eyes that Ibrahim formed whole companies of one-eyed and left-handed soldiers. This, however, is certain, that about that time a good many young men hired themselves as grooms and table-boys to Europeans, in whose houses they were at that time regarded as protected; and Sa'id was one of these, serving in the house of an American missionary.

XXI—4

The best proof his fidelity as a servant was that his master, on leaving the country, recommended him to a brother missionary, and he again to a third, and so on for several years, till Sa'id came to regard himself as having a sort of claim on the kindness of the *mishleriyyeh*, as he called the missionaries. A little incident of that early period of his life, which Abu 'Omar was fond of relating, will show what his idea of fidelity as a servant was. One day the *khowadjah* (*i.e.* the gentleman or master of the house) came home tired and hungry. Sa'id was at the gate to hold his stirrup as he dismounted, and led the horse away to the stable, while the rider walked into the house. A few minutes afterwards the master, becoming impatient for his dinner, which it was Sa'id's duty to serve, called to his servant rather sharply, and demanded the cause of the delay. "Have patience, sir," was the reply. "You have the power of speech to ask for what you wish; but the poor dumb horse might be neglected, if I did not serve it first."

The time came when Sa'íd's friends thought it was the proper thing for him to take a wife. It is a mere matter of arrangement by friends. Had it been a matter of courtship it is not likely—yet who knows?—that he would have married the woman he took; but of this more anon. A household servant, if he is honest, can hardly afford to keep a house, and as a matter of fact few householders in those parts keep married servants. And so Sa'íd, after receiving one increase of wages after another till his fellow-servants became jealous, was advised to open a little shop, his friends the missionaries promising their patronage. And so he opened a shop, which he continued to have till the day of his death; and it was evident from the frequent repetition of this portion of his history that he considered the promise of his first patrons to be binding on their successors in all time coming.

Sa'íd's marriage was, as has been hinted, not a happy one. At the time I knew him his wife had been dead some years, and he would occasionally speak of her without reserve. "She was industrious," he would say, "very industrious—in fact never idle; she kept the house in good order and attended to all my wants; but she could not agree with her neighbours, nor with any one; her temper was something wonderful." And when it is a question of a woman's temper we had better leave it thus vaguely described in his own words. A Muslim of less prudence would have got rid of her at any cost; but Abu 'Omar was of a different mind. Once only, when sorely tried by her, he thought of divorcing her, but went first to consult his *sheikh*, or religious adviser. "No," said the old man, "do not put her away; if God sees good He will change her disposition, or else He will remove her from you, or, at least, He will give you patience to bear with her; and," he added, "who knows? you might get a worse." And so Abu 'Omar had patience; but he found in her an illustration of a saying he often repeated—"The temper lies deeper than the life, and cannot depart till the life departs." At length she determined to make the pilgrimage to Mecca, though her husband could not undertake the journey. When she said she would go, go she must, even without him; but she caught a bad fever on the way, of which she died, leaving 'Omar and three daughters, I believe, to be brought up by the father.

'Omar turned out badly; his father thought he inherited his mother's disposition; he would settle at nothing, would not learn a trade, would not help in the shop, showed no signs of sense, and was, in short, a good-for-nothing. The daughters, of course, I never saw, except veiled; but I know that one was married, and had to return to her father's house on account of the cruelty of her mother-in-law—no uncommon thing in the East—and that many a weary journey Abu 'Omar made to the husband's house, in the effort to bring about a reconciliation. When we condemn the iniquitous marriage laws of Islam for the degrading position they assign to women, we do not always remember the misery they also bring upon husbands and fathers.

Notwithstanding this experience Abu 'Omar did not think himself too old, even when some of his children had grown up, to marry a second time. According to a story he was wont to repeat, he would not marry a widow, who would always be talking in the *past tense*, but followed the advice of the proverb: "Take the roundabout road, roundabout though it be, and marry the young woman, penniless though she be." He married a wife as young as his own daughters, and according to his own account of the matter, he was very happy. "For instance," he would say by way of illustrating his domestic peace, "if at any time I propose to bring her a new dress, she will never allow me to do so, unless I first bring dresses for my daughters." The young wife and the daughters seemed in short to live together like sisters.

With the business of his little shop, Abu 'Omar combined, like a good many in his circumstances, various other occasional occupations. Being a good judge of animals, it was his custom in the spring, when green food was abundant, to buy a young donkey, which he would sell again at the end of the season. Such a transaction had a double advantage, as during the warm season he lived in the gardens outside the town, and thus could ride into town to his business. He kept his eyes open also to any other good bargains that could be made; and his skill as a buyer, with great tact in the management of affairs, made him trusted in many ways as a general broker or go-between, an office of great importance in a country where negotiations are conducted with great tediousness and delicacy. The great advantage of employing him in such transactions was that one could be sure that no mean or dishonest tricks were resorted to. It was a triumph of pure diplomatic skill, and no Blue Book of the Foreign Office could be more instructive than his careful reports of the conclusion of some bargain as to the purchase of a horse or the hiring of a house. He was, moreover, employed by several families to buy stores of firewood, oil, soap, and such articles as are laid in for winter use, transactions in which the ordinary household servant, from inexperience or other reasons, is not always to be trusted. The way in which he was paid for these various services was peculiar. First of all, he expected his friends to patronise his shop, and then, on the conclusion of a business, it was the custom, though there was no fixed commission, to give him something, which was supposed to be counted by neither party. But his favourite mode of being paid was as follows:—About the beginning of winter he would make an evening call. After the usual formalities he would begin with a graver air than usual, telling the old story how he had first become acquainted with the missionaries, and how the shop had been opened on the faith that his friends would not forget him. He would then say that this was the best time for him to buy his winter's stock of sugar. But it was not very easy for him to buy a cask or two for cash ; to borrow money on interest was an expensive matter. His friend, the doctor, had kindly, on several occasions, lent him a small sum without interest, and if I also could spare five pounds or so it should be repaid in spring, and the loan would be a greater favour than the paying of the interest on the money. I do not think he ever failed in these applications ; he was careful to give a note for the amount ; and when his own time came the money was always faithfully repaid.

But it was not merely for his business capabilities that Abu 'Omar was valued. He had the art of making even an unpleasant business amusing, and, when business was over, it was a rare pleasure to enjoy his company and hear him talk. Many an evening, when wearied with the day's work and unable to study, I would hear the welcome patter of his donkey's feet, and the old man would walk into the court, slip off his shoes, enter the room, and sit quietly down on the divan to spend an hour or two in conversation. He was the type of a perfect gentleman, knew when to speak, knew exactly how long to stay, and, simple as he was, could have conducted himself with propriety and dignity in the best society. There was no prying curiosity in his questions, and he used to prefix his questions with " excuse me for saying so ; " but he could be trusted with any confidence and consulted on the most delicate subjects. It was very interesting to watch the carefulness with which he answered any difficult question proposed to him. He would take a whiff or two of his cigarette, pull up his one foot more closely under him as he sat, and deliver himself of some proverb or story, the drift of which was not at first clear, but whose point always exactly hit the case in hand. No Oriental could tell a story better, and that is saying a good deal ; and his stories were so well selected that they not only interested the hearer but conveyed reproof or instruction in the most delicate form.

Though he could neither read nor write, Abu 'Omar could think ; and by a shrewd observation of the world as far as he had seen it, and by intercourse with men, he had formed his own opinions, which, however, were not elaborated in systematic form, but embodied in pithy parables or legendary stories which contained political, religious, and moral truth in the mass. His political views, as might be expected, were not of an advanced type. He took no trouble to understand the various forms of government which he was told prevailed in the West; and for our civil liberties of which we are so proud, he expressed no particular admiration. To him it was all one what name the ruler of a people bore, provided he ruled in the fear of God ; and the one thing in our Western institutions that he never ceased praising was the impartial administration of justice. All rule that was just was good; all else was simply oppression. Many a story he had to tell, showing how God in His own time most certainly brought oppression to an end; but equally pointed was the stories which showed that a good and honest people are the stability of a country. Like all old men, he was fond of dwelling on the good times when men like the first Caliphs lived in simplicity, heard the cause of rich and poor alike, and regarded themselves as God's instruments for the good of the people. Those were the times when men cared less for wealth than for peace, and were great, not in their outward circumstances but in their love and practice of justice.

Though he lived for many years in the houses of missionaries, and was all his life on intimate terms with many of them, I never heard that he had been classed as an " inquirer," or suspected by his co-religionists of leaning towards Christianity. No doubt he had been much influenced by what he saw and heard. His mind had been cleared of the prejudices which unthinking Muslims entertain; and he knew that there was a Christianity which does not consist in a round' of ceremonies combined with a loud boast of orthodoxy. But he was a religious man, and his religion was eminently of a practical kind. He attended to the prayers and rites of his own creed with quiet stead-fastness, and was not ashamed, in the presence of educated Europeans, to avow his Muslim faith. But he had no faith in mere outward performances, had come to the conclusion that "in every nation he that feareth God and worketh righteousness is accepted of Him," and like a true Muslim hoped to be saved at last by the mercy of God. If he did not give up his own religion I believe it was simply because he believed he had not done all that his religion required of him. I remember him once speaking on this subject with unusual earnestness. It was in the month of November, and during the fast of Ramadhan. The usual autumn rains had not fallen, an eclipse of the moon had taken place the night before, and a hot dry wind was blowing as Abu 'Omar came in. "Well," said I, "do you see any signs of a change of wind?" "Sir," he said promptly, "there will be no change in the weather till there is a change in men's hearts. These winds, and clouds and skies all betoken rain; but so long as people remain as they are, it is a matter of perfect uncertainty whether God will be gracious to us or not, it depends entirely on His good pleasure." Then followed a story the point of which was, that if men prayed with sincere hearts their prayer was answered as soon as it was uttered, otherwise it was a matter of uncertainty, so far as man knew, whether the blessing would be given or not. Finally he added abruptly, "And these rulers—God deliver us from them—for their rule is not according to truth and justice." On his asking me what news I had from England, I told him what I had read in the last papers of failures and frauds and speculations. Whereupon he continued, "According to us, it is the last time; and we are told that in the last times evil men will increase and good men be few, and children will not help their fathers, nor fathers love their children. Such is the case now, and it becomes those who would be prepared for approaching evil to do their duty quietly, to attend to their own affairs and to do good as they have opportunity.

But my opinion is that we are all under sin —the whole of us—and these blessings that come to us, showers, and sunshine, and provisions, I do not know whether God sends them for the sake of the brute creation and speechless children, for it cannot be because we deserve them."

It is true that with his religion there was mixed up much that was childish and super-stitious; and it is needless to speculate what he might have been had he known the power of a better faith. But his religion, such as it was, was mixed up with his every-day life, made him an upright man, and enabled him to bear a lot that was not easy with wonderful fortitude. Judged as a man among his fellow-men, one might say of him as of Lessing's Nathan, "Ein besserer Christ war nie."

My last money transaction with him was characteristic and in keeping with all I had ever seen of him. On the day I sailed from Syria he had received a commission to buy for me some little articles I was to take with me. When I passed by his shop in the course of the day to pay the account, his brother Ibrahim was in charge, wrote out an account, received in payment a twenty-franc piece, which for a year at least had stood at the fixed value of a hundred piastres, and gave me the change. In the afternoon Abu 'Omar himself appeared to say farewell, but began first by saying, "There was a little mistake in the accounts to-day. The things bought came to two and a quarter piastres less than you were charged, and the lira has risen in value to-day a quarter of a piastre; here are your two piastres and a half," handing me the sum, about 5d., in a piece of paper. I was disposed to smile at his carefulness, but he rebuked me by saying gravely, "Sir, that is your *right*;" and then he said, "How long have you known Abu 'Omar?" I replied, "Eleven years." "And did you ever in all that time see any difference between this"—extending his hand with the palm upward—"and that?"—turning it with the palm downwards. "No," said I, "I have always found you an upright and honest man." "Then," said he "we can part as friends in peace," and he kissed me first on one cheek and then on the other with tears in his eyes, and I saw him no more.

Shortly after my arrival in this country, I heard of his death. The fast of Ramadhan, a month of daily abstinence from sunrise to sunset, which he carefully observed, was too much for one at his years and with the daily work he had to do. He went down one day to open the shop as usual, and was found soon after by some of his neighbours, lying in peace.

I wish I had been present when his body was laid out for burial. On such an occasion, after the corpse has been carefully washed according to the rites of the Muslim creed, the presiding *sheikh* stretches his hand out over the departed and, addressing the by-standers, says, " What do you say of him ?" and all with one voice reply, " God will have mercy on him !"

JAMES ROBERTSON.

THOUGHTS FOR NEW YEAR'S DAY.

THERE is no inconsistency between the innocent merriment with which it is customary to usher in the first day of the year, and the serious reflections which the season naturally suggests. Even when we are most conscious of thoughts that lie " too deep for tears," we may join with all our hearts the bright faces gathered in the old home, where, amid the laughter of youth and the smiles of age, friend meets friend with the familiar greeting of " A good new year !"

True religion does not frown on scenes like these. They are among the most human and beautiful that I know. The stroke of the bell which " rings out the old, rings in the new," probably sounds very differently in the ears of youth and of age. To the one it may seem wholly a merry peal telling how—

" The new year, blyth and bold,
Comes up to take his own."

To the aged it may summon the past more than the future, and even while there is the ready smile of welcome to all around, the heart goes back to bygone scenes, and other faces and other voices are seen and heard. But it is just this mingling of diverse emotions which imparts its touching interest to such meetings as these.

There is a tendency at such times to take a wider survey than usual of life, looking backwards to the influences which have hitherto affected us, and forwards to the solemn possibilities of the future. Through such reflections we may certainly gain wisdom for daily direction. But while this conduct is proverbially characteristic of man as a rational being, it is injurious to keep the eye so fixed on the distant horizon as to forget the all-important character of the duties that lie beside us. The melancholy which broods on the past, or the sanguine hopefulness which dwells ever in the future, is apt to hinder present energies. The burdens of anxiety which oppress us, and the frivolities which spring from over-confidence, are equally detrimental. And so we find that Scripture forbids rather than encourages an idle forecasting of events. " Take no thought for the morrow—for the morrow shall take thought for the things of itself." " I would have you without carefulness." " Ye know not what shall be on the morrow." " Whatsoever thy hand findeth to do, do it with thy might, for there is no work, nor device, nor knowledge in the grave whither thou goest."

For we are not, in a sense, responsible for the future, but only for the use we make of the present. The point at which we stand is that where the threads of opportunity as they come to us are beat into the unchangeable web of history. All before us is pliable, all behind us is fixed. We are each weaving character, the pattern of which is determined by every stroke of volition. Each day brings its own " now or never." As there are certain seasons granted for the fulfilment of particular kinds of work—springtime appropriate for sowing, summer for culture, and autumn for reaping—and as the wise farmer knows that his harvest is affected by the delay of a week or even a day when the weather is " seasonable," so is it in the higher sphere of character. The man can never properly recover in riper years the opportunities which were appropriate to his school-days, for even if he does make up on his fellows it is at a cost which represents a proportionate loss for the time being. Our religious progress is similarly determined. Each day brings a certain combination of circumstances which can never recur. Like the marvellous variety in nature, whereby amid the millions of our race no two faces are exactly the same, nor two minds absolutely identical, so every new day brings a particular series of events which is never repeated. And it is by the use we make of these that our characters are proven. What we are to-day is to an appreciable extent determined by the manner in which the temptation of yesterday was met, or by the advantage we took of opportunities for prayer or active usefulness. The common-place nature of our duties does not lessen the important consequences which depend on their due performance. As it is attention to the every-day drill, with its monotonous and tiresome details, which makes the true soldier on whom alone reliance can be placed amid the excitement of battle, so is all moral or spiritual goodness the consequence of an infinite number of apparently trifling particulars. Character is but the condensed result of the faithful or unfaithful use of multitudinous opportunities, which we must perforce employ for good or evil.

For we are not as ships afloat in a stagnant sea, but as those ceaselessly exposed to diverse winds and tides, and which can advance towards the true haven only by such wise use of every chance as to make all powers favourable that would otherwise retard. And yet even amid things prosaic there may come demands which call for the highest moral heroism. The duty to which conscience points may be very humbling. It is not easy for a proud or stubborn man to confess a fault which no one suspects, to seek reconciliation with an enemy, to ask forgiveness for an injury, or to bridge over some family quarrel. It is hard for a successful man to give up the demoralizing business, or to sacrifice the habit of trade which custom condones, but which he knows to be really dishonest although profitable. There is a certain type of religionism which evades these common tests, and hides itself under the letter of dogma while it denies the spirit of all religion. Self-examination, however, on matters like these, and decided action regarding them, are surely healthier spiritual exercises at the commencement of a new year than indulging in vapourish sentimentalities regarding the brevity or sadnesses of life.

Natural temperament makes another range of duties peculiarly difficult. The shy man, for example, can hardly summon courage enough to speak faithfully to a friend, or it may be to his own child; he shrinks from beginning family worship, or has not firmness to drop a bad companionship. The greatest trials and the truest victories are those which are discovered by him who tries to bring the influences of the Christian spirit into the every-day details and worries of life—to overcome irritability or impatience under provocation, and to learn gentle considerateness; to subdue the sloth or dilatoriness which hinders the discharge of duty, and to do the least as well as the greatest with unswerving faithfulness; to repress unkindly judgments, and to

sweeten all life with a noble courtesy and generous charity. Yet these are the qualities which, springing from the love of God and loyalty to Christ, really advance the influence of religion as showing its power in the actual redemption of character. The true Christian can, therefore, draw no distinction between secular and sacred, for all duties become consecrated by the spirit in which he fulfils them. He cannot regard the office or the farm as belonging to a different world from the Church or the Lord's day. And so it is that in the strictest sense the merchant who buys and sells, the man who ploughs the field, the mechanic who wields the hammer, the servant who sweeps the room, the mistress in charge of the household, the landlord with his tenantry, or the statesman who governs an empire, can glorify God, and make their daily tasks a continual worship by bringing the highest principles to the discharge of common duties.

One lesson, therefore, which the beginning of New Year's day ought to teach us, is the importance of the opportunities each future day will bring. We need not summon visions of joy or anticipate sorrows which may never, in God's providence, be experienced by us. Our wisest plans, that already seem freighted with success, may be shipwrecked by circumstances we do not now foresee. Our most anxious fears may be removed by some turn in the stream of events which we have never imagined possible. These things are not within our control. But if we are willing to walk humbly and obediently in the way of duty as God calls us thereto daily, then we know that "all things will work together for our good." It is best to calculate life not by the long periods, but the short; not by the year, but by the day. Our journey is most safely accomplished when we reckon it step by step, and resolve that each one shall be taken steadfastly, and all passing opportunities grasped with the strong hand of faith. If we begin the new year by thus yielding ourselves to God in all sincerity, then we may rest assured that whatever changes may come none can separate us from Himself and in Him from any true good. " Cast thy burden on the Lord and He will sustain thee." " He will never suffer the righteous to fall." " Yea, though I walk through the valley of the shadow of death, I will fear no evil: for Thou art with me, Thy rod and Thy staff they comfort me. Surely goodness and mercy shall follow me all the days of my life; and I will dwell in the house of the Lord for ever."

DONALD MACLEOD.

THE EAR AND ITS MECHANISM.

BY PROFESSOR J. G. McKENDRICK, M.D.

THE recent inventions of the telephone, phonograph, and microphone have excited the attention of all classes of the community. Some have been attracted by the apparent utility of these inventions; others by the insight which a study of their phenomena gives into certain dim regions of acoustics, magnetism, and electricity; whilst many have regarded them more from the physiological point of view, as instruments exhibiting in a marvellous manner the delicate susceptibility of the human ear to vibrations of sound. These inventions also naturally lead us to the study of the mechanism of the ear, perhaps the most intricate and elaborate organ of sense we possess. No doubt there are some people who derive little or no pleasure from the contemplation of the structure of the "fine wrought eye and the wondrous ear," * and they shrink from investigating the how or why of any operations going on in the body. They are content in ignorance, and any information on such subjects is shut out mainly from a morbid dread that they may know too much of matters which, in the good old times, were almost the exclusive property of members of the medical profession. Happily, such narrow views are becoming rarer every year, and there is now a prevalent opinion that a knowledge of the general facts of physiology ought to form a part of the culture towards which we strive. The courses of physiological lectures now delivered in many of our large cities, the introduction of physiological teaching into our schools, and the publication of many excellent manuals of physiology and of biology, suitable for non-professional readers, are doing good service. The knowledge thus sown broadcast will in due time exercise its influence on the opinions formed upon many· theological, social, and hygienic questions.

But apart altogether from the obvious utility of such studies, I venture to assert that they have a high æsthetic value, and that they cannot be engaged in in a right spirit without elevating the thoughts, or without giving one a glimpse of what may be termed the poetry of science. It is a mistake to suppose that to be scientific demands that one is to be satisfied merely with the accumulation of facts, or with the construction of hard theories and dry hypotheses; that he is to shut himself out from the realms

* Shelley, "On Death."

of imagination, and that he is not to attempt to see and appreciate the beautiful in the fields of science. Not so. Science simply gives a man an increased range of vision; she gives him a glimpse into things which otherwise he could not see; she asks him to contemplate nature, not merely as shown to the unassisted eye and ear, but as revealed by all her methods. The love of such natural objects as the floating, fleecy cloud, the mountain covered with purple heather, the grassy bank set off by buttercups or hyacinths, the broad expanse of the sea, woods, trees, flowers, animal forms, is not lost or even injured by knowing something of the natural history of these objects. It is rather enhanced; it becomes deeper and fuller; the mind does not cease to regard them as objects of wonder and of admiration; scientific knowledge does not remove the mystery surrounding all natural objects, but it only lets us see a little deeper and permits us to take a wider visual sweep. I believe the time will come when poets will find material for their art, not only in the more obvious phenomena of nature, nor only in the play of human passion, and the lights and shadows of human existence, but also in many of those beautiful forms and wonderful mechanisms which at present are studied only in the cooler light of science. After all, the microscope, the scalpel, chemical analysis, and all the methods of science, only increase our perceptive powers, and they do not necessarily injure or destroy the sense of beauty and of perfection which we experience when we gaze on a glorious landscape or on an object faultless in form and colour. If we fix the ideas thus obtained from the more minute study of nature into stereotyped scientific forms, or associate them with a hard nomenclature, no doubt we may lose something which appeals to our emotional nature; just as one might be disturbed in the contemplation of rounded hills,—lovely with the bloom of heather, green sward, and graceful curves, —by the suggestion of glacial action, submergence, denudation, &c. ; but the one state of sensuous and dreamy enjoyment need not be incompatible with the other of intellectual appreciation. We have been accustomed to walk more in the one path than in the other, and we may be somewhat disturbed by the effect of contrast. But if we could take a broader view, might we not reach a state of purest pleasure in which both the emotional and the intellectual would be blended, and thus nature would appeal to our whole being? If so in landscape, why not in fields of contemplation of a narrower area? Let us leave the broad expanse and come to something of narrower bounds. Instead of studying the effect of masses, let us go to particulars, and from systems of things let us study things themselves. Even in these, simple as they may at first sight appear, we will find enough to excite wonder and admiration; and are not these feelings two of the mainsprings of poesy?

With such thoughts, it is my object to describe the arrangements of the human ear, one of the most wonderful of all mechanisms. This will be somewhat difficult, inasmuch as few organs of the body have been more minutely described by anatomists, who have attached to it numerous technical terms which repel a beginner in the study of this organ. However, with the aid of diagrams, it may be possible to convey an intelligible notion of its structure and mechanism.

Only a portion of the ear is seen externally. Part of it, and that by far the more important part, is situated deeply in the head. The term "ear" is often applied only to what is external, but physiologically it ought to be applied to the whole organ. The ear is divided

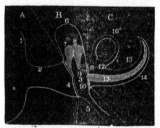

Fig. 1.—Diagrammatic view of the ear :—A, external ear; B, middle ear; C, internal ear. The dotted lines indicate the division of the ear into three parts :—1, auricle, or external portion; 2, external canal, or passage; 3, tympanum, or drum; 4, drum-head, or membrana tympani; 5, Eustachian tube, communicating with the throat; 6, cavities in the bone immediately behind the ear; 7, 8, 9, small bones of the ear; 10, round window, and 11, oval window, communicating with the internal ear; 12, central part of internal ear, called the vestibule; 13, cochlea, or snailshell, in which part of the auditory nerve terminates; 14, 15, spaces above and below 13, called staircases or scalæ; 16, semicircular canals.

anatomically into three parts :—(1) The *external ear*, formed of the *shell* or *auricle*, which we see externally, and of a canal or tube passing a short distance into the head, called the *external auditory canal*, and which

is closed at the bottom by a membrane called the *drum-head* of the ear; (2) the *middle ear* or *tympanum*, a cavity in the bone filled with air, shut off from the external ear by the drum-head, but communicating with the back of the throat by a tube called the *Eustachian tube*; and (3) the *internal ear* or *labyrinth*, a very complicated structure, specially connected with the endings of the auditory nerve. Strictly speaking, the third portion, or internal ear, is the true auditory apparatus, the other two being arrangements for transmitting sonorous vibrations to this portion. The various parts just mentioned are shown in the accompanying diagram (Fig. 1), which represents a plan of the apparatus. It should be studied with the aid of the description of the figure.

I.—STRUCTURE AND FUNCTIONS OF EXTERNAL EAR.

The external ear is formed of cartilage or gristle covered with skin. Its external surface, which receives waves of sound from without, is marked by many elevations and depressions, the most remarkable being the deep one, called the *concha*, into which the auditory canal opens. It is supplied with little muscles which, although feebly developed in man, attain considerable size and power in some animals. The power of moving the ears is usually absent in man, and it has been supposed that as man advanced in civilisation, the power of moving the ears voluntarily gradually became less and less until it was lost. Sometimes, however, persons are met with who can still voluntarily move their ears. It is narrated of Albinus, who was Professor of Medicine in the University of Leyden about the middle of last century, that he was in the habit of removing his wig in order to demonstrate to his class the power he possessed of moving his auricles at will. The power which many animals have of directing their ears towards the supposed source of sound, or of erecting them in an act of attention, is familiar to every one. To many animals the external ear no doubt acts as a kind of artificial hearing-trumpet, so that ordinary sounds may be augmented and faint sounds rendered audible. The auricle is small in moles, seals, and walruses, but it is largely developed in some bats and in the African elephant. The ears of the mouse and of the hedgehog are delicate organs of touch. In birds, the auricle is wanting. It is remarkable, however, that in nocturnal birds, such as many owls, the feathers can be elevated round the ear-opening so as to form a kind of external ear. In some aquatic mammals, such as in certain seals, the sea-otter, &c., the opening of the ear is merely a slit. It would seem, speaking generally, that a fully formed auricle is found only in mammals whose habits are terrestrial, and that it is reduced in size, or, it may be, is absent in mammals living underground or in water. It was once supposed that it had no function in man, and it was stated that those who had lost the external ears from accident or injury did not appear to suffer any diminution in the power of hearing. Recently, however, it has been shown, more especially by Dr. Burnett of Philadelphia, that the external ear, instead of being useless, has an important influence in the perception of quality of tone, and that it acts as a kind of resonator, lengthening the external auditory canal, so as to make certain tones more audible than they would otherwise be. It is well known that nearly every sound consists of a number of partial tones, and that the number and intensity of these give to our consciousness the "colour," "timbre," or "klang" of that particular sound. These tones are of different pitch—some high, others low. Burnett has found that the peculiar form of the external ear strengthens the higher partial tones. "By holding the hand behind or around the ear we have the power of adding a still deeper column of air and its resonance to that of the external ear. Hence the deaf person involuntarily places his hand to his ear, to increase by resonance the ordinary sound falling upon it. His hearing is thus strengthened, especially for those tones of high pitch and short wave-length to which the human voice owes its peculiar timbre or klang-tint." * Helmholtz has already observed in his great work on "Sensations of Tone,"—"It is, indeed, remarkable that the human voice should be so rich in over-tones for which the human ear is so sensitive." †

It appears, therefore, that in the peculiar conformation of the external ear we have a delicate resonator for tones of short wave-length in which the human voice is rich, and to which it owes its special quality. These interesting observations of Burnett show us how careful we ought to be in coming to the conclusion that any organ of the body should be placed in the catalogue of "inherited"

* Burnett's " Treatise on the Ear," 1877, p. 36.
† Helmholtz's " Tonempfindungen," 1870, p. 176.

organs, no longer possessing functions. This is specially true of any portion of an organ of sense, inasmuch as apparently trivial anatomical peculiarities may exercise an important influence on function. They also indicate to us that many sounds, such as those of the human voice, may not be appreciated by animals having movable or pendulous ears, such as the dog or cat, as they are by man. Then when the dog erects his ears, according to Burnett, the higher partial tones of certain sounds will be strengthened, and the quality of the sound will be more or less affected.

The position, form, and direction of the external canal will be understood from Fig. 2.

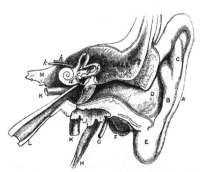

Fig. 2.—Transverse section of the entire auditory apparatus on the left side. A, helix; B, anti-tragus; C, anti-helix; D, concha; E, lobule; F, mastoid process; G, portio dura; H, styloid process; K, internal carotid artery; L, Eustachian tube; M, tip of petrous process; N, external auditory meatus; O, membrana tympani; P, tympanum; c, placed on the vestibule of the labyrinth; d, the cochlea; e, f, and g. the semicircular canals; h, facial nerve, the molar nerve of the face; and k, the auditory nerve.

The canal extends from the bottom of the concha to the drum-head. It is about one and a quarter inches in length, whilst its average width is about a quarter of an inch. Lined with skin, which is continuous with that covering the auricle, it resembles the finger of a glove, the finger-tip being the position of the drum-head. In this infolded skin there are from one thousand to two thousand minute glands, which secrete the wax of the ear. This wax is gradually pushed out of the canal as it is formed. It is remarkable that the tendency of the wax is always to move outwards, so that there is no necessity in a healthy state for removing it artificially. Those who try to clear it out with pins, push in more than they draw out, and also run the risk of injuring the delicate drum-head. The canal is usually somewhat tortuous, but occasionally it is so straight and wide as to permit one to look directly down on the drum-head. It is scarcely necessary to point out that in the healthy state the drum of the ear shuts off all communication between the external air and the middle ear, so that insects cannot penetrate into the head without rupture of the drum. Many tales of earwigs and other insects going into one ear and out by the other are entirely fictitious.

When sonorous waves impinge on the external ear, some will be reflected and practically lost, whilst others may be directed by the inequalities on its surface into the canal. Other waves may directly enter the canal, and be conveyed by it to the little drum-head at the bottom. Vibrations may also no doubt be conveyed directly by the walls of the canal, without the intervention of the air.

II.—STRUCTURE AND FUNCTIONS OF THE MIDDLE EAR.

The middle ear, tympanum, or drum, is an irregularly shaped cavity, about half an inch in height and one or two lines deep, placed between the external auditory canal and the labyrinth (see Fig. 2, P). It communicates with numerous little cavities or cells in the mass of bone which may be felt with the finger behind the ear; and, as already mentioned, it also communicates with the back of the throat by the Eustachian tube. If we could imagine ourselves in this little cavity, we would find the outer side of it partly formed by a membrane, the inner surface of the drum-head; the inner side would present two openings, one round, the other oval, both closed by membrane during life, and both communicating with the internal ear; whilst traversing the cavity we would discern a chain of three minute bones, called the *bones of the ear*. We would also observe a funnel-shaped opening, that of the Eustachian tube. The tympanum is lined by a membrane which is a continuation of that of the throat, nose, and Eustachian tube, an anatomical fact which explains how inflammations of these parts may affect the middle ear.

The important point to observe regarding the middle ear is that through it vibrations are conveyed by the chain of bones, and partly also by the air it contains and by its walls, from the drum-head to the internal ear. The drum-head, or *membrana tympani*, is itself a very remarkable structure. Somewhat elliptical in form, it is constructed of three layers of tissue—an external, which is

continuous with the skin lining the external canal; an internal, formed by the lining of the middle ear, whilst between the two are layers of fibrous tissue, some of the fibres radiating from a point towards the circumference, whilst others are arranged in a circular manner. This little membrane is stretched obliquely across the end of the auditory canal, and it is drawn inwards, so as to present a somewhat convex shape towards the middle ear (see Fig. 1, A).

The chain of bones stretches from the drum-head to the oval window already mentioned as communicating with the internal ear. It consists of three little bones shown in Fig. 3.

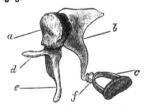

Fig. 3.—The Bones of the Ear. *a*, malleus or mallet; *b*, incus or anvil; *c*, stapes or stirrup; *d*, short process of malleus; *e*, long process of malleus, fixed to drum-head; *f*, point between incus and stapes. The short process of incus (above *b*) is fixed to wall of tympanum.

It will be observed that the chain is very irregular in form, and that the individual bones composing it have characteristic shapes. Proceeding from without inwards, the first, attached to the drum-head, is called the *malleus* or mallet; this is connected by a distinct joint with the second or middle bone, known as the *incus*, or anvil, which in turn is united by a minute joint at the end of one of its processes with a small bone shaped like a stirrup, and hence called the *stapes* or stirrup-bone. The base or foot of the stirrup fits into the oval window. Hence it will be seen that any movement made by the drum-head will be conveyed to the internal ear through the chain of bones to the oval window. But why should it be a *chain* of bones? It has already been mentioned that the base of the stirrup is inserted into the oval window, opening communicating with the internal ear. Now, the area of the drum-head is about fifteen to twenty times larger than that of the oval window. The internal ear on the other side of the oval window is full of fluid, and it is manifest that a far greater amount of pressure will be necessary to cause this fluid to oscillate backwards and forwards than was required for the movements of the air in the auditory passage. On the other hand, in consequence of the small size of the internal ear, and more especially considering that the appendages and terminations of the auditory nerve are of microscopical size, the extent of the oscillations of the fluid in the internal ear must be relatively very small. The mechanical problem, therefore, that might be propounded to an engineer desirous of constructing a similar apparatus, is to transform a motion of considerable amplitude and of little force, as it occurs at the drum-head, into one of small amplitude and great force, as occurs at the oval window. To accomplish this, as pointed out by Helmholtz, mechanical appliances, such as levers, trains of pulleys, or cranes might be employed. Actual observation of the movement of the bones, and a careful measurement of them, have shown that they really constitute a lever having a long and a short arm. The tip of the handle of the hammer, attached to the drum-head, is about one and a half times as far from the centre of rotation as that point is from the base of the stirrup, and consequently the pressure at the base of the stirrup will be one and a half times as great as that which drives the hammer. By an ingenious series of experiments made by Dr. Burnett, he succeeded in measuring the extent of movement of a bright speck on the drum-head, when a sound was conducted to it, and in comparing it with the amount of movement of a similar speck on the base of the stirrup. The experiments were performed on nine fresh preparations of the ear; of these, seven were from man, one from a calf, and one from a horse. Fixing the bone containing the internal ear firmly in a vice, an opening was made into the middle ear by chiselling away a portion of its wall. Thus the chain of bones was exposed. These were lightly sprinkled with powdered starch, a powerful beam of light was thrown into the dark cavity, a microscope of low power was directed towards the bones, and thus the particles of starch appeared as minute, shining specks. When in these circumstances the sound of an organ-pipe was conveyed directly to the drum-head, the chain of bones was seen to vibrate in excursions bearing a fixed relation to each other. The little bright specks then became short and brilliant lines, and the length of the line indicated the extent of movement of the illuminated point. By this method he ascertained that the amplitude of movement of the stirrup was about one-third that of the drum.

Helmholtz has further shown that the shape of the drum-head itself also assists in obtaining this result. Instead of being flat, it is somewhat curved, its middle part being drawn inwards by the handle of the mallet-bone, so as to present a funnel-shape. Curiously, however, the sides of the funnel are not straight, but are curved, being slightly convex on the outer side. Thus a considerable movement of any part of the sides of the funnel will cause a much smaller movement of its apex, to which the handle of the hammer is attached.

By these exquisite arrangements, therefore, dependent on the form of the drum-head, and on the mechanism of the chain of bones, the movements of the oscillating air in the auditory passage are reduced in extent, but increased in efficient power, before they reach the minute structures in the internal ear.

In the middle ear, there are two minute muscles, one, called the *tensor tympani*, the action of which is to tighten the drum-head, and the other, the *stapedius*, attached to the little stirrup bone. The precise action of the latter muscle is not clearly understood; but the ear has, in these two muscles, an apparatus for accommodating itself to various sounds. According to Professor Lucae, the first muscle aids in the perception of low musical tones by tightening the drum-head, whilst the *stapedius* performs the same function for high unmusical tones; and he states that abnormal contraction of one or other muscle may produce a modified state of perception, which he terms "low hearing" and "high hearing;" that is, the person may have a degree of acuteness for low sounds, or for high sounds, which is abnormal; or, on the other hand, his power of perceiving such sounds may be diminished.

The chief function of the Eustachian tube * appears to be to regulate pressure on the drum-head. It is generally supposed that during rest the tube is open, and that it is closed during the act of swallowing. As this action is frequently taking place, not only when food or drink is introduced, but also when saliva is swallowed, it is evident that the pressure of the air in the tympanum will be kept in a state of equilibrium with that of the external air, exerted on the outer surface of the membrana tympani, and that thus the latter will be rendered independent of variations of atmospheric pressure, such

* First described by Vesalius, who was Professor of Anatomy in Padua, about 1540. It was more carefully described by Bartholomew Eustachius, an Italian physician, about 1570.

as may occur within certain limits—as when we descend the shaft of a mine or ascend a high mountain. By a forcible expiration, the mouth and nose being closed, air may be driven into the middle ear, while a forcible inspiration will draw air from that cavity. In the first case the membrana tympani will bulge outwards; in the second case inwards; and in both, from excessive stretching of the membrane, there will be partial deafness, especially for sounds of high pitch. Permanet occlusion of the tube is one of the most common causes of deafness.

(To be concluded in next number.)

"WILL FAITH BE LOST?"

"Nevertheless, when the Son of Man cometh, shall He find faith on the earth?"—LUKE xviii. 8.

A Sermon preached at the Chapel Royal, St. James's, by the Rt. Rev. the Lord Bishop of Rochester.

CRITICISM has a question to ask about this word *faith*. What faith is it? Is it the faith within a man, what may be called the prehensile force of the soul, by which he lays hold of something outside him, and through grasping it makes it his own? Or is it something without him, be it a person to be adored, or a doctrine to be believed, or a fact to be explained, which, when this inward faculty of apprehension has seized and assimilated it, and in exact proportion to the completeness of such seizure becomes its very substance and life? You may say, if you will, that the question is immaterial, for, plainly, the two kinds of faith just spoken of imply and require each other; either alone is inoperative. Yet for exactness' sake, and for the full comprehension of the Divine Teacher's warning, we should learn, I think, from the context, that it is the inward faculty of belief, rather than the objective thing to be believed, that Christ refers to here. What had made that poor widow woman at once so vehement in the pleading of her suit, and so successful in winning it? Was it not her overpowering sense of necessity, fortified by a supreme instinct of justice, that, like the blow of a hundred pairs of mailed hands, broke down the barrier of a hard selfishness, and conquered for her her rights? And how does Christ point His own tale? To urge and press faith. "Shall not God avenge His own elect, which cry day and night unto Him, though He bear long with them? I tell you He will avenge them speedily. Nevertheless" (however earnestly man may plead, and God bless), "when the Son of Man cometh shall He find faith on the earth?"

This question, my brethren, which, as you will observe, Christ did not answer (He never answered His own questions), about which certainly He was not very hopeful, I propose to you to-day. It is the supreme question of our own time. Everything else dwarfs into an utter insignificance by the side of it. It is a question for the Church as much as for the world; for the clergy as well as for the laity. This is certain: that if in the heart of the living Church of God there were burning now with anything of a clear and steady flame the fire of love to God and to man as the offspring of God, we preachers would not have so often, and to so little purpose, to beseech and even push the Church to evangelise Paganism. This, too, I confess, that of all strange and saddening inconsistencies that an honest minister of Jesus Christ most constantly encounters, and most sorrowfully deplores in his own spirit, is the slight hold these grand and overwhelming realities have of his will and heart. While his entire being and life should be possessed and inflamed by them, as if there was nothing else in the world so much worth thinking about, he is conscious of accepting them with but a languid assent; and again and again, when Jehovah bids Jonah go to Nineveh to deliver His message, the prophet flees to Tarshish from the face of the Lord.

First we will glance at the peril, and then at the safeguard.

The peril is that of losing faith.

"When the Son of Man cometh, shall He find faith on the earth?"

Now, faith in reference to questions of revelation has three degrees, and only the last represents it in its completeness, though, indeed, as things go now we are apt to accept even and only the first with a sort of thankful surprise. First, there is faith in a personal God, maker and owner of the universe, who, in the far distant past, in the mystery of His infinite power and wisdom, summoned everything into being. "In the beginning God created the heavens and the earth." What theology calls by the cold name of Deism, is, however, far beyond the reach of some thinkers now. Because science cannot discover God, reason is pertly bidden to treat Him as if He could not be discovered. The dogmatism of physical philosophers, so far more intolerable, because so much more inconsistent than that of theologians, arrogantly narrows the area of reliable knowledge within the limits of physical experiment, and shuts up to the thinker all roads but one.

Then there is another table land, whereon faith recognises not only the being of God, but also His government; refuses to suppose that, exhausted with the labours of creation, He has ever since left the universe to take its own course, or if after a fashion governing it, handcuffed by His own laws. That a Divine Providence is over us all caring, thinking, providing for the very humblest of His creatures, is, indeed, incredible in its sublime blessedness—until the lens of the microscope, displaying the inexhaustible skill lavished on an insect's wing, makes it cease to be improbable that He who took such pains to create would be at less pains to preserve.

If Moses has told us of the Creation, and a later prophet assures us how He reserves the appointed weeks of the harvest, David has set to music the grand hymn of an over-ruling Providence.

"He causeth the grass to grow for the cattle, and green herbs for the service of men. The young lions roar after their prey, and seek their meat from God. These wait all upon Thee, that Thou mayest give them their meat in due season. The glory of the Lord shall rejoice for ever: the Lord shall rejoice in His works."

The third and final stage of Christian faith is where the spirit of man worships the God of the creeds—God, that is, revealed and reconciled in His incarnate Son, who, after He had perfected our redemption by His death, rose from the grave and went back to heaven; from whence He sent His Holy Spirit to build up his Church among men, until in the end of the days He comes back with His holy angels to judge both the quick and the dead.

And, my brethren, it is this faith—with a few all of it, with many some of it—that seems now to be perishing out of our midst, so as already to justify the Saviour's mournful question, "When I come back, who will there be to believe on me?"

There are many causes for this; happily none of them without remedy.

One is that dense, and coarse, and almost brutal ignorance, in which the toiling masses of the people who have outgrown the Church's grasp—not, we trust, her conscience—are permitted to live and die, of all that touches their salvation, and explains their destiny. To hundreds of thousands of our fellow-countrymen Almighty God is practically an unknown Being except as the substance of a hideous oath: Jesus Christ, in His redeeming love and human sympathy, as distant as a fixed star.

Then, there is another phase of unbelief, which may be said to spring chiefly from a cynical indifference to the whole subject. Thousands of partially educated men and women will not even exert themselves to reflect about what they once learned superficially in their childhood, but which has lost all interest for them now. The world to come seems a long way off; this world is close at hand, and absorbing, and filled with keen delights. Here the pursuit of gain, there the fever of pleasure; with one person the slow paralysis of an engrossing indulgence, with another the instinctive consciousness that on the whole it may be better that there should not be another world with its inevitable retribution, and its awful revelations, and its terrible partings, and its unspeakable remorse, presently settles the already biassed judgment into the conviction that there is none.

People tell us now that one hopeful phenomenon of modern scepticism is that its disciples are blameless in their moral conduct; and it may be hopeful, though I am not so sure of it. This I am sure of, that human nature in the masses is substantially the same all down the ages; and that when sinful man is forced to hide himself from the face of his Maker because he knows he has disobeyed Him, it is a pleasant and an easy delusion to arrive at, that perhaps there is no God, from whom he need be at the pains to flee. But there is yet one cause more, the peculiar growth of the present day, and what goes by the new word of agnosticism. In other words, it is the mental and moral condition that waits, and puts off deciding about God, and the world to come, and its own future, and prefers to keep what it calls its judgment in suspense; and feels it a kind of offence against reason, and the results and masters of reason, to have an opinion of its own, until they give it leave; and so they stand by the bank of the Church's life, lazily and voluptuously watching it flow past them, little conscious that they themselves are on the bosom of a yet mightier tide, that is hurrying them to the unveiling of the great secret, in every breath they draw, and every moment they live; and that while they are ready with the least possible amount of evidence quickly and finally to decide on mundane questions, which when put into the scale with these Divine things are like a child's game against the battle that decides an empire, about God, and the soul, and the future, and what comes after death, they think it no loss, no baseness to say, "I cannot tell."

But see what will come of it. All that the religion of Christ has given the world, is still giving it, must go, if faith goes. The serene and sweet elevation of conduct and life that comes from the hope of immortality—that must go; and it would be worse than death to millions of beautiful lives.

The absorbing and regenerating forces that flow from the contemplation of Jesus Christ—His life, and death, and words, and character: these will be all dried up, as a river when it is lost in the sands, and with nothing in its place.

For these friends of ours, who ruthlessly cut down the Tree of Life before our eyes, tell us while they do it, that they know of no other to plant in its place. That indeed is not their business. "Your Jesus of Nazareth was but a beautiful dreamer. Get rid of your dreams; live at your best; then face death, without hope or fear."

And yet two more things must go—go for ever—if faith goes. I mean morality and benevolence.

Mind, I do not say that all morality will go. Society will always have self-interest enough to know how to protect life and property; civilisation of a certain sort in material things, perhaps increasingly refined and complete, will always remain; nay, for generations it may retain the subtle and inextinguishable aroma of the recollection of Christ. But purity—you must not expect to keep that, if you banish from your homes and your lives Him whose first great beatitude was pureness of heart; whose religion was the first among men to declare that the body is the temple of God. Unchristianised England would soon need a second Juvenal to scarify the world's conscience with the revelation of her guilt.

And philanthropy would perish when there was nothing to feed it with. Rome, Athens, Sparta knew nothing of the hospital or the workhouse, of kindness to the poor, or pity for the orphan. To lose faith might, indeed, be to get free from restraints that curb license, and from shadows that check levity, and from a Holy Presence that is a felt barrier to self-will, and from the thought of a judgment swift to righteousness.

But you would have in its place—and it is doubtful if it would be as well worth having —wives whom you could not trust, children whom you would not train; toil with no Sabbath; poverty with no almsgiving. As for the Bible—would the starch primers of science help the weary to be patient, and the tempted to be steadfast? Partings by the grave would have no sweet hope of a tearless and sinless meeting; an age of reason, certain of its reaction in a gloomy, and perhaps cruel superstition, would have its earliest harvest in an elysium of vice.

"When the Son of Man cometh, shall He find faith on the earth?"

Such is our peril: from which good Lord deliver us!

But what is our safeguard?

First, while we look round us and discern the signs of the times, let us discard on the one hand a shallow optimism that counts all to be right just because we wish it to be; on the other hand we will resist the spirit of despair as if the Church was on the rocks; and lifting up our heads, though sailing over a sea white with breakers, be brave and calm, for our ship which has weathered many storms already shall yet get safe to land. God is not asleep, and Christ is not dead; and the Church is awake, and because she is awake is feared, hated, and opposed. The student of history, as he looks back over the long space between the Ascension and to-day, sees times when there was far more cause to fear for truth and godliness even than the present; breathes again, for he is inspired by a living hope. But we must each do the work given him to do, each be at his post. What is this work? First let us, each of us, more thoroughly master, more minutely examine, more devoutly study, more sincerely love the great doctrines of our religion, never treating them as if they were something to be ashamed of, unfit for reasoning men and this superior time. Then not only will our souls be more filled with a grateful and absorbing impression of their beauty and suitableness, but we shall be in a far better position to explain and maintain them with others. Never was there a time when it was more necessary for every true Christian man to qualify himself, at least in his own family and neighbourhood, to be a champion of the hope that is in him. Never was there a time when there was less excuse for either ignorance or helplessness. To our hand, at our very door, there are provided for us readable and compact treatises compiled from the latest sources, and by very able pens, on the bulwarks of our faith, and on the reasonableness as well as the divineness of our religion. I say, let us use them, as those who are summoned to fight for God. For it *is* a reasonable religion : and if you could sweep it away with a scornful phrase to-morrow, it would be a far harder task for reason to explain its history and its results on the hypothesis of its being a delusion, than to maintain it on the theory of its being true.* If only a little of the patience and ingenuity, and erudition that are so lavishly displayed on behalf of the destructive theorists against our faith could be exercised by them on its behalf against the unsubstantial speculations of imperfect observers, religion for once would have justice done her, and the Cross would prove a safe resting-place for perplexed spirits waiting for more light, but consenting to use the light they have.

Then let us use and enjoy and deepen our faith by sharing it with others. If anywhere within the sphere of human life no man liveth to himself, and no man dieth to himself, it is in the matter of religion. If in any one of our possessions selfishness is an utterly unreasonable and monstrous and wicked thing, it is with the faith of Christ—Christ who has redeemed the world, and set the Church in its midst, to be salt and light to it, and who says to each soul that, conscious of His goodness, looks up to Him for orders, "Go tell these souls that they are dear to me, for they are bought with my blood." Shall I tell you the secret of a cold, and pulseless, and languid, and halting religion ? It is *uselessness.* "Unprofitable servants !" You remember what the parable did with them. The soul that cares only for its own salvation, and leaves to a small handful of professional teachers the blessed duty of confessing Christ before men—it *may* be saved ; but it will have a poor time of it, and it will be saved "as by fire." The brightest and bravest, and strongest and blessedest souls, are those which feel their religion a trust ; their faith a profession before many witnesses ; their warfare not only fighting for themselves, but contending for their Master ; their crown, when it comes to them from

* Any one who would like to see how the recent hostile theories on the origin of the Synoptic Gospels have been utterly pulverised by the simple process of letting them destroy each other, should read with care the Archbishop of York's introduction to the three first Gospels in the "Speaker's Commentary."

the King's hand, sparkling beyond the brightness of the firmament, with the precious salvation of a brother's soul.

In conclusion, this question of Christ's includes three thoughts of paramount value.

One is Christ's absence, as implied in the fact of His coming back after having been so long away. "When the Son of Man cometh," which first of all meant He is going away. In a most real sense Christ *is* away. No one sees or hears Him. He does not interfere in the world's affairs. He does not assert His life, when men deny it, nor vindicate His justice, when they impugn it ; He does not protect His disciples when they are persecuted ; He does not rout His enemies when they are insolent. His kingdom is invisible, and invisibly administered over an empire of souls. This is why it is so plausible to deny His existence altogether, and to repeat the cheap scoff we have heard so often, that if there was a living Christ still, the Christ we read of in the Gospels, how is it to be reconciled with the state of the world now ? Well, He foresaw it all, and He has neither forgotten it nor left it to itself, but He rules it by His Spirit ; He will not overpower the free operation of the understanding by supernatural interference. He will not check physical discovery to protect the weak faith of timid or ignorant followers. He will suffer Himself to be discovered only by the faith of the heart. He, the Son of Man, knows what is in man, pities it, bears with it, makes the best of it, hopes the best for it, and, knowing His purpose, waits. For He is coming back. Wonderful thought ! though not more wonderful than the other wonderful things of the gospel story. Supernatural, yet not more supernatural than His being born of a virgin, and rising again from the dead ; final, for it will be in the end of the days ; supreme, for it will be the last revelation of the glory of God on earth. My brethren, I pray you to take this into your inmost heart and soul, and to saturate your entire spiritual consciousness with the truth of it, and to make it increasingly at once the motive of your life, and the hope of your glory, that Christ is coming back ; coming in the clouds ; coming with the angels ; coming to be glorified in His saints ; coming to judge the world ; coming to reveal iniquity ; coming to crown faithfulness ; coming to manifest God, and to reign for ever and ever. And He is coming to us, to you and me. Will He find faith in us? The faith that has believed His word, trusted His providence, tasted His love, used His grace, finished His work, borne His cross, confessed his name!

Shall I tell you whom He will most welcome then? Those who did most to spread His gospel. Shall I tell you who will most rejoice to see Him then? Those who, with all humility, but singleness of heart, laid their lives at His feet. Shall I tell you who will find heaven most heavenly? Those who will meet the greatest number of souls shown the way there. Shall I tell you how you may find out if He will then find in you what He will wish to find? Only in one way. Does He find it now?

HEALTH AT HOME.

By B. W. RICHARDSON, M.D., F.R.S.

PART I.

THE old saying, "There is no place like home," has a singularly happy meaning, when it is applied to health and the benefits which spring from health that is good and beautiful. We who are engaged in forwarding sanitary work may labour our lives out, and still do little service, until we can get each home, however small it may be, included in the plan of our work. The river of national health must rise from the homes of the nation. Then it will be a great river on which every blessing will be borne.

When I, as a physician, enter a house where there is a contagious disease, my first care is to look at the surroundings. What are the customs of the people there? Are they wholesome? Are they unwholesome? If the answer be, "Wholesome and common sense," then I know that the better half of success in the way of treatment and prevention is secured. If the answer be, "Unwholesome, slovenly, disorderly, careless," then I know that all that may be advised for the best will be more than half useless, because there is no habit on which any dependence can be truthfully placed, and because habit in the wrong direction is so difficult to move that not even the strongest ties of affection are a match for it even in times of emergency.

If we could then get wives, mothers, and daughters to learn the habitual practice of all that tends to health, we should soon have an easy victory, and should ourselves cease to be known as the pioneers of sanitary work, the work itself being a recognised system and a recognised necessity to be practised by everybody.

To me it always seems that no point in the warfare against disease is anything like so important as that of getting the women of the household to work heart and soul with us sanitarians. I am never tired of repeating this fact, and I never shall be until the fact is accomplished. We always look to women for the cleanliness and tidiness of home. We say a home is miserable if a good wife and mother be not at the head of it to direct the internal arrangements. We speak of slovenly women, so much importance do we attach to orderly women, twenty times to one more frequently than we do of slovenly men. A slovenly woman is a woman of mark for discredit, and there can be no doubt that the natural excellences of women in respect to order and cleanliness have, without any distinct system or mode of scientific education, saved us often from severe and fatal outbreaks of disease. In the cholera epidemics which I have twice witnessed, and in which I have taken visiting charge of affected districts, I have found the women by far the most useful and practical coadjutors. The men sat by the fire if they were at home; the women truly bestirred themselves. They saw that the water intended for drinking purposes was boiled before it was used for drinking purposes; they attended to details relating to ventilation and general cleansing; they washed the clothing and bedding of the affected persons; they attended in the sick rooms; they prepared the food. In a sentence, they were acting forces for the suppression of the epidemics, and their devotion, and I say it faithfully, their readier and superior appreciation of details, were the great saving factors in relation both to preventive and curative art.

That which we sanitarians want, therefore, to see, is the scientific education of women to prepare them to meet emergencies at once, and not only so, but to prevent, by forethought and intelligent prevision, the necessity for emergencies. We wish them to understand the principles which suggest the details, instead of having to learn the details in moments of much excitement and anxiety and dread, when details, however important they may be, seem new, obscure, involved, and all but impossible, when habits which have been acquired have to be given up or much modified, and when new habits have to be, as it were, improvised and enforced with regularity at a moment's notice. For it is as true as it is simple that good health is after all, and bad health is after all, a matter of habit to an extent which few persons in the slightest degree acknowledge or comprehend.

To the domestic cleanliness which most women by habit learn to acquire, it should be easy to tack on many of the other forms of cleanliness which the physician wishes to enforce, but which the general public does not altogether or readily recognise. It is in relation to this further cleanliness, this more than commonplace cleanliness—but which should be commonplace for all intents and purposes—that I wish to draw attention, and the attention of the women of the nation particularly, in these papers on Health at Home. I promise to put forward not one suggestion that cannot be carried out. I will in these essays—

"Imagination's airy wing suppress,"

and give nothing more than plain rules for plain people of every grade of life.

SUNLIGHT AT HOME.

Whether your home be large or small give it light. There is no house so likely to be unhealthy as a dark and gloomy house. In a dark and gloomy house you can never see the dirt that pollutes it. Dirt accumulates on dirt, and the mind soon learns to apologise for this condition because the gloom conceals it. "It is no credit to be clean in this hole of a place" is soon the sort of idea that the housewife gets into her mind; the "place is always dingy, do what you may," is another similar and common idea; and so in a dark house unwholesome things get stowed away and forgotten, and the air becomes impure, and when the air becomes impure the digestive organs become imperfect in action, and soon there is some shade of bad health engendered in those persons who live in that dark house. Flowers will not healthily bloom in a dark house, and flowers are, as a rule, good indices. We put the flowers in our windows that they may see the light. Are not our children worth many flowers? They are the choicest of flowers. Then again light is necessary in order that the animal spirits may be kept refreshed and invigorated. No one is truly happy who in waking hours

XXI—5

is in a gloomy house or room. The gloom of the prison has ever been considered as a part of the punishment of the prison, and it is so. The mind is saddened in a home that is not flushed with light, and when the mind is saddened the whole physical powers soon suffer; the heart beats languidly, the blood flows slowly, the breathing is imperfect, the oxidation of the blood is reduced, and the conditions are laid for the development of many wearisome and unnecessary constitutional failures and sufferings.

Once again, light, sunlight I mean, is of itself useful to health in a direct manner. Sunlight favours nutrition; sunlight favours nervous function; sunlight sustains, chemically or physically, the healthy state of the blood. Children and older persons living in darkened places become blanched or pale; they have none of the ruddy, healthy bloom of those who live in light. We send a child that has lived in a dark court in London for a few days only into the sunlight, and how marked is the change. We hardly know the face again.

Let us keep, then, this word in our minds, light, light, light; sunlight which feeds us with its influence and leaves no poisonous vapours in its train.

Before I leave this subject, I want to say a word about light in relation to the sick. A few hundred years ago it became a fashion, for reasons it is very hard to divine, to place sick people in dark and closely curtained bedrooms. The practice to some extent is continued to this day. When a person goes to bed with sickness it is often the first thing to pull down the blinds of the windows, to set up dark blinds, or if there be Venetian blinds to close them. On body and spirit alike this practice is simply pernicious. It may be well, if light is painful to the eyes of the sufferer, to shield the eyes from the light, or even shut the light off them altogether; but for the sake of this to shut it out of all the room, to cut off wholesale its precious influence, to make the sick-room a dark cell in which all kinds of impurities may be concealed day after day, is an offence to nature which she ever rebukes in the sternest manner.

This remark presses with special force in cases where epidemic and contagious diseases are the affections from which the sufferers are suffering, for these affections, as they live on uncleanliness, require for their suppression the broadest light of day. Moreover, I once found by experiment that certain organic poisons, analogous to the poisons which

propagate these diseases, are rendered innocuous by exposure to light. Thus, in every
point of view, light stands forward as the
agent of health. In sickness and in health,
in infancy, youth, middle age, old age, in all
seasons, for the benefit of the mind and for
the welfare of the body, sunlight is a bearer
and sustainer of health.

To secure the entrance of sunlight, every
house should have a plentiful supply of large
windows, and not an opportunity of any kind
should be lost to let in light to every room.
It is very easy to exclude light when it is too
bright: it is very hard to let it in when by
bad building it is systematically excluded.
Lately, by an architectural perversity which
is simply astounding, it has become a fashion
to build houses like those which were built
for our ancestors about two centuries ago,
and which are called Queen Anne houses or
mansions. Small windows, small panes, overhanging window brows, sharp long roofs enclosing attics with small windows: these are
the residences to which I refer; dull, red, dark,
and gloomy. I am told that their excellence
lies in their artistic beauty, to which many
advantages that we sanitarian artists wish for
must necessarily be sacrificed. I would be
the last to oppose either the cultivation of
art in design or of art in application, and I
do not for one moment believe that such
opposition is necessary. But these beetle-
browed mansions are not so beautiful as
health, and never can be. I am bound to
protest against them on many sanitary
grounds, and on none so much as on their
interference with the work of the sun. They
produce shade, and those who live in them
live in shadow.

In many residences where there is plenty
of window space there is much neglect in
keeping the windows clean. Windows should
be cleaned once a week at least, and a great
desideratum is to bring into general use a simple mechanical contrivance by which the window sashes can be easily removed and turned
into the room, so as to enable the cleaning to
take place without the perilous process of
standing outside on the window-sill. Amongst
the poor who cannot afford to have a professed window-cleaner the windows often
become quite obscured, because the women
of the household cannot get at them, as they
say, on both sides, and the men are not at
home in the day to give them assistance.
Baker's new ventilating window promises to
answer best for the object here stated. The
sashes of this window hang on centres instead
of sliding up and down. When they are

closed the sashes fit neatly and exclude
draughts and wet effectually; and when they
are opened they can be set at any required
angle to admit air. The greatest advantage
of all is that each window sash can be turned
over, so that it may be cleaned with equal
facility on its inside and outside surfaces
without exposing the cleaner to the risk of
standing outside at any stage of the cleaning
process.

The introduction of daylight reflectors has
been, in late years, a very great and useful
advance. The dark basements of town
houses can be so often completely lighted by
these reflectors, that I wonder they are not
universally demanded in places where their
action is effective. The light they afford is
steady, often actually bright, and always
pure.

SLEEP AT HOME.

I have been speaking about sunlight, and
am led by this to refer to another and allied
topic, I mean night and hours of sleep. If
it be good to make all possible use of sunlight,
it is equally good to make as little use as
possible of artificial light. Artificial lights,
so far, have been sources of waste, not only
of the material out of which they are made,
but of the air on which they burn. In the
air of the closed room the present commonly
used lamps, candles, and gaslights, rob the
air of a part of its vital constituent, and
supply in return products which are really
injurious to life. Gaslight is in this respect
most hurtful, but the others are bad when
they are long kept burning in one confined
space. The fewer hours after dark that are
spent in artificial light the better; and this
suggests, of itself, that within reasonable
limits the sooner we go to rest after dark the
better. We require in the cold season of
winter, when the nights are long, much more
of sleep than we do in the summer. On the
longest day in the year, seven hours of sleep
is sufficient for most men and women who are
in the prime of life. On the shortest day, nine
hours of sleep is not overmuch, and for those
who are weakly, ten or even twelve hours may
be taken with real advantage. In winter,
children should always have ten to twelve
hours of sleep. It is not idleness to indulge to
that extent, but an actual saving, a storing
up of invigorated existence for the future.
Such rest can only be obtained by going to
bed very early, say at half-past eight o'clock
or nine.

It is wrong as ever it can be that our

legislators should often be sitting up, as we know they do, times after times, in the dead of night, trying against life to legislate for life. It is most foolish that public writers, who hold so many responsibilities in their hands, should be called upon to exercise their craft at a time when all their nature is calling out to them—rest, rest, rest! It is said I am foolish for declaring these things. Is it so? I am standing by Nature, speaking under her direction, and, without a thought of dogmatism, I am driven to ask: May it not be the world that is foolish?—the world, I mean, of fashion and habit, which could, if it would, change the present systems as easily as it criticizes the view that it ought to make the change. Anyway, this I know, and it is the truth I would here express, that in every man, woman, and child there is, at or about the early time I have named, a persistent periodical desire for sleep, which steals on determinately, which, taken at the flood, leads to a good sound night's rest, and which resisted never duly returns, but is replaced by a surreptitious sleep, broken by wearing dreams, restless limbs, and but partial restoration of vital power. I have said before, *make the sun your fellow-workman*. I repeat the saying now. I do not say, go to bed at all seasons, with the sun and rise with it, because in this climate that would not be, at all seasons, possible; but I say, as a general principle, as closely as you can, make the sun your fellow-workman; follow him, as soon as you are able, to rest, and do not let him stare at you in bed many hours after he has commenced his daily course. Teach your children, moreover, this same lesson, and the practice of it, whereupon there will be, in a generation or two, even in this land of fogs and dulness a race of children of the sun, who will stand, in matter of health, a head and shoulders above the children of the present generation.

BEDROOMS AND BEDS.

From the subject of sleep I am led by as easy and natural a transition to the subject of bedrooms and beds, as I was before led from the subject of light to the subject of sleep. But perhaps some one will say, Why, in speaking of a home and fireside topics, should you begin with bedrooms? There is the drawing-room, surely, first to be thought of; that room in which the company gathers when company comes together; that room in which the lady of the house takes the most pride, shows the most taste, feels most at home. There is also the dining-room, or sitting-room, or breakfast-room, or study. Again, there is the kitchen—of all rooms, surely, the most important in every sanitary point of view?

We will enter all these rooms in good time; but let us go into the bedroom first, and get that in order, because, after all, it is really the most important room in the house, by far and far again. I know it is not commonly thought to be so. I am quite aware from my daily observations, for over thirty years, that this is one of the least popular notions about bedrooms. I often think, as I wend my way up ever so many different kinds of stairs daily, that a doctor's usual journey would be something like that on a treadwheel, were it not for the fact that there is always some new ending to his ascents, and that on his mission of freedom and usefulness he is carrying the blessings of the services his brethren are giving to him, for dispensation, into the sanctuaries of sorrow. But one fact would lighten my heart very much more, I mean the fact, if it were as fully as it were easily realisable, that I should always find the bedrooms in sickness or in health befitting their office and the purpose to which they are assigned.

As a rule I regret to record that from want of appreciation of what is most healthy, in opposition to a keen appreciation of what is most fashionable, the bedroom is too often the part of the house that is least considered. It may be in any part of the house. There is no room too much out of the way or too little cared for that may not be a bedroom. "This is only a bedroom," is the commonest observation of the woman who is deputed to show you over an empty house that stands to be let. "We can turn the dressing-room into a bedroom whenever we like," is not unfrequently a housewife's, and even a good housewife's, expression. "Give me a shake-down somewhere," is the request of the unexpected traveller or visitor who wants to stay with you all night. "Anywhere will do, so long as it is a bed." "This is only an attic; but it is large enough for one servant, you know, and two have slept in it many a time before now." These are the kind of ordinary terms that are applied to bedrooms as apologies for something that is confessedly but observedly wrong about them. The language itself implies error; but it is far from expressing the whole of the error that really exists.

When we enter the bedroom we too often find it, though it may be a good-sized room,

altogether unsuited as a sleeping apartment.
It may be situated either at the back or the
front of the house; it may or may not have
a fireplace, and if it should have a fireplace
the register may or may not be open. The
windows may be large or small, according
to mere caprice of the builder, or of accident,
or of necessity; and whether the window will
open or shut from the top or the bottom
sash, or from both, is a matter of smallest
consequence. As a rule the bedroom windows
that have a double sash open only from the
bottom, and it is the most usual occurrence
to find the sash-lines out of gear altogether,
or the frames in a bad state, so that the
sash has to be supported with care, or
"humoured," whenever it has to be opened
or closed. Then to the window, that the
room may look snug and comfortable, must
be muslin blinds (half blinds), roller blinds,
and very often heavy curtains. When the
window is opened the roller blind blows out
like the sail of a boat, or blows in, at the risk
of knocking down the looking-glass. Sometimes Venetian blinds, which are never in
order for two months together, take the
place of roller blinds, and it becomes quite
an art to manage the laths, though these
blinds are on the whole the best. Then the
walls of bedrooms are in most instances
covered with paper, and of all rooms in
the house they are least frequently papered.
"The lower rooms must be papered, they look
so very dirty; the bedrooms are dingy, but
they may stand over another year; nobody
sees them." To carry out further the idea
of snugness, the bedrooms are carpeted, it
may be over their whole surface right up to
the walls of the rooms, and the carpet is
nailed down, so that it may be swept without
being dragged out of its place.

Again, the bedroom is too often made a
kind of half lumber-room—a place in which
things that have to be concealed are carefully
stowed away. "Under the bed" is a convenient hiding-place. It is the fact, that
once in a public institution for the sick which
I inspected there existed an arrangement by
which each new patient who came in to be
cured had his every-day clothes, after they were
taken off his body, put into a rickety old box
and pushed under his bed, to remain there until
he was able to put them on again when he
"left the house," or until he died, if his disease ended fatally, and his relatives claimed
them. I found eighteen of these boxes of
clothes secreted systematically under eighteen
beds in one insalubrious sick-room, or ward,
of this establishment. In private houses this
same plan of stowing away old clothes, old
boots and shoes and the like, is too frequently
put in practice.

I notice once again that the occurrence of
damp or wet in the ceilings and walls of a bedroom is much more readily tolerated than it
is elsewhere. If a pipe bursts and the drawing-room or dining-room ceiling is covered
with a dark patch, ever so small, that must
be at once attended to, it looks so very bad.
But a patch of similar character, though it
look like a map of the United Kingdom, with
the Straits of Dover and the coast of France
as an opposing outline, may remain on the
ceiling of the bedroom until it dries, and then,
being dry, may still remain, because if the water
should come in again the condition will be
as bad as ever.

I will say no more about bedrooms to
their disparagement. The errors I have
pointed out when they are present are unpardonable in regard to the healths of those
who permit them, and inasmuch as the health
of these is of far greater moment than their
equanimity of sentiment, I must run the risk
of disturbing the temper that I may assist
the health. I feel the less compunction
on this head because what I am about to
propose in the way of remedy means nothing
but economy of reconstruction along the
whole line. I will tender in a few rules what
are the essentials of a healthy bedroom. If
they cannot all be carried out in every case,
many of them can be without any serious
difficulty.

The reason why I give these rules in respect to bedrooms the first place in domestic
sanitation is obvious enough, if but a few
moments' consideration be given to the importance of the bedroom as a centre of the
household. In this room, if a due proportion
of sleep be taken, the third part of all the
life is passed, thirty years out of a life that
reaches to an age of ninety. In what other
room in the house is so much of the life
passed without change? In the sitting-rooms
we move about, we have the doors frequently
open, and in numerous ways we change the
air, and change our own relations to it. In
the bedroom we are shut up closely, we are
unconscious of what is going on silently
around us. If the air becomes close we do
not notice it, and it may become positively
poisonous without our knowledge. Moreover,
during sleep we are most susceptible to influences which act detrimentally upon us.
We are breathing slowly, and we are not
casting off, or eliminating, freely the products
of animal combustion.

Rules for Bedrooms.

I.

The bedroom should, by preference, have its window either on the southern side of the house, the south-eastern, or the south-western. Of the three positions, the bedroom that has a south-western view is the most fortunate in our country. The winds from the south-west are the most frequent, and so the room can be most frequently ventilated by them, from the open window, during the day. These winds, moreover, are soft winds, and compare favourably with the eastern winds, from which it is always good to be protected as much as possible. The bedroom having a south-western aspect gets the longest share of light during the day. The early morning light soon feeds it with a subdued and agreeable light, and in the evening it gets the later rays, almost the last rays of the life-giving sun.

II.

The bedroom should in all cases be shut off from the house during the time it is occupied, so that the emanations from the rooms may not enter into it. It should be ventilated, I mean, independently. In our present houses the bedrooms are actually the traps, or bell-jars, into which, in too many cases, the air of the lower rooms, charged with the gaseous or vaporous products made during the day, are laid up. In these instances the occupants retire to sleep in an atmosphere of their own emanations, to say nothing of what comes from the kitchen, from gas, and from other sources of impurity. It is most easy to ventilate the bedroom independently. Nothing more is wanted than to remove one or two bricks in the outer wall beneath the flooring, and to carry up a wooden tube four inches square for a room of very moderate size—say eighteen feet long, fourteen wide, and twelve high—into the room from that opening. This tube should ascend into the room six to eight feet. It may be covered at the top with a layer of gauze or muslin if the current of air is too strong. The tube should be six feet from the bed. The bed may be protected from a draught by a light curtain or screen placed between it and the tube.

In some houses it is not difficult to bring a four-inch wooden tube through the whole length of a partition from the top to the bottom floor of a house, and to let a supply of air enter that tube at the upper part, and distribute air to every room that lies in its course.

On rising in the morning the bedroom windows should be opened at the top and bottom equally, and, except when the weather is very wet, they should remain open until the sun begins to go down. It is a bad practice to leave the windows open late in the day, and this especially in the winter. The air becomes charged with damp, and a damp air is really as dangerous, if not more dangerous, than a close air. To sleep in damp air is quite as bad as to sleep in damp sheets, and is a most common cause of rheumatism, neuralgia, and chronic cold or catarrh. When the windows of the bedroom are closed the door ought also to be closed, and the entrance of air into the room be allowed to take place only through the communication with the external air.

While provision is made for the entrance of air, an equal provision should also be made for the escape of air. This is best effected by an opening in the chimney shaft near to the ceiling where there is, as there ought always to be, a fireplace and shaft. The opening for the exit of air up the shaft may be protected by an Arnott's valve.

The late Dr. Chowne invented a process of exit ventilation which answers well for bedrooms, and to which he gave the name of "syphon ventilation." The name was very unfortunate, because there is no syphon principle in it, and owing to this the plan received very severe handling by the late Dr. Neil Arnott. The plan nevertheless is very good and cleanly, and when from an Arnott valve smoke and dust issue, as they often will in rooms placed at the upper part of a house, the Chowne tube is excellent. A three or four-inch piece of stove piping is let into the wall from the ceiling down to the mantel-piece. Near the ceiling the tube opens into the room. At the mantel-shelf the tube is made to turn at a right angle into the chimney. At all times there is a current of air down this tube into the chimney, and when there is a fire in the grate the exit current is extremely sharp and effective, while there is always freedom from soot and smoke in the room, an advantage which recompenses for the extra friction and resistance caused by the tube. Chowne's plan is so effective and simple that I have often brought it temporarily into action in closed rooms by simply turning a piece of stove piping into a chimney at the fireplace, and running a straight piece of tubing from the elbow up to near the ceiling, and temporarily fixing it against the wall.

When exit ventilation cannot be carried out by a chimney shaft owing to the circumstance that there is no fireplace or shaft, it is next best to carry it out into the staircase by a diaphragm opening made over the door of the room. An opening twelve inches long and four inches wide is made vertically through the wall, in the space over the door. Into this opening is placed a metal frame as wide as the thickness of the wall, with a partition or diaphragm of thin metal planted vertically in the centre of it. When this metal frame is fixed in the wall a current of air will be found to pass, after the room is closed, into the room on one side the diaphragm, and out of the room on the other side. This secures an outer current, which is better by far than none at all, but it also admits a current into the room from the house, which to a certain extent is objectionable.

It has been recommended by some sanitarians to ventilate the bedroom from the window by the plan of costless ventilation of Dr. Peter Hinches Bird. In this plan the lower sash of the window is raised a few inches, the space between the window and the window sill being filled up by a solid piece of wood. A space is in this way left between the two sashes up which flows a constant current of air. I have tried this method, and I have modified it by letting the upper sash down, and filling up the space between it and the top part of the window frame with board, which is, I think, the better arrangement, and for staircases I do not think anything is so good. But in bedrooms, the windows of which are opened and closed so frequently, and which have blinds, the plan does not answer so well as the tube of which I have spoken. There are more frequent draughts from the window, and not, I think, so regular a supply of air.

In my next paper I shall continue the rules relating to the bedroom.

A GOOD OLD MAN.

"Children, you will soon lay me in the ground. Then you are to be cheerful, and drink some of this wine; for I have lived a joyful life before God all my days."—*Life of Ernst Maurice Arndt.* London. 1879. P. 38.

THE old man sate beside the fire,
His years fourscore and two,
His locks were thin and wintry-white,
But his eyes were bright and blue.

His children's children round him stood,
His face with joy did shine;
And he called for a glass, and placed on the board
A pint of the ruby wine.

And he said, "Now list to me, brave boys:
I've lived a life, thank God!
Full of bright hours and happy days,
And soon beneath the sod

"Your hands must lay my head. This glass
I fill with thanks to Him
Who made my cup through fourscore years
With joy to overbrim.

"There might be clouds; but they have passed;
For this I surely knew—
Behind the clouds there dwelt a sun
And a dome of glorious blue.

"There might be frets; but not with me
Might fret and murmur dwell;
For God, I knew, was judge of all,
And still He judgeth well.

"Then fill the sparkling glass, brave boys,
And quaff the wine with me,
His gift whence flows to men all light
And love and liberty!

"And keep a stout heart in your breast,
And trust in God, brave boys;
And march right forward without fear,
And evermore rejoice.

"And when you lay my head, brave boys,
Beneath the cool green sod,
Remember how I walked in strength
And joy before my God."

JOHN STUART BLACKIE.

THE MYSTERY OF THE GOSPEL.

WHEN we speak of anything which we cannot explain we call it mysterious. Many things in nature are mysteries. In a sense the whole world and all connected with it, as life, death, birth, growth, and decay, however common and familiar they may be, is a mystery. There is no subject we can exhaust, no matter we can fully explain, everything has a *beyond*. It is allied to something else, and that to another branching out into the infinite. If it is so in nature, we may expect the same in the gospel. The subject is God, man, and redemption. Though the gospel be a revelation, and on one side comprehensible, yet the more we study it, the deeper we go, the more we cry out, "Oh, the depth!" Everywhere there is a background of mystery. Infinity meets us on every side. Even time itself, which seems so definite, merges into eternity.

When theologians speak of the mysteries of Christianity they mean doctrines or dogmas hard or impossible to be understood, but in this sense the word mystery does not seem to be once used in the New Testament. Another common use of the word is to apply it to the Christian Sacraments. In the English service the bread and wine representing the body and blood of Christ are called "these holy mysteries." In the Eastern Church the Seven Sacraments are the Seven Mysteries. But this use of the word is also without any authority from the New Testament. Like the word sacrament itself it is purely Pagan, and the idea is derived from the mysteries of the old Pagan religions. Mystery in the New Testament means something once hidden but now revealed, unknown to some but known to others, and which might be known to all. Christ speaks of its being given to His disciples to know the mysteries of the kingdom, while to others they were represented by parables. In the Epistle to the Ephesians St. Paul speaks of the mystery being made known to him, and of his knowledge of the mystery of Christ, and the thing called a mystery in this case is not anything dark or difficult to be understood, but only something unknown until it was revealed. It was simply the calling of the Gentiles, and he asks the Ephesians to pray for him that utterance might be given to him that he might make known to others the mystery of the gospel. In the Epistle to the Romans, St. Paul says that he did not wish them to be ignorant of this mystery, which he describes as revealed to him. To Timothy he wrote that without controversy the mystery of godliness was great, but so far was he from meaning by mystery any abstruse doctrine or dogma, that he explains the mystery of faith as consisting of what is revealed concerning the manifestation of God in the flesh. The mystery of the faith is identical with the revelation of the gospel. It was once a mystery, but now the mystery is unveiled. It was hid for ages, but revealed to Christ's disciples, and the apostles were to publish it to the world.

St. Paul always used the strongest language when he described the actual state of the heathen. They were not merely strangers from the commonwealth of Israel, but they were without God in the world, and by nature children of wrath. He did not mean that they were born reprobates, or that even in a state of nature they were of necessity depraved, but that by long continuance in evil they had come to the very worst. In respect of mere morality the gospel was a mystery to the Gentiles. They had been so long in darkness that they could not look upon the light. Holiness as revealed in the gospel was unknown to them. They were so immersed in the pleasures of sense that they could not understand spiritual joys. They were dead in trespasses and sins, dead to righteousness.

The character of God as revealed in the gospel was a mystery to the Gentiles. Once they knew God, but they did not like to retain the knowledge of Him in their minds. They changed the glory of the incorruptible God into the image of corruptible man, and of birds and creeping things and four-footed beasts. This lapse into the vilest idolatry was not originally through want of light, but the result of their evil lives. They had so long delighted in sin that they became vain in their imaginations, and their foolish hearts were darkened. God as manifested to reason, God as revealed to the pure in heart, God as the eternal, the infinite, the absolutely righteous, was not the object of their worship, but gods with human passions, gods corrupt like themselves, of immoral lives and served with impure rites.

To the Gentiles the greatest gospel mystery was the revelation of God in Christ. As they knew nothing of a perfect God, so had they lost the idea of a perfect man. But though the idea was obliterated, the capacity for it was not gone. Plato had spoken of a perfectly just man, but such a character was so opposite to that of the society in which he lived that if, he said, this just man were to arise he would be scourged, racked, and crucified. When the perfection of man, as realised in Christ, is set before the minds of men, their first feeling is the impossibility of their ever reaching it. The brighter the light shines, the more a man sees the darkness in which he is involved. When the soul becomes really conscious of its defilement it is overwhelmed with remorse and despair. The more a man knows of the perfection which God's law requires, the more he cries out, "Oh, wretched man that I am, who shall deliver me from the body of this death?" The gospel is the mystery of forgiveness unveiled to the soul. It proclaims the mercy of God, the taking away of sin by Jesus Christ, and it gives grace and strength for the new life.

The mystery of the gospel is the revelation of man's relations to God. The Gentiles did not know that they were God's children. They were prodigals, indeed, in a far country in want and destitution, but they knew not that they had a Father in whose house there was enough and to spare. Christ revealed the Father. He told us that we were not orphans, that though strangers from the commonwealth of Israel we were still of the household of God. The rite of baptism is the declaration of this sonship. Its realisation is in the Christian life, our return to our Father's house, and submission to His will in all things.

St. Paul was very zealous to make known the mystery of the gospel. To himself it had been a revelation of light and life, and what it had been to him he knew it could be to others. But to many who have heard the gospel it is still a mystery. It is one thing to hear, and another to know. We speak of the mysteries of a trade or profession, and often we know a great deal about them without really knowing them. A mystery is not known till what it conceals is revealed.

To know the mystery of Christianity is not then to know some abstruse doctrine. It is not to give consent to some incomprehensible propositions resting on some supposed external authority. It is to know and realise what is plainly taught in the gospel. It is to feel the truth of what is revealed, to have a sense that we have come out of darkness into light, to know that God is a Being of the greatest perfection, that He is manifested in Christ the perfect man, that we may be delivered from all sin and conformed to the Divine image. And the more earnest we are to learn, the more we shall know; the better we are, the more the mystery shall be revealed to us. St. Paul, writing to the Corinthians, says : " We speak the wisdom of God in a mystery, even the hidden wisdom which God ordained before this world to our glory, which none of the princes of this world knew, for had they known it they would not have crucified the Lord of glory. But as it is written—eye hath not seen nor ear heard, neither have entered into the heart of man, the things God hath prepared for them that love Him. But God hath revealed them unto us by His Spirit, for the Spirit searcheth all things, even the deep things of God."

JOHN HUNT.

A VISIT TO THE PRISONS OF CAYENNE.

In Good Words for November, 1878, in an article entitled " A Visit to one of the Prisons in Cayenne," I drew attention to the case of a young French convict, Adolphe Jean Pétrel, who had been sentenced to penal servitude at Cayenne for eight years, on a charge of manslaughter ; but who had, when I saw him (in 1875), been there thirteen, or some five years beyond his proper time, because he could not muster the sum of 600 francs to enable the Government to send him well provided to another country. Indeed, we were told, on good authority, that if this amount were not forthcoming in his behalf he would need to spend the remainder of his life in a degrading and soul-destroying exile. I also mentioned that an attempt, made by some of the gentlemen on board our vessel, the Hooper, to buy the man his freedom had proved a failure, by reason of the Hooper suddenly leaving the place on telegraph work.

Soon after the publication of that article I received, through the Editor of Good Words, a number of letters from different parts of the country manifesting a deep interest in Adolphe Jean, and offering money to procure him his liberty. These letters were apparently from persons of all classes : one gentleman very generously promised the entire sum required (£24) ; another promised half of it ; and a working-man declared in round terms that he would give all he could spare.

On receipt of these letters I availed myself of the kind assistance of my friend, Mr. Edward Almack, Secretary of King's College Hospital, Lincoln's Inn Fields, who had taken the leading part in trying to effect the prisoner's release before, and a letter was written to the Governor of Cayenne stating the case, and setting forth our desire to liberate Pétrel if he were still alive. A courteous reply came informing us that he was still living, but had been removed from the prisons of the Salut Islands to the town of Cayenne, which, however, he was not permitted to leave, unless the sum of 800 francs (or 200 more than was asked before) were handed to the Governor, and permission obtained from some neighbouring country, such as Brazil, Demerara, or Trinidad, to allow him to live there.

The sum of £36 was then collected from the two gentlemen I have referred to, and dispatched by Mr. Almack to the Governor, with the request that Pétrel should be sent to Trinidad, an English colony, where we thought he would readily find work at his trade of mechanical fitting. An introduction to a civil engineer in Port of Spain was also enclosed for Pétrel, in order that he might not arrive there quite friendless.

In due course a response came from the Governor acknowledging the receipt of the money, and assuring us that as soon as the permission of the Governor of Trinidad arrived Pétrel would be sent thither. More recently another letter, of which I subjoin a translation, conveyed to us the welcome intelligence that the man was at last set free :—

"PENITENTIARY ADMINISTRATION OF FRENCH GUIANA
"(CABINET DU DIRECTEUR), CAYENNE,
"August 28th, 1879.

" SIR,—I have the honour to inform you that M. the Governor of Trinidad, having given his acquiescence to the residence of the discharged convict Pétrel, the latter has been booked for Trinidad by the packet of the 3rd September.

" The sum put so graciously at the disposal of Pétrel has been given to him, with the exception of 200 francs, which have been deposited at the Transportation Office, conformably to the regulations in force, and which can be reclaimed by Pétrel after he reaches his destination.

" May he recognise, by a worthy return, the signal favour of which he has been the object.

" Receive, Monsieur, the assurance of my
"high consideration,
(Signed)   " EADBERT (?), Director of the Penitentiary
"Administration.

" M. Ed. Almack."

[Since this letter came we have heard from Port of Spain that Pétrel arrived there on October 8, and began work the next day.]

I may also add that the Howard Association sent a copy of the article in Good Words to the French Government, who thereupon caused an inquiry to be made into the state of the prisons of Salut.

4, Montague Road, W. Croydon,   J. MUNRO.
October 6th.

BRETON PEASANTS GOING TO MASS ON CHRISTMAS EVE.
A Study in Black and White by G. Montbard.

Page 77.

SARAH DE BERENGER.

By JEAN INGELOW.

CHAPTER IV.

GREAT schemes may be reasoned out, and great sacrifices already made in thought while leaning her face on her hand, a heartsick woman sits brooding, with her feet on the fender.

Uzziah Dill's wife had tried hard to forgive him, and, while at peace in present freedom, had persuaded herself that she need not tremble, thinking of the day that would bring her into his presence and under his dominion again.

Uzziah Dill's wife now gave him up for good and all. She suffered in so doing from no sense of wrong, any more than of unkindness, towards him. Clearly he did not want her, and he had sinned against her in that one only way which made her, by all law, divine and human, free to depart and be loosed from him for ever.

But then she wanted to save her children, not only from the disadvantage and disgrace of knowing that they had a convict for their father, but from self—the costly and consoling fruit of her great mistake? For their sake, in spite of the sorrow and fear it had brought her, she always found it impossible to wish the past undone.

If she was, indeed, never to retrieve the mistake, could she not still so act as to take

that acquaintance with wickedness, evil living, and shame that they could not escape if she went into Court so soon as he was free, and laid all her wrongs open in order to obtain a divorce.

How could she save these that were her all—these, so much dearer to her than her-all its weight upon herself? She longed, as true love must, to shield her children from the cruel robbery of affection that she had proved—from exposure to contaminating examples, from want and blame.

To this end, she effaced herself utterly, and left her name behind her. When she was again seen by one who knew her, she showed herself that she might learn how to deprive the vicious father of his children, to secure which she was willing to rob herself of them also.

At first, restless and wretched, she could not mature her plan, but journeyed from one little seaside place to another, never calling herself by her husband's name, but using any other, indifferently, that came into her head.

Mr. Bartlett, during those three or four months, heard frequently from Hannah Dill, and forwarded money to her as she required it. Before he got rid of the whining old mother-in-law, and the helpless young girl, he had wished many times that he had never taught her to run away.

And then there was a drunken father-in-law, who tormented him for more money, and said it was on his conscience that Hannah ought to be advertised for, and made to come back to her own husband's relations, that were so willing to look after her and the children.

Mr. Bartlett said they might advertise if they liked, and make her come back if they could. He added, in such a convincing way, that he did not care what they did, that in the end they believed him, and gave him up, as the "wrong-headedest" and "hard-heartedest" gentleman they had ever met with. They then departed.

At last, but not for some time after this, Mrs. Dill appeared one morning at Mr. Bartlett's office, sent up a note, and was straightway admitted to an interview.

It was evident that she had gone through great trouble; her eyes were hollow, and her features thin. Her children had both been ill, she told him, but she acknowledged nothing else afflictive, and after a few commonplaces of condolence from him, she broke in with—

"I came to ask your opinion, sir, about some things I don't fairly understand."

"Well, Mrs. Dill, I am at your service."

"I wish, sir, to know how people came first by their surnames. I have made out, by a book of history, that we did not always have such."

"Certainly not."

"People took them, I fare to think, mainly for convenience."

"Quite true."

He then went over familiar ground with her—described how some names grew out of the trades of those first called by them, others came from the father's Christian name, others, again, from localities.

"But you do not need that I should tell you this," he broke off to say; "you have studied the subject, I find."

"Yes, sir," she answered. "Then what they took for convenience, I should say they may change for convenience."

"They very commonly do—for the sake of some property, for instance, left on that condition."

"I know it, sir. Well, it would hurt my conscience to live in a lie. If I call myself by another name than poor Dill's, do I lie? Mayn't I take a name for myself, as my fore-ancestors did?"

"That depends, I should say, partly on the motive. If you meant, by such an act, to prevent your husband from claiming you and his children when he gets free, and also to keep from him, if you can, the money that you have inherited, and to which he will have a clear right——"

Mrs. Dill's silence appeared to show that she did so intend.

"It would be every way wrong," he presently added. "It would deprive him of his wife, while, being unable to prove your death, he could not marry again."

"No, but that would be no worse for him than for me. I could never marry again, either."

"You propose to interfere with your husband's clear legal rights."

"Sir, sir!" she interrupted. "Of course a man must be expected to take the man's side. I don't resent that ; so it is, and always will be, just as sure as that a woman will take against a woman. But if he has behaved to me so bad and so base, that no laws—not God's, nor even man's—would give me back to him——"

"Mrs. Dill, you must tell me something more."

Mrs. Dill did tell more. For the first and last time she unfolded her many wrongs, and told all. This was not a common case, and the husband had not cared to conceal either his unfaithfulness or his cruelty. She ended, with many heart-sick tears, "I never will live with him again. He may claim me, but he shall never get me. Rather than that, I'll spend every shilling of my money to get free."

("Your money!" thought Mr. Bartlett.) "I must and will save his children and mine. And that's why I want to have another name, sir; and you, having treated me almost as if I was a friend——"

"You want a friend's opinion?"

"I want to know, first, if I can be punished for doing it?"

"Why, my good woman, of course not, *unless you are found out.*"

"And would you tell me, as a friend, am I living in a lie? Is it a moral wrong to take a new name?"

"I answer, as a friend, decidedly not. But it is a great risk; for your husband will be able to get your money, though it will prevent him from getting you."

"Yes; I've been to Mr. Gordon, and he said so."

"The money is, in fact, now lying in my hands. The executor did wish to sell the property, and it is to be reinvested."

"You will not let me have even half of it?"

"No, because you cannot give me a receipt that would not still leave me liable to have your husband come upon me. Mr. Gordon cannot give it to you either."

"No, sir; Mr. Gordon was saying, though, that the money might be invested in a way not generally allowed—laid out, I mean, in stocking a shop."

Mr. Bartlett here looked steadily into Hannah Dill's clear, honest eyes. "I half expected this," he thought. "Well, Mrs. Dill?"

"He said, if I could keep a shop——"

"Yes, if you could keep a shop?"

"But I said I was afraid; and if I lost the money, Dill would be so angry."

"It was to be kept under your own—I mean your husband's name?"

"I never mentioned it to him about going by another."

"Humph!"

"He said my husband could not object nor come on you or him afterwards, even if any money was lost; on the other hand, I might make money by trade, and that surely would not belong to Dill?"

"What did you answer?"

"I did not take to the notion, and I was thinking about changing my name."

"Oh, that was all. Well, now, as regards Mr. Gordon's remarks, you tell him from me that he had better look out."

"But I did say that I was afraid to keep a shop."

"No matter; tell him I say he had better look out. But as to changing your name, I

believe I should change mine under like circumstances."

"Oh, thank you, sir, for saying it; now, indeed, I fare to see it cannot be wrong."

"But you must remember, Mrs. ——" He paused half an instant, wondering what name she would take.

"Sir, my name is Snaith," she exclaimed. So quick to take the advice she had longed for, so afraid some one should enter and hear her old name.

A clerk at that instant did enter.

"But you must remember, Mrs. Snaith," he replied, slowly and steadily; then paused to receive and return a message, and when his clerk had shut the door, went on, "You must remember, Mrs. Snaith, that you have many years yet of freedom before your husband can come and take the income."

"But I have to hide all from his children, and I want to begin from the first."

"Then begin by taking leave of me."

"Sir, sir, I mean to do it, though you have been the best and kindest friend I have had for a long time."

He then explained to her how she could receive her income at a distance from the place where she lived.

She went away, and the next afternoon Mr. Gordon desired to speak with him.

("Oh, my prophetic soul!") "Well, show him up," said Mr. Bartlett.

Mr. Gordon explained that he had come about Mrs. Dill's affairs.

"Where is Mrs. Dill?"

"She is gone back to the seaside, sir, with fifty pounds in her pocket as I drew for her."

"You seem to have had some conversation with her, Mr. Gordon."

"Well, I have, sir. But Goodrich's niece is that soft and that straightforward, that she's hardly to be trusted with her own interest."

Mr. Bartlett repeated to the executor that he had better "look out."

The other replied that he had looked out, he had been looking out for some time; and as to the matter of the reinvestment, he had a great wish to spend a portion of the money in buying the goodwill of a business that he had heard of, and in the stock of a man about to retire—"a friend of mine, at Bristol," he began—"a very honest man."

"At Bristol?"

"Ay, sir. A long way off, but a very honest man."

"Hannah Dill has no wish to keep a shop."

"She have altered her mind, sir. She have taken into consideration that I, being an old friend and fellow-townsman of Goodrich's, and, as I have said to her, I know he would wish it——"

"Now, what might you mean in this case by an honest man?"

"Well, I might have said to an old friend, 'Jem Gravison, I am in a fix with poor Goodrich's niece that have married a convict, and have been ill-used by him in a shameful way. Poor Goodrich,' I might have said, 'have made me his executor, to take care of his money, and he left word that it might be laid out in buying the stock and the goodwill of a business, shoe trade preferred.' I might have said, 'Jem Gravison, have you such to sell?' and being a right-down honest man, he might have made answer, 'Old boy, I have not.'"

At this unexpected conclusion of the sentence, Mr. Bartlett looked up, surprised.

"But yet, you see, it's a fine thing to carry out the blessed laws of the land, and the provisions of poor Goodrich's will; and when he and him had corresponded together, he might have said, 'It's true I did mean to sell, as witness my advertisement in the paper;' and if as well as that he had said—which he may have done—that if he sold to a worse than widow for more than orphans he would take no advantage—me knowing that well enough before—I should call him an honest man."

"And you really mean to tell me," said Mr. Bartlett, with a stolid face, "that you think this man's shop and trade and stock will be a good investment?"

"I do, sir. And I mean to have everything properly gone into—the books, the vally of the goods, bad debts, and what not."

"You had better take a little time to consider this."

"Yes, sir; and I shall want it done in the most legal way. Nothing like fencing yourself round with the law, sir. The will says a part of the property. It never specifies what part."

"No."

"It may be anything short of the whole, then."

Mr. Bartlett, being a little out of temper, answered shortly that it might.

His client took some days to consider, some more to decide how to act, but in the end the stock-in-trade, shop, and goodwill of a certain shoe trade, lately the property of James Gravison, were duly bought and paid for by the executor of the late H. Goodrich, on behalf of his niece and her husband, the said niece to keep the shop.

Mr. Bartlett did not much like the affair,

he therefore took the more care to conduct it with all legal formality; and when all was arranged, it seemed to him to be rather a suspicious circumstance that the executor had left that precise portion of property in his hands which paid what must be called hush-money to the Goodrich family, and which, as Mr. Bartlett remarked, would of course be claimed by the convict husband when he came forth, the wife's resolution not binding him at all to dispose of it thus.

"I have not mentioned that to Goodrich's niece yet, sir," said Mr. Gordon.

Mr. Bartlett said nothing; he had noticed the peculiar emphasis on the word *yet*.

Mr. Gordon informed him, with a certain open cheerfulness of manner, that he had caused Hannah Dill's name to be painted up on the shop; he also pulled out a Bristol paper, wherein Hannah Dill advertised herself as having bought the stock of the late Thomas Gravison, of his brother James Gravison, of the United States of America, and Hannah Dill hoped, by unremitting attention to business, to merit the patronage of the public.

"That advertisement goes into unnecessary details," said Mr. Bartlett. "Did Mrs. Dill indite it?"

"Well, no, sir; she have not that turn for business that I could wish. At present she do not intend to serve in the shop herself, the children being still so sadly." So saying, Mr. Gordon gravely folded up the paper and put it in his pocket.

In the meantime Mrs. Snaith, as she must now be called, quite unaware of the various manœuvres being carried out for her benefit,—Mrs. Snaith went back to her children with fifty pounds in her pocket, besides the money she had obtained by the sale of all her best and handsomest clothes. She bought for the two little ones some very handsome frocks, ribbons, and toys, spent two or three days in picking every mark from their clothes and her own, then packed all up in boxes, with the name of Mrs. Snaith on them, and departed, not leaving even at her lodgings any address, or account of what she might be going to do.

The children were too young to imperil the success of her scheme; neither could talk. They did not know their own names, nor where they had come from.

In a short time the convict husband's day came for writing again. He knew now, through his brother, of his wife's good fortune, therefore, of course, his letter this time was to her.

It had been such an astonishing piece of news that it had wrought in him a certain change. He had a profound contempt for his wife mainly on account of the love which had induced her to throw herself away upon *him*. He believed he had only to flatter her to have back her heart.

He wanted her to believe that he was a reformed character. His letter, therefore, besides being affectionate in language, was full of cant, such cant as is commonly learned in a prison. He meant, when he had a chance, to show what a changed character he was; he even gave her religious and moral advice, as one already in such matters her superior. Then, after lamenting that this money had not come in time to prevent him from throwing himself away, he proceeded to assure his wife that he would make her a happy woman yet, and with unparalleled impudence he continued, that he knew it was hard on her to be away from him so long, but she was not the woman, he was sure, to go out of the paths of virtue, and she must take care of the money, and keep herself respectable for his sake.

Uzziah Dill sent this letter through his brother, as he had done the first. He hoped to write to each of the women once a year, and to keep it secret from both that this was the case. So, not knowing his wife's address, he trusted to his brother, directing to him and asking him to read the letter before sending it on, that his dear parents might know how he was.

Jacob Dill saw the game his brother was trying to play, and felt what a bad fellow he was; but he justified what Hannah Dill had said. He took the man's side, being swayed also by the desire to pacify and conciliate the woman who had brought money into the Dill family.

Jacob Dill sent the letter to Mr. Gordon, asking him to let Hannah have it. Mr. Gordon, who exhibited great fearlessness in acting for others, returned it, informing him that he did not know where Mrs. Dill was, and that they need not trouble themselves to send any more letters to him, as she had means of drawing money without letting him know where she lived.

This was bad news for the Dills. That Mr. Gordon could not send on the letter was possible, that he would not was evident. In fact, so bad was the news considered, that the drunken old father was sobered by it for the time being, and shaking his head over this " dispensation of providence," actually went to work at his trade again.

Mr. Gordon did not inform them that he had copied the letter; he did, however, muttering to himself as he folded it and put it in his desk, " For Goodrich's niece is that soft, that she may relent towards the convict after all. This'll help to keep her straight towards doing what's right by her uncle."

CHAPTER. V.

It was now the middle of July; the inhabitants of a beautiful little sea-side place in the south-west of England were cleaning their windows, hanging up their fresh white curtains, and putting out placards of the lodgings they had to let.

There was a smell of paint and tar about; the pleasure boats had just been put into first-rate order, and run up on the beach in a tempting phalanx, while the sentimental or patriotic names on their little pennons hung almost unmoved in the sunny air. The landladies grumbled, as they always did every year, said " how short their season was, and that the visitors were long of coming."

The prettiest little terrace boasted as yet of but one lodger, and she, her landlady said, was but a servant—a nurse with some children. " However," continued the good woman, " those that sent her must have sent good money with her, for she pays like her betters, I will say. But she keeps herself mighty close, and has no notion of being asked any questions." This she said to her next-door neighbour, as the two stood to gossip on their respective door-steps. " And so particular about the children's eating! She's almost worse than a lady at that."

In about a week matters mended. The neighbour let her drawing-room floor, several families appeared on the beach, flower-girls began to pervade it, a band played in the evening, and more bathing-machines were pushed down. Soon there were many groups of children dotted about in cheerful proximity to one another, some with nurses, some with mothers, and they all pleased themselves with the same time-honoured toys, buckets, and wooden spades.

A very respectable-looking and plainly dressed nurse was sitting one morning on the beach a little apart from any of these groups. She was at work, just beyond high-water mark, and two lovely little children were playing beside her. One, scarcely a year old, seated on the nurse's gown, was complacently patting the shingle with a wooden spade; the other had a small cart, and had attained to such a degree of intelligence as enabled her to fill it with shells and seaweed, and drag it on a little way, when it generally turned over, and the same operation had to be performed again.

These children were fair, of very refined appearance, rather delicate, with pure complexions, deep-blue eyes, and black lashes.

Some ladies who lodged next door had several times noticed them and their nurse. They evidently had no one else with them. She always kept them delicately clean in their dress. In the morning they wore flapping white sun-bonnets, but in the evening, after their early tea, she used to dress them up in broidered frocks, and take them forth upon the little parade, in all their infantine bravery of pink or blue sashes and ostrich feathers.

"That woman looks as proud of the children as if they were her own," observed one of the ladies; "their parents may well trust her with them."

"And how very plainly and neatly she dresses," replied the other. "I wish any one of our servants was like her. A clean print gown in the morning, a neat coburg in the evening. The children's dress looks twice as handsome, hers being so unpretending. I wonder whose children they are."

The nurse, Mrs. Snaith, not at all aware of the notice and approval she had attracted, seated herself the following morning nearly in her previous place, while, in a profound calm, the tide was softly coming up.

She looked almost happy, for she was beginning to feel safe, and accustomed to her new name. Her position as nurse to the children had been taken for granted the moment she appeared; she had already overheard remarks made on their lovely and refined appearance, and her own evident respectability.

This pleased her. She liked also to observe the beauty of the shore, and went on leisurely working and watching

"And all the fishing craft hanging about . . . . looked as faint as grey ghosts."

the water and the two graceful little creatures beside her.

No air stirred but such as was set in motion by the slight action of the oncoming wave; and presently, in the perfect calm of the morning, a sea mist began to rise, and as she looked, the somewhat distant bathing-machines were already in it.

Presently she herself was in it, and all the fishing craft hanging about in the harbour looked as faint as grey ghosts; but each boat, being clearly reflected in the water, seemed to stand up an unnatural height, it was hard to distinguish it from its image. The mist did not reach very high; all above was blue and full of light. She put down her work to look, and, half unconsciously, to listen. A crier was pacing up and down the little terrace behind her, with his bell. " Oh yes! oh yes! a bracelet was lost on the beach—a gold bracelet in the form of a snake." The nurse turned, and, as a flat, neutral-tinted outline, could just discern the figure of the crier, as he passed out of hearing. " Oh yes! oh yes ! " she heard him begin again, and then his voice became faint in the distance, and gave way to other sounds. There was a strange kind of creaking and a flapping over the water, but nothing could be seen; the fishing-boats were quite invisible.

It interested her inquiring mind to notice now how all outlines were melting away into the mist. What could that creaking be? There was nothing to make it. Why, yes, there was! An enormous high pole, all aslant, was pushing on right towards her, and two vast sheets hung aloft behind it. Why, this was a ship. She could see the two gaunt masts now, and the ropes, some hanging slack, and the mainsail flapping and coming down. Sailors were swarming about up there, and now the beachmen came running on to meet the vessel.

The tide was almost at the height, and this must be the coal brig that had been expected, coming up to be beached.

The tall bowsprit appeared to be nearly hanging over her, before the beachmen got up to the brig's bows; and then there was shouting and splashing in the shingle, and she rose and moved backward with the children, for the almost formless wave was washing up close to her feet.

" Oh yes! oh yes!" repeated the crier, now become audible again. " Oh yes! a gold bracelet was lost—a bracelet in the form of a snake, with pearls for eyes. Whoever would bring the same to the hotel on the east cliff, should receive two guineas reward."

She sat down higher up on the shingle, and hearkened as the crier's message waxed loud, and then faint again; and she watched how the heavy rope from the brig was made fast to a clumsy wooden windlass, and, with stamping and chanting, the beachmen began to turn this round. All was new and fresh to her, and the mist, which generally turns with the tide, had already fallen back a little, dropping behind the nearest fishing-vessels, and giving them and their shadows back to the sunshine before she tired of gazing; and chancing to look round, noticed on her right, and almost close at hand, one of the ladies next door, who, seated also, was smiling on the elder child and trying to attract her.

"She is not shy, ma'am," said Mrs. Snaith; "she will come to you. Shake hands with the lady, missy."

Steps were now heard behind, crashing through the shingle.

" Mrs. Snaith," cried a young girl, "mother says she can get no milk this morning; and what is she to make instead of the pudding, for your little ladies?"

"Dear me!" exclaimed the nurse, "no milk? And so fanciful as the dears are! You must tell your mother to boil them each an egg, and to mind they are as fresh as fresh."

"They are delicate?." asked the lady.

"Yes, ma'am, bless them ! very delicate."

In the meantime, the elder child had broken loose from the stranger's caresses.

" Pretty dears ! " said the lady. " What is their name ? "

"That one's name is Amabel."

" Oh, I meant their surname."

A sudden bound at the nurse's heart; for an instant a pause. Then, recovering herself, " Missy, missy ! " she cried, starting up, " don't go too near the edge ; you'll wet your precious f__ee__t.—Now, to think of that question coming so soon, and me not ready for it !" she muttered ; and she hastened al__o__ng the shingle with the younger child in her arms ; and, setting her down, took up the elder, who, by various acts of infantile rebellion, did what she could to continue the fascinating play of slapping the water with a long banner of dulse.

In the meantime the little òne filled both her hands with what she could find, and the two were shortly carried up by Mrs. Snaith, one under each arm.

" I must take them in at once, ma'am," she

remarked, as she hastily passed the lady. "Missy is so wet."

Her face was flushed, and when she got to a safe distance from her questioner, she sat down to take a short rest.

The mist had almost melted away. How grand the brig looked! She thought she had never seen anything more beautiful than the shape of her bows, with reflections of the receding water wavering all over them.

Something nearer than the wave was sparkling. The baby had something fast in her dimpled fist, and was recklessly striking the stones with it, uttering little cries of pleasure when she saw it flash as she knocked it about.

A costly toy! The gold bracelet, the snake with pearls for eyes!

That same evening, when Mrs. Snaith had put her two little nurslings to bed, she left them in charge of her landlady's daughter, and, dressed in her neatest and plainest habiliments, set forth to find the hotel on the east cliff, and return the bracelet to its owner.

There was never seen a better embodiment of all that a servant ought to be (from the mistress's point of view), than she appeared on that occasion. She was very desirous to have certain things taken for granted, that she might be asked no questions. "Are these your children?" would have been an awkward inquiry. She had made it a very unlikely one. She was so unassuming, so quiet, so respectable in her manner, so unfashionable and economical in her attire, that the position in which she stood toward them had appeared to be evident to every one; but during the whole of this evening walk, even to the moment when she found herself sitting in the hall of the hotel, while a waiter went up-stairs to announce her errand, she kept revolving in her mind the question of the morning, and wishing she could decide on a name for the children.

For, as has before been said, this woman in somewhat humble life, and used to common fashions, had thoughts not common, not humble. She had indulged a high ambition. A form of self-sacrifice that most mothers would shrink from as intolerable, had fully shaped itself in her mind, and become a fixed intention. She had deliberately planned to wait on her own children as their nurse, as such to bring them up, and never let them know that they were hers.

For the next eleven years at least she could bring them up in comfort, and educate them well; after that, she had every hope that their wretched father would not be able to find her. But, lest such should be the case, she meant to give them a name different from her own, almost at once; to begin to earn money, so that before there was a chance of a ticket-of-leave for her husband, she could put them to a good school, and having found a guardian for them, leave money enough in his hands to last till they were of an age to go out themselves as governesses. Having made this arrangement, she intended to leave them, deliberately deciding to hear of them and to see them no more.

She would then, indeed, have lost her children. If she were unhappy enough to be found by their wretched father, she would tell him so.

With her mind full of all this, she sat in the hall of the hotel, and her only half-attentive eyes rested on some boxes, with a name painted on them—

"Captain de Berenger, Madras, N.I."

The owner was evidently on his way to the east, and the name of the ship he was to sail in was painted on them also.

Presently a lady and gentleman came down, and began to excuse themselves for having kept her waiting, on the ground that they were in a hurry—just off.

They seemed to be a newly married couple, and while the lady expressed her pleasure at getting the bracelet back, the gentleman was evidently fumbling in his purse for the reward.

"It seemed so hard to lose it," said the lady, clasping the trinket on slowly, as if to give her husband time. "I had quite given it up, for we are off almost directly by the express for Southampton. We cannot wait. —Tom!"

Tom was still not ready. "What did we say?" he whispered. "Two, or three?"

"Sir," cried Mrs. Snaith, now perceiving the state of affairs, "indeed I could not think of such a thing."

"Oh, but we offered a reward!" exclaimed the lady. "Captain de Berenger offered a reward. Pray take it."

"No, ma'am; I don't need it. Indeed, you are kindly welcome."

"Well, at least shake hands, then, and thank you very much indeed;" and all their boxes being already placed on a fly, the lady and gentleman drove off in a hurry, nodding and repeating their thanks till the fly turned a corner.

"De Berenger," thought Mrs. Snaith; "now, that name seems as if it really would

"He sat down beside her on the shingle."

do. It has a kind of a foreign sound. It's uncommon. I fare to take to it, and it's not too uncommon neither. There's De Berenger, the baker, at Bristol, and there's a shop at Pentonville with that name on the door. These people, too, are off to India; they'll never know I borrowed their name from their boxes. I shall not forget how it was spelt, nor how it goes. And I must be quick, for to-morrow the man will come round again to print the visitors' names in the paper. Mine must not go in again 'Mrs. Snaith and *two children*.'"

So that evening Mrs. Snaith overhauled the children's toys. On one little wooden spade she printed in clear letters, "Amabel de Berenger;" on the other, "Delia de Berenger."

Her eldest child she had named after the young lady whose maid and reader she had been, and had always called her "Missy," as she had called her namesake. Her younger child she had named Delia, partly in remembrance of a tender little song that her husband had sung during the few kind days that

had followed their marriage, partly because she had a natural ear for pleasant sounds; and she felt that this now disregarded name was a very beautiful one. Their baptismal names, therefore, the children retained, and received the new surname of De Berenger.

The remainder of the evening she spent in marking some of their pinafores and other clothing; and this done, without any assertion of their name, she let things take their course.

It was only a very few days after this that Mrs. Snaith was startled by an elderly man, who, stopping short in front of her, accosted her with, "Well, and how are you, ma'am? Finely, I hope. You look so."

"Mr. Gordon!"

"Don't be startled," he continued; "there's not a soul within earshot—not even my friend that came with me. I wouldn't go to 'your lodgings. We have been about on the beach looking for you. Nobody in life "— seeing her look disturbed—"nobody in life know your address but me only. I said in life, for we have no reason to think that H.

Goodrich know what I am about to do—I wish he did—and thereby you may be sure it's all right and straight."

Mrs. Snaith said she was sure of that; and he sat down beside her on the shingle, admired the children, one of whom was asleep, and the other eating some luncheon, and then went on—

"Now, look here, H. Goodrich's niece. I told you the will would allow of my buying a stock-in-trade on your behalf, and I sent you the document here to be signed as legal as could be. It cost twenty pound, that transaction did. I bought the stock. 'Twill cost you seven pound ten more, for I had to go to Bristol on your affairs and come here this day, which I cannot afford on my own cost, as H. Goodrich was well aware."

"I'll pay it, sir, and thank you too."

"Well, having bought this stock-in-trade for you, I have nothing more to do with that part of the trust money (as I hope), the part that bring in one hundred and fifty pound a year. But a party that knew your uncle, and have come down here—and let me say would on no hand wrong the widow and the orphan —he have something to say to you. You know what *payable to bearer* means?"

"Yes, I believe I do."

"Such things you know of, as foreign bonds. Say United States bonds. Those are very good securities, and are made payable to bearer. They'll pass from hand to hand like a bank-note; you just show 'em and you take your money. That would be the best thing for you to have."

"Better than the stock-in-trade?"

"Better by half."

"But, bless you, sir, why did you buy the stock-in-trade for me, then; and make out it was such a fine thing to do?"

"Why did I? That's where it is. That's where it is, H. Goodrich's niece. And this I call you, seeing you want to keep your name to yourself. You couldn't get at your money, you perceive, before I did that."

"No. But can I now?"

"I should calculate you bought the stock-in-trade, meaning, in the way of trade, to sell it again. Retail or wholesale—or wholesale," he repeated presently, when she remained silent.

"Well, sir, I was afraid the person you put in to sell would be a great expense to me. Then you think, if I gain ever so little, I ought to sell wholesale if I get a chance?"

"You won't gain anything at all. A docu-

ment being wanted, you'll lose several pound. And *I've* no advice to give you, H. Goodrich's niece." The twinkle in his eyes seemed to show joy and triumph. He beckoned to a man near at hand. "There he is. If you want to have what you paid for the stock-in-trade (all but what I specified) in your own hand, payable to bearer, United States bonds, there's the man that will buy your shoes of you, and that have a document in his pocket, and a ink-bottle and pen, that you may sign handy. All I need add is, I wish H. Goodrich was here to see his money rescued from the grasp of a convict."

"Are you sure it's legal, and won't get you into any trouble?" exclaimed H. Goodrich's niece, when the other man had come up, and from a bundle of papers was sorting out one for her to sign.

"Well, so far as we can make out, it is. He"—pointing out his friend—"he have no call to quake, and· I expect the thing will hold. All I shall ask is, H. Goodrich's niece, that you keep your distance, and never let me know anything about me. I can get into no trouble for eleven year at the least. If I should then (and not likely), you'll promise me you'll always, wherever you be, take the *Suffolk Chronicle;* and if I'm in life then, and you see an advertisement in it letting you know I've got into trouble, then you'll have to write to me. But I'm not afraid. There's a pretty little income—over thirty pounds a year—left in my hands, and if a certain party made himself unpleasant and wanted the rest of it, he could be threatened with a suit in the Divorce Court, and I think he'll be glad enough to let things be."

"The purchase was legal, ma'am," observed the stranger; "your executor has the papers to prove it."

"And where our friend is going to take the boots and shoes is neither here nor there," proceeded Mr. Gordon.

"You'll take notice, though," continued the stranger, "that bonds and what not, made payable to bearer, are in one sense very ticklish property to keep. If they get burnt you've no remedy, if you lose them you've no remedy, or lose one, and whoever finds it holds it and gets the money. And I don't mean to say as you can always reckon on the same sum for them, not to a shilling or even a pound, because the dollar varies slightly in value, you know."

"I'll sign the paper," said Hannah Dill at last. "I fare to understand that I'm a free woman for good and all, and I'm deeply obliged to you both."

CHAPTER VI.

AND now the document which sold her
stock-in-trade to J. Gravison having been
duly signed by Hannah Dill (who for many a
long day never used that name again), a large,
awkward-shaped bundle of papers having
been consigned to her, and Mr. Gordon
having again remarked " that where those
boots and shoes were going, and where the
purchaser might be going, was neither here
nor there," the two friends make as if they
would withdraw, but this did not at all suit
the notions of the convict's wife.

She longed to give them, at least, a dinner,
and after a little pressing they agreed that
she should; and she left them on the beach,
while she hastened to her lodgings with her
children and the papers, where, having secured the latter, and taken out money for
her executor's expenses, she got her landlady to take charge for a few hours of the
former.

" Certain," quoth the landlady, " I'll see to
your little ladies, ma'am, with the greatest
pleasure; don't you worrit about them."

So Mrs. Dill came forth again, and conducted the two friends to a respectable
public-house, much frequented by sea captains and farming people.

Here, while they sat in a green bower out-
of-doors and smoked, she ordered and assisted to produce such a dinner as might be a
credit to her taste and her generosity, and a
thing to be remembered ever after.

It was not ready till half-past three, the
two guests having been more than ready for
some time.

First appeared dishes for which the place
was famous—soused mackerel at one end,
and at the other hot lobsters, served whole,
with brown bread and butter and bottled
porter.

After this came a rumpsteak pie with fresh
young onions, also a green goose, and abundance of peas and kidney potatoes. With
this course the company drank beer. One
of the guests observed with conviction that
even a Guildhall dinner could not beat this,
and the other remarked that it was what he
called " a square meal."

Next came an apricot pudding with a jug
of cream, and a dish of mince pies, blue with
the spiral flame of the lighted rum they were
served in.

All this took time, but at every fresh call
on their efforts the guests fell to again,
nothing daunted; there was no flagging but
in the conversation.

With the cheese and dessert appeared port,
and the affair concluded with more pipes in
the arbour, and some gin and water.

It was a great success.

In the cool of the evening they said they
must depart, and each giving an arm to H.
Goodrich's niece, they walked in high good
humour, and very steadily on the whole, to
the railway station, she seeing them off, with
many thanks on her part for their kindness,
and on theirs for her hospitality.

Mrs. Snaith then hastened to her lodgings.
Already her peculiar position had made her
cautious and reserved. She seldom began a
conversation, or volunteered any information,
however trifling, which gave others an opening for asking questions.

She found the children asleep and well,
thanked her landlady, and, seeing her weekly
bill on the table, paid it, and said she should
stay on.

The landlady retired. She began to understand her lodger; she found her a just woman
to reckon with, though not one to waste words.

" Why, if she bought her words by the
dozen," thought the good woman, " and was
always considering how to use them to the
best advantage, and make them go as far as
they would, she could not any way be more
mean with them."

Mrs. Snaith, asking no questions, did not
hear how much " the little ladies" had been
admired that day, nor how much curiosity
they had excited.

For the small place being very full of
visitors, the landlady and her young daughter
had amused themselves during their lodger's
absence by sitting in the open window of
her pleasant parlour, which was down-stairs,
and watching " the company," while little
Miss Amabel and Miss Delia played about
the room with their toys.

It was a pride and joy to them to see the
place so crowded, and to observe the new-
comers looking about for lodgings.

Little Amabel in the meantime was setting
out a row of wooden tea things on the sill of
the window, and the baby Delia, who could
but just walk alone, trotted up to her to admire, and presently began to toss some of
them out on to the pavement below.

This was a fine thing to have done, and
the little creatures looked on with deep interest, while the landlady's daughter, called
'Ria, went down the steps of the street-door
and fetched them in again.

Little Delia, having tasted the joy of this
small piece of mischief, now threw out her
shore-spade, while Amabel, not to be out-

done, filled a toy wooden bucket with the animals from a Noah's ark, and one by one sent them after it, the long-suffering 'Ria going out, with unwise patience, to collect and bring them back, as if the vagaries of children were no more under human control than are the rising of the wind or the changes of the moon.

"How tiresome gentlefolk's children are, mother!" she said at last, when, to the amusement of the ladies next door, who were reading novels on a bench, she came forth for the eleventh time and picked up two elephants and a canary; "why, they give ten times the trouble that we do when we're little."

"Ay," answered the mother, with a sage air of conviction, "it's all very well to say they're the same flesh and blood as we are; there's that difference anyhow. You won't easy deceive me; I'll undertake to tell a gentleman's child by it anywhere. They've no responsibility in 'em either. Why, a big child five years old will run away from her nurse, and her nurse just has to run after her, while at that age you took the baby as then was on the beach, and had Tom to take care of with you."

"But they're minded," said the girl; "that's why they can't *seem to grow any responsibility* of their own."

"There!" said one of the ladies to the other, "that girl is putting away the Noah's ark and giving the child a doll to play with. I wonder she did not think of doing so before. Look! there comes the spade again."

Two lovely little faces looked out as before, and some infantile babble was heard, but no landlady's daughter came forth to bring it in; so, lest it should be lost to its small possessor, one of the ladies, before she went indoors, picked it up, intending to bring it to the window.

"Amabel de Berenger!" she exclaimed, reading the name. "Why, Mary, these children are De Berengers! I wonder which branch of the family they belong to?"

"Not to the old baronet's," observed the other. "His sons are unmarried; at least, Tom de Berenger was only married a few weeks ago, and was here till lately on his wedding tour."

"They may be strangers from another neighbourhood," observed the first. "The name is not so very uncommon;" and she came to the outside of the window, giving the spade to its dimpled owner, remarking to the landlady that she was intimate with one family of De Berengers, and asking where these children came from.

"Amabel was now six years old."

The landlady did not know, and little miss was backward with her tongue, as delicate children often were. They only had a nurse with them, she said, and she looked at the spade with just a little touch of curiosity.

"Dear me!" said the lady. "I should like to see that nurse again; but, unfortunately, we go away this evening. Perhaps these are Mr. Richard de Berenger's children, and their parents may be coming."

"I think not, ma'am," replied the landlady. "I have not heard of it."

Thereupon, having kissed the children, this lady departed, and the landlady said to her daughter, "Well, 'Ria, my girl, only think how I have wished to ask Mrs. Snaith who the children were, and didn't seem to think she would like it, she being so close, and yet all the time here was their name as plain as print for anybody that liked to look at it!"

"You didn't know their name, mother?" cried the girl.

"No; I say I didn't. Did you?"

"Well, I don't know as I gave it a thought that she hadn't mentioned it, till one night (last week I think it was) I noticed it on some pinafores that she sent to the wash."

"It just shows what fancies folks take in their heads," observed the landlady. "I felt as sure as could be she didn't want to tell who they were, and so I never asked her; and now look!" She held up the spade and laughed.

"They might be that parson's children," said the girl; "him that was here three summers ago, mother, in our house, with his boy brother and his aunt."

"Hardly," answered the mother; "he was not a married man then, I know."

"My!" cried the girl, "how those two used to teaze that aunt, the lady that would always be talking of her will. I was so little then, they used to go on while I was waiting, and not mind me. Well, to be sure, what a silly old thing she was!"

"And you were always as handy as could be. To see you wait, little as you were, has made many a lodger laugh," observed the mother, with pleasant pride in her offspring.

Here the conversation ended, Mrs. Snaith never hearing the questions that had been asked concerning the children, nor of the reminiscences of 'Ria and her mother. The half of either, if duly reported, would have changed her plans entirely, and changed her children's destiny and her own.

Mrs. Snaith quickly found that she was living very much beyond her income, so she very soon went away from that little seaside place; but her delicate children had improved during their stay so much, that she proposed to come back again when the season was quite over, and rooms might be had for an almost nominal rent.

She thus betrayed to the landlady her expectation that these children would be some time under her sole charge and control. The good woman was all the more deferential to her in consequence, and finding her more reticent day by day, took care to let her depart without asking her a single question.

Mrs. Snaith thought what a nice hardworking woman she was—one who minded her own business, and had no idle curiosity—and she was perhaps beguiled by this opinion into the only piece of confidence she offered: that she had brought these children from London.

She established herself about twelve miles inland, in a small village, where she found a little cottage to let. She wanted to save money, that she might send her darlings, when they were old enough, to a good school; but, meanwhile, she dressed them well and waited on them with the devoted love of a mother.

It was enough to satisfy and make happy and cheerful a mind constituted as hers. She grew stout, looked well and serene, and month by month her darlings became fresher and fatter; only little Delia, as she fancied, sometimes limped a little, and this made her anxious, considering the child's parentage.

There were no mothers in the village whom she could consult excepting the wives of two small farmers, and they both recommended that little miss should be taken to the shore to paddle in the salt water. They were sure that was what the father would approve.

It had come to be thought there—a thought which had grown out of the remarks of the villagers one to another—that the children's father was abroad: that they had lost their mother seemed to be evident.

Mrs. Snaith—her security in that obscure place having been so complete—did not think of stepping forth again into the inquisitive world without a pang. She had taken up her new name and position in a far more confident spirit than she now felt. Month by month she became more afraid of ultimate detection, not so much by the wretched father, as by the children themselves.

She had lived in her tiny cottage two years, and their infantile intelligence was equal already to the perception (a false one, but not the less tenaciously held) that there was a difference of rank between them and their dear nurse. They could by no means have expressed this, but every one about them helped it to unconscious growth.

Amabel was now six years old. In her sweet humility the mother considered herself not equal to teaching even the alphabet to a child destined to be herself a teacher.

She had tried hard to divest herself of her provincial expressions, some of which her dear lady had pointed out to her. In many cases she had succeeded, but her grammar was faulty, and certain peculiarities of language clung yet to her daily English. She wanted little Amabel to speak well from the first, and she went to a poor, but well-educated old lady—the late clergyman's sister, who boarded in a farmhouse near her cottage—and proposed to her to teach the child for two or three hours a day. Miss Price said she should be delighted to teach little Miss de Berenger, and she instilled into her mind, while so doing, various notions not out of place considering the position she supposed her to hold. She must remember that she was a young lady. She must never talk in a sing-song tone, as her good nurse did; that was provincial. Her dear papa would be much vexed if she used such and such expressions. No doubt she often thought about her dear papa, and wished that he should be pleased with her on his return.

Little Amabel was a docile child; she did begin to wish to please this dear papa. In her infantile fashion she felt a strange attraction toward him, and set him in her mind far above the tender woman whose care and pride she was, while, like most children who have a governess and a nurse, she gave her kisses to the nurse, and talked like the governess.

But little Delia, in case her ankle was really weak, must have every advantage, whatever happened. So Mrs. Snaith wrote to her former landlady, asking the price of rooms, and was told that if she could come at a particular time mentioned, between two other " Lets," she should have some cheap. She felt, when she appeared at the door with the children, that she had not gained courage, though she had been on the whole very happy; she knew the day must come when she would be confronted by awkward questions. She had often rehearsed in her mind the words she would use in reply. They were to be very few and simple, and long reflection had made her aware that her danger of self-betrayal would lie most in the way she met matters that were taken for granted.

The landlady thought her more "close" than ever. "I did not expect to see your little ladies so much grown and so rosy," she remarked. "I thought, ma'am, you said Miss Delia was not well."

"It was only that I thought her ankle was weak," said Mrs. Snaith anxiously. "I fared to think she turned one of her feet in more than the other when she walked."

This conversation took place while the landlady cleared away breakfast the day after Mrs. Snaith's arrival. "Many children do that," quoth the good woman, impelled, spite of her own interest, to make a suggestive observation. "Why, dear me, ma'am, their father will be a strange gentleman if he is not satisfied, when he returns, that you have done the best anybody could for them."

She was rewarded for once. Mrs. Snaith coloured all over her honest, homely face; concealment did not come easily to her. She answered that she had no reason at all to think he would not be satisfied, and her reply, considering the character of this said father, seemed to herself almost ridiculous; she knew well that he cared for their welfare not a straw. And the landlady, not having been contradicted, supposed herself to know that the children's father was abroad.

Mrs. Snaith fell easily into her old habit of sitting at work on the beach while she watched the children playing at the edge of the wave. They were very much grown. Both were lovely, and in all respects unlike herself. She instinctively kept apart from the other nurses and children. Her quiet life went on in a great silence, yet she was happy; love and service contented her. She was safe for a long while to come from the husband whose drunken brawls had made life a misery, and whose crimes had kept her in constant fear. She was freed from want, and that was enough to make her wake every morning in a conscious state of thankfulness.

The fortnight she had meant to stay had almost come to an end, and she was watching Delia one afternoon, and feeling almost contented with her pretty little white ankles. That slight something, whatever it had been, habit or weakness, had almost disappeared, and, lovely and rosy, the little creature was paddling in the water with her sister, when clearly rang a voice that she recognised, as its owner came up briskly to her side.

"Why, there's that nurse again, the person that I told you of! And the children with her. There they all are, I declare!"

Mrs. Snaith turned slowly and saw the lady who had asked the children's name two years ago. She had never forgotten her, nor that her landlady had called her Miss Thimbleby. They hurried up.

"You have forgotten me, perhaps?"

"No, ma'am."

They sat down near her. "I saw the children's name on their spade," said Miss Thimbleby. "This"—pointing out the other lady with an air, as if she was giving some intelligence that must be most welcome—"this is Miss de Berenger."

"Indeed, ma'am," said Mrs. Snaith, with slow and quiet caution; and she lifted attentive eyes to the stranger, who nodded and smiled.

"Yes, I am Miss de Berenger. You have heard him speak of me, no doubt?"

"Him?"

"He was always my favourite," continued the lady, who seemed both glad and excited, "and of course he must have mentioned me. Indeed, I am sure of it."

This was rather a startling speech.

"I don't understand you, ma'am," said Mrs. Snaith slowly. She looked again at Miss de Berenger. It did not require much penetration to see that she was not a wise woman; her style of dress alone might have suggested this thought, if there had been nothing else about her to do it.

"And I have looked for you repeatedly, and told my nephew Felix all about you; but we never could find you, either of us."

"Looked for us! Indeed, ma'am, may I ask why?"

"Why? why?" exclaimed Miss Thimbleby, with reproachful astonishment. "Do I really hear you asking why?"

A little useful resentment here rising in Mrs. Snaith's breast enabled her to answer rather sharply, "Yes, you do." And she looked again at the lady who had been mentioned as Miss de Berenger.

She was a slender, upright little woman of between fifty and sixty, nearer to the latter age. Her hair, not precisely red, was yet too near that colour to pass for golden. It was abundant for her time of life, free from grey, and dressed in long loose curls, so light and "fluffy," that they blew about with the slightest movement in the air. Her dress was of that reddish purple which makes orange look more conspicuous. She had a green parasol, wore a deal of jewelry, had a jaunty air, and might have passed for little more than forty—so brisk and youthful was she—but that her cheeks were streaked with the peculiar red of an apple that has been kept into the winter—a bright, fixed hue, which early in life is scarcely ever seen.

The other lady was very plainly dressed, and seemed to be under thirty. She started up on hearing Mrs. Snaith's last word, and going to the edge of the wave, brought back with her the two children, who, a little surprised by Miss de Berenger's gay appearance, stood gazing at her for a moment, their bare feet gleaming white on the sand, and their rosy mouths pouting with just the least little impatience at being taken from the water.

"The very image of him!" exclaimed Miss de Berenger, shaking back her curls and clasping her hands. "Come and kiss me, my pretty ones."

The children, with infantile indifference, gave the required kisses, looked at the lady, looked at Mrs. Snaith; but the one was drying her eyes, the other watchful, to discover what this might mean. She turned cold, but did not look at her darlings, so they took the opportunity to slip away and run back to the water.

"Where is their father now?" asked Miss de Berenger. "Ah, I was very fond of him. If he had only stopped at home, I should have left him everything." A twinkling in her eyes seemed to promise tears. She wiped them again, though these proofs of feeling had not come. "Where is he?"

"I don't know, ma'am," said Mrs. Snaith, who now laid down her work, to hide the trembling of her hands.

"He is abroad, of course?"

"Ma'am, I am not sure."

Both answers perfectly true.

The reluctance to speak was evident; it seemed to astonish Miss de Berenger, even to the point of making her silent.

"Why, surely," exclaimed the other lady, with a certain air of severity, as if by the weight of her disapproval she hoped to oppress Mrs. Snaith into giving her testimony—"surely you can have no objection to answer a few questions—such natural questions as these, nurse!"

"Perhaps she has had her orders," murmured Miss de Berenger.

Mrs. Snaith for the moment was much surprised at this question. Under whose orders could they think she was?

"Unless that is the case," said Miss Thimbleby, with uncivil directness, "I cannot understand what reason you can have for concealing anything from Miss de Berenger —what *good* reason."

Again indignation came to the aid of Mrs. Snaith. She rose, took up the children's shoes and socks, and turning her back on the two ladies, went to the water's edge and called her little treasures to come to her.

A Scene in Greenland—1875.

AN ICE HERO.

By Captain ALBERT HASTINGS MARKHAM, R.N.

He must greatly lose who would greatly gain,
Turn from friends and home to the wandering main ;
To ice-fields of the north and its long, long night,
And weary days bereft of all delight.

TO those readers of GOOD WORDS who have been, more or less, interested in the work of Arctic Research during the last quarter of a century, the name of Hans Hendrik, the Greenland Eskimo, will be familiar, for he has, with only one exception, accompanied every expedition that has been dispatched for the exploration of the unknown north, by Baffin Bay and Smith Sound, during that period.

His exploits whilst so engaged have fairly earned for him the title I have given to this article, and he may, without affectation, lay claim to be considered a veritable ice hero in the truest acceptation of the term.

His adventures during these voyages have recently been published in an interesting little work written entirely by himself.

For quaintness and originality of expression this memoir vies with the publications of that grand old divine Hakluyt, or his successor Purchas.

It would be unfair to classify Hans as an ignorant savage, although it must be acknowledged that the extent of his education was decidedly limited, and that his mode of existence was by no means of the most refined order. He was, however, able to write a little in Eskimo, and the result of this accomplishment, aided by a good memory, is the naively-expressed little work, which has recently been published by Dr. Rink, late Danish Inspector of South Greenland, and which has afforded me material for the subject of my sketch.

The Greenlanders of the present day have taken kindly to school instruction, and those who have had the advantage of being educated at any of the Danish settlements situated on the west coast of Greenland, are invariably skilled in both reading and writing the Eskimo language.

Although, comparatively, so little known, few countries possess such an interesting history as Greenland.

Discovered more than eight hundred years ago by an Icelandic chief, such a glowing description was published of the fertility of the land, and its admirable adaptability for colonization, that the simple-minded people of Iceland and Norway were easily induced to leave home and country for the purpose of establishing themselves in this newly-found territory.

We read that in the year 986 no less than twenty-five ships sailed for the new colony, fourteen of which, however, only reached their destination, the remainder having been either lost during the voyage, or compelled to put back by stress of weather.

The site selected by the colonists was on the south-west extreme of the continent; two settlements being there formed, called respectively the East and West "Bygds," or parishes.

The ruins of these ancient settlements, including a church, with several Runic stones, are still to be seen.

The spirit of maritime enterprise that led to the discovery, and afterwards to the colonisation, of Greenland, did not diminish amongst the settlers, two of whom may fairly lay claim to being the discoverers of America, four hundred years prior to the memorable voyage of Columbus. In a northerly direction the latitude of 73° N. was reached by some unknown wanderer from the colony; this has been plainly indicated by the recent discovery of a Runic stone, found upon an island in that position, lately transferred to the Museum of Northern Antiquities in Copenhagen. This stone has the names of three Norsemen inscribed upon it, and a date which, although nearly illegible, is supposed to be the year 1236.

Christianity was introduced into Greenland by Lief, who had previously been converted during a visit paid to King Olaf of Norway.

On his return from the old country, the colonists listened to his preaching, and were readily induced to embrace the Christian faith. The first bishop was sent out by the Pope in 1126. At that time the people were ruled by a kind of republican organization, similar to the government then existing in Iceland; but in 1261 a new bishop, who appeared to devote more of his time to political affairs than to his ecclesiastical duties, instigated the colonists to swear allegiance to the King of Norway, and from thenceforth, until the extirpation of the settlers, Greenland became a dependency of that country.

The condition of the colony was, apparently, flourishing up to the fourteenth century, when communication between it and the mother country, partly caused by the outbreak of plague or "black death" in Norway, almost entirely ceased.

In the early part of the fifteenth century tidings from the far-away colony grew more rare and obscure, until they ceased altogether in about the year 1448, from which date all knowledge of the old Norse colony is lost in obscurity.

Greenland was not again visited until John

Davis, during one of his famous voyages for the discovery of a north-west passage, landed in 1585, in latitude 64° N., and bartered with the natives. The reports brought home by this energetic navigator revived in Denmark the memory of their long-neglected settlements, and induced that nation to send out an expedition in order to effect communication with their almost-forgotten countrymen. But, alas! no traces of the old Norsemen and their families could be discovered. It is true that the sites of the old settlements were found, with the ruined remains of the cathedral, but no vestiges of the descendants of those gallant people who had accompanied Erik the Red in his grand work of colonization.

From a few traditional tales that have been preserved amongst the Eskimos of Southern Greenland, it is generally supposed that a sudden descent was made on the Norsemen by the Eskimos, whom they called Skrellings, which ended in the absolute extermination of the colonists. This is the generally accepted belief regarding the total annihilation of the inhabitants of the East and West Bygds. From this time, although the Norsemen had disappeared, the Eskimos seemed to have resided and flourished in South Greenland, and along the west coast even to a high latitude. It was the conversion of these poor heathens to the Christian faith that again brought to our knowledge this hitherto little known and so long-neglected land.

The person who resolved, with the blessing and aid of Divine Providence, to undertake this good deed, was a Moravian missionary named Hans Egede, a man alike conspicuous for his fervent devotion as for his indomitable will and energy. This remarkable man landed in Greenland with his wife and children in the year 1721, and after years of incredible difficulties and hardships, not unmixed with danger, he had the extreme gratification of knowing and seeing that his teachings were listened to, and that his exertions were being rewarded by success.

Not only did Hans Egede succeed in his spiritual ministrations, but he also established that system of barter between the Danes and Eskimos, which is carried out to the present day with beneficial effect to both sides.

The Danish Government viewed with approbation the good work begun by this devoted man, and taking the colony under their especial protection, established settlements along the coast presided over by Danish Governors, under the immediate

XXI—7

supervision of a Royal Inspector, an officer selected by the king as his representative and superintendent of trade in Greenland.

Dr. Rink, by whom this post was held for many years, in the preface of an admirable work descriptive of Greenland and its interesting inhabitants, uses the following words— "As regards Greenland life, no one will deny that it would be very interesting to see it pictured by the Greenlanders themselves."

By a curious coincidence, Dr. Rink, not very long after writing the above, is the medium of presenting to the public the memoirs of a Greenlander written by himself, for it was Dr. Rink who undertook the task of translating from the Eskimo language, and publishing, the interesting life of the hero of this article.

In his introduction he tells us that although Hans Hendrik did not keep a regular diary, there are indications of his having kept extensive notes; and where these failed, he was aided by a retentive memory, to which is due the compilation of the greater part of the narrative.

Hans, who must have been born about the year 1835, was brought up at the little trading establishment of Fiskernaes. Although the winters there are very severe, its position is not more northerly than many places in Norway, and it is situated well outside the Arctic circle.

Lichtenfels was the neighbouring Moravian missionary station, from the resident pastor of which Hans received his first ideas of religion, and learnt to place that firm belief in a merciful God, which afterwards strengthened and supported him during many trials.

He was but a lad of eighteen years of age when Dr. Kane, the distinguished American Arctic explorer, put in to Fiskernaes, on his way northward in command of the brig *Advance*, which, at the expense of Mr. Grinnell of New York, had been equipped and dispatched in order to prosecute the search for Sir John Franklin and his missing comrades. As Kane was in want of an Eskimo hunter and dog-driver, he readily accepted the offer of Hans to accompany him in that capacity.

Hans seems to have had some little trouble in getting away from his relations, for he tells us that, after he had accepted Dr. Kane's offer, he went to inform his mother, but, " she gainsaid me and begged me not to join them. But, I replied, If no mischief happen me I shall return and I shall earn money for thee." This answer of his had due weight with his parent and he was allowed to go.

The *Advance* was unable to reach a very high position, notwithstanding the energy and perseverance displayed by Dr. Kane in his attempts to push through the heavy ice peculiar to Smith Sound. The vessel was eventually secured in winter quarters in a snug land-locked bay, which was called Rensselaer harbour.

Hans, who was an excellent hunter and a capital shot, at once entered upon his own particular avocations, and with such success, that he was frequently able to diversify the ordinary ship fare by a haunch of venison, a hare, or a seal steak. It must be recollected that, Fiskernaes being situated south of the Arctic circle, Hans had hitherto never experienced a day on which the sun had not made its appearance above the horizon, therefore it is not surprising to hear that he was ludicrously frightened at the long night, of nearly four months' duration, which he now for the first time realised. He alludes to this circumstance in the following words : " Then it really grew winter and dreadfully cold, and the sky speedily darkened. Never had I seen the dark season like this ; to be sure it was awful, I thought we should have no daylight any more. I was seized with fright, and fell a-weeping. I never in my life saw such darkness at noontide. As the darkness continued for three months, I really believed we should have no daylight more."

The return of the sun dispelled the inactivity which the winter had necessitated, and enabled our hero to resume that active life to which he had been inured from childhood.

Not only was the chase, for which Hans had a passionate liking, diligently and successfully followed up, but he was also continually employed during the spring and summer in exploring the surrounding country in a dog-sledge. He it was who was the sole companion of Morton when that officer reported his wonderful discovery of an open Polar Sea, seen from Cape Constitution, but which has, alas ! been recently proved to have no existence.

That they saw a large water space is evident, not only from Morton's report, but also from Hans, who says, " we fell in with a large open water," but that this pool should have been magnified into an open Polar Sea appears almost incredible, for the channel is only at this promontory eighteen miles broad, whilst land extends in a northerly direction, bounding on each side a narrow channel for over one hundred miles ! The range of vision on the day of Morton's wonderful discovery must have been remarkably limited, if nothing was visible to the north-ward but a boundless ocean !

All efforts to release the *Advance* from her icy bondage during the autumn proved in-effectual ; she was immovably frozen up, and her unhappy crew were compelled to pass another drear and monotonous winter in her.

The term unhappy is here used advisedly, for it is well known that this vessel left America wretchedly equipped, and ill pro-vided to guard against the severities and exi-gencies of an Arctic winter. To add to their sufferings scurvy made its appearance, the Commander himself being one of the earliest and greatest sufferers. Indeed, it is highly probable that none would have survived to relate the tale of their extremities had it not been for the kindness of a tribe of Eskimos, who visited them and kept them supplied with seal and walrus meat—a sure and effi-cacious remedy against scurvy.

As the prospect of ever releasing the ship was a very doubtful one, it was determined at the end of the second winter to abandon her, the whole party, with the exception of Hans, proceeding to the south in their boats directly the weather admitted of travelling. After enduring great hardships, they even-tually reached one of the Danish settlements, whence they returned to America. The cause of our hero's parting with his companions is better related in his own words—

" My companions began to think of aban-doning their vessel and repairing to Uperni-vik. I did not believe they would be able to reach it. At the same time I happened to visit the natives in order to get hares. The day after I had come to them I set out for the chase in a gale from the north. A heavy squall suddenly carried me off, hurting me against the hard frozen snow. My native friends led me by the hands to the sledge, and carried me back to their houses, where I recovered during a stay of several days.

" As these men behaved so kindly to-wards me, I began to think of remaining with them. It was my intention to return, but I began to envy the natives with whom I stayed, who supplied themselves with all their wants and lived happily. At length I wholly attached myself to them, and followed them when they removed to the south. I got the man of highest standing among them as my foster-father, and when I had dwelled several winters with them I began to think of taking a wife, although an unchristened one. First I went a-wooing to a girl of good morals, but I gave her up, as her father said,

' Take my sister.' The latter was a widow, and ill reputed. Afterwards I got a sweet-heart whom I resolved never to part with, but to keep as my wife in the country of the Christians. Since then she has been bap-tized and partaken of the Lord's Supper; but I was greatly delighted at taking along with me one of the unchristened when I re-turned to a Kavdlunak [Danish] settlement."

It is greatly to be feared, even from Hans's own showing, that he deserted his party at a very critical moment, when, in fact, his ser-vices as a hunter were more than ever re-quired.

These events happened in the year 1855, and for the next five years Hans remained with these Northern Eskimos, a tribe that never ventured farther south in any of their migratory wanderings or hunting excursions than Cape York, the northern extreme of Melville Bay.

In his autobiography he furnishes us with an interesting account of his newly found friends and their means of subsistence, and he also tells us of his own efforts to con-vert them to the Christian faith; but in his zealous explanation of the tenets of Chris-tianity he appears to have succeeded more in, frightening his hearers than in bringing them round to the true faith. He says, " It is a great pity that people there in the north have no idea of a Creator. Only by me were they informed about the Maker of heaven and earth and everything else, of all animals, and even of ourselves ; also about His only be-gotten Son, who came in the flesh for the sake of sinful men for the purpose of saving them, teaching them faith, and performing wonderful deeds amongst them, and after-wards was killed on a wooden cross, and arose from the dead on the third day, and will come down again to judge the living and the dead. On hearing this the Northlanders were rather frightened as to the destruction of the world in their life as well as in their death."

Our hero's domestic felicity remained un-broken until August, 1860, when Dr. Hayes, who had served as a subordinate in Kane's expedition, put into Cape York for the ex-press purpose of seeking him, and, if suc-cessful in his search, inducing him to join his ship in the same capacity that he held in the *Advance*. This expedition of Dr. Hayes, it will be remembered, was undertaken with the hope that the open Polar Sea, in whose existence many theorists firmly believed, would be reached, whence many interesting observations would be made, and a large tract of hitherto unknown land and sea would be explored.

One of the conditions made by Hans on joining the *United States*, the name of Dr. Hayes's schooner, was that his wife and baby should be allowed to accompany him; a permission that was readily granted, as it was thought the woman would be of great use in the preparation of skins and their conversion into wearing apparel.

Dr. Hayes was not even so fortunate as Dr. Kane in reaching a high latitude in his ship, being unable to do more than just enter the portals of Smith Sound, where he secured his vessel in winter quarters in Hartstene Bay. No spot could have been better selected in which to pass the winter, for, in addition to its possessing a well-sheltered anchorage, the hills and valleys in the neighbourhood abounded with animal life in the shape of reindeer and hares; in fact it well deserves the name of an "Arctic Paradise," which has not unfrequently been bestowed upon it.

Here, such a keen sportsman as Hans was naturally in his element; he says himself, " I felt very happy that now I had got something to do;" and before the winter had set in Dr. Hayes records that "the carcases of more than a dozen reindeer were hanging in the shrouds, whilst rabbits and foxes were suspended in clusters from the rigging."

But with the disappearance of the sun the troubles of Hans appear to have commenced.

Whether it was that he was of a more reticent and stolid disposition than the three other Eskimos that were on board the *United States*, or whether it was that, having his wife and family on board, he did not associate so much with the remainder of the crew, he certainly, whatever the cause, lost in favour with all on board the schooner, from the commander downwards. Dr. Hayes goes so far as to accuse him of jealousy of the other natives and sulkiness, and declares that "he is a type of the worst phase of the Eskimo character."

These traits in his character may have been produced and intensified by the treatment he received on board; for on the two subsequent expeditions in which Hans served, during one of which he was personally known to the writer of this article, he was particularly free from anything of the sort, although he would at times be subject to fits of despondency, imagining that some of the crew had evil designs regarding him. These impressions were doubtless occasioned by his inability to understand what was said by those around him, and from his interpreting dark looks into meaning threats. This is not to be wondered at when it is remembered that Hans was suddenly transplanted from his own quiet mode of existence to live in the midst of a strange people of a different tongue, whose habits and customs were totally at variance with anything that he had been accustomed to.

(To be concluded in next number.)

JOHN THE BAPTIST BEFORE HEROD.

By the Rev. H. R. HAWEIS, M.A.

"THE conscience of the king"—others speculated, when they heard of the new Nazarene Prophet and his miracles, it was Elias, or one of the many fanatics abroad about this time, or an old Hebrew seer risen from the dead—but Herod *knew*, "It is John, whom I beheaded."

"Conscience makes cowards of us all." Men whisper together; you think they are talking about you. One tells a tale of how another robbed the till, maltreated his wife, did some time ago, in secret, an act of villany. Your look betrays you. "All the world's a stage," and your own hidden life-drama is incessantly being played out before your eyes. You see what others cannot see; you hear what others cannot hear.

At last the strain becomes intolerable.

You spring, like Claudius, King of Denmark, from his seat, in that palace where sits by his side the guilty paramour; in the place of the murdered Banquo—you will see no more—and yet you can see nothing but your crime till the day of your death.

The drama is eternally recurrent; it belongs neither to Hamlet nor to Herod. A man will give himself up to the gallows twenty years after the treacherous stroke. Nero was haunted by the ghost of his mother, whom he had put to death. Caligula suffered from want of sleep—he was haunted by the faces of his murdered victims. We can still see the corridors recently excavated on the Palatine Hill. We can walk under the vaulted passages where his assassins met him. "Often weary with lying awake," writes Suetonius, "sometimes he sat up in bed, at others walked in the longest porticos about the house, looking out for the approach of day." You may see the very spot where his assassins waited for him round a corner. Domitian had those long walls cased with clear agate. The mark of the slabs may still be seen. The agate reflected as in a glass any figure that might be concealed round an angle, so that a surprise was impossible.

It is said that Theodoric, after ordering the decapitation of Lysimachus, was haunted in the middle of his feasts by the spectre of a gory head upon a charger. And how often must a nobler head than that of Lysimachus have haunted a more ignoble Prince than Theodoric as he sat at meat and muttered shudderingly aside, " It is John whom I beheaded !"

The Gospel narrative begins with the spiritual state of Herod after the murder. It sounds at once the note of an accusing conscience. We have now to look back and suppose for ourselves the lesson which leaps forth with a certain fiery and bloody emphasis as we proceed step by step.

Herod Antipas was a son of Herod the Great, set over Galilee and Judea, with the title of Tetrach, or one of four governors— not king. It has been said that " he was a man in whom were mingled the worst features of the Roman, the Oriental, and the Greek" (Farrar), but this is probably too severe a judgment.

Herod was a weak man, not without a sense of the dignity and functions of a Roman Governor. He was zealous in repairing the cities of Betharam and Sepphoris, and recalled the glories of the Great Herod in the magnificence of the city of Tiberias, founded in honour of the Roman Emperor.

He was easily swayed—now by John the Baptist, whom he heard gladly and obeyed willingly up to a certain point; now by Herodias; and lastly by the looks and opinions of those who sat at meat with him. Weakness, vanity, and the family failings of restless ambition were the poisonous blossoms of character which ripened into the more bitter fruits of incestuous adultery and cowardly murder.

The provincial kings and governors of the Empire were often to be found at Rome paying court to the Emperor, at this time Tiberius Cæsar, under whom Jesus Christ was crucified. It was at Rome that Herod Antipas became enamoured of Herodias, his brother Philip's wife. Philip was a Herod ; but he was not a king, not even a governor.

Herodias seized her opportunity. She was the grand-daughter of the Great Herod. The Herods had no scruples; the women of the family were ambitious, cruel, unscrupulous, and, in their own estimation, born to be queens. The marriage tie, sacred to the Jew, sat lightly upon the Roman. Herodias snapt it rudely and left Rome with Herod Antipas. Being divorced herself, she required Antipas to divorce the Arabian Princess whom he had married. But before the unfaithful husband reached his kingdom the unhappy woman had already fled to the strong fortress of Makaur. There she met her father, the Emir or King of Petra, and from that moment Herod's frontier never ceased to be harassed by his indignant and dishonoured relatives.

The Tetrach returns to his kingdom, but he has committed his first great public crime, and he has forfeited for ever the esteem of his people, the friendship of his allies, and the integrity of his character.

Irritable, irresolute, wavering, no longer his own master, a puppet in the hands of a violent woman, he turns upon the one defenceless figure that has courage in this critical hour to tell him the truth. He hears the murmur of the people in silence. He cannot still the tongue of an angry woman ; but he can cast into prison the dauntless man of the desert, who thunders forth the terrible veto, " It is not lawful for thee to have thy brother's wife."

Perhaps he thought the prophet might relent beneath the blandishments of court favour and flattery, or, yielding to the terror of a lonely cell and the loss of freedom, pronounce a verdict of acquittal, or at least keep silence. How little he knew of John ! The Baptist was made of sterner stuff. His purpose was firm as the desert rocks; his heart as clear and simple as the Jordan water. We are apt to excuse crime in high places, to smile on the foible of the wealthy and powerful, whilst showing no quarter to the poor, the frail, and the tempted ! But no threat or cajolery could change the irrevocable verdict which had blasted the reputation of the Tetrarch from Nazareth to Arimathea, " It is not lawful for thee to have thy brother's wife."

But those who cannot be silenced may be destroyed. As Henry II. craved to be rid of Beckett, as Mary Queen of Scots fretted to be quit of John Knox, so did Herodias watch like a panther for the opportunity to spring upon her victim. It came but too soon.

In the strong fortress of Makaur, built by Herod the Great, the very fortress so lately occupied by the fugitive Princess in her first agony of despair and indignation—the fortress at that very moment the prison house of John the Baptist—there was a sumptuous banqueting-hall. Like Dover Castle, Makaur was long a royal residence as well as fortress; and Herod kept his birthday there, and feasted the great lords of the Galilean estates.

By a fatal irony, so often illustrated in history—as when the inventor of the gallows died on the gallows, the inventor of the guillotine is beheaded by the guillotine—the scene of Herod's third and last great crime is indissolubly associated with his first and second—the irregular marriage and the base imprisonment.

How often do men choose their Makaur as the scene of those giddy dissipations in which they strive to quench the light of the soul! Forget, they cannot; then there is but one remedy—face it out, brazen it out, sear "the conscience with a hot iron."

In these corridors *she* walked, on this couch *she* reclined, here *she* ate, and drank, and slumbered—the woman who is gone, dishonoured and unwept; and yonder, in a cell deep down, yet almost within hearing of the revelry, lies the coarse, rude man of the desert, who is *her* friend. "The enemy of my incomparable Herodias; the woman I love no more; the Censor I will hear no more; both are out of the way. Let us eat and drink, and be merry." "Herod made a supper to his lords, high captains, and chief estates of Galilee."

The Herodian women were famed for their beauty. The charms of the mother had first seduced the affections of Antipas. The beauty of Salome, her daughter, was to complete his moral ruin. Shall we say that every step in the coming bloody drama was carefully prepared? Shall we say that Herodias had looked forward to this day—had planned this banquet—had even chosen the convenient site within a stone's throw of her victim—had drilled with fierce and eager interest the lithe and graceful motions of a young girl who, in the first glow of her beauty, might well recall to the eyes of Antipas her own fading charms?

The thing was all too subtle and well done to be a common birthday surprise. The sacred historian allows the serpent in the grass to rear its venomous head in that one sentence, "Therefore Herodias had a quarrel against him, and would have killed him, but she could not." Nay, she could, and she would.

No feast in those corrupt days was complete without some oriental performers—an Egyptian conjuror throwing up eggs; a necromancer from Persia or Arabia; Eastern girls trained in all the lax motions of the Ionic dance. Herodias decided the moment; she has doubtless watched the progress of the feast.

No common dancing is to be here, but the lovely grand-daughter of Herod the Great—herself a future queen—is to be presented to the assembled guests, well skilled to perform one of those refined figures which, in Syria, M. Renan tells us, are not thought unbecoming, even to people of high rank.

It was a surprise to men accustomed to the coarse routine exhibitions of Eastern dancing-girls. The doors are thrown open. Salome, herself scarcely more than a child, bursts in upon them. She glides over the shining and tesselated floors; she stands for a moment perchance a little dazzled and confused by the glare of light, the sound of applause; she gazes timidly at the magnificent banquet-table groaning with gold and silver chargers, at the royally robed revellers reclining in the cloth of gold, the wealth of Arabian perfume, the spotless Egyptian linen; her eyes pass from the glitter of ruby and emerald to walls richly tapestried, velvet carpets, and tall window-curtains glowing with the Tyrian dye. And as the applause begins almost to terrify and at the same time intoxicate her, she plunges with childlike abandon into her well-practised steps.

Oh, for a weight of lead to stay those light and tinkling feet! Oh, for a sudden stroke to stiffen those fair and agile limbs! Oh, for the pallor of death to wither the roses in those flushed cheeks, and quench the fires in Salome's eyes. But no; the girl's dance and the prophet's life are wearing fast away to the bitter end. "She danced, and pleased Herod and them that sat at meat with him."

Herodias, the wily mother, listens. In savage transport she hears Herod's drunken vow, "Whatsoever thou shalt ask of me, I will give it thee, to the half of my kingdom." The girl is speechless. She had not then been told; the burden of her terrible reward had been kept from her. Could she have danced so lightly with murder clogging her heels? But now, excited, flushed with exercise and giddy with delight, she rushes to her mother, the woman who knew her own mind, who would take a life or blast a character with equal thoroughness, who could bide her time and strike.

The doors close on the glittering banquet-hall. Salome passes with dazzled eyes into the faintly-lit corridor. She can hear still the subdued hum and murmur of delight and admiration behind her; she meets the eager Herodias. Four words from Salome: "What shall I ask?" Five words from Herodias: "The head of John Baptist." Was ever dialogue so full? Was ever play so foul, so brief?

In she comes. What will she ask? All heads are turned, all eyes and ears are strained. A casket of jewels—an Arab charger—a yacht 'like Cleopatra's—a chariot like the Empress Julia's—a pleasure island like that of Capræ, where Tiberius at that moment held his revels? Through the dead pause and silence of expectation breaks the clear voice of the young girl, as fatally drilled as her ready limbs, to the very syllable: "I will that thou give me by-and-by in a charger the head of John the Baptist."

Had any there present been baptized by John in Jordan? If so, they kept silence. But the King was staggered; he was over-taken with a sudden revulsion of feeling. For a moment he was alone once more, with the prophet's warning voice in his ear. Such flashes of sanity come to evil men—for an instant "they are very sorry," they "see clear." In that moment the life of the greatest of the prophets was in the balance. Would the King recant his promise? Ought vows to be recanted? They ought. On what principle? On the principle that one offence cannot be wiped out by the commission of another.

But for such meditation Herod had no time, nor was he "in the vein" for it. Conscience is convenient. The conscience which had kept silence when he took Herodias from Philip, now importuned him to keep his vow to Salome, "for his oath's sake." He thought it was conscience; or thought that he thought it was. What was it really? The beauty of Salome, the fear of Salome's mother, and, last and meanest, the "opinion of those who sat at meat with him."

What goes not to the wall in this world for that? In a few years, when Caligula de-throned Antipas, did one of these revellers protest? But they could flatter and fawn now; he hung upon their suffrages, he courted their protection, he bribed them for their smiles, nor could he face the least affront put upon his own vanity in the open banquet-hall.

So it is in the world—honour, justice, conscience, manhood, everything that might redeem or ennoble human conduct goes down, in a moment, beneath a sneer, a look, a whisper, from those "who sit at meat with us."

Remember this when the time for moral courage comes—the giddy moment is not all, the blaze and jubilee, the feast will not last for ever, you must be alone, you must face the consequences of what you do and say; there the easy way runs steep down to the slippery ruin. But the damsel waits. The cloud of indecision and remorse quickly passed. "He would not reject her."

Can we not hear the tumult and applause which then burst forth from that luxurious circle, whose daily lives were condemned, and whose master was thwarted, by the man of the desert?

How unimportant did the fate of that troublesome fanatic seem; how strange that good Herod had borne with him so long! It seemed so easy to do away with him, and yet fear, craven fear of the mob had stood in the way!

"And immediately the King sent an executioner and commanded his head to be brought."

Is he asleep? Through the narrow rift in the thick dungeon-walls the moon falls full upon the Baptist's worn face. There he lies, perchance as he had stationed himself before watching and fatigue relaxed in sleep his spare and sinewy limbs.

The free man of the desert caged at last! What solace for the captive but to mark from his cell the stars as they sailed by the narrow slit, like golden lamps suspended in the black-blue night of the East, or watch the rising moon as it stole round to visit his dungeon floor, and bathe his wasted form with its un-earthly radiance.

Months and years of confinement—far from friends, sympathy, occupation, activity, will shake at times the most dauntless soul. And John had been shaken. He had "decreased." He was debarred from watching the "in-crease" of his Master. Was He—the Lamb of God—too, destined to wane and go down like so many an eager enthusiast? Would He, too, one day languish in a prison, His work only half done? What was He doing then? Had His power and popularity not yet waned, would He not, could He not exert Himself to rescue the friend of His youth, the man whose baptism He had received in the Jordan waters?

Apparently no news, or little, from the outer world was permitted to reach John in prison. Depression, failing health, disappointment, a body enfeebled by ascetic practices, a mind for years sustained by the enthusiasm of crowds now left to prey upon itself. Is it strange if some dark doubts came upon him? Was the man whom he had baptized really Christ? Had he been a true forerunner? At last he had found the means to reach Christ. He sent to ask Him whether He was indeed the Christ, and whether the results of His ministry corresponded thereto.

The answer, full, glorious, decisive, came. The Messianic wonders accompanied each step of the New Ministry, and John from that moment felt that his work was done. He could sleep; he could dream, perchance of freedom, once more surrounded by the rocks he loved, and the unlovely wastes of white calcareous soil, once more beside the crystal wave in which men were baptized unto repentance, and once more above him the bright vision of the heavenly dove which spoke to his inmost heart of the baptism of fire.

And nothing breaks the silence, and nothing mars the deep peace of that unconscious smile as the prophet sleeps where angels might well keep watch.

But, hark! in the dead of night a distant footfall sounds in a remote corridor. He hears it not. Other steps now sound louder. The jailor's well-known tramp; the Roman soldiers are there too, for a distant clash of swords and staves against mailed cuirass and buckler now rattles nearer in the passage. But still he sleeps.

Suddenly they stop outside the Baptist's cell—the bolt is shot, the door flies open, a glare of torches drowns the pale moonlight, the prophet starts. But his is no drunken sleep; in a moment he is awake and ready. The hour is come for which he has waited week by week, day by day. It is the hour of his release. No more watching, no more unavailing protest, no more battling with doubt, no more struggling with a perverse generation, no more long weary hours of loneliness and silent wasting and suspense. Slowly he rises. Quickly he bows the neck whose soul was never bowed to a tyrant's will. The sharp scymetar flashes and falls, and the head of Israel's greatest prophet rolls upon the bloody pavement.

Let us draw a veil over the last ghastly appearance of Salome as she carries to her mother on a charger, with natural childish loathing, the head of a corpse.

That a thoughtless girl should have thus suddenly imbrued her hand in innocent blood; that a scene of light festivity and a dance in which she at least may have taken an innocent pride and pleasure should have ended in so foul a murder, and that her young life's threshold should have been thus stained—these are amongst the secondary shadows in this dark narrative.

It remains for us briefly to trace Herodias and her husband to their end.

The restless ambition that had sacrificed already an innocent woman and an illustrious saint could not rest. Herod found himself unequal to the defence of his own dominions, and he was invaded by an indignant father-in-law at the very time when he was being urged to Rome by his wife to seek for higher distinctions. Caligula continued to heap favours upon his brother, Herod Agrippa, and Herodias, madly jealous, craved for her husband at least the title of King in exchange for that of Tetrarch. Agrippa resisted her designs by intrigue, accused Antipas of sedition, and he was soon deposed and banished with his wife to Gaul, in the year 39, where both died in neglect and poverty.

In the eyes of "the lords and the high captains" of that day, the lives both of John and of Antipas seemed failures; but we see in the degradation of Herod his just and irrevocable sentence, whilst the martyrdom of John irradiates with its foreshine even the hill of Calvary.

Failure? Yes! so seemed the life of Christ when He breathed His life out upon the cross—only a few women to weep for Him, and not a disciple but what forsook him and fled. It is the old cheat of appearances; but only sin is failure. The humblest work done for Christ will win. No cup of cold water given to a disciple shall fail of its reward; no falchion shall sever from Christ the heart that loves and follows him, however humbly. Sacrifice is victory, and through the grave and gate of death we rise to the life immortal. When the Baptist's head fell, his work was already done, and the crown of glory was hung up for him beyond the reach of Herod and his executioner—above the stars.

CHARITY.

'TIS better to give than to get,
　When the heart with the gift goeth fair:
For Pity, as treasurer set,
　Relieveth while sharing the care!

Oh, the bliss of the magical touch
　That gaineth whene'er it would spend,
Knowing nought of the sad overmuch
　That only hath loss to the end.

The poorest have riches to win
　In the giving that wasteth no store,
When the oil and the wine pourèd in
　Flow graciously back to the door.

The cruse of the widow hath still
　Fullest record in hearts that are pure,
Who arise in their grace to fulfil
　The law of the Lord that is sure.

E. CONDER GRAY.

HEALTH AT HOME.

By B. W. RICHARDSON, M.D., F.R.S.

PART II.

THE BEDROOM (continued).

IN my last part I dwelt on the ventilation of the bedroom. I pass now, still keeping to the bedroom, to the questions of warming and ventilating.

III.

It is always a matter of great moment to maintain an equable temperature in the bedroom. A bedroom, the air of which is subject to great, and frequent, and rapid changes of temperature, is always a trap for danger. To persons who are in the prime of life, and who are in robust health, this danger is less pronounced, but to the young and the feeble it is a most serious danger. It is specially dangerous to aged people to sleep in a room that is easily lowered in warmth. When the great waves of cold come on in these islands, in the winter season, our old people begin to drop off with a rapidity that is perfectly startling. We take up the list of deaths published in the *Times* during these seasons, and the most marked of facts is the number of deceased aged persons. It is like an epidemic of death by old age. The public mind accepts this record as indicative of a general change of external conditions, and of a mortality therefore that is necessary as a result of that change. I would not myself dispute that there is a line of truth and sound common sense and common observation in this view, but when we descend from the general to the particular we find that much of the mortality, seen in such excess amongst the aged, is induced by mistakes on the subject of warmth in the bedroom.

The fatal event comes about somewhat in this way. The room in which the enfeebled person has been sitting before going to bed has been warmed probably up to summer heat; a light meal has been taken before retiring to rest, and then the bedroom is entered. The bedroom perchance has no fire in it, or if a fire be lighted provision is not made to keep it alight for more than an hour or two. The result is that in the early part of the morning, from three to four o'clock, when the temperature of the air in all parts is lowest, the glow from the fire or stove which should warm the room has ceased, and the room is cold to an extreme degree. In country houses the water will often be found frozen in the hand-basins or ewers under these conditions.

Meanwhile the sleeper lies unconscious of the great change which is taking place in the air around him. Slowly and surely there is a decline of temperature to the extent, it may be, of thirty or forty degrees on the Fahrenheit scale; and though he may be fairly covered with bedclothes he is receiving into his lungs this cold air, by which the circulation through the lungs is materially modified.

The condition of the body itself is at this very time unfavourable for meeting any emergency. In the period between midnight and six in the morning, the animal vital processes are at their lowest ebb. It is in these times that those who are enfeebled from any cause most frequently die. We physicians often consider these hours as critical, and forewarn anxious friends in respect to them. From time immemorial those who have been accustomed to wait and attend on the sick have noted these hours most anxiously, so that they have been called by one of our old writers, " the hours of fate." In this space of time the influence of the life-giving sun has been longest withdrawn from man, and the hearts that are even the strongest beat then with subdued tone. Sleep is heaviest, and death is nearest to us all in " the hours of fate."

The feeble, therefore, are most exposed to danger during this period of time, and they are most exposed to one particular danger, that of congestion of the lungs, for it is the bronchial surface of the lungs that is most exposed to the action of the chilled air; and, in the aged, that exposure is hazardous.

One of the ablest writers on the Hygiene of Old Age, M. Reveillé-Parise, attaches so much importance to the function of the lungs in the aged that he comes to the conclusions, first, that old age commences in the lungs; and, secondly, that, as a rule, death commences in the lungs in the aged. He reasons in this manner : " If we reflect that it is from the blood that life derives the principles which maintain and repair it, that the more vigorous, plastic, and rich in nutritive principles the blood is, so much the more organic life increases and manifests itself, and that the organ of sanguinification is the organ of respiration, we shall be compelled to admit the opinion that the age of general decline commences with the decay of the lungs, and that the one is the result of the other."

Flourens, from whose work on Human Longevity I copy this extract, demurs to the conclusion drawn by Reveillé-Parise. He will admit it in part only. "Old age," he asserts, "does not commence in any organ. It is not a local, but a general phenomenon. All our organs grow old, and it is not always at the same organ that we feel the first effects of age; it is sometimes one, sometimes another, according to the individual constitution."

I agree for my part with both these authors, because I think there is nothing in experience which is different or is in opposition to either of their views. Flourens is correct in saying that all the organs grow old together. Reveillé-Parise is correct in suggesting that the lungs more usually go first, because they are at one and the same time most exposed and most vital.

It is not in the least degree irrelevant to my present discourse to dwell on this argument. It shows better than any other argument could show how easily the depressing influence of cold tells on the vital organs, and specially on the lungs of the sleeper, whose vital capacity is already impaired by age. The minute vessels of the lung, in the pulmonary circuit of blood over the lung, are paralyzed by the cold so easily that congestion of blood in them is an almost natural result if they be long exposed to cold. And this, in truth, is the most common event in the aged, leading to that bronchial irritation and obstruction which is called congestive bronchitis, from which so many are recorded as having died when winter shows its face.

The practical question that comes out of this discussion is, How shall the danger of congestion of the lungs be avoided in the sleeping apartments of the enfeebled?

Our forefathers replied to this question in a very plain and striking manner. They shut themselves up in a warm tent. The old four-posters and the old tent bedsteads are the still extant witnesses of the ways and means for keeping out the cold in the old times. In country houses one sometimes finds still the massive four-post bedstead with its heavy damask curtains and snug enclosure. Advocate of fresh air as I am, I confess still to a lingering liking to this snug enclosure when I see it on a cold midwinter night. I met with it not very long ago and I crept into it with a sort of quiet glee as if feeling unusually safe and comfortable in so cosy a retreat.

I won't let mere likings tempt me to say that the plan is a good one. It is really not commendable, or only so when nothing better is at hand. If in a large room with cold walls and floors on a cold night I were obliged to sleep in a fireless room and had choice of two beds, one a curtained four-poster and the other a camp bedstead, I would no doubt, under the special circumstances, choose the four-poster, but not as a general principle by any means.

In our modern bedrooms, furnished according to modern taste and fashion, the best plan to adopt is that of admitting air freely to the sleeper, at the same time taking care that throughout the whole of the night the air shall be kept, within a few degrees, at the same temperature. I repeat, at the same temperature, for uniformity of warmth during all the hours of sleep is as essential as warmth. To have an overheated atmosphere at one time of the night and a low temperature at another, is just the kind of change that is attended with most hazard. Indeed, I doubt whether an equable cold atmosphere is not on the whole safer than one in which there is frequent and marked fluctuation.

The safest method is to have the air of the room, a short time before it is occupied, brought up to an uniform temperature of from 60° to 65° Fahr. It should never fall five degrees below 60° and never rise above 65° under ordinary circumstances. In cases where the occupant of the room is extremely enfeebled it may be necessary to raise the temperature to a higher point, but I am thinking at this moment of sleepers who are in fair health, and for whom no such special provision is required.

A mistake is sometimes made in observing the temperature. The reading of the thermometer is taken in one part of the room only, perhaps in the warmest part, that is to say, over the fireplace or from the mantle-shelf. This is not a fair observation, for a room at that part may be very warm while it is very cold in other parts. The temperature should, properly, be taken at the bed's head, about two feet above the pillow, and that is the best position in which to keep the thermometer, with which every bedroom ought to be furnished. An ordinary thermometer suffices as a general index, but a registering instrument is most advantageous when particular care is demanded in observation.

I now come to consider what is the best mode of warming the bedroom and of maintaining the equal warmth, on which so much has been insisted.

The simplest of all plans with which I am acquainted is that which brings air from the outside through a small chamber or pipe that can be heated by a fire or by gas, and which allows the air, after it has been warmed, to diffuse steadily into the room.

A stove called the Calorigen, invented by Mr. Webb George, is, in my opinion, best adapted for use in the bedroom. It burns either with coal gas or coal; or, more correctly speaking, a calorigen stove can be obtained either for gas or for coal. The stove has this great advantage, that it warms and ventilates at one and the same time. The stove contains within its outer cylinder or case a spiral iron tube, which by its lower end communicates with the outer air, and by its upper end opens into the room. The heat generated in the stove communicates heat to the spiral tube, and the air in the spiral is heated and ascends into the room. The ascension of warm air causes a draught from below, and so a current of warm air is at all times diffusing through the room so long as the fire of gas or coal is burning. At the same time the products of combustion from the stove are conveyed away by another pipe into a flue or chimney.

When one of these stoves is in good action the air of an apartment may be kept pure and warm for any length of time, and the temperature can be maintained at the same uniform degree all the while. There is also about the method the immense advantage that it secures freedom from cold draughts from doors and from windows. The copious influx of warm air from the stove is, indeed, so effective that when the stove is heated to its full, and the room is of moderate size, there is a draught or current of air out of the room by the doors when they are opened a little way, unless there be a provision for a fixed ventilating outlet. Properly there ought always to be a ventilating outlet, even when the room is steadily charged with fresh and warm air, for a current is always desirable.

My friend, Mr. Henry C. Stephens, in an excellent paper which he has written on Ventilation, maintains, with much force, that no mode of ventilation is actually perfect unless by precise mechanical means air be actually drawn into an apartment in duly measured quantities. He suggests a system of supply of air by a mechanism moved and regulated by weight and balance, so that the air through a house may be systematically supplied with all the accuracy of good and effective clockwork; or if this be not appli-

cable, he favours the admirable waterwheel ventilation which has lately been brought out by Messrs. Verity, of Regent Street. There is much to be said in favour of Mr. Stephens's argument, and if I were constructing a house from the first I should introduce Verity's ventilating system into every room; but we have to deal with houses everywhere that were originally erected without the slightest regard to sanitary rules, and we must therefore adapt what is best and cheapest to improve if not to perfect. In the bedroom, the stove I refer to is of these adaptations the best I know of. It is really automatic in action when it is once started, and it can be put up anywhere where there is a chimney for the exit pipe for consumed air. Lastly, it is quite safe in the bedroom: the fire being enclosed no sparks can fly from it, and the fuel makes no dust within the room.

In my laboratory I have had one of the Calorigen stoves in work for several years, and I have found it so manageable and good I can recommend it on the best of all recommendations, its practical value. In the Annerley Industrial Schools, which I visited at the time of the Sanitary Congress, held last October, at Croydon, I found that the stoves were in common use, and that they were as much approved of by the school authorities as they are by my own experience of them.

There is one precaution which I would suggest to those who are going to introduce a Calorigen into their bedroom. When the stove is fixed it is usual for the man who fixes it to push the air-feeding pipe through the floor of the room so as to get the supply of air from under the floor. No arrangement can be better if due care be taken, but it is essential to make sure of three things in carrying out this plan. Firstly, it is essential to see that there is a free opening from the outer wall by a perforated brick or grating under the floor, so that the air chamber beneath gets a due supply of fresh air from without. Secondly, it is well to see that there is no gaspipe running beneath the floor from the joints of which gas could escape and be drawn by the stove into the air of the room above. Thirdly, it is important to have the space below the floor made quite free of old rubbish, and to have it made thoroughly dry. All these steps are really essential, for if there be no admission of air beneath the floor from without, the stove will exhaust, and the space will be recharged with air from the room through openings and chinks in the flooring; if there be any escape of gas beneath the floor the stove will diffuse the gas into the room; if there be decomposing matter or dust beneath the floor the stove will also diffuse them, and if there be damp it will diffuse the damp.

I name these possible errors because I have seen them all made, and, actually, in one instance, I saw removed from beneath the floor of a bedroom and dressing-room twenty barrow-loads of dust and débris which had been lying there for nearly a century. The workmen in building houses care little about leaving dust and rubbish on ceilings that are covered by floors. In this case the rubbish consisted of shavings, sawdust, and sundry other things, such as old slippers and shoes, which had been lying there ever since the house was built.

If it be impossible, or if it be too expensive, to lift up the floor-boards and clean the whole of the space beneath, the next best thing to do is to take up a floor-board and under it to carry a box one foot deep between the joists of the floor from the point where the air-pipe of the stove pierces the floor-board to the outlet in the wall in which the air-brick or grating is inserted. The floor-board will form as it were the lid of this box, and the air, drawn by the stove, will be through the box direct from the outside. The box should be made of pine wood, and neatly planed on its inner surface. That surface should be polished with beeswax and turpentine so soon as the box is laid in, and from time to time the floor-board should be removed and the polishing should be repeated. The air passing over the surface of wax and turpentine is made singularly healthy and pure. It is as if it had been subjected to ozone before entering the chamber, and if it enter the chamber at a temperature of 60° to 65° Fahr., the fresh odour is distinguishable in the room after it has been for a short time unoccupied. These plans are all very simple to carry out when they are simply explained, and as a bedroom that is well and easily warmed and well and easily ventilated is of priceless value, I make no apology for spending so much time on this one topic.

IV.

THE FLOOR COVERINGS OF THE BEDROOM.

The bedroom can hardly have too good a floor, and after all no floor is so good as one of wood. If the wood is smooth and well planed it may be treated all over with wax and turpentine without being either stained or painted; or it may be stained all over and varnished; or if it be rough and will not take stain well, as is not uncommon in cases where the floors are very old, the boards may be covered with a good layer of zinc—white paint, coloured according to the taste of the owner, and afterwards well varnished. My own predilection is for Stephen's wood stain, when the boards will admit of the application, and taking it all in all a light oak stain is, I think, the best. The stain may be applied by any person who is at all deft at such artistic work. The floor is, in the first place, well cleansed by dry scrubbing with clean sawdust, and any great roughnesses and irregularities are planed or otherwise smoothed down. Then the whole surface is covered with a layer of thin size, which is allowed to dry. The stain is next prepared by mixing sufficient of it with water to get the required depth of tint, and sufficient is made to cover all the surface without recourse to a new solution. The stain is lightly and evenly laid on with a piece of sponge, and that also is left to dry. Finally, a good layer of varnish is laid on with a brush over the stained surface, and when that is dry, the next best floor to a floor of real and of polished oak has been obtained by the trouble and cost expended on the work. The floor prepared either by varnish simply, or by staining and varnishing, or by paint and varnish, should afterwards be kept clean by dry rubbing, and by beeswax and turpentine. There is nothing really so clean, and nothing so healthy. After a short time the varnished floors take the wax very well, and by that firm and smooth surface nothing is absorbed to create bad air. The floor is easily dusted. Loose particles of dust, feathers, and woollen fluff are readily detected, and the fact that there is any collection of dust or dirt on the floor is at once made obvious. There are no crevices or rough places in which the dust and fluff can be concealed.

There cannot, I think, be a doubt that for the bedroom floor dry cleansing is always the best. Water destroys the varnish on stained and painted floors, making them patchy and dirty-looking; water destroys the evenness of surface; water makes the adoption of the waxed floor almost impossible; water when it is used often percolates into the joints of the floor-boards, causing them to separate and become holders of dirt; and, lastly, if water be used for cleansing the chances are many in the course of a year that the room will be left damp and chilly. The floor will be washed on some damp and foggy days, the boards will dry imperfectly, and though, at bed-time, they may be to appearance dry they will not be so entirely, while the air of the room will be still charged with moisture; so that although the sleeper does not get into a damp bed he does get into a damp bedroom, which in some respects is equally injurious.

I have seen such very bad results from damp sleeping-rooms in which the dampness of the air has been caused by washing the floors, that I do not press the lesson I wish to enforce at all too forcibly or earnestly.

When from any circumstance the floor of the bedroom cannot have given to it a varnished or waxed surface; when, for example, the floor is constructed simply of deal planks, it may seem to be absolutely necessary to clean the surface with water. These floors, moreover, are just the floors that hold water the longest, and for all reasons are least adapted for water cleansing. How then, it will be said, are such floors to be cleansed? They are most easily cleansed in one dry way, viz., by dry scrubbing with sawdust. The servant takes up a small pailful of clean, fresh sawdust, and, taking it out by handfuls, spreads it on the floor, and with a hard, short-bristled brush scrubs with the sawdust as if she were using water itself. When the whole surface has been scrubbed in this way, she sweeps up the sawdust, and finds beneath it a beautifully clean and dry floor; or if there be left any part still dirty she easily remedies the defect by an additional scrub at that part. When all is finished she carries the dirty sawdust away, and destroys it by burning it in the kitchen fire. White sand may be used instead of sawdust for this same purpose, but it is not so convenient, and is not so quick a cleanser as sawdust. The same sand, if sand be used, can be applied several times if it be cleansed, by washing and afterwards heating it over the fire until it is quite dry.

I have to speak next about carpets in bedrooms. I need hardly insist on the fact that the old-fashioned plan of covering every part of the bedroom with carpet stuff, so as to make the carpet hug the wall, is as bad a plan as can possibly be followed. In these days everybody is beginning to recognise this truth, and the change which has taken place within the last ten years, in the matter of carpets for bedrooms, is quite remarkable. In some instances I notice that an extreme change, which is neither wanted nor warranted, has been instituted; that is to say, instead of the carpet that at one time covered all the surface of the floor with the greatest nicety of adaptation, there is no carpet at all. This extreme change is not at all desirable. It is

good to have carpets in every part of the room where the feet must regularly be placed. It is bad to have carpets in any part of the room where the feet are not regularly placed. These two rules govern the whole position, and the most inexperienced housewife can easily remember them. By these rules there should be carpet all round the bed, carpet opposite the wardrobes or chests of drawers, carpet opposite the washing-stand, carpet opposite the dressing-table, but none under the beds, and none for a space of two to three feet around the room, that is to say two or three feet from the walls of the room. The carpets that are laid down should be loose from each other, each one should be complete in itself, so that it can be taken up to be shaken with the least trouble, and each one should be arranged to lie close to the floor, so that dust may not easily get underneath.

Carpet stuff for bedrooms should be made of fine material closely woven, and not fluffy on the surface. Felt carpet stuff for bedrooms is what is commonly recommended in the shops for bedroom service, and after that Axminster. The first is all wrong; it never lies neatly, it very quickly accumulates dust, and it is really not in the end economical. Axminster is more free from these objections, but it is not so good as Brussels. There was a form of Brussels carpet called "tapestry," which some years ago was very largely used. It was as warm as the thickest blanket, and it was almost like wire in fibre; in fact, it was tough enough to last half a lifetime, and it was the best carpeting for bedrooms I ever remember. Fluff adhered to it very slightly, it held an exceedingly small quantity of dust, and it was always in its place on the floor. As a matter of course, "tapestry" went out of fashion in due time and season.

The advantages of small carpets in the bedroom are many. They cause the footsteps to be noiseless, or comparatively noiseless, they prevent the feet from becoming cold while dressing and undressing, they make the room look pleasant, and when used in the limited manner above suggested they save trouble in cleansing by preventing dust and dirt from being trodden into the floor.

And now, having seen to the lighting of the bedroom, to the position of it in regard to aspect, to the ventilation, to the warming, and to the construction and covering of the floor, I ought to pass on to the walls, and the curtains, and the beds. But I must ask the reader to wait until next article for the final instalment on the bedroom.

SOCIAL PLAGUES.

I.—ADVICE AND CONDOLENCE.

ON the chance that the readers of Good Words, accustomed to be largely fed on the milk of kindness, may accept an occasional acid alterative, I propose briefly to call their attention to a few of the grievances or minor afflictions of our time, which make our life less worth living. Considering with which to start, the memory of the saying, "If you ask advice and don't follow it the giver hates you; if you do follow it he despises you," suggests my text.

All of us, I presume, have suffered from advice, asked or unasked. In the former instance there is no real ground of complaint, as, however offensive the result, the asker has set the trap for himself. There are, indeed, a number of persons, martyrs of indecision, who make it their business to go from door to door on errands of mental beggary, desiring to shift on to other shoulders their own proper responsibilities. These are, among the dangerous classes of society, not the least pestilent. When a man about to perpetrate a poem, or deliver a speech, or marry a fool, insists on and obtains your downright opinion, you have most likely made a mortal enemy; but through no fault of your own. Being constituted the temporary legal adviser of the fraudulent client—fraudulent because he only wants to be confirmed in his folly—you run the risk of your position. But the volunteer of counsel about my manuscript, or my food, or my wife, should be rigidly ostracised.

Nothing is more common than literary advice, nor, as a rule, more useless. If we require it after leaving school and college, literature is not our calling; the modest man who does not require it is hampered; to the self-confident it is a mere irritation. The offence assumes various forms according as it is committed before or after the fact. The candid friend who would prevent your writing at all, in the hope it may be of keeping more elbow-room for himself, probably does no injury to the world. But the other who persuades you to write to his dictation, to ride his hobby in place of your own, to cast a book according to his plan, is a malefactor; for because of him your work is spoilt and brought before the reader in a twisted and unnatural shape. A third hurries you into premature production by reminding you of the shortness of life, then "nags" at your style, and demands alterations. Much so-called "English" is doubtless bad enough, but it is the duty of the public censor to suppress, chastise, or mend it; it will gain little by private clipping. Further varieties are:—the witty adviser, who tells you "petulanti splene cachinno," as if he were making a new point worthy of Heine, to "cut out all the finest passages;" the solid critic who, if you dabble in verse, recommends you, with his hands behind his back and his back to the fire, to "stick to prose;" the pedant who exhorts you to be learned, when your pride is in knowing your ignorance; the pure Saxon who objects to a Latin quotation, because he can't construe it; the jester who admonishes you to be smart when you feel serious; the sententious prig to whom every approach to epigram, which you consider your forte, is a censurable flippancy; the wary man, who fences every sentence of his own with "but," "however," "notwithstanding," "although," and trembles lest you should commit his respectable paper to an honest assertion; and, lastly, the rare, sensible friend who bids you take your own time and theme and be yourself.

Advice on "taking part in public affairs" is on a par with that about literary ventures, except when it is worse. The noes, ever cautious overmuch for all, will hinder you from exposing some absurdity. The ayes, cautious only for themselves, are commonly monkeys who make you play the part of the cat and laugh at your burnt fingers. If you are ridiculously silenced on the hustings, find yourself, permanently discredited, in a contemptible minority, and are at a loss to meet your printers' bills, the good-natured friend will observe, with a twinkle in his eye, that the affair has its humorous side.

But, hurrying from the dangerous ground of politics and their penalties, we come to the tribe of advisers on matters more strictly personal. A section on the strength of remote relationship or other ties assume the authority of your professional men. Those who recommend investments, or the sale of stock, or legal proceedings, or the reverse, may be commonly utilised as lighthouses are. He prospered who, asking advice of ten women, and getting ten different answers, adopted the only remaining course which none of them had recommended. Others who would regulate your habits of life as to diet, drugs, sleep, and exercise, you are, if neither a drunkard nor a glutton, entitled to address in the words of the "pretty maid." The most pertinacious in proffering this sort of advice *gratis* are, by the way, very commonly maids, the function of whose later life it is to matronize both sexes. So also with those who claim to take part in the management of your family, dictate the profession of your sons, the education and even the dresses of your daughters, the company you are to keep, your selection of a clergyman or a confidant, your choice of a dentist, an upholsterer, or a cook. The bad cook will only spoil your dinner, but the friend or enemy made by request may mar your career.

Such interference is, however, more commonly stupid or tedious than consciously impertinent, and in fair weather it may be borne without an overstrain on one's philosophy; but it should be a maxim of manners that only intimates have a right to condole. A man in trouble does not easily brook the patronage of chance acquaintants. There is no question here of the greatest of calamities. Bereavement is universally revered, and serious illness calls forth only genuine solicitude. It is otherwise with chronic weakness, or pain without present danger. One scarcely finds a perfectly healthy person who does not at the bottom of his heart think that every one with a cranky constitution is somehow to blame, or who has not an undercurrent of sympathy with Hazlitt's confession that he hated sick people. It is hard for an invalid to have this undefined censure added to the long worry of a life in which it is a perpetual struggle for him to discharge his duties. Let it be an occasion for the exercise of charity. Stalwart men, gaining strength to-morrow from putting forth strength to-day, and going easily onward, if not upward, cannot help these judgments. Their half-pitied, half-censured opposites must bear with the moral imperfection which is one result of extreme robustness.

Failure in health sometimes commands sympathy, failure in work "hardly ever." 'Tis scarce in human nature to refrain from saying that bunglers should have been better advised, for they reflect discredit on their backers. The publication of a book is a touchstone of friendship. Then is the hour for the man whom, by some indiscretion of manner or speech, you have unwittingly offended, to have his revenge in the anonymous review, and for the true friend to grieve that he has failed to anticipate the assassin. Then is the hour for the shallow or jealous ally to indulge his condolence, and to make sure that the murderous *Quarterly* or the provincial

lampoon has not escaped your notice. He carries the attack in his pocket, deprecates it, but pulls it out and is distressed to find that you are somehow unpopular. Whatever amount of disdain you either feel or affect, he yet retires satisfied, convinced that you are secretly as sore as in the circumstances he would be himself.

But the misfortune which brings into strongest and most salient relief the curiosities of society is the loss of money. Those who can understand nothing else can understand this. The merest human beaver estimates, and sometimes overestimates, the evil of being robbed or swindled by brigands or by banks; but he is not always much afflicted: if he has himself been down in the world, he cannot help reflecting that your turn has come, and he on whom your sunshine has at any time cast a shade is apt to exhibit a somewhat radiant regret. Another is sincerely sorry; but his idol is wealth, and, however innocent you may be, he cannot help thinking worse of you for having let it go. A financial catastrophe is the signal for manifold intrusiveness. Counsellors, reticent about themselves, curious about their neighbours, inquire regarding your losses that they may ascertain your property and appraise your belongings. Some make capital of the disaster, and proffer assistance in public on intolerable conditions. Others expose the immorality of attempts to assist you, and, their own withers being unwrung, bid you "grin and bear it." A casual correspondent, who claims acquaintance on some trivial ground, writes with a croak that the result is likely to prove worse than it seems. Another sits beside you and groans. All obtrude advice good, bad, contradictory, and mostly futile; but their motives, besides those of genuine benevolence, are rarely malicious. Officious conduct is mainly the outcome of a meddlesome temper and a restless self-assertion that never realises the idea of self-respect conveyed in the sentence of a wise writer, "In all things I would have the island of a man inviolate." Finally, such crises have their comforts. Your true friend, who has rejoiced in your successes and mourned over your failures, reminds you that there are possessions dearer to you left intact. He is secretly working to do you a substantial service, he sharpeneth your spirit in the battle as iron sharpeneth iron, and the grasp of his hand is like the hold of an anchor.

W. ROSS BROWNE.

THE TRUMPET-MAJOR.

By THOMAS HARDY, AUTHOR OF "FAR FROM THE MADDING CROWD," ETC.

CHAPTER V.—THE SONG AND THE STRANGER.

THE trumpet-major now contrived to place himself near her, Anne's presence having evidently been a great pleasure to him since the moment of his first seeing her. She was quite at her ease with him, and asked him if he thought that Buonaparte would really come during the summer, and many other questions which the gallant dragoon could not answer, but which he nevertheless liked to be asked. William Tremlett, who had not enjoyed a sound night's rest since the First Consul's menace had become known, pricked up his ears at sound of this subject, and inquired if anybody had

seen the terrible flat-bottomed boats that the enemy were to cross in.

"My brother Robert saw several of them paddling about the shore the last time he passed the Straits of Dover," said the trumpet-major; and he further startled the company by informing them that there were supposed to be more than a thousand of these boats, and that they would carry a hundred men apiece. So that a descent of one hundred thousand men might be expected any day as soon as Boney had brought his plans to bear.

XXI—8

"Lord ha' mercy upon us!" said William Tremlett.

"The night-time is when they will try it, if they try it at all," said old Tullidge, in the tone of one whose watch at the beacon must, in the nature of things, have given him comprehensive views of the situation. "It is my belief that the point they will choose for making the shore is just over there," and he nodded with indifference towards a section of the coast at a hideous nearness to the house in which they were assembled, whereupon Fencible Tremlett, and Cripplestraw of the Locals, tried to show no signs of trepidation.

"When d'ye think 'twill be?" said Volunteer Comfort, the blacksmith.

"I can't answer to a day," said the corporal. "But it will certainly be in a down-channel tide; and instead of pulling hard against it, he'll let his boats drift, and that will bring 'em right into Weymouth Bay. 'Twill be a beautiful stroke of war, if so be 'tis quietly done."

"Beautiful," said Cripplestraw, moving inside his clothes. "But how if we should be all abed, corporal? You can't expect a man to be brave in his shirt, especially we Locals, that have only got so far as shoulder firelocks."

"He's not coming this summer. He'll

never come at all," said a tall sergeant-major decisively.

Loveday, the soldier, was too much engaged in attending upon Anne and her mother to join in these surmises, bestirring himself to get the ladies some of the best liquor the house afforded, which had, as a matter of fact, crossed the Channel as privately as Buonaparte wished his army to do, and had been landed on a dark night over the cliff. After this he asked Anne to sing; but though she had a very pretty voice in private performances of that nature, she declined to oblige him; turning the subject by making a hesitating inquiry about his brother Robert, whom he had mentioned just before.

"Robert is as well as ever, thank you, Miss Garland," he said. "He is now mate of the brig *Pewit*—rather young for such a command; but the owner puts great trust in him." The trumpet-major added, deepening his thoughts to a profounder view of the person discussed, "Bob is in love."

Anne looked painfully conscious, and listened attentively; but Loveday did not go on.

"Much?" she presently asked.

"I can't exactly say. And the strange part of it is that he never tells us who the woman is. Nobody knows at all."

"He will tell, of course?" said Anne, in the remote tone of a person with whose sex such matters had no connection whatever.

Loveday shook his head, and the tête-à-tête was put an end to by a burst of singing from one of the sergeants, who was followed at the end of his song by others, each giving a ditty in his turn; the singer standing up in front of the table, stretching his chin well into the air, as though to abstract every possible wrinkle from his throat, and then plunging into the melody. When this was over one of the Foreign Hussars—the genteel German of Miller Loveday's description, but who called himself a Hungarian, and in reality belonged to no definite country, performed at Trumpet-major Loveday's request the series of wild motions that he denominated his national dance, that Anne might see what it was like. Miss Garland was the flower of the whole company; the soldiers one and all, foreign and English, seemed to be quite charmed by her presence, as indeed they well might be, considering how seldom they came into the society of such as she.

Anne and her mother were just thinking of retiring to their own dwelling when Sergeant Stanner of the —th Foot, who was recruiting at Weymouth, began a satirical song :—

"When law'-yers strive' to heal' a breach',
And par'-sons prac'-tise what' they preach',
Then lit'-tle Bo'-ney he' 'll pounce down',
And march' his men' on Lon'-don town' !

Chorus.—Rol'-li-cum ro'-rum, tol'-lol-lo'-rum,
Rol'-li-cum ro'-rum, tol'-lol-lay'."

Poor Stanner! In spite of his satire, he fell at the bloody battle of Albuera a few years after this pleasantly spent summer at Weymouth, being mortally wounded and trampled down by a French Hussar when the brigade was deploying into line under Beresford.

While Miller Loveday was saying "Well done, Mr. Stanner!" at the close of the thirteenth stanza, which seemed to be the last, and Mr. Stanner was modestly expressing his regret that he could do no better, a voice was heard outside the window shutter :—

"Rol'-li-cum ro'-rum, tol'-lol-lo'-rum,
Rol'-li-cum ro'-rum, tol'-lol-lay'."

The company were silent in a moment at this phenomenon, and only the military tried not to look surprised. While all wondered who the singer could be somebody entered the porch; the door opened, and in came a young man in the uniform of the Yeomanry Cavalry.

"'Tis young Squire Derriman, old Mr. Derriman's nephew," murmured voices in the background.

Without waiting to address anybody, or apparently seeing who were gathered there, the young man waved his cap above his head and went on :—

"When hus'-bands with' their wives' a-gree',
And maids' won't wed' from mod'-es-ty',
Then lit'-tle Bo'-ney he' 'll pounce down',
And march' his men' on Lon'-don town' !

Chorus.—Rol'-li-cum ro'-rum, tol'-lol-lo'-rum," &c., &c.

It was a verse which had been omitted by the gallant Stanner, out of respect to the ladies.

The new comer was of florid complexion, red-haired, and tall, and seemed full of a conviction that his whim of entering must be their pleasure, which for the moment it was.

"No ceremony, good men all," he said; "I was passing by, and my ear was caught by the singing. I like singing; 'tis warming and cheering, and shall not be put down. I should like to hear anybody say otherwise."

"Welcome, Master Derriman," said the miller, filling a glass and handing it to the yeoman. "Come all the way from quarters, then? I hardly knowed ye in your soldier's clothes. You'd look more natural with a spud in your hand, sir. I shouldn't ha' known

"Welcome, Master Derriman."

Page 106.

ye at all if I hadn't heard that you were called out."

"More natural with a spud!—have a care, miller," said the young man, the fire of his complexion increasing to scarlet. "I don't mean anger, but—but—a soldier's honour, you know!"

The military in the background laughed a little, and the yeoman then for the first time discovered that there were more regulars present than one. He looked momentarily disconcerted, but expanded again to full assurance.

"Right, right, Master Derriman, no offence —'twas only my joke," said the genial miller. "Everybody's a soldier nowadays. Drink a drap o' this cordial, and don't mind words."

The young man drank without the least reluctance, and said, "Yes, miller, I am called out. 'Tis ticklish times for us soldiers now; we hold our lives in our hands. . . . What are those fellows grinning at behind the table? I say, we do."

"Staying with your uncle at the farm for a day or two, Mr. Derriman?"

"No, no—as I told you, billeted at Dorchester. But I have to call and see the old, old——"

"Gentleman?"

"Gentleman!—no, skinflint. He lives upon the sweepings of the barton; ha, ha!" And the speaker's regular, white teeth showed themselves like snow in a Dutch cabbage. "Well, well, the profession of arms makes a man proof against all that. I take things as I find 'em."

"Quite right, Master Derriman. Another drop?"

"No, no. I'll take no more than is good for me—no man should; so don't tempt me."

The yeoman then saw Anne, and by an unconscious gravitation went towards her and the other women, flinging a remark to John Loveday in passing. "Ah, Loveday! I heard you were come; in short, I came o' purpose to see you. Glad to see you enjoying yourself at home again."

The trumpet-major replied civilly, though not without grimness, for he seemed hardly to like Derriman's motion towards Anne.

"Widow Garland's daughter!—yes, 'tis surely. You remember me? I have been here before. Festus Derriman, Yeomanry Cavalry."

Anne gave a little curtsey. "I know your name is Festus—that's all."

"Yes, 'tis well known, especially latterly." He dropped his voice to confidence pitch.

"I suppose your friends here are disturbed by my coming in, as they don't seem to talk much? I don't mean to interrupt the party; but I often find that people are put out by my coming among 'em, especially when I've got my regimentals on."

"La! and are they?"

"Yes; 'tis the way I have." He further lowered his tone, as if they had been old friends, though in reality he had only seen her three or four times. "And how did you come to be here? Dash my wig, I don't like to see a nice young lady like you in this company. You should come to some of our yeomanry sprees in Dorchester or Blandford. Oh but, the girls do come! The yeomanry are respected men, men of good substantial families, many farming their own land; and every one among us rides his own charger, which is more than these cussed fellows do." He nodded towards the dragoons.

"Hush, hush! Why, these are friends and neighbours of Miller Loveday, and he is a great friend of ours—our best friend," said Anne with great emphasis, and reddening at the sense of injustice to their host. "What are you thinking of, talking like that? It is ungenerous in you."

"Ha, ha! I've affronted you. Isn't that it, fair angel, fair what do you call it—fair vestal? Ah, well! would you was safe in my own house! But honour must be minded now, not courting. Rollicum-rorum, tol-lol-lorum. Pardon me, my sweet, I like ye. It may be a come down for me, owning land; but I do like ye."

"Sir, please be quiet," said Anne, distressed.

"I will, I will, love. Well, Corporal Tullidge, how's your head?" he said, going towards the other end of the room, and leaving Anne to herself.

The company had again recovered its liveliness, and it was a long time before the bouncing Rufus who had joined them could find heart to tear himself away from their society and good liquors, although he had had quite enough of the latter before he entered. The natives received him at his own valuation, and the soldiers of the camp, who sat beyond the table, smiled behind their pipes at his remarks, with a pleasant twinkle of the eye which approached the satirical, John Loveday being not the least conspicuous in this bearing. But he and his friends were too courteous on such an occasion as the present to challenge the young man's large remarks, and readily permitted him to set them right on the details of camping and other military routine, about which the troopers seemed willing to let persons hold any opinion whatever, provided that they themselves were not obliged to give attention to it; showing, strangely enough, that if there was one subject more than another which never interested their minds, it was the art of war. To them the art of enjoying good company in Overcombe Mill, the details of the miller's household, the swarming of his bees, the number of his chickens, and the fatness of his pigs, were matters of infinitely greater concern.

The present writer, to whom this party has been described times out of number by members of the Loveday family and other old people now passed away, can never enter the old living-room of Overcombe Mill without seeing the genial scene through the mists of the seventy or eighty years that intervene between then and now. First and brightest to the eye are the dozen candles, scattered about regardless of expense, and kept well snuffed by the miller, who walks round the room at intervals of five minutes, snuffers in hand, and nips each wick with great precision, and with something of an executioner's grim look upon his face as he closes the snuffers upon the neck of the candle. Next to the candle-lights show the red and blue coats and white breeches of the soldiers—nearly twenty of them in all, besides the half-fledged Derriman—the head of the latter and the heads of all who are standing up being in dangerous proximity to the black beams of the ceiling. There is not one among them who would attach any meaning to "Vittoria," or gather from the syllables "Waterloo" the remotest idea of their own glory or death. Next appears the correct and innocent Anne, little thinking what things Time has in store for her at no great distance off. She looks at Derriman with a half-uneasy smile as he clanks hither and thither, and hopes he will not single her out again to hold a private dialogue with—which, however, he does, irresistibly attracted by the white muslin figure. She must, of course, look a little gracious again now, lest his mood should turn from sentimental to quarrelsome—no impossible contingency with the yeoman-soldier, as her quick perception had noted.

"Well, well; this idling won't do for me, folks," he at last said, to Anne's relief. "I ought not to have come in, by rights; but I heard you enjoying yourselves, and thought it might be worth while to see what you were up to; I have several miles to go before bedtime;" and, stretching his arms, lifting his

chin, and shaking his head, to eradicate any unseemly curve or wrinkle from his person, the yeoman wished them an off-hand good-night, and departed.

"You should have teased him a little more, father," said the trumpet-major drily. "You could soon have made him as crabbed as a bear."

"I didn't want to provoke the chap—'twasn't worth while. He came in friendly enough," said the gentle miller without looking up.

"I don't think he was overmuch friendly," said John.

"'Tis as well to be neighbourly with folks, if they be not quite onbearable," his father genially replied, as he took off his coat to go and draw more ale—this periodical stripping to the shirt sleeves being necessitated by the narrowness of the cellar and the smeary effect of its numerous cobwebs upon best clothes.

Some of the guests then spoke of Fess Derriman as not such a bad young man if you took him right and humoured him; others said that he was nobody's enemy but his own; and the elder ladies mentioned in a tone of interest that he was likely to come into a deal of money at his uncle's death. The person who did not praise was the one who knew him best, who had known him as a boy years ago, when he had lived nearer to Overcombe than he did at present. This unappreciative person was the trumpet-major.

CHAPTER VI.—OLD MR. DERRIMAN OF OVERCOMBE HALL.

AT this time in the history of Overcombe one solitary newspaper found its way into the village. It was lent by the post-master at Weymouth (who, in some mysterious way, got it for nothing through his connection with the mail) to Mr. Derriman at the hall, by whom it was handed on to Mrs. Garland when it was not more than a fortnight old. Whoever remembers anything about the old farmer-squire will, of course, know well enough that this delightful privilege of reading ancient history in long columns was not accorded to the Widow Garland for nothing. It was by such ingenious means that he paid her for her daughter's occasional services in reading aloud to him and making out his accounts, in which matters the farmer, whose guineas were reported to touch five figures—some said more—was not expert.

Mrs. Martha Garland, as a respectable widow, occupied a twilight rank between the benighted villagers and the well-informed gentry, and kindly made herself useful to the former as letter-writer and reader, and general translator from the printed tongue. It was not without satisfaction that she stood at her door of an evening, newspaper in hand, with three or four cottagers standing round, and poured down their open throats any paragraph that she might choose to select from the stirring ones of the period. When she had done with the sheet Mrs. Garland passed it on to the miller, the miller to the grinder, and the grinder to the grinder's boy, in whose hands it became sub-divided into half pages, quarter pages, and irregular triangles, and ended its career as a paper cap, a flagon-bung, or a wrapper for his bread and cheese.

Notwithstanding his compact with Mrs. Garland, old Mr. Derriman kept the paper so long, and was so chary of wasting his man's time on a merely intellectual errand, that unless she sent for the journal it seldom reached her hands. Anne was always her messenger. The arrival of the soldiers led Mrs. Garland to dispatch her daughter for it the day after the party; and away she went in her hat and pelisse, in a direction at right angles to that of the encampment on the hill.

Walking across the fields for the distance of about a mile, she came out upon the high road by a wicket-gate. On the other side of the way was the entrance to what at first sight looked like a neglected meadow, the gate being a rotten one, without a bottom rail, and broken down palings lying on each side. The dry hard mud of the opening was marked with several horse and cow tracks that had been half obliterated by fifty score sheep tracks, surcharged with the tracks of a man and a dog. Beyond this record of earlier nomadic tribes appeared a carriage-road nearly grown over with grass, which Anne followed. It descended by a gentle slope, dived under dark-rinded elm and chestnut trees, and conducted her on till the hiss of a waterfall became audible, when it took a bend round a swamp of fresh watercress and brooklime that had once been a fishpond. Here the grey, weather-worn front of a building edged from behind the trees. It was Overcombe Hall, once the seat of a family now extinct, and of late years used as a farmhouse.

Benjamin Derriman, who owned the crumbling place, had originally been only the occupier and tenant-farmer of the fields around. His wife had brought him a small fortune, and during the growth of their only son there had been a partition of the Overcombe estate, giving the farmer, now a widower, the opportunity of acquiring the building and a small portion of the land attached on exceptionally low terms. But two years after the purchase the boy died, and Derriman's existence was paralyzed forthwith. It was said that since that event he had devised the house and fields to a distant female relative, to keep them out of the hands of his detested nephew; but this was not certainly known.

The hall was as interesting as mansions in a state of declension usually are, as the excellent county history showed. That popular work in folio contained an old plate dedicated to the last scion of the original owners, from which drawing it appeared that in 1750, the date of publication, the windows were covered with little scratches like black flashes of lightning; that a horn of hard smoke came out of each of the twelve chimneys; that a lady and a lap-dog stood on the lawn in a strenuously walking position; and a substantial cloud and nine flying birds of no known species hung over the trees to the north-east.

The rambling and neglected dwelling had all the romantic excellencies and practical drawbacks which such mildewed places share in common with caves, mountains, wildernesses, glens, and other homes of poesy that people of taste wish to live and die in. Mustard and cress could have been raised on the inner plaster of the dewy walls at any height not exceeding three feet from the floor, where the stain ended; and mushrooms of the most refined and thin-stemmed kinds grew up through the chinks of the larder paving. As for the outside, nature, in the ample time that had been given her, had so mingled her filings and effacements with the marks of human wear and tear upon the house, that it was often hard to say in which of the two, or if in both, any particular obliteration had its origin. The keenness was gone from the mouldings of the doorways, but whether worn out by the rubbing past of innumerable people's shoulders, and the moving of their heavy furniture, or by Time in a grander and more abstract form, did not appear. The iron stanchions inside the window panes were eaten away to the size of wires at the bottom where they entered the stone, the condensed breathings of generations having settled there in pools and rusted them. The panes themselves had either lost their shine altogether or become iridescent as a peacock's tail. In the middle of the porch was a vertical sundial, whose gnomon swayed loosely about when the wind blew, and cast its shadow hither and thither, as much as to say, "Here's your fine model dial; here's any time for any man; I am an old dial; and shiftiness is the best policy."

Anne passed under the arched gateway which screened the main front; over it was the porter's lodge, reached by a spiral staircase. Across the archway was fixed a row of wooden hurdles, one of which Anne opened and closed behind her. Their necessity was apparent as soon as she got inside. The quadrangle of the ancient pile was a bed of mud and manure, inhabited by calves, geese, ducks, and sow pigs surprisingly large, with young ones surprisingly small. In the groined porch some heifers were amusing themselves by stretching up their necks and licking the carved stone capitals that supported the vaulting. Anne went on to a second and open door, across which was another hurdle to keep the live stock from absolute community with the inmates. There being no knocker she knocked by means of a short stick which was laid against the post for that purpose; but nobody attending she entered the passage, and tried an inner door.

A slight noise was heard inside, the door opened about an inch, and a strip of decayed face, including the eye and some forehead wrinkles, appeared within the crevice.

"Please I have come for the paper," said Anne.

"Oh, is it you, dear Anne?" whined the inmate, opening the door a little farther. "I could hardly get to the door to open it, I am so weak."

The speaker was a wizened old gentleman in a coat the colour of his farmyard, breeches of the same hue, unbuttoned at the knees, revealing a bit of leg above his stocking, and a dazzlingly white shirt-frill to compensate for this untidiness below. The edge of his skull round his eye-sockets was visible through the skin, and he had a mouth whose corners made towards the back of his head on the slightest provocation. He walked with great apparent difficulty back into the room, Anne following him.

"Well, you can have the paper if you want it; but you never give me much time to see what's in en. Here's the paper." He held it out, but before she could take it he drew it back again, saying, "I have not had my share o' the paper by a good deal, what with my weak sight, and people coming so soon for en. I am a poor put-upon soul; but my Duty of Man will be left to me when the newspaper is gone." And he sank into his chair with an air of exhaustion.

Anne said that she did not wish to take the paper if he had not done with it, and that she was really later in the week than usual, owing to the soldiers.

"Soldiers, yes—rot the soldiers. And now hedges will be broke, and hens' nests robbed, and sucking-pigs stole, and I don't know what all. Who's to pay for 't, sure? I reckon that because the soldiers be come you don't mean to be kind enough to read to me what I ha'n't had time to read myself."

She would read if he wished, she said; she was in no hurry. And sitting herself down she unfolded the paper.

"'Dinner at Carleton House?'"

"No, faith. 'Tis nothing to I."

"'Defence of the country?'"

"Ye may read that, if ye will. I hope there will be no billeting in this parish, or any wild work of that sort; for what would a poor old lamiger like myself do with soldiers in his house, and nothing to feed 'em with?"

Anne began reading, and continued at her task nearly ten minutes, when she was interrupted by the appearance in the quadrangular slough without of a young man in the uniform of the yeomanry cavalry.

"What do ye see out there?" said the farmer with a start, as she paused and slowly blushed.

"A soldier—one of the yeomanry," said Anne, not quite at her ease.

"Scrounch it all—'tis my nephew!" exclaimed the old man, his face turning to a phosphoric pallor, and his body twitching with innumerable alarms as he formed upon his face a gasping smile of joy with which to welcome the new-coming relative. "Read on, prithee, Miss Garland."

Before she had read far the visitor straddled over the door-hurdle into the passage and entered the room.

"Well, nunc, how do you feel?" said the young man, shaking hands with the farmer in the manner of one violently ringing a hand-bell. "Glad to see you."

"Bad and weakish, Festus," replied the other, his person responding passively to the rapid vibrations imparted. "Oh, be tender, please—a little softer, there's a dear nephew! My arm is no more than a cobweb."

"Ah, poor soul!"

"Yes. I am not much more than a skeleton, and can't bear rough usage."

"Sorry to hear that; but I'll bear your affliction in mind. Why, you are all in a tremble, Uncle Benjy!"

"'Tis because I am so gratified," said the

old man. "I always get all in a tremble when I am taken by surprise by a beloved relation."

"Ah, that's it!" said the yeoman, bringing his hand down on the back of his uncle's chair with a loud smack, at which Uncle Benjy nervously sprang three inches from his seat and dropped into it again. "Ask your pardon for frightening ye, uncle. 'Tis how we do in the army, and I forgot your nerves. You have scarcely expected to see me, I dare say, but here I am."

"I am glad to see ye. You are not going to stay long, perhaps?"

"Quite the contrary. I am going to stay ever so long!"

"Oh, I see. I am so glad, dear Festus. Ever so long, did ye say?"

"Yes, ever so long," said the young gentleman, sitting on the slope of the bureau and stretching out his legs as props. "I am going to make this quite my own home whenever I am off duty, as long as we stay out. And after that, when the campaign is over in the autumn, I shall come here, and live with you like your own son, and help manage your land and your farm, you know, and make you a comfortable old man."

"Ah! How you do please me!" said the farmer with a horrified smile, and grasping the arms of his chair to sustain himself.

"Yes, I have been meaning to come a long time, as I knew you'd like to have me, Uncle Benjy; and 'tisn't in my heart to refuse you."

"You always was kind that way."

"Yes, I always was. But I ought to tell you at once, not to disappoint you, that I sha'n't be here always—all day, that is, because of my military duties as a cavalry man."

"Oh, not always? That's a pity!" exclaimed the farmer with a cheerful eye.

"I knew you'd say so. And I sha'n't be able to sleep here at night sometimes, for the same reason."

"Not sleep here o' nights?" said the old gentleman, still more relieved. "You ought to sleep here—you certainly ought; in short, you must. But you can't!"

"Not while we are with the colours. But directly that's over—the very next day—I'll stay here all day, and all night too, to oblige you, since you ask me so very kindly."

"Th-thank ye, that will be very nice!" said Uncle Benjy.

"Yes. I knew 'twould relieve ye." And he kindly stroked his uncle's head, the old man expressing his enjoyment at the affec-

tionate token by a death's-head grimace. "I should have called to see you the other night when I passed through here," Festus continued; "but it was so late that I couldn't come so far out of my way. You won't think it unkind?"

"Not at all, if you couldn't. I never shall think it unkind if you really can't come, you know, Festy." There was a few minutes' pause, and as the nephew said nothing Uncle Benjy went on: "I wish I had a little present for ye. But as ill-luck would have it we have lost a deal of stock this year, and I have had to pay away so much."

"Poor old man—I know you have. Shall I lend you a seven-shilling piece, Uncle Benjy?"

"Ha, ha!—you must have your joke; well, I'll think o' that. And so they expect Buonaparty to choose this very part of the coast for his landing, hey? And that the yeomanry be to stand in front as the forlorn hope?"

"Who says so?" asked the florid son of Mars, losing a little redness.

"The newspaper-man."

"Oh, there's nothing in that," said Festus bravely. "The gover'ment thought it possible at one time; but they don't know." Festus eagerly went on to explain that even if the enemy came at all, it might not be at their part of England, and certainly would not be till later in the summer. As for him, Festus, he wished Boney might come; but no such good luck. The fact was, he said, that the actual reason for the arrival of the troops at this particular time was not altogether fear of Boney's landing just there, but that the king was coming again to Weymouth during the summer, and it became necessary to keep a good guard in the vicinity on his account.

Festus turned himself as he talked, and now said abruptly. "Ah, who's this? Why 'tis our little Anne!" He had not noticed her till this moment, the young woman having at his entry kept her face over the newspaper, and then got away to the back part of the room. "And are you and your mother always going to stay down there in the mill-house watching the little fishes, Miss Anne?"

She said that it was uncertain, in a tone of truthful precision which the question was hardly worth, looking forcedly at him as she spoke. But she blushed fitfully, in her arms and hands as much as in her face. Not that she was overpowered by the great boots, formidable spurs, and other fierce appliances

Page 110.

of his person, as he imagined; simply she had not been prepared to meet him there.

"I hope you will, I am sure, for my own good," said he, letting his eyes linger on the round of her cheek.

Anne became a little more dignified, and her look showed reserve. But the yeoman on perceiving this went on talking to her in so civil a way that he irresistibly amused her, though she tried to conceal all feeling. At a brighter remark of his than usual her mouth moved, her upper lip playing uncertainly over her white teeth; it would stay still—no, it would withdraw a little way in a smile; then it would flutter down again; and so it wavered like a butterfly in a tender desire to be pleased and smiling, and yet to be also sedate and composed; to show him that she did not want compliments, and yet that she was not so cold as to wish to repress any genuine feeling he might be anxious to utter.

"Shall you want any more reading, Mr. Derriman?" said she, interrupting the younger man in his remarks. "If not I'll go homeward."

"Don't let me hinder you longer," said Festus. "I am off in a minute or two, when your man has cleaned my boots."

"Ye don't hinder us, nephew. She must have the paper: 'tis the day for her to have'n. She might read a little more, as I have had so little profit out o' en hitherto. Well, why don't ye speak! Will ye or won't ye, my dear?"

"Not to two," she said.

"Ho, ho! hang it, I must go then, I suppose," said Festus, laughing; and unable to get a further glance from her he left the room and clanked into the back yard, where he saw a man; holding up his hand he cried, "Anthony Cripplestraw!"

Cripplestraw came up in a trot, moved a lock of his hair and replaced it, and said, "Yes, Maister Derriman." He was old Mr. Derriman's odd hand in the yard and garden, and like his employer had no great pretensions to manly beauty, owing to a limpness of backbone and speciality of mouth, which opened on one side only, giving him a triangular smile.

"Well, Cripplestraw, how is it to-day?" said Festus, with socially-superior heartiness.

"Middlin' considering, Maister Derriman. And how's yerself?"

"Fairish. Well, now see and clean these military boots of mine. I'll cock my foot up on this bench. This pigstye of my uncle's is not fit for a soldier to come into."

"Yes, Maister Derriman, I will. No, 'tis not fit, Maister Derriman."

"What stock has uncle lost this year, Cripplestraw?"

"Well, let's see, sir. I can call to mind that we've lost three chicken, a tom-pigeon, and a weakly sucking-pig, one of a fare of ten. I can't think of no more, Maister Derriman."

"H'm, not a large quantity of cattle. The old rascal!"

"No, 'tis not a large quantity. Old what, did you say, sir?"

"Oh, nothing. He's within there." Festus flung his forehead in the direction of a right line towards the inner apartment. "He's a regular sniche one."

"Hee, hee, fie, fie, Master Derriman!" said Cripplestraw, shaking his head in delighted censure. "Gentlefolks shouldn't talk so. And a officer, Mr. Derriman! 'Tis the duty of all calvery gentlemen to bear in mind that their blood is a knowed thing in the country, and not to speak ill o't."

"He's close-fisted."

"Well, maister, he is—I own he is a little. 'Tis the nater of some old venerable gentlemen to be so. We'll hope he'll treat ye well in yer fortune, sir."

"Hope he will. Do people talk about me here, Cripplestraw?" asked the yeoman, as the other continued busy with his boots.

"Well yes, sir; they do, off and on, you know. They says you be as fine a piece of calvery flesh and bones as was ever growed on fallow-ground; in short, all owns that you be a fine fellow, sir. I wish I wasn't no more afraid of the French than you be; but being in the Locals, Maister Derriman, I assure ye I dream of having to defend my country every night: and I don't like the dream at all."

"You should take it careless, Cripplestraw, as I do; and 'twould soon come natural to ye not to mind it at all. Well, a fine fellow is not everything, you know. Oh no. There's as good as I in the army, and even better."

"And they say that when you fall this summer, you'll die like a man."

"When I fall?"

"Yes, sure, Maister Derriman. Poor soul o' thee! I shan't forget 'ee as you lie mouldering in yer soldier's grave."

"Hey?" said the warrior uneasily. "What makes 'em think I am going to fall?"

"Well, sir, by all accounts the yeomanry will be put in front."

"Front! That's what my uncle has been saying."

"Yes, and by all accounts 'tis true. And naterelly they'll be mowed down like grass; and you among 'em, poor young galliant officer!"

"Look here, Cripplestraw. This is a reg'lar foolish report. How can yeomanry be put in front? Nobody's put in front. We yeomanry have nothing to do with Buonaparte's landing. We shall be away in a safe place, guarding the possessions and jewels. Now can you see, Cripplestraw, any way at all that the yeomanry can be put in front? Do you think they really can?"

"Well, maister, I am afraid I do," said the cheering Cripplestraw. "And I know a great warrior like you is only too glad o' the chance. 'Twill be a great thing for ye, death and glory. In short, I hope from my heart you will be, and I say so very often to fokes—in fact, I pray at night for't."

"Oh! drown you! You needn't pray about it."

"No, Maister Derriman, I won't."

"Of course my sword will do its duty. That's enough. And now be off with ye."

Festus returned to his uncle's room and found that Anne was just leaving. He was inclined to follow her at once, but as she gave him no opportunity of doing this he went to the window, and remained tapping his fingers against the shutter while she crossed the yard.

"Well, nephy, you are not gone yet?" said the farmer, looking dubiously at Festus from under one eyelid. "You see how I am. Not by any means better, you see; so I can't entertain 'ee as well as I would."

"You can't, nunc, you can't. I don't think you are worse—if I do, dash my wig. But you'll have plenty of opportunities to make me welcome when you are better. If you are not so brisk inwardly as you was, why not try change of air? This is a dull, damp hole."

"'Tis, Festus; and I am thinking o' moving."

"Ah, where to?" said Festus, with surprise and interest.

"Up into the little garret in the north corner. There is no fire-place to the room; but I sha'n't want that, poor soul o' me."

"'Tis not moving far."

"'Tis not. But I have not a soul belonging to me within ten mile; and you know very well that I couldn't afford to go to lodgings that I had to pay for."

"I know it—I know it, Uncle Benjy. Well, don't be disturbed. I'll come and manage for you as soon as ever this Boney alarm is over; but when a man's country calls he must obey, if he is a man."

"A splendid spirit!" said Uncle Benjy with much admiration on the surface of his countenance. "I never had it. How could it have got into the boy?"

"From my mother's side perhaps."

"Perhaps so. Well, take care of yourself, nephy," said the farmer, waving his hand impressively. "Take care! In these warlike times your spirit may carry ye into the arms of the enemy; and you be the last of the family. You should think of this, and not let your bravery carry ye away."

"Don't be disturbed, uncle; I'll control myself," said Festus, betrayed into self-complacency against his will. "At least I'll do what I can, but nature will out sometimes. Well, I'm off." He began humming "Brighton Camp," and promising to come again soon, retired with assurance, each yard of his retreat adding private joyousness to his uncle's form.

When the young man had disappeared through the porter's lodge Uncle Benjy showed preternatural activity for one in his invalid state, jumping up quickly without his stick, at the same time opening and shutting his mouth quite silently like a thirsty frog, which was his way of expressing mirth. He ran up-stairs as quick as an old squirrel, and went to a dormer window which commanded a view of the grounds beyond the gate, and the foot-path that stretched across them to the village.

"Yes, yes!" he said in a repressed scream, dancing up and down. "He's after her: she've hit en!" For there appeared upon the path the figure of Anne Garland, hastening on at some little distance behind her, the swaggering shape of Festus. She became conscious of his approach, and moved more quickly. He moved more quickly still, and overtook her. She turned as if in answer to a call from him, and he walked on beside her till they were out of sight. The old man then played upon an imaginary fiddle for about half a minute; and, suddenly discontinuing these signs of pleasure, went down-stairs again.

CHAPTER VII.—HOW THEY TALKED IN THE GREEN PASTURES.

"You often come this way?" said Festus to Anne, rather before he had overtaken her.

"I come for the newspaper and other things," she said, perplexed by a doubt whether he were there by accident or design.

They moved on in silence, Festus beating the grass with his switch in a masterful way. "Did you speak, Mis'ess Anne?" he asked.

"No," said Anne.

"Ten thousand pardons. I thought you did. Now don't let me drive you out of the path. I can walk among the high grass and giltycups—they will not yellow my stockings as they will yours. Well, what do you think of a lot of soldiers coming to the neighbourhood in this way?"

"I think it is very lively, and a great change," she said with demure seriousness.

"Perhaps you don't like us warriors as a body."

Anne smiled without replying.

"Why, you are laughing!" said the yeoman, looking searchingly at her and blushing like a little fire. "What do you see to laugh at?"

"Did I laugh?" said Anne, a little scared at his sudden mortification.

"Why, yes; you know you did, you young sneerer," he said like a cross baby. "You are laughing at me—that's who you are laughing at. I should like to know what you would do without such as me if the French were to drop in upon ye any night?"

"Would you help to beat them off?" said she.

"Can you ask such a question? What are we for? But you don't think anything of soldiers."

Oh yes, she liked soldiers, she said, especially when they came home from the wars, covered with glory; though when she thought what doings had won them that glory she did not like them quite so well. The gallant and appeased yeoman said he supposed her to mean chopping off heads, blowing out brains, and that kind of business, and thought it quite right that a tender-hearted thing like her should feel a little horrified. But as for him, he should not mind such another Blenheim this summer as the army had fought a hundred years ago, or whenever it was—dash his wig if he should mind it at all. "Hullo! now you are laughing again; yes, I saw you!" And the choleric Festus turned his blue eyes and flushed face upon her as though he would read her through. Anne strove valiantly to look calmly back; but her eyes could not face his, and they fell. "You did laugh!" he repeated.

"It was only a tiny little one," she murmured.

"Ah—I knew you did," said he. "Now what was it you laughed at?"

"I only—thought that you were—merely in the yeomanry," she murmured slily.

"And what of that?"

"And the yeomanry only seem farmers that have lost their senses." .

"Yes, yes; I knew you meant some jeering o' that sort, Mistress Anne. But I suppose 'tis the way of women, and I take no notice. I'll confess that some of us are no great things; but I know how to draw a sword, don't I?—say I don't, just to provoke me."

"I am sure you do," said Anne sweetly. "If a Frenchman came up to you, Mr. Derriman, would you take him on the hip, or on the thigh?" .

"Now you are flattering!" he said, his white teeth uncovering themselves in a smile.

"Well, of course I should draw my sword— no, I mean my sword would be already drawn; and I should put spurs to my horse—charger, as we call it in the army; and I should ride up to him and say—no, I shouldn't say any-thing, of course—men never waste words in battle; I should take him with the third guard, low point, and then coming back to the second guard——"

"But that would be taking care of yourself —not hitting at him?"

"How can you say that!" he cried, the beams upon his face turning to a lurid cloud in a moment. "How can you understand military terms who've never had a sword in your life? I shouldn't take him with the sword at all." He went on with eager sulki-ness—"I should take him with my pistol. I should pull off my right glove, and throw back my goat-skin; then I should open my priming-pan, prime, and cast about—no I shouldn't, that's wrong; I should draw my right pistol, and as soon as loaded, seize the weapon by the butt; then at the word 'Cock your pistol,' I should——"

"Then there is plenty of time to give such words of command in the heat of battle?" said Anne innocently.

"Noe!" said the yeoman, his face again in flames. "Why, of course I am only telling you what *would* be the word of command *if* —there now! you la——"

"I didn't; 'pon my word I didn't!"

"No, I don't think you did; it was my mistake. Well, then I come smartly to pre-sent, looking well along the barrel—along the barrel—and fire. Of course I know well enough how to engage the enemy! But I expect my old uncle has been setting you against me."

"He has not said a word," replied Anne; "though I have heard of you, of course."

"What have you heard? Nothing good, I dare say. It makes my blood boil within me!"

"Oh, nothing bad," said she assuringly. "Just a word now and then."

"Now, come, tell me, there's a dear. I don't like to be crossed. It shall be a sacred secret between us. Come, now!"

Anne was embarrassed, and her smile was uncomfortable. "I shall not tell you," she said at last.

"There it is again!" said the yeoman, throwing himself into a despair. "I shall soon begin to believe that my name is not worth sixpence about here."

"I tell you 'twas nothing against you," re-peated Anne.

"That means it might have been for me," said Festus, in a mollified tone. "Well, though, to speak the truth, I have a good many faults, some people will praise me, I suppose. 'Twas praise?"

"It was."

"Well, I am not much at farming, and I am not much in company, and I am not much at figures, but perhaps I must own, since it is forced upon me, that I can show as fine a soldier's figure on the Esplanade as any man of the cavalry."

"You can," said Anne; for though her flesh crept in mortal terror of his irascibility, she could not resist the fearful pleasure of leading him on. "You look very well; and some say, you are——"

"What? Well, they say I am good-look-ing. I don't make myself, so 'tis no praise. Hullo! what are you looking across there for?"

"Only at a bird that I saw fly out of that tree," said Anne.

"What? Only at a bird, do you say?" he heaved out in a voice of thunder. "I see your shoulders a-shaking, young madam. Now don't you provoke me with that laugh-ing. It won't do!"

"Then go away!" said Anne, changed from mirthfulness to irritation by his rough manner. "I don't want your company, you great bragging thing! You are so touchy there's no bearing with you. Go away!"

"No, no, Anne; I am wrong to speak to you so. I give you free liberty to say what you will to me. Say I am not a bit of a soldier, or anything! Abuse me—do now, there's a dear. I'm scum, I'm froth, I'm dirt before the besom—oh yes!"

"I have nothing to say, sir. Stay where you are till I am out of this field."

"Well, there's such command in your looks that I ha'n't heart to go against you. You will come this way to-morrow at the same time? Now, don't be uncivil."

She was too generous not to forgive him, but the short little lip murmured that she did not think it at all likely she should come that way to-morrow.

"Then Sunday?" he said.

"Not Sunday," said she.

"Then Monday—Tuesday—Wednesday, surely?" he went on experimentally.

She answered that she should probably not see him on either day, and, cutting short the argument, went through the wicket into the other field. Festus paused, looking after her; and when he could no longer see her slight figure he swept away his deliberations, began singing, and turned off in the other direction.

VICTORIA TO WINNIPEG *VIA* PEACE RIVER PASS.

NO. I.—BRITISH COLUMBIA.

FROM Ottawa to San Francisco by rail, and thence by steamer to Vancouver Island, a journey in all of about four thousand miles, was a requisite preliminary to our more interesting journey from Victoria across Northern British Columbia, through the Rocky Mountains by the Peace River Pass, and over the prairies to Winnipeg.

The railway trip to Frisco—for life is too short and business too pressing to allow Californians to use the longer name when speaking of their capital—has been so frequently described that we need not linger over it; and the sea voyage to Victoria, a distance of 750 miles, in a commonplace steamer was too much like ordinary sea voyages to merit special mention. But before proceeding up the coast to the point where we leave the Pacific, it may be well to spend a little while in the southern part of British Columbia.

Although Vancouver Island was constituted a Crown colony in 1849, it was little known outside of the ledgers of the Hudson's Bay Company and the official documents of Downing Street until 1858, when the discovery of gold on the Fraser River attracted thousands to Victoria, and when the mainland portion of what is now the province of British Columbia was first erected into a colony. The two colonies were united in 1866, the one giving the name, British Columbia, the other giving the capital, Victoria, to the united colony. On the 20th July, 1871, the colony was confederated as one of the provinces of the Dominion, and Canada was thus extended to the Pacific.

Victoria is British Columbia in much the same way as Paris is France. Originally an Indian village gathered around a post of the Hudson Bay Company, then a small settlement of traders, &c., it sprang forward rapidly under successive waves of excitement; first in 1858 when gold was found on the lower Fraser, again in 1860 when new and most profitable gold-fields were opened in Cariboo, and subsequently with spasms and at intervals until the discovery of new mines at Cassiar in 1873. Its population—a motley crowd from every land — like all prosperity, has fluctuated, at one time swelling to 12,000, but now shrunk to less than half that number. Although some parts of it, especially those occupied by the Chinese and Indians, have a worn-out look, yet it is upon the whole a pretty little city, with delightful drives, taste-ful gardens, comfortable homes, a charming public park; and views of the snow-capped Olympian range, that seem on a warm day refreshing as a cool breeze from the hill-tops. The surroundings of the city are very attractive, the foliage being rich and varied, the shrubs including species seldom seen in the Eastern Provinces, and never grown there as here in the open air, such as holly, ivy, arbutus, &c., while the yew and the scrub-oak give additional charms to the scenery.

Many causes have been at work to retard the progress of Victoria, causes that have similarly affected the whole province. It has suffered largely from the fact that many of its temporary citizens have come with the intention of leaving as soon as they had made their "pile," and have therefore taken no interest in the settlement or development of the country. The mining excitement has slackened. More capital and cheaper labour are required to work both gold and coal mines to advantage, as well as to make use of the vast iron deposits now lying almost untouched. Although eight million pounds sterling have been taken out of the gold-mines of British Columbia within the past twenty years, there is very little in the province to-day to represent that amount. Many have carried their money away; many others have left the country "dead broke;" and while in Ontario and other provinces the fortunate remained because of their success and the disappointed also remained because unable to leave, and while all thus settled, worked and developed the resources of those provinces, men who were successful in British Columbia often left to enjoy their wealth elsewhere, and the disappointed could easily cross to California to repair if possible their shattered fortunes, so that a large number of its former citizens have left the province rather the worse for their having lived in it.

Labour is still dear notwithstanding the presence of a large Chinese element, against which the chief accusation laid by the anti-Chinese agitators is that it keeps down the price of labour and so impoverishes the white man. Household servants receive from three pounds to six pounds sterling per month, farm servants from four pounds to eight pounds sterling per month, with board and lodging, and other white labour is paid in proportion. The two great classes of labourers, however, in British Columbia are the Indians and the

Chinese. Many of the Indians work admirably on steamers, in saw-mills, in salmon canneries, &c. They are active, strong, good-tempered, with little self-restraint if liquor is within reach, and with a great contempt for Chinamen. Some of them have excellent farms, with comfortable cottages, while a number of Lillooet Indians, on the lower Fraser, raise cattle and hay for market. White settlers have no trouble from them.

The other chief labourer of British Columbia, though as yet found almost exclusively in the southern part of the province, is the Chinaman. It is not merely within recent years that men have come from the land of the Celestials across the Pacific to our western coast. There is ample evidence that at some past period the blood of Asiatics was blended with the blood of our Indians. Many of the Pacific Indians are of such a marked Mongolian type of face that you can scarcely distinguish them from the Chinamen except by the difference of dress or of language, or by the absence of the pig-tail, which, however, the Chinaman often wears coiled up under his cap. As late, indeed, as 1834 Japanese junks were found stranded on our western shores; and whether the arrival of men from that farther west, which is commonly spoken of as the far east, was the result of accident or of set purpose, one consequence has been an infusion of Asiatic blood among some of our Indian tribes. The immigration, however, of Chinamen for trade and labour is a thing of recent date. As yet their presence can hardly be said to provoke much hostility, but as the number that have already arrived may be only the advance-guard of a large army of workmen, it is possible that this province may yet witness a conflict between white and Chinese labour similar to that which already has seriously disturbed the peace of California.

From whatever quarter the labourers come, many labourers must soon be required here, not only in the construction of the Canadian Pacific Railway—one hundred and twenty-five miles of which, in southern British Columbia, are now under contract—but also to work in the mines, forests, fisheries, and farming districts which must be rapidly developed when cheaper labour and increased facilities of transport are provided. Some of the gold-fields which have been largely abandoned are estimated still to contain extensive deposits, but future mining operations will involve deep digging and quartz-crushing, and will require more capital, improved machinery, and cheaper living. Of

some of the Cariboo mines, which have been among the richest ever known, Mr. G. M. Dawson, of the Geological Survey, states that "it would not be extravagant to say that the quantity of gold still remaining in the part which has been worked over is about as great as that which has already been obtained." Extensive areas of the best bituminous coal have been discovered in Vancouver Island: of one of these—the Comox coal-district alone—it is stated in the report of the Geological Survey of Canada, that the coal-producing area is three hundred square miles, and the estimated quantity of coal underlying the surface is set down at twenty-five thousand tons per acre, or sixteen million tons per square mile. And yet, as if this were not a sufficient quantity of coal to warm the world for years, and to enrich Vancouver for ages, it would seem from the Reports of the Geological Survey that much of the island, so far as the dense timber forests permit examination, is underlaid with rich coal-measures, while there are known to be extensive beds of anthracite coal in the Queen Charlotte Islands. In the island of Texada, between Vancouver and the mainland, excellent iron ore has been found with such tokens of abundance as would almost warrant the belief that the greater portion of the island is a mass of ore; and this deposit of iron is within twenty-five miles by water of the coal-fields of Comox and Nanaimo, and in the immediate vicinity there are forests sufficient to make charcoal for generations. The fisheries of this province are among the richest in the world; salmon swarm in its rivers in almost incredible numbers, so that an Indian, or any who will follow his example, can in less than a month catch and cure enough to form his chief article of food for the year. Along the coast halibut, herring, and cod are found in large quantities, while in the northern waters the seal and the otter abound. The forests yield the largest of all Canadian timber, the Douglas pine, which sometimes grows to a height of one hundred and eighty feet, with a diameter of eleven feet at the base. Excellent for ordinary use, this wood is specially suited for the manufacture of spars, &c., where toughness, lightness, and durability are essential. Only in respect to farming does British Columbia fall short of its sister provinces of the Dominion, though some of its large valleys afford good arable farms and stock-raising ranches. Its climate near the coast is as moderate as that enjoyed ten degrees farther south on the Atlantic, for it has no cold stream from the Arctic flowing down upon it, while its shores are washed by a warm oceanic current that keeps its ports open at all seasons, and that gives to the southern portions of the province a climate not unlike that of the south of England.

It would be unreasonable to question the future prosperity of such a province. The tariffs of other countries may for a time delay its development; they cannot permanently prevent it. Its time must come, when the restless and speculative spirit created by the gold fever, and still too palpably present, shall give place to steady labour; when industry shall unfold the resources of which as yet only the outskirts have been grasped; and when possessions, in some respects similar to those that secured the material prosperity of the mother country, shall make British Columbia one of the wealthiest, most populous, and most influential provinces of Canada.

But we must hurry northward. We left Victoria in the commodious and comfortable steamer *Olympia*, belonging to the Hudson Bay Company. Our course lay eastward, through the Haro Straits, between Vancouver and San Juan. The sight of this latter island can hardly fail to rouse Canadians to indignation and regret at the way in which our interests have suffered in any dispute with the United States about our boundaries. A large portion of the State of Maine, on our Atlantic coast, was lost through the indifference of the British commissioners engaged in the Ashburton treaty, or Ashburton capitulation, as it has been sometimes called. Washington Territory, and part of Oregon, on the Pacific, were lost to us through reckless ignorance; because it had been reported to the then Premier of England that the country was not worth contending for, as the salmon in the Columbia River would not rise to the fly; and apparently he acted on this report. And surely there must have been culpable deficiency in the evidence and arguments submitted to the Emperor of Germany when, as arbitrator, he decided that the Americans should possess San Juan, to which recently they laid no claim. Not long ago there died in San Juan an aged servant of the Hudson Bay Company, a Scottish Highlander who, with a brother and sister, had come there when the island belonged to Britain. It was the dying wish of the old man, as well as the desire of his only surviving relations, that his remains should not lie in a foreign land. At some difficulty and expense they were removed to Victoria,

where the brother and sister told their story to the Rev. S. McGregor, who could speak to them in their native Gaelic. The little funeral procession of two, accompanied by the minister, passed from the wharf to the graveyard, and there they left the dust of the old loyalist beneath the protection of the flag he loved.

After steaming through the Straits of Haro we passed northward between Vancouver and the smaller islands that stud the Straits of Georgia, until, leaving the northern extremity of Vancouver, we enter the series of channels that divide the mainland from the long succession of islands which fringe the coast with scarcely any interruption as far as Alaska. This land-locked strip of ocean that stretches almost unbroken along our Pacific coast from San Juan to Port Simpson, some five hundred miles, is one of the most singular water-ways in the world. On the western shores of Vancouver and of the chain of islands lying to the north the waves of the Pacific break with an unceasing roll; but here, inside the breastwork of islands, and between them and the mainland, the sea is commonly as smooth as a canal. It is deep enough for the largest man-of-war, even within a short distance of the shore, and yet the tiniest steam-yacht runs no risk of rough water. For commercial purposes, when the mines along the eastern seaboard of Vancouver become more fully developed and the coasting trade increases, the value of such water communication, possessing all the advantages of deep-sea navigation, yet protected by a line of breakwaters from all the dangers of the sea, can hardly be overestimated. Only at two places is it exposed to the gales of the Pacific, and there only those from the west, viz. from the north end of Vancouver Island as you round Cape Caution, a distance of about thirty miles, and again for about ten miles when passing Millbank Sound.

Beyond the shelter of Vancouver the climate became, as we had expected, decidedly moist. A drizzling rain obscured, for most of the time, our views of what, from occasional glimpses, we inferred must be magnificent scenery. When the leaden mist would lift we could see the hills, now bare and precipitous, now wooded and sloping, now torrent-carved and snow-capped, sometimes like a wall of adamant defying the waves, and again cleft by deep narrow fiords or gorges. The whole country seemed to be wrapped in silence, with scarcely a sign of life, except some salmon-canning establishments or a few small Indian villages that had grown up in localities well favoured for shooting or fishing, or that had clustered around the posts of the Hudson's Bay Company.

We were to leave the coast at Port Essington, a village at the mouth of the Skeena, but it was necessary for us to go about twenty-five miles farther north to Metlahkatlah, to secure canoes and Indian crews for our journey up the Skeena. This settlement is chiefly known through the remarkable mission established here, in connection with the Church of England, by Mr. William Duncan. Other missions to the Indians, both Protestant and Catholic, exist in British Columbia, but it is no disparagement to them to say that none of them have proved so successful as the mission at Metlahkatlah. The Tsimpseans, as the Indians of that district are called, were at the time when Mr. Duncan came among them, seventeen years ago, as fierce, turbulent, and unchaste as any of the other coast tribes, not excepting the Haidahs; whereas now the chastity of the women, the sobriety and steady industry of the men, the thrift and cleanliness of all render their settlement the equal, in these respects, of almost any place of the same size in the eastern provinces. Mr. Duncan desired from the first to draw in the Indians from scattered districts along the coast to one centre—a plan which might work well in this quarter, where the Indians live chiefly by fishing, although it could not be carried out in the same way among the Indians of the woods or of the prairies, who live chiefly by hunting. He chose as the centre of operations the little Indian village of Metlahkatlah, where at that time about fifty persons were living, and he has already gathered around him Indians from the districts to the number of about a thousand, upon whom he has been able to exert a strong and steady influence. He learned their language, made it a written language, and now teaches them it grammatically, while instructing them also in English. He learned several trades that he might teach them, and sent some of them to Victoria to learn trades that they might in turn become artisan teachers. The fruits of their labour, beyond what are required for their own maintenance and comfort, are exchanged for such commodities in the way of clothing, provision, &c., as they can procure from Victoria, and these are furnished at an excellent shop in the village, which, under the missionary's direction, is managed by Indian clerks. A large and beautiful church,

a commodious school-house, an extensive trading store, comfortable dwellings, a saw-mill, and numerous workshops are among the outward and visible evidences of the success of the mission. We engaged two crews here, and found them to be excellent fellows, active, honest, and kindly; they were accustomed each evening to have prayers in their own language, and the man who led their devotions was the bravest, best-tempered, and most skilful boatman of them all.

North of Metlahkatlah about twenty-five miles is Port Simpson, the best harbour of British Columbia, and spoken of at one time as a possible terminus of the Canadian Pacific Railway; but as it is accessible from the east only by a route that would traverse a large extent of unprofitable country, and as it is too far north to serve the general interests of the province, the idea of making it a railway terminus has been abandoned, and our transcontinental line will touch the Pacific at Burrard Inlet, near the mouth of the Fraser. Having visited Port Simpson, and having caught a glimpse of Alaska, we returned to Port Essington, our point of departure from the coast. Our proposed route was by the river Skeena to the village of Hazelton, or Forks of Skeena, one hundred and fifty miles from the sea, then across country to Babine, up Lake Babine, and down Lake Stewart to Fort St. James. This would be our first stage. The second stage would be from Fort St. James across country to Fort McLeod, seventy miles, and thence by water through the Rocky Mountains to Dunvegan. The third stage would be from Dunvegan across the prairies to Winnipeg.

We had secured excellent crews and canoes at Metlahkatlah. The boats are spoken of as "canoes," but they are very different from the birch-bark canoes to which in our eastern provinces that name is commonly applied, for these are made of wood, sound and strong as any ordinary boat, though neither carvel or clinker built. They are simply "dug-outs" of capacious size and graceful model, each made of a cedar log. When the log has been shaped and hollowed it is filled with water, into which highly heated stones are dropped, the steaming process being assisted by a gentle fire beneath the boat. The sides in this way become pliable, and are extended so as to give breadth of beam. Seats are forced in, and the thin, tough shell of cedar, retaining this shape, forms an excellent boat. Sometimes these canoes are as much as sixty feet long, and capable of carrying several tons of freight, made of the large cedar-trees that are found along our Northern Pacific coast ; and they are so safe that the Indians of Queen Charlotte Islands use them in whale-fishing. We had two, each being twenty-five feet keel, with about four feet eight inches beam.

Our most essential stores were flour, bacon, beans, and tea ; these form the staple food of travellers through the interior of British Columbia. Of these it was necessary for us to take a goodly quantity, for we could not expect to add to our supplies for several weeks ; we might meet with accidents and many unforeseen delays ; and, besides, some extra provisions are valuable in dealing with the Indians, as a little flour or tea, or, what is often more acceptable, a piece of tobacco, is frequently better than money for securing the services of an Indian, or for purchasing any commodity, such as salmon, that he may have to barter.

The Skeena, like all the rivers along our Canadian Pacific coast, is very rapid ; our ascent, therefore, was slow, usually at the rate of ten to twelve miles a day after we had left tide water, and that even though our canoeing hours were from seven A.M. till four P.M., and each canoe was manned by a crew of five stalwart Indians. We required other means besides paddles to make head against the current. Sometimes, when a favourable beach gave opportunity, the men "tracked," that is, dragged the canoe by a tow-rope as is done with a canal boat. When, however, as in most cases, the bank was too precipitous, or the growth of brush and timber too dense to allow of tracking, "poling" became necessary. Each man is provided with a hemlock pole, from ten to fourteen feet in length, while some extra ones are kept on hand in case of loss or breakage. A strong steering oar has been lashed to a crossbar at the stern, for in some parts of the current a paddle would be useless as a feather for steering, and if the canoe were to sheer an upset would immediately follow. The men lay themselves to their work, poling against the stream as if straining their strength to the utmost, and the poles seem to grip the gravelly bottom while the current makes them quiver and rattle against the canoe.

Occasionally we pass an Indian village, consisting of a few rude houses made of rough cedar boards. Each house accommodates two or more families, and in some of the villages each house is adorned by a curiously carved door-post. The figures ingeniously cut upon these door-posts are supposed to be the heraldic bearings of the family ; but to the uninitiated the heraldry of these Indians is as mysterious as the heraldry of the English nobility. Frogs, bears, beavers, whales, salmon, seals, eagles, men, sometimes men tapering into fish like the fabulous merman, are the figures most frequently seen. Several of these may be found on each post, the post being about thirty feet high, and two feet in diameter at the base. In many cases more labour is expended on this post than upon all the rest of the house ; sometimes it is large enough to admit of a hole being cut through it sufficient to serve as a doorway, and in this case the opening is usually by some quaint conceit made to represent the mouth of one of the carved figures ; frequently, however, it is quite distinct from the house, standing in front of it like a flag-staff.

Near almost every village we found men engaged in fishing, for, as we passed here about the middle of June, the first run of salmon had already commenced, and salmon is the staple, almost the exclusive article of food among these Indians. When the salmon fails, as it has sometimes done, the distress and destitution are very great, for the natives seldom raise any kind of vegetables, the character of the country, as well as of the people, being adverse to agriculture. When, however, the salmon can be taken in their ordinary abundance, a man may in less than a month lay in his supply of food for the year.

The salmon are cured, after being cleaned, simply by being dried in the sun ; and, as the curing-ground is usually near the beach, quantities of sand are blown over the fish. One result of this is that the teeth of the Indians are gradually ground down by the sand which has been incorporated with their food, so that you can approximately tell the age of an Indian by "mark of mouth," the teeth of the young being but slightly affected, while those of the aged have, in most cases, been worn down to the gums. The dried salmon are stored in a *cache*, a large box or casing made of rough-hewn cedar boards, and usually built around a tree at some distance from the ground. No Indian will interfere with another man's salmon-cache: it is as safe as if it were guarded by a regiment.

Having reached the village of Hazelton, or the Forks, formerly known by the name of Kitunmax—an Indian community with three white families—we bade good-bye to our crews and their cedar canoes. As no horses nor mules were to be found at Hazelton, and as there is no waggon-road in any

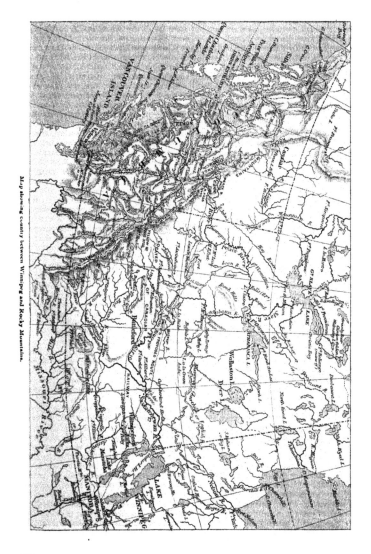

Map showing country between Winnipeg and Rocky Mountains.

direction from the village, we employed a number of men to "pack" for us, that is, to carry all our stores, tents, blankets, baggage, &c., while we accompanied them on foot to Lake Babine, forty-five miles distant. It is surprising how easily these Indians and their wives carry large burdens, although they do not look very robust. Their capacity for this kind of work seems to lie in their power of preserving their balance accurately, rather than in great muscular strength. The "pack" rests on the back, chiefly between the shoulders; it is kept in position by a "tump-line," which passes in a broad band across the forehead, and the ends of which are fastened across the chest. Sometimes the "packer" may have difficulty in raising his burden, or rather in raising himself with his pack from his sitting posture in which he has fastened it on; but once erect he moves off quite easily.

After leaving the Forks—so called from the junction at this point of the Skeena and Watsonquah—our course for a short distance lies along what is known as the "telegraph trail." Not that there is a telegraph line in operation in this part of the province, but a very extensive line was once projected in this direction. The Western Union Telegraph Company of America, in 1865, commenced explorations with a view towards the construction of an overland telegraph, which, by way of Behring Straits, was to unite the Old and New Worlds. After the expenditure of three millions of dollars the scheme was abandoned owing to the success of the Atlantic cable. To construct and maintain this telegraph it was necessary to clear a wide track on either side of the proposed line, and this track is now known as the telegraph trail. It extends for some distance north of Hazelton to a point known as Fort Stager; and before the project was abandoned the line had been built through a large portion of British Columbia, part of it, as far north as Quesnelle on the Fraser, being now in operation, the property of the Canadian Government.

Soon after leaving the telegraph trail our course led up the valley of the Susqua and of the Oo-atz-an-li, tributaries of the Watsonquah, over low rolling hills that are covered with rampikes, as the fire-swept, branchless trees are called. From these hills, looking westward, we can see to great advantage the snowy peaks and serrated ridges of the Cascade Range. Sometimes the scenery becomes Alpine in character, though it has not the sustained grandeur of the mountains of Switzerland. Farther south, along the valley of the Homathco, the Cascade Range is said to be grander than on the Skeena, while the Rocky Mountains are much higher near our southern boundary than they are near the Peace River. Here and there we saw patches of land that might be cultivated, and some of the hillsides, where cleared of timber, abound in pea-vine, wild hay, and bushes, affording excellent pasture, while the valleys of the Susqua and Watsonquah grow abundance of luxuriant grass; but the climate of this part of the province is unfavourable for agriculture, even where the soil is fit for cultivation. Potatoes, oats, and barley, however, are grown successfully in some parts, especially on the flats that fringe the lakes.

At Babine village, near the foot of Lake Babine, we secured, after some delay and difficulty, crews and canoes to take us up the lake. Our difficulty was caused by a very natural though ludicrous mistake. On our arrival at the lake-side the villagers from the opposite shore at once came across to interview, examine, and inspect, as they always do with the liveliest curiosity. Among them was one whose coat was gaily adorned with buttons, and to whom, on account of his appearance, we paid special deference, thinking he was the chief. At the same time the old chief, wrapped in a well-worn blanket, was quietly looking on, and soon retired in indignation. When we tried to hire men and canoes we found that we had been "booin'" to the wrong man," as the chief raised the price on us. A deputation waited on him, and by a special offer for the use of his own canoe secured reduced rates, giving him at the same time, at his own urgent request, some medicine and some tobacco. These Babine Indians have the poorest reputation for honesty of any of the British Columbia tribes.

From Babine village a trail leads eastward towards Omenica, a district which, like many other parts of the province, was almost unknown except to Indians and to Hudson's Bay Company officials, until it was explored by gold miners. Gold was found there in 1872; for a time there was the usual rush to the new diggings; supplies were required; Indians were employed as porters to carry in provisions, &c., and times were brisk about Babine. But the mines have not realised the hopes formed regarding them; they have been deserted for Cassiar in the remote north, and only a few of the eager crowd are left there now.

The lake, which is 100 miles in length, is

very beautiful, its banks rising gently from the water's edge, the wooded slopes being backed by undulating hills which give place occasionally to tracts of good pasture land. Were it not for the lofty summits seen here and there in the background, one would have little idea that he was travelling through a country which has, for the most part, been fitly described as a "sea of mountains." Crossing from Lake Babine to Lake Stewart, a distance of eight miles, we were surprised to find at the eastern end of the portage a tolerably good farm, owned and cultivated by an Indian, who had some excellent stock, as well as crops of hay, oats, and vegetables. Continuing our course down Stewart's Lake, which is forty miles in length, we reach, at the foot of the lake, Fort St. James, the centre of the Hudson's Bay Company's posts in northern British Columbia, a district formerly known as New Caledonia. The fort is beautifully situated on a broad plateau about thirty feet above the beach, with a commanding outlook, and with views of scenery that remind one greatly of the Scottish Highlands. There are no snow-capped summits visible, but, look in any direction you may, there is a background of hills that in some parts border on the lake, and in others are separated from it by wooded plateaux or undulating slopes, while under the prevailing westerly winds the waters of the lake break upon the beach with the musical monotone of the sea. Here we were met by friends who had come up from Victoria, or rather from Yale, by the great highway which follows the Valley of the Fraser through central British Columbia. They were accompanied by a mule-train laden with stores, &c.; so at Fort St. James we rest for a day to replenish and rearrange our supplies, to write letters to our friends in the east, which will go by way of Victoria and San Francisco, and to prepare for the next stage of our journey, which will include a ride with a mule-train to Fort McLeod and a voyage by boat through the Rocky Mountains, borne onward by the broad waters of the Peace River.   DANIEL M. GORDON.

FOOD FOR THE ECONOMICAL.
By J. MILNER FOTHERGILL, M.D.
II.

IN a previous contribution I pointed out several food combinations of high food value and little cost, in which the composition of the *erbswurst* of the German army of 1870—1871 was followed. This sausage consisted of pea-meal and pig fat, the richest and cheapest combination of albuminoids and fat possible. It was readily made into a soup, to which a turnip sliced added the necessary antiscorbutic quality. The value of this sausage as a food was widely recognised at that time and since; and this sausage is a type of what a cheap food of high food value should be.

Another food of high food value is cheese, which is now produced of very good quality, and at a very cheap rate, from Canada and the United States. The great objection to cheese has been that it is reputed to be indigestible. This is unfortunately true of cheese as ordinarily cooked, and especially so of cheese made with skimmed milk and new milk. Rich cheeses are made by adding cream to new fresh milk. Such cheeses can now be bought for 8d. a pound; and as such cheese is rich in a very digestible fat, and in albuminoids, in the form of caseine, it should form a considerable factor in cheap dietaries.

As Welsh rarebit, as toasted cheese, as macaroni cheese, and, still more, as cheese souffiet made with eggs, cheese is indigestible. Why? Because it is not sufficiently finely subdivided before it enters the stomach. It is impossible to so masticate hot cheese as to render it acceptable to many stomachs; it must then be cooked in such a manner that it reaches the stomach in a finely divided form. To achieve this, rice may be boiled and then a quantity of milk added, while some cheese finely chopped, as suet is for a pudding, is mixed up with it; and the whole put into a stewpan or a dish in the oven. This is good, but a better plan is to use hominy. Hominy is Indian corn, not ground, but finely cracked, so that each piece is about the size of a very small pin's head. It is sold in five-pound bags at 2d. per pound. To make a sufficient meal for one person half a pound of hominy should be placed in water overnight, next day it should be boiled; then half a pint of milk (1d.) should be added, and half a pound of cheese finely chopped be mixed with it very thoroughly. The whole may then be placed in a dish in the oven or a saucepan, and cooked for fifteen minutes. When served up the smell and taste of the cheese are retained, but it is lost to view, so finely is it subdivided. To the taste this is excellent, and the food value is high; it is also most digestible, and can be eaten by a dyspeptic without discomfort. It lacks, however, antiscorbutic properties, and therefore should be preceded by lentil soup; and the combination of the two makes an excellent and very cheap dinner. This cheese pudding is sure to soon become a very favourite dish, for it is most palatable. I should like to discuss at further length the combination of cheese with farinaceous matters, but space will not permit it.

The preparation of vegetable soups in which legumes take the place of meat is a matter which must attract the attention of housewives in the future. Either lentils (Egyptian) or split peas may be used, in the proportion of half a pound to two quarts of water. The legumes are first picked and washed, and then boiled for four hours, by which time they are quite soft, and can be pressed through a colander, and again put in the liquor. Various vegetables may be added to this "stock," for such it is—a large onion sliced, a carrot and a turnip chopped up, or a head of celery and some parsnips. A little pepper and salt are necessary; and a dessert-spoonful of brown sugar is an agreeable addition, according to Miss Orlebar's interesting little book ("Food for the People; or Lentils and other Vegetable Cookery"). Such soup is very agreeable to the palate, is eminently digestible, and is very cheap; while its food value is as high as most soups made with meat. The vegetables other than the legumes furnish the desired antiscorbutic quality. Such soup followed by cheese pudding is quite sufficient food for a meal for most persons.

The reader will perhaps wonder that all along bread has never been mentioned. Of course it is taken for granted that bread will be eaten with all the dishes mentioned. It is not necessary to say anything further on the subject. Bread eaten with bacon or with cheese is the staple food of the working classes, especially the field labourer. A very poor meal may be eked out by a slice of bread and cheese, and thus a good food value be given to it. Even in the houses of the poorest labourers the vegetable soup given above and bread and cheese are attainable. Bread and cheese do not possess antiscorbutic properties, but the vegetable soup provides them. A large variety of vegetable soups could easily be furnished by variations from the formula just given, the main lines laid down here being followed.

At this point something may be said on economical food for others than those to whom cost of material is the primary object. The subject of the rational use of farinaceous foods may profitably engage our attention. The good old plan of rearing children on oatmeal porridge, which made bone, it was said, obtained in the north of England, as well as Scotland, up to the time of my childhood, and it is a pity that such porridge is going out of fashion; but oatmeal porridge does not agree with every stomach, and with some persons produces acid eructations and heartburn. For such persons hominy is the proper substitute. Though retaining an affectionate remembrance of oatmeal porridge, my allegiance is now transferred to hominy porridge. Hominy soaked in water over night and boiled in milk, in the proportion of two ounces of hominy to a pint of milk, boiled for twenty minutes, is delicious to breakfast. It may, like oatmeal porridge, be eaten with milk or cream, with treacle, with butter and sugar, or with butter alone. It also agrees with dyspeptics.

And now a few words on maize, or Indian corn. Even at the present low price of wheat, corn flour is cheaper than wheat flour by 25 per cent., and that, too, white corn flour; the yellow form, "the yellow male" of the Irish famine, being still cheaper. There are several misconceptions about maize. It is thought to induce skin affections; and in some parts of Italy where the food is almost exclusively maize it appears there is some foundation for the statement; but others, as Americans, both North and South, and Zulus, eat maize in large quantities without any evil consequences. Then it is thought that maize is nearly pure starch, but such is not the case. Maize contains as much nitrogen, or albuminoids, as the best wheaten flour; and more fat even than oatmeal. Consequently for food value it stands at the head of the *Farinaceæ*. The appearance of the London Omnibus Company's horses has much improved since Indian corn was substituted for oats. Maize is very fattening, and is used by farmers to finish off their fat stock. It is too fattening for fowls, who do not lay well on it. Pavy says of it, "Maize, or Indian corn meal, is not adapted for making bread on account of its deficiency in gluten, without the admixture of wheaten or rye flour." But this very fact is in favour of maize flour for many other purposes. It is largely used in making biscuits. Pastry made with maize flour is less tenacious than that made with wheaten flour, and therefore more digestible.

For ordinary pie-crusts, pastry-crust, and boiled puddings maize is better, as well as cheaper, than wheaten flour. I know a lady who cannot eat a suet-pudding without indigestion, unless her cook mixes powdered dried bread crumbs with the flour. What does this tell us? When wheaten flour has once been cooked it will not make bread. The gluten has been so altered that the particles will not adhere as before. All the baby-foods in vogue consist more or less of baked flour, because such flour will not cohere and form masses in the stomach, but dissolves entirely like a biscuit. Now, for all such puddings, batter-puddings, rollypollies, &c., maize flour alone, or with a small quantity of wheaten flour, may be used with advantage; it is cheaper to buy and is rich in fat. "As regards this quality none of the other *cerealia* exhibit even an approach to it. Properly prepared it furnishes a wholesome, digestible, and nutritious food for man; but with those, it is said, who have been unaccustomed to its use, it is apt to excite a tendency to diarrhœa." (*Pavy.*) This last quality of maize flour indicates its extensive use in the nursery along with milk, which has a tendency to constipate the bowels.

For ordinary households where there are children hominy or oatmeal porridge should be the staple of breakfast, furnishing a readily digestible food on which the child can start the day; after which other food, as a little fried bacon or an egg, may be eaten. Then, again, milk puddings should be more largely eaten than they are, for they are very digestible. Lentil flour added to a corn-flour pudding gives a dish of high food value; the lentils furnishing a large percentage of albuminoids. Then milk puddings with stewed fruit should be more often seen than they are, especially where there are dyspeptics. The remains of the milk pudding and stewed fruit may be eaten cold at breakfast, especially by those whose appetite is defective or fastidious in the morning. The ordinary British housewife usually stands aghast with astonishment at the suggestion of such a breakfast; but, nevertheless and notwithstanding, such a breakfast is very nice indeed, especially in warm weather. For those who cannot eat the ordinary English breakfast cold stewed fruit with cream or a milk pudding will be found very appetising. In addition to the excellent tinned and bottled fruits now coming over from the United States, I have privately received some tins and bottles of cream from Iowa; the latter are all that could be wished; and probably will soon be in the market at a price far below that of the present cost of cream.

There is another vegetable production which is worth consideration by the economical, and that is the date. The date is rich in sugar, and possibly in albuminoids; but Dr. Pavy has not yet settled this latter point, he writes me. As sold, pressed in masses, it costs about twopence a pound. When picked and stewed, the date is very palatable, eaten with a milk pudding. The costly dessert dates are too dear to be thought of as economical in any sense.

These combinations of milk pudding are very desirable where there are children. Whatever may be the reason or reasons, children at present do not take to fat very readily, and certainly a large proportion of them reject the fat of joints; consequently it becomes very desirable that they have dishes provided for them which are fairly rich in fat which is not visible to the eye. Such dishes were considered in the first article in last month's issue; and are to be found in milk puddings when a piece of butter has been put into them. Butter is not an extravagant article of diet even at its price; and is a fat which is usually well borne by the most delicate stomach, and assimilated readily by the feeblest digestive organs, provided always that it is not swallowed in masses, but is taken in a finely divided form. Many children who cannot take butter well in the form of thick slices of bread with a comparative thick layer of butter, can take it famously when the slice of bread is thin, and the butter well rubbed in—company bread and butter, in fact. In the latter form the butter is finely subdivided, and in mastication is thoroughly mixed with the bread, so that it reaches the stomach in an acceptable form; while in the other form the stomach resents its presence. When added in generous quantity to a pudding consisting of milk and some form of farina, butter can be given to delicate children in practically sufficient quantities. Many children would be all the better if they were taught to eat puddings of all kinds with butter, or with butter and a little sugar, instead of the jam and preserves now in such common use. A more economical form of fat is beef suet, and suet puddings, especially if made with treacle, are readily eaten by children, and should be more largely used even than they are at present. Such puddings made with maize flour cost little, are very palatable, and have comparatively a high food value. In the present condition of the digestive organs of children, it is eminently desirable to provide them with a sufficient quantity of fat for proper tissue nutrition, without offending their palates or their stomachs. Much dyspepsia, much phthisis ultimately, would be avoided if the problem of how to successfully introduce fat into the stomachs of children could be practically solved; as there is reason to believe it might be if the combinations given above were generally adopted. The general objection to fat *en masse* is shown by its absence from the tinned meats which now come in such large quantities from abroad. No matter whence they come, or in what form almost, they are sadly deficient in fat. The best forms are minced meat, and the baked beans and pork of New England. The latter are exceedingly good, either "hotted" or eaten cold, and are a cheap food. The minced meats, either pork sausage meat or beef, as minced collops, or the minced mutton, can readily be "hotted," and eaten with potatoes; and as such are digestible. But the ordinary tinned meats are only adapted to be eaten cold; they are already sufficiently cooked, or rather, even over-done, so that they cannot be heated or converted into hashes without detriment to their digestibility. All that was said in the first article about re-cooked meat holds good of tinned meats. Though the sale of these tinned meats is now very great, the problem of cheap food is not successfully solved by tinning masses of meat. The hashes made with legumes and a little fresh meat are better in every way. Certainly it would be possible to make a hash purely of vegetables, and add some minced meat just before serving up. By so doing, the objections to re-cooked meat would be largely obviated.

As to tinned fruits, they are very good, but can scarcely be regarded as cheap food. Dried apple rings are, however, cheap, and when stewed are excellent with a milk pudding. Mushrooms in tins are very good, and might be tinned with advantage in other countries than France; and larger mushrooms might be used than the French button mushrooms. As to fish, whether fresh, dried, or tinned, I am utterly unable to suggest any form as a cheap food. Contrasting the cost of fish with its low food value, it is expensive; too expensive for persons with whom economy is a consideration. One day at Victoria Park Hospital, I had a Whitechapel fish-curer's wife as a patient. I asked her if ever her family had fish dinners for economy. She replied decisively that they had fish dinners sometimes, but not for cheapness. "The fish are too dear to buy for that," she added. Well, if Whitechapel fish-curers cannot buy fish cheap, there is not much prospect of other people doing so. Of course, there are certain places along our coasts where fish may be cheap; but compared with butcher's meat or bacon, fish is an expensive food.

In penning the above remarks, the writer does not suppose that the subject of cheap food is treated here at all exhaustively. Far from it. It is a mere outline of the subject as a guide to the reader on the matter. It is a mere skeleton—the osseous framework of a rational economical dietary. It is left for the different readers to clothe it with flesh in the form of varieties of the typical combinations here limned out. These articles, however, may suggest to medical men, and to ladies interested on the subject, the lines on which they should proceed in studying the subject. And such study is very desirable. These combinations of foods could be varied, and the results given at the evening readings now so general. Medical men could have the matter experimented upon at home, by which their own domestic expenses could be lessened; their acquaintance with food increased, to the advantage of their patients; and they could instruct their neighbours, who would be grateful. If once the subject could be set agoing at penny readings, the rational study of food would soon become general. Ladies, then, could take up the subject, try the different constituents of a meal in a variety of combinations, and point out the most acceptable. Such treatment of the subject would bring it under the notice of those most concerned, but who see least of the subject, viz., the housewives of the lower middle-class and artisan orders. They attend these evening readings, and the benevolently disposed would find that by introducing the subject of Food and How to Cook it to these evening readings, knowledge on the subject could soon be widely spread. A medical contemporary concluded a series of articles on Rational Cheap Dietaries lately, as follows:—"With the increase of physiological knowledge on the one hand, and unlimited supplies of food at a low price coming in from abroad, on the other, the dietary of the inhabitants of Great Britain may be profoundly modified, made at once attractive and nutritive; money may be saved, appetites and digestions improved, tempers sweetened, and tissues better nourished, if the housewife would only be induced to lend her ear to the charmer."

.HOLLAND.

PART II.

Hour-Glass Stand.

ALTHOUGH Walcheren is so old-fashioned and averse to every kind of innovation, yet it has a bathing-place or seaside Pension at Domburg, on the east coast. To reach this a carriage must be hired, and then comes a lively experience of old-fashion travelling, probably with a farmer to drive; if so, so much the better, as local information is valuable.

We were sorry to leave Flushing, with its cheerful carillons, the working of which is shown in the small illustration on page 128. The kindness of the consul had made an impression upon us, and when away from home little attentions and civilities are much prized and thought of.

Our driver was cheerful, very great on the immensity of Dutch dykes, the vast sums of money originally spent on their construction, and the annual cost of repairs. We passed near one, the "West Kapelle Dyke;" to this he referred with honest pride as the largest dyke in the world, and the view as we drove by was curious to any one but a Dutchman, for above the long skyline of the dyke we saw the topsails of a brigantine running before the wind in the German Ocean. The time seemed to fly as our coachman gave us his

Light beyond the Grave, Domburg.

views on all kinds of subjects. One thing surprised us: he thought it very extravagant to shoe horses all round, as in Zeeland they never put shoes on the hind feet, only on the fore. Domburg is supported by a few families who stop at the Pension on the Duines, the village being seldom visited save by people who are anxious to post their own letters. To this class I belonged, and found a companion every evening. It was some time before it oozed out that we were both writing daily to our wives, and keeping up a good old custom which once started is seldom relinquished. I soon discovered my companion's love of nature and admiration of cattle. No wonder he saw beauties in cows and polders, for he was no less than De Haas, a Dutch painter, who has done

Veere.

grand work of remarkable power and fresh-ness.

Soon after our arrival at the Pension we betook ourselves to the bathing department; the warm weather and dusty roads made the very idea of a bath refreshing. Here again we had a surprise. The bathing machines are faithfully drawn in the sketch, and are really diligences which, having performed as much perfunctory duty as they were capable of on land, had been told off to finish their days in the amphibious mission we found them in. How the poor horses who dragged them up on the sand must have wished they had been of lighter draught and more scientific construction! Most likely they had never had pleasanter experiences of bathing machines, and so worked away with plodding content-ment.

Whilst staying at Domburg an oppor-tunity presented it-self of visiting an old Dutch family and mansion at Overduin. I had heard much of them, of their love of art, their family hospitality, the re-fined taste of every-thing about the house, the library and almost perfect collection of Ja-cobus Catz' works, and grounds, and perfect farm-build-ings. To arrive at

The Carillons, Flushing.

Overduin it was necessary to walk along the sands for some considerable distance before turning inland over a spot where the camp of English in 1809 is easily traceable, and the cooking-places of the troops undisturbed. This had a saddening association naturally, as so many of our men were carried off by fever, and so many others returned with germs of sickness which could never be eradi-cated.

Another association of far earlier date, however, was in store. In walking by the shore we naturally kept as near as possible to the receding water, as the foothold is so much better than on the dry and loose sand, which fatigues terribly. It happened to be an unusually low tide, and seeing some stumps sticking up we waded to them; on nearer approach we found a skeleton half-buried in sand, then another, and a third, with remains of wood round them. The whole thing seemed a mystery; one, how-ever, that soon cleared up on our describing what we had seen and the bearings of the spot visited. "Why, you have seen the graves of Dom-burg," said our kind host—"Roman re-mains but rarely seen, even at the lowest tides."

Really, the Romans seem to have been everywhere; we hardly expected to have such a find under the water in Holland. Some years ago two altars were dug up at the same spot, and some bronze fibulæ found also; it was not, however, our good fortune to find any relic that was portable.

Our visit to Overduin was delightful; so kindly all the members of the family, such charming simplicity with all the dignity of château life and old family status. Almost all the Dutch painters of modern times were represented in the different rooms, and a fine collection of water-colours was hidden away in portfolios. How astonished we were, too, to find the finest collection of nearly all the different editions of Jacobus Catz, a writer so dear to all Dutchmen whether at home or abroad; and last, but not least, the stables were so good. There we had a good opportunity of seeing and thoroughly examining all the details of Zeeland costume, the farmers near the house being very well to do, and farmers' wives and daughters in Holland do not go with the times; their manners, customs, and costumes are the same as their grand-
XXI—10

Boy Smoking.

Fisherwoman, Arnemviden.

fathers before them, and quite good enough they consider them to be for them. The old silver handed down to them is prized, almost revered and much more valued than any modern work; as they keep to the same form in their boats, so in their outline of dress. We heard one farmer described as being a little foppish, because he had a boat built a few inches less in beam than the old pattern generally; and the number of petticoats worn by farmers' wives is as unalterably kept to as the law of the Medes and Persians. We found two characteristics in the Zeelanders. They carried silver-handled knives in a special pocket on the right side, the handle much ornamented and rather of a yatagan form, with a blade of about seven inches; and their hair is cut square right across the forehead. The houses are painted here with blue and red distemper outside round the door; the shutters, green with white panels, giving a remarkably bright look; especially as the crockery of Holland is so beautiful in colour (particularly some of the tones of green glaze), and their varieties of brass work and cooking utensils perfectly endless. An endeavour to sketch in colour their unusual combination of colour in house-painting elicited a quaint remark from the "Basena," or farmer's wife; pointing to the sketch she said, "Are those English colours? I do not think much of them!" In the twinkling of an eye she returned with two spoons full of dry colour, one red the other blue. Emptying them on to the sketch she exclaimed, "That's Dutch colour;" and it was certainly brighter than modern chromo-lithographs, which is saying something. Before leaving this farm we must refer to a remark made by the daughter, who was very good-looking, handsome we may say, of the Spanish type, very neatly costumed, with the usual corkscrew pendants dangling from her temples. Wishing to make a careful drawing, I apologised rather and hoped she

The Hall of Justice, Veere.

would excuse my looking at her. Her reply was admirable. "I never mind being looked at by a gentleman." It is superfluous to refer to smoking; but the instance of the lad nursing the doll, with a long pipe hanging down over it, was considered too authentic a record of early smoking to pass by unnoticed. We must not linger—we must press on for Veere, *via* Middleburg.

Middleburg is the capital of Walcheren and famous in history, with its fine Town Hall and Spanish remains of street architecture and one notably fine twelfth-century house. These, however, deserve an article to themselves, but we cannot now refer to them in detail, as Veere demands our attention. Veere was a fortified city, small but important; at its zenith during Maximilian's time. What a contrast now! Grass grows in the streets; it is quite deserted, and some people say that

State pensioners are offered houses there, as the fever is sure to prove fatal. The centre of interest now is the Town Hall.

Elegant in form and well preserved, outside the principal door hang two remarkable weights, shown in the sketch. They each weigh eight pounds, and were used to be placed hanging from the necks of unfaithful wives, when they were paraded through the town for punishment at the hands of the citizens. The bronze handles of the doors are ornamented with the Royal motto, "Honi soit qui mal y pense," encircling the cross of St. George, surmounted by a Royal crown. The Hall was built 1491 A.D., and the Emperor Maximilian presented the city with a beautiful gold cup in 1541 A.D. It is still preserved, and sometimes shown, together with his autograph. The form of the cup is shown on the table in the Justice-room, illustrated by the large woodcut in this number. There is something weird and time-worn about this chamber of justice. The great brass rod is very prominent as a warning to offenders, and over the fireplace are several bronze hands, holding hammers, or knives, or whatever instrument had been used in celebrated murders. Veere is now silent, gloomy and forsaken. "Ichabod" at every turn seems to stare at all points.

Water Tower, Veere.

Veere had five gates in olden days; three on the land side, two on the sea. One, known as Arnemviden Poort, is now especially associated with the supply of fish for Middleburg and Flushing, and it is from that locality that we have the illustration of the over-petticoated fish-wife in this part. It may be well to impress upon the reader that this really is a portrait carefully rendered to give true character. Veere has been so great in its day that we must at all events give a few data of its past. As early as the thirteenth century it flourished, associated with the name of the Graf Floris den Vijfden, then Wolfaart van Borselen, and the Heer van Beveren. The Heere of Veere was an important title and high position, for Wolfaart van Borselen was a man of might, and in 1444 A.D. brought Maria Stuart, daughter of James I. of Scotland. In this way the Scotch made a firm footing and obtained great privileges for trading. In 1540 A.D. Maximilian of Burgundy built a large arsenal during the time that he was Heere of Veere, and did much for the development of the place without interfering with the Scotch interests, which seemed to have prospered under his *régime;* for 1620 A.D. found that community more thriving than ever, and seems to have been a foreshadowing of that Scotch success which, in these modern days, thrives everywhere, for where most people would starve the Scotch, by careful living

Zeeland Peasants.

and steady perseverance, often lay the foundations of future fortune. Who can tell but that they first introduced schnapps into Holland as an anti-fever medicine and wholesome tonic?

Whilst in this delightful atmosphere of modern Dutch art and the old masters, can we do better than pay a tribute of respect to both classes, and congratulate the Dutch on the state of their modern school, recognising at the same time with pleasure and gratitude the large-hearted noble way in which they welcome a foreign painter amongst them? At the Hague and at Amsterdam

A Sketch from Nature.

are two societies, admirably organized and most agreeably carried out in all their details. Their evenings are most enjoyable and instructive; for instance, take an evening at Amsterdam, at the "Ars et Amicitia," the President sitting at the head of the table. It is an evening for sketches, two narrow tables run down like the prongs of a fork. At these sit the members, each with a friend sitting next to him (here we have the Amicitia). Good lights from above illumine the whole; and now the President, after a few kindly words of welcome to the guests, and explanation to the members, opens a portfolio, takes out a drawing, and starts it round. In a few minutes another is under way, and the procession is kept up until the last arrives and is returned to the portfolio. Let us notice some of these drawings by living men. We have already referred to the bold, powerful painting of De Haas, cows and landscapes, fresh and vigorous; now what a change when we see a Josef Israels before us, low in tone, beautiful in harmony, sombre in colour, pensive in subject. Next, perhaps, may come

Herman Tenkate. Here we are carried back to the costumes, manners, and customs of the seventeenth century swashbucklers and arms. How vividly he brings before us the stirring scenes of Holland's greater struggle for independence against Spanish tyranny! Next may come some of Verveer's work, full of energy, like himself; and then, what we naturally expect from Holland, some marine work, stamped with unmistakable practical knowledge. This is Heemskerk van Best, who has been in the Dutch navy, but nature's gift steered him into the pleasant haven of successful art. Long may he enjoy his delightful home at the Hague! Another change, David Bles, President of the Pulchri Studio at the Hague, brings us to a very finished phase of *genre* painting, combining refinement and exquisite finish. The space here will not admit of justice being done to the many good men now upholding the national art of Holland; still we must refer to the bold, good work of Stortenbeker, the able secretary of Pulchri Studio, &c.; and the rich work of Bischop, whose glory is luscious colour, and whose perfect taste is shown in every part of his picturesque house overlooking the canal at the Hague. Amongst the younger men too we had the pleasure of meeting Bloomers, full of energy and art-power; not to forget the gentle Ph. Sadée, with his tender, pearly greys, the very poetry of sea-side morns and Dutch landscapes. Personally we desire to testify not only to the talent of the present Dutch school, but to the hearty welcome they offer to those brother-brushes who chance to go amongst them.

R. T. PRITCHETT.

Bathing Machine.

THE CHILDREN'S CREED.

Preached on the Eve of Innocents' Day (St. John's Day), 1879, in Westminster Abbey.

BY A. P. STANLEY, D.D., DEAN OF WESTMINSTER.

"I have no greater joy than to hear that my children walk in truth."—3 JOHN, 4.

AS once before, so now, we have brought you together on St. John's Day because Innocents' Day falls on a Sunday. Those words which I have read from St. John well express what all of us ought to feel—"We have no greater joy than that our children, than that the rising generation, should walk in truth." And I have, therefore, thought it useful to set forth what are the religious truths which we should try to teach our children, and which our children should try to learn. Some of what I say will chiefly be addressed to parents and friends; some of what I say will be chiefly addressed to children. But most will find—some in one part, some in another—something to instruct them.

There are two points to be mentioned at the outset which might seem difficult to reconcile, but which in fact wonderfully agree, and are a support to each other. On the one hand, what we teach to children should be truths which will stand the wear and tear of time as they grow up. Solomon says, "Train up a child in the way he should go, and when he is old he will not depart from it." That is very true, but in order that he should not when he is old depart from it, it must be a way which, when he is old, he will find to be as good for him as it was when he was young. On the other hand, we must try to teach a child what he will understand, in the simplest and not in the hardest words, in the words which sink deepest into his soul and lay most hold on his heart. This, perhaps, we might think, cannot be the truth in which the child will feel most delight when it grows older. Not perhaps in the very same forms; but we may be sure, and our Saviour himself has told us, that the instruction which is most suitable for a little child is also the most suitable for the oldest and wisest of men.

I.—What then shall we teach our children to believe which when they grow up they may find that later experience does not require them to alter?

(1.) We must teach them that beyond what they feel and see and touch there is something better and greater which they can neither feel nor see nor touch. Goodness, kindness to one another, unselfishness, fairness and uprightness — these are the best things in all the world. It is true that goodness and kindness have no faces that we can kiss—no hands that we can clasp; but these are certainly close to us, both in the midst of our work and our play. And this goodness and kindness which, except in outward acts, we cannot see, is something which existed before we were born. It is from this that we have all the pleasant things of this world—the flowers, the sunshine, the moonlight—all these were given us by some great kindness and goodness which we have never seen at all. And this Goodness and Love are the Great Power out of which all things come, which we call by the name of God. And because God is so much above us and so good to us, we call Him by the name which is most dear to us of all earthly names—our Father. When a father goes away from home, still his children know that he is somewhere, though they cannot see him, and they know what to do in order to please him. So it is with the great unseen Father of us all. Let us then teach our children that God is Goodness and Justice; that the rules which He has laid down for the government of the world are His will and wish for us; even frost and cold, even sickness and pain, are for our good, and we must trust that He has some good reason for it, perhaps to make us strong, and brave, and healthy. It is for this reason that you see in the Abbey, on the monument of Sir John Franklin, who was so long shut up in the ice, the words "O ye Frost and Cold; O ye Ice and Snow; bless ye the Lord; praise Him and magnify His name for ever." This then, in various ways, is our way of expressing our belief in our Father in heaven.

(2.) But this highest kindness and fairness are like what we have seen and heard of in the world. Children can see it in their good parents, their good uncles and aunts, their good brothers and sisters; and as they grow older they will find that there have always been good people, and they will hear that there was once one Child, one Man, so good to all about Him, so good to little children, that He has shown us better than any one else what is the true likeness of that unseen Goodness which we call God, and which we still hope to know in heaven. Children should be taught what Jesus Christ did and said when He went about doing good, and should be made to understand that only so far as we are like to Jesus Christ, or like what Jesus Christ taught when He was in the world, that we can be His friends or followers. He was good, and He went through all sorts of trouble and pain even to His death on the Cross, for no other reason but to make us good. This will help us to understand why He is called the Son of God, the Saviour of Men.

(3.) And children should learn to know that there is in the heart of every one of us something which tells when we have done right or wrong, which makes the colour come into our cheeks when we have said what is not true, which we must treat with honour both in ourselves and others. What is-this? There are many names by which you will hear it called in after life, but there is one name which we speak of almost in a whisper, because we do not like to think or speak of it as if it were a common thing. We call it "the voice of God," the invisible Power all around, which also is within us—the "Breath" or the "Spirit of God," which we cannot see any more than we can see our own breath or spirit—and because it is so good we call it "the Holy Spirit of God." And from this "Breath or Spirit of God" comes all the Good not only in ourselves but in other people; and children cannot learn too early to admire and love all that is admirable and lovable in the men, women, and children that they see around them. They may, perhaps, also be able to learn the great lesson that there are things to be admired and loved in people they do not like, in people that hurt and annoy them, or even in those whom they ought to avoid. And if, as sometimes happens, children are brought up in other countries where they do not see the people always go to the same church, or utter the same prayers as they and their parents, they may learn thus early a lesson which they never will forget, namely, that our Heavenly Father has those who serve Him and do good in many different ways, but still in and by the same Good Spirit.

II.—These are the chief things which we ought to learn from our catechism as to what the young should *believe.* And now, what must we teach them as to what they should *do?* St. John, when he was a very old man, so old that he could not walk, and could hardly speak, used to be carried in the arms of his friends into the midst of the assembly of Christians, and then he would lift himself up and say, "Little children, love one another;" and again, "Little children, love one another;" and again, "Little children, love one another." When asked, "Have you nothing else to tell us?" he replied, "I say this over and over again, because if you do this there is nothing more needed." Now, that is something like what I would say to you. What you have to be told to do is very simple. It is that you should be kind and loving to one another, for then you will be loving towards · God, because you will be doing that which He most desires. Try not to vex or tease your smaller brothers or sisters; try to help them when they are in difficulty; do not be jealous of them; do not tell stories against them; above all, do not lead them into mischief, because the worst harm you can do to a young child is to tempt him to do what is wrong. If he once begins you cannot stop him, and many years afterwards he will remember with bitter grief and indignation that you were the first to lead him astray into evil ways. A lie that is told, a deceit that is practised, a bad word that is heard, a bad act that is lightly spoken of, often enters into the mind of a young child, and remains there all his life. There is a proverb which says, "Little pitchers have long ears," and it means that little children often hear more than you think they hear, and keep in their memory things which you think they must have forgotten. It is the same, in other words, as a Latin proverb which those boys who understand Latin will translate for themselves—*maxima debetur pueris reverentia.* The greatest reverence, the greatest fear, should restrain us from doing anything by false, or vulgar, or foolish words to spoil the conscience, or the taste, or the character of a little boy. You know what you mean by a spoiled picture, or a spoiled book—the colours are slurred, the leaves are rumpled. That is what we mean by a child whose character is spoiled or stained by the foolish indulgence or neglect of those about him. Parents, try not to spoil your children. Children, try not to spoil one another; and take care not to be spoiled yourselves. That is one of the most important ways of fulfilling St. John's precept both for old and young, "Little children, love—do not spoil—one another." And there is another part of this precept which children should be taught : it is that love and kindness include not only our brothers and sisters and relatives, but also poor people who are in suffering or want; and not only these, but also the poor dumb creatures that depend upon us. Never be rude to any poor man or woman because they are in rags, or because they look and talk differently from ourselves. Never be cruel to any dog, or cat, or bird. There was once a very cruel Roman emperor—cruel to men, women, and children—who, when he was a little boy used to amuse himself by tormenting flies. Perhaps if he had been stopped then he would not have had his heart hardened against his fellow men.

III.—And, now, how are you to be strengthened to believe and to do these things? There are many ways, but I will mention only two. By reading good books and by learning good prayers.

(1.) Good books. First of all, the best parts of the Bible; for even in the best of all books, the Bible, there are some parts more useful, more easy, more likely to stand the trials of time than others. Learn these, teach these, and you will then find that the more difficult parts will not perplex those who in their early childhood have had a firm grasp of those parts of which the truth and beauty belong not to the vesture that is folded up and vanisheth away, but to the wisdom and grace which endure for ever. And of other good books, let the stories of the good and great men of our own or former times be fixed in our remembrance. How many such stories there are which, as Sir Philip Sidney said of Chevy Chase, stir our souls and spirits as with a trumpet! How many are there which will make our blood boil against the evil-doer, or our hearts beat with admiration for generous and noble deeds! There was a famous French soldier of bygone days whose name you will see written in this Abbey on the gravestone of Sir James Outram, because in many ways he was like Bayard. Bayard was a small boy, only thirteen, when he went into his first service, and his mother told him to remember three things. "First, to fear and love God; secondly, to have gentle and courteous manners to those above him; and, thirdly, to be generous and charitable,

without pride or haughtiness, to those beneath him;" and these three things he never forgot, which helped to make him the soldier "without fear, and without reproach." These are the stories which are part of the heritage of all the families of the earth, and ought to be cherished from the first to the last.

(2.) And what must we teach, what must be learnt about prayer? Let no parent forget, let no child forget, to say a prayer, however short, at morning and at evening. It will help to make you better all the day. The Lord's Prayer will never fail you. The child will be able to understand it, the old man will find it expressing all that he wants. And there is also that form of prayer which is expressed in hymns. There are hymns which can be remembered better than anything else, and which in restless, sleepless nights of pain and suffering will come back to our minds, many, many years after they were learnt in childhood. Amongst these let me recommend the Morning and Evening Hymns, written by one of the best of Englishmen, Bishop Ken—the first beginning, "Awake, my soul, and with the sun," and the other, "Glory to Thee, my God, this night." Not long ago I was visiting an aged and famous statesman, and he repeated to me, word by word, "The Evening Hymn," as he had learnt it, he told me, from his nurse ninety years before. So may it be with you, my dear children, not only with hymns, but with the other good things which you may learn now, and perhaps when you are like that old, very old man, grown grey in the service of his country, and full of years and honours, you may remember that when you were a child you heard something which you have not forgotten on the festival of St. John, on the eve of Innocents' Day, in Westminster Abbey.

VIGIL.

SLEEP, little flow'ret! with fragrant flowers sleeping,
　　Serene on earth's breast.
Close, weary eyelids! with folded leaves closing—
Symbol their languorous bliss while reposing,
　　O rest with these, rest!
　　While the night dews are weeping.

Smile, little angel! with still water's smiling,
　　Beneath the white moon.
Dream, little soul! with their rapturous dreaming—
Image their heaven-bosomed beauty, and seeming—
　　O wake not too soon!
　　To the daylight defiling.　　ALLISON HUGHES.

EDUCATIONAL PROGRESS.

IT is difficult to realise how great has been the change in public opinion, since the century began, on the subject of educating the people. In olden days it was generally deemed an enviable accomplishment to read and write, with the exception of the brief space during which Jack Cade is said to have declared that an "honest, plain-dealing man" made his mark instead of writing his name. But the approval of education as a good thing in itself did not move the legislature to insist, till our own day, upon its being imparted to every child in the land. Indeed, the population of England was long divided into two classes, the members of the one having received at least a tincture of book-learning, the members of the other being unashamed to admit that they could neither read nor write. The former were in a small minority. If the diffusion and acceptance of sound ideas on the subject had not been followed by personal and parliamentary action, the mass would have still remained as ignorant and helpless as savages. The passage of the Act establishing board schools, and rendering education imperative, demonstrated how much wiser and more practical the present generation has become than the generations which are commonly praised because they are credited with meaning well. The conviction that such legislation was indispensable, which preceded and caused its adoption, will insure it against reversal. School boards may sometimes have blundered or been the objects of adverse criticism; yet they are great and firmly established facts, which it is easier to attack than to overthrow. They owe their establishment to a recognised necessity, and they will be justified by their works. Every child that leaves a board school in the possession of knowledge which might not have otherwise been acquired, is an argument in their favour, and may be relied upon hereafter as an advocate for their existence.

Though it has long been a truism in enlightened circles that every child ought to go to school, yet it is only now that the philanthropist can feel assured that every English child receives school training. At the close of the last century and the beginning of the present one the delusion was widespread that reading, writing, and other branches of education were unsuited for the children of the poor. It was then held that, in their case, any knowledge was dangerous. They were sent into the world, it was argued, to work with their hands. Their highest duty was supposed to be thorough contentment with the lot in which Providence had placed them. They were regarded as praiseworthy if they passed their lives from youth to their last breath in unceasing labour, varied only by eating and drinking no more than would keep them alive, and sleeping as little as would fit them for resuming their daily routine. The more closely they resembled very docile and industrious animals, the greater praise did they receive as good citizens and true patriots. The labourer who read books was commonly regarded as on the high road to become a rebel. It was assumed to be the privilege of his betters to cultivate their minds; his part consisting in cultivating the land or toiling in mines or factories, in manning merchant vessels, men-of-war, or fighting for his country as a soldier. It was even accounted dangerous and improper to interfere with what was held to be the established order of nature in this particular. Hannah More and her sisters made the attempt towards the end of the eighteenth century, and they did so at the risk of misapprehension and in the face of artificial obstacles. The country was then in a state of chronic panic lest what were styled French principles should take root, germinate, and bear fruit. The French poor, who had suffered grievous oppression, and who were in a state of the densest ignorance, had been impelled by hunger, superadded to misgovernment, to rebel against their rulers. Bad laws iniquitously administered were the leading causes which engendered that terrible and sanguinary uprising which is known as the First French Revolution; yet, had not a failure of the crops reduced the people to the verge of starvation, they might have continued to suffer in silence as they had done during many grievous years. They achieved a ghastly triumph, after perpetrating innumerable acts of folly and wickedness. The rest of Europe shuddered at the spectacle. A general dread prevailed among the governing classes on the Continent lest French principles should prove infectious, and lest the suffering poor in other lands should imitate the worst and most blame-worthy doings of the French. The richer and better-educated class in this country was smitten with the like dread, and trembled for the safety of all established institutions. It is scarcely possible to credit the nature and the extent of the delusion on this head. The fact is certain, though almost incredible, that the commonly approved plan for hindering the people from copying the French was to prevent them from being educated at all. The contention was that the monarch and the Church, Parliament and the courts of law, the nobility, and social order itself, would all be endangered, if not immediately overthrown, once the body of the people could read and write. Hannah More, who shares with Mr. Raikes, the founder of Sunday-schools, and with Bell and Lancaster, the reformers of rudimentary education, the credit of having contributed largely to excite a desire for learning and of helping to satisfy it, had her labours greatly increased owing to the ignorance and opposition of those persons who ought to have known better. She was even suspected of disloyalty—though no one was more ardently attached to the constitution, its abuses and shortcomings included, than herself—owing to her unwearied exertions in teaching neglected children.

Hannah More's own account of her efforts to elevate the condition of the people among whom she lived seems to readers now as the story of one who had been cast among African barbarians. Her first beginnings are narrated in a letter to Wilberforce. Living in Somersetshire she found that, in many large parishes there, no provision had been made for education, and scarcely any for religious ordinances. In thirteen adjoining parishes there was no resident curate. In one case three curates had to do duty in eight churches. She began her work in the village of Cheddar, which contained two thousand inhabitants, most of whom were very poor. There were a dozen wealthy farmers whom she calls "hard, brutal, and ignorant." She and her sister took a lodging at a little public-house, and then set out to visit these farmers. The result can best be given in her own words:—
"We visited them all, picking up at one house (like fortune-tellers) the name and character of the next. We told them we intended to set up a school for their poor. They did not like it. We assured them we did not desire a shilling from them, but wished for their concurrence, as we knew they could influence their workmen. One of the farmers seemed pleased and civil; he was rich, but covetous, a hard drinker, and his wife a woman of loose morals, but good natural sense; she became our friend sooner than some of the decent and the formal, and let us a house, the only one in the parish that was vacant, at £7 per annum, with a good garden. Adjoining was a large ox-house; this we roofed and floored, and by putting in a couple of windows, it made a good school-room. While this was doing, we went to every house in the place, and found each a scene of the greatest ignorance and vice. We saw but one Bible in all the parish, and that was used to prop a flower-pot. No clergyman had resided in it for forty years. One rode over three miles from Wells to preach once on a Sunday; but no weekly duty was done, or sick persons visited, and children were often buried without any funeral service. Eight people in the morning, and twenty in the afternoon, was a good congregation. We spent our whole time in getting at the characters of all the people, the employment, wages, and number of every family; and this we have done in our other nine parishes. On a fixed day, of which we gave notice in the church, all the women, with all their children above six years old, met us. We took an exact list from their account, and engaged one hundred and twenty to attend on the following Sunday. A great many refused to send their children, unless we would pay them for it! and not a few refused, because they were not sure of my intentions, being apprehensive that at the end of seven years, if they attended so long, I should acquire a power over them, and send them beyond sea. I must have heard this myself in order to have believed that so much ignorance existed out of Africa." In a journal kept at the time, Hannah More makes a few additions to the foregoing account. Some of the farmers whom she visited explained their opposition to children being taught anything by expressing their belief that the result would be the ruin of agriculture. Others who were more tolerant, if not much wiser, approved of children going to school, for they thought it would prevent them robbing orchards. Her experience among the miners of the Mendips was still more trying. She ventured to prosecute her self-imposed and self-denying mission in places where a constable dared not go to apprehend a criminal. Risking her life as well as spending her substance, she had the satisfaction of effecting much good. She not only instructed children in the elements of education, but she established classes at which girls were taught sewing, knitting, and spinning. A special inducement was held out to these girls to be regular in their attendance and diligent in learning. Each girl who had complied with the rules received on her wedding-day a gift of five shillings, a pair of

white stockings, and a new Bible. Before Hannah More's labours ended she had established schools over a tract of country covering ten miles, in which twelve hundred children, who would otherwise have grown up utterly ignorant, received no inconsiderable amount of instruction. Such is a brief outline of Hannah More's services in this respect. The difficulties which she had to surmount cannot here be set forth in their full magnitude. But what was least easy for her to bear, and that is astounding to readers now, is the suspicion excited by her good works. It was actually supposed that her attachment to the established order of things could not be very strong or genuine, seeing that she exerted herself so much in founding and filling schools. She declares herself obnoxious to both Dissenters and High Churchmen, because she belonged to no party and inclined to moderation. A friend, who was a High Churchman, sent her a letter containing advice which is a startling sign of the spirit which then prevailed. This candid friend advised her "to publish a short confession of her faith, as her attachment both to the religion and the government of the country had become questionable to many persons."

Quite as noteworthy as the experience of Hannah More, in showing the alteration which public opinion has undergone during the present century on the subject of popular education, is the testimony of William Cobbett. He was a man who owed his success in life, and his influence over his fellows, to the pains which he had taken in educating himself. The son of a small farmer, his education as a boy was very imperfect. He could read and write, but that was all. Running away from home, he aspired to make his fortune in the great world of London. He had only a few pence in his pocket, and was very hungry, when he saw a copy of Swift's "Tale of a Tub" for sale, and he bought it, instead of getting a dinner with his money, and read it till he forgot his hunger. This was the beginning of a career every step of which was marked by patience in learning and perseverance in following a plan, but of which Cobbett could not have taken in the upward path a single step had it not been for his good fortune in having been taught the rudiments of education in boyhood. He was never ashamed of his humble origin; on the contrary, he was disposed to boast of having laboured in the fields at an early age. He had a practical acquaintance with the peasant's life in its rudest form, and he knew

by experience that education was power. It would be supposed that such a man might have been counted upon as an advocate for popular education. The strange thing is that, as his manner was when he disliked a novelty, he opposed it with all his might. Few things, except perhaps potatoes and tea, did Cobbett denounce more vehemently as wholly injurious and indefensible, than the education of young children. His remarks on the subject are contained in his "Cottage Economy," a small work which was written with a view to render the labouring class happier and more thrifty. He said that children were "solid advantages" to a labourer if they were turned to proper account. He maintained that they should not be educated in book-learning till after they had been trained "to get their living by labour," by which time they would find it doubly difficult, and be strongly disinclined to learn from books. Holding this eccentric opinion, he was "wholly against children wasting time in the idleness of what is called *education*." I need not waste time, in turn, by exposing the absurdity of Cobbett's notions. They were hurtful as well as ridiculous, and, though they are not now proclaimed with the like emphasis, they are still entertained by many persons of less experience and capacity. It is not long since Colonel North, one of the members for Oxfordshire, intimated to the Banbury Agricultural Association that he could not help thinking " the country had run perfectly wild on the subject of the value and blessing of education." There is a good deal of method in the country's madness on this score, and it is a form of madness which the majority of the people cannot distinguish from entire sanity.

It is pleasing and satisfactory to learn, by the comparison which I have made, how complete has been the change in regarding the duty of imparting education to the people at large. Any one who now ventures to talk in the strain of Hannah More's adverse critics, or of Cobbett himself, is commonly listened to with a feeling of pity for an aberration charitably regarded as involuntary. The few who may still think as their prejudiced fathers did, cannot succeed in retarding the movement which gains force every day. That all children should learn reading, writing, and arithmetic is accounted good and necessary. But, it is added in many quarters, let this be the consummation. Anything taught in board schools in excess of the minimum is not only objected to as superfluous, but is stigmatized as wicked waste. Limitation of the education of the poor is the cry of the persons whose forefathers denied that the poor should be educated at all. The professed aim is economy. Nothing, however, is less to be desired than an ignorant nation. Physical causes limit the amount of teaching which the poorer children can receive ; the greater the need, then, for rendering the education which is imparted to them as complete as possible. In these days of international competition a great problem occupies the thoughts and tasks the energies of all wise and energetic men. Physical force alone can accomplish but a tithe of that which physical force, guided by a trained intellect, can achieve. The dominion of the world must fall to the most worthy, and the worthiest are the best educated. It is a consolatory sign of the times that the nation at large has become alive to the conviction that, unless all its constituent parts are in harmony, and are able to perform their functions thoroughly, the whole must suffer. While a rapid glance over the years which have elapsed since the education of the people was a topic of discussion suffices to show the progress which has been made in our educational notions, a right understanding of existing conditions and future possibilities serves to impress on the mind how infinite is the progress which must be made before the philanthropist can rest contented with the result.

T. WALKER.

A PLEA FOR THE DUMB ANIMALS.

YE call them dumb ; and deem it well,
  Howe'er their bursting hearts may swell,
They have no voice their woes to tell,
  As fabulists have dreamed.
They cannot cry, " O Lord, how long
Wilt Thou, the patient Judge and strong,
Behold Thy creatures suffer wrong
  Of those Thy blood redeemed ? "

Yet are they silent ? need they speech
His holy sympathies to reach,
Who by their lips could prophets teach,
  And for their sakes would spare ;
When, wrestling with his own decree,
To save repentant Nineveh,
He found, to strengthen mercy's plea,
  " So many cattle " there?

Have they no language ? Angels know,
Who take account of every blow ;
And there are angel hearts below
  On whom the Eternal Dove

His pentecostal gift hath poured,
And that forgotten speech restored
That filled the garden of the Lord
  When Nature's voice was love !

Oh, blest are they the creatures bless !
And yet that wealth of tenderness,
In look, in gesture, in caress,
  By which our hearts they touch,
Might well the thoughtful spirit grieve,
Believing—as we must believe—
How little they from man receive,
  To whom they give so much !

They may be silent, as ye say,
But woe to them who, day by day,
Unthinking for what boon they pray,
  Repeat, " Thy kingdom come,"
Who, when before the great white Throne
They plead that mercy may be shown,
Find awful voices drown their own—
  The voices of the dumb !

ANNA H. DRURY.

THE EAR AND ITS MECHANISM.

By Professor J. G. McKENDRICK, M.D.

III.—Structure and Functions of the Internal Ear.

WE come now to the most complicated, but at the same time the essential part of the organ of hearing. On account of its complexity, it is often termed the *labyrinth*. It consists of a bony portion or case, containing a membranous portion. The bony part, if chiselled out of the surrounding bone, or if a cast were taken of it by pouring molten metal into a dried specimen, would present the appearance seen in Fig. 6. It consists of a

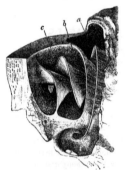

Fig. 4.—Osseous part of the cochlea of right side opened. *b*, central pillar, around which (*a*, *c*) a spiral partition of bone is twisted.

central portion called the *vestibule*, communicating anteriorly with a coiled structure like a twisted shell, called the *cochlea* (Fig. 4), and posteriorly with tubes which, from their form, are known as the *semicircular canals*. As seen in Fig. 6, *d*, the wall of the vestibule is pierced by an opening, the oval window already alluded to, into which the base of the stirrup bone is adjusted. Thus the movements of the base of the stirrup must be

Fig. 5.—Membranous labyrinth.

communicated to the structures in the interior of the osseous labyrinth.

In the osseous labyrinth there is a membranous structure of the form seen in Fig. 5. This consists of two sacs—the *utricle, u*, communicating with the semicircular canals, and the *saccule, s*, opening into *c*, the *ductus cochlearis*, a tube lying in the cochlea or shell. The cochlea may be regarded as a tube tapering to one end, twisted spirally two and a half times about a bony pillar. Imagine this tube to be partially divided into two parts by a thin plate of bone springing from the central column. This twisted osseous partition is seen in section in Fig. 4. Further, sup-

Fig. 6.—External view of a cast of the left osseous labyrinth. *a*, junction of superior and posterior semicircular canals; *b*, external canal; *c*, end of superior canal; *d*, position of oval window; *f*, position of round window; *g*, cochlea.

pose that a thin membrane is stretched from the bony partition to the side of the tube, and it will then be apparent that the tube is divided into two cavities. As already stated, the tube twists round the central column, causing the cochlea to assume the shell-like form. In consequence of this arrangement, the old anatomists compared the two divisions of the tube, as they ascended to the apex of the column, to staircases. The upper one, as it started from the vestibule, was termed the *vestibular staircase*, and the lower, as its base was found to correspond to the round opening or window seen on the inner wall of the tympanum or middle ear, near the oval window, was termed the *tympanic staircase*. It was also found that the two staircases communicated with each other at the apex of the cochlea. If, then, one could reduce himself to microscopic dimensions, and enter the vestibule, he might ascend the vestibular staircase to the apex of the cochlea, pass through a door at this point, and then descend the tympanic staircase, at the bottom of which he would find a round membrane which would prevent his escape into the middle ear.

But this is not all. It has been found

that the membranous part of the partition dividing the tube into two portions is not single but double, and that, consequently, a third and intermediate cavity is situated between the vestibular and tympanic staircases. The floor of this cavity, supposing we were in the tympanic staircase, is formed of a thin membrane called the *basilar membrane*, as seen in Fig. 7, *b*, and its roof (which would

Fig. 7.—Diagram showing a section of tube of the cochlea. Ls, spiral lamina; sv, vestibular staircase; st, tympanic staircase; v, Reissner's membrane; DC, cochlear duct; *b*, basilar membrane, on which (dotted lines) organ of Corti rests.

be part of the *floor* of the vestibular staircase) by another thin membrane, *v*, termed *Reissner's membrane*, after the anatomist who first described it. Thus the tube of the cochlea is divided into three parts, namely, the vestibular staircase, communicating with the vestibule; the tympanic staircase, communicating with the tympanum or middle ear by the round window; and between these, a space which is really the cochlear duct, seen in Fig. 5, *c*. It will be observed that this duct is triangular in form, the base being formed by the basilar membrane, and the two sides by the membrane of Reissner and the side of the tube respectively. On the basilar membrane we find one of the most remarkable structures met with in the body, a series of minute arches, formed of irregularly shaped rods, placed against each other like the couples in the roof of a house. It was first described by an Italian nobleman, the Marchése di Corti, in 1851. Each arch is formed of two rods, an inner and an outer, as seen in Fig. 8. It need scarcely be said

that these rods are of microscopical size, and that they can only be seen by using microscopes capable of magnifying an object to at least three hundred times its real size.

At this point, I can imagine the reader wondering how it is possible to reach such minute things hidden in a mass of bone and of tissue. It is one of the characteristics of scientific progress that it devises new methods of overcoming obstacles that lie in the way of research. The structures I speak of are so small as scarcely to be visible to the naked eye, even under favourable circumstances. They are placed in an apparently inaccessible portion of the head, surrounded by masses of bone and other tissues, and they are soft, transparent, easily destroyed, and of a perishable nature. How, then, can they be got at? Not directly. Knife and forceps are far too coarse, and methods must be devised by which they may be kept in position and rendered firm and resistant, so that they may be cut into thin slices suitable for being examined under high powers. This is accomplished by immersing the portion of bone containing the internal ear in an acid which will dissolve out the earthy matter of the bone, and thus render it soft; the softened tissue is then embedded in gum and frozen, so as to make it firm and resistant, but at the same time capable of being cut; thin sections can then be cut with a razor, and stained with a solution of such a substance as carmine. Such a section, if a good one, is laid on a strip of glass, perhaps in a drop of glycerine; a thin bit of glass is laid over it, and then it is fit for examination. I mention these facts to show how complicated are the methods now employed for examining minute structures of the body. Just as in the manufacturing or chemical arts, much ingenuity has been displayed in contriving methods, machinery, and chemical appliances to separate the metal in a state of comparative purity, or to produce the manufactured article required, so in that path of science in which men scrutinise the minute structure of the tissues of the plant or of the animal, numerous methods have been devised by which we can see and describe what otherwise would lie beyond our ken.

To return from this digression. When Corti found those arches formed of rods, he looked upon them from above, and when he saw them lying side by side, the comparison to a series of strings of different lengths, like those of a piano or of a harp, was almost irre-

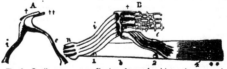

Fig. 8.—Corti's organ. A, profile view of two rods: *i*, internal; *e*, external. B represents in position five complete arches resting on the basila membrane *b*.

sistible. He supposed that here we have an apparatus consisting of strings tuned to tones of different pitch. Now we know that if we sing a note before the uncovered wires of a piano, the wires corresponding to the note or notes we sing will give the sound back to us. If we place two tuning-forks side by side, both tuned to precisely the same pitch, and sound the one, the other will in an instant be set into vibration also, so as to give out a corresponding sound. Thus, by "sympathetic" vibration, as it is termed, suppose two bodies capable of vibrating are tuned to vibrate, or move backwards and forwards, in the same periods of time, if the one is set a-going the other will soon perform the same movements. Apply this to the ear. Imagine that we had in this organ of Corti, a series of arches, each capable of vibrating for a tone of a certain pitch : when a tone was produced outside it would be picked up by its corresponding arch; if then each arch were connected by a filament of nerve with the brain, we can suppose that this filament would be excited, and that a message, a thrill, a molecular movement, a "something," would pass along it to the brain, where the message would be construed by the mind into a tone of that particular pitch.

Such was the theory of hearing that seemed to spring out of Corti's observations. It was accepted by Helmholtz, and, indeed, it was largely owing to his advocacy that it came to be generally adopted. It is a theory that at once commends itself to one's common sense. Hence it is, I suppose, that it is a theory older than Corti or Helmholtz. The older anatomists and physiologists—and it must be remembered that these are brethren in science, united by the closest bonds— could not help thinking of the probable analogy of the cochlea to such an instrument as a harp or a piano, with long and short strings.

Imagine two harps in a room, with the same number of strings, and each string perfectly attuned to a corresponding string in the other. Touch a string in one, and the corresponding string in the other will give out the same sound. Try another string, and its corresponding tone will be sounded. So with all the strings. So with any combination of the strings. It would not matter how you played the one harp, the other would respond. No doubt the response would be weaker. That is what one would expect ; but the response, as regards pitch and quality, would be almost perfect. Now substitute for one harp a human ear, and the conditions would, according to theory, be the same, except that the responsive mechanism of the

ear is much smaller than that of the responsive harp. In the ear there are minute cords, rods, or something, in such a state of tension, as to be tuned to tones of various pitch ; sound a tone, its corresponding rod or cord in the ear will respond, perhaps feebly, but still with energy sufficient to excite the nerve-filament connected with it ; the result is a nervous current to the brain, and a sensation of a tone of a particular pitch.

There can be no doubt that this theory of the ultimate mechanism of hearing is one likely to be correct ; the difficulty lies in squaring it with the facts in our possession. My reason for asserting that it is likely to be correct is that there is no other theory than one involving the principle of sympathetic vibration conceivable in the present state of science. The questions then are, Do those rods or arches really vibrate ? are they of such a structure, so far as one can make out by the microscope, as to lead one to suppose that they could vibrate? are they of unequal lengths, and are their lengths proportioned like those of the strings of a harp, so as to lead to the inference that they are tuned to tones of different pitch ?

The first question cannot be answered. It is impossible, in the circumstances, to make such *direct* observations as to warrant us in stating that the arches or rods are capable of vibrating, or not. In the next place, from their position and structure, it does not appear likely that these rods or arches vibrate. They are firmly fixed, and apparently rigid. Again, it cannot be made out that they are of such varying lengths as to justify us in stating that they are tuned to tones of different pitch. Then, comparative anatomy contributes the quota of evidence that there are animals apparently capable of appreciating pitch, or height or depth of tone, which have a cochlea containing no such rods or arches. Is it possible, then, that these, after all, may not be vibrating structures ?

Suppose an elastic body, such as a strip of whalebone set in a socket of wood, and that the free end was plucked, it would vibrate vigorously backwards and forwards for a certain time. Now imagine such a rod (reduced, however, to microscopical size) vibrating backwards and forwards at a certain rate, through very minute distances. You would then have an idea of the movements of a class of minute structures found in the body called *cilia*, met with in the air passages and in other parts. Similar structures are found, according to the observations of Hensen, of the Physiological Institute of Kiel, upon the organ of hearing in crustaceans. He found that in the *mysis*, or opossum shrimp, there were hairs which vibrated sympathetically when certain notes were sounded on a horn. Thus a hair, or set of hairs, vibrated with a certain tone and with no other, and the inference, of course, is that these hairs, or sets of hairs, were tuned to that tone or tones and to no other. Now, if we imagine that each hair, or tuft of hairs, was connected with the brain by means of a nerve-filament, we can understand so far how a tone of a particular pitch might be generated. The to-and-fro movements of the hair might irritate the nerve; a nervous disturbance would be carried by the nerve to the brain, with the result of arousing a sensation of a particular tone.

It is remarkable that in the ears of mammals and of man such hair-like appendages have been actually discovered. On the inner side of the arched roof formed by the arches of Corti, there is a single row of minute cells, each carrying a few hairs, and on the outer side there are five rows of such ciliated cells. Stretched over the surface of these arches and cells, there is a beautiful net-like structure, through certain of the meshes of which the tufts of hair pass. It has been conjectured that possibly this membrane may act as a kind of *damping* apparatus for arresting the vibrations of the hairs, and thus preventing the stimulation of the nerve for too long a time.

From this study of the anatomical arrangements of the internal ear, it would appear that in each of the cavities of the labyrinth, namely the vestibule, semicircular canals, and cochlea, the extremities of the auditory nerve are furnished with special apparatuses, in the form of hairs, which by their consistence and elasticity are ready to receive vibratory movements communicated to them either by the external ear and middle ear, or by the bones of the head. In the utricle and saccule (portions of the membranous labyrinth situated in the vestibule) the vibratory hairs are frequently in close contact with small masses of crystals, called *otoliths*, or ear-stones. It is evident that any movement occurring in the fluid in which these are immersed, will be readily communicated to the hairs; but such movements can only be irregular, inasmuch as the ear-stones will tend to arrest any regular vibration. From these considerations, some have supposed that this part of the internal ear is specially connected with the perception of sounds, without reference to pitch or quality —indeed, what may be termed *noises*. The special organ for the perception of musical tones is the cochlea.

Let us remember that the three staircases or compartments described in the cochlea are full of fluid, and that one of these compartments, the vestibular staircase, is in communication with the vestibule. It is evident then that any variation of pressure transmitted to the fluid in the vestibule by the base of the stirrup bone at the oval window will be communicated along the vestibular staircase to the apex of the cochlea, and will descend towards the round window by the tympanic staircase. Now sonorous vibrations produce rapid augmentations and diminutions of pressure, and these must evidently act so as to determine a regular periodic movement of the basilar membrane, on which we found the organ of Corti, already described. It is impossible to say precisely what the function of the membrane is. Is it merely a support for the arches of Corti; or does it act, as now suggested by Helmholtz, as a system of parallel fibres, stretched transversely and with different degrees of tension, and of lengths gradually diminishing from its widest part at the base to its narrowest at the apex of the cochlea?

Imagine each transverse segment of the basilar membrane to carry a couple of rods forming one of Corti's arches. Such an arch would support the hair-cells previously alluded to, and by reason of its rigidity it would be well fitted for communicating to the ciliated cells any vibratory movement of the segment of basilar membrane. According to this view, the ultimate recipients of vibratory movements would be the *ciliated cells;* and it is remarkable that this view is supported by recent histological evidence, which is to the effect that the filaments of the auditory nerve terminate in these cells. Such a theory also is consistent with the facts of comparative anatomy. Thus, in the cochlea of birds there are no arches of Corti, but the cells are placed

Fig. 9.—Portion of the cochlea of a pigeon, showing hair-cells. *a,* basilar membrane; *b* and *c,* nerve cells; *d,* cells bearing hairs.

directly on the basilar membrane, as seen in Fig. 9. The older theory, that the rods were the vibrating structures, was inconsistent with this fact, as we could not suppose that birds were incapable of appreciating variations of pitch and of quality of musical tones.

According to Kölliker, the cochlea of each human ear contains 3,000 arches of Corti. Suppose that each is situated upon two fibres of the basilar membrane, the number of such fibres must then be at least 6,000. Is that a sufficient number for all the "hearing" possibilities of the human ear? We are informed that highly trained musicians may distinguish a difference of pitch of only the one-sixty-fourth part of a semitone. In 7 octaves, of 12 semitones each (the usual range of our musical instruments), there must be 5,376 gradations of pitch, each corresponding to the one-sixty-fourth part of a semitone. But we have seen that there are at least 6,000 fibres in the basilar membrane; that is 624 fibres more than are sufficient for appreciating differences of pitch between the extreme limits found in musical instruments. These 624 fibres are probably influenced by sounds placed above or below these limits.

Thus we have in the cochlea a wonderful apparatus for the recognition of *pitch* of tone. It follows that it also must be the apparatus by which we appreciate *quality*. When a simple vibration reaches the ear, it excites sympathetically the fibre of the basilar membrane, which is tuned for its proper number of vibrations. If, then, different fibres are tuned to tones of different pitch, it is evident that we have here a mechanism which, by exciting different nerve fibres, will give rise to sensations of pitch. When the vibration is not simple, but compound, in consequence of the blending of vibrations, corresponding to various harmonics or partial tones, the ear has the power of resolving this compound vibration into its elements. It can only do so by different fibres responding to the different vibrations of the sound; one for the fundamental tone being stronger, and giving the sensation of a particular pitch to the sound, and the others corresponding to the upper partial tones, being weaker, and causing special though undefined sensations,

which are so blended together in consciousness as to terminate in a complex sensation, or a tone of a certain *quality* or timbre.

Nothing has been said as to the functions of the semicircular canals, because, so far as physiological science knows at present, they seem to have nothing to do, strictly speaking, with the sense of hearing, but with that sense of *equilibrium* by which we regulate the carriage of the body and the movements of the head. From their intimate anatomical connection with the internal ear, it is difficult to admit that they have nothing to do with hearing, and possibly it may be discovered that there is a physiological relationship between our perception of the direction and intensity of sounds and those co-ordinated movements by which we maintain our equilibrium.

Such, then, is a brief description of the structure and mechanism of the human ear. In writing such a description, one always feels how inadequate language is to give a true idea of the beauty of the apparatus. No machine of human construction exhibits such nicety of adjustment and delicacy of finish, and none can perform such efficient work by parts of such small dimensions. All the ultimate structures,—rods and hairs and filaments of nerves,—are of microscopical size, and they cannot be seen except by the use of most refined methods and appliances.

The next time we listen to musical tones of any kind, it will not disturb our appreciation of their beauty by knowing something of the arrangements by which our body is fitted to receive them; nor will a knowledge of such arrangements make the mystery less of how it is these bodily changes and mechanisms communicate with the soul. Here, as in many other regions of thought, it is presumptuous to dogmatise. Rather let us cherish what we know—a heritage of knowledge transmitted by our fathers, and constantly receiving additions from every earnest worker in science—and let us use those faculties God has given us in attempting to get a little further into a knowledge of his works.

THE HAUNT OF THE IBIS ON THE EUPHRATES.

A STUDY IN BLACK AND WHITE BY IRVING MONTAGU.

THE TRUMPET-MAJOR.

By THOMAS HARDY, Author of "Far from the Madding Crowd," etc.

CHAPTER VIII.—ANNE MAKES A CIRCUIT OF
THE CAMP.

WHEN Anne was crossing the last field, she saw approaching her an old woman with wrinkled cheeks, who surveyed the earth and its inhabitants through the medium of brass-rimmed spectacles. Shaking her head at Anne till the glasses shone like two moons, she said, "Ah, ah; I seed ye! If I had only kept on my short ones that I use for reading the Collect and Gospel I shouldn't have seed ye; but thinks I, I be going out o' doors, and I'll put on my long ones, little thinking what they'd show me. Ay, I can tell folk at any distance with these—'tis a beautiful pair for out o' doors; though my short ones be best for close work, such as darning and catching fleas, that's true."

"What have you seen, Granny Seamore?" said Anne.

"Fie, fie, Miss Nancy! you know," said Granny Seamore, shaking her head still. "But he's a fine young feller, and will have all his uncle's money when 'a's gone." Anne said nothing to this, and looking ahead with a smile passed Granny Seamore by.

Festus, the subject of the remark, was at this time about three-and-twenty, a fine fellow as to feet and inches, and of a remarkably warm tone in skin and hair. Symptoms of beard and whiskers had appeared upon him at a very early age, owing to his persistent use of the razor before there was any necessity for its operation. The brave boy had scraped unseen in the out-house, in the cellar, in the wood-shed, in the stable, in the unused parlour, in the cow-stalls, in the barn, and wherever he could set up his triangular bit of looking-glass without observation, or extemporise a mirror by sticking up his hat on the outside of a window-pane. The result now was that, did he neglect to use the instrument he once had trifled with, a fine rust broke out upon his countenance on the first day, a golden lichen on the second, and a fiery stubble on the third, to a degree which admitted of no further postponement.

His disposition divided naturally into two, the boastful and the cantankerous. When Festus put on the big pot, as it is classically called, he was quite blinded *ipso facto* to the diverting effect of that mood and manner upon others; but when disposed to be envious or quarrelsome he was rather shrewd

than otherwise, and could do some pretty strokes of satire. He was both liked and abused by the girls who knew him, and though they were pleased by his attentions they never failed to ridicule him behind his back. In his cups (he knew those vessels, though only twenty-three) he first became noisy, then excessively friendly, and then invariably nagging. During childhood he had made himself renowned for his pleasant habit of pouncing down upon boys smaller and poorer than himself, and knocking their birds' nests out of their hands, or overturning their little carts of apples, or pouring water down their backs; but his conduct became singularly the reverse of aggressive the moment the little boys' mothers ran out to him, brandishing brooms, frying-pans, skimmers, and whatever else they could lay hands on by way of weapons. He then fled and hid behind bushes, under faggots, or in pits, till they had gone away; and on one such occasion was known to creep into a badger's hole quite out of sight, maintaining that post with great firmness and resolution for two or three hours. He had brought more vulgar exclamations upon the tongues of respectable parents in his native parish than any other boy of his time. When other youngsters snowballed him he ran into a place of shelter, where he kneaded snowballs of his own, with a stone inside, and used these formidable missiles in returning their pleasantry. Sometimes he got fearfully beaten by boys his own age, when he would roar most lustily, but fight on in the midst of his tears, blood, and cries.

He was early in love, and had at the time of the story suffered from the ravages of that passion thirteen distinct times. He could not love lightly and gaily; his love was earnest, cross-tempered, and even savage. It was a positive agony to him to be ridiculed by the object of his affections, and such conduct drove him into a frenzy if persisted in. He was a torment to those who behaved humbly towards him, cynical with those who denied his superiority, and a very nice fellow towards those who had the courage to ill-use him.

This young gentleman and Anne Garland did not cross each other's paths again for a week. Then her mother began as before about the newspaper, and though Anne did not much like the errand, she agreed to go

XXI—11

for it on Mrs. Garland pressing her with unusual anxiety. Why her mother was so persistent on so small a matter quite puzzled the girl; but she put on her hat and started.

As she had expected, Festus appeared at a stile over which she sometimes went for shortness' sake, and showed by his manner that he awaited her. When she saw this she kept straight on, as if she would not enter the park at all.

"Surely this is your way?" said Festus.

"I was thinking of going round by the road," she said.

"Why is that?"

She paused, as if she were not inclined to say. "I go that way when the grass is wet," she returned at last.

"It is not wet now," he persisted; "the sun has been shining on it these nine hours." The fact was that the way by the path was less open than by the road, and Festus wished to walk with her uninterrupted. "But, of course, it is nothing to me what you do." He flung himself from the stile and walked away towards the house.

Anne, supposing him really indifferent, took the same way, upon which he turned his head and waited for her with a proud smile.

"I cannot go with you," she said decisively.

"Nonsense, you foolish girl! I must walk along with you down to the corner."

"No, please, Mr. Derriman; we might be seen."

"Now, now—that's shyness!" he said jocosely.

"No; you know I cannot let you."

"But I must."

"But I do not allow it."

"Allow it or not, I will."

"Then you are unkind, and I must submit," she said, her eyes brimming with tears.

"Ho, ho; what a shame of me! My wig, I won't do any such thing for the world," said the repentant yeoman. "Haw, haw; why I thought your 'go away' meant 'come on,' as it does with so many of the women I meet, especially in these clothes. Who was to know you were so confoundedly serious?"

As he did not go Anne stood still and said nothing.

"I see you have a deal more caution and a deal less good-nature than I ever thought you had," he continued emphatically.

"No, sir; it is not any planned manner of mine at all," she said earnestly. "But you will see, I am sure, that I could not go down to the hall with you without putting myself in a wrong light."

"Yes; that's it, that's it. I am only a fellow in the yeomanry cavalry—a plain soldier, I may say; and we know what women think of such: that they are a bad lot—men you musn't speak to for fear of losing your character—chaps you avoid in the roads—chaps that come into a house like oxen, daub the stairs wi' their boots, stain the furniture wi' their drink, talk rubbish to the servants, abuse all that's holy and righteous, and are only saved from being carried off by old Nick because they are wanted for Boney."

"Indeed, I didn't know you were thought so bad of as that," said she simply.

"What! don't my uncle complain to you of me? You are a favourite of that handsome, nice old gaffer's, I know."

"Never."

"Well, what do we think of our nice trumpet-major, hey?"

Anne closed her mouth up tight, built it up, in fact, to show that no answer was coming to that question.

"Oh, now, come, seriously, Loveday is a good fellow, and so is his father."

"I don't know."

"What a close little rogue you are! There is no getting anything out of you. I believe you would say 'I don't know' to every mortal question, so very discreet as you are. Upon my heart there are some women who would say 'I don't know,' to 'Will ye marry me.'"

The brightness upon Anne's cheek and in her eyes during this remark showed that there was a fair quantity of life and warmth beneath the discretion he complained of. Having spoken thus he drew aside that she might pass, and bowed very low. Anne formally inclined herself and went on.

She had been at vexation point all the time that he was present, from a haunting sense that he would not have spoken to her so freely had she been a young woman with thriving male relatives to keep forward admirers in check. But she had been struck, now as at their previous meeting, with the power she possessed of working him up either to irritation or to complacency at will; and this consciousness of being able to play upon him as upon an instrument disposed her to a humorous considerateness, and made her tolerate even while she rebuffed him.

When Anne got to the hall the farmer as usual insisted upon her reading what he had been unable to get through, and held the paper tightly in his skinny hand till she had agreed. He sent her to a hard chair that she could not possibly injure to the extent of a pennyworth by sitting in it a twelvemonth, and watched her from the outer angle of his near eye while she bent over the paper. His look might have been suggested by the sight that he had witnessed from his window on the last occasion of her visit, for it partook of the nature of concern. The old man was afraid of his nephew, physically and morally, and he began to regard Anne as a fellow-sufferer under the same despot. After this sly and curious gaze at her he withdrew his eye again, so that when she casually lifted her own there was nothing visible but his keen bluish profile as before.

When the reading was about half-way through the door behind them opened and footsteps crossed the threshold. The farmer diminished perceptibly in his chair, and looked fearful, but pretended to be absorbed in the reading, and quite unconscious of an intruder. Anne felt the presence of the swashing Festus, and stopped her reading.

"Please go on, Miss Anne," he said. "I am not going to speak a word." He withdrew to the mantelpiece and leaned against it at his ease.

"Go on, do ye, maidy Anne," said Uncle Benjy, keeping down his tremblings by a great effort to half their natural extent.

Anne's voice became much lower now that there were two listeners, and her modesty shrank somewhat from exposing to Festus the appreciative modulations which an intelligent interest in the subject drew from her when unembarrassed. But she still went on, that he might not suppose her to be disconcerted, though the ensuing ten minutes was one of disquietude. She knew that the bothering yeoman's eyes were travelling over her from his position behind, creeping over her shoulders, up to her head, and across her arms and hands. Old Benjy on his part knew the same thing, and, after sundry endeavours to peep at his nephew from the corner of his eye, he could bear the situation no longer.

"Do ye want to say anything to me, nephew?" he quaked.

"No, uncle, thank ye," said Festus heartily. "I like to stay here, thinking of you and looking at your back hair."

The nervous old man writhed under this vivisection, and Anne read on; till to the relief of both the gallant fellow grew tired of his amusement and went out of the room. Anne soon finished her paragraph and rose to go, determined never to come again as long as Festus haunted the precincts. Her face grew warmer as she thought that he would be sure to waylay her on her journey home to-day.

On this account, when she left the house, instead of going in the customary direction, she bolted round to the north side, through the bushes, along under the kitchen-garden wall, and through a door leading into a rutted cart-track, which had been a pleasant gravelled drive when the fine old hall was in its prosperity. Once out of sight of the windows she ran with all her might till she had quitted the park by a route directly opposite to that towards her home. Why she was so seriously bent upon doing this she could hardly tell; but the instinct to run was irresistible.

It was necessary now to clamber over the down to the left of the camp, and make a complete circuit round the latter—infantry, cavalry, suttlers, and all—descending to her house on the other side. This tremendous walk she performed at a rapid rate, never once turning her head, and avoiding every beaten track to keep clear of the knots of soldiers taking a walk. When she at last got down to the levels again she paused to fetch breath, and murmured, "Why did I take so much trouble? He would not, after all, have hurt me."

As she neared the mill an erect figure with a blue body and white thighs descended before her from the down towards the village, and went past the mill to a stile beyond, over which she usually returned to her house. Here he lingered. On coming nearer Anne discovered this person to be Trumpet-major Loveday; and not wishing to meet anybody just now Anne passed quickly on, and entered the house by the garden door.

"My dear Anne, what a time you have been gone!" said her mother.

"Yes, I have been round by another road."

"Why did you do that?"

Anne looked thoughtful and reticent, for her reason was almost too silly a one to confess. "Well, I wanted to avoid a person who is very busy in trying to meet me—that's all," she said.

Her mother glanced out of the window. "And there he is, I suppose," she said, as John Loveday, tired of looking for Anne at the stile, passed the house on his way to his father's door. He could not help casting his eyes towards their window, and, seeing them, he smiled and looked conscious.

Anne's reluctance to mention Festus was such that she did not correct her mother's error, and the dame went on: "Well, you

John Collier

are quite right, my dear. Be friendly with him, but no more, at present. I have heard of your other affair, and think it is a very wise choice. I am sure you have my best wishes in it, and I only hope it will come to a point."

"What's that?" said the astonished Anne.

"You and Mr. Festus Derriman, dear. You need not mind me; I have known it for several days. Old Granny Seamore called here Saturday, and told me she saw him coming home with you across Park Close last week, when you went for the newspaper; so I thought I'd send you again to-day, and give you another chance."

"Then you didn't want the paper—and it was only for that! Goodness gracious!"

"He's a very fine young fellow; he looks a thorough woman's protector."

"He may look it," said Anne.

"He has given up the freehold farm his father held at Pitstock, and lives in independence on what the land brings him. And when Farmer Derriman dies, he'll have all the old man's, for certain. He'll be worth ten thousand pounds, if a penny, in money, besides sixteen horses, cart and hack, a fifty-cow dairy, and at least five hundred sheep."

Anne turned away, and instead of informing her mother that she had been running like a doe to escape the interesting heir-presumptive alluded to, merely said, "Mother, I don't like this at all."

CHAPTER IX.—ANNE IS KINDLY FETCHED BY THE TRUMPET-MAJOR.

AFTER this, Anne would on no account walk in the direction of the hall, for fear of another rencontre with young Derriman. In the course of a few days it was told in the village that the old farmer had actually gone for a week's holiday and change of air to Weymouth, at the instance of his nephew Festus. This was a wonderful thing to hear of Uncle Benjy, who had not slept outside the walls of Overcombe Hall for many a long year before; and Anne well imagined what extraordinary pressure must have been put upon him to induce him to take such a step. She pictured his unhappiness at the bustling watering-place, and hoped no harm would come to him.

She spent much of her time indoors or in the garden, hearing little of the camp movements beyond the periodical Ta-ta-ta-taa of the trumpeters sounding their various ingenious calls for watch-setting, stables, feed, boot-and-saddle, parade, and so on, which made her think how clever her friend the trumpet-major must be to teach his pupils to play those pretty little tunes so well.

On the third morning after Uncle Benjy's departure, she was disturbed as usual while dressing by the tramp of the troops down the slope to the mill-pond, and during the now familiar stamping and splashing which followed there sounded upon the glass of the window a slight smack, which might have been caused by a whip or switch. She listened more particularly, and it was repeated. As John Loveday was the only dragoon likely to be aware that she slept in that particular apartment, she imagined the signal to come from him, though wondering that he should venture upon such a freak of familiarity.

Wrapping herself up in a red cloak, she went to the window, gently drew up a corner of the curtain, and peeped out, as she had done many times before. Nobody who was not quite close beneath her window could see her face; but, as it happened, somebody was close. The soldiers whose floundering Anne had heard were not Loveday's dragoons, but a troop of the York Hussars, quite oblivious of her existence. They had passed on out of the water, and instead of them there sat Festus Derriman alone on his horse, and in plain clothes, the water reaching up to the animal's belly, and Festus's heels elevated over the saddle to keep them out of the stream, which threatened to wash rider and horse into the deep mill-head just below. It was plainly he who had struck her lattice, for in a moment he looked up, and their eyes met. Festus laughed loudly and slapped her window again; and just at that moment the dragoons began prancing down the slope in review order. She could not but wait a minute or two to see them pass. While doing so she was suddenly led to draw back, drop the corner of the curtain, and blush privately in her room. She had not only been seen by Festus Derriman, but by John Loveday, who, riding along with his trumpet slung up behind him, had looked over his shoulder at the phenomenon of Derriman beneath

Anne's bedroom window, and seemed quite astounded at the sight.

She was quite vexed at the conjunction of incidents, and went no more to the window till the dragoons had ridden far away and she had heard Festus's horse laboriously wade on to dry land. When she looked out there was nobody left but Miller Loveday, who usually stood in the garden at this time of the morning to say a word or two to the soldiers, of whom he already knew so many, and was in a fair way of knowing many more, from the liberality with which he handed round mugs of cheering liquor whenever parties of them walked that way.

In the afternoon of this day Anne walked to a christening party at a neighbour's in the adjoining parish of Springham, intending to walk home again before it got dark; but there was a slight fall of rain towards evening, and she was pressed by the people of the house to stay over the night. With some hesitation she accepted their hospitality; but at ten o'clock, when they were thinking of going to bed, they were startled by a smart rap at the door, and on it being unbolted a man's form was seen in the shadows outside.

"Is Miss Garland here?" the visitor inquired, at which Anne suspended her breath.

"Yes," said Anne's entertainer, warily.

"Her mother is very anxious to know what's become of her. She promised to come home." To her great relief Anne recognised the voice as John Loveday's, and not Festus Derriman's, as she had feared.

"Yes, I did, Mr. Loveday," said she, coming forward; "but it rained, and I thought my mother would guess where I was."

Loveday said with diffidence that it had not rained anything to speak of at the camp, or at the mill, so that her mother was rather alarmed.

"And she asked you to come for me?" Anne inquired.

This was a question which the trumpet-major had been dreading during the whole of his walk thither. "Well, she didn't exactly ask me," he said rather lamely, but still in a manner to show that Mrs. Garland had indirectly signified such to be her wish. In reality Mrs. Garland had not addressed him at all on the subject. She had merely spoken to his father on finding that her daughter did not return, and received an assurance from the miller that the precious girl was doubtless quite safe. John heard of this inquiry, and having a pass that evening, resolved to re-

lieve Mrs. Garland's mind on his own responsibility. Ever since his morning view
of Festus under her window he had been on
thorns of anxiety, and his thrilling hope now
was that she would walk back with him.

He shifted his foot nervously as he made
the bold request. Anne felt at once that
she would go. There was nobody in the
world whose care she would more readily be
under than the trumpet-major's in a case like
the present. He was their nearest neighbour's son, and she had liked his single-
minded ingenuousness from the first moment
of his return home.

When they had started on their walk Anne
said in a practical way, to show that there
was no sentiment whatever in her acceptance
of his company, "Mother was much alarmed
about me, perhaps?"

"Yes; she was uneasy," he said; and then
was compelled by conscience to make a
clean breast of it. "I know she was uneasy,
because my father said so. But I did not
see her myself. The truth is, she doesn't
know I am come."

Anne now saw how the matter stood; but
she was not offended with him. What woman
could have been? They walked on in
silence, the respectful trumpet-major keeping
a yard off on her right as precisely as if that
measure had been fixed between them. She
had a great feeling of civility toward him this
evening, and spoke again. "I often hear
your trumpeters blowing the calls. They
do it beautifully I think."

"Pretty fair; they might do better," said
he, as one too well-mannered to make much of
an accomplishment in which he had a hand.

"And you taught them how to do it?"

"Yes, I taught them."

"It must require wonderful practice to get
them into the way of beginning and finishing
so exactly at one time. It is like one throat
doing it all. How came you to be a trumpeter, Mr. Loveday?"

"Well, I took to it naturally when I was
a little boy," said he, betrayed into quite a
gushing state by her delightful interest. "I
used to make trumpets of paper, elder-sticks,
eltrot stems, and even stinging-nettle stalks,
you know. Then father set me to keep the
birds off that little barley-ground of his, and
gave me an old horn to frighten 'em with.
I learnt to blow that horn so that you could
hear me for miles and miles. Then he bought
me a clarionet, and when I could play that
I borrowed a serpent, and learned to play a
tolerable bass. So when I listed I was picked
out for training as trumpeter at once."

"Of course you were."

"Sometimes, however, I wish I had never
joined the army. My father gave me a very
fair education, and your father showed me
how to draw horses, on a slate I mean. Yes,
I ought to have done more than I have."

"What, did you know my father?" she
asked with new interest.

"Oh yes, for years. You were a little
mite of a thing then; and you used to cry
when we big boys looked at you, and made
pig's eyes at you, which we did sometimes.
Many and many a time have I stood by
your poor father while he worked. Ah,
you don't remember much about him; but
I do!"

Anne remained thoughtful; and the moon
broke from behind the clouds, lighting up
the wet foliage with a twinkling brightness,
and lending to each of the trumpet-major's
buttons and spurs a little ray of its own. They
had come to the old park gate, and he said,
"Do you like going across, or round by the
lane?"

"We may as well go by the nearest road,"
said Anne.

They entered the park, following the half-
obliterated drive till they came almost opposite the hall, when they entered a footpath
leading on to the village. While hereabout
they heard a shout, or chorus of exclamation,
apparently from within the walls of the dark
buildings near them.

"What was that?" said Anne.

"I don't know," said her companion. "I'll
go and see."

He went round the intervening swamp of
watercress and brooklime which had once
been the fish-pond, crossed by a culvert the
trickling brook that still flowed that way, and
advanced to the wall of the house. Boisterous noises were resounding from within, and
he was tempted to go round the corner,
where the low windows were, and look
through a chink into the room whence the
sounds proceeded.

It was the room in which the present owner
dined—traditionally called the great parlour
—and within it sat about a dozen young men
of the yeomanry cavalry, one of them being
Festus. They were drinking, laughing, singing, thumping their fists on the table, and
enjoying themselves in the very perfection of
confusion. The candles, blown by the breeze
from the partly opened window, had guttered
into coffin handles and shrouds, and, choked
by their long black wicks for want of snuffing,
gave out a smoky yellow light. One of the
young men might possibly have been in a

maudlin state, for he had his arm round the neck of his next neighbour. Another was making an incoherent speech to which nobody was listening. Some of their faces were red, some were sallow; some were sleepy, some wide awake. The only one among them who appeared in his usual frame of mind was Festus, at the head of the table, enjoying with a serene and triumphant aspect the difference between his own condition and that of his neighbours. While the trumpet-major looked, a young woman, niece of Anthony Cripplestraw, and one of Uncle Benjy's servants, was called in by one of the crew, and much against her will a fiddle was placed in her hands, from which they made her produce discordant screeches.

The absence of Uncle Benjy had, in fact, been contrived by young Derriman that he might make use of the hall on his own account. Cripplestraw had been left in charge, and Festus had found no difficulty in forcing from that dependent the keys of whatever he required. John Loveday turned his eyes from the scene to the neighbouring moon-lit path, where Anne still stood waiting. Then he looked into the room, then at Anne again. It was an opportunity of advancing his own cause with her by exposing Festus, for whom he began to entertain hostile feelings of no mean force.

"No; I can't do it," he said. "'Tis underhand. Let things take their chance."

He moved away, and then perceived that Anne, tired of waiting, had crossed the stream, and almost come up with him.

"What is the noise about?" she said.

"There's company in the house," said Loveday.

"Company? Farmer Derriman is not at home," said Anne, and went on to the window whence the rays of light leaked out, the trumpet-major standing where he was. He saw her face enter the beam of candlelight, stay there for a moment, and quickly withdraw. She came back to him at once. "Let us go on," she said.

Loveday imagined from her tone that she must have an interest in Derriman, and said sadly, "You blame me for going across to the window, and leading you to follow me."

"Not a bit," said Anne, seeing his mistake as to the state of her heart, and being rather angry with him for it. "I think it was most natural, considering the noise."

Silence again. "Derriman is sober as a judge," said Loveday, as they turned to go. "It was only the others who were noisy."

"Whether he is sober or not is nothing whatever to me," said Anne.

"Of course not. I know it," said the trumpet-major, in accents expressing unhappiness at her somewhat curt tone, and some doubt of her assurance.

Before they had emerged from the shadow of the hall some persons were seen moving along the road. Loveday was for going on just the same; but Anne, from a shy feeling that it was as well not to be seen walking alone with a man who was not her lover, said—

"Mr. Loveday, let us wait here a minute till they have passed."

On nearer view the group was seen to comprise a man on a piebald horse, and another man walking beside him. When they were opposite the house they halted, and the rider dismounted, whereupon a dispute between him and the other man ensued, apparently on a question of money.

"'Tis old Mr. Derriman come home!" said Anne. "He has hired that horse from the bathing machine to bring him. Only fancy!"

Before they had gone many steps farther the farmer and his companion had ended their dispute, and the latter mounted the horse and cantered away, Uncle Benjy coming on to the house at a nimble pace. As soon as he observed Loveday and Anne, he fell into a feebler gait; when they came up he recognised Anne.

"And you have come home from Weymouth so soon, Farmer Derriman?" said she.

"Yes, faith! I couldn't bide at such a ruination place," said the farmer. "Your hand in your pocket every minute of the day. 'Tis a shilling for this, half-a-crown for that; if you only eat one egg, or even a poor windfall of an apple, you've got to pay; and a bunch o' radishes is a halfpenny, and a quart o' cider a good tuppence three-farthings at lowest reckoning. Nothing without paying! I couldn't even get a ride homeward upon that screw without the man wanting a shilling for it, when my weight didn't take a penny out of the beast. I've saved a penn'orth or so of shoe-leather to be sure; but the saddle was so rough wi' patches that 'a took twopence out of the seat of my best breeches. King George hev' ruined Weymouth for other folks. More than that, my nephew promised to come there to-morrow to see me, and if I had stayed I must have treated en. Hey—what's that?"

It was a shout from within the walls of the building, and Loveday said—

"Your nephew is here, and has company."

"My nephew *here!*" gasped the old man. "Good folks, will you come up to the door with me? I mean—hee—hee—just for company. Dear me, I thought my house was as quiet as a church."

They went back to the window, and the farmer looked in, his mouth falling apart to a greater width at the corners than in the middle, and his fingers assuming a state of radiation.

"'Tis my best silver tankards they've got, that I've never used! Oh, 'tis my strong beer! 'Tis eight-candles guttering away, when I've used nothing but twenties myself for the last half year!"

"You didn't know he was here, then?" said Loveday.

"Oh, no!" said the farmer, shaking his head half-way. "Nothing's known to poor I! There's my best rummers jingling as careless as if 'twas tin cups; and my table scratched, and my chairs wrenched out of joint. See how they tilt 'em on the two back legs—and that's ruin to a chair! Ah! when I be gone he won't find another old man to make such work with, and provide goods for his breaking, and house-room and drink for his tear-brass set!"

"Comrades and fellow-soldiers," said Festus to the hot farmers and yeomen he entertained within, "as we have vowed to brave danger and death together, so we'll share the couch of peace. You shall sleep here to-night, for it is getting late. My scram blue-vinnied gallicrow of an uncle takes care that there shan't be much comfort in the house, but you can curl up on the furniture if beds run short. As for my sleep, it won't be much. I'm melancholy! A woman has, I may say, got my heart in her pocket, and I have hers in mine. She's not much—to other folk, I mean—but she is to me. The little thing came in my way, and conquered me. I crave that simple maid! I ought to have looked higher—I know it; what of that? 'Tis a fate that may happen to the greatest men."

"Whash her name?" said one of the warriors, whose head occasionally drooped upon his epaulettes by accident, and whose eyes fell together in the casual manner characteristic of the tired soldier. (It was really Farmer Stubb, of Duddle Hole.)

"Her name? Well, 'tis spelt, A, N—but nay, I won't give ye her name here in company. She don't live a hundred miles off, however, and she wears the prettiest cap-ribbons you ever saw.—Well, well; 'tis weakness. She has little, and I have much; but I do adore that girl, in spite of myself!"

"Let's go on," said Anne.

"Prithee stand by a old man till he's got into his house!" implored Uncle Benjy. "I only ask ye to bide within call. Stand back under the trees, and I'll do my poor best to give no trouble."

"I'll stand by you for half an hour, sir," said Loveday. "After that I must bolt to camp."

"Very well; bide back there under the trees," said Uncle Benjy. "I don't want to spite 'em."

"You'll wait a few minutes, just to see if he gets in?" said the trumpet-major to Anne as they retired from the old man.

"I want to get home," said Anne anxiously.

When they had quite receded behind the tree-trunks, and he stood alone, Uncle Benjy, to their surprise, set up a loud shout, altogether beyond the imagined power of his lungs.

"Man a lost! man a lost!" he cried, repeating the exclamation several times; and then ran an'd hid himself behind a corner of the building. Soon the door opened, and Festus and his guests came tumbling out upon the green.

"'Tis our duty to help folks in distress," said Festus. "Man a lost, where are you?"

"'Twas across there," said one of his friends.

"No; 'twas here," said another.

Meanwhile Uncle Benjy, coming from his hiding-place, had scampered with the quickness of a boy up to the door they had quitted, and slipped in. In a moment the door flew together, and Anne heard him bolting and barring it inside. The revellers, however, did not notice this, and came on towards the spot where the trumpet-major and Anne were standing.

"Here's succour at hand, friends," said Festus. "We are all king's men; do not fear us."

"Thank you," said Loveday; "so are we." He explained in two words that they were not the distressed traveller who had cried out, and turned to go on.

"'Tis she! my life, 'tis she!" said Festus, now first recognising Anne. "Fair Anne, I will not part from you till I see you safe at your own dear door."

"She's in my hands," said Loveday civilly, though not without firmness, "so it is not required, thank you."

"Man, had I but my sword——"

"I'd throw it over that elm," said Love-day.

"Hey?" said Festus.

"Come," said Loveday, "I don't want to quarrel. Let's put it to her. Whichever of us she likes best, he shall take her home. Miss Anne, which?"

Anne would much rather have gone home alone, but seeing the remainder of the yeomanry party staggering up she thought it best to secure a protector of some kind. How to choose one without offending the other and provoking a quarrel was the difficulty.

"You must both walk home with me," she adroitly said, "one on one side, and one on the other. And if you are not quite civil to one another all the time, I'll never speak to either of you again."

They agreed to the terms, and the other yeomen arriving at this time said they would go also as rear guard.

"Very well," said Anne. "Now go and get your hats, and don't be long."

"Ah, yes; our hats," said the yeomanry, whose heads were so hot that they had forgotten their nakedness till then.

"You'll wait till we've got 'em—we won't be a moment," said Festus eagerly.

Anne and Loveday said yes, and Festus ran back to the house, followed by all his band.

"Now let's run and leave 'em," said Anne when they were out of hearing.

"But we've promised to wait," said the trumpet-major in surprise.

"Promised to wait!" said Anne indignantly. "As if one ought to keep such a promise to drunken men as that. You can do as you like, I shall go."

"It is hardly fair to leave the chaps," said Loveday reluctantly, and looking back at them. But she heard no more, and flitting off under the trees was soon lost to his sight.

Festus and the rest had by this time reached Uncle Benjy's door, which they were discomfited and astonished to find closed. They began to knock, and then to kick at the venerable timber, till the old man's head, crowned with a tasseled nightcap, appeared at an upper window, followed by his shoulders, with apparently nothing on but his shirt, though it was in truth a sheet thrown over his coat.

"Fie, fie upon ye all for making such a hullaballoo at a weak old man's door," he said. "What's in ye to rouse honest folks at this time o' night?"

"Scrunch it—why—it's Uncle Benjy! Haw-haw-haw!" said Festus. "Nunc, why how's this? 'Tis I—Festus—wanting to come in."

"Oh, no, no, my clever man, whoever you be!" said Uncle Benjy in a tone of incredulous integrity. "My nephew, dear boy, is miles away at quarters, and sound asleep by this time, as becomes a good soldier. That story won't do to-night, my man, not at all."

"Upon my word 'tis I," said Festus.

"Not to-night, my man; not to-night! Anthony, bring my blunderbus," said the farmer, turning and addressing nobody inside the room.

"Let's break in the winder-shutters," said one of the others.

"My wig, and we will!" said Festus. "What a trick of the old man!"

"Get some big stones," said the yeomen, searching under the wall.

"No; forbear, forbear," said Festus, beginning to be frightened at the spirit he had raised. "I forget; we should drive him into fits, for he's subject to 'em, and then perhaps 'twould be manslaughter. Comrades, we must march. No; we'll lie in the barn. I'll see into this, take my word for 't. Our honour is at stake. Now let's back to see my beauty home."

"We can't, as we haven't got our hats," said one of his fellow-troopers—in domestic life Jacob Noakes, of Muckleford Farm.

"No more we can," said Festus, in a melancholy tone. "But I must go to her and tell her the reason. She pulls me in spite of all."

"She's gone. I saw her flee across park while we were knocking at the door," said another of the yeomanry.

"Gone!" said Festus, grinding his teeth and putting himself into a rigid shape. "Then 'tis my enemy—he has tempted her away with him! But I am a rich man, and he's poor, and rides the king's horse while I ride my own. Could I· but find that fellow, that regular, that common man, I would—"

"Yes?" said the trumpet-major, coming up behind him.

"I," said Festus, starting round, "I would seize him by the hand and say, 'Guard her; if you are my friend, guard her from all harm!'"

"A good speech. And I will, too," said Loveday heartily.

"And now for shelter," said Festus to his companions.

They then unceremoniously left Loveday, without wishing him good night, and proceeded towards the barn. He crossed the park and ascended the down to the camp, grieved that he had given Anne cause of complaint, and fancying that she held him of slight account beside his wealthier rival.

CHAPTER X.—THE MATCH-MAKING VIRTUES OF A DOUBLE GARDEN.

ANNE was so flurried by the military incidents attending her return home that she was almost afraid to venture alone outside her mother's premises. Moreover, the numerous soldiers, regular and casual, that haunted Overcombe and its neighbourhood, were getting better acquainted with the villagers, and the result was that they were always standing at garden gates, walking in the orchards, or sitting gossiping just within cottage doors, with the bowls of their tobacco-pipes thrust outside for politeness' sake, that they might not defile the air of the household. Being gentlemen of a gallant and most affectionate nature, they naturally turned their heads and smiled if a pretty girl passed by, which was rather disconcerting to the latter if she were unused to society. Every belle in the village soon had a lover, and when the belles were all allotted those who scarcely deserved that title had their turn, many of the soldiers being not at all particular about half an inch of nose more or less, a trifling deficiency of teeth, or a larger crop of freckles than is customary in the Saxon race. Thus, with one and another, courtship began to be practised in Overcombe on rather a large scale, and the dispossessed young men who had been born in the place were left to take their walks alone, where, instead of studying the works of nature, they meditated gross outrages on the eyes, noses, teeth, backs, and other parts of the brave men who had been so good as to visit their village.

Anne watched these romantic proceedings from her window with much interest, and when she saw that even dashing officers did not scorn to pass the time in chatting and strolling with any handsome girl who chose to encourage them, she was filled with a melancholy sense of her own loneliness. To see round-faced Miss Mitchell, the navy-surgeon's daughter, tiny Susan Comfort, and crabbed Sarah Beach walk by on the gorgeous arms of Lieutenant Knockheelmann, Cornet Flitzenberger, and Captain Klaspenkicken respectively, of the thrilling York Hussars, who swore the most picturesque foreign oaths, and had a wonderful sort of estate or property, called the Vaterland, in their strange and unknown country across the sea—to see these girls walk by in the company of such distinguished men with as much ease and confidence as if they were merely Tom Penny or Jack Halfpenny, who worked and muddled in the next parish, made Anne think of things which she tried to forget, and to look into a little drawer at something soft and brown that lay in a curl there, wrapped in paper. So, thus beholding the happiness that prevailed without, she felt what a dismal place one's own room is to pass a day in, and at last could bear it no longer, and went down-stairs.

"Where are you going?" said Mrs. Garland.

"For a walk, to see the folks, because I am so gloomy."

"Certainly not at present, Anne."

"Why not, mother?" said Anne, blushing with an indefinite sense of being very wicked.

"Because you must not. I have been going to tell you several times not to go into the street at this time of day. Why not walk in the morning? There's young Mr. Derriman would be glad to——"

"Don't mention him, mother, don't!"

"Well then, dear, walk in the garden if you must walk."

So poor Anne, who really had not the slightest wish to throw her heart away upon a soldier, but merely wanted to displace old thoughts by new, turned into the inner garden from day to day, and passed a good many hours there, the pleasant birds singing to her, and the delightful butterflies alighting on her hat, and the screamingly delightful ants running up her stocking.

This garden was undivided from Loveday's, the two having originally been the single garden of the whole house. It was a quaint old place, enclosed by a thorn hedge so shapely and dense from incessant clipping that the mill-boy could walk along the top without sinking in, a feat which he often performed as a means of filling out his day's work. The soil within was of that intense fat blackness which is only seen after a century of constant cultivation. The paths were grassed over, so that people came and went upon them without being heard. The grass harboured slugs, and on this account the miller was going to replace it by gravel as soon as he had time; but as he had said this for thirty years without doing it, the grass and the slugs seemed likely to remain.

The miller's man attended to Mrs. Garland's piece of the garden as well as to the larger portion, digging, planting, and weeding indifferently in both, the miller observing with reason that it was not worth while for a helpless widow lady to hire a man for her little plot when his man, working alongside, could tend it without much addition to his labour. The two households were on this account even more closely united in the garden than within the mill. Out there they were almost one family, and they talked from plot to plot with a zest and animation which Mrs. Garland could never have anticipated when she first removed thither after her husband's death.

The lower half of the garden, farthest from the road, was the most snug and sheltered part of this snug and sheltered enclosure, and it was well watered as the land of Lot. Three small brooks, about a yard wide, ran with a tinkling sound from side to side between the plots, crossing the paths under wood slabs laid as bridges, and passing out of the garden through little tunnels in the hedge. The brooks were so far overhung at their brinks by grass and garden produce that, had it not been for their perpetual babbling, few would have noticed that they were there. This was where Anne liked best to linger when her excursions became restricted to her own premises; and in a spot of the garden not far removed the trumpet-major loved to linger also whenever he visited his father's house.

Having by virtue of his office no stable duty to perform, he came down from the camp to the mill almost every day; and Anne, finding that he adroitly walked and sat in his father's portion of the garden whenever she did so in the other half, could not help smiling and speaking to him. So his epaulettes and blue jacket, and Anne's yellow gipsy hat, were often seen in different parts of the garden at the same time; but he never intruded into her part of the enclosure, nor did she into Loveday's. She always spoke to

him when she saw him there, and he replied in deep, firm accents across the gooseberry bushes, or through the tall rows of flowering peas, as the case might be. He thus gave her accounts at fifteen paces of his experiences in camp, in quarters, in Flanders, and elsewhere; of the difference between line and column, of forced marches, billeting, and suchlike, together with his hopes of promotion. Anne listened at first indifferently, but knowing no one else so good-natured and experienced, she grew interested in him as in a brother. By degrees his straps, buckles, spurs, badges, and rings of brass lost all their strangeness and were as familiar to her as her own clothes.

At last Mrs. Garland noticed this growing friendship, and began to despair of her motherly scheme of uniting Anne to the wealthy Festus. Why she could not take prompt steps to check interference with her plans arose partly from her nature, which was the reverse of managing, and partly from a new emotional circumstance with which she found it difficult to reckon. The near neighbourhood that had produced the friendship of Anne for John Loveday was slowly effecting a warmer liking between her mother and his father.

Thus the month of July passed. The troop horses came with the regularity of clockwork twice a day down to drink under her window, and, as the weather grew hotter, kicked up their heels and shook their heads furiously under the maddening sting of the dun-fly. The green leaves in the garden became of a darker dye, the gooseberries ripened, and the three brooks were reduced to half their winter volume.

At length the earnest trumpet-major obtained Mrs. Garland's consent to take her and her daughter to the camp, which they had not yet viewed from any closer point than their own windows. So one afternoon they went, the miller being one of the party. The villagers were by this time driving a roaring trade with the soldiers, who purchased of them every description of garden produce, milk, butter, and eggs, at liberal prices. The figures of these rural sutlers could be seen creeping up the slopes, laden like bees, to a spot in the rear of the camp, where there was a kind of market-place on the greensward.

Mrs. Garland, Anne, and the miller were

conducted from one place to another, and on to the quarter where the soldiers' wives lived who had not been able to get lodgings in the cottages near. The most sheltered place had been chosen for them, and snug huts had been built for their use by their husbands, of clods, hurdles, a little thatch, or whatever they could lay hands on. The trumpet-major conducted his friends thence to the large barn which had been appropriated as a hospital, and to the cottage with its windows bricked up, that was used as the magazine; then they inspected the lines of shining dark horses (each representing the then high figure of two-and-twenty guineas purchase-money), standing patiently at the ropes which stretched from one picket-post to another, a bank being thrown up in front of them as a protection at night.

They passed on to the tents of the German legion, a well-grown and rather dandy set of men, but with a poetical look about their faces which rendered them interesting to feminine eyes. Hanoverians, Saxons, Prussians, Swedes, Hungarians, and other foreigners were numbered in their ranks. They were cleaning arms, which they leant carefully against a rail when the work was complete.

On their return they passed the mess-house, a temporary wooden building with a brick chimney, where, in wet weather, the officers could spend the day if they chose. As Anne and her companions went by, a group of three or four of them were standing at the door talking to a dashing young man, who was expatiating on the qualities of a horse that one of the officers was inclined to buy. Anne recognised Festus Derriman in the seller, and Cripplestraw was trotting the animal up and down. As soon as she caught the yeoman's eye he left the knot of officers and came forward, making some friendly remark to the miller, and then turning to Miss Garland, who kept her eyes steadily fixed on the distant landscape till he got so near that it was impossible to do so longer. Festus looked from Anne to the trumpet-major, and from the trumpet-major back to Anne with a dark expression of face, as if he suspected that there might be a tender understanding between them.

"Are you offended with me?" he said to her in a low voice of repressed resentment.

"No," said Anne.

"When are you coming to the hall again?"

"Never, perhaps."

"Nonsense, Anne," said Mrs. Garland, who had come near, and smiled pleasantly on Festus. "You can go at any time, as usual."

"Let her come with me now, Mrs. Garland; I should be pleased to walk along with her. My man can lead home the horse."

"Thank you, but I shall not come," said Miss Anne coldly.

The widow looked unhappily in her daughter's face, distressed between her desire that Anne should encourage Festus, and her wish to consult Anne's own feelings in the matter, which she imagined to be in favour of John Loveday.

"Leave her alone, leave her alone," said Festus, his gaze blackening. "Now I think of it I am glad she can't come with me, for I am engaged with these noblemen." And he stalked away to where the officers of dragoons were still surveying the horse in various oblique directions.

Anne moved on with her mother, young Loveday silently following, and they began to descend the hill. Mrs. Garland was a woman who could not help looking round when she had passed anybody who occupied her thoughts, and she turned her head now.

"Don't, mother; it is so vulgar," said Anne quickly.

"Mr. Derriman and the officers are watching us," said the widow. "Now I wonder what in the world they are doing that for?"

"It is no concern of ours," said Anne.

But Festus at least was watching them seriously, and in spite of his engagement with the noblemen he did not take his eyes off our party till they were hidden from his sight by the roundness of the ground. Then Mrs. Garland cast about her eyes again. "Well, where's Mr. Loveday?" she asked.

"Father's behind," said John.

When she could do so without Anne noticing, Mrs. Garland looked behind her again; and the miller, who had been waiting for the event, beckoned to her.

"I'll overtake you in a minute," she said, and went back, her colour, for some unaccountable reason, rising as she did so. The miller and she then came on slowly together, conversing in very low tones, and when they got to the bottom they stood still. Loveday and Anne waited for them, saying but little to each other, for the rencontre with Festus had damped the spirits of both. At last the widow's private talk with Miller Loveday came to an end, and she hastened onward, the miller going in another direction to meet a man on business. When she reached the trumpet-major and Anne she was looking very bright and rather flurried, and seemed sorry when Loveday said that he must leave them and return to the camp. They parted in their usual friendly manner, and Anne and her mother were left to walk the few remaining yards alone.

"There, I've settled it," said Mrs. Garland. "Anne, what are you thinking about? I have settled in my mind that it is all right."

"What's all right?" said Anne.

"That you do not care for Derriman, and mean to encourage John Loveday. What's all the world so long as folks are happy! Child, don't take any notice of what I have said about Festus, and don't meet him any more."

"What a weathercock you are, mother! Why should you say that just now?"

"It is easy to call me a weathercock," said the matron, putting on her face the look of a good woman; "but I have reasoned it out, and at last, thank God, I have got over my ambition. The Lovedays' are our true and only friends, and Mr. Festus Derriman, with all his money, is nothing to us at all."

"But," said Anne, "what has made you change all of a sudden from what you have said before?"

"My feelings and my reason, which I am thankful for."

Anne knew that her mother's sentiments were naturally so versatile that they could not be depended on for two days together; but it did not occur to her for the moment that a change had been helped on in the present case by a romantic talk between Mrs. Garland and the miller. But Mrs. Garland could not keep the secret long. She chatted gaily as she walked, and before they had entered the house she said, "What do you think Mr. Loveday has been saying to me, dear Anne?"

Anne did not know at all.

"Why, he has asked me to marry him."

VICTORIA TO WINNIPEG *VIA* PEACE RIVER PASS.

II.—THROUGH THE ROCKY MOUNTAINS BY BOAT; PEACE RIVER DISTRICT.

IN 1793 Sir Alexander Mackenzie, having made a previous journey from Montreal to the mouth of the great river, since known by his name, that falls into the Arctic Sea, passed through the Rocky Mountains by way of Peace River, reaching the Pacific at Cascade Channel, an arm of Dean Inlet. He was the first to cross this northern portion of the continent. His purpose was partly to explore the country and partly to extend the fur trade of the North-West Company, with which he was connected, and which was subsequently amalgamated with the Hudson's Bay Company. The record of his journey contains the earliest account we have of that Peace River country, through a portion of which we purpose in this article conducting our readers. We have still, however, seventy miles to travel from Fort St. James, the central Hudson's Bay depôt of northern British Columbia, before we touch, at Fort McLeod, the waters that flow into the Peace, where we shall begin our journey by boat through the Rocky Mountains. The only route connecting these two forts is a bridle-path, which leads sometimes over low hills, sometimes by the margin of small lakes, sometimes through thick woods or over treacherous swamps, where we were frequently delayed by the necessity of "brushing" the trail, that is, of laying large branches across the path, so as to afford some footing for our horses and for our pack-mules. As there are many parts of British Columbia to which goods can be transported only by means of mule-trains, this mode of conveyance is very frequently adopted. Ours had come up from Yale by the great waggon-road which runs along the valley of the Fraser to Quesnel, and thence by trail to Fort St. James, carrying the supplies required by us for our farther journey. Our progress was slow, for even on a good trail fifteen miles a day is considered fair travelling, when each mule carries from two hundred to three hundred pounds, and the trail in this case was not uniformly good; yet, being well mounted, we found it for the most part very pleasant, even though sometimes the woods were so thick that both hands were required to press aside the branches, which would otherwise strike the face. The country through which we were passing seems quite unfit for agriculture, not only on account of the character of the soil, but also on account of the climate and the altitude above sea level. With few exceptions an elevation of 2,000 feet above the sea may be regarded as the maximum altitude for cultivable land in British Columbia, while here we range from 2,200 feet at Fort St. James up to 2,700 feet at the height of land between Fort St. James and Fort McLeod. And while unfit for agriculture, beyond the growth of barley and potatoes, this northern part of the province has not, as the southern portion has, much mineral wealth, for the gold fields of Omenica have ceased to attract much attention, and are almost entirely abandoned, while the timber, where it has been spared by fire, is usually of an inferior quality. It is valuable chiefly for its fur-bearing animals, bear and beaver being the most abundant. It may therefore be expected to remain for many years in much the same condition as at present, a condition that probably does not differ much from that in which Mackenzie found it nearly a century ago.

We reached Fort McLeod on the 14th July, having taken seven days from Fort St. James. The name "fort" applied to these Hudson's Bay posts is frequently imposing in more ways than one. It naturally suggests a picture of strong walls, formidable gateways, fortified residence, &c., but often, as in the case of Fort McLeod, the reality is very different from the vision. A small single-story dwelling made of hewn logs, little better than the rude shanty of a Canadian backwoodsman, a trading store as plain as the dwelling, a smoke-house for curing and storing fish or meat, and a stable, constitute the whole establishment. The fort is said to have had its days of greatness, when it was surrounded by a palisade and had other visible signs of importance, but it is now one of the smallest posts in British Columbia. The manager, a young English gentleman, who has whiled away some of his lonely hours by sketching for the *Graphic*, has named the post "Fort Misery," a name indicative of many a dreary day.

At Fort McLeod our party was divided, some proceeding through the Rocky Mountains by way of Pine River Pass, accompanied by the mule-train with supplies for continued explorations east of the mountains, the rest of us proceeding by boat down the Peace River, both parties expecting to rendezvous at Fort Dunvegan, the central Hudson's Bay depôt of the Peace River district, east of the Rocky Mountains.

We were fortunate enough to procure at Fort McLeod a capacious boat—40 feet keel, 9 feet beam—which, although old and well worn, was, by a little caulking and somewhat frequent pumping, fitted for our purpose. The fort stands at the foot of Lake McLeod, whose waters are emptied into the Peace River by a stream called Pack River, about fourteen miles in length. Passing down this stream we enter on the Parsnip River, the great southern tributary of the Peace, whose head waters lie near the head waters of the Fraser on the western slopes of

the mountains. Here, and for many miles below this, the Parsnip is about one hundred and fifty yards in width, with a current of from three to four miles an hour. Its course, until it meets the Finlay, the other main tributary of the Peace, is a little west of north. Sometimes the banks are bare and steep, with exposures of sand, clay, and gravel, and occasional croppings of sandstone and of limestone; sometimes they are pleasantly varied by levels of pasture land or by low wooded hills. The river is dotted by numerous islands, at the upper ends of which it sometimes divides so evenly that it is difficult to distinguish the main channel. The voyageurs observe changes in it from year to year. The soil, being light and sandy, is easily washed down by the current in spring, when the river rises fifteen or twenty feet above its lowest summer level, the shores are cast into new curves, the islands are worn away above and increased by deposits farther down, and the slopes and benches along the banks have in some places been swept by fire, while in others they have been covered by new growths of bush or tree.

While borne steadily and pleasantly along we met some fur-traders, struggling up stream with their cargoes *en route* to Victoria by way of McLeod Lake, the Giscombe Portage, and the Valley of the Fraser, engaged in the very precarious task of competing with the Hudson's Bay Company.

We met also, while floating down the river, straggling miners engaged in prospecting—in one case a solitary Frenchman, in another three Scotchmen. Many a time the miner will start off alone to seek new "diggings," trusting to his own brain, bone, and sinew, taking some small supplies to stand between him and starvation, lest he might find no game nor any human habitation in his wandering. Onward he goes, washing a pailful of sand from this "bar," and then passing on to the next, until he finds sufficient gold to tempt him to prolong his search at some particular point, as a "colour"—that is some tiny particles of gold just large enough to be seen in the dark sand—may be found in any river in British Columbia. Smiling at dangers and difficulties that would make less resolute men despair, restless in their rambling as the Wandering Jew, broken it may be in fortune, sometimes broken in health, but never broken in hope, these men have pierced the country from Kootenay to Cassiar. The Indians could not, and the Hudson's Bay Company would not, tell the outer world what they knew of this northern

Junction of Nation and Parsnip Rivers, looking West.

land: the miners came, they opened the gates, and the world rushed in. Let this solitary Frenchman or these three Scots find a good bar to-day, and make it known at Fort McLeod or Fort St. James, and the news would spread like wildfire: ere autumn hundreds would crowd in from every centre of population between Alaska and San Francisco, and a large community would soon be gathered amid these unpeopled solitudes. Indeed, there are several bars on this river, especially between the Nation and the Finlay, where gold has been found year after year, probably borne down from the rocks in the neighbourhood of Omenica. Some of these were worked with small yet steady returns for a number of seasons by two men, Nigger Dan and Pete Toy, of whom Major Butler speaks in his interesting account of a winter trip through Peace River country in 1873, given in his "Wild North Land."

Nearly half-way between the Pack River and the Finlay the Nation River flows in from the west, receiving the waters of numerous lakes that lie south of Omenica, between Lake Babine and the Parsnip, a region not yet surveyed, hardly even explored, and little known except to the natives. Not far from the mouth of the Nation lignite has been discovered so pure and compact as to be of value as fuel, if further examination should disclose sufficient quantities. Landing near this on the right bank, we found the soil excellent, covered with a rich crop of hay and pea-vine, indicating that the flats and slopes along the river, and possibly also some of the plateaux and rolling country farther back, might afford good and abundant pasturage.

Approaching the forks where the Finlay and Parsnip meet, some seventy-five miles below Pack River, we caught to the north-east our first glimpse, high up among the hill-tops, of the gap through the mountains that forms the Peace River Pass, the hills being here more rugged and more densely massed than anything we had seen since we left the Skeena, while occasionally snow-peaks could be seen glistening among them. The Finlay, so named from the first white man that ascended it, drains a great portion of Omenica by one branch, while by another it receives the waters of an unexplored region to the north of Omenica. For fully three hundred miles it has twisted and coiled itself by many a rugged mountain and through many a rocky canyon, receiving as its tributaries streams whose sands glitter with gold. Here its flow is gentle, but thirty miles off we can see bold snow-capped hills that tell of the character of the country through which it has carved its way. And the Parsnip, ere the two rivers blend, has flowed nearly as far as the Finlay. As they meet their waters broaden into a

From a Photograph by]   Mount Selwyn, Peace River.   [A. R. C. Selwyn.

small smooth lake, and then rush down a rough and stormy current nearly half a mile in length and some two hundred and fifty yards in width, known as the Finlay Rapids. Here the names Parsnip and Finlay are dropped, and from this onward until it meets, near Fort Chipewyan, the waters that empty Lake Athabasca, a thousand miles from this, the united river is known as the Peace. The Sicanies of northern British Columbia call it the Tseta-i-kah—" the river that goes into the mountains." The Beaver Indians who live east of the Rocky Mountains call it the Unchagah, that is, " The Peace," for on its banks was settled once for all a feud that had long been waged between them and the Crees. About a mile below the rapids the river, with its forces now united from the south and west, turns suddenly eastward. At this bend it is fringed on both banks by gentle slopes and irregular benches, beyond which rise the hills, at first not more than from two thousand to two thousand five hundred feet in height, some scarped by ravines, some castellated by regular strata of rock, but for the most part lightly wooded. This is the beginning of the Peace River Pass.

Almost immediately below the entrance to the pass Mount Selwyn rises to the right, four thousand five hundred and seventy feet above the river, six thousand two hundred and twenty feet above the sea. It is a massive pyramid XXI—12

flanked by a ridge of rock on either side; its lower slopes formed by the detritus washed down from side and summit, partly covered by burnt timber and tinted by frequent patches of grass; its upper slopes in part moss-covered, in part bare as polished granite, broken and irregular as if shattered by fire and frost; its sides now shelving, now precipitous, grooved and seamed by torrent and by avalanche; its edge ragged and serrated until it terminates in a snow-clad peak. Along the northern side the hills are grouped in endless variety of form, the irregular masses looking as if they had been flung there at some terrible convulsion of nature, to show into how many shapes mountains might be cast. To the right and left, alternately, in broad curves, sweeps the river, which is here from two hundred to two hundred and fifty yards in width, while the ridges between which it flows seem to be interlaced and dovetailed as you look down the pass. The river changes with each bend of the current; here a rugged shoulder, bare and hard as adamant, butting upward for recognition; there a frowning precipice with no trace of vegetation, or a wooded knoll, solid beneath but with a fair green surface; here a wild ravine, there a great shell-shaped valley; while stretching far up are the peaks that form a resting place for the eagle and the cloud. The day being fine, there was a perpetual play of light and shade on river and hill; and so, as we were swept on by the current, cloud, mountain and river, peak, bluff and wooded bank were woven into countless and ever-changing combinations. Gradually as we were borne onward we found the character of the hills changing. Instead of being bold and peaked and serrated, they were rounded and wooded to the top. The valley widens. To the right stands Mount Garnet Wolseley (so named by Butler), the last of the range that seems with sharp edges to cleave the sky. Though the width of the river continues much the same, yet plateaux on either side broaden until the hills are set about two miles apart from north to south, summit from summit. We recognise that we have pierced from west to east the Rocky Mountain Range, through a pass about twenty-two miles in length, borne pleasantly along in a large boat by the waters of the great Unchagah.

After passing the Clearwater and some other small tributaries, whose crystal purity is in marked contrast with the turbid, greyish colour of the Peace, we ran the Parle-pas Rapid, so called because it is not heard far up the river, though it speaks loudly enough when you are once in its grasp and cannot retrace your course. Our pilot, who had gone forward to examine it before venturing to run it, held the long "sweep" that was lashed astern to serve as the steering oar, for an ordinary rudder would be useless here; the four oars were vigorously manned, and then into the boiling current we went. We had taken the first plunge when, midway, we were caught by an eddy; the bow swung around a little; had it swung much farther we must soon have been swamped; the men bent themselves to their oars; the helmsman let out some of his reserve strength. It was only the work of an instant; the boat swung back into its true course, and the next moment we were in calm water, wishing we had another rapid to run.

Below this there are flats and benches in almost unbroken succession stretching between the river and the now receding hills, while on both sides there are numerous terraces in tier upon tier, sometimes with their edges as clearly cut as if they had been meant for fortresses. Those on the right bank are almost uniformly timbered, while those on the north bank are grassy and smooth, their slopes occasionally seamed by old buffalo trails; for though buffalo are no longer found in this district, yet this was once the pasture land for large herds that found here their western limit. The general appearance of the country as we approached the Canyon of Peace River, particularly of that on the north side, is that of a pastoral country. Some of the flats might furnish arable farms, others might be suited for stock-raising, while the low grassy hills remind one of some of the sheep-farming portions of the south of Scotland.

Were it necessary to run a railway line to the Pacific as far north as this, a practicable route through the mountains is offered by way of the Peace River Pass. The chief difficulty would be, not in the Rocky Mountains, but at the canyon, where the river sweeps round the base of a solitary massive hill, known as the Mountain of Rocks, or the Portage Mountain, just above Hudson's Hope. For any railway line, however, that would follow a northern route to the Pacific, the Pine River Pass, a little south of this, which is known to be quite practicable, would be preferable to one by way of Peace River.

The Canyon of Peace River, which at its upper extremity is about fifty miles east of the Rocky Mountains, is about twenty-five miles in length, and the river is here a wild, broken torrent some two hundred feet in width, which, so far as known, has never been navigated, except by the dauntless Iroquois crew that accompanied Sir George Simpson on his expedition to the Pacific in 1828. The cliffs are in some places broken into terraces; in others they rise sheer and precipitous for over two hundred and fifty feet. The course of the river is always curved as it dashes alternately to right and left, while from end to end the canyon forms one great curve around the base of the Portage Mountain. This canyon is the only obstruction to the navigation of the river for several hundred miles. From the head of the canyon to Pack River, that empties the waters of McLeod Lake, that is, about one hundred and fifty miles, and even farther up the Parsnip, the river is navigable for steamers of light draught. The Parle-pas and the Finlay are the only rapids of any importance, and while these can be run with safety they could be surmounted without much difficulty by warping the boat up stream, as is done on the heavier and more tortuous rapids of the Fraser and the Columbia. From Hudson's Hope at the lower end of the canyon, which is twelve miles by the Portage trail from its upper extremity, there is no obstruction whatever to steam navigation until the falls below Vermilion are reached, nearly five hundred miles lower down; and below this another break in the navigation occurs at a place called Five Portages on Slave River. When that is passed the river (which is known as the Slave River between Lake Athabasca and Great Slave Lake, and as the Mackenzie from Great Slave Lake to the sea) is open to large steamers down to the Arctic Ocean. There are thus only three places at which continuous steam navigation would be interrupted from above the mouth of Pack River, down the Parsnip, the Peace, the Slave, and the Mackenzie (which, though differing in name, are in reality one), that is, from British Columbia through the Rocky Mountains, by the fertile Peace River district, to the Northern Sea, a distance in all, by water, of not less than between two and three thousand miles.

We were forced to abandon our boat at the head of the canyon, but were fortunate enough to procure the horses of some Indians to convey our supplies, baggage, &c., across to Hudson's Hope. For our further journey by the river we had to make a raft, on which we drifted down to Dunvegan, one hundred and ten miles below the canyon. Life on a raft is not very exciting, but ours, on this occasion, was varied by the novelty of watching the bears, both black and grizzly, that are found in large numbers throughout this district, and that in summer frequent the lofty banks of the river to feed on the saskatum, or service-berry, which grows in abundance. They were generally beyond the range of our rifles, or, at least, of our riflemen; but had we been able to spend some time here in hunting we might have secured, not only a large number of bears, but also of moose, for the Peace River district is the best moose country in Canada. Here the moose is to the Indian almost everything that the buffalo is to the hunter of the plains. The flesh is his chief article of food; the skin when tanned is the great material for dress, at least for winter costume, while untanned it is used for a great variety of purposes, among others as the covering for his tent, or tepee; and, cut into strips (in which form it is known as shaganappi), it serves in almost every manufacture, and for all kinds of repairs. While such large game continue plentiful it is vain to expect that the Indians will take to a settled life, or will cultivate the soil, as some of the Indians of the plains are being forced to do by the gradual extinction of the buffalo. Even at the Hudson's Bay posts throughout this district, where most of the vegetables and cereals grown in Ontario can be raised with success, the agents and half-breeds are almost entirely dependent on their hunters

for food. They could raise cattle and crops very easily, for cattle at Dunvegan require to be housed and home-fed only from the latter part of November until about the middle of March; wild hay is plentiful in the vicinity of many of the forts; the return of potatoes is frequently as high as forty to one, twenty-five kegs of potatoes at Dunvegan having yielded one thousand kegs; the horses winter out, being able to paw away the light snow, beneath which they find abundance of grass; and yet many of the Hudson's Bay agents depend for their supply of food very largely on the labours of the Indian hunters that are attached to each post. Their neglect of agriculture is due, no doubt, to the policy which the Company have long pursued of keeping the country as a fur-bearing preserve, furs being of more importance to them than farming; and it is due also, in some degree, to the frequency with which their agents are moved from one post to another, which discourages them from making any improvement on the land, or from undertaking work from which they may probably reap no results. One consequence, however, of this dependence upon their hunters for supplies is, that when, as has sometimes occurred, several weeks pass in winter without any snow, and there is no chance of tracking the deer, the people at some of the posts may be reduced to the verge of starvation.

The Hudson's Bay posts, a few mission stations, and two or three "free-traders'" establishments are the only places occupied by white men throughout this vast northern country that we speak of as the Peace River district, and these are uniformly found on the fertile flats near the river's edge. On those flats the soil is usually of the richest character, while the climate at those inhabited parts is such that wheat thrives at almost all the Company's posts from Hudson's Hope to Fort Simpson on the Mackenzie, lat. 64° north, and cucumbers flourish at Dunvegan, Vermilion, and elsewhere. The agricultural resources of this district, however, are not confined to those alluvial river-flats, for, properly speaking, the district consists of the vast plateau which, with few interruptions, extends for many miles in almost unbroken level to north and south, at an altitude at Dunvegan of about eight hundred feet above the river, an altitude that gradually diminishes to about fifty feet, five hundred miles farther down the river. This plateau, through which the Peace winds with a gentle current, and as uniformly as a canal, is narrow near Hudson's Hope, but widens as it stretches eastward. South of Dunvegan it embraces one of the most fertile tracts of the north-west, known as La Grande Prairie, while to the south-east of this, in a line crossing the Athabasca toward Edmonton, the greater portion of the soil is good. Along the north bank of the river, for a width varying from twenty-five to seventy miles, the land is known to be very fertile, partly well timbered, partly covered with light poplar, partly prairie land ready for the plough, with rich herbage, luxuriant wild hay, and pea-vine, at least as far as the Salt Springs on the Slave River. As yet, in the absence of actual experiment, the fitness of the climate of this plateau for the growth of wheat is not fully assured. Some parts of the country are subject to occasional summer frosts, but apparently frost rarely occurs before August, when wheat would not suffer much injury from it; some parts, however, such as La Grande Prairie, may even already be pronounced fitted for successful wheat culture. In Canada the agricultural value of any portion of the country is measured chiefly by its wheat-producing power. As yet we have not sufficient data to institute a comparison between the Peace River district and other fertile portions of the North-West Territories, nor can we as yet give a reliable estimate of the extent of wheat-growing land in the district, but sufficient is known of the character of the soil, of the luxuriance of the herbage, and of the success that has here hitherto attended any attempts at the cultivation of wheat, to warrant the conviction that this must yet become a great wheat-raising province. In addition to its agricultural resources it possesses abundance of good coal and of excellent timber, while the facilities for steam navigation afforded by the Peace and the large size of several of its tributaries must furnish easy communication throughout the country.

Every traveller through the Peace River district is surprised at the mildness of the climate. Although the winter is somewhat severe, yet the summer is as warm as that usually enjoyed ten degrees farther south in Ontario and Quebec, without the discomfort of oppressively warm nights. There is in this respect a marked change between the climate on the east and that on the west side of the Rocky Mountains, due probably to the fact that the prevailing westerly winds from the Pacific have, by the time they come so far inland, been relieved of much of their moisture, first by the Cascade Range, and then by the Rocky Mountains, and have thus been raised in temperature, while at the same time the general level of the country

here is much lower than that of northern British Columbia.

We reached Dunvegan on the 1st of August, a fortnight after leaving Fort McLeod. The name recalled a scene very different from any to be met with on the banks of the Peace. Far away, on the north coast of Skye, a rocky steep washed by the wild Atlantic, stands Dunvegan, the castle of McLeod. From that land of wild scenery and weird legend came one of the McLeods many years ago with fond recollections of his northern home, and as he planted this fur-trading post he named it after the chief castle of his clan. It stands on a broad low flat, in a large bend on the northern bank of the river. Behind it rises an abrupt ridge, broken by grassy slopes and knolls, and leading to the rich pasture-land of the plateau that spreads its vast expanse eight hundred feet above the fort.

At the time of our visit the Beaver Indians from the surrounding country had come in for supplies for their autumn hunt, and as they passed on the Sabbath morning to the Roman Catholic mission one could see almost every variety of Indian dress and fashion, except the war paint. Some wore the old Hudson's Bay capote of navy-blue cloth with brass buttons; some wore skin coats richly tasselled; some were gorgeous in embroidered leggings or in hats trimmed with feathers and gay ribbons; while the women were dressed chiefly in tartans, the bright patterns being evidently preferred, as if Scottish taste prevailed in the selection of imported goods as well as in the naming of the forts.

Père Tessier, the Roman Catholic missionary at Dunvegan, one of the Oblat Fathers, told us that he has observed some improvement among the Indians, which he ascribes to the influence of the mission, especially in their increasing regard for the marriage tie, and their carefulness in observing the Sabbath, things not only good in themselves, but probable indications of improvement in other respects.

It was necessary for our party to spend several weeks in explorations through this Peace River country; explorations, however, which, as they affected chiefly the Canadian Pacific Railway, need not here be further referred to. By the 1st of September the members of the party, having met at Dunvegan to compare notes regarding the portions of country traversed by them, parted, some returning to Victoria, the others taking various routes eastward.

DANIEL M. GORDON.

SUNDAYS IN MANY LANDS.

By JAMES CAMERON LEES, D.D.

II.—IN CATHOLIC SPAIN.

SPAIN would be a good country to travel in if—there were clean hotels, and no garlic, and no oil, and no cold winds from the sierra, and no dust, and no rushing to catch trains at unearthly hours in the morning, and no chance of being robbed when taking a quiet stroll, and no beggars clamouring for cuartos, and no—— There is one thing to put against all this catalogue of ills, and that is, picturesqueness. It more than outbalances them all. A peculiar grace and charm meet you everywhere, in city and in country, in railway and by road, in church and out of it, in the peasant with his bright girdle and gracefully folded cloak and purple umbrella, in the gallegos with their charmingly shaped water jars, in the Murillo groups of the great city squares, that seem as if they had come out of one of the great master's pictures, in the patios with their flowers and fountains, in the slim-made senoritas that go gliding along, on their heads the mantilla, in their hands the fan—and we know whence that picturesqueness has come. The Moors have been in Spain, and have left everywhere behind them the grace of the Orient.

Here we are this Sunday morning in Seville, after a long and uncomfortable journey. We have been groaning and grumbling all the morning, never was there such an execrable country, never such an execrable hotel; and so we step on to a great square filled with fruit and flower sellers, amid heaps of oranges and pomegranates, and stalls filled with roses and lilies and carnations, and wander thence through narrow streets, and look in at grated doorways into courts blazing with flowers, and listen to the plash of fountains and see the graceful Sevillanas moving along with their prayer-books in their hands and their duennas behind them, and come to a regular Moorish horseshoe gate, like a bit of Damascus, and enter a court planted with orange-trees. The air is balmy, and there is a perfume of orange-flowers, and a blending of colours, and a sculptured fountain, and an old grey cathedral in the background. We are soothed, we are in dreamland—who could be angry here?

Now in the court aforesaid there is a stone pulpit, from which, an inscription tells us, a certain St. Vincent de Perier and other eminent preachers in this city " prelected with good fruit ;" and seated below this pulpit, as demurely as if he was a clerk waiting to begin the service should any of these preachers make their appearance, is a tall well-built man in a jaunty jacket, and breeches covered with buttons, and a broad slouched hat, a red belt wound round his waist, out of which peeps a formidable clasp-knife, and a cigarette, of course, in his mouth. He is looking straight away into the orange grove, but he grows alert at our appearance ; he makes a graceful obeisance as if welcoming us to his own kingdom ; he informs us that his name is Pedro, he has been in the service of Englishmen at the mines, he speaks English very well, he loves the English, he will be charmed to be our guide while we are in Seville. We could not resist such grace, so we accept the services of Pedro. " Go along, you sons of dogs !" he cries, in musical Andalusian, to the swarm of beggars who were closing around. The beggars hobble away, and we feel we have got hold of a very capable man.

Now I do think that if I were able to perform the happy theological dispatch, if I could summon before me the Pope and all the councils, and the writings of the fathers, and pronounce sentence upon them after long examination, research, and study, and then, after having performed this great act of private judgment, go into the Church of Rome, and kick over the ladder that brought me there, and bid good-bye to the right to think for myself for ever, I would make straight for Seville and haunt this cathedral for the rest of my days. It is a place where there seems no call to think at all ; no ghosts of old controversies would rise before me. I could dream life away most pleasantly in company with these charming priests' in red and white and gold, surrounded with the glorious pictures of Murillo and Alonso Cano, and amid these orange groves. The Cathedral of Seville combines the beauty of a mosque with the quiet of a mosque ; for it was a mosque once, and as things are said to go by the law of circularity, it may be one again. It would not surprise me to see a turbaned Turk resuming his sandals at that horseshoe door, and frowning at the unbeliever who had invaded his precincts. High over everything towers the famous and most exquisite Giralda tower. It is the work of the Moors, and was built by Geber the Arabian, with whose productions of another kind schoolboys have considerable and painful acquaintance, for he is said to have been also the inventor of algebra. From this tower, in the days when it was surmounted by the crescent, the muezzin, or call to prayer, used to be sounded over the city. It is now crowned by a statue of Faith, of which the Sevillians think much as a work of art; but as it serves for a weather-cock, and turns about with every wind that blows, it may be doubted whether this symbol of the Christian grace is in its proper position. Pedro leads us in at the horseshoe door and along an arched corridor, and we are in the great building. It is very grand. Spaniards, comparing it with the other two cathedrals of the peninsula, say, "La de Sevilla la grande, la de Toledo la rica, y la de Leon la bella," and the comparison is just. Led by Pedro we thread our way to the end of the nave. If it were not for the *coro*, or choir, which is in the middle of the church, the view would be magnificent. The choir is one mass of painting and carved wood, but it sadly mars the perspective. The interior of this cathedral recalls Milan, but it is altogether finer. It is very sombre—so dark as to be oppressive. The arches are of immense height, the interior spacious, the furniture rich, the pictures simply magnificent. Perhaps the finest of these is the celebrated St. Antony of Padua by Murillo. The kneeling saint is looking heavenwards with outstretched hands, and the infant Christ descends in answer to his prayer. Beside him is a bunch of lilies placed in a vase, which is so natural that birds, it is said, come and peck at the flowers. Others than the innocent birds have been attracted by it. One fine morning the guardians of the cathedral found the frame vacant and the picture stolen. A thrill of horror ran through Spain. Prayers were offered for the recovery of the treasure, and a large reward promised. The result, perhaps, of both was that the picture was discovered in New York and brought back again. "It was a great miracle," says Pedro with a laugh; but Pedro is not a Catholic. He is, he says, a Protestant; but being further interrogated calls himself a Materialista. There are many like Pedro in Spain. Look round this splendid cathedral. Forty masses are going on. There are numbers of women present, but no men save ourselves, the priests, and a few beggars; yet the service here is very fine, and when the priests go up to the high altar, and there are clouds of incense, and glorious streams of colour, and a voice crying as if from another world, the effect is overpowering. I

would require to be well used to it before I would cease to be affected by it. We have been standing at the west end of the cathedral, near the grave of the son of Columbus. On the stone is engraved the ship in which the discoverer crossed the Atlantic, with many oars and a great square lantern at the stern. How such a craft could ever have crossed the sea it is hard indeed to understand. It would be a risky thing to sail in her round the Mull of Cantire. A bombastic inscription states, "A new world to Leon and Castile gave Colon." Fortunately that new world has been given to a few countries besides. We now go to the east end of the church, where in a silver sarcophagus reposes St. Ferdinand, who wrested Seville from the Moors—a thorough-going saint, whose zeal for religion was such, that on more than one occasion he carried with his own hand faggots of wood for heretical bonfires. This species of sanctity has largely characterized Spanish religion. As I stand at this saint's shrine stories of the Inquisition and the Quemadero, with their horrors, come vividly to remembrance. The Catholic Church of Spain was at the Reformation the most powerful of all European Churches. The expulsion of the Moors and the discovery of America had given it unbounded wealth. It stamped the Reformation out by sheer physical force. In one night eight hundred Protestants were thrown into the prisons of Seville, and for days the fires blazed in the chief Spanish cities. A short time ago a drain was cut through the field near Madrid where the Protestants were burnt. The workmen laid open a deep layer of black, shining dust, mixed with calcined bones and pieces of charcoal. It was the remains of those who perished at the bidding of the Church. Since then, until lately, she has had it all her own way, but retribution has at last reached her. The Spanish Church is in a state of utter decay. Her convents have been suppressed; her wealth has been taken from her; her priests are in poverty. The masses whom she allowed to grow up utterly uneducated and uncared for treat her with contempt. Men will keep on their hats when the host passes. They laugh at the clergy and regard them as their natural enemies. But a priest enters the pulpit, crosses himself, and begins his sermon. There are many eloquent men, I understand, among the Spanish preachers. Their sermons are generally on political topics, or rather upon those political topics which border on the ecclesiastical. In the country the cura will speak in the most familiar manner to his parishioners. One of them was lately, we were told, preaching that "God made everything perfect," when a hunchback, stepping up to the pulpit, pointing to his hump, asked the orator what he called that. "I call it," replied the ready cura, "as perfect a hump as I have ever seen!" We couldn't understand our preacher of Seville, so we go. Pedro speaks of him with a sneer. "He is always preaching about the captivity of the Pope, and telling us that he has only straw for his bed. Many a better man hasn't even that," says Pedro. He is very independent of priests, this bold Spaniard, in his ragged capa; and as we go along he tells us, with many gesticulations, that he would rather walk the streets on his own legs, though he might sometimes stumble, than be wheeled about in a chair, and have everything done for him; by which simile he indicated his preference for individualism over ecclesiasticism. There are vast multitudes in Spain of Pedro's way of thinking. They have given up the Church; they hate the priest; they wander in darkness. "Our Church," says our loquacious guide, "is the café, and our cathedral the Plaza de Toros."

In the evening, after our Sabbath rest, we again wander out under the Andalusian sky. The streets are gay and festive; the tinkling music of the guitar and the clatter of castanets is heard on every side. As we saunter along, groups of señoritas lean over the balconies and wave their fans. In a courtyard we see through the gateway a family at their evening meal, reclining on cushions and listening to music—a pretty picture it is. So we pass on, breathing the delicious air. Suddenly, as we are opposite the porch of a church, we hear sweet singing, and, strange to say, it is to a familiar Scotch tune. We inquire what church it is of a ragged urchin on the doorstep, and are told it is that of the "Holy Trinity." We enter into a spacious building and find regular-built pews, a pulpit where an altar should naturally have been, and in the pulpit a dark-bearded man in spectacles, arrayed in black gown and bands. We had gone back in a moment to Scotland. The congregation finish their hymn, and the sermon begins. It is in Spanish, and is delivered with great energy and much gesticulation. I can just make out clearly that he is having a good fling at the Pope. The congregation, numbering about two hundred, are evidently very much pleased with the clergyman's endeavour. An old Spanish crone

looks at me significantly and cries, "Bueno! bueno!" "Bueno!" say I, taking it for granted that it is all right. The old woman then nudges up an old man, and there is a little chorus of "Buenos" all round. The church was a very handsome one, and I believe belonged to one of the suppressed convents. There was unmistakable earnestness about both pastor and people. The sermon was very long, my companions wearied, and we came away with some of the congregation who were leaving, but I was glad to have had even a passing glimpse of a sower of good seed in that great city. I heard he is a good man, and God be with him! A Protestant Church has risen in Spain, it is tolerated by Government, and looks like life.[*] It is Presbyterian in government, has kirk sessions, presbyteries, synods, and general assemblies, and a Confession of Faith, consisting of thirty-five chapters, similar to that of Westminster, and almost as minute in its definitions. It will be curious to see whether the ecclesiastical polity and creed of hard-headed, dogmatic Scotland will suit the fiery Andalusian. I fear we might almost as well expect him to give up his cooling wine for Glenlivat, or his boiled vegetables flavoured with garlic for our honest oatmeal porridge! Perhaps even the religious world may learn a lesson from these instances of natural adaptation.

Revolving these things as we found our way quietly homewards, we were invited by a pleasant-looking man to enter his house. So pleasant was his invitation that it seemed discourteous to decline it, and we found ourselves in a little square room, full of dark-browed, sash-begirt, truculent-looking men. Seated in the centre of the room on an upturned tub was a man clothed in a coat of many colours, and manipulating the veritable chanter of a veritable bagpipe; a tambourine and castanets were held in reserve. At the sounds, which were of a caterwauling character, some of the men commenced a sort of jig, amid the bravos of the on-lookers. Canas, or small glasses, of wine were handed round, but there was no excess, no drunkenness. During all our wanderings in Spain we never saw a drunken man. The chief virtues of the Spaniard are sobriety and courtesy—his chief vices passion and cruelty. His knife is unsheathed at any moment, and he will take life on very little provocation. Murders of the most brutal kind are plentiful. The Spaniard, however, has noble qualities, and would be a pleasant companion if his love for

[*] "Daybreak in Spain," by the Rev. J. A. Wylie, LL.D.

Puerta del Perdon, Cathedral, Sevilla.

fighting and for garlic were not so great. Garlic and tobacco smoke were very pronounced in this Spanish interior, not to speak of the bagpipe and tambourine, and as the spectacle generally was very unedifying we beat a retreat as soon as we could with common politeness. The host bowed us out of the dingy apartment in the most effusive manner.

"What future is there for people like these?" we say to one another when we emerge on the street. Never was there a nation calling itself Christian lower down in the scale of civilisation than Spain is at present. Politically her people have lost all stability, and seem to be the dupes of any clever schemer who takes them in hand; and yet politics are what seems to interest them most. Go and talk to any of those lazy-looking fellows loitering about in the square about the existing government, its virtues or its misdeeds, his cigarette is allowed to go out, his hands gesticulate, his eyes flash, and in a few moments he has worked himself up to a passion of excitement. Provoke him by abusing his favourite political leader, or his pet political newspaper, and he will have his knife out in a twinkling. And such a knife! clasped, and half a foot long. Yet no government seems to retain its popularity for any length of time. Revolution follows revolution, each leaving the country poorer and more hopelessly embarrassed. Never was there a kingdom in some respects more highly favoured than Spain. She has grand harbours on two seas, broad navigable rivers, great mineral wealth, fertile soil, and yet she seems utterly bankrupt, and to have lost all power of recuperation. It is usual with Protestants to blame the Church of Rome for the degenerate state of the country, but that Church has lost its hold, at least in southern Spain, upon the people, and there is still no sign of improvement. They are happy, idle, unprogressive. Their wants are few—a piece of bread, a bunch of grapes, a few vegetables, garlic of course, and little more is needed for the daily meal. A halfpenny calabash will support a family for a day. There is no inducement to labour. The soil is scratched, the seed sown, and the crop is often unvisited until it is to be reaped. It is a strange thing to think of, that Spain was more prosperous under the Moors than she has been under Christian rulers. Her government was more liberal, more tolerant, more cultured, her people better educated, her land better culti-

vated. Since the Moors have been driven out Spain has almost continuously retrograded. Let us hope the darkest hour has now been reached. At present few of the population are educated—out of sixteen millions two only are able to read or write—but common schools are being started in a feeble way, and as education advances things may grow better. Perhaps the saddest feature in Spanish life is that which, in more ways than one, we have had vividly brought on this Sunday before us—the falling away of the people from religious belief. Many profess open infidelity, but the largest number are what are called *Indiferentes*—they look upon religion as altogether outside of their life, a thing with which they have nothing whatever to do. Some can see hope in the utter chaos of doubt and unbelief that prevails—earnests of better things to come; but I confess I can see none.

In the *sala* of the hotel, when we got back, sat a regular John Bull with his friend, a Spanish wine-merchant from Cadiz. We had seen him going forth in the morning rejoicing, clad in an ample white waistcoat, and a flaming carnation in his button-hole. He had been to Jeres, to a bull fight, and had just returned in a very depressed condition. The heat, the crowd, the spectacle, had all been too much for him. Loud was his denunciation of the great national Spanish amusement. It was cruel in the extreme. The horses were miserable hacks and were fearfully used—made to go up to the bull with their entrails trailing on the ground. Two bulls had been killed after being fearfully tortured. The whole spectacle was disgusting to any one who cared to see fair play. His impressions regarding the chulos, and the picadores, and the espadas, and all the bull-ring frequenters, were most thoroughly emphatic. When he saw the bull gore the first horse and lay open his side he nearly fainted, but a lady beside him was loud in her applause. "I tell you what, Don Alfonso," said he, turning to his friend, "this country of yours is a strange place."

"Quien no ha visto Sevilla
No ha vista maravilla," *

says the Don with a laugh, in reply, as he finishes his bottle of Malaga seca—and he was right.

---

* " He who hath not Sevilla seen
Hath not seen strange things I ween."

FAITH AND VIRTUE.

By the BISHOP OF TASMANIA.

2 Peter i. 5.

SAFETY rather than life, deliverance from the results of sin rather than from sin itself, is the end proposed by much of the religious teaching of the day. "Believe and you are safe" is the Alpha and Omega of popular Christianity. This, which is in effect the idolatry of faith—that is with many a mere variable emotion—leads them to cherish notions of Divine favouritism, and to an unconscious dangerous inference that, if they have once believed, actual conduct and growth in the religious life may be disregarded. But, in truth, faith is but the coming to Christ, Who came to restore us to the broken communion with God, and to sanctify us through the truth, and so to reunite the broken strings of the human heart. Our Maker looked upon His own work, after sin had entered the abode of man, and, behold, it had become evil! He is restoring it by the revelation of His goodness, that He may look upon "a new earth and a new heaven," and pronounce it once more "very good." The disease, as a deadly cancer, must be eradicated. That disease is self-will. We see its symptoms on every side in many-sided misery and moral death. In crowded cities and the dark places of the earth they appear in open lawlessness and vice. In higher circles of society the same sins are there, only more refined ; the same misery, only more disguised. Man is separated from man, family from family, nation from nation, by motives of selfish interest. Each has self for its centre, and self is opposed to self. The self-sacrifice of Christ is the remedy provided, and so far is salvation from being a selfish escape from danger, which is but another form of selfishness, that it is a *dying unto self*, and living unto God. It is a consequence of this extravagant exaltation of the merits of faith that the emphatic witness of Holy Scripture to the necessity of a life-long struggle with evil is lost sight of. The message which many, who assume to teach others, proclaim among an ignorant population, that everything has so been done for them, that they have nothing themselves to do but to believe, has produced in many parts of this and other countries the most careless laxity of morals. The work of Christ *for* us is insisted upon, while the work of Christ *in* us is not insisted upon. All those passages of Scripture which speak of uniting man's work and man's suffering with Christ's work and suffering speak of truths they fail to apprehend. What means St. Paul's statement that "our light afflictions *work* for us an eternal and exceeding weight of glory," or that "we should fill up that which is lacking in the sufferings of Christ"? To those who stop short with Christ's work *for* us, those Scriptures might never have been written which teach us that we must be united to, and become partakers of, His glorified humanity—"Bone of His bone, and flesh of His flesh." And what value can we put upon the Holy Communion, if it is regarded only as an occasion of commemorating what He has done *for us*, instead of regarding it as a sacramental means by which we lay hold upon His very humanity, dying with Him unto sin that we may live unto righteousness? What a dead letter to most of us who are satisfied with a modern and superficial theology is that higher strain of Holy Writ which speaks of "Christ *in* us, the hope of glory," not Christ *instead of* us, but *in* us, conforming us to His own likeness. How can we "glory in our infirmities," or "rejoice in tribulations," unless we unite them to Christ's own sufferings, and by presenting them at His Cross make them, through His merits, "work together for our good"? How many, again, are ready enough to see in the Cross a selfish escape from the fear of death and punishment. But how few feel called to take up their own cross and follow Him, "denying themselves ungodliness and worldly lusts," resisting passion, idleness, the selfish love of money or pleasure. How many are content to rest upon a barren and indolent faith, or something they mistake for faith, instead of "adding to their faith virtue," and all those manly and Christian graces implied in the very name and derivation of the word virtue —the manliness that does right.

Those who are in danger of making faith an object of worship are apt to place stress on St. Paul's controversy with the Judaising Christians of his age, but they never think of reconciling St. Paul with St. James, nor St. Paul with himself, nor both with their common Master. No sooner, however, was St. Paul converted than he cried, "Lord, what wilt Thou have me to *do?*" So far from adopting the deceptive phrase "once a believer, always a believer," he laboured more abundantly than they all, under an awful sense that he might become himself " a castaway." He was "instant in season, out of season." He was "instant in prayer." He had exalted views of sacramental grace. He thought and taught that the bread which we break was the *communication* of *the body of Christ*, and that the wine that we drink was the *communication* of the *blood of Christ.* Christ *in* us was a more prominent thought with this Apostle than Christ *for* us. His idea of the gospel came to this, "God in Christ, and Christ in man." He believed in One Who was called, even before His birth, "Jesus," for He should save us *from* our sins, and deliver us from their power, as David was delivered from the paw of the lion, or "as the bird from the hand of the fowler."

It is an alarming feature of the age when men call themselves after the name of Christ, and neglect and break the laws of Christ, taking refuge under the delusion that they are believers, *i.e.* are conscious now, or were some time ago conscious, of a certain emotion. But in whom are they believers? "Believers in Jesus," they reply. But do they really believe in the Jesus of the Gospels, or a Jesus of their own creation? Is it in that Jesus Who said, "Why call ye Me Lord, Lord, and do not the things which I say?" Is it in Him Who said on the mountain-side to those that cherished feelings of anger and revenge, "Love your enemies, do good to them that despitefully use you"? Is it in Him Who said to those that bought and sold and got gain, "Whatsoever ye would that men should do unto you, even so do unto them"? Is it in Him Who warns those that call themselves disciples, but are only hearers, and listen gladly, but never obey, "Not every one who saith unto Me Lord, Lord, shall enter into the kingdom of heaven"? No; the age needs to learn that "the Word of God, which liveth and abideth for ever," must be inscribed, not in the letter of a written record, but on the fleshy tables of the hearts of men, who obey the Will of God.

But is not salvation ascribed to faith? Yes, but so it is to repentance, baptism, confession, obedience, but only in a secondary sense, and never on the ground of merit. Salvation can only be ascribed to one source, and that is *the free, spontaneous love of God* in and through the Saviour. None of these subordinate agencies, working in or by ourselves, can be dispensed with, whether they be the moral faculties of the soul or the positive institutions of Christ, or of His Church. But He Himself is the door. By Him we enter in. To know the Father in Him is to have life. "This is life eternal, to *know* Thee, the only true God, and Jesus Christ, Whom Thou hast sent." But as knowledge of the art of bread-making cannot feed us, or listening to a lecture upon medicine cannot heal us, or to know the history of a great man implies no personal intimacy with him, so no mere theoretical knowledge of the way of salvation can save us. To know God in Jesus Christ is to *acquaint* ourselves with Him, and to be at peace. It is to be on intimate relations with Him—"I will sup with him, and he with Me."

Again, when popular writers confine their theology to a few favourite texts which insist on faith, they lose sight of the great truth of the unity of the Christian communion in an intense individualism. Even Churchmen, untaught in the faith and "in the whole counsel of God," catch the spirit of the age, and utter without meaning, "I believe in the communion of saints," or "I believe in the Holy Catholic Church." The Church to them is some "fortuitous concourse of atoms," units of individual men, who say, or think, that they believe in Christ. Such individual believers, so long as their belief is one of the soul, and not of the understanding only, we cannot doubt, draw virtue from the touch of Christ's garment. But it is the life of the single stem that ends in itself; not the life of the vine, which, drawing its sap from the soil, has an interdependent life from branch to branch. It is not the realisation of St. Paul's idea, when with his large vision he speaks of Christ, as One "in Whom the whole family in heaven and earth is named," that "speaking the truth in love, we may grow up unto Him in all things, Which is the Head, even Christ; from Whom *the whole Body*, fitly joined together, and compacted by that which every joint supplieth, according to the effectual working in the measure of every part, maketh increase of the Body, unto the edifying of itself in love." The Church is not to them " the fulness of Him that filleth *all in all.*"

The view in which we have presented the gospel places the work of Christ in its proper relation to all that proceeds from ourselves. *Confession, contrition, repentance, faith, good works* or *obedience*, have their due and relative position. None is distorted, like the ray refracted through the mist of one-sided apprehension. The sacraments, which Christ instituted in His Church, are not disparaged or weakened, nor yet extravagantly exalted. Neither sacraments nor faith are objects of idolátry. With the majority of modern sects the Sacraments have no positive significance whatever; and when their significance is even allowed, their grand witness to a world-wide, universal love is not recognised. But their true witness is that assigned to them in the corporate Church, which retains its primitive and catholic character as "the pillar and ground of the truth." According to its teaching, Baptism is the legal instrument of the new Covenant assuring us of better promises than those of the older. It proclaims aloud an universal capacity of salvation in man, *as man;* it places in his hands the title-deeds of a share in an unlimited Redemption, and of an election to privileges which nothing but unbelief can wreck. And it gives to the blessed Sacrament of the Eucharist its full significance. It does not regard it as the mere commemoration of salvation, much less of one limited to a few, but as a pleading of the promises of the Father through Christ to all. On the part of believers, it is a dedication and a surrender of all we *have* and *are,* for all time and hereafter—riches, poverty, life, death, children, friends—to Him Who has redeemed us by His blood.

Now, in all that I have said, do I under-value faith? No! but I warn you only against worshipping the means instead of the end—faith instead of Christ, the Object of faith. Faith to many is an unsubstantial notion; to others a formal creed; to others a transient feeling. But we know nothing of faith unless it leads us to Christ in such a sense that He is to us Light and Life; not the Deliverer from a future hell, but a present and eternal Life. Our souls are abodes of darkness until their windows are opened, and the true Light enters. Faith is nothing more than the hand that opens those windows of the soul to let in the Light of the world. Man cannot create this Light any more than he can create his own eye; yet the unbelief of man may close the eye, and keep it closed. But with the entrance of the Light comes life. He Who is "the Light that lighteth *every man* that cometh into the world," said Himself, "I am the Way, the Truth, and the *Life.*" Before the Light enters the heart, all is frozen, cold, dead. But when the true Light has entered, the eye kindles; the life-blood flows; hope and love unfold themselves; the heart moves under the warmth of a new affection. This is salvation; this is "eternal life." It is not something future; it is a present possession. "He that *hath* the Son hath life," for he is a "partaker of the Divine nature."

SNAILS AND SLUGS.

BY THE REV. J. G. WOOD, M.A.

SNAILS.

WHAT is a snail? Scientifically, it is called a terrestrial, pulmobranchiate, gasteropodous, conchiferous, heterogangliate animal. "These be brave words," but we cannot define a snail without them or their equivalents.

As this account of the snail is intended to be a life-history rather than a scientific treatise, I shall lay more stress on its biography than its anatomy, merely employing the latter as a means of elucidating the former.

That snails are usually ranked among the molluscs, every one knows who has the least smattering of zoology, but if he were asked to define the term, he would find himself rather at a loss to do so. The fact is, the word mollusc, which signifies a soft-bodied animal, is really a very inadequate one, as the softness of the body is a very slight and unimportant characteristic in their structure. The nervous system, and not the softness or hardness of the tissues among which the nerves are distributed, is now accepted as the real distinction between the molluscs and the articulates. Consequently, the name of heterogangliata (*i.e.* creatures possessing dissimilar ganglia, or nerve-centres) has now been substituted for the original term. For convenience' sake, however, I shall make use of the familiar word mollusc, in lieu of the more correct, though little known, "heterogangliata."

Few persons would think, or believe when they are told, that the oyster, which remains in one spot, and has neither limbs nor head, occupies a far higher place in the animal kingdom than do the butterflies, bees, and ants, the recognised types of beauty, industry, and intelligence among insects. Yet such is the case, and a brief examination of the nervous system will prove the truth of the statement.

There seems to be a wonderful dislike to snails in this country, partly on account of their cold, slimy skins, and partly because they consume fruit and vegetables. Perhaps there may be some grounds for this dislike; but, in spite of all prejudices, the snail is a wonderful being, not without a certain grace and beauty, and possessing an organization quite as complicated as that of the cockroach, which has already been described.

The snail's first entrance into the world is made underground, where its composite parent has left it in the shape of a small, spherical, semi-transparent egg. These eggs may be found an inch or two below the surface of the earth, clusters of twenty or thirty being generally seen in each cavity.

Even in the egg state, the snail is worthy of examination. Thin-skinned and fragile as are these eggs, their vitality is astonishing. Though a sudden heat will kill them, they may be exposed gradually to heat which dries them so completely that they shrivel into flat spangles, and may be crumbled into dust between the fingers. Yet, if placed in a damp atmosphere, they will gradually absorb the moisture of the air, swell out afresh to their former plumpness, and produce the young in perfectly good condition.

Cold seems to have absolutely no effect upon the eggs, except that so long as they are kept below a certain temperature they cannot be hatched. They may be frozen into ice, left in that state for any length of time, and, when the ice has melted, will be found uninjured.

From the very first moment that the living snail can be seen through the transparent envelope of the egg, it is seen to be covered with a shell. It is a remarkable fact, that not only the slugs, which do possess a tiny shell, but many of the absolutely shell-less relatives of the snail, are furnished, while in the egg, with a singularly beautiful shell, much resembling that of the chambered nautilus.

Just before it issues from the egg, we shall have an admirable opportunity of studying the manner in which the shell and its tenant are united. The shell is then nearly transparent, as the snail has not as yet eaten the earthy matters which render it opaque, and so the body, which is also nearly transparent, can be seen through it. It will then present an appearance not unlike the accompanying Fig. 1.

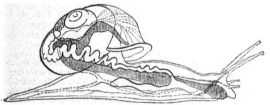

Fig. 1.

First, it will be seen that, in common with all molluscs, the entire animal is enveloped in a thick membrane. This is analogous to the skin of a human being, and is capable of almost indefinite expansion and contraction. Thus, the entire snail can withdraw so far into the coils of the shell, that scarcely any of it can be seen; or it can extend itself to such a degree that the shell looks quite insignificant when compared to the body.

It can be modified into various forms, so as to suit different purposes; and the most important of these is the so-called "foot," on which the snail glides along. The foot is, in fact, nothing but the lower surface of the mantle, much thickened, and capable of being crumpled into an infinite number of transverse wrinkles.

These wrinkles act instead of feet, and indeed, when in action, they bear a wonderful resemblance to the legs of the millipedes. Let a snail crawl along a flat plate of glass so that the under surface of the foot may be visible. Then a string of waves may be seen rippling along the foot from the head towards the tail. If one of these waves be watched, it will be seen to traverse the whole length of the foot, each wrinkle rising and falling in regular succession.

Hold a fine comb with the points of the teeth upwards. Now draw a stout needle along the side of the comb, and the tooth-points will be seen to follow it like a little wave, as they bend and rise again. So although the wrinkles do not themselves change their position, they produce the same optical effect as is seen in the waves of the sea.

As the foot, and, indeed, the whole body of the animal, is lubricated with slime, the creature glides slowly and regularly on its course, being held tightly to the object on which it crawls, not by any muscular clasp, but by the pressure of the atmosphere.

A very familiar example of the power of the pressure of the atmosphere as utilised by a mollusc, is shown by the common limpet. Every one who has visited a rocky sea-coast must have seen the limpets sticking so firmly that they seem almost to be part of the rocks themselves. But, push a wire or needle under the shell, and it comes off at once.

The fact is, that the limpet presses the edge of its foot against the rock, and then, by muscular force, draws the centre into the body. The air is therefore exhausted, just as is done by a boy's sucker, and the pressure of the atmosphere, averaging some twenty-five pounds weight on a large limpet, holds the animal in its place. The needle, however, makes a passage for the air, and, in consequence, the limpet loses its hold of the rock.

As the snails, slugs, limpets, and a host of other molluscs have the lower surface of the mantle thus converted into a foot, they are called gasteropoda, i.e. belly-footed creatures.

Another important office of the mantle is the formation of the shell. This needful portion of the snail's structure is secreted from the surface of the mantle. First, a simple cell is produced, and this is afterwards filled with calcareous matter, extracted by the wondrous chemistry of animal life from the vegetables on which the snail has fed. These vegetables, in their turn, have first extracted it from the earth.

It is therefore evident that the shells of snails must differ in accordance with the soil. About Sheffield, I am told that snails are extremely rare, while on chalk downs they absolutely swarm, existing in such number that the celebrated "Southdown" sheep are thought to derive the peculiar flavour of their flesh from the snails which the sheep are obliged to consume while grazing.

In the formation of the shell, it is found that the edge of the mantle is employed in the enlargement and colouring of the shell, while the other portions are used in thickening it. Thus it is, that the interior layers of the shell, which are deposited by the central part of the mantle, have no colour, and are simply white. If a portion of a snail's shell be broken away, the gap can be effectually mended in point of thickness. But the colouring matter will be either wholly or partially absent, and so there will be a gap in the pattern.

The whole subject of the colouring of shells is a very interesting one, but it penetrates too deeply into the arcana of chemistry and optics to be suitable for the present paper. The same may be said of the snail's blood. Any one, however, who wishes to investigate this subject, will find that the researches of the President of the Geological Society, Dr. H. C. Sorby, have cleared away many of the difficulties which surrounded this subject.

The same distinguished investigator told me that the azure hue of the snail's blood and the blue tint of the sky were both owing to the same cause, i.e. that certain constituents of that blood and of air absorbed the red and yellow rays of light, but allowed the blue rays to pass almost unaltered. Some of the molluscs have opalescent blood, and in this case the coloured rays are irregularly absorbed or rejected.

"Hæmoglobin" is also found in the blood of snails, but as few of the readers of this journal are likely to take any very great interest in hæmoglobin, I merely refer to Dr. Sorby's paper in the Quarterly Journal of Microscopic Science, vol. xvi. (New Series), p. 77.

The mention of blood brings us to the circulation, which is quite unlike the same functions in the insects and other articulates. In them, the place of the heart is taken by the "dorsal vessel," a pulsating tube furnished with valves, and running along the back. In the snails and slugs, however, there is a much nearer approach to a heart; and, indeed, as the organ in question consists of a well-defined auricle and ventricle, it may be fairly considered as a heart, though an imperfect one when compared with the same organ in the vertebrated animals.

There are arteries through which the blood is driven from the heart, and there are veins to bring it back again, and send it through the respiratory system in which it is purified. But the blood is not confined within the walls of distinct tubes, as in the higher animals, but wanders through the various structures of the body, without even following any definite track. This may be proved by injecting any part of the mantle, even the foot, the coloured particles of the injection fluid diffusing themselves without following the course of any blood-vessels.

Respiration has been mentioned. In many gasteropoda, especially those which inhabit the sea, the respiration is conducted by means of gills. But in the snails and slugs, which inhabit the land, respiration is conducted by means of an air sac, traversed by the vessels which have been already mentioned. These vessels constitute a tolerably perfect lung, and, therefore, all this group of molluscs is termed pulmobranchiata, *i.e.* lung-gilled animals. In the illustration on page 173, the lung sac is indicated by the radiating dotted lines on the upper part of the shell.

The reader is not, however, to imagine that all the lung-gilled molluscs are terrestrial. Many of them, such as the common water snails, are aquatic, and can remain submerged for a long time, but are obliged to make periodical visits to the surface for the purpose of respiration. In fact, they are to the land snails what the whales, seals, &c., are to terrestrial mammals.

As to the nervous system which has been briefly mentioned, there is an approach to a brain. In insects, the nervous system consists of a number of "ganglia," or nervous knobs, running along the lower part of the body, and joined by a double nervous thread.

In the slugs and snails, however, there is a distinct approach to a brain. It is a collar of nervous substance which encircles the gullet and gives off branches to various parts of the body. This, then, is the vulnerable part, not only in snails but in the cuttles, which rank next to the vertebrates in the animal kingdom.

Even the natives of Polynesia are aware of this fact.

When they hunt after the cuttles they attract their prey by a bait, over which the cuttle flings its arms, so as to hold it while it drives its sharp beak into it. The fisherman then smartly pulls the line and bait out of the sea, so that the cuttle falls ashore or into the canoe before it can loosen its grasp.

Sometimes it attacks its captor, and might inflict no small harm did not the man know something of its anatomy. He always has a sharp stick ready to hand, and as soon as he can find an opportunity he thrusts the point into the cuttle's body just at the junction of the arms. The nerve-collar is severed by the stroke, and the arms collapse as completely as would the limbs of a man if his brains were knocked out.

This brief history of the snail not being an anatomical treatise, we must omit many details of the nervous system. One portion of it, however, viz. that which has reference to the visual organs, requires mention.

Every one must have noticed the four tentacles, or "horns," as they are properly called, of the snail, that they can be protruded or withdrawn at will, and that the upper pair are very much longer than the lower. At the tip of these upper tentacles is a tiny black speck. It is the eye, which is necessarily protruded and withdrawn into the body together with the tentacle.

Fig. 2.

If a snail be watched while in the act of crawling, especially when viewed against a strong light, the remarkable mechanism of the tentacle and eye can easily be seen. Supposing the snail to be crawling along with all its tentacles extended, a slight touch upon one of them will cause it to be slightly contracted. Presently, however, it will be extended afresh, and, as it is protruded, the little black eye-speck will be seen to pass up and down, just a little way below the tip.

The fact is that the tentacle is inverted, and so gradually tucked into the head. A tolerable idea of the movement of the tentacle and eye may be obtained by fastening a thread to a black spiral bead in order to represent the eye, and passing the thread through the tip of a glove-finger, which does duty for the tentacle. Then, if the thread be pulled, the finger will be gradually inverted and drawn into the palm of the glove, carrying with it the black bead.

As the distance of these eyes from the brain varies so greatly, it is evident that some special structure of the optic nerve must exist in these creatures. This nerve is of just sufficient length to stretch from the brain to the tip of the tentacle when the latter is extended to its utmost, but it is so constructed that when the tentacle is retracted it falls into coils between the base of the tentacle and the brain. These neat coils can be seen with an ordinary pocket lens, but require some management of the light before they can be distinguished from the shadows thrown by the granulated surface of the tentacle.

If the reader would like to try this experiment for himself, he can easily do so, even though the season be winter and the snail be ensconced in its shell.

First put the snail into a cup filled with water warmed to a temperature of 70° or thereabouts. Then take a piece of thin wood or stout cardboard, and cut a slit in it about an inch long and a quarter of an inch wide. In a few minutes the snail will protrude itself from its shell, and, roused to exertion by the genial warmth and moisture, will begin to crawl upon the cup. Now, dip the board in the water and put the snail upon it, so that its head may be an inch or so below the slit. For a moment or two it will collapse, but it will soon resume its journey.

As soon as it begins to crawl, the board should be held up against a strong light—daylight is incomparably the best—and, as the tentacles slowly pass over the slit, their structure can easily be seen.

The ears of snails are not so easy of detection as the eyes. They are situated near the base of the tentacles, and consist of two delicate membranous bags, or sacs, in which are some tiny crystalline bodies analogous to the ear-bones or "otoliths" of fishes, and evidently performing a similar office. They are always in rapid movement, spinning round and round, and darting about the sac in which they are contained, as if endowed with life.

As to the sense of smell, there is no doubt that they possess it. For example, the whelks, which are simply sea-snails, can smell a sunken bait at wonderful distances, and come crawling to it from all directions. Then, as all entomologists know to their cost, the slugs, as well as moths, can smell their "treacles," and will find them almost as soon as the moths do. Yet I believe that anatomists have not as yet discovered where the organs of smell are placed. We know their position in the insects, but, in the molluscs, which rank so much higher in the scale of creation, their locality is unknown.

(*To be concluded in next part.*)

IRISH BALLAD.

COLLEEN OGE ASTORE.

AIR: "*Callino Casturame.*"

[NOTE.—"It is evidently to this tune that Shakespeare alludes in the play of *Henry the Fifth*, Act iv., Scene 4, where Pistol on meeting a French soldier exclaims, 'Quality! Calen o custure me.' In the folio we find 'Calline custure me,' which has been turned, in the modern editions, into 'Call you me? Construe me.' Malone found among 'Sundry new Sonets in a Handefull of Pleasant Delites,' 1584, a sonnet of a lover in praise of his lady, to 'Calen o custure me,'—sung at every line's end. In Mr. Lover's 'Lyrics of Ireland,' he notices the resemblance of the first word to the name 'Caillino,' speaking of Mrs. Fitzsimon's beautiful poem, 'The Woods of Caillino;' and adds, 'Mr. Boswell, in his edition of Shakespeare, says that Mr. Finnegan, Master of the school established in London for the education of the Irish, says the words mean, "Little Girl of my heart, for ever and ever."' Now this is not the meaning, and I cannot but wonder that, with so much literary discussion as has taken place on the subject, the true spelling, and consequently the meaning of the burden, have remained till now undiscovered. The burden, as given in the 'Handefull of Pleasant Delites,' and copied by Malone, is 'Calen o custure me,' which is an attempt to spell, and pretty nearly represents the sound of 'Colleen oge astore,' and these words mean, 'Young Girl, my Treasure'."—Stokes's "Life of Petrie," page 431, quoted by Hoffmann in his "Ancient Music of Ireland."] This air is taken from Queen Elizabeth's "Virginal Book." It has already been published by Mr. W. Chappell, in his work on "Popular Music of the Olden Time," and is reprinted in Hoffmann's Collection by his permission.

WHEN I marched away to war,
How you kissed me o'er and o'er,
Weeping, pressed me,
Sobbing, blessed me,
Colleen, Colleen oge astore!

I was wounded, wounded sore,
Dead your father falsely swore;
Set to harry
You to marry
One with miser gold in store.

Ah! but when you dreamed me dead,
Forth you flew a wildered maid;
Ever grieving,
Ever weaving
Willow, willow for your head.

"Nay! he lives," your mother said;
But you only shook your head.
"Why deceive me?
Ah! believe me,
Mother, mother, he is dead!"

So you pined, and pined away,
Till, when in the winter grey,
Home I hasted,
Wan and wasted,
Colleen, Colleen oge, you lay.

"'Tis his lonesome ghost," you said,
"Come to call me to the dead."
Nay; discover
Your dear lover
Longing now at last to wed.

Then your cheek, so pale before,
With the rose of hope once more
Faintly, slowly,
Brightly, wholly,
Blossomed, Colleen oge astore.

Till upon the chapel floor,
Side by side we knelt and swore
Duty dearest,
Love sincerest,
Colleen, Colleen oge astore.

ALFRED PERCEVAL GRAVES.

SARAH DE BERENGER.

By JEAN INGELOW.

CHAPTER VII.

MRS. SNAITH had no sooner got away from the two ladies, than she began to wonder why she had been so much alarmed. She had hardly understood at first that Miss de Berenger claimed the children as relations. "And why," she thought, "should this have frightened me? I have no presence of mind at all. I should have told her she was mistaken, and there would have been an end. Folks cannot take them from me; and if I make it seem to everybody that I am their nurse, and allow that their father is living, it's natural—I fare to see now—that people should think I must be under his orders."

She turned while seated on the sand, fitting on little boots. Miss de Berenger was behind her.

"We did not mean to offend you," she exclaimed, shaking back her curls. "I am sure, nurse, you are doing your duty by the darlings, but——"

"I am not offended with *you*, ma'am," answered Mrs. Snaith, when she stopped short. "Anybody can see that you are quite the lady, and had no thought of being rude."

"Then I wish you would be a little more open, nurse. You say you do not know where their father is, but you might at least tell me how long it is since you heard from him."

Mrs. Snaith pondered, then gave the truth. "Two years and three months, ma'am. But will you sit down a minute? Run on, my pretty ones."

The children, nothing loth, obeyed. Miss de Berenger sat down.

"Ma'am, you make it plain that you think these children must be related to you."

"Of course; I am sure of it."

"Well, ma'am, then it is my duty to tell you that they are not. You don't owe them any kindness, I do assure you. They are not related to you at all."

"Not that you know of," said Miss de Berenger, in correction. "But," she continued, "there might be family reasons, you must allow—very important family reasons—for not telling you everything about them."

She was perfectly polite in her manner, but this pertinacity alarmed Mrs. Snaith again. What should she say next? She had not decided, when Miss de Berenger went on—

"Did he tell you to bring them here? Because, if he did, it must have been on purpose that I or some of us might find them out, and acknowledge them."

Here was at least a suggestion which could be met and denied.

"Nobody told me to bring them here, ma'am. I do assure you I did it wholly to please myself, and out of my own head."

"Well, well, Felix must be told of this," said Miss de Berenger, not at all convinced. She twisted one of her curls over rather a bony finger. "I shall consult Felix, and he will soon get to the root of the matter."

"I don't think Felix will," thought Mrs. Snaith, and a furtive smile, in spite of herself, gleamed in her eyes.

"But, surely," continued the good lady, "you can have no motive for being more reticent with me than with the person in whose lodgings you are. She knows that you brought the children first from London, that their father is away, and that they have lost their mother, for she told us so."

"Did she, ma'am?" said Mrs. Snaith; and pondering the matter in her mind, she felt sure she had never said they had lost their mother.

"You are intrusted with the entire charge of them," was the next question; "is it not so?"

"Yes; they have no one to look after them but me."

"They are very like the family, and so my friend remarked, when she saw them here some time ago."

"Do you mean that person who was with you just now?" quoth Mrs. Snaith. She was still offended with her.

"She is quite a lady," exclaimed Miss de Berenger instantly, losing sight of the matter in hand to defend this person. "It is true that she has married Mr. de Berenger's fellow-curate, which was a most imprudent thing to do (and everybody said so), particularly as he had been plucked at college till he had hardly a feather left on him; but she would have him, and they were married, and had twin children with lightning rapidity. She is come here with me to get cured, if possible, of a bad cough that she has had ever since some months before their birth. But, indeed, what could she expect, going out as she did when the roads were blocked up with snow, and the thermometer yards below zero?"

The lady in question now made herself audible, as she came pounding down through the shingle to join them. It was evident to her keen observation that no fresh information had been obtained.

Mrs. Snaith rose, and, preparing to follow the children, made a bow to Miss de Berenger, whereupon the mother of twins said coldly—

"Miss de Berenger is very much hurt, and very much surprised too—that I can plainly see—by the way in which you have repelled her kind advances. The children's true interests are evidently very far from your thoughts. You can only think of your own."

"Good afternoon, ladies," said the nurse, tossing her head rather haughtily; and she passed on, half frightened again. There was a self-satisfied air of authority in the speaker, and something threatening in her tone, which, under the circumstances, was very ridiculous, and yet a certain effect was produced on her who knew those circumstances best.

Not even a mother could seriously believe that any one wanted to steal her children. Mrs. Snaith did not reach that point of folly; but she felt uneasy and insecure, as if, having ceased to admit her maternity, she had lost power over them.

Her boxes were already packed, she having always intended to go away by that evening's train; and she was truly glad that the little chaise was at the door and the two children in it, when Miss de Berenger coming up with her friend, she noticed the puzzled look of the one and the displeasure of the other.

She had bid her landlady good-bye, and had directed her driver to the station, when the voice of the late Miss Thimbleby struck on her ear. "Why, the woman's actually running away!"

"Drive on," said Mrs. Snaith.

"Running away, ma'am!" cried the landlady, looking after the chaise as it bore off her late lodgers. "Quite the contrary, I do assure you. Mrs. Snaith would have been very thankful to stay, if I could have kept her. As it is, I've let her stop on till I'm very hard drove to clean up for my next 'let.' Nobody ever 'runs away' from this place; and goodness knows there's little need, so healthy and bracing as it is."

Miss de Berenger hastened to say something complimentary concerning the place, and, in return, the landlady obliged her with the address of her late lodger.

About ten days after this, while Mrs. Snaith, already calmed by a sense of remoteness from observation, was pleasing herself with the certainty that her little Delia walked now as well as other children, Miss de Berenger took an opportunity to open her

" ' Four-and-sixpence each, I should think,' she reflected."

Page 179.

mind to her nephew, and fill him with a vague sense of responsibility towards these children.

Felix de Berenger was seven-and-twenty, a bachelor. He had lately been presented to a living, a very small one in point of income, but having a good-sized and comfortable house attached to it; a most excellent garden, two fields, an orchard, and a poultry yard.

To this place he had thankfully removed what little furniture he possessed, together with his books and his two brothers; also the nurse who had brought up the younger of these, and now, with a village girl to help her, did all the work of the parsonage, including the care of a cow and a pig.

His circumstances were peculiar. While he was yet almost in infancy, his father's regiment had been ordered to India, and he had been left behind. Several children, born to his parents during the next few years, had died in early childhood, and they had returned to England for the year's leave with one only, a boy just eight years younger than Felix.

The mother made great lamentation over the loss of her children, from the hot climate not suiting them. She left the second son behind also, and returning to India with her husband, the same misfortune overtook her again—her infants died; and it was not till after her final return to her native country that the youngest of her surviving children was born. He was now between seven and eight years old—a delicate little fellow, child-like in appearance, fully nineteen years younger than his eldest brother, and, being already orphaned, wholly dependent on the said brother both for maintenance and affection.

Miss de Berenger, a woman of good fortune, had come to stay with her dear nephew Felix, and, in her own opinion, to help him. She loved to scheme for other people, but out of her ample means she afforded them nothing but schemes.

Yet she was not accounted mean, for she was perfectly consistent. If people render help to those near to them at intervals, which are felt to be remote, or if their frequent presents are considered to be inadequate, they are thought ungenerous; but if they never give anything at all, they often escape from such an imputation. The minds of others are at rest concerning them, the looking out for needed assistance not being connected with them.

The late Mrs. de Berenger had considered her husband's only brother to be extremely mean; and this was mainly because once, when her little Dick was a baby, he had caused his wife, with profuse expressions of good-will from him, to bring the child a handsome little merino coat.

Miss de Berenger, having come to stay with her dear nephew Felix, was waiting in his pleasant dining-room till he should appear to breakfast.

He had been away from home when she arrived; sitting up with a sick parishioner, whose bedside he had not left till late in the night. She had not, therefore, seen him, and was now occupied in looking about her.

There were only six chairs in the room; these were of a very light description. "Four-and-sixpence each, I should think," she reflected; "certainly, not more." Then there were two large, solid book-cases, which were so disposed as to make the most of themselves. A square of carpet was spread in the middle of the room, and on this stood the table; all uncovered parts of the floor being stained brown. This scanty furnishing made the large room look larger. It looked, also, rather empty—for it was rather empty.

She walked to one of the windows, and, gazing out, saw what pleased her better. On the right, but a good way off, was a very high and thick yew-tree hedge, with a square place in front of it paved with small cogglestones. In this grew two fine walnut-trees. Nearer to her, and only divided from the paved yard by a line of artificial rock-work scarcely a foot high, was a large, beautiful garden, which, close to the house, was planted with rose-bushes, lilies, tree-peonies, and many lovely old-fashioned plants, called by modern gardeners "herbaceous rubbish." Those pernicious weeds, the scarlet geranium and the yellow calceolaria, had not found their way into it. As this garden sloped away from the house, large fruit-trees of fine growth appeared among the flower borders; climbing clematis, white or purple, was folded round the trunks of some. Farther off still, but not divided by any hedge from the flowers, excellent crops of various vegetables might be seen.

A second window in the dining-room showed her a mossy old lawn, in which grew two immense fir-trees, and between them was visible the broad, low tower of a village church.

Felix came down, his young brother Amias followed; a few words of welcome were said, then the bell was rung for prayers, and in came the two servants, the little brother Dick, and Miss de Berenger's maid.

If Felix had not been thinking of his sick parishioner, he must have noticed the restlessness of his aunt. As it was, he proceeded, after prayers, to help her to her breakfast, with nothing to break the force of his surprise, when, after little Dick had shut the door behind him, she flung back her curls and exclaimed, with an air of triumph—

"Yes! Well, now, Felix, well, now, Amias, what do you think? I've discovered the most astonishing family mystery that you ever heard of. It's enough to make your hair stand on end."

They were both well used to their aunt's sensational speeches: to do her justice, it was their habit of insisting on not being astonished at what she had to say, which mainly led to her constantly making her statements more and more startling.

Amias continued to cut the bread quite calmly, but Felix paused with his fork in the bacon. His aunt's bright red cheeks had taken a clearer dye than usual; she was evidently excited herself, not merely trying to excite them.

"I told you," she exclaimed, tossing back her curls to cool her face—"I told you I believed I was on the track of John's children. Poor John! Yes, I've found them, Felix. And their nurse, being alarmed at something (what, I don't know), positively stood me out, and declared that they were no relations of ours. Poor little waifs, they are the very image of him; and unless we show a parent's heart towards them, Felix, I really do not know what is to become of them."

Felix, unequal to the task of cutting the bacon, left the fork sticking upright in it.

"John's children!" he exclaimed. "Why, John's not married; at least, I never had a hint that he was, much less that he had a family."

"Nor had I, Felix; but I always suspected that, when he quarrelled with his father and went away, he *did* marry that young person. And I have no doubt, whatever the nurse may say, that he sent her to D—— on purpose that I might fall in with the children. Her conduct was most peculiar; she no sooner found out that they were relations of mine, than she rushed off with them. But she had better mind what she is about. I am going to write to her, for I have her address, and I shall tell her that if I go to law with her, it will certainly be brought in 'abduction of an heiress.'"

"An heiress!" exclaimed Felix. "She cannot be John's child, then."

"She is a very lovely little girl; and if I make a will in her favour, she will turn out to be an heiress. And then, as I said, that nurse had better look out, or she will get herself transported for carrying her off as she has done."

At this point the two brothers seemed to lose their interest in the matter, and to find their wonder subside, so that they could begin to eat their breakfast.

She then gave an account of what had passed, but at the same time taking so much for granted, and so piecing together what she had been told, what she thought, and what the landlady had thought, that Felix, in spite of himself, could not help believing that these children must be John de Berenger's daughters.

John de Berenger was the third son of old Sir Samuel de Berenger, who, having married late in life, was the father of a family very little older than Felix de Berenger, the son of his nephew.

The baronet's eldest son, for whom he had never cared much, was a confirmed invalid, spending most of his time at Algiers or in Italy. He was a married man, but childless. The second son, Tom, had just married, and gone to join his regiment in India. The third, John, who was not without certain endearing qualities, was no credit to any one belonging to him. He was reckless of opinion, extravagant, and so hopelessly in debt, that he would certainly have been outlawed, but that there was only one healthy life between him and the baronetcy; and his father, moreover, was both rich and old. So that it seemed to his creditors wise to wait on the chance of his inheriting, at least, enough to pay his debts, provided they did not make his father aware how great these were.

"I cannot bear to hear poor John called the reprobate of the family," exclaimed Miss de Berenger, "and threatened with outlawry, dear fellow!"

It was partly on account of the word "outlaw" that Miss de Berenger took a romantic interest in John. No halo hangs about vulgar debt, but outlawry brings to mind the Lincoln green, bows and arrows, and a silver horn to blow upon under the greenwood tree.

"I wish you would not tease the *old man* about these children," said Amias. "Hasn't he enough to think of just now? I'm the reprobate of the family. I repudiate John; he's an impostor."

"Yes, indeed, Amias," cried Miss de Berenger instantly, remembering that she ought to bear her testimony against the youth's behaviour. "Yes, very sad. I've heard of your conduct. Sir Sam wrote to me in a rage. I hear you've turned teetotaler as well, on purpose to insult him; and I'm informed that you said brewing was not a proper trade for a gentleman."

"I said drunkenness was the cause of almost all the misery in the country. I said there was hardly a judge on the bench who had not declared that it had to do with nine-tenths of the crime that came before him. I said——"

"Now, look here," exclaimed Felix, suddenly rousing up, "I can stand a good deal, but I can't and won't stand a temperance lecture on the top of John's children!" Then thinking, perhaps, that he had been a little too vehement, he added and half laughed, "It's all right, my boy."

"The *old man* has a great deal to worry him just now," said Amias, excusing his brother's sudden heat to his aunt.

"And after he had been so kind—I mean, Sir Sam had been so kind—and proposed to take you into the concern, and in time give you an interest in it! Yes, it is very sad."

"Well, you would not have had me be such a sneak, I suppose, as not to tell Uncle Sam what I'd done? Everybody else knew. I'd been bursting with rage some time to think how we were actually the ruin of people. But that was not why I did it, I can tell you; I did it for fun. When that temperance fellow came into the village, and stood on a kitchen chair ranting, a lot of people soon got round him, and some of them cheered and some jeered me as I came calmly by and stopped to listen."

"Ah! stopped to listen, Amias. That shows what comes of tampering with evil. Well?"

"Well, presently two drunken men came reeling up, and insisted on shaking hands with me. And the people hauled out another chair from a cottage, and declared that I must mount it and answer him. I had not known at first what it was that he was ranting about, with 'dear brethren,' and 'dear sisters,' and 'dear fellow-sinners.' By the time I did know they would not let me off; they stamped and cheered, and said it was election time, and I must and should speak up for the old concern."

"Well, Amias, well."

"Why, the tide turned against the temperance man; they hooted him down. And (I was excited at first, you know, it seemed such fun) so I got on the chair and imitated the man, his cockney talk and cant. I did him capitally; I ranted till they all shrieked with laughter. And then I stopped, for I knew I was doing the devil's work. I stopped, I tell you, and I told them the temperance man was quite right, and asked them if they didn't know it, and all that; and then Felix coming up, I felt that I was stumped, and I jumped down and ran off. I could hear every step I took on the grass, the people were so still; I suppose it was with astonishment."

"Very sad," said Miss de Berenger again. Felix smiled.

"So," continued the boy, "I thought the next day I had better go and tell it all to Uncle Sam. The *old man* thought so too; so I went and did for myself, for, of course, he sent me packing. And here I am."

"Well," said Miss de Berenger, with some bitterness, and what was meant for irony, "then, I hope the *old man* made you welcome."

"Yes," said Felix calmly, "I did."

"You needn't shake your head, aunt," proceeded the boy. "I'm glad I did it."

Miss de Berenger had sense enough to see that what she might say on this subject could have no effect. She returned to her former theme; she did not see how poor John's children were to be educated.

"The proper person to tell this to is old Sam himself," observed Felix.

"Oh, I have written to him, my dear Felix. I have laid the whole matter before him, and——"

"And what?"

"And he repudiates them utterly! But if he could see them, beautiful little creatures, and such a respectable nurse, I'm sure it would soften his heart."

"How can John afford a nurse? His father allows him very little to live on."

"Very little. I thought it so touching to see them handsomely dressed when John must be almost in want. It shows his heart is in the right place. And then, no doubt, he had them thrown in our way, hoping we should take them up."

"If that is the case, why, in the name of common sense, did their nurse carry them off?"

"Why, my dear, she might not know his motive, or she was afraid, perhaps, that my penetration, or some unexpected question of mine, might lead her to betray what she is probably aware must not be told—that is, where John's abode is."

"It sounds queer," said Felix.

Miss de Berenger took no notice of this remark, but dashed into what seemed a perfectly different subject.

"And what about poor little Dick? He has had no lessons at all since you came here. Yes, he ought to have a governess, for he is far too delicate to go to school."

"Aunt, you know very well that I cannot afford a governess just yet."

"But, Felix, I have matured a scheme. Yes, I have thought it out. I wish I was more thankful for this talent committed to me of planning for others. You know dear Cecilia's sister, Ann Thimbleby, of course?"

"Of course," said Felix, without any enthusiasm.

"Dear Cecilia would like so much to have her near at hand. But then, you know, Ann has to educate her little sister, and she finds it extremely difficult to meet with any one who will take a governess and a ten-years'-old sister with her."

"I should think so!"

"Ann Thimbleby asks forty pounds a year salary."

"Oh!"

"Felix, do listen."

"Ann Thimbleby asks forty pounds a year salary, you said."

"Yes, Felix; but she and the child are vegetarians. Just think of your garden. It would cost you a mere nothing to feed them, with the eggs, too, that you have from the poultry yard, and the milk from your cow. You would still (when your family was supplied) have fruit and vegetables to exchange for groceries, as I explained to you was commonly done. If you would give her little sister board and lodging, and let Ann teach her with Dick, Ann would take ten pounds a year and be thankful. I know she would, for she has twenty pounds a year of her own."

"I could not afford even that. I should still be out of pocket."

"Yes, you would — perhaps almost as much as twenty pounds a year. Yes. But, then, there are these little De Berengers. I have ascertained that their nurse pays a certain Miss Price twenty pounds for teaching them. Now, Felix, if that woman would come and live in the village, you could agree with Ann to teach the four children together, and you, receiving the twenty pounds, would get Dick educated for nothing. You would keep a kind of co-operative store for the benefit of all parties, the goods being children."

Felix was struck with surprise.

"You actually propose to me to encumber myself with a governess, a girl, and two children, in order to get little Dick taught his lessons?"

"Well, Felix, can you think of a better plan? It would be bringing these darlings close to their own family, and getting Dick looked after and taught for nothing. I do not mean to say that Mary Thimbleby is a nice child—far be it from me to deceive you. She is a stupid, uncomfortable girl, and how their mother, who was the sweetest woman — so managing, too — contrived to have such an uncomfortable child, I cannot think. It is something quite new in that family to produce a variety of the sort. But these subjects," continued Miss de Berenger, pushing back her loose curls, and putting on an air of wisdom and cogitation—"these subjects are as intricate as all others on the origin of species."

A gleam of joy shot across the dark face of Felix, but he remained silent, and his aunt continued.

"And as for Cecilia's marrying Carlos Tanner, of course that was very imprudent; but I cannot help taking an interest in him, considering, my dears, that I ought to have been his mother, and that, but for the fickleness of mankind, I should have been."

This was an old story.

"Never mind, Aunt Sarah," said Amias. "His father's wife lost all her fortune after he married her, and everybody said that served him right."

"And she had been a widow twice before he took her," observed Felix.

"Yes," said Aunt Sarah, much consoled; "and she was married in a brown gown—actually, my dears, in a brown gown. If he had married me, I should have had a white one."

"Well, then, I hope the wedding cake, instead of white, was done with brown sugar," continued Felix.

"For consistency's sake it should have been," answered Sarah; "but, my dears, we cannot expect consistency in this world! Yes!"

CHAPTER VIII.

THIS plan of Miss de Berenger's appeared to her nephew so preposterous, that he gave it no better reception than a somewhat ironical smile; then he finished his breakfast, and what more his aunt had to say he heard without receiving the sense. Yet, in less than one month, he was glad to carry out the whole scheme, almost to the letter.

In about a week he found that he was living precisely up to his income, and had nothing to spare for such contingencies as illness, nor anything to spend on Dick's education. At the same time, Miss de Berenger having said vaguely that no doubt little Dick would soon have a governess, a widow lady, a friend of hers, who lived half a mile off, came and proposed advantageous terms, if her son might come as a day pupil, and take his lessons with Dick. Her boy, she said, was lonely; he was delicate; he was her only child. Might he ride over on his pony? She was sure they should agree about terms.

On this hint Miss de Berenger spoke again, and got leave from Felix to write to Mrs. Snaith; which she did, proposing to the poor woman to come and live in a little cottage then vacant, and pay twenty pounds a year for the education of the two children.

Mrs. Snaith did not often laugh, but she laughed heartily when she got that letter; felt as if she had been politely invited to step into the lion's den, and put it aside, taking nearly a fortnight for considering the precise terms in which she could decline it.

But lo, at the end of that term scarlet fever broke out in the farmhouse where Miss Price the governess lived, and she felt at once a longing desire to get away from the place. She only took her little cottage by the week; she could hire a cart to carry away her furniture to the station. She had spent a good deal of money on her late trip to the shore, and could not possibly afford another. How cheap this plan was—how easy! And, after all, no one but herself had any power over the children; no one could possibly prevent her taking them away again from these De Berengers whenever she chose.

She drew out the letter again. There was no time to be lost; one more day brought her news of another case of fever, and without loss of an hour she wrote a respectful letter to Miss de Berenger, setting forth that she would appear with the children the very next evening, and what little furniture she had should come with them.

Miss de Berenger had seldom been happier. She rushed to accept the widow's proposition, then she flew to arrange matters with Miss Thimbleby, which she did in such a satisfactory fashion, that this young lady was to receive a small salary for her services, together with vegetarian board, lodging, and leave to educate the little sister; Felix, on his part, taking the remainder of what Mrs.

Snaith and the widow lady were to pay, so as to reimburse himself for his outlay, and pay also for the small quantity of cheap furniture that had to be bought, his main advantage being that he was to get his little brother taught and looked after for nothing.

It was an anxious and trying day for Mrs. Snaith that took her, her children, and her goods, to the new home. Several times during the course of it imagination transported her among the people she was going to. How would they receive her? What questions would they ask? She thought of them as excited also, as busy about her affairs, for Miss de Berenger had assured her that the little cottage should be swept down for her, and that she should find a comfortable supper ready there for herself and her little charge.

There was a certain amount of bustle, and some excitement also, that day at the parsonage; not in the minds of Felix or his brother, for they were gone out for the day; and not concerning Mrs. Snaith. If she could have known what it was that effaced her from their thoughts, it would have helped her, as such things always do, to realise how small the place was that she filled in creation.

It is hard sometimes, when one had thought that one's self and one's affairs were filling the minds of others, to find that one has been utterly forgotten; but it is positively humbling to discover, as is sometimes our lot, what a small, what an utterly worthless thing it was that blotted us out.

However, in this case, it cannot be said to have been a small thing—quite the contrary, it was a very large thing; there was the oddness of the matter. And how so large a thing could possibly be lost, missing, or mislaid, in such a scantily furnished house, was the whole mystery. The thing, in short, for sake of which Mrs. Snaith passed out of mind, was a clothes-basket.

Jolliffe, the servant, had looked all over for it, and was out of breath. A girl who had been blamed, and had wept in consequence, was now helping the others to express the common astonishment, and counting off on her fingers, as Jolliffe enumerated them, all the places, likely and unlikely, that had been looked into in vain.

A large bundle of clothes, ready tied up to be put into this basket, was lying in the mean time on the clean kitchen floor, and the washerwoman sat in judgment upon it, deciding that it was too heavy to be carried as it was, even with the help of her little boy, who, with his legs hanging down, sat

regarding it with a sheepish and shamefaced air, as one so used to be accused, when any sort of mischief had been perpetrated, that he was expecting every moment to hear the loss of the basket confidently laid at his door.

Just then a youth, who had been hired to weed, came clattering across the paved yard in his hobnailed boots.

"I forgot the loft," said Jolliffe; and she put her head out at the casement window. "Andrew, you go and look in the loft over the stable if the big clothes-basket is there."

"I know it can't be there, mem," answered the boy.

"I didn't ask you what you knew," said Mrs. Jolliffe with the dignity of full conviction. "If it's not in a likely place, it stands to reason that it must be in an unlikely. You go and do as I bid you."

"Yes, mem," said the boy; and he burst into a chuckling laugh, and instantly was grave again.

"That boy Andrew is the awkwardest in the parish," continued Mrs. Jolliffe; "but when I say the basket couldn't have gone without hands, I don't mean but what his hands are clean, in a manner of speaking."

"It ain't there," said Andrew, returning, and chuckling again. Whereupon he was reproved by all parties for things in general, including his having been frequently seen to laugh even at his work, as if nothing was of any account; which, they observed, had very probably emboldened some tramp to carry off the missing article. He was then made to fetch the lightest wheelbarrow from the potato garden, and in that the clothes for the wash were solemnly wheeled away.

The soft shadows of evening were coming on, and everything about the parsonage was very still, when Miss de Berenger came bustling up to the kitchen door, calling for Dick.

"I cannot find him anywhere, Jolliffe. I want him to come this minute and see his little cousins. They have just arrived at the cottage with their nurse, and I told them they should see him."

Jolliffe had been leaning out at the dairy window, talking to a market gardener who also kept a shop in the neighbouring town, in which he sold both fruit and grocery, and with whom Felix, under Miss de Berenger's advice, had made an agreement to exchange some of his superfluous fruit for tea and other groceries. She now started forth, suddenly remembering that she had not seen Dick for a long time, the gardener following.

"Wherever can the dear child be!" she exclaimed. "I should have looked after him before, if I hadn't had those lettices on my mind. They've all come to their hearts at once; the dairy floor is all over green things that master cut for fear their heads should spread."

"That comes of the vegetable ladies," observed the gardener. "I'm sure I don't grudge anything its growth—not but what I shall lose by all those apricots being ripe together."

"Wherever can the dear child be?" repeated Jolliffe. "Master Dick!" she shouted, "where are you? Come, it's supper time, and your aunt wants you, lovey."

A childish whoop answered, and was echoed from the old church tower, which was close to the garden.

"I can't tell where he is," she observed; "the sound seemed to come from all round." Then she turned to the east, and exclaimed, "Why, goodness!—why, good gracious me, if ever I saw anything so strange in my life, Mr. Bolton! There's ever so many stars shining in the chestnut tree."

Mr. Bolton looked. There stood the great horse-chestnut tree, in all the splendour of its rich, deep foliage, and there certainly was a light shining between the leaves. Not the moon, for she hung a yellow crescent, that yielded no light at all; not Venus, for she, of all stars, was the only one out; but a warm orange, steady light that illuminated the whole centre of the tree, and shone through the leaves as well as between them.

The soft veil of the gloaming came on, and made this light every moment brighter; while such a silence seemed to gather and rise from under the trees, that Jolliffe and her companion, as they slowly and cautiously approached, did not care to speak. Then the woman hung back, the light looked so strange; and the man went under, looked up, and came back with a smile.

"I'll give you two guesses regarding what's up in that tree!" he exclaimed.

"Can't I see that it's a light?" cried Mrs. Jolliffe with much impatience. "I don't see, though you have bought the fruit off the very walls, that I've any call to pick out answers for your riddles in master's own garden, at this time o' night."

"Of course it's a light," replied Mr. Bolton, "but what's the light in? Well, if you don't like to come any nigher, in regard of its being so close to the old churchyard, I'll tell you. It's in the old clothes-basket."

Jolliffe's surprise made her good-tempered. Again she came under the tree, and looked up. "This must be one of the dear child's antics," she observed; "but however in the world did he get it up there? Must be fifteen feet high. What a horrid dangerous trick!"

"I don't see that," answered Mr. Bolton. "He can climb like a cat. What he's done is this: he's drawn it up, do you see, by that long dangle of clothes-line to the fork where those three branches spread out, and there, as he stood above, he's managed to land it pretty steady, and he's tied it with the rope in and out among the boughs, and then he's fetched the stable lantern."

"And that boy Andrew helped him, I'll be bound!" exclaimed Mrs. Jolliffe. "I shouldn't wonder if he's in it now. Master Dicky, dear, you'll speak to your own Jolly, won't you?"

A good deal of creaking was now heard in the wicker-work of the basket, but there was no answer.

"Oh, well, Mr. Bolton," remarked Mrs. Jolliffe in a high-raised voice, "it's a clear case that he ain't here; I'd better go in and tell his brother that he's lost."

A good deal more creaking, and something like a chuckle, was now heard in the basket, and presently over the edge peered the face of a great owl, a favourite companion of the child's.

It was dusk now under the tree, and the creature's eyes glared in the light of the lantern. Mrs. Jolliffe, being startled, called him a beast; but he looked far more like the graven image of a cherub on a tomb, for nothing of him could be seen but his widespread wings and his face, while he looked down and appeared to think the visit of these two persons intrusive and unseasonable.

"Well, old goggle-eyes," quoth Mr. Bolton, "so you're there too, are you? If you know where your master is, which appears likely—for you're as cunning as many Christians, and full as ugly—you'd better tell him that, as sure as fate, we're going to fetch his brother out if he doesn't come down."

"Ay, that we are," added Mrs. Jolliffe. "Why, it'll be dark presently, and how is he to get down in the dark?"

The round, rosy face of little Dick was now reared up beside the face of the owl. He looked like a cherub too, but with a difference.

Mr. Bolton shook his head, and said rather gruffly, "Now, what are we to think of this here behaviour? What with getting yourself lifted off your legs a-ringing the church bells, and what with setting yourself fast in the chimney, climbing after jackdaws' nests, and what with sailing in the wash-tub, and what with getting yourself mixed up with the weights of the parish clock, you're a handful to your family, I do declare, and a caution to parties about to marry."

Instead of looking at all penitent, the little urchin only said, "But you won't *tell*, Jolly, dear—you won't really tell?"

"Yes," answered Mrs. Jolliffe stolidly, "I shall tell; so now you know. And how anybody that's only to eat lettices and green meat generally is ever to conquer *you!* Of course I shall tell."

"Well, then, just throw up the cord," said the little fellow, "and I'll be down in a minute."

"I shouldn't wonder if that boy Andrew has been helping you," observed Mrs. Jolliffe. "If he has it may be as much as his place is worth."

It was never worth more than ninepence a day; but the discussion was just then cut short by the sound of voices. Felix and his brother came down the grass walk.

"What's all this?" said Felix; but before Mrs. Jolliffe and Mr. Bolton had explained, he had taken in the whole matter, and, what was more, he evidently thought nothing of it.

Amias brought a fruit-ladder, Felix called the little fellow down from his wicker nest, and when he was upon it and conveniently near, gave him a not unfriendly slap on his chubby person. "You had better look out, you little monkey," he remarked in a casual and general sort of way. Little Dick said he would, and Felix, mounting the ladder, looked into the basket, saw the owl and the lantern, and a quantity of mown grass; also two books of fairy tales which Dick had been reading. He brought these last down and put out the light. "The basket is a good-for-nothing old thing," he observed to Jolliffe as he descended; "the child may as well be allowed to keep it."

Mrs. Jolliffe almost held up her hands. "Is that the way to bring up a child?" was her mental answer. "Well, after this week we shall wash at home, so it does not so much signify."

Felix was not half so fond of his little brother as a parent would have been, but he was, on the whole, nearly as indulgent. Dick, while he slowly retreated, heard permission given for him to keep the clothes-basket, but a ready instinct assured him that he would do well to retire from observation. He had other pieces of mischief on his mind beside the building of that child-nest in the tree, so he evaded his aunt when he heard her calling him, and creeping up to his little room, tumbled into bed and went to sleep as fast as possible.

He slept sweetly. So did not Mrs. Snaith, though she was much fatigued; a foreboding thought of impending questions haunted her. And as, between ten and eleven o'clock the next morning, she came forth from her tiny cottage to bring her little girls to the vicarage, her senses seemed to be sharpened both by the new scene and the leisure given her for remarking it.

Miss de Berenger had asked her to bring the children. As well then, she thought, as at some future time. The little creatures, exquisitely neat and clean, with sunny locks flowing under their limp white hats, walked on before her, while she, very plainly clad, came after, all in sober brown. She entered the parsonage gate, and there stood the vicar in his white gown; he had just been marrying a rustic couple at the church, and was leisurely divesting himself of this long white garment, which was so clean that, between the two great dark fir-trees on the lawn, it seemed almost to shine.

Felix came up when he saw the children, met them just as they reached the front door, and gave a hand to each; then addressed the nurse pleasantly. But, hardly noticing her answer, he seated himself on the outside of the dining-room window and cast attentive glances at his two little guests, who, unabashed and calm, looked at him with wide-open eyes of the sweetest blue-grey, and found it interesting to notice how the clerk was folding up that long white gown, and how a tame jackdaw had come hopping up to Felix, and was perching herself on his knee. Sometimes the children answered when Felix spoke, sometimes the nurse, but an inward trembling shook her. She had thought the shy anxieties of those few moments would soon be over; but no—far otherwise. She looked earnestly at the clergyman, at this Mr. Felix de Berenger, and she saw in his face no recognition, but a growing conviction made her more aware that she did not see him for the first time. A dark, thin man of middle height, a pleasant face—though rather an anxious one—thin features. And the hair? Well, what of the hair? Felix took off his hat presently for the morning was warm; then,

rising, he turned the other side of his head towards her, as he called up at an open window, "Dick, Dick! Come down, you little monkey. Come; I want you." Yes, there it was, visible enough—one lock, narrow and perfectly white, among the otherwise umber waves of thick, dark hair.

The nurse felt for the moment as if her heart stood still, and all was up with her. The curate! It was the curate who had been kind to her in her worst adversity, who had given her a shilling in the hop-garden.

He showed no signs of recognition. How, indeed, should he know her again, or she fail to know him again? He was not altered in the least, and had, as she instantly remembered, seen many and many a poor creature since such as she had been. But she—her lean, gaunt figure was changed by several years of peace, comfort, and good living. She was inclined, for her age, to be rather stout now. She was very neatly and becomingly dressed, for in place of that flimsy, faded clothing, she wore plain, dark colours, and her shining hair was disposed in two close bands down her face.

She looked well into his eyes, impelled by her very fear to seek the worst at once. He did not know her. And now a lovely little boy in a pinafore was coming up; a dimpled creature as brown as a berry—hair, and eyes, and face—excepting where the clear crimson of the cheek showed through a little.

He was inclined to be very shamefaced. Amabel was not. She came up to him and gave him the usual greeting of infancy, a kiss. Then Delia slipped off Mr. de Berenger's knee, and, after inspecting Dick for an instant, she also kissed him; and then the children smiled at one another all over their little faces, and, taking hands, walked off among the trees chattering.

Pretty little Dick! he was supremely happy that morning. The joy of their presence was as if two little child-angels had come to play with him. He made them welcome to all his best things; he also took them up the fruit-ladder to his nest. For more than four years after this, those beautiful nestlings spent their happiest hours in it.

But on this first climb into it they were aided by Andrew, who had originally helped Dick to tie the basket safely, and was now very impressive with all the children. "They were on no account to go up, nor down neither, without his help; they were to promise solemnly that they never would—to promise *as sure as death.*" So they did, knowing and caring about death nothing at all. But they knew they were happy—Dick especially—and he fell easily and at once under the influence of their sex, and never so long as he lived escaped from it any more.

The leaves were very thick underneath them, so that they could not be seen from below. But they could see the great shining face of the church clock, the rooks leading off their second brood, the white road winding on through the heathery common, and far beyond a little hill in old Sir Sam's park, on the slope of which does and fawns were lying half hidden by the bracken.

In the mean time Mrs. Snaith, little aware what they were about, had been introduced by Jolliffe to the clean kitchen, and there, after a good deal of polite haggling, as, "Well, ma'am, I'm sure it's a shame," and "Well, ma'am, I couldn't bear myself sitting with my hands before me," had been accommodated with an apron, and allowed to make herself useful by stringing and slicing beans. The party had been invited to an early dinner at the parsonage, and there were rabbits and parsley sauce to prepare, and there were late red currants to strip from the stalks for a fruit pudding. Aided by the circumstance that they had something to do, the ladies soon became friendly, and talked of such subjects as really interested them.

"Well, it *is* a very small cottage, ma'am; there you're right."

"And in lodgings you're saved a vast of trouble, so that if it wasn't for the dripping——"

"Ah, indeed; you may well mention that, ma'am. Why, not one in ten of those landladies is to be depended on."

Mrs. Snaith assented.

"And to sit in your parlour," she continued, "and know as well as can be that they're making their own crusts with your dripping, and that you mayn't go down to see it, is enough to spoil the best of tempers and the least particular."

They were rather a large party at dinner, for the new governess and her young sister had arrived, and Felix, as he sat at the head of the table, had only just marshalled them, said grace, and begun to wonder how the one young servant of the establishment would wait upon them all, when Mrs. Snaith appeared, carrying in the first dish, which she set before him and uncovered, as if she was performing some ordinary and looked-for duty.

"Mrs. Snaith!" he exclaimed.

"I should wish it, if you please, sir, whenever my young ladies is here," she replied calmly.

A very convenient wish, and she began to carry it out with a quiet and homely dignity that he much admired, every now and then giving the gentlest motherly admonition to the children, including little Dick. Felix had a certain fear of a lady; womanhood was sufficiently alarming to him without fine clothes, accomplishments, and a polished and self-possessed manner. He found himself most attracted by a good woman who was without these extraneous advantages; this homely dignity and unruffled humility pleased him, and commanded his respect. He let Mrs. Snaith alone, and under her auspices

the dinner went on pleasantly to its conclusion.

Little Amabel and her sister won great approval by their sweet looks and pretty behaviour at that dinner. They had been well taught, and could conduct themselves perfectly well at table.

Felix regarded them with attention; they were graceful, they were fair, but he saw no special likeness to old Sir Sam's family.

The children had in fact been helped, by their mother's intense sympathy, to the inheritance of a certain pensive wistfulness that was in their father's soul and countenance; the reflection of it was in their faces—only in their faces—and even there it appeared more as the expression of a sentiment than of a passion, that abiding passion of regret for his lameness that the bad, beautiful youth was always brooding over. When their lovely little faces were at rest, and no smiles rippled over them, their mother could often see that look, a witness to their father's sorrow and their mother's pity; it gave a strange, and to her a very touching, interest to both the children. There was an unusual contrast between the still deeps in their lucid, grave blue eyes, and the rosy lips, so dimpled and waggish, so ready to soften and smile, and show a mouthful of pearls.

"Well, Felix; well, Amias," said Miss de Berenger, when this dinner was over, and she was left alone with her two nephews, "I suppose you will both admit that I have brought a treasure into the family. Yes! How well that woman waits! What a sight the great heaps of potatoes must have been for her, and the cabbages and the buttered beans that Ann and Mary consumed! I call to mind now your dear father asking me if I remembered a dinner we were at once, at their mother's. 'Remember it!' I exclaimed. 'Ay, thou poor ghost of a meal, while memory holds her place in an empty stomach.' I was inspired to say it, just as Shakespeare was at first, though in general I am not at all poetical. And then the tipsy cake she gave us in the evening! It was a tremendous falsehood to call it by such a name. Tipsy, indeed! How was a whole cake to get tipsy on one glass of South African wine? You need not look so wise, Amias; a degrading thing, I suppose you'll say, to make fun of even a dumb cake, when it's drunk," proceeded Miss de Berenger, after a pause. "As if there could be real fun in the inebriation of anything whatever. Yes! Why, how very ridiculous you two are! I never saw such risible fellows in my life. And you a clergyman, too, Felix! What can you be laughing at now?"

While this conversation took place in the garden, and while the children played together, and the vegetarians, walking between thick hedges of peas and beans, and ridges of new potatoes, felt that they had come into a land of fatness and plenty, Mrs. Snaith, helping to wash the glass in the neat kitchen, was made welcome to a good deal of information that no amount of questioning would have procured for those in a different station of life to her informers.

These were Mr. Bolton, who had just stepped up to gather some early summer jennetings, but out of delicacy forbore to take them under the eyes of Felix, and so waited till he should come in; and Mrs. Jolliffe, who in dismissing the washerwoman, after counting out the clean clothes she had brought home, took occasion, with patronising suavity, to recommend her to the newcomer as a very honest woman, and a good hand at getting up children's clothes.

Mrs. Snaith said she would employ her, and the grateful and respectful thanks that she and Jolliffe both received opened the heart of the latter still further, so that as the little woman retreated across the yard her praises followed her.

"An honest little woman, and industrious too, Mrs. Snaith; and has lately got the laundry work of the clerks at the brewery. Still, as she said to me, 'Mrs. Jolliffe,' said she, 'there's no sweet without its bitter, and most of those gentlemen air such extra large sizes, that I feel it hard I should hev to do justice to their shirts, at twopence-halfpenny apiece, when I should hev had the same money if they'd been smaller.'"

"Her present husband is not to complain of for size," observed Mr. Bolton.

"No, but that was a conveniency," quoth Mrs. Jolliffe; "and, for aught I know, the conveniency helped to decide her, as such things very frequently do, and no harm neither."

Mrs. Jolliffe spoke with such a meaning smile, that Mrs. Snaith testified some curiosity, whereupon she continued:—

"For, as I said, a prudent little woman she was. Her first husband's Sunday coat was laid by as good as new; so she took and cut it smaller for her second to be married in, and very respectable he looked in it, and it saved money. And why not, Mr. Bolton?" she inquired, with a certain sharpness of reproof in her voice.

"Why not, indeed!" answered Mr. Bolton,

hastening to agree, though at first his face had assumed a slightly sarcastic expression. Then, on reflection, he veered round to his first thought. "But it don't seem a feeling thing to do, neither."

"Feeling!" quoth Mrs. Jolliffe, in the tone of one who makes a telling retort. "You and I can't talk together about feelings, and hope to agree at all. Some folks have most feeling for that that can hold up its head and stop at home, which is my case. I don't pretend to understand them whose feeling is for that that must run away."

Here both Mrs. Jolliffe and Mr. Bolton laughed, and Mrs. Snaith was appealed to in words that confused and startled her, for they seemed to hint at her wretched husband's condition, as if the speaker knew all about it.

"When the law has got hold of a man, that man is not, therefore, to be cried down by me, and never shall be. No, nor by you neither, ma'am, as your actions make evident."

Mrs. Snaith flushed and trembled, but said nothing, and with what relief, and what gratitude for it, she heard the rest of the conversation, neither of those who marked her rising colour could have the least idea.

"Now, my feelings go across the water. What's old Sam to me?"

"That you should talk of him so disrespectful, almost at his own gates!"

"Why not?" replied Mr. Bolton. "Do I owe him for a single drop of his beer, either given me or sold to me?"

"Right well you know that he'd have lost his seat if he'd given any away at the last election."

"Right well I do know it. For all that, old Sam, as I was saying, never gives a pleasant word to his neighbours. And never was a freer, friendlier man than Mr. John, and free and friendly is he treated now by me and by others. Does he find any difficulty in getting intelligence of all he wants to know? I should say not. Why, Mrs. Snaith, Mr. John has more than one correspondent here, that knows as much about him as maybe I do, and maybe as you do."

"Mr. John?" exclaimed Mrs. Snaith, now breathing freely. "Oh, Mr. John de Berenger it were that you spoke of?"

"Why, yes," said Mr. Bolton, looking at her with some admiration for what he considered an excellently feigned surprise. "Mr. John de Berenger, of course. Who else?"

CHAPTER IX.

OLD Sir Sam, as people called him, otherwise Sir Samuel Simcox de Berenger, was in some respects a particularly agreeable man. He had some undesirable qualities, but from the first he had been so strangely dealt with by circumstances, by nature, and by Providence, so drawn on through the natural openings made by other men's mistakes, that if he had been any better, he would have been a hero; and that he certainly was not.

Most people thought he was a great deal richer than he ought to have been, and yet he had never taken a shilling but what the laws of his country accorded to him.

His own father, having two sons, had taken him, the elder, into partnership, and given him a share in his great brewery business. The younger had gone into the army, obtaining the father's consent, though it was very reluctantly given.

This second son had married very young, and left three children, one of whom was the father of Felix, and another his aunt, Sarah de Berenger. To her the old grandfather had given a handsome fortune during his lifetime—had, in short, settled upon her a small estate, which had come into the family by the female side, so that she was much better off than her two brothers; for when, after his younger son's death, the old man also died, it was found that, owing to some fatal informality in the will, the representatives of the younger branch could not possess themselves of that interest in his business and his property which he had always expressed himself as intending to leave them.

Sir Samuel, without a lawsuit, was evidently master of all. He took immense pains to get the best legal opinions, and confidently expected that his two nephews would try the case. Being a pugnacious man, he looked forward to a fair fight, not without a certain amount of pleasure and excitement.

Perhaps the two nephews took counsel's opinion also; but however that might be, they never gave him a chance of fighting. Instead of going to law, they took themselves off, left him to swallow up all, and maintained themselves independently of him and his business.

There is little doubt that he would have been, to a great extent, the conqueror, if there had been a suit. In such a case he would have held his head high, and also have done something for his late brother's family; but when he found that he was left master of the situation without a suit, and also without a reconciliation, he felt it. To win in open fight is never so necessary to the comfort and pride of the winner, if he is right, as if he is wrong.

While Sir Samuel was considering that, though these nephews could make good no claim at law, yet they ought to have *some thing*, one of them chanced to die without a will, and he chose to consider himself the young man's heir-at-law. That is to say, he reflected that the dead nephew, having been the elder of the two, ought to have had, if he had lived, a double share; he would certainly have given him a double share. So he divided off that portion of his possessions as having been destined for his nephew, and he always called it, "What I came in for, in consequence of poor Tom's premature death." Thus that claim settled itself.

The other nephew, the father of Felix, never quarrelled with him, but rather seemed to set him at nought. Yet he felt that he must do his duty by him. To that end he informed him that he should take his second son, then an infant, into the business; which in due time he did, with what results has already been explained.

He never had any thanks from the father of the baby, who went to India before the future brewer could run alone; but he occasionally called the child "Small-beer," by which he made it evident that Sir Samuel had leave to carry out his noble intention if he pleased. Sir Samuel felt that too; for though he retained all the material advantage that had come of the unlucky will, he none the less fretted under a sense of contempt that he knew his nephew held him in, and was always particularly cautious what he said, lest he should provoke an answer.

So he lived in the exercise of a certain self-control, feeling it, in general, politic to be bland and obliging to his nephew; and this, to a man of his choleric nature, was galling. At the same time, he took all opportunities of being affectionate and useful to his niece Sarah, who, being herself very well off, felt her brother's poverty the less keenly, and was often inclined to identify herself with the rich side of the family, as finding riches a great thing to have in common. Sarah lost both her brothers in their comparative youth. As for Felix, her nephew, his was a grievance once removed—an old story. His great-uncle, for a time, had been very kind to Amias—had, in fact, shown a decided affection for him; it was as well now to let the old great-grandfather's will be forgotten.

Felix was helped in his wish to let it pass into the background by his liking for old Sir Samuel's sons, the youngest of whom was only one year his own senior; for Sir Samuel had married somewhat late in life, so that his sons and his great-nephews were contemporaries.

And now two little girls had appeared upon the scene, to Sir Samuel's great surprise and very natural annoyance. His great-nephew had been the cause of their coming; and Miss de Berenger had told him pointedly that they were his grandchildren.

He was secretly enraged with Felix—would like to have had an encounter with him about it; the more so as he felt inclined to believe it was so.

No one knew so well as himself how utterly in the wrong his favourite son had always been in his quarrels with him. In fact, his affection for the scapegrace had enabled him to endure a vast deal that any father would have found hard, and in hope of winning, and then retaining him, to be almost subservient and long-indulgent.

But the favourite had got into debt many times after being brought home and freed. Finally, the father had been obliged to send him from home on an allowance, and John had actually gambled away great part of his interest even in that.

His father knew he had somehow deeply entangled himself, but knew not all. Sometimes he got a hint from Felix, to whom, at rare intervals, John still wrote, for as boys the two had been friends. When Sir Samuel found that Felix was arranging for the education of these little De Berengers, he felt how hard it was that his son should confide in a cousin rather than in himself, and he waited a week, in confident expectation that Felix would lay a case before him, declare that these were his grandchildren, and make some demand on him for money; he intended to dispute every inch of the ground, not give a shilling unless the fact was fully proved, and, even then beat Felix down to the lowest sum he could possibly be induced to accept. But the week came to an end, and Felix said not a word.

Everybody declared that these two little girls were the image of John. He felt a devouring anxiety to see them, for he was an affectionate old fellow. He had vowed to himself that they were none of his, and that, as John had acknowledged no marriage, it

could be no duty of his to take upon him the great expense of their maintenance; but here they were at his gates, and he longed to see them.

He asked Felix whether they had asked after him.

"How should they, uncle," exclaimed Felix, "when they never heard of your existence?"

"Why—why," stuttered Sir Samuel, "don't they know anything at all about—the family?"

"Evidently not. One of them can talk plainly, and she seems, so far as I can judge, to know nothing about any of us."

"I would have done well by them, John," muttered the old man, as he drove home with an aching heart; "but you never had any bowels towards your old father. Why, look here! he flings his children at me, without so much as asking me for my blessing on them!"

The next day, about one o'clock, little Amabel and little Delia were seated on two high chairs at the table, in their tiny cottage, and waiting for their dinner, when an old gentleman looked in at the open door, smiled, nodded to them, and then came inside, taking off his hat and putting it on the window-sill among the flower-pots. A nice old gentleman, with white hair and white eyebrows. The little girls returned his nod and smiles, then the elder lifted up her small, high voice, and called through the open door that led to the little back kitchen, "Mrs. Naif, Mrs. Naif!" A cheery voice answered, and then the younger child tried her skill as a summons. "Mrs. Naif, dear! Make haste, Mrs. Naif! Company's come to dinner."

Mrs. Snaith presently appeared with a good-sized rice pudding, and set it on the table, which was graced with a clean cloth.

Sir Samuel greeted her when she curtsied. "Good morning, ma'am. You are the nurse here, I presume?"

"Yes, sir, I am."

"Will you be seated, and allow me just to look on awhile."

Mrs. Snaith sat down, and helped the little ones to their pudding. The elder was inclined to be slightly shy, the younger, pulling Mrs. Snaith by the sleeve, pointed at Sir Samuel with her spoon, and whispered some loving confidences in her ear.

"What does she say?" asked Sir Samuel.

The nurse smiled. "She says, sir, 'Give the company some pudding.'"

"Does she, pretty lamb?" exclaimed the old baronet, with a sudden access of fervour; then recollecting himself, and noticing that the nurse was startled, and coloured slightly, he said, by way of continuing his sentence, "I didn't exactly catch your name, I think?"

"Mrs. Snaith, sir."

"Yes, her name's Mrs. Naith every day," said the little Amabel, "but when she's very good we call her Mamsey."

"Her name's Mamsey when she gives us strawberries and milk," the other child explained. "But she hasn't got a black face, company," she continued, addressing him earnestly, as if it behoved him to testify to the truth of her words.

"A black face!" exclaimed the puzzled guest.

Mrs. Snaith explained. "There were some American children with a black nurse, sir, at the seaside where we've been. They called her Mamsey, and so these little dears imitated them."

By this time it was evident that the nurse was ill at ease; she perceived the deep interest with which her unbidden guest watched the children's words and ways. Her pride as a mother was not deceived with any thought that this was a tribute to their beauty or infantile sweetness; she knew this must be the rich man, the great man of the place, who was held in that peculiar respect which merit and benevolence can never command. People say of eastern nations, that those who would hold sway over them must needs make themselves feared, and they do not enough consider that this is almost as true at their own doors as it is at the ends of the earth. When the villagers had nodded and whispered in her presence, mysteriously hinting that anybody at a glance could see who these children were, though she would not answer any questions, she had inwardly felt that the great and proud man whom they had in their thoughts would know better, that he would write to his son, who would at once reply that he knew nothing about these children, and there would be an end.

But here sat Sir Samuel, gazing at Amabel and Delia with a scrutiny sometimes keen, sometimes almost tender. He was making them prattle; he was at last actually drawing his wooden chair to the table, and, at their desire, partaking of the new potatoes which concluded their meal.

He took so little notice of her that she had no need to speak; and that homely dignity which was natural to her coming to her aid, she rose and began to wait on the children and their guest, moving in and out between the little front room where they were dining and the tiny kitchen behind; marking all the old man's efforts to please the small coquettes, and how easily they were won, and how engaging they were; and how noisy the canary was, bustling about in his cage, and singing every time they laughed, as if he longed for some attention too; how the pale, overblown roses outside let their dropping leaves float in and drift over the table-cloth.

For the first time in her life, as she stood in the back kitchen, with hands pressed in one another, listening, she felt a jealous pang, not of her darlings themselves, but of the refined grace and delicate beauty which had so played into her hands as to make the part she had chosen for herself easy.

It was easy to play the part of their nurse—she had elected to play it—and yet her mother's heart resented its being always taken for granted that she could be nothing more.

"I fare almost afraid they'll despise me when they get a bit older," she thought. "If they do, dear lambs, I must take them away from these gentlefolks before it's too late."

Sir Samuel calling her, she came in and found Amabel on his knee. The brown face of little Dick was seen; he was leaning in at the casement, and Delia, leaning out, was kissing him.

Beautiful little Dick was as happy about that time as anything that breathes can be. When they saw him Sir Samuel lost the attention of the other children.

They must have their sun-bonnets on. Mamsey must reach them down.

"Did they love him? Would they like to see him again?"

Oh yes, they liked him, they liked him very much, but they wanted to go now with Dick; and presently they all three set forth together down the quiet road to the vicarage, leaving Sir Samuel and Mrs. Snaith alone.

He was sitting in the Windsor chair, lost in thought, and looking after the children as well as the clustering rose-branches would let him.

She stood a moment expecting him to speak, but he did not; and, unable to bear inaction, she fetched in a tray, and when he looked round, she was quietly clearing the table, placing the remains of the simple dinner upon it.

He got up and she paused.

"You have behaved with great discretion," he said with energy: "and the reticence which I hear you have displayed—the refusing, I mean, to answer people's idle questions—has my entire approval,—I may say, commands my respect."

Mrs. Snaith was silent.

"I am quite aware," he continued, "of all that passed between you and Miss de Berenger. I do not see that even she had a right to expect a full account of matters from you; but—but"—here he paused, baffled by the nurse's grave silence—"but the excellent care with which you fulfil your trust deserves my thanks, and, as I said before, your refusal to answer idle questions commands my respect."

"Thank you, sir. It is my wish to keep quiet, and I don't fare to think I have any call to answer questions."

"But if I asked you some," he answered, a little startled, "of course it would be different."

"I beg your pardon. Not at all different, sir."

"I am Sir Samuel de Berenger, Mr. John de Berenger's father. Now what do you say?"

"Nothing, Sir Samuel."

"Nothing! You're ordered to keep silence, even to me?"

"Sir, I never said I were under orders. I am not."

"Nonsense."

"And I ask your pardon, sir; but if you know all I said to Miss de Berenger, you know all I ever shall say."

"Why, you foolish woman, you are enough to provoke a saint! You quite mistake your employer's meaning. What are you afraid of? What do you mean? Do you think you are to deny to *me* whose and what these children are? It's contrary to all reason—contrary to my son's obvious meaning; clean against their interest. Why, it's—— I never met with such folly in my life!"

Here Sir Samuel launched into certain violent denunciations against folly in general, and this fool in particular; but as she did not further enrage him by making any reply, but helplessly gazed at him while he stormed at her, on the other side of the table, he soon managed to calm himself sufficiently to recur to the matter in hand.

"And whatever may be your motive, I tell you, there's no more use than there is reason in your present line of conduct. It's no use your denying to *me* that these are my grandchildren, I can see it in their faces. It's no use your denying to *me* that they were thrown in my niece's way on purpose that I might hear of them. No, don't speak, woman—it's my turn to speak now. I tell

XXI—14

you all that stuff is of no use; I am not to be deceived."

In the energy of his indignation he leaned over the table and shook his fist at her, and reddened to the roots of his snowy hair; while she, pale and doubtful, continued to find safety only in silence. Every moment for thought seemed to be something won; but she won many, and he had checked himself, and sat down again in his Windsor chair, and was fuming there in more quiet fashion, while, still standing with her hand upon the tray, she was searching for some reply.

At last he said with a sigh, as if something in his own mind had checked him as much as her behaviour, "Perhaps the poor lambs were not born in wedlock."

"Oh yes, they were," she answered, sharply and decidedly; "that's a question I'd answer to anybody, let him be who he would."

"You can prove your words!"

"I could, if there was any need, Sir Samuel."

"Makes nothing of me—cares nothing what I think. But you never did, John. *If there was any need!*"

"You have a son, sir, *by what I can make out*," said the nurse, finishing her sentence with a certain emphasis.

"Oh yes—a son; his conduct looks like a son. You know well enough that I have a son. What of him?"

"If you'll give me leave to advise you, sir——"

"Well?"

"Well, sir, though I don't know the gentleman, I fare to think that if you wrote to him he would answer like a gentleman, and tell you——"

"Tell me what?"

"What would get the mistake out of your head, sir."

"I don't know where to find him."

"Indeed, sir," she answered slowly; "then worse luck for me! And yet," she continued, as if in deep cogitation, "there are those not very far off that do know."

Sir Samuel did not at all doubt her word, but he answered with the surprise he really felt at her making such an admission.

"You don't say so!"

"Yes, sir, I do."

"If I write a letter to my son and bring it to you, will you promise to direct it to him?" exclaimed the old baronet.

He regarded this admission as tantamount to a confession of all, and she, considering, on the contrary, that the letter would be so answered as to put an end to all, gave her consent.

"I'm not that certain about it, sir, that I can promise, but I will do my best."

He sat a few minutes longer, thinking and calming himself, then rose and put on his gloves, looking at her, almost with a smile in his eyes. "You are a remarkably inconsistent woman," he observed, but not rudely.

"Sir!"

."I said, Mrs. Snaith—— But, pooh! what is the good of arguing? Do you want any money?" he added sharply, and at the same time pulling out his purse.

"No, sir," she answered, colouring and drawing back.

"Well, if you should, you'll know whom to come to; and I'll send you down the letter to-morrow. Good morning."

"Good morning, Sir Samuel," said Mrs. Snaith. And even to those simple words she seemed to impart an air of thoughtfulness and caution.

He went away without the shadow of a doubt in his mind that these little girls were his grandchildren; and he did not consider, what was not the less perfectly certain, that if their nurse had made a claim on him, and come to the village demanding that he should acknowledge and assist them, he would have required ample proof of their rights in him, and perhaps not have been at all cordial to them at first, though this had been forthcoming.

As to the likeness. His son was a small, fair man. Absence and love had done a good work for his face in his father's recollection. These small, fair creatures were like what he had been in complexion as a child, but their dimpled features and dark eyelashes were far different. Yet Sir Samuel, reflecting on their sweet little faces, absolutely felt, not only that they recalled his son's childhood, but that he had almost forgotten, till he saw them, what a pretty and engaging little fellow his son had been as a child.

ABOUT FLAGS.

IT is a matter with which we should be all familiar, yet how few of us know what the national colours are, what the Union is, what the Royal Standard is. Not to speak of civilians, are there many officers in either the army or the navy who, without a copy before them, could accurately construct or describe the flag of the nation under which they fight, or tell what its component parts represent? I doubt it. And, after all, they would not be so much without excuse, for even at the Horse Guards and the Admiralty there is some confusion of ideas on the subject. I have before me "The Queen's Regulations and Orders for the Army," issued by the Commander-in-chief, in which flags which can be flown only on shore are confounded with flags which can be flown nowhere but on board ship. Yet the subject is really an interesting one, and, connected as it is with national history, it is deserving of a little study.

Flags are of many kinds, and they are put to many uses. They are the representatives of nations, they distinguish armies and fleets, and to insult a flag is to insult the nation whose ensign it is. There are national flags, flags of departments, and personal flags; and as signals they are of the greatest value as a means of communication at sea.

In the Middle Ages almost every flag was a military one, the principal varieties being the pennon, the banner, and the standard. The pennon was a purely personal flag, pointed or swallow-tailed, borne below the lance-head, and charged with the arms of the knight who carried it. The banner was the flag of a troop. It was square in form, and was borne by knights—called after it bannerets—and by those above them in rank. It was the custom, after a battle, for the commander of the host to reward the distinguished services of a knight bearing a pennon by tearing off the "fly," or outer part of that flag, and by so doing giving it a square form, thus making it a banner and its bearer a knight banneret.

But it is of our present flags only that I intend to speak. In a paper like this I cannot go into much detail, but I propose to give a short popular account of them, avoiding as far as possible heraldic technicalities.

First of all comes the national flag, the Union, so called because it is formed by a combination of the flags of the three nations: the red St. George's cross of England, the white St. Andrew's cross, or saltire of Scotland, and the red St. Patrick's cross, or saltire of Ireland. After the union with Scotland, the St. Andrew's cross was conjoined with the cross of St. George, the ground of the flag—the "field," as the heralds call it—being at the same time changed from white to blue, which was the colour of the Scottish flag. And at the union with Ireland the cross of St. Patrick was added to the other two. The St. George's cross remained as it was, but the saltires of Scotland and Ireland were placed side by side, but "counter-changed"—that is, in the first and third divisions or quarters the white, as senior, is uppermost, and in the second and fourth the red is uppermost. The "verbal blazon," or written description, is very distinct, but in making the flag, or rather in showing pictorially how it was to be represented, a singular and very absurd error occurred, which, in the manufacture of our flags, has been continued to the present day, and which it may be interesting to explain.

The verbal blazon is contained in the Minute by the King in Council and in the proclamation which followed on it, issued on 1st of January, 1801. I need not give the technical words; suffice to say that the flag is appointed to be azure, with the three crosses, or, rather, the one cross and two saltires combined. And in order to meet a law in heraldry, that colour is not to be placed on colour, or metal upon metal, it is directed that where the red crosses of England and Ireland come in contact with the blue ground of the flag they are to be "fimbriated"—that is, separated from the blue by a very narrow border of one of the metals, in this case silver or white. Of heraldic necessity this border of both the red crosses fell to be of the same breadth. To use the words of the written blazon, the St. George's cross is to be "fimbriated as the saltire;" a direction so plain that the merest tyro in heraldry could not fail to understand it and be able to paint the flag accordingly.

Let me premise another thing. It is a universal rule in heraldry that the verbal blazon is alone of authority. Different artists may, from ignorance or from carelessness, express the drawing differently from the directions before them, and this occurs every day; but no one is or can be misled by that if he has the verbal blazon to refer to.

Now, in the important case of the Union flag it so happened that the artist who, according to the practice usual in such cases, was instructed to make a drawing of the flag on the margin of the King's Order in Council, was either careless or ignorant or stupid. Most probably he was all three, and here is how he depicted it. The horizontal lines represent blue and the perpendicular red; the rest is white.

Now here, it will be observed, the red saltire of Ireland is "fimbriated" white, according to the instructions; and this is done with perfect accuracy, by the narrowest possible border. But the St. George's cross, instead of being fimbriated in the same way —which the written blazon expressly says it shall be—is not fimbriated at all. The cross is placed upon a ground of white so broad that it ceases to be a border. The practical effect of this, and its only heraldic meaning, is that the centre of the flag, instead of being occupied solely by the St. George's cross, is occupied by *two crosses*, a white cross with a red one superinduced on it. So palpable is this that Mr. Laughton, the accomplished lecturer on Naval History at the Royal Naval College, in a lecture recently published, suggests that this is perhaps what was really intended. "A fimbriation," he says, "is a narrow border to prevent the unpleasing effect of metal on metal or colour on colour. It should be as narrow as possible, to mark the contrast. But the white border of our St. George's cross is not, strictly speaking, a fimbriation at all. It is a white cross of one-third the width of the flag surmounted of a red cross." And his hypothesis is that it may have been intended to commemorate a tradition of the combination of the red cross of England with the white cross of France. The suggestion is ingenious and interesting, but it has clearly no foundation. There might have been something to say for it had there been only the drawing to guide us. In that case, indeed, the theory of Mr. Laughton, or some one similar, would be absolutely necessary to account for the two crosses. But Mr. Laughton overlooks the important facts, first, that we possess in the verbal blazon distinct written instructions; secondly, that where such exist no drawing which is at variance with them can possess any authority; and lastly, that in this case the verbal blazon not only is silent as to a second cross, but it expressly prescribes that there shall be only one, that of St. George. To that nothing is to be added—nothing, that is, but the narrow border or fimbriation necessary to meet the heraldic requirement to separate it from the blue ground of the flag, the same as is directed to be done, and as has been done, with the saltire of Ireland.

Some years ago I called the attention of the Admiralty to this extraordinary blunder, and I pointed out then, just what Mr. Laughton has done in his recent lecture, that the flag, as made, really shows two crosses in the centre. The Admiralty referred the matter to Garter King of Arms, but Sir Albert Woods, while he had not a word to say in defence of the arrangement, would not interfere. "The flag," he said, "was made according to the drawing" (which was too true), "and it was exhibited," he added, "in the same way on the colours of the Queen's infantry regiments;" and, naturally enough, he declined the responsibility of advising a change. And so it remains. I may observe, however, that in one, at least, of the Horse Guards' patterns, to be afterwards noticed, the arrangement of the tinctures is not, as Sir Albert supposes, according to the original drawing, and it is quite different from the pattern prescribed by the Admiralty.

There is another error in the flag as now worn. The breadth of the Irish saltire is less than that of the white cross of Scotland. For obvious reasons, and according to the written blazon, they ought to be the same. Indeed, all the three crosses should be of the same breadth.

It is to be hoped that heraldic propriety will prevail over a practice originating in obvious error, and that our national flag will be flown according to its true blazon. The correction would be very easily made. The reduction of the breadth of the border and the slight increase in the width of the Irish saltire would not be noticed by one in a thousand, while, besides correcting obvious errors, it would have the advantage of bringing the flag, in one important respect, into conformity with the design as represented on the coinage. On the reverse of our beautiful bronze coins the St. George's cross on Britannia's Shield is fimbriated as it ought to be, that is, by the narrow border prescribed by the written blazon.

But if the penny is right in that respect, it exhibits another extraordinary example of our slipshod heraldry by a variation of a different and more startling kind. My complaint against the flag, as made, is, that it represents four crosses, but on the penny there are only two. This was all right when the design was first made in the reign of Charles II., but when the third cross was added to the flag it should have been added also on the coin. A desire to adhere to the original design cannot certainly be pleaded, for there have been many changes in this figure of Britannia. She was first placed there by Charles II. in honour of the beautiful Duchess of Richmond, who sat to the sculptor for the figure. But her drapery on the coin of those days was very scanty, and her semi-nude state was hardly in keeping with the stormy waves beside which she was seated. Queen Anne, like a modest lady as she was, put decent clothing on her, and made her stand upright, and took away her shield, crosses and all. In the subsequent reigns she was allowed to sit down again, and she got back her shield, with the trident in her left hand and an olive-branch in the right. On the present coinage the drapery of Queen Anne is retained, but the figure is entirely turned round, and faces the sinister side of the coin instead of the dexter, as at first, and the olive-branch (*absit omen*) has been taken away. But with all these changes there remain only two crosses on the shield—the Union with Ireland notwithstanding. The reader will naturally suppose, however, that the omission consisted in not adding the Irish saltire to that of Scotland, which had been there from the first. But no. In this instance there was certainly no injustice to Ireland, for the extraordinary thing is, that the St. Andrew's cross has been taken away altogether, and the saltire of Ireland, distinguished by its fimbriated border, has been put in its place, Scotland being not now represented on the coin at all.

But to return to our flags. The Union Jack is a diminutive of the Union, and, although of the same pattern, it is a totally different flag, although the two are often confounded. For example, in the Queen's Regulations for the Army a list of stations is given "at which the national flag, the Union Jack, is authorised to be hoisted." And in a general order issued from the North British Head-quarters as to the arrangements to be observed on the last occasion of the sitting of the General Assembly in Edinburgh, it was stated that "the Union Jack" would be displayed from the Castle and at the Palace of Holyrood. But the Union Jack is never flown on shore. It is peculiarly and exclusively a ship flag; and is only flown at the Jack-staff, a staff on the bowsprit, or fore part of a ship of war. The Union is the shore flag, and, except personal flags, the only one which is displayed from fortresses and other stations. On board her Majesty's ships it is sometimes displayed, but only on special occasions. It is hoisted at the mizen top-gallant-masthead when the Queen is on board, the Royal Standard and the flag of the Lord High Admiral being at the same time hoisted at the main and fore top-gallant-mastheads respectively. And an Admiral of the Fleet hoists the Union at the main top-gallant-masthead. The Army Regulations, however, referring to the presence of the Queen on board ship, again confound the two flags, and prescribe that a salute shall be fired by forts whenever a ship passes showing the flags which indicate the presence of the sovereign, and among these is specified "the Union Jack at the mizen top-gallant-masthead." If the commandant of a fortress acted on this, her Majesty might pass every day of the year without a salute, as he would certainly never see the Union Jack in that position. The mistake is the more curious as the Regulations elsewhere distinguish the Union Jack from the Union by speaking of the latter as the "Great Union."

The Jack when flown from the mast with a white border is the signal for a pilot. In this case it is called the Pilot Jack. When flown from the bowsprit of a merchant ship it must have a white border.

It has been said that the term "Jack" is derived from the name of the sovereign James I., in whose reign it was constructed. This is the legend at the Admiralty, but it is of doubtful authority. The Oxford Glossary says there is not a shadow of evidence for it, and traces the word to the surcoat worn of old by the soldiery called a *Jacque*—whence jacket. But this also is doubtful.

The Union, or junction of the three crosses, is used in other cases in the Royal navy, and also in the merchant service, not by itself, but in certain combinations.

The Royal Standard is a personal flag, being used only by the sovereign in person, or as a decoration on Royal fête days. There are depicted on it the royal arms, which are also those of the nation. The arms of William Duke of Normandy emblazoned on his standard were two lions, and they were borne by him and his successors as the Royal arms of England till the reign of Henry II. That monarch married Eleanor, daughter and co-heiress of the Duke of Aquitaine, whose arms —one lion—Henry added to his own. Hence the three lions borne ever since as the ensigns of England. These now occupy the first and fourth quarters of the standard, but they did not always do so. The Fleurs de Lis of France were, till a comparatively recent period, quartered with the English arms, having been first borne by Edward III. when he assumed the title of King of France. Many noble families, both in this country and on the Continent, have quartered the French lilies to show their origin, or in acknowledgment of the tenure of important fiefs there. Among the last may be mentioned Sir John Stewart of Darnley, who obtained from Charles VII. the lands and title of Aubigny, and the right to quarter the arms of France with his own. But in all these instances the Fleurs de Lis occupied a secondary place. So if Henry II. had desired merely to show his French connection by maternal descent, he would have placed them in the second and third quarters. But he placed them in the first quarter as arms of dominion, to indicate that he claimed the kingdom by right, and our sovereigns continued this idle pretence till so late as the reign of George III. It was not till the union with Ireland that it was discontinued.

On the accession of James I. the Royal Standard was altered. The arms of France and England quarterly appeared in the first and fourth quarters, those of Scotland in the second, and the Irish harp in the third. George III. when he left out the ensigns of France marshalled those of his Germanic states in an escutcheon of pretence—a small shield in the centre point. This was omitted on the accession of Queen Victoria, who bears on her standard the arms of England in the first and fourth quarters, Scotland in the second, and Ireland in the third.

The Royal Standard is never carried into action even though the sovereign in person commands the army. A heraldic manuscript of the sixteenth century prescribes that the Royal Standard "shall be sett before the kynges pavillion or tente, and not to be borne in battayle, and to be in length eleven yardes." The Royal Standard is never hoisted in ships except when her Majesty is on board, or a member of the Royal family other than the Prince of Wales. When the latter is on board his own standard is hoisted. It is the same as that of the Queen except that it bears a label of three points, with the arms of Saxony on an escutcheon of pretence. Wherever the sovereign is residing the Royal

Standard is hoisted; and on Royal anniversaries and State occasions it is hoisted at certain fortresses or stations—home and foreign—specified in the Queen's regulations, but nowhere else.

The flag under which all our 'ships sail is the Ensign, of which there are three; the white, the blue, and the red. It is a large flag of one of the colours named, with the Union in a square or canton at the upper part of the hoist. I may explain that the portion of a flag next the staff or rope from which it is flown is called the hoist, the next is called the centre, and the outer portion the fly. Besides the Union in the canton the white ensign has the St. George's cross extending over the whole field. Although the Union flag of Great Britain was appointed by Royal order in 1606, it was not till long afterwards that it came to be worn in the Ensign.

The history of the Ensign is curious, but I have not space to go into it. In the Royal navy, not always, but for some time previous to 1864, the fleet consisted of three divisions called the White, the Blue, and the Red Squadrons, each carrying its distinctive Ensign, and each having its admiral called after the colour of his flag. But this proved puzzling to foreigners, and it was found inconvenient in action. It was for this last reason that Lord Nelson, on going into action at Trafalgar, ordered the whole of his fleet to hoist the White Ensign, and it was under that flag, the old banner of England, but with the Union in the upper corner, that that great victory was gained. In 1864 the classification of the navy under the three denominations mentioned was discontinued, and now the White Ensign only is used by all her Majesty's ships in commission. Previous to this it had been ordered by Royal proclamation in 1801, that merchant ships should fly only the Red Ensign, and this is still the rule; but since 1864, when the three divisions of the fleet were abolished, the Blue Ensign is allowed to be used by British merchant ships when commanded by officers of the Royal Naval Reserve, provided ten of the crew be men belonging to the Reserve. By permission of the Admiralty the Blue Ensign is also allowed to be used by certain yacht clubs; and the members of one club—the Royal Yacht Squadron—have liberty to use the White Ensign.

In going into action it is the custom with the ships of all nations to hoist their national colours. Nelson at Trafalgar carried this to excess, for he hoisted several flags lest one should be shot away. The French went to the opposite extreme, for they hoisted no colours at all till late in the action, when they began to feel the necessity of having them to strike. Nelson on that occasion ran his ship to board the *Redoutable*, a large seventy-four gun ship, and fought her at such close quarters that the two ships touched each other. Twice Nelson gave orders to cease firing at his opponent, supposing she had surrendered, because her great guns were silent, and as she carried no flag there was no means of instantly ascertaining the fact. It was from the ship which he had thus twice spared that Nelson received his death wound. The ball was fired from the mizen-top, which, so close were the ships, was not more than fifteen yards from the place where he was standing. Soon afterwards the *Redoutable,* finding further resistance impossible, hoisted her flag only to haul it down, in sign of surrender, within twenty minutes after the fatal shot had been fired.

The flag of the Lord High Admiral is crimson, having on it an anchor and cable, and it is hoisted on any ship of which that high officer is on board. It is also hoisted at the fore top-gallant-masthead of every ship of which the Queen may be on board. The flag of an admiral is white with the Cross of St. George on it. It is only flown by an admiral when employed afloat, and then at the main, fore, or mizen top-gallant-masthead, according as he is a full, vice, or rear-admiral.

The Union and the Blue Ensign are, with the addition of certain distinctive badges, used as personal flags by certain high officers, and also in particular departments of the service. For example, the flag of the Lord Lieutenant of Ireland is the Union with a harp in the centre on a blue shield; and the Governor-General of India has the Union with the Star of India in the centre surmounted by a crown. There are also differences in the Ensign with distinctive badges for our colonies and consuls, and other offices and departments.

The Pendant is a well-known flag in ships of war. It is of two kinds, the long and the broad. The first is a long, narrow, tapering flag—the usual length being twenty yards, while it is only four inches broad at the head. Its origin is generally understood to have been this:—After the defeat of the English fleet under Blake, by the Dutch fleet under Van Tromp, in 1652, the latter cruised in the Channel with a broom at the masthead of his ship, to signify that he had swept his enemies off the sea. In the following year the English fleet defeated the Dutch, whereupon the admiral commanding hoisted a long streamer from his masthead, to represent the lash of a whip, signifying that he had whipped his enemies off the sea. Hence the pendant, which has been flown ever since. It is of two colours—one white with a red cross in the part next the mast; the other blue with a red cross on a white ground. The first is flown from the masthead of all her Majesty's ships in commission when not otherwise distinguished by a flag or broad pendant. The other is worn at the masthead of all armed vessels in the employ of the Government of a British colony.

The broad pendant or "burgee" is a flag tapering slightly and of a swallow-tailed shape at the fly. It is white with a red St. George's cross, and is flown only by a commodore or the senior officer of a squadron to distinguish his ship.

Signal flags are of various shapes and colours, each flag representing a letter or number, so as to enable communication to be kept up between vessels at a distance from each other. By a recent arrangement a universal code has been adopted by which vessels of different nations can now communicate.

The yellow flag is the signal of sickness and of quarantine.

Such are the principal naval flags. Of the uses to which they are put, and the circumstances in which they may or may not be legitimately used in naval warfare, some interesting stories might be told. When a ship is taken, the hoisting her ensign under that of her captor is the direct way of announcing the capture, and in one instance a mistake in this produced disastrous results.

A flag of truce is white both at sea and on land, but on board ship it is customary to hoist with it the national flag of the enemy—the white flag at the main and the enemy's ensign at the fore.

The Ensign and Pendant at half-mast are the recognised signs of mourning. Sometimes also it is an expression of mourning to set the yards at what seamen call "a cock bill," that is all the yards topped up different ways on each mast; but this is chiefly done by foreigners, who, on Good Friday and other occasions, set their yards thus.

It is not within my purpose to speak of foreign flags, but it may be interesting to notice that the first flag worn as a national ensign by ships of the United States of America after their Declaration of Independence, and which consisted of thirteen horizontal stripes—white and red—had still in the upper canton the British Union. The origin of the American stripes is not known, but it was not an original flag. It was for a long time a well-known signal in the British navy, being that used for the Red Division to draw into line of battle.

I have left myself little space to speak of the flags of the army. Every regiment of infantry has two flags, both of silk; in this differing from sea flags, which are usually made of bunting. With the exception of the Foot Guards, the first or Queen's colours of every regiment is the Union or National Flag, with the Imperial crown in the centre and the number of the regiment beneath in gold. The second or regimental colours are, with certain exceptions, of the colour of the facing of the regiment, with the Union in the upper corner. The second colours of all regiments bear the devices or badges and distinctions which have been conferred by Royal authority. The first or Royal colours of the Foot Guards are crimson, and bear certain special distinctions besides those authorised for the second colours—the whole surmounted by the Imperial crown. The first battalion of the Scots Fusilier Guards possesses the high distinction of carrying on their first colours the Royal arms of Scotland. The second or regimental colours of the Foot Guards is the Union, with one of the ancient badges conferred by Royal authority. The colours of infantry are as a rule carried by the two junior lieutenants.

In the cavalry the standards of regiments of Dragoon Guards are of crimson silk damask, embroidered and fringed with gold, and their guidons—a swallow-tailed flag—are of crimson silk. Each is inscribed with the peculiar devices, distinctions, and mottoes of the regiment. The standards and guidons of cavalry are carried by troop sergeant-majors. The Hussars and Lancers have no standards. They were discontinued, for what reason I do not know, by William IV., and their badges and devices are now borne on their appointments. The Royal Engineers have no colours. Neither have the Royal Artillery; nor is it necessary that they should have any on which to record special services, for the Artillery is represented in every action. Their appropriate motto, *Ubique*, is borne on their appointments.

On all fortresses and military stations the Union flag is flown. At the Royal Arsenal and a few other stations it is displayed daily. At others, such as Sandgate Castle and Rye, it is flown only on anniversaries. At Tilbury, Edinburgh Castle, and other places it is hoisted only on Sundays and anniversaries. And there are similar rules for foreign stations.

The Queen's and regimental colours always parade with the regiment. On march they are cased, but they are always uncased when carried into action.

For military authorities "when embarked in boats or other vessels," there is a special flag. It is the Union with the Royal initials in the centre on a blue circle, surrounded by a green garland, and surmounted by the Imperial crown. For this flag there is a regulation pattern, a copy of which is before me, in which the proportions of white and red in the Union are quite different from the regulation pattern prescribed by the Admiralty. Among other things the breadth of the Irish saltire is reduced so as to be no more than the breadth of the so-called border of the cross of St. George.

In regard to the use of the national ensign by private persons, there is a positive rule as to marine flags, but none, so far as I am aware, as to its use on shore. I have occasionally seen it flown on shore with a white border, under an impression, apparently, that this difference was necessary, but it is unmeaning, and there is no authority for it. In numberless instances we see one or other of the marine ensigns hoisted on shore over gentlemen's houses, or used in street decoration on the occasion of public rejoicings; but nothing could be more absurd, as the ensign is exclusively a ship flag.

Any private individual entitled to armorial bearings may carry them on a flag. In such cases the arms should not be on a shield, but filling the entire flag. The flags and banners represented in works on heraldry have almost invariably a fringe; but this is optional. If a fringe is used it should be composed of the livery colours, each tincture of the arms giving its colour to the portion of the fringe which adjoins it.

To every true patriot the national flag must be a subject of pride. What it is to the sailor and the soldier when it is shaken out on going into battle none but the soldier and the sailor can realise. At the interment of Lord Nelson, when his flag was about to be lowered into the grave, the sailors who assisted at the ceremony ran forward with one accord and tore it into small pieces, to be preserved as sacred relics. "I know," says Charles Kingsley—in those "brave words" which he addressed to our soldiers then fighting in the trenches before Sebastopol—"I know that you would follow those colours into the mouth of the pit; that you would die twice over rather than let them be taken. Those noble rags, inscribed with noble names of victory, should remind you every day and every hour that he who fights for Queen and country in a just cause is fighting not only in the Queen's army, but in Christ's army, and that he shall in no wise lose his reward."

A. MACGEORGE.

A FACT.

VIDE *GRAPHIC* OF 27TH DECEMBER, PAGE 627.

"'TWAS a dull November day
   Off Bayonne, where we lay,
And the wind had died away
   About noon.
A French barque came drifting near,
And when the crew could hear,
We hailed them with a cheer,
   Answered soon.

Whilst we were still agaze,
To our horror and amaze,
Up burst an awful blaze
   Through her deck,
Swift followed by a roar
That re-echoed from the shore,
And the ship from aft to fore
   Was a wreck !

Through the smoke the red flame gleamed,
And the wretched women screamed
As the liquid fire streamed
   O'er the sea ;
But our brave old captain spoke :
"Now, my lads and hearts of oak,
We must go and save these folk ;
   Who's with me ?"

Then the sailors, at the sight
Of that dreadful flaming light,
Shrunk back—as well they might—
   In dismay ;
But the blood within me boiled
To see that these recoiled,
And our country's honour soiled,
   On that day.

I'd no call to be a sailor :
I was carpenter and nailer,
And they called me the ship's tailor
      Oft in joke ;
But I jumped into the boat
When the captain was afloat,
And our oars the water smote
      Stroke for stroke.

How the fearful fire flashed
As through it all we dashed,
And the flame and water splashed
      From the bow ;
But we rescued not a few
Of that wild despairing crew,
Although many more we knew
      Sank below.

To our ship we back returned,
With our hands and faces burned,
But I felt that I had earned
      My good name ;
And the deed was much applauded—
Far and widely 'twas recorded,
And with medals well rewarded,
      And much fame.

But in helping thus to save
These poor folks from fire and wave
'Twas my livelihood I gave
      And my pow'r,—
For my hands were burnt too sore
For rough labour evermore
On ship-board or a-shore
      From that hour.

I but ask to win my bread
By light work of hand and head,
To ward off disgrace and dread
      From my life ;
And to keep a roof above
The two dear ones that I love,
My trembling little dove,
      And my wife.

They can't live on fame and praise :
Will no man a finger raise
To ward off the evil days,
      And to save
These poor things from want and wail,
From grim hunger, gaunt and pale,
From the workhouse—or the gaol—
      Or the grave ?

WM. A. GIBBS.

XXI—15

LUNG CAPACITY AND TIGHT-LACING.

By JOSEPH FARRAR, L.R.C.P.,ED., ETC.

BY " lung capacity" is meant the amount or volume of air which the lungs are capable of containing at one time, and which varies according to circumstances. The chief of these being the height of the individual ; the position or attitude of the body at the time the test is applied ; the person's weight, age, and the presence or absence of disease. The greatest quantity of air which a man can expel from his lungs at one time, by the greatest voluntary effort immediately succeeding the greatest voluntary inspiration of air, is technically termed the VITAL VOLUME or VITAL CAPACITY ; and this is easily determinable by the "spirometer," invented for the purpose, into which the individual, after having first loosened the clothes about his chest and taken as deep an inspiration as possible, empties his lungs through a mouth-piece. An indicator attached marks off the number of cubic inches of air blown into the apparatus by the single expiratory act, and we thus at once ascertain the capacity sought for.

It appears from a large number of experiments, instituted with the view of ascertaining what condition is the most general or constant that regulates the " vital capacity " of an individual, that the *height* of the person is the chief. In the erect position the average number of cubic inches which a man of 5 feet 9 inches in height, for example, can expire immediately after the deepest inspiration is 246 ; while another person of 5 feet 10 inches in stature, and whose condition, except that of height, is the same in every, respect as that of the former, would expire about 254 cubic inches ; and another man, again, one inch taller than the last, would give us about 262 cubic inches ; or an increase in each case of 8 cubic inches for each additional inch in height of the individual. And this cubical increase of capacity according to the progressive height of the individual (between 5 feet and 6 feet in height, at any rate) is the very general rule ; that is, *for every inch of stature between 5 and 6 feet*, 8 *additional cubic inches of air, at the usual temperature of* 60° *F., are given out by the deepest expiration immediately following the deepest inspiration.* Of course, this rule applies only to persons in good health ; for, as we have already remarked, the " vital capacity " is also influenced by disease, and more especially by disease of the lungs, of which more will be said presently.

By carefully taking the stature of an individual, and comparing this with the " vital capacity " obtained, as indicated by the spirometer, the medical man may be led in certain doubtful cases to form an opinion of considerable importance in the examination of that person, and one of the greatest value, both to the man himself and to his friends, not to mention its pecuniary worth to life insurance companies, &c., in cases where a policy is being sought from them. Say, for example, that the person under examination stands 5 feet 9 inches, and on taking his vital capacity we find this to be, say, 160 cubic inches instead of 246 cubic inches, the volume which, as we have seen, a man of the stature given should, in health, be able to expire, we should at once suspect serious mischief within the chest ; and on examination by the usual physical methods we should almost certainly discover disease therein.

As the imperial gallon contains about 277 cubic inches (277·274), we learn the fact that a man of 6 feet in stature should, if his lungs be in a normally healthy condition and no other impediment, mechanical or otherwise, be present, expel from his lungs by one forcible expiration nearly this quantity of air —almost 8 pints ! A far greater volume than the majority of people would have thought possible.

The manner in which *weight* affects the " vital capacity " is chiefly by the presence in the individual of an excess in the amount of fat, the weight being therefore augmented. This excess in fat tissue acts upon the " vital capacity " mainly in a mechanical manner. It surrounds the lungs, for example, and breathing tubes, in masses so large as to interfere with 'their full expansion during inspiration ; and as the quantity of air expired, or capable of being expired, is strictly regulated by the quantity inhaled, and as this latter is regulated by the degree to which the chest can expand, we see at once how this excess operates. When, moreover, this condition (excess of fat) has become far advanced by reason either of some peculiar diathesis, or by approaching old age, a still more efficient cause comes into operation, and one of far more serious import, since it is much less amenable to treatment. We allude to what is termed *fatty degeneration* of the various structures of the body, including, of course, the degeneration of the muscles, and of those, therefore, concerned in the movements of the chest-walls. In such case the muscles, whose duty it is to raise the ribs, by means of which the act of inspiration is performed, become changed in structure by the disappearance of their muscular fibres, and the substitution for these latter of globules of fat. In other words, the substitution of matter possessing no *lifting* power for matter whose very essence is one of active mechanical force. The ribs, therefore, fail in such case to be raised to the full extent, the chest does not expand sufficiently, less air enters the lungs, and hence there is a proportionate diminution in the amount capable of being expired; that is, there is diminished "vital capacity." There are other ways, too, in which excess of fat, or fatty degeneration, operates prejudicially to the "vital capacity." It surrounds the breathing tubes themselves, for example, and becomes infiltrated into their muscular walls. Large quantities of fat are found loading the heart and surrounding the large blood-vessels within the chest, and pressing upon and interfering with the lungs in a mechanical manner. There is this overloading, too, in the abdomen, and this impedes, more or less considerably, the descent of the diaphragm, a muscular partition, whose duty consists, not only in dividing the cavities of the chest and abdomen from each other, but in carrying on abdominal respiration. The lungs being thus mechanically pressed upon from every side; the organs themselves being more or less incapacitated by the metamorphosis of the muscular walls of their air tubes, &c.; the loss of power in the muscles, whose duty it is to raise the ribs that air may rush into the chest; and the loss of elasticity, both of the lungs and the ribs, by which the air is expelled from the chest, must of necessity, and *do*, as the reader will readily understand, act with a potency more or less marked in diminishing the vital volume.

The only other abnormal factor obnoxious to the integrity of the "vital capacity" to which we shall refer, is that consequent upon the presence of disease within the chest, but particularly to what is termed pulmonary consumption. In this disease, which, it need scarcely be said, is disease of the substance of the lung, the diminution in the vital volume is sometimes enormous. Thus, a man standing, say, 5 feet 10 inches, and who in a state of health should, by the rule given, expire, by one forcible act, about 254 cubic inches of air, might, if suffering from pulmonary consumption, give no more than 170 —a loss of 84. But the loss is not infre-

quently much greater; the capacity being in cases still farther advanced, as low, perhaps, as 145 cubic inches; and occasionally—as in the last stage of the disease—no more than 119—a loss, respectively, of 109, and 135! In simple inflammatory affections of the contents of the chest—as of the lungs—or the pleura, &c., the decrease is often very striking. A man may, for example, have but one lung at his command, the other lung having been rendered impervious to air by reason of the changes which sometimes take place in it as a result of an inflammatory attack; in which case the "vital capacity" must, of course, be very considerably diminished. But enough has already been said perhaps to convey to the reader a proper understanding of our subject.

That the reader is fully persuaded that it is highly advantageous, and even important, to the individual, that his "vital capacity" should be as great, or at least as near to the average as possible, we will take for granted. With the vocalist, indeed, or the performer upon such wind instruments as require to be played upon by blowing air through the operator's mouth, this will not be questioned. To these, as well as to ministers of religion, public speakers, &c., it is surely of the last importance, both to their own comfort and to that of their hearers, that the performer should have great command over his respiratory movements; but this he cannot have, to any great extent, if his "vital capacity" be greatly reduced. What, for example, is more painful to the auditor than to be compelled to sit beneath a puffing, asthmatic, broken-winded speaker? And what more difficult of accomplishment than for a speaker to pour forth a telling, thrilling oration under the adverse conditions just named? Or, again, how futile the attempts of a vocalist to attain to a high mark of distinction, where the power is wanting of prolonging such musical notes as require to be thus sustained, and which power depends so entirely upon the possession of a large "vital capacity"! In short, setting entirely aside all sanatory considerations, it cannot be doubted that, for comfort and convenience alone, it is highly desirable and necessary that the "vital capacity" should be up to the average, or at least not far below it.

By careful and temperate exercise of the respiratory muscles—as by a proper use of dumb-bells, well-directed singing exercise, blowing upon some wind instrument, &c.— the "vital capacity" may not only be kept up to the average, but may be actually increased. And especially does this remark apply to persons before they have attained the middle period of life; and with the utmost benefit, also, to the general health. There are, of course, certain diseases or conditions of the system, during the presence of which it would be inadvisable to practise certain of the foregoing exercises, and which conditions are easily detected by the medical adviser; but, generally speaking, the temperate and intelligent exercise of the respiratory function is attended with the happiest results. And not only as regards the improvement to the "vital capacity," but likewise to the general health of the individual. Some physicians have even gone so far as to affirm that where the dreaded disease just named has shown a tendency to take up its abode in the system, careful and regulated exercise, under proper surveillance, of the respiratory organs, as by singing, &c., has been the means not only of arresting, but of totally eradicating, the evil, and of restoring the hitherto tottering constitution to a condition of robust health. Dr. Burg, for instance, a French physician, is a most ardent advocate for well-directed exercise on wind instruments. In a little book expressly written on this subject, he remarks: "Many philanthropists on seeing our young military musicians wield enormous wind instruments, have sorrowed over the few years the poor fellows would have to live. Well, they are mistaken. All the men whose business it is to try the wind instruments made at the various factories, before sending them off for sale, are, without exception, free from pulmonary affections. I have known many who, on entering upon this calling, were very delicate, and who, nevertheless, though their duty obliged them to blow for hours together, enjoyed perfect health after a certain time. I am myself," he continues, "an instance of this. My mother died of consumption; eight children of hers fell victims to the same disease, and only three of us survive, and we all three play wind instruments." So much, then, for this part of our subject.

If the preceding pages have been read and thought over, even cursorily, it can scarcely be necessary to point out to the intelligent reader the evils of that now fashionable custom of tight-lacing. For of all the evils which woman brings upon herself in the name of fashion few, if any, equal this in the injury it inflicts upon her animal economy. By reference to the accompanying figure (Fig. 1), it will be seen that Nature designed that the walls of the chest should gradually increase

in circumference from above downwards. But look at the contour brought about at the dictate of fashion, as seen in Fig. 2. Here the arrangement is turned topsy-turvy, the broad end being uppermost, and the apex meeting the apex of another cone, also artificially induced, giving to the entire body the shape of a huge, highly magnified egg-boiler! And the more this constriction and narrowing of the waist can be effected, the more "fashionable" is the possessor of it supposed to be, and the more enviable does she become to her "fashionable" sisters. Look, too, at the distortion of the ribs, and the fearful havoc made with the backbone! But fashion

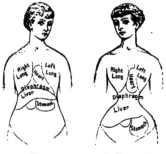

Fig. 1.
Natural Form.

Fig. 2.
With Tight-lacing.

is an arbitrary and severe ruler, and cares neither for beauty of feminine form, for comfort and convenience, nor, what is most to be deplored, the health and happiness of those who foolishly become her slaves. But let us consider how the question affects our particular subject.

The circumference, then, of the waist in a woman of medium height and dimensions, measures, on an average—when not cramped and distorted by the practice under consideration—about 30 inches; but in those who have long adopted tight-lacing, it may measure no more than 20 inches and sometimes even much less. Now what becomes, in these latter cases, of the several organs contained within the chest and abdomen? They are, of course, compressed, and pushed, and squeezed out of their natural shapes; and made to protrude into places in which they have no business, because never meant to occupy such places. It was intended by nature as a matter of course that the chest and abdomen should respectively hold their various contents in their allotted and relative positions, occupying certain portions of space, and having ample room for the due performance of their individual duties, without that jostling and interference with one another which necessarily accompanies disorder and bad arrangement. But, on the other hand, there is no vacuum or empty space in either of the two cavities—there is no region without its own particular organ or part; and each organ or part, though provided by nature with ample room for the needful and unobstructed discharge of its special function, it has yet not much to spare. When, then, any one particular organ is, by the system of tight-lacing, &c., unduly pressed upon, and pushed and squeezed, it must, like a man in a crowd—since it cannot get out of the way—be seriously hampered in its movements, and its important duties imperfectly discharged, to the no small injury and suffering, sooner or later, of the foolish self-torturer. And this, in proportion to the unnatural pressure and squeezing to which the organ has had to submit. The excessive crushing, however, which results from this much-to-be-deplored custom, as well as the consequences arising from it, is not confined to one organ only, but it is transmitted to those lying in its immediate proximity—these having to bear the pressure from the organs which are *directly* implicated, though they themselves may be entirely removed from the direct load. The practice of tight-lacing brings about this crushing and displacement of organs most completely and effectually—hampering and thwarting them in the performance of their assigned and indispensable duties, and with the consequent production of a whole host of very serious troubles, and not a few real and grave diseases. There are few natural diseases, indeed, which so thoroughly displace, and jam, and wedge together so great a number of the internal organs, and so generally disseminate amongst them incapacity for the discharge of their multifarious duties, as does this positively sinful practice of tight-lacing. Shortness of breath, congestion and even inflammation of the lungs, congestion of the liver, of the kidneys, &c.; palpitation and subsequent disease of the heart; faintings, bronchitis, indigestion, jaundice, obstruction of the bowels, rupture, &c., are a few only of the many evils arising from the custom which we are so emphatically condemning; a list, one would think quite formidable enough to cause the most thoughtless and the most fashion-beridden subject to immediately renounce all allegiance to a practice so fraught with mischief; and one, moreover, which has not a single redeeming point, even in the occasionally foolish eyes of the sterner sex, in its favour.

Where this folly of tight-lacing is kept up, and where the evils just enumerated show themselves, it cannot, of course, be expected that the "vital capacity" can remain normal, much less that it can possibly become increased. How *can* the chest expand when harnessed round with a coat or case as unyielding as the jaws of an iron vice? And if it cannot expand to allow the proper amount of air to enter the lungs, these organs necessarily fail to become sufficiently dilated; the air cannot enter them, and it cannot, therefore, be expired—that is, the "vital capacity" is reduced to a fraction of what it should be.

The remedy is self-evident. First of all, lay aside the pinching corset—"swan-bill" or any other "bill"—which is designed to effect a reduction in the circumference of the waist. And if corsets or "stays" *must* be worn, let them be wide enough and laced lax enough to allow the poor crushed ribs by their elasticity to have every chance of resuming the original contour impressed upon them by their Maker. Next, do everything possible to assist the chest in this work of re-establishing its pristine beauty of form, and its consequent power of fulfilling to the utmost its numerous important duties, one of the most indispensable of which is that of expansion and contraction, whereby the function of respiration is mainly carried on. Plenty of out-door exercise, particularly walking—but not riding in luxurious carriages; horseback exercise; dilation of the chest by frequent acts of deep and forcible inspiration, especially in the open air; the proper use of the dumb-bells; boating, though not by sails or steam, but by handling the oars; and many other exercises of a similar character, in which the arms are brought into action and the ribs raised, are some of the means by the regular adoption of which we shall best succeed in undoing the work which our folly or thoughtlessness has unfortunately effected.

And then will be initiated a movement which will bring in its train such a host of comforts and blessings, that the now happy possessor will always laud and honour the day when she had the courage and good sense to forswear the practice of tight-lacing.

Monnikkendam—Waterland.

HOLLAND.

III.—MARKEN AND MONNIKKENDAM.

AMONGST the many good songs which have been selected and handed down to us by our forefathers there is one ever popular one, which has done much to keep Holland pleasantly and cheerfully fresh in our memory. Who is not influenced by hearing the words, "Deep as the rolling Zuyder Zee"? and immediately a whole host of associations rise up before our minds of Mynheer Van Dunck and his surroundings—taking the good things of life judiciously, for he never got drunk when he took his brandy-and-water gaily. We are now going to visit the Zuyder Zee, and do so with a special interest when we think that the stupendous work of pumping it out has not only been proposed, but has been commenced, and is now at this very moment in its transition state, similar to the Haarlemer Meer, which has been pumped out effectually,

Marken Fisherman.

and converted into "polder" lands and comfortable thriving farms. This, however, is nothing compared with the gigantic work of the Zuyder Zee. Our start was made from Amsterdam, our route laid out for Monnikkendam and Marken. It was a lovely summer day as we left the Capital of Holland, founded *arc.* A.D. 1200, about which time the castle was built. The River Ÿ is always full of interest, with its variety of boats, its quaint old dredging machines, the merchantmen, the market boats, the women rowing the men, the beautiful blending of fresh vegetables with brass milk-cans, Dutchmen with immense bags for breeches, sabots of every variety of colour, some green, some painted white, with a few flowers; and then the great charm of cleanly costume, which as we approach North Holland seems to concentrate its charms about the forehead; it seems the ambition of North Holland ladies to cover their foreheads either with sprays of diamonds or silver plates. Crossing the river affords a good general view of the city of Amsterdam, and in the distance looms that marvellous collection of wind-mills known as Zaandam, near the house of Peter the Great. Wind-mills are used in Holland to pump water, grind grain, cement, snuff, saw timber, and do everything that motive power can be applied to. The mills in the distance naturally attract attention, as few travellers are accustomed to see three or four hundred wind-mills whizzingly rotating. Apart from reminding us how perseveringly these good Dutchmen utilise the power of the elements, we could not resist thinking how thoroughly this would have been the place for Don Quixote to spend a happy day. By this time we have landed on the opposite side of the river, and find waiting for us the national conveyance of Holland — the "Trek-schuyt." Everything worked together for good, everything harmonized; the perfect repose of everything, even the summer haze, was not oppressive. Be-

Dutch Furniture.

seats on the top for fine weather and the general comfort of the travellers. The tow rope is out on the bank of our Dutch canal; the small wiry horse, with the lad standing by him ready to jump on to his back and start off, looks round occasionally to see how soon we shall be off. A few more passengers come, and at last we are away.

Soon the smoke of Amsterdam begins to fade away, and we are getting into North Holland and Waterland, flat as flat can be, yet beautiful in repose and warm greys. The perspective of the vast flat, however, is remarkably graduated by the black and white cows, which abound in Holland: in fact all cows, we may say, in Holland are black and white. Then we have more wind-mills, of varied form and size; long "slooten" or ditches dividing the farms, or an avenue of well-trained black poplars, or abeles, leading up to a farm; sometimes a steeple, sometimes a white mill came to the rescue, and sparkled up the hazy distance; while these charms were alluring us without, there was much that was interesting within. As the trek-schuyt moved down the canal almost every one

fore starting, let us describe a trek-schuyt. Most of our readers have seen the canal boats on the Grand Junction Canal, with painted tiller, painted cabin, the water can and bucket, all floral ornamentation with prominent roses and plenty of paint. The length and beam similar; the chief difference is the fitting. The canal boats in England are not passenger boats, the trek-schuyts are. They are therefore divided into two classes, fore and aft cabins; the larger boats having pulled out his pipe; that is to say the male population on board. The conversation took a turn on the blessings of home, and family peace and contentment. One dear old Dutch lady, with silver plates on her forehead, lace cap, and a straw bonnet on the top of that, a very handsome silver *gibecière* at her side, and large silver buckles on her black velvet shoes, told me that "every thousand guilders brought more avarice." She seemed perfectly saturated with proverbs: Quarle's Emblems and Jacob Catz. Again, she seemed to throw in these proverbs, as a kind of chorus, after any remark. Some of them were very good, but singularly inappropriate, like giving tracts to the wrong people; sometimes the quotations did fit in. For instance, a good old farmer made a slight stumble, after having some schiedam and schnapps; the opportunity was not lost: " Better the wine 'n the flagon than in the head." " Idleness is the devil's pillow" seemed to be always ready for active service, whether the occasion called it forth or not. " He who drains the last drop will get the lid on his nose," this being equivalent to "serve him right." Our afternoon was most enjoyable, and we reached, in good time, a village, the name of which is well known in guide books and Murray as " Broek ;" the cleanest place in creation, and really a show place. We were conducted to one house in particular; as the climax of purity and correctness, in old days visitors had to take their shoes off and leave them outside—a relic of the usual custom in Dutch farm-houses. Pressure of business, however, does not now allow of this being done. If persisted in, what confusion there would be outside at the height of the season! It would be almost as bad as trying to get one's umbrella at the Royal Academy. The charm of Broek has rather passed away; it is all very well for people who do not care to take the trouble, or give the time, to seeing real Dutch cleanliness in all its genuine originality, to be content with this artificial

Water Tower, Monnikkendam.

specimen, for artificial it must be when we discover that directly we admire anything very much, we are informed that we can become the possessor of the article admired provided we pay the price of it. Still Broek should be seen. It has been the show place for nearly one hundred years; it therefore has claims on the attention of travellers. Soon after leaving Broek we see looming in the distance an object which reminds us much of the fens of Lincolnshire at Crowland, nearly the same outline of wood and abbey, dyke and canal, same herons and wildfowl. In the large wood right a-head of us lies Monnikkendam, and beyond that the Zuyder Zee, whither we are bound. About a mile from the town the canal abruptly stops; our trek-schuyt is alongside a kind of landing place. The few passengers left on board go off to different farms, and my friend and myself are directed into the town. We make for the church surrounded by a large wood. It is late on a fine summer evening, and the chatter and noise of the thousands of birds, congregating at the close of day, was far beyond anything we had experienced before; in numbers and density they exceeded the flights on the downs, just before migration, and as for *bruit* devoid of melody, they were unequalled. The noise was perhaps enhanced by the ghostly stillness of everything else around. The trek-schuyt travelling was noiseless save the ripple, and the occasional cry of the boy encouraging the trek pony. When we approached the abbey, we heard no sound ; we walked in, found no one ; walked into the principal street of Monnik-kendam, saw no one. Was it one of the cities of the dead ? We found an inn ; entered, no one there. At last we discovered a young person, and most thankful we were to learn that we could not only have food, but a bed, and everything with Dutch cleanliness and comfort. Later in the evening, the Dutch servant came and sat in the room with us. It required some tact to elicit why this to us unusual attention was shown, and at last we were informed that it was only to prevent our being kept waiting in case we needed her services. So perfectly deserted a city re-minded us at once of Veere, in Zeeland, in the South of Holland ; and there was another resemblance, the Water Tower or Watch

Pile Houses in Marken.

Tower, which is similar, and used for the same purpose, especially as a land mark. Monnikkendam was originally a city of monks, as monks no longer thrive in Holland, the whole place is desolate ; grass grows in the streets ; the houses totter almost for want of repair, and the only use for the place now seems to be that of a point of departure for Marken. The most interesting view of the city is obtained from the Dyke running out beyond the Water Gate, as from this point we see the Water Tower in the centre, the grand old wind-mill which is a glorious relic of the past, and in the distance we see the wood with the abbey nestling in the midst of it.

Much as the song says of " Deep as the rolling Zuyder Zee," we must remember that

Het Dikkertje.

the whole of the bottom of it was originally farm land, the area of surface being much increased about A.D. 1400, just before the great inundation near Dordrecht, when some one hundred thousand lives were lost. The Zuyder Zee being the result of inundation is really only about 10 feet deep, save where the channels have been deepened, so that when the pumping shall have been completed the land will be quite Dutch and perfectly level. The most curious feature of this will perhaps be that there are certain islands now, such as Marken, Urk and Schokland, the inhabitants of which will not have much to do with the mainlanders, and after some four hundred years of history are proud of their insular position; but the day is coming, slow and sure, like the sword of Damocles, when their boats will be superfluities, and they will find their dykes unnecessary, and their night watchers can turn in comfortably instead of pacing long hours in stormy nights, waiting to give the signal that the dyke has burst and their island deluged. Leaving Monnikkendam we came down through some old buildings and by-ways, which must have been built originally to facilitate smuggling and smugglers—notice the ins, outs, and round-the-corner construction of the building in our illustration. The whole atmosphere seems suggestive of stores of adventure and contraband goods. As we came down to the land-

ing place, the question was, whether we could get any boat to take us over. The wind was fair both ways. The Zuyder Zee was not rolling, there was only a nice breeze. No one even asked us if we would like to go. Several Marken men were standing about, fine tall men, clean-shaven, with silk handkerchiefs tied as Garibaldi wore his generally, their breeches very short, half-way from the hip joint to the knee, very full indeed, fastened at the waist by two large buttons. Their boats are of the Schokker class, but the Marken mainmast is farther aft, giving a larger foresail, and the mainsail is hoisted on a gaff. The sails are deep tan, with a light cloth inserted every now and then as required. After conversation and pipes it seemed agreed and decided that we should be allowed to visit Marken, and we started in one of these crafts, with a good breeze, and soon we were bowling along gloriously. No sooner had we arrived than the news soon spread that foreigners were paying a visit. The first thing that struck us was, looking down from the dyke and finding the island lying as it were in the bottom of a saucer, the dyke round being the edge of the saucer. The houses are built on piles, as shown in the illustration, so that when the dyke gives, the water-level is just below the floors of the houses; and as they contain some delightful bits of old furniture, &c., it is well that they should be preserved. We were fortunate in being allowed to interview the principal person of

The Queen of the Island, Marken: Widow Klok.

the island, a widow, who was, and we hope is still, queen of the island. She helps the fishermen in bad times. She is beloved by all, and her kindly influence seems to have done much good. She and her handsome daughter wear the costume of the island, which is very curious, particularly the head-dress, very much like the Parsee form, but white with a little lace on the front, and two long curls, one on each side; these are indispensable—if not supplied by nature then they must be obtained from the mainland. The little children are very picturesque indeed; as the coiffure offers no protection for the

Back Entrance to Shop, Monnikkendam.

eyes, in summer-time a pink shade is sometimes adopted.

We were introduced to one young Marken lady who was remarkably well covered—almost too plump; she was, however, very happy and contented, and seemed to think that she had rather the best of it. It is, however, rather conspicuous to be shown to visitors as "Het Dikkertje van Marken," or

the Thick One of Marken. In the rooms of the houses everything seemed so well cared for and so good; no shoddy left by those who had gone before; everything was as good and useful for the next generation as the last, and that is more than we can say for some of the things purchased in the present day by young housekeepers. The sheets and pillow-cases particularly struck us as being edged with such admirable patterns; some only picked out with black, others more intricate. The same kind of borders are used in red and white to bind their jackets with and some part of their scarlet waistcoats, still worn by the women. The lamps were so quaint and picturesque on their carved oak stands, and show the long clay pipes so cunningly arranged in their stand, the brass *comfoortje*, so original a mode of warming the feet, which are placed on a carved square box containing this apparatus, that we have put them all in one family group. R. T. PRITCHETT.

Early Morning off Marken.

JOSEPH AND HIS BRETHREN.

A Lecture.

IT is not often in history that we are able to point to four such distinct types of men in four successive generations as Abraham, Isaac, Jacob, and Joseph. Abraham is the type of the elder world of men, the pastoral chieftain, enthusiast in faith, severe and simple in life, rapid as lightning in war, courteous in peace and of a noble chivalry, in his relations with men, unworldly in heart, the wise patriarch of the tribe, the loving husband and father, and keeping through every relation of life a desert grandeur of character which makes him one of the greatest figures in history.

Isaac is the type of the contemplative man, inactive in the world, active in the world of his own heart; the Wordsworth of the Old Testament. Jacob is different from both, the type of the worldly-wise business man, changing under higher influences, but very slowly, into the man wise with the wisdom of the world to come. When we come to Joseph, all is changed. He is the type of the man of genius; not that which is made, as some are made, by education, but the born genius, one who is always right he knows not why; who is always master of events and of himself, and whom every event makes greater; who attracts the love of all and is not harmed by it; who keeps the heart, the humility, and the impulse of childhood in the midst of the experience of manhood and the glare of success, wise as the serpent, harmless as the dove.

He passed his childhood wrapt in the mantle of his father's regret. All that Jacob had felt for Rachel was given to her eldest son, and a special and passionate love has a strange power in the development of genius; partly in this case because it isolated the boy; partly because it made him rapidly feel what he was, yet without thinking of it; and partly because it made him feel at home and secure in the world. The pastoral peace of his father's dwelling, where he lived alone, the silence in which he walked, his absence from the practical and noisy life of his brothers with their wandering flocks made him the dreamer, and the short visits he paid them kindled his imagination and gave fuel to his dreams. In those prophetic dreams of his, in which the unconscious aspirations of the day realised themselves in fantastic forms at night, the temperament of genius first revealed itself. The boy felt in the rushing life within him his coming greatness, but he did not understand what his feeling meant. Naturally, without any thought that the spontaneous audacity of inspiration was in his dreams, he told them to his brothers with the unconsciousness of genius. But his brothers saw what they were. They never had had dreams.

We see how fine his genius was when we find that he could turn his hand to anything, and succeed at once. He saw that his brothers did not manage the cattle well, and with the one weakness of his life he brought to his father an evil report of them. No sooner is he in Potiphar's house than he becomes the best steward in Egypt; no sooner is he in the prison than he emerges from disgrace and the whole arrangement of it is given into his hands, and everything succeeds. The prisoners cannot resist his charm and tell their tales to him; he has the secret of making men speak to him and believe in him. No sooner is he released than the kingdom is intrusted to his rule, and the slave and the prisoner becomes at one step the astute, far-seeing and trusted prime minister, leading the country through the dangers of prosperity and adversity with the same undisturbed wisdom, and keeping, without one sacrifice of principle, his place till the close of life; and all this right in the teeth of the disadvantage of his being a stranger, and belonging to a people with whom the Egyptian court would not eat.

The trust that he won from all men is proved in service and the prison; it is still more delightful to see the universal love and honour he received when his position might have kindled envy. Nowhere is this attractiveness which marks the highest genius of a man who has to do with men, more delightfully shown than when the whole court, and the king himself, are filled with joy at the news that Joseph's father and brethren are come. This man, placed over all heads in a day, rising from the ranks of the slaves, had not one apparently in the whole court who was not his friend. When any good happened to him, the world was pleased.

Again, having so marked a character and powers so great, he could not help having adventures. An uncommon character makes an uncommon life, and in the power it has of awaking enmity as well as friendship and love, creates adventure. Even his father feels that he is marked from mankind and distinguishes him from the rest by the coat of many colours. His brothers hate him, conspire to slay him, feeling that he is greater than they, though some among them, even at the last, are subdued by his charm and desire to save him. Adventure meets him again in Egypt, and before he is thirty years old his life is a romance.

His first adventure threw him on the world. The peace of the shepherd home was exchanged for the roar of the great city, the love that watched every movement for rough slavery, the prophetic dreams, poor boy! ended in a fall that might have sobered the wildest visions. Young, alone, inexperienced, he was cast upon the world in a strange land. What will he do, and what become?

It is a question many of us in youth and afterwards have had to ask ourselves. The answer depends on character, and character, so far as we can make it, on the way we meet circumstances. Look back to the hour when you first started on your own responsibility; look around you now that you have to begin life again. What do you see within; how does your heart beat; with what powers have you faced, or do you face, life at this moment? I do not ask whether you have been successful, or can bode success; I ask what you are, strong or weak, brave or trembling, ready to command life, or to sink under its weight; honest and clear of heart, or afraid of yourself. That is the question before God, and the end of life depends on how you can answer it.

Yes, character tells. If you had passed, that day the Ishmaelites arrived, through the chief city of Pharaoh, and seen, as one might still see lately in the eastern market-place, the slaves exposed for hire, and among them the beautiful Hebrew stripling, perhaps a thought of pity, perhaps a sense of shame, might have touched your heart, but scarcely the imagination that before a few years were over the boy would be a prince, and the thoughtful brain that now mused upon his fate be the directing power and the salvation of Egypt. Potiphar passed by; the quiet sorrow and the beauty of the boy touched him; he saw the upright face and the clear eye and bought the youth to do his work. And in his new life Joseph's character made its way. Step by step he rose, till at last all things were done by his hands, and all things prospered in them.

That success was due to genius, but to genius made powerful for good by moral and religious character. The moral force is

shown in the healthy way in which he set to work. If any man might have been embittered or made morbid it was Joseph. Almost murdered, sold as a slave by his very brothers! Why, it were no wonder if he had thought that all men were false, and all the work of the world hateful. Nothing of the kind. He must have felt the blow sorely. There was no lack of affection in him who wept over and forgave his brothers, and remembered his father with tears; but the vivid nature in him, borne up by moral courage, and the new and quick interests in life which his conquest of revengeful feeling allows him to feel with all their power, set him to work, and made him rejoice in his work. Youth, intellect, moral strength were all on his side, and behind them the unknown force of genius. What wonder he succeeded!

Along with these, another element in his success was a religious spirit. "The Lord gave him favour," we are told. It is another way of saying that at the root of his genius was love of God, that his powers were sanctified by worship of the Highest. All men recognised this. Pharaoh and the council said, the spirit of God is in this man. And it is worth saying that in these early times no one seems to doubt that genius is the direct inspiration of God. We look upon it as only of the man himself; it is even part of our idea that its inspiration is not from God at all. We have secluded inspiration to certain sacred books and certain sacred businesses. So that when a great artist, statesman, or philosopher arises he does not hear from the world that the spirit of the Holy God is in him, but only that he is a great man. Hence no sacred ideal necessarily dignifies his work; he does not habitually refer his powers to God, nor is he taught to use them with a reference 'to Divine purposes. Often hearing that his inspiration is profane, he works it for unholy ends and degrades it. It might be different if we were to say to men who have the magical gift of genius with Pharaoh, This man has in him the spirit of God. It is a great and ruling thought to possess. For half the irreligion of the world arises from our separation of our gifts from God and of the work we do with them from the Divine character. He who, with genius, has God's spirit also, makes his life and his work more noble, as Joseph did.

It is a question much debated whether goodness of life has any influence on genius. Will a vicious person, if he has great gifts, build, or paint, or carve, or compose poetry or music, or think clearly in science, or rule a nation less well, because of his life being without goodness? Not so, at first, for the glow of genius is too strong for the inward baseness, the Divine in it struggles long against its enemy. But as time goes on, the evil influence, whatever it be, tells. The sensibility to beauty goes; the clear judgment fails; the selfish interest steps in and spoils the execution. The power used for base purposes, for money, or self-interest, or mere fame, becomes itself base; the corrupt life corrupts the heart and stains the imagination, and we see, even though the power may remain, that it has become unable to do good to man or to give an enduring pleasure.

And what is true of genius is true in a less degree of every true work. If it is to be true, faithful, and enduring, the inspiration of God in the brain and heart should be matched by the inspiration of God in the spirit. We should be worthy like Joséph of the favour of the Lord by striving to be like the Lord, and by adding to the gifts of God the graces of God.

Being such, Joseph, wherever he went, had power. His character spoke for itself. As steward, prisoner, prime minister, he was thoroughly trusted; and though a master might naturally suspect a slave, a jailor a prisoner, and a king one whom the people worshipped—yet all the world believed in him, everywhere his righteous uprightness and clear soul shone like a star. Truth of character begets trust, wins its way to some usefulness, no matter in what circumstances.

It is a glorious thing to aspire to and to win; to be so manly that wherever you are, men may recognise you as their strength; to be so upright that your life may create uprightness around you; so noble and true of heart that you may not only always hear the voice of God within, but also in apparent ruin, poverty, suffering, through slander and denial of the world, may make men feel that they have a king among them.

These are the men who really rule the world. They may be poor, unknown, despised. They may never have Joseph's chances, but they have had power, they have done more than many of those who are called great and famous. Half the progress of the world is due to unknown persons who have been true men in their obscurity, who have lived as Joseph, while slave and prisoner, as faithful children of the Eternal Righteousness. Character tells always for enduring results, but it must be character that daily grows up into likeness to God's character.

The whole truth of this is made more vivid for us when godlike character, as in Joseph, is united to genius. Able to do anything well, he was led by God and circumstances to be a statesman. The experience of many kinds of life which he had had in Palestine among the shepherds, in the slave caravan, in the stewardship, in prison, had fitted him for this work. Young as he was he knew men and women, and the insight he had into human character, an insight born of that quick sympathy that loses itself to do anything for the fate and dreams of others (nothing is more forcibly brought out in the story than this), fitted him still more for his work. And the natural dignity he shows before Pharaoh, the rapidity with which he sees and chooses at once the right means to meet the coming famine, the faith he possesses in the future and in himself, the quickness and roundness of his ideas, the care with which he assumes and fills his new post, the fearless way in which, in a moment, he rises to a vast responsibility, all betray the born statesman.

The measures he adopts are masterly, but one is surprised that no one seems to challenge them. But there is no need for surprise, for here character comes in. It was his unstained hónour, his incorruptibility that brought him universal acceptance. In his position nothing could have been easier than to enrich himself by a few politic turns, and one may be sure that many were on the watch to catch him tripping. He kept the confidence and love of Egypt to the end, because his was the spirit of honour in his doings with men, and the spirit of moral duty in his secret life with God. Who does not recollect his speech to the wife of Potiphar in which both are contained, How can I deceive my master who has trusted me? how can I do this great wickedness and sin against God?

Yes, these are the things which in man or woman, gifted or ungifted, really act upon the world. You may have the personal charm which makes a host of friends; the wit, knowledge, brilliancy, that attract society; the wealth or rank that secures its flattery; the passionate enthusiasm that kindles admiration and love—they are all useless to keep the lasting reverence and love of men, unless they repose on faithfulness to honour and fidelity to God; unless you can put aside temptation to indulgence when it injures the least of men who are Christ's brothers; unless you can sternly reject, even though your rejection bring worldly ruin with it, the act or the thought which in sinning against truth or purity or mercy sins against the righteous will of God. Would you keep, as Joseph did, the trust and affection of men; would you ennoble your genius or transfigure into beauty the common gifts you have—be faithful to honour, be faithful to your high birth as a son of the King of Righteousness.

Through a long life Joseph was true to God and man. The times of his trial had now gone by, and we find him as the Viceroy of Egypt. A new life now opened on the much-tried man. He who had been betrayed, sold, tempted, falsely imprisoned, was now the second person in the land. Married into the highest priestly family, in full flush of youthful manhood, with enjoyment made deeper by the sorrow of the past, with the highest work possible to do and with equal powers and opportunities, Joseph stands before us in the full blaze of the sunshine of prosperity. Surely, we say, trial is over now; God will let His servant rest. Yes, if prosperity be rest and not rather the severest trial. It is not so difficult (once God has been loved) to keep close to Him in illness, or poverty, or bereavement; one is driven to the invisible comforter when visible things decay; but in health, happiness, and when all goes well, the visible usurps the invisible. God drifts from our sight, and we lie open to a thousand temptations; our moral force is enervated, our spiritual life is seized with sleep. So the prayer of the Litany is, "In all time of our tribulation, in all time of our wealth—our welfare—good Lord deliver us."

Prosperity is our time of trial; it is well for some of us who are at ease to realise that. Too often, having got the portion of goods which falleth to us, we set off into the far country to waste our substance, to enjoy without serving, to rest, not from excitement, but from duty; to be free to do our own will, not to be free in doing the will of God, to lose in the noise of amusement the still small voice of Him who whispers in our slumbering ear, "Watch and pray, lest ye enter into temptation." "Be sober and watch to the end."

There are two things that protect the soul in prosperity, keep it true to God and humble in itself. One is prayer. We see that Joseph had got the habit of referring all to God. Nothing can be quieter than his sayings when the dreams of the king are told to him. There was no pride, no thought of self. "God will give Pharaoh an answer of peace," was all he said. The man who could then so speak, the imprisoned slave before the great king, was one who so habitually lived in the presence of God that all earthly sovereigns were dwarfed in his presence—and such a constant consciousness of God's presence is to live a life of prayer. No adversity, no prosperity could do hurt to the noble soul who took both as the gift of Him who would take away or confirm them when He thought it right for His follower's highest life. At every action of his life, he looked up and God was before his eyes, and he bowed his head, and said, "Lord God, thou seest me, look on my work and bless it."

This is the guard of life.

The other guard Joseph had in prosperity was that his work was for man. Idleness is a common danger of prosperity; and idleness does not live alone. It is a king and keeps its court, and if it has got into your life it brings with it its counsellors, which are impure thoughts, and its queen which is folly, and its followers which are envy and slander, gossiping and mischief; and the more idleness you indulge in the worse all these become, till their final result is corruption. An idle man or woman rots away. Neither intellect, nor imagination, nor memory, nor even the affections can endure its crawling poison. As to the spirit, it loses all true humanity, all true relation to God, and becomes the victim of diseased and hateful hysteria. There is no worse evil in the world than to let prosperity bring idleness.

On the other hand, the prosperous man is often a hard worker. His danger is not idleness, for prosperity urges him to gain more prosperity; but it is this, that he begins to think of himself, of his and his family's success alone. Nothing more than that, and that is ruin. When there is no thought for others, no expansion of his wealth beyond his own circle, no life in the great interests of mankind, no ideas that make his thoughts fly with sympathy and practical help to nations or tribes struggling for freedom or truth, no care that his labour or his money should bless the future and give a swifter motion to the wheels of human progress—then the man is as much ruined by prosperity as the idle man. "No," he says, "I am a practical man; charity begins at home; I am too sensible to try and do good to people of whom I know nothing, and to care for interests too indefinite for me." That sounds like sense, but is nonsense. Charity may begin, but does not end, at home. You are not a practical man, but a dull man when you never pass beyond your own circle, and dulness does not improve your business—and common sense of this sort is nothing more than stupid hardness of heart. There is nothing worse in the world than selfish prosperity. As to religious life—to live for your own interests alone in the midst of this vast brotherhood, is to live without God in the world, because you are living without man in the world. For in what words is given, at the end, the last judgment? "Inasmuch as ye did it not to the least of these my brethren, ye did it not to me."

Joseph escaped from this fate. His work for fourteen years was wholly for his adopted country, and when the seven years of plenty had seen his wise economy, he could save not only Egypt, but all the countries round from the plague of famine. His prosperity bore on the wants, the interests, the happiness and progress of mankind.

That is the kind of thing we want now. We have plenty of rich men, rich far beyond their needs. How do they spend their money? Is it in self-aggrandisement, in rising in the world, in adding to the power of their family, in laying field to field, that they may be alone in the midst of the earth? in building larger and larger nests that their people may continue from generation to generation? Is it only in these things that wealth is spent? —then it becomes corrupt and the rich man's life contemptible. To provide for one's self and family is necessary, but it is only one use of great wealth. There are other uses, for the interests of mankind, which ought to be fulfilled if wealth is to be made righteous and poetical. You who are rich have only to look round and ask yourself what men want; and there are many noble and poetic things to do, things which will send your name down to ages to come with a lustre round it which will ennoble it. Have you founded a college for poor students at the university?

Have you given ten thousand pounds to the education and training of girls and women for higher work than they can do at present for want of the keys of learning, for want of knowing that method in work which unlocks the gates of usefulness? Have you endowed research? There are at this moment a number of branches of knowledge and art that only want a thousand a year for a few years to produce incalculable use to men, and incalculable additions to their happiness! Have you bought beautiful things, and set them forth in the sight of those who cannot buy them? Have you made a great library in your county town, or in a great centre of human activity; have you built baths for the poor; have you brought fresh water to a fever-ridden town; have you sought out and helped without their knowledge struggling men of genius; have you said to the school-master of the common school, or to the head of one of the great schools, "Let me know if you have a scholar whom I may send to the university"? Have you established places where recreation may be given to the wearied? Have you sent help over the world to nations that are struggling for freedom, to bodies of men who are striving for ideas useful to mankind? Is your wealth like the stagnant lake in your grounds, or is it flowing like a great river through the world, blessing and fertilising mankind? Have you wrought like Joseph, or have you lived like him who said, "I will pull down my barns and build greater, and there shall I bestow all my fruits and my goods." But God said to him, "Thou fool, this night shall thy soul be required of thee, then whose shall those things be that thou hast provided?"

STOPFORD A. BROOKE.

SEEKING REST.

THUS saith my soul, "The path is long to tread,
 Behind me far it stretches, far before;
 Wearily, drearily, sight travels o'er
Leagues that have lengthened as the slow days sped,
And wearily o'er leagues untraversèd
 Which I must traverse ere I gain the door
 That shuts not night nor day. What need I more
Than to find rest at last in that last bed?"

Is it well said, O soul? The way *is* long,
 Weary are heart and brain and aching feet,
But 'mid thy weariness thou still art strong,
 And rest unearned is shameful; so entreat
This one thing—that at last the conqueror's song
 May echo through a sleep divinely sweet.

J. ASHCROFT NOBLE.

A CORNER OF THE BOIS DE CHAUMOUR, BURGUNDY.
A STUDY IN BLACK AND WHITE BY G. MONTBARD.

SARAH DE BERENGER.

By JEAN INGELOW.

CHAPTER X.

THE next morning Sir Samuel's carriage stopped again at the door of the tiny cottage. A footman got down, went in, and soon came back to his master, with "The nurse's respects, Sir Samuel, and I was to say, if you wished to see the young ladies, they are up at the vicarage doing their lessons."

"I should like to see *her*."

"She hopes you'll excuse her, Sir Samuel: she is making bread, and has her hands in the dough."

Sir Samuel alighted, with the smallest of brown paper parcels in his hand, and sought Mrs. Snaith in her little clean back kitchen. "I thought, Mrs. Snaith, I need not trouble you to go all the way—a mile or more—to the post with this. I can post it for you."

"Oh, sir, it will be no trouble, thank you kindly; I have to walk over to the shop."

"If you'll give me pen and ink, I'll direct it, then." He looked about, but saw nothing excepting the copper before which Mrs. Snaith was standing, with both hands plunged into the bread-pan.

Mrs. Snaith, blushing, said she had no pen and ink, but, if he would leave the letter, it would go all right. "It's not often I have to write anything," she continued, as if excusing herself; "and my little ladies do their copies at Mr. de Berenger's."

He half smiled, perceiving that his device for obtaining the direction had for the present failed.

"I'll see that it go all right, sir," she repeated.

He was too proud to sue for what he wanted.

"So be it, then," he answered; took a letter from the brown paper covering and laid it on the clean edge of the copper. "I shall be much obliged to you," he said, as he retired. "You'll let me pay for the stamp, of course?"

"How simple she is!" he thought. "She might just as well have told me my poor boy's address, considering how easy it will be for me to find it out at the post-office."

But it did not prove so easy. In less than a quarter of an hour Mr. Bolton passed, with a light cart full of vegetables that he had brought from the parsonage, and Mrs. Snaith, coming out to him, asked him if he would oblige a neighbour by getting that letter sent to Mr. John de Berenger.

Mr. Bolton turned the letter over and over

several times, and looked critically at the paper and curiously at Mrs. Snaith.

"I'll never breathe a word to any soul, if you will, Mr. Bolton, how it was, or who it was that got it done for me," she pleaded.

Still Mr. Bolton paused and seemed to cogitate.

So she urged him further. "I've been that annoyed lately about him, that I can't bear myself till I get things explained."

"Well, you'll observe," answered Mr. Bolton, answering what he supposed to be her thought, but in fact only his own false supposition—"you'll observe that there's no post-office in nature equal to ours for sureness; and likewise, if you want a letter to be forwarded, you must write *that* in their foreign words; also you should never put 'esquire' on a letter that's to go abroad— they're apt to mistake the word for a man's name. And you've always got to prepay a foreign letter."

Mrs. Snaith produced a shilling, and to her surprise received only sixpence change, but she was too polite to make any remark; and, having given Mr. Bolton the letter, hastened to escape from a subject almost sure to lead to questioning.

"And how is your good lady, Mr. Bolton? I saw her on Saturday in the shop, looking as fresh as a rose."

"Fresh she is!" answered Mr. Bolton with enthusiasm. He had lately married a wife many years younger than himself. "Fresh she is, and always pleased. What her father said has come true. 'Cornelius,' says the old gentleman (he's in the shoe line), 'Cornelius, you'll find her a rare one to make you laugh; her cheerful temper is as good as a daily blow out.'"

Mrs. Snaith, considering this a vulgar compliment, instinctively drew herself up; but the proud husband was spared any observation of her silent disapproval, for at that instant the horse, perhaps thinking he had waited long enough in the sun, suddenly started down the road at a good pace, and Mr. Bolton, after calling to him in vain to stop, had to run after him. Mrs. Snaith only remained outside till he was seated and had the reins in his hand, then went in, glad to have got the letter forwarded, but with a lowered opinion of Mr. Bolton, as rather countrified and common, considering what a good shop he had, and that he kept the post-office.

Sir Samuel, who was not at all in the habit of shopping, went into Mr. Bolton's shop the next day, feigning to want some melon-seed, of which he ordered a ridiculously large quantity, and then asked Mrs. Bolton what foreign letters had been posted that day, or the day before.

It appeared that no foreign letters whatever had been posted for more than a fortnight.

Sir Samuel brought himself to say, "I have lost my son's (Mr. John de Berenger's) address; if one directed to him should be posted, will you kindly copy the address for me?"

"I will, Sir Samuel," said young Mrs. Bolton; and when her husband came in she related to him what had passed.

"Lost the address, have the old gentleman?" quoth Mr. Bolton calmly. "Well, now, his gardener won't put those melon-seeds in, I know, but they must be sent. Only think of old Sam's losing the address!"

"It's a pity but what he was more careful," observed Mrs. Bolton; and so few letters passed through her hand, that it gave her no trouble to keep this request in mind.

Four days passed. "John's not in England," thought Sir Samuel, "or I should have had an answer before now." Two more days passed. "John's not in France," thought Sir Samuel. A fortnight. "John's not in Italy, nor in Germany either." Six weeks. "John's not in the States—at least, anywhere near the sea-board — nor in Canada."

Three more months, and a letter from Ceylon, in John's handwriting, was lying on his table. It was dated from a small place up the country, among the coffee plantations; was a very satisfactory letter on the whole, but the father soon saw, both by the date and the contents, that his son had not yet received the important letter. With a certain moderation of compunction which, however, satisfied Sir Samuel, he expressed his regret that his family, and his father in particular, had no better reason to be proud of him. He hoped to do better; had got employment that maintained him, and should write from time to time. This was a very hot place—steaming hot; in fact, he had to have a black boy standing beside him while he shaved, to wipe the dew that every few minutes gathered and clouded the looking-glass. The boots he took off at night were covered in the morning with mould. But there was plenty of alligator shooting; he and some other fellows had shot two the week before. This was on the third page. His father went on to the end, which, with a description of how the other fellows who were newly come out "funked" when they saw a serpent, ended rather abruptly, "Your affectionate son, JOHN DE BERENGER."

Sir Samuel's heart was appeased; both his pride and his affection soothed themselves over this letter. "The boy has not forgotten me; and he means to do better. Well, well, he has sown his wild oats. He will make me proud of him after all. Been in Ceylon six weeks, after stopping at Heidelberg all the winter. Ah!"

In the meantime Ann Thimbleby fulfilled her task of education as well as she knew how; she was lucky enough to take sufficient interest in it to induce her to make experiments, and when one failed she tried another. At that time her inquisitive mind was much exercised on the subject of etymology, but the pains she took to instil some liking for it into the minds of her two elder pupils bore no fruit, except to make them like playing with words, while the little ones became familiar with a few uncommon expressions, which they used glibly in their childish talk.

"He's a greedy, *nefarious* boy," said Amabel to Sir Samuel, speaking of Dick; "and we're not friends with him."

Sir Samuel had come to see the children; he was seated in a chair on the parsonage lawn when she said this, and a slight stirring five feet from the ground, in the great fir tree, made him cast up an inquiring glance, and observe Dick looking out, shamefaced and red.

"What has he been about?" asked the old man, more to make the fair little creature talk than with any interest in Dick's delinquency.

"Coz gave each of us a sugared almond," said Amabel, pouting. "I said, 'Dick, you may take a bite of mine,' and he—— Oh, Dick, you *in-principled* boy, you gobbled it all up—and now," she continued, with deep melancholy, "I can never get it back."

Dick felt at that moment as much shame as mortals can feel for any delinquency whatever, shame being born with us full grown, and beginning, as a rule, to wax feeble before we have the truest cause to feel it. He wondered how it could have come to pass that he had done an action so utterly to be despised—wondered whether it would be forgotten by the time he was grown up—and felt, though he was not equal to the expression of such a thing, that his future prospects were blasted, and his young life nipped as by a spring blight. How could he ever show his face again!

He moved uneasily on his branch, hiding himself among the thick greenery, and with dreary compunction listened to the conversation below, which was very friendly and confiding. But could he believe his ears? In spite of what had unfortunately occurred, the old uncle in a very few minutes was actually calling to him.

"Come down, you little scaramouch; come here, I say. Do you see what this is?"

A whole shilling! Not a new one, it is true, but good for buying things with. Evidently for him! There was a reprieve. He descended, blushing with beautiful confusion, took it, darted out of the gate with it to a cottage below Mrs. Snaith's, and returned, almost able to hold up his head, with a goodly quantity of "bull's-eyes" screwed up in paper.

These articles of commerce have almost disappeared from any but village shops. They are round lumps of sugar, flavoured with peppermint, and marked across with blue and red bands.

Dick squatted down beside Amabel and opened the screw of paper. Sir Samuel was just thinking that she was a far lovelier child than *her father* had ever been.

"No," said the little creature, declining this peace-offering, "I don't like them, Dick; when I open my mouf they make my tongue feel so cold."

She turned away her face—but "*how useful it is to have money!*"

"You're cross," said Dick. "I'm very sorry. Do kiss me this once and make it up."

"I don't want to kiss you," said Amabel.

"Do," pleaded Dick. "Well, if you will, *I'll give you the other sixpence!*"

There was the sixpence in his hand. Amabel looked at it—paused, relented. "If you'll go with me to the shop to spend it," she said, "I will."

Thereupon the two children kissed each other, and being now good friends again, left the bull's-eyes on the grass and ran off together through the vicarage gate; while the giver of the shilling was left to amuse himself with little dimpled Delia, who, seated on his knee, answered his questions about the sea-side, and her lessons and Mamsey, as well as she knew how.

A certain tenderness towards the children softened his heart, and made him feel younger again. The love of money gave way before it to a sufficient degree for the decision which he had formed, that they should never want

"Sir Samuel was thinking that she was a lovelier child than *her father* had ever been."

for anything. Little Delia's lisping tongue reminded him of the infantile talk of his own sons in their childhood. He had taken no interest in, and made few observations on, other children, therefore, when the behaviour of Amabel and Delia stirred in him slumbering recollections of his own nursery, he regarded this as a proof of likeness to his family, and did not know that such were the common ways and wiles, and this was the ordinary English of childhood in general.

"But the motive," thought Sir Samuel, when, having mounted his horse, he went slowly along the shady road that led from the vicarage past the nurse's, and past two or three other cottages, towards his own gate— "the motive. No human being acts without a motive, and I cannot see the motive, however mistaken, that induces this woman to deny that these are John's children. Why, they're as like him as they can stare; and I could declare, when I see their little ways

and hear them lisp, that it's my own boys over again." He paused, then went on slowly. "He might, to be sure, have threatened her that, if she told, he would stop the supplies—for, of course, he was always in imminent danger of being arrested whenever he came to see them ; but he sailed about the time that she brought them here, no doubt by his orders. Well, I must wait. It is still *just possible* they may not be his, after all (pooh ! it's not possible, though). However, he will not be long in letting me know. And considering that I've offered to take the whole charge of them, and provide for them too, if they are—— Here comes Felix, looking as if he had the weight of the world on his shoulders. Well, nephew parson, how are you ? "

Felix observed a certain familiar way in the greeting, a cordiality that he was not accustomed to. Not to be outdone, he shook hands with his uncle when the old man stopped his horse, and asked where he could have been riding during the hottest hours of such a hot day.

Sir Samuel told him; went a little from the subject to remark, in a casual way, that one of the little girls looked pale, and then said abruptly, "I suppose I shall have to send her to the sea."

Now, Felix knew that John de Berenger had written to his father. "Has John acknowledged them, then?" he exclaimed with vehemence.

Sir Samuel admitted that he had not, "though, putting this thing and that thing together, nephew parson," he continued, "I no more doubt the fact than you do."

Felix paused; his conduct certainly appeared to show that he did not doubt it. His aunt Sarah had taught the children to call him Coz, and he had not forbidden it. While he was considering what answer to make, Sir Samuel repeated his former argument with himself.

"But, then, no human being acts without a motive, Felix."

"Certainly not."

"What motive can that woman have, nephew parson, in declaring that these children are none of mine?"

"I do not see that a *motive* is very far to seek," observed Felix, "if that is what you want."

"Nephew parson, that precise thing is what I do want."

"She is all-powerful while she receives whatever John allows the children, and spends it as she pleases."

"True—true."

"She has an excellent situation, and an almost independent one. I have a good opinion of her. I think it probable she does not know the children are anything to you. John may have chosen her through an agent; through an agent he may correspond with her. If you take them up, you make her place a sinecure, perhaps in the end dismiss her. How natural she should be hard to persuade that you have any right to them."

"But she knows that John is my son—and —and the fact is, she undertook, before I had his address, to get a letter sent to him."

"She did!" exclaimed Felix.

Sir Samuel nodded. Mrs. Snaith, in the opinion of Felix, forthwith went down; he was rather sorry.

"Now, as you are good at motives," continued the old man, "find me a motive for John's behaviour, nephew parson; there is that to think of also."

"Very true," said Felix, and he went on slowly. "John's motive, I should say, is transparent enough. It is evident that he has no claim, unless these are the children of a marriage."

Sir Samuel seemed to wince a little here.

"The only marriage I ever heard of that John wanted to make was one that you most violently opposed."

"I always shall oppose it," cried Sir Samuel, very red in the face. "I always will oppose it, to the last breath I can draw. Why— why, the fools had nothing to live upon— nothing at all."

"No," said Felix, rather coldly; "and yet it may have taken place, and these may be the offspring of it."

"A dissenting minister's daughter!"

"Yes. Well, all that supposed, one may suppose also that John thinks these children have a better chance of pleasing you, if he does not force them on your notice, than if he does; but it is quite a work of supererogation to make out motives either for him or the nurse. The wisest course, I should say, is to regard everything as absolutely uncertain till next mail day, when all will be set at rest."

"Extraordinary!" he thought, when the two had parted, and were going different ways. "So proud as old Sam is, that he should have demeaned himself to communicate with his own son, through the favour of a servant!

"*The fools had nothing to live on.* Of course not. He brought up John to no profession, and made him no regular and proper allowance; now he smarts for it, and perhaps for preventing that marriage as well. He might have maintained John married for half what he has cost him single. As far as I know, John never went wrong till the quarrel about that poor girl.

"I have never believed there was any instinctive drawing in the heart of a parent towards a stranger child. Is it possible that I see it here? He will have it so. He is determined to believe that these little creatures are his grandchildren.

"They are no trouble about the place, but I feel, and I suppose I shall feel, that their probably being something to him makes me no better inclined to regard them as something to me."

Felix spoke with a touch of bitterness. Sir Samuel had never so much as asked after Amias, the young nephew whose boyish escapade had deprived him of an excellent opening and future provision. Felix, being absolutely honest with himself, admitted mentally that, if the boy had settled to the brewery business, it would not have hurt his own conscience: people must have beer, just as they must have money; the abuse of either, or both, is their own affair. But now that the youth had broken away from his uncle, had given such reasons for the rash act, and was taking the consequences, on the whole, well and humbly, Felix would have denied himself every comfort in life rather than have interfered with his conscience.

"So you met Uncle Sam?" observed Amias that evening. "I am glad I did not."

"Why?"

"Because you say he was cordial, and that aggravates me. I don't like to think he is happy and jolly, *helping everybody to get drunk;* and I am not happy because——"

"Well?" said Felix, with a smile.

Amias paused.

"You, at least, may wish him well," said Felix; "he has never shown anything but kindness to you."

"But I hope it will stick in his conscience," observed Amias, "how all the judges talk against publicans and public-houses. Why, I was reading only this morning, that in some of the great towns two-thirds of the public-houses are brewers' property, and that they buy up the rubbishing old tenements and let them out at a low rent, on condition that all the stuff sold in them shall be of their own brewing. I hate the publicans."

"That's a fine Christian sentiment. Do you think there's no such thing as intemperance excepting in the case of strong drink? or can you really think that nobody is to blame for the drunkenness that degrades the country excepting the distillers, the brewers, and the publicans?"

"Why, what do *you* think, Felix?"

"I think they are no worse than other people, excepting when they make direct efforts to keep up the present state of things, after having had the misery of it pointed out to them. We are all to blame, we and our fathers."

"No worse?—the publicans no worse?"

"Unless they adulterate."

"But they do. We know they put aquafortis in. And do you call oil of juniper, and cocculus Indicus, and photo-phosphate of iron proper things to drink? Did you never hear of these drugs? And are you not aware that at many public-houses you can hardly get such a thing as unadulterated beer, and that they put salt in- it on purpose to make people thirsty?"

"Your voice is a little cracked at present, which makes me think you may be rather young just yet to lecture with good effect, on this or any other subject."

"You are always so abominably calm, Felix. Well, anyhow, what I don't know yet about temperance, I shall find in my copy of 'The Publican's Mixing and Reducing Book.' I shall learn it all by heart, with its vile receipts for purifying tainted gin, &c. But you have no zeal; you are always making game of a fellow."

"On the contrary, your enthusiastic desire to do some good, and your ardent indignation against evil practices, are the qualities I like most in you. What I find ridiculous is that you are so positive."

"I certainly do wish that most of the breweries and distilleries had accidentally got blown up; and I wish most of the public-houses were forcibly shut up—prohibited."

"But not all?"

"No, there must be some."

"How the 'some' would thrive! Many people, however, see great danger in legal restraints. That a thing should be dangerous and wrong, gives it often attraction enough; that it should also be forbidden, so far as is possible, might give it an extra charm."

"But that is not your view?"

"Perhaps not. Others reason thus. The French are a very sober people: every man of them may make his own wine, any man may sell it anywhere. What we should try for, rather than restriction, is freedom."

"I never thought of that."

"But you should think; and you should learn all that can be known on all points beforehand. And you must give up wholesale charges and exaggerations. There is also a certain thing that you would do well to settle forthwith, which is, whether it would give you most delight to reclaim two or three drunkards, or to make old Sam ridiculous in his own neighbourhood, and to know that everybody blamed him, and talked of the feud between you."

"Two or three, Felix! You might at least allow a fellow two or three dozen. Am I to give up riches and independence, and perhaps a seat in Parliament, for two or three?"

"You may be fairly said to have given these things up for nothing, for no principle whatever—merely for a ridiculous joke."

"Well, it was rather hard upon you, old man; I know that."

"And it seems to me that you live upon the hope that you shall one day justify that joke."

"So I do."

"I consider that a low motive—anything but heroic, anything but philanthropic."

"Well, I cannot be such a prig as to pretend that I think of nothing but philanthropy. 'There's a mixter, sir,' as Bolton said; 'you can't expect to find no tares at all in the best bag of seed-corn.' But perhaps you think the 'mixter' consists of a few grains of corn in a bag of tares?"

"I wish you to go away, not thinking of yourself as a martyr to principle, but simply as having made a joke and paid for it, and having now got to earn a living, if possible, in a manly, commonplace fashion. As for your zeal in the cause of temperance, I shall think something of it when you propose to begin to work for it in London, and nothing at all, so long as the joy of it depends on some great commotion made in our little town, just at our old uncle's gates. As I said to you just now, we are all—that is, all this nation which calls itself Christian—to blame for the present state of things; it is the selfishness of the whole community—the crowding up of the poor in foul air, where they crave stimulus, because they have not enough oxygen. It is the sordid way in which we have let them live, without any sort of culture, without ennobling amusements, without enough of anything—enough variety of food, enough light, enough warmth, enough joy, enough kindly fellowship with those that are better off,—it is our whole attitude toward them which has helped, not to make them a drunken people—for that they always were—but to keep them one. Our fathers drank deeply; we have, during the last three generations, been slowly struggling upward toward sobriety. We had every help; we only give them one help—the pledge. Do you think that if every drop of whisky, gin, and ale could be sunk into the sea, and the trade in liquor stopped, it would make people sober? No. It might, with every other aid that could possibly be thought of, put an end to half the drunkenness; but it is a natural instinct in man to long for stimulus when he is overworked, or weary, or sick, or sad, or when he has been used to have it; and the other half of the drunkards would all turn brewers and distillers on their own account. You cannot undo the evil work of many generations with a few rough-and-ready schemes; you must be patient and painstaking, and you must not try to shove off the blame on other men's shoulders."

"All right, old man," said Amias, almost humbly.

He was to go away to London the next morning, at a very inconveniently early hour, by a third-class train, Felix having, after great efforts, at last got him into a Government office, at a salary on which it was hardly possible for him to be wholly maintained. He was to take with him rather a large hamper of potatoes and other roots, with a few green vegetables also, so as to eke out his first attent.pt at providing for himself in his lodgings. Felix was to send him fruit and vegetables now and then. This was by their aunt Sarah's advice, and was worth while, as she explained to the brothers, because the lodgings Amias was to occupy were close to the railway station. "You can give your landlady a vegetable marrow or two," she observed; "but, whether or not, you will probably, for reasons of her own, find her always willing to send for your hamper. The children might have gathered you more currants if Ann had superintended properly, but, if you'll believe me, I found her among the cabbages, telling them that those tiresome white butterflies were considered by the Greeks to be emblems of your soul, and hunting out with dictionaries the derivations of a slug."

CHAPTER XI.

So Amias was gone. And Sir Samuel, when he quite by chance discovered this, felt somewhat aggrieved. It was manifest that he ought to have been told, and if the matter had been laid before him in a proper spirit, he should have given Amias something towards the needful expenses. He said so to his niece Sarah. "But I am not asked," he continued, with bitterness, "not consulted at all. Oh dear, no; that family is much too proud to take any help from me."

"Why doesn't he give it without being asked? Why doesn't he send Amias a cheque now?" thought the good lady. "He always reminds me of an onion (for we all, as it is said, resemble in some degree one or other of the inferior animals). His conscience is wrapped round with as many layers to cover it from the light, as the heart of an onion. The outside layer is avarice. Yes; very thick. Peel that off, you come to a layer of self-conceit; peel again, you come to his scruples—a sort of mock conscience. He must not do anything so wrong as to help Felix unless Amias first humbles himself."

It never occurred to Miss de Berenger for a moment that she ought to help her nephew Felix herself. And as he had been used to her all his life, and been accustomed to accept her at her own valuation of herself, it never occurred to him either. One duty was strongly impressed on her mind; this was the duty of paying her bills. She generally incurred debts to the full amount of her income. Her course was plain; she must pay them.

But she frequently came and stayed with Felix, kept his house for the time, and paid her exact proportion of the expenses, besides almost always suggesting some plan by which he saved something or gained some advantage.

She was always welcome. He found her inconsequent speeches and simple shrewdness in action decidedly attractive and refreshing. Family affection is so far from following in the wake of esteem, that merely to be sure of it and depend on it, is often to have it. Those who are loved, not for any special qualities in themselves, but just because they are human beings, and stand near to us, are almost sure to retain affection; for they always will be human beings, and the longer they stand near to us the more at ease we shall feel with them. What so comfortable, what so delightful, as perfect ease? Nothing in the world can surpass it but perfect love, and that we cannot all expect.

When Felix, the very first time he entered his empty rectory house, found his aunt there before him, inspecting the cupboards and having one cleaned out, he did not interfere with her, did not even ask her a question; in a man's indolent way, he thought she knew what she was about.

"Yes," she presently observed, "you've got dozens of empty pickle bottles and empty marmalade pots over at your lodgings. I shall have those beer bottles saved too, and put in here till we want them."

Felix was surprised, but he let her alone, and she locked the closet and took away the key.

A good while after this she drove up in her pony-carriage, saying she had come to stay a week, and producing a great parcel of sugar, for which Felix was to pay. "Bolton will not buy the common gooseberries and cherries at all; they are so cheap this year." And she forthwith bustled into the garden and set everybody, excepting the rector, to work to gather fruit. "I shall have a quantity of jam made of the gooseberries," she observed to her nephew; "it will scarcely cost you threepence a pot. And the gooseberries could not be bottled, because the beer bottles have such narrow necks; they would stick in them. I shall bottle the red

currants. There are sixty bottles; I counted them. I shall save out one dozen for mulberry syrup." Thereupon she produced the big key of the cupboard, and before the week was over, there was a fine store of jam and excellent bottled fruit in the house.

Felix, of course, was glad; he knew enough about his own affairs to be sure that this would be a saving in his housekeeping, and also make his table more various. But he did not thank his aunt; he was just as well aware that it was a great joy to her to intermeddle in his matters, as she was that she might avail herself of the privilege, and yet count on his belief that all her intermeddling was for the best.

But to return to Sir Samuel and his important letter. The mails had now gone by, and there was no answer. He wrote again, and in case the first should have miscarried, he entered on all the particulars once more in a second letter.

Then it occurred to him that Mrs. Snaith might, in all good faith, have sent the first letter to Heidelberg, not being aware of his son's change of address. He wrote, and after complying with certain forms, got it back from the *poste restante*. He hardly knew whether to be most annoyed or relieved—so much time lost. But, then, his son had not received a letter from him that he had neglected to answer.

It was now Christmas; he knew that he must wait till March, and felt that he must not make himself ridiculous meanwhile by having the two little girls to his house, or by in any other way seeming to acknowledge them before the time.

But he accepted and returned nods and smiles, even at the church doors; sometimes the parties exchanged kisses in less public places. The children liked to see his white head. Once Amabel climbed upon the seat of the pew at church, when the sermon was long, and looked over the high back, as if to ascertain whether he was in his place. Miss Thimbleby, who was in charge of her and the other two children, quietly took her down, but the entire congregation saw the pretty smile with which she had greeted the old man, and his involuntary answer to it.

Felix wrote constantly to his brother, and gave him all manner of good counsel, which Amias was assisted to follow by his very straitened circumstances. He said as little as he possibly could in answer concerning this want of money, but the discipline of life was very strict upon him that winter and

"And set everybody, excepting the rector, to gather fruit."

of those choice spirits, his companions, without the faintest thought of influencing their habits in regard to strong drink, but simply to delight them by reproducing the ridiculous action and uncultivated language of certain zealots whom he now and then went to hear. He was a water-drinker, but escaped ridicule, because it was felt that this was not from high principle, but from indignation against his uncle for repudiating him. In the meanwhile it came in his way, for no better reason than has been given, to accumulate a vast amount of information concerning the misery and crime arising from drunkenness, the almost incredible sums paid by the poor for the drinks that are their ruin, and the constant temptations set before them on all sides. These facts, when he had time to think them over, sometimes impressed him a good deal.

Early in April a letter from Felix let him know that old Sam was in great affliction; the news had just reached him that his son John had died of fever in Ceylon, and he could not hold up his head at all.

"Poor old boy!" thought the inconsequent youth. "Well, after all, malt liquor (if only it could be got good and pure) is very wholesome; it's the public-houses that want doing away with." So he schooled his mind for a little while into less intemperate thoughts upon temperance.

John de Berenger, in fact, never read his father's important letter. The news of his death was communicated by a friend, a young

spring. He was poorer than any of the young fellows with whom he was associated. During the first week of his sojourn his story came out, and he passed for a kind of hero among them; though almost all thought him a fool for his pains, and would have thought him a prig too, but for the open and boyish sincerity with which he made his love of temperance depend on his anger against his old uncle. Many and many a temperance lecture was rehearsed in the presence

man who was staying with him when his short illness came on, and who wrote of him very kindly, assuring his father that everything had been done for his comfort. Also, the letter was returned. The stranger apologized for having opened and read it, as a means of discovering to whom he should send the sad news. In consequence of the questions asked in it, he had collected every scrap of writing and every letter that he could find among John de Berenger's effects, and now forwarded them. He had not read them, but thought it right to tell Sir Samuel that, though the sick man had talked freely of his past life during the earlier stages of his illness, he had uttered no word that seemed to bear at all on such a matter as his father's letter unfolded.

Sir Samuel mourned for his son, and said to himself, " In a very short time I shall know all. The news of poor John's death will fall on that woman like a thunderbolt. Has she received it yet? Evidently not. I am left to tell it to whomsoever it may concern."

He searched the few letters that had been sent through and through; most of them contained pressing requests for payment of certain debts. There was not one that could possibly have come from Mrs. Snaith, or that seemed to concern the two little girls in any way whatever.

" But I have the whip-hand of her now," thought Sir Samuel. " She will see his death in the paper, even if the whole village is not eager to tell it to her beforehand. As he has left absolutely nothing behind him, no more supplies can reach her. She will be glad enough soon to come to me and tell the whole truth. I shall not make the first move."

Mrs. Snaith knew that ample time had passed since the sending of her letter for an answer to reach Sir Samuel from any part of the world. He had not told her that he had received one—in fact, he had not spoken to her since she had taken the letter from his hand. She had often met him in the road, but had never accosted him. If he was quite satisfied now that he had made a ridiculous mistake, there was no need to make him own it, and thus, perhaps, bring on herself the dreaded question, " These children, not being my son's, why are they here? Whose are they?"

She always took refuge in silence, and tried to efface herself as much as possible from the thoughts of others. Sometimes she thought she would steal away from her cottage, and

again take the children among strangers: but then careful reflection seemed to assure her that where she now was people had got used to her, and had ceased to wonder at her. There had seemed to be a mystery, but all the villagers considered that they had solved it, and all the same way; there was no difference of opinion. What talk there still was chiefly concerned what old Sam would do, and why the family, who doubtless knew all, were so silent about it. Besides, the children were well, happy, receiving a very good education, and were already too familiar with these De Berengers ever to forget them. Moreover, if she fled, it would not only rouse curiosity to the utmost, but Miss de Berenger would be almost certain to start in pursuit, and in all probability would eventually find her.

The foolish have us far more in their power than the wise. If it had not been for Sarah de Berenger, Mrs. Snaith felt that she could have confided the whole truth to Felix, got him to keep it absolutely secret, and also help her to get away; but nothing could possibly be confided to Sarah, or it would come out; and if it was not confided, she would search for the children, meanwhile raising such a commotion that the matter was sure to get into the newspapers as a strange and romantic story. Sarah would, perhaps, be silly enough to publish descriptions of the children, with their Christian names; these alone would be sufficient to rouse the suspicions of any person whatever among her old friends. Finally, some hint of it would reach the Dills, and, through them, the dreaded convict husband.

Sarah was away from her home when the news of John's death reached her. She came back and flew to Mrs. Snaith, asking where the darlings were.

" At the vicarage, ma'am, doing their lessons."

" And their mourning—is that ordered ? Sir Samuel will, of course, expect to see them in proper mourning."

It was no use pretending to misunderstand, but Mrs. Snaith felt confident of her ground, and was determined to hold it. " No, ma'am," she answered. " You have no call to trouble yourself any further about that mistake. I take leave to tell you that Sir Samuel expects nothing of the kind."

That was on Tuesday. Miss de Berenger considered that there would be plenty of time to get mourning ready for Sunday, and she wrote to Sir Samuel about it.

" The woman wants money already," he

thought; "let her come and ask for it." And he wrote to his niece more curtly than kindly, desiring her not to interfere.

Mrs. Snaith did not apply for money, and at the end of the week Sir Samuel went to London, feeling that this was only a question of time.

In the meanwhile, knowing that whatever she did would make fresh talk, Mrs. Snaith dressed the children on Sunday in clean white frocks and white hats as usual, and sent them up to the vicarage, but had not courage to attend the morning service herself.

When the children came home to dinner, each had a black sash on. Cousin Sarah had sent them, they said, in answer to her questions, and Miss Thimbleby had put them on.

Mrs. Snaith shed a few quiet tears of vexation then. Sarah's folly had mastered her again.

To be in London a full year before he could hope for a holiday. This was the lot of Amias, and what a long, slow, dark, and dirty year it seemed.

Occasionally, towards the end of it, he began to dream of the old church-tower, and the rooks floating high above it in the clear elastic air, and to dream of scarlet strawberries ripening on their beds, and meadows full of buttercups, and hay being cut in the clear heat of noon, and of other common country sights and sounds which had never impressed him at all while he lived among them. Also of Felix and of that little monkey Dick. Like those of many another boy, his affections had slumbered a good deal since his childhood. They were waking. He found that he was rather attached to his elder brother; and when Dick sent him letters of wholly intolerable badness, as regarded both the writing and the orthography, he read them over with a certain keenness of pleasure, recalled the beautiful little brown face, imagined that he had always been very fond of Dick, and wondered whether the little fellow was grown.

April, May, and June went by. Sir Samuel, still in London, received no application from Mrs. Snaith; "but," he argued, "she may have been paid a quarter's allowance for the children just before my poor son's death."

. He wrote to Felix, requesting him not to lend her any money.

"She may think," he considered, "that poor John has left money in the hands of his agent, and that through him she shall receive it. She cannot know as I do that he left nothing whatever behind him but his debts, and that I have his papers in my hands, which prove it fully. I wish I knew my dear boy's motive, though."

So he deluded himself. The human mind is always inexorable in demanding a motive for all human actions. It is only himself that each man permits to act without one, and avails himself of the privilege with astonishing frequency; sometimes letting a momentary caprice push itself in and snatch a reasonable motive out of his hand; sometimes, from mere indolence or inattention, failing to make out what he means to do till the thing does itself, and he, still hesitating, looks on and lets it alone.

Sir Samuel kept hesitating, and failing to make out what he wanted in this particular instance. The children were receiving an excellent education, were taken very great care of by their nurse, and—he was not asked for a shilling. He did not distinctly put this and that together, but waited on occasion and let things drift. When he thought of future expense, he hardly knew what he believed concerning these little girls; when he thought of his dear dead son, he did know. But his asking questions would not make them any more his grandchildren, if such they were, while it would, as he thought, bring him their bills to pay. No, it would be dangerous to investigate. He should *now* not encourage that woman to talk. He elected to leave things alone, and he had to take the consequences.

Thus the days and weeks went by, till that happy time arrived when Amias was to go home for his destined holiday.

A slow third-class train was alone within his means, and the nearest station being seven miles from his brother's house, he was not to be met, but to send his box on by a carrier, and walk over himself.

It was about eight o'clock in the evening of a very hot day when he stepped forth for his walk, first across a good many fields, then over the end of a great common, next through Sir Samuel de Berenger's wood, and finally along the winding country lane that went past his brother's gate.

He was still half a mile from it. The slow dusk had begun to gather; large flowers of the bindweed, trailing over the low wayside hedge, were mere specks of milky whiteness; he could but just distinguish between them and the dog-roses, could hardly detect the honeysuckle but for its fragrance.

" Delightful ! " he thought, as he strode

on. "The smell of things in this lane is worth all the sights in London put together. Whew! what's that?"

He stopped. No cottage within a hundred yards, and yet a pungent, powerful whiff of something worse than London fog or smoke came past him, and lost itself among the honeysuckle: a smell of burning. He wondered—strode on—admitted to himself, almost with fear, that it was odd no one had come even thus far to meet him. Then, all on a sudden, behold a great gap! Some slight thing fell with hardly a sound, and up mounted a shower of sparks. He ran on, shouting out in the dusk—

"Why—why, there's something wrong! What's up? What can be the matter? Mrs. Snaith's cottage is gone!"

Mrs. Snaith's cottage was gone indeed—its place was vacant; it was burnt to the ground. A few singed hollyhocks leaned forlornly forward to the road, two elms, with all their leaves shrivelled up, held out bare and ghastly arms, a puff of smoke came now and then from a dark heap of ashes, and a few sparks would mount when fanned by evening air.

Amias rushed on, dashed through a scattered group of people who seemed to be watching the rectory gates, and, encountering his aunt in the hall, demanded vehemently to be assured that Felix was all right.

"Yes, yes," quoth Sarah, "he's in his room, changing his singed clothes. You needn't bang at his door like a burglar," she panted, for she had pursued him up-stairs.

"Mrs. Snaith's cottage is gone!"

"I knew he would be in the scrimmage," cried Amias, as Felix, opening his door a little way, let his brother in. "And where's Dick?" shouted Amias through the keyhole, having satisfied himself at once that his brother was none the worse. He opened the door about an inch to receive his aunt's answer.

"He never was near the fire," quoth Miss de Berenger. "As soon as I heard of it I ran into the garden, and there I found him enjoying the prowl of innocence, his cat and his owl after him. He's safe in bed now, very sulky to think what fun there has been and he not in it."

"Anybody hurt?" asked Amias, as he

was proceeding down a passage to look at Dick.

"Yes; Mrs. Snaith a little, foolish woman. And old Nanny Fothergill was frightened almost into a fit, seeing the flames through her window."

"Oh, she's alive yet?"

"Yes," quoth Miss de Berenger. "She's not at all an irreligious woman, though she *has* lived to be ninety-four. I don't know how she reconciles that with 'the days of our life,' you know, 'are three-score years and ten.' At the same time," she continued, falling into thought, "I am quite clear that it would not be right of her to hasten matters."

AMÉLIE-LES-BAINS.

A New Wintering-Place.

EVEN in these days of wandering, there is still one sheltered nook of Southern France that is not so well known as it deserves to be for a winter station—a nook so guarded from all wintry weather, that on last New Year's Day, when many other "health resorts" were visited with unusual mist and frost, and even snow, the invalids at this favoured spot spent several hours out of doors, with open sunshades, listening to the singing of the birds, and watching the lambs playing in the meadows by the river-side. The sky was cloudless; the air fragrant with the odour of lavender; our hearts joined in the *Jubilate* of the robins; for thoughts of pain we found no time; our senses drank in the view, the warmth, the perfume, and the joyous sounds; and the mere consciousness of living was a pleasure. Ah, yes! on such a day, with carnal sense so feasted, it felt easy to understand being "joyful," serving "with gladness," and coming "before His presence with a song!" I think the widest gate to memory is that of smell; and the scent of lavender will always recall to me that day, those rugged, parched mountains, and the little white town of Amélie-les-Bains.

Amélie-les-Bains is situated in the Department of the Pyrénées Orientales, about eighteen miles from the Mediterranean in a direct line, and the same distance from the town of Perpignan, the nearest railway station. It lies in a narrow valley at the southern foot of Canigou, the third highest of the Pyrenees. Quite surrounded by lofty mountains, it is sheltered from cold winds; and being elevated on a rocky base at the height of about seven hundred feet above the sea, the air is pure and bracing, and yet only moderately exciting. The "mistral" wind is unknown; rain and fogs are rare. The eminent French physician who recommended me to go to Amélie, considers it much to be preferred to Nice or Mentone for rheumatic and gouty patients, on account of its situation at some distance from the sea, as well as its more equable temperature; also the great advantage of its hot sulphur springs—similar to those of Aix-les-Bains—and which, owing to the mildness of the climate, can with safety be used for drinking and bathing all through the winter. For full information about Amélie and its waters, medical men can read the little work written by its talented physician, Doctor Bouyer.[*]

The mineral baths are at the two principal hotels, Thermes Romains and Pujade, and many of the rooms in these houses are heated by pipes of the naturally hot water. Owing to this, and to the completely sheltered situation close under the mountain cliffs, the temperature is equal in every room, and, except for the cheerfulness, it does not in the least matter whether you have a southern aspect or not. The hotel people of Amélie, and, indeed, everywhere in the Pyrénées Orientales, as far as my experience goes, are very pleasant to deal with, just and obliging. Living in hotels and apartments is reasonable, and everything fairly good for such an out-of-the-way region; but, of course, at present there are some drawbacks for English people, though they are only things that will right themselves in time. For instance, at Amélie there is no Protestant service of any kind—no English chaplain, no French pastor to visit the sick and the dying. Then there is no English doctor, nor any French physician who can speak English. Some knowledge of French is absolutely needful for the visitor, as not even in the hotels can any one of the people understand a word of English.

At the lower end of Amélie there are several villas and apartments for letting in charming, sunny, and sheltered situations. It is a pity that some enterprising person does not build a really first-class hotel at that end, suited to persons who merely require a mild climate and not the thermal waters. Close to that part of the town lies the 'favourite promenade, " La Petite Provence "—a road completely sheltered from every wind, and yet in full sunshine all day. Along this road are many delightful sites; and also at the village of Palalda,' which is perched on the mountain-side about a mile and a half from Amélie. Palalda is a dirty Catalan village, with scarcely a decent house. A carriage road leads to it from Amélie, but stops at the entrance. The houses are huddled close together; the lanes merely wide enough for mule traffic, and some of them simply flights of rude steps. Still I expect a bright future for Palalda, with its excellent springs of pure

* " Etude Médicale sur la Station Hivernale d'Amélie-les-Bains." : Par le Docteur Achille Bouyer. Paris. Librairie Germer-Baillière, 17, Rue de l'Ecole de Médicine.

water, its dry rock sites (at the northern end), and the glorious view—not to say anything of its charming aspect—full south, with a crescent-shaped mountain behind, sheltering it from east, north, and west.

The parish priest assured me that every encouragement would be given to any one with money who would build a hotel there. The neighbourhood abounds in limestone, marble, and wood of various kinds (pine, oak, &c.) for building purposes; and supplies of all sorts can easily be got from Perpignan. It is expected that before long there will be a railway made to Amélie, as there is a very important military hospital there (the largest in France, I believe), with beds for about five hundred men.

first impressions of Amélie-les-Bains were not favourable. I had come from Hyères— lovely, beaming Hyères!— where, although it was the beginning of November, everything but the fruit-trees seemed almost summer-like: the vines still green, the flowers

Hôtel Pujade.

blooming under the waving palms; and then the outlook over the island-studded sea and the soft lilac mountains. Ah! after Hyères, Amélie felt to me cramped up; a doleful, dreary place to spend the short winter days.

I went out and stood on a foot-bridge,

staring in dismay at the bare vines, the yellow trees, the rugged, brown mountain-sides —so close around—and the shallow stream down below making as much clamour as it could in its wide, rocky bed. Tears of disappointment rushed to my eyes; I felt shocked and forlorn, and neither· saw nor heard that an old French gentleman had hobbled along the bridge with the help of two sticks, and stood beside me.

"Madame is admiring this charming view of those beautiful mountains, is she not?"

Admiring! Nothing was farther from my thoughts; and in rage I turned round, quite forgetting what a fool I looked, with blurred eyes and wet cheeks. "No! oh, *no!* Monsieur. It is *horrible!* It is *frightful!*"

"Ah!" in an oily voice, "Madame is suffering from home-sickness, and thinks no place beautiful but her England!"

"Indeed you are wrong, Monsieur," and I pulled a little photograph of the Hôtel des Iles d'Or at Hyères from my pocket, and held it before him. "*There!* Look at that lovely place and those palm-trees! How can I like Amélie, coming from there?"

Monsieur glanced contemptuously at the photograph (I could have pulled his sticks from under him); he shrugged his shoulders and said carelessly, "Yes, yes, yes; I know Hyères well."

"But the palm-trees, Monsieur?"

"Madame can see orange-trees here," and he pointed to a garden down by the river where, it is true, there were a couple of orange-trees, aggravatingly flourishing, and covered with fruit in spite of the gloom.

"Oh, Monsieur! just think of Hyères and the wide prospect and beautiful blue sea."

"I can think of nothing but the mistral there, and the pain that it caused to my rheumatisms. Does not Madame feel the air softer here?"

"I am sure it must be very damp. See those walls of rock shutting out the sun, and that river down there!"

"Ah, Madame will think differently after one week. This is my fourth winter at Amélie, and I have never found any other place so dry and so free from cold. To me it is the most beautiful of all places, because I have less pain here."

I felt ashamed and penitent, for now that he called my attention to it, I remarked that I had actually no pain, and my joints had been always aching for months, so that I had become used to constant suffering. I had to confess and to thank poor old "Monsieur;" and when I looked after him, as he hobbled

along the bridge, leaning so heavily on his sticks, and thought of how cheery and contented he was, and of how slight were my little aches in comparison with his, he seemed to be glorified to my eyes into an angel who had been sent to reprove me and to teach me the wickedness of my own heart. After that hour I saw Amélie-les-Bains in a different light—the "blue spectacles" were cast away, and I set off to explore the place calmly and in good-humour.

A nice, clean little village it proved to be; fresh and white and pure, in spite of its many springs of hot sulphur water. Here flows one warm streamlet (a cold one also) from under the very foundations of the church, and women, with funny little, thick, white caps without borders, are fetching the water in curious earthen and copper vessels. There are other fountains too in the tiny market-place, and they are all double—jets of hot sulphur and of cold pure water flowing side by side from the same fountain. Then the girls and children are blooming advertisements of the place, so healthy and plump; so very pretty too as many of them are, and the close caps, that all wear, so becoming. The men also look extremely picturesque with their red sashes and caps; and the old people — how active they appear to be, climbing up the steep steps to their homes on the cliff-side, with heavy burdens on their heads! Surely *they* cannot suffer from rheumatism! And so I go on and on, and suddenly it strikes me that I have been walking just twice as much as ever I had been able to do at Hyères!

Three days after I walked fully six miles, and before the end of the week I would have been very sorry to go back to Hyères, for during the weeks I had spent there I had been scarcely able to walk, and at night could not sleep from pain. Now I could scramble easily up the mountain paths, and enjoyed unbroken rest at night.

The artist and botanist may find continual enjoyment at Amélie; and for those who like mountain climbing there are endless beautiful walks and excursions, many lovely drives too; and even the invalid that is unable for more exertion than just going out to sit in the sunshine, can walk from the Hôtel Thermes Romains direct—from the first and second floors by a passage and bridge—to one of the upper terraces of its garden, which lies on the hill-side below the fort.

To me the winter passed pleasantly by, in the daily enjoyment of out-of-door exercise.

In November and December there were altogether but two days that we could not go out. One morning before Christmas, snow lay on the ground—a rare thing, happening only once in three or four years—but it was a mere sprinkling and soon thawed away, and after that the " vent d'Espagne," the south wind, set in, and we basked in warmth and sunshine till the end of January. By that time I could no longer resist undertaking a step that I had projected from the first week after my arrival, namely, to lodge at Palalda.

When I spoke of it to my English friends at the Thermes Romains, they groaned, and implored me at least to give up the idea until the days should be getting longer. I should "find the evening so lonely," &c., &c. As for the French people, they thought me quite insane to think of such a thing. " No lady, not even a native, had ever been known to stay at Palalda, and how then could an Englishwoman go there? Why, the peasants of the village could not speak French, only Catalan! Supposing Mademoiselle were to get ill there—what would she do? And even if well, how could she get her meals cooked? Could she eat garlic, and soup made with oil?" And so on, and so on. Even the coarseness of the sheets I should get on my bed was spoken of to deter me; but I held to my own opinion, and would not be discouraged. Every day that I walked over to Palalda I felt more and more charmed with the air. It seemed always warm there, always bracing and dry, and there was a great deal more sunshine than at Amélie, as well as a more beautiful open prospect; more subjects for sketching, too, within easy reach, and all the charms of a real country life. I had been for seven months living at hotels, and the long table d'hôte meals had become a weariness to me. I lost my appetite, and grieved over the wasted time spent at table. Even loneliness, I thought, would be a pleasant change, or, at least, the society of unsophisticated simple peasants; and I heard at Amélie that the people of Palalda were so sober, honest, and quiet—nothing at all to object to except that they only spoke Catalan and were not clean. I hovered about Palalda day after day with my sketch-book, just like a moth round a candle. At last, one afternoon, in I plunged, into the middle of the flame. "Where did Monsieur le Curé live?" I soon found some one who could understand me, and a little girl led me up a flight of rude steps to a queer little door, opening into a kind of vaulted place, which proved

to be at the top of the priest's house, for a nice, kind-eyed woman, in peasant's dress, conducted me down a winding stair and into a tiny parlour, where she introduced me to her brother, the Curé. I apologised, and asked him if he knew of respectable people with a clean house, where I could lodge, and he answered promptly that there was just one house with an apartment for letting, very clean, and the people excellent. Mademoiselle, the sister, most kindly offered to go and make the bargain for me, and, suffice it to say, I went back to Amélie possessing actually three rooms at Palalda !

What a clamour my friends at Amélie made when they heard I was going to Palalda ! They told me all sorts of brigand stories, and insisted that Spanish robbers with blackened faces had attacked a farmhouse close by only a few nights before. It turned out that the plundered house was a cottage high up on the side of the opposite mountain, close to the frontier of Spain ; and, of course, in a village, and not far from the high-road, I had nothing to fear. Still, these stories made me rather unhappy when leaving the hotel, so I arranged to go back there at the end of a week if not quite comfortable. But instead of only one week I stayed six weeks at Palalda, and even then it was with a sharp pang that I tore myself away. The people are charming, and, except the old women and the little children, they can almost all speak French. Where I lodged, the street was clean and the air thoroughly pure—perfection, in fact—and in a few days I got the appetite of a beast of prey, and thoroughly enjoyed the simple English dishes cooked by my own hands.

My rooms were on the second floor of the house of a rich peasant proprietor—at least, they were second floor in front; but the house clings to the hill-side, and an olive branch tapped against my kitchen window. Of course, in a less favoured climate this would be unhealthy, but the air felt fresh and dry all over the house, as it faces the south.

A flight of tiled stairs led up to the dingy little kitchen—like that of a peasant's *chaumière*—through which I had to pass into the small room that served me for meals, a mere passage to the bedroom beyond, where I generally received my friends ; for there I had an old arm-chair and writing-table by the window, which commands a view that makes up for everything else, even the unsightly wooden floors and scant furniture.

Next door lived a maker of espadrillos—the sandalled and embroidered white cotton

PALALDA.

slippers, with hemp soles, worn by the peasants, men as well as women—the only shoes indeed they wear, a proof of the dryness of the climate. I arranged with the espadrillo-maker's daughter, Angélique, to attend me, just for a few hours, morning and evening. She fetched water from the spring, and did all the scrubbing, and sweeping, and "cleaning up," but, of course, I had to undertake the chief part of the cooking myself; this, however, was an amusement in the evening. The village postman brought me everything that I needed from Amélie. I had only to write a note to Madame Abdon Mary, grocer, and a most enterprising woman, and she bought the meat, bread, or whatever I required, and sent all to me neatly packed in a basket. Vegetables of all kinds could be got at Palalda; amongst them, by-the-bye, wild asparagus, which grows on the mountains, and is delicious in an omelette. My landlord, Monsieur D——, supplied me with excellent wood. He and his wife are delightful people, so kind and obliging. But I could prose on about them and about Palalda

for a month! How pig-killing time came just after my arrival, and horrible cries resounded; and how everybody was helping everybody to make sausages and salt the meat, and many little acts of kindliness were shown. And then all the carnival mummeries, with the evening dance in the little "Place," where the chief musician "modulated in the Doric style" on a pipe, and at the same time beat a tiny drum fastened to his shoulder; and the boys and girls wound round the "pole of liberty" in the graceful intricacies of the Catalan dance, with a mixture of vivacity and of dignity entirely Spanish; the parents and old people sitting on chairs close by the walls. No loud laughter, no noise; just as perfect propriety and politeness as there could be in a Paris drawing-room! Yonder see, a man with the air of a stage prince, dressed in a matador's jacket of scarlet and gold, with sleeves slashed with white satin, and, holding his hand in the dance, comes the belle of belles (for almost all the girls are pretty). And here comes a lad in his simple blouse leading my hand-maid, Angélique, who smiles and bows to me, and looks gorgeous, arrayed in a dress of white calico trimmed with red, glazed cotton stuff, and on her head a Catalan cap, embroidered elaborately by her own plump little hands. She came to me that evening beforehand to show me her gown, as radiant and happy as if it were of satin, instead of being made cleverly out of an old petticoat;

and she implored me to go see the dance, because "Mademoiselle might never have an opportunity of seeing so beautiful a sight again."

Then there was the double wedding that came off before Lent; the brides wearing wreaths of orange-flowers round the crowns of their caps; and devout women standing outside the church door making money for the priest and the "Sainte Vierge," by the sale of hideous favours of artificial flowers to the guests, and by stopping the bridal pairs with a crimson silk sash with gold fringed ends, which they held across the steps until the bridegrooms put silver on the offering-plate, when the sash was raised for them and their brides to pass under. And the doors of this old church! How curious they are, with the Saracen horse-shoes nailed on in every available space between the scroll-work of the hinges. But I must stop.

Only one word more. On the mountains

Peasants of the district.

round Amélie, and especially on that above Palalda, grows every kitchen-garden herb I know of: thyme and rosemary, sage and basil, marjoram, balm, &c., &c.; and as for lavender, acres of it amongst the thistles and thorns, withering and lavishing its sweetness everywhere. The Amélie doctors consider that this aromatic air contributes largely to the cure of their consumptive patients, in conjunction with the vapour of the sulphur water which they are advised to inhale. But I feel bound to mention that I saw no persons with delicate lungs look as if they were recovering at Amélie, except those suffering from bronchitis; and certainly one English lady, who the winter before, at Cannes, had never been well enough to dine at the table d'hôte, passed four months at Amélie in excellent health, and left greatly improved in strength, which improvement she attributed, not only to the climate, but to inhaling the steam of the mineral water. The consumptive

patients seemed to get worse very rapidly. However, probably they had come to Amélie when they were past cure; and I was told the air was only of use before absolute disease set in.

After the middle of April the climate of Amélie becomes unhealthy. The south wind prevails, and consequently the air is hot and relaxing. We were then recommended by the doctor to go to Prades, a small town in a lovely valley at the north side of Canigou. A mule-path leads over a shoulder of the mountain to Prades; but of course the only way for a delicate person to reach it is by the railway from Perpignan. Prades is a charming little place, there are so many beautiful excursions to be made from it, and Canigou towers up, with its snowy crest, so near. But no one who is not strong should venture too early in the year to Prades, for it is exposed to the mistral, and the spring comes nearly a month later than at Amélie.

One great attraction at Prades is the "Hotel January." Old Mademoiselle Julie January is the perfection of a hostess. I do think her chief pleasure in life is to set before her guests every dainty that she can possibly procure, and the greatest *gourmet*

Shepherd of the district.

could not find a fault with any of her dishes. Strangest of all is the excellent quality of the beef. At Amélie it is almost always tough; at Prades it melts like a bonbon in your mouth. But words fail to describe Mademoiselle Julie and her table d'hôte lunches and dinners. The dear old thing helps to wait on her guests herself. She toddles round the table, smacking her lips, presses you to eat in the most insinuating tones, and asks you, with such an air of delight, "N'est-ce pas qu'il est délicieux?" And you eagerly say "yes," for perhaps it is a dish of chicken's livers, baked with sweet herbs, or a superb *mayonnaise*, or some unknown delicacy tasting like ambrosia. The terms for these feasts and a comfortable bedroom are as reasonable as at the hotels of Amélie. If only Mademoiselle Julie and her hotel could be transported over Canigou, and planted at Palalda, that spot would be a little paradise!

L. F. B.

JOSEPH AND HIS LIFE AND DEATH.

WE left Joseph master of all the land of Egypt, the favourite of Pharaoh, married into the family of the greatest subject in Egypt, the genius whom all recognised, the far-seeing statesman who was to save the country. A mighty change from the prison and from slavery! We shall see now how his life went on, and how his character grew, and how he died; and I collect what I have to say around the names he gave to his sons, Manasseh and Ephraim.

In those days names had meaning. Mother and father, in the hour when the child was born, when their hearts were full of thoughts of the past or of the future—when they were moved by such deep feeling as Joseph must have had when, remembering all his sorrow and toil, and contrasting them with his happiness, he looked on the face of his first-born—threw into the name they gave their child the concentrated essence of their thoughts. And Joseph, standing by his wife's bedside, and feeling the blessing of home, and looking backward and forward as he heard his son's cry, said, "I will call him 'forgetting,' for God hath made me forget all my toil and my father's house."

1. "All my toil :"—Joseph looked back on all his sorrow in Egypt and it seemed to him a dream in this reality of joy. But of course it was not absolute forgetfulness—that was impossible—but the forgetfulness which comes of deep delight after great pain. His life had been like a thirsty strand long exiled from ocean, its companion, baked by frost and sun, and weary of its long desire. At last, one day, the barrier that has held the sea back is overthrown, and the fresh and leaping waves rush in, rejoicing and rejoiced. Their life, their joy, their dew penetrates every thirsty atom of the sand, and makes them sing with happiness. And the weary strand forgets in the flow and rapture of waters all the dead days of pain. It lives in the present joy, but half its joy has been made by the previous pain. The toil is not forgotten, only the bitterness of the toil is drowned in sweet content.

It is often in this way with men, and it was so with Joseph. All his toil was loosed from its bitterness, but the toils themselves were not forgotten. It is better not to forget the toils, for did we forget, there would be no many-sided character, and no gratitude. It is the labours of the soul against varied toils and trials that weave the many-folded web of a strong character. Each labour adds a colour, each resistance a new symbol, to the pattern ; each conquest strengthens the whole web, till to study a much-tried character is like studying a great book. When we have conquered and when joy comes, we forget the pain, but we remember the struggle, and we know that the victory is sweet. It adds its inward sweetness to the outward joy, and we are content with God. " God," we say, "has made us forget our toil."

It is the memories of the past in contrast with the present that give birth to thankfulness such as Joseph had. We look back on the tumbling ocean from the quiet haven and thank God. We see His hand in many an escape, and we are happy in the thought that He has never left our side. We see Him even in the fiercest storm we have borne, and we are full of trust in Him for the future ; because we know now that through the tempests He was training us for strength and fitting us for rest. The pain has changed into pleasure, for the sense of victory is itself delight; the pain has passed into strength, and the sense of moral force is one of our deepest joys. He who climbs an Alp upon a burning day knows what I mean, and that it is the same with human life if we have climbed its mountain steadily. We conquer its troubles at last, reach its summit, and sit down to rest. Joy fills our heart as we look down on the way we have come, and we think with pleasure of the difficult places and the nooks where we rested. A deeper joy fills our heart as the mist steals over the lower landscape, and in the calm of evening we wait for death. The night comes, the stars steal out, we hear the whisper of God, and looking up we thank Him for life and death. Then He comes and touches us, and we die with His words in our ears, "Well done, good and faithful servant." And entering into the joy of our Lord, at home with Him, all our toils are at last forgotten.

2. "My father's house :"—It was not only his toils that Joseph had forgotten, it was also his father's house. They are strange words. Do they mean that he had forgotten his father's love, the tenderness of that protected infancy, and all the thoughts that touch on home? No! these things were not lost. They survived deep below in his heart. What pathos, what depth of long remembrance in the words spoken long after this time to his brothers !—" Is your father well,

the old man of whom ye spake? Is he yet alive?" Yet, some sense of oblivion must now have stolen over him, for he was young, and his new home, and new ties, and new love rushed upon him, and in the new, the old home life faded towards dreamland. And it is natural and wise that this should be. There is a necessity for passionate feeling in order to work a new life well, and if passionate feeling belongs also to the old life, it troubles the movement of the new. It is better that for a time at least the old be somewhat forgotten, laid into the background of life, put by, like a book which we have loved and read, upon its shelf, and suffered to rest there undisturbed.

There are many who spoil new lives from over-sentimental clinging to the old, who try to make two passions coalesce, who do not say when they are first married, "God has made me forget my father's house," or, when they are married a second time, "God has made me forget my past." It will not do. If they take up new lives they are bound to do so with sufficient joy to lay the past aside, not as neglecting or despising it, not as not being grateful and loving towards it, but as losing its passion in a deeper passion. Else it is wise to form no new ties at all, for we form them only to spoil them, and to spoil the old as well.

It is better to accept frankly the facts of life, and to put by the bygone life. It may sound a little hard to say so, but in truth it is not. All the pure beauty and quiet tenderness and old delight we had in our home and in our vanished life remain untouched, and reappear later on in life to increase the beauty of remembrance. Fondness gathers afterwards round them, and they do not then interfere with the new life which we have now secured. But it is folly to regret them, folly to dwell on them and compare them with the new, folly to let any passionate feeling brood upon them. And it is unjust to the new, and its injustice will work bitter sorrow. No; let life be natural and true. Say, "God hath made me forget."

But there were reasons other than these that Joseph had for thanking God he could forget his father's house. We trace in the phrase that he had suffered. Even his beautiful nature had felt the sting of the bitter memories of his father's house. It was no wonder. A brother, he had been betrayed by brothers; not one voice was raised to save the lonely boy from the hideous fate of a freeman sold to slavery. Many would have been soured for life, would never have trusted man again. For there are some things which corrupt life and fill the heart brimful with gall. The very kindliest and most merciful nature cannot endure some treacheries, and become hard and unforgiving. Love is changed to hatred, tenderness to contempt, the very kindnesses and joys of many years become hateful memories. The injured friend thinks that the untruth and selfishness of the injurer has been, unknown to him, an element of the past friendship. The whole of life is then made a burning misery.

Joseph was too young to consider this so deeply; its worst bitterness belongs to middle age. Moreover, along with the reactiveness of youth he had a beautiful soul which let evil slide away from it. In Potiphar's house, in the prison, the same kindly, trustful spirit appears, as full of sympathy as if it had never been deceived. Falsely accused by his master's wife, forgotten by the chief butler, these things were added to his brothers' treachery—and yet Joseph's heart came out gold, unrevengeful, believing in man, making allowance for the weakness of men, not imputing their trespasses to them. Yet, for all that, he must have felt in some sort the sting of so much treachery. He must have been miserable at some times, asking himself bitterly, "Is home affection an error; is love folly, and friendship feigning?"

We are often cured, when we have so suffered, as Joseph was cured, by true love and joy. The heart, if it have vigour and truth in it, cannot long live in a poisonous atmosphere. It seeks for faithfulness that it may forget betrayal, for love that its hatred may be healed, for honest and natural ties that it may forget, as Joseph forgot, the unnatural injury. There is nothing else but love to cure it, and so wonderfully made is the human heart, and so powerful is this medicine, that I have seen a man's unexpected discovery of suddenly found faithful love heal in an hour the bitterness and misanthropy of years. "God has made me forget," he cried, "my misery."

It was in this way the heart of the great Hebrew was healed. He found true love: a wife clung to him, children blest him, the king loved him, and the people. All men were glad when they saw him. It fell like balm upon the wounded heart, and he was made ready to forgive his injuries. "God has made me forget my father's house."

In so much forgetting, in all this novel joy, there was one whom Joseph did not forget. He remembered, nay, he never forgot God. As he looked on his first-born, one might say he would have thought first of Pharaoh or of

Egypt. Was it not to them that all his happy pride was due? *Not* in his eyes. His praise is rendered to God. The favour of the king, wealth, his home, his child and fame were laid at the footstool of God's love. In the midst of pomp and royal favour his soul was as humble as a child.

It is too much the fashion to apply the warnings of the Scriptures to rich men indiscriminately, as if they were of necessity proud and selfish, and to think of the poor as always humble and self-devoted. It is a matter of character, not of circumstance alone. If poverty is a burden that often subdues the heart and leads it to seek God for comfort, wealth is often no less a burden that drives a conscientious man to God in deep humility. Many a poor man is as proud as Lucifer and with less cause; many a rich man carries beneath a costly life a gentle and lowly spirit. Many a poor man, who descants on the hardness of the rich to the poor, is cruel and selfish in his own household, and wealth would make him a deeper curse than he is. Many a rich man, flattered by the world, with every temptation to thoughtlessness, suffers the flattery as inevitable—how can he help the baseness of the base—we cannot cure a worm of slime—but spends his days in eager effort to do right with his wealth, because he holds it in trust for God and in trust for man.

Thus it was with this enriched young statesman. For the bowed knee and the court paid him, Joseph did not care. It was his faith that whatever of worth there was in the outward show of life was due to God, who was using him for a great purpose. He felt he was but the instrument of a higher power than that of Egypt. We know that from his speech to his brothers. Alone in his heart, Joseph, the prince, laid all his life in meekness and lowliness before God, and found rest to his soul. Rest! and he needed it.

Some men know well—if they have genius or talent, if they are statesmen, or poets, or philosophers, if, in one word, they have the qualities that command success in anything—how the thought of what men will say of them, how the world's blame or desire of its praise spoil the peace of life and make them chafe within till they become irritable without, a distress to themselves and others. There is no remedy for that unquiet vanity or pride, but Joseph's—the humility that feels, "I am nothing; God within me is all. To be true to the voice and thought of God, that is all I have to think of, all I need care for much." Life then becomes at rest. What the world says does not matter one whit; the

man is of the truth, and the truth has made him free from the itch of wounded self-conceit. All things are his, for he has joy in his heart, and his meekness inherits the earth. Undazzled in wealth, calm in poverty, using all his powers nobly, in the perfect peace of duty he can at last say with Christ, "My meat and drink is to do my Father's will and to finish his work."

Then, if one of those great calls to righteous and loving action comes on him in life, in which the full powers of good and evil meet in battle array, his choice of goodness will be easy, for his soul has been prepared by living close to God. When the great demand was made on Joseph, he answered finely to its call. God brought at last the traitor brothers to his feet, and Joseph had beautiful mercy on them. It is true he had been prepared to forgive them by years of happiness; ere they came, the calm pleasure of domestic life and honoured manhood had softened the memory of wrong; but still, he might have grudgingly forgiven them and made them feel the bitterness of his wrong. On the contrary, the forgiveness was frank and loving and mingled with no reproach. At first he was somewhat hard in seeming. Benjamin was not with them. Where was he? Was it possible that the jealousy of the sons of Leah of the sons of Rachel had gone beyond himself to injure Benjamin? His own wrong was forgivable; but had they done this other wrong, justice should have its way. But when he saw Benjamin at last, when he found that Judah loved him, when he heard their own words in which they remembered their sin against himself and repented of it—then, nothing is more beautiful in the Bible than the scene when Joseph, crying, "Let every man go forth from me," broke into tears, revealed himself to his brothers, and made that Divine excuse for the wrong he had suffered— "Now therefore be not grieved, nor angry with yourselves, that ye sold me into Egypt: for God did send me before you to preserve life." That was princely forgiveness, princely courtesy. He turned his wrong into a good—and the statesman's sense of his duty to the race—"sent by God to preserve life"—gives dignity to the forgiveness. Joseph was great throughout. The noble genius, conscious of itself, shines side by side with the forgivingness of his character. Nor did his forgiveness fail as time went on. His brethren feared when their father died, with the cowardice of conscious wrong, that he would then requite their evil. Little they knew that generous nature! "Am I in the place of God?" he answered, referring as usual all things to God. "Fear not; ye thought evil against me, but God meant it unto good, to save much people alive. Now therefore fear not: I will nourish you and your little ones." And he comforted them, and spoke kindly to them. That was true nobility. That was the triumph of the spirit of Christ before Christ came. And nothing is higher in this world than to remember injury only to forget it, in order that we may keep our hearts open, and free to do good to man. Had Joseph cherished revenge he could never have saved much people alive. The heart that broods over wrong cannot love men, or act for humanity.

3. Round Ephraim's name clusters the rest of what we have to say. Ephraim means fruitful. "For God," said Joseph, "hath caused me to be fruitful in the land of my affliction." Years, we see, had only deepened his sense of God as the source of all good. As in his first son God had spread sunshine over the past, so in the second he saw God illumining for him the future. "Against hope," he might have said, "here in the land of my affliction I suddenly rise to power. What may not be the fortune of these boys? In them I look forward to becoming a people."

Fruitful! fruitful! it was the one Jewish cry. That profound and impelling sense of their race that Abraham, Isaac, and Jacob had, that mastering desire of becoming a great people which seemed born with every Hebrew child, had seized on Joseph now. But how was he to realise it, he, made half Egyptian by circumstance, alone in the world, divided from his father's house?

We may be sure that the passion of the continuance of his race had wrought in his imagination for the years before he saw his brethren. Then the famine brought his brothers to Egypt, and Joseph knew them. The old times came back at their sight. He thought of the little knot of people who looked forward to being a nation, to whom the land of Canaan was given. In his mind's eye he saw his father waiting and enduring in the faith of Abraham and Isaac. The deep feeling of early love of home came back as he thought of Benjamin and his mother. It was the first reknitting of old tribal ties. He felt that he was not the Egyptian but the Hebrew. Only one thing agitated his hopes—was Benjamin alive? Had the sons of Leah rooted out the sons of Rachel? If so, he might have abjured his race. But when he heard that Benjamin was alive, he wept with joy, and felt the Hebrew longing in his heart. All his effort now played round his desire to get

his people round him. He kept Simeon, and when he saw Benjamin, and found that he was so much loved that Judah offered himself as a bond slave in his place, pride in his race was still more deeply kindled. These brothers of his loved one another; though they had hated him, they lived for their father, felt him to be their chief and master; there was a family tie between them that could not be broken, and Joseph felt he must become one of them again. The thought of sorrow that he was outside this little circle, the thought of joy that he might become one of it again, both made him weep. He could not refrain himself; the passion of reunion with his people seized his heart and broke out in his words, "I am Joseph; doth my father yet live?" "I am Joseph your brother, whom ye sold into Egypt." I am one of you; take me back again. Haste and go to my father, bring down my father hither. And when the long-divided son and father met, and Joseph fell on his father's neck and wept on his neck a good while, the tie of race was felt in every moment of the silence of that embrace. Abraham's people were all once more together. We see this feeling of race in all that Joseph said and did. He took care to isolate his people from the Egyptians. He watched over them and nourished them. Apart from them, he was one of them. In the most fruitful part of Egypt, he watched them growing. "Ephraim, Ephraim," he said to himself, as he saw them multiply, "God has made me fruitful." Nor did the feeling die in its fulfilment. He brought his two sons to his father's deathbed and Jacob adopted them as his own in solemn words, and bound them up with his race and with the promise. He fell in with his father's desire of burial, not in Egypt but with his fathers in Canaan, and the prime minister of Egypt gave seven days to a burial ceremony which must have stamped the feeling of their race on all the Hebrews who witnessed it. And when he died himself, his last words to his brethren were, "I die; and God will surely visit you, and bring you out of this land into the land which he sware to Abraham, to Isaac, and to Jacob." And Joseph took an oath of the children of Israel, saying— "God will surely visit you, and ye shall carry up my bones from hence."

Every one who cares for his nation and feels the living tie of race will sympathize with that; we English above all, for beyond our love of home, and indeed founded on it and growing from it, is our love of race. We cling together as the Jews cling. That passion which glowed in the heart of Joseph and made him feel that Egypt was not his home, though all he loved was there, that made him long for the little patch of ground where by the field of Machpelah, the sole possession of his people in Canaan, his father lay ; which made him see in that place his true home, is, and has been always, the English passion. And all our race has shared it. To this little spot of earth, shut in by the inviolate sea, from Australia, New Zealand, Canada, India, from Africa and the Far West, men turn their eyes and think of home with swelling hearts. Even the great American people, severed from us by many years of a vast national life, look back with fondness to the cradle of their race, and own the motherhood of England. " Ephraim," we may say with Joseph, " God has made us fruitful;" and with force and passion equal to his, Joseph's words are echoed in the hearts of all of English blood when they think of England— " the land of my fathers."

Lastly, in a still higher way we are filled with ideas similar to those that the Israelites possessed. That great conception given to Abraham that he was to live in order to found a people, that all his descendants were to live for the thought of their race, never ceased to influence the Jews profoundly and influences them still. Nothing in the lives of any of these patriarchs depressed them too much, because faith in this magnificent idea supported them. It ran through every act, every thought of their lives. It knit them together, so that every Israelite was a brother. It kept them pilgrims in strange lands, and isolated them from the ties which might make them forget that their true home was far away. It filled their life with hope, and hope made their intense energy and wrought at last their deliverance. With these thoughts Joseph lived and died in Egypt.

With these thoughts we should live and die in this world. Our Master has given us the same conceptions. We too have the magnificent thought that all our effort builds up a great people — the spiritual humanity, the multitude whom no man can number of God's redeemed. We know that all shall be brought home at last, and the vast nation of mankind be perfect in God — one Divine and glorious whole. We live, knowing that a destiny is being wrought out for us, and for all, by God. Our lives, built on that thought, grow great in it. Every action is made noble, every work eternal, every thought important. We can never be too much depressed, never despair, never fold our hands in sloth. We must be worthy of our lineage, worthy of our high vocation, worthy of the future, for everything we do helps our race forward to the Canaan of its perfection.

And do we not too feel the tie of race? In it we are all brothers. Beyond the tie of family, beyond the tie of nationality, rises for us the tie of mankind. Every human soul is God's child, therefore every man is our brother. We look round and feel ourselves bound with an eternal bond to all men who breathe and act, and knit to them as Joseph was knit to his people. It is the greatest human thought that is thought on earth. Only one is greater. It is that which extends the same conception to all the dead and all the unborn men and women of mankind. All who have gone before are now living in God and are at one with us; all who shall be born, will also be at one with us. There is but one humanity, and it lives and will live for ever, each part as intensely as the whole, in God. Let modern philosophies match that thought. When they do, then we may turn from Christianity to consider them, but not till then.

Nor, lastly, is this world our true home any more than Egypt was to Joseph. We dare not rest here save as pilgrims. We do not isolate ourselves from the work of the world, for it is God's work, and we are bound to do it, as Joseph did his work in Egypt, with all our might. But we look for a better country, a nobler and more beautiful home. We live in its hope and faith. A little while and it shall be ours, and death bring us out of Egypt into Canaan. When the time comes, and our eyes grow dim, it will be joyful to look backward at our work in this world and say with Joseph, " God has made me forget my toils. God has made me fruitful in the land of my affliction ;" as joyful also to look forward and to say to all men as we die, " God will surely visit you and bring you out of this land into the heavenly country he has sworn through Jesus Christ to our fathers and to you."

STOPFORD A. BROOKE.

SNAILS AND SLUGS.

BY THE REV. J. G. WOOD, M.A.

PART II.

OF the voracity of the snail it is needless to speak, as all florists or fruit-growers are only too practically acquainted with the fact. Strawberries, which necessarily lie close to the ground, are especially liable to their attacks, and even the fruit on standard trees suffers greatly. Wall-fruit is also much eaten by snails, and in neither of these cases is it easy to keep the depredators away. Sawdust scattered thickly round the strawberry-beds answers well enough so long as the weather is dry, but a shower of rain soon converts the sawdust into a pleasantly moist path, over which the snails are sure to make their way.

As to fruit-trees, whitewashing the trunks may be useful for a short time, but it must be perpetually renewed, to be of any lasting service. A highly scientific plan of securing walls and trees from slugs and snails was once promulgated. Nothing could be more promising on paper, but, unfortunately, it was anything but effective in a garden. It was called, if I recollect rightly, the "Galvanic Barrier," and was made by fastening a strip of copper along the wall or round the tree-trunk, and a band of zinc about half an inch above it. As, in order to pass this barrier, the animal must of necessity complete the circuit between the two metals, a galvanic shock would ensue, and the snail be repelled.

Undoubtedly, there is a galvanic shock, but the snail does not seem to be much affected by it. The creature passes over the copper without noticing it. As soon as its tentacles touch the zinc, it draws back for a moment, as if surprised, but does not fall to the ground as was expected. Presently, it makes another attempt, and recoils again. But, after sustaining one or two shocks, it seems to become used to them, and glides onwards without appearing to suffer any inconvenience.

Such at least has been my own experience. I have lately seen an electric manger which gives a shock to a horse that attempts the dangerous practice of crib-biting, and am told that it is wonderfully successful, the horse soon learning that to seize the edge of the manger involves a bewildering and mysterious punishment. But, snails and slugs seem to care little for a shock, if indeed their nervous system be capable of transmitting it, and so they set the Galvanic Barrier at defiance.

The jaw-system, if I may so call it, by which the snail devours its food, is a marvellous structure. That a snail should possess about eleven thousand teeth is almost incredible. Such, however, is the case, and the teeth can be seen by means of an ordinary pocket lens, although to show their formation a microscope is required.

If the mouth of a common snail be removed, and carefully opened, a large, horny, deeply edged tooth is seen. This tooth is shown in Fig. 5, and its office is that of biting

off the morsels on which it feeds. The scooped tracks of this tooth can easily be seen in any strawberry which a snail has attacked.

This tooth, however, is not sufficient for the necessary attrition of the food, and so the snail is furnished in the floor of the mouth with a wonderful apparatus called the "tooth-ribbon," scientifically known by the name of "Odontophore." A moderately magnified view of the tooth-ribbon is given at Fig. 6.

Along this organ are set successive rows of very minute and most beautifully formed teeth, the number of rows varying greatly in different individuals. A double row of these teeth, as they appear under a rather powerful pocket lens, is shown at Fig. 2. At Fig. 3 some of these teeth are shown when viewed from above through a microscope, and a profile view of five teeth is given at Fig. 4.

The best mode of distinguishing the exquisite formation of these teeth is to employ the polarizing apparatus in the microscope, as by its aid the teeth glow with every prismatic hue, while the membranous tongue in which they are set remains uncoloured.

The action of the tooth-ribbon is precisely that of the cordon or chain-saw ; the resemblance, indeed, being so close, that it is hardly possible to think that the inventor of the cordon-saw must not have taken the idea from the tooth-ribbon. By reason of their almost perpetual action, the teeth are worn away at the tip of the ribbon. But, as fast as they disappear, fresh teeth are supplied from behind, being developed in a little sac into which the base of the ribbon passes.

As to the food of the snails, it is mostly vegetable, but they are apt to be carnivorous on occasions, and will eat the dead bodies of their own kind. All the whelk tribe are essentially carnivorous, feeding mostly upon other molluscs, and by means of this wonderful tooth-rasp, boring holes through the hardest shells, and licking out the bodies of their occupants.

Here I may mention that if the reader wishes to study the anatomical structure of the snail, the creature is easily killed by chloroform. Immersion in boiling water causes instantaneous death, but, as it alters some of the tissues, I recommend the chloroform. Both snails and slugs will keep well if immersed in spirits, and their tissues will be firmer than if they had been dissected immediately after death.

In the winter time the food supply fails, and then, like many other creatures, the snail retires to winter quarters, such as a crevice in a rock, a hollow tree, or angles of old ruins. The snail prepares itself for its winter's sleep after a very curious manner.

Drawing its body just within the shell, it traces a ring of slime round the edge. This ring soon dries into a flat quoit-like circular disc about the twelfth of an inch wide. A second ring is then drawn within the first, a third within the second, and so on, until a complete plate of tough hardened slime is formed upon which the concentric rings look very much like those of a target. It is worthy of remark that several of the wood-boring bees make the floors of their cells in a similar fashion, using masticated wood-fibres instead of slime.

Having made one of these slime-plates, or "epiphragms" as they are called, the snail withdraws a little farther into its shell, and then makes a second epiphragm. A third and a fourth follow, and then the snail abandons itself to its long repose. The object of the successive epiphragms is obvious. Between each pair of epiphragms a layer of air is enclosed, and, as air being a non-conductor of heat, the three air-plates effectually shield the enclosed snail from the cold.

When warm weather arouses the snail from sleep, it softens the edges of the epiphragms with fresh slime, pushes them off, and leaves them on the object over which it happened to be crawling.

The number and density of the epiphragms depend much on the locality in which the snail hibernates. If it can find a hollow tree, or similar refuge, it is often content with a single epiphragm, and takes no other precautions. But where no such shelter is to be found, it is obliged to make one, utilising for that purpose dry earth, dead leaves, moss, and similar substances. These it agglutinates together with slime, and thus forms a dome-like chamber, so admirably concealed by its resemblance to surrounding objects that scarcely any foe can discover it.

The hedgehog is, perhaps, the worst of its enemies, for it is itself a hibernator, waking occasionally when a warmer day than usual enlivens the winter. On such days, or rather evenings, the hedgehog awakes from sleep and feels hungry after its long fast. It then sets off in search of food, and seldom fails to discover any snails that may be hibernating in its neighbourhood. Next to the hedgehog in the long list of the snail's enemies comes the thrush, and even during the hardest frosts the constantly renewed heaps of broken snail-shells that may be seen near some large stone afford evidences of the work which the thrush does in the winter.

I do not know whether it has been ever observed that hibernating snails are infested with mites, or, at all events, accompanied by them. Yet I have found in almost every hibernating snail which I have examined, several mites closely resembling the cheese-mite in form, but being rather whiter, smaller, and infinitely more active.

They traverse the body of the snail with wonderful speed, and run about between the shell and mantle with perfect ease. If the snail be irritated, and pour out the liquid secretion which it can abundantly produce in such cases, the mites are by no means incommoded, but run on the surface of the liquid as easily as on the body of the snail.

Their capture is consequently a very difficult task. They are so minute, and their bodies are so fragile, that to pick them up without destroying them seems almost impossible. Even if one of them be shaken out of the shell together with the liquid, and transferred to a glass slide, it still baffles the microscope by its incessant activity.,

At last, however, I managed to procure one, uninjured and quiescent, as a specimen. I dipped the point of a needle in chloroform and touched the mite with it. The creature became instantly motionless, and was taken up together with a small drop of the liquid which the snail poured out on feeling the touch of the chloroform.

As a rule English people would feel horrified at the idea of eating these creatures, and the same person who would eat a boiled periwinkle or whelk, or a living oyster or mussel, would turn away with disgust from a snail. Yet there is nothing but prejudice which inhibits snails as a recognised article of food. They are at all events cleaner feeders than the whelks, which delight in garbage and revel on human corpses; they and the crabs, lobsters, prawns, and shrimps, and not the fishes, being the usual consumers of drowned sailors.

In some parts of England, however, they are still eaten. At Newcastle there used to be, and may be still, a custom among the glass-blowers of holding an annual snail feast. It is said also that vast quantities of snails are exported to the United States for human consumption, but I rather doubt the statement, and think that they are intended for the food of birds and not of man.

On the Continent, however, snails are largely eaten. I have often seen the French peasants cooking their snail dinners on an iron plate, and have much wondered how our own peasantry, even if they were dying from starvation, could afford to waste so much excellent and appetising food.

The ancients knew better than to reject such food, and we find many references to it in the classic authors, both Greek and Latin. There is, for example, the well-known story of the boy who was cooking snails on an iron plate, and who, on hearing the hissing sounds produced in the cooking process, called them silly creatures for singing while their houses were burning.

Then we have references to the great Edible Snail (*Helix pomatia*), which the Romans brought over with them when they were masters of this country, nearly two thousand years ago, and the descendants of which may still be found near the sites of the old Roman settlements. In this country it does not attain any very great size, but it may be easily distinguished from the common snail by its pale, yellowish-grey colour, traversed by four rather indistinct brown bands.

The ancient Romans, however, delighted in fattening for the table several creatures which have almost been forgotten, such as dormice, which they fed in special houses, called Gliraria; and muraenæ eels (wrongly called lampreys), which they sometimes fed on unsatisfactory slaves. The Edible Snail was another of these artificially fattened creatures, and it increased to such an enormous size when fed upon meal mixed with wine that three snails were considered a sumptuous supper for two persons. The places in which this fattening process was conducted were called Cochlearia.

In this country, however, the snails are seldom eaten except for their supposed medicinal effects. Sometimes they are cooked, but are mostly pounded up with new milk into a sort of a paste. Consumptive patients and other sufferers from lung diseases are thought to derive much benefit from a snail diet. I well recollect, when a child, being greatly horrified at the preparation of this medicine. The old "yarb" woman collected snails of every kind, and when she had procured a large clothful she used to break away the shells, extract the snails, put them into a cambric handkerchief, and then pound them with a large round stone, pouring milk by degrees into the vessel.

As to killing the poor creatures before pounding them, she never would do it, one of the essential points being that the snails should be pounded alive. Fortunately for themselves, however, snails seem to have but a slight sense of pain, and even while they are being eaten by the various creatures which feed upon them, appear rather to be annoyed than to suffer pain as we understand the word.

SLUGS.

In many respects the life history of the slug much resembles that of the snail, and therefore I shall only mention a few salient points of slug life.

The popular idea of a slug is, that it is a kind of snail without a shell. This definition is partially, but only partially correct, as nearly all the slugs possess shells hidden under the mantle, and some have an external shell so conspicuous that they derive from it the generic name of testacella, or little shell.

Every one knows the slugs and their voracity, but every one does not know that they are the real authors of much mischief which is attributed to the little birds. Slugs are essentially nocturnal beings. During the day they hide themselves in any convenient crevice, often below the surface of the ground, contracting their bodies into rounded lumps that bear no resemblance to the shape of the creature as it appears when crawling. Consequently they are not seen so frequently as the snails, and their depredations are not so well known.

For the ravages which are usually ascribed to the small birds, the slugs are mostly to blame. They hide under the earth during the day-time, and come out to feed at night. I never fully appreciated this fact until I kept a family of tame blindworms. Living at the time in the heart of the City, I was obliged to visit the suburbs for convenient hunting grounds for the small garden slug (*Limax agrestis*), on which the blindworm almost entirely feeds. A garden at Blackheath was the usual place selected for this purpose, and I used to visit it on damp warm nights, when the slugs were likely to be abroad. Their numbers were astonishing, a few minutes sufficing to fill my jar with slugs enough to feed the blindworms for a fortnight.

Newly sown pea-beds are terribly injured by the slugs, who nibble off the young leaves as soon as they spring from the soil. As the bite of the slug very much resembles that of a bird's beak, it is no wonder that the gardener, who sees the little birds among the peas in the early morning, but who does not see the slugs which are ensconced beneath the ground, should lay the fault on the former.

Crossed strings, flapping feathers, scarecrows, and wire guards are not of the least use, for they only keep off the birds and cannot have any effect on the slugs, pea-beetles, woodlice, and other creatures which the birds would have eaten if they had been allowed free access to them.

That this is the case I can prove from my own experience. At one time I was rather an enthusiastic cultivator of peas, and when I sowed my new crops I determined to follow Mr. Waterton's plan, which I had seen at work at Walton Hall, and encourage the birds instead of driving them away. A neighbour, with whom I waged a friendly war in pea-growing, warned me that I should not have a pea left in the ground. His garden was within fifty yards of mine, and we used to pay daily visits of inspection. He took all kinds of precautions, even going to the expense of covering each row of peas with wire guards. I chose exactly the opposite course, and en-

couraged the birds as much as possible. The result was, that he had to sow nearly all his peas three times over, while my crop was a perfect success.

I have mentioned that the slugs are as troublesome to entomologists as to gardeners. The great grey slug (*Limax maximus*) is the chief offender in this respect. It smells the " treacles " at a considerable distance, and dozens of these slugs may generally be seen before the treacle has been exposed for an hour. In their eagerness to reach the treacle they stretch their bodies to an extent that seems almost incredible, and they lick it off the trees with a rapidity that is extremely annoying to the moth hunter. If they be knocked off the tree-trunks and crushed, a stream of treacle issues from them, and is sure to be found and surrounded by their companions. In fact, if a slug-bait be needed, nothing is better than treacle mixed with rum, such as is employed by entomologists.

Like snails, the bodies of slugs are covered with slime. Its secretion is much more copious than in the snail, and, indeed, serves it as a defence, but not in the manner that is usually supposed.

The slime is said to be given it as a protection against birds and other foes. This I do not believe. Very few birds ever see a slug in the course of their lives, on account of its nocturnal habits. But, when the warm rain attracts the slugs abroad by day, the ducks, who equally approve of such weather, are certainly not repelled by the slime. Neither is the blindworm, which also is a nocturnal creature, and catches the slugs in spite of all their slime.

But, in many cases, the slime is as efficient a protection to the slug as is the shell to the snail, and enables it to escape the effects of many noxious substances. When I first began to keep a garden, I was told that quicklime would be instantaneously fatal to slugs. Accordingly, having taken a great number by a cabbage-leaf bait, I threw a quantity of quicklime over them. There was a great hissing and bubbling, and I thought that every slug was dead. But, in a few minutes, they emerged one by one from the lime, leaving a still hissing and bubbling trail of slime behind them. They were reduced to half their size, but otherwise seemed to be little the worse for their sojourn under the lime.

On examining the lime-heap from which they had escaped, it was found that each slug had formed a sort of slight tunnel in it, the slime being secreted in such quantities that it threw off the lime and kept it from actual contact with the skin.

A weak solution of ammonia, however, appears to be fatal to the slug, which cannot throw it off as it does the solid substance of the lime. I may also mention that when dead, the bodies of the slugs can be mixed with earth, and form a valuable compost for florists.

There is another use for the slime, which may often be seen exemplified in the treacle-eating slugs which have been mentioned. Very often, especially in pollard trees, the slugs fix their nocturnal resting-places at the junction of the branches with the trunk. At night, when they smell the treacle, and are in a hurry to reach it, they do not take the trouble to crawl down the tree, but lower themselves by means of a slime thread, just as is done by many caterpillars with their silken threads. I have many a time seen them descending by means of these slime-cords, but never saw them ascend.

The eggs of the slug are quite common, though they often escape observation. They are gelatinous, small, oval, long in proportion to their width, and a very pale yellow in colour. They are mostly laid on the surface of the ground among grass, and are deposited in little masses of ten or fifteen in number.

Lastly, we come to the shell of the slug.

Few persons seem to know that the slug has a shell, although the slug-shells were esteemed objects in the pharmacopœia of past days, when they were thought to be efficacious in the cure of epilepsy. But together with other strange medicines, such as powdered mummy, "crab's-eyes," woodlice, and dried frogs, they have disappeared from the druggists' shops, and their very existence has been forgotten except by naturalists.

The shell of the slug is very small, flattish, and of an irregular oval. It is situated in a sac on the back of the creature, where its place is designated by a sort of hump. When first taken out of the sac it is semi-transparent, and so fragile that it can be torn like wet tissue paper. As it dries, however, it becomes dull, opaque white, and is so brittle that it can be easily reduced to powder, in which state it was given as medicine.

What purpose the shell serves is not known, for it simply lies in the sac within which it is formed. It is too slight to act as a protection to the respiratory organs over which it is placed, and it does not act as an attachment to any muscles.

One slug there is, which does possess an external shell. This, however, is rather horny than calcareous, and is set nearly at the tip of the tail. The scientific name of testacella, or little shell, which is given to these slugs, alludes to this structure.

The testacella is essentially carnivorous, and its tooth-ribbon is most formidably armed with teeth, which are arranged in fifty rows. It will eat other molluscs, but mostly feeds upon the earth worms, which it follows into their burrows. As it pursues its course through the worm holes, the little hard shell stops up the passage behind it, and acts as a shield against any foe that might follow it. Whether this be the real object of the shell and its peculiar position, I do not venture to say, but it certainly does fulfil that purpose.

PLAIN-SPEAKING.

PRELIMINARY.

IT has been remarked, "You may say anything, to anybody, if you only know *how* to say it." That is, with kindliness, good temper, and calm justice : free from "bumptiousness," and above all from the smallest suspicion of envy, malice, and all uncharitableness. Under such conditions, the act of "speaking one's mind," usually so obnoxious, is shorn of much of its harmfulness; and fault-finding becomes less a weapon of offence than a surgeon's lancet, used not for injury; but cure.

Therefore, if in this or succeeding papers I say somewhat hard things, I beg my readers to believe that it is not out of a hard heart, careless of giving pain, but a sad heart, knowing that pain must be given, and that if bitter truths need to be spoken, they are better spoken by an optimist than a pessimist: by a straightforward Christian woman than by a cynic or a laughing philosopher.

Also let me wholly disclaim intentional personalities. If there be a cap which fits any one, and he likes to put it on his own head, and fly into a passion about it, that is his fault, not mine. I accuse no one, let people's own consciences accuse themselves. If by looking into this silent glass, they see their own image, and go away, not forgetting but remembering and amending it —for our moral beauty or ugliness depends very much upon ourselves—then this plain-speaking of mine will be no offence, nor shall I have spoken altogether in vain.

I.—THE TIDE AT THE TURN.

"There is a tide in the affairs of men
Which, taken at the turn, leads on to fortune."

"WHY, this is like a bit out of 'Cranford,'" said I to a friend as we came out into the clear winter twilight, from a house where she had taken me to pay a call.

"Yes; Mrs. Gaskell would have made a charming picture out of that cosy little parlour, with Miss Sarah sitting alone there, so round and fat and comfortable-looking." ("Pretty, too," interposed I; "she must have been pretty when she was young.") "That parrot, too, it is as good to her almost as a child, and as troublesome." (My friend does not believe in the delightfulness of children.) "And Miss Phillis makes as much of the parrot as her sister. I wish you had seen Miss Phillis; but she is always out of afternoons."

And then I learnt how, at the other end of the town, lived an old gentleman, very helpless and infirm, whom Miss Phillis for years had gone to see every day, spending an hour or two in reading or talking to him.

"In summer I often used to meet her walking beside his Bath-chair. She is not at all like Miss Sarah, but very tall and thin, and decidedly active for her years. This winter I hear poor Mr. White cannot go out at all, but Miss Phillis never misses a day in going to see him."

"Is he a relation?"

"Oh, no; only a very old friend. An old bachelor, too—quite solitary. People do say —have said it any time these thirty years— that he had better have married Miss Phillis, and that she would not have objected; but one never knows the truth of these things. They have been most steady friends, anyhow."

Here, truly, was a chapter out of "Cranford," or out of human life generally. Once I had myself chanced to see Mr. White—a funny little old man in a brown Brutus wig— it was difficult to make a sentimental hero of him. Still——

"I have always been rather fond of Miss Phillis," continued my friend. "She would have made a good man's fireside very bright. Perhaps Mr. White was one of those who are always missing their chances, who cannot 'take the tide at the turn.' If so, it was a pity. So many let happiness slip by them, and regret it when too late. Not that I am aware of Miss Phillis's regretting anything. She is a very cheerful-minded woman, and is invaluable now to old Mr. White."

We were neither of us in a moralising mood, being also cheerful-minded women, and bent on enjoying as much as possible our brief winter holiday—"gently but kindly," like our own advancing age—so the conversation dropped.

Since, however, it has often recurred to me, in noticing how very common is this fatal peculiarity of not being able to "take the tide at the turn," especially in love affairs. That of Miss Phillis and Mr. White may never have existed at all, except in the imagination of their friends; but I have known several other instances in which a little honest rashness would have been the best wisdom.

One case especially: a young couple— playfellows from childhood—all their friends agreeable to and expecting their engagement, nay waiting, somewhat anxiously, for the gentleman to "make up his mind" and say the final word, which from pure shyness he delayed doing. At last, one Sunday—the young lady was going away on Monday—he determined to speak during their usual evening walk home from church. But—— "I'll go to church with you to-night," said an unconscious, well-intentioned friend. Alas! "two is company, three is none." The proposal was not made—never made. Three days after the lady accepted a long-persistent suitor, who years before had made up *his* mind—and declared it. Well, no hearts were broken apparently. She married, but her old playfellow is a bachelor still. He comes now and then to see her, romps with her children, plays chess with her husband, and does not look at all miserable. But perhaps, when he goes back to his handsome empty house, he wishes things had been a little different.

However, love, if it be the heart of life, constitutes only a small portion of it externally, to a man at least. On many other matters besides love-matters this inability to take the tide at the turn is most fatal. How many a man owes his whole success in life to the faculty of being able to see the golden moment and catch it ere it flies! " All things come alike to all." That is (with very rare exceptions), every man has a certain number of chances—the distinction between success and failure is that one grasps them, another lets them slip by. An unanswered letter, an appointment broken, a train missed, may for all we know change the colour of our whole existence. All the more because we do *not* know; until, looking back, we see upon what trivial things — mere accidents apparently — hinged the most important events of our lives. A situation applied for at once, and gained "just at the nick of time;" a first invitation accepted, not neglected; a business letter answered without delay; an appointment kept, with trouble and pains, yet still kept: these small things have many a time proved the key-stone of the arch on which a young man has built his fortunes. "Only a quarter of an hour!" said an old man to a young one who was apologising carelessly for having kept him waiting thus long. "My friend, to that quarter of an hour I owe everything in life!"

Between the courage which seizes an opportunity and the sanguine rashness which snatches at everything and grasps nothing, is as wide a difference as between bravery and foolhardiness. Sometimes one may make a mistake. A lady once told me how she stood before a post-office with a letter in her hand—a momentous letter, written on the impulse of the moment, and with a strong conscientious desire to do the right—all the more because it was painful — how twice, three times, she seemed to feel some invisible hand restraining her own, how she looked helplessly up to the silent sunset sky—then with a sort of desperation dropped the letter into the box—and repented it to her dying day.

But these difficult crises seldom happen. On the whole, far more harm is done by irresolution than by precipitation: even, as I have heard it said, and I agree thereto, weakness is worse than wickedness. At any rate,

it is more dangerous. The man who never can make up his mind, who lets chance after chance go past him, is always a little too late for everything, and never knows that kindly Fortune has touched him till he catches the last sad sweep of her garment as she glides by—for ever!—the misery which this man creates, and inflicts—for it is a fallacy that any one can be nobody's enemy but his own —is, in the aggregate, much greater than that caused by the strong bad man. Him we recognise at once, and against him we can protect ourselves a little; against the other we never can. Our very pity takes up arms against our judgment. For, alas! we know the certain end—

> " He that will not when he may,
> When he would he shall have nay."

Only for a single hopeful minute is the tide on the turn; when once it *has* turned, it has turned for ever, and

> " Leaves him at eve on the bleak shore alone."

All thorough business men and women— for women require to be good "men of business" too in this our day—know that the aptitude for seeing the right moment to do a thing, and doing it, without rashness, but also without delay, is a vital necessity of success—success in anything. He who puts off till to-morrow what can be done—or ought to be done—to-day, is most hopeless as a clerk, a servant, or in any position where regular systematic work is required. More fatal still is such a quality in a master or mistress—for the real heart of a family is almost always the mistress. If *she* cannot "take the tide at the turn," judge the fittest moment for domestic decisions of all kinds, and carry them out, woe betide her! There may be no actual shipwreck, but her household barque will be a very helpless, helmless vessel at best.

This habit of dilatoriness and indecision is so much of it mere habit that children cannot be too early taught, first the necessity of making up one's mind, and then of acting upon it. The trick of "hanging about," of wasting minute after minute, hour after hour, in work as in play—for idlers never even play conscientiously—is often acquired in mere infancy, and too often, alas! in imitation of elders and betters, never to be got rid of to the end of life. What is in the boy or girl pure carelessness, becomes in the man and woman a confirmed peculiarity, which haunts them like a curse, causing no end of misery to themselves and all belonging to them.

For we know our gains and achievements; our losses, our failures, we never fully know. But we may dimly guess at them, by our despair over some application thrown aside and neglected, till the lost chance of benefiting ourselves or our neighbour can never be recalled; our remorse over an unanswered letter, when the writer has suddenly gone whither no kindly word can reach him any more; our regret over cordial visits left unpaid, and pleasant meetings unvalued, till friendship, worn out, dies a natural death, or burns itself to ashes like a fire without fresh coals. Then we may lay the blame on Providence, luck, circumstances; anything or anybody except the true sinners, ourselves—but it is too late.

"We cannot help it," we plead, and after a certain time we really cannot help it. There is a disease called paralysis of the will, an actual physical disease, though its results are moral, and every one who cultivates, or rather does not strive with all his might to eradicate, the habit of indecision, lays himself open thereto. A baby—even a dumb infant who "knows its own mind," and stretches out the little impetuous hand, quite certain whether it is the doll or the waggon which it wants to play with, and eager to snatch it, without wasting a minute—is a personage not to be despised, but encouraged. The gift of being able to enjoy to-day, not to-morrow or next week, but to-day, which alone is our real property, and also (the one faculty involves the other) of doing resolutely each day's work within the day, is one of the greatest blessings that can fall to the lot of any human being. Let us, who are parents, try by all conceivable means to secure it to our children.

For the young can learn; the old seldom can. "Redeeming the time because the days are evil" is very difficult when the days have become "evil;" when the glow has gone out of life, and instead of the rosy flush of hope the grey twilight of endurance settles over all things; when we smile at "taking the tide at the turn," knowing that no more tides will ever turn, for us at least;—but they may for our children.

Let us teach them, whether or not we have learnt it ourselves, "whatsoever thy hand findeth to do, do it with thy might." And do it *at the time*. Not "to-morrow," or the day after, or "by-and-by when I am in the mood for it," but at once, at the moment when it presents itself to be done. For the tide will turn, and you never know the moment of its turning. Be first clear-sighted, cautious, prudent, and then be decided. Make up your mind; but having made it up, act upon it. Do not—

"Linger shivering on the brink,
And fear to launch away"—

but take the tide at the turn; plunge boldly in; do your best, and trust the rest.

There is an old English verse, part of a love poem, I think; but it applies to many another crisis in life besides love—

"He either fears his fate too much,
Or his deserts are small,
Who dare not put it to the touch,
To win or lose it all."

And without defending either folly, recklessness, or rashness, I think we may safely say that the man who *dare* "put it to the touch" is the man most likely to prosper through having taken "the turn of the tide."

THE AUTHOR OF "JOHN HALIFAX, GENTLEMAN."

NOVANTIA.

I.

PERHAPS no common wilderness—
  Forsaken garden's lonely place,
Forgotten but for loneliness,
  Or ruined hamlet's lingering trace
In orchards leafless all the year—
Would please me by its cheerless cheer.

II.

But thou, Novantia, set within
  Thy lake, incomparable isle,
Remote from fever, and from din
  Of modern life and strife and guile,
Thou should'st not be a garden trim—
A tradesman's manufactured whim.

III.

Here is a garden; here the years
  Refuse submission to a plan;
Disowned are human hopes and fears
  In man's inheritance from man,
And nature's bounty overrules
Precepts of prim artistic schools.

IV.

With ivy clad, with ivy crowned,
  Old walls are reddened by the dawn,
Whose stones surrender to the ground
  Dead boughs from rusty nails withdrawn,
While o'er their height—time's sere regrets—
Waves stalwart grass its bannerets.

V.

The beaten road from beaten ways
  That led wayfaring men to God,
The peace of God of mortal days
  Ended in peace beneath the sod,
O'er which, with breath of eve and morn,
The breath of orisons is borne,—

VI.

That beaten road no longer leads
  From common ways to sacred earth ;
Sunk deep beneath the roots of weeds,
  Whereof redundant death was birth,
It heeds not, nor, forgotten, knows
If dead or living comes or goes.

VII.

Memorial of a common life
  Lived sordidly an age ago,
In care of sheep and oxen rife,
  With scorn of popery aglow,
That old grey stone sinks out of sight,
Garnished with Scripture, into night.

VIII.

It had its day, that old grey stone ;
  Done is the work device could do
To rescue from oblivion
  A churl's desire to live anew,
And daily cursed the Man of Sin,
A golden crown and harp to win.

IX.

Henceforth no difference of fate
  By difference of creed is made
Between the monk of ancient date
  Here near his oratory laid,
And him who placed in God his hope
As mighty to confound the Pope.

X.

Their hatred and their love forgot,
  The churl above, the monk below,
Submissive to the common lot—
  To be and to oblivion go—
Forgiven, forgiving heretics,
Ashes with alien ashes mix.

XI.

Men and their works together lose
  Remembrance of themselves—to-day
Brightest the foxglove's beauty glows,
  Rankest the nettle's rank array,
Where holy fane of vanished men
Has crumbled into dust again.

XII.

It is not meet that any art,
  Skilful alone to pare and square,
Should enter here and do its part
  To show how well by human care
Nature's variety may be
Reduced to blank monotony.

XIII.

Fit is it that where ages meet
  Which each to each were flower and weed,
And men collect whose sour and sweet
  Were opposites of deed and creed,
Nature should still have man's consent
To be his varied monument.

XIV.

Consider how the lilies grow,
  And thistles with the lilies spring ;
While garden roses bud and blow
  Wild roses too are blossoming :
For flower and weed there is a place
In nature's comprehensive grace.

XV.

Various as these the race of man,
  Garden and desert it may be,
With weeds and flowers confused the plan
  And absent uniformity.
It may be that, for good and ill,
Good is the all-prevailing will.

XVI.

Even as shadows on the grass,
  That hides the dust restored to dust,
Novantia, thy owners pass,
  And pass thy lovers also must :
Comes soon, alas ! the rueful hour
Which ends another shadow's power.

XVII.

His shall not be the evil fame—
  That he was but a learned fool,
Who fresh from school to Nature came
  And ordered Nature back to school,
Impaired by rule thy loveliness
To show a petty skilfulness.

XVIII.

Still may thy lake thy beauty woo,
  And silence lend to solitude !
Still may thy girdling beeches, too,
  Shade peace with leafy amplitude !
That Eden, yet uncursed, may be
By purer ages seen in thee !

                              J. SERVICE.

THE TRUMPET-MAJOR.

By THOMAS HARDY, Author of "Far from the Madding Crowd," etc.

CHAPTER XL—OUR PEOPLE ARE AFFECTED BY THE PRESENCE OF ROYALTY.

TO explain the miller's sudden proposal it is necessary to go back to that moment in the narrative when Anne, Festus, and Mrs. Garland were talking together on the down. John Loveday had fallen back so as not to interfere with a meeting in which he was so decidedly superfluous; and his father, who guessed the trumpet-major's secret, watched his face as he stood. John's face was unmistakably sad, and his eyes followed Mrs. Garland's encouraging manner to Festus in a way which plainly said that every parting of her lips was tribulation to him. The miller loved his son as much as any miller or private gentleman could do, and he was pained to see John's gloom at such a trivial circumstance. So what did he resolve but to help John there and then by precipitating a matter which, had he himself been the only person concerned, he would have delayed for another six months.

He had long liked the society of his impulsive, tractable neighbour, Mrs. Garland; had mentally taken her up and pondered her fifty times in connection with the question whether it would not be for the happiness of both if she were to share his home, even though she was a little his superior in antecedents and knowledge. In fact he loved her; not tragically, but to a very creditable extent for his years; that is, next to his sons Bob and John, though he knew very well of that ploughed-ground appearance near the corners of her once handsome eyes, and that the little depression in her right cheek was not the lingering dimple it was poetically assumed to be, but a result of the abstraction of some worn-out nether millstones within the cheek by Rootle, the Weymouth man, who lived by such practices on the heads of the elderly. But what of that, when he had lost two to each one of hers, and exceeded her in age by some eight years. To do John a service, then, he quickened his designs, and put the question to her while they were standing under the eyes of the younger pair.

Mrs. Garland, though she had been interested in the miller for a long time, and had for a moment now and then thought on this question as far as, "Suppose he should," "If he were to," and so on, had never thought much farther; and she was really

taken by surprise when the question came. She answered without affectation that she would think over the proposal; and thus they parted.

Now her mother's infirmity of purpose set Anne thinking, and she was suddenly filled with a conviction that in such a case she ought to have some purpose herself. Mrs. Garland's complacency at the miller's offer had, in truth, amazed her. While her mother had held up her head, and recommended Festus, it had seemed a very pretty thing to rebel; but the pressure being removed an awful sense of her own responsibility took possession of her mind. As there was no longer anybody to be wise or ambitious for her, surely she should be wise and ambitious for herself, discountenance her mother's attachment, and encourage Festus in his addresses, for her own and her mother's good. There had been a time when a Loveday thrilled her own heart; but that was long ago, before she had thought of position or differences. To wake into cold daylight like this, when and because her mother had gone into the land of romance, was dreadful and new to her, and like an increase of years without living them.

But it was easier to think that she ought to marry the yeoman than to take steps for doing it; and she went on living just as before, only with a little more thoughtfulness in her eyes.

Two days after the visit to the camp, when she was again in the garden, soldier Loveday said to her, at a distance of five rows of beans and a parsley-bed—

"You have heard the news, Miss Garland?"

"No," said Anne, without looking up from a book she was reading.

"The King is coming to-morrow."

"The King?" She looked up then.

"Yes; to Weymouth; and he will pass this way. He can't arrive till long past the middle of the night, if what they say is true, that he only reaches Andover by supper-time," continued Loveday, encouraged by her interest to cut off the parsley-bed from the distance between them.

Miller Loveday came round the corner of the house.

"Have ye heard about the King coming, Miss Maidy Anne?" he said.

Anne said that she had just heard of it,

XXI—18

and the trumpet-major, who hardly welcomed his father at such a moment, explained what he knew of the matter.

"And you will go with your regiment to meet 'en, I suppose?" said old Loveday.

Young Loveday said that the men of the German Legion were to perform that duty; his regiment had nothing to do with the reception. And turning half from his father, and half towards Anne, he added, in a tentative tone, that he thought he might get leave for that night, if anybody would like to be taken to the top of the hill over which the cavalcade was going to pass.

Anne, knowing by this time of the budding hope in the gallant dragoon's mind, and not wishing to encourage it, said, "I don't want to go."

The miller looked disappointed as well as John.

"Your mother might like to!" he said.

"Yes; I am going indoors, and I'll ask her if you wish me to," said she.

She went indoors, and rather coldly told her mother of the proposal. Mrs. Garland, though she had determined not to answer the miller's question on matrimony just yet, was quite ready for this jaunt, and in spite of Anne she sailed off at once to the garden to hear more about it. When she re-entered, she said—

"Anne, I have not seen the King or the King's horses for these many years; and I am going."

"Ah, it is well to be you, mother," said Anne, in an elderly tone.

"Then you won't come with us?" said Mrs. Garland, rather rebuffed.

"I have very different things to think of," said her daughter with virtuous emphasis, "than going to see sights at that time of night."

Mrs. Garland was sorry, but resolved to adhere to the arrangement. So the night came on; and it having gone abroad that the King would pass by the road, many of the villagers went out to see the cavalcade. When the two Lovedays and Mrs. Garland were gone, Anne bolted the door for security, and sat down to think again on her grave responsibilities in the choice of a husband, now that her natural guardian could no longer be trusted.

A knock came to the door.

Anne's instinct was at once to be silent, that the comer might think the family had retired.

The knocking person, however, was not to be easily persuaded. He had in fact seen rays of light over the top of the shutter, and, unable to get an answer, went on to the door of the mill, which was still going, the miller sometimes grinding all night when busy. The grinder accompanied the stranger to Mrs. Garland's door.

"The daughter is certainly at home, sir," said the grinder. "I'll go round to t'other side, and see if she's there, Master Derriman."

"I want to take her out to see the King," said Festus.

Anne had started at the sound of the voice. No opportunity could have been better for carrying out her new convictions on the disposal of her hand. But in her mortal dislike of Festus, Anne forgot her principles, and her idea of keeping herself above the Lovedays. Tossing on her hat and blowing out the candle, she slipped out at the back door, and hastily followed in the direction that her mother and the rest had taken. She overtook them as they were beginning to climb the hill.

"What! you have altered your mind after all?" said the widow. "How came you to do that, my dear?"

"I thought I might as well come," said Anne.

"To be sure you did," said the miller heartily. "A good deal better than biding at home there."

John said nothing, though she could almost see through the gloom how glad he was that she had altered her mind. When they reached the ridge over which the highway stretched they found many of their neighbours who had got there before them idling on the grass border between the roadway and the hedge, enjoying a sort of midnight picnic, which it was easy to do, the air being still and dry. Some carriages were also standing near, though most people of the district who possessed four wheels, or even two, had driven to Weymouth to await the King there. From this height could be seen in the distance the position of the town, an additional number of lanterns, lamps, and candles having been lit to-night by the loyal burghers to grace the royal entry, if it should occur before dawn.

Mrs. Garland touched Anne's elbow several times as they walked, and the young woman at last understood that this was meant as a hint to her to take the trumpet-major's arm, which its owner was rather suggesting than offering to her. Anne wondered what infatuation was possessing her mother, declined to take the arm, and contrived to get in front with the miller, who mostly kept in the van to guide the others' footsteps. The trumpet-major was left with Mrs. Garland, and Anne's encouraging pursuit of them induced him to say a few words to the former.

"By your leave, ma'am, I'll speak to you on something that concerns my mind very much indeed?"

"Certainly."

"It is my wish to be allowed to pay my addresses to your daughter."

"I thought you meant that," said Mrs. Garland simply.

"And you'll not object?"

"I shall leave it to her. I don't think she will agree, even if I do."

The soldier sighed, and seemed helpless. "Well, I can but ask her," he said.

The spot on which they had finally chosen to wait for the King was by a field gate, whence the white road could be seen for a long distance northwards by day, and some little distance now. They lingered and lingered, but no king came to break the silence of that beautiful summer night. As half-hour after half-hour glided by, and nobody came, Anne began to get weary; she knew why her mother did not propose to go back, and regretted the reason. She would have proposed it herself, but that Mrs. Garland seemed so cheerful, and as wide awake as at noonday, so that it was almost a cruelty to disturb her.

The trumpet-major at last made up his mind, and tried to draw Anne into a private conversation. The feeling which a week ago had been a vague and piquant aspiration, was to-day altogether too lively for the reasoning of this warm-hearted soldier to regulate. So he persevered in his intention to catch her alone, and at last, in spite of her manœuvres to the contrary, he succeeded. The miller and Mrs. Garland had walked about fifty yards farther on, and Anne and himself were left standing by the gate.

But the gallant musician's soul was so much disturbed by tender vibrations and by the sense of his presumption that he could not begin; and it may be questioned if he would ever have broached the subject at all, had not a distant church clock opportunely assisted him by striking the hour of three. The trumpet-major heaved a breath of relief.

"That clock strikes in G sharp," he said.

"Indeed—G sharp?" said Anne civilly.

"Yes. 'Tis a fine-toned bell. I used to notice that note when I was a boy."

"Did you—the very same?"

"Yes; and since then I had a wager about that bell with the bandmaster of the North Wessex Militia. He said the note was G, I said it wasn't. When we found it was G sharp we didn't know how to settle it."

"It is not a deep note for a clock."

"Oh, no. The finest tenor bell about here is the bell of Peter's, Dorchester—in E flat. Tum-m-m-m—that's the note—tum-m-m-m." The trumpet-major sounded from far down his throat what he considered to be E flat, with a parenthetic sense of luxury unquenchable even by his present distraction.

"Shall we go on to where my mother is?" said Anne, less impressed by the beauty of the note than the trumpet-major himself.

"In one minute," he said tremulously. "Talking of music—I fear you don't think the rank of a trumpet-major much to compare with your own?"

"I do. I think a trumpet-major a very respectable man."

"I am glad to hear you say that. It is given out by the King's command that trumpet-majors are to be considered respectable."

"Indeed! Then I am, by chance, more loyal than I thought for."

"I get a good deal a year extra to the trumpeters, because of my position."

"That's very nice."

"And I am not supposed ever to drink with the trumpeters who serve beneath me."

"Naturally."

"And, by the orders of the War Office, I am to exert over them (that's the government word) exert over them full authority; and if any one behaves towards me with the least impropriety, or neglects my orders, he is to be confined and reported."

"It is really a dignified post," she said, with, however, a reserve of enthusiasm which was not altogether encouraging.

"And of course some day I shall," stammered the dragoon—"shall be in rather a better position than I am at present."

"I am glad to hear it, Mr. Loveday."

"And in short, Mistress Anne," continued John Loveday bravely and desperately, "may I pay court to you in the hope that—no, no, don't go away!—you haven't heard yet—that you may make me the happiest of men; not yet, but when peace is proclaimed and all is smooth and easy again? I can't put it any better, though there's more to be explained."

"This is most awkward," said Anne, evidently with pain. "I cannot possibly agree; believe me, Mr. Loveday, I cannot."

"But there's more than this. You would be surprised to see what snug rooms the married trumpet and sergeant majors have in quarters."

"Barracks are not all; consider camp and war."

"That brings me to my strong point," exclaimed the soldier hopefully. "My father is better off than most non-commissioned officers' fathers; and there's always a home for you at his house in any emergency. I can tell you privately that he has enough to keep us both, and if you wouldn't hear of barracks, well, peace once established, I'd live at home as a miller and farmer—next door to your own mother."

"My mother would be sure to object," expostulated Anne.

"No; she leaves it all to you."

"What, you have asked her?" said Anne, with surprise.

"Yes. I thought it would not be honourable to act otherwise."

"That's very good of you," said Anne, her face warming with a generous sense of his straightforwardness. "But my mother is so entirely ignorant of a soldier's life, and the life of a soldier's wife—she is so simple in all such matters, that I cannot listen to you any more readily for what she may say."

"Then it is all over for me," said the poor trumpet-major, wiping his face and putting away his handkerchief with an air of finality.

Anne was silent. Any woman who has ever tried will know without explanation what an unpalatable task it is to dismiss, even when she does not love him, a man who has all the natural and moral qualities she would desire, and only fails in the social. Would-be lovers are not so numerous, even with the best of women, that the sacrifice of one can be felt as other than a good thing wasted, in a world where there are few good things.

"You are not angry, Miss Garland?" said he, finding that she did not speak.

"Oh no. Don't let us say anything more about this now." And she moved on.

When she drew near to the miller and her mother she perceived that they were engaged in a conversation of that peculiar kind which is all the more full and communicative from the fact of its definitive words being few. In short, here the game was succeeding which with herself had failed. It was pretty clear from the symptoms, marks, tokens, telegraphs, and general by-play between widower and widow, that Miller Loveday must have again said to Mrs. Garland some such thing as he had said before, with what result this time she did not know.

As the situation was delicate, Anne halted awhile apart from them. The trumpet-major, quite ignorant of how his cause was entered into by the white-coated man in the distance (for his father had not yet told him of his designs upon Mrs. Garland), did not advance, but stood still by the gate, as though he were attending a princess, waiting till he should be called up. Thus they lingered, and the day began to break. Mrs. Garland and the miller took no heed of the time, and what it was bringing to earth and sky, so occupied were they with themselves; but Anne in her place and the trumpet-major in his, each in private thought of no bright kind, watched the gradual glory of the east through all its tones and changes. The world of birds and insects got lively, the blue and the yellow and the burnished brass of Loveday's uniform again became distinct; the sun bored its way upward, the fields, the trees, and the distant landscape kindled to flame, and the trumpet-major, backed by a lilac shadow as tall as a steeple, blazed in the rays like a very god of war.

It was half-past three o'clock. A short time after, a rattle of horses and wheels reached their ears from the quarter in which they gazed, and there appeared upon the white line of road a moving mass, which presently ascended the hill and drew near.

Then there arose a huzza from the few knots of watchers gathered there, and they cried "Long live King Jarge!" The cavalcade passed abreast. It consisted of three travelling-carriages, escorted by a detachment of the German Legion. Anne was told to look in the first carriage—a post-chariot drawn by four horses—for the King and Queen, and was rewarded by seeing a profile reminding her of the current coin of the realm; but as the party had been travelling all night, and the spectators here gathered were few, none of the royal family looked out of the carriage windows. It was said that the two elder princesses were in the same carriage, but they remained invisible. The next vehicle, a coach and four, contained more princesses, and the third some of their attendants.

"Thank God, I have seen my King!" said Mrs. Garland, when they had all gone by.

Nobody else expressed any thankfulness, for most of them had expected a more pompous cavalcade than the simple tastes of the king cared to indulge in; and one old man said grimly that that sight of dusty old leather coaches was not worth waiting for. Anne looked hither and thither in the bright rays of the day, each of her eyes having a little sun in it, which gave her glance a peculiar golden fire, and kindled the brown curls grouped over her forehead to a yellow brilliancy, and made single hairs, blown astray by the night, look like lacquered wires. She was wondering if Festus were anywhere near, but she could not see him.

Before they left the ridge they turned their attention towards Weymouth, which was visible at this place only as a portion of the sea-shore, from which the night-mist was rolling slowly back. The sea beyond was still wrapped in summer fog, the ships in the roads showing through it as black specks suspended in the air. While they looked and walked a white jet of smoke burst from a spot which the miller knew to be the battery in front of the King's residence, and then the report of guns reached their ears. This announcement was answered by a salute from Portland Castle and the ships in the neighbouring anchorage. All the bells in the town began ringing. The King and his family had arrived.

During the whole of that day travelling-carriages of all kinds and colours climbed and descended the road over the hill that led towards Weymouth. Some contained those personages of the King's suite who had not kept pace with him in his journey from Windsor; others were the coaches of aristocracy, big and little, whom news of the King's arrival drew thither for their own pleasure; so that the highway, as seen from the hills about Overcombe, appeared like an ant-walk—a constant succession of dark spots creeping along its surface at nearly uniform rates of progress, and all in one direction.

Anne, who had all that romantic interest in court people and pageantry which was natural to an imaginative girl of her tastes, frequently bent her eyes on this microscopic spectacle from the field near the front of her house, and allowed her fancy to paint the portraits and histories of those who moved therein. That speck was a coach, perchance full of ladies of resplendent charms, leading fairy lives in some gorgeous palace, and accustomed to walk in gardens of bewildering beauty. Those rattling dots of horsemen were perhaps gallant nobles and knights who had the privilege of jesting with kings; that figure on the horizon, about the 'size of a pin's head, was perhaps composed throughout of royal blood. That, as a matter of fact, the several coaches contained the elderly Countess of A——, of placid nature, plain features, and dowdy dress; the virtuous and homely Lady B——; the strange-tempered Marchioness of C——, and so on: that the horsemen were puffy, red-faced General D——, a couple of grey and bald-headed colonels, a diminutive diplomatist, and numbers of commonplace attendants on the court, made no difference whatever to the transcendency of her mental impressions.

CHAPTER XII.—HOW EVERYBODY, GREAT AND SMALL, CLIMBED TO THE TOP OF THE DOWNS.

As the days went on, echoes of the life and bustle of Weymouth reached the ears of the quiet people in Overcombe hollow—exciting and moving those unimportant natives as a ground-swell moves the weeds in a cave. The traffic and intelligence between camp and town passed in a measure over their heads. It being summer-time the miller was much occupied with business, and the trumpet-major was too constantly engaged in marching between the camp and Gloucester Lodge with the rest of the dragoons to bring his friends any news for some days.

At last he sent a message that there was to be a review on the downs by the King, and that it was fixed for the day following. This information soon spread through the village and country round, and next morning the whole population of Overcombe—except two or three very old men and women, a few babies and their nurses, a cripple, and Corporal Tullidge, ascended the slope like a flock of sheep and awaited the events of the day.

The miller wore his best coat on this occasion, which meant a good deal. An Overcombe man in those days would have a best coat, and keep it as a best coat half his life. The miller's had seen five-and-twenty summers, chiefly through the chinks of a clothes-box, and was not at all shabby as yet, though getting singular. But that could not be helped; common coats and best coats were a distinct species, and never interchangeable. Living so near the scene of the review he walked up the hill, accompanied by Mrs. Garland and Anne as usual.

It was a clear day, with little wind stirring, and the view from the downs, one of the most extensive in the county, was unclouded. The eye of any observer who cared for such things swept over Weymouth and Deadman's Bay beyond, and Portland, lying on the sea to the left of these, like a great crouching animal tethered to the mainland. On the extreme east of the marine horizon, Saint Alban's Head closed the scene, the sea to the southward of that point glaring like a mirror under the sun. Inland could be seen Badbury Rings, where a beacon had been recently erected; and farther to the left Bulbarrow, where another beacon stood. Not far from this came Nettlecombe Tout; to the west, Dogberry Hill, and Black'on near to the foreground, where there was yet another beacon, built of furze faggots thatched with straw, and standing on the spot where the monument now raises its head.

At nine o'clock the troops marched upon the ground—some from the camps in the vicinity, and some from quarters in the different towns round about. The approaches to the down were blocked with carriages of all descriptions, ages, and colours, and with pedestrians of every class. At ten the royal personages were said to be drawing near, and soon after the King, accompanied by the Dukes of Cambridge and Cumberland, and a couple of generals, appeared on horseback, wearing a round hat turned up at the side, with a cockade and military feather. (Sensation among the crowd.) Then the Queen and three of the princesses entered the field in a great coach drawn by six beautiful cream-coloured horses. Another coach, with four horses of the same sort, brought the two remaining princesses. (Confused acclamations, "There's King Jarge!" "That's Queen Sharlett!" "Princess 'Lizabeth!" "Princesses Sophiar and Meelyer!" &c., from the surrounding spectators.)

Anne and her party were fortunate enough to secure a position on the top of one of the barrows which rose here and there on the down; and the miller having gallantly constructed a little cairn of flints, he placed the two women thereon, by which means they were enabled to see over the heads, horses, and coaches of the multitudes below and around. At the march-past the miller's eye, which had been wandering about for the purpose, discovered his son in his place by the trumpeters, who had moved forwards in two ranks, and were sounding the march.

"That's John!" he cried to the widow. "His trumpet-sling is of two colours, d'ye see; and the others be plain."

Mrs. Garland too saw him now, and enthusiastically admired him from her hands upwards, and Anne silently did the same. But before the young woman's eyes had quite left the figure of the trumpet-major they fell upon the figure of Yeoman Festus riding with his troop, apparently to mark the ground on the other side, and keeping his face at a medium between haughtiness and mere bravery. He certainly looked as soldierly as any of his own corps, and felt more soldierly than half-a-dozen, as anybody could see by observing him. Anne got behind the miller in case Festus should discover her, and regardless of his monarch rush upon her in a rage with, "Why the dickens did you run away from me that night—hey, madam?" But she resolved to think no more of him just now, and to stick to Loveday, who was her mother's friend. In this she was helped by the stirring tones which burst from the latter gentleman and his subordinates from time to time.

"Well," said the miller complacently, "there's few of more consequence in a regiment than a trumpeter. He's the chap that tells 'em what to do, after all. Hey, Mrs. Garland?"

"So he is, miller," said she.

"They could no more do without Jack and his men than they could without generals."

"Indeed they could not," said Mrs. Garland again, in a tone of pleasant agreement with any one in Great Britain or Ireland.

It was said that the line that day was three miles long, reaching from the high ground on the right of where the people stood to the turnpike road on the left. After the review came a sham fight, during which action the crowd dispersed more widely over the downs, enabling widow Garland to get still clearer glimpses of the King, and his handsome charger, and the head of the Queen, and the elbows and shoulders of the princesses in the carriages, and fractional parts of General Garth and the Duke of Cumberland; which sights gave her great gratification. She tugged at her daughter at every opportunity, exclaiming, "Now you can see his feather," "There's her hat," "There's her Majesty's India muslin shawl," in a minor form of ecstasy, that made the miller think her more girlish and animated than her daughter Anne.

In those military manœuvres the miller followed the fortunes of one man; Anne Garland of two. The spectators, who, unlike our party, had no personal interest in the soldiery, saw only troops and battalions in the concrete, straight lines of red, straight lines of blue, white lines formed of innumerable knee breeches, black lines formed of many gaiters, coming and going in kaleidoscopic change. Who thought of every point in the line as an isolated man, each dwelling all to himself in the hermitage of his own mind? One person did, a young man far removed from the barrow where the Garlands and miller Loveday stood. The natural expression of his face was somewhat obscured by the bronzing effects of rough weather, but the lines of his mouth showed that affectionate impulses were strong within him—perhaps stronger than judgment well could regulate. He wore a blue jacket with little brass buttons, and was plainly a seafaring man.

Meanwhile, in the part of the plain where rose the tumulus on which the miller had established himself, a broad-brimmed tradesman was elbowing his way along. He saw Mr. Loveday from the base of the barrow, and beckoned to attract his attention. Loveday went half-way down, and the other came up as near as he could.

"Miller," said the man, "a letter has been lying at the post-office for you for the last three days. If I had known that I should see ye here I'd have brought it along with me."

The miller thanked him for the news, and they parted, Loveday returning to the summit. "What a very strange thing!" he said to Mrs. Garland, who had looked inquiringly at his face, now very grave. "That was Weymouth postmaster, and he says there's a letter for me. Ah, I now call to mind that there *was* a letter in the candle three days ago this very night—a large red one; but foolish-like I thought nothing o't. Who *can* that letter be from?"

A letter at this time was such an event for hamleteers, even of the miller's respectable standing, that Loveday thenceforward was thrown into a fit of abstraction which prevented his seeing any more of the sham fight, or the people, or the King. Mrs. Garland imbibed some of his concern, and suggested that the letter might come from his son Robert.

"I should naturally have thought that," said miller Loveday; "but he wrote to me only two months ago, and his brother John heard from him within the last four weeks, when he was just about starting on another voyage. If you'll pardon me, Mrs. Garland, ma'am, I'll see if there's any Overcombe man here who is going to Weymouth to-day, so that I may get the letter by night-time. I cannot possibly go myself."

So Mr. Loveday left them for awhile; and as they were so near home Mrs. Garland did not wait on the barrow for him to come back, but walked about with Anne a little time, until they should be disposed to trot down the slope to their own door. They listened to a man who was offering one guinea to receive ten in case Buonaparte should be killed in three months, and to other entertainments of that nature, which at this time were not rare. Once during their peregrination the eyes of

the sailor before mentioned fell upon Anne; but he glanced over her, and passed her unheedingly by. Loveday the elder was at this time on the other side of the line, looking for a messenger to Weymouth. At twelve o'clock the review was over, and the King and his family left the hill. The troops then cleared off the field, the spectators followed, and by one o'clock the downs were again bare.

They still spread their grassy surface to the sun as on that beautiful morning long ago; but the King and his fifteen thousand armed men, the horses, the bands of music, the princesses, the cream-coloured teams—the gorgeous centrepiece, in short, to which the downs were but the mere mount or margin, have been dead and gone for years and years; lying scattered about the world as military and royal dust, some at Talavera, Albuera, Salamanca, Vittoria, Toulouse, and Waterloo; some in home churchyards; and a few small handfuls in a royal vault.

In the afternoon John Loveday, lightened of his trumpet and trappings, appeared at the old manor-house door, and beheld Anne standing at hers.

"I saw you, Miss Garland," said the soldier gaily.

"Where was I?" said she smiling.

"On the top of the big mound—to the right of the King."

"And I saw you; lots of times," she rejoined.

Loveday seemed pleased. "Did you really take the trouble to find me? That was very good of you."

"Her eyes followed you everywhere," said Mrs. Garland from an upper window.

"Of course I looked at the dragoons most," said Anne, disconcerted. "And when I looked at them my eyes naturally fell upon the trumpets. I looked at the dragoons generally, no more."

She did not mean to show any vexation to the trumpet-major, but he fancied otherwise, and stood repressed. The situation was relieved by the arrival of the miller, still looking serious.

"I am very much concerned, John; I did not go to the review for nothing. There's a letter a-waiting for me at Weymouth, and I must get it before bedtime, or I sha'n't sleep a wink."

"I'll go, of course," said John; "and perhaps Miss Garland would like to see what's doing there to-day? Everybody is gone, or going; the road is like a fair."

He spoke pleadingly, but Anne was not won to assent, though she wanted to go.

"Anne and the Trumpet-major were left standing by the gate."

"You can drive in the gig; 'twill do Blossom good; he is getting fresh, and wants exercise," said the miller.

"Let David drive Miss Garland," said the trumpet-major, not wishing to coerce her; "I would just as soon walk."

Anne joyfully welcomed this arrangement, and a time was fixed for the start.

CHAPTER XIII.—THE CONVERSATION IN THE CROWD.

IN the afternoon they drove off, John Loveday being nowhere visible. All along the road they passed and were overtaken by vehicles of all descriptions going in the same direction; among them the extraordinary machines which had been invented for the conveyance of troops to any point of the coast on which the enemy should land; they consisted of four boards placed across a sort of trolly, thirty men of the volunteer companies riding on each.

The borough was in a paroxysm of gaiety. Weymouth town was quite overpowered by Weymouth district and country round, much to the town's delight and profit. The fear of invasion was such that six frigates lay in the roads to insure the safety of the royal family, and from the regiments of horse and foot quartered at the barracks, or encamped on the hills round about, a picquet of a thousand men mounted guard every day in front of Gloucester Lodge, where the King resided. When Anne and her attendant reached this point, which they did on foot, stabling the horse on the outskirts of the town, it was about six o'clock. The King was on the Esplanade, and the soldiers were just marching past to mount guard. The band formed in front of the King, and all the officers saluted as they went by.

Anne now felt herself close to and looking into the stream of recorded history, within whose banks the littlest things are great, and outside which she and the general bulk of the human race were content to live on as an unreckoned, unheeded superfluity.

When she turned from her interested gaze at this scene, there stood John Loveday. She had had a presentiment that he would turn up in this mysterious way. It was marvellous that he could have got there so quickly; but there he was—not looking at the King, or at the crowd, but waiting for the turn of her head.

"Trumpet-major, I didn't see you," said Anne demurely. "How is it that your regiment is not marching past?"

"We take it by turns, and it is not our turn," said Loveday.

She wanted to know then if they were afraid that the King would be carried off by the First Consul. Yes, Loveday told her; And his Majesty was rather venturesome. A day or two before he had gone so far to sea that he was nearly caught by some of the enemy's cruisers. "He is anxious to fight Boney single-handed," he said.

"What a good, brave King!" said Anne.

Loveday seemed anxious to come to more personal matters. "Will you let me take you round to the other side, where you can see better?" he asked. "The Queen and the princesses are at the window."

Anne passively assented. "David, wait here for me," she said; "I shall be back again in a few minutes."

The trumpet-major then led her off triumphantly, and they skirted the crowd and came round on the side towards the sands. He told her everything he could think of, military and civil, to which Anne returned pretty syllables and parenthetic words about the colour of the sea and the curl of the foam, a way of speaking that moved the soldier's heart even more than long and direct speeches would have done.

"And that other thing I asked you?" he ventured to say at last.

"We won't speak of it."

"You don't dislike me?"

"Oh, no!" she said, gazing at the bathing machines, digging children, and other common objects of the sea-shore, as if her interest lay there rather than with him.

"But I am not worthy of the daughter of a genteel professional man—that's what you mean?"

"There's something more than worthiness required in such cases, you know," she said, still without calling her mind away from surrounding scenes. "Ah, there's the Queen and princesses at the window!"

"Something more?"

"Well, since you will make me speak, I mean the woman ought to love the man."

The trumpet-major seemed to be less concerned about this than about her supposed superiority. "If it were all right on that point, would you mind the other?" he asked, like a man who knows he is too persistent, yet who cannot be still.

"How can I say, when I don't know? What a pretty chip hat the elder princess wears!"

Her companion's general disappointment extended over him almost to his lace and his plume. "Your mother said, you know, Miss Anne——"

"Yes, that's the worst of it," she said. "Let us go back to David; I have seen all I want to see, Mr. Loveday."

The mass of the people had by this time noticed the Queen and princesses at the window, and raised a cheer, to which the royal personages waved their embroidered handkerchiefs. Anne went back towards the pavement with her trumpet-major, whom all the girls envied her, so fine-looking a soldier was he; and not only for that, but because it was well known that he was not a soldier from necessity, but from patriotism, his father having repeatedly offered to set him up in business: his artistic taste in preferring a horse and uniform to a dirty, rumbling flour-mill was admired by all. She, too, had a very nice appearance in her best clothes as she walked along, trying to look as if she wore them always—the sarcenet hat, muslin shawl, and tight-sleeved gown being of the newest Overcombe fashion, that was only about two years old in Weymouth, and in Paris three or four. She could not be harsh to Loveday and dismiss him curtly, for his musical pursuits had refined him, educated him, and made him quite poetical. To-day he had been particularly well-mannered and tender; so, instead of answering,

"Never speak to me like this again," she merely put him off with a "Let us go back to David."

When they reached the place where they had left him, David was gone.

Anne was now positively vexed. "What *shall* I do?" she said.

"He's only gone to drink the King's health," said Loveday, who had privately given him the money for performing that operation. "Depend upon it, he'll be back soon."

"Will you go and find him?" said she, with intense propriety in her looks and tone.

"I will," said Loveday reluctantly; and he went.

Anne stood still. She could now escape her gallant friend, for, although the distance was long, it was not impossible to walk home. On the other hand, Loveday was a good and sincere fellow for whom she had almost a brotherly feeling, and she shrank from such a trick. While she stood and mused, scarcely heeding the music, the marching of the soldiers, the King, the dukes, the brilliant staff, the attendants, and the happy groups of people, her eyes fell upon the ground.

Before her she saw a flower lying—a crimson sweet-william—fresh and uninjured. An instinctive wish to save it from destruction by the passengers' feet led her to pick it up; and then, moved by a sudden self-consciousness, she looked around. She was standing before an inn, and from an upper window Festus Derriman was leaning with two or three kindred spirits of his cut and kind. He nodded eagerly, and signified to her that he had thrown the flower.

What should she do? To throw it away would seem stupid, and to keep it was awkward. She held it between her finger and thumb, twirled it round on its axis and twirled it back again, regarding and yet not examining it. Just then she saw the trumpet-major coming back.

"I can't find David anywhere," he said; and his heart was not sorry as he said it.

Anne was still holding out the sweet-william as if about to drop it, and, scarcely knowing what she did under the distressing sense that she was watched, she offered the flower to Loveday.

His face brightened with pleasure as he took it. "Thank you, indeed," he said.

Then Anne saw what a misleading blunder she had committed towards Loveday in playing to the yeoman. Perhaps she had sown the seeds of a quarrel.

"It was not my sweet-william," she said hastily; "it was lying on the ground. I don't mean anything by giving it to you."

"But I'll keep it all the same," said the innocent soldier, as if he knew a good deal about womankind; and he put the flower carefully inside his jacket, between his white waistcoat and his heart.

Festus, seeing this, enlarged himself wrathfully, got hot in the face, rose to his feet, and glared down upon them like a turnip-lantern.

"Let us go away," said Anne timorously. "I must go home now; I'll walk."

"I'll see you safe to your own door, depend upon me," said Loveday. "But—I had near forgot—there's father's letter, that he's so anxiously waiting for! Will you come with me to the post-office? Then I'll take you straight home."

Anne, expecting Festus to pounce down every minute, was glad to be off anywhere; so she accepted the suggestion, and they went along the parade together.

Loveday set this down as a proof of Anne's relenting. Thus in joyful spirits he entered the office, paid the postage, and received his father's letter.

"It is from Bob, after all!" he said. "Father told me to read it at once, in case of bad news. Ask your pardon for keeping you a moment." He broke the seal and read, Anne standing silently by.

"He is coming home *to be married*," said the trumpet-major, without looking up.

Anne did not answer. The blood swept impetuously up her face at his words, and as suddenly went away again, leaving her rather paler than before. She disguised her agitation and then overcame it, Loveday observing nothing of this emotional performance.

"As far as I can understand he will be here Saturday," he said.

"Indeed!" said Anne quite calmly. "And who is he going to marry?"

"That I don't know," said John, turning the letter about. "The woman is a stranger. —Now shall we walk up the street again?"

At this moment the miller entered the office hastily, and seeing John went across to him, in his earnestness abstaining from anything like a general glance round.

"Come, John, I have been waiting and waiting for that there letter till I was nigh crazy."

"It is only from Robert," said the trumpet-major; and his father took the letter and read.

"To be married! . . . Still, it is no such bad news as I thought. Why have ye been so long, John? There have I been thinking

" Before her she saw a flower lying."

perhaps 'tis this, and perhaps 'tis that, and at last could do no otherwise than follow ye."

John was very sorry, and replied in rather lame tones that they had been looking at the King; while the miller took off his hat and wiped the exact line where his forehead joined his hair, saying that since 'twas as 'twas it did not matter, and that he must get home again at once, and read the letter over quiet to himself, and so get more of the true sense of it than he could in this noisy place, and think what was to be done.

Anne had been very glad to see John's father, for it relieved her of her difficulty in getting home; and it was arranged that as David was nowhere to be found she should take the spare seat beside Mr. Loveday.

They walked up the street, leaving John to return alone. The miller was so absorbed in his mental perspective of Bob's arrival that he saw nothing of the gaieties they passed through; and Anne flung a fearless look towards the inn occupied by Festus and his friends as she marched past it, fortified by the miller.

CHAPTER XIV.—LATER IN THE EVENING OF THE SAME DAY.

WHEN they reached home the sun was going down. It had already been noised abroad that miller Loveday had received a letter, and his cart having been heard coming up the lane, the population of Overcombe drew down towards the mill as soon as he had gone indoors—a sudden flash of brightness from the window showing that he had struck such an early light as nothing but the immediate deciphering of literature could require. A letter was a matter of public moment, and everybody in the parish had an interest in the reading of those rare documents; so that when the miller had placed the candle, slanted himself, and called in Mrs. Garland to have her opinion on the meaning of any hieroglyphics that he might encounter in his course, he found that he was to be additionally assisted by the opinions of the other neighbours, whose persons appeared in the doorway, partly covering each other like a hand of cards, yet each showing a large enough piece of himself for identification. To pass the time while they were arranging themselves, the miller adopted his usual way of filling up casual intervals, that of snuffing the candle.

"We heard you had got a letter, Maister Loveday," they said.

"Yes; 'Southampton, the twelfth of August, dear father,'" said Loveday; and they were

as silent as relations at the reading of a will. Anne, for whom the letter had a singular fascination, came in with her mother and sat down.

Bob stated in his own way that having, since landing, taken into consideration his father's wish that he should renounce a seafaring life and become a partner in the mill, he had decided to agree to the proposal; and with that object in view he would return to Overcombe in three days from the time of writing.

He then said incidentally that since making his voyage he had been in lodgings at Southampton, and during that time had become acquainted with a lovely and virtuous young maiden, in whom he found the exact qualities necessary to his happiness. Having known this lady for the full space of a fortnight he had had ample opportunities of studying her character, and, being struck with the recollection that, if there was one thing more than another necessary in a mill which had no mistress, it was somebody who could be one with grace and dignity, he had asked Miss Matilda Johnson to be his wife. In her kindness she, though sacrificing far better prospects, had agreed; and he could not but regard it as a happy chance that he should have found at the nick of time such a woman to adorn his home, whose innocence was as stunning as her beauty. Without much ado, therefore, he and she had arranged to be married at once, and at Overcombe, that his father might not be deprived of the pleasures of the wedding feast. She had kindly consented to follow him by land in the course of a few days, and to live in the house as their guest for the week or so previous to the ceremony.

"'Tis a proper good letter," said Mrs. Comfort from the background. "I never heerd true love better put out of hand in my life; and they seem 'nation fond of one another."

"He haven't knowed her such a very long time," said Job Mitchell, dubiously.

"That's nothing," said Esther Beach. "'Nater will find her way very rapid when the time's come for't. Well, 'tis good news for ye, miller."

"Yes, sure, I hope 'tis," said Loveday, without, however, showing any great hurry to burst into the frantic form of fatherly joy which the event should naturally have produced, seeming more disposed to let off his feelings by examining thoroughly into the fibres of the letter paper.

"I was five years a-courting my wife," he

presently remarked. "But folks were slower about everything in them days. Well, since she's coming we must make her welcome. Did any of ye catch by my reading which day it is he means? What with making out the penmanship, my mind was drawn off from the sense here and there."

"He says in three days," said Mrs. Garland. "The date of the letter will fix it."

On examination it was found that the day appointed was the one nearly expired; at which the miller jumped up and said, "Then he'll be here before bedtime. I didn't gather till now that he was coming afore Saturday. Why, he may drop in this very minute!"

He had scarcely spoken when footsteps were heard coming along the front, and they presently halted at the door. Loveday pushed through the neighbours and rushed out; and, seeing in the passage a form which obscured the declining light, the miller seized hold of him, saying, "Oh, my dear Bob; then you are come!"

"Scrounch it all, miller, don't quite pull my poor shoulder out of joint! Whatever is the matter?" said the new-comer, trying to release himself from Loveday's grasp of affection. It was Uncle Benjy.

"Thought 'twas my son!" faltered the miller, sinking back upon the toes of the neighbours who had closely followed him into the entry. "Well, come in, Mr. Derriman, and make yerself at home. Why, you haven't been here for years. What ever has made you come now, sir, of all times in the world?"

"Is he in there with ye?" whispered the farmer with misgiving.

"Who?"

"My nephew; after that maid that he's so mighty smit with?"

"Oh, no; he never calls here."

Farmer Derriman breathed a breath of relief. "Well, I've called to tell ye," he said, "that there's more news of the French. We shall have 'em here this month as sure as a gun. The gunboats be all ready—near two thousand of 'em—and the whole army is at Boulogne. And miller, I know ye to be an honest man."

Loveday did not say nay.

"Neighbour Loveday, I know ye to be an honest man," repeated the old squireen. "Can I speak to ye alone?"

As the house was full, Loveday took him into the garden, all the while upon tenterhooks, not lest Buonaparte should appear in their midst, but lest Bob should come whilst he was not there to receive him. When they

had got into a corner Uncle Benjy said, "Miller, what with the French, and what with my nephew Festus, I assure ye my life is nothing but wherrit from morning to night. Miller Loveday, you are an honest man."

Loveday nodded.

"Well, I've come to ask a favour—to ask if you will take charge of my few poor title-deeds and documents and suchlike, while I am away from home next week, lest anything should befall me, and they should be stole away by Boney or Festus, and I should have nothing left in the wide world. I can trust neither banks nor lawyers in these terrible times; and I am come to you."

Loveday after some hesitation agreed to take care of anything that Derriman should bring, whereupon the farmer said he would call with the parchments and papers alluded to in the course of a week. Derriman then went away by the garden gate, mounted his pony, which had been tethered outside, and rode on till his form was lost in the shades.

The miller rejoined his friends, and found that in the meantime John had arrived. John informed the company that after parting from his father and Anne he had rambled to the harbour, and discovered the *Pewit* by the quay. On inquiry he had learnt that she came in at eleven o'clock, and that Bob had gone ashore.

"We'll go and meet him," said the miller. "'Tis still light out of doors."

So, as the dew rose from the meads and formed fleeces in the hollows, Loveday and his friends and neighbours strolled out, and loitered by the stiles which hampered the foot-path from Overcombe to the high road at intervals of a hundred yards. John Loveday being obliged to return to camp was unable to accompany them, but Widow Garland thought proper to fall in with the procession. When she had put on her bonnet she called to her daughter and asked if she was ready to come too. Anne said from up-stairs that she was coming in a minute; and her mother walked on without her.

What was Anne doing? Having hastily unlocked a receptacle for emotional objects of small size, she took thence the little folded paper with which we have already become acquainted, and, striking a light from her private tinderbox, she held the paper, and curl of hair it contained, in the candle till it was burnt. Then she put on her hat and followed her mother and the rest of them across the moist grey fields, cheerfully singing in an undertone as she went, to assure herself of her indifference to circumstances.

CONFLICT AND VICTORY.

OH ! Refuge of men worn and weary,
　　With suffering and sin oft distressed,
Could'st Thou leave 'mid surroundings so
　　dreary
　　Thy peace as a dying request ?

To Thine ear comes the cry of sharp sorrow
　　That rings through this pitiless world ;
And know'st Thou how oft with the morrow
　　To a deeper despair we are hurled ?

For the dawn brings no light that can lead us,
　　The birds sing no songs that can cheer,
Nor does harvest give food that can feed us,
　　And the winter's gloom reigns thro' the
　　year.

We've felt strange 'mid our kindred and
　　neighbours,
　　Been lonely in thick haunts of men,
Had to rest on a stone from our labours,
　　And no visions to comfort us then.

We've been lured by the voice of the siren
　　And caught in her cruel embrace,
Have found that the heart may be iron,
　　Tho' beauty may shine in the face.

We are weary with chasing the shadows
　　And bearing our burdens of care,
For our way has not lain through the mea-
　　dows,
　　We have chosen the dust and the glare.

Yet, Saviour, on Thee in our anguish
　　We'll pillow our sore-stricken head,
For in sorrow of soul Thou did'st vanquish
　　The foes that fill life with such dread.

We have lived for ourselves 'stead of others,
　　Sought in temples of pleasure our shrine,
Held no cup to the lips of our brothers,
　　Or with gall often mingled our wine.

We bless Thee who cam'st down in glory
　　To suffer, to succour, to save ;
By Thy Cross to shine bright in life's story
　　And triumph o'er death and the grave.

We'll fret with the world then no longer ;
　　It can bring to us nothing but bliss,
Were love in our heart only stronger
　　To God and to man than it is.

　　　　　　　　　　　　JOHN GLASSE.

THE OSPREY IN ONE OF HIS HIGHLAND HAUNTS.

By WILLIAM JOLLY, H.M. INSPECTOR OF SCHOOLS.

THE Osprey is one of our rarest visitors, even in the wilds of Scotland, once his chosen and appropriate home. This interesting bird now nestles only in two, or at most three, places there, and it is to be feared that modern tastes in shooting, collecting, and scenery-seeking will entirely banish so shy a creature from even the loneliest scenes; and that, like the reindeer and the beaver, his connection with the country will merely be a historical fact. Still, however, it is happily an existing reality, and fortune recently favouring the writer with an unusual insight into his haunts and habits, simple gratitude, as well as love of birds, compels him to tell the tale.

At the head waters of the northern Dee towers the granitic mountain group, crowned by Ben Macdhui, known from the more popular peak as the Cairngorms. These mountains approach the Spey in the middle of its course, greatly contracting its valley at Rothiemurchus, opposite Craigellachie, the rocky hill that furnished the Grants with their war-cry.

Close in under their western skirts lies a small romantic lake called Loch-an-Eilan. It occupies a deep hollow between them and the limestone hill of Tor Bain, that is, the White Hill, so called from its brighter aspect. It is a true alpine basin, the great mountains rising right from its shores. It is enclosed on all sides by a dark pine forest, the trees on the west next Tor Bain being remnants of the great Caledonian forest of old that once covered all the land and sheltered our fierce forefathers. This is one of the few spots where these ancient pines are worthily represented, Rothiemurchus itself having received from this fact its strange-looking name, the Fort of the Big Firs. These trees are magnificent specimens of vegetable life, towering with their great bare trunks from fifty to eighty feet in height; their upper portions bright with the warm glow of their rose-coloured bark, and crowned by an umbrageous spread of evergreen foliage. Stretching into Loch-an-Eilan on the rocky headlands, and rising in picturesque groups to the crest of Tor Bain, they give to this wild lake a unique charm, which has engaged the pallettes of many a painter—Horatio Macculloch eminent among these—and the efforts of many a pen. As a picture, it possesses also the point of unity necessary for perfection in such a scene, in a solitary castle rising in ruins from its waters. These occupy the whole surface of an island about thirty yards from the western shore, and this being the dominant feature has given name to the lake, the Loch of the Island. The walls are adorned with trees and bushes, which relieve their grey sternness with a poetic greenery. They present an almost unbroken face to the west, the sole openings being the entrance gate, approachable only by boat, and a small window high in the northern tower. This water-warded keep was one of the lairs of that old scourge of the Highlands, the Wolf of Badenoch, whose story is so grandiloquently told by Dick Lauder, a haunt to which the fierce marauder occasionally retired from his palatial pile in the treeless Lochandorb, some twenty miles to the north-west. Since the time of the Red Comyn, the castle has been tenantless, except by occasional wild wanderers, and by a race of birds whose inoffensive habits form a marked contrast to the stern cruelties of their human predecessor—that of the Osprey, or Fishing Eagle. On the top of the southern turret, in easy sight of the shore, rests a huge nest of rough sticks, as large as a cart and several feet in height, the gathering of generations.* This bird frequented this solitary spot till lately, undisturbed and fearless. His nest was visited, in 1824, by Macculloch, the eminent geologist and delineator of the Highlands, who described the scene with unwonted enthusiasm, and reverently refrained from moving even a twig in the eyrie. All went well with the feathered clan till seven years ago, when a noble lord, filled with the noble thirst for slaughtering our wilder innocents, wantonly shot one of the birds, and frightened this shyest of eagles from the home of his ancestors. The nest has since been deserted till the present year, when a pair once more risked their lives in the old castle tower.

The opportunity of seeing so rare and interesting a bird in a habitat so old and romantic was too valuable to be lost, and I repaired to the spot in May last; not, however, for the first time, for it is a favourite resort of all that have once seen it. In com-

* The accompanying picture (page 264), which is from a new photograph by my friend, shows the castle from the west, with the nest on the top of the right-hand or southern tower.

pany with a friend, I reached the lake late on a dull afternoon. We were fortunate in finding the female at home, brooding in silence, in the face of a cold wind blowing strongly down the glen. When we emerged on the shore we heard a scream, and beheld the great creature rise slowly in the air and sweep in a wide curve down to the lower end of the loch. She then returned, beating heron-like over the water and, soaring to a great height, slowly descended to her eyrie, where she settled as at first, evidently disturbed, however, by the sight of the intruders. We watched her long, rousing her at intervals in order the better to observe her form and flight, our cries being increased by a good echo from the walls. While brooding, she continually turned her head on all sides in restless apprehension, her natural fears not yet being dispelled. When she stood erect, she appeared to be about three feet in height, and seemed a handsome specimen of the race. Her general plumage was a beautiful brown, except on the breast, where a pure white relieved the sober hue. Her pinions were broad, extending as wide as the arms of a man, and bore some resemblance to the heron's, induced by her similar fishing habits, but they had the acuteness, style, and swiftness of the falcon. Her eagle affinities were also apparent in the hooked beak, the deep-set eye, the short, thick, powerful legs, the curved talons, and pointed wings, which were longer than the body, and in her power of easy curving, swooping, poising, and floating with motionless feathers in upper air.

The osprey feeds exclusively on fish, being the only eagle that confines itself to such mild diet, always choosing his eyrie with reference to such prey; though it is rumoured that want sometimes compels him to touch other flesh, at the best a rare departure from usual habit in so good a fisher. He catches his silvery food by sweeping along the surface of the water, being able to discover it from a great height, when he descends sheer as a bolt, not headlong like the solan, but feet foremost, seizing the luckless fish with his powerful talons, the lower surface of which are roughly scaled to prevent its escape. He prefers to build on the summit of a high rock, headland, or castle wall, either by the sea-shore or in a loch, close to good fishing ground. He is frequently obliged, however, to nestle on a tree, doing so always on its very head, and therefore generally selecting a fir with a flat top, on which his great nest may lie, in order to command a free outlook for observation and safety, dear to a creature so shy. Even here he settled for several years on a tall pine at the farther side of the lake. Scorning all protection from wind and weather, however fierce and inclement, the hardy bird sits calmly with beak to the rudest blast and under the heaviest deluge. Singularly inoffensive and mild in disposition, he attacks no other bird or beast ; though he is as brave as the fiercest of the falcons, not fearing the heaviest odds. Indeed the osprey would seem to be a kind of Gunnar among the birds, big, strong, mild, and dauntless as Njal's son, with a like devotion to duty which, as we shall see, is as beautiful as it is interesting.

I was disappointed at not seeing the male bird at this visit, as he had likely retired for the night. The coming darkness compelled us reluctantly to leave the scene, determined, however, to return. This I was soon able to do in June, when I spent the greater part of two days watching the birds and enjoying the scene. For Loch-an-Eilan is one of those spots that never pall on the seer, it varies so greatly and so rapidly in character : now wild, weird, and melancholy, anon bright, warm and beautiful, again dark, cold and seething in the storm ; but always alpine, picturesque and powerful, amidst its enclosing mountains and their ancient pines. On this occasion I was accompanied by another friend, who lives in a pleasant hollow not far from the lake, in sight of the Cairngorms, and is proud of the castellated loch and its rare dwellers. We ascended to the top of a spur of the fair Tor Bain. From this point of vantage we commanded a full view of the loch. With the aid of a good telescope we could look down on the nest as well as if we had been near it, and could literally see into the deep-set eye of the bird. The object glass certainly presented a pretty picture, with the castle in the centre, surrounded by a circle of sparkling water, a striking medallion of one of nature's rarer sights.

When we took our place on this rock, the female was seated on the eyrie. All that was then visible of her was her brown back on a level with the twigs, and her erect head and flashing eye, which she constantly turned with the restless watchfulness of all predatory birds. She was looking up the loch when we arrived, a position she seemed to prefer, but successively faced in all directions. She formed an interesting sight, with her grey crest and head and the darker line round the neck, which gave her the appearance of wearing a cowl, her pure white breast and the long hair-like feathers of the upper body blown picturesquely about by the wind. She generally sat quietly on the nest gazing round, now re-adjusting the bleached sticks of her nest, then changing her attitude, to settle down again in watchful repose. The extraordinary devotion of so wild a creature to the trying duties of motherhood was most impressive. She seldom left the nest day or night, being supplied with necessary nourishment by her loving and unwearied partner. Happily her confidence in the security of the position seemed now almost complete, for she could scarcely be made to rise at all, as she did with ready alarm at my first visit. During these two days, she never once soared into the air, contenting herself when roused with merely rising in the nest, standing on its edge, and flapping her broad wings. An artist and his wife had lately taken quarters at the farm near the castle, and the inhabitants in this and other cottages there, as well as numerous visitors, did not seem to disturb her in the least. We saw the artistic pair seated on the beach opposite the tower, the one with white umbrella, easel, and other paraphernalia, the other with a rustling newspaper, while the creature sat calmly looking on. The proprietor had greatly contributed to this feeling of security, for, justly proud of his rare visitors, he had rigidly refused the use of a boat on the lake, for fear of scaring the birds.

While we sat on the rocky height a sudden movement turned our attention upwards, where we observed the male bird high in air, approaching from the south. He swept round in narrowing circles, and finally settled on the nest beside his mate. It was the first time I had seen him, and I was in luck. She rose at his approach and stood beside him, her greater size and height becoming distinctly apparent, as in many other birds of prey. While on the wing he showed nothing in his talons, which were hidden in the longer feathers beneath ; but he came not empty-handed, for he laid on the broad edge of the nest a shining fish, and this she proceeded at once to consume. The generous provider remained beside her for a little, and then, rising vertically, swept towards the mountains on the other side of the loch, where he perched on the top of a pine, to watch her, as his custom was, while thus engaged, evidently to prevent her being unwittingly surprised. When the two met on the nest, they made no demonstrations of affection beyond some quiet chirruping, having evidently passed the exuberant period of love, and, like old married folks and good

Haunt of the Osprey—Loch-an-Eilan.

householders, attending discreetly to domestic duties. His behaviour to his wife was at all times modest, dignified, and attentive, as befitted a bird of quiet tastes, good character, and aquiline rank. As he stood amid the dark green of the firs, his white breast caught the eye, although he was about a mile distant. When the mother had finished her mid-day meal she settled down once more to her brooding, and he then flew away to the lower end of the loch, wheeling, swooping, gyrating, floating, soaring, and skimming, sometimes high above the outline of Cairngorm, in evident enjoyment of the airy exercise. He never stayed long on the nest, which, big as it was, had room only for one in its hollow, but gave abundant standing space for both on its broad brim. Though smaller, he looked stronger and more athletic than she, sweeping wider, soaring higher, flying swifter, and indulging in more distant excursions. The solitary nest on the tower having fewer claims on his attendance, he could take a freer range ; which, moreover, he required to do, for his own sake and hers, for, as bread-winner to the household, he had to seek the necessary provision in distant lakes, Loch-an-Eilan not being good ground for either the human or the falcon fisher.

By-and-by we descended to the loch opposite the keep. Just as we reached the shore the sudden flapping of a startled wild pigeon alarmed the osprey, and made her stand erect, showing to advantage her fine form and wide-spreading pinions ; but she soon settled down again while eyeing us on the banks. We sat long observing the devoted mother, but tried in vain to rouse her to flight. The castle itself had a fairer aspect than formerly, the shrubs and trees round it being in full leaf, but too low to afford any shelter to the hardy bird, which seemed positively to rejoice in the fiercest blast that battered on her exposed perch.

We wandered along the side of the loch under the craggy front of Tor Bain, enjoying the exquisite effects of the afternoon sky through the natural pines that crest its summit, as we walked through the remnants of the ancient forest once the glory of the lake and the pride of Strathspey ; on towards the picturesque hill of Creag-an-Chait, or the

Crag of the Wild Cat, with its bold, rocky face, the very name suggesting the wildness of the scene. On our way homewards, we passed the bird unwearied at her maternal duties. Later in the evening, when the dying sunset glorified the pines on Tor Bain and shed a warm glow on the grand mountains beyond, we returned to the spot. After remaining till dusk, retired for the night, admiring the beautiful constancy of the lonely bird, and feeling genuine respect for her kindly guardian, perched in her sight, on the far edge of the loch, his white breast, brighter from the sunset light, revealing his position amidst the darkness of the forest.

On the following morning we were early on the scene. The loch was then as glassy as a mirror, reflection perfect, and the inverted image of the ruined tower in the stainless surface unusually fine. The osprey was alone on the nest, silent and patient as ever. We found the artist and his wife already settled on the beach, evidently painting the castle and its occupant. We skirted the loch along the north and east, opposite Tor Bain, thus making its entire circuit, to catch its varied aspects. The day, however, became less propitious, and it rained a good deal, sending us for shelter under the tall trees, but rewarding us with new effects and refreshing odours. On this side the road winds through a close forest of modern trees, good for the coming axe and saw, but poor compared with the pines that gave name to Rothiemurchus. The views here are interesting and varied, but inferior to those from the other side; for the Cairngorms are distant above you, the castle is distant, and Tor Bain, though picturesque, wants the mass, height, and impressiveness of the greater mountains, which give the loch its special alpine character.

We were again rejoiced by a sight of the male osprey, returned from a kindly foray for his home-bound companion. As we entered the forest we observed him soaring high above Tor Bain, and saw him, after several wide sweeps, descend to his lady-love and lay a fish at her feet. After depositing his gift he retired at once to a tree on the shore, just above the artist group—a pleasing proof of growing confidence in the dreaded human species, their greatest and, perhaps, only enemies in this country. She soon dispatched the prey, and settled down to her wonted repose. After waiting for some time he swept up and down the water in a grand and easy style, and then perched in a tree near us. We watched him for a while from a projecting promontory, and then entering the forest, saw him no more. We continued our walk along the shore till we came to the upper end, where both lochs can be seen from a height that commands an expansive view. Then keeping the Crag of the Wild Cat on our left, we emerged through the ancient pines on Kinrara and the Spey, and left the scene of the eagles' eyrie to its own solitariness. I returned to my distant home, carrying with me indelible memories of its picturesqueness and grandeur, and its rare and attractive tenants. My friend continued regularly to visit the loch, and to watch the happy pair with growing pleasure and interest, which became heightened when two eaglets appeared in the great nest. The solicitude of the mother increased, and the father had to redouble his efforts in foraging for his enlarged home circle; a task for which he was easily competent, though the young creatures devoured an astonishing quantity of food. By-and-by they were fully fledged; and one morning in the beginning of August he found the nest deserted, the whole family having taken flight to distant and unknown regions—to return, it is to be hoped, for many years to come, with renewed confidence as to a secure home in this wild seat of their ancestors, on the old castle tower under the protection of the Cairngorms.

THE FINAL TRIUMPH OF GOOD.

By the BISHOP OF TASMANIA.

ROMANS xii. 21.

IT is part of the purpose of the gospel to proclaim the glad tidings that good will eventually triumph over evil. The end will fulfil the prediction given from the beginning—"The seed of the woman shall bruise (or break) the serpent's head." A glance over the world, over the pages of past history and the records of the Church, and into our own hearts, will show to us the struggle of two great principles for the mastery. To account for this conflict the heathen have everywhere adopted the theory of two divinities, the divinity of good and the divinity of evil. The gospel, which is a revelation of light, has scarcely yet dispelled the heresy that Satan is a co-ordinate, miracle-working, omniscient deity. I lately found a Christian mother reading the "Pilgrim's Progress" to her child; and coming to that part which describes the combat of Christian with Apollyon, the child raised the startling difficulty that, if she tried to be good, and to keep God's commandments, perhaps she might make Apollyon angry! The anecdote from real life shows the necessity of carefully protecting our children from heathen notions, and from the bad habit of investing the impersonation of evil with the attributes that belong exclusively to God.

The work of Christ is to overcome evil, to hurl down Dagon, and to set up the throne of God within the hearts that He has made. By "evil" is meant war with the Will of God; and what aspect of evil can be more alarming than this—that it is war with good, for God is and must be good. All science, i.e. the knowledge of God's laws, by which He governs the universe, teaches us that order means happiness, disorder misery. Obey these laws, and then enjoyment; disobey, and then suffering. The same everlasting law holds in the moral sphere. Let there be disobedience or revolt, then comes disorder and contradiction; let there be obedience, then harmony of the passions and peace of mind. The difference is between what God made us and what we have made *ourselves*; between what we *might* be and what we *are*. It is in perfect harmony with these everlasting distinctions that our Lord has not made faith, or repentance, but obedience, the end of His work. Indeed, the main end of Christ's mission was not to save men, but to unite their wills with the Will that is Divine. It is written, "the soul that sinneth, it shall die;" and this is the verdict, remember, not of vengeance but of unalterable law. It is a matter of necessity, for God is a law unto Himself. Man, unless restored to harmony, must die; must perish, if law be law and God be God. Whatever death may mean, the sinner must *return* to a state of obedience or he must *die*. He must die; not the body's death merely, for all things living *so die*, but the "second death," the death of unrepented sin and blighted hopes; the death that comes from the memory of ill-deeds done and great opportunities lost for ever. It is the death of those who have seen God and cannot live; the death symbolized by the ancients, who pictured the lost as climbing up the trelliswork of Paradise, longing for the fruits and enjoyments they had lost for ever; the death

of souls who, in the words of Holy Scripture, are cast into the outer darkness, beyond the precincts of the banquet chamber, on which is written, "Ye cannot enter in."

In man's *recovery* from his ruin, and his deliverance from the punishment that comes from broken laws, God works still, as ever, by law. Evil in man's moral nature must be overcome by good, as darkness by light, and hatred by love. "God was in Christ, reconciling the world unto Himself." The Father has placed in the hands of His Christ the sceptre of His love and pity, and bid Him sway it over the vast empire of human souls. All the promises and all the preparations before Christ's Advent show this.

From the human cry of the Holy Babe at Bethlehem, from His pure childhood passed in the village home of Nazareth, from the three years of His ministry spent in works of mercy and words of wisdom in the Holy Land, from that entire devotion to His mission which marked every step of our blessed Redeemer's life, giving health to the sick, bread to the hungry, life to the dead, until we see the surrender of His Will on the night of the Agony, and hear on the Cross His prayer for those that reviled Him, what lesson do we learn from it all, but that He was "overcoming evil with good."

There is no other way than this, whether we would be won to God or win our enemies to ourselves. When we are told to overcome evil in our fellow-men by doing them good, we are only asked to do what God does to us. What but this drew to Himself the love and lives of sinful men and women, as Zaccheus the oppressor, the woman convicted of impurity, the Roman captain. So " Christ came not to condemn, but to save;" to win men back to obedience by the proclamation of the free, unconditional forgiveness of the Father, and in the power of His own Love to draw them to the path in which He had Himself led the way.

And now we come to a most deeply interesting question. Have we hope that this mission of the world's Redeemer will succeed? Men are asking, "Lord, are there *few* that shall be saved?" But He does not answer that question. Whether God's purposes of love will eventually so far overcome evil that *all* shall sooner or later yield their wills to God as the Supreme Good is hard for us to pronounce; it is a doctrine favoured by some statements of Holy Scripture, but difficult to reconcile with others.

If we take Holy Scripture for our guide, we must be careful not to read its figurative language in a too literal sense. If we avoid that error, we shall at once get rid of those hard and material views of future sufferings which Roman Catholic and Calvinistic theologies have alike adopted. I could give you parallel passages from the writings of both which shock me for their blasphemous pictures of the physical torments of the finally condemned. I know not how I could smile again if I believed them. "Only conceive," says a popular teacher, in his pictorial language, "that poor wretch in the flames who is saying, 'Oh, for one drop of water to cool my parched tongue!' See how his tongue hangs from between his blistered lips! How it excoriates and burns the roof of his mouth, as if it were a firebrand! . . . I will not picture the scene. Suffice it for me to close up by saying, that the hell of hells will be to thee, poor sinner, the thought that it is to be for ever. . . . When the damned jingle the burning irons of their torments, they shall say, 'for ever!' When they howl, echo cries 'for ever.'" I would place side by side with this picture another drawn by a Roman Catholic writer, but it is too harrowing to contemplate, describing, as it does, the fate of a mere child beating her head against the bars of a red-hot prison.

The truth is that Holy Scripture uses fire figuratively, as the most terrible element we know, to represent the physical, social, and mental misery of those who have deliberately chosen the evil and rejected the good. But this is the point on which I wish to lay stress. If we are compelled to receive such passages as represent this misery in their most literal sense, we must consistently do the same with other passages of a different character, that speak of an *universal restitution* and the final victory of good over evil. Amidst such conflicting testimonies to an universal restoration on the one hand, and never-ending torments on the other, we, as Churchmen, may well rejoice that our Church, true to its rule of taking the teaching of primitive Christianity as its guide, has refused to dogmatize. In the early Church it was held that in the intermediate state which shall intervene between death and the Judgment, the spirits of the good are purified from remaining dregs of evil while they anticipate the perfection of their bliss. But whether the all-loving Father, for Christ's sake, will bring fresh influences upon the impenitent during that interval, or in the endless ages beyond, which shall win them into obedience, it is difficult to show from Holy Scripture. This we know, that unless so won, they cannot be saved or enter Christ's kingdom; that "without holiness no man shall see the Lord;" and that sin unrepented of and unforsaken, must inflict ruin while it lasts. We know that the soul that never turns to God must abide in night, but whether it be a night of bitter memories and a discipline of penal constraint, where souls are punished with the few or many stripes, with whom the discipline of love had hopelessly failed; or whether it be a night from which there is no awakening —the doom of absolute extinction out of God's renovated universe, passed upon souls over which the powers of evil triumphed, it is for none of us to say. Enough for us to know that the God of love cannot be cruel; the God of all the earth cannot but do right, and He whose Name is Love "*will* have all men to be saved." This much, however, we may positively say, that there is nothing in Holy Scripture, and nothing in the teaching of the sub-apostolic age, or in that of the Church of England, to support the popular doctrine, held in common by Romanist and Puritan theologians, of a hell involving endless awful physical torture. As the tongue of Dives was in a flame, and yet his whole body was still in the grave, the language was clearly figurative. The communions that have placed this awful doctrine with the articles of their belief, have done so from a mistaken tendency to cross the limits of human judgment, and so obscure the judgment and character of God. All that revelation, seconded by conscience—"God's vicegerent of the soul in man"—and the moral sense of mankind require of us to believe is this, that "without holiness no man shall see the Lord;" that sin, *i.e.* continued and obstinate disobedience to the everlasting law of righteousness, whether here or hereafter, unless and until it be overcome by love, shall bring with it a terrible condemnation. The condemnation of such a soul shall be "the *pœna damni*, by which the ancients meant the loss of the presence of God and of the beatific vision;" whether in the whole forfeiture of existence, as we suppose it is with the lower creatures, or in the misery of those who choose to remain for ever beyond the reach of good and the softening influences of grace, self-elected to evil, who shall say? Enlightened hope clings to better and more complete triumphs, and looks to a time when there shall be "a restitution of *all things*," and when good shall so far overcome evil that men shall yield their own wills to the supreme good, and "God shall be all in all."

Alas! how little, it must be confessed, does

the present state of the world seem to justify these sanguine hopes! How little, at least, were it not that we believe in an all-loving Will that can subdue *all things* unto itself! We now behold astir a great reaction from popular beliefs, whether in the insupportable pretensions of the Church of Rome or the private interpretations of a reactionary and disorderly Protestantism, rejecting the lawful claims of authority from the domain of religion. It comes more surely still from the degrading conceptions of God, whether mediæval or modern, from which thoughtful men, students of nature, irreligious against their will, are struggling to free themselves. Many of those who have recoiled from popular beliefs find themselves as men bereaved, and shudder as they look to a dismal, impersonal Nature as their teacher, and find her, if I may quote the language of a prominent atheistic writer, "too vast to praise, too inexorable to propitiate; with no ear for prayer, no heart for sympathy, no arm to save." Oh ! what a terrible blank is this, for which wrong ideas of "the God and Father of our Lord Jesus Christ" may be so much to blame ! How many hearts, whom possibly we might have directed and comforted, have been left to cry—

"Ah, welladay, for we are souls bereaved!
Of all the creatures under Heaven's wide cope,
We are most hopeless, who had once most hope,
And most beliefless, who had once believed."

The remedy is the proclamation of the gospel as glad tidings to all men. This bold proclamation of the Church's Creed, "I believe in the forgiveness of sins," opens the heart of man for the infusion of a new blood "which cleanseth from all sin," and makes us holy in our lives, as well as happy in our conscience. This free and unconditional proclamation will put to the credit of God what men are putting to their own credit, viz., their repentance, their faith, their prayers, their penances, their obedience, their offerings and oblations. This love will sanctify each of them, and unduly elevate none. Favouritism, caprice, and cruelty, which belong to heathen deities, and are transferred to our heavenly Father by mediæval and Calvinistic creeds, will cease to shock the conscience of mankind. The love of God will be' welcomed as the air we breathe and the sun which shines. It will encircle the whole earth, and penetrate cot-

tage and palace alike. Baptism will recover its witness to "the forgiveness of sins," and admit, upon the strength of that witness, "every creature" into a state of potential purity. Faith, even with imperfect light, will become *that state of mind* which makes these blessings that flow from forgiveness possible and real. The gaoler who was told, "Believe in the Lord Jesus Christ and thou shalt be saved," had still to be shown "the way of the Lord;" for what did he yet know of Him in whom he was told to believe? Enough at first for him to believe in "the forgiveness of sin." *Repentance* followed in its rightful place—the effect of belief and the consciousness of a forgiven life. "Return unto me, for I have redeemed thee" (Isaiah xliv. 22). "The Lord *hath* put away thy sin" (2 Sam. xii. 13). "I am the Lord; I change not; *therefore* ye sons of Jacob are not consumed."

And, lastly, the doctrine of the "forgiveness of sins," while it places the human affections of faith and repentance in their proper and subordinate relation to it, as "the glad tidings," does not displace from the Christian creed a future judgment. On the contrary, the very fact of an universal pardon and unconditional love makes such a judgment imperative. Judgment is the award to those that put from them God's mercy. They who refuse to accept God's love for love of the present world will hear the sentence, "Behold, ye despisers, and perish !" "The glorious Gospel of the Blessed God has appeared unto *all men*, teaching us that, denying ungodliness and worldly lusts, we should live soberly and righteously and godly in this present world, looking for that blessed hope and the glorious appearing of the great God and our Saviour Jesus Christ, who gave Himself for us, that He might redeem us from all *iniquity*, and purify unto Himself a peculiar people, *zealous of good works*." "These things," adds the inspired writer, "speak, and exhort and rebuke with all authority." That exhortation I have endeavoured to obey. With such a revelation of the Father in Christ, "how shall we escape if we neglect so great salvation?" See how the loadstone of the Cross attracts, "Come unto Me." But *inverted* see how it repels. If the Love that sought us was so great, how shall we dare to obscure it for others or turn from it ourselves?

AN ICE HERO.

II.

ONE of the other three natives on board the schooner was named Peter, and between him and Hans, according to Dr. Hayes, a ludicrous rivalry existed. This at last reached such a height that, one night in November, Peter disappeared and was no more heard of, in spite of the energetic exertions of all on board to discover traces of the missing one. His fate remained a mystery for some months, when his dead body was found in an old deserted Eskimo hut, situated about forty miles south of their winter quarters. His reasons for thus leaving the ship will ever remain a mystery; but Dr. Hayes was decidedly under the impression that Hans was at the bottom of it, and that the lad had deserted in consequence of mysterious hints thrown out by him regarding the intentions of the sailors towards him.

In the search that ensued Hans took a very active and prominent part, and, from his own account, really seems to have felt the loss of his countryman. He writes: "His memory left a deep impression upon me, he being the only friend whom I loved like my brother."

Dr. Hayes himself testifies to the zeal displayed by Hans during the search, and remarks that "he looked the picture of innocence itself, and did not appear to have upon his mind any other thought than that of sorrow for Peter's unhappy condition."

In all probability, the charitable conclusion arrived at by Mr. Sonntag (the astronomer of the expedition) was the correct one: namely, that "Peter, provoked by some slight put upon him by one of the crew, went off to cool his anger at Etah, or in a snow hut."

Should this be the case, the poor fellow's burst of petulance had indeed a tragical termination.

This was not the only fatal event with which our hero was doomed to be connected, the succeeding one being the death of another member of the expedition, his sole companion on a sledging journey.

It happened in this wise. A disease, having the appearance of a species of rabies, broke out amongst the dogs with which Dr. Hayes had been furnished at the Greenland settlements for sledging purposes. This malady invariably ended fatally, and so reduced his team in number that the doctor determined to attempt a communication with a tribe of natives, which Hans declared would be found about a hundred miles to the southward, in the hope that he might be able to replenish his rapidly diminishing pack by purchasing some from these people. With this object in view, Mr. Sonntag left the ship four days before Christmas, in a dog sledge, with Hans as his driver and companion; they carried with them provisions for twelve days. They took no tent, intending to rely solely upon their own skill in the construction of snow huts. The events connected with the death of Mr. Sonntag, which occurred during this journey, are thus alluded to by Hans:—

"We arrived at a small firth and crossed it, but on trying to proceed by land on the other side, it proved impassable, and we were obliged to return to the ice again. On descending here, my companion fell through the ice, which was nothing but a thick sheet of snow and water. I stooped, but was unable to seize him, it being very low tide. As a last resort, I remembered a strap hanging on the sledge poles. This I threw to him, and when he had tied it around his body I pulled, but found it very difficult. At length I succeeded in drawing him up, but he was at the point of freezing to death; and now, in the storm and drifting snow, he took off his clothes and slipped into the sleeping-bag,* whereupon I placed him upon the sledge, and repaired to our last resting-place.

"Our road being very rough, I cried from despair for want of help; but I reached the snow hut, and brought him inside. I was, however, unable to kindle a fire, and was myself overpowered with cold. My companion grew still worse, although placed in the bearskin bag, but with nothing else than his shirt. By-and-by his breathing grew scarcer, and I too began to feel extremely cold, on account of now standing still after having perspired with exertion. During the whole night my friend still breathed, but he drew his breath at long intervals, and towards morning only very rarely. When, finally, I was at the point of freezing to death, I shut up the entrance with snow; and as the breaking up of the ice had rendered any near road to the ship impracticable, and the gale continued violently, I set out

* This sleeping-bag was made of bear's skin.

for the south in search of men, although I had a wide sea to cross."

Although mention of his dissolution is omitted, poor Mr. Sonntag had, ere this, breathed his last. Nothing human, in such a low temperature, could survive the immersion that he was subjected to; more especially as he was unprovided with a change of clothing, and there was no fire by which he could either warm himself or dry his wet and frozen garments. Still, however much we may admire our hero, we cannot fail to be struck with his apparent apathy on this occasion. He does not attempt to chafe the poor sufferer's frozen limbs and thus restore circulation; nor does he seem to have deprived himself of any of his own warm clothing for the relief of his patient. He appears simply to have sat with stolid indifference, until the sufferings of his fellow-traveller terminated in death. This conduct may probably be characteristic of the Eskimo nature. It, however, forms a striking contrast to the noble efforts displayed by those two gallant young officers in Sir George Nares's expedition when attending the poor Dane, Petersen, who was suffering in the same terrible manner as Mr. Sonntag.

On the death of his companion, Hans blocked up the entrance to the hut with blocks of frozen snow, in order to keep off bears and other beasts, and started for the Eskimo settlement, to reach which had been the ultimate object of their journey. His escape from a death similar to that of which he had already been an eye-witness, during this long, lonely, and cheerless drive, seems marvellous, for several times was he almost succumbing from the combined effects of hunger, cold, and exhaustion. Once he was so overcome with weariness, and his dogs so fatigued as to be unable to drag any longer, that he threw himself down in front of a high cliff, awaiting and hoping for death.

"When here I lay prostrate, I uttered, sighing, 'They say that some one on high watches over me too;' and I added, 'Have mercy on me, and save me, if possible, though I am a great sinner. My dear wife and child are in such a pitiful state; may I first be able to bring them to the land of the baptized!' I also pronounced the following prayer:—

'Jesu, lead me by the hand;
While I am here below,
Forsake me not.
If Thou dost not abide with me I shall fall,   ·
But near to Thee I am safe.' "

The repetition of these prayers revived his drooping spirits, and after much suffering he succeeded in reaching the Eskimo settlement,

where he was well looked after and entertained. Thence, instead of returning to the ship to communicate the disastrous result of the journey—although, as he says, he was greatly concerned about his dear wife and child, who were left on board—he travelled farther to the southward, until he reached the tribe whom he had joined, and from which he had taken his wife.

In all probability he was then afraid to return, uncertain as to the reception he would get, and fearful lest he might be suspected of the murder of Mr. Sonntag.

Six weeks elapsed before our hero could sum up sufficient courage to return to his ship; when he did so his welcome by the sailors was anything but a warm one, for they, not unnaturally, attributed the death of their shipmate to a want of attention on the part of Hans. Dr. Hayes, however, with a greater sense of justice, after putting him through a severe cross-examination, sums up in the following words, " It is idle to speculate about the matter; and since Hans's interests were concerned in proving faithful to the officer who, of all those in the ship, cared most for him, it would be unreasonable as well as unjust to suspect him of desertion."

The remainder of Hans's services on board Dr. Hayes's schooner were of an uneventful nature ; he was not employed in any of the sledging expeditions dispatched from the vessel in the spring, and never having succeeded in making himself popular with the men, he was not at all sorry to be landed at Upernivik during the summer, when that port was touched at by Dr. Hayes on his homeward journey.

Here Hans lived a peaceful, quiet life for ten years, sometimes being engaged as a labourer, and sometimes being employed, under the auspices of the priest, in teaching the children at the neighbouring settlement of Kingitok. We may be sure that his spare moments were also devoted to the chase, for Hans was a true sportsman, a keen and successful hunter.

The quiet repose of his life was at last disturbed by the arrival, at Upernivik, of the American exploring ship *Polaris*, in 1871, under the command of the lamented Hall.

In the *Polaris* was Mr. Morton, an officer who had previously served in Dr. Kane's expedition, and was the identical one who, with Hans, had reported the famous discovery of the open Polar Sea!

. On Hans becoming acquainted with this fact, he was easily induced to accept the invitation offered to him by Captain Hall, of accompanying the expedition, especially as he was permitted, as on the last occasion, to take his wife and children. Another Eskimo, who belonged to a tribe living on the west side of Baffin Bay, named Joe, with his wife and child, were also on board the *Polaris*.

The season being a remarkably open one, and the vessel having the advantage of steam-power, a quick run was made northwards up Smith Sound, and on the 2nd of September, they had the satisfaction of knowing that they had carried the American flag farther north by sea than any ship had ever before been. On this date, however, they were stopped by heavy ice, and they were compelled to secure the ship in winter quarters on the east side of the channel in a small indentation of the land, which went by the name of Polaris Bay.

Immediately the winter quarters of the ship was decided upon, the two Eskimos were actively employed scouring the surrounding country in search of game, happily with successful results.

They also accompanied their leader on the last sledging journey that enthusiastic explorer was ever fated to take part in.

It will perhaps be in the recollection of our readers how Captain Hall returned from a reconnoitring expedition to the northward, after an absence from his ship of fourteen days, and how he was almost immediately seized with an apoplectic fit, to which he succumbed in a few days.

The death of their leader was a sore blow to the members of the expedition, who had, previous to his death, been kept together by his cheery spirit and enthusiastic zeal in the cause which he had espoused.

During the summer Mrs. Hans presented her husband with an increase to his family. This little child has the honour of having the most northern birthplace of any known person in the world.

On the break up of the ice in the summer of 1872, the *Polaris* took her departure from Thank God Harbour and steamed down Kennedy Channel. Before getting very far, however, she was entirely beset by the ice, with which she drifted helplessly to the southward. So critical was her position, from the constant nips to which she was exposed, that it was deemed advisable to make such preparations as would guard against fatal consequences to the crew, in case the vessel should be totally destroyed, an event that appeared more than likely. Provisions were accordingly transferred from the ship to a large ice-floe which was pressing against her; fuel and other stores were also deposited on it.

On the 15th of October a furious gale raged, causing the vessel, with the surrounding ice, to drift with great rapidity. The blinding snow-drift that whirled around them wrapped everything in obscurity, whilst the severe blows from the ice and the increased pressure were only too sure indications of a catastrophe which they felt powerless to avert. Preparations were made to abandon the ship at a moment's notice ; nearly everything had been removed to the upper deck, and each man had his little bag of personal effects ready to pass out. During the night the gale increased, and such a pressure was brought to bear upon the vessel that she was raised bodily out of the water and thrown over on her port side. The groaning of her timbers was dreadful to listen to, whilst her sides seemed to be breaking in.

Escape from destruction seemed impossible.

The fury of the storm, the black murky darkness of the night, and the crashing of the ice added to the horrors of the situation.

The loss of the ship appeared inevitable, so the order was given to save as much as possible. Then ensued a busy scene—casks, cases, tins, and packages of all descriptions were thrown out on the ice with great rapidity. Coal, large barrels, boxes, and even beds and bedding were hurriedly disgorged from the ship ; books also, in the hope of being preserved, many containing the valuable observations of the past winter, were also indiscriminately flung out upon the ice. Two boats were also lowered and placed on the floe. Suddenly, whilst the majority of the officers and men were collecting all the articles that had thus been summarily ejected from the ship, and depositing them in a heap together, a more than usually violent gust burst upon them, the ship broke loose from the floe, and in an instant was lost sight of, and nineteen human beings found themselves adrift on an ice-field on a wild stormy night, with no hope of succour, and the bitter miseries attendant on an Arctic winter in their most horrible form staring them in the face.

With these castaways were all the Eskimos belonging to the *Polaris*, and as it will be this party whose fortunes we shall follow, it will be as well to state here that those remaining on board the ship, fourteen in number, succeeded in running their vessel on shore, in a sadly dilapidated condition, the next day ;

A prime shot for Hans.[1]

and that, after spending a second winter near the entrance of Smith Sound, they were eventually rescued by an English whaler and reached America in safety, towards the latter end of the year 1873.

Hans relates their separation from the ship in the following words :—"It was a pitch-dark night, when the ice began moving northward, and the floes were jammed and pushed over each other. At last our ship began to crack terribly from their pressure. I thought she would be crushed.

"On perceiving this we brought our wives and children down upon the ice, and hurried to fetch all our little luggage, and remove the whole to a short distance from the ship. Then the ice broke up close to the vessel, and her cables broke; but in the awful darkness we could only just hear the voices on board, and when the craft was going adrift we believed she was on the point of sinking. Here we were left—ten men, our wives and children, and the Tuluks, making nineteen in all, and having two boats, no boat remaining with the ship. When the others* drifted from us we thought they had gone to the bottom, while we ourselves were in the most

* Those in the ship.

miserable state of sadness and tears. But especially I pitied my poor little wife and her children in the terrible snowstorm. I began thinking : 'Have I searched for this mysel by travelling to the north? But no; we have a merciful Providence to watch over us.' At length our children fell asleep, while we covered them with ox-hides in the frightful snow-drift."

The provisions, on which depended their salvation, were carefully collected together and stored in a snow house, whence the allowance was served out every day by weight. Three other snow huts were built—one for the white men, one for Hans and his family, and one for Joe and his wife and child.

Our hero thus records the construction of his house : "The next day we built a snow hut in the middle of the ice-floe. Fancy! this was to be our settlement for the whole winter."

The sun took its departure on the 28th of October, shedding its rays, for the last time for the space of eighty days, on those helpless beings whose fate it was to be cast away on an ice-floe, at the mercy of drifting currents and cold tempestuous gales.

They spent their days in a simple manner, the greater part of their time being passed in their snow houses. It was too dark to walk about, and it was also too cold. Exercise was avoided as much as possible as a matter of economy, for the greater the amount of exercise, the greater the appetite.

The reliance of the party, however, was firmly fixed on the two native hunters, who, in spite of cold and darkness, were constantly away for hours together searching for seals or bears, and who rarely returned empty-handed. Indeed, it is not too much to say that the white men owed their lives to the skill and ardour of Hans and Joe as hunters, for without their help they would inevitably have perished of starvation.

In this way was the winter of 1872 passed, during which time they were being drifted rapidly to the southward. But as summer approached a new danger threatened them. The increasing warmth of the air and water, and the motion of the latter as they drew near the Atlantic, began to have a perceptible influence upon the floe, which worked and cracked in a most alarming manner. These causes so diminished the floe that on the 1st of April it was found necessary to abandon it and take to the boats. Hans thus alludes to this event: " As we advanced far south, we had a heavy swell, and, in a pitch-dark night, the floe, our refuge, split in two. At length the whole of it was broken up all around our snow huts. When we rose in the morning, and I went outside, the sea had gone down, and the ice upon which stood our house had dwindled down to a little round piece. Wonderful! There must be an all-merciful Father! At last we made up our minds to go in search of land, although none at all was in sight. We started in the boat, which was heavily laden. For some days we pushed on pretty well. When the seas came rolling they looked as if they were going to swallow us up, for which reason at intervals we landed on ice-floes."

At length, after unheard-of sufferings and miraculous escapes from death, in more ways than one, this forlorn party was rescued, on the 30th of April, by the English steamer *Tigress*, employed in the sealing trade. They had been exposed to the vicissitudes of an Arctic winter in its very worst form for a period of 197 days, during which time they had drifted the almost incredible distance of 1,500 miles.

Their rescue seems little less than a miracle!

On the 12th of May the *Tigress* landed the poor wanderers at St. John's, Newfoundland, whence they were conveyed to Washington in the U.S. steamer *Frolic*.

Here Hans for the first time became acquainted with the realities of civilised life; his surprise at everything he saw is easier imagined than described. He says:—

"Here for the first time we saw horses used for draught—a very strange thing indeed to me and my wife and children, though we had heard talk about it."

On their arrival at Washington they were all examined regarding the death of Captain Hall.

"When we had come ashore the officer[*] next in command to the chief of America, questioned me. 'From what sort of disease did All[†] die?' I answered, 'I did not know his sickness quite, but it was similar to stitch; first he improved for a while, but then he had a relapse and suddenly died. When I went to look at him, he tried to grasp his left side. This is all I have to say.' He also asked me, 'What dost thou prefer: to settle down here, or to return home?' I answered, 'I wish to return to Upernivik when I can get an opportunity.' He replied, 'Thou wilt soon return;' and he added, 'Come to my house all of you to-night.' Then, again, we went down a broad staircase below the surface of the earth, where we entered a large room. Here he regaled us, and treated us very politely. He also gave us some images,[‡] his own portrait, and that of the chief."

The description of his first journey by rail is thus related:—

"Then our train arrived, and we took seats in it. When we had started and looked at the ground, it appeared like a river, making us dizzy, and the trembling of the carriage might give you headache. In this way we proceeded, and whenever we approached houses they gave warning by making big whistle sound, and on arriving at the houses they rung a bell and we stopped for a little while. By the way we entered a long cave through the earth, used as a road, and soon after we emerged from it again. At length we reached our goal, and entered a large mansion, in which numbers of people crowded together." He likens the people going out of the railway-station to " a crowd of church-goers, on account of their number."

Hans's stay in America, which lasted some eight or nine weeks, was one continual round of astonishment and pleasure; all with

---

[*] The Secretary of the Navy is here probably meant.
[†] Captain Hall.
[‡] Photographs (?).

whom he came into contact did their utmost to point out and explain the wonders of civilisation to him, and he was kindly and hospitably entertained wherever he went. At length he, with his wife and family, embarked on board a ship in which they were safely carried to Greenland, when Hans again settled down to his ordinary quiet life at Upernivik.

What wondrous tales he must have had to narrate to an admiring and astonished, but almost incredulous, Eskimo audience. Not of his hair-breadth escapes in the far north, or his miraculous drift on an ice-floe—these would be thought every-day occurrences by his hearers, and would scarcely be listened to with interest—but of the wonderful large houses in which the white men dwelt, their enormous cities, the railways running through the bowels of the earth, and, above all, the horses, cows, and sheep, with other strange animals that he had seen; the stories of these marvellous things would indeed excite their wonder and test their credulity.

Hans was not allowed to remain long undisturbed, for less than two years after his return to Upernivik, the English Arctic expedition, under Sir George Nares, arrived at that port on its way northwards, and Hans readily complied with the wish of Sir George that he should accompany the expedition. As an Eskimo, named Freddy, had already been entered on board the *Alert*, Hans was shipped as one of the crew of the *Discovery*. On this occasion he was unaccompanied by his wife and family; his parting with them is thus touchingly expressed:—

"But as I was now going to depart, I pitied my wife and my little children, who were so attached to me, especially my only son, who would not cease crying, as he preferred me to his mother. Thereupon I left Kangersuatsiak, making my fourth visit to the north with the Tuluks.* When we put to sea, and I looked at the people on shore through the spy-glass, I discovered my little daughter, Sophia Elizabeth, lying prostrate on the top of a big stone and staring at us. It was a sad sight, which made me shed tears from pity. But I felt consoled by thinking that if no mischief should happen me or her, we should meet again. I also got sight of my wife standing amongst the crowd and looking after us. I said to myself, with a sigh, 'May I return to them in good health!'"

The progress of the ships through Smith Sound until their winter quarters were reached

is so well known, and has already been described in GOOD WORDS, that it is unnecessary here to revert to it.

The winter quarters of the *Discovery* were situated a few miles farther north than the position in which the *Polaris* had passed her first winter.

Whilst the officers and ship's company of the *Discovery* were busily engaged in the multifarious duties connected with the preparations for an Arctic winter, our hero was scouring the adjacent hills for musk oxen, hares, and other game, and with such good and successful results as to be able to furnish his shipmates with several fresh meat meals during the long winter that ensued.

In the spring and summer of 1876 Hans did good sledging work, being employed on several journeys with the dogs. During one of these trips he visited the *Alert*, and thus had an opportunity of renewing his acquaintance with the other Eskimo, Freddy, who, he says, "appeared to him like a brother." He was afterwards employed on the opposite coast of Greenland, where his skill and energy as a hunter tended very materially to restore the health of Lieutenant Beaumont's scurvy-stricken party. His conduct on this occasion deserves the highest praise.

On the return of the expedition to the southward, Hans was landed at Disco, as was also his companion Freddy. Here he was allowed to reside, and was very kindly treated by the Inspector, at whose instigation he was induced to write the interesting memoir, a brief *résumé* of which we have here attempted to sketch. This is alluded to by Hans, for, in concluding his little book, he says, referring to the Inspector, "He desired me to write what I had seen, and though unskilled in composition, I have tried to give this account of my voyages while engaged thrice with the Americans and once with the Tuluks.* Four times in all I travelled to the north. And now I bid farewell to all who have read my little tale. I minded my business, sometimes under hardships, sometimes happy. May all who read this live happily in the name of the Lord! Written in the year 1877."

Hans Hendrik is now employed as boatswain and labourer at one of the Greenland settlements, his principal duties being the conveyance of oil and skins from various parts of the coast to one or other of the storehouses established at each of the settlements. The accumulation of the pay that

---

* White men.

* In this instance meaning British.

he received whilst in the service of the Americans and English amounted to a considerable sum, which, being put out at interest, gives our hero a very comfortable competence ; indeed, Hans may be regarded as a very wealthy Greenlander. Let us hope he will long live to enjoy the little fortune which he so richly deserves, and which he acquired at so much self-sacrifice, and at the risk of great dangers.

ALBERT HASTINGS MARKHAM.

THE POETRY OF THE SCOTTISH HIGHLANDS.

A Lecture delivered at Oxford

BY PRINCIPAL SHAIRP, LL.D.

I.—THE OSSIANIC POETRY.

IT is strange to think how long, and up to how late a date, the world of the Scottish Gael lay outside of the political and the intellectual life not only of England, but even of their neighbours, the Scottish Lowlanders. From the time A.D. 1411, when on the field of Harlaw it was finally decided whether Celt or Saxon should rule in Scotland, down to the time of Montrose and Claverhouse, that is for two centuries and a half, the Highlanders lay almost unheeded within their own mountains, except when by some marauding or avenging raid they made their existence for a moment felt beyond them. The first appearance of the clans in modern history took place when they rose in defence of the dethroned Stuarts, and enabled Montrose to triumph at Inverlochy, Viscount Dundee at Killiecrankie. When they rose again in the same cause in the Fifteen and the Forty-five, especially in the latter, they so alarmed the minds of English politicians, that in the rebound after the victory of Culloden these exacted from the helpless Gael a bloody vengeance, which is one of the darkest pages in England's history. During the century when the Gael were throwing themselves with all their native ardour into the political struggle, they were making no impression on England's literature. This was first done nearly twenty years after the Forty-five, when James MacPherson published his translation of the so-called " Epics of Ossian." Of the great storm of controversy which MacPherson's Ossian awakened, I shall say nothing at present. But whether we regard the Ossianic Poems as genuine productions of the ancient Gael, or fabrications of MacPherson, there cannot be a doubt that in their publication the Gael for the first time came forward, and were recognised on the field not only of England's but of Europe's literature. Henceforth Highland scenery and Celtic feeling entered as a conscious element into the poetry of England and of other nations, and touched them with something of its peculiar sentiment. How real and penetrating this influence was let the eloquent words of Mr. Arnold in his delightful lectures on Celtic Literature declare. " The Celts are the prime authors of this vein of piercing regret and passion, of this Titanism in poetry. A famous book, MacPherson's Ossian, carried in the last century this vein like a flood of lava through Europe. I am not going to criticize MacPherson's Ossian here. Make the part of what is forged, modern, tawdry, spurious, in the book, as large as you please; strip Scotland, if you like, of every feather of borrowed plumes which, on the strength of MacPherson's Ossian, she may have stolen from that *vetus et major Scotia*—Ireland ; I make no objection. But there will still be left in the book a residue with the very soul of the Celtic genius in it ; and which has the proud distinction of having brought this soul of the Celtic genius into contact with the nations of modern Europe, and enriched all our poetry by it. Woody Morven, and echoing Lora, and Selma with its silent halls ! we all owe them a debt of gratitude, and when we are unjust enough to forget it, may the Muse forget us ! Choose any one of the better passages in MacPherson's Ossian, and you can see, even at this time of day, what an apparition of newness and of power such a strain must have been in the eighteenth century."

In his work on " The Study of Celtic Literature," from which I have just quoted, Mr. Arnold lays his finger with his peculiar power on the Celtic element which exists in the English nature, and shows how it is the dash of Celtic blood in English veins, which has given to it some of its finest, if least recognised quality; how the commingling of Celtic sentiment and sensibility with Saxon steadiness and method has leavened our literature. I know nothing finer in criticism than the subtle and admirable tact with which he traces the way in which the presence of Celtic sentiment has heightened and spiritualised the genius of our best poets, has added to the imagination of Shakespeare a magic charm which is not found even in the finest words of Goethe. This line of thought, true and interesting as it is, has reference to the unconscious influence of the Celtic spirit on Englishmen, who never once, perhaps, thought or cared for anything Celtic. It would be a humbler and more obvious task to trace how the direct and conscious infiltration of the Celtic genius from the time of MacPherson's Ossian has told on our modern poets. But from this I must refrain to-day; and in what remains confine myself strictly to the Gael of the Scottish Highlands and their poetry. I shall not venture to speak of the Celts in general, much less of that very abstract thing called "Celtism." For Celt is a very wide word, covers several very distinct peoples with very marked differences.

What is true of the poetry of Wales is not true of the poetry of Ireland. What is true of the poetry of Ireland cannot be said of the poetry of the Scottish Gael. In all our talk about Celts, let us never forget that there are two main divisions of the great Celtic race—the Cymri and the Gael. Each of the two great branches had its own distinct cycle of legends—or myths, if you choose—on which were founded their earliest heroic songs or ballads. The story of Arthur and his knights sprang from the Cymri, and had its root probably in some vicissitudes of their early history, when the Saxons invaded their country and drove them to the western shores of Britain. Latin chroniclers and French minstrels took up the history of their doings, and handed it on, transformed in character and invested with all the hues of mediæval chivalry. It is, in fact, an old Cymric legend, seen by us through the haze which centuries of chivalric sentiment have interposed. But, however transfigured, vestiges of the Arthurian story linger to this day in all lands where descendants of the Cymri still dwell—in Brittany, in Cornwall, in Wales, in the old Cymric kingdom of Strath-Clyde. Merlin lies buried at Drummelzier on Tweed; Guenvre at Meigle, close to the foot of the so-called Grampians; Arthur's northernmost battle was fought, according to Mr. Skene, near the foot of Loch Lomond. But there all traces of Arthur cease; beyond the Highland line he never penetrated.

That Highland line, namely, the moun-tain barrier which stretches from Ben Lomond in a north-eastern direction to the Cairn-gorms, and the Deeside Mountains, encloses a whole world of legend as native to the Gael of Scotland and Ireland as the Arthurian legend is to the lands of the Cymri. Where Arthur's story ends, that of Fion and his Feinne begins. Within that mountain barrier, all the Highlands of Perthshire, of Inverness-shire, and of Argyll are fragrant with memories of an old heroic race, called the Feinne, or Fianntainean. Not a glen, hardly a mountain, but contains some rock, or knoll, or cairn, or cave, named from Fenian warriors, who people those mountains like a family of ghosts. The language of the native Gael abounds with allusions to them, their names are familiar in proverbs used at this hour.

Who were these Feinne? To what age did they belong? Mr. Skene, our highest authority on all Celtic subjects, replies that they were one of those races which came from Lochlan, and preceded the Milesian Scots, both in Erin and in Alban. Lochlan is the ancient name given in Irish annals to that part of North Germany which lies between the mouths of the Rhine and the Elbe, before the name was transferred to Scandinavia. From that North German sea-board came the earliest race that peopled Ireland, and Alban or the Scottish Highlands. During their occupation, Ireland and the north of Scotland were regarded as one territory, and the population passed freely from one island to the other at a time "when race, not territory, was the great bond of association." Hence it came that the deeds and memories of this one warrior race belong equally to both countries. Each has its songs about the Fenian heroes; each has its local names taken from these, its "Fenian topography." The question, therefore, often agitated, whether the Fenian poetry belongs of right to Ireland or to Scotland, is a futile one. It belongs equally to both, for it sprang from the doings and achievements of one warrior race, which occupied both lands indifferently. I leave Ireland to speak for itself, as it does very effectually through the lectures of the late Professor O'Curry, and other native writers. In the Western Highlands, I may say, in the words of Mr. Skene, "The mountains, streams, and lakes are everywhere redolent of names connected with the heroes and actions of the Feinne, and show that a body of popular legends, whether in poetry or prose, arising out of these, and preserved by oral recitation, must have existed in the country where this topography sprang up." But whether the events associated with particular local names originally happened in Scotland or in Ireland must be left undetermined.

That songs about the Feinne, which had never been committed to writing, had been preserved from time out of mind by oral recitation among the native Gael, no candid man who has examined the question can doubt. Yet the great Dr. Johnson would not believe this on any evidence. But as one among innumerable witnesses tells us, "It was the constant amusement or occupation of the Highlanders in the winter time to go by turns to each others' houses in every village, either to recite, or hear recited or sung, the poems of Ossian, and other songs and poems." Almost all the native Gael could recite some parts of these, but there were professed Seannachies, or persons of unusual power of memory, who could go on repeating Fenian poems for two or three whole nights continuously. I myself have known men who have often heard five hundred lines of Fenian poetry recited on end at one time.

A little after the middle of the last century, when James MacPherson began his wanderings in search of such songs, the Highlands were full of such Ossianic poetry, and of men who could recite it. I am not going to retail the oft-told history of MacPherson's marvellous proceedings, much less to plunge into the interminable jungle of the Ossianic controversy. Those who may desire to see the facts clearly stated will find this done in Mr. Skene's Introduction to the book of the "Dean of Lismore," published in 1862, and in the very clear and candid Dissertation prefixed by Dr. Clerk to his new and literal translation of the Gaelic Ossian, published in 1870. I endeavoured myself to give a condensed view of the present state of the question in a paper published in *Macmillan's Magazine*, in June, 1871. Since this last date new contributions have been made to the subject, especially by the publication of Mr. J. F. Campbell's "Book of the Feinne," in which he advocates a view entirely opposed to that taken in the three publications already named. Without at all entering into the controversy I shall just note the crucial point round which the whole question turns. MacPherson published in 1762 an English translation of Fingal, an epic which he attributed to Ossian. The next year, 1763, he published Temora, another Ossianic epic. On the appearance of these two epics the controversy broke out. MacPherson never published the Gaelic originals while he lived, but he left them in MS., and after many vicissitudes they were published by the Highland Society in 1807. There these two now lie side by side, the English and the Gaelic Ossian, and the question is which of the two is the original, which the translation. Mr. Skene and Dr. Clerk strongly maintain that the Gaelic shows undoubted signs of being the original, and the English of being a translation. These two are among the most eminent Gaelic scholars now alive. On the other hand Mr. J. F. Campbell, an ardent collector of Gaelic tales and antique things, if not so accurate a Gaelic scholar as the former two, contends as strongly for the English being the original, from which he says the Gaelic has evidently been translated. Again, supposing, with Mr. Skene and Dr. Clerk, that the Gaelic is the original, who composed the Gaelic? Among those who agree in holding the Gaelic to be the original, there are two divergent opinions. Some hold that the Gaelic was mainly the composition of MacPherson, who incorporated into it here and there certain ancient fragments, but composed the larger portion of it himself. They further believed that when he had thus composed the Gaelic, he rendered it into the stately, if sometimes tawdry, English, which we know as Ossian. Others maintain that by far the larger portion of the Gaelic is ancient, and that MacPherson supplied only a few passages here and there to link together his ancient originals. Hardly any one, however, is prepared to argue that the long epics of Fingal and Temora came down from a remote antiquity in the exact form in which MacPherson published them. The piecing together of fragments, often ill-adjusted and incongruous, is too transparent to allow of this.

The English and the Gaelic Ossian, as I said, lie before us. Is it too much to hope that criticism may yet decide the question? that some future Porson or Bentley may yet arise, who shall apply to the documents the best critical acumen, and pronounce a verdict which shall be final, as to which of the two is the original, which the translation. If some one were to assert that he had discovered a lost book of Homer, and were to publish it with an English translation, the resources of Greek scholarship are quite competent to settle whether the Greek were authentic or a forgery. Why should not Gaelic scholarship achieve as much? But even if we were to cancel all that has passed through MacPherson's hands, whether Gaelic or English, enough still is left of Ossianic poetry, both in the Dean of Lismore's book, that dates from early in the sixteenth century, and also in the gleanings of other collectors, whose honesty has never been questioned, to prove that the whole Highlands were formerly saturated with heroic songs about the Feinne, and to enable us to know what were the characteristics of this Fenian poetry. I believe that the last reciters of such poetry have scarcely yet died out in the remoter Hebrides.

Who was this Ossian, and when did he live? His exact date or even century we cannot name; but the undoubtedly genuine fragments refer to a very dim foretime, even to the centuries when Christianity was yet young, and was struggling for existence against old Paganism in Erin and in Alba.

The conception of Ossian, not only in MacPherson, but in the oldest fragments and in universal Highland tradition, is one and uniform. He is the proto-bard, the first and greatest of all the bards. Himself the son of the great Fenian king Fion, or Finn, and a warrior in his youth, he survived all his kindred, and was left alone, blind and forlorn, with nothing but the memories of the men he loved to cheer him. There he sits in his empty hall, with the dusky wilderness around him, listening to the winds that sigh through the grey cairns, and to the streams that roar down from the mountains. No longer can he see the morning spread upon the hill-tops, nor the mists as they come down upon their flanks. But in these mists he believes that the spirits of his fathers and his lost comrades dwell, and often they revisit him waking or in dreams. One only comfort is left him, Malvina, the betrothed of his hero son, Oscar, who had early fallen in battle; and the best consolation she can minister is to raise her voice in the joy of song. As the sightless old man sat in the last warmth of the setting sun, the days of other years would come back to him, and he would sing a tale of the times of old. And his song was of his father Fion, the king of the Fenians, and of his deeds of prowess when he led on his peers to battle against the invading hosts of Lochlan. These peers were the "great Cuchullin with his war chariot, the brown-haired and beautiful Diarmid, slayer of the boar by which himself was slain, the strong and valiant Gaul, son of Movni, the rash Conan—a Celtic Thersites—the hardy Ryno, the swift and gallant Cailta." These all stand out before the imagination of the Gael as individual in their deeds and their characters, as did the Homeric heroes before the minds of the Greeks. All of them died before Ossian, and, most pathetic of all, Oscar, his own son, the pride and hope of the Feinne, died, treacherously slain in the first bloom of his youth and valour.

As a sample of the average Ossianic style, let me give a few lines of one of those fragments which MacPherson published in 1760. These he translated before he knew they would have any literary value, and before he brought out his epics, so that, as Mr. Skene says, there is little reason to doubt that they are genuine ancient fragments. The one I am about to give he afterwards incorporated as an episode in the first book of "Fingal," but this version is the literal unadorned rendering of Dr. Clerk.

A warrior, called Du-chomar, meets a maiden, called Morna, alone on the hill, and thus addresses her—

> "'Morna, most lovely among women,
>   Graceful daughter of Cormac,
> Why by thyself in the circle of stones,
> In hollow of the rock, on the hill alone?
> Streams are sounding around thee;
> The aged tree is moaning in the wind;
> Trouble is on yonder loch;
> Clouds darken round the mountain tops;
> Thyself art like snow on the hill—
> Thy waving hair like mist of Cromla,
> Curling upwards on the Ben,
> 'Neath gleaming of the sun from the west;
> Thy soft bosom like the white rock
> On bank of Brano of foaming streams.'
>
> "Then said the maid of loveliest locks,
> 'Whence art thou, grimmest among men?
> Gloomy always was thy brow;
> Red is now thine eye, and boding ill.
> Sawest thou Swaran on the ocean?
> What hast thou heard about the foe?'"
> *   *   *   *   *

He replies that he has seen or heard nothing, and then goes on—

> "'Cormac's daughter of fairest mien,
>   As my soul is my love to thee.'
> *   *   *   *   *
> 'Du-chomar,' said the gentle maiden,
> 'No spark of love have I for thee;
> Dark is thy brow, darker thy spirit;
> But unto thee, son of Armin, my love,
> Brave Cabad, Morna cleaves to thee.
> Like gleaming of the sun are thy locks,
> When rises the mist of the mountain.
> Has Cabad, the prince, been seen by thee,
> Young gallant, travelling the hills?
> The daughter of Cormac, O hero brave,
> Waits the return of her love from the chase.'
>
> "'Long shalt thou wait, O Morna,'
>   Said Du-chomar, dark and stern—
> 'Long shalt thou wait, O Morna,
> For the fiery son of Armin.

Look at this blade of cleanest sweep—
To its very hilt sprang Cabad's blood.
The strong hero has fallen by my hand;
Long shalt thou wait, O Morna.
I will raise a stone o'er thy beloved.
Daughter of Cormac of blue shields,
Bend on Du-chomar thine eye;
His hand is as thunder of the mountain.'

"'Has the son of Armin fallen in death?'
Exclaimed the maiden with voice of love—
'Has he fallen on the mountain high,
The brave one, fairest of the people?
Leader of the strong ones in the chase,
Foe of cleaving blows to ocean strangers?
Dark is Du-chomar in his wrath;
Bloody to me is thy hand;
Mine enemy thou art, but reach me the sword—
Dear to me is Cabad and his blood.'"

He gives her the sword, she plunges it in his breast. Falling, he entreats her to draw the sword from his wound. As she approaches he slays her.

One of the standing arguments used by Dr. Johnson and others, to prove that MacPherson's Ossian was a shameless imposture, was the generosity, the nobility of nature, and the delicacy and refinement of sentiment which pervade those poems attributed to Fingal and his comrades, who must have been, if they lived when they were said to have lived, ferocious savages. This, no doubt, was a natural objection. But one fact is worth a world of such hypothesis. Here is the description of Finn, as it is found in one of the fragments of Ossianic song, about which no doubt can be raised, for it has been preserved in the book of the Dean of Lismore, and that was written about 1520. The fragment when thus written down by the Dean was attributed to Ossian, who then was reckoned a poet of unknown antiquity. The following is the bare literal translation of it:—

" Both poet and chief,
Braver than kings,
Firm chief of the Feinne,
Lord of all lands.
Foremost always,
Generous, just,
Despised a lie.
Of vigorous deeds,
First in song,
A righteous judge,
Polished his mien,
Who knew but victory.
All men's trust,
Of noble mind,
Of ready deeds,
To women mild,
Three hundred battles
He bravely fought.
With miser's mind
Withheld from none.
Anything false
His lips never spake.

He never grudged,
No, never, Finn.
The sun ne'er saw king
Who him excelled.
Good man was Finn,
Good man was he;
No gifts ever given
Like his so free."

This may not be very great poetry, but it is an image of noble manhood.

I do not know how much acquaintance even with MacPherson's English I may reckon on in my present audience. If I thought that many who hear me had even a very moderate acquaintance with it, I should shrink from quoting, or even alluding to, the well-known address or hymn to the Sun, as being quite a commonplace with students of Ossian. But the passage is so remarkable in itself, and is of such undoubted antiquity, having been recovered from many other sources besides MacPherson, that I shall venture to presume on the ignorance of some present, and once more to quote it :—

"O thou that travellest on high,
Round as the warrior's hard full shield,
Whence thy brightness without gloom,
Thy light that is lasting, O sun?
Thou comest forth strong in thy beauty,
And the stars conceal their path,
The moon, all pale, forsakes the sky,
To hide herself in the western wave;
Thou, in thy journey art alone;
Who will dare draw nigh to thee?
The oak falls from the lofty crag;
The rock falls in crumbling decay;
Ebbs and flows the ocean;
The moon is lost aloft in the heaven;
Thou alone dost triumph evermore,
In gladness of light all thine own.

"When tempest blackens round the world
In fierce thunder and dreadful lightning,
Thou, in thy beauty, wilt look forth on the storm,
Laughing mid the uproar of the skies.
To me thy light is vain,
Never more shall I see thy face,
Spreading thy waving golden-yellow hair
In the east on the face of the clouds,
Nor when thou tremblest in the west,
At thy dusky doors, on the ocean.

"And perchance thou art even as I,
At seasons strong, at seasons without strength,
Our years, descending from the sky
Together hasting to their close.
Joy be upon thee then, O sun!
Since, in thy youth, thou art strong, O chief."

This hymn to the Sun marks the highest reach of the Ossianic poetry; if I may venture to say so, only a little below the description of the Sun in the opening verses of the 19th Psalm.

I wish I could go on to give more specimens of this ancient poetry, for there are many more to give. This only I will now say, that the people who in a rude age could create poetry like that, and could so love it as to preserve it from generation to generation in their memories, merit surely some better fate than the contempt and ill-treatment they have too often received from their prosaic Saxon neighbours.

I have throughout indicated that I regard the body of Ossianic poetry, which belongs partly to the Scottish Highlands, partly to Ireland, as a genuine ancient growth. Even were we to set down all that MacPherson published as fabricated by himself, we should still have in the fragments preserved in the Dean of Lismore's book, in those collected by the Highland Society, and in pieces gathered by other collectors of undoubted veracity, enough to prove that it belonged to a remote antiquity. How remote I do not venture to say, only I am inclined to believe that it belonged to a time far back beyond the mediæval age. Neither have I said a word as to the existence of one Ossian. Mr. Skene has distinguished three separate and successive stages in the creation of this poetry. At each stage it assumed a different form.

In its oldest form there are pure poems of a heroic character, each poem complete in itself, and formed on a metrical system of alliteration and of rhyme, or correspondence of vowels. For the other two forms I must refer to Mr. Skene's Introduction. The poems of the oldest form are attributed to one mythic poet; but whether one or many, I should suppose that there must originally have been one master-spirit who struck the key-note of a poetry containing so much that was original, exalted, and unique.

It remains now only to notice its chief characteristics.

The exquisite, penetrating sensibility which has been so often noted as the basis of Celtic character, is fully reflected in these Ossianic poems. That quickness to see, quickness to feel, lively perceptions, deep, overpowering, all-absorbing emotions, this which is the exact opposite of the tough, heavy, phlegmatic Saxon temperament, is found nowhere more powerfully than in the Scottish Gael, and in that early poetry which rose out of their deepest nature, and has since greatly reacted on it. This liveliness of eye and sensitiveness of heart have been noted as main elements of genius, and no doubt they are.

One side of this sensibility is great openness to joy—a sprightly, vivacious nature,

loving dance and song; the other side is equal openness to melancholy, to despondency. Gleams intensely bright, glooms intensely dark—exaltations, agonies—these are the staple of the Gael's existence, and of his poetry.

Turned on human life, this high-toned sensibility makes the Gael, in poetry as well as in practice, venerate heroes, cling to the heroic through all vicissitudes; never mind though the heroes fall, die, and disappear, still he remains faithful to their memories, loves these, and only these. This fervid devotion to the memory of all the Fenian warriors whom he had known, is a characteristic note in Ossian, but it becomes a quite passionate tenderness towards "the household hearts that were his own," towards his father Fion, his brother Fillan, his son Oscar. The laments he pours over this latter exceed in their piercing tenderness anything in Greek or Roman poetry, and recall some Hebrew strains.

These feelings of devotion to their chiefs, and tenacity of affection to their kindred, which we find in their most ancient poetry, reappear in the Gael throughout all their history, down to the present hour.

Again, this same sensibility made a lofty ideal of life quite natural to the Gael, even before Christianity had reached him; made his heart open to the admiration of the generous and the noble, and imparted a quite peculiar delicacy of sentiment and courtesy of manner—qualities which, even after all he has undergone, have not yet forsaken him. These qualities enter largely into the Ossianic ideal. It is wonderful how free from all grossness these poems are, how great purity pervades them. There is, of course, the dark side to this picture: ferocity of vengeance when enraged, recklessness of human life. As the counterpart of this devotion to the high and the heroic, is the Gael's aversion to the commonplace routine of life, his contempt for the mechanical trades and arts. To this day the native Gael in his own glens thinks all occupations but that of the soldier, the hunter, and, perhaps, the shepherd, unworthy of him. He carries down to the present hour something of the Ossianic conception which recognises only the warrior and the hunter.

Turned upon nature, this penetrating sensibility is quick to seize the outward aspect of things, but does not rest there, cannot be satisfied with a mere homely realism; is not even content with the picturesque attitude of things, but penetrates easily, rapidly to the secret of the object, finds its affinity to the soul; in fact, spiritualises it. This is that power of "natural magic" which Mr. Arnold makes so much of in his book on Celtic literature. The impressionable Gael were from the earliest time greatly under the power of the ever-changing aspects of earth and sky. The bright side is in his poetry: the sunrise on the mountains, the sunset on the ocean, the softness of moonlight, all are there touched with exceeding delicacy. But more frequently still in Ossian, as befitted his country and his circumstances, the melancholy side of nature predominates. His poetry is full of natural images taken straight from the wilderness, the brown heath, the thistle-down on the autumn air, the dark mountain cairns, the sighing winds, the movements of mist and clouds—these are for ever recurring in impressive monotony. Even to this day, when one is alone in the loneliest places of the Highlands, in the wilderness where no man is, on the desolate moor of Rannoch, or among the grey boulders of Badenoch, when

> "the loneliness
> Loadeth the heart, the desert tires the eye,"

at such a time, if one wished a language to express the feeling that weighs upon the heart, where would one turn to find it? Not to Scott; not to Wordsworth, though the power of hills was with him, if with any modern. Not in these, but in the voice of Cona alone would the heart find a language that would relieve it. It is this fact, that there is something which is of the very essence of the Highland glens and mountains, something unattained by any modern poet, which the old Ossianic poetry alone expresses—this, if

nothing else, would convince me that the poetry which does so is no modern fabrication, but is native to the hills, connatural, I had almost said, with the granite mountains among which it is found.

Lastly, this sadness of tone in describing nature is still more deeply apparent when the Gaelic poet touches on the destiny of his race. That race, high-spirited, impetuous, war-loving, proud, once covered a great portion of Europe. It has been for ages pushed westward before a younger advancing race, till now and for centuries they have retained only the westernmost promontories and islands. To these they still cling, as limpets to their rocks, and feel, as they gaze wistfully on the Atlantic ocean, that beyond it the majority of their race has already gone, and that they, the remnant, are doomed soon to follow or to disappear.

> "Cha till, cha till, cha till mi tuille."
>
> "I return, I return, I return no more."

This is the deepest feeling in the heart of the modern Gael; this is the mournful, ever-recurring undertone of the Ossianic poetry. It is the sentiment of a despairing and a disappearing race, a sentiment of deeper sadness than any the prosperous Saxon can know.

These two facts are enough. The truthfulness with which this old poetry reflects the melancholy aspects of Highland scenery, the equal truthfulness with which it expresses the prevailing sentiment of the Gael and his sad sense of his people's destiny, these two internal witnesses are enough. I need no other proofs that the Ossianic poetry is a primitive formation, and comes from the ancient heart of the Gaelic race.

GETHSEMANE.

I WILL go into dark Gethsemane,
    In the night when none can see;
I will kneel by the side of Christ my Lord,
    And He will kneel down with me.

I will bow my head, for I may not look
    On that brow with its bloody dew,
Nor into those eyes of awful pain,
    With the dread cross shining through.

Then my soul rose up, as a man will rise
    Who hath high, stern words to speak,
And said, " Now what wilt thou do by Him
    With that sweat on brow and cheek?

" Canst thou drink from the cup He proffers thee?
    Canst thou quaff it at a breath?
For the dregs are sorrow and scorn and shame,
    The crown of thorns and death.

" Stand thou from afar, for thou canst not know
    That hour in Gethsemane.
Thou canst only know, in thine own dim way,
    That He strove that night for thee."

So I stand afar, and I bow my head;
    But I dare not look into those eyes,
Whose depths have the depths of the night around,
    With the starlight in the skies.

And my soul, as a friend will talk to a friend,
    Still whispers and speaks unto me,
"'Thou canst only know in thine own dim way
    That hour in Gethsemane."   ALEXANDER ANDERSON.

HEALTH AT HOME.

BY B. W. RICHARDSON, M.D., F.R.S.

PART III.

V.

FROM the floors of the bedroom, which were considered in my last paper, we may pass to the walls and ceiling. These should be covered in every case in such a manner that they may be at any time effectively cleaned at as little possible expense and trouble as is possible. We have been accustomed for a long series of years past to use papers for the covering of bedroom walls, and in the shops for the sale of wall-papers it is the usual thing for the salesman to offer for inspection a distinct series of bedroom papers, the patterns of the paper and the quality of the papers being specially displayed in order to meet the tastes of the purchasers. There is no doubt that extremely beautiful and artistic papers are to be bought, but for my part I object to paper altogether in the bedroom. Paper has one recommendation, that of presenting for selection a variety, and it may be a beauty of pattern, and at first this is an enticing suggestion. After a short time, however, the most beautiful pattern causes weariness. The sight every night and morning of just the same lines and series of objects, so many groups, so many figures, so many flowers, so many singular or imaginary designs, becomes in a short time a wearisome process, and in the bedroom is often intolerable. This sameness, which becomes an objection even to a handsome paper, is a minor objection when it is compared with others which have to be mentioned. In some instances the paper itself is unwholesome owing to the surface of it containing arsenic, which, having been used for colouring purposes, is given off in fine dust, is disseminated through the air, and is breathed by the occupant of the room to his decided injury. The common view held on this subject is that the papers called flock papers, and papers of green colour, are those only which give off arsenical dust; but this is not strictly true, for Dr. Leonard Sedgwick found that a blue paper gave off arsenical dust into a bedroom, and that for a long time the sleepers in the room were suffering from the irritation caused by arsenic without discerning the true cause. They suffered from irritation of the throat, from dyspepsia, and from considerable *malaise* until the cause was discovered and removed.

Of course it would not be difficult to select in every case a paper for the walls of the bedroom which is quite free of arsenic, and as the trouble and expense of such proof is comparatively slight, I do not dwell on this objection with any pertinacity, I name it merely as an objection of an accidental kind which cannot fairly be omitted.

The argument usually offered for the adoption of paper as a wall covering is the economical argument that the paper lasts so long. Once put up it is not necessary to touch the wall again with a new covering for five or even seven years. In some leases and agreements there is a clause directing that the walls shall be papered every five or seven years, and the tenant makes it a point never to do more at any rate than just carry out the said agreement. The paper being once up on the walls looks clean and nice. "It will last another year very well." It is getting dingy certainly, but then it is such a nuisance to have in the paper-hanger, and go through the worry of emptying the room for him. So month after month the long doomed paper is allowed to hang until from actual necessity it is removed and replaced, or re-covered with a new paper.

Imperceptibly, but surely, a room, the walls of which are covered from year to year with the same paper, is a room the air of which is dirty, so that the very temptations to delay renewal, and the very arguments of economy, become the strongest of objections to papers altogether. When the air of the room is damp the paper gets damp. In the damp state it absorbs readily the dust that is in the air. When the weather gets dry and warm, or when the room is warmed by a fire, the dust becomes dry on the paper, and is then easily wafted and distributed through the air of the room, while if the paper be at all rough or raised the small irregular spaces are at all times receptacles for dust. This is a strong objection to the paper covering for the wall.

A final objection to the paper covering is the mode in which it is put on the walls. As a common practice layer is laid on layer until six or seven or more layers are sometimes put one over the other. And I have recently seen a room stripped of no fewer than ten layers of paper before the wall was reached. By this plan the room becomes lined with coating after coating of paste, which in course of time is decomposed, is turned into fine organic dust, and is itself, whenever the paper is torn away so as to allow of an escape of dust, a decided source of danger to health. Let sickness take place in a room the walls of which are treated in the manner now described; let the particles of the poison of a contagious disease disseminate in such a room, and almost of a certainty some minute portion of the particular poison will be cased up behind the new paper that is laid on, to remain a source of danger for after occupants of the room for years and years to come.

For these reasons, and I think they are sound and good, I think the common system of paper for the walls of the bedroom is not the best. If a paper could be invented which, once laid on, would present a permanent surface, and a surface that would admit of

systematic cleansing by means of soap and water or by dry scrubbing, then I should not have a word to say against it, and such an invention will, I should hope, one day be brought into common use.

The nearest approach I have ever seen to perfect success in the direction named was in a room in the house of my good friend Dr. Thursfield, of Leamington. Dr. Thursfield had a room very carefully papered with a good fine paper of oak pattern. This paper he coated with coachmakers' varnish until the complete surface was in truth as hard as the panel of a carriage itself. This wall could be washed with the greatest ease, and was as perfect as need be. Sometimes in the halls and on the staircases of houses we see oak and marble papers which are varnished, and which bear to be washed very well, but I have never seen those walls so perfect as the walls of the room I specially name, and certainly I have seen no approach to anything of the kind within a room.

Presuming that paper is used for the walls of a bedroom, there are certain rules which ought to be followed in respect to the process. The first of these is that the paper selected should not be a flock paper; next, it ought not to have a raised or rough surface; thirdly, the pattern should be of the plainest possible kind, and, if I may so express it, patternless; the colour should be grey or a sea-green; and lastly, the paper should be frequently renewed — it should be changed every three years at least. Moreover, in changing the paper there should be no slipshod method of putting on a new paper before the removal of the old. The old paper should be entirely stripped off, the wall should be well cleansed of dry paste, and the new paper should be put on with paste that is quite fresh and pure. The introduction of a little alum into the paste is always good practice.

In cases where a person has suffered from any one of the contagious diseases, and has occupied a room the walls of which are covered with paper, there should be no hesitation, when the room is relieved of its occupant, in clearing every particle of paper from the wall at once, also making the clearance as complete as possible. I usually direct, in those cases, that the paper, while it is still on the wall, should be saturated with water that is at boiling heat, the water being applied with a small flannel or woollen mop. In this manner two purposes are served : the heat disinfects, and the paper is made to peel off with great readiness and completeness. When the paper is thus removed down to the solid walls, the walls may be fumigated with sulphurous acid vapour and afterwards washed down, sponged, and allowed to dry. After such cleansing the new paper may be laid on, the ceiling having been previously cleansed and coloured.

If paper be not used for the covering of the wall of the bedroom recourse may be had to one or other of the following plans.

In a newly-built house there can be no better outlay than that which would be devoted to the plan of making the walls of the bedroom quite impermeable and smooth, by covering them with a firm cement like parian. The walls ought to be made so readily cleansable that they can at any time be scalded and washed, just as a piece of crockery can be scalded and washed. The simple plain surface is better than the tiled surface; it is more easily cleansed, and it does not weary by a pattern that is immovable. It has been objected to this plan that when it is adopted the wall becomes covered with moisture whenever the air is charged with moisture. The objection would be sound if the air must, by necessity, be so charged with moisture as to produce the effect stated; but, in truth, this ought not to be the case. If the air of a room is so damp that water will condense on the walls it does not signify whether those walls be permeable or impermeable, for the air will be damp all the same. The only difference will be in what is seen. If the walls be impermeable the condensed water will be visible, and will run down the walls, whereby it will be known as a fact that the air is, or has been, loaded with moisture. If the walls be coated with a permeable substance the water, truly, will not be seen, but it will be there all the same, for it will have passed into the permeable covering of the walls, and will remain until it is given up again to the air of the room as a drier time or season arrives. We may observe this fact well illustrated from the looking-glasses in a damp room, or from the moisture on a damp permeable wall. The wall may seem as dry as a bone, but the glass may be so covered with moisture that there is no reflection at all from it. The wall here is not less damp than the glass, but it holds the damp, and is, therefore, the more dangerous. Supposing, then, that a room with an impermeable wall shows signs of moisture on the wall, the evidence is definite that such a room is not properly ventilated, or that water vapour has access to it, or that it is so cold that water easily condenses upon it; whereupon the effort should

be, not to make the wall porous, but to keep the air of the room warm and dry.

In houses that are already built and that have simply plaster walls, the plan of covering the walls with an impermeable cement may be too expensive or otherwise undesireable. In these instances we may have recourse to paints or to distemper; ordinary old-fashioned lead paint for walls, when it is laid on properly and is of best quality, is always good. It is expensive at first, but it is very durable; it admits of ready cleansing, and when it is well varnished the surface of it may be washed many times without injury. If the paint has been simply flatted it may also be washed very often, provided that neither soda nor other alkaline substance be used with the water. I have, within the last nine years, used the new substance called silicate paint with much advantage for the bedroom wall. This paint gives, I think, a little more trouble than the ordinary lead paints in its application, and many painters are much prejudiced against it. One of these who was working for me was, indeed, so opposed to the use of the silicate paint that he actually threw up his tools and went away, leaving the men who were working under him without a leader. Nevertheless I let the work go on, and a better result could not have been wished for. The extra trouble with the silicate paint lies in the fact that it does not "cover," to use the term that is employed by the artisan. Two layers of the ordinary sound lead paint are, they say, equivalent to four of the silicate. The paint also has to be laid on with more care than the lead paint to prevent it from showing the lines caused by the brush. When, however, it is completely laid on and the requisite number of layers are applied so as to cover thoroughly, it yields a surface which is at once fine, impermeable, and clean. The surface can be washed with soap and water as freely as if it were a surface of cement, and, as far as I can see, so far it wears effectually. With these advantages the objections of the workmen pass away, and they ought to be fairly considered by the workmen themselves, seeing that in the use of the silicate paint the health is not endangered. The risk of being poisoned by the lead which is present in the lead paints, to which from long custom the workman so rigidly pins his faith, does not exist.

If neither paper nor paint be used for the bedroom wall, there remains the old and simple plan of colouring with distemper, and really, after all, this cheap and easy method is as good as any. Distemper colour is wholesome as a covering, it is cheap, and it suggests more than paper does, a frequent renewal.

It is worth noting that in instances where the wall has been covered with paper, and where the paper is not broken or torn away at any part, and where, for any reason, it is not felt to be desirable to remove the paper, one or two coats of distemper may be laid on the paper after a coating of size as a preliminary. If the paper be smooth the pattern of it will entirely be covered by the wash; if the paper be not smooth—if, I mean, it has on it a raised pattern—the distemper will give an outline of the pattern which, though quite distinct, is not disagreeable to the sight.

Whatever be the substance used for covering the wall, whether lead paint, silicate paint, or distemper, the colour should, I think, be the same as was suggested for paper, namely, a light green, what is, I believe, called a "sea-green" colour. This colour, taking it all in all, is more pleasant to the sight, as a colour to be regularly gazed at. When the eye meets it on awaking it offers no resistance or sense of unpleasantness, and it bears to be looked at more frequently than other colours. In this respect it resembles the grass of the fields, the verdure of the forest, and the surface of the sea. After the green, grey, or russet red colour is most to be desired.

While I have advocated a perfectly plain surface for the walls of the bedroom—that is to say, an absence from anything like a staring permanent pattern—I would earnestly encourage the ornamentation of the walls by objects of good art that are easily removed and changed. Good pictures, statuettes, and other ornaments are excellent in the bedroom. At the same time it is wise and wholesome practice to break the uniformity of decoration from time to time. The health of the body is very much modified by the tone and turn of the mind, and whatever creates a pleasurable diversion of mind, however simple it may be, is wholesome to the body not less than to the mind itself.

The ceiling of the bedroom is the next consideration after the walls. This should be attended to more frequently than is customary in most households. The ceiling should be coloured regularly once a year at least, either with ordinary white or lime-wash, with distemper, or with zinc white. Zinc white, which has lately been introduced by Mr. Griffiths, as a paint, answers excellently for ceilings; it covers well, gives a smooth surface, and is very little more expensive than common lime-wash. The colour of the bed-room ceiling should not be pure white, it should be slightly toned towards blue or green.

The bedroom is now lighted, ventilated, warmed, floored, and carpeted, and its walls are coloured, and, it may be, decorated. It is ready to receive its furniture, and to the furniture we will therefore direct our attention.

FURNITURE, BEDS, AND BEDDING.

It may be taken as a general rule that a bedroom should have in it the least possible amount of furniture, and that whatever furniture there is in it should be as free as possible of all that can hold dust and fluff.

I cannot do better than commence what I have to say concerning beds and bedding by protesting against the double bed. The system of having beds in which two persons can sleep is always, to some extent, unhealthy. No two persons are so constituted as to sleep naturally under the same weight of bedclothes and on the same kind of bed or mattress. But sleep to be perfect and profound and restorative should be so prepared for, that not a single discomfort should interrupt it. A good illustration of the fact to which I am directing attention is shown at the Industrial Schools at Annerley. The visitor to those schools, in which children most unhealthily born are reared into a condition of health which is singularly good, and which seems to prove that even hereditary evils may be educated out of the body almost in one generation—the visitor to those schools will find in the dormitories there that each child has its own little bed. It will be asked perhaps—in fact, I heard it asked—whether this plan is not very expensive and troublesome, causing double bed-making, double bed-airing, double laundry work, and double cost of bed linen and coverings. Well, the reply was, that there is an extra cost in regard to those particulars, but that, on the whole, there is an untold saving in relation to health. The children rise from their beds really refreshed and in every way better for the separate occupation. In this manner the sick list is kept free to a great extent; and as one sick child in its infirmary sick-couch is an anxiety by night as well as by day, and as one sick child confined to its bed by its sickness is more trouble and anxiety than half-a-dozen healthy children occupying each a separate bed during sleeping hours, there is a positive saving of trouble and of expense in the course of the year from the practice of the single-bed system. It is not difficult to discover the reason of the saving of health. The fact that no two persons are constituted to require the same kind of clothes and the same kind of bedding has been already adverted to, to which may be added the further fact that no children or persons can sleep under the same covering without one being a cause of some discomfort to the other, by movement, position, or drag of clothing. Beyond these discomforts, moreover, there is the question of emanations from the breath. At some time or other the breath of one of the sleepers must, in some degree, affect the other; the breath is heavy, disagreeable, it may be so intolerable that in waking hours, when the senses are alive to it, it would be sickening, soon after a short exposure to it. Here in bed with the senses locked up the disagreeable odour may not be realised, but assuredly because it is not detected it is not less injurious.

I need not pursue this subject much further, common sense will tell everybody who will reflect on the subject with common sense that I am correct, and that it is best for persons of every age to have to themselves the shelter within which they pass one-third of their whole lives—thirty years of life if they live to be ninety years old. I dwell, therefore, only on one point more in favour of the single bed, and that is to enforce the lesson that under the single-bed system it is rendered impossible to place very old and very young persons to sleep together. To the young this is a positive blessing, for there is no practice more deleterious to them than to sleep with the aged. The vital warmth that is so essential for their growth and development is robbed from them by the aged, and they are enfeebled at a time when they are least able to bear the enfeeblement.

The single bed for every sleeper determined on, the size of the bedstead and the number of bedsteads in the room, according to space, should be considered. For ordinary adult persons the bedstead need not exceed 3 feet 6 inches in width by 6 feet 6 inches in length; and in no room, however well it may be ventilated, should a bedstead be placed in less than a thousand cubic feet of breathing space. A bedroom with two single beds should not measure less than 16 feet long by 12 feet wide and 11 feet high. There are some sanitarians who would not be satisfied with those dimensions for a room to be occupied by two persons, and I frankly admit the dimensions are close to the minimum, though with good ventilation they may, I think, suffice. With bad ventilation they are confessedly out of court, and I name them

merely for the sake of meeting the necessities of the limited bedroom space that pertains to the houses of great cities. In my own mind I do not consider twice the amount of space named at all too much, even with the ventilation as free as I have suggested in previous chapters of this essay.

There can be no mistake that the bedstead should be constructed of metal, of iron or brass, or of a combination of those metals. Wooden bedsteads are altogether out of date in healthy houses. They are not cleanly, they harbour the unclean, and they are not cleansible like a metal framework. The framework of the bed should be so constructed that the bed or mattress is raised two feet from the floor of the room, and the whole framework should be steady and so well knit together that the movements of the sleeper shall cause neither creaking nor vibration.

A good deal of controversy has been raised on the matter of curtains for beds. From the old system of curtains all round the bed, like a tent, there has been a reaction to an entire abolition of the curtains. I am of opinion that this complete change is not beneficial. Two light side head-curtains, with a curtain at the back of the head and a small tester, are, I think, very good parts of a bedstead. The curtains fulfil a doubly useful purpose; they shield the head and face of the sleeper from draughts, and they enable the sleeper to shut out the direct light from the window without in any way necessitating him to shut the light out at the window itself. The room may be filled with light, and yet the sleeper may be shielded from the direct action of it upon his eyes if he have the curtain as a shield.

The kind of bed on which the body should rest is a question on which there is extreme divergence of opinion. Whenever we leave our own bed to go to sleep elsewhere, in an hotel or in the house of a friend, it is almost certain we shall find a bed differing from that to which we are accustomed. We may find a bed of down so soft that to drop into it is like dropping into light dough; we may find a soft feather bed, or a soft mattress, or a spring mattress, a moderately hard mattress, or a mattress as hard, I had nearly said, as the plank bed for which our prisons are now so unenviably notorious. These differences are determined by the taste of the owner of the bed without much reference to principle, or to the likings of any one else in the world; not a very good or satisfactory state of things. There ought to be some principle for guidance in a trial so solemn as that which settles the mode in which our bodies shall rest for a third of our mortal existence.

I fear it is hard to fix on definite principles, but there is one principle, at any rate, which may be relied on, and which, when it is understood, goes a long way towards solving the question of the best kind of bed for all sleepers. The principle is, that the bed, whatever it be made of, should be so flexible, if I may use the term, that all parts of the body may rest upon it equally. It ought to adapt itself to the outline of the body in whatever position the body may be placed. The very hard mattress which yields nothing, and which makes the body rest on two or three points of corporeal surface, is at once excluded from use by this principle, and I know of no imposition that ought to be excluded more rigorously. On the other hand, the bed that is so soft that the body is enveloped in it, though it may be very luxurious, is too oppressive, hot, and enfeebling; it keeps up a regular fever which cannot fail to exhaust both physical and mental energies, and at the same time it really does not adapt itself perfectly to the outline of the body.

The best kind of bed, taking everything into consideration, is one of two kinds. A fairly soft feather bed laid upon a soft horsehair mattress, or a thin mattress laid upon one of the elastic steel-spring beds which have lately been so ingeniously constructed of small connected springs that yield in a wave-like manner to every motion. It is against my inclination to try to write out the time-honoured old feather bed and mattress, but I am forced to state that the new steel-spring bed is, of necessity, the bed of the future. It fulfils every intention of flexibility; it is durable; it goes with the bedstead, as an actual part of it, and it can never be a nest or receptacle of contagion or impurity.

On the subject of bed-clothes, the points that have most to be enforced are that heavy bed-clothing is always a mistake, and that weight in no true sense means warmth. The light down quilts or coverlets which are now coming into general use are the greatest improvements that have been made, in our time, in regard to bed-clothes. One of these quilts takes well the place of two blankets, and they cause much less fatigue from weight than layer upon layer of blanket covering.

As to the actual quantity of clothes which should be on the sleeper, I can lay down no rule of numbers or quantities, because different people require such different amounts. I can, nevertheless, offer one very good practice which every person can learn to apply. It should be the rule to learn so to adapt the clothing that the body is never cold and never hot while under the clothes. The first rule is usually followed, and need not be dwelt on; the last is too commonly broken. It is a practice too easily acquired to sleep under so much clothing that the body becomes excessively heated, feverishly heated. This condition gives rise to exhaustion, to disturbing dreams, to headache, to dyspepsia, and to constipation. It is so injurious that it is better to learn to sleep with even too little than with too much clothing over the body. This, specially, is true for the young and the vigorous. It is less true for the old, but in them it holds good in a modified degree.

The position of the bed in the bedroom is of moment. The foot of the bed to the fireplace is the best arrangement when it can be carried out. The bed should be away from the door, so that the door does not open upon it, and it should never, if it can be helped, be between the door and the fire. If the head of the bed can be placed to the east, so that the body lies in the line of the earth's motion, I think it is in the best position for the sleeper.

The furniture of the bedroom, other than the bed, should be of the simplest kind. The chairs should be uncovered, and free from stuffing of woollen or other material; the wardrobe should have closely fitting doors; the utensils should have closely fitting covers; and everything that can in any way gather dust should be carefully excluded.

In a word, the bedroom, the room for the third of this mortal life, and that third the most helpless, should be a sanctuary of cleanliness and order, in which no injurious exhalation can remain for a moment, and no trace of uncleanliness offend a single sense.

(To be continued.)

THE HAUNTED GLEN.

'TWAS on a summer's evening,
　　Just darkening was the sky,
That through Glen Tanar homeward rode
　　My little steed and I.

Around us stretched the moorland
　　In many a purple fold;
Before us rushed a sparkling burn,
　　All bubbling, white, and cold.

The scene was such as would right well
  The artist's brush repay;
The glen was wild and picturesque,
  On all sides beauty lay.

Anon, as I was musing
  Upon the good in store
For hungry man and hungry beast,
  Who soon should fast no more,

My little steed pricked up his ears,
  And as he roughly shied,
I, waking from my hungry trance,
  His cause for fear espied.

Across the burn were passing
  A herd of fine red deer;
In countless numbers on they passed
  Over the waters clear.

With wondering eye I watched them,
  Much puzzled when I found
That as they crossed the rushing burn
  They made no splashing sound.

In perfect silence on they passed
  In never-ending stream;
So strange a thing it seemed to me,
  Methought it was a dream.

At length I called them loudly,
  But never turned they round.
I called again; they showed no sign
  That they had heard the sound.

I looked again; their number
  Seemed never to decrease;
It was the gloaming, and I wished
  Their silent march would cease.

The sight was unaccountable;
  It made my flesh to creep,
And in the lonely glen I felt
  I could no longer keep.

So while the herd still streamed across
  The merry, laughing burn,
I spurred my gallant little steed,
  And made him homeward turn.

Arrived at home I kept my tale
  A secret in my breast,
For fear lest I a laughing-stock
  Should be to all the rest.

But much I pondered thereupon,
  Yet could not make it clear,

Nor understand whence came that herd
  Of never-ending deer.

* * * *

'Twas some time after that I rode
  Once more in Tanar Glen;
A friend was riding by my side,
  The moon rose o'er the fen.

" Know you that 'tis the ' Haunted Glen '
  Through which we ride to-night?"
The question greatly startled me,
  Heard in the still moonlight.

" I knew it not, my friend," I said;
  " Yet *I* could tell a tale
Of what with mine own eyes I've seen
  In this same Tanar vale.

" But tell me what the spirits are
  Which here are wont to roam?
Unless so weird, 'twill make us wish
  We both were safe at home!"

" It is no tale of horror,"
  With smile my friend replied.
" The ghosts of all the red deer killed
  Upon this mountain-side

" Are said to haunt this lonely glen,
  And often have been seen,
Though not by me, by those I know.
  True is the tale, I ween."

Now much I marvelled at the news,
  And marvelled, too, my friend,
When I described the herd *I*'d seen
  Of red deer without end.

We looked across the little burn;
  No deer were then in sight;
Perhaps their spirits stay at home
  When the moon shines so bright.

But some day, in the gloaming,
  We'll through Glen Tanar ride,
Once more to see the spirits
  Of all the deer who've died,

A death of pain and terror,
  By hand of cruel man.
My tale is true; like me, my friends,
  Make of it what you can.*

EMILY GRACE HARDING.

---

* This ghost story is a true one; the vision of the red deer
having been actually seen by a nobleman in Scotland, in the
manner above described, he not being aware at the time that
the glen was popularly known to be haunted by the spirits of
the slaughtered red deer.

SARAH DE BERENGER.

By JEAN INGELOW.

CHAPTER XII.

THE return of Amias had, indeed, followed closely on the conclusion of an exciting occurrence.

It was Thursday evening; Felix always had full service then, and a sermon.

This was the favourite religious occasion of the week, and (except during the harvest) very well attended: a time-honoured institution, the ringers ushered it in with a cheerful peal. Then, when days were long, the outlying hamlets, and not unfrequently the adjacent parishes, contributed their worshippers; and even some people from the little town (former parishioners of Felix) would walk over to join, and see how he fared. Then every old woman, as she came clattering up the brick aisle, felt some harmless pride in herself; she knew she must be welcome, helping to swell the congregation. She looked at Felix, as he stood gravely waiting at the desk, and he looked at her.

Then were given out long-winded hymns, dear to all the people. Then the rustic choir broke out into manifold quavers, and sang with a will. Then shrill, sweet voices of children answered, and farmers' wives put in like quavers (but more genteelly), while the farmers themselves, and the farmers' men, did their share with a gruff heartiness not untuneful. Then, also, the "Methody folk," having no "Bethel" of their own, came to church, and expressed their assent to the more penitential prayers by an audible sigh and an occasional groan. They said of Felix that he was a gracious young man, and knew how to hit hard; which two qualities they considered to be strictly harmonious.

But his own people gave him a good word

as well. He had inherited this service from his predecessor, and finding it at a convenient hour and popular, kept it up with loyal and dutiful care. They said of him that "he had no pride; he didn't mind shouting for a poor man. Preached just as loud and just as long, he did, in bad weather, when he had nobbut a few old creeturs and poor Simon Graves the cripple for congregation, as when the most chiefest draper and his lady walked over from the town to attend, as well as Mr. Pritchard the retired druggist, that kept his own gig, and was said to be worth some thousands of pounds."

It is hardly needful to record that Felix did not find the singing ridiculous. It was far from perfect praise, but he supposed it must be more acceptable than city music led by an organ and sung by a paid choir.

There is something very pathetic in the worship of the poor and rustic. They often think they oblige the clergyman by coming to church. And the old have a touching humbleness about them; they feel a sincere sense of how worthless they are in this world, which they could hardly have attained unless the young had helped them to it. The rich mix the world with their prayers, so do the poor thus—they feel that they come and say them with their betters.

So this was a Thursday evening. Felix felt the solemn sweetness of the hour. It was a clear, hot time of year, and all the doors and windows were open. He had an unusually large congregation, and had just mounted into the pulpit and given out his text, when, to the astonishment of the people, instead of beginning to preach, he stood bolt upright for an instant; then his eyes, as it seemed involuntarily, fell on Mrs. Snaith (who sat just facing him) with a look of such significance that she instantly started up and rushed out at the chancel door.

She thought of the little girls, naturally; what had she in life but them?

The amazed congregation gaped at him. He turned to the schoolmistress, and saying, "Keep all those children in their places," closed his Bible, and exclaimed to the people generally, "My friends, remember that there are fire-buckets under the tower, and that the nearest water is in my pond. Mrs. Snaith's cottage is on fire."

The red light from it was already flaring high, and making pink the whitewashed walls and his gown. It had passed for a sunset flush, till from his height he saw what it meant, and saw the two little girls running hand in hand down the dusty lane, with loose hair flying. They were making their way, clad only in their white night-gowns, towards the church, for there they doubtless knew that Mamsey was.

Thanks to the way in which he had arranged his sentence, the mass of the people, as they rushed out of church, ran round to the tower, and when he himself descended, he met the two little girls, neither hurt nor frightened, running up to the door. Each had a great doll—her best doll—under one arm; but when they saw him, with childish modesty they sat down on a grassy grave, and tucked their little feet into their gowns. It was such a very hot night that there was no risk of their taking harm from their evening excursion. Not that any one thought of that, or thought much about them, excepting Felix, who, fearing that Mrs. Snaith might not have seen them, and might risk her life for their sake, followed on after her at the top of his speed, leaving them behind with his aunt Sarah.

"Yes!" exclaimed Sarah, when describing the scene afterwards to Amias. "There are occasions when decorum and dignity are forgotten. If you had seen what Felix looked like, rushing down the lane with his surplice flying!" An exaggerated owl suggested itself, or a ghost pursued by its creditors. These are the things that give Dissenters such a hold when they cry out for Disestablishment. However, by the time he overtook the clerk he had got it off; he flung it over the old man's arm, who folded it up and laid it on the grass under a fir-tree.

Felix on this occasion found little scope for the exercise of courage, and no opportunity of giving aid. The dry thatch was sending out an even breadth of flame to the very middle of the road; there was (as he supposed) no approaching. There was great shouting; women as well as men were eagerly handing on fire-buckets, while he searched the crowd for Mrs. Snaith, and was told, to his amazement, that she was inside the blazing premises. He had scarcely heard it when she emerged from them with a box under her arm. He and Mr. Bolton advanced to help her forward. Her gown was smoking, and some buckets of water were thrown all over them without ceremony, as their bearers, running up with them from the pond, saw the state of the case. Mr. Bolton, dripping as he was, could not forbear to moralise. "Now didn't I tell you, ma'am, 'twas too late? Your things were all alight. This is one of the occasions

"Felix had scarcely heard the words, when Mrs. Snaith emerged from the burning house with a box under her arm."

Page 290.

when folks may·be glad their goods ain't worth much, 'stead of risking their precious lives to save them. Sit down, there's a good creature," he continued, as he and Felix conducted her to a grassy bank.

Mrs. Snaith put a small box into the hands of Felix, then sat down and wiped her face.

" Your gown's no better than tinder," continued Mr. Bolton, taking a mean advantage of her inability to answer. " Choked a'most, I can see. And you've got me a good suit of clothes spoilt very near, and the water, that's black as ink, running over me and Mr. de Berenger, and right into our shoes, just because you must needs save your Sunday bonnet. There's nothing better in that box, I'll be bound. And I did tell you your Windsor chairs were safe outside, before ever we got out of church, and your eight-day clock, and your best fender and fire-irons. Here he gave himself a shake, and a pool of water enlarged itself at his feet.

" Let her alone," said Felix compassionately. " She thought the children were inside."

" No, sir," said Mrs. Snaith, recovering her voice, " I didn't."

Having thus dissipated his sympathy, she got back her box from him, and he also felt for the first time how wet he was. He, too, felt inclined to moralise.

A good many buckets of water had by this time been flung at the fire, but it seemed to send all out in steam again, and before even a straw of the thatch was wet, and just as the sunset flush faded, all that had once been a habitation had gone up or gone down. It *was not*. A thick black cloud of pungent smoke brooded still among the trees, and a soft wet heap of ashes was lying in the garden. The shouting and excitement were over. It had been a very old cottage, and built of wood and plaster; dry weather had made the thatch ready for a spark,'which had come from the chimney. Well, it had been a strange thing to see how fast it had melted down, or with what a rage of haste the flame and smoke of it had ascended; but, after all, the people considered it had not been what any one could call a tragical sight: nobody was injured, and there was hardly any property in it worth mentioning.

Felix was a little hoarse the next morning, after his wetting, when Mrs. Snaith knocked at his study door and asked if she might speak with him.

She and her children had slept at the rectory; her eight-day clock had been accommodated in the kitchen, and was diligently ticking and striking against the clock of the house. Her Windsor chairs, also her fender and fire-irons, some bedding and a few toys, were disposed about a large empty room. No need to apologize for their presence in it ; they made it look more habitable.

These things had been saved by the first man who discovered the fire, and who had carried the two little girls down-stairs before he gave the alarm.

Mrs. Snaith, over and above a sort of contrition for the trouble her goods had caused in their burning—or saving, as the case might be—was much vexed at the drenching Mr. de Berenger had got, and the cold it had evidently given him.

Felix had fortunately been only arrayed at the time in a rusty old camlet cassock ; it was still in course of being slowly dried at the kitchen fire. Jolliffe said it could take no damage ; it was past that. This was a secret source of comfort to Mrs. Snaith. But she longed to explain matters, and she wanted to know what had been done with her box. As Felix opened the door to let her enter, she felt a certain hint of disapproval in his voice, hoarse though it was.

" If you please, sir," she began, " might I see if the things in my box are safe ?"

" Oh, your box," he answered, looking about him. " What did I do with it ? There it is—just inside the fender. You risked a great deal for that box, Mrs. Snaith."

He was sitting now at his writing-table, and, pointing with his pen at the scorched and smoky article, was surprised to see the eagerness with which she darted upon it, as she replied, " Well, yes, sir ; but what else could I do ? If I'd lost that, I should never have 'forgave myself. I didn't ought to have kept it in the copper, but I thought it was a safe place, too."

She set it on the table before him.

· " This is a sort of thing that people call a bandbox, is it not?" he inquired. " You surely kept nothing valuable in it?"

" Yes, sir, I did. I thought, in case of thieves, they would never think of looking in a bandbox for what I'd got. It's full of papers and things, sir. All I have for maintaining the children, and schooling them, and that."

Felix was struck with astonishment when she opened it and began to lay its contents before him.

" Why, this is property !" he exclaimed,

taking up a paper. "This is a United
States bond, payable to bearer. If this had
been burnt the money it brings in would
have been lost, forfeited, and, as far as I
know, irreclaimable."

"Yes, I know, sir. I was fully warned."

"By whom?"

Mrs. Snaith was not to be caught; she
made an evident pause here, choosing her
words.

"By him that gave them over to me, sir.
He advised me to turn them into another
kind of property as soon as I could. But I
never could exactly make out how. And
I was afraid it might be found out."

She stopped and coloured, as if vexed with
herself, when she had said these last words.
He made as if he had not heard them; and
she had such trust in him, and in his gentle
manhood, that, observing this, she felt safe
again, as if she had not made that little slip
of the tongue.

"Where is the list? You have a list of
the papers, of course," continued Felix; and
he had scarcely any doubt that he should be
shown his cousin John De Berenger's handwriting.

"I have no list, sir."

Felix, full of surprise, paused again. He
had set a chair for her opposite to himself,
and as she took out paper after paper, and
handed them to him across the narrow table,
he received each and scanned it with curiosity and interest.

"Would you like me to make a list for
you?" he said at last.

"I should be much obliged to you, sir.
Most of them have numbers—I've noticed
that; and I have some of the numbers in my
memory."

"Do I understand that no list, even of
the numbers, was given you?"

"No, sir," she replied, as if apologizing
for the donor. "It were a rather hasty thing,
and a legal document cost money."

"A legal document! Well, Mrs. Snaith"
—here he paused; he would not mention a
name, she having so carefully and pointedly
refrained from doing so —"well, Mrs.
Snaith, _he_ showed great confidence in you
that gave these papers over to your charge."

"He hadn't any choice, sir," she put in,
but rather faintly. ("I'll be bound he
hadn't!" thought Felix.) And she continued
her sentence, "And it was no more than my
due to have them."

"Still, as I said, it was a great mark of
confidence," continued Felix, "and far be it
from me to show less. But I may say, and

I do, that it was a strange act of imprudence
in you to keep this property by you in such
a form, specially though (as you admit) you
were expressly warned not to do so. Since
you lived here you have, as I remember,
taken a journey several times. Did you
carry this box with you?"

"Yes, sir; I went to get what they call
the dividends paid. I feared to think I ought
not to trouble _you_ about this, but now you
have come to know——"

"Well, Mrs. Snaith?"

"Perhaps you wouldn't mind the trouble
of letting me understand how to turn them
into something safer — invest them over
again. You see, sir, if I were to die, it
would be very awkward."

"Very, indeed," said Felix, gravely; "because, for anything that appears to the contrary, this property is absolutely yours; so
that, if you died, not a shilling of it could
be claimed for the children. I say," he continued, seeing her look amazed, "that the
two children, being no relation to you, could
not, in case of your death, claim to possess
what is only payable to Hannah Snaith.
Your own relations might claim it, you see,
and the children would actually be cut out."

Mrs. Snaith, on hearing this, turned extremely pale. She saw that she herself was,
in case she died, so acting as to cut her children out of the money which she only cared
to have for their sake. What had she not
sacrificed already for them? How should she
learn to do anything more?

"But surely there is a will," continued
Felix, the strangeness of John's supposed
conduct growing on him. "No doubt,
though you may not be aware of it, some
other person, some other guardian, must have
been appointed to meet such a case."

Mrs. Snaith, still very pale, was silent. If
she had only said so much as "I do not
know," he would have been better satisfied.

"I take for granted that the person,
whoever he was, that made over this property to you, did so in full confidence that
it would be faithfully spent on and for these
children."

To this appeal she still made no reply. She
had for some time seen no cause to fear that
her wretched husband would ever find her;
she had left behind her, at present divided
among her own relations, so much of the income as she felt it her duty to let him take,
and she meant the children to inherit the
remainder. "I may die any day," was the
thought now pressing on her, "and so sure as
I die, they would advertise for my relations,

let them have it, and, unless they found out the truth, which would be still worse, my dears would be left penniless."

"Sir," she said at last, "if it please the Lord, I hope I shall live to see my—dear—young ladies grow up."

The slight, the undefinable air of disapproval daunted her. She was so much puzzled, so much agitated by the perception of how nearly she had lost everything, and by his remark as to the children not being related to her, that she had no intelligence at liberty for noticing that disapproval was an odd sensation for a man to exhibit concerning a matter that was no affair of his. Still less did she think of Sir Samuel's former notion, as perhaps shared by Felix. She never doubted that the old man had received a letter from his son, which had set the matter at rest. She often thought he had gone away because he was proudly angry that he ever should have been so deceived, and should have demeaned himself to come and question her.

There was Sarah, to be sure—the children were still allowed to call her Coz—but Sarah was so inconsequent, so wrong-headed, that she and her doings hardly seemed to count.

"I have been very foolish, I own, sir," she said at last, in a tone of apology, for, as has just been explained, the reason of his disapproval was hidden from her. "What do you think it would be best for me to do now?"

"I am not a very good man of business," Felix answered, "but I think this property could not be invested in the names of the two children—only by guardians or trustees, for their benefit." Then he paused to think. "I am the more likely to be right in this notion, because it has not been done already; but I can easily ascertain. If you consent to its being invested for them," he continued, "I will agree to be one of the guardians, you being the other."

Amazing kindness! remarkable condescension! Mrs. Snaith could not hear it and keep her seat. She rose and curtsied. "Sir, you are very kind; I am deeply obliged to you," she answered, very highly flattered, and also very much flustered. "I never could have hoped for such goodness; but it's just like you, sir."

Why was it "like" in Mrs. Snaith's opinion? Because Felix stood godfather to half the children baptized in his parish; because he let himself be called, at all untimely hours, to comfort the sick; because he had housed her goods, and helped to

carry them in as a matter of course; because she had more than once seen him carry the market basket of a poor rheumatic old woman, and lend her the aid of his arm as well to help her home—these were some of the reasons why it was "like him" to propose being guardian to her little treasures.

Felix looked up when, again seating herself, she pushed the papers towards him, as if giving them over to his charge for good and all.

The shadow of a smile crossed his face. He did not see that it was so very kind; but the tinge of disapproval vanished.

"You consent, then?"

"Yes, sir, I consent, and thank you kindly; but I am that circumstanced, as I can only say I consent unless *he* should interfere that may be able to interfere."

"Now, what does she mean by that?" thought Felix, still strong in the notion that he was to be guardian to John de Berenger's children. "Can she mean old Sam? I suppose she does."

But though his face was full of cogitation, the sunshine of approval had come back to it—he was even feeling that he had wronged her; and when she said would he lock the papers up in some safe place, and do as he pleased about investments, he felt suddenly that he did not want such perfect liberty as that. "I shall do nothing without consulting a lawyer," he said, "and you will be so good as to take care of the list I have made."

"Hadn't you better keep it, sir?" she answered, in her simplicity; "it would save you the trouble of making another."

"No, Mrs. Snaith," he answered, and laughed and held out his hand, as he generally did to his parishioners. So she shook hands with him and left the room, feeling as if she should like to serve him all her days.

When she had retired, Felix again looked over the papers. "All made payable to bearer—that bearer, Hannah Snaith." Now, if John de Berenger had made that money over to her during his lifetime, it must have been to protect it, so that it could not be recognised as his, and claimed by his creditors. He must have trusted her; and she had proved worthy of his trust as regarded her honesty. As regarded her prudence—no!

Felix leaned his chin on one hand, and turning over those papers with the other, began to puzzle himself with a problem which he stated wrongly, and which, consequently, could have no right answer.

The problem was this.

"As John de Berenger had died deeply in debt, could this money (invested in the name of Hannah Snaith) be considered in fairness to belong to *his* children; was it not the property of his creditors? Had he not proved, by the course he had taken, in order to conceal or protect it from them, that it was in justice theirs?"

"That depends," Felix presently thought, "on how John got the money. Wait a minute. This woman, Hannah Snaith, has repeatedly declared that she knew nothing about John. After all, why may not this be true? Why may not the money have come through his wife, whoever she was?

"No, that won't do. 'By *him* that made them over to me,' she said. Well, why should it not have been the wife's father?

"Let me think this out. If John did marry, as I suppose is certain (at least, one of the few things Hannah Snaith has positively declared, is that these children were born in wedlock and that she could easily prove it if necessary)—as he did marry, I will therefore say he must be supposed to have married that poor, pretty young creature, the Baptist minister's daughter, whom he harped upon to me for years, fell in love with when she was only fifteen, as he saw her passing to and from school — Fanny Tindale (neither child is called Fanny, by-the-bye). Well, let us say that after her father moved away to somewhere in Lincolnshire, I think it was, John went and married Fanny Tindale. I know she died some time ago. Suppose her father, a vulgar old fellow, but not particularly poor, that I am aware of, saved, or at any rate died possessed of, what I now see before me—I am sure I have heard that he too is dead—of course his care would be to prevent John from ever touching his money; but if he died before his daughter, he may have feared lest somehow it might be got hold of by the creditors, and may have chosen to trust it to a person whom he knew, and no relation, in the faith of her honesty. Her being more of his class in life than of John's, is much in favour of the theory. And this is in favour of it too, that by all I know of her—and I know her now pretty well—I seem to be assured that she is not a person who would lend herself to any scheme that she knew to be dishonest."

Felix de Berenger, having thus stated his problem, thought the better of himself for finding an answer to it so convincing and so complete.

"I wonder I never thought of this before,"

he observed, as with a satisfied air he locked up Hannah Snaith's papers. "Poor little waifs! Yes, I see it all."

An uncomfortable reflection sometimes presses on us, to the effect that the world is full of people who think they have an answer to most of the problems of life, or at least to such as more especially concern their own lives. Who think so—but we are sure they are mistaken. And is it not possible—just possible—though to the last degree improbable—that we, we ourselves, may be? No, that flash of intelligence crossing the shady chambers of thought, is soon put out; of such reflections the human mind is always impatient.

Yet a great many of us know no more of the answers to such problems as lie close about us, and most concern us, than did the Reverend Felix de Berenger in this recorded instance, and nevertheless we, perhaps, as he did, bring a great deal of good out of the mistaken circumstances.

CHAPTER XIII.

HANNAH SNAITH'S money was soon reinvested, and she herself made joint guardian with Felix to Amabel and Delia de Berenger.

But even before that was accomplished she found herself in a different, in a lower, position. In fact, this was the case from the day she gave it up—almost from the hour; for she was staying at the rectory-house, and made welcome to remain as long as she liked. She, therefore, began at once to help Jolliffe with all the household duties, which were greater than usual by the presence of Amias, her two little girls, and last, but not least, of Miss be Berenger with her maid.

Sarah had been invited to come and help to welcome "Ames," as she always called him. She perceived and mastered the facts of this new situation at once. Mrs. Snaith's cottage was down. There was no cottage empty in the village; there were no lodgings to be had near enough to admit of the children's daily attendance at the rectory to take their lessons. If she let them and their nurse depart, her scheme would all tumble into ruins. Felix would lose a certain small amount of profit that he derived from it, there would be no one to educate Dick, nothing to keep his "grandchildren" in the view or the mind of Sir Samuel, and an interesting mystery, which she herself had brought into notice, might be withdrawn.

She walked about the garden nodding at

her own thoughts, and saying "Yes" many times. She was excited, but, after a while, her movements became calmer. She resolved on action. "Dear Felix! Yes; how stupid men are! Better off, he says, than he could have expected—finds his income go further. Why, how should it be otherwise? He receives money, and pays in kind. It's true Bolton pays at less than market price, but Felix has the land for nothing, and does the labour himself, too; so he pays for little but for seed. The same with Ann Thimbleby. She educates Dick, and takes 'green meat' for her young sister instead of much of the coin she would, but for it, get for herself—— Yes, I'll do it now." Accordingly, with what for her was almost a languid air, she went indoors, and, in the course of conversation, asked Felix what was the exact income produced by the shares, &c., which had been made over to him.

Felix told her.

That he was to be joint guardian with her to these children had been gratefully mentioned by Mrs. Snaith herself, and was not a secret. Sarah revolved the sum in her mind as she slowly proceeded down the long passages of the house to an almost empty room, where Mrs. Snaith was sitting at work. To do her justice, she considered that whatever she proposed must certainly include a maintenance for the nurse, who, though she had been so very imprudent as very nearly to lose the children's money, had still meant so well by them that she had a full right to remain their attendant.

It certainly did occur to her, however, that this was a disadvantage. "She will be a very expensive servant," was her thought, "and difficult to manage, perhaps, for she has been long independent. But for her undeniable claims, I could make Felix—yes! get a much less expensive person."

Mrs. Snaith was counting over and mending some clothes of her own and of the children's, which had fortunately been at the wash when her cottage was burnt. This gave Sarah a natural opening for what she wanted to say. She sat down, took up a little frock, and admired it.

"Yes! Mrs. Snaith, how nice the little girls always look—so neatly and prettily dressed. I like your taste. Do you mind telling me what their clothes cost?"

"About thirteen pounds a year each, ma'am. I'm glad you like the looks of them."

"And you give twenty for their schooling?"

"Yes; and the rent was six pounds yearly. I reckoned that very cheap."

"I almost wonder how you managed."

"Oh, ma'am, very well indeed. I can get them to eat but little meat at present, bless them! so I took care they had plenty of milk and eggs, and those are cheap here."

"Then there is your own dress; you always look the picture of neatness."

This interest rather flattered the nurse. "Well, ma'am, I got the whole of the eatables paid for, and sometimes a little beer, out of the rest of the income, and I had about twenty pounds left for myself, as I may call it."

Sarah was silent; she was cogitating.

Mrs. Snaith went on with her confidences. "The washing were the expense I could not stand, so I took it home and almost always did it; but the last fortnight, thank goodness, I had put it out, because Jolliffe, being unwell, I wished to come and help her up at the rectory. But for that I should have lost all our clothes."

"Every word she says makes the matter easier," thought Sarah. "Yes. Twenty-six pounds for the children's dress, twenty pounds for what I'll call her wages, twenty for the schooling, sixty-six. Set aside four for doctors or a visit to the sea—that would leave eighty. Felix could do it—just do it. Thirty for her board, twenty-five for each child. In fact, it would be a profit to him (mem. not to tell him so). Yes; because I shall soon get the *girl* dismissed. Of course Mrs. Snaith could attend to the children, Dick included—do needlework; I know her. She would never sit with her hands before her. She and Jolliffe would do everything: and instead of the wages and board of that girl, who eats more than anybody in the house, Felix might have that active little washerwoman to come every Saturday as a charwoman and do what scrubbing or cleaning there could be that they objected to. She brings home the clothes on Friday. Yes. Why, Felix would be a great gainer by it. Is there a chance, now, that it might be done? Two such capable women in the house—if only they were not jealous of one another! He would save nearly forty pounds a year by that girl's food and wages and breakages; and he'll never know how that's managed, unless I tell him. Such are men!"

She got up rather abruptly, putting down the pretty little frock with a thoughtful air and walking away in deep cogitation, her bright red cheeks requiring to be cooled by frequent throwing back of the long curls.

"They sat down on a grassy grave, and tucked their little feet into their gowns."

Felix was just setting off to hold a service in an outlying part of the parish, where a schoolroom had been licensed for the purpose. Amias was with him. Sarah walked a little way beside them, the better to unfold her plan, in which she did not mention the eventual dismissal of the young servant then in the house, but only explained to Felix that he would lose nothing, and be a gainer, by the excellent services of Mrs. Snaith.

"What, come and live here as a servant," exclaimed Felix, "and accept twenty pounds a year! I am sure she would never think of such a thing. Why should she, aunt?"

"Why, she gets nothing but board and lodging and twenty pounds a year now," said Sarah.

"And independence," observed Felix, his aunt's words impressing him so little that he went on talking to his brother as if she had not interrupted him.

Sarah waited for a pause, and then she too went on as if she had not been interrupted. "But that was a very nasty little cottage that she lived in—always smelt of the dry rot. Only think how different it would be to live in a nice rectory-house like yours! You might let her have that empty room on the ground floor as a kind of sitting-room for herself; it opens into the kitchen. And there are large rooms up-stairs that you make no use of."

"You'd better dismiss it from your mind, aunt," said Felix.

"It's no use talking to the old man when he's going to one of his services," said Amias.

Felix strode on ; Sarah trotted beside him. Amias, meandering now before, now behind, jerked up a stone into the clear air, and his aunt thought it came down rather dangerously near to his feet.

"Oh yes, dismiss it, of course, Felix! And you, Amias, bring yourself to an untimely end, if you like, before my eyes ! Pray don't mind *me*. Why, how is Ann Thimbleby to be paid, unless these children are here to be taught? and what house is there here now but yours? *Yes, you won't get a congregation for your saints' days service,*

I can tell you, if you send away Ann Thimble-by and Mrs. Snaith, your best attendants!"

Miss de Berenger knew that this last remark would tell. It did. Felix, for a moment, stood stock still.

"You'll have to shut up the church pretty often," she continued, "because you know it's not lawful to have a service without a congregation."

"Well?" said Felix dreamily.

"And you don't like that."

"No."

"What can you be thinking of, Felix? You do not seem to consider the importance of my words."

"Why, he's thinking," observed Amias, "that Mrs. Snaith cannot be expected to accept twenty pounds a year, and become a servant, in order that he may have a congregation on saints' days."

Here, coming near a stile, by which they had to enter the field they were to cross, Amias measured its height with his eye, took a short run, and sprang over it. "This time last year," he said to Felix, "you shirked that stile." Felix looked at him steadily, then he also took a short run and cleared it easily.

"Before my very eyes!" exclaimed Sarah. "O youth, youth! how thoughtless! Yes."

"You'd better dismiss it from your mind, aunt," repeated Felix, turning and regarding her from the other side of the stile. "I cannot think about it till after to-morrow. Perhaps something will turn up."

Then the brothers proceeded on their way together, and Sarah, who was arrayed in a salmon-coloured gown, returned slowly to the house.

"The fact is, a different generation is never to be depended on to understand one," thought Sarah. "I'm sure Felix seems earnest and serious enough as a rule, and then all on a sudden, when you think you've got him, he shows the cloven foot of youth. The experience and wisdom that come with years oppress young people. To-morrow's Sunday. Let me see."

Sarah proceeded slowly to the house, and entered it by the back way.

Jolliffe, in the clean kitchen, was cutting thick bread-and-butter.

"How are you to-day, my good creature?"

"Better, ma'am, thank you kindly. Mrs. Snaith has been doing for me right and left."

"Ah, what a comfort she is in the house!"

"You may say that, ma'am; whereas with a girl you never know where you are. They make more work than they do, and they eat their heads off. I never looked to have to spend my precious strength cutting bread-and-butter for a servant-girl, but for all that I know better than to let her cut it for herself."

"Yes," said Miss de Berenger, who was very friendly with Jolliffe. "I wish there was a chance of your having Mrs. Snaith here always."

"Oh, ma'am," answered Jolliffe, "no such luck."

So her sentiments were ascertained. Miss de Berenger went again into the room where the nurse was sitting. Her own clock, her chairs and table, her best fender, and two or three other articles that had been saved, were arranged in it. Mrs. Snaith was darning socks now, and Sarah observed some of Dick's among them.

"How comfortable you look, Mrs. Snaith, with all your things about you—quite at home."

"Yes, indeed, ma'am. It were a kindness I never can repay Mr. de Berenger, taking me in till I can look round; it relieve me from so much discomfort."

"I should not at all mind seeing you always here," observed Sarah. "Nor would my nephew; but he seems to think you would not like the notion—in fact, he said I had better dismiss it from my mind. And yet as I said to him, I cannot see where else you can possibly be; for it is not to be thought that, now my nephew has undertaken to be a guardian to the children, he would consent to them being taken quite away."

"Ma'am!" exclaimed the nurse, colouring deeply and putting down her work. She looked like a creature which has suddenly found out that it is tethered: the grass close around had proved so abundant and so sweet, that it had not hitherto stepped out far enough to feel the tugging of the string.

She took up the sock again and tried to go on with her work, but her hand trembled. There were going to be discussions; they would argue with her, and question her, even if they did not interfere.

Sarah, observing her discomfort, thought what a nervous woman she was. She had not seriously supposed, when she made that last speech, that Mrs. Snaith would consent to her whole plan; her uttermost hope was that, if higher wages were offered, she might agree to remain for a time, and then, by some further plan for her advantage, be induced to stay on.

Sarah had such a just confidence in her own powers of scheming, that she depended on herself to bring a further plan to light when it should be wanted, and her general way of proceeding was to state the matter at its worst, and then, if the conflicting party rejected it, to yield to objections and show advantages.

"Yes," she continued, "I had been wondering what you would do." Then she unfolded the plan she had concocted, adding, "Of course, if you lived here, you would not be called a servant; and, as you have told me, you only get board and lodging and about twenty pounds a year as it is. However, my nephew remarked that I had better dismiss it from my mind."

Sarah made and propounded many schemes, and had long ago learned to be philosophical as to the utter rejection of some of the best and most impartial, as well as to receive without obvious elation the adoption of some of those most to her own advantage. She propounded, and then observed.

Mrs. Snaith, as usual, took refuge in silence, so Sarah presently perceived that there was some hope of her consent. She therefore went on—

"This room is very like a nursery. It could be yours if you came. I never liked the miserable little attic—no air in it—where the darlings slept in that cottage. They could have a room five times as large here, and three times as high. So, of course, *they* would be better off here; there is no doubt it would be for *their* advantage to remain. Yes? Well, of course, if that is so, and as you are fond of them, you would, I conclude, wish them to stay; and then you would stay too? You would not like to leave them; you are too fond of them for that? Still, as my nephew said, something might turn up."

Mrs. Snaith was not startled by this hint of a possibility that she might leave the children for their own good, for so the questioning tone made her read the meaning of these words. She noticed that Sarah still stuck to the notion that the children were her relations, but her mind was too much on the stretch now for such a feeling as surprise. Was there not a course open to her which would provoke no discussion at all, admit of no opposition, lead to no questioning? Yes, there was; and yet was it not such a manifestly disadvantageous course for her, that, if she fell into it at once, Jolliffe and all her acquaintances of her own class would wonder at her?

She looked about her, and felt the truth of what had been said; the accommodation was much better—so much more air and space. She was shrewd enough to notice that it was Miss de Berenger, and not the rector, that had thought of this plan. She observed, with the quickness of one used to money matters in a small way, that though the children would live better than they had done, and only the same sum be spent on their board by her, yet, as an abundance of milk, eggs, and vegetables came from the rectorial cow, poultry-yard, and garden, the rector would be a considerable gainer. He had the land required for this produce free of rent. Now, what was she asked to give up besides her independence? Her heart fluttered, her colour changed, her hand trembled, as she thought this over. She was willing to efface herself utterly, if need were, but not to dare discussion.

"Ma'am," she said at last, "such a—such a kind offer as this require some time to think over."

"Oh, certainly," answered Sarah, greatly surprised, and inclined, by the expression "kind," to believe that the proposition really might be as good a one for Mrs. Snaith as for Felix—or, at any rate, that she thought so.

"I can stay, and no questions asked," thought the other. "And if I had to leave them—if poor Uzziah came out, and there was any fear of his finding me—where could I leave them so safe as they are here, leave the money behind for them as well? Yes, my precious dears, mother 'll do this for you too."

In the rectory house that night, housed in a large, comfortable room, Mrs. Snaith lay awake all night considering matters. It was bitter to give up her independence, but there was safety in it. First, because no one belonging to her would believe that she would give it up and look for her in domestic service. Secondly, because it would mark and make wider the apparent difference of station between her and the children. They would be in the parlour, and she in the kitchen. What between these cogitations and the effects of her late alarm and excitement, which, after an interval of slumber, were roused again by this second cogitation, she was very restless and nervous all Sunday, and laid herself down again at night dreading inexpressibly what she had to do, and yet, as the weary, wakeful hours bore on, deciding more fully that it should be done, and that she would do it.

Felix was rather an intellectual man, but by no means intelligent; that is, he could think better than he could observe. He liked to cogitate over principles, and he disliked details. His own habits were most simple, self-denying, and economical; but he had no notion how to cut down household expenses, and in all domestic matters he was quite at the mercy of the womankind about him.

Hannah Snaith, while she perceived that Miss de Berenger had made a scheme which was very much to her nephew's advantage, was quite sure he did not know it, and naturally would not be enlightened by his aunt. Everybody understood Miss de Berenger better than Felix did. Jolliffe and Mr. Bolton had confidently declared that Miss Sarah would go home on Tuesday. Mrs. Snaith was also sure she would. Why? For this reason. Miss de Berenger had driven herself over on the previous Wednesday in her pony-carriage, and had not brought a bag of oats in the back of the vehicle for the creature's food, as usual; there was nothing found there but a longish cord for a tether. For behind the little paved court once before mentioned, was a small turfed drying-ground, containing about four perches. The grass was rather long. Miss de Berenger had the pony tethered to a tree in one corner of it, that this excellent feed might not be wasted. The pony was not proud; he was accustomed to get his living where he could. Miss de Berenger added threepence a day to the boy Andrew's wages to attend him. He had already consumed the grass in the four corners of the drying-ground; on Monday he would be tethered on the little bit in the middle that he had not been able to reach, and, therefore, on Tuesday evening, when he had eaten all, Miss de Berenger, it was certain, would go away.

Miss de Berenger had no scruple in taking this grass, since Felix would not permit the cow to be turned in on it, because she was too restless to bear the tether, and if at large she got into the garden.

On Monday morning Hannah Snaith was admitted again to the rector's study. She began, " If you please, sir, Miss de Berenger—she propose a scheme. I've thought it over, and——"

" Oh yes, yes," said Felix, setting a chair for her, and feeling as if his aunt had taken a liberty; " pray dismiss that from your mind. I believe my aunt felt that it would be awkward for me to be guardian to these little ones unless they were near at hand." He forgot that his whole household would fall to pieces if she withdrew, but that was because he was thinking of her side of the question, not his own.

She answered simply, and without taking the chair, " Yes, sir; and that's what I feel too."

Felix looked at her.

" If my dear young ladies have a chance of living in your house, brought up with your little brother, sir, I seem to think I ought not to deprive them of it."

" But the fact is," said Felix, a slight tinge of red showing in his dark cheek, " I am not well off; a proportion of their money would have to go to pay me for their board."

She saw he did not like discussing the money with her.

" Sir," she answered, " when I'm your servant—as I hope to be—I can never talk so freely, and that, as I can now. So I'll say once for all, I expect I shall be lodged and boarded better than I have been, and I look to get the same sum for myself—twenty pounds. That is what Miss de Berenger thought."

" Yes," said Felix, looking at her. As she did not choose to seat herself, he was standing also. " Well, Mrs. Snaith, I suppose you know your own business best." And yet he seemed doubtful.

" I suppose I do, sir; but there's one thing it's fair I should say—it's my great confidence in you, sir, make me think I may."

" It's coming at last," thought Felix. " I will respect your confidence, Mrs. Snaith, whatever it may be."

" I'm not a widow, sir."

" No?" said Felix, in a tone of pity and inquiry.

" No, sir; my poor husband's alive. I fare to think people would look down on me if they knew the truth—but not you, sir—not you."

All in a moment, after years of silence, she had been surprised into saying these words. His trust in her was so complete, he was so honourable—as far as he knew—that he had overcome her, and sick at heart, and choked with sobs, she sat down of her own accord, and wept and bemoaned herself before him with passionate, irrepressible tears.

" My poor husband is a convict, sir; he was sentenced for fourteen years," she said, when she recovered herself. " If I live under your roof, I fare to think you have a right to know it. But when I came into this room, I didn't mean to tell it, neither." She dried her eyes and almost coldly rose ; her passion and sorrow was over.

"My poor friend," said Felix. "I am sorry."

That was all, but often afterwards the words, so quietly spoken, were a comfort to her. He meant them, and his pity would last.

"My poor friend. I am sorry."

"You'll keep it to yourself, sir ? "

"Yes."

She had not told him what he had expected to hear, but her sudden grief had made him forget this. He had certainly thought of her as a widow, perhaps on account of that very phrase that she sometimes used, "My poor husband ! " So in those parts of the country they always speak of the dead. The same phrase had made others also think of her as a widow, and if any had disparaging thoughts concerning her, they certainly never supposed she had a living husband to conceal, but rather that perhaps she had no right to the ring. For, of course, she had to pay for her great silence ; her cautious reticence could not but be noticed, and why should people be so wonderfully chary of their words unless they have some secret to keep that is not to their advantage ?

CHAPTER XIV.

Now, Amias always comforted himself with a flattering conviction that he was no prig.

He would not touch strong drink because he knew that the abuse of it made his countrymen wicked and poor, and he had thrown up his prospects, and made no use of opportunities to have them back.

He abstained, not that he was quite sure, but that he supposed, every instance of absti-nence was likely to do good. He had thrown up his prospects on the spur of the moment, and almost before he had fully made up his own mind.

His conscience had, as it were, tricked him into action ; it was afterwards that, revolving the matter, his reason approved.

It is a fearful thing for a young man to be thought a prig—almost as bad, so to speak, as being suspected of burglary. The com-panions of Amias were so kind as to admit that he certainly was no prig. What, then, is a prig? They did not exactly know, or at any rate they could not in so many words have characterized what here, in default of a better, receives this definition.

A prig is one who makes, and prides him-self on making, such confident and high pro-fession of his opinions, whatever these may be, that though he should act upon them never so consistently, his words will, notwith-standing, tower above and seem to dwarf his actions.

If this definition is a fair one, then Amias was the perfect contrary, the fine reverse of a prig.

With little more than an instinct towards the right, and on the first admonishing of conscience, he had plunged into action ; much as a man will plunge into a river to save some drowning person. When this last has been safely brought to the brink, his bold deliverer, with a quart at least of cold water in his own stomach, may reflect that the stream was stronger than he had supposed, the water deeper, that he is not a first-rate swimmer himself. What if they had both gone down together ?

But when his sister says to him, "Tom," or "Dick," as the case may be, "you were rash, you might have been drowned," he has already had time to think the matter out and justify the action by the result.

"Nonsense, my dear," he answers. "I am all right. I am glad I did it. I would do it again ! "

And he would do it again. He knows enough of himself now to be sure that he certainly should do it again. Does he there-fore, to keep himself out of danger, eschew the banks of the river? No, but in more perfect and accomplished style, he learns to swim.

There is nothing like action to show a man what he really is. It may have been hidden from this very young fellow's eyes that he cared enough for his own brother, the one he liked best, to risk his life for him. Till the decisive moment came he had not perhaps the remotest suspicion that he cared for human life in the abstract ; and here he stands dripping, having risked his own to save that of an absolute stranger. For the future he knows all. He perceives the awful and mysterious oneness of humanity, how it draws the units to the whole. He is not in-dependent, as he may have thought ; he is a part of all.

This is why a man who has saved life hardly ever boasts of it, or prides himself on it. Such, particularly the uneducated, will not unfrequently try to slink away, going silently, as if some knowledge or feeling had come to them that was not perfectly welcome.

On the Sunday after the fire a remarkable circumstance occurred. Sir Samuel de Berenger invited Amias to dinner. Sir Samuel had only returned to his country place a few days previously. He went to church in all state, as he commonly did on a Sunday morning, and behold, there was Amias in the rectory pew. He was growing up to be a fine young fellow, taller than Felix, well made, and brown. He was looking about him as if he was pleased to be at home again, and not in the least conscious that he had made a fool of himself. Perhaps he hadn't, but it cannot be expected that his uncle or the congregation generally would think so.

Sir Samuel looked at him several times; quite naturally, and as if it could not be helped, their eyes met. "Young dog," thought the old man, not at all displeased; "how perfectly he carries it off! You would have me think you don't care, would you!"

Amias, of course, could not know how many hundreds of times the old great-uncle had wished him back again. John was dead, Tom was gone; but that was not all. The old fellow constantly told himself, how the longer he lived the more his conscience became enlightened, and the more he suffered from the perversity of his father's descendants, who would not let him be just and generous to them. All that he meant, however, to do at present, was to make a clerk of Amias, and give him a salary; in fact, to condone the past.

He was always wishing to have him back again, and if Amias had known from the beginning that such was the case, it might have had a great effect upon him. That he did not know appears, therefore, to be a good thing or a bad thing, according to the judgment one may form of his conduct.

In the porch, after service, old Sam greeted his niece Sarah and the two little girls. He then spoke to Amias, who was behind, and, with a cordiality the more pleasant because it was unexpected, invited him to dinner.

Amias accepted. He was pleased that old Sam should thus make overtures of peace. His pride was flattered, for though he took special care not to seem aware that he was reckoned a foolish, wrong-headed young fellow, he felt it. When the wind blows strongly in one's face, it is difficult not to put down one's head.

Amias told no one in the house excepting Felix, who instantly said, "Why didn't he ask me too?"

"It was rude of him," answered Amias, "and queer; I was just now thinking so. If you like I'll send and decline."

Felix paused. It was no ridiculous feeling that he himself had been neglected which had led to the sudden exclamation.

"He's a mean old boy," said Amias disrespectfully. "I hear he pays the fellow he got in my place even less than he paid me."

"That alone would be enough to decide him against what I suspected," thought Felix. "How absurd I am!—You had much better go," he said aloud. "Only keep clear of the matter you quarrelled about. It does not become you to dispute with such an old man, and at his own table."

"Oh!" said Amias, "you don't think I shall have a chance, do you? Most likely he has a dinner party, and wants me to make the table even."

When Amias arrived, however, he found himself the only guest, and felt that he could have enjoyed his dinner more if his dress-coat had not been so exceedingly tight; in fact, he had not worn it for a year. And, having been accustomed for that period to take his chop alone in his dingy lodgings, he was at first uncomfortably conscious of the footmen's eyes, their stealthy movements, and constant assiduities.

He had just been making a firm resolution that he would go out to dinner no more till he could afford a new dress-coat, when the last servant withdrew, after the meal, as quietly as a cat, and shut the door behind him. Then Amias began to perceive, as by a kind of instinct, that his old uncle had been waiting for this occurrence, that he had something to say, and was now about to speak.

So far as appeared, Amias was rather young for his years—as a rule, thoughtless. He still had a boy's delight in mischief. He did not love work; a boat race would rouse him to a ridiculous pitch of enthusiasm; a cricket match was far more important than a Government defeat, or anything of that sort. As he now sat waiting, he again felt how tight his coat was, took up a particularly fine strawberry, and, while cogitating with discomfort as to what could be coming, appeared to gaze at it with interest, and almost with curiosity.

"Amias," said Sir Samuel, with a serious and slightly pompous air, "your brother Felix has, of course, been made aware of my invitation?"

"Oh yes, uncle," answered Amias, diligently eating his strawberries.

"What remark did he make upon it?"

Amias, taken by surprise, looked up. It seemed out of the question to repeat the remark in question, and, of course, he had not forgotten it.

"What remark did he make upon it?" repeated the old man. He saw that Amias looked a little confused.

"It was nothing particular that he said, uncle," replied Amias, in a blundering fashion. "I couldn't exactly repeat it to you."

"Why not?" asked Sir Samuel. He himself was not so much at his ease as usual. He never doubted that Felix had expressed pleasure at this move towards a reconciliation. Perhaps he had told his young brother he must make some sort of apology for the past. If Amias shirked the repetition of such a speech (and what other could Felix have made?), Sir Samuel did not see how he could continue the conversation. He looked hard at Amias, with an air of reproof and admonition; whereupon a slight tinge of red showed itself through the healthy brown of the cheek, and Amias blurted out—

"What Felix said was, 'Why didn't he ask me too?'"

"Very natural, nephew parson," thought the old man. "You see what I am about, and would like, if I take the boy back, to tie me down as regards the future; but I think I'll manage it myself, nephew parson, if you have no objection. You would like to come back again into the country, I dare say, Amias, among your own people, and that sort of thing?" he continued aloud.

"Yes, I should, uncle, of course; I hate London."

"I take it for granted that you regret the foolish escapade which—which led to your being sent away."

Amias looked up. The manner was rather kind; but he thought, "This is mean of the old boy; he is going to give me a wigging at his own table;" and instead of making a set answer to Sir Samuel's suggestion he followed his own thoughts to a point where they became urgent for utterance, and then blurted out, "If I hadn't told you myself what I'd done, nobody else would have told you. You might never have found it out to this day."

"Quite true," answered the old uncle still more graciously and pompously. "I have thought the better of you ever since for that proper straightforwardness. I have frequently said, when people have remarked to me on your folly, 'But there was much

that was gentlemanlike in my nephew's behaviour. I am not altogether displeased with him.' I say again, Amias, would you like to come back?"

"Back here?" exclaimed Amias, at last understanding him—"back to *the concern!* —back to you?" And his air of astonishment threw Sir Samuel off his guard.

"Yes, back here. Why not, if I am content to forget the past and you are anxious to retrieve it?"

"You couldn't have a fellow back who is a teetotaler—a fellow that would stand on the beer-barrels and preach at the people not to buy the stuff!"

"*You* stand on the beer-barrels! *You* preach at people!" exclaimed Sir Samuel, so astonished at the grotesque picture that he could not be very angry yet. "Do you mean to tell me that you are so lost to all sense of what befits your age, and your rank in life, and your future respectability, that you can stand on a beer-barrel and rant like a demagogue?"

Amias, in spite of himself, for he was very nervous, burst into a short laugh. "You are very kind, uncle," he answered; "and —well, I never expected it. No, I never lectured yet, excepting that once. But I should if I came here. I am sure I could not help it! I am a great deal worse than I used to be; for now I wish all the gin-palaces were blown up, and I should be glad if half the beer-barrels were kicked into the sea. When I went away, uncle, I felt as if it was extremely hard that I should be obliged to think about strong drink in such a way as to ruin my prospects; but now—I— I don't care. There must be some fellows to think the inconvenient things and do them; in fact, if there were not, the world would never get better. But I did not suppose you could be so kind and forgiving. I am very much obliged to you."

At the commencement of this speech Sir Samuel felt such rage and amazement that he was speechless. As Amias went on, much more slowly and taking more thought, a sudden revulsion, caused by what seemed the strangeness of his words, made the old man shiver.

All was useless. Why had he thus demeaned himself? His money was nothing, his kindness was set at nought; he was mastered by a mere youth, who had not a shilling. But when with boyish simplicity, and a sort of whimsical pathos, Amias went on to say how he had at first considered it hard that he should be obliged so to think as to ruin his prospects, and when he added, "But now I don't care," then Sir Samuel, worldly and shallow though he might be, believed that he was hearing of somewhat to be feared and not gainsaid; something not of this world, though familiar to the Christian 'creed. It had asserted itself and been obeyed. It was very inconvenient, but it was always to have its way, and Amias did not seem to recognise it by name, or know what its strivings meant.

Rather a long pause followed. Sir Samuel poured himself out a glass of claret, and sipped it slowly. Amias having no wine to occupy him, and no fruit on his plate, looked hard out of the window into the lovely, peaceful park, and towards a wood. Little more than a year ago he had robbed several feathered mothers there. He wished it was spring; and oh, how he wished this dinner was over! Oh, that Felix had indeed been invited to it also, for then he should not have had to tell him of it afterwards. And why did not old Sam speak? Was he so *stumped* with astonishment that he disdained to say a word more?

Amias would have been much surprised if he could have read his old uncle's thoughts just then, and how, not without a certain reverence, he revolved in his mind a familiar sentence which begins, "Lest haply——"

He was rapidly calming. The matter had settled itself. He must find out some other way to benefit that family. Amias would be of no use to him as he was, and he would not take the responsibility of trying to change him.

When he did speak, it was so kindly that the words gave Amias a click in his throat that made him miserably uncomfortable. He resented that too—would have liked a "wigging" better. Sir Samuel observed that he was in low spirits, and got more and more dull as the evening went on.

"I'd better go," he said, as the darkness came on, "if you'll excuse me, uncle. I've got to tell Felix."

"Felix will be vexed?" asked Sir Samuel, in quite a friendly tone.

"Yes," said Amias gloomily; "of course."

Then the old man acted in a way to surprise his nephew and himself. He remarked to Amias, that about a year and a half ago he had promised to give him a nag. Amias remembered the promise, and how he had felt that the beast had received this somewhat disparaging name that no very high expectations might be formed as to his merits.

"I shall give you the money instead," quoth the old uncle; and, preceding Amias into the lighted library, he actually sat down to his writing-table and then and there wrote a cheque for the sum of £38 10s. "Just such a nag as I meant to give you was sold out of my stable a week ago for that sum," he said. "There, Amias, you will understand that any displeasure I may have felt against you has ceased."

Amias accepted the cheque humbly. It was so unexpected, under the circumstances, and so unlike the donor to give it, that he felt as if he had been put in the wrong utterly. He seemed to have made himself ridiculous and to be forgiven. He had thrown away his prospects now twice, and yet he had to feel like a sneak; he could not do it with a high hand. What amount of fun there might have been in the future must now be thrown after those prospects, and lost as they were, for of course he could never come and oppose old Sam in the town 'or in his own neighbourhood now. No. And yet he did not even *wish* that his peculiar notions had ever made a lodgment in his breast. Some fellows must have inconvenient thoughts; so it was, and so it would be.

The old man and the young took leave of one another. Amias went off toward home, telling himself what a lucky dog he was to have thirty-eight pounds ten shillings in his pockets, keeping up a smart run, and every now and then raising a boyish whoop or shout. He scarcely allowed to himself that he wanted to keep up his spirits, and was defying himself and fate; but when he left the open carriage drive, which was white and clear in the moonlight, and had to find and slowly feel his way under the trees in the solemn darkness of the summer night, he began to feel that ominous click in his throat again. One or two whoops meant to be hilarious came out in feeble and wavering style, and when at last he emerged from the wood, and saw lying in its shadow the great fallen trunk of a tree lately felled, he was fain to throw himself upon it and cry out—

"I know the old man will think this hard." He meant his brother Felix; and having so said, he dropped his face in his hands and sobbed for about two minutes as if his heart would break.

Moaning, and yet enraged and deeply ashamed of himself—"To think that at my age I should demean myself to howl!"—he dried his eyes. Something moved before him, and, startled, he sprang to his feet. A man stood just beyond the shadow, covered with moonlight—Felix.

"Oh, it's you, old fellow."

"Yes. Don't knock me down."

"How did you know I was here?" exclaimed Amias, choking down the heavings of his chest with a mighty sob.

"I was coming to meet you, and saw you go into the wood. I shall think it hard, shall I?"

"Felix, you know I like you better than any one in the world—far better."

"Yes; but what shall I think hard? Has old Sam been proposing to you to come back? I thought he would."

"Did you, Felix?" said Amias ruefully.

"If you accepted I shall think it hard."

Amias immediately sprang at him and hugged him.

"How could you think otherwise, you young scamp?" said Felix when he was released.

"It's all right then," exclaimed Amias, immensely relieved. The last remainder of the storm rolled off with a final heaving of the chest. "I was miserable because I thought you would be so vexed. If I'd only known,"

he added, with deep disgust against himself, "I wouldn't have made such a muff of myself. You'll—of course you will never mention it?"

"Certainly not," said Felix affectionately.

Owls were hooting all round them; the valley was full of mysterious shadows and confusing shafts of moonlight; little hollows had ghostly white mists lying in them. Presently a large white creature, with eyes like a cat's, skimmed past them close to the grass, silent as a dream; a fluffy bunch of down, her newly fledged young one, after her. They disappeared in the wood. Amias, with a great whoop, gave chase, and Felix shouting after him with all his might to remember the pond and keep well up the side of the hollow, the whole place seemed to wake up and fill itself with echoes, as if twenty De Berengers instead of two were in it, and were throwing their voices at one another.

When Echo repeats a man's voice she always gives it with a difference. Felix could have declared it was his dead father crying out to Amias to beware of the water, and John de Berenger, who was lying in the Ceylon forest, that answered with fainter repetitions, "It's all right—all right—all right."

VICTORIA TO WINNIPEG *VIA* PEACE RIVER PASS.

III.—DUNVEGAN TO WINNIPEG: THE PRAIRIES.

DURING the first half of the present century much was done to explore the extreme north of what is now the Dominion of Canada, and to map out the country along the Arctic coast; but there is a vast territory between that remote north-land and the western United States which was almost entirely unknown to any except the Hudson's Bay Company officials and Indians until 1857, when Captain Palliser made an expedition from Lake Superior to the Rocky Mountains. The lonely regions of the north may long continue to be, as they have been for ages, the home of the musk-ox, the summer resort of the elk, the hunting ground of the Indian, and the preserve of the fur-trader, unless indeed their minerals should prove of sufficient value to attract capital and population; but this more southern and more central territory, about which the outer world was long kept in ignorance while those who held it on lease retained it for buffalo and beaver and other fur-bearing animals, is one of the most fertile parts of our empire, and may soon become one of the chief granaries of the world.

This district, which is sometimes called the Prairie Region of Canada, and which includes the best portion of the North-West Territories, may be roughly described as a great triangle, one side stretching for one thousand miles along the international boundary line—the 49th parallel; another extending from the boundary northward, in part along the foot of the Rocky Mountains, for about eight or nine hundred miles; while the base of the triangle is formed in a broken and irregular way by the chain of lakes that stretch from the Lake of the Woods, a little east of Manitoba, north-westward to Great Slave Lake. The estimated area of this prairie region is not less than three hundred millions of acres, that is, about ten times the size of England. Manitoba, covering nine millions of acres in the south-east corner of this vast triangle, is, as compared with the whole territory, little more than one square on the chessboard. It is unwatered by a great system of rivers that flow into the chain of lakes which bound it along the north-east, and these lakes, in turn, are emptied by another river-system that flows through the remoter north land into the Arctic Ocean and Hudson's Bay. The Peace and the Athabasca cut across the northern portion of this territory; the Saskatchewan cleaves its way for a thousand miles through the rich central districts; while through the south-eastern portions flow the Assiniboine and the Red River, which unite their waters at Winnipeg, the capital of Manitoba and present gateway of the North-West.

This territory, with all the country to the north and the north-east, was transferred to Canada in 1870, having formerly been held by the Hudson's Bay Company under charter from the Crown. When the Canadian Government had thus acquired a clear title to this territory, and when provision had been made for the efficient maintenance of law and order by the appointment of a Lieutenant-Governor and Council, and by the establishment, at widely scattered points, of the North-West Mounted Police, it became necessary to increase the facilities of access and communication. As yet Manitoba is accessible from the east for ordinary travel only by the aid of United States railways. There is, however, in course of construction, to be completed in 1882, a railway from Winnipeg to Thunder Bay, on Lake Superior, which by means of the Lake steamers will be connected with the railway system of Ontario, so that ere long travellers may pass by steamer and railway, through Canadian territory, from Halifax or Quebec to Winnipeg.

Means of communication throughout the North-West are furnished to some extent by its great system of rivers, and already steamers ply, during the open season, on Red River, the Assiniboine and the Saskatchewan, running up the latter river as far as Edmonton, near the foot of the Rocky Mountains. These rivers, however, provide facilities of communication for a comparatively small portion of the country, and even this limited communication is available only for the six or seven months during which they are not frost-bound. The prairie carts and sleighs are already inadequate for the traffic to and from the interior. Railway communication must, therefore, be provided, and the Government, recognising this when they acquired possession of the territory, took steps at once towards the construction of a railway from Winnipeg to the Rocky Mountains.

In older countries settlement usually precedes railways, and it is only when busy communities exist, and when people have been massed in considerable numbers, that railway construction is undertaken. In Canada,

XXI—22

however, as in the western portions of the United States, railways often precede settlement, and it is after facilities of communication have been provided that people enter and develop the resources of the country. For purposes of settlement, therefore, a railway must be built across this fertile prairie region, from which in due time branch lines will extend to north and south. And while the settlement of the North-West requires the extension of a railway to the foot of the Rocky Mountains, other reasons, such as the interests of British Columbia, the closer union of the Canadian Provinces by lines of traffic, and the development of commerce with Asia, demand railway extension to the western seaboard. The Government, recognising on these and other grounds the necessity of a Canadian Pacific Railway, have, after a careful and exhaustive survey, adopted a line that shall pass through Edmonton and that, crossing the Rocky Mountains by the Yellowhead Pass, shall touch the Pacific at Burrard Inlet. Already a hundred miles of this railway are in course of construction from Winnipeg westwards, to be finished before the close of the present year; one hundred and twenty-five miles of the British Columbia section are under contract; and it is confidently hoped that the extension of the line across the prairie region will proceed at the rate of a hundred miles per year, and that by the close of this decade our transcontinental line will be complete.

The construction of the Canadian Pacific Railway may well be regarded as a work of Imperial as well as of Canadian importance. It concerns the welfare of the empire both as a colonisation road and as part of a transcontinental highway. The settlement of the North-West must very soon and very seriously affect the wheat supply of the mother country. At present that supply is drawn largely from the United States and from Russia, and as these countries, being foreign, might become unfriendly, the receipt of breadstuffs from these sources might any season be imperilled. Seeing this, Sir Samuel Baker and others have advocated wheat culture on an extended scale in Egypt. Canadians, however, invite the attention of the empire to their vast prairies, which are peculiarly suited to the growth of grain, confident that if these be developed the policy of foreign countries could not seriously disturb the wheat market of Britain. At the same time the welfare of the empire is concerned in the extension of this line of railway to the western seaboard, as it would not only provide speedy com-

munication through British territory with British possessions on the Pacific, but would supply the great missing link in a rapid route from England to Eastern Asia that would be safe against foreign interference.

The prairie region has been opened for settlement on the most liberal terms.. The land is laid off into townships of six miles square, each of the thirty-six square miles being called a section. Within a belt of one hundred and ten miles on each side of the proposed line of the Canadian Pacific Railway every alternate section is reserved for railway lands, and is offered for sale at prices varying from one dollar (4s. 2d. sterling) to five dollars per acre, according to the proximity of the land to the railway. The remaining lands in this belt are open for homestead and pre-emption. Any person who is the head of a family, or who has attained the age of twenty-one years, is entitled to be entered on these unappropriated lands for a homestead of a quarter-section—that is, one hundred and sixty acres—and, on his compliance with certain requirements in the way of settlement and cultivation of the soil, he receives a Crown patent confirming him in absolute proprietorship. In addition to this free homestead the settler may acquire another block of one hundred and sixty acres by pre-emption; that is, he has the right of purchasing the quarter-section adjoining his homestead, so that he may thus become proprietor of a farm of three hundred and twenty acres, the price of the pre-empted land varying from one dollar to two dollars and a half per acre, according to its proximity to the line of railway.

The value of this vast tract of unoccupied land where a free homestead is offered to the settler, come whence he may, is greatly enhanced by the admission, on the part of competent authorities in the United States, that nearly all the free agricultural lands in that country have been taken up. Thus the Hon. D. A. Wells, in July, 1877, stated that "the quantity of fertile public lands suitable for farm purposes which can now be obtained by prescription or at a nominal price (in the United States) is comparatively limited, if not nearly exhausted."

To the same effect Major Powell, of the United States Geological Commission, writes, "All the good public lands suitable for settlement are sold. There is not left unsold in the whole United States, of land which a poor man could turn into a farm, enough to make one average county in Wisconsin. The exception to this statement, if it is open to any, may perhaps be found in Texas or the Indian Territory; elsewhere it is true."

It is not claimed that this great prairie region of the Canadian North-West is uniformly good. On the contrary, there are parts that present few attractions to settlers. In the northern portion, for instance, there is a large expanse of country enclosed between the Peace and the Athabasca, north of Lesser Slave Lake, which is covered by a network of swamps, lakelets, and streams, and which, however much it might be improved by drainage, is at present the best beaver country in Canada. And yet excellent wheat is grown at Lesser Slave Lake, while specimens of wheat and barley grown at the Chipewyan Mission, Lake Athabasca (58° 42' north lat., or about 600 miles north of Winnipeg) received a medal at the Philadelphia Centennial Exhibition of 1876. In the southern portion, again, there are poor lands, that seem to be a continuation of the American desert, for some distance north of the boundary line; while in crossing the prairies by the common route from Edmonton *viâ* Ellice to Winnipeg one traverses some tracts of poor soil, and occasional short stretches of alkali land. Yet even on some of the seemingly poorest soil, near Battleford, excellent wheat has been grown; and it is probable that when the salt or alkali lands are covered with trees, as they may easily be upon the general settlement of the country, the character of the soil will be very greatly improved. It must be remembered, too, that the prairie trails usually follow the ridges or the gravelly soil, where such can be found, as good soil makes bad roads: so that good land may very frequently lie a little to the north or south of that which, judging by what is seen from the trail, might appear hopelessly unproductive. For some time after the transfer of the North-West territories it was customary to speak of a "fertile belt," this name being used to designate that portion of the prairie region south of the north branch of the Saskatchewan, between the Rocky Mountains on the west, and Lake Winnipeg and the Lake of the Woods on the east; and many were led to suppose that the country so described was uniformly good, while that to the north was thought to be comparatively worthless. But further examination discloses occasional poor land in this generally fertile belt and numerous tracts of excellent soil to the north of it, so that the good arable land appears to lie in districts that are interspersed with lands of less value. Very much of the land, however, that is unfit for wheat is admirably adapted for grazing, and stock-raising may be as important as wheat-growing. In the Bow River district, for instance, which embraces about 20,000 square miles in the south-western portion of the prairie region, cattle are raised in large numbers, the climate being such as to admit of their wintering out, as the seasons are mild and the snowfall extremely slight. Other districts, such as that which is unwatered by the Qu'appelle, are said to be well suited for sheep-farming, although housing and home-feeding would be necessary during part of the winter. Others, again, are rich in lumber, as there are large forests easily accessible from the upper waters of the Saskatchewan and of the Athabasca; while on these two rivers and on several of their tributaries coal of superior quality and in large quantity is found, giving promise of abundant fuel for the millions that must yet people this territory.

Attempts have been made to estimate the extent of wheat-growing land in this great North-West. Professor Macoun, of the Canadian Geological Survey, sets it down at 200,000,000 of acres. Colonel Taylor, the United States consul at Winnipeg, comparing the Canadian prairies with the Western and North-western States, says that "four-fifths of the wheat-producing belt of North America will be found north of the international boundary." These estimates may be premature; and yet each year, with its ampler examination of the country by surveyors and its increasing testimony from settlers, tends rather to confirm than to refute these figures.

Many thought, however, as many still think, that the climate in those northern latitudes must be unfavourable for wheat-farming, no matter how excellent the soil; but experience is proving that the climate, unless in the farther north, is thoroughly suited to the growth of grain, while even in such remoter portions as the Peace River country summer frosts may disappear when the soil is cultivated, or may prove to be local and comparatively harmless. Careful observations made at Battleford show that the average temperature there from April to August—the wheat-growing months—is higher than it is at Toronto during the same months; so that, even though the average for the year may, on account of the severe cold of winter, be lower than in Western Ontario, the temperature is more favourable as far as the growth of grain is concerned; and Battleford has much the same climate as any part of the country along the line from Edmonton to Winnipeg. Besides, in those northern latitudes there is a much larger proportion of sunlight during the summer than there is farther south, a fact that must tell very greatly in favour of our Canadian prairies, and that may, in some measure, account for what climatologists have often observed, that the quality of wheat improves the more closely you approach the northern limit of wheat-growing lands.

In travelling from Dunvegan, where we left the reader in our last article, to Winnipeg, as the writer did, by way of Edmonton, Battleford, and Touchwood Hills, one passes through much of the finest portion of our prairie country. Having floated down Peace River on a raft fifty miles to the Smoky River depôt, where we procured horses to convey us to the Hudson's Bay Company's Fort at Lesser Slave Lake, we caught the Company's boats on one of their freighting trips down the Lake and Lesser Slave River and the Athabasca to a point called the Athabasca Landing, from which we came by a comfortable conveyance over a good waggon-road to Edmonton. The traveller in the North-West, at least in the remoter districts, is largely dependent on the Hudson's Bay Company, and although in the summer season you may meet on the more frequented trails long bands of carts belonging to independent freighters, or may at some points find that the "free-traders" can forward you more quickly and more comfortably than the Company, yet the assistance of the Hudson's Bay Company officials, who are almost invariably energetic, hospitable, and courteous, is of material importance in traversing the lonely north. At nearly every post of the Company a large number of horses are kept, for the keep of horses throughout this wide region costs nothing, as they can winter out, pawing away the light snow and finding abundance of grass beneath. If the agent at any post has no horses under his charge he can usually make arrangements with half-breeds or with white settlers for forwarding travellers, many being able to furnish not only good horses and strong prairie carts, but also comfortable buck-boards and waggons; and thus you are passed on by stages, with perhaps four or five changes of driver and conveyance between the Rocky Mountains and Winnipeg.

For winter travel dogs have hitherto been largely used, as with light loads they are swifter than horses. To drive a team of dogs it is said that one must be able to swear in English, French, or Cree, while to be a first-rate dog-driver requires a fluent command

of profanity in the three languages. Some years ago a well-known Winnipeg ecclesiastic was making an extended winter trip; the dogs, though frequently whipped, made little progress, so the bishop remonstrated with the driver. That functionary replied that he could not make them go unless he swore at them; absolution was therefore given him for the trip, and the dogs, hearing the familiar expletives, trotted along briskly. Dog-driving, however, is passing out of use in the North-West, as it is becoming much more expensive to keep dogs than it is to keep horses. While buffalo were abundant and every post and wigwam could have unlimited pemmican it was easy for any man to keep a kennel; but as the buffalo are rapidly disappearing, and as the dogs must be fed throughout the whole year while the horses can forage for themselves at all seasons, horses are being used almost entirely on the prairies, except in the more northern districts where game and fish are very abundant.

Edmonton, which has for many years been an important depôt of the Hudson's Bay Company and a distributing point for a large circle of trading-posts, is the centre of an extensive district of peculiar fertility, probably the most attractive in the North-West. Nowhere do settlers reap larger crops "off the sod,"—that is, the first season that the soil is ploughed. In some parts of the country the land yields little or nothing the first summer, and the settler can only plough it up that the grass-roots may rot and the soil be ready for seed the following spring. In most parts of the Saskatchewan Valley, however, good crops may be raised on newly broken land. As the Canadian Pacific Railway will pass through Edmonton, and as a line of steamers ply between this and Winnipeg, the district will be easy of access, and its facilities of communication must attract towards it the traffic of the Bow River grazing country to the south and of the Peace River district to the north. Already the little settlement gathered here has two churches, a school, an hotel, and a telegraph station connecting it with the world's 4,000,000 miles of wire.

In six days of prairie travel along the north bank of the Saskatchewan we reached Fort Pitt, passing over excellent soil almost the whole way, much of it well wooded and well watered; and three days more brought us to Battleford, where Governor Laird and his Council administer the affairs of the North-West Territories. Prairie travel means —at least, in the shortening days of October, when we made acquaintance with it—an average of about thirty-five miles a day. You have your saddle-horse, or, if you prefer it, you take a seat with your half-breed attendant in the waggon or buck-board, your tent, baggage, provisions, &c., being piled up on the rear of your waggon, or stowed away in an accompanying cart. You cannot lose your way, unless at some forks or cross-roads, for the track has been clearly grooved by the traffic of years ; and near any centre, such as a farming settlement or a Hudson's Bay post, the converging trails remind one of the railway lines near any dépôt. Occasionally you meet immigrants, or trains of freighters with their bands of prairie-carts, at first almost as rare as a ship on mid-ocean, but more frequent as you move eastward, like the increasing number of vessels as you draw near port. You need have no difficulty in keeping the pot well supplied with game, for abundance of duck may be found in the numerous lakelets that border the trail, and prairie chicken are plentiful in all except the more settled districts. As day after day passes you become more and more in love with the climate, as well as with the country ; you can understand how it should be noted for its peculiar healthfulness, and specially for its freedom from fevers and from diseases of the throat and lungs. There is a continual freshness and interest in your journey, and if you have some pleasant travelling companions your prairie trip may be like a prolonged picnic.

Continuing from Battleford, by way of Carlton, Touchwood Hills, and Ellice, to Winnipeg, you pass over stretches of country which rival Manitoba in the attractions they offer to settlers, and out of which new provinces must ere long be carved. Soon after entering Manitoba you may find a change come over your half-breed driver. Beyond the limits of that province the sale of intoxicants in the North-West is strictly forbidden, and the law is rigidly enforced ; any who desire to import wines or spirits for private use requiring a special permit for that purpose from the Lieutenant-Governor. In Manitoba, however, there is no such restriction upon the liquor traffic ; your driver will be sure to find a good camping-ground near the first hamlet you come to after entering the province. In the morning you may find the poor fellow rather unfit for work ; you must watch him pretty closely for the rest of the way ; and, as you approach Winnipeg— or Garry, as they all call it, from the old Hudson's Bay fort round which the city has clustered—his face will beam with delight at the vision of unrestricted whisky.

We reached Winnipeg from the west. How fares it with the immigrant approaching it from the east ? His passage from Liverpool, by way of Quebec, Sarnia, and Duluth, has taken about fifteen days, and has cost him from £9 to £28 sterling, according to the accommodation he has chosen by steamer and rail. From previous information he knows where to settle, and at once procures his "location" from the Dominion land agent ; or, perhaps, he can afford a little time to look about him. If he has arrived early enough in the year, and has settled on land that yields a good return off the sod, he may be able to raise a crop his first season. If not, he must content himself with breaking up his land, to have it ready for the following spring, and with building his "shanty" and barn, providing himself with stock, and laying in winter supplies. He has availed himself of the liberal homestead law, and has pre-empted an adjoining quarter-section, so that he is now the possessor of a farm of 320 acres, having brought out his family, procured his land, and started with sufficient stock and implements for a new settler, at a total outlay of less than a single year's rental for a wheat-farm of a similar size in the mother country. He will find an abundant market for all that he can raise, whether it be stock or cereals. New settlers will require food and seed : the Hudson's Bay Company may be a large purchaser of his produce, and the Government will buy extensively on behalf of the Indians, who must for some years be assisted at the public cost, until they adopt a more settled life. Indeed, there is every prospect that, for several years, the bulk of the grain raised in the North-West will be required for local consumption ; and by the time that settlers are ready to export grain the means of communication will be so much increased, and the cost of freight so much reduced, that they will be able to compete on most favourable terms for the supply of the British market. Competent authorities estimate that within two years, as soon as the railway is completed from Winnipeg to Thunder Bay, on Lake Superior, grain can be taken from Manitoba to Liverpool at a total outside cost of 45 cents per bushel. Wheat is grown in Manitoba at a cost that does not exceed, if it reaches, 40 cents per bushel ; so that it will be grown in Manitoba and delivered in Liverpool at a cost to the producer, including all charges for transport, of 85 cents (that is,

3s. 6d. sterling) per bushel, or £1 8s. 4d. per quarter. As the average price of wheat in England for the thirty years, from 1849 to 1878, was £2 13s. sterling per quarter—the lowest in that period being, in 1851, £1 19s. 7d. sterling—a sufficiently broad margin is left for the Canadian wheat-grower.

And if such facilities of transport be not sufficient to secure for our North-West, where land yields from thirty to sixty bushels of wheat per acre, the chief supply of the British market, other and shorter lines of transport may yet be opened. Already a new route is projected, and a company is being formed to construct a railway, a little over 300 miles in length, from the northern extremity of Lake Winnipeg down the valley of the Nelson River to Port Nelson on Hudson's Bay. This port is twenty-one miles nearer Liverpool than New York is. It appears that the valley of the Nelson offers a practicable route for a railway, although the river is too broken to be navigable, and the navigation of Hudson's Bay and Hudson's Straits can be relied on for at least three months in the year, probably for a longer period. This would allow of the shipment of a very large amount of grain from the Canadian North-West and also from the north-western portions of the United States by this route. Even if the year's crop could not be shipped the same season that it was harvested, yet the difference in cost of transport would probably make it worth while to hold much of it over until the following summer rather than send it by the more expensive southern routes.

But whether the grain of our North-West reaches the Atlantic by way of the St. Lawrence or by way of Hudson's Straits, it seems almost inevitable that it must soon become a powerful, and perhaps a controlling, factor in regulating the wheat markets of the world.

The development of this great prairie region cannot be long delayed. Its vast wheat-lands, its rich pastures, its coal measures and its woods, combined with its increasing nearness to the markets of Europe, must insure its rapid settlement. As you traverse the country, as you hear the unvarnished tales of men who, starting on their homesteads two or three years ago with little stock and no reserve capital, are now in comfort and on a fair way to wealth ; as you examine the prospects that lie before the sober and industrious, and as, in fancy, you connect the toiling tenant-farmers and agricultural labourers of the mother country with these broad, fertile acres, it is scarcely possible, even for the least sanguine, to refrain from visions of a time when this vast territory will be the home of many millions. Canadians ask the men of other lands, they specially ask the farmers of the fatherland, to examine, as some of them have already done, their wide and inviting prairies. They know that an impartial verdict must be in their favour. They have the utmost confidence in their country, in its capacities, and in its future ; and they believe that, ere long, a cluster of rich and loyal provinces will extend from the Red River to the Rocky Mountains.

DANIEL M. GORDON.

"AM MEER."

(Schubert.)

I.

THE long moan of the monotonous sea,
  And ceaseless wash of never-ending waves ;
The roll of foaming billows thro' dim caves
Skirting the unknown shores ; and hushfully
The lisp of lapping wavelets in soft glee
  About the moonlit sands. No wild wind raves
Above the solemn waste ; the night is still
Save the sea-sound and casual sea-bird's shrill.

Hark ! the moan grows into a troubled cry,
  The billows plash more suddenly, and leap
Like startled herds that plunge before they fly ;
  A weird wind riseth swiftly and doth sweep
The salt sand from each wave-top towards the sky,
And the great sea awaketh from its sleep.

II.

The wild wind wails above the foaming seas,
  The billows break in swirling clouds of white,
The sickly moon, cloud-hidden, scarce gives light,
And the dense mists are blown to shreds of fleece ;
The whole sea panteth for a wild release,
  Like some great brute with fleeing prey in sight ;
And the harsh echo from the surf-beat shore
Blends with the boom where the great caverns roar.

Hush ! the wind shivers, moans, and dies away !
  The foam-wreath'd billows now no longer flee
Along the dismal track of swirling spray.
  The stars come forth and shimmer mournfully.
There is no sound at all but the soft sway
  Of long waves breathing on the sleeping sea.

WILLIAM SHARP.

Mogador.

FROM MOGADOR TO MOROCCO.

BY RALLI STENNING.

PART I.

OUR journey is to the Antipodes—not the secondary one of geography, but to the primary one of people, customs, and civilisation. The world affords no contrasts more striking and complete than the cities of London and Morocco. From London to Gibraltar, from Gibraltar to Tangiers, from Tangiers to Saffi—the most picturesque town on the Morocco coast—from Saffi to Mogador—this is our way. At Mogador we start for Morocco, the city.

Mogador is a port, enjoying the questionable honour of having been made such by the decree of a sultan, not by the laws of nature—partly surrounded by sand hills, with a distinctively fine climate, and, what is more rare in Moorish cities, a good sewer. A handful of the two thousand Europeans said to be found in the coast towns of Morocco reside here. It is remarkably healthy: life to the dying is said to be in its breezes. Why do not invalids go there? Let the food answer. If we could at any time live on air, we cannot when we are ill. Moorish sauces may pass muster with the strong. Something, however, seems to disagree with the Jews we see here. Surely a more cadaverous set of faces in a bright and breezy world is not to be found.

It is afternoon, and to-morrow we are to start for Morocco. We wander about the streets of the town, curious, charmed, dismayed. New and indescribable sensations possess us at the very first turn of the street which conceals our quarters and companions. Dress here is a combination of nun, monk, and showman : free white flowing robes, long pointed monastic hoods, broidered gowns and girdles, turbans and scimitars. It is an animated picture-book, and nobody in it seems astonished. All are familiar with what seems to us as strange as men in the moon. We gaze on dreamy, moon-stricken faces; figures slowly sailing about, as under less severe gravitation than of our own familiar world. We listen to their speech, as if it could tell us something about the melancholy forms which move along with an air somewhat between that of a carnival and a funeral. We dare not go far in a world like this. It is a place to dream of, not to live in. A glance up a narrow, long passage, which we come eventually to know as a Moorish street; a vague sense of sleeping Arabs, flat upon the ground, propped against the wall, or rolled up, ball-like, in a corner; pluckings of fowls, lumps of mud-concrete, rags, cabbage-stalks, cracked walls, loop-holes, low archways, blacks and beggars, half-naked children, smothered-up women, faint smells—these and the like will long combine in the memory of this first impression of a Moorish town. The white houses in the intense sunlight add to the daze of this waking dream. Since this glimpse of barbarism, finding ourselves once more in the boarding-house (though that preserves but little of European civilisation), we seem to have returned to a real world again.

Mogador is a thorough-going Moorish town, its European doctor and foreign sewer notwithstanding; though of its fifteen thousand inhabitants six thousand are Jews. The uncommon regularity of its streets, which seems to have won for it the name of *Sueraa*, meaning beautiful, may show that latent capacity of order in the Moorish mind survives its centuries of confusion.

There are no "tourist sights" in Mogador; the most picturesque the town in the clear moonlight. A dreamy flatness of white house-tops, scarcely broken by turret or tower, sur-

An Arab of the Soudan.

rounded by sea and hill, has a peculiarly charming effect. The houses — sometimes looking like houses piled upon houses—consist of one or two stories of rooms surrounding the verandah and balcony of a *patio* or courtyard, which is entered by a covered gateway. The windowless streets are all narrow, some long and straight. Private houses, merchants' warehouses, hostelries, all are of one generic type, save those found in blind alley and slum. In business quarters there is little or no appearance of business. A caravan of camels is seen bringing merchandise from Timbuctoo : the procession, which moves slowly, gravely, with silent foot, heightening our sense of mystery, suddenly turns down a gateway scarcely wide enough to admit it, into the central court of a warehouse, and is out of sight. We follow through the archway, to find these "ships of the desert" moored to their quay with freights of almonds, gums, ivory, gold-dust, and ostrich feathers which might be of little value, for they are tied much as we tie up bundles of waste paper, letting the paper be its own covering. The outer feathers of the bales are broken and dirty. Imagine London with all its drays out of sight in invisible warehouse squares! Such is the condition of commerce in Mogador. These camel trains are the poetry of trade, a living link to patriarchal and modern times. They have a look of immense sadness, as though willing to close their long-enduring history.

As we leave the *patio*, a solitary street cry attracts our attention. A man is leading a girl of about sixteen years of age. He cries her qualities, for she is being hawked before her auction. This is the second day; to-morrow she will be brought to the hammer, when, as she is good-looking, well-made, and healthy, she will probably fetch £18 or £20. The jaded, rag-covered Arab who leads her bought her "a spec" in the market of Timbuctoo, to which Arab robbers had brought her from some quiet Soudan village they had sacked and burned, killing the old and sick, and turning the well-grown and healthy into money. With what emotion do those large white eyes look out upon these strange streets and people !

There is a European dispensary in Mogador, established by Sir Moses Montefiore's benevolent interest in his Jewish brethren ; but Moors, we are told, prefer charms to medicine—at least to European medicine. Their own practitioner, who sits in the market-place, is usually a naked fanatic of some religious order, with whom sewage is an occasional specific, and a tramp along the patient's backbone, as he lies face to face with the ground, a professional operation.

Turkish baths are much in vogue here; many establishments exist. They consist of long, low, dark, stuffy, dismal, stinking rooms, at least to European eyes and nose. Men are admitted till mid-day at what is equal to a half-penny each, and women from mid-day to night-fall, for twice that sum. We are attracted by a fine-looking figure of fifty years of age, riding a handsome Arab horse, with a triumphal train of attendants. The pace, the attitude, the look, betoken authority. It is the Governor of Mogador. Old men seek his benediction. Women lift children to kiss his hands. He passes out of the gate, and we reflect upon a glimpse of rank · and state which, as we are told, has a stipend of five shillings a day! Yet a governor maintains barbaric magnificence, and sends money presents to his caid, pasha, and sultan! Here is scope for financial ingenuity. No wonder that Moorish prisons are filled with small and unlucky farmers who do not meet their extortionate taxes. Strange how all the world loves authority, and none the less when it is invested in one man who can flog it if he please.

* * * * *

A Governor and his People.

We start for Morocco amid a crowd of audacious old idlers and chattering street-boys, entertained doubtless by the most consciously unbecoming dress, which from considerations of safety we have been driven to adopt. Though the *caic* and turban—loose foldings of white muslin about the body and the head—are not unbecoming to Bedouin or Moor, on the European they look utterly grotesque. Our own dress might attract the wandering robbers who chance to be near our path. Europeans are regarded as plump and fair game for their sport. We are urged to wear Moorish slippers, but they prove to our inflexible English feet impossible; so we are compelled to keep our own boots. We have preferred mules to ride, because they are docile, sure-footed, and capable of great endurance, and these Morocco mules are the first of their kind. With a necessary detachment of native soldiers, provided with influential letters of introduction to the governors, caide, and other officials on the line of route, our cavalcade of mules, donkeys, camels, and men, all in the best of spirits, defiles up the long straight street leading across the town from the gate of the Ben-Yantor, by the markets and government workshops, through the Morocco gate out by the Moorish cemetery into the country. Our way at first lies through loose sand covered with white broom, next across a band of richer-soiled country, dotted with a tree peculiar to Morocco — the Argan tree—which looks like the rugged gnarled olive, its timber being as hard as the iron wood. Occasionally it presents a charming picture. Goats, leaving the parched coarse herbage of the ground, climb nimbly up into its straggling branches and nibble the leaves from its twigs. As we proceed, the scattered trees gather into a forest which extends for miles. Beyond this we enter upon a tract of country not unlike that of an English park, bounded in the distance by some soft Surrey hills. On the whole the prospects of the journey are uninteresting, and, until we reach the palm groves which belt Morocco, certainly are not beautiful. Tufts of stunted fan-palms (palmettos), exaggerated white broom, ugly dwarf-

thorn bushes, straggling over land now gravelly, now sandy, always barren, do not charm. Certain quarrelsome, thievish tribes of Arabs from the Sahara, however, find spots even here on which to exist. Their square group of black tents, known as a *duar*, are often visible from our track. From ten to twenty families, generally nearly related, inhabit them. A gaily painted chest, a hand corn-mill, distaff, weaving loom, a few jars, a lamp, long musket, dagger, saddle and bridle, together with a few goat-skins and mats, are generally found within each tent; and outside, a little garden of scratched soil, an oven of a couple of bricks, a few poultry, milch goats and cows, with as many horses as they have been lucky enough to steal. The males are all thieves from eight years old. The women and girls spin, weave, cook, and lead a fairly busy life. The clothes, tents, and ropes of their dwellings are all homespun.

The two principal towns on our route are Sidi Mokhtar and Rasbat el Udaia, both of which are situated on branches of the Tensift, several of whose tributaries we cross. At such points the eye delights in the beauties of watered vegetation. The shade of olives, palms, and oleanders make a little paradise, a charming close to a long day's ride over scorching arid waste. Nights are spent in the *inzella*—a sort of

The Cemetery by the Morocco Gate.

travellers' fold, made of high mud walls or impassable thorn fences, into which we go, mules, camels, donkeys, servants, and all, for safety from certain freebooters, who might prove more than even our guard could defend us from. These places provide nothing.

A Moorish Town on the way.

Servants, soldiers, cooks, all rush about till the tents are pitched, dinner served, and the weary animals fed. Then the night—dogs bark, camels groan, drivers snore, a restless ass stumbles over the tent-cord, cocks crow, and unaccustomed sounds of every pitch and degree alternately aid our slumbers. Then the dawn, the bath, breakfast, and the start. A whole day's march without one living thing, another with a mounted courier or solitary camel carrying goods from Morocco to the coast. Save by the inhabitants of the inzellas, and clusters of mud huts which straggle about it, the country proper seems unoccupied. The specimens of horse-flesh we see in these places contrast awkwardly with our school-day imaginings of the "Arabian steed." Arab horses, as seen here, are little better than those found in English gipsy camps. But the Arab farmer is not our man. It is the governor, the pasha, the sultan, men whose extortions accumulate these poor fellows' wealth, who own the typical Arab horse, which is as rare and as costly as the English candidate for the Newmarket. Perfection of breeding is confined to the extreme south of the country by the borders of the Great Sahara. On food of camels' milk and dates it attains its greyhound slimness, speed, and grace. With confined stable and dry bean-food it soon loses both slimness, grace, and speed.

Near the villages we sometimes pass little plots laid out as gardens and farms, in which vegetables grow luxuriantly ; a radish attains the size of our carrot, and a single cabbage vies with the proportions of an umbrella, but even here cultivation is at its lowest pitch. Exported harvests might produce immense wealth, but the Moor seems unconquerably lazy. He loves money, but he more loves ease. His faith comes of his character, as most other people's ; with " If it please God to send rain, there will be enough for myself and my family," he does not strive to lay up even against the possibility of its not pleasing God to send rain; actual famine does not convert his laziness. " Never run when you can walk " is his national motto; while other people strive, he idles down to ruin. After miles of weary jogging over rough dreary plains, the eye alights on these little belts of village cultivation with restful delight. Patches of corn, figs, and pomegranates ; green lanes of shrubs, climbing plants, and olives refresh one as a kind of vegetation sea-bath. These pleasures at length culminate in the extensive gardens and palm groves which flank the walls of the city of Morocco. The gardens, surrounded by mud walls (tabia) in various stages of decay, are stocked with orange, fig, citron, and lemon-trees, but a glance shows no sign of flowers. Before us is Morocco in the soft rosy light of the setting sun, surrounded by its twenty-feet mud-wall defences, flanked here and there by turrets. After eight days of caravan life in ardent heat and suffocating dust, we exult in the prospective comforts of " a city that hath foundations." The mortal weariness of wandering in a country like this is necessary to understand such a figure of the soul's last resting-place. We look and are enlightened: in sunbeams and fancies, it is transfigured.

Passing under the massive gateway with its guard-house, we catch the glimpse of a countenance which makes us shudder. It is one of the guard; ferocious, immovable, inhuman. One word, and you are a dead man. We quickly turn our gaze into the street; yet that face has impressed us for ever. Its phantom in the memory strikes horror. The street! Yes; we look at the street which gives entrance to the city. Our spirits sink; we are overcome with melancholy; the effect is dismal: a long narrow passage of flat, windowless, yellow walls, topped here and there with lumbering stork nests, and banked up on either hand with filth and nameless abominations. We are told it passes the Sultan's palace wall!—it might be a city dust-yard. Even the narrower path down which we defile is encumbered with rubbish, which makes it difficult to proceed. This first impression is utterly distressing— nothing but filth and desolation.

We turn and twist and twine as in the mazes of a labyrinth—down passages six feet wide; between ruins of fallen buildings; through dark gateways, and long low-covered alleys, in the deepening twilight. Abominable smells, flies, dust; din of shouting boys shaking clenched fists at "the Christians;"

one old hag lifting up an arm of bone, screaming curses out of an almost toothless grinning skull; a dead horse; a heap of bones; a woman flitting by in spectral robe; a turbaned lord, sleek and leering—these are the confused abiding pictures of our first steps in Morocco.

Our cavalcade is at length conducted, by the escort the Governor has sent us, through an archway into a kind of sluggard's garden, forming a large central court to a square of rooms in two stories, with verandah supported on carved wooden pillars, and carrying a balcony which runs on every side—picturesque doubtless, yet in our present mood and in the gathering darkness dismal in the extreme. A small fountain forms the centre of this weedy place, dry and dilapidated; yet we are just cheerful enough to ejaculate at the sight, "What a pity! something might be made of this." Here are to be our stables, kitchens, bedrooms, dining-room, &c., &c. A few unglazed latticed windows and a larger number of curtained doors open on to the verandahs and balconies. We dismount and survey our quarters. Every room is a long narrow arrangement of four bare walls, dark, stuffy, and furnitureless; but we must not "look a gift horse in the mouth." The accommodation, such as it is, is provided by the grace of the Governor in response to our letters; and

A Duar,

there is no option in hotels. We left the last faint trace of civilisation on leaving Mogador; here is uncorrupted barbarism. Without the courtesy of the authorities we must have camped outside the walls, or rather, we must have stopped at Mogador. And after all we have come here for new experiences, and are we not having them? In no time, mats, &c., are spread, and a cup of tea, which the tact of our cook is quick to serve, puts a new complexion on things. We light up—affairs, after all, don't look so bad. We quite enjoy the discovery that the ceiling of our sitting-room is decorated with arabesques, which develop to our wider-opened or more accustomed eyes delicate tints of green and red. More lights! The doorways prove to be surrounded with stucco in Moorish style, and a band of devices in pale Pompeian red runs round the walls both at floor and ceiling. Familiarity does not breed contempt! Dinner is served, accompanied by complimentary dishes from the Governor's table, with polite offers of an expert cook for our stay. Moorish politeness in such matters is, however, dangerous, so we thank the Governor in the extravagant manner of the country and decline. European visitors are fanatical Moors' abominations, and Governors are obliged to listen to their peoples' demands. Unpopularity may find a ready way to popularity in driving out "the infidels," and a cook can accomplish this desirable exodus in a triumphantly Moorish way. Mild doses of poison, administered in a favourite dish, brings on indisposition, awakens suspicions, and the infidel departs. How excellent may prove the services of a Governor's cook! The night falls; lights are extinguished; sleep is courted. The buzzing ears, tingling necks, burning brows, sensations everywhere!

Lights are rekindled. We make a night sortie, with victorious results. It is again dark, and the eyes close; but the enemy returns reinforced! The attack is one of revenge; from head to foot we are assailed and wounded. "Powder" is of no avail; the countless army braves its dangers. "Lights!" we cry; but the mischief is done; bloodthirsty fleas, bugs, mosquitoes, a grand alliance, have carried the day—or night—and rush off, laden with booty. We had thought we were at least in a clean house—property of the Sultan, granted by his Grace! But vermin are Republican; so are Moors. Political opinions are not supposed to have any natural connection with men asleep; but here is clearly an exception. The Moorish creed of equality brings all classes into contact. "Saint," filthiest of the filthy, elbows the Governor; the Bedouin jostles the merchant; Moorish vermin, therefore, enjoy a commonwealth. But the Moors' theory of equality has a better side. A slave may rise to the highest position of the State; his blood has coloured a Sultan; but this good side of his creed is evidently for the aspiring negro, and thirsty vermin, certainly not for the sleepy traveller. To these poisonous pests, a clean man asleep is a fête—a carnival! Telegraphic news of the event excites the whole neighbourhood, which under some entomological Mr. Cook takes a trip to the scene.

The dawn, the bath, fresh air and certain skin-soothers with which we are provided, fit us for increased acquaintance with this venerable city. Our breakfast is taken in the open air of our garden, on Moorish carpets spread in the shade of an olive-tree, a situation in which there is a certain picturesqueness and novelty.

GOTHENBURG AND SWEDEN.

September, 1879.

THE handsome and growing seaport of Sweden has gotten itself a name for something else than its picturesque situation and roomy harbour; a man may care little about the merits of various licensing systems, but it has become worth while to understand what that system is with which the name of Gothenburg is now associated all over Europe.

In the report laid before Parliament on the 24th of March, 1879, by the Select Committee of the House of Lords on Intemperance, the general character of the system is stated in a few words:—

"The civil authority in Gothenburg was the first to avail itself (in 1866) of the power given by the new law of letting their licenses to a company or Bolag. This was the result of the deliberations of a committee, which recommended the organization of the liquor traffic on an entirely new principle, viz., that no individual, either as proprietor or manager, should derive any private gain from the sale of spirits. The whole public-house traffic was transferred to a limited liability company, consisting of the most respected members of the community, who undertake by their charter not to derive any profit from the business, or allow any one acting under them to do so, but to conduct the business solely in the interests of temperance and morality, and to pay to the town treasury the whole profits beyond the ordinary rate of interest on the paid-up capital."—*Report*, p. xlii.

The system is no longer theory, but an experiment of twelve or thirteen years' standing, and we found the testimony of well-informed citizens, on a recent visit, to be unanimously favourable; though with one or two reservations. There are certain houses, among which are the hotels, not yet in the hands of the company; these do a thriving café business, free from the restrictions imposed on the other houses. The grip of the community on the liquor traffic is already firm, and could, on occasion, be made firmer; and it may be that those interested in houses meanwhile exempted are tormented before the time. It would not, however, be right to say so much without adding that there was no reason, from anything we saw or heard, to think that the principal hotels are not conducted at least as well as the best of those at home. But one of the exempted houses, a music-hall on the Skeppsbron (quay), was as ugly as might be. At half-past eight at night it was full of men—no women—drinking freely, and listening to impure songs sung to them by four tawdrily dressed girls. It was some comfort, after watching the scene for ten minutes, to be told that the new law had reduced such abominations to this unit, and might one day extinguish that also.

Public men of the town, earnest friends of the system, were anxious that strangers should not approach Gothenburg with too high expectations. Its peculiar licensing law does not profess to be a specific for the cure of drunkenness in the individual, nor a means of promptly banishing intemperance from a community. No law and no police can secure these high results; the good which the Gothenburg system has, in the judgment of its friends, effected, does not extend so far, nor did they ever expect that it would. It is only fair to place this disclaimer in the front of an impartial statement, such as the present is intended to be.

We went out to inspect, under the guidance of Mr. Reubenson, a gentleman well known in the town for his interest in philanthropic works. The hours chosen were from 5 to 7 P.M., these being the hours of greatest indulgence, and we encountered four cases of drunkenness in the first few minutes. One of these was seen at the door of a public-house in a back street. The man seemed to have some tipsy glimmering of our errand, and was anxious to give us the benefit of his large experience. The other three cases were found at the Polis Vaht Kontor. A foreign sailor was locked up, helpless; another man, native, was brought in while we were there; and a very wretched woman, who had been brought in at noon, was coming to herself in an adjoining cell. The effect was shocking, for we had not had the forethought to make similar visits to police offices at home, where we would have seen a much larger number of incapables. The woman was, we found, an old offender.

The houses are unattractive, inside and outside, a circumstance which arrests a British stranger. There are no signs, no plate-glass, no gilding, no blaze of light, no marble tables or cushioned seats, no over-dressed and smirking barmaids; but plain sanded floors, counters of dull lead, small deal tables, chairs with painfully short backs, and men-waiters in leathern jackets. This description applies to the houses where bränvin is retailed to the lower classes. Bränvin is a muddy white spirit, distilled from corn or potatoes, costing less than a penny a glass, and nasty in the extreme, if one may judge by the smell. That is the only intoxicating drink sold, except a cheap brandy, which a very few persons seemed to take in the form of toddy. Most of the customers seemed to be only a minute in the shop at a time. They hurried in, drank their glass, paid their six öre—for sale on credit is strictly forbidden—and hurried out again. Little knots of half-a-dozen, who had been doing some piece of work on the docks together, would sit down to share the payment that had been put into the hands of one of their number. Men engaged on exhausting work will, we are told, visit the public-house ten or twelve times in the course of the day, spending ninepence or tenpence on the stimulant; cases in which this quantity is exceeded are rare.

These retail shops are open from 7 A.M. till 9 P.M. on week-days. The law with reference to Sundays is that they are closed from 6 P.M. on Saturday to 8 A.M. on Monday; and the same law applies to holidays. The eating-houses are open for two hours on Sunday afternoon, but all "bar business" is prohibited.

Under the same roof with most of the public-houses there are eating-houses and cafés. In the latter those who can afford to pay more are supplied with the diet to be found in any European restaurant; in the former, good and well-cooked food is sold to the working classes at very low prices. A warm meal of beef or pork with potatoes costs 25 öre—rather less than 3½d.; soup, coffee, or an exceedingly small beer, can be had for 10 öre more. On the one hand, we were told that the company, in their desire to make the houses places for eating as well as drinking, had fixed these rates rather under the figures of remuneration; but on the other hand, it is certain that before the post of manager is many hours vacant, there are fifty applicants eager to get it. As the law makes it impossible for a manager to derive profit except from food and unintoxicating drinks, it is probably the café and restaurant business, where prices are not fixed by law, that pays. And a singular detail of the system should be noticed in this connection. After 6 P.M. the sale of drink without food is illegal. We were shown an exceedingly substantial sandwich, of flad-brod, butter, and ham, which goes with each glass, the consumption of which must prove a highly satisfactory condition of the digestive organs.

Besides the retail houses for consumption of spirits on the spot, there are a certain number of shops, seven, I think, in which quantities of not less than two quarts are sold. In these the average of daily transactions is represented by 50 kronas, £2 16s.; but on Saturday, the market day, the amount is ten times greater. The smaller sum indicates the consumption of bränvin in the houses of the common people of the town; the larger sum indicates what is used by the population of ten surrounding parishes. For the company's monopoly now extends so far, and there are no shops for the sale of liquor except in the town.

We were assured that all these provisions of the law are enforced by a growingly careful inspection on the part of the company and the police. "There seems to be no doubt," says the Committee of the House of Lords, "that this experiment has worked well."

Mr. Bædaker, in his admirable Guidebook to Norway and Sweden, says, "It is at least certain that drunkenness has diminished greatly of late years" (p. 271).

The truth seems to be that the state of things in Sweden prior to 1855 was fearfully bad. The production and sale of strong drink were under no restraint; and crime and immorality had become such as to make vigorous measures imperative. The following items, in which the philanthropic portion of the Gothenburg community recognise distinct gains as accruing from its new licensing law, are gathered chiefly from notes of a lengthened interview in which Mr. S. A. Hedlung, editor of the leading newspaper and a member of the Upper House of the Swedish Legislature, was good enough to put us in possession of the results of his long and intelligent observation.

1. No individual now derives profit from his neighbour's indulgence in strong drink.

2. The company do their best to secure that the spirits sold shall be pure.

3. Twenty-seven towns in Sweden—there are only twenty-eight—having a population of 5,000 and upwards, have followed the example of Gothenburg; and so have nineteen towns in which the population is smaller.

4. In the capital, Stockholm (fairest and brightest of cities!) the system was adopted in 1877, after much discussion, and notwithstanding large expense in buying up vested interests. The population of Stockholm is close on 170,000; yet the experiment there is thus far satisfactory. The statistics showed five hundred and seventy-eight cases of delirium tremens in 1875, whereas last year (1878) they had fallen to less than half that number, two hundred and sixty-three. And Bædaker says, "The police statistics show that drunkenness and crime have already decreased."

5. The number of licensed houses in Gothenburg has been diminished. There were sixty when the new law came into operation in 1866; there are now forty-one; and this number includes the shops of wine-merchants, the hotels and cafés, and the shops for the sale of bränvin off the premises. Meanwhile the population, which was under sixty thousand when the experiment began, has grown to seventy thousand.

6. Every year the system remains in force the traffic becomes more distinctly under legislative control. The minds of men get familiar with this important idea; vested interests lapse, and more vigorous measures of repression, if such should appear to the community to be required, could be now enforced with less difficulty.

7. The fact on which both friends and others place most emphasis is that the profits of the traffic, which formerly went into the pockets of one hundred and nineteen publicans, now go to the civil authority to be used for the public good. This circumstance is exposed to the obvious criticism that magistrates might be tempted to encourage

the traffic for the sake of increasing revenue and saving rates; to which the answer made is that the temptation is less to a representative body than to an individual; and that, supposing the temptation yielded to, the resulting evil is less.* Besides, it would be easy, if necessary, to transfer the profits to the imperial treasury, and let them be disposed of as the nation should judge best.

But we are not to discuss here what the friends of the system say for it. We wish rather to describe what is being done with the large sum, fully £50,000 last year, accruing from the traffic in Gothenburg.

A portion of the money goes to the agricultural societies in the adjacent parishes; and the remainder is not used to lighten local rates but is spent on public parks, on docks, and particularly on schools. These are admirable. Seven thousand children are educated at the public cost. Not five children are untaught, the compulsory act being now virtually displaced by the willingness of the parents. The order, airiness, and general heartiness of these schools leave nothing to be desired. Each boy spends a certain portion of the day in the industrial department, and his class work loses nothing by the arrangement. Last year was only the second of the practice school's existence, yet the money value of the boys' work was nearly £1,000, all the bookbinding and joiner's work being done on the premises. The philanthropic citizens point you to such things and say, There is the good of our licensing system. We have no wish to reduce our rates; but instead of our being left to meet the cost entailed by the crime and poverty which intemperance produces, we get their taxes from the drinkers at the fore-end and the profits of the publicans to boot; and we spend them, as you see, in works fitted to make the community intelligent, healthy, industrious, and virtuous.

The town is distinguished for philanthropic efforts. A school for the training of girls from the age of sixteen to eighteen, under the care of Miss Amelia Arvedson, was specially interesting. There we saw a *crèche*, where some of the girls were caring for thirty fat babies; a kitchen, where a savoury dinner was being cooked for thirty boys from the adjacent gymnasium; a bakery, where all sorts of bread is made and readily sold to the best families; a laundry, in which fine and remunerative work is done; a dor-

mitory, where everything was exquisitely white and fresh; and a bright common room, where the inmates gather after work hours.

Reference has been made to the very general adoption of the Gothenburg system recently throughout Sweden. It only remains to mention the refreshment rooms at the railway stations. We passed over the length of the country from Helsingborg to Jönköping and Gothenburg, and again from the Norwegian frontier, through Stockholm, to Malmö, at all hours of day and night, with a uniform and striking experience. At no station is anything sold stronger than a light beer, and that must be asked for. Out of dozens of travellers you will not see more than four or five taking this native öl, and none of these have their glasses replenished; all go to side-tables and help themselves to tea or coffee—the latter, first-rate—with bread and cakes, taking as much as they choose and paying 35 öre. If it is the time of day for lunch, or dinner, or supper, the long central table is laden with all manner of solid food, warm and toothsome. Each traveller helps himself and drinks as much fresh milk as he cares for, making a uniform payment of about 1s. 7d. for what at Crewe or Rugby would cost 3s. at least. The only peculiarity is the provision of the national whets—sardines, salt ham, raw herrings and other dreadful morsels—without which no native, man or woman, thinks of beginning a substantial meal. Among these, in towns and at home, is a dram of the cheap and nasty spirit; but at railway stations the law is supposed to forbid schnapps. It winks at it, however, to a certain very mild extent, for the custom of drinking this thimbleful of spirit before eating seems to be one from which adult males in Sweden cannot be weaned suddenly. You may, therefore, if you are put up to the thing, see three or four men out of as many dozens, after gulping the whet and before settling to the more serious part of dinner, open a door inside which the bottle of bränvin is found, and help themselves to a raw dram. No more is taken and no payment is made. There can hardly be said to be any secrecy about the singular transaction, but it is gone through quickly and in silence. Anything like indulgence, or a single person affected by drink, was not to be seen in the many hundreds of miles over which our journey extended. The contrast to the state of things on our railways and in Holland and Germany is remarkable.

A. MACLEOD SYMINGTON.

FALLS OF THE LOCHY, PERTHSHIRE.
A STUDY IN BLACK AND WHITE BY E. JENNINGS

THE TRUMPET-MAJOR.

BY THOMAS HARDY, AUTHOR OF "FAR FROM THE MADDING CROWD," ETC.

CHAPTER XV.—"CAPTAIN" BOB LOVEDAY, OF THE MERCHANT SERVICE.

WHILE Loveday and his neighbours were thus rambling forth, full of expectancy, some of them, including Anne in the rear, heard the crackling of light wheels along the sunken curved lane to which the path was the chord. At once Anne thought, "Perhaps that's he, and we are missing him." But recent events were not of a kind to induce her to say anything; and the others of the company did not reflect on the sound.

Had they gone across to the hedge which hid the lane and looked through it, they would have seen a light cart driven by a boy, beside whom was seated a seafaring man, apparently of good standing in the merchant service, with his feet outside on the shaft. The vehicle went over the main bridge, turned in upon the other bridge at the tail of the mill, and halted by the door. The sailor alighted, showing himself to be a well-shaped, active, and fine young man, with a bright eye, an anonymous nose, and of such a rich complexion by exposure to ripening suns that he might have been some connection of that foreigner who calls his likeness the Portrait of a Gentleman in galleries of the Old Masters. Yet in spite of this, and though Bob Loveday had been all over the world from Cape Horn to Pekin, and from India's coral strand to the White Sea, the most conspicuous of all the marks that he had brought back with him was an increased resemblance to his mother, who had lain all the time under Overcombe aisle wall.

Captain Loveday tried the house door; finding this locked he went to the mill door: this was locked also, the mill being stopped for the night.

"They are not at home," he said to the boy. "But never mind that. Just help to unload the things; and then I'll pay you, and you can drive off home."

The cart was unloaded, and the boy was dismissed, thanking the sailor profusely for the payment rendered. Then Bob Loveday, finding that he had still some leisure on his hands, looked musingly east, west, north, south, and nadir; after which he bestirred himself by carrying his goods, article by article, round to the back door, out of the way of casual passers. This done he walked round the mill in a more regardful attitude, XXI—23

and surveyed its familiar features one by one —the panes of the grinding room, now as heretofore clouded with flour as with stale hoar-frost; the meal lodged in the corners of the window-sills, forming a soil in which lichens grew without ever getting any bigger, as they had done since his smallest infancy; the mosses on the plinth towards the river, reaching as high as the capillary power of the walls would fetch up moisture for their nourishment, and the penned millpond, now as ever on the point of overflowing into the garden. Everything was the same.

When he had had enough of this it occurred to Loveday that he might get into the house in spite of the locked doors; and by entering the garden, placing a pole from the fork of an apple-tree to the window-sill of a bedroom on that side, and climbing across like a monkey, he entered the window and stepped down inside. There was something anomalous in being close to the familiar furniture without having first seen his father, and its silent, impassive shine was not cheering; it was as if his relations were all dead, and only their tables and chests of drawers left to greet him. He went down-stairs and seated himself in the dark parlour. Finding this place, too, rather solitary, and the tick of the invisible clock preternaturally loud, he unearthed the tinder-box, obtained a light, and set about making the house comfortable for his father's return, rightly divining that the miller had gone out to meet him by the wrong road.

Robert's interest in this work increased as he proceeded, and he bustled round and round the kitchen as lightly as a girl. David, the indoor factotum, having lost himself among the quart pots of Weymouth, there had been nobody left here to prepare supper, and Bob had it all to himself. In a short time a fire blazed up the chimney, a tablecloth was found, the plates were clapped down, and a search made for what provisions the house afforded, which, in addition to various meats, included some fresh eggs of the elongated shape that produces cockerels when hatched, and had been set aside on that account for putting under the next broody hen.

A more reckless cracking of eggs than that which now went on had never been known in Overcombe since the last large christening; and as Loveday gashed one on the side, another at the end, another longways, and another diagonally, he acquired adroitness by practice, and at last made every son of a hen of them fall into two hemispheres as neatly as if it opened by a hinge. From eggs he proceeded to ham, and from ham to kidneys, the result being a brilliant fry.

Not to be tempted to fall to before his father came back, the returned navigator emptied the whole into a dish, laid a plate over the top, his coat over the plate, and his hat over his coat. Thus completely stopping in the appetizing smell, he sat down to await events. He was relieved from the tediousness of doing this by hearing voices outside; and in a minute his father entered.

"Glad to welcome ye home, father," said Bob. "And supper is just ready."

"Lard, lard—why, Captain Bob's here!" said Mrs. Garland.

"And we've been out waiting to meet thee!" said the miller as he entered the room, followed by representatives of the house of Cripplestraw, Comfort, Mitchell, Beach, and Snooks, together with some small beginnings of Fencible Tremlett's posterity. In the rear came David, and quite in the vanishing-point of the composition, Anne the fair.

"I drove over; and so was forced to come by the road," said Bob.

"And we went across the fields, thinking you'd walk," said his father.

"I should have been here this morning; but not so much as a wheelbarrow could I get for my traps; everything was gone to the review. So I went too, thinking I might meet you there. I was then obliged to return to Weymouth for the luggage."

Then there was a welcoming of Captain Bob by pulling out his arms like drawers and shutting them again, smacking him on the back as if he were unwell, holding him at arm's length as if he were of too large type to read close. All which persecution Bob bore with a wide, genial smile that was shaken into fragments and scattered promiscuously among the spectators.

"Get a chair for 'n!" said the miller to David, whom they had met in the fields and found to have got nothing worse by his absence than a slight slant in his walk.

"Never mind—I am not tired—I have been here ever so long," said Bob. "And I——" But the chair having been placed behind him, and a smart touch in the hollow of a person's knee by the edge of that piece of furniture having a tendency to make the person sit without further argument, Bob sank down dumb, and the others drew up other chairs at a convenient nearness for easy analytic vision and the subtler forms of good fellowship. The miller went about saying, "David, the nine best glasses from the corner cupboard!"—"David, the corkscrew!"—"David, whisk the tail of thy smockfrock round the inside of these quart pots afore you draw drink in 'em—they be an inch thick in dust;"—"David, lower that chimney-crook a couple of notches that the flame may touch the bottom of the kettle, and light three more of the largest candles;"—"If you can't get the cork out of the jar, David, bore a hole in the tub of Hollands that's buried under the scroff in the fuel house; d'ye hear?—Dan Brown left en there yesterday as a return for the little porker I gied en."

When they had all had a thimbleful round, and the superfluous neighbours had reluctantly departed, one by one, the inmates gave their minds to the supper, which David had begun to serve up.

"What be you rolling back the tablecloth for, David?" said the miller.

"Maister Bob have put down one of the under sheets by mistake, and I thought you might not like it, sir, as there's ladies present."

"Faith, 'twas the first thing that came to hand," said Robert. "It seemed a tablecloth to me."

"Never mind—don't pull off the things now he's laid 'em down—let it bide," said the miller. "But where's Widow Garland and Maidy Anne?"

"They were here but a minute ago," said David. "Depend upon it they have slinked off 'cause they be shy."

The miller at once went round to ask them to come back and sup with him; and while he was gone David told Bob in confidence what an excellent place he had for an old man.

"Yes, Capm Bob, as I suppose I must call ye; I've worked for yer father these eight-and-thirty years, and we have always got on very well together. Trusts me with all the keys, lends me his sleeve-waistcoat, and leaves the house entirely to me. Widow Garland next door, too, is just the same with me, and treats me as if I was her own child."

"She must have married young to make you that, David."

"Yes, yes—I'm years older than she. 'Tis only my common way of speaking."

Mrs. Garland would not come in to supper, and the meal proceeded without her, Bob recommending to his father the dish he had cooked, in the manner of a householder to a stranger just come. The miller was anxious to know more about his son's plans for the future, but would not for the present interrupt his eating, looking up from his own plate to appreciate Bob's travelled way of putting English victuals out of sight, as he would have looked at a mill on improved principles.

David had only just got the table clear, and set the plates in a row under the bakehouse table for the cats to lick, when the door was hastily opened, and Mrs. Garland came in, looking concerned.

"I have been waiting to hear the plates removed to tell you how frightened we are at something we hear at the back-door. It seems like robbers muttering; but when I look out there's nobody there!"

"This must be seen to," said the miller, rising promptly. "David, light the middle-sized lantern. I'll go and search the garden."

"And I'll go too," said his son, taking up a cudgel. "Lucky I've come home just in time!"

They went out stealthily, followed by the widow and Anne, who had been afraid to stay alone in the house under the circumstances. No sooner were they beyond the door when, sure enough, there was the muttering, almost close at hand, and low upon the ground, as from persons lying down in hiding.

"Bless my heart!" said Bob, striking his head as though it were some enemy's: "why, 'tis my luggage. I'd quite forgot it!"

"What?" asked his father.

"My luggage. Really, if it hadn't been for Mrs. Garland it would have stayed there all night, and they, poor things! would have been starved. I've got all sorts of articles for ye. You go inside, and I'll bring 'em in. 'Tis parrots that you hear a muttering, Mrs. Garland. You needn't be afraid any more."

"Parrots?" said the miller. "Well, I'm glad 'tis no worse. But how couldst forget so, Bob?"

The packages were taken in by David and Bob, and the first things unfastened were three of cylindrical shape, wrapped in cloths, which being stripped off revealed three cages, with a gorgeous parrot in each.

"This one is for you, father, to hang up outside the door, and amuse us," said Bob. "He'll talk very well, but he's sleepy to-night. This other one I brought along for any neighbour that would like to have him. His colours are not so bright; but 'tis a good bird. If you would like to have him you are welcome to him," he said, turning to Anne, who had been tempted forward by the birds. "You have hardly spoken yet, Miss Anne,

but I recollect you very well. How much taller you have got, to be sure!"

Anne said she was much obliged, but did not know what she could do with such a present. Mrs. Garland accepted it for her, and the sailor went on—"Now this other bird I hardly know what to do with; but I dare say he'll come in for something or other."

"He is by far the prettiest," said the widow. "I would rather have it than the other, if you don't mind."

"Yes," said Bob, with embarrassment. "But the fact is, that bird will hardly do for ye, ma'am. He's a hard swearer, to tell the truth; and I am afraid he's too old to be broken of it."

"How dreadful!" said Mrs. Garland.

"We could keep him in the mill," suggested the miller.

"Yes; perhaps that's the best thing to do. It won't matter about the grinder hearing him?" said Bob.

"Not at all," said his father.

"The one I have given you, ma'am, has no harm in him at all. You might take him to church o' Sundays as far as that goes."

The sailor now untied a small wooden box about a foot square, perforated with holes. "Here are two marmosets," he continued. "You can't see them to-night; but they are beauties—the tufted sort."

"What's a marmoset?" said the miller.

"Oh, a little kind of monkey. They bite strangers rather hard, but you'll soon get used to 'em."

"They are wrapped up in something, I declare," said Mrs. Garland, peeping in through a chink.

"Yes, that's my flannel shirt," said Bob apologetically. "They suffer terribly from cold in this climate, poor things! and I had nothing better to give them. Well, now, in this next box I've got things of different sorts."

The latter was a regular seaman's chest, and out of it he produced shells of many sizes and colours, carved ivories, queer little caskets, gorgeous feathers, and several silk handkerchiefs, which articles were spread out upon all the available tables and chairs till the house began to look like a bazaar.

"What a lovely shawl!" exclaimed Widow Garland, in her interest forestalling the regular exhibition by looking into the box at what was coming.

"Oh, yes," said the mate, pulling out a couple of the most bewitching shawls that eyes ever saw. "One of these I am going to give to that young lady I am shortly to be married to, you know, Mrs. Garland. Has father told you about it? Matilda Johnson, of Southampton, that's her name."

"Yes, we know all about it," said the widow.

"Well, I shall give one of these shawls to her—because, of course, I ought to."

"Of course," said she.

"But the other one I've got no use for at all; and," he continued, looking round, "will you have it, Miss Anne? You refused

the parrot, and you ought not to refuse this."

"Thank you," said Anne calmly, but much distressed; "but really I don't want it, and couldn't take it."

"But do have it!" said Bob in hurt tones, Mrs. Garland being all the while on tenterhooks lest Anne should persist in her absurd refusal.

"Why, there's another reason why you ought to!" said he, his face lighting up with recollections. "It never came into my head

till this moment that I used to be your beau in a humble sort of way. Faith, so I did, and we used to meet at places sometimes, didn't we—that is, when you were not too proud; and once I gave you, or somebody else, a bit of my hair in fun."

"It was somebody else," said Anne quickly.

"Ah, perhaps it was," said Bob innocently. "But it was you I used to meet, or try to, I am sure. Well, I've never thought of that boyish time for years till this minute! I am

sure you ought to accept some one gift, dear, out of compliment to those old times!"

Anne drew back and shook her head, for she would not trust her voice.

"Well, Mrs. Garland, then you shall have it," said Bob, tossing the shawl to that ready receptacle. "If you don't, upon my life I will throw it out to the first beggar I see. Well, now, here's a parcel of cap ribbons of the splendidest sort I could get. Have these —do, Anne!"

"Yes, do," said Mrs. Garland.

"I promised them to Matilda," continued Bob; "but I am sure she won't want 'em, as she has got some of her own; and I would as soon see them upon your head, my dear, as upon hers."

".I think you had better keep them for your bride if you have promised them to her," said Mrs. Garland mildly.

"It wasn't exactly a promise. I just said, 'Til, there's some cap ribbons in my box, if you would like to have them.' But she's got enough things already for any bride in creation. Anne, now you shall have 'em—upon my soul you shall—or I'll fling them down the mill tail."

Anne had meant to be perfectly firm in refusing everything, for reasons obvious even to that poor waif, the meanest capacity; but when it came to this point she was absolutely compelled to give in, and reluctantly received the cap ribbons in her arms, blushing fitfully, and with her lip trembling in a motion which she tried to exhibit as a smile.

"What would Tilly say if she knew!" said the miller slily.

"Yes, indeed—and it is wrong of him!" Anne instantly cried, tears running down her face as she threw the parcel of ribbons on the floor. "You'd better bestow your gifts where you bestow your l—l—love, Mr. Loveday—that's what I say!" And Anne turned her back and went away.

"I'll take them for her," said Mrs. Garland, quickly picking up the parcel.

"Now that's a pity," said Bob, looking regretfully after Anne. "I didn't remember that she was a quick-tempered sort of girl at all. Tell her, Mrs. Garland, that I ask her pardon. But of course I didn't know she was too proud to accept a little present—how should I? Upon my life, if it wasn't for Matilda I'd—— Well, that can't be, of course."

"What's this?" said Mrs. Garland, touching with her foot a large package that had been laid down by Bob unseen.

"That's a bit of baccy for myself," said Robert meekly.

The examination of presents at last ended, and the two families parted for the night. When they were alone, Mrs. Garland said to Anne, "What a close girl you are! I am sure I never knew that Bob Loveday and you had walked together: you must have been mere children."

"Oh yes—so we were," said Anne, now quite recovered. "It was when we first came here, about a year after father died. We did not walk together in any regular way. You know I have never thought the Lovedays good enough for me. It was only just—nothing at all, and I had almost forgotten it."

It is to be hoped that somebody's sins were forgiven her that night before she went to bed.

When Bob and his father were left alone, the miller said, "Well, Robert, about this young woman of thine—Matilda what's her name?"

"Yes, father—Matilda Johnson. I was just going to tell ye about her."

The miller nodded, and sipped his mug.

"Well, she is an excellent body," continued Bob; that can truly be said—a real charmer, you know—a nice good comely young woman, a miracle of genteel breeding, you know, and all that. She can throw her hair into the nicest curls, and she's got splendid gowns and head-clothes. In short, you might call her a land mermaid. She'll make such a first-rate wife as there never was."

"No doubt she will," said the miller; "for I have never known thee wanting in sense in a jineral way." He turned his cup round on its axis till the handle had travelled a complete circle. "How long did you say in your letter that you had known her?"

"A fortnight."

"Not very long."

"It don't sound long, 'tis true; and 'twas really longer—'twas fifteen days and a quarter. But hang it, father, I could see in the twinkling of an eye that the girl would do. I know a woman well enough when I see her—I ought to, indeed, having been so much about the world. Now, for instance, there's Widow Garland and her daughter. The girl is a nice little thing; but the old woman—oh no!" Bob shook his head.

"What of her?" said his father, slightly shifting in his chair.

"Well, she's, she's—— I mean, I should never have chose her, you know. She's of a nice disposition, and young for a widow with a grown-up daughter; but if all the men had been like me she would never have had a husband. I like her in some respects; but she's a style of beauty I don't care for."

"Oh, if 'tis only looks you are thinking of," said the miller, much relieved, "there's nothing to be said, of course. Though there's many a duchess worse-looking, if it comes to argument, as you would find, my son," he added, with a sense of having been mollified too soon.

The mate's thoughts were elsewhere by this time.

"As to my marrying Matilda, thinks I, here's one of the very tip-top sort, and I may as well do the job at once. So I chose her. She's a dear girl; there's nobody like her, search where you will."

"How many did you choose her out from?" inquired his father.

"Well, she was the only young woman I happened to know in Southampton, that's true. But what of that? It would have been all the same if I had known a hundred."

"Her father is in business near the docks, I suppose?"

"Well, no. In short, I didn't see her father."

"Her mother?"

"Her mother? No, I didn't. I think her mother is dead; but she has got a very rich aunt living at Salisbury. I didn't see her aunt, because there wasn't time to go; but of course we shall know her when we are married."

"Yes, yes, of course," said the miller, trying to feel quite satisfied. "And she will soon be here?"

"Ay, she's coming soon," said Bob. "She has gone to this aunt's at Salisbury to get her things packed, and suchlike, or she would have come with me. I am going to meet the coach at the King's Arms, Dorchester, on Monday, at one o'clock. To show what a capital sort of wife she'll be, I may tell you that she wanted to come by the Mercury, because 'tis a little cheaper than the other. But I said, 'For once in your life do it well, and come by the Royal Mail, and I'll pay.' I can have the pony and trap to fetch her, I suppose, as 'tis too far for her to walk?"

"Of course you can, Bob, or anything else. And I'll do all I can to give you a good wedding feast."

CHAPTER XVI.—THEY MAKE READY FOR THE ILLUSTRIOUS STRANGER.

PREPARATIONS for Matilda's welcome, and for the event which was to follow, at once occupied the attention of the mill. The miller and his man had but dim notions of housewifery on any large scale; so the great wedding cleaning was kindly supervised by Mrs. Garland, Bob being mostly away during the day with his brother, the trumpet-major, on various errands, one of which was to buy paint and varnish for the gig that Matilda was to be fetched in, which he had determined to decorate with his own hands.

By the widow's direction the old familiar incrustation of shining dirt, imprinted along the back of the settle by the heads of countless jolly sitters, was scrubbed and scraped away; the brown circle round the nail whereon the miller hung his hat, stained by the brim in wet weather, was whitened over; the tawny smudges of bygone shoulders in the passage were removed without regard to a certain genial and historical value which they had acquired. The face of the clock, coated with verdigris as thick as a diachylon plaster, was rubbed till the figures emerged into day; while, inside the case of the same chronometer, the cobwebs that formed triangular hammocks, which the pendulum could hardly wade through, were cleared away at one swoop. Mrs. Garland also assisted at the invasion of worm-eaten cupboards, where layers of ancient smells lingered on in the stagnant air, and recalled to the reflective nose the many good things that had been kept there. The upper floors were scrubbed with such abundance of water that the old-established death-watches, wood-lice, and flour-worms were all drowned, the suds trickling down into the room below in so lively and novel a manner as to convey the romantic notion that the miller lived in a cave with dripping stalactites.

They moved what had never been moved before—the oak coffer, containing the miller's wardrobe—a tremendous weight, what with its locks, hinges, nails, dirt, framework, and the hard stratification of old jackets, waistcoats, and kneebreeches at the bottom, never disturbed since the miller's wife died, and half pulverized by the moths, whose flattened skeletons lay amid the mass in thousands.

"It fairly makes my back open and shut," said Loveday, as, in obedience to Mrs. Garland's direction, he lifted one corner, the grinder and David assisting at the others. "All together: speak when ye be going to heave. Now!" And they heaved.

The pot covers and skimmers were brought to such a state that, on examining them, the beholder was not conscious of utensils, but of his own face in a condition of hideous elasticity. The broken clock-line was mended, the kettles rocked, the rose-tree nailed up, and a new handle put to the warming-pan. The large household lantern was cleaned out, after three years of uninterrupted accumulation, the operation yielding a conglomerate of candle-snuffs, candle-ends, remains of matches, lamp-black, and eleven ounces and a half of good grease—invaluable as dubbing for skitty boots and ointment for cart-wheels.

Everybody said that the mill residence had not been so thoroughly scoured for twenty years. The miller and David looked on with a sort of awe tempered by gratitude, tacitly admitting by their gaze that this was beyond what they had ever thought of. Mrs. Garland supervised all with disinterested benevolence. It would never have done, she said, for his future daughter-in-law to see the house in its original state. She would have taken a dislike to him, and perhaps to Bob likewise.

"Why don't ye come and live here with me, and then you would be able to see to it at all times?" said the miller as she bustled about again. To which she answered that she was considering the matter, and might in good time. That as for the house, she could have done no less than clean it for him in common humanity. (He had previously informed her that his plan was to put Bob and his wife in the part of the house that she, Mrs. Garland, occupied, as soon as she chose to enter his, which relieved her of any fear of being incommoded by Matilda.)

The cooking for the wedding festivities was on a proportionate scale of thoroughness. They killed the four superfluous chickens that had just begun to crow, and the little curly-tailed barrow pig, in preference to the other; not having been put up fattening for more than five weeks it was excellent small meat, and therefore more delicate and likely to suit a town-bred lady's taste than the large one, which, having reached the weight of fourteen score, might have been a little gross to a cultured palate. There were also provided a cold chine, stuffed veal, and two pigeon pies. Also seventy rings of black-pot, a dozen of white-pot, and twenty-five knots of tender and well-washed chitterlings, cooked plain, in case she should like a change.

As additional reserves there were sweetbreads, and five milts, sewed up at one side in the form of a chrysalis, and stuffed with marjoram, thyme, sage, parsley, mint, groats, rice, milk, chopped egg, and other ingredients. They were afterwards roasted before a slow fire like martyrs, and eaten hot.

The business of chopping so many herbs for the various stuffings was found to be aching work for women; and David, the miller, the grinder, and the grinder's boy being fully occupied in their proper branches, and Bob being very busy painting the gig and touching up the harness, Loveday called in a friendly dragoon of John's regiment who was passing by, and he, being a muscular man, willingly chopped all the afternoon for a quart of strong, judiciously administered, and all other victuals found, taking off his jacket and gloves, rolling up his shirt-sleeves and unfastening his collar in an honourable and energetic way.

All windfalls and maggot-cored codlins were excluded from the apple pies; and as there was no known dish large enough for the purpose, the puddings were stirred up in the milking-pail, and boiled in the three-legged bell-metal crock, of great weight and antiquity, which every travelling tinker for the previous thirty years had tapped with his stick, coveted, made a bid for, and often attempted to steal.

In the liquor line Loveday laid in an ample barrel of Dorchester "strong beer." This renowned drink—now almost as much a thing of the past as Falstaff's favourite beverage—was not only well calculated to win the hearts of soldiers blown dry and dusty by residence in tents on a hill-top, but of any wayfarer whatever in that land. It was of the most beautiful colour that the eye of an artist in beer could desire; full in body, yet brisk as a volcano; piquant, yet without a twang; luminous as an autumn sunset; free from streakiness of taste; but, finally, rather heady. The masses worshipped it, the minor gentry loved it more than wine, and by the most illustrious county families it was not despised. Anybody brought up for being drunk and disorderly in the streets of its natal borough, had only to prove that he was a stranger to the place and its liquor to be honourably dismissed by the magistrates, as one overtaken in a fault that no man could guard against who entered the town unawares.

In addition, Mr. Loveday also tapped a hogshead of fine cider that he had had mellowing in the house for several months, having bought it of an honest down-country man, who did not colour, for any special occasion like the present. It had been pressed from fruit judiciously chosen by an old hand—Horner and Cleeves apples for the body, a few Crimson-Kitties for colour, and just a dash of Old Fivecorners for sparkle—a selection originally made to please the palate of a well-known temperate earl who was a regular cider-drinker, and lived to be eighty-eight.

On the morning of the day appointed for her coming Captain Bob Loveday set out to meet his bride. He had been all the week engaged in painting the gig, assisted by his brother at odd times, and it now appeared of a gorgeous yellow, with blue streaks, and tassels at the corners, and red wheels outlined with a darker shade. He put in the pony at half-past eleven, Anne looking at him from the door as he packed himself into the vehicle and drove off. There may be young women who look out at young men driving to meet their brides as Anne looked at Captain Bob, and yet are quite indifferent to the circumstances; but they are not often met with.

So much dust had been raised on the highway by traffic resulting from the presence of the Court at Weymouth that brambles hanging from the fence, and giving a friendly scratch to the wanderer's face, were dingy as church cobwebs; and the grass on the margin had assumed a paper-shaving hue. Bob's father had wished him to take David, lest, from want of recent experience at the whip, he should meet with any mishap; but, picturing to himself the awkwardness of three in such circumstances, Bob would not hear of this; and nothing more serious happened to his driving than that the wheel-marks formed two beautiful serpentine lines along the road during the first mile or two, before he had got his hand in, and that the horse shied at a mile-stone, a piece of paper, a sleeping tramp, and a wheelbarrow, just to make use of the opportunity of being in bad hands.

He entered Dorchester between twelve and one, and putting up at the Old Greyhound, walked on to the Bow, and waited till he saw the mail coach rise above the arch of Grey's Bridge, a quarter of a mile distant, surmounted by swaying knobs, which proved to be the heads of the outside travellers.

"That's the way for a man's bride to come to him!" said Robert to himself with a feeling of poetry; and as the horn sounded and the horses clattered up the street he walked down to the inn. The knot of hostlers and inn-servants had gathered, the horses were dragged from the vehicle, and the passengers for Dorchester began to descend. Captain Bob eyed them over, looked inside, looked outside again; to his disappointment Matilda was not there, nor her boxes, nor anything that was hers. Neither coachman nor guard had seen or heard of such a person at Salisbury; and Bob walked slowly away.

Depressed by forebodings to an extent which took away nearly a third of his appetite, he sat down in the parlour of the Old Greyhound to a slice from the family joint of the landlord. This gentleman, who dined in his shirt-sleeves, partly because it was August, and partly from a sense that they would not be so fit for public view farther on in the week, suggested that Bob should wait till three or four that afternoon, when the road-waggon would arrive, as the lost lady might have preferred that mode of conveyance; and when Bob appeared rather hurt at the suggestion, the landlord's wife assured him, as a woman who knew good life, that many genteel persons travelled in that way during the present high price of provisions. Loveday, who knew little of travelling by land, readily accepted her assurance and resolved to wait.

Wandering up and down the pavement, or leaning against some hot wall between the waggon-office and the corner of the street above, he passed the time away. It was a still, sunny, drowsy afternoon, and scarcely a soul was visible in the length and breadth of the street. The office was next door to All Saints' Church, and the afternoon sermons at this church being of a dry and metaphysical nature at that date, it was by a special providence that the waggon-office was placed close to the ancient fabric, so that whenever the Sunday waggon was late, which it always was in hot weather, in cold weather, in wet weather, and in weather of almost every other sort, the rattle, dismounting, and profane noises outside completely drowned the parson's voice within, and sustained the flagging interest of the congregation at precisely the right moment. No sooner did the charity children begin to writhe on their benches and adult snores grow audible than the waggon arrived.

Captain Loveday felt a kind of sinking in his poetry at the possibility of her for whom they had made such preparations being in the slow, unwieldy vehicle which crunched its way towards him; but he would not give way to the weakness. Neither would he walk down the street to meet it, lest she should not be there. At last the broad wheels drew up against the kerb, the waggoner with his white smock-frock, and whip as long as a fishing line, descended from the pony on which he rode alongside, and the six broad-chested horses backed from their collars and shook themselves. In another moment something showed forth, and he knew that Matilda was there.

Bob felt three cheers rise within him as she stepped down; but he did not utter them. In dress, Miss Johnson passed his expectations—a green and white gown, with long, tight sleeves, a green silk handkerchief round her neck and crossed in front, a green parasol, and green gloves. It was strange enough to see this verdant caterpillar turn out of a road-waggon, and gracefully shake herself free from the bits of straw and fluff which would usually gather on the raiment of the grandest travellers by that vehicle.

"But, my dear Matilda," said Bob, when he had kissed her three times with much publicity—the practical step he had determined on seeming to demand that these things should no longer be done in a corner —"my dear Matilda, why didn't you come by the coach, having the money for't and all?"

"That's my scrimping!" said Matilda in a delightful gush. "I know you won't be offended when you know I did it to save against a rainy day."

Bob, of course, was not offended, though the glory of meeting her had been less; and even if vexation were possible, it would have been out of place to say so. Still, he would have experienced no little surprise had he learnt the real reason of his Matilda's change of plan. That angel had, in short, so wildly

"Bob did not hurry the horse, there being many things to say and hear."

spent Bob's and her own money in the adornment of her person before setting out, that she found herself without a sufficient margin for her fare by coach, and had scrimped from sheer necessity.

"Well, I have got the trap out at the Greyhound," said Bob. "I don't know whether it will hold your luggage and us too; but it looked more respectable than the waggon, and if there's not room for the boxes I can walk alongside."

"I think there will be room," said Miss Johnson mildly. And it was soon very evident that she spoke the truth; for when her property was deposited on the pavement, it consisted of a trunk about eighteen inches long, and nothing more.

"Oh—that's all!" said Bob, surprised.

"That's all," said the young woman assuringly. "I didn't want to give trouble, you know, and what I have besides I have left at my aunt's."

"Yes, of course," he answered readily. "And as it's no bigger, I can carry it in my hand to the inn, and so it will be no trouble at all."

He caught up the little box, and they went side by side to the Greyhound; and in ten minutes they were trotting up the Weymouth Road.

Bob did not hurry the horse, there being many things to say and hear, for which the present situation was admirably suited. The sun shone occasionally into Matilda's face as they drove on, its rays picking out all her features to a great nicety. Her eyes would have been called brown, but they were really eel-colour, like many other nice brown eyes; they were well-shaped and rather bright, though they had more of a broad shine than a sparkle. She had a firm, sufficient nose, which seemed to say of itself that it was good as noses go. She had rather a picturesque way of wrapping her upper in her lower lip, so that the red of the latter showed strongly. Whenever she gazed against the sun towards the distant hills, she brought into her forehead, without knowing it, three short vertical lines—not there at other times —giving her for the moment rather a hard look. And in turning her head round to a far angle, to stare at something or other that he pointed out, the drawn flesh of her neck became a mass of lines. But Bob did not look at these things, which, of course, were of no significance; for had she not told him, when they compared ages, that she was a little over two-and-twenty?

As Nature was hardly invented at this early point of the century, Bob's Matilda could not say much about the glamour of the hills, or the shimmering of the foliage, or the wealth of glory in the distant sea, as she would doubtless have done had she lived further on; but she did her best to be interesting, asking Bob about matters of social interest in the neighbourhood, to which she seemed quite a stranger.

"Is Weymouth a large city?" she inquired when they mounted the hill where the Overcombe folk had waited for the King.

"Bless you, my dear—no! 'Twould be nothing if it wasn't for the Royal Family, and the lords and ladies, and the regiments of soldiers, and the frigates, and the King's messengers, and the actors and actresses, and the games that go on."

At the words "actors and actresses," the innocent young thing pricked up her ears.

"Does Elliston pay as good salaries this summer as in ——?"

"Oh, you know about it, then? I thought——"

"Oh no, no. I have heard of Weymouth —read in the papers, you know, dear Bob, about the doings there, and the actors and actresses, you know."

"Yes, yes, I see. Well, I have been away from England a long time, and don't know much about the theatre at Weymouth; but I'll take you there some day. Would it be a treat to you?"

"Oh, an amazing treat!" said Miss Johnson, with an ecstasy in which a close observer might have discovered a tinge of ghastliness.

"You've never been into one, perhaps, dear?"

"N—never," said Matilda flatly. "Whatever do I see yonder—a row of white things on the down?"

"Yes; that's a part of the encampment above Overcombe. Lots of soldiers are encamped about here; those are the white tops of their tents."

He pointed to a wing of the camp that had become visible. Matilda was much interested.

"It will make it very lively for us," he added; "especially as John is there."

She thought so too, and thus they chatted on.

CHAPTER XVII.—CONTAINING TWO FAINTING FITS AND A BEWILDERMENT.

MEANWHILE Miller Loveday was expecting the pair with interest; and about five o'clock, after repeated outlooks, he saw two specks the size of caraway seeds on the far line of ridge where the sunlit white of the road met the blue of the sky. Then the remainder parts of Bob and his lady became visible, and then the whole vehicle, end on, and he heard the dry rattle of the wheels on the dusty road. Miller Loveday's plan, as far as he had formed any, was that Bob and his wife should live with him in the mill-house until Mrs. Garland made up her mind to join him there; in which event her present house would be made over to the young couple. Upon all grounds, he wished to welcome becomingly the woman of Bob's choice, and came forward promptly as they drew up at the door.

"What a lovely place you've got here!" said Miss Johnson, when the miller had received her from Bob. "A real stream of water, a real mill-wheel, and real fowls, and everything!"

"Yes, 'tis real enough," said Loveday, looking at the river with balanced sentiments; "and so you will say when you've lived here a bit as mis'ess, and had the trouble of claning the furniture."

At this Miss Johnson looked modest, and continued to do so till Anne, not knowing they were there, came round the corner of the house. Bob turned and smiled to her, at which Miss Johnson looked glum. How long she would have remained in that phase is unknown, for just then her ears were assailed by a loud bass note from the other side, causing her to jump round.

"O la! what dreadful thing is it?" she exclaimed, and beheld a cow of Loveday's, of the name of Crumpler, standing close to her shoulder. It being about milking-time, she had come to look up David and hasten on the operation.

"O what a horrid bull!—it did frighten me so. I hope I shan't faint," said Matilda.

The miller immediately used the formula which has been uttered by the proprietors of live stock ever since Noah's time. "She won't hurt ye. Hoosh, Crumpler! She's as timid as a mouse, ma'am."

But as Crumpler persisted in making another terrific inquiry for David, Matilda could not help closing her eyes and saying, "Oh, I shall be gored to death!" her head falling back upon Bob's shoulder, which—seeing the urgent circumstances, and knowing her delicate nature—he had providentially placed in a position to catch her. Anne Garland, who had been standing at the corner of the house, not knowing whether to go back or come on, at this felt her womanly sympathies aroused. She ran and dipped her handkerchief into the splashing mill-tail, and with it damped Matilda's face. But as her eyes still remained closed, Bob, to increase the effect, took the handkerchief from Anne and wrung it out on the bridge of Matilda's nose, whence it ran over the rest of her face in a stream.

"Oh, Captain Loveday!" said Anne; "the water is running over her green silk handkerchief, and into her pretty reticule."

"There—if I didn't think so!" exclaimed Matilda, opening her eyes and starting up.

Promptly pulling out her own handkerchief, she wiped away the drops, assisted by Anne, who, in spite of her background of antagonistic emotions, could not help being interested.

"That's right," said the miller, his spirits reviving with the revival of Matilda. "The lady is not used to country life; are you, ma'am?"

"I am not," replied the sufferer. "All is so strange about here."

Suddenly there spread into the firmament, from the direction of the down:—

"Ra, ta, ta! Ta-ta-ta-ta-ta! Ra, ta, ta!"

"Oh dear, dear; more hideous country sounds, I suppose?" she inquired, with another start.

"Oh no," said the miller cheerfully. "'Tis only my son John's trumpeter chaps at the camp of dragoons just above us, a-blowing Mess, or Feed, or Picket, or some other of their vagaries. John will be much pleased to tell you the meaning on't when he comes down. He's trumpet-major, as you may know, ma'am."

"Oh yes; you mean Captain Loveday's brother. Dear Bob has mentioned him."

"If you come round to Widow Garland's side of the house, you can see the camp," said the miller.

"Don't force her; she's tired with her long journey," said Mrs. Garland humanely, the widow having come out in the general wish to see Captain Bob's choice. Indeed, they all behaved towards her as if she were a tender exotic, which their crude country manners might seriously injure.

She went into the house, accompanied by Mrs. Garland and her daughter; though before leaving Bob she managed to whisper in his ear, "Don't tell them I came by waggon, will you, dear?"—a request which was quite needless, for Bob had long ago determined to keep that a dead secret; not because it was an uncommon mode of travel, but simply that it was hardly the usual conveyance for a gorgeous lady to her bridal.

As the men had a feeling that they would be superfluous indoors just at present, the miller assisted David in taking the horse round to the stables, Bob following, and leaving Matilda to the women. Indoors, Miss Johnson admired everything: the new parrot and marmosets, the black beams of the ceiling, the double corner-cupboard with the glass doors, through which gleamed the remainders of sundry china sets acquired by Bob's mother in her housekeeping—two-handled sugar-basins, no-handled tea-cups, a tea-pot like a pagoda, and a cream-jug in the form of a spotted cow. This sociability in their visitor was returned by Mrs. Garland and Anne; and Miss Johnson's pleasing habit of partly dying whenever she heard any unusual bark or bellow added to her piquancy in their eyes. But conversation, as such, was naturally at first of a nervous, tentative kind, in which, as in the works of the poet Keats, the sense was considerably led by the sound.

"You get the sea breezes here, no doubt?"

"Oh yes; when the wind is that way."

"Do you like windy weather?"

"Yes; though not now, for it blows down the young apples."

"Apples are plentiful, it seems. You country-folk call St. Swithin's their christening day, if it rains?"

"Yes. Ah me! I have not been to a christening for these many years; the baby's

" Her head fell back upon Bob's shoulder."

name was George, I remember—after the King."

" I hear that King George is still staying at Weymouth. I hope he'll stay till I have seen him."

" He'll wait till the corn turns yellow; he always does."

" How fashionable yellow is getting for gloves just now ! "

" Yes. Some persons wear them to the elbow, I hear."

" Do they ? I was not aware of that. I struck my elbow last week so hard against the parlour door that I feel the ache now."

Before they were quite overwhelmed by the interest of this discourse the miller and Bob came in. In truth, Mrs. Garland found the office in which he had placed her—that of introducing a strange woman to a house which was not the widow's own—a rather awkward one, and yet almost a necessity. There was no woman belonging to the house except that wondrous compendium of usefulness, the intermittent maid-servant, whom Loveday had, for appearances, borrowed from Mrs. Garland, and Mrs. Garland was in the habit of borrowing from the girl's mother. And as for the demi-woman David, he had been informed as peremptorily as Pharaoh's baker that the office of housemaid and bed-maker was taken from him, and would be given to this girl till the wedding was over and Bob's wife took the management into her own hands.

They all sat down to high tea, Anne and her mother included, and Bob sitting next to Miss Johnson. Anne had put a brave face upon the matter—outwardly, at least—and seemed in a fair way of subduing any linger-ing sentiment which Bob's return had revived. During the evening, and while they still sat over the meal, John came down on a hurried visit, as he had promised, ostensibly on pur-pose to be introduced to his intended sister-in-law, but much more to get a word and a smile from his beloved Anne. Before they saw him, they heard the trumpet-major's smart step coming round the corner of the house, and in a moment his form darkened the door. He appeared in his full-dress laced coat, white waistcoat, and breeches, and towering plume, the latter of which he in-stantly lowered, as much from necessity as good manners, the beam in the mill-house ceiling having a tendency to smash and ruin all such head-gear without warning.

"John, we've been hoping you would come down," said the miller, "and so we have kept the tay about on purpose. Draw up, and speak to Mrs. Matilda Johnson. . . . Ma'am, this is Robert's brother."

"Your humble servant, ma'am," said the trumpet-major gallantly.

As it was getting dusk in the low, small-paned room, he instinctively moved towards Miss Johnson as he spoke, who sat with her back to the window. He had no sooner noticed her features than his helmet nearly fell from his hand; his face became suddenly fixed, and his natural complexion took itself off, leaving a kind of yellow in its stead. The young person, on her part, no sooner looked closely at him than she said weakly, "Robert's brother," and changed colour yet more rapidly than the soldier had done. The faintness, previously half counter-feit, seized on her now in real earnest.

"I don't feel well," she said, suddenly rising by an effort. "This warm day has quite upset me."

There was a regular collapse of the tea party, like that of the Hamlet play scene. Bob seized his sweetheart and carried her up-stairs, the miller exclaiming, "Ah, she's terribly worn by the journey; I thought she was when I saw her nearly go off at the blare of the cow. No woman would have been frightened at that if she'd been up to her natural strength."

"That, and being so very shy, too, must have made John's handsome regimentals quite overpowering to her, poor thing!" added Mrs. Garland, following the catastro-phic young lady up-stairs, whose indisposition was this time beyond question. And yet, by some perversity of the heart, she was as eager now to make light of her faintness as she had been to make much of it.

The miller and John stood like straight sticks in the room the others had quitted, John's face being hastily turned towards a cari-cature of Buonaparte, that he had not seen more than a hundred and fifty times before.

"Come, sit down and have a dish of tea, anyhow," said his father at last. "She'll soon be right again, no doubt."

"Thanks; I don't want any tea," said John quickly. And, indeed, he did not, for he was in one gigantic ache from head to foot.

The light had been too dim for anybody to notice his amazement; and not knowing where to vent it, the trumpet-major said he was going out for a minute. He hastened to the bakehouse; but David being there, he went to the pantry; but the maid being there, he went to the cart-shed; but a couple of tramps being there, he went behind a row of French beans in the garden, where he let off an ejaculation: "Heaven! what's to be done?"

And then he walked wildly about the paths of the dusky garden, where the trickling of the brooks seemed loud by comparison with the stillness around; treading recklessly on the cracking snails that had come forth to feed, and entangling his spurs in the long grass till the rowels were choked with its blades. Presently he heard another person approaching, and his brother's shape appeared between the stubbard tree and the hedge.

"Oh, is it you, John?" said the mate.

"Yes. I am—taking a little air."

"She is getting round nicely again; and as I am not wanted indoors just now, I am going into the village to call upon a friend or two I have not been able to speak to as yet."

John took his brother Bob's hand. Bob rather wondered why.

"All right, old boy," he said. "Going into the village? You'll be back again, I suppose, before it gets very late?"

"Oh yes," said Captain Bob cheerfully, and passed out of the garden.

John allowed his eyes to follow his brother till his shape could not be seen, and then he turned and again walked up and down.

THE FIRSTBORN OF EVERY CREATURE.

By JOHN HUNT, D.D.

THESE words are in the Epistle to the Colossians. Their nearest parallel is in the Revelation of St. John, where Christ is called the beginning of the Creation of God. Colosse was a town in Phrygia, in Asia Minor. It was situated in the valley of the Lycus, a tributary of the Meander, and was very near two other cities mentioned in the Epistle to the Colossians, Laodicea and Hieropolis, in both of which there were Christian Churches. The valley was remarkable for its fertility, and these cities in St. Paul's time were flourishing cities of commerce. It is a question if, when St. Paul wrote this epistle, he had ever been at Colosse, or if he only heard of the faith of the Colossians from Epaphras, who came to Rome to visit him in his first imprisonment, and who may have been one of his Ephesian converts. These cities were closely allied with Ephesus, so that Epaphras may have been their first evangelist.

The subject of the Epistle to the Colossians is the pre-existence of Christ. It is a difficult subject, stretching back into the depths of the Godhead, and this is the only epistle in which St. Paul treats expressly of it. In the Ephesians the subject is Christ glorified, but here it is Christ in the glory which He had with His Father before the world was.

The epistle was evoked by the progress of some heresy in the Colossian Church. It is not easy to point out what the heresy was, for we have no guide to it beyond St. Paul's words, and from these we infer that it was a kind of Gnosticism mixed with Judaism. The Gnostic doctrine concerning Christ was that Christ was one of the mighty beings that had emanated from God. The Gnostics had many theories about the heavenly hierarchies or different orders of beings that had proceeded from the Godhead, and they said that Christ, before his incarnation, was one of these beings. But the peculiarity of the Colossian heresy was the mingling with it of a Judaic element. The necessity of circumcision, with all other Jewish ordinances, was inculcated on the Christian converts. It seems as if a party of Jews, who had embraced Christianity, had embraced also some of the old Pagan speculations about the creation of the world and the origin of evil. And as they made evil to be a necessary result of the existence of matter, they enjoined abstinence from all bodily pleasures to the extent of a rigid asceticism, and sometimes they ran into the contrary extreme of giving the reins to all desires, because of their entire indifference to what concerned the body.

In the epistle St. Paul has before him all these errors, both the speculative and the practical. He tells the Colossians of their freedom as Christians from all Jewish observances. They did not require the Jewish circumcision, for they had received the circumcision not made with hands; they were warned lest any man should spoil them through philosophy, or vain deceit; to beware of a voluntary humility and worship of angels, and they were exhorted to mortify the members which are upon the earth, which is explained by a catalogue of sins which they were to avoid. Other religions may be indifferent to morality, but Christianity concerns the whole of man's nature. It does not regard the body as absolutely evil, however common may be the case that it is made the instrument of sin.

The foundation of the Colossian heresies was a mistake as to the divinity of Jesus Christ. They did not deny His pre-existence, nor did they say that He was a mere man, but they made him one of the beings that had proceeded from God, and their conception of matter as something necessarily evil led to the denial of His humanity also, for the Gnostics supposed that He was a man in appearance only. St. Paul announced that He was not merely a perfect man, but that he was the Firstborn of every creature, not merely one of the beings that proceeded from God, but the fountain of all procession, for by Him all things were created, whether they be thrones, or dominions, or principalities, or powers. These were some of the names which the Gnostics gave to the emanated beings of whom they said Jesus was one, but of whom St. Paul says, He is above them all.

But it has been objected, if He is the firstborn of every creature, He must be Himself created. This is apparently a fair inference from the apostle's words. He could not be the firstborn of creation if he were not created. There is a similar speech in Milton, where he calls Eve the fairest of all her daughters. Critics have objected to the expression; but Milton was striving to set forth Eve's beauty, without wishing to say that she was one of her own daughters, which was impossible. · So St. Paul was striving to express the pre-eminence of Christ, but did not wish to say that He was one of the created beings. As the firstborn had the inheritance, to be the firstborn came to mean supremacy or dominion, so that when Christ is called the firstborn of every creature, the object is to express His supremacy over all creatures. He created all, and therefore could be no more one of those created than Eve could have been one of her own daughters.

But now that the apostle has got thus far he does not attempt to go farther. The Godhead is not explained. It remains a mystery. Christ, before His incarnation, was God; that is enough for us. The rest of the mystery may be beyond our faculties, and so incapable of being revealed to us in our present state. It is strange that St. Paul, supposing he did not write the Epistle to the Hebrews, never calls Christ the Word, as St. John did, and as was done by the philosophers when they spoke of God, considered as Creator or as manifesting Himself to men. But though St. Paul does not call Christ the Word, he yet ascribed to Him all that St. John ascribed to the Word. He is before all things, and by Him all things exist.

Christian writers, and, indeed, the Christian Church in general, have spoken too much of Christ's divinity, as if it were something meant to confound and humble human reason. In fact, they have explained the Godhead in a way that has some likeness to the old Gnostic speculations; that is, they have intrenched on that which is not revealed; but the divinity of Christ as it is set forth by St. Paul is the true remedy for our deliverance from all fanciful speculations like those of the Gnostics concerning God.

And as Christ is the head of the natural creation, so is He the head of the new creation. As He is God and made the world, so the world cannot be necessarily evil, and being the Head of the new creation, He gives it life. As He was before creation and made it, so was He before the Church, which received its life from Him. As He was the firstborn of every creature, so is He the firstborn from the dead, in all things having the pre-eminence.

MY LITTLE WOMAN.

A HOMELY cottage, quaint and old,
Its thatch grown thick with green and gold,
  And wind-sown grasses;
Unchanged it stands in sun and rain,
And seldom through the quiet lane
  A footstep passes.

Yet here my little woman dwelt,
And saw the shroud of winter melt
  From meads and fallows;
And heard the yellow-hammer sing
A tiny welcome to the spring
  From budding sallows.

She saw the early morning sky
Blush with a tender wild-rose dye
  Above the larches;
And watched the crimson sunset burn
Behind the summer plumes of fern
  In woodland arches.

My little woman, gone away
To that far land which knows, they say,
  No more sun-setting!
I wonder if her gentle soul,
Securely resting at the goal,
  Has learnt forgetting?

My heart wakes up, and cries in vain ;
She gave me love, I gave her pain
    While she was living ;
I knew not when her spirit fled,
But those who stood beside her, said
    She·died forgiving.

My dove has found a better rest,
And yet I love the empty nest
    She left neglected ;
I tread the very path she trod,
And ask,—in her new home with God
    Am I expected ?

If it were but the Father's will
To let me know she loves me still,
    This aching sorrow
Would turn to hope, and I could say,
Perchance she whispers day by day,
    " He comes to-morrow."

I linger in the silent lane,
And high above the clover plain
    The clouds are riven ;
Across the fields she used to know
The light breaks, and the wind sighs low,
    " Loved and forgiven."
                 SARAH DOUDNEY.

FOUNDERS OF NEW ENGLAND.

I.—WILLIAM BRADFORD.

THE settlement of New England may be classed among the most notable occurrences in the history of the North American continent. That settlement was effected under peculiar conditions ; its consequences have been remarkable and enduring. New England was colonized by reformers in civil government as well as in ecclesiastical discipline, whose ideal was a Church without a bishop and a State without a king. They prepared the way for the accomplishment of their design on a much larger scale than they had contemplated ; the great Republic of North America is a visible and splendid product of their teaching. They command the respect of all unprejudiced and appreciative persons for having achieved grand results in the face of great obstacles, and at sacrifices such as cannot easily be paralleled. The tendency is to exaggerate and give undue prominence to their failings. It is indisputable that their ways are not those which our contemporaries regard with unqualified approbation. It is easier to acknowledge than to admire their excellences ; their virtues lacked sweetness, and their lives lacked geniality. Hawthorne's comment upon them is both appropriate and pointed. He considered it highly gratifying to count the founders of New England among his ancestors, while feeling sincerely thankful not to live under their rule.

The Puritans of Massachusetts were disciplinarians of the severest type. They had a rigid code of conduct, of morals, and of belief, and they would not even tolerate criticism upon the precepts by which they governed themselves, and which they compelled others to observe under a heavy penalty for noncompliance. What they accounted heresy was punished as ruthlessly as any Spanish Inquisitor would have punished what he would have deemed their heresy. Religious toleration was sinful laxity in their eyes. They have not only been blamed for these things, but a charge of inconsistency has also been leveled against them. They were only too consistent and uncompromising. It is a mistake to infer that, because they left the Old World on account of the persecution which they endured there, their purpose was to establish in the New World a home for all who were desolate and oppressed. Their real object was to form a community in which their own views should be supreme, and in

which their interpretation of Scripture and their mode of self-government should neither be subject to question nor exposed to overthrow. When contemporary critics of the Puritans of Massachusetts and their system arose in the persons of Roger Williams, Ann Hutchinson, and zealous quakers, the critics were banished or hanged. This short, sharp, and most effectual reply to criticism was quite in accordance with their original purpose. They did not consider themselves persecutors even when mercilessly persecuting their opponents. They held that they were doing God a service by valiantly defending what they conceived to be the truth and the ordinances which had His sanction. If they had been less consistent they would have received praise from critics who now condemn their inconsistency. They were excellent persons in many respects ; they were men whose vocation may be said to have been the settlement of New England, men whom a New Englander may well glory in numbering among his ancestors, while agreeing with Hawthorne in being thankful that their system has passed away with themselves. However unattractive they may appear as a body, they improve when singled out for personal study. Many of them were men with whom it would be a pleasure to converse ; none of them were wanting in worldly wisdom, nor would it be easy to find among the "smartest" men of the New England of to-day shrewder and wilier men of business, keener hands at a bargain, and better adepts at combining the practice of piety with success in life, than its revered founders. Conspicuous among those of them deserving the highest commendation and whose closer acquaintance is a pleasure to make, stands William Bradford, who, for thirty years, was Governor of New Plymouth.

William Bradford was born in the small Yorkshire village of Austerfield in 1590. His parents and relatives were yeomen, possessing and tilling farms which rendered them independent. He was left an orphan in early life. The death of an uncle increased his patrimony, so that, on attaining man's estate, he was in easy circumstances. When a lad he was greatly impressed by the preaching of the Rev. Richard Clifton, rector of Babworth. He went to Babworth, which is six miles distant from Austerfield, to profit by Mr. Clifton's preaching. His native village is said to have sunk very low in the moral and religious scale ; none of the inhabitants had a Bible, and the clergyman was lukewarm.

At Scrooby, in Nottinghamshire, which is not far from these places, a Church of Separatists, or Nonconformists, as they would now be called, had been established. The vigour with which the Rev. Richard Clifton inculcated his puritanical tenets having subjected him to ecclesiastical censure, he thereupon resigned his rectory ; young Bradford became a member of the Scrooby Nonconformist body. He was then very young, being under eighteen. The chief member of this congregation was William Brewster, who had been private secretary to Mr. Davidson, one of Queen Elizabeth's Secretaries of State and an avowed Puritan, who had filled the office of postmaster in Scrooby for several years. The meetings of the Separatists often took place in Brewster's house. These meetings rendered Brewster and others liable to punishment. The Archbishop of York set the Ecclesiastical Court in motion with the result that, in 1608, three Separatists, Richard Jackson, William Brewster, and Robert Rochester, of Scrooby, were fined £20 each for the offence of worshipping God in their own fashion. These poor people and their associates deemed it hard, as the Covenanters did at a later day, that they could not carry out what they held to be the logical doctrines of the Reformation, without being molested and punished. Their state became at length so desperate that they resolved, at any sacrifice, to escape from the sufferings to which they were subjected by their tormentors. What they suffered and what they determined to do cannot be set forth more clearly and effectively than in Bradford's own words. He describes how the Separatists were " scoffed and scorned by the profane multitude," and otherwise illtreated during many years, and then how " they were hunted and persecuted on every side, so as their former afflictions were but as flea-bitings in comparison of these which now came upon them. For some were taken and clapt up in prison, others had their houses beset and watched night and day, and hardly escaped their hands ; and the most were fain to fly and leave their houses and habitations and the means of their livelihood. Yet these and many other sharper things which afterward befell them, were no other than they looked for, and therefore were the better prepared to bear them by the assistance of God's grace and spirit. Yet seeing themselves thus molested, and that there was no hope of their

continuance there, by a joint consent they resolved to go into the Low Countries, where they heard was freedom of religion for all men ; as also how sundry from London and other parts of the land had been exiled and persecuted for the same cause, and were gone thither, and lived at Amsterdam and in other places of the land. So after they had continued together about a year, and kept their meetings every Sabbath in one place or other, exercising the worship of God among themselves, notwithstanding all the diligence and malice of their adversaries, seeing they could no longer continue in that condition, they resolved to get over into Holland as they could ; which was in the year 1607 and 1608."

Before the members of the Scrooby congregation determined to go to Holland, several Puritans had accompanied the expedition which proceeded to colonize Virginia in 1606. Others were desirous of joining them, but Archbishop Bancroft frustrated their project by causing a proclamation to be issued forbidding the departure of emigrants without a royal license. When Robinson, Brewster, Bradford, and others had made ready to depart for Amsterdam, had disposed of their farms and the goods which they could not carry with them and had hired a vessel to convey them from Boston, in Lincolnshire, to their destination, they found that they were not to be allowed to depart in peace. The proclamation which had been designed to hinder the emigration of Puritans to Virginia was employed to hinder the Scrooby congregation finding an asylum in Holland. The master of the vessel, which they had hired at an exorbitant rate, betrayed them to the authorities after they had gone on board, taking their portable property with them. The search officers made them return on shore in the ship's boat, having first ransacked their boxes and rifled their persons for money, subjecting the women to immodest treatment, and then, after landing, they cast them into prison. After being imprisoned for a month, all of them, with the exception of seven who were committed for trial at the assizes, were liberated in obedience to an order in council, and sent to the places whence they came. This disastrous miscarriage of their design occurred at the end of 1607. In the spring of 1608 they made a second attempt. They found the master of a Dutch vessel at Hull to whom they explained their case and their desire, and who bade them be of good cheer and trust him to do what they wished. It was agreed that they should embark at an unfrequented common between

Hull and Grimsby. The women and children sailed to the appointed place in a small bark, the men proceeded by land. The bark arrived a day too soon, and, as the sea was rough and the women very sick, the sailors hearkened to the entreaties of the women that they should run the bark into a creek where it would be aground at low water. The Dutch vessel appeared the following morning, but the bark could not be set afloat till the tide rose at noon. The Dutchman, seeing men walking about the shore, sent a boat to bring them on board. After the first boat-load had arrived, and when the boat was about to return, the master saw a host of armed men approaching the shore with the intent of seizing the Puritans ; thereupon he swore an oath, weighed anchor, hoisted sail and put out to sea. Some of the men who had been left behind escaped from their pursuers, others and the poor women and children were carried before the magistrates. The latter were puzzled what to do ; they could not inflict punishment on the forlorn women, nor could they order them to return home, seeing that they were destitute and homeless. In the end the magistrates were glad to get rid of them on any terms, the result being that these women and their little ones passed over the sea, rejoining at Amsterdam the husbands, fathers, or brothers, who had arrived there before them. It was no pleasure trip which these men had enjoyed. They were seventeen days on the sea ; during the half of that time they were in peril of shipwreck. Their persecutors had not foreseen that the sufferings to which the fugitives were subjected would attract attention to their doctrines. Many persons being struck with their meek and Christian behaviour had joined their Church, so that they were able to celebrate their safe arrival at Amsterdam with exulting hearts. The Rev. John Robinson, Brewster, and Bradford were he last to reach Holland.

Bradford writes that, when the Scrooby congregation reassembled in Amsterdam, its members had attained security in their desired haven, yet that the feeling of thankfulness which first predominated in their breasts was speedily exchanged for one of apprehension as to their future lot. They were poor refuges in cities which seemed to them rich in all the things. To use Bradford's picturesque phrase, " It was not long before they saw the dim and grisly face of poverty coming upon them like an armed man, with whom they must buckle and encounter, and from whom they could not fly." While it was a

serious problem for them how to get daily bread, they had another source of deep tribulation. Two English congregations of Puritans had settled in Amsterdam before them; the one had come from London twelve years previously, the other, which preceded them a short time, had come from Gainsborough. These congregations were bitterly antagonistic, the semi-conformity of the one being accounted heresy by the absolute Nonconformists of the other. Bishops of the Church of England considered all Nonconformists as equally blameworthy, while the Nonconformists themselves were divided in opinion as to whether they could hold any fellowship with that Church, or whether they were to break with it absolutely, treating the Church of England as unscriptural in all things as the Church of Rome. The Rev. John Robinson and the members of the Scrooby congregation took the view that separation from the Church of their fathers was to be confined to those points and practices which they considered to be unwarranted by Scripture, but that in all other things they were ready to co-operate with that Church; they had not separated from any particular Church, but from the corruptions of all Churches. Not desiring to take sides in a dispute between the two other congregations, the Scrooby Nonconformists determined to quit Amsterdam and settle in Leyden. Accordingly, in February, 1609, they accomplished their removal, and for twelve years after this time the Scrooby congregation remained at Leyden, with the Rev. John Robinson as its pastor and William Brewster as its ruling elder.

Bradford came of age during the sojourn of the congregation at Leyden. He then sold his property in England, but, owing to mismanagement of the proceeds, he was obliged to resume labouring for his bread, as he had done on arriving at Amsterdam. He chose the trade of silk-dyeing. He added to his cares by marrying Dorothy May, who is supposed to have been a member of one of the Amsterdam Churches. Brewster resorted first to teaching, and afterwards to printing, for a livelihood, and he obtained both money and reputation in the latter capacity. Sir Dudley Carleton, then English Ambassador at the Hague, was incensed on account of Brewster printing with impunity, at Leyden, books which could not be openly printed and sold in England. On Brewster visiting London, in 1619, an attempt was made to arrest him, but this attempt happily miscarried. Brewster's son then conformed, established himself as a bookseller at the sign of the Bible in Fleet Street, prospered, and rose to be treasurer of the Stationers' Company. He was not an exception. Indeed, the members of the congregation at Leyden lamented that many of their children had become backsliders. This was a most grievous trial as well as a mischief not easily remedied. Bradford records that some of the young men "became soldiers, others took upon them far voyages by sea, and others some worse courses, tending to dissoluteness and the danger of their souls, to the great grief of their parents and dishonour of God." What these godly parents bitterly mourned over was the prospect of their posterity becoming degenerate and corrupt. Hence, they resolved to leave Leyden and seek for a new home where their liberty to worship God as they pleased would be preserved, and where the temptations to sin would be lessened. Many considered that they would find an earthly paradise in Guiana, alleging, on the authority of Robert Harcourt, who had travelled thither and who wished to form a settlement there, that "the country was rich, fruitful, and blessed with a perpetual spring and a flourishing greenness; where vigorous nature brought forth all things in abundance and plenty without any great labour or art of man." Others preferred Virginia, on the ground that Englishmen "had already made entrance" there, that its climate would agree better with them than that of hot countries, and that it was prudent to avoid the danger of proximity to the Spaniards, of whom the French Huguenots in Florida had been the victims. The main objection to Virginia was that, if under English dominion there, "they would be in as great danger to be troubled and persecuted for the cause of religion as if they lived in England, and it might be worse." However, it was finally determined "to live as a distinct body by themselves, under the general government of Virginia."

After the decision to leave Leyden was arrived at, many difficulties had to be surmounted before the Rev. John Robinson's congregation could start for America. But the necessary arrangements were completed, including an advance of funds wherewith to meet the outlay. It was agreed with some English merchants to form a joint-stock company, whereof all the members who emigrated should work for seven years for the common benefit, and that, at the expiry of the term, a division of the property should be effected according to a specified scale. These Merchant Adventurers, as they were called, numbered seventy, and the subscribed

capital was £7,000. Bradford, Brewster, Carver, and others who had money of their own, contributed liberally to the undertaking. Two vessels were provided to carry them across the Atlantic. The one named the *Speedwell*, of 60 tons burden, was bought and fitted in Holland; the other named the *Mayflower*, of 180 tons burden, was chartered in London. The departing members of the Leyden congregation set sail in the *Speedwell* from Delftshaven for Southampton, where they arrived at the end of July, 1620. They were detained at Southampton till the middle of August. They found it necessary to buy some things there, and, in order to do so, they had to sell four firkins of the butter which they brought from Leyden. They were, indeed, put to great extremities, as they stated in a letter addressed to their partners in London, "Scarce having any butter, no oil, not a sole to mend a shoe, nor every man a sword to his side, wanting many muskets, much armour, &c." The day before sailing, a letter was read from the Rev. John Robinson, who had remained at Leyden with the intention of leaving it along with the rest of his congregation, after the members who had departed were settled in their new homes. If no other writings of Robinson than this letter were extant it would suffice to stamp him as a man of great practical wisdom. He specially exhorts them to live on good terms with each other and be patient under trials, to have their hearts as well as their hands bent upon promoting the general advantage, concluding with a piece of advice which merits quotation: "Whereas you are become a body politic, using among yourselves civil government, and are not furnished with any persons of special eminence above the rest, to be chosen by you into office of government, let your wisdom and godliness appear, not only in choosing such persons as do entirely love, and will diligently promote, the common good, but also in yielding unto then all due honour and obedience in their lawful administrations, not beholding in them the ordinariness of their persons, but God's ordinance for your good; not being like unto the foolish multitude, who more honour the gay coat than either the virtuous mind of the man, or glorious ordinance of the Lord."

When the Pilgrims set sail from Southampton for the Western land, they were mistaken if they supposed that their perplexities were over. A week later they had to call at Dartmouth on account of the unseaworthiness of the *Speedwell*. Again they set sail, and, when the two ships had got a hundred leagues beyond the Land's End, it was found necessary to put back into Plymouth to repair the *Speedwell;* and then it was determined to abandon that vessel and transfer to the *Mayflower* the passengers who still desired to go. Several were ready and anxious to return home, the result being that the passengers who eventually embarked numbered one hundred and two. For the third time the *Mayflower* sailed from the English coast, with a fair wind, on her Atlantic voyage. The voyage lasted sixty-five days. The weather was frequently stormy, and the danger seemed so great in mid-ocean that it was debated whether the prudent course would not be to return. One of the vessel's beams had given way, but as a passenger had brought "a great iron screw out of Holland," which served to repair the beam and strengthen the hull, it was decided to continue the voyage. Two deaths occurred on board, one among the passengers, the other among the crew. The sailor's death struck Bradford and others as a retribution for his conduct. He was "a proud and very profane young man, ... of a lusty, able body, which made him the more haughty." This sailor mocked the poor sea-sick passengers, made merry over their sufferings, and cursed and swore bitterly when gently reproved by any of them. Moreover, he expressed a hope that he might help to cast half of them overboard before the voyage ended. In mid-Atlantic he was smitten with a grievous disease, of which he died, "and so was himself the first that was thrown overboard." The passenger who died was William Bullen, the servant to Samuel Fuller, this vacancy in the number that started being supplied by Oceanus Hopkins, who was born at sea. Bradford chronicles the narrow escape of John Howland, "a lusty young man," who fell overboard when the ship gave a lurch, and who, clutching the top-sail halyards which touched the water, was drawn on deck again.

The destination of the *Mayflower* was a spot near the Hudson River in what is now the State of New Jersey. On the morning of the sixty-fourth day after leaving Plymouth the Pilgrims espied the white sand banks which surround Cape Cod. This was not considered accidental at the time, and there is good reason for supposing that the master, Thomas Jones, had accepted a bribe to carry the Pilgrims to New England instead of landing them in Virginia. He died five years later with the reputation of having robbed the Indians of New England and committed piracy on the Spaniards. However, the Pilgrims accepted their lot and made judicious arrangements for settling on the place to which they were conveyed. They had acted for years in Holland as a body politic, and their design was to continue this form of self-government on a wider scale and on a more certain basis. That something should be determined as to the political status of the community was indispensable, seeing that strangers to their church, but shareholders in their joint-stock company, had joined them at Southampton, and refused to submit to the rule of Mr. Carver, who had been elected governor. They indulged in mutinous speeches during the voyage and intimated that they would act as they pleased after landing. As the Pilgrims had no patent for the locality where they found themselves obliged to settle, the majority resolved to remedy the inconvenience and hinder subsequent misunderstanding by entering into a solemn covenant. The document is unique in history. If Rousseau had known of it, he would have cited it as a practical illustration of his theory about a social contract being entered into when human society first originates. It runs thus : "In the name of God, Amen. We whose names are under-written, the loyal subjects of our dread sovereign Lord, King James, by the grace of God, of Great Britain, France, and Ireland, King, Defender of the Faith, &c., having undertaken, for the glory of God, and advancement of the Christian faith and honour of our king and country, a voyage to plant the first Colony in the northern parts of Virginia, do by these presents solemnly and mutually in the presence of God and one of another, covenant and combine ourselves together into a civil body politic, for our better ordering and preservation and furtherance of the ends aforesaid; and by virtue hereof to enact, constitute, and frame such just and equal laws, ordinances, acts, constitutions, and offices, from time to time, as shall be thought most meet and convenient for the general good of the Colony, unto which we promise all due submission and obedience." This document, which was signed by the adult males on board, served for many years as the charter of New Plymouth:

On the 21st of November the *Mayflower* was anchored off Cape Cod; it was not till the 21st of December that the passengers went on shore to take formal possession of the site on which to erect their dwellings. Much labour had been expended in exploring the coast, and, in despair of finding a more suitable place, that on which Plymouth now stands had been chosen. An Indian village called Patuxat stood here till, having been depopulated by an epidemic, the survivors were induced to move away. Several encounters with the Indians had occurred, but no lives had been lost. A fortunate discovery of seed-corn, stored up in an Indian granary, provided the Pilgrims with a thing which they omitted to bring with them, and without which they could not count upon reaping a harvest in the following year. A girl was born whilst the ship lay at anchor; she was named Peregrine White. Her antique cradle is one of the curiosities which New Englanders treasure as a precious relic of their forefathers. This birth was followed by a death, the victim being Bradford's wife, who fell overboard and was drowned during his absence in a small boat on a voyage of exploration. He married again two years afterwards; his second wife was Alice Southworth, a widow. He had a son by his first marriage, two sons and a daughter by the second. His second wife survived him thirteen years.

Soon after the landing of the Pilgrims, the life of Bradford was in such imminent danger from a sudden attack of cramp, due to a chill which he had received, that his death was expected; however, he rallied, and recovered his wonted health. Many of his companions who were struck down also were less fortunate. Before the winter months had passed away the half of the Pilgrims were laid in graves, which were carefully concealed lest the Indians might learn how greatly the band had been weakened. Several of the *Mayflower's* crew had died also, so that, when that vessel returned home in April, 1621, the seamen on board were but half as numerous as when she left England. Immediately after the vessel sailed Governor Carver died suddenly. Bradford, though ailing himself, was elected his successor, with Isaac Allerton as assistant. The strongest proof of the constancy with which the Pilgrims endured their trials is the fact that not one took advantage of the sailing of the *Mayflower* to return to the old home. But they had many instances of good fortune, as well as much to bear with patience and fortitude. The Indians proved friendly. A visit from one named Samoset was the most startling of their early experiences. He walked into their rude town, advanced boldly to the first person whom he saw, held out his hand and exclaimed, "Welcome, Englishmen." Squanto, who came after him, was an Indian who had not only formed an acquaintance with the traders who visited the coast, but had been kidnapped, carried to Spain, whence he escaped to England, had dwelt in London with Master John Slanie, a merchant of Cornhill, and had been re-conveyed to America. He caught fish for the Pilgrims, who had omitted to provide themselves with fishing-tackle. When they first landed they had eaten the shell-fish with which the shore was strewn, and had suffered so severely that, for some time after, they were rather chary about eating fish at all. However, the eels caught by Squanto were pronounced "fat and sweet," and were eaten with pleasure. He also taught them how to sow Indian corn, an art of which they had no knowledge, and he was the medium of their entering into a treaty of peace and friendship with Massasoit, the Chief of the Indians there. They prospered during the first year of their sojourn, so that at the end of 1621 one of their number, Edward Winslow, could write in the following terms to a friend in England: "I never in my life remember a more seasonable year than we have here enjoyed; and if we have once but kine, horses, and sheep, I make no question but men might live as contented here as in any part of the world. For fish and fowl we have great abundance, fresh cod in the summer is but coarse meat with us; our bay is full of lobsters all the summer, and affordeth variety of other fish; in September we can take a hogshead of eels in a night, with small labour, and can dig them out of their beds all the winter; we have mussels and othus [cockles?] at our doors; oysters we have none near, but we can have them brought by the Indians when we will; all the springtime the earth sendeth forth naturally very good salad herbs; here are grapes, white and red, and very sweet and strong also. Strawberries, gooseberries, raspas, &c. Plums of three sorts, white, black, and red, being almost as good as a damson; abundance of roses, white, red, and damask, single, but very sweet indeed; the country wanteth only industrious men to employ, for it would grieve your hearts if (as I) you had seen so many miles together by goodly rivers uninhabited, and withal to consider those parts of the world wherein you live, to be even greatly burdened with abundance of people." Nearly two hundred and sixty years have elapsed since the foregoing words were penned, the population of England is six times greater now than it was then, and yet the fact of the land being overburdened with people seems to have been as much a subject of complaint early in the first quarter of the seventeenth century as it is in the last quarter of the nineteenth.

The brilliant prospect depicted by Edward Winslow was soon overcast; the harvest failed the Pilgrims, and for two years they had to subsist chiefly on fish. In 1623 a change for the better occurred, and from this time forward they had not to dread or endure the misery of famine. They suffered, however, from the system which condemned them to labour in common for the benefit of the Merchant Adventurers in London. The conditions proved so onerous that several attempts were made by Bradford to procure a mitigation of them. He complained of the hard measure meted out by the London merchants, who charged as much as 70 per cent. profit on the goods which they supplied, and demanded as much as 50 per cent. interest for the money which they advanced. In 1626 it was agreed to dissolve the contract with the Merchant Adventurers, the Pilgrims paying them £1,800 in nine annual instalments, Bradford and seven others undertaking to be responsible for the fulfilment of the engagement. Then the land was parted among the settlers by lot, and the cattle also was divided among them, every thirteen persons receiving a cow and two goats. It was not till 1641 that the debt to the London merchants was finally liquidated; this caused so heavy a loss to Bradford and his associates that they even contemplated removing to a place where their labour would yield a better return. However, they had too many ties to New Plymouth ever to leave it. The surviving brethren of the Church at Leyden had all joined them; unhappily the Rev. John Robinson was not spared to cross the Atlantic; he died in 1625, to the great grief of his attached friends on both sides of the ocean. Brewster died in 1643 at the age of fourscore, and his decease gave Bradford the opportunity of writing a beautiful and touching eulogium on his friend and colleague. Though a devout man, Brewster was no ascetic; on the contrary, he was "of a very cheerful spirit, very sociable and pleasant among his friends." When Bradford notes these things in his friend's praise, he lets the reader infer that he himself was akin in temperament; he would not have commended a trait which was foreign or repugnant to his nature. His own death occurred on the 19th of May, 1657, when he was in his sixty-eighth year. He set himself in his old age to study Hebrew. He could read Latin and Greek, he could speak Dutch and French; but his great desire was to understand the ancient language and holy tongue in which the oracles of God are written, and he had the satisfaction of recording that, though he did not become a proficient in Hebrew, yet he was refreshed with a glimpse of what he desired, just "as Moses saw the land of Canaan afar off." He was a wise and judicious governor. Thirty times was he elected governor of New Plymouth, and he would have been elected thirty-five times had he not begged to remain out of place during five years. He urged that, if it were a distinction to be governor, others ought to have their turn, and that, if it were burdensome, others ought to take their share in the labour.

Not many personal particulars of Bradford are extant; but the following story, which he narrates in his "History of New Plymouth," gives a notion of his shrewdness combined with kindliness as a man. He is relating what happened in 1621, and says at the end, that he remembers but one thing more to be noted, and this "is rather of mirth than weight. On the day called Christmas-day the Governor called them out to work (as was used), but the most of this new company excused themselves, and said it went against their consciences to work on that day. So the Governor told them that if they made it matter of conscience, he would spare them till they were better informed. So he led away the rest and left them; but when they came home at noon from their work, he found them in the street at play, openly; some pitching the bar, and some at stool-ball, and suchlike sports. So he went to them and took away their implements, and told them that was against his conscience that they should play and others work. If they made the keeping of it matter of devotion, let them keep their houses; but there should be no gaming or revelling in the streets."

Cotton Mather records that when Bradford died he was lamented by all the colonies of New England, as a common blessing and father to them all. No other settler in North America has merited or received higher praise. Though many of William Bradford's contemporaries and successors may have surpassed him in natural talents and attainments, yet he has an incontestable claim to a foremost and most enviable place alike among the founders of New England and old English worthies.

W. FRASER RAE.

AN OLD FRENCH CITY.

By KATHERINE S. MACQUOID.

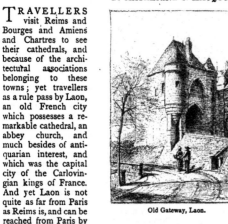

Old Gateway, Laon.

TRAVELLERS visit Reims and Bourges and Amiens and Chartres to see their cathedrals, and because of the architectural associations belonging to these towns; yet travellers as a rule pass by Laon, an old French city which possesses a remarkable cathedral, an abbey church, and much besides of antiquarian interest, and which was the capital city of the Carlovingian kings of France. And yet Laon is not quite as far from Paris as Reims is, and can be reached from Paris by railway in a few hours. The country between Laon and Reims is very flat, but all at once as one journeys along the monotonous plain, first one sees the towers, and then the grand cathedral of Laon, surrounded by its towers, appears standing abruptly on the end of a range of lofty hills. It forms a most striking picture for some time before one reaches the station. On leaving the station the road begins to mount towards the town, zigzagged up the steep rock. The omnibus was full of Laon people

returning home, who showed much interest in our visit to their city. As we ascended we could see open country on either side between the rows of chestnut and acacia trees that bordered the dusty road, but soon a steep rocky bank rose upon the left, though on the right the level plain seemed as if it might stretch away to Amiens.

Suddenly, above the rocky heights on the left we saw the imposing group of the cathedral towers; and in a few moments we drove into Laon under an arched gateway, seemingly of the Empire period. The streets looked narrow and quaint, and our inn, the Hôtel de la Hure, which stands in the principal street, has a huge sow's head hanging from a quaint bracket of ornamental ironwork, which projects halfway across the street.

Close by this inn de la Hure there stood, till 1831, the famous great tower or towers of Louis d'Outremer, the tower in which Charles of Lorraine took refuge when the

Château near Laon.

town of Laon was treacherously yielded to Hugh Capet by its bishop, Adulberan.

But we were roused from historic memories by the sight of our dark-eyed landlady, who stood just below the ancient sign, beaming with smiles of welcome; though she was in despair at having only one large bedroom to offer.

"It is not my fault, mesdames," she said ingenuously; "it is that of the house, it has only one large chamber."

All this time there stood slightly behind this bright-eyed little woman, but close at her elbow, a most ambiguous-looking creature wriggling about and twisting his hands together. He was dressed like a man, but his hands, his voice, and his gestures were those of a woman. He wore white trousers, a white apron with a bib, and a blouse; he moved as gently and purred as softly as a cat, as he followed us up-stairs, assuring us that in spite of the smallness of some of the rooms we should find them "Tout-à-fait bien."

We certainly found the rooms clean and comfortable; and we found, too, an excellent luncheon ready before we sallied forth to explore the town.

Not far from our inn we saw the ancient and curious Porte de Chenezelles. The best view of this is to be had from the garden of the photographer.

As we went through the old grass-grown streets to the cathedral we noticed several quaint signs supported by ornamental iron work of the same fashion as that dangling from our inn.

It was disappointing to find the grand old building, Notre Dame de Laon, in process of restoration—the interior completely given up to scaffolding and workpeople—but the effect even under these disadvantages was

very grand and striking, the total length of the interior being three hundred and thirty-one feet. This church is very severe and pure in style, and is said to have been built early in the twelfth century. It is also said to have taken only two years in building,

View of the Cathedral from the Walls.

but the date of much of it is seemingly a century later. Its most striking external features are its four towers, with open lights, two at the west end and two at the transepts. These towers have huge oxen at each corner, said to be placed there to commemorate a pious legend concerning the oxen who dragged up hill the stone and other materials for building the church. The west porch is also very remarkable, much more severe and more simple in character than the exquisite portal of

Reims which we had only left that morning,
but still very imposing.

All round the interior of the church is a series
of small chapels, with elaborate open work six-
teenth-century screens shutting them in from
the aisles. We went up into the lower tri-
forium (there are two), and this lower gallery
is spacious, making a fine promenade; from
it we had a good view of the interior. It
is certainly very imposing, and seems in
excellent preservation. There is a curious
painting, intended to represent the impression left on the handkerchief of St. Veronica,
in the sacristy. While we were up in the
gallery the master mason showed us a tomb
which had been found during the repairs,
a kind of stone box, with this inscription:—

"Ici repose Guillaume d'Harségney, médecin de
Charles VI, bienfaiteur de la Cathédrale et de la
ville de Laon."

The doctor's bones were within.

Coming out at the west door we went down
a street on the left beside the cathedral.
We hoped to get a clear view of the building, but it is almost entirely surrounded
by houses. However, not far from the door
into the transept we saw a striking picture.
The grand old towers rise above the tiled
roof of a quaint, low, Gothic stone house,
which abuts on the church itself. Under a
niche at the angle of this house is a sun-dial.
A vine grows luxuriantly over the wall below
in exquisite harmony and contrast with the
rich greys and oranges of the old stone wall.
We went in at an open door in this range of
building—part of which is occupied by the
sacristan—and we found ourselves in a picturesque little court, one side formed by the
side of the cathedral.

Farther on down the street, Rue du Cloître,
is an interesting old stone building with
pointed gables and three Gothic windows.
As we went along we got peeps through
arches and doorways of pretty gardens full of
green plants and bright flowers.

We found our way, up and down and in
and out of narrow grass-grown streets, to what
was once an old church of the Templars, a
very curious little round building, with a
porch or narthex at the west end and a small
projecting chancel at the east. It now belongs to the Frères Chrétiens, and stands in
the enclosure of their garden. One of the
brothers received us very kindly. He had
been busy gathering fruit from a sunny wall,
but came cheerfully down the ladder to greet
us. He guided us through the pretty garden,
one part of which was surrounded by a hedge

of golden nasturtiums trained over a trellis,
with a tempting plot of artichokes for
centre.

Laon is a perfectly orthodox old French
town with regard to pavement, and we had
been trotting for some time over its round,
unevenly set stones till our feet ached, when
all at once we came to a gate surmounted
by a green arch formed by some trailing
plant, through which showed the prettiest of
little gardens. On the left a high wall was
green up to its very top with a wealth of
varied and graceful leafage—a fig-tree, climbing roses, clematis, and on a shelf among
these a gigantic cereus flung down huge
knotted limbs, while the garden plot below
was at once gay and rich with blossoms.
A narrow path divided this in two unequal
portions, and led up to the porch of the
house. Another bower of choice creeping
plants sheltered a double row of blue lilies
and deeply coloured carnations, while flame-
like gladioli and crimson fuchsias glowed on
each side of the path. We all stood still,
longing to enter this little Paradise. It
seemed like a fairy tale, when as we looked a
pleasant-faced, dark-eyed gentleman came
from beneath the bowered porch and smiled
at our admiration.

He came forward and we apologised for
staring, upon which he bowed, assured us of
his cordial sympathy, and, opening the gate,
bade us all come in.

He said that he tended his flowers himself, and told us interesting little particulars
about them; but when he found that we
knew the names of the plants and flowers,
and were acquainted with his precious
darlings, his eyes grew brighter still — he
was quite excited with delight.

"Ah, mesdames and monsieur," he cried,
"come in, come in, I beg of you; there is
something better worth seeing within than
flowers even."

With this he led us into a narrow passage,
also full of flowers and plants, and, flinging
open a door at the end of it, we saw through
the open window opposite a fine view of the
surrounding country lying many feet below.
It was like a stage effect, to come suddenly
out of the narrow, closely built street to this
immense vista of far-off plains and hills. But
as we followed our host into a brightly furnished little room with pictures and gilt
mirrors and engravings on the walls, and
tables covered with books and gay knick-
knacks, we saw through the window that we
had reached the edge of the old town, the
part built within the walls, and that our

polite friend's house stood on the ramparts. Just below us was the picturesque old wall, and on the right the Porte Royer or Ardon, a very interesting gate tower of the thirteenth century, founded on an ancient Roman gateway, of which the foundation stones still remain in huge uncemented blocks of stone.

When we turned round from the window and the lovely landscape glittering in sunshine, we saw that some one else had come into the room—a tall grey woman dressed very plainly in black, wearing a large muslin cap tied under her chin. She looked very grave, and seemed like a shadow in the midst of this bright little casket and its green nest; but she smiled amiably when our impromptu host presented her as his mother in the affectionate tone one hears so often from the lips of Frenchmen.

"My mother lives with me," he said simply. "She helps me to bring up my little daughter and to take care of my garden."

He sighed and looked grave for an instant, but he was soon smiling again and expatiating on the charms of his autumn *marguerites*. They were just over, but he said they had been most abundant. The old lady received our compliments on her flowers with a stately and smiling courtesy.

We heard afterwards that he had suffered much from the loss of his wife, who had died a year before. He held an official post in the town.

The bright little episode—not a rare one in pleasant France—had made us forget our fatigue, but after this we were glad to make our way back to the Hôtel de la Hure, passing several interesting old relics of the past on our way. Laon had once sixty-three churches and chapels and a great reputation for sanctity. St. Béat seems to have been its first apostle, about the close of the third century; but two centuries later St. Remy, Archbishop of Reims, a native of Laon, baptized Clovis, the Pagan husband of Saint Clotilda, and obtained from the Frankish king, among other grants, the creation of a bishopric for his native city of Laon.

The city itself is of very ancient origin, and is said undoubtedly to have been built on the site of the famous Bibrax mentioned by Cæsar as having opposed so formidable a resistance to the army of 300,000 Belgians sent to dislodge the Romans, who were advancing to that part of Gaul.

While we rested at our inn there was a tap at the door, and in answer to our "Entrez," came in the ambiguous garçon de chambre.

His head drooped forward, his shoulders seemed drawn together in a deprecating fashion, and he rubbed his small womanish-looking hands fondly together.

"Madame," he put one hand before his imploring mouth and gave a little cough—we began to fear some accident must have befallen our luggage—"Madame, I have come to entreat that you will ring your bell when you want anything; remember, madame, that I am always here, ready to bring you hot water—what do I say? all you wish—I am devoted to your service. Madame, there is the bell-rope. Parfaitement, Madame."

Our fellow-traveller told us he had put himself at her service in just the same devoted fashion. He looked so earnest, so tenderly solicitous, that it was very hard not to laugh; with all his kindness and attention, he was certainly a trial to our gravity; he met us on the stairs, everywhere, indeed, with offers of service, always with the same pathetic entreaty in his face. I think he suffered from a secret consciousness that we should prefer a female chambermaid, and he wished he were a woman for our sakes; but he was genuinely kind, and we shall always have a friendly memory of that pathetic-faced chamberman at Laon; he is a relic of a fashion passing away.

When we had rested we drove to the abbey church of St. Martin, and then round the town; and it takes some time to do this, for the road is cut on the side of the steep descent, and is both rough and dangerous; but the fragments of wall and bits of fortress peeping out among the houses, and garlanded with vines, are most picturesque and interesting. The old wall near St. Martin's is said to have been built from a legacy of Guillaume d'Harségney, whose coffin we had seen in the cathedral.

The abbey buildings of St. Martin are now used for the Hôtel-Dieu. The patients are nursed by Sisters of Charity. Close by is the venerable abbey church; its entrance, some centuries later in style than the rest of the building, has a bas-relief over the portal in which St. Martin cuts his cloak in two with his sword, so that he may give half to the Evil One in the form of a beggar.

The chancel, the oldest part of the church, is very beautiful, and it is altogether a striking building of the twelfth century, full of good effects of light and shade.

Near the entrance are two very remarkable tombs—one in white marble, that of an abbess of the convent of Sanvoir sous Laon, said to be Jeanne of Flanders, widow of Enguerrand de Coucy. It was once in the

Church of Sanvoir, and was removed and buried in a garden to save it during the Revolution, and then placed in this abbey church. The other, in black Ardennais marble, represents a knight in armour, said to be that of a Sire de Coucy. Tradition relates that a Sire de Coucy having resolved to end his days in prayer, begged permission of the monks of St. Martin to enter their convent. The monks consented on condition that after his death certain lands belonging to him, notably the forest of Samoussy, should be given to them. De Coucy consented, and proceeded to the abbey. Feeling hungry as soon as he arrived, he asked for food, and a couple of eggs, the usual collation of the monks, was served to him. But as soon as he had eaten he fell sick, and soon after died; not, however, till he had executed a deed willing the promised bequest to the monks of St. Martin. But the Sire de Coucy was a Huguenot, and there had not been time to convert him; the monks felt sorely puzzled. The forest of Samoussy and its revenues would be a most welcome addition to their resources, at that time greatly impoverished, but they were too conscientious to bury a heretic within the church. A chapter was called, and it was decided that the dead nobleman should be buried outside the sacred building. The interment took place. But the dead man had powerful relations, and these, hearing of the deed of the monks of St. Martin, instituted a suit against them which threatened the deprivation of the rich bequest. It was therefore decided to build out this portion of the abbey church so as to bring the tomb within its walls. This legend is, however, disputed, as the effigy on the tomb is said not to be a De Coucy at all, but probably that of Roger, Lord of Pierrepont and Montaigu, who died in the abbey of St. Martin, after two years of residence, about 1130. The ruin of Château de Coucy, near Laon, is a very fine specimen of a castle of the Middle Ages.

This is also a fine château given in our engraving, a few miles out of Laon, which is worth a visit.

We did not go into the Hôtel-Dieu, though we heard that there is a fine staircase to be seen there. After leaving St. Martin we drove outside the town, seemingly on the verge of the steep hill, to see the Creuttes de St. Vincent. We passed many fragments of old wall, picturesque with wild plants and vine sprays, and came to a very curious leaning tower called La Tour Penchée, and also

Cloister of the Archbishop's Palace.

Tour de la Dame Eve. The Creuttes are most curious dwellings scooped in the side of the rock itself, with earthen fronts. They are said to be of great antiquity, but some of them are evidently still inhabited, for we saw clothes hanging out to dry. Just beyond these singular dwellings we came to the venerable enclosure of the once famous abbey of St. Vincent, said to have been founded in 590 by Queen Brunehaut. The last remains of this abbey were destroyed in 1794, but much of the wall is unquestionably very old. The road became wider with trees planted on each side, making pleasant boulevards and charming shaded walks for the townspeople—for the view on all sides is most extensive. Presently we came to a magnificent point: a huge hollow, called La Cuve St. Vincent, divides the portion of hill on which we were from the steep rock on which the cathedral is built. The massive old towers and spire stand up grandly from among the houses and trees, and with the sweeping curve of the ground in front make a very striking picture.

Old Gateway.

Our driver pointed down the valley a little way on, and asked us if we could see a church nestling beside the hill. Yes, we saw a church, and at some distance we made out a village. There seemed to be a tree-shaded walk of some length between the church and the houses.

"Do you see," our driver pointed with his whip, "near the church, in the hollow of the hill, a farmhouse?"

We looked again: there was certainly a small house standing by itself, with a few trees near it.

Our driver stopped his horses, and turned round so as to look into the carriage.

"If mesdames will listen," he said, "I will tell what happened down there a few years ago."

We felt interested and begged him to go on.

"The mistress of the farm down yonder," he pointed again, "died, and she left only a daughter to take her money. She had another child, a son, but every one had forgotten him. Ah, he was a good-for-nothing! He broke his father's heart, and then he ran away to sea; if any of us remembered him, *dame*, it was only to hope that the devil had got his own. Well, mesdames, the old woman died; she had been a good old body, and Monsieur le Curé used to go and see her daughter, and masses were said for the old woman's soul, all as they should be, when one evening, a fortnight after, home comes the good-for-nothing. The sister was frightened; she was alone in the house, and it was long since she had seen the 'vagabond; she could not tell what he might not have become. 'What do you want?' she asked; 'our mother is dead.'—'I know that she is dead, and I am come for her hoards,' he said. 'Do you suppose I mean you to keep them? I heard of her death by accident, and I have come many miles to claim my own.' His sister told him he was mistaken; already much of his mother's money had been robbed by him on his last visit to the farm. 'And what was left,' she said, 'I have paid to Monsieur le Curé for the funeral and for masses for our mother.' He swore loudly, and the poor girl said he looked at her like a devil. 'Is this true?' he said. 'I warn you not to tell me a lie.'—'It is as true as that you are here. Do be reasonable, Michel,' she said. 'I have no money for you.' He looked all round, but he could see nothing worth taking; then he ground his teeth and swore a fearful oath. 'I will settle Monsieur le Curé's reckoning myself,' he said, and he went away.

"Next morning was Sunday, and the girl went as usual to mass at eight o'clock; so did the rest of the villagers. Monsieur le Curé did not leave the building till the little chorister who served had departed. Usually he and the child walked back together to the presbytery. It so happened that one of the villagers wanted to speak to Monsieur le Curé that morning, and came up from the village very soon after the priest had left the church. As he went on past the building just there, you see, before reaching the presbytery, he saw something black under a tree, and there was Monsieur le Curé lying on the ground dead as a stone, shot through the head."

"Was the murderer taken?" we asked, for our driver paused with a sigh; indeed, he had not told his story at all in the matter-of-fact style of a man who told it every day.

"Yes, he was taken, and his sister testified against him, and he was executed. Allez!" he said to his horses, and soon we had left the boulevards and were again on the narrow rampart of the walled part of the city, looking at the picturesque group formed by the archbishop's palace, now turned, into the Palais de Justice, crowned by the cathedral towers. The entrance into this palace is by an archway near the cathedral; through this we reached the cloister garden. The view of the cathedral is very fine from this point, and the cloister arcade itself is very good; the capitals of the columns are skilfully carved and varied in design. Within the building the *salle* is a disappointment, as it has been divided into courts of justice, but the chapel is very interesting, and so is the crypt below it.

We left Laon next day, impressed with the belief that there was much more to see in the town than we had discovered in our brief visit, and rejoiced to have added another to our list of quaint and deeply interesting old French cities.

We had parted from our landlady and her strange domestic at the inn door, in the midst of compliments and expressions of good-will. But we had not seen the last of the man-*femme de chambre*. Just as we were on the point of starting by the train, he came flying into the station, pale, with staring eyes, and out of breath, holding in his hand some artist-materials which one of our party had left behind. He had run all the way down the steep hill with them. At first he could not speak, but when his breath came back he said, "I would have run farther still, if necessary, to oblige Monsieur."

The last thing we saw was his sensitive, twitching face.

THE BORDER LAND.

IN fleshly weakness as abed I lie,
   And through the casement catch the gentle swing
Of emerald boughs against the sapphire sky,
   And list the sweet wild birds their vespers sing,

I have no wish but my tired soul to lay
   Upon the bosom of the Good and Great;
To fold my hands in meek content and say,
   "Well if thou bid'st to come, well if to wait."

One word, "Forgive," embraces all past years,
   With praise for present gifts my heart runs o'er,
While through the mist of silent, tranquil tears
   Gleams the far vision of a golden door.

Stands it ajar for me this summer night?
   To greet me there are my lost angels met?
Am I so soon to share their pure delight?
   Hark! a soft voice responsive saith, "Not yet.

"Go back once more a simple child to school—
   The world's wide battle school of toil and heat;
Follow no law but Christ's most loving rule,
   And bring each day new trophies to His feet:

"Some selfish aim subdued, dark passion slain,
   Some sweet forgiveness of a bitter wrong,
Some tender solace of a brother's pain,
   Some sorrow bravely borne in duty strong.

"And aye the more you wrestle on to know,
   And knowing, walk the path the Master trod,
Your all of hope in lowlier homage throw
   Upon the mercy of the perfect God."

Ah, yes! When sickness unto death goes by,
   The border land should be a holy place—
A glorious mount of pause 'twixt earth and sky,
   Whose finer airs give souls a deeper grace.

So be it mine henceforth in chastened mood
   To wear my lengthened years, forgetting never
The Pisgah height where I this night have stood,
   And glimpsed afar the home beyond the river!

                        JANE C. SIMPSON.

THE TEN COMMANDMENTS.

By A. P. STANLEY, D.D., Dean of Westminster.

"There was nothing in the ark save the two tables of stone, which Moses put there at Horeb."—1 Kings viii. 9.

I PROPOSE to consider the Ten Commandments, both in their original meaning and as explained by the new light of the Spirit of Christ.

Let us ask what were the Ten Commandments in their outward form and appearance when they were last seen by mortal eyes as the ark was placed in Solomon's Temple; and why they were regarded as of such immense importance—why the two tables of stone, and nothing else, were enshrined thus in the Most Holy Place.

I. First, then, their actual form.

1. They were written on two tables or blocks of stone or rock. The mountain of Sinai, from which they were taken, is of red and white granite. On two blocks of this granite rock—the most lasting and almost the oldest kind of rock that is to be found in the world, as if to remind us that these Laws were to be the beginning and the end of all things—were the Ten Commandments, the Ten Words, written. They were written, not as we now write them, only on one side of each of the two tables, but on both sides, so as to give the idea of absolute completeness and solidity. Each block of stone was covered behind and before with the sacred letters. Again, they were not arranged exactly as we now arrange them. In the Fourth, for example, the reason for keeping holy the seventh day is, in Exodus, because God rested on the seventh day from the work of creation; in Deuteronomy it is to remind them that they were once strangers in the land of Egypt. Probably, therefore, these reasons were not actually written on the stone, but were given afterwards, at two different times, by way of explanation; so that the first four Commandments, as they were written on the tables, were rather shorter than they are now. Here, as everywhere in the Bible, there may be many reasons for doing what is right. It is the doing of the thing, and not the particular occasion or reason, which makes it right: "He that doth righteousness is righteous." Another slight difference was that the Commandments were not divided exactly as they are now. Probably they were divided into two equal portions, so that the Fifth Commandment, instead of being, as it is with us, at the top of the second table, was at the bottom of the first. The duty of honouring our parents is so like the duty of honouring God, that it was put amongst the same class of duties. Our parents on earth are to us so nearly the likeness of our Father in heaven that they are not divided.

I mention these little differences between the original arrangement and the arrangement as it is now,—first, because it is interesting to have before us as nearly as we can the exact likeness and figure of those very old Commandments, and because it is useful to remember how even these most sacred and ancient words have undergone some change in their outward form since they were first given, and yet still are equally true and equally venerable. Religion does not consist in counting the syllables of the Bible, but in doing what it tells us. Inspiration does not lie in the letter, but in the spirit of what is written.

2. When the Christian Church sprang out of the Jewish Church, it did not part with those venerable relics of the earlier time, but they were still used to teach Christian children their duty, as Jewish children had been taught before. There were different arrangements introduced in different parts of the world. St. Augustine divided them so that the First and Second stood together and made one Commandment, and the Tenth was divided into two, so that the Ninth Commandment was—"Thou shalt not covet thy neighbour's wife," and the Tenth, "Thou shalt not covet thy neighbour's house." This was the division followed by the Roman Catholic Church, and also by the Lutheran. The other was the division such as we have adopted, which was followed by the old Churches of the East and also by all the Churches commonly called the Reformed, including the Church of England. Whichever division we adopt makes little matter as to the sense. Here, again, the various arrangements give us a good lesson, as showing us how the different parts of our doctrine and duty may not be quite put together in the same way, and yet be still the same. And also it may remind us how the very same arrangements, even in outward things, may be made by persons of the most opposite way of thinking; so that we ought always to be prevented from judging any one by the mere outward sign or badge that they wear. No one could be

more unlike to the Roman Catholic Church than the Reformer Luther, and yet the same peculiar arrangement of the Ten Commandments was used by him and by them. No one could be more unlike to the old Eastern Church than John Knox or Calvin, or Cranmer, and yet their arrangement of the Ten Commandments is the same. These facts are constant warnings: "Judge not according to appearance, but judge righteous judgment."

II. What are we to learn from the place which the Ten Commandments occupied in the old dispensation?

We learn what is the true foundation of all religion. The Ten Commandments are simple rules; any child can understand them. But still they are the very heart and essence of the old Jewish religion. But they occupy a very small part of the Books of Moses. The Ten Commandments, and not the precepts about sacrifices, and passovers, and boundaries, and priests, are the words which are said to have been delivered in thunder and lightning at Mount Sinai. These, and not any ceremonial ordinances, were laid up in the Most Holy Place, to show what God most cares for. "There was nothing in the ark save the two tables of stone, which Moses put there at Horeb."

Do your duty. This is what they tell us. *Do your duty to God and your duty to man.* Whatever we may believe or feel or think, the main thing is that we are to do what is right, not to do what is wrong. Therefore it was that they occupied so sacred a place in the Holy of Holies in the Jewish Temple. Therefore it is that in the Church of England and in the Reformed Churches of the Continent they are still read in the most sacred parts of the service, as if to show us that, go as far as we can in Christian light and knowledge, make as much as we will of Christian doctrine or of Christian worship, still we must never lose hold of the ancient everlasting lines of duty.

III. But it may be said, Were not those Ten Commandments given to the Jews of old? Do they not refer to the land of Egypt and the land of Palestine? *We* love and serve God, and love and serve our brethren, not because it is written in the Commandments, but because it is written on the tables of our hearts by God's Holy Spirit in our spirits and consciences. Yes, but Christ Himself has told us what their use is to be.

In the Sermon on the Mount He took two or three of these Commandments, and explained them Himself to the people. He took the Sixth Commandment, and showed that for us it is not enough to remember, "Thou shalt not kill," but that the Commandment went much deeper, and forbade all angry thoughts and words. This is what we should apply to all the other Commandments. It is not in their letter but in their spirit that they concern us, and this, no doubt, is what is meant by the prayer which in the Church of England follows after each of them, and at the end of all of them, "Incline our *hearts* to keep this Commandment," "Write all these Commandments in our *hearts*, we beseech Thee."

1. Let us take them one by one in this way. The First Commandment is no longer ours in the letter, for it begins by saying, "I am the Lord thy God, who brought thee out of the land of Egypt." He did not bring us up out of the land of Egypt, and so completely has this ceased to apply to us, that in the Commandments as publicly read the Church of England has boldly struck out these words altogether. But the spirit of the Commandment still remains; for we all need to be reminded that there is but one Supreme Mind and Lord of all, whose praise and blame are, above all, worth having, seeking, or deserving.

2. The Second Commandment is no longer ours in the letter, for the sculptures and paintings which we see at every turn are what the Second Commandment in its letter forbade, and what the Jews, therefore, never made. Every statue, every picture, not only in every church, but in every street or room, is a breach of the letter of the Second Commandment. No Jew would have ventured under the Mosaic dispensation to have them. When Solomon made the golden lions and oxen in the Temple, it was regarded by his countrymen as unlawful. The Mahomedan world still observes the Second Commandment literally. The Christian world has certainly set it aside. But in spirit it is still most important. It teaches us that we must not make God after our likeness or after any likeness short of the most absolute moral perfection. Any fancies, any doctrines, any practices which lead us to think that God is capricious or unjust or untruthful, or that He cares for any outward thing compared with holiness, mercy, and goodness—that is the breach of the Second Commandment in spirit. Every attempt to purify and exalt our ideas of God is the keeping of the Second Commandment in spirit, even although we live amidst pictures and statues and sculptures of things in heaven and things in

earth and things under the earth. For the spirit is greater than the letter—the letter killeth and the spirit giveth life.

3. The Third Commandment. Here the original meaning of the Commandment is more elevated and more spiritual than that which is perhaps commonly given to it. Many see in it only a prohibition of profane swearing or false swearing. It means this—but it means much more. It means that we are not to appeal to God's name for any unworthy purpose. It is a protest against all those sins which have claimed the sanction of God or of religion. "O Liberty!" said one of the victims of the French Revolution, "how many are the crimes which have been committed in thy name!" "O Religion!" "O Lord God!"—so the Third Commandment says to us—"how many are the crimes that have been wrought in thy name!" Think not that the plea and pretext of God's name will avail as an excuse for cruelty or hypocrisy or untruthfulness or undutifulness. No; the Lord will not hold him guiltless who taketh His name in vain—that is, who brings it to an unjust or unrighteous cause. All the wicked persecutions carried on, all the wicked wars waged, all the pious frauds perpetrated in the name of the Holy God are breaches of the Third Commandment, both in its letter and in its spirit.

4. The Fourth Commandment. Here, as in the Second Commandment, there is a wide divergence between the letter and the spirit. In its letter it is obeyed by no Christian society whatever, except the Abyssinian Church in Africa, and the small sect of the Seventh-Day Baptists in England. They still keep a day of rest on the Saturday, the seventh day of the week. But in every other Church in the world the seventh day is observed only by the Jews, and not by the Christians. And again, only by the Jews, and not by Christians anywhere, are the Mosaic laws kept which forbade the lighting of a single fire, which forbade the walking beyond a single mile, which forbade the employment of a single animal, which visited as a capital offence the slightest employment on the seventh day. And again, the reasons given in the two versions of the Fourth Commandment are passed away. We cannot be called, as in Deuteronomy, to remember that we were strangers in the land of Egypt, for many of us were never in Egypt at all. We cannot be called, as in Exodus, to remember that the earth was made in six days, for we most of us know that it took, not six days, but millions of

XXI—25

ages, to bring the earth from its void and formless state to its present condition. The letter of the Fourth Commandment has long ceased. The very name of the Lord's Day and of the first day of the week is a protest against it. The very name of Sabbath is condemned by St. Paul. The Catechism of the Church of England speaks of the duty of serving God all the days of our life, and not of serving Him on one day alone. But has, then, the principle which lay at the bottom of the Fourth Commandment passed away? No. Just as the prohibition of statues in the Second Commandment is now best carried out by the avoidance of superstitious, unworthy, degrading ideas of the nature of God, so the principle of the observance of the Sabbath in the Fourth Commandment is aimed against worldly, hard, exacting ideas of the work of man. The principle of the Fourth Commandment enjoins the sacred duty of rest—for there is an element of rest in the Divine Nature itself. It enjoins also the sacred duty of kindness to our servants and to the inferior animals—"for remember that thou wast a servant in the land of Egypt." How this rest is to be carried out, within what limits it is to be confined, what amount of innocent recreation is to be allowed, how far the Continental notions have erred on the one side or the Scottish notions on the other side, in their mode of observance, whether the observance of the English Sunday is exactly what it ought to be, or in what respects it might be improved—these are questions which we do not here discuss. It is enough to say that amidst all the variations in the mode of observing the Sunday, it is still possible, and it is still our duty to bear in mind the principle of the ancient Law. "I was *in the Spirit* on the Lord's Day:" that is what we should all strive to attain, what we should all be thankful for—to be raised at least for one day in the week above the grinding toil of our daily work—above the debasing influence of frivolous amusements—above the jangling of business and controversy—raised into the high and holy atmosphere breathed by pure and peaceful lives, bright and beautiful thoughts, elevating and invigorating worship. Although the day has been changed from the seventh day to the first day everywhere—nay, even had it been further changed, as Calvin intended, from Sunday to Thursday—even had it yet been further changed, as Tyndale, the foremost of the English Reformers, proposed, from the seventh day to the tenth day—yet still there would survive the solemn obligation founded, not on the Law of Moses, but on the Law of God in Nature—the obligation of rest and of worship as long as human nature remains what it is, as long as the things which are temporal are seen, and the things which are eternal are unseen.

I pass on more rapidly through the other Commandments.

5. The Fifth. Here, again, the letter has ceased to have any meaning for us. "That thy days may be long in the land which the Lord thy God giveth thee." We have no claim on the inheritance of the land of Canaan. No amount of filial reverence will secure for us the possession of the goodly heights of Lebanon, or the forests of Gilead or the rushing waters of Jordan. But the ordinance of affection and honour to parents has not diminished, but grown with the years which have passed since the command was first issued. The love of son to mother, the honour of children to parents, is far stronger now than in the days of Moses.

It is often discussed in these days whether this or that principle of religion is natural or supernatural. How often is this distinction entirely without meaning ! The Fifth Commandment — that sacred to the dearest, deepest, purest, noblest aspirations of the heart—is natural because it is supernatural, is supernatural because it is natural. It is truly regarded as the symbol, as the sanction of the whole framework of civil and religious society. Our obedience to law, our love of country, is not a bond of mere expediency or accident. It is not, as some of our own day represent it, a worldly, unspiritual ordinance, to be rejected because it crosses our own religious fancies or interferes with some theological allegory. It is binding on the Christian conscience, because it is part of the natural religion of the human race and of the best instincts of Christendom.

6. The Sixth Commandment. The crime of murder is what it chiefly condemns, and no sentimental feelings of modern times have ever been able to bring the murderer down from that bad pre-eminence as the worst and most appalling of human offenders. It is the consummation of selfishness. It is the disregard of the most precious of God's earthly gifts— the gift of life. But the scope of the Commandment extends much further. In the sense in which we shall speak of it, he is a breaker of the Sixth Commandment who promotes quarrels and jealousies in families, who indulges in fierce, contemptuous words, who fans the passions of class against class,

of church against church, of nation against nation. In the horrors of war it is not the innocent soldier killing his adversary in battle, but the partisans on whatever side, the ambitious in whatever nation, the reckless journalists and declaimers of whatever opinions, who have fostered and fanned the angry passions of hatred, that are the true responsible authors of the horrors which follow in the train of armies and in the fields of carnage. In the violence of civil and intestine discord, it is not only human life that is at stake, but that which makes human life precious. "As well kill a good man as a good book," was the saying of Milton, and so we may add in thinking of those who care neither to preserve nor to improve the inheritance which God has given us, "As well kill a good man as a good institution."

7. The Seventh Commandment. Of this it is enough to say that here also we know well in our consciences that it is not only the shameless villain who invades the sanctity of another's home and happiness that falls under the condemnation of that dreadful word which the Seventh Commandment uses. It is the reader and writer of filthy books ; it is the young man or the young woman who allows his or her purity and dignity to be soiled and stained by loose talk and loose company.

8. I pass on to the Eighth, " Thou shalt not steal." That lowest, meanest crime of the thief and the robber is not all that the Eighth Commandment condemns. It is the taking of money which is not your due, and which you are forbidden to receive ; it is the squandering money which is not your own on the racecourse or at the gambling table ; it is the taking advantage of a flaw or an accident in a will which gives you property which was not intended for you, and to which others have a better claim than you. He is the true observer of the Eighth Commandment not only who keeps his hands from picking and stealing, but he who renders just restitution, he who, like the great Indian soldier, Outram, the Bayard of modern times, would not claim any advantage from a war which he had victoriously conducted, because he thought the war itself was wrong ; he who is scrupulously honest, even to the last farthing of his accounts, with master or servant, with employer or employed ; he who respects the rights of others, not only of the rich against the poor, not only of the poor against the rich, but of all classes against each other— these, and these only, are the Christian keepers of the Eighth Commandment.

9. The Ninth: "Thou shalt not bear false witness." False witness, deliberate perjury, is the crown and consummation of the liar's progress. But what a world of iniquity is covered by that one word, *Lie!* Careless, damaging statements, thrown hither and thither in conversation; reckless exaggeration and romancing, only to make our stories more pungent; hasty records of character, left to be published after we are dead; heedless disregard of the supreme duty and value of truth in all things—these are what we should bear in mind when we are told that we are not to bear false witness against our neighbour. A lady who had been in the habit of spreading slanderous reports once confessed her fault to a good and wise man of her acquaintance, and asked how she should cure it. He said, "Go to the nearest market-place, buy a chicken just killed, pluck its feathers all the way as you return, and come back to me." She was much surprised, and when she saw her adviser again, he said, "Now go back, and bring me back all the feathers you have scattered." "But that is impossible," she said; "I cast away the feathers carelessly; the wind carried them away. How can I recover them?" "That," he said, "is exactly like your words of slander. They have been carried about in every direction; you cannot recall them. Go, and slander no more."

10. The Tenth: "Thou shalt not covet." The form of the Commandment speaks only of the possessions of a rude and pastoral people—the wife of a neighbouring chief, the male and female slaves, the Syrian ox, the Egyptian ass. But the principle strikes at the very highest heights of civilisation and at the very innermost secrets of the heart. Greed, selfishness, ambition, egotism, self-importance, money-getting, rash speculation, desire of the poor to pull down the rich, desire of the rich to exact more than their due from the poor, eagerness to destroy the most useful and sacred institutions in order to gratify a social revenge, or to gain a lost place, or to make a figure in the world—these are amongst the wide-reaching evils which are included in that ancient but most expressive word "covetousness." "I had not known sin," says the Apostle Paul, "but for the law which says, *Thou shalt not covet.*" So we may all say. No one can know the exceeding sinfulness of sin who does not know the guilt of selfishness; no one can know the exceeding beauty of holiness who has not seen or felt the glory of unselfishness.

IV. These are the Ten Commandments—the summary of the morality of Judaism, the basis of the morality of Christian creeds. We have heard it said of such and such an one with open, genuine countenance, that he looked as if he had the Ten Commandments written on his face. O blissful passport through this world's crooked ways! We have heard it said by an honest, pious soul, on whom a devout but feeble enthusiast was pressing the use of this and that small practice of devotion, "My devotions are much better than those. They are the devotions of the Ten Commandments of God."

In the Reformed American Church and in the Reformed Churches of France, and intended by the last reformers of the English Liturgy, though they failed to carry the point, after the Ten Commandments are read in church comes this memorable addition, which we ought all to supply in spirit and memory, even although it is not publicly used:—"Hear also what our Lord Jesus Christ saith:" This is what is taken as the ground of the explanation of the Commandments in the Catechism. Everything in what we call the first table is an enlargement of that one simple command, "Thou shalt love the Lord thy God." Everything in the second is an enlargement of the second—"Thou shalt love thy neighbour as thyself." The two together are the whole of religion. Each of itself calls our attention to what is the first and chief duty of each of the two tables. God, the supreme goodness, and the supreme truth—God is to be served with no half service; it must be a service that goes through our whole lives. We must place Him above everything else. He is all in all to us. Truth, justice, purity are in Him made the supreme object of our devotion and affection. Man is to be served also—with a love like that which we give to ourselves. Selfishness is here made the root of all evil; unselfishness the root of all goodness. Whatever else there is in the Law or the Prophets, it must be comprehended in these two sayings and subordinated to them.

If any Church existed which in reality and in spirit put forth those two Commandments as the sum and substance of its belief, as that to which all else tended, and for the sake of which all was done, it would indeed take the first place amongst the Churches of the world, because it would be the Church that most fully had expressed the mind and intention of the Founder of Christendom.

There was, indeed, one addition which the English divines of the time of William III.

wished to make to the recital of the Ten Commandments in church, and which suggests one concluding thought. It was that, on the three great festivals, instead of the Ten Commandments of Mount Sinai should be read the Eight Beatitudes of the Mountain of Galilee, in order to remind us that beyond and above the Law of Duty, there is the happiness of that inward spirit which is at once the spring and the result of all duty — the happiness, the blessedness which belongs to the humble, the sincere, the unselfish, the eager aspirant after goodness, the generous, the pure, the courageous.

That happiness, that solid inward happiness, is the highest end and aim of all religion. Most blessed are they who can attain to it by the natural gift and grace of God. But blessed are they who can advance towards it in the lowly way of walking in the path of God's Commandments, even although in the innermost ark of their minds and hearts there be nothing besides the Ten Commandments of Moses. For in these Ten Commandments and in the Two Commandments we have the ends to which, first in the Jewish and then in the Christian religion, everything else must tend.

THE INFLUENCE OF ART IN DAILY LIFE.

By J. BEAVINGTON ATKINSON.

INTRODUCTION.

I PROPOSE in these papers to show in how many ways the arts serve for pleasure and profit, how they embellish the house and bring joy to the home, how they refine daily life and add grace and finish to individual character. The inquiry has naturally a twofold bearing : the one outward, the other inward ; the one dealing with houses and tenements, with furniture, dress, decoration, pictures, and other visible and tangible objects of beauty. This is the concrete, the actual branch of the subject. While the converse side concerns conditions of mind, desires of imagination, taste, and the sense of the beautiful. This is the abstract, the mental, and what may be called the æsthetic phase. To picture one side exclusively would be to present only one-half of the subject ; while to combine the two into a whole brings into view the arts as they exist in the world bodily, and as they affect man mentally. Cause and effect here move in a circle : the inborn love of beauty begets art, and then again art, when brought into daily life, feeds the finer faculties of the mind. Art is a pervading atmosphere which colours common things, giving, as Lord Bacon says of poesy, " some shadow of satisfaction to the mind of man in those points wherein the nature of things doth deny it, the world being in proportion inferior to the soul." The end to strive for is, to raise life to the level of art, not to sink art to the level of the common world.

A man's home is something more than a protection against the elements : in fact, his house in relation to his life may be compared in some sort to the connection between body and soul. The analogies are many ; indeed, the windows of a dwelling have been sometimes likened to the outlooking senses, the eyes being as the windows of the mind. And next in import to the health and comeliness of the fleshly tabernacles we inhabit, are the houses we make our homes—their light, air, and beauty ; the colours, forms, and ornaments that growing into daily life percolate the thoughts and flow into the current of the domestic affections. One reason why a man is seldom quite comfortable in lodgings is that the surroundings are foreign to himself : hence the endeavour to make his house in some good degree an integral part of his life.

It has been aptly said that " a house is in a certain sense an outer garment, which should bear the impress of the owner's peculiarities ; " and it may be further observed that as a single dwelling represents an individual, so does a collective style or concerted mode of construction and decoration, correspond to a race, a nation, or a period. A historic style, whether it be exemplified by a temple, church, palace, or ordinary private house, is an accumulative growth. In domestic architecture the first germ may be said to be a chamber or room, a shelter from the elements, which as barbarism passes into civilisation gradually grows ; and so in the course of time have been matured the Greek and Roman house, the Italian villa, the French château, the German schloss, the English castle and manor-house. Each type in turn was moulded on the actual life, and, having served its end, was succeeded by a new form accommodated to changed circumstances. Moreover, these historic styles and architectural structures have risen in the presence of nature—that nature which in its beauty colours the mind of man; they reflect conditions of climate, they make provision for summer's heat and winter's cold, they respond to the daily wants of great families of mankind, they embody an idea and satisfy a desire. And thus these forms and decorations become more living than inanimate stone; they are vital as organic tissues, they share a growth with nature and a grace with the human figure and flowing draperies. I deem it rather important here at starting to indicate how the manifold phases of art which in these latter days have grown complex and perplexing, had at first a simple origin in the forms of nature and in the wants of man; how they stand as tangible effects of more or less ascertainable causes, and accordingly are appreciable to reason and common-sense. This line of thought invites to further study.

Domestic architecture in England sprang out of the social state of the people. The arrangements were once feudal and servile, but at length the local arts, like the national laws, wrested as it were a Magna Charter of liberty. In mediæval times the distinctive domestic feature was the dining-hall, but after the fifteenth century expanded into importance dormitories and other chambers, including the ladies' "withdrawing-room." These structural changes were made to meet the advance in the social and moral condition of the English nation, the object being to minister to the convenience, comfort, and privacy of domestic life. Mr. Parker sums up the case clearly; he shows that the English house in the Middle Ages, as well as in subsequent times, was not the individual contrivance of any one builder, but the continuous accretion of centuries. "Side by side with the gradual development of the civilisation, wealth, and power of England, grew the domestic habitations of the country, in each age reflecting not only the manners and customs of the people, but the position and prosperity of the English as a nation; each progressive step in the gradual development of the style and plan being but an illustration to a page of history."

Whether the British Islands possess any one style that can be called expressly national is doubtful, and yet beyond question our structural and decorative arts have grown out of and respond to our national life. Our laws are said to be the perfection of reason, and our arts, though not very ideal, are little short of perfect in their adaptation to practical ends. Like our liberties, they are the heritage of our people. Of the Englishman's house, the boast has been made that though the winds of heaven may blow through it, the king cannot enter. Against our political constitution the fault has been found, that it holds so loosely together that a carriage and six can be driven between its clauses, and yet it works well. And so with the domestic economy of our art: it may be wanting in symmetry and consistency, and yet it keeps out weather and insures comfort. The Englishman's house, as the race inhabiting these islands, is compounded of divers constituent elements; like the spoken language, it is composed of many roots, and yet it has shaken into goodly shape, and reconciles in great degree variety with unity. An Englishman true to his birthright might as a motto inscribe over his door "Liberty with order, heaven's first law;" the corner stone might serve as the symbol of stability, the keystone as the bond of a union insuring repose.

Architecture is the parent art whence all the auxiliary arts spring; and the reason of this is obvious, not only because a structure must be raised before it can be decorated, but also because the conditions of man and the surroundings of nature which mould the architecture act with equivalent forces on all subsidiary creations. Hence sculpture and painting, born as twin sisters, acknowledge architecture as a parent entitled to govern and to guide. Cognate, if not identical, principles of construction, composition, and ornament prescribe the style of a building, of a statue and wall decoration; like laws regulate the fashion of a stone façade, of a wood cabinet, of a wall-painting, and a woollen carpet. I do not wish to underrate the difficulty an unprofessional person may find in mastering these principles with their practical applications. But it may be well to recognise that without some knowledge a householder's judgment must be all but worthless; that wanting the first rudiments he will fall a victim to blind caprice and unreasoning fashion. Such misadventures, which have brought upon the arts in all their aspects incalculable evils, may, I think, in great part be averted even by the most elementary tuition. Art education, fortunately, becomes day by day more widely extended; and casting aside what is false, florid, and meaningless, people are taught to revert to a simplicity akin to nature and appreciable to clear reason and common-sense. Nor is it hard to gain a sound groundwork by aid of the plain and practical books which treat of the orders of architecture and the principles of design and decoration ; and such teachings may receive pleasant illustration by visits to public museums and schools wherein national styles and chronological developments are exemplified by leading historic examples. The mind thus recipient of light will crave for clearer vision, difficulties will vanish, and soon, if I mistake not, the learner will readily accept as helps to further advancement some such propositions as Owen Jones, in his " Grammar of Ornament," lays down to the following effect :—

Architecture is the material expression of the wants, the faculties, and the sentiments of the age in which it is created. Style in architecture is the peculiar form that expression takes under the influence of climate and with the materials at command. The decorative arts arise from, and should properly be attendant upon, architecture. All the decorative arts must possess, like architecture, fitness, proportion, harmony; the result of all which is repose. As in every perfect work of architecture a true proportion will be found to reign between all the members which compose it, so throughout the decorative arts every assemblage of forms must be arranged on certain definite proportions; the whole of each particular member should be a multiple of some simple unit. Those proportions are usually the most beautiful which the eye detects with most difficulty. Thus the proportion of a double square, or 4 to 8, is less pleasing than the more subtle ratios of 3 to 5, 3 to 7, 5 to 8.

What is the style, Italian, Gothic, or otherwise, which an Englishman may best select for his dwelling ? In the majority of cases this is decided for him, and not by him. In a city, at all events, the chances are that he will have to content himself with " the common square house," which he must make the best of. But, of course, the ideal condition is that a man possessed of some modest independence shall begin at the beginning, and first construct the house which he will afterwards proceed to decorate and furnish. Thus in due course the inside grows in harmony with the outside, all is of one type and pattern, and will turn out a consistent and complete work of art. This I have known done successfully—of course under professional advice, for I need scarcely say that the man who acts as his own architect has a fool for his client. Happily it is not difficult in the present day to find a well-trained and trusty adviser. Now, as in the best epochs, the divisions are broken down between high and low, great and small ; the artist is not above

industries, while the artisan is raised by legitimate aspirations. Our modern architects, treading without servility in the foot-prints of Giotto, Orcagna, and other masters of the revival, deign to decorate, at least by proxy, the structures they design, and thus, as by a guild or brotherhood of art, the home is brought into harmony. Art, as Thomas Carlyle says of poetry, " is the attempt which man makes to render his life harmonious." Very salutary is the close fellowship that has sprung up among skilled labourers. We may possess no " Gardens of the Medici," but we have at least the Schools of South Kensington. And throughout the country in the same Government institutions are seen studying together the architect, the sculptor, the painter, and the art workman. And it is no slight gain that among the pupils may be counted the sons of capitalists and of private gentlemen. Nothing, it is well known, tended more in the immediate past to the degradation of the arts than the ignorance and false taste of the middle and the higher classes ; but now when art culture, at least in its rudiments, is possessed by all conditions in life, professional men may, with advantage, take council with patrons and connoisseurs. Such relations between employers and employed have in the best epochs led to salutary results. The dilettante is the man of ideas, of imaginings sometimes over visionary it may be, and the artist comes with skilled hand to fashion the conceptions into form and colour. And the hope would seem not unreasonable that the architect and decorator may be incited to rarer beauty and subtler utility by the well-to-do, well-read, and widely travelled Englishman who not unreasonably requires that his house in its plan and appointments shall minister to his highly wrought sensibilities. It is through such reciprocities that the domestic arts have ever blended with the habit and complexion of the times, and it is yet possible that new and improved adaptations may follow, when the artist shall find equivalent expression for the better thought of man and the higher phases of life.

Never were the facilities greater for bringing domestic surroundings into keeping with the mind's imaginings. The sage advice has indeed been given to " leave the goodly fabrics of houses meant for beauty only to the enchanted palaces of the poets who build them with small cost." To count the cost were certainly wise before any one should venture to realise Tennyson's description of " the Palace of Art "—

> " Full of great rooms and small the palace stood
> All various, each a perfect whole
> From living Nature, fit for every mood
> And change of my still soul."

But fortunately " the thing of beauty " is not costly in proportion to the joy it brings, and while the necessaries of life have grown year by year dearer, elegancies, and even luxuries, have come within the reach of moderate means. Therefore the solecism is less than ever inevitable, that a poet should write in a garret, an artist paint in a barn, or a man stricken with the love of beauty live in an ugly tenement. Sometimes, nevertheless, strange incongruities subsist, as when a certain literary man, hypercritical to a fault, was known to tolerate within his own house whatever might seem expressly to refute the principles he propounded. It may be observed that there are typical characters which appear to fit typical houses ; on the other hand, incongruities arise between tenants and tenements, as signified by the supposititious blunder of putting a square man into a round hole. It may be readily conjectured that there exist certain angular, crotchety, serrated individuals to whom gable ends, barge-boards, and cork-screw chimneys prove most congenial ; while there are others of symmetric proportion, balanced thought, and finished manner, who might feel most at home within a geometric and ideal villa as designed by Palladio and Sansovino. What greatly to be desired is, that art shall express character of some sort, for in these days, especially in city-life, the bane has been that houses, like their inhabitants, are characterless. Artists, however, of late years, both at home and abroad, have set a good example ; they have raised habitations which, breaking aloof from dull routine, are picturesque as their own manners are unconventional. It may be invidious to single out examples, and yet, among many others, recur to mind the houses of Mr. Birket Foster, Mr. William Burgess, and Mr. G. H. Boughton. Studios are naturally built and adorned in response to the arts they shelter. I have known many in England and on the Continent, some in London and its suburbs, others in Munich and in Düsseldorf, quiet retreats secluded from the busy world in gardens among shadowy trees, or shut off from noisy city life by tapestries, and otherwise far removed from senseless fashion by old treasures—painted glass, cabinets, carvings, costumes, and embroideries, which transport the fancy to periods historic and picturesque. A studio fitly reflects the style of an artist's compositions ; a library, in like manner, echoes an author's thoughts, and each will generally be found to yield material for a picture. Indeed scarcely any better test can be made of the felicity, or otherwise, of any structure or decoration than by asking the simple question, Will it compose well ; will it add beauty to the landscape ; will the whole arrangement make a pleasing picture ? Many such paintings live within the memory. Take as examples Lord Lytton and Charles Dickens, each seated among books in his library ; or, again, the studios of great artists surrounded by the works their genius has called into being. Each man, though but a small unit in a large world, impresses his mind indelibly on his home, and something more than idle curiosity leads a traveller to search out the haunts and habitations of Coleridge, Wordsworth, and Shakespeare— of Goethe and Schiller. Matter impressed by mind becomes art.

The reverence for antiquity, the love for what is old, has made our century a period of revivals. And there is a reason under the law of reaction why men suffering from the pressure, the turmoil, and perpetual motion of modern civilisation, should seek refuge in the tranquil and poetic past. Young men rush to the city, while older men have retired to the country, only too happy if amid the beauties of nature could be found repose in—

> " an English home—where twilight pour'd
> On dewy pastures, dewy trees,
> Softer than sleep—all things in order storod—
> A haunt of ancient peace."

The country seats of old England gave place to palladian villas, not of native growth, but exotics transplanted from abroad. Then ended for a time, at any rate, the national type, and houses were raised for pride and ostentation. The successive architectural styles, often named from the reigning sovereign, which took root in British soil were, it must be confessed, far from legitimate in descent ; the Elizabethan was followed by the Jacobean, and in due course came Queen Anne and the Georges. Nothing can be more melancholy than the degradation and corruption into which the arts had fallen, when at last the notion happily seems to have occurred that it might be well to revive the old styles in their purity. Hence the resuscitation of the Gothic, not only for ecclesiastical, but for secular uses ; a revival which, notwithstanding some extravagancies and follies, brings to our English homes manifold forms of fantasy and beauty. Since have followed other phases, and one of the latest and most favoured of ideas is that the Queen

Anne style, though somewhat mongrel, bids best for the art of the future. These several revivals have the advantage of being sustained by research. Archæology, a study which has done good service in correcting "modernism," is a rich mine wherein our artists have dug sufficiently deeply to bring again to the light of day forms which, though decked as the newest, are virtually the oldest. And so critical has been the study of historic masterpieces, that the care-taking revivals of Classic, Gothic, or Renaissance types reproduce the style, purged from late corruptions, in the chastity of the best period. Thus there is good ground to hope that shams have had their day; indeed there cannot be a doubt but that the domestic arts have gained greatly in purity, simplicity, and truth. In fine, the time has come when art permeates all conditions of society, ministering to the luxuries of the rich as well as to the necessities of the poor. The aim should be in all our works to approach the completeness and fitness which mark the more perfect ways of creation, making our homes, the furniture of our houses, the clothes of our bodies, part of that large economy in which uses intermingle with beauties.

MY LITTLE BOY THAT DIED.

BY THE AUTHOR OF "JOHN HALIFAX, GENTLEMAN."

LOOK at his pretty face for just one minute!
  His braided frock and dainty buttoned shoes—
His firm-shut hand, the favourite plaything in it–
  Then tell me, mothers, was't not hard to lose
    And miss him from my side—
    My little boy that died?

How many another boy, as dear and charming,
  His father's hope, his mother's one delight,
Slips through strange sicknesses, all fear disarming,
  And lives a long, long life in parents' sight.
    Mine was so short a pride!—
    And then—my poor boy died.

I see him rocking on his wooden charger;
  I hear him pattering through the house all day;
I watch his great blue eyes grow large and larger,
  Listening to stories, whether grave or gay,
    Told at the bright fire-side—
    So dark now, since he died.

But yet I often think my boy is living,
  As living as my other children are.
When good-night kisses I all round am giving,
  I keep one for him, though he is so far.
    Can a mere grave divide
    Me from him—though he died?

So, while I come and plant it o'er with daisies —
  (Nothing but childish daisies all year round)--
Continually God's hand the curtain raises
  And I can hear his merry voice's sound,
    And feel him at my side—
    My little boy that died.

" Sho was standing before the looking-glass, apparently lost in thought."

Page 361.

THE TRUMPET-MAJOR.

By THOMAS HARDY, Author of "Far from the Madding Crowd," etc.

CHAPTER XVIII.—THE NIGHT AFTER THE ARRIVAL.

JOHN continued his sad and heavy pace till walking seemed too old and worn-out a way of showing sorrow so new, and he leant himself against the fork of an apple-tree like a log. There the trumpet-major remained for a considerable time, his face turned towards the house, whose ancient, many-chimneyed outline rose against the darkening sky, and just shut out from his view the camp above. But faint noises coming thence from horses restless at the pickets, and from visitors taking their leave, recalled its existence, and reminded him that, in consequence of Matilda's arrival, he had obtained leave for the night, a fact which, owing to the startling emotions that followed his entry, he had not yet mentioned to his friends.

While abstractedly considering how he could best use that privilege under the new circumstances which had arisen, he heard Farmer Derriman drive up to the front door and hold a conversation with his father. The old man had at last apparently brought the tin box of private papers that he wished the miller to take charge of during Derriman's absence; and it being a calm night, John could hear, though he little heeded, Uncle Benjy's reiterated supplications to Loveday to keep it safe from fire and thieves. Then Uncle Benjy left, and John's father went up-stairs to deposit the box in a place of security, the whole proceeding reaching John's preoccupied comprehension merely as voices during sleep.

The next thing was the appearance of a light in the bedroom which had been assigned to Matilda Johnson. This effectually aroused the trumpet-major, and with a stealthiness unusual in him he went indoors. No light was in the lower rooms, his father, Mrs. Garland, and Anne having gone out on the bridge to look at the new moon. John went up-stairs on tip-toe, and along the uneven passage till he came to her door. It was standing ajar, a band of candlelight shining across the passage and up the opposite wall. As soon as he entered the radiance he saw her. She was standing before the looking-glass, apparently lost in thought, her fingers being clasped behind her head in abstraction, and the light falling full upon her face.

XXI—26

"I must speak to you," said the trumpet-major.

She started, turned, and grew paler than before; and then, as if moved by a sudden impulse, she swung the door wide open, and, coming out, said quite collectedly and with apparent pleasantness, "Oh, yes; you are my Bob's brother! I didn't, for a moment, recognise you."

"But you do now?"

"As Bob's brother."

"You have never seen me before?"

"Never," she answered, with a face as impassible as Talleyrand's.

"You mistake; I'll remind you," he said. And he did remind her at some length.

"Never!" she again said desperately.

But she had mistaken her man. Five minutes after that she was in tears, and the conversation had resolved itself into words which, on the soldier's part, were of the nature of commands, tempered by intense pity, and were a mere series of entreaties on hers.

The whole scene did not last ten minutes. When it was over, the trumpet-major walked from the doorway where they had been standing, and brushed moisture from his eyes. Reaching a dark lumber-room, he stood still there to calm himself, and then descended by a Flemish ladder to the bakehouse, instead of by the front stairs. He found that the others, including Bob, had gathered in the parlour during his absence and lighted the candles.

Miss Johnson, having sent down some time before John re-entered the house to say that she would prefer to keep her room that evening, was not expected to join them, and on this account Bob showed less than his customary liveliness.

As for the trumpet-major, his mind was in such a state that he derived no pleasure even from Anne Garland's presence, though he held a corner of the same book with her, and was treated in a winsome way which it was not her usual practice to indulge in. She saw that his mind was clouded, and, far from guessing the reason why, was doing her best to clear it.

At length the Garlands found that it was the hour for them to leave, and John Loveday at the same time wished his father and Bob good night, and went as far as Mrs. Garland's door with her.

He had said not a word to show that he

was free to remain out of camp, for the reason that there was painful work to be done, which it would be best to do in secret and alone. He lingered near the house till its reflected window-lights ceased to glimmer upon the mill-pond, and all within the dwelling was dark and still. Then he entered the garden and waited there till the back door opened, and a woman's figure timorously came forward. John Loveday at once went up to her, and they began to talk in low yet dissentient tones.

They had conversed about ten minutes, and were parting as if they had come to some painful arrangement, Miss Johnson sobbing bitterly and turning to re-enter the house, when a head stealthily arose above the dense hedgerow, and in a moment a shout burst from its owner.

"Thieves! thieves!—my tin box!—thieves! thieves!"

Matilda vanished into the house, and John Loveday hastened to the hedge. "For heaven's sake, hold your tongue, Mr. Derriman!" he exclaimed.

"My tin box!" said Uncle Benjy. "Oh, only the trumpet-major!"

"Your box is safe enough, I assure you. It was only "—here the trumpet-major gave vent to an artificial laugh—" only a sly bit of courting, you know."

"Haha, I see!" said the relieved old squireen. "Courting Miss Anne? Then you've ousted my nephew, trumpet-major! Well, so much the better. As for myself, the truth on't is that I haven't been able to go to bed easy, for thinking that possibly your father might not take care of what I put under his charge; and at last I thought I would just step over and see if all was safe here before I turned in. And when I saw your two shapes my poor nerves magnified ye to housebreakers and Boneys and I don't know what all."

"You have alarmed the house," said the trumpet-major, hearing the clicking of flint and steel in his father's bedroom, followed in a moment by the rise of a light in the window of the same apartment. "You have got me into difficulty," he added gloomily, as his father opened the casement.

"I am sorry for that," said Uncle Benjy. "But step back; I'll put it all right again."

"What, for heaven's sake, is the matter?" said the miller, his tasseled nightcap appearing in the opening.

"Nothing, nothing!" said the farmer. "I was uneasy about my few bonds and documents, and I walked this way, miller, before

going to bed, as I start from home to-morrow morning. When I came down by your garden-hedge, I thought I saw thieves, but it turned out to be—to be——"

Here a lump of earth from the trumpet-major's hand struck Uncle Benjy in the back as a reminder.

"To be—the bough of a cherry-tree a-waving in the wind. Good-night!"

"No thieves are like to try my house," said Miller Loveday. "Now don't you come alarming us like this again, farmer, or you shall keep your box yourself, begging your pardon for saying so. Good night t' ye!"

"Miller, will ye just look, since I am here—just look and see if the box is all right? there's a good man. I am old, you know, and my poor remains are not what my original self was. Look and see if it is where you put it, there's a good man."

"Very well," said the miller good-humouredly.

"Neighbour Loveday! on second thoughts I think I will take my box home again, after all, if you don't mind. You won't think it ill of me? I have no suspicions, of course; but now I think on't there's rivalry between my nephew and your son; and if Festus should take it into his head to set your house on fire in his enmity, 'twould be bad for my deeds and documents. No offence, miller; but I'll take the box, if you don't mind."

"Faith! I don't mind," said Loveday. "But your nephew had better think twice before he lets his enmity take that colour." Receding from the window, he took the candle to a back part of the room and soon reappeared with the tin box.

"I won't trouble ye to dress," said Derriman considerately: "let en down by anything you have at hand."

The box was lowered by a cord, and the old man clasped it in his arms. "Thank ye!" he said with heartfelt gratitude. "Good night!"

The miller replied and closed the window, and the light went out.

"There, now I hope you are satisfied, sir?" said the trumpet-major.

"Quite, quite!" said Derriman; and, leaning on his walking-stick, he pursued his lonely way.

That night Anne lay awake in her bed, musing on the traits of the new friend who had come to her neighbour's house. She would not be critical, it was ungenerous and wrong; but she could not help thinking of what interested her. And were there, she silently asked, in Miss Johnson's mind and person such rare qualities as placed that lady altogether beyond comparison with herself? Oh yes, there must be; for had not Captain Bob singled out Matilda from among all other women, herself included? Of course, with his world-wide experience, he knew best.

When the moon had set, and only the summer stars threw their light into the great damp garden, she fancied that she heard voices in that direction. Perhaps they were the voices of Bob and Matilda taking a lover's walk before retiring. If so, how sleepy they would be next day, and how absurd it was of Matilda to pretend she was tired! Ruminating in this way, and saying to herself that she hoped they would be happy, Anne fell asleep.

CHAPTER XIX.—MISS JOHNSON'S BEHAVIOUR CAUSES NO LITTLE SURPRISE.

PARTLY from the excitement of having his Matilda under the paternal roof, Bob rose next morning as early as his father and the grinder, and when the big wheel began to patter and the little ones to mumble in response, went to sun himself outside the mill-front, among the fowls of brown and speckled kinds which haunted that spot, and the ducks that came up from the mill-tail.

Standing on the worn-out mill-stone inlaid in the gravel, he talked with his father on various improvements of the premises, and on the proposed arrangements for his permanent residence there, with an enjoyment that was half based upon this prospect of the future, and half on the penetrating warmth of the sun to his back and shoulders. Then the different troops of horses began their morning scramble down to the mill-pond, and, after making it very muddy round the edge, ascended the slope again. The bustle of the camp grew more and more audible, and presently David came to say that breakfast was ready.

"Is Miss Johnson down-stairs?" said the miller; and Bob listened for the answer, looking at a blue sentinel aloft on the down.

"Not yet, maister," said the excellent David.

"We'll wait till she's down," said Loveday. "When she is, let us know."

David went indoors again, and Loveday and Bob continued their morning surv$_{ey}$ by ascending into the mysterious quivering recesses of the mill, and holding a discussion over a second pair of burr-stones, which had to be re-dressed before they could be used again. This and similar things occupied nearly twenty minutes, and looking from the window, the elder of the two was reminded of the time of day by seeing Mrs. Garland's tablecloth fluttering from her back door over the heads of a flock of pigeons that had alighted for the crumbs.

"I suppose David can't find us," he said, with a sense of hunger that was not altogether strange to Bob. He put out his head and shouted.

"The lady is not down yet," said his man in reply.

"No hurry, no hurry," said the miller with cheerful emptiness. "Bob, to pass the time we'll look into the garden."

"She'll get up sooner than this, you know, when she's signed articles and got a berth here," Bob observed apologetically.

"Yes, yes," said Loveday; and they descended into the garden.

Here they turned over sundry flat stones and killed the slugs sheltered beneath them from the coming heat of the day, talking of slugs in all their branches—of the brown and the black, of the tough and the tender, of the reason why there were so many in the garden that year, of the coming time when the grass walks harbouring them were to be taken up and gravel laid, and of the relative exterminatory merits of a pair of scissors and the heel of the shoe. At last the miller said, "Well, really, Bob, I'm hungry; we must begin without her."

They were about to go in, when David appeared with haste in his motions, his eyes wider vertically than crosswise, and his cheeks nearly all gone.

"Maister, I've been to call her; and as 'a didn't speak I rapped, and as 'a didn't answer I kicked, and not being latched the door opened, and—she's gone!"

Bob went off like a swallow towards the house, and the miller followed like the rather heavy man that he was. That Miss Matilda was not in her room, or a scrap of anything belonging to her, was soon apparent. They searched every place in which she could possibly hide or squeeze herself, every place in which she could not, but found nothing at all.

Captain Bob was quite wild with astonishment and grief. When he was quite sure that she was nowhere in his father's house, he ran into Mrs. Garland's, and telling them the story so hastily that they hardly understood the particulars, he went on towards Comfort's house, intending to raise the alarm there, and also at Mitchell's, Beach's, Cripplestraw's, the parson's, the clerk's, the camp of dragoons, of hussars, and so on through the whole county.

But he paused, and thought it would be hardly expedient to publish his discomfiture in such a way. If Matilda had left the house for any freakish reason he would not care to look for her, and if her deed had a tragic intent she would keep aloof from camp and village.

In his trouble he thought of Anne. She was a nice girl, and could be trusted. To her he went, and found her in a state of excitement and anxiety which equalled his own.

"'Tis so lonely to cruise for her all by myself!" said Bob disconsolately, his forehead all in wrinkles; "and I've thought you would come with me and cheer the way?"

"Where shall we search?" said Anne.

"Oh, in the holes of rivers, you know, and down wells, and in quarries, and over cliffs, and like that. Your eyes might catch the loom of any bit of a shawl or bonnet that I should overlook, and it would do me a real service. Please do come!"

So Anne took pity upon him, and put on her hat and went, the miller and David having gone off in another direction. They examined the ditches of fields, Bob going round by one fence and Anne by the other, till they met at the opposite side. Then they peeped under culverts, into outhouses, and down old wells and quarries, till the theory of a tragical end had nearly spent its force in Bob's mind, and he began to think that Matilda had simply run away. However, they still walked on, though by this time the sun was hot and Anne would gladly have sat down.

"Now didn't you think highly of her, Miss Garland?" he inquired, as the search began to languish.

"Oh yes," said Anne; "very highly."

"She was really beautiful; no nonsense about her looks, was there?"

"None. Her beauty was thoroughly ripe —not too young. We should all have got to love her. What can have possessed her to go away?"

"I don't know, and, upon my life, I shall soon be drove to say I don't care!" replied the mate despairingly. "Let me pilot ye down over those stones," he added, as Anne began to descend a rugged quarry. He stepped forward, leapt down, and turned to her.

She gave him her hand and sprang down. Before he relinquished his hold, Captain Bob raised her fingers to his lips and kissed them.

"Oh, Captain Loveday!" cried Anne, snatching away her hand in genuine dismay, while a tear rose unexpectedly to each eye.

"I never heard of such a thing! I won't go an inch farther with you, sir; it is too barefaced!" And she turned and ran off.

"Upon my life I didn't mean it!" said the repentant captain, hastening after. "I do love her best—indeed I do—and I don't love you at all. I am not so fickle as that! I merely just for the moment admired you as a sweet little craft, and that's how I came to do it. You know, Miss Garland," he continued earnestly, and still running after, "'tis like this: when you come ashore after having been shut up in a ship for eighteen months, women-folks seem so new and nice that you can't help liking them, one and all, in a body; and so your heart is apt to get scattered and yaws a bit; but of course I think of poor Matilda most, and shall always stick to her." He heaved a sigh of tremendous magnitude, to show beyond the possibility of doubt that his heart was still in the place that honour required.

"I am glad to hear that—of course I am very glad!" said she, with quick petulance, keeping her face turned from him. "And I hope we shall find her, and that the wedding will not be put off, and that you'll both be happy. But I won't look for her any more. No; I don't care to look for her—and my head aches. I am going home!"

"And so am I," said Robert promptly.

"No, no! Go on looking for her, of course—all the afternoon, and all night. I am sure you will, if you love her."

"Oh, yes; I mean to. Still, I ought to convoy you home first."

"No, you ought not; and I shall not accept your company. Good morning, sir!" And she went off over one of the stone stiles with which the spot abounded, leaving the friendly sailor standing in the field.

He sighed again, and observing the camp not far off, thought he would go to his brother John and ask him his opinion on the sorrowful case. On reaching the tents he found that John was not at liberty just at that time, being engaged in practising the trumpeters, and leaving word that he wished the trumpet-major to come down to the mill as soon as possible, Bob went back again.

"'Tis no good looking for her," he said gloomily. "She liked *me* well enough, but when she came here and saw the house, and the place, and the old horse, and the plain furniture, she was disappointed to find us all so homely, and felt she didn't care to marry into such a family."

His father and David had returned with no news. "Yes, 'tis as I've been thinking, father," Bob said. "We weren't good enough for her, and she went away in scorn!"

"Well, that can't be helped," said the miller. "What we be, we be, and have been for generations. To my mind she seemed glad enough to get hold of us."

"Yes, yes—for the moment—because of the flowers, and birds, and what's pretty in the place," said Bob tragically. "But you don't know, father—how should you know, who have hardly been out of Overcombe in your life?—you don't know what delicate feelings are in a real refined woman's mind. Any little vulgar action unreaves their nerves like a marline spike. Now I wonder if you did anything to disgust her?"

"Faith! not that I know of," said Loveday, reflecting. "I didn't say a single thing that I should naturally have said, on purpose to give no offence."

"You was always very homely, you know, father."

"Yes; so I was," said the miller meekly.

"I wonder what it could have been," Bob continued, wandering about restlessly. "You didn't go drinking out of the big mug with your mouth full, or wipe your lips with your sleeve?"

"That I'll swear I didn't," said the miller firmly. "Thinks I, there's no knowing what I may do to shock her, so I'll take my solid victuals in the bakehouse, and only a crumb and a drop in her company for manners."

"You could do no more than that, certainly," said Bob gently.

"If my manners be good enough for well-brought-up people like the Garlands, they be good enough for her," continued the miller, with a sense of injustice.

"That's true. Then it must have been David. David, come here! How did you behave before that lady? Now, mind you speak the truth!"

"Yes, Mr. Captain Robert," said David earnestly. "I assure ye she was served like a royal queen. The best silver spoons were put down, and yer poor grandfer's silver tanket, as you seed, and the feather cushion for her to sit on——"

"Now I've got it!" said Bob decisively, bringing down his hand upon the window-sill. "Her bed was hard!—and there's nothing shocks a true lady like that. The bed in that room always was as hard as the Rock of Gibraltar!"

"No, Captain Bob! The beds were changed—wasn't they, maister? We put the goose bed in her room, and the flock one, that used to be there, in yours."

"Yes, we did," corroborated the miller. "David and I changed 'em with our own hands, because they were too heavy for the women to move."

"Sure I didn't know I had the flock bed," murmured Bob. "I slept on, little thinking what I was going to wake to. Well, well, she's gone; and search as I will I shall never find another like her! She was too good for me. She must have carried her box with her own hands, poor girl. As far as that goes, I could overtake her even now, I dare say; but I won't entreat her against her will—not I."

Miller Loveday and David, feeling themselves to be rather a desecration in the presence of Bob's tender emotions, managed to edge off by degrees, the former burying himself in the most floury recesses of the mill, his invariable resource when perturbed, the rumbling having a soothing effect upon the nerves of those properly trained to its music.

Bob was so impatient that, after going up to her room to assure himself once more that she had not undressed, but had only lain down on the outside of the bed, he went out of the house to meet John, and waited on the sunny slope of the down till his brother appeared. John looked so brave and shapely and warlike that, even in Bob's present distress, he could not but feel an honest and affectionate pride at owning such a relative. Yet he fancied that John did not come along with the same swinging step as he had shown yesterday; and when the trumpet-major got nearer he looked anxiously at the mate and waited for him to speak first.

"You know our great trouble, John?" said Robert, looking stoically into his brother's eyes.

"Come and sit down, and tell me all about it," answered the trumpet-major, showing no surprise.

They went towards a slight ravine, where it was easier to sit down than on the flat ground, and here John reclined among the grasshoppers, pointing to his brother to do the same.

"But do you know what it is?" said Robert. "Has anybody told ye?"

"I do know," said John. "She's gone; and I am thankful!"

"What!" said Bob, rising to his knees in amazement.

"I'm at the bottom of it," said the trumpet-major slowly.

"You, John?"

"Yes; and if you will listen I'll tell you all. Do you remember what happened when I came into the room last night? Why, she turned colour and nearly fainted away. That was because she knew me."

Bob stared at his brother with a face of pain and distrust.

"For once, Bob, I must say something that will hurt thee a good deal," continued John. "She was not a woman who could possibly be your wife—and so she's gone."

"You sent her off?"

"Well, I did."

"John!—Tell me right through—tell me!"

"Perhaps I had better," said the trumpet-major, his blue eyes resting on the far-distant sea, that seemed to rise like a wall as high as the hill they sat upon.

And then he told a tale of Miss Johnson which wrung his heart as much in the telling as it did Bob's to hear, and which showed that John had been temporarily cruel to be ultimately kind. Even Bob, excited as he was, could discern from John's manner of speaking what a terrible undertaking that night's business had been for him. To justify the course he had adopted the dictates of duty must have been imperative; but the trumpet-major, with a becoming reticence which his brother at the time was naturally unable to appreciate, scarcely dwelt distinctly enough upon the compelling cause of his conduct. It would, indeed, have been hard for any man, much less so modest a one as John, to do himself justice in that remarkable relation, when the listener was the lady's lover; and it is no wonder that Robert rose to his feet and put a greater distance between himself and John.

"And what time was it?" he asked in a hard, suppressed voice.

"It was just before one o'clock."

"How could you help her to go away?"

"I had a pass. I carried her box to the coach-office. She was to follow at dawn."

"But she had no money."

"Yes, she had; I took particular care of that." John did not add, as he might have done, that he had given her, in his pity, all the money he possessed, and at present had only eighteenpence in the world. "Well, it is over, Bob; so sit ye down, and talk with me of old times," he added.

"Ah, Jack, it is well enough for you to speak like that," said the disquieted sailor; "but I can't help feeling that it is a cruel thing you have done. After all, she would have been snug enough for me. Would I had never found out this about her! John, why did you interfere? You had no right to overhaul my affairs like this. Why didn't you tell me fairly all you knew, and let me do as I chose? You have turned her out of

the house, and it's a shame! If she had only come to me! Why didn't she?"

"Because she knew it was best to do otherwise."

"Well, I shall go after her," said Bob firmly.

"You can do as you like," said John; "but I would advise you strongly to leave matters where they are."

"I won't leave matters where they are," said Bob impetuously. "You have made me miserable, and all for nothing. I tell you she was good enough for me; and as long as I knew nothing about what you say of her history, what difference would it have made to me? Never was there a young woman who was better company; and she loved a merry song as I do myself. Yes, I'll follow her."

"Oh, Bob," said John; "I hardly expected this!"

"That's because you didn't know your man. Can I ask you to do me one kindness? I don't suppose I can. Can I ask you not to say a word against her to any of them at home?"

"Certainly. The very reason why I got her to go off silently, as she has done, was because nothing should be said against her here, and no scandal should be heard of."

"That may be; but I'm off after her. Marry that girl I will!"

"You'll be sorry."

"That we shall see," replied Robert with determination; and he went away rapidly towards the mill. The trumpet-major had no heart to follow—no good could possibly come of further opposition; and there on the down he remained like a graven image till Bob had vanished from his sight into the mill.

Bob entered his father's only to leave word that he was going on a renewed search for Matilda, and to pack up a few necessaries for his journey. Ten minutes later he came out again with a bundle in his hand, and John saw him go diagonally across the lower fields towards the high road.

"And this is all the good I have done!" said John, musingly readjusting his stock where it cut his neck, and descending towards the mill.

CHAPTER XX.—HOW THEY LESSENED THE EFFECT OF THE CALAMITY.

MEANWHILE Anne Garland had gone home, and, being weary with her scramble in search of Matilda, sat silent in a corner of the room. Her mother was passing the time in giving utterance to every conceivable surmise on the cause of Miss Johnson's disappearance that the human mind could frame, to which Anne returned monosyllabic answers, the result, not of indifference, but of intense preoccupation. Presently Loveday came to the door; her mother vanished with him, and they remained closeted together a long time. Anne went into the garden and seated herself beneath the branching tree whose boughs had sheltered her during so many hours of her residence here. Her attention was fixed more upon the miller's wing of the irregular building before her than upon that occupied by her mother, for she could not help expecting every moment to see some one run out with a wild face and announce some awful clearing up of the mystery.

Every sound set her on the alert, and hearing the tread of a horse in the lane she looked round eagerly. Gazing at her over the hedge was Festus Derriman, mounted on such an incredibly tall animal that he could see her to her very feet over the thick and broad thorn fence. She no sooner recognised him than she withdrew her glance; but as his eyes were fixed steadily upon her this was a futile manœuvre.

"I saw you look round!" he exclaimed crossly. "What have I done to make you behave like that? Come, Miss Garland, be fair. 'Tis no use to turn your back upon me." As she did not turn he went on— "Well, now, this is enough to provoke a saint. Now I tell you what, Miss Garland; here I'll stay till you do turn round, if 'tis all the afternoon. You know my temper —what I say I mean." He seated himself firmly in the saddle, plucked some leaves from the hedge, and began humming a song, to show how absolutely indifferent he was to the flight of time.

"What have you come for, that you are so anxious to see me?" inquired Anne, when at last he had wearied her patience, rising and facing him with the added independence which came from a sense of the hedge between them.

"There, I knew you would turn round!" he said, his hot angry face invaded by a smile in which his teeth showed like white hemmed in by red at chess.

"What do you want, Mr. Derriman?" said she.

"'What do you want, Mr. Derriman?'— now listen to that! Is that my encouragement?"

Anne bowed superciliously, and moved away.

"I have just heard news that explains all that," said Festus, eyeing her movements with somnolent irascibility. "My uncle has been letting things out. He was here late last night, and he saw you."

"Indeed he didn't," said Anne.

"Oh, now! He saw you and Trumpet-major Loveday courting in that garden walk; and when he came you ran indoors."

"It is not true, and I wish to hear no more."

"Upon my life, he said so! How can you do it, Miss Garland, when I, who have enough money to buy up all the Lovedays, would gladly come to terms with ye? What a simpleton you must be, to pass me over for him! There, now you are angry because I said simpleton!—I didn't mean simpleton, I meant misguided — misguided rosebud. That's it—run off," he continued in a raised voice, as Anne made towards the garden door. "But I'll have you yet. Much reason you have to be too proud to stay with me! But it won't last long; I shall marry you, madam, if I choose, as you'll see."

When he was quite gone, and Anne had calmed down from the not altogether unrelished fear and excitement that he always caused her, she returned to her seat under the tree, and began to wonder what Festus Derriman's story meant, which, from the earnestness of his tone, did not seem like a pure invention. It suddenly flashed upon her mind that she herself had heard voices in the garden, and that the persons seen by Farmer Derriman, of whose visit and reclamation of his box the miller had told her, might have been Matilda and John Loveday. She further recalled the strange agitation of Miss Johnson on the preceding evening, and that it occurred just at the entry of the dragoon, till by degrees suspicion amounted to conviction that he knew more than any one else supposed of that lady's disappearance.

It was just at this time that the trumpet-major descended to the mill after his talk with his brother on the down. As fate would have it, instead of entering the house he turned aside to the garden, and walked down that pleasant enclosure, to learn if he were likely to find in the other half of it the woman he loved so well.

Yes, there she was, sitting on the seat of logs that he had repaired for her, under the apple-tree; but she was not facing in his direction. He walked with a noisier tread, he coughed, he shook a bough, he did everything, in short, but the one thing that Festus did in the same circumstances—call out to her. He would not have ventured on that for the world. Any of his signs would have been sufficient to attract her a day or two earlier; now she would not turn. At last, in his fond anxiety, he did what he had never done before without an invitation, and crossed over into Mrs. Garland's half of the garden, till he stood before her.

When she could not escape him she arose, and saying, "Good afternoon, trumpet-major," in a glacial manner unusual with her, walked away to another part of the garden.

Loveday, quite at a loss, had not the strength of mind to persevere further. He had a vague apprehension that some imperfect knowledge of the previous night's unhappy business had reached her; and, unable to remedy the evil without telling more than he dared, he went into the mill, where his father still was, looking doleful enough, what with his concern at events and the extra quantity of flour upon his face through sticking so closely to business that day.

"Well, John; Bob has told you all, of course? A queer, strange, perplexing thing, isn't it? I can't make it out at all. There must be something wrong in the woman, or it couldn't have happened. I haven't been so upset for years."

"Nor have I. I wouldn't it should have happened for all I own in the world," said the dragoon. "Have you spoke to Anne Garland to-day—or has anybody been talking to her?"

"Festus Derriman rode by half an hour ago, and talked to her over the hedge."

John guessed the rest, and, after standing

John Collier

on the threshold in silence awhile, walked away towards the camp.

All this time his brother Robert had been hastening along in pursuit of the woman who had withdrawn from the scene to avoid the exposure and complete overthrow which would have resulted had she remained. As the distance lengthened between himself and the mill, Bob was conscious of some cooling down of the excitement that had prompted him to set out; but he did not pause in his walk till he had reached the head of the river which fed the mill-stream. Here, for some indefinite reason, he allowed his eyes to be attracted by the bubbling spring whose waters never failed or lessened, and he stopped as if to look longer at the scene; it was really because his mind was so absorbed by John's story.

The sun was warm, the spot was a pleasant one, and he deposited his bundle and sat down. By degrees, as he reflected, first on John's view and then on his own, his convictions became unsettled; till at length he was so balanced between the impulse to go on and the impulse to go back, that a puff of wind either way would have been well-nigh sufficient to decide for him. When he allowed John's story to repeat itself in his ears, the reasonableness and good sense of his advice seemed beyond question. When, on the other hand, he thought of his poor Matilda's eyes, and her, to him, pleasant ways, their charming arrangements to marry, and her probable willingness still, he could hardly bring himself to do otherwise than follow on the road at the top of his speed.

This strife of thought was so well maintained that, sitting and standing, he remained on the borders of the spring till the shadows had stretched out eastward, and the chance of overtaking Matilda had grown considerably less. Still he did not positively go towards home. At last he took a guinea from his pocket, and resolved to put the question to the hazard. "Heads I go; tails I don't." The piece of gold spun in the air and came down heads.

"No, I won't go, after all," he said. "I won't be steered by accidents any more."

He picked up his bundle and switch, and retraced his steps towards Overcombe Mill, knocking down the brambles and nettles as he went with gloomy and indifferent blows. When he got within sight of the house he beheld David in the road.

"I've been out looking for ye, captain," said that retainer. "Have you been able to hear anything of her?"

"Nothing."

"Well, it is of no consequence at all, and no harm will be done. Maister and Mrs. Garland have made up a match, and mean to marry at once, that the wedding victuals may not be wasted. They felt 'twould be a thousand pities to let such good things get blue-vinnied for want of a ceremony to use 'em upon, and at last they have thought of this."

"Victuals—I don't care for the victuals!" said Bob, in a tone of far higher thought. He went on to the house, an interest in the announcement growing up in his mind in spite of his assertion of indifference.

His father appeared in the opening of the mill-door, looking more cheerful than when they had parted. "What, Robert, you've been after her?" he said. "Faith, then, I wouldn't have followed her if I had been as sure as you were that she went away in scorn of us. Since you told me that, I have not looked for her at all."

"I was wrong, father," Bob replied, throwing down his bundle and stick gravely. "Matilda, I find, has not gone away in scorn of us; she has gone away for other reasons. I followed her some way; but I have come back again. She may go."

"Why is she gone?" said the astonished miller.

Bob had intended, for Matilda's sake, to give no reason to a living soul for her departure. But he could not treat his father thus reservedly; and he told.

"She has made great fools of us," said the miller deliberately; "and she might have

made us greater ones. Bob, I thought th' hadst more sense."

"Well, don't say anything against her, father," implored Bob. "'Twas a sorry haul, and there's an end on't. Let her down quietly, and keep the secret. You promise that?"

"I do." Loveday remained thinking awhile, and then went on—"Well, what I was going to say is this: I've hit upon a plan to get out of the awkward corner she has put us in. What you'll think of it I can't say."

"David has just given me the heads."

"And do it hurt your feelings, my son, at such a time?"

"No—I'll bring myself to bear it, anyhow. Why should I object to other people's happiness because I have lost my own?" said Bob, with saintly self-sacrifice in his air.

"Well said!" answered the miller heartily. "But you may be sure that there will be no unseemly rejoicing, to disturb ye in your present frame of mind. All the morning I felt more ashamed than I cared to own at the thought of how the neighbours, great and small, would laugh at what they would call your folly and mine, when they knew what had happened; so I resolved to take this step to stave it off, if so be 'twas possible. And when I saw Mrs. Garland I knew I had done right. She pitied me so much for having had the house cleaned in vain, and laid in provisions to waste, that it put her into the humour to agree. We mean to do it right off at once, afore the pies and cakes get mouldy and the blackpot stale. 'Twas a good thought of mine and hers, and I am glad 'tis settled," he concluded cheerfully.

"Poor Matilda!" murmured Bob.

"There—I was afraid 'twould hurt thy feelings," said the miller, with self-reproach: "making preparations for thy wedding, and using them for my own!"

"No," said Bob heroically, "it shall not. It will be a great comfort in my sorrow to feel that the splendid grub, and the ale, and your stunning new suit of clothes, and the great table-cloths you've bought, and all the rest of it, will be just as useful now as if I had married myself. Poor Matilda! But you won't expect me to join in—you hardly can. I can sheer off that day very easily, you know."

"Nonsense, Bob!" said the miller reproachfully.

"I couldn't stand it—I should break down."

"Deuce take me if I would have asked her,

then, if I had known 'twas going to drive thee out of the house! Now, come, Bob, I'll find a way of arranging it and sobering it down, so that it shall be as melancholy as you can require—in short, just like a funeral, if thou'lt promise to stay?"

"Very well," said the young man. "On that condition I'll stay."

CHAPTER XXI.—THE DEPARTURE OF THE DRAGOONS.

HAVING entered into this solemn compact with his son, the elder Loveday's next action was to go to Mrs. Garland, and ask her how the toning down of the wedding had best be done. "It is plain enough that to make merry just now would be slighting Bob's feelings, as if we didn't care who was not married, so long as we were," he said. "But then, what's to be done about the victuals?"

"Give a dinner to the poor folk," she suggested. "We can get everything used up that way."

"That's true," said the miller. "There's enough of 'em in these times to carry off any extras whatsoever."

"And it will save Bob's feelings wonderfully. And they won't know that the dinner was got for another sort of wedding and another sort of guests; so you'll have their good-will for nothing."

The miller smiled at the subtlety of the view. "That can hardly be called fair," he said. "Still, I did mean some of it for them, for the friends we meant to ask would not have cleared all."

Upon the whole the idea pleased him well, particularly when he noticed the forlorn look of his sailor son as he walked about the place, and pictured the inevitably jarring effect of fiddles and tambourines upon Bob's shattered nerves at such a crisis, even if the notes of the former were dulled by the application of a mute, and Bob shut up in a distant bedroom—a plan which had at first occurred to him. He therefore told Bob that the surcharged larder was to be emptied by the charitable process above alluded to, and hoped he would not mind making himself useful in such a good and gloomy work. Bob readily fell in with the scheme, and it was at once put in hand and the tables spread.

The alacrity with which the substituted wedding was carried out, seemed to show that the worthy pair of neighbours would have joined themselves into one long ago, had there previously occurred any domestic incident dictating such a step as an apposite expedient, apart from their personal wish to marry.

The appointed morning came, and the service quietly took place at the cheerful hour of ten, in the face of a triangular congregation, of which the base was the front pew, and the apex the west door. Mrs. Garland dressed herself in the muslin shawl like Queen Charlotte's, that Bob had brought home, and her best plum-coloured gown, beneath which peeped out her shoes with red rosettes. Anne was present, but considerately toned herself down, so as not to too seriously damage her mother's appearance. At moments during the ceremony she had a distressing sense that she ought not to be born, and was glad to get home again.

The interest excited in the village, though real, was hardly enough to bring a serious blush to the face of coyness. Neighbours' minds had become so saturated by the abundance of showy military and regal incident lately vouchsafed to them, that a wedding of middle-aged civilians was of small account, excepting in so far that it solved the question whether or not Mrs. Garland would consider herself too genteel to mate with a grinder of corn.

In the evening, Loveday's heart was made glad by seeing the baked and boiled in rapid process of consumption by the kitchenful of people assembled for that purpose. Three-quarters of an hour were sufficient to banish for ever his fears as to spoilt food. The provisions being the cause of the assembly, and not its consequence, it had been determined to get all that would not keep consumed on that day, even if highways and hedges had to be searched for operators. And, in addition to the poor and needy, every cottager's daughter known to the miller was invited, and told to bring her lover from camp, an expedient which, for letting daylight into the inside of platters, was among the most happy ever known.

While Mr. and Mrs. Loveday, Anne, and Bob were standing in the parlour, discussing the progress of the entertainment in the next room, John, who had not been down all day, entered the house and looked in upon them through the open door.

"How's this, John? Why didn't you come before?"

"Had to see the captain, and—other duties," said the trumpet-major, in a tone which showed no great zeal for explanations.

"Well, come in, however," continued the miller, as his son remained with his hand on the door-post, surveying them reflectively.

"I cannot stay long," said John, advancing. "The route is come, and we are going away."

"Going away! Where to?"

"To Exeter."

"When?"

"Friday morning."

"All of you?"

"Yes; some to-morrow and some next day. The King goes next week."

"I am sorry for this," said the miller, not expressing half his sorrow by the simple utterance. "I wish you could have been here to-day, since this is the case," he added, looking at the horizon through the window.

Mrs. Loveday also expressed her regret, which seemed to remind the trumpet-major of the event of the day, and he went to her and tried to say something befitting the occasion. Anne had not said that she was either sorry or glad, but John Loveday fancied that she had looked rather relieved than otherwise when she heard his news. His conversation with Bob on the down made Bob's manner, too, remarkably cool, notwithstanding that he had after all followed his brother's advice, which it was as yet too soon after the event for him to rightly value. John did not know why the sailor had come back, never supposing that it was because he had thought better of going, and said to him privately, "You didn't overtake her?"

"I didn't try to," said Bob.

"And you are not going to?"

"No; I shall let her drift."

"I am glad indeed, Bob; you have been wise," said John heartily.

Bob, however, still loved Matilda too well to be other than dissatisfied with John and the event that he had precipitated, which the elder brother only too promptly perceived; and it made his stay that evening of short duration. Before leaving he said with some hesitation to his father, including Anne and her mother by his glance, "Do you think to come up and see us off?"

The miller answered for them all, and said that of course they would come. "But you'll step down again between now and then?" he inquired.

"I'll try to." He added after a pause, "In case I should not, remember that Revay will sound at half-past five; we shall leave about eight. Next summer, perhaps, we shall come and camp here again."

"I hope so," said his father and Mrs. Loveday.

There was something in John's manner which indicated to Anne that he scarcely intended to come down again; but the others did not notice it, and she said nothing. He departed a few minutes later, in the dusk of the August evening, leaving Anne still in doubt as to the meaning of his private meeting with Miss Johnson.

John Loveday had been going to tell them that, on the last night, by an especial privilege, it would be in his power to come and stay with them until eleven o'clock, but at the moment of leaving he abandoned the intention. Anne's attitude had chilled him, and made him anxious to be off. He utilised the spare hours of that last night in another way.

This was by coming down from the outskirts of the camp in the evening, and seating himself near the brink of the mill-pond as soon as it was quite dark; where he watched the lights in the different windows till one appeared in Anne's bedroom, and she herself came forward to shut the casement, with the candle in her hand. The light shone out upon the broad and deep mill-head, illuminating to a distinct individuality every moth and gnat that entered the quivering chain of radiance stretching across the water towards him, and every bubble or atom of froth that floated into its width. She stood for some time looking out, little thinking what the darkness concealed on the other side of that wide stream; till at length she closed the casement, drew the curtains, and retreated into the room. Presently the light went out, upon which John Loveday returned to camp and lay down in his tent.

The next morning was dull and windy, and the trumpets of the —th sounded Reveillée for the last time on Overcombe Down. Knowing that the dragoons were going away, Anne had slept heedfully, and was at once awakened by the smart notes. She looked out of the window, to find that the miller was already astir, his white form being visible at the end of his garden, where he stood motionless, watching the preparations. Anne also looked on as well as she could through the dim grey gloom, and soon she saw the blue smoke from the cooks' fires creeping fitfully along the ground, instead of rising in vertical columns, as it had done during the fine weather season. Then the men began to carry their bedding to the waggons, and others to throw all refuse into the trenches, till the down was lively as an anthill. Anne did not want to see John Loveday again, but hearing the household astir, she began to dress at leisure, looking out at the camp the while.

When the soldiers had breakfasted, she saw them selling and giving away their superfluous crockery to the natives who had clustered round; and then they pulled down and cleared away the temporary kitchens which they had constructed when they came. A tapping of tent-pegs and wriggling of picket-posts followed, and soon the cones of white canvas, now almost become a component part of the landscape, fell to the ground. At this moment the miller came indoors, and asked at the foot of the stairs if anybody was going up the hill with him.

Anne felt that, in spite of the cloud hanging over John in her mind, it would ill become the present moment not to see him off, and she went down-stairs to her mother, who was already there, though Bob was nowhere to be seen. Each took an arm of the miller, and thus climbed to the top of the hill. By this time the men and horses were at the place of assembly, and, shortly after the mill-party reached level ground, the troops slowly began to move forward. When the trumpet-major, half buried in his horse-furniture, drew near to the spot where the Lovedays were waiting to see him pass, his father turned anxiously to Anne and said, "You will shake hands with John?"

Anne faintly replied "Yes," and allowed the miller to take her forward on his arm to the trackway, so as to be close to the flank of the approaching column. It came up, many people on each side grasping the hands of the troopers in bidding them farewell; and as soon as John Loveday saw the members of his father's household, he stretched down his hand across his right pistol for the same performance. The miller gave his, then Mrs. Loveday gave hers, and then the hand of the trumpet-major was extended towards Anne. But as the horse did not absolutely stop, it was a somewhat awkward performance for a young woman to undertake, and, more on that account than on any other, Anne drew back, and the gallant trooper passed by without receiving her adieu. Anne's heart reproached her for a moment; and then she thought that, after all, he was not going off to immediate battle, and that she would in all probability see him again at no distant date, when she hoped that the mystery of his conduct would be explained. Her thoughts were interrupted by a voice at her elbow: "Thank heaven, he's gone! Now there's a chance for me."

She turned, and Festus Derriman was standing by her.

"There's no chance for you," she said indignantly.

"Why not?"

"Because there's another left!"

The words had slipped out quite unintentionally, and she blushed quickly. She would have given anything to be able to recall them; but he had heard, and said, "Who?"

Anne went forward to the miller to avoid replying, and Festus caught her no more.

"Has anybody been hanging about Overcombe Mill except Loveday's son, the soldier?" he asked of a comrade.

"His son the sailor," was the reply.

"Oh—his son the sailor," said Festus slowly. "Hang his son the sailor!"

THE WORLD AS I FIND IT.

THEY say the world's a weary place,
  Where tears are never dried,
Where pleasures pass like breath on glass,
  And only woes abide.
It may be so—I cannot know—
  Yet this I dare to say,
My lot has had more glad than sad,
  And so it has to-day.

They say that love's a cruel jest;
  They tell of women's wiles—
That poison dips in pouting lips,
  And death in dimpled smiles.

It may be so—I cannot know—
  Yet sure of this I am, .
One heart is found above the ground
  Whose love is not a sham.

They say that life's a bitter curse—
  That hearts are made to ache,
That jest and song are gravely wrong,
  And health a vast mistake.
It may be so—I cannot know—
  But let them talk their fill;
I like my life, and love my wife,
  And mean to do so still.

FREDERICK LANGBRIDGE.

IN THE GLOAMING, SCHEVENINGEN.

Page 373.

Storm on the Beach at Scheveningen.

HOLLAND.

IV.—SCHEVENINGEN, THE HERRING FISHERY.

SCHEVENINGEN is by far the best sea-side place to visit in Holland, especially as it combines the real fisherman's life with all the attractions of the "Grand Hôtel des Bains," about a mile off; its bathing, with real European machines, not the "diligences" of Domburg, which we described in a previous paper; the promenade on the hard sands; the large summer-house straw cabin chairs to keep the dust and sun off either invalids or lovers, as the case may be; sweet music, dances, representations of operas, military bands, and even fireworks with set pieces. What a programme! All this is easily accounted for. Scheveningen, sometimes written Scheveling, is hardly three miles from the Hague, and connected with it by a long avenue of trees, by the side of which runs a tramway, so that the traffic between the two places is considerable, and in addition to this there are trek-schuyts from the "Grands Bains." These, however, take longer, and passengers have to disembark some distance from the centre of the city, whereas the tram carriages run right into the principal Place, close to the Vyverberg.

As our space is small we will leave the "Grands Bains" for those who prefer conventional sea-side manners and customs to the simple fishing life, which we are especially anxious to investigate, now that so admirable an opportunity presents itself.

Emerging from the avenue we come upon the village; rounding the church sharply we pass the "pinck" building yard, and are soon out in the open again. Fortunately at this point the tramway is well protected by the dyke, running along the top of which is a paved way, generally known as the "Klinkers." This paved way connects the fishing village at the south end with the baths at the north end, and forms a good dry promenade, and a splendid hoop-course for the young visitors.

To see this, however, at its best, Sunday should be chosen, and a fine one, just after church, for the Scheveningen people are great in costume. Saturday is the day for cleaning or "schoon-maken," and Sunday is the great result; not that it is the result of pride or conceit—not at all—they like to have everything good and clean, they have been brought up to it, and they like the reaction from the dirt and disagreeables of carrying fish during the week, and enjoy purity on Sundays.

The costume of the women is very distinct. Their immense straw hats are very curious; the size probably is to save drippings from anything in the baskets above, as they carry everything on their heads. Next, the cap is put on over a silver plate which comes round the back of the head and terminates in two horns, as shown in Petronella's sketch. From these hang, on full-dress occasions, ornaments or dangles, which sometimes are very beautiful in design. Very little hair is shown—if any it is turned back over a small roll on the forehead; the white cap being fixed with two pins left prominently up. The small low bodice, very short-waisted, is exceedingly pretty, and then we approach the series of "jupons" which make Scheveningen women what they are. The correct list for Sunday's wear is, I believe, as follows; and I am indebted to Petronella for the details, who explained to me that the petticoats set better by running tucks in them at different distances from the waist, the object being to fill them well out. Details generally thus: 1, dark; 2, blue; 3, red; 4, black and white, vertical stripe; 5, blue; 6, brown.

A rich silk handkerchief is generally worn over the shoulders, a red coral necklet with gold clasp fits closely round the neck. The petticoats all rather short, and on the feet is worn a kind of slipper called "meulen." These have a wonderfully natural tendency to come off; it is, however, of rare occurrence, although there is no leather round the hinder part to keep it on the foot. To complete this costume, having already mentioned the large straw hat, we have only to add the cloak of strong brown home-made stuff, generally lined with red flannel, and surmounted by a stiff huge collar, fastened at the neck by a silver clasp. This is the "schoor-mantel." Sabots are generally worn on week-days, the "meulens" on Sundays.

Scheveningen.

Scheveningen Church.

Having accorded "place aux dames," the men next deserve attention. The old men generally wear tall hats with rather wide brims, which are most prominent when kept on by them during Divine service at the church, as shown in our woodcut. The fishermen have leather boots and trousers all in one for sea work, above which rises a garment only seen, I believe, at this place, and called a "kusack." It is of black woollen stuff with a high collar, of the same family as that of the schoor-mantel; its sleeves are short, enlarging below the elbow, and show the brown jacket underneath, together with the three silver buttons worn at the wrist; round the neck a black handkerchief is tied, but so arranged as to display the gold buttons worn at the throat.

During the herring season the beach at Scheveningen is all bustle. 1st. The row of pincks or boms, in all their variety of gay ornamentation, nets drying, sails of every hue hanging in every conceivable form of festoon. 2nd. The picturesque herring carts, painted green, generally containing seven thousand herrings in each. These are hurrying backwards and forwards, the horses labouring hard as they come to the loose sand, and rise to the village by the church. Knots of fish-women waiting for the tide to go down, some resting until the tide rises. Nearly every object here is of local interest; few foreigners come beyond the church or the Zee-rust, hotel and res-

taurant. Then a whole family comes down to start off a fisherman. Perhaps a vessel may be taken up for repair, in which case nearly all the horses are collected to haul on her. It would be a very stirring scene if it were not for the poor quality of horse, which is painful to behold. The whole "Plage" is of immense extent, and affords some very interesting studies of perspective.

One thing strikes the Englishman especially—the absence of small boats. The "boms," being flat-bottomed, and standing bolt upright directly they touch the bottom or sand, naturally draw but little water, for their total length is 40 feet, beam 20 feet, and depth from deck to keel 10 feet; and no small boats are used because directly the vessel touches the sand the crew get out and walk on shore. The steersman alone is privileged to be carried, and occasionally, for a treat, the boys. Some of the Dutch boats put into Lowestoft at the end of the season, and on their return take over some apples with them sometimes. The crew may be seen distributing their favours, and throwing them to the girls on the beach, deriving much amusement from the girls' anxiety to obtain the much-wished-for fruit without wetting their feet.

The variety of life on the beach is endless. We have already referred to it on a fine day. Let a breeze come up at low water—for at that time the expanse of sand is much

Church Service—Evening.

Petronella.

one's back on the sea and take to the avenue, with its tram and characteristic dog-carts—not dog-carts in the English sense of the word, but carts drawn by dogs, every dog looking at every Englishman with an appealing eye, as much as to say, "If you do not belong to the Society for the Prevention of Cruelty to Animals, do, and come to the rescue!"

Towards the end of the summer, breezes become gales. The beach becomes more roughly active, the pincks roll and bump more as they take the ground, and the rollers, coming in with their usual double bank, burst with more force and more bang over the fishing vessel, as she bumps up again with the rising tide. At this time two men are always centres of attention on the beach. The "Lynhaler" is the man who rides on trusty steed out to the vessel when she takes the ground, and catches a light line thrown to him. This line he brings on shore, and, being attached to a hawser on board, the beach crowd soon hawl the hawser on shore and fasten it to an anchor, whilst the crew work the capstan or spill on board.

The horse ridden by this man has evidently seen better days, and takes to his work with all the intelligence and perseverance of a

greater—the dry sand begins to move; the lower extremities of all the people about are lost to sight. Should the wind be steady, so much the better, but if gusty it is hard work. The natives turn their aprons over their heads; the whole atmosphere is sand, the very meals at table "servis au sable." No tooth-powder required in packing for Scheveningen—no sooner taken out than the tooth-brush becomes sufficiently charged. The effect of the lower part of the body being lost in the seething sand took a curious turn one morning. Six artillerymen were coming down the Duines to the "Plage" or beach. Some were smoking large pipes, some cigars in long bones. The only parts visible were their heads, pipes, or cigars, and bodies below the waist nothing. They were, in fact, vignetted, with no more bodies than are accorded to some pictures, which are generally all heads and wings. The Dutch artillerymen would have required immense wings.

This sand disturbance settles down after a time. The loose sand is driven, according to the strength of the wind, in wreaths. At the end of the season the Klinkers, or paved way connecting the fishing and bathing quarters, are covered in some places many feet deep, and the only way is to turn

The Flagman.

broken-down gentleman. The Lyn-haler does his work well, but the horse is an important agent, and dodges the breaking rollers with a marvellous instinct, the sure result of a long experience.

The other personage referred to is the " Flagman." Of these good functionaries there are six, men all above sixty, old fishermen generally, deserving old salts, and their duty is to indicate to each pinck, as she arrives, the proper place to make for and the position she should take upon the beach. As the flagman comes down from the Duines, he is generally followed by the relations of the fishermen expected, for the keen and long-accustomed eye of the old flagman can generally pick out some individuality in the craft, which gives a clue as to what she probably is. As a rule, the top of the mast is painted with distinctive bands of colour. They are all exactly the same size, length, and beam, so no information can be gained from that;

The Sandstorm.

still, they do know each vessel long before she is near enough even for telescopes to decide; and these good old gentlemen never use a telescope or modern invention of that kind.

The flagmen have much to do at the end of the herring season, if it blow hard, and many vessels come back together, for some ninety pincks belong to Scheveningen; many more than one would suppose, for in the early summer one may go and find the beach without a vessel on it—all away after herring, and just at the close of the season there may be ninety, before they dismantle for the winter. The way they hibernate is very curious. They are dismantled, and then carried up and run on rollers through the village, and so laid up until the next season.

XXI—27

The Sunday is well kept here, the church well attended. The most striking part of the service is perhaps to see the old men come in with their tall hats, unless the singing of the hymns and psalms be noticed. In that case the visitor will be struck by the shrill voices of the women, and may possibly recognise some that he has heard during the week. Our old friend Petronella had a voice like the shrill trumpet of a buck elephant in thick jungle. These voices in church make a point of following each other, and the organist considerably waits at the end of each verse for the stragglers to come up, ready for a fresh start in the next verse. And all this is done seriously and in a devout spirit; for there is much reverence and deep feeling amongst these fisher-folk. A certain melancholy pervades the whole village every time a pinck goes away. She may be a week or six weeks, or never return, never heard of. These are anxious times ; long nights of patient hope, hope deferred and the heart sick, refusing to be comforted. And so the wives sit out on the Duines, watching and longing, trusting and hoping ever.

Before leaving this interesting spot, where we had spent many happy days, we experienced a surprise which is so indicative of the wholesome state of the minds and religious feeling of the old flagmen, that I cannot do better than insert here a literal translation of the address. The village dialect is quite different to other patois. Some difficulty occurred to obtain a fac-simile of the real sentiment in English words. It is now reliable, and the original is much treasured by all to whom it refers. May the kind wishes of the good old men redound to their own happiness !

COPY OF ADDRESS.

November 4th, 1869.

To Weel E. Heer, whose name we know not.
A wish for Blessing to the Honourable, and highborn, and noble Heer and his dear wife, including his sweet children. Oh! that God may keep you safe over The Great Waters ; that you, by his grace, may be led to your native place ; and when you have, by God's grace, arrived at the Haven of your wishes, may you give Him the praise for it ; may you live still many years, noble Heer and dear lady, in good health and prosperity for your family's sake. But is this all we wish ? No ! we go further ; we wish prosperity to your Soul ; and when the house of the Tabernacle will be broken, that with Jesus you may land safely for ever in heaven above.

This is the wish and prayer of the Twelve Old Fishers of Scheveningen.

		Jaar.
(Signed)	H. Groen, oud.	76
	A. Bal	77
	Ad. Toor	70
	P. Pronk, oud.	76
	D. Jager	68
	Evd. Knoutter	69
	C. Heyer	68
	M. Bronsveld	69
	Con. Pronk	69
	G. Kraa	75
	J. Kinders	66
	G. Spaan	65

and Stijn Bol, Lyn-haler.

The good old men little knew, when they came up to take their farewell of us, how deep an impression their kind words would make, that they would be carefully handed down as a lesson and guide for those who come after us.

So grows the grain of mustard-seed, and works wheel within wheel ; in this case Good Words within "GOOD WORDS."

La Plage.

PUSHING.

WE all know what a pushing person is like. In fact, the very meaning of push is to keep one's self prominently before the eyes of others ; so that a pushing man is one of the best known of human types, just because he is one of the most conspicuous. He has a way of always coming to the front, and of taking the lead. If he is in business he manages to get people to talk about his large undertakings, and his wide foreign connections. If he is a man of society he always turns up in the best drawing-rooms on special evenings, and figures generally as a leader in conversation and social entertainment. The pusher never lets you lose sight of him. He button-holes you on all manner of occasions for the purpose of impressing you more deeply with his numerous claims to general recognition. While the man destitute of push stands aside in a corner overlooked and forgotten, the pusher seems to be a ubiquitous sort of being who invariably happens to be a prominent figure in the $f_0r_eg_r_0un_d$ of the social picture.

Pushing is carried on with very unequal degrees of skill. There is a clumsy and an adroit kind. Just as a man may physically push his way through a crowd in a rough fashion, calling everybody's attention to his exertions, while another will get through quite as effectively without any disturbance or appearance of effort, so with the man of push in a figurative sense. Some people have a knack of coming to the front and absorbing attention easily and naturally as though by royal right. Others again have to force their way into notice by dint of strenuous exertion. Indeed, pushing is an art that admits of very different degrees of proficiency. Some persons seem to be born with an aptitude for push, while others never reach even a respectable degree of skill. The saying that it is the part of true art to conceal art applies to pushing. A genuine expert knows how to further himself in your good opinion without the least appearance of solicitude. Thus he will begin to talk on an indifferent subject and yet manage to bring in, carelessly and at hap-hazard as it seems, references to his big acquaintances, or to his growing professional practice.

The pusher meets us in all departments of life. He is everywhere the same type, though his appearance will vary slightly, according to the medium through which he has to push. Thus the pushing broker on the Stock Exchange has a somewhat different gait from that of the pushing talker in a London drawing-room. One kind of push is required by the medical man who has to ingratiate himself with timorous mammas, another by the barrister who is concerned to make his mark on the mind of the judge before whom he usually pleads. The pushing young clergyman displays his powers by winning the notice of his seniors, if promotion is to come from above, or, if from below, by displaying his powers of persuasion at the ladies' tea party. The pushing artist manifests his skill by gathering the right sort of people to a lunch in his studio. The pushing writer studies the weak points of editors, to whom, in spite of rebuffs, he is never weary of submitting new contributions.

One or two varieties of the pusher are familiar figures in modern society. The loud man who carries everything before him by sheer self-confidence and audacity in the club or drawing-room is known to all. Then there is the ambitious lady of questionable descent, who is determined to force her passage into a higher social stratum, a character that our leading comic journal has of late been hitting off with a clever hand. Another variety which many of us have reason to remember is the pushing young Miss in her teens who is ambitious to be thought a young woman, and who forces her way into adult conversation with all the confidence and coolness of a practised member of society.

It is to be added that pushing is not confined to the obtrusion of one's own personality and doings on the notice of others. A person may display very much the same kind of disposition and ability in relation to any subject that is specially taken under his care. Thus we have the familiar figure of the man or woman who is continually urging the claims of some pet scheme of charity or social amelioration. Even a speculative idea may be pushed in the shape of a doctrine, and modern society is invaded by a whole swarm of zealous pushers of new theories in science, philosophy, &c. Finally, it may be observed that a good deal of pushing has the promotion in public esteem of some other person besides the pusher. As a general rule it is far easier to push some second person than to push one's self, and most people have one or two friends whom they are anxious to bring on in the world. A not infrequent figure in contemporary society is the lady who makes a special protégé of some " promising young man," and never loses an opportunity of giving him a friendly push. She has an eloquent way of appealing to your sympathies, which, for the moment at least, makes you look on her protégé as a most interesting person, and one who has the strongest claims on the gratitude of the generation which is so fortunate as to have him in its midst.

It is supposed to be a mark of a refined mind to greatly dislike pushing and pushers. And there is no doubt that the irrepressible pusher, whether the object of his promotion be himself or somebody else, is apt to be a bore. An unskilful pusher is pretty certain to tire people by the very monotony of his theme. And it is plain besides that this theme can never be one of supreme interest to the majority of mankind, otherwise there would be no need of enforcing it so energetically. More particularly in our languid age, when it is a mark of good breeding never to be excited to a pitch of intense interest about anything, the pusher is exceedingly likely to disgust his audience, for he is by profession an enthusiast, and it is his direct object to kindle something of his own enthusiasm in others.

In point of fact, pushing is looked on in good society as "bad form." It is seen to be egoistic, conceited, and rude, to wish to force one's own petty interests on others whether they will or not. Consequently, the pusher is a well-marked personage in genteel society, and his advent in a drawing-room is commonly the signal for the most fastidious of the company to retire to some inconspicuous nook where they may hope to escape his keen and vigilant eye.

Yet if the pusher is an unpopular person he is at least successful. Even if the pushing process is apt to be fatiguing it generally effects its object. Sometimes, indeed, it does this through the very fatigue it induces. When a man has been hammering at you off and on for a month or so respecting some new project, you are disposed to accord him a measure of recognition if only to put a stop to the process of dinning. So if an ambitious lady continues to persecute a hostess a little above herself, placing herself in her way at most inopportune moments, and hanging on, so to speak, to the hem of her robe, the latter may probably decide that she will be less bored in the future if she gives the importunate person the coveted entrée into her circle. There is little doubt that a good bit of pushing attains its object through an appeal to this motive of avoiding the weariness which all importunity is apt to produce.

Yet this kind of success cannot be called complete. It is not the result which the pusher commonly aims at. What he really wishes is to convince his hearers of the importance of the subject he advocates, and his triumph can only be called perfect when he does actually beget this conviction. And notwithstanding the prejudice of the fastidious few against the pusher, he is for the most part successful in this larger sense. The indefatigable advocate of his own claims or of those of others does, as a rule, win over his hearers to his own view. And he does so just because the majority of people are easily infected by the contagion of enthusiastic belief. If a talker or writer only gives the impression of being very much in earnest in his views, people are disposed to think there must be something in them. It is an old saying that the man who wants others to believe in him must show that he believes in himself, and he who vigorously pushes his own claims exactly fulfils this condition. And when the pushing is of a more disinterested character it is easier for the hearer's impulses of sympathy to come into play and accelerate the process of conviction. Even the sensitive people who are soon bored by the operation of pushing, are, sometimes in spite of themselves, constrained to acknowledge the merits of the case thus painfully obtruded on their attention.

It is thus seen that readiness to push and skill in pushing are prime qualifications for success in life. Without this, real ability often fails to make itself known, while with them the most ordinary mediocrity may attain a certain brilliancy of reputation. Nay, mere stupidity itself, if vigorously backed by eloquent advocacy, may now and again rise to an imposing altitude and assume all the aspect of profound wisdom. In every department of life in which success is largely determined by personal reputation, that is to say, in politics, in the learned professions, in literature and art, and in society, the advantages resulting from push are manifest. And the increase of competition which marks our age obviously serves to extend the range of this art. For pushing is simply self-assertion, and in the struggle for existence, physical or social, self-assertion means readiness to jostle others out of the way.

Nevertheless, it is possible to over-estimate the practical value of push. We have all known men who somehow managed to get along without pushing themselves, though their abilities were certainly not of the first order. Now and then, indeed, sterling worth in its remote retreat succeeds in making its soft lustre visible through all the harsh glare of nearer and bolder lights. Yet this possibility is too precarious to have much effect on practical calculation. A more important consideration is one suggested by our slight study of pushers, namely, that a man often has the choice between pushing himself and letting others push him. We have all known the young man of pleasant, ingratiating manners, whose love of ease makes pushing a disagreeable operation to him, and who considerately leaves this to be done by his friends. It would seem that if a man can only count on a thoroughly devoted and energetic friend's doing his pushing for him, he will be as well off as if he does it for himself, and at no cost of personal exertion.

There are, however, definite risks connected with this alternative of doing one's pushing by proxy. It may happen that the devoted friend will grow weary of his task, or otherwise fail when his exertions are still needed. And this is the more likely to happen because a man in indolently trusting to others to advance him is very apt to become generally inert, and so to discontinue those very exertions which form the only reasonable basis of recommendation. If a man pushes himself he must do something to give colour to his self-recommendation, and the fact of his making the first kind of effort is some sort of guarantee that he will make the second kind also. But if a man leaves it to others to bring him forward he very naturally drifts into total idleness ; and then the friendly pusher is pretty certain to become tired of his hopeless task. Even the devoted and untiring wife may, in this way, wake up to the illusoriness of her fond aspirations, and cease to push the man whom she has hitherto tried so hard and so resolutely to believe in as one specially unfortunate and unappreciated. It is an evil moment for one who has got into the way of thus leaning on others when their eyes are opened to his real merits.

Allowing, however, for these risks, the policy of delegating one's pushing to others has very much to be said in its favour. If a man of easy nature and fortunate in the possession of devoted friends only succeeds in keeping up an appearance of merit, and so supplies to his friends a bare ground of recommendation, he may enjoy a kind of life that suits him far better than one of severe exertion. And as a matter of fact there are a good many of such spoilt men in the world who manage to thrive fairly well on the exertions of vicarious pushers, and who probably laugh in their sleeve at the feverish endeavours of their more ambitious rivals.

It may be said, then, with confidence that in this age ordinary men cannot do without . pushing, either their own or that of somebody else. This being so, it would seem to be foolish to be over-fastidious and to shrink from every form of advancement by this means. People generally show this fastidiousness with respect to self-advancement. They would like to be thought too modest and too dainty to get success in this noisy, vulgar fashion. A good deal of this delicacy of mind strikes one as somewhat forced, for if a man honestly believes in his own merits one cannot see why he should shrink from making them known just because they happen to be his own. It is noticeable, too, that some of the sensitive people who thus dread to vulgarise themselves by self-assertion, have not the least compunction in letting others sound abroad their praises. And yet one would say that this latter course is the much more undignified of the two, growing positively contemptible when, as often happens, it is made an excuse for personal indolence.

Still, there is no doubt that a refined mind will shrink from the coarser forms of self-assertion, just as a manly mind will shrink from relying on others' advocacy. And this being so, an unscrupulous man will often have an advantage in the struggle. Accordingly, it must hold good in the case of men of ordinary powers that great moral sensitiveness and refinement are unfavourable to the attainment of lofty prizes. A highly sensitive man of average ability must be content to aim comparatively low, and leave the most tempting rewards to his less scrupulous competitors.

It seems to follow that great refinement of moral sensibility is not for ordinary and mediocre men. This endowment is a luxury in which only the few of unmistakable power can indulge. It is often said that there are penalties attached to the possession of genius, and this is probably true. But genius has its own rewards, and among these not the least is immunity from the harsher conditions of ordinary human success. The man of transparent talent, whose fitness to reign among men nobody can overlook, needs neither to push himself nor to be pushed. He, and he alone, can afford to look down on the rude conflict with something like calm contempt. It is only the man destined to be eminent by virtue of great natural endowments who has any right to the highest degrees of moral sensibility. The harder the exertion necessary to success, the less room for delicacy of feeling. In this, as in many other things in this odd world of ours, the rule holds good, that to him that hath shall be given.

JAMES SULLY.

·HEALTH AT HOME.

By B. W. RICHARDSON, M.D., F.R.S.

PART IV.

IN speaking of beds and bedding in my last paper, I neglected to state one fact, which it is of moment to remember, namely, that in the cleansing of the feathers which are used to fill pillows and bolsters, the utmost care ought to be taken never to put the feathers back into the tick until they are thoroughly dried. If only a little moisture attach to the feathers they decompose; they give out ammoniacal and sulphuretted compounds, and they become in this manner not only offensive to the sense of smell, but sometimes an insidious source of danger to health.

A few years ago I went with my family to a well-known seaside place, where during the season we were obliged to take what we could get in the way of house accommodation. I was myself located in a small bedroom, which was scrupulously clean and comfortable, and, as bedrooms go, well ventilated. The first night after going to bed I awoke in early morning with the most oppressive of headaches, with a sense of nausea, and with coldness of the body. The thought that these unpleasant symptoms arose from smallness of the room and close air led me to open the window. I was soon somewhat relieved, but could sleep no more that morning, so I dressed, took a walk, and after a few hours felt fairly well, and as wanting nothing more than a few hours of extra sleep. The next night I took the precaution to set the window open, but again in early morning I woke as before, and even in worse condition. I now canvassed all possible causes for the phenomena. Had I contracted some contagious disease? Was this bedroom recently tenanted by a person suffering from a contagious malady? Had I taken some kind of food or drink which had disagreed with me? The answer to each of these queries was entirely negative. All I could get at was that I had a sense of an odour of a very peculiar kind, which came and went, and which seemed to have some connection with the temporary derangement. On the third night I went to bed once more, but rather more restless and alert than before; and an hour or two after I had been in bed I woke with a singular dream. I was a boy again, and I was reading the story, so I dreamt, of Philip Quarles, who, like Robinson Crusoe, was lost on a desolate island, and who could not sleep on a pillow stuffed with the feathers of certain birds which he had killed, and the feathers of which he had used for a pillow. The dream led me to examine the pillow on which my own head reclined. It was a soft, large downy cushion, with a fine white case and a perfectly clean tick; but when I turned my face for a moment on the pillow and inhaled through it, I detected the most distinct sulphur-ammoniacal odour, which was so sickening I had no difficulty in discovering mine enemy. The bolster I found to be the same. I put both away, made a temporary pillow out of a railway rug, went to sleep again, and woke in the morning quite well. It turned out that the pillow and bolster had been recently made up with imperfectly dried feathers, and some of these were undergoing decomposition.

This experience of mine is a good illustration detected, as it happened, on the spot. It is by no means singular. Little children are often made sleepless, dreamful, and restless in their cots from a similar cause.

BED VENTILATION.

In treating of bed and bedding I have dwelt on the importance of allowing the clothes so to lie on the sleeper that they shall not too closely wrap him up in his own cutaneous exhalations. What I wished to convey by this teaching was, that the bed should be ventilated not less than the room. Benjamin Franklin used to take what he called an air bath, which consisted in walking about in an open room, sharply, for a short time in a loose dress, so that the air might come well and briskly on to the surface of his skin and exert its purifying and cleansing influence on the cutaneous envelope. The good and refreshing effect of this simple measure of cleanliness is well experienced by those who resort to it, and part of the value of the Turkish bath is due to Franklin's method, which is there of necessity carried out. But there is no doubt that an improvement might be made in beds themselves by a process of ventilation of them, and I am glad to say that this principle has been introduced lately by a clever and simple invention, called O'Brien's Bed-ventilating Tube. The late Dr. Chowne showed that the ordinary motion of the air through tubes vertically placed and open at each end is in one continued upward direction, the air enclosed within the tubes being always of slightly higher temperature than that outside. I saw many of Dr. Chowne's experiments on this subject, and although I could never see what he called the syphon principle which he supposed to be in action, I am bound to admit that he could in the most equable and even atmosphere cause a current of air to circulate down a short arm of a vertical tube, and up a longer arm of another tube connected with the shorter by a joint or bend. Mr. O'Brien, taking advantage of this fact, has then invented a tube which ventilates the bed while the sleeper is in it. A tube of two inches diameter at the foot of the bed opens just under the bed-clothes; it passes beneath the frame of the bed to the bed's head, and runs up at the bed's head until it nearly reaches the ceiling, or when convenient passes into a flue. Through this tube a current of air, entering the bed at the upper part and passing over the sleeper, is made to circulate out of the bed by the ventilating tube, carrying with it the watery matter that is exhaled by the skin, and keeping up, in fact, a perfectly ventilated space, in which the body for so many hours reposes. The quantity of fluid from the skin which condenses in this tube in the course of a night is, to common observation, quite remarkable, consisting of several ounces. I consider the O'Brien tube to be a marked hygienic improvement in the construction of bedsteads and bedding. It ought to be fitted to every bedstead, and in the beds of all sick-rooms and wards of hospitals it should have an immediate and settled introduction.

WINDOW CURTAINS AND WINDOW BLINDS IN THE BEDROOM.

There is much difference of opinion on the question of window curtains and window blinds in the bedroom. Some persons who have been unhealthily educated are unable to sleep except when the room is entirely dark, the faintest ray of light being sufficient to break their repose. Others can sleep when light enters into the room in the fullest degree. I have no doubt those are most healthy who can sleep without any window shade whatsoever, and I am sure that every one can be trained so as to sleep without blinds if the training do but commence early enough in life. Light purifies and invigorates; and children that sleep in darkness, by their blanched faces alone, may be distinguished from those who sleep in a well-lighted room. More than this, the admission of daylight early in the morning tends to create a habit of early rising, which is so conducive to health. He who hails the sun instead of letting the sun hail him is the wise man. Those who sleep like moles in a hole, though they may grow sleek and fat, are not sun-healthy; they are feeble, subject to headaches, excitable, pale, and nervous. For these reasons I would, therefore, teach that the half-blind of muslin is all that is sufficient for the bedroom window, and that the roller-blind should only be used to prevent the actual glare of the sun, or to shut out the view into a room that is exposed to other houses that overlook it. Heavy curtains for bedroom windows, or curtains of any kind, are altogether out of place, except as mere ornamental appendages, and they, when present for appearance' sake, should never be drawn except on emergency, in seasons of extreme cold or heat.

A light green colour is best for the muslin blind and the roller-blind.

ANSWERS TO SOME INQUIRIES.

Before I leave the bedroom it is well for me to take the opportunity of replying to one or two of a great number of inquiries that have been sent to me respecting the various points that have been mooted in these papers.

1. For daylight reflectors Chapuis's are, I think, up to this time, without a rival.

2. For the floors of bedrooms, in cases where the wooden flooring is bad, an oil-cloth covering is in all particulars good. The oil-cloth can be cleaned by the dry method perfectly well.

3. A portion of stove piping carried from the calorigen stove to the outer air for the purpose of admitting fresh air answers fairly well; but no plan is so good as to clear away all rubbish from beneath the floor of the room, make plenty of opening from the outer air to beneath the floor, and then let the tube for feeding the fresh air to the stove perforate the flooring into the space beneath.

4. The open gas fire-place in the bedroom is perfectly safe so long as there is a good chimney draught, but if there is anything like a down draught the stove is very dangerous to health. The product which injures most from the gas fire is not carbonic acid, but carbonic oxide. On the whole, I think the chimney-cowl called the "Empress," made by Messrs. Ewart, of the Euston Road, is the best for preventing down draught in the chimney shaft. The gas fire in good action, and planned on a proper principle, such as Verity's, has great advantages over a coal stove. It causes no dust, which is a considerable advantage of itself, and it saves much labour. But the

great advantage of the gas fire is that it maintains an equal temperature. With the coal fire, unless it be under almost impossible observation, there is no equality of warmth in the apartment it vivifies. It goes nearly out, leaving the room chilly and uncomfortable; it burns up, making an undue warmth, and hurrying in draughts; and then it cools, temporarily, to what may be considered the proper temperature. The gas fire on the other hand is entirely manageable. With a little practice the temperature of a room, in every part, may be set for the night, and the variation need not exceed five degrees Fahr. The only objection I know of in the open gas fire is its cost. It is, with all care, at least double the expense of a coal fire. That at all events is my experience.

5. The mean temperature of the bedroom should be from 60° to 65° Fahr. This is easily maintained by the calorigen stove, and at a very moderate expense. The calorigen that burns with coal is perhaps the steadiest of the varieties of coal stoves which warm and ventilate at the same time.

6. A paper, for walls, which "will wash like linen," as one of my correspondents suggests, is not at all out of the question. Indeed, since these essays have been in progress, Dr. Scoffern has sent me a small specimen of his cupri-ammonium prepared paper which can even be boiled or steamed without being destroyed. A little improvement in a paper of this construction, so as to make it more artistic, would give a basis for a perfectly healthy wall paper, which could be put up, in panel, without paste, on a glazed wall, and permit of being taken down, at any time, for cleansing, as easily as a picture.

7. There is, it must be acknowledged, a great difficulty in admitting air into the bedroom from the outside, and at the same time excluding damp. In foggy weather, in such seasons as the one we have just passed through, this difficulty is almost insurmountable, and we are unfortunately placed between Scylla and Charybdis in relation to it. I have tried several plans for drying air in its course from the outside into the room, but only with partial success. When the air of the room is well and equally warmed, the injury arising from moisture is greatly lessened, and it is therefore of moment, in foggy seasons, to keep up a considerable temperature in the room by which the water vapour will be removed, if there be at the same time free exit ventilation. But all plans of artificial drying are partial or mischievous. To stretch a layer of porous and dry woollen stuff over

the opening that lets air into the room is the only mechanical plan I can suggest that is of real value. This at all events filters the air. It might be supplemented by introducing into the ventilating tube some loosely packed charcoal in good-sized pieces, over which the air would pass on its entrance into the chamber. Dr. Stenhouse has suggested this plan as a means of purification of air, and it is a good suggestion in that particular.

THE STAIRCASE LANDING.

We may leave the bedroom now, and pass to the landing of the staircase outside. This space, or landing, is, as a rule, a terrible trouble to the sanitary mind. It is a rialto on which varied kinds of sanitary difficulties combine. It often is deficient in light. On it is placed the receptacle, necessary but fearful, of the housemaid's cupboard or closet. On it is placed the sink and water-butt. Worst of all, in nearly every London house, it is the place for the water-closet. When there are two landing floors in the house these convenient inconveniences are usually divided, but frequently, in houses less fortunately placed, they are all in conjunction.

Good Light and Costless Ventilation.

It is essential on the landing of the bedroom floor first of all to have abundance of light. The window should be made as large as is consistently possible, and it should be kept specially clean. When light is deficient here the reflector ought to be brought into immediate use. In a large and newly-built house in this metropolis, into which I was, lately, led by a professional summons, an artificial light had actually to be kept for a portion of the day, and for the whole day when the sky was clouded, in order that the passage could be sufficiently illuminated for ordinary purposes. A great blank of dead wall opposite the window kept up a perpetual eclipse. I suggested a reflector, and as soon as it was in position the passage became actually brilliant with light, to the immense comfort of the occupiers of the house.

After light on the landing of the staircase comes the admission of air by the window, and here I can have no hesitation what to recommend. The costless system of ventilation introduced by Dr. Peter Hinckes Bird is for all intents the best. Dr. Bird's plan is simplicity itself. The lower sash of the window is lifted up about three inches, and in the space between the sill and the sash a piece of wood is introduced to fill up the space. The lower sash at its upper part is thus brought a few inches above the lower part of the upper sash, which it by so much overlaps. In this manner there is left in the middle between the two sashes an open space, up which the air is constantly passing from the outside into the house. At all times the air is finding its way, and, as the current is directed in an upward course, draught is not felt even when the air blows in freely. At the same time the sashes can be opened or closed as may be desired without altering the arrangement for ventilation.

I have recommended and employed Dr. Bird's costless ventilation so many years with such excellent practical results, I hardly like to venture on a shade of suggestion for its modification. There is, however, one change in it which, while it adheres entirely to the principle, is, I venture to think, an improvement in detail. This consists simply in letting the lower sash remain unchanged, and in bringing down the upper sash three inches, so as to let it by that distance overlap the lower. The space above on the upper part of the top sash has then to be filled up, and I recommend for this purpose a permanent bar of wood, against which the upper sash can close. The advantages of this detail are, that the window looks better; that light at the lower part is saved; that lower blinds are not interfered with; that the interposed piece of wood is out of the reach of the servants, so that it cannot be taken away without great trouble; and, that if there be a draught at the space where the sash touches the interposed portion of wood, it is at the top instead of the bottom sash, and is not felt by those who are passing the window on ascending the stairs.

The costless ventilation once effected, it should be in operation all the year round. It is true that in cold weather it causes a lower temperature on the landing than would exist if the window were absolutely closed; but this must be met by increasing the warmth within the house, not by the process of excluding the outer air.

It will be soon detected in windows in which the costless ventilation is set up, how large a quantity of dust there is in the air which finds its way into the dwelling-house of the great city. The space through which the air passes is very quickly charged with dust, some of which settles on the panes of the window and the framework, and requires removal at short regular intervals. It is raised by some as an objection to the system of costless ventilation that the dust enters so freely through the permanent opening as to become, in its turn, a nuisance. Hence, we often find the opening partly filled up with a sandbag, or else with a plate of perforated zinc, the openings of which are quite closed up with dust. Both these practices are bad; the open space should never be closed. In spite of the acknowledged inconvenience of dust, it is far better to have a free admission of air than to exclude the air. In practice, moreover, the dust nuisance is less than would be expected. It is only occasionally present, while bad air, if outer air be kept out, is always present.

The floor of the landing should be treated precisely in the same manner as the floor of the bedroom. In the course of the tread in the centre of the landing, for a width, say, of from eighteen inches to two feet, a line of carpet may be laid down, but the floor space on either side of the carpet should be uncovered, and if it be of wood it should be dry scrubbed and treated with wax and turpentine, when the boards will allow of it. Where the staircase and landing are of stone, nothing is more healthful than the stone itself duly cleaned and whitened. When the floor surface is of indifferent wood or stone, it may, with advantage, be covered with oil-cloth, with the centre carpet. In no case should the whole of a landing be carpet-covered so as to make the carpet hug the wall. A floor covered in that manner holds the dust, and keeps the air charged with dust, every step and every gust of air that moves the carpet from beneath tending to waft some particles of dust into the air above.

Of oil-cloth as a covering for landings, passages, and outer parts of bedroom floors, nothing can be said that is unfavourable, granting always that it is laid down with skill and care. As a rule it should be closely fitted to the floor, and well glued and nailed down at the edges, so that it cannot become a coating for a thick layer of dust beneath it. Fixed firmly in its place in such a way as to form part of the floor itself, oil-cloth can be cleaned with as much facility as can a boarded floor, and can be waxed as perfectly. It does not retain dust; it shows the presence of dust and dirt, and it is a good non-conductor of heat. The substance called linoleum is, in some particulars, an improvement on oil-cloth, because it is a better non-conductor. Kamptulicon is more enduring than either, but it does not admit of such perfect cleaning; it catches the dust more, and it never looks so bright and cheery as the others do. We are told that it is so much more serviceable, and that is true ; but then it is not good to have for ever in view a structure that is unchangeable and practically indestructible. An occasional change of structure is a positive relief, and when it can be obtained at slight cost is a useful luxury.

The walls of the landing, like those of the bedroom, should be covered with a paint or paper that will readily admit of being washed. Failing this, they should be distempered.

ASCENDING VENTILATING SHAFT.

It is always good practice wherever it is practicable to make an opening from the stair-landing into, and out of, the roof of the house, or into the stack of the chimney. If the landing be just under the roof, then it is good to get a direct opening through the roof, or the cock-loft leading to it, so that there may be an immediate communication with the outer air above. In most houses this upper landing-place is connected by the staircase with the whole of the lower part of the house. The house from below ventilates into it, and if upon it there be no efficient outlet it is in a bad position indeed. Should there be an intervening floor between the floor and the roof of the house a small shaft should be carried up, and beneath that shaft a gas-burner may with much advantage be suspended, so as to make the shaft a chimney for the conveyance of the products of the gas and of air, away from the interior of the house.

THE WATER-CLOSET ON THE STAIRCASE LANDING.

In the houses of crowded cities the worst sanitary difficulty of all lies in the arrangement of the water-closet on the landings of the staircases. Some sanitarians propose to meet these difficulties by introducing the dry earth-closet system, or by some other special system distinct from what is in general use. I do not object to such suggestions where they are practicable ; but my business, at this time, is to indicate the safest mode of meeting the present objectionable system, and, until a better mode of construction is effected, to improve to the utmost the water-closet as it now exists. I will deal with the earth-closet in the next paper.

It cannot be denied that great danger attends the water-closet system in many houses. The closet itself is placed so as to be in the centre of the sleeping part of the domicile. It is most imperfectly ventilated and lighted. The flow from it is often exceedingly bad; the leverage and the water supply are apt to get out of order; the pans soon become unclean, and, whatever care the housekeeper may exercise, there is an odour from the closet which will pervade the floor of the house in which the closet is placed, and will declare the unwholesomeness of the arrangement.

To meet these unfortunate conditions, the first care should be to secure an absolutely free course from the pan of the closet into the soil-pipe, and from the soil-pipe into the sewer, in such a manner that at some point before it reaches the trap leading to the sewer the pipe shall be open to the air. I shall explain in a future paper how this may be done ; but for the present I point it out as a necessity. The second care is to secure a good and steady supply of water, so that the pan of the closet can always be thoroughly flushed and charged with water. The third care is to have a closet apparatus that shall let the water completely empty the pan, and shall afterwards leave a good supply of water there. Underhay's plan is one of the best for securing this advantage ; it gives a free fall of water when the trap is raised, and it fills, if it may so be said, as it empties, thereby rendering the return of air from the soil-pipe all but impossible.

These plans secured, the next step consists in arranging for the purification of the closet itself; for the free ventilation of it specially.

When there is a ready means of making a window or direct shaft from the closet into the open air the difficulty of finding an exit opening is fairly solved, and I need only to say of such an opening that it can hardly be too large or too free. The great obstacles are found when the closet is in the centre of the floor, and there is no means of direct communication with out-door air. In many of our London houses so circumstanced it is actually not uncommon to see a window from the water-closet opening into the staircase, a plan as bad as can possibly be imagined. To avoid that, I would offer the following arrangement, which I have carried out with very satisfactory results.

To ventilate freely under the conditions named it is requisite to make an opening through the ceiling of the closet, and to secure an outlet, so as to allow the air of the closet to find free exit. This is best done when the closet is under the roof of the house by carrying a three or four inch tube into the space under the roof, and either running it from there into a chimney shaft, or direct out on to the roof by a chimney of its own. In cases where there is an intervening floor it is necessary to carry the opening through the ceiling of the closet into the space between the ceiling and the floor above, and from that, by a tube laid between floor and ceiling, to the side wall, and through that wall into the open air by an exit shaft. Or else to carry a tube through the ceiling and floor direct up to and through the roof, or into a chimney shaft. If gas be at hand it is well to have a burner put into the closet, and to allow the light to be suspended immediately beneath the ascending exit air-tube. By this method the escape of air from the closet is always well secured and part of the difficulties are overcome.

Following, however, upon this it is necessary to let air freely into the closet, so that there may always be a free current of air circulating through it. To effect this object one step more must be taken. Through the floor of the closet in front of the seat, at either or at both ends, there must be cut a free opening into the space between the floor and the ceiling of the room below. From this opening another free communication must be made to the outer air by an opening made through the wall of the house. It may be necessary here to carry a tube from the opening in the outer wall to the closet, but, as a rule, it is only requisite to insert a few perforated bricks in the wall on the level of the space between the floors and the ceilings of the rooms beneath. This space then becomes an air chamber, which feeds the closet with air in the freest manner. The air introduced should pass also freely under the seat of the closet.

By the simple plan now detailed I have seen a closet in the centre of a floor rendered free of all odour, and so flushed with air that it was purer than some closets are which are placed out of doors.

Recently a very ingenious invention has been brought out by the Deodorizing Water-closet Company, in the Harrow Road, by which the pan of the closet is kept free of odour. Under the seat of the closet, but quite concealed by the front of the seat, there is placed an apparatus which contains a large supply of permanganate deodorizing solution. A tube from this apparatus enters from above into the basin of the closet, and after water has been allowed to flow through the pan, just as the lever descends to shut off the water, a portion of the deodorizing solution is pumped into the water that remains in the basin, and is left there. The water is coloured red by the solution, and not only deodorizes, but becomes a test of the cleanliness of the closet itself. If the pan of the closet be very unclean the water is almost immediately decolorized; if, on the other hand, the closet be in a wholesome state the water retains the colour of the solution for several hours. I have had this apparatus set up in my own house, and find it to answer excellently. It will, I suspect, become a necessity in hotels, convalescent homes, and hospitals.

The walls of the water-closet should either be painted so that they may be washed frequently, or they should be coated with distemper often renewed. All porous coverings for the walls are particularly objectionable.

The closet should be frequently cleansed throughout, and once in a twelvemonth, at least, the pan should be taken out, and it and all the parts and tubes beneath should be systematically cleansed and purified. Once every week the closet should be thoroughly flushed with water; and through the seat, over the handle of the lever that lifts the plug to let in the water, an opening should be cut so that the handle can be raised during the flushing, while the lid of the closet is closed down.

(*To be continued.*) ·

[*Erratum.*—In the April number of GOOD WORDS, article "Health at Home," page 284, column 2, line 19, for *nine* years read *three* years.]

THE TORRENT.

YEA, like to some torrent which, severed in twain,
  By cruel rock sundered, meets never again
    With tumult of music and mirth,
But river-ward roameth, all silent and lone,
    Till in the commotion
    Of wild wind and ocean,
      Escaped from the trammels of earth—
The parted, commingling, for ever are one!

So, my soul and thy soul are severed in twain,
  By cruel fate sundered, nor ever again
    Love's joyful communion shall know—
But linger, with silence and distance between—
    Till life's fierce commotion
    Be lost in that ocean
      Whence essence to essence forth flow,
And unite—in Eternity's endless Serene!

ALLISON HUGHES.

HAGAR'S LIFE.

IT is very pleasant sometimes, when we are overweighted with the close atmosphere of our too-busy and too-crowded days, to turn to the records of the earlier world and keep company with a franker and simpler life. Civilisation is often too much for us; the world is too much with us. We are wearied out with intellectual disputes, with social questions, with the daily rush of news upon us from all quarters of the world. The desire comes on us to leave it and bury ourselves in solitude, or to go far into some wild country, where we may renew the dreams of youth and be at rest from the ceaseless demands made on heart, and brain, and spirit by the contentions of society, knowledge, and religion. It is a growing need among us, because we are civilised too largely towards the work of the intellect and the work of the world, and not enough towards the leisure of wise enjoyment and the pleasure of noble imagination.

One way, however, of escaping at intervals from this close air is to throw ourselves, in fancy, into the life of the young world. Many cannot do that in company with Homer, but all can do it in imaginative reading of the stories of the Book of Genesis. There are no stories more simple, human, full of the fresh childhood of the world, than the stories of Abraham, Isaac, and Jacob. A clear wind seems to blow upon our faces as we read, and a charm of youth to move in our veins. We live with men and women, yet they are as simple as children. They are wise in humanity, but they know nothing of our knowledge. They are great in war, and courteous in their society, and prudent in government of men, but the war, and the society, and the government are as simple as ours are complex.

The land, too, in which they lived was as lonely as ours is crowded. A few villages and forts rested on its hills; a few encampments were seen upon its plains; a few wells marked where the wandering tribes rested on their way as they changed the feeding-places of their flocks; but for the most part the land was as empty as the outskirts of the Australian belt of population, where the sheep farms lie scattered miles asunder. Half of it was the wild wilderness, and the bright stars looked down on a country nearly as uninhabited as their own. Here and there a few figures moved among clustered tents and wandering cattle. Who were they? They were the men and women from whom flowed the great Jewish and Arab races, the ancestors of the religion of mankind. When we enter their pastoral encampment we stand at the fountain-head of nations. We pass with a long sigh of relief out of our complicated, worried, problem-ridden, sceptical, fashionable, and worn society into another where the ways of life are simple, where faith is undoubting, where men could be quiet, where government was paternal, and society moved on a few well-known lines of obedience and courtesy, where a deep impression on the heart or a new idea was a voice of God, where so small was experience that everything new was marvellous. Into such an atmosphere and such a society the story of Hagar brings us. It has its own profound humanity in the midst of its simplicity. Whatever criticism may be applied to it, there is that in it which is for ever independent of criticism—the revelation of the human heart.

But there is something more. The Bible is not only the book of human nature, it is also—and it is in this that its true inspiration is partly found—the book that tells of the human heart in its relation to God. This element in it remains untouched. It is a constant quantity in every page. It does not matter whether the whole drama of the Book of Job be an invented or an historical record of real conversations; whether the men who speak are characters of history or imagination—the record of the spiritual dealings of God with a heart made passionate by grief, the record of the spiritual struggle of a heart with the most awful problem of the universe, is equally instructive on either supposition. The struggle was a real one in the heart of him who wrote the book; the doings of God with him were real.

Our Bible stories have, then, a double interest—one purely human, the other (which makes them religious) Divine and human—one the doings of man, the other the doings of man and God together.

The story of Hagar is the subject of this lecture, and it illustrates both these aspects of the Bible.

She was a bondwoman: a bondwoman, and yet the intimate care of God. That is the first revealed truth, and it is a revealed truth because it was not a truth that had then grown up in the uneducated human heart. To forbid slavery then would have been too much for the untrained conscience of the world. What could be wisely done was done. A tale like this was enshrined in the sacred books. In an age when the slave was despised, all the Hebrews were made to know that the fate of a bondwoman was the special interest of God. No master, no slave could hear without many working thoughts that a slave was the mother of a mighty people, that she twice heard God speaking to her, that she was His personal care. It was one of those stories which are the seeds of future civilisation. It had its weight in after Jewish history. It ought to have its weight with us. There are no slaves in England, but how many employers, and foremen, and masters, and mistresses say to themselves, " Those who serve us for hire are equal to us in God's sight. He takes care of them. To them He speaks; for them He watches as faithfully, as certainly as He does for us." Were we always so to speak and so to think, there would not be so much to change in the relation of master to servant, and of servant to master, of capitalist to workman, and of workman to capitalist.

Again, she was an Egyptian, not one of the chosen people; and yet the care of God. It marks the principle that though the Bible chooses the Hebrews for special treatment, because they were to give a religion to the world, that choice does not exclude, but asserts, God's care of other nations. Where there is election there is not exclusion. The choice of the Jews represents the truth that what God was doing for them he was also doing for Persia, and Greece, and Rome, and is doing for Europe and England. It was a representative, not an exclusive choice.

What are we told here in this first book of the Bible? Only that Abraham was to be the father of the Jews according to the will of God? No; we hear also that it was by His will, and by His direction, that the Arab people grew. " I will make," God says, " of Ishmael a great nation." It is no light thing for us to know that God is at the root of all nations, of the order of their migrations, movements, settlements, and progress; and it is one of those revealed truths which mark the true inspiration of the Bible.

What has it to do with us? Why, everything. If it be true, then, when the first English bands landed on our shores, it was God who came with them to found the great English nation, and we may believe that He has never ceased to be with us as much as He was with the Jews. We have had our psalmists, and prophets, and poets, and great

men inspired by Him to do their national work. We are not only, as persons, sons of God, we are sons of God as citizens of the nation He has made.

It is the truest patriot note to strike, for it enhances all the others. It does us good to look back to our wild origin, more than 1,200 years ago, and to think that the Creator of nations led our forbears forth, and saw hidden in them the noble literature ; the firm, fixed freedom, the inspiring and resolute national character, which has done so much for the world; the vast colonising and governing enterprise that has replenished the East and the West and the tracts of the under world with English-speaking peoples. When God made England He made not only a nation, but a mother of nations. Yes, it is a high and religious thought to have, that all we have been and are was contained in His idea who chose us for this work. For then a Divine conception knits our history together, a soul and a conscience is given to it, and all our national work past and present becomes religious. Nor is the past only religious, but also the future. We look forward, having the glorious aim, collectively as a people, individually as citizens, of comprehending and fulfilling the idea that God gave to the English people to work out for the use, and progress, and pleasure of mankind. As long as we are true to that, we shall never perish ; as long as we cling fast to the great English ideas (and they lie before us in all our history, and are Divine in evidence), and sacrifice for them selfish glory, and selfish ease, and the viler lust for wealth ; as long as we think more of what we are bound to do for Man than what we are bound to do for our own interests —so long will England live and be great, in her truth to Him who has made her seed as the stars of heaven, and as the sand of the sea-shore for multitude. So long, and only so long, will she live. Her fate is sealed when she is wholly false to this work. When she forgets her origin in God, and the duties it involves, she will perish, and it will be better she should perish.

It is not apart from our subject to speak of nations, for with Hagar we stand side by side with the mother of a nation. It is a fact on which history rests that character is transmitted from generation to generation; and in Hagar's character we can trace something of the character of that Arab people who have never been enslaved. The Jews to this day are Jacob; the Arabs to this day are Hagar and Ishmael.

In her met the nobleness and the evil

of the oriental nature, modified by those elements of quick intelligence and fiery temper which are found where the glowing sun of Egypt nourishes natures swiftly. We see how quickly her passionate blood, aroused by her master's preference and her mistress's anger, was provoked to storm, and we think of a hundred Arab stories. We see how quickly, when driven into the wilderness, and the victim of depression following on fierce excitement, her oriental nature gave way. When a certain point in endurance had been reached, Hagar, in a hopeless surrender to fate, cast her boy under a shrub and went apart not to see him die. An Englishwoman would have struggled on till she died to save the lad. All the fatalism of the Arab is there.

Again, above all, we trace in her the natural, wild, almost fierce love of freedom we know so well in her race. With Abraham this freedom was developed, partly by the life of wandering liberty, partly by her elevation in the household, partly by her conceiving a child. When she saw that she had conceived, her mistress was despised in her eyes. Nor is that touch of scorn apart from her national character. In a moment, in thought, she set herself free; and then, because contempt was with her freedom, the worse side of her freedom had its way, a natural but an ignoble way. Had her love of freedom been always bound up with scorn, she would never have grown into a noble freewoman. But it was not so. She learnt the lesson that makes freedom firm, the lesson of obedience; she learnt the lesson that makes freedom loving, the lesson of humility. When she had done her wrong, been punished and fled away, God touched her—she repented and returned to submit herself to ·Sarah. That was very noble of her; not many would have done it. Not many, after such an exile, after the haughty violence of a wronged mistress had spent itself in passionate words, would have had the sense or the nobleness of submission.

Mark, too, how quickly her intellect seized the meaning of God's revelation; how readily she saw that the promise of the great future of her son would enable her to bear the present; how patiently, for her son's sake, she endured the life that Sarah made her bear; how rapid was the change from pride to humbleness; how faithfully, how deeply she was touched to better things through the noble passion of motherhood—in all not far apart from that great Arab nature, whose wild liberty and wild war, and subtle intelligence and strange mingling of pride and humility, of passive obedience and scornful

rule, whose poetic imagination and poetic religion, whose passionate work and passionate love, whose passionate submission when supported by great ideas, whose power of waiting on the future and faith in the future, have wrought so mightily upon their own world and the world of Europe. We look on the fountain and prophesy the stream.

How was she educated? That is our next question. How did God deal with such a character? We connect our answer with her two flights into the desert.

The first flight was not without good reason. Hagar conceived and despised her mistress; natural anger awoke in Sarah, and Abraham could not take the girl's part against his life-companion. The wrong lay in Hagar. She presumed on God having given her that which was denied her mistress to despise misfortune. She used God's kindness as a means of unkindness, and turned her gift into a curse. It is one of our commonest and worst sins.

Had Hagar been left thus, she had been a lost woman. But God does not leave us to our wretched selves, and He met her in her sorrow. She had fled, miserable, into the wilderness, and thought herself deserted of all the world. Footsore, weary, and despairing, as she lay with a broken heart beside the desert fountain, she heard in her soul the voice of God : "Hagar, Sarai's maid, whither wilt thou go?" And she said, "I flee from the face of my mistress Sarai." And then the trial was given her. Return, submit thyself to one whom thou hast wronged. She was commanded to ask pardon for her contempt, to bend her pride, to unlearn it and her unkind heart, in a life which would be grief to her free and fiery spirit.

Yet with the stern trial was given a great comfort. A magnificent thought] was made her companion. The promise, dearer than all else to an Eastern woman, was given her, that she should bear a son whose race should be a multitude, whose name should enshrine for her the sympathy of God. "Ishmael—God shall hear." It was a double consolation which strengthened and irradiated life. When Sarah's sarcasm was bitter, when the enslaved life was hard to bear, when Hagar stood alone, apart from the upper and the lower ranks alike of the household, isolated by her position, she could repose on and take courage from these two great ideas : My son shall be the father of a numberless people—and I am listened to and loved by the God of Abraham.

Such is the way God often deals with us.

We misuse our gifts, and we are punished, not in an arbitrary way, but by reaping the harvest we have sown. We fly from our punishment, and find ourselves in the wilderness, remorse, astonishment, or anger in our hearts. We are not the better off, but the worse, for flying like Jonah from our duty. God meets us there. Have we not heard His voice, telling us to go back? Who has not heard it, as sharply as Hagar heard it? " Whither wilt thou go?" " I flee from the face of my mistress—Duty." And if we listen to God's voice, He sends us back to work out our punishment, for the only way to get rid of punishment and to turn it into education is to confess its justice and to undergo it.

Suppose we have—I take an analogous case to Hagar's—made our life at home hard by our own bad temper, and, as is common, resent the hardness of it as if it were the fault of others and not our own, and flee away from our natural punishment, which is to stay at home, into a solitary life. Shall we be better or more at ease? Certainly not. We get into a drearier wilderness than our home. Our bad temper increases in the moodiness of solitude; we have not the chance we have at home of doing loving things, and so of making our ill-nature less. Solitary ill-nature multiplies its evils, till the very springs of love are parched.

There is nothing for it in this case, as in others, but to return as God commands, and submit, and take up our life with a new impulse towards loving kindness. Let us see what charity will do towards covering our own faults and those of others, and restoring happiness to life. And then we shall have the help that Hagar had from God. We shall be, like her, conscious of a Divine presence with us, who, in loving us, will make us love others. To feel one's self loved makes it easy to love, and, more than that, very pleasant and easy to do good. It is when the air around us is full of coldness, of ill-temper, of violence, or of jars, that we feel it hard to love. But the question is, have we made that air ourselves? When we change ourselves, we change the air ; and to love and be kind is soon easy. Great ideas are then ours, as they were Hagar's, for comfort and support in a life which is certain to be difficult. We shall know then that children of our life will be given to us; that our faithfulness to love will bear its fruit in others. A multitude of acts of love will flow from our acts of love. Numbers yet unborn may bear the traces of our life, and rise and call us blessed.

For who can measure the reproductiveness of love? Its seed is like the sand of the sea-shore for multitude.

Those are some of the lessons of the first exile, which was voluntary. The second, of which I now speak, was not voluntary, but enforced.—Fifteen years had passed away, years of monotonous submission, during which Hagar's free spirit must have pined, and at last, perhaps, sunk into a growing apathy, when, on a festal day, Ishmael, inheriting his mother's scoffing spirit, mocked the heir whom Abraham had gotten from God, and the Egyptian and her boy were driven into the desert. The morning soon passed, and now the merciless brightness of the sun poured on the plain of sand and stones, dotted with dry shrubs and bitter flowers. The two wandering figures passed on weeping—and sorrow doubles weariness and thirst and pain. The water was spent in the bottle—for a mother cannot resist her child's cry—and at last the poor boy could go no further, and Hagar suddenly lost all hope; and she cast the child under one of the shrubs, and went and sat down over against him a good way off, as it were a bow-shot, for she said, " Let me not see the death of the child ; and she lift up her voice and wept."

Then we are told that God spoke to Hagar. " And the angel of God called to Hagar out of heaven, and said unto her, What aileth thee, Hagar? Fear not, for God hath heard the voice of the lad where he is. Arise, lift up the lad and hold him in thine hand ; for I will make of him a great nation. And God opened her eyes, and she saw a well of water. And God was with the lad, and he grew and dwelt in the wilderness, and became an archer." So God proved Himself to be the Ever Near.

That was Hagar's last recorded trial, the last lesson in her education.

It seems a cruel experience. One would say, at first, that God had been hard upon her ; but not so, if we look deeper. As in the case of many sorrows, bitter in the present, the end of which we cannot see, but which years after become blessings, so here we see how thoughtful and delicate was God's care of Hagar. Had she remained with Sarah now exultant in her son, her life, if she kept to the end her wild-heartedness, would have been miserable, and her son's life a baffled career. Fancy Hagar a slave to the end ! It could not be ; God removed her, and made her the free-woman of the desert. Or, perhaps, from long submission of her free character against her nature, she might have become apathetic, have sunk down into the nurse of the family. Oh, what a pity it is when the eager heart dies down, and the interests, once the interests of a winged youth, are set into the mould of a few daily commonplaces! What joy was Hagar's when she was saved from that cruel fate! Can we imagine that she regretted the enslaved drudgery of the encampment—did not feel one day of the desert liberty better than ten years of the tent of Abraham!

Yes; even we can see that God did well for her. And observe, how He no longer said, "Return, submit." Hagar had learnt that lesson; her character, now strengthened, was fit to do its work and train her son. And now she had her boy to keep her company. "Arise, hold the lad in thine hand, for I will make of him a great nation." God renewed the promise that was like living courage in her heart, and bound Himself up in her soul with all the love of motherhood. Wherever now she looked she saw God, whatever she did she felt Him with her, the All-seeing to rebuke, the Ever Near to comfort; the God of her freedom, the God of her child, the God of her past, her present, and her future; the God who loved her for her motherhood. And with that Divine presence felt all around her, and in the fresh liberty in which she renewed her youth, the oriental heart was at last at peace. And before long, with peace, charity crept in. The interests of the families no longer clashed, and they were reconciled. Ishmael and Isaac often met, and both stood together over their father's grave. The education of Hagar was fulfilled.

How the whole story comes home to us! After our first trial, our first tempest in life, we have often years of quiet monotony. At last, when we are in danger of becoming undeveloped, when our peace threatens to be the peace of an apathetic life, a swift break occurs. Something happens—trial, bereavement, a rush of joy or passion—and in a moment we are loosed from our anchorage, swept out to sea, and in the midst of a raging tempest. Wonder-stricken, in wild pain, unfit, we think, to bear the storm, we half despair like Hagar. Bitter is our cry. The last hope, the last aspiration, the last joy we cling to and have taken with us, we cast away, as Hagar did Ishmael, and make ourselves ready, in our despair, to die.

Then, if we listen, we shall hear God speaking to us, and telling us He is the Ever Near; as near us, and nearer, in this our new and wild experience, than in the lost life of pleasure or self-indulgence, or in the apathetic peace in which we were growing stagnant. Better this, He says, than that brain and heart and spirit should be enslaved to the world, or rust for want of use; better this wild and desert sea in which you are awake, than the slumber of the soul; better this hunger and thirst and difficulty than a life in which you cannot grow to know either yourself or me, in which you forget that your home is not on earth, but in a vaster world.

Therefore, instead of despair, He bids us rise and exert the strength of God within us. "Take up," He speaks in our heart, "the abandoned hopes of life again. Resume the battle with new power, which a few weeks of energy will win out of your trial. Out of that very difficulty that casts you down will come your strength. Arise, I am with you, and will make of your changed life a multitude of interests. Open your eyes, and beside you is a well of water. Drink in it a new life. The new duties and the new things will make your years once more full of fresh interest." It is true it cannot be the old freshness of youth, but it will be to breathe a freer and keener air than we did in our sleepy quietude. And, so awakened, we are not left comfortless. Two mighty thoughts are with us. First, we know, more intensely than before, that God is with us, our very inmost friend, the abiding presence of our heart. With that faith, after a time, our happiness becomes secure; we look forward with almost a youthful hope; peace enters in, love to all is born in us, and soothes and comforts life by its exercise. And, secondly, we have a great future and great hopes in it. We pass on to the better land, like Hagar, feeling that our life, lived in God, will become the parent of thoughts that will endure and become a great multitude in others; of acts which will reproduce themselves in a harvest of love and blessing to our family, our friends, perhaps to Man. Our education is completed.

STOPFORD A. BROOKE.

"Visions of lingering over book-stalls."

SARAH DE BERENGER.

By JEAN INGELOW.

CHAPTER XV.

FELIX, intending to take new inmates, and finding that it was just a year since he had received the last, went over his accounts during the hours that Amias spent with Sir Samuel, and found, to his pleasure, that, having paid all his bills, he was actually the possessor of twenty pounds.

When, therefore, Amias emerged from the wood without having been able to capture the wisp of flying flue, the brothers, while they sauntered home, compared notes, and felt as if their worst days of restriction and poverty were over. Amias could get his watch out of pawn, and have new clothes. Felix could come up and spend a parson's week in London, find out how Amias was really lodged, and how he fared; also could enjoy himself after the peculiar fashion of zealous and painstaking young clergymen. "Always supposing that he keeps the money," thought Felix. "He is so full of scruples already that I shall suggest no fresh ones to his conscience; but if he doesn't see his inconsistency here very soon, I am much mistaken."

Amias exulted as he walked; and visions of lingering over book-stalls, and picking up old divinity very cheap, of attending many services, going to hear all manner of sermons, XXI—28

and sitting for hours and hours at religious meetings, flitted through the brain of Felix. What a pleasure it is to think that somebody here and there enjoys such meetings, and gets hints from them!

The brothers separated for the night in good spirits, and the next day Felix spent some hours in digging, while Amias, with a spud in his hand, sauntered about, enjoyed the country air, and chopped at *dent-de-lions* and thistle-roots in the slightly disordered lawn.

Felix did most of the digging and raking, the real hard work that had to be done in the garden. He was extremely fond of that kind of exercise, but he would not weed or attend to the flowers; there he drew the line. He had one very large plot a good way from the house, containing about two rods of ground, in which he seldom planted anything, and which he, notwithstanding, dug over at least once a month. Sometimes, lost in thought, he would pause and pensively hang over the spade; then, with a certain fervour of industry, he would dig on with perfect enthusiasm, and slap the squares of mould, as he threw each into its place, as if he lived by this work and his master was looking at him. This was, in fact, his out-of-door study. Over this plot he mainly composed his sermons.

"You're filling my house," he said to his aunt, when she came to him on Tuesday afternoon, just as he left off digging—came to take leave, for, of course, she *did* go on Tuesday.

Amias, who had brought out a chair, was now sitting close at hand, looking somewhat moody, and at his leisure mending an old cherry-net.

"Yes, it's all settled," answered Sarah, who continued to feel a good deal surprised at the success of her plan. "And I've left an excellent long piece of strong cord behind. I brought it for the pony, to tether him with."

Felix looked surprised.

"Because," continued Sarah, "I have no doubt now that you will get most of the washing done at home; and it will be useful as a clothes-line. The drying-ground is cropped short, and all ready."

"Oh," said Felix. His ideas on the subject of a family wash were exceedingly hazy.

"Mrs. Snaith is a capital ironer. She likes nothing better than ironing, and has told me so," continued Sarah.

"Oh," said Felix again; and his aunt, observing a certain absence of mind, in fact a kind of helplessness about his air in the face of these household matters, suddenly heaved up such a deep sigh as recalled him to himself, and he cast on her a glance of surprise.

She sighed again. "For indeed, under the present sad circumstances—sad indeed! —every yard of cord, and everything else, may well be said to matter."

"Sad circumstances?" said Felix, a little surprised.

Amias smiled furtively.

"Sad indeed! Amias so lost to everything!"

Felix began to dig softly.

"And as for you, Felix, I never would have believed, if I hadn't seen it, that you don't seem to care. I feel as if I had never known till now what you really were."

"There are many people in the world," answered Felix, rather dreamily, "who don't know what they really are till circumstances show them."

All this time Amias netted on, and neither of them took any notice of him.

"And a very good thing too," she exclaimed, "for some of us. If the pepper-castor could know what it really was, it would always be sneezing its top off."

"Some of us!" repeated Felix, gravely pleased with this illustration, which seemed to claim humanity for the pepper-castor.

"I only wish Amias had never found himself out," she persisted, "but had continued to think he was something quite different—and to act accordingly," she went on, after a pause, during which Amias preserved a discreet silence.

"I consider," observed Felix, "that every man has a right to his own conscience, and the more so as you cannot take it from him."

"Felix! Yes, I know your parishioners, some of them, believe the most extraordinary things."

"And I let them alone. One believes that Christian people ought not to eat pork, thinks the Mosaic law perfect wisdom for all men on sanitary matters, says almost all foul disease comes of our eating pork. I thought a great deal of her conscience till I found she fattened pigs for the eating of other people."

"Is that the woman who married an old man, and after she had escorted him to the grave took a mere boy?"

"Even so."

"Well, Felix, I wish you were as tolerant to the poor publicans as to your parishioners. What right have you to interfere with the liberty of the subject?"

"Not the least. Have I any to interfere with the slavery of the subject?"

"That is merely a play of words, Felix— not worthy of you as a clergyman and a man of sense. Why should not the publican stand on his rights like other people?"

"Whether he stands on them or not," said Felix, laughing, "there is no doubt in my mind that the present generation will sit upon them!"

"There! you meant that for a joke. Yes! the notions of Amias are actually infecting you."

"What are his notions?"

"He is extremely one-sided," replied Sarah; "everybody must allow that. While he is considering how to reform the drunkards he quite forgets what is to become of the publicans. Thousands of them as there are —thousands and thousands."

"They are much to be pitied. But still, if it is the will of Providence, they will have eventually to go to the wall."

"Providence," said Sarah, not irreverently, "must be allowed to do as it pleases. But I do not and cannot see how you find out what that pleasure is till it is made manifest. I cannot see what right you have to run on in your own thoughts, and be so sure what Providence is going to do, and so eager to help before the event. Yes! I call that patronising Providence."

"You are vexed, my dear aunt, that Amias should have, as you consider, thrown away his prospects again. That is what this means, is it not?" said Felix.

"And you are not vexed?"

"Well, no," said Felix dispassionately. "Amias must, as the saying is, 'have the courage of his opinions.' I did not put them first into his head—it is inconvenient to me that he should hold them so strongly—but I should heartily despise him if he threw them over to serve his own interests. And, after all, I suppose that even you have no doubt that two-thirds of all the misery and three-fourths of all the crime in the country really and truly and persistently do come of strong drink, and from nothing else."

"Oh, very well," exclaimed Sarah, in a high, plaintive tone: "pray fly out against your own family, if you like. Just as if the politicians did not frequently say that the country could not pay its way but for the duties on what you unkindly call strong drink!"

"Strong drink is not the only thing the country has to answer for. I hope to see the day when we shall take the making of opium, and the traffic in it, and especially the monopoly of it, to heart;" and thereupon he turned up the edge of the spade to his somewhat short-sighted eyes, and, as if he wished to shirk further discussion, remarked that it was rather blunt, and began to dig again.

Sarah heaved up another deep sigh and shook her head, but neither of her nephews said anything; so, after a few moments, she exclaimed, with a somewhat theatrical start, "Well, I do not know, Felix, how much longer I am expected to look on while you dig. How many of these useless rods are there?"

"Three," said Amias, "including the one in pickle that you brought with you, aunt."

It did not suit Sarah to take direct notice of this speech; but Amias had lost his advantage of silence, and was made welcome to a good deal of advice, and to many comments on his conduct. "And so kind as my dear uncle has been to you, Amias!" she continued. "I know all about it. Yes."

"It does seem a shame, doesn't it?" answered Amias; "but it cannot be helped—I wish it could," he added hastily. Then, when Felix looked at him with surprise, and Sarah with pleasure, he paused in his netting, and said with deliberation, "No, I don't; that was a lie—at least, I forgot myself. Well, good-bye, Aunt Sarah; you'd better

forgive me, for I shall never be any different."

Sarah took leave of him, and soon after this departed, Felix driving her home, and a chorus of laughter in the kitchen breaking out as her wheels left the yard, she having just explained the use that was to be made of an old hen-coop, which was to be turned upside down, she said, and play the part of a clothes-basket, the only one belonging to the establishment being still up a tree.

Felix had not gone forth to meet the temperance question, he had only accepted it when it came to seek him. He found it in his study when he came home.

Amias was there, so was Sir Samuel de Berenger, and they both looked so extremely serious that he was quite startled. "What is the matter now?" he exclaimed.

Sir Samuel looked a little flustered, but not in the least angry. When he spoke, his whole manner was decidedly conciliatory.

"The fact is, this young gentleman met me in the road, said he had something to tell me—asked me in here—and now he has nothing to say."

Amias laughed, but he looked very much ashamed of himself. "I am such a fool!" he exclaimed; and he certainly looked very foolish. "I am such a fool—nobody would believe it. I can hardly believe it myself."

"Sit down," said Felix; "we both know what you mean. Out with it."

Amias sat down and said humbly, "I beg your pardon, uncle."

Instead of asking what for, the old man continued to look pleasant. "Nonsense!" he said. "Say no more, and think better of it."

"I hope you'll forgive me, and try to forget this," said Amias, reddening, at the same time pushing a crumpled piece of paper towards Sir Samuel without looking at him.

The old man took it up. It had cost him a an to give that cheque, and now here it was in his hands again. His first thought was one by which he often cajoled himself. "How extraordinarily difficult it is to do anything for this family!" His next thought corrected this. It was not worth while to keep it; it would make his conscience so uneasy. The more he did for Amias, the less weight, he instinctively felt, these temperance notions of his would have over him. Besides, Amias was a great favourite. He would give him another chance.

"You see," said Amias, as if excusing himself, "I have no right to cry out against—against anything, and then show myself ready to accept a benefit from it. It seems almost as mean as taking a bribe. No, I did not mean that; but I'm so blunder-headed I don't know what I say. I'm sure you meant nothing of the kind, uncle."

Sir Samuel at that moment knew that he had meant it, and that he would willingly offer one far heavier if by its means he could get rid of these scruples on the part of Amias; who, seeing the old man still looking kindly at him, went on, "I certainly did want that money, but I'm not half as badly off as you think. I've got an old necklace that Felix thinks I can sell when I go back to London, so that I hope I shall get on—and not be any expense to you, Felix."

"An old necklace!" exclaimed the baronet, as if he failed to understand the value of such property.

Felix explained that his mother had left several articles of jewelry in her dressing-case, that he had had them valued, and divided into three shares, one of which was for Amias.

"Sentiment would lead a man to keep his mother's ornaments," continued Felix, "but the poor cannot afford to indulge sentiment. Amias must sell his share. He never saw our mother wear this necklace."

"What is it worth?" asked Sir Samuel.

"My father bought it in India, and my Aunt Sarah says she remembers hearing him say that it cost forty pounds."

"Then it is fully worth that now in this country, old jewelry being so fashionable," thought Sir Samuel. "Does it matter who buys it?" he inquired.

"No," answered Amias, in a dispirited tone, and without deriving any hope of a customer from this speech.

"Well," said Sir Samuel, with real kindness of manner, and still trifling with the cheque, "I'll buy the necklace. I will give the forty pounds."

Amias sprang up. "Uncle, you don't mean it!"

"Yes, I do. It's partly out of regard to Felix, who is likely to have enough on his hands with you and your scruples, and partly because, you young dog, your astonishing impudence amuses me. Nothing that breathes ever insulted me as you have done!" Here he laughed. "But you have the grace to be heartily ashamed of yourself, and somehow you make me feel that you cannot help it. There, fetch the beads." Amias left the room.

"I suppose *this* transaction will stand?" he continued, addressing Felix, still looking more amused than irate.

"I suppose so," was all Felix answered.

Amias presently returned with a small red leathern case, which he gravely opened, and displayed before the customer a faded white satin lining, on which was lying a delicate necklace of gold filigree work, with a few emeralds sparkling in its centre.

Then Sir Samuel drew forth his purse and pushed back the cheque to Amias, together with a sovereign and ten shillings.

"Give me a receipt," he said, for his habitual caution did not leave him; and he felt when he took it that he had done a noble action, for he certainly did not want the necklace. Also he felt as if he had got it for one pound ten, for even if it had not been mentioned, he must have found some way of benefiting that family, at least to the extent of his original gift.

A glad satisfaction swelled his heart as he put the case in his pocket; and as for Amias, he felt that, his whole fortune being in his hand, he should certainly be no expense to Felix for the next two years, for he could well live on it, together with his small salary.

When Sir Samuel was gone, Amias looked furtively at his brother. How would he take the matter? What would he say now they were alone? As Felix took no notice of him, but continued for some time to mend the stumps of some remarkably bad old quill pens, Amias at last said, in rather a humble tone, "You'd better take care of this, hadn't you, Felix?" He put the cheque before him, continuing, "The one pound ten will get my watch out of pawn, and you might want to use some of this."

Felix put his hand in his pocket for his keys. "I shall want nothing of the kind," he answered. "But, just after a fire, I don't much like taking care of valuable bits of paper. Suppose we should have another? This must be changed into gold as soon as may be." He unlocked a drawer in his table and laughed. "Still, if it got burnt, I suppose the old boy would, if the thing was fully proved, give you another or return the necklace."

Amias was greatly relieved at hearing him laugh; he longed to subside into ordinary talk without any discussion about his having renounced the present. But he altered his mind when Felix went on. "It's my belief that Uncle Sam is actually developing a conscience. It is very young and feeble at present, and if you had kept that money much longer, you might thereby have almost snuffed out its young life."

"And yet you said nothing to me."

"I thought nothing just at first."

"And when you did?"

"I do not always think that logic is to be used to force on a waiting soul."

"Then you do not think it would have been wrong in me to keep the money."

"No; but it would have been mean—that is, if he did offer it as a species of bribe—and it would have been ridiculous, because it would have been so inconsistent."

"But now, Felix, if we had originally received our proper share of our grandfather's money? Of course we should have lived on it."

"No doubt we should."

"Would there have been any harm in that?"

"You had better say, would there have been or would there now be any good, if you had it, and your flinging your share of it away?"

"Yes, that's what I mean."

"But where would you fling it to? Not to beggars, I hope—beggars, in any sense; for I for one believe that is to do infinitely more harm than good."

"Almshouses—workhouses?"

"Almshouses, and even workhouses, are full of old people whose own children are guilty before God, and are losing all sense of those feelings that raise families and hold them together, because they leave them there. Every right and natural responsibility of which you relieve a man, taking it on yourself, makes him less able to bear those responsibilities that nothing can relieve him of. If you could take all his duties from him, as we sometimes do, it would only make it certain that he would not then even do his duty by himself."

"I often puzzle over this kind of thing, Felix. If nobody is to inherit or use any money or anything that has not been earned with perfect honesty, and also by some noble trade or honourable means that does good and no harm, how are any of us to have anything—anything, I mean, but what we earn ourselves?"

"And yet," observed Felix, in his most dispassionate tone, "if, after a man's death, his relations were to sit in judgment on him, and were to bring out and make a great heap of all the things they thought he had not earned with perfect honesty, and were to allow the unscrupulous to have a free fight over them, each appropriating what he could for his own benefit, would that make the world any better than it is?"

Amias laughed. "And then there is the land," he observed.

"Quite true. How little land was ever originally appropriated with anything like honesty! Often first got by violence, often long kept by violence, or extortion—Church land just the same as others."

"We are a bad lot."

"You have just discovered it?"

"No, I was always peaceably aware of it. But what is the good of that? Why am I obliged to be constantly thinking of such things? Everything in my lot turns them up for my consideration. I must think on them; and yet I know quite well that, even if I could do away with a wrong, it would not make a right."

Felix, who was still mending his pens, smiled with good-humoured sarcasm, and, beginning to answer in a tone of banter, got more grave as he went on. "My dear young friend, I hope you don't think that the harbouring of such thoughts shows anything original in the cast of your mind. I went through the same experiences at your age. That expression, 'He cannot call his soul his own,' has deep meaning in it, that the first utterer never knew of. Whence the soul is derived we have been informed, and some of us believe it; but many of us, to the last, decline to believe in any influence over it from its Source, other than what we are pleased to call a *religious* influence; and yet, comparing the soul to an inland sea, imprisoned as it were within us, we must allow that it often flings up on its strand, for our senses and observation to exercise themselves on, things out of its depths that we never knew to be there. You cannot call your soul your own; but on the whole, it pleases me greatly to find that you are getting over the wish to do so—more satisfied to give way to these 'inconvenient thoughts,' which, if they were of a more solemn nature, and made you feel unhappy, you would more easily acknowledge for what they are."

"There's nothing in my being satisfied *now*."

"What do you mean?"

"Why, I've got forty pounds by honest trade, and I not only feel now that I shall not be a burden to you, but I find that you by no means blame me. Why," continued Amias, with boyish self-scorn, "I hope you don't think I would be such a prig as to whine about the giving up of my *own* prospects. I wouldn't have our fellows know how much I cared the other night even about your supposed annoyance—no, not for the whole price of that necklace. But, I say, Felix——"

"Well?"

"When you come up to London, you shall hear something that you don't expect."

"Not a temperance lecture from you, I hope!" exclaimed Felix, suddenly suspicious.

"Why not?"

"Because you are much too young."

"Well, I've promised our fellows."

"What have they to do with it?"

"You need not look so vexed. I tell you it will be a real one—perfectly solemn, and all that. Why, they have subscribed to give a tea to the people. We shall issue 1d. tickets for it. It will be the best lark I ever had. No; I mean no harm. It will be a capital lecture, though I say so. Several of our fellows helped me to get it up. And we expect you to take the chair."

"Do you mean to tell me that you are all taking this up out of real desire to do good, and in serious approval of the temperance cause?"

"No, Felix, I don't. We're going to give a tea-drinking at the beginning—there's no harm in that; then a temperance lecture in the middle—short and strong; and then we shall wind up with a few transparencies and a couple of songs. The tea will be just as good for the poor old women as if we were all in earnest, instead of only one of us."

"Why, you have just this moment told me that you should consider it a great lark!" exclaimed Felix.

"Well, so I shall; but do you mean to tell me, just after talking in the serious way you have, that when I am doing a thing I earnestly wish to do, because I fully believe it will produce good, and when I am willing to give up all sorts of things for its sake, I am not to see, or even to suspect, what fun it will be to us as well? You need not be at all afraid, Felix—we are going to have it in Baby Tanner's parish. Mrs. Tanner approves, so I leave you to judge whether it will be right and serious enough."

Mrs. Tanner was the Miss Thimbleby who had married imprudently, and frightened Mrs. Snaith by her severe remarks. Becoming tired of the bucolic poor, she had caused her husband to take a miserable perpetual curacy in one of the worst parts of London, and they were both struggling with their duties there in the most heroic fashion.

CHAPTER XVI.

Amias, after his short holiday, accompanied Felix to London, and the temperance tea-drinking duly came off.

Finding that the reverend gentleman who has been called Baby Tanner looked forward to it in all good faith as something likely to elevate his people, and that he expected his old friend to take the chair, Felix agreed to do so—admired the simple industry of the good man, and the painstaking efforts of his ponderous wife to get the place into order.

"Everything is left to us," she explained. "None of the fashionable people run after Carlos."

"No wonder," thought Felix, when he saw this rosy-faced, single-minded saint trotting about after his school-children.

"But," the wife continued, "it is because we are so far from the fashionable localities that I never get any ladies to come and help us."

Mrs. Tanner knew very well that the youths who were going to entertain her poor women expected to entertain themselves as well, but it was very difficult to fill her mother's meetings and get the women to church, or the children to school, if she never had any kind of treat to give them. All the tickets were to be in her hands, and she had the buying of the bread and the butter, and the ordering of the cakes and the tea; so she took care that there should be plenty of these commodities, and gladly agreed that the schoolrooms should be at the service of the "committee" for this great occasion.

She had been governess to the head of the committee in his childhood, and Amias she had known slightly all his life; so she hoped they might be trusted—particularly "Lord Bob," who, as Felix was told by one of the committee when he inquired, was "a son of the Duke of Thingumy."

"And here he is with the bag," cried the youth, dashing down-stairs on the eventful evening, while Felix with Amias and three of the committee were enjoying a "meat tea" in the little lodgings.

"Where's the prisoner?" exclaimed a tall, dark youth, rushing in and holding up a large camlet bag.

"He's all right," cried the second committee man.

"Not funking in the least," said the third.

"He'd better not. Escape is now impossible."

"Come on," quoth Lord Bob, seizing Amias; and the two disappeared into the small chamber beyond. There were no less than twelve committee men. This move enabled some to enter who had been standing on the tiny landing. The room was now absolutely full, but shouts of laughter being heard issuing from the chamber, the youths soon pulled its door open, and a man was seen within — rather an elderly man, with rough grey hair and a fine white beard. He was then in course of being arrayed in a black coat, which sat loosely, for it was a good deal too big. Lord Bob was buttoning it for him up to the throat. His linen collar was large and limp, and he had on a pair of loose black kid gloves. Shrieks of laughter greeted his appearance. Felix did not recognise him till he made a step or two forward.

"Amias!" he then exclaimed angrily; but his voice was drowned in acclamation.

"What a jolly go!"

"He looks fifty!"

"Nobody could possibly know him!"

"Doesn't he look *respectable*?"

"My friends," said Amias, gazing mildly round and wiping a large pair of spectacles on a white handkerchief—"my friends, this riot and these peals of laughter are unseemly. Yes, Felix, it's no use your looking furious; you don't suppose my lecture would be listened to if I only looked nineteen? My friends, let us go forward."

Twelve against one, and that one silent from displeasure, was too great odds. Felix mechanically allowed himself to "go forward;" that is, he was among the youths as they thundered down the narrow staircase. The landlady, who was holding the door open, curtsied to Amias, not recognising him. Felix, almost without his own choice, found himself in a spare omnibus, which had been hired for the occasion. He put off deciding what to do till he reached his destination. The driver and the conductor, both devoted teetotalers, had been exhorted by Lord Bob to attend the meeting, for the room was expected to be very empty. These zealous individuals promised so to do, and the youths, swarming outside and inside, caused them deep edification by lustily singing temperance songs. One gave such especial pleasure that they respectfully begged the young gentleman to repeat it. It began, "No, we are not ashamed of the cause—oh, we are not ashamed of the cause!"

Amias, a little daunted by the gravity and displeasure of Felix, tried to check them; but he could not say much, for he had taught them that song himself, having heard it sung by some excellent and single-minded folks, who pronounced it, "We *air* not ashamed," and having imitated that, as well as the peculiar burr sometimes imparted to

their vocal exercises by the uneducated. The committee, of course, gave the song as they had learned it; and Felix had just decided how to act so as best, when he was called to the chair, to overpower the ridiculous element which at present was uppermost, when the vehicle stopped in a shabby street opposite the parish schools.

Remarkable fact!—a good many men, whose hands were not too clean, welcomed the committee with especial cheerfulness, almost with hilarity. Some insisted on shaking hands with them.

"We had a thought of taking the hosses out and dragging yer in," said one gentleman. Others declared their intention of attending the meeting, "so soon as the ladies had finished their tea."

No fewer than two public-houses and a small gin-palace were visible, and placards of the intended meeting were ostentatiously posted up all over them.

Felix, being the last to descend, noted these circumstances, and had a short conversation apart with the driver and conductor, both of whom assured him that they were wide awake, and promised to act on his directions.

He then entered the large boys' schoolroom. "Remarkable fact!" exclaimed the Rev. Carlos Tanner. "It shows how deeply the minds of the masses are stirred on this great subject. Why, the very publicans, to please them, are advertising our meeting!" His eyes then fell on Amias, and Lord Bob had the impudence, without mentioning his name, to introduce him with much apparent respect as an eminent friend to the "cause."

All the committee then hastened up-stairs to the girls' schoolroom, where one hundred poor women, all looking meek, most of them pale, and many old, were waiting for their tea.

The committee, having piled up their hats in a corner, fell at once, and without a struggle, under the dominion of Mrs. Tanner. The noisiest spirits became calm; the number of babies materially helped to daunt them. Mrs. Tanner called one and another to cut up cakes; others had to tilt the great kettles, and carry round the teapots; some handed sugar, others put in milk. Pity and respect awoke in their young minds; they all behaved like gentlemen, and took real delight in seeing the enjoyment of the guests over the steaming tea and excellent viands.

Work was found for all, excepting Lord Bob and Amias, each of whom fell under the eye of Mrs. Tanner, and knew that she knew all about it. She detected Amias at once under his disguise; she knew that Lord Bob had done it. These two young gentlemen were therefore fain to sneak away from her "severe regard" of control, and press their services on such of the ladies as sat in corners, or had been quickest in dispatch of victuals.

The guests had just arrived at that point when, to their regret, they were obliged to leave off eating and drinking from sheer repletion; and the committee, having divided the considerable quantity of food that was left into portions, were helping the ladies to wrap them up in handkerchiefs, or get them into their pockets, when Felix came up, and had no sooner said grace, by Mrs. Tanner's desire, than Mr. Tanner followed, with a beaming countenance.

"My dear, the room below is so full—so absolutely full! Not one seat vacant, and people outside. It passes my utmost hope. In fact, we must have a second meeting for you, my friends, up here."

"Yes," said Felix, to the surprise of Mrs.

"Amias began to speak."

Tanner, suddenly taking on himself to order matters. "It would be a good plan if I went down with you, Tanner, and the *lecturer*: and the committee was left up here to sing the temperance songs, and afterwards show the transparencies."

The members of the committee were nothing loth, excepting Lord Bob, who, prescient of some fun or mischief, declared that he ought to go down with the lecturer. The others, who had expected to sit through the lecture and have nothing to do till it was over, were naturally not averse from a plan which enabled them to begin at once, and the poor women, very warm and comfortable by this time, were right glad to stay where they were.

Mr. Tanner led the way to the boy's schoolroom. He entered first, then Felix. It was packed full. A low laugh of ecstasy broke out here and there, and was gone like summer lightning, while a voice cried out in tones of delight, "Here comes vicar, and here comes the temperance man. My! don't he look as if he never got a drop of anything comfortable!" This compliment was intended for Felix, whose face, naturally dark and thin, was never embellished by ruddy hues, and now looked especially grave.

The crowd was so hilarious that both the reverend gentlemen felt the impossibility of opening such a meeting with prayer.

Felix wondered whether Amias would have nerve enough to address an assembly so manifestly enjoying some secret joke. But he need not have troubled himself; nothing was further from their minds than to let the lecturer be heard at all.

Felix was, however, successfully called to the chair; but he had no sooner introduced the lecturer than a deafening round of applause broke out, and was not appeased till four policemen stood up in different parts of the room, and, without regarding any individuals in the seated crowd, appeared to be looking with interest at the doors and the tallow candles in the chandeliers.

The five or six people who had actually come to the meeting from some misguided notion that they should improve their knowledge, or inflame their zeal by means of it, must have found such outrageous enthusiasm very inconvenient.

Amias began to speak, but at the end of his first sentence the cheers broke out again, so that he seemed to be acting in dumb show. Not a word was heard beyond the platform. Dust rose and caused a good deal of coughing, and presently there was cuffing and struggling in one corner, during which half the meeting turned round. Rough voices encouraged, some one, some the other combatant, but they were soon hauled asunder by two policemen, and successfully marched out at two different doors.

"Go on!" shouted Felix to Amias.

A good many men and lads followed the combatants; the doors banged incessantly, and two more policemen came in, which seemed to cause a slight lull, so that a sentence was distinctly audible.

Amias had, of course, learned his lecture by heart, and now delivered himself of this most inappropriate sentence—

"For I have a right to suppose, my friends, from your attendance here, and your attention on this occasion, that your feelings are in harmony with that great cause which I have the honour——"

"Harmony!" shrieked a voice, far louder than his. "Bless you, sir, there never was anything like the harmony as pervades this assembly."

"Give the gentleman a hearing," cried a real sympathizer, very much put out.

"Give him three cheers," shouted another.

Amias was obliged to go on. It was trying work, for several men, in a high state of good-humour, had mounted on the benches to propose resolutions; others kept pulling them down again.

"We air not obligated to hear the gentleman," cried one.

"Not by no means," shouted a policeman; "you air only obligated to keep the peace." This was said while a drunken man was being assisted to make his exit.

"It's a plot," shouted Mr. Tanner to Felix, hardly making himself heard amid the cheering and scraping of feet.

"Of course," shouted Felix in reply. "They've been treated by the publicans. Can't you see that many are half tipsy?"

"Then what are we to do-o?" shouted Mr. Tanner.

"Let them alone," shouted Felix, "till they're tired of it. Go on," he continued to Amias. "If you stop, and we try to retreat, there'll be a riot."

Amias never forgot the next half-hour as long as he lived — the dust, the sudden draughts of air, the banging doors, the guttering candles, the stand-up fights with fisticuffs that came off now and then in corners, and occasionally the sound of his own voice when there was a lull. Now and then came words of encouragement from Felix, together with a charge to go on; and he did so, half mechanically, not feeling any nervousness about his lecture. Why should he, when so little of it was heard? At last he could not but notice that the room was less crowded. The dust being thick, there was more coughing and less cheering, and the spirits of the audience seemed to flag. Not being interfered with in any way worth mentioning, they began to think they had had enough of their joke. Portions of the floor became visible; there was even more noise now in the street than in the room. Amias having involuntarily stopped to cough, one of the audience chose to suppose that the meeting was over, and, jumping on a form, proposed a vote of thanks to the chair.

"Wind up now," said Felix, and he made his bow.

The vote was responded to by a considerable show of hands.

"Those," continued the proposer, "whose opinion is contrary to him, hold up theirs."

About an equal show for this side of the question.

"This meeting thanks the chairman, and likewise the lecturer," proceeded the orator, "and they air respectfully invited never to come here any more."

The police were slowly moving from the centre of the room towards the doors, and now that it was half empty it became manifest that nobody liked to be last; there was a sudden rush, during which a respectable-looking man, who had been standing with

his back to one of them, enjoying the scene, got knocked down and hurt; but they soon had him up again; and just as the last of the audience disappeared, and the doors were bolted behind them, the first of the committee came down-stairs and appeared at the back of the platform.

It would be a waste of time to attempt to describe how sulky the committee were when they found what a "row" there had been, and they not in it. The resources of the English language cannot convey the darting flashes of eleven pairs of eyes, set in the brows of eleven youths between the ages of seventeen and twenty-one, which, with natural indignation, they hurled at the back of Felix, as he stood in the front talking to the policemen.

"Well, I hope you're satisfied, gentlemen, with this temperance work of yours," observed the most important of the two policemen still present, while he wiped his hot forehead.

"You see, sir, you're new to the work," remarked the other, accosting Mr. Tanner; "but this elderly gentleman," pointing to Amias, "he did ought to have known better."

The light was none of the best. The policemen went on, first one, then the other.

"There's two cases for the lock-up, and a broken arm. You saw that respectable man knocked down? I expect you'll have to go before the magistrates and give your evidence."

"I dessay you don't expect to go triumphing home atop of that vehicle of yourn?"

The committee looked as if they did.

"It's now a-waiting for you outside. I consider you'd better not be drawed out of the neighbourhood. What breaches of the peace we'd hed already would be nothing to speak of compared——"

"Now then, gentlemen, if you please," they both exclaimed, as there was a thundering knock at the principal door. "They're all ready for you there, so you follow us out at the back, as fast as your legs will carry you."

The committee, deeply disgusted, had to obey. They came out into a playground. One of the policemen had a key, and after fumbling awhile at the lock of the door, let the party out into a miserably dark and shabby court, marching them through its empty length, and through several winding ways, till they found themselves in a considerable thoroughfare, and close to a metropolitan station.

Whilst waiting for the train Amias was divested of his wig and beard, and all the party, very much disgusted with things in general, set forth in a silence that for some time was absolutely unbroken.

Lord Bob spoke at last, after deep cogitation. "If it hadn't been for Mr. de Berenger we should all have got ourselves into a jolly row."

But Amias was dull in his spirits; he did not like the hint that had been dropped by the policeman, that he might be called on to give evidence before the magistrates. He had seen the fighting and scuffling, and he had seen the man knocked down.

"Bob," he said, "do you think the magistrates can do anything to us if it turns out that I was disguised, and that we did it all for a lark?"

Lord Bob was sixteen months older than Amias. Sixteen months count at that time of life. He reassured his young friend. "I do not see that they can. It was straight and fair. Mr. de Berenger says he knew the moment he saw the placards that the publicans would have the best of it. There were two larks, you see, and they both flew up, as it were, and met, and had a tussle · in the air. Neither lark was prepared for the other. The publicans thought we were ordinary temperance fogies. They did not want us, of course, and they treated a lot of fellows to cheer themselves hoarse, and utterly quench us with applause. Still, though the publicans outwitted us, our lark came down without loss of a feather, and theirs got badly pecked."

"If it hadn't been for my wig," said Amias doubtfully, "I could have looked any magistrate in the face."

"Did the meeting find it out, though eighteen 'dips' illuminated it?"

"No."

"I heard Mrs. Tanner say to Baby, 'Dark, my dear! How can the room be dark, when there are eighteen dips in the chandeliers, exclusive of the four on the platform?' Baby was all in his glory, excited quite out of himself, and reckless of tallow; but when he found she was inexorable, and would have no more melted for this great occasion, he trotted gently away. Well, you allow that the meeting did not find it out. Did the police, then—I ask you that?"

"Not one."

"When you appear in court in your ordinary rig, they'll declare you are not the man. You will then fall on your knees and confess the whole. The magistrates will inquire of me, 'Why did you aid and abet this young fellow in disguising himself?' I shall reply, 'To make him look respectable.' They will answer, 'Nothing can do that.' I shall desire leave to show the contrary. We retire. Tableau in court. You, in your wig and beard, your loose gloves and spectacles; I with my arm out as a sign-post point. Two policemen faint, crying out, ''Tis he!' You immediately begin your lecture. The court listens enthralled, and before they know where they are, three attorneys have taken the pledge."

"Bob, it's no use. I feel like a fool."

"So do I. I almost always do. I think the reason must be——"

"What?"

"Why, that I *am* a fool. But," he continued, "if you think I am a greater fool than yourself, or if you think I think that I am, I can only say you never were more mistaken."

Felix was seated in the same compartment with these two, and, with hands thrust into his pockets, was deep in thought; but when Amias said, "Do you think the magistrates can do anything to us?" surprise arrested his attention, and the shadow of a smile flitted over his face. He felt what a strangely boyish speech this was, and did not care to comfort his brother and Lord Bob on the occasion. Felix was vexed, not having sufficiently remarked that the finest characters are never of rapid growth. He thought Amias ought to have done with childhood; but he was a graduate in nature's university. Nature is wiser than the schoolmaster; she educates, but she never crams. Her scholars do not go up to take their degrees; their degrees come to them.

CHAPTER XVII.

THE Rev. Felix de Berenger was called upon to appear before the magistrates and give evidence as regarded various scuffles and riotous crowds, which had resulted in some broken bones, and which were directly caused by, or at any rate had taken place at, a temperance meeting over which he had presided.

It however came out that the three publicans in the immediate vicinity had freely distributed a great deal of liquor, and had encouraged their customers to give a lively reception to the lecturer; also to take heed not to let his voice be heard, but to do this in a cheerful, fair, and unexceptionable fashion. They had likewise encouraged the crowd to take out the omnibus horses, one of which, being frightened, had become unmanageable, got away, and dashed through the window of a sausage-shop, whence he withdrew his head with a necklace of sausages where his collar should have been. A long string of sympathizers with the publicans had got a rope and hoped, by means of it, to draw the omnibus down the street, and a great assembly, whose best friends could hardly have called them sober, hung about waiting to help them; and when at last they discovered that the lecturer and committee, instead of mounting the machine, had gone out another way, they were indignant, and went and smashed the windows of the smaller public-house.

Why this? Well, it appeared that the landlord of this very public-house had lent the rope, though it was declared by several ringleaders that he must have known what the police were after; for, in short, when they came round and remarked that the gentlemen were off, they were seen to wink at him—*ergo*, he must have meant by means of this rope to occupy the people, and at the same time baulk them of a very innocent piece of fun.

The policemen here earnestly declared that he had not winked, and the magistrate crushed him. At the same time, he was very pleasant with Felix, and let it be evident that he considered the temperance cause rather ridiculous than otherwise.

Amias and Lord Bob were within call, but the inquiry seemed nearly over, and Felix hoped that a sarcasm or two directed against himself would be all the temperance cause, as represented by the late affair, would have to suffer; but at last an unlucky question was asked, to which he could not frame a true answer without exciting surprise. Another followed, and thereupon both the youths were called, and the whole ridiculous affair came out.

But they were not dealt with in the same fashion as the publicans or the chairman had been. They were both very fine, pleasant-looking young fellows; there was something boyish and ingenuous about them. They excited amusement, and they took pains to remind the court that no one had found out the wig; it therefore could have had nothing to do with the riotous proceedings. This was so manifest, that they got nothing but the very slightest of reprimands, and that was half lost in the cheering, which, however, was instantly put down by the presiding magistrate.

This was a great occasion for Amias, though he little thought so at the time. He and Lord Bob were retiring, both feeling more foolish by half than they had done the previous night, when the latter was accosted by his maternal grandfather.

This old gentleman, whose sole distinction in life was that the duke's sons were his grandsons, was allowed by them all to be the best grandfather going. He was specially proud of this one, and when he saw him giving his evidence, screening his friend and letting it be seen, in a blundering and ingenuous fashion, how little he cared for the temperance cause, and how much he loved a lark, then the grandfather felt that of all the dozens of larks after which his grandsons had craved aid of him and got it, not one had come before his notice that was so innocent.

No; they looked indeed for a temperance lecture, and Amias had stipulated that the first half of his should be given in sober sadness, and should contain as many trenchant sentences against drink as he, with all care and much elaboration, had got into it. But the second half?

They came down, as they thought, in plenty of time to hear the second half. Amias, being a great mimic, fully intended to give them the treat of hearing capital imitations of no less than three lecturers with whom he had made them more or less familiar.

There was to be an interval; the lecturer, making his bow, was to sit down and partake of his cold water, while the committee was to be called on by the chairman for some songs.

They counted on having a very dull, stupid audience, who would never get as far beyond surprise as to reach suspicion, and would not find out how the lecturer, beginning again in the style and with the voice of the great Smith, and imitating his anecdotes and his frown, would gradually and cautiously develop himself into the more stately and gentlemanly Jones, with his glib statistics and

"Here are two politicians."

see-saw motion of the hands; and then toning down Jones in delicate gradations, would carefully take up a third voice and work it up, and work himself up, till, with coat-tails flying, and eyes ready to start from his head, he concluded with the impassioned screams of the fervid Robinson.

And the parson-brother of Amias—what an element of joy it added to the pro-gramme, that it would be impossible for him to remonstrate, or in any way to interfere!

There he would be, seated in all state, looking every inch a parson. He would not find out at first. They should behold his air of startled puzzlement, then his awakened intelligence, not unmixed with indignation, and finally his vain attempts to look stolid, and his alarm lest the audience should perceive that they were being made game of.

What might occur after this they left to the event, but they by no means wished that their little plot should be discovered. No; they trusted that Amias and his brother, the parson, would manage better; for, if not, the entertainment could hardly come off again. If Mr. Tanner found out, it was of no consequence, they thought, unless he told Mrs. Tanner.

No wonder they were sulky as they drove home; circumstances had been hard upon them.

But to return to the grandfather. Felix escaped to his book-stalls when the inquiry was over, and he drove Lord Bob and Amias to his house to lunch, where he was disturbed to see that neither of them drank anything but water. The slightest of Scotch accents emphasized his words not unbecomingly. "Ye were as thin as a lath always, Robert; and if ye drink nothing but water, ye'll be just liable to blow away."

"Quite true. Why, I am so light that the wind almost takes me off my legs now. I must be weighted, to keep me down." He plunged his hands in his pockets. "I must put some pieces of lead in these," he observed; "or perhaps gold would do, grandpapa. Have you any about you handy?"

They always called him grandpapa when they wanted money, and he always laughed and thought it droll.

Lord Robert received ten sovereigns in his palm. "And now, grandpapa, when you pay the bill——" he observed as he counted them.

"What bill?" cried grandpapa with pretended sharpness.

"Why, the omnibus horse fell down and broke his knees. If you will go in for these larks, like a rare old bird as you are, why, you must pay for them. And the man who broke his arm used to earn thirty shillings a week when he was sober, though he never thought of working on a Monday. I'm afraid you're in for that thirty shillings a week till his arm's well. I don't know what you think, but that's my view, grandpapa."

"Yes, yes," said the grandfather, still rather pleased at this dependence on him than grieved to part with his cash. "Noblesse oblige, Robert, when it has a grandfather."

"Quite my view again."

"But I'll need to investigate these claims before I pay anything."

"Oh, yes," answered the grandson; and now he naturally looked on his liabilities in this matter as settled to the satisfaction of all parties; that is, he felt that honour demanded that, as he was the eldest of the committee by several months, as well as the ringleader and the one of highest rank, the proper person to pay was *his* grandfather.

The story of Amias was already known to the grandfather. It had been told, however, with a difference, as thus :—"He was heir to his uncle, a baronet, and a jolly old brewer, the richest man in the county; had been allowed to spend as much as he liked, you know. And the old boy had such covers! Never expected him to go in for work, excepting about as much as a fellow might rather like than otherwise. Well, and then he happened, entirely for fun, to pull down a temperance lecturer, and mount the beer

barrel he was standing on and lecture himself. And the old uncle was in such a rage; he said he was insulted, and disinherited him, and turned him out of doors. It is thought he will leave his money to his granddaughters. And now, you know, De Berenger has nothing but his beggarly pay. He told me the other day that he often got his dinner at an eating house for elevenpence— it was either elevenpence or thirteenpence, I know; and yet he's one of the jolliest fellows going. I came to know him through little Peep. He was one of little Peep's chums."

The young man called little Peep was one of Lord Bob's second cousins, and had been his schoolfellow. He was little physically, but as a fool he was great.

Amias had been duly warned that little Peep was never to be chaffed, reasoned with, or remonstrated with at all, it having been found by experience that there was much more fun to be got out of him by letting him alone.

But, sad to relate, little Peep's career in the same Government office which had the advantage of young De Berenger's services had been cut short; in fact, he had been called on to take possession of a moderately good estate in the north of Scotland, in consequence of the death of a distant cousin, and the end of this was that he fell under the dominion of two elder sisters, and, as far as could be now known, he was, to the grief of his old friends, conducting himself almost like other people.

And yet it had come to pass that little Peep had introduced Amias to Lord Bob, just before he took his lamented departure for the north, and then it had come to pass that Lord Bob had introduced him to the grandfather, who not only carried him home to lunch, but liked him, and pressingly invited him to dinner.

Amias had got his dress clothes now, and did not care who invited him. He went to dinner several times, and there he met people of all sorts—radical members, rising barristers, authors, newspaper editors, and dandies of fashion. They fed his opening mind with large discourse, they stimulated his sense of humour by their oddities; the radicals helped his plastic mind to the certainty that he was a conservative; the authors drew him to themselves. As for the newspaper editors, he regarded them almost as kings, and would have long gone on doing so, if some of them had not made it plain to him that they shared, and rather more than shared, his views concerning them.

Does it really matter nothing to the possessors whether their rank and standing came first a mark of grace or of disgrace? Apparently not. And these sons and these cousins, who have inherited a great name in science or in literature? The dear progenitor sits, as it were, like an Egyptian of old, at all their feasts. He never gets any rest in his grave; they have got him out, and are all hanging on behind him, using his dead body as a rammer with which they push. Strange that, because he was wise, they should think he must ram a hole for them to enter, and show themselves fools where they please.

And here are two politicians. They have been having a battle royal, each for his party. One of them almost flew at the other's throat, in the papers, and now they meet with undisguised pleasure. So they only quarrelled for their constituents then, and now they revert to friendship and their fishing.

Amias found plenty to feed his observant mind the first time he dined at grandpapa's house. The next visit afforded him just as much interest and as many speculations.

During the third evening he came to honour. An editor spoke to him! He was sitting quietly and hearkening to the discourse with modest attention, when with a certain kindliness, as the conversation ended and the other converser moved away, this royal personage turned and said, "I dare say you have been very much bored. Eh?"

Amias brusquely declared the contrary. The subject was one that was just beginning to interest people. He had read a book or two already that bore on it, and he made such intelligent comments on them and the conversation, that the editor said, "Not bad."

And then somebody else coming up to talk, he kindly admitted Amias to the conversation, and once called on him for his opinion. He gave it with his natural fervour, and with a touch of humour which was always ready to his hand. When they parted, he somehow believed himself to understand that if he wrote a letter on the point in question, for this said editor's journal, it might possibly appear in print.

This was only a hint, but Amias had heard earlier that the matter wanted "airing."

Two days after a letter actually appeared in the journal. Amias, with a leap of the heart, saw his signature, "A. de B." He read the letter with greedy eyes, and a dread lest it should have been altered that would have taken away half his pleasure. But no;

it was put in just as he had written it, and he sighed with joy and pride.

In the joy of his heart Amias sent the newspaper down to his brother. In a few days other letters appeared; some of them referred to "A. de B." and agreed with him. Amias wrote a second letter, but as he was reading it, with the peculiar delight that it always gives a young writer to see himself in print, a letter came from Felix, full of affectionate remonstrance. Felix admonished his young brother that he ought not to interfere in matters too high for him, nor to set his heart on influence, before he had learned to get a bare living. Most religious people who are restricted to certain places, and particular lines of duty, as well as kept back by small means, are beset with such fears for the more adventurous spirits about them, not considering how much more dangerous it is for youth to lack a worthy interest, and find low things tempting, because life is empty and poor. High things to each mind are the things above it. Let each put forth his hand for those on its own level. It is difficult to think of things as high in the abstract.

And so it came to pass that, through Lord Bob's grandfather, Amias first met a number of interesting people, and then found his own level, which was a much more important matter. He soon went to visit his newspaper friend, and from him had introduction to all sorts of men—got among painters and authors, from great historians and poets to the merest literary hacks, and commenced dabbling in literature himself, picking up a few guineas here and there for articles in periodicals and magazines. The aristocracy of culture began to take him up; the Bohemians, luckily, would have none of him, and he soon dropped away from the world of fashion.

Lord Bob, however, continued his fast friend. They suited each other too well for severance to be possible. How young they were when they began to lecture in public (not by any means always on the temperance question), whether they dared to disguise themselves or not, whether they succeeded to their satisfaction, and how many allies and accomplices they had, are not matters that it is needful to enlarge upon here.

At the same time, it would not be violating any confidence to inform the reader that little Peep, keeping up a correspondence with his old "chums" in the Government office, and having the celebrated lecture sent down in manuscript to read, wrote in reply, to the intense delight and astonishment of all concerned, and informed them "that he saw things in a new light, and he and his second sister intended to take the pledge."

"Good little fool!" exclaimed Amias, with such a sense of shame and compunction as almost forced tears into his eyes. He remembered with what gravity he and Lord Bob had pressed into little Peep's hand at parting a long letter on his duties as a landlord; and this he had taken in good part, though he owned that at first he was so elated, what with a moor of his own, and real gillies, &c., &c., that he had not read it.

"Innocent little Peep!" exclaimed Lord Bob to Amias. "Only think of his giving himself the airs of a reformed rake! And he thinks we are all in earnest as well as himself. I must write and undeceive him—let him down gently."

"You had much better let him alone. I don't see that you have any right to interfere with my first convert," answered Amias.

And Lord Bob, reverting to the known power of little Peep to act himself best when not interfered with, did let him alone, and the consequence of that was that little Peep wrote very soon to ask if he might deliver the lecture himself in the next town. His sister thought he was quite old enough, and he thought it might do good.

Amias curtly consented, feeling very much ashamed; but Lord Bob, to whom the correspondence had, of course, been shown, wrote and counselled little Peep to return the lecture first, that "the usual directions" might be written on it. This was accordingly done, and sent back marked here and there, "Now drink a whole tumbler of water, to show your zeal for the cause;" "Here shed a few tears—three or four will do;" "Here stamp—the right foot is the proper one to use," &c., &c.

Amias never knew that this had been done till little Peep returned the lecture, having read it in three neighbouring towns with great pride and joy. He said he wished the directions had been simpler, for he found it almost impossible to carry them out; but Amias would be glad to hear that several people had signed the pledge, and he supposed that was the principal matter.

"It is a blessed thing to be an ass!" said Amias, on reading this to Lord Bob. "Little Peep has got more than twenty people to leave off drinking, and we have never got one."

THE EDWARD STANLEYS OF ALDERLEY.

THE Dean of Westminster has furnished us with the means of knowing something of four good lives—those of his father and mother, a brother and a sister. They are lives which would have been worth knowing in any case; they have a peculiar interest as aiding us to mark the progress of religious thought and life in one large portion of the English nation during this century, and as conveying lessons useful to be considered in this its distracted close. The nineteenth century has witnessed very large changes in matters political, theological, ecclesiastical; but there are certain things which have not been moved by these changes.

EDWARD STANLEY's public life carries us through precisely the first half of the century. Born on the first day of 1779, he attained manhood on the first day of the century. The second son of a baronet and the youngest of seven children, he was destined to the family living as his heritage. His own choice of a profession would have been the navy, the passion for the sea being so singularly strong in him that "as a child he used to leave his bed and sleep on the shelf of a wardrobe, for the pleasure of imagining himself in a berth on board of a man-of-war." The love of ships and salt water never left him, but at the age of eighteen he achieved his first victory of decision, by setting aside conclusively the dream of spending his life on them. He went to Cambridge, and worked so heartily as to make up for lost time in great measure, and acquired a respectable fitness for service in the Church. He missed, indeed, that foundation of scholarship and scholarly habit which is required for eminence in classics or in theology; but the early victory over himself was worth more than any such distinctions, and prepared him for winning many a battle in his parish and diocese.

Even one who knows a little about the low condition of some parts of Cheshire, both rural and urban, can scarcely conceive the almost utter neglect of the parish of Alderley when Edward Stanley became its rector in 1805. His predecessor's boast was that he had never set foot in a sick person's cottage; and of the thirteen hundred inhabitants seldom enough came to church to make a congregation. The children were untaught; drinking and prize-fighting were the common pleasures. Disregarding "the reproach of singularity and even of Methodism," the new rector set himself to an earnest work of reformation. Not public opinion but duty gave him law and impulse ; difficulties were for him things to be overcome. He visited every house systematically, striving to win the confidence of man and woman ; he took unflagging interest in the education of the children, and made them feel how real was his love for them ; he established weekly lectures in different parts of the parish ; he lent books, and sold blankets under cost price ; indeed, whatever things had become common and respectable in the third quarter of the century, these Edward Stanley did in the first quarter, without any example to copy and in the face of considerable opposition from those who felt themselves rebuked by his zeal. Some things also he did which are not yet common. He " issued printed or lithographed addresses to his parishioners on Observance of the Sabbath, on Prayer, on Sickness, on Confirmation ; " he hung on the walls of public-houses exhortations to sobriety and religion, and placarded his parish with vigorous denunciations of drunkenness ; he stopped drunken brawls by going in among the combatants. One instance tells us much : a desperate prize-fight was in pro-

Mrs. Stanley.

gress, the spectators covering a field and clustering in the trees, when the rector rode briskly up ; "in one moment it was all over; there was a great calm ; the blows stopped ; it was as if they would all have wished to cover themselves up in the earth ; all from the trees dropped down directly, no one said a word, and all went away humbled." Next day he talked to the men by themselves, giving a Bible to each; and the brutal practice was no more heard of in his neighbourhood.

Carefully studying the Bible rather than books of theology, he taught earnestly what he believed earnestly, and had his reward so far in a full church and steady increase of communicants. Other and higher forms of reward came later, when the love of his people was revealed by his separation from them ; and his chief reward is not registered here. His son, returning from the Continent not many years ago, met with a gentleman who told him that he had been one of eight barefooted boys who wandered in to hear a lecture given by him on Geology in Macclesfield; that he had then got the impulse which led to a " prosperous commercial life ; " and that he had retained through fifty years " an undying interest in his benefactor and his benefactor's son."

XXI—29

Lord Melbourne did well to press such a man to become a bishop; for he needed to be pressed: the "Nolo" was with him unfeigned. He had already put aside overtures in regard to the new See of Manchester, and no minister could say with more truth that he had given his heart to his people. Life for him was "life in earnest;" but he had also the genuine humility and candour of soul which save earnestness from degenerating into either bigotry or ambition. The struggle nearly broke down his health and spirits, but at length he yielded to what he judged the call of duty, and was made Bishop of Norwich in 1837, being in the fifty-ninth year of his age. The sundering of ties that had been multiplying and strengthening for more than thirty years was full of pain on both sides. He made a point of taking farewell of each parishioner; he promised an annual visit, a promise faithfully kept; he stipulated that his successor should not be a stranger; and he gave an example of ministerial devotedness which, so far as we remember to have read or heard, is quite unique, in the preparation of two solemn and loving addresses, intended to be *posthumous*, "one to the parishioners, the other to the school-children of Alderley." These were "written about a year before he was removed to the See, and counter-signed by him about seven years afterwards, with a request that a copy of each might be sent after his death to every house in the parish."

It was the sphere only, not the man or his work, that was changed by his removal to East Anglia. Instead of 1,300 persons, he had now 900 benefices to care for; and the extreme age of his predecessor (Dr. Bathurst) had helped these to get, for the greater part, into a miserable condition. In correcting large abuses of non-residence and neglect of ordinances, in establishing schools and ragged schools, in preaching to sailors at Yarmouth, and facing chartist mobs in his own city, the same energies were employed that had formerly gone forth against ignorance and sottishness at Alderley. He took delight in visiting the poor, his habitual courtesy and thoughtfulness toward them winning for him from these—who are probably the best judges in the matter—the character of "a gentleman."

Bishop Stanley was among the first of the liberal bishops—using that word in reference to political, and, so far as it can be fitly used, to ecclesiastical matters. His moral courage was so displayed in connection with his high public position that those who at first mistook it for combativeness were hardly to be blamed. Arnold, then conspicuous for his reforming efforts, was his friend, and must preach his consecration-sermon. Archbishop Howley objected that Arnold "would be very ill-received by the clergy in general," and asked him to nominate another; but that the Bishop would not do, and the exclusion of Arnold was left to the Archbishop himself. In his second charge (1846), he attacked the doctrine of apostolical succession as "the very fountain-head from which originally flowed the late extravagancies" of the Anglican party; and when preaching the annual sermon for the Propagation Society, in 1844, "he took the opportunity to disavow this doctrine in the presence of the assembly of bishops and of metropolitan clergy," fairly earning the praise of having delivered "the boldest sermon that had ever been delivered in St. Paul's Cathedral." Westminster witnessed the same display of independent courage when the Nestor of African Missions, Robert Moffat, appeared there one 30th of November at the invitation of its Dean.

What the Bishop of Norwich was as a theologian may be gathered from a single instance.

"Read the Gospel of St. John," he would say to one troubled with sceptical doubts, "and ask whether that book could have proceeded from any but a Divine source."

What he was as a man, in his family and before God, may be seen in the following extract from his private journal, written on the eve of his sixty-fourth birthday, after having had all his five children gathered about him for the last time. One of them, Charles, had just left.

"I have closed the evening by family prayer; all assembled save my dear Charles. God knoweth how earnestly my heart yearned to him, and how warm was the blessing I in secret offered for him. The scriptural reading for the night was the conclusion of St. John's Gospel; the passages to which I alluded, 'Lovest thou me?' 'Feed my sheep,' 'What is that to thee?' 'Amen.' And my private prayer shall be that we may, while life is granted to us, each pass that life in closest bonds of affection, uniting it with as sincere and devoted a love for the Saviour as can be excited and can exist between a finite and an infinite being, whose full and perfect character and sacrifice we can only know in all its height and depth when our mortal shall have put on immortality." *

He died well, having for many years died daily, and having enjoyed the full use of his powers for the three-score years and ten. In

* "Memoirs of Edward and Catherine Stanley." Edited by their Son, A. P. Stanley, D.D., p. 99. London: John Murray, 1880.

the autumn of 1849 he was induced to take a rest in the far north of Scotland. Cholera was then in the country, and he stipulated, "The moment it breaks out," in Norwich, "I return instantly to be at my post." He died in Ross-shire after a brief illness, on the 6th of September, and—almost with dramatic fitness, considering how his youthful longing for the sea had been set aside—his remains were brought home to Yarmouth with difficulty through a severe gale. All mourned for him sincerely, the people of Alderley not least.

Of CATHERINE STANLEY we have scarcely any memoir, but such extracts from her journal and letters as prove a noble character. We would not think we were paying these writings a compliment if we called them masculine; they are womanly through and through, yet strong in brain and truth, in purity and love. There is a measure of severity about them also, here and there; but in this poor world purity and love need to be severe. We do not find these without the severity except in Thorwaldsen's marble of St. John, and there the Evangelist's eye is soaring higher than his eagle's. Some of these extracts are racy with touches of recent observation; but for the most part they have that abstract and reflective character which will give the book a lasting interest.

For example:—

"Excellencies and Defects of Churches, 1831:—
"UNITARIANISM:—*Good* tendencies: toleration, liberality, active usefulness in all benevolent and charitable purposes, high attainments in science, universal philanthropy. *Deficiencies:* want of spirituality, humility, Christian zeal and love, literature, and scholarship. *Evil* tendencies: indifference, want of reverence, scepticism, coldness, not caring for the souls, only bodies, resting in outward moral works not in inward unction and holiness.
"CATHOLICISM:—*Good* tendencies: devotion, submission, faith, reverence, self-sacrifice. Saints, Sisters of Charity. *Evil* tendencies: superstitions, inward corruptions, moral sense destroyed or vitiated by the distinction between venial and mortal sins, by interposing virtually, though not nominally, between ourselves and God, by the continual sacrifice of sense and perception to the absurdities of the Mass, and the equivocations necessary to keep hold the fallible doctrines of an infallible Church.
"EVANGELICALISM:—*Good* tendencies: spirituality, zeal, liberality as to the boundaries of the Church, willing for its extension, and for co-operation with all who unite in the great fundamentals of the Gospel, dwelling on the Church of Christ rather than the Church of England. *Evil* tendencies: over-zeal as to doctrine as compared with work, consequent deficiency in common points of moral conduct, and exclusive in phraseology, habits and intercourse narrow."—Pp. 281, 282.

Daughter of a neighbouring clergyman, and

elder sister of that Mrs. Augustus Hare whom many have learned to love through her memoirs, Mrs. Stanley represents a very valuable class of English women—cultured, high-principled, with a religious life rising by its earnestness quite out of the restraints of form, however much these may have been valued, and with great desire of doing good. Too few; yet as we are permitted to know of another and another to be classed with the Baroness Bunsen, Mrs. Tait, Lady Augusta Stanley, and others still living, we recognise a leaven from which much may be hoped.

Mrs. Stanley was married at eighteen and lived on to her sixty-ninth year. During the twelve years that she survived her husband "the happiness and energy of her existence were concentrated on the son and the two daughters who were still left to her." She died on the Ash Wednesday of 1862, a date which her son now associates with the Ash Wednesday of 1876, when "he stood by the death-bed of her by whose supporting love he had been 'comforted after his mother's death,' and whose character, although cast in another mould, remains to him, with that of his mother, the brightest and most sacred vision of his earthly experience."

Of their five children, only two remain. When the good old Bishop died he was spared the distress of knowing that his youngest son, CHARLES, had been suddenly cut off by fever in Tasmania. He was a Captain of the Royal Engineers, and had earned the love of those who knew him best.

In Captain OWEN STANLEY the father's passion for the navy at length made a way for itself. Within his short life of thirty-eight years he gave to his country intelligent and, indeed, heroic service in one Arctic voyage, in securing our possession of the Middle Island of New Zealand, in the survey of Torres Straits and New Guinea. He was found dead in his berth while the ship he commanded lay in Sydney harbour, and in February 7, of 1850, was laid in the ground where Commodore Goodenough was laid twenty-five years afterwards.

MARY STANLEY gave herself to devoted Christian labour among the poor in Norwich. When the Crimean war came, she followed Florence Nightingale to the shores of the Bosphorus as leader of a second band of nurses, well content to fulfil a saying of her mother's, "Remember, Mary, your lot in life is to sow for others to reap." Her brother says—

"In 1856 she joined the Roman Church, of which she remained a faithful member to the end. But her natural sincerity was not touched. . . . Unlike many converts, she insisted on making the largest not the narrowest use of whatever liberties the rules of her new form of faith permitted; and she regarded not proselytism, but abstention from proselytism, as her sacred duty." Last year she visited, on his ninety-third birthday, the venerable Lord Stratford de Redcliffe, her friend and protector at Constantinople, who told a story of his having said to one of the Popes, "You are not my sovereign and I am not your subject: you are a Catholic and I am a Protestant: but it cannot be wrong for me to ask or for you to give me your blessing." Whereupon Mary Stanley said, "Lord Stratford, you are not my sovereign and I am not your subject: I am a Catholic and you are a Protestant: but it cannot be wrong for me to ask or for you to give me your blessing." She died on the 26th of November last, and was buried by her brother and brother-in-law, the Dean of Llandaff, beside her mother in Alderley churchyard.

Dean Stanley, "warned by the lengthening and deepening shadows of life," has thought it well to give to "this age of transition" these lives, as expressing "thoughts of which we may be sure that, as they preceded our present conflict of opinions, so they will long survive it." That is true. He probably had it not in view to teach old-fashioned Evangelical Puritans a lesson of charity in a kindly way; nevertheless he will be glad to be assured by one of these that the lesson has been taught by this book.

R. D. N.

MAN'S JUDGMENT.

ST. PAUL, writing to the Corinthians, says, "It is a small thing for me to be judged of by you, or by man's judgment." There is something defiant in this language. All men naturally wish to have the good opinion of their fellow-men, and to stand well with the world. One of the things of which we are most careful is to have our actions and our motives rightly judged. And this disposition is so highly and so frequently commended in Scripture that it is converted into a principle. Jesus said, "Let your light so shine before men, that they may see your good works;" and St. Paul himself speaks of walking circumspectly, so as to have a good report even among those who are not of the Christian community; and again he said, "Let not your good be evil spoken of."

St. Paul's words are all the more startling in that he was speaking of himself in his character of an apostle or minister of Christ. No class of men are more subject to criticism than the teachers of religion. Of necessity their profession is great, and the eye of the world is ever upon them to see if their practice corresponds to their profession. They are liable to suffer from detraction, but they may also be injured by elevation or flattery. Men who are themselves above the spirit of party may be made party leaders by weak and injudicious followers. It was so at Corinth; Paul, Apollos, and Cephas, as well as Christ, had their different partisans, who boasted of their leaders as if they had all been opposed to each other, instead of all working for one object. It was hard on Paul that in the Corinthian Church, which he had been the means of forming, there were some who disowned him as an apostle, and others who made him merely the head of a party. He had begotten them in the gospel, but they were perverse children. In this epistle he remonstrated with them, telling them that he and the other apostles were merely their servants. Christ was the head of the Church, and the apostles were ministers, or, to translate the Greek word literally, *under-rowers*. As if he had said, we do not want these invidious positions as party leaders. You may over-estimate us, or you may under-estimate us. It is a small matter comparatively for us which way. Our business is to be faithful to our Master. "Therefore judge no man before the time till the Lord come, who will bring to light the hidden things of darkness."

Though the approbation of our fellow-men be a laudable thing for us to desire, yet it has its dangerous side in seeking the praise of men. There is here a vanity which is altogether opposed to the spirit of Christianity. The Corinthians were a fickle, volatile people; it was hard to wean them from the follies of the world. They were not, before their conversion to Christianity, elevated in their morals; and their delight, when they rose above the pleasures of sense, was in contending about their favourite philosophers and rhetoricians. The same spirit showed itself after they became Christians. Each party had its apostle to be raised above the others, and to be thus made the occasion of strife. Oftentimes men of no religion fight for their religious party or their favourite preachers, and men who neglect the first principles of morality will boast, in a spirit of partisanship quite opposed to the spirit of the gospel, that they are of Christ. The failing of the Corinthians is not unknown among ourselves, and the apostle's corrective is that the ministers of the Christian dispensation are not philosophers or rhetoricians standing up on their own account and craving the suffrages of the people, but servants of Jesus Christ and stewards of the mysteries, that is teachers of the things revealed in the gospel.

And it is required of a steward that he be found faithful. He is not to be guided by people's opinion of him. He is to be above that, and independent of it. However much he may desire to win men, he is not to please them by any want of fidelity to his charge. Approbation from man is a small thing compared with the approbation of God, as man's judgment is a small thing compared with God's judgment.

St. Paul adds, "I judge not mine own self." Another very startling declaration. Are we not recommended to examine ourselves, to try ourselves, and to accuse and condemn ourselves? Who of all the sacred writers has said more about conscience than St. Paul? And what is conscience but the judge within? Yet St. Paul says, "I judge not mine own self." The reason is that he had a higher judge. He knew nothing specially against himself. He was conscious of integrity, fidelity, and sacrifice in the service of Christ; yet that does not justify him. It might justify him to himself, but there was another tribunal before which he must stand. He might be deceived even as to his own motives, but when the Lord cometh He will bring to light the hidden things of darkness —perhaps things of which the apostle himself was ignorant.

Man's judgment is defective, and therefore it is small compared with God's. Many men are deceived with themselves; they mistake their own characters. This is done in two ways: some take themselves to be much better than they are; others, doubtless a smaller number, think themselves worse than they are. To both the apostle's principle is safe, not to judge themselves, always to remember that there is a fuller judgment than they can make, and by One to whom all things are known. Men's judgments of each other are

equally defective with their judgments of themselves. There are many things which blind our eyes to our neighbour's goodness, as well as to his faults. It is an often-quoted saying of Archbishop Tillotson's that there will be two wonders in heaven: one that we shall find so many there whom we did not expect to find; and the other that we shall miss so many whom we expected to find there.

This part of this Epistle to the Corinthians is read during Advent, because it speaks of judgment to come. The Lord will bring to light the hidden things of darkness. There is nothing that the wicked have more cause to dread, and nothing which the just have more cause to desire. A day of judgment in which the hidden thoughts of every heart shall be revealed is what the world needs. Without judgment God could not be just, and without justice God could not be God.

If our neighbours cannot judge us, and if we cannot judge ourselves, it may be objected that we have no rule of life. But we have. Our knowledge may not be unerring, yet it is sufficient to guide us. So long as we have an honest purpose, are walking in uprightness, and striving to have a conscience void of offence, we may leave the rest to the day of judgment, with the same confidence that St. Paul had, that he should be justified when the Lord cometh and bringeth to light the hidden things of darkness.

So long as we have a good conscience we need not trouble ourselves about the judgment of others, except for the sake of righteousness, that our good be not evil spoken of, otherwise men may doubt the very existence of goodness. We need not put our light under a bushel, but on a candlestick, for light reaches others. Goodness has the power of attracting men to it.

The apostle speaks with certainty of the judgment. He felt that it must come. His conviction of its truth was so strong that he lived with a continual reference to it. It is men of strong convictions who are men of great deeds. We only half believe, and so we pass our lives doing nothing with decision. St. Paul had faith; he believed, and therefore he spoke, and his words ever since he uttered them have been ringing in the world's ears. He was certain that his Lord would come to judgment, and therefore it was a small matter for him to be judged by men—yea, he did not judge his own self.

JOHN HUNT.

SOME NOXIOUS INSECTS.

PART I.

NOXIOUS insects may be briefly defined as those insects which injure man.

Obviously they may do this in two ways. Either they inflict direct injuries on his person, or they indirectly injure him by damaging his property. In either case, they are the result of civilisation.

To the genuine savage no insects are noxious, not even those bloodthirsty parasites which we call by the general name of "vermin." A savage cares nothing for vermin of any kind, and it is not until man is far removed from savages that he begins to object to their presence.

One African traveller, for example—I think the late Mr. J. Baines—was hospitably entertained in the hut of a Kafir chief. During the night he was awakened by the most intolerable pricking sensations all over his body. On starting up he found that his host, with the kindest intentions, had spread his own kaross, or fur cloak, over his guest. The kaross was swarming with vermin, and they had taken full advantage of their good fortune in finding such a victim. He was obliged to go out of the hut into the open air, and clear himself and his clothes of his tormentors before he could hope for rest. Yet the owner of the kaross could have felt no inconvenience from them, or he would not have transferred them to his guest.

A curiously similar incident is recorded in the "Arabian Nights" (Lane's edition).

In the story of Noureddin and the Fair Persian, the Caliph is represented as meeting a fisherman, and exchanging clothes with him for the purpose of disguising himself more effectually. Scarcely had the change been effected than the Caliph felt himself bitten in all quarters, and cried out with pain. The fisherman, accustomed from childhood to consider the presence of vermin as a necessary adjunct of existence, simply advises the Caliph to take no notice of them, but to allow them to go on biting until he was accustomed to them, and would feel them no longer.

In Knight's "Historical Parallels" the same idea is inferred.

There was a certain Swedish hero, named Starcharetus, who is represented as having lived about the beginning of the Christian era, but is evidently a wholly fictitious character. He performed a series of exploits, was gigantic in form, and lived to three times the usual age of man, dying at last a violent death intentionally procured by himself.

The following adventure befell him in his old age.

"Nine warriors of tried valour offered to Helgo, King of Norway, the alternative of doing battle against the nine, or losing his bride upon his marriage-day. Helgo thought it best to appear by a champion, and requested the assistance of Starcharetus, who was so eager for the adventure that, in following Helgo to the appointed place, he performed, in one day and on foot, a journey which had occupied the king, who travelled on horseback, twelve days.

"On the morrow, which was the appointed day, ascending a mountain, which was the place of meeting, he chose a spot exposed to the wind and snow, and then, *as if it were spring*, throwing off his clothes, he set himself to dislodge the fleas that had nestled in them."

Here the narrator expresses no surprise at the presence of the fleas. He assumes that the hero's clothes would be full of them, and that the operation in question would have been the usual employment in spring. He only calls attention to the remarkable fact that Starcharetus took the trouble of performing it in winter.

That the hardy champion disdained or was unacquainted with "the flimsy artifices of the bath," as Thackeray puts the point, is self-evident. Clean skins and clothing are inconsistent with vermin; and, indeed, a theory has not been wanting that the parasites in question are directly beneficial to the non-washing races of mankind, by serving as a succedaneum for soap and water, and, by the irritation which they cause, keeping up a healthy action of the skin.

As to secondarily noxious insects, a savage has no conception of them. He does not till the earth, and consequently has no crops to be devoured. He possesses neither flocks nor herds, and therefore even such insects as the tzetze-fly and gad-fly have no terrors for him. Neither does he wear clothes, so that he is not even aware of the existence of the clothes moth.

Take, for example, the most noxious insect which an agriculturist fears, namely, the locust, and see how it affects a savage, say a Bosjesman.

To the South African farmer the locust is the most fearful of pests. A swarm of locusts will mean absolute ruin, for the creatures will

Migratory Locust.

destroy in a single night the harvest on which the owner depends for subsistence.

But to the Bosjesman the locust-swarm is an unmixed blessing. He has no crop that the insects can destroy, but he finds in the locust-swarm an abundant store of food without the trouble of hunting for it. He hails the approach of the distant swarm, and as long as it remains in his neighbourhood he enjoys to the full the chief luxury of savage life, *i.e.* eating to repletion day after day, and only sleeping off the effects of one meal to begin another.

Take, again, the great Palm Weevil (*Calandra palmarum*), the huge jaws of which are so destructive to the palm-trees, and so noxious to the cultivator.

The savage exults when he sees the traces of the "gru-gru," as this larva is called, for it forms one of his most dainty articles of food,

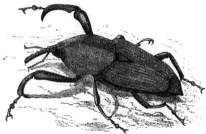

Palm, or Gru-gru, Weevil.

and all the more valuable because it requires no cooking. The gru-gru is simply cut out of the tree, held by the head, and eaten alive, as we eat oysters in this country. Many

a savage, and white man also, when leading a savage life, has been indebted for his very existence to the Palm Weevil. To the cultivator of the palm this weevil is one of the worst of noxious insects. To the same man, when travelling out of the reach of civilisation, it is a priceless boon.

Then there are the various Termites, the terror of civilised man, the destroyers of his furniture, books, and papers, the devourers of every piece of woodwork in his house, and sometimes the underminers of the house itself.

The savage values them for the various ways in which they contribute towards his livelihood.

In the first place he eats them.

In this country we revolt at the idea of eating insects, but in savage lands the Ter-

Great Termite, male.

mite is eaten, not as a matter of absolute necessity, but of choice. Indeed, a savage king, to whom a traveller presented some apricot jam, declared it to be the best food he knew next to Termites.

Then, the nests which these insects rear are of great service to the savage. There are several animals, popularly called Ant Bears, which feed chiefly on the Termites, or White Ants, as they are wrongly called. These creatures are furnished with enormous claws, with which they tear out the whole interior of the nest, leaving nothing but the shell of clay, baked as hard as brick in the sunbeams.

Such empty nests serve several purposes. In the first place they are utilised as ovens, in which the native hunters can cook the animals killed by them.

Then, such savages as build huts find that

nothing makes so good a floor for their houses as Termites' nests ground into a powder mixed with water, beaten down until quite smooth and level, and left to harden in the rays of the tropical sun.

Lastly, they serve as tombs for the dead. The corpse is thrust into the empty nest

Termite, female.

through the hole left by the Ant Bear, the aperture is closed with stones and thorns, and there the body may remain undisturbed by any foe except man.

As to the services rendered by the Termites to civilised man, I shall have something to say before the conclusion of this article.

Every reader of this magazine has, I presume, seen the common Water-Boatmen insects, which are shaped so much like boats, swim on their keel-shaped backs, and use their long hind legs as oars. All of them possess sharp, strong beaks, capable of penetrating the human skin, and depositing in the wound a poisonous secretion, which causes a dull, throbbing pain lasting for several hours.

There are many species of Water-Boatmen, but those which belong to the genus *Corixa*, and can be known by the flattened ends of their bodies, have the sharpest beaks, the most virulent poison, and consequently are the most noxious when handled. Even in England these Corixæ are apt

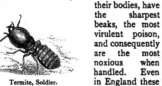

Termite, Soldier.

to be rather unpleasant insects, but there are some parts of Mexico where the lakes swarm with Corixæ of very much larger dimensions than any British species.

Yet these insects, noxious as we might think them, are very useful to the comparatively uncivilised natives, who eat, not the Corixæ, but their eggs.

At the proper time of the year the natives sink large bundles of reeds in the water. In a week or two the reeds are thickly covered with Corixa eggs, which are scraped off and the reeds returned to the water. In fact the Corixa is treated very much like the mussel in the French breeding beds. The eggs, after being scraped off, are pressed into cakes, which are cooked and used for consumption, under the name of " haoutle.",

Even the dread mosquito, the only insect which a savage can have an excuse for ranking as noxious, is really of direct value to some savage tribes.

Livingstone mentions that the shores of the Lake Nyassa swarm with mosquitos. The late Mr. Baines told me that no one who has not seen the mosquito swarms that hang on the banks of these African lakes, can form even a conception of their multitude. They fill the air so that they seem to be an almost solid mass. If a lamp be lighted, they put it out by settling on it, while the hum of their wings is almost like the roaring of the sea in the ears of a diver.

Yet the natives can utilise even these terrible pests, which are so venomous that not even a mule could stray on the banks of the lake and live through the night. But the mosquito never seems to travel to any great distance from the water in which it passed through its previous stages of existence, and the natives can avoid it by sleeping in spots far removed from the water's edge.

They do more than this; they sweep the mosquitos into large bags, press them together and form them into cakes, just as is done with the eggs of the Corixa. These cakes go by the name of "kungo." They are circular, about eight inches in diameter, and an inch or so in thickness. When eaten they are said to bear some resemblance to caviare in flavour.

Before quitting this part of the subject, we must not lose sight of the fact that none of the so-called noxious insects, even though they cause direct annoyance to man, were created for that purpose. Take, for example, the mosquito swarms above mentioned. Man is not the normal food of the mosquito, which can and does maintain existence without ever seeing a human being. But when man presents himself in the tract already inhabited by the mosquitos, he becomes an intruder and has to suffer the penalty of his intrusion.

I mentioned at the beginning of this essay

that the noxiousness of insects is in direct ratio to the civilisation of the men whom they annoy.

In the uncivilised days of England the carrot, the turnip, the asparagus, the cabbage, the celery, and other garden plants, were mere weeds, and, in consequence, the insects which fed upon them were unheeded by man. Our semi-savage predecessors could find no fault with the cabbage caterpillars, with the turnip grub, the celery fly, or the asparagus beetle, simply because the plants on which they fed had not been brought into cultivation, and their destroyers could not be ranked among noxious insects.

So at the present day we do not cultivate the stinging nettle, ranking it among the weeds, and, in consequence, we rather look upon the insects which feed upon it as our benefactors. But if some clever gardener, "with Doric accent and high wages," were to develop the stinging nettle into a garden vegetable, the beautiful Tortoiseshell, Atalanta, and Peacock butterflies would be placed among our noxious insects, inasmuch as their larvæ feed upon the plant. Perhaps the gardeners of Dreepdailie, who, according to Andrew Fairservice, cultivated that vegetable under forcing glasses, held precisely the same opinion of the insects.

Then there comes the question of counterbalancing qualities.

There are several insects to which all civilised nations confess themselves indebted. The bee, for example, furnishes us with honey and wax, and so we praise it for its industry, though we have no word of commendation for the common wasp, which is quite as industrious and unselfish as the bee, or the sand wasp, which works infinitely harder.

The silkworms are almost venerated, because we use the silk which they produce. Yet there is not a caterpillar, either of butterfly or moth, that does not produce silk of some kind.

The cochineal insect is almost as important to man as the silkworm, and, tiny as it is, it furnishes the means of existence to thousands of human beings. Two of its near relatives are also of exceeding value, one furnishing a wax equal in many respects to that of the bee, and the other producing the "lac" so invaluable for lacquer work, sealing-wax, and varnish.

Yet, were it not that we have learned the value of their counterbalancing qualities, every one of these creatures would be justifiably ranked among the noxious insects.

Take the bee. A child, who is ignorant of the character of the bee, seizes it, is stung, and has very good reason for considering it as a very noxious insect.

Afterwards, when he learns that the bee furnishes the sweet honey which tickles his palate, he pardons the sting which has hurt his hand. He has learned one of the counterbalancing qualities of a noxious insect. As he increases in knowledge and civilisation, he learns that the wax, which as a child he would have flung after draining it of the honey, is by far the more valuable product of the two, and that some of the arts—metal statuary, for example—could not be conducted without it.

Take the silkworm. It destroys the leaves of the mulberry-tree, and injures the crop of fruit which man wants for himself, so that, to a race of men sufficiently civilised to cultivate the mulberry-tree, it would be classed among the noxious insects.

But further knowledge about the habits of the creature enables mankind to understand its counterbalancing qualities, and so, although the silkworm consumes far more mulberry foliage than it did when it was considered merely as a noxious insect, we have learned to compare the value of the silk which it produces with that of the leaves which it devours, and prize the silkworm as a source of national wealth.

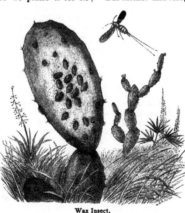

J. C. WOOD.

Wax Insect.

THE INFLUENCE OF ART IN DAILY LIFE.

By J. BEAVINGTON ATKINSON.

II.—INTERIOR DECORATION OF THE HOUSE.

NOTHING can be more fatal than the notion that a man, in the decoration of his house, has only to know what he likes, and to do with his own as he chooses. Without some guiding principles the farther he goes the more wide will be his departure from true standards. In the present day the mere diversity of doctrines and multiplicity of appliances, each with some show of truth and beauty in its favour, become perplexing. The conflict between styles, the rivalry among fashions, old and new, the impatience as to methods handed down from time immemorial, the effort to throw off all bondage to traditional arrangements, and the not unlaudable desire to strike out something original and to assert private judgment within the dwelling, have in these latter times too often divided the house against itself and brought upon the domestic arts confusion, not to say anarchy. I shall be glad if the simple suggestions made in the sequel may serve to restore order.

The first thing in the art-treatment of the interior of a house to decide on is a well-considered scheme of decoration. And, of course, must be taken into account all the conditions—such as the use, size, and number of the rooms; the several requirements of hall, library, breakfast, dining, and draw-ing-rooms, of boudoirs and bedrooms; their aspects as regards the sun; the distribution of windows and doors, with the means of approach and intercommunication. Certain characteristics all rooms possess in common: they are interiors, and are bounded by walls, floors, and ceilings. These, then, are the surfaces calling for decoration. "The scheme" should primarily provide for the "general effect," whether grave or gay, qui-escent, animated, or festive. It should also secure an agreeable sequence among the varied members of the house, so that one room may lead on pleasantly to its next-door neighbour, and the whole suite, whether large or small, combine in harmonious va-riety. This scheme of the whole and the altogether, which may be called the decora-tive idea or motive, is of vital import; if happily conceived, the interior is an assured success.

Next to be considered is the means that may best conduce to the required effect; and herein it should be borne in mind that the decorator can employ but three agents or instruments of expression—form, colour, and material. The form is the design or pattern; the colour is the harmony of tone; the material, whether stone or wood, paint or paper, woollen, cotton, or silk, gives quality or texture of surface, involves cost or economy, and concerns utility, durability, richness, or plainness of decorative effect. Among these three means of ornament, ma-terial is of least moment; it is comparatively an accident, while higher and subtler ele-ments subsist in form and colour—form lying close upon thought, and colour being in correspondence with emotion. Thus by the play and interchange of the one with the other over walls, floors, and ceilings, the interior of the house is made responsive to the mind's desires. In the use of these appliances the decorator's purpose, stated in the general, should be to exclude all that is ugly and to embrace every attainable beauty; the one removes all that is disagreeable, the other brings into the house the colours and the forms that give most pleasure. As to colour, let gravity be free from gloom, and let cheerfulness not degenerate into levity or garish gaiety. Domestic decorations should come as genial accompaniments to domestic affections; they are scarcely re-quired, like ecclesiastical decorations, to move to solemn emotion. They need not, as works of high art, convey definite ideas to the intellect; they attain for the most part their end sufficiently well when, by pleasing impressions, they conduce to tranquil tones of feeling and states of mental felicity.

The principle can hardly be too often insisted upon that decoration is the obedient, though not the servile, handmaid to the master art of architecture, and therefore like that art must conform to symmetry, propor-tion, order. The geometric construction of an arch, whether round or pointed, the flat lintel of a door or the horizontal line of a cornice, will severally impose accordant com-positions in ornament. The decoration must likewise in its scale be apportioned to the size of the rooms and to the wall-spaces to be filled: the ornament should be evenly balanced and disposed over the entire sur-face, conveying the impression of intention and method. The decoration of a dwelling is indeed little else than the application to flat surfaces of the laws of ornament. And the style of any ornament may be compared to, and has the significance of, handwriting; ornament is handiwork, and like writing gives expression to thoughts and sentiments; it takes from nature what is most lovely in form and colour, it responds to the craving in the human mind for beauty, it thus brings to our homes in a thousand ways pleasures for the eye and the fancy. Ornament is a language, and its varied styles are as divers tongues spoken from age to age by the great human families. And ornament is no less a history: its developments mark the transition from states of barbarism to civilisation; it is an index to culture; and thus it becomes of all the more import what decorative modes, whether Greek, Romanesque, Byzantine, Gothic or Renaissant, we admit within our dwellings. The fundamental rules which regulate all ornament, whether of walls, floors, or ceilings, of paper-hangings, carpets, curtains or furniture, have been epitomized by the Government Department of Science and Art in substance as follows:—

The true office of ornament is the decoration of utility. Ornament should arise out of, and be subservient to, construction; it requires a specific adaptation to material, and therefore the decoration suited to one fabric needs re-adjustment to another. True ornament does not consist in the mere imitation of natural objects, but rather in the adaptation of the essential or generic beauties of form or colour found in nature to decorative uses, and such adaptation must be in conformity with the material, the laws of art, and the necessities of manufacture.

The decoration of an ordinary dwelling is a comparatively simple affair, provided only a few elementary principles be borne in mind. Domestic decoration, unlike the monumental painting formerly in the service of the State or of princely families, is not usually prompted by patriotism, poetry, or other phases of lofty thought. The cases are rare in which an Englishman can follow the example of the Roman banker who called to his aid Raphael, Giulio Romano, and Giovanni da Udine to adorn the Palazzo Farnesina with poetic scenes from the Greek Parnassus. Still, within recent years private houses have with happy results been intrusted to the decorative skill of many of our English artists, such as G. F. Watts, R.A., E. J. Poynter, R.A., E. Armitage, R.A., H. S. Marks, R.A., W. B. Richmond, Burne Jones, Albert Moore, W. B. Scott, Walter Crane, and H. Holiday. These are among the best signs of our times, and there seems reason to hope that, emulating the example of the great art epochs, the decorative works of our painters may, like the poetry of our best authors, become as household words the near companions of our daily lives. And it may not be amiss just to mention that money can hardly be laid out more profitably. The wall decorations of Italy are simply priceless, and there can be no doubt that the contemporary works ventured upon in England are year by year gaining a value in excess of the first outlay.

The themes for such decorations cannot be better suggested than by our English poets and writers of romance. And I have long had a favourite idea that the poetic and graceful designs of Flaxman, such as he made for Wedgwood, might with suitable modification work effectively as friezes or panels for our rooms. The designs can be got for nothing, and the execution by hand or by a printing process need not cost much. It has also been with some a cherished idea that our English classics might be turned to good decorative account by furnishing quotations to be illumined on friezes or borders. One advantage accruing from such inscriptions is that decorations which give delight primarily to the senses might be made to appeal also to the understanding and to convey positive truths. Mere ornament may be compared to pantomime or dumb show, but such intermingling of choice quotations from our best authors might seem to break the silence by speech. It may be fitly left to individual taste to determine what literary extracts can best give verbal expression to the art motive; but perhaps a library or a studio might echo the latent thought within by some such extracts, treated decoratively, as the following:—

"Reading maketh a full man, Conference a ready man, and Writing an exact man."

"In Reading we hold converse with the wise; in the business of life generally with the foolish."

"Calm let me live, and every care beguile,
Hold converse with the great of every time,
The learn'd of every class, the good of every clime."

"Order is Heaven's first law, and the way to Order is by Rules that Art hath found."

"The course of Nature is the Art of God."

Many are the methods and materials used in past and present days for the decoration of dwellings. In by-gone ages rooms were not only painted and coloured, but were hung with tapestries, damasks, silks, and embossed leathers. But now, for many reasons, for economy, cleanliness, and convenience, most other modes have given place to paper-hangings. And in point of taste there is no great loss, inasmuch as some of our chief artists have designed patterns which fulfil the true conditions of surface decoration. But the difficulty constantly arises as to a wise choice among the perplexing multiplicity of styles and patterns. In former days wall designs were made for some actual locality or room, and became part and parcel of the freehold and inheritance; but paper-hangings, the reverse of mural paintings, belong to no spot in particular, and are in their habits as itinerant as easel-pictures. Yet the principles which underlie all wall decorations alike remain for ever unchangeable, and therefore in the selection of a paper-hanging it is not sufficient to look to the beauty of the design in the abstract, but to its suitability to the uses, scale, and proportions of the actual apartment. Opinions differ as to the rules which should guide the choice, and indeed considerable latitude is permissible; the following laws, though not to be insisted upon too dogmatically, may be of service:—

Paper-hangings bear the same relation to the furniture in a room that a background does to the objects in a picture. The decoration, therefore, should not invite attention to itself, but be subdued in effect, without strong contrasts either of form, colour, or light and dark. The decorative details should be arranged on symmetric bases, and nothing should be introduced to disturb the sense of flatness. Colour is not to be in positive masses, but should be broken over the whole surface, so as to give a general negative hue and an impression of retiring quietude.

In direct dissonance with such placidities are the eminently pictorial paper-hangings which come conspicuously from Paris. A peacock disporting the attractions of his tail on a terrace is just one of those mural placards which the French love to put up in corridors. Neapolitan peasants dancing the tarantella in the foreground, with the blue Bay of Naples and Vesuvius flaming in the distance, are likewise chosen to give to interiors a festive and out-door aspect. In Venice I have seen rooms painted freehand, with fancy figures in masks, or revealing gay costumes as they peep out from the ambush of columns. Perhaps it may not be easy quite to justify such vagaries even in decoration, which avowedly is a field for fancy and frolic. But at least these extravaganzas meet the popular taste, and when all is in keeping it were hard to prohibit what pleases. Indeed, almost everything may be permitted that is beautiful in itself and is rightly placed. Yet war needs to be waged perpetually against the follies of fashion and the eccentricities and conceits which pass for strokes of genius.

What is chiefly to be desired is that each decorative system shall be clearly understood in its character and its conditions, and that then it shall be consistently carried out to its legitimate consequences. In the present day the public are divided into opposing parties, and the utmost diversity of opinion can indeed be tolerated, the golden rule in art ever being, liberty free from license. Some authorities, as just seen, lay down the law that wall decorations shall be retiring and comparatively insignificant, while others would make them conspicuous and self-asserting. Which of the two alternatives may be preferable will greatly depend upon whether the wall relies on its own surface decoration, or whether it will receive additional adorning from easel pictures, drawings, or engravings. The general substitution in modern times of movable pictures in frames for mural paintings attached to the structure, has brought about a radical revolution in the ornamentation of our rooms. Large, obtrusive paper patterns are of course destructive of the delicate tones of pictures. On the whole, small, quiet designs are obviously the safest. Colour is yet another perplexed problem. With some authorities colour has assumed the certitude of a creed, with others it is still subject to controversy. This complex question will in the sequel call for special consideration; in the meanwhile, let it be premised that here likewise stand face to face two opposing schools. The one favours strong positive pigments applied boldly, though of course in balance; the other beats a timid retreat behind quiet, retiring tones. Each party claims specific successes: the adventurous course has most to gain, the cautious line has least to lose. It need scarcely be added that the treatment of the furniture will have to be reversed with each revolution in the wall decoration. It may further be observed that paper-hangings or other mural adornings can either be in monochrome or polychrome; if of one colour, then the pattern will have to be thrown up from the ground by either a lighter or a darker tone of that colour. Or if the decoration be of two or more colours, then a simple and favourite arrangement is to use some complementary hues, such as green for the ground, and red for the patterns, a harmonious contrast exemplified by nature in the red flower of the geranium rising out of a green mass of leaves. It is well that a room should be so decorated that the walls, when looked at near, offer forms of simple beauty pleasingly varied, and when viewed at a distance present as a whole, both in design and colour, a composition which falls into prevailing unity and repose.

Floor-coverings, whatever be their material, should be made to accord with the general rules already laid down for wall-clothings. Indeed the difference in position and use between a floor and a wall would seem to demand that these laws be here enforced with all the greater rigour. Floors are for walking on, therefore they should seldom be embellished with objects that it is outrageous to trample under foot. They moreover serve as the resting-place and support of furniture, and therefore whatever be the materials or fabrics employed, whether mosaics, tiles, marquetry, or carpets, the impression conveyed should be that of a stable and sustaining surface. A floor likewise being the lowest member in a room and the nearest to the ground, should not advance upon the eye, and even when serving as a foreground should appear in shade rather than in sunshine. These considerations incline to sombre colouring and to unostentatious designs. But here again there are no rules without occasional exceptions, and I am not one of those stern critics who would prohibit, for instance, such freedoms as the strewing of floors with flowers. Fra Angelico in his pictures scatters flowers on paths leading to Paradise, and if our homes can in anywise be made heaven-like, art will in good degree fulfil its mission. But as to the placing or misplacing of flowers I remember that at the Imperial fête given by the Düsseldorf artists in Jacobi's Garden, now the Malkasten Club, the Empress of Germany started from her seat, exclaiming, "I am trampling lovely flowers under my feet, remove the chair on one side." We may recall, however, on the other hand, how at a certain sacred triumph on the road leading from the Mount of Olives to Jerusalem "a very great multitude spread their garments in the way; and others cut down branches from the trees and strewed them in the way." Enthusiasm and love which in religion inspire to acts of devotion, need not be denied humble service in arts of decoration. Yet in our times a cold and barren rationalism would restrain fancy in her innocent sport with things of beauty.

But to return to plain matter of fact, it may be of use to sum up the general rules for floor coverings; they are briefly these :—

The surface of a carpet serving as a ground to support all objects, should be quiet and negative, without strong contrast of either form or colour. The decorative designs must be flat, without shadow or relief; flowers and foliage from nature must be conventionalised to meet the exigencies of art, and the pattern should be distributed evenly over the whole floor. The entire composition must be brought into balance of lines and masses, and into harmony of colour.

Ceilings, which have been strangely neglected or defaced, claim more than a moment's consideration, did space permit. They have sometimes been surrendered to a negative, sanatory, and undecorative coating of whitewash, and then again they have been heavily weighted with constructional beams serving to give stability to ponderous ornament. As to whitewash, the remedy is easy and inexpensive. Let some colour be added to the wash which shall harmonize with the tone of the upper walls. One purpose in the preceding remarks has been to show that the disposition of light, shade, and colour within a house may be reduced to certain elementary principles. And a rudimentary axiom is that dark should gravitate downwards, while light ascends upwards. Hence in part the reason why floors should be dusk and shadowy. And while the floor or ground represents the earth, the ceiling or vault leads up into air and space. Some persons, indeed, have pushed the comparison so far as to maintain that ceilings are best dealt with when, after the practice of the ancient Egyptians, they are coloured as the blue sky, spangled with golden stars. Others again have pushed the atmospheric idea to the extreme of covering the expanse of the ceiling with floating clouds; and a member of the Royal Society has not inappropriately employed a well-known artist to compose an astronomical ceiling, with the sun in the centre and the seasons and signs of the zodiac around. Other householders, inclining to botany and floriculture, train over their heads flowering creepers and climbing roses, making the ceiling a bowery canopy, attractive to butterflies and winged birds of bright plumage. At this point the transition becomes easy to Italian-like compositions wherein Cupids and genii float in mid heaven; but it is well to stop somewhere ere the sublime runs into th ridiculous. However, suffice it to say, that ceilings present spheres for diversions of fancy inviting to minds cherishing the laudable ambition of redeeming a dwelling from ordinary commonplace by some pretty spurts of poetry.

When the floor, walls, and ceiling are brought into harmony the decorations of a room are complete. Each part, I repeat, must be in studied relation of design and colour to the rest; the floor must sustain the walls, and they in turn must lead up to and support the ceiling. Yet while all are brought into unity, it is well when each is kept distinct. Accordingly fitting divisions and boundary lines are usually provided structurally in the skirting-board, the dado, the frieze, and cornice. These several members it is wise to pronounce more or less decisively, such points of demarcation in the decorative arts being comparable to punctuation in written compositions, serving, like commas, dashes, or full-stops, as pauses and spaces for rest. In the decoration of a room the crowning victory is in the successful coming of the whole together. And although simplicity is, for ease and economy, to be commended, yet, on the other hand, the greater the complexity and the difficulty challenged and overcome, the more signal will be the triumph gained, and the more subtle the pleasure imparted to the mind. Tyros in any art are timid; experts daring. Elementary forms and negative colours may be safe; but designs highly developed and colours lustrous as light will, in a master hand, secure decorative evolutions and effects comparable to the harmonies evoked by a full orchestra.

One or two general considerations may be added. It is not unworthy of remark that the house of the north necessarily differs from the house of the south. In the south protection is sought from heat, from the tyranny of the sun and the blaze of day, accordingly the classic house and the Italian villa provided open courts, cool corridors, and balconies of free outlook, while the walls and floors were clothed with plaster, marbles, or mosaics. But in the north the conditions are reversed; comfort and coziness are desired, and thus the northern house secures

closed rooms safe from the assaults of the elements, and provides snug curtains, warm carpets, and tight casements. In northern cities, too, a crying need is for more light within the dwelling. "The dark ages" were dark in more senses than one, and dirty into the bargain, and when modernism swept away the cobwebs of mediævalism, light entered as the herald of truth. Architecture, in its onward and upward growth, has been seeking to secure more light. Early structures are shadowy and cavernous; but at length buildings learnt to spring from the earth into the heavens, and courted companionship with the day. And light seeks association with the bright sisterhood of colour, and all in concert strive to compensate for the darkness and dulness of our northern clime, in the absence or shyness of the sun.

A like current of thought is suggested by the contrasted conditions of a town house and a country house. In England a country seat may be fitly designed for the summer and the sun. It is often in close proximity to nature; the windows possibly command a pleasing landscape; the daily life comes in hourly contact with gardens, trees, meadows; and in proportion as it thus shares in the simplicity of nature can the helps and allurements of art be dispensed with. But the town house is surrounded by opposite conditions. To shut out the external world, the noise of the street, and the gaze of the neighbour, is an end to be gained. And to make the home-life within all the more self-sustaining and satisfying, the mind seeks as a substitute for converse with nature, the companionship of literature and art. The complexities of modern society oust the artlessness of more primitive life, and the converse of cultured intellects, the contact of minds highly wrought, the companionship of books and music, demand that the dwelling shall be decorated to like concert pitch. In fine, in towns and northern latitudes, where the sky is overcast and the life of man sad, it peculiarly behoves us to make our homes lightsome and cheerful, so that in dark days witness shall not be wanting to the promise that, though "weeping may endure for a night, joy cometh in the morning."

"WHY ART THOU CAST DOWN, O MY SOUL?"

BY THE AUTHOR OF "SELINA'S STORY."

" HE has forsaken me, and I am weary
  Of journeying on a path so dark and dreary."

" And wherefore is it drear ? The birds are singing
  From boughs that shadows on the shine are flinging."

" I hear no music when one Voice does fail me ;
  My light is quenched ; can day's high noon avail me ? "

" And wherefore did He leave thee in thy sorrow ?
  He will return and comfort thee to-morrow."

" Alas, my sins me from His love did sever !
  His chidings I thought hard, repining ever."

" But He is gracious ; quick is His relenting,
  From far He sees the signs of thy repenting."

" Alas, too late I mourn ! He'll let me wander
  Cheerless, alone, my lost estate to ponder."

" For His forsaking, He more close will press thee
  Where the sword pierced, and surely there will bless thee."

" Ah, no ! His foes His footstool are, kept under
  By Him, whose hand had plucked their bars asunder.

  He wipes the tears from off the children's faces,
  And with the kiss of peace the bride embraces."

" O sorrowing soul ! such grief might be thy token,
  'Tis not the slave's will, but the child's heart broken ;

  'Tis not the rebel by His wrath o'ertaken,
  It is the bride one little hour forsaken.

  The rebel frets not that his lord's afar,
  The slave holds revel 'neath the morning star ;

  But spouse and children yearn for His returning,
  And keep to welcome it the hearth-fires burning."

MODERN GAELIC BARDS AND DUNCAN MACINTYRE.

A Lecture delivered at Oxford.

TO those who feel that poetry is a thing older than all manuscripts and books, and in its essence independent of them, there is something very refreshing in the poetry of the Gael. They will find there a poetry which, both in its ancient and more modern forms, was the creation of men who were taught in no school but that of nature; who could neither read nor write their native Gaelic; who, many of them, never saw a book or a manuscript; who had no other model than the old primeval Ossianic strains which they heard from childhood; and who sang only when inborn passion prompted—but then songs of genuine inspiration. What they com- posed they never thought of committing to writing, for writing was to them an unknown art. The great body of Highland poetry, both in old and in modern times, has come down to us preserved mainly by oral tradition. This is a fact which can be proved, let learned criticism believe it or not. I have already spoken of that great primitive background of heroic songs and ballads known as the Ossianic poetry, which had lived for centuries, only on the lips of men, before it was committed to writing. That was the nurse and school by which all after Gaelic poets were formed. To-day let us turn to the post-Ossianic, or modern poetry of the Gael, which reaches from the Middle Age almost down to our own time.

"In a land of song like the Highlands," says one who knew well what he spoke of, "every strath, glen, and hamlet had its bard. In the morning of my days," he goes on to say, writing in 1841, "it was my happy lot to inhale the mountain air of a sequestered spot, whose inhabitants may be designated children of song, and in a state of society whose manners were little removed from that of primitive simplicity. I had many opportunities of witnessing the influence of poetry over the mind, and I found that cheerfulness and song, music and morality, walked almost always hand in hand." Making allowance for the warmth of feeling with which a man looks back on a childhood spent among the mountains, these words are, I believe, true. One may be forgiven if one doubts whether the School Boards and the Code with its six Standards which have superseded this state of things, and are doing their best to stamp out the small remains of Gaelic poetry, are wholly a gain.

The writer from whom I have quoted, Mr. John Mackenzie, was a native of the west coast of Ross, and to him those who still cherish Gaelic poetry owe a great debt; for in 1841 he published his "Beauties of Gaelic Poetry," which is a collection of the best pieces of the best modern Gaelic bards. They are but a sample of what might have been dug from the vast quarry, but they are a good sample. In many cases he had to gather the poems of some of the best bards, not from any edition of their works, or even from manuscripts, but from the recitation of old people who preserved them in memory. Mackenzie's book contains more than thirty thousand lines of poetry on all kinds of subjects, from the heroic chant about—

> "Old unhappy far off things,
> And battles long ago!"

down to the—

> "More humble lay,
> Familiar matter of to-day."

To this book and its contents I shall confine myself to-day when I speak of the modern poetry of the Gael.

It is divided into three parts. First, a few poems of the Mediæval age, which form a sort of link between the Ossianic and the modern poetry. The second, and by far the largest, part consists of the poems of well-known bards from the Reformation down to the present century. The names of these are given with their works, and some account of their lives. The third portion consists of short popular songs well known among the people, but without the name of the authors attached to them.

Of the thirty bards, whose poems Mackenzie has preserved, I might give the names and a few facts about their lives and writings, but this, which is all I could do within my prescribed space, would not greatly edify any one. I might tell you of Mary Macleod, the nurse of five chiefs of Macleod, and the poetess of her clan; of Ian Lom McDonald, the first Jacobite bard, who led Montrose and his army to Inverlochy, pointed out the camping ground of the Campbells, then mounted the castle ramparts, watched the battle, and sang a fiery pæan when the victory was won; of McDonald, the second great Jacobite bard, who joined Prince Charlie's army, shared his disaster, and preserved the memory of that time in songs of fervid Jacobite devotion. But I would do little good by giving you merely bare lists of names, facts, and a few notions about Rob Donn, or Mackay, the poet of the Reay Country, a bitter and powerful satirist; of Dougal Buchanan, the earnest and solemn religious poet of Rannoch; and William Ross, the sweet lyrist of Gairloch, on the western shores of Ross, and many more. If any one desires to know more about these bards of the Gael, let me refer him to the brief biographies given of each of them in the book I have already spoken of, "Mackenzie's Beauties of Gaelic Poetry," and also to the very animated commentary on the contents of that book contained in my friend Professor Blackie's lively and interesting work on "The Language and Literature of the Scottish Highlands."

One characteristic of these Gaelic bards must be mentioned. They were most of them satirists as well as lyrists and eulogists. It was a true instinct that made the Chief of Macleod forbid his poetic nurse to sing praises of himself and his family, for the bard who is free to praise is also free to blame. Enthusiasm in admiration and love has as its other side equal vehemence of hatred. And this bitter side of the poetic nature found full vent in the poetry of many Highland bards. Biting wit, invectives often exceeding all bounds—these, but not humour, characterize the Gael. Humour, which is a quieter, more kindly quality, generally comes from men fatter, more well-fed, in easier circumstances than most of the Highland poets were. Satire abounds in both the Macdonalds, above all in Rob Don, who carries it often to coarseness. It is not wanting in the kindlier nature of the poet of whom I am now to speak; for I think I cannot do better than take as a sample of the Bardic Brotherhood one whom I have most studied, and who is, I believe, recognised as one of the very foremost, if not quite the foremost, of the Highland minstrels.

Any one who of late years has travelled by the banks of Loch Awe must have seen by the wayside, a short distance above Dalmally, a monument of rude unhewn stones cemented together. It stands very near the spot where Wordsworth, in his famous tour, first caught sight across the loch of the ruined Castle of Kilchurn, and shouted out impromptu the first three lines of his Address to the Castle :—

"Child of loud-throated war! the mountain stream
Roars in thy hearing, but thine hour of rest
Is come, and thou art silent in thine age."

That monument has been raised to the memory of the Bard of Glenorchy, Duncan MacIntyre, or "Donacha Ban nan Oran," Fair Duncan of the Songs, as he is familiarly called by his Highland countrymen. If ever poet was a pure son of nature, this man was. Born in a lonely place called Druimliaghart, on the skirts of the Monodh Dhu, or Breadalbane Forest of the Black Mount, of poor parents, he never went to school, never learnt to read or write, could not speak English, knew but one language—his own native Gaelic. His only school was the deer forest, in which he spent his boyhood. His lessons were catching trout and salmon with his fishing-rod, shooting grouse, and stalking deer with his gun. His mental food was the songs of the mountains, especially the great oral literature of the Ossianic minstrelsy. He tells us that he got a part of his nursing at the shealings; and I remember once, in a walk through the mountains of the Black Forest, beside a grass-covered road that leads down to Loch Etive, having the ruins of the bothy pointed out to me to which Duncan Ban used to come to spend his early summers. Those shealing times, when the people from the glens used to drive their black cattle and a few small sheep to pasture for the summer months on the higher Bens, are still looked back to by the Highlanders as their great season of happiness, romance, and song. Duncan had just reached manhood when the rising of the clans in the Forty-five broke out. Like all true Highlanders, his heart was with the Stewarts, but, as he lived on the lands of the Earl of Breadalbane, he was obliged to serve on the Hanoverian side as a substitute for a neighbouring taxman. This man supplied Duncan with a sword, which in the rout of Falkirk Duncan treated as Horace did his shield, and either lost or flung away. His earliest poem was composed on this battle, and in it Duncan describes with evident relish the disgraceful retreat, hinting that had he been on the Prince's side he would have fought with more manhood. The man as whose substitute he served in that battle refused to pay the sum promised because Duncan had lost the sword; so the poet took care to give him a sidelong satiric thrust in the poem. Fletcher, for that was the man's name, fell upon the poet and thrashed him with his walkingstick, telling him to go and make a song upon that. But Duncan had a friend in the Breadalbane of the day, who came to his aid and forced Fletcher to pay down the money to the man who had risked his life on his account. This first poem soon became known and made Duncan famous and Fletcher despised.

Early in life the bard married a young girl of somewhat higher station and richer parents than himself. There is nothing more pleasing in the loves of any of the poets than this courtship. In a beautiful lyric called "Mairi Bhan òg," or "Fair Young Mary," he tells how he wooed and won her. Her home was within less than a mile of his own, but their condition in life was so dissimilar that for long he despaired. Her father was baron bailiff, or under factor, and a freeholder, and she had some cows and calves of her own for a dowry. Duncan was the son of poor people, and had no patrimony. He tells how he used from his own door to watch her as she went about her household work, and how, when at last he ventured to address her, her kindness of demeanour gave him confidence. After praising her beauty, he says, the thing that most took him was her firmness in good, and her manners that were ever so womanly. And he concludes by wishing to take her away and hide her in some place where decay or change might never reach her. This song, we are told, is regarded, "on account of its combined purity and passion, its grace, delicacy, and tenderness," as the finest love song in the Gaelic language.

After his return from soldiering, his patron, Lord Breadalbane, made Duncan his forester, first in Coire Ceathaich, or the Misty Corrie, in the forest of Maam-lorn; at the head of Glenlochy; then on Ben Doran, a beautifully shaped hill at the head of Glenorchy, looking down that long glen towards Loch Awe. For a time, too, he served under the Duke of Argyll as deer forester on Buachail

XXI—30

Etie, or the Shepherd of Etive, a gnarled peak facing towards both Glen Etive and Glencoe. Duncan has made famous Coire Ceathaich and Ben Doran by two of his best poems. The poem on Coire Ceathaich has been translated by a living poet, Mr. Robert Buchanan, in his book called "The Land of Lorne." His version gives a very good notion of it, with its minute realistic description :—

> "My beauteous corrie! where cattle wander,
> My misty corrie! my darling dell!
> Mighty, verdant, and covered over
> With tender wild flowers of sweetest smell;
> Dark is the green of thy grassy clothing,
> Soft swell thy hillocks, most green and deep,
> The cannach flowing, the darnel growing,
> While the deer troop past to the misty steep."

But of all Duncan Ban's poems the most original, the most elaborate, and the most famous is that on Ben Doran. It consists of five hundred and fifty-five lines, and is unique in its plan and construction. It is adapted to a pipe-tune, and follows all the turns, and twirls, and wild cadences of the pibroch with wonderful skill. It falls into eight parts, alternating with a sort of strophe and antistrophe, one slow, called "urlar," being in stately trochees; another swift, called "siubhal," being a sort of galloping anapæsts. In Ben Doran, as in Coire Ceathaich, the bard dwells with the most loving minuteness on all the varied features and the ever-changing aspects of the mountain which he loved, as if it were a living creature and a friend. But besides this, in no poem one ever heard of have all the looks, haunts, habits, and manners of the deer, both red-deer and roe, been pictured so accurately and so fondly by one who had been born and reared among them, and knew them as his chosen playmates.

Professor Blackie has made a very spirited rendering into English of this most difficult poem, to which I would advise any one to turn who cares for poetry fresh from nature. I venture at present to give some passages from a translation I made years ago to beguile hours of wandering among the Highland hills. Be it remembered, however, how different a thing is a wild Celtic chant adapted to the roar and thunder of the bagpipe from a literary performance meant only to be read by critical eyes in unexcited leisure. Here is the opening stave :—

> "Honour o'er all Bens
> On Bendoran be!
> Of all hills the sun kens,
> Beautifullest he;
> Mountain long and sweeping,
> Nooks the red deer keeping,
> Light on braesides sleeping;
> There I've watched delightedly.

> Branchy copses cool,
> Woods of sweet grass full,
> Deer herds beautiful,
> There are dwelling aye.
> Oh! blithe to hunting go,
> Where white hipped stag and hind,
> Upward in long row,
> Snuff the mountain wind.
> Jaunty follows sprightly,
> With bright burnished hide,
> Dressed in fashion rightly,
> Yet all free from pride."

The poem is, as I have said, made for a pibroch tune, and is, like the pibroch, full of repetitions. It returns again and again upon the same theme, but each time with variations and additions. Thus the grasses, and plants, and bushes that grow on Ben Doran are more than once described, as if the poet never tired of thinking of them. The red-deer, the stag and the hind, with their ways; the roe-deer, buck and doe, with their ways; each are several times dwelt on at length.

I shall now give but one specimen of the description of each kind of deer. Here is a picture of the red-deer hind and the stag, her mate :—

> "Hark that quick darting snort!
> 'Tis the light-headed hind,
> With sharp-pointed nostril,
> Keen searching the wind;
> Conceited, slim-limbed,
> The high summits she keeps,
> Nor, for fear of the gun-fire,
> Comes down from the steeps.
> Though she gallop at speed
> Her breath will not fail,
> For she comes of a breed
> Were strong-winded and hale.

> "When she lifteth her voice,
> What joy 'tis to hear
> The ghost of her breath,
> As it echoeth clear.
> For she calleth aloud,
> From the cleft of the crag,
> Her silver-hipped lover,
> The proud antlered stag.
> Well-antlered, high-headed,
> Loud-voiced doth he come,
> From the haunts he well knows
> Of Bendoran, his home.

> "Ah! mighty Bendoran!
> How hard 'twere to tell
> How many proud stags
> In thy fastnesses dwell.
> How many thy slim hinds,
> With woe calves attending,
> And their white-twinkling tails
> Up the balloch ascending,
> To where Corrie-Chreetar
> Its bield is extending.

> "But when the mood takes her
> To gallop with speed,
> With her slender hoof-tips
> Hardly touching the mead,
> As she stretcheth away
> In her fleet-flying might,
> What man in the kingdom
> Could follow her flight?
> Full of gambol and gladness,
> Blithe wanderers free,
> No shadow of sadness
> Ever comes o'er their glee.
> But fitful and tricksey,
> Slim and agile of limb,
> Age will not burden them,
> Sorrow not dim."

· · · · ·

"How gay through the glens
  Of the sweet mountain grass,
Loud sounding, all free
  From complaining they pass.
Though the snow come, they'll ask
  For no roof-tree to bield them;
The deep Corrie Altrum,
  His rampart will shield them.
There the rifts, and the clefts,
  And deep hollows they'll be in,
With their well-sheltered beds
  Down in lone Aisan-teean."

Again in an urlar or slow trochaic strophe he returns to the same theme—

"O! sweet to me at rising
  In early dawn to see,
All about the mountains,
  Where they've right to be,
Twice a hundred there
  Of the people without care,
Starting from their lair,
  Hale and full of glee;
Clear-sounding, smooth, and low,
  From their mouths the murmurs flow,
And beautiful they go,
  As they sing their morning song.

*   *   *   *   *

Sweeter to me far,
  When they begin their croon,
Than all melodies that are
  In Erin—song or tune—
Than pipe or viol clear,
  More I love to hear,
The breath of the son of the deer,
  Bellowing on the face
Of Bendoran."

Our last sample shall be the description of the roe :—

"Mid budding sprays the doe
  Ever restless moves—
Edge of banks and braes,
  Haunts that most she loves.
Young leaves, fresh and sheen,
  Tips of heather green—
Dainties fine and clean
  Are her choice.
Pert, coquettish, gay,
  Thoughtless, full of play,
Creature, made alway
  To rejoice.
Maiden-like in mien,
  Mostly she is seen
In the birk-glens green
  Where lush grasses be.
But sometimes Crag-y-vhor,
  Gives her refuge meet,
Sunday and Monday there
  In a still retreat.
Bushes thick and deep
  Close there round her sleep,
And far from her keep
  Rude north-winds blowing,
In bield of Doire-chro,
  Lying down below
The Sron's lofty brow,
  Where fresh shoots are growing.
There well-springs clear and fine,
  With draughts more benign
Than ale or any wine,
  Always are flowing.
These, as they pour
  Their streams unfailing,
Keep her evermore
  Fresh and free from ailing.

"Yellow hues and red,
  Delicately spread,
O'er her figure shed
  Loveliness complete.
Hardy 'gainst the cold,
  Virtues manifold,
More than can be told,
  In her nature meet.

"At the hunter's sound
  Sudden whirling round,
How lightly doth she bound
  O'er rough mountain ground,
Far and free.

Quicker ear to hear
  Danger drawing near,
Fleeter flight from fear,
  In Europe cannot be."

This long hunting pibroch, of which I have given a few samples, is a prime favourite with all Gaelic-speaking men, and is to them what such songs as "Gala Water" or the "Holms of Yarrow" are to the ear of the Lowlander. Duncan Ban will ever be remembered among his countrymen as the chief minstrel of the deer, the chase, and the forest. As a deer-stalker he had lived much in solitude,—

"—had been alone
Amid the heart of many thousand mists."

When he was forester on Ben Doran, in Coire Ceathaich, and on Buachail Etie, these were his best hours of inspiration. But solitude left no shade of sadness on his spirit; there is in his song nothing of the Ossianic melancholy. He was a blithe, hearty companion, fond of good-fellowship, and in several of his songs he has praised boon-companionship with right good-will. But though he enjoyed such things he never lost himself in joviality.

When his foresting days were over he joined a volunteer regiment called the Breadalbane Fencibles, in which he served for six years, till they were disbanded in 1799. After his discharge from the Fencibles he served for some time in the City Guard of Edinburgh, which Walter Scott has described in one of his novels. The third edition of his poems was published in 1804, and in 1806 he was able to retire from the City Guard and to live for the remainder of his days in comparative comfort on the return which this third edition brought him. He died in 1812 in Edinburgh, in his eighty-ninth year, and was buried there.

Born at Druimliaghart, on the skirts of the Black Mount, at the head of Glenorchy; laid in Gray Friar's Churchyard, Edinburgh; beloved in life; honoured after his death by his countrymen with a monument placed at the foot of his own Glenlochy, of him we may say more than of most of the Sons of Song—that "he sleeps well."

Once or twice he wandered through the Highlands to obtain subscriptions for a new edition of his poems. I knew a Highland lady who remembered to have seen him in her childhood on one of these occasions, when he visited her father's house in Mull. He was wandering about with the wife of his youth, Mairi Bhan òg, still fair, but no longer young. He then wore, if I remember aright, a tartan kilt, and on his head a cap made of a fox's skin. He was fair of hair and face, with a pleasant countenance, and a happy, attractive manner. An amiable, sweet-blooded man, who never, it is said, attacked any one unprovoked; but when he was assailed, he could repay smartly in that satire which seems to have been a gift native to all the Highland bards.

After he had settled in Edinburgh he paid one last visit to his native Glenorchy in 1802, where he found that those changes had already set in which have since desolated so many glens, and changed the whole aspect of social life in the Highlands.

In the close of his pathetic farewell Duncan Ban has touched on what has since become a great social question—I mean the clearing of the glens, the depopulation of the Highlands. This great change—revolution I might call it—began early in this century, and our bard saw the first fruits of the new system. The old native Gael who used to live in groups or hamlets in the glens, each with so many small sheep and goats and a small herd of black cattle which they pastured in common on the mountains, these were dispossessed of the holdings they had held for immemorial time, to make way for Lowland farmers with large capital, who covered hill and glen with large flocks of bigger sheep. These a few shepherds, often Lowlanders, tended on those mountains from which the old race had been expelled, and the land became indeed a wilderness. One question only was asked—What shall most speedily return large rents to the lairds; and what shall grow the largest amount of mutton for the Glasgow and Liverpool markets? Tried by this purely commercial standard, the ancient Gael were found wanting, and being dispossessed, went to America and elsewhere. Great Britain thus lost thousands of the finest of its people irrecoverably.

Since Culloden, the Highlands have received from the British Government only one piece of wise and kindly legislation. That was when the elder Pitt gave the chiefs or their sons commissions to raise regiments from among their clansmen. The result was the Highland regiments, who bore themselves all know how, in the Peninsula and at Waterloo. Their name and the remembrance of their achievements remain to this day a tower of strength to the British army, although in many of the so-called Highland regiments there is now scarcely one genuine Gael. In the glens which formerly sent forth whole regiments you could not now set a single man to wear her Majesty's uniform.

But to return from these matters economical and political to our bard. It is a noteworthy fact that as he could neither read nor write, he had to carry the whole of his poetry, which amounts to about six thousand lines, in his memory, which was also stored with a large equipment of Ossianic and other ancient lays. After Duncan had retained his poems for years on the unwritten tablets of his heart, a young minister took them down from the bard's recital, and so preserved them for us. Facts like these, and they could easily be multiplied, tend to show how short-sighted is the view of critics who refuse to believe in the preserving power of oral tradition. They also show how far culture can go wholly unaided by books. Any one who reads with an open heart the poetry of our bard must acknowledge that here we have a man more truly replenished with all that is best in culture, than most of the men who are the products of our modern School Board schools, or even than some of their teachers.

McIntyre has sometimes been called The Burns of the Highlands. Burns and he lived at the same time, but McIntyre's life overlapped that of Burns at both ends. He was born thirty-five years before Burns, and outlived him by sixteen years. It is strange, and shows the great separation there then was between the Highlands and the rest of the world, that there is no evidence that either poet knew of the existence of the other. Yet McIntyre must have heard of Burns when he passed his old age in Edinburgh. Though McIntyre has been compared to Burns, there is little likeness between them, except in this. Both were natural, spontaneous singers; both sang of human life as they saw it with their own eyes; each is the darling poet of his own people. Here the likeness ends. McIntyre had not the experience of men and society, the varied range, of Burns. The problem of the rich and poor, and many another problem which vexed Burns, never troubled the Bard of Glenorchy. He accepted his condition, and was content; had no jealousy of those above him in rank or wealth. He was happier than Burns in his own inner man, and had no quarrel with the world and the way it was ordered, till they expelled the deer and brought in the big long-wooled sheep. But if McIntyre knew less of man than Burns, he knew more of nature in its grand and solitary moods. He took it more to heart; at every turn it more enters into his song and forms its texture.

McIntyre's poetry eminently disproves,— as indeed all Gaelic poetry does—that doctrine of the schools, that love of nature is necessarily a late growth, the product of refined cultivation. It may be so with the phlegmatic Teuton, not so with the susceptible impassioned Gael. Their poets, and above all McIntyre, who were never inside a school-room, never read a book, love their mountains as passionately as Wordsworth loved his, though with a simpler, more primitive devotion.

Mr. Arnold concluded his lectures delivered here on Celtic Literature by pleading for the foundation in Oxford of a Celtic chair. He thought that this might perhaps atone for the errors of Saxon Philistines, and send through the gentle ministrations of science a message of peace to Ireland. Oxford since then has got a Celtic chair, though how far this has propitiated Ireland seems doubtful.

Another Celtic chair is just about to be founded in Edinburgh University, thanks to Professor Blackie, who by his own right hand, and the advocacy of years, has raised more than £11,000 for its endowment. But the foundation of Celtic chairs will be of little avail, unless the younger generation takes advantage of them. In Oxford, if anywhere, there are surely some who have leisure, linguistic faculty, and some love of poetry. To such let me say that if they will but master the language of the Gael and go into the great background of their native song, they will find there to repay their efforts much that is weird and wild, as well as sweet and tender, thrilling with a piercing tenderness wholly unlike anything in the Saxon tongue. There they may not only delight and reinvigorate their imagination, but they may fetch thence new tones of inspiration for our English poetry.

And more than this, they will find there sources of deep human interest. The knowledge of the Gaelic language will be a key to open to them the hearts of a noble people as nothing else can. England does owe a real debt to the Scottish Gael, if not so claimant as her debt to Ireland. A debt for the wrongs done last century after Culloden battle—a debt still unrepaired, perhaps now unrepairable. A debt, too, for the world of pleasure which English people annually reap in the Scottish Highlands. The native Gael are capable of something more than merely to be gillies and keepers to rich brewers and to aristocratic pleasure-seekers. Beneath those dim smoky shealings of the west beat hearts which contain feelings which the pushing and prosperous Saxon little dreams of. The race whose fathers in the last century sheltered and defended with their lives their outlawed prince, and while they themselves were poor and starving, and £30,000 was offered for his head, never once thought of betraying him, though many hundreds of them were in the secret—that race contains in their heart something of finer quality which Englishmen and Lowland Scots might learn to recognise and to love with benefit to themselves.

J. C. SHAIRP.

CITY COURTS AND COUNTRY LANES.

By KATHARINE S. MACQUOID.

" One touch of nature."

SIR ARTHUR HELPS said in one of the last books he wrote that nowadays, if a working-man wants to breathe pure air, he must walk ten miles out of the heart of London to reach it.

One has got into a way of thinking that only the purely animal or the purely spiritual side of the poor of London need be cared for; whereas the indirect influences that affect both matter and spirit—influences that arise from pleasant impressions and emotional causes—are apt to be much overlooked in dealing with our badly clothed and badly fed brothers and sisters. I am convinced that the imaginative side of a working man's or woman's brain should be cultivated in childhood, not by trashy and stimulating literature, but by the yearly refreshment of seeing what is pure and beautiful in the sweet invigorating air of the country; in flower-pied meadows, with the sight of fair trees; the glories of sunrise and sunset; and all the exquisite charms that make the country, just the country, with its deep stillness, its leisureful repose, its fragrant air and fresh pure breezes, and the almost magical benefit effected by change of air and change of surroundings, such a haven of bliss for the cultivated worker. It would be worth while at least to try the experiment, and then see in the next generation whether we have less drunkenness and wife-beating, and possibly happier lives and homes, in the heart of our great city. There are so many who live in its crowded lanes and courts who tell you they have no friends in the country. Not long ago I was in some of these crowded White-chapel courts, and I think only one of the many children I talked to told me he had country friends to go to.

When one thinks of the exquisite joy that the mere sight of the country gives, how one's whole being seems to expand as one drinks in the fresh loveliness of unstained leafage, of luxuriant grass, of pure daisies and golden buttercups; the fragrance of honeysuckle hedges or of a newly-mown hay-field; or perhaps, a little later in the year, of a rosy clover-field, enamelled by a moving awning of butterflies; then the lark singing all day long; the cuckoo, that cheerful, mellow-voiced companion of our walks; the old twisted stiles we have to climb heedfully lest long hard red bramble arms in the hedge hard by tear us before we gain the other side. Just think how few of these pale-faced, shrunken-limbed East-end children have ever seen a bramble! one of the most beautiful sights in nature—beautiful in leaves and flowers and fruit.

> " For dull the eye, the heart is dull
> That cannot feel how fair,
> Amid all beauty beautiful,
> Thy tender blossoms are ;
> How delicate thy gauzy frill,
> How rich thy branchy stem,
> How soft thy voice when woods are still
> And thou sing'st hymns to them."

It is a flower, too, as the Corn-law Rhymer goes on to tell us, that is to be found when

> " The primrose to the grave has gone,
> The hawthorn flower is dead,
> The violet by the mossed grey stone
> Hath laid her weary head ;
> But thou, wild bramble, back doth bring,
> In all their beauteous power,
> The fresh green days of life's fair spring,
> And boyhood's blossomy hour."

" Blossomy hour "—scarcely metre, but how full of meaning when one thinks of the squalor and dirt and drunkenness, and, in summer, the stifling air in which our East-end children have been reared, and how little of freshness or brightness they have known! They play, when they do play, in the narrow paved courts, surrounded by small overfilled houses, which reek of close air and old clothes; and though some of the children have rosy cheeks, and brighter eyes than could be expected, yet if you feel their little hands and arms their flesh is flabby and nerveless ; and when they play there is utter monotony in their surroundings, the only relief from the dull houses being a line full of wet linen across the court, or, perhaps, a bird-cage or a pot-

flower outside a window. Some pots of prim-roses I saw gleamed out like jewels from the dull walls. Yet, spite of their foul surroundings and the dull ugliness of their daily lives, the poor generally show, if you give them a chance, a love for the beautiful. The success of the flower-shows and window-gardening prizes attest this ; still more, the longing, hungry-eyed glances with which any London child greets the sight of flowers. An East-end worker told me that in some of the City courts a bunch of bright flowers, as a peace-offering, had gained her an entrance into houses hitherto shut against her. Not long ago she was distributing bunches of spring flowers to a crowd of eager-eyed, pale-faced little ones; the flowers were all given, and yet she saw craving little hands stretched out towards her. What could they want? The poor little things wanted the fallen petals which strewed the table and the basket in which she had taken the flowers. They were full of delight to get these crumbs of the feast of beauty. It is, of course, possible to develop this love of the beautiful in any class into a mere hollow, soul-destroying æstheticism, by making self and the senses its centre and aim. But surely in the country the very serenity and peace of all outward things must teach wholesome lessons ; a lesson—

> " Which bids us see in heaven and earth,
> In all fair things around,
> Strong yearnings for a blest new birth,
> With sinless glories crown'd.

> "Which bids us bear at each sweet pause
> From care and want and toil,
> When dewy eve her curtain draws
> Over the day's turmoil,

> "In the low chant of wakeful birds,
> In the deep weltering flood,
> In whispering leaves, those solemn words,
> 'God made us all for good.' "

Certainly I believe that if the plan tried last year with so much success by the Rev. Miles Atkinson, of St. Jude's, Whitechapel, for some of the poorest children of his flock, can be organized in future every year on a much larger scale for the whole of the East-end of London, it will not only bring a large supply of health and happiness into the most wretched districts, but may eventually raise the tone and character of our London poor.

A few years ago a City clergyman, much troubled by the pale faces and meagre limbs of some of his closely-housed flock, hired a house in a country village, and sent the children down to recruit in small batches at a time. This was a good beginning; but in 1878 Mr. Barnet, of St. Jude's, Whitechapel, made a yet more successful experiment. He began at the other end, wrote to all the country clergymen and country gentlemen he could think of, and asked them to find room in their villages for so many children, for each of whom five shillings would be paid weekly.

His appeal was successful. In the course of the summer he sent down about thirty-four children for change to villages in Huntingdonshire, Cambridgeshire and elsewhere. Last year a lady anxious to get country air for a little sickly *protégé*, heard of Mr. Barnet's successful experiment, and gladly joined the good work which Mr. Atkinson was preparing to begin on a much larger scale. Country clergymen and squires were besieged wherever any clue could be found to them, and the appeal was always most willingly and cordially answered. There were many arrangements and conditions. The kind country helpers in the work made themselves responsible for good, clean, and healthy homes, and Mr. Atkinson and his London helpers promised to send down clean and safe children. In every case where it was possible, the parents were asked to contribute towards the travelling expenses and to take their children to the railway station and see them off, so as to give them a personal interest in the work; but much lecturing and supervision was needed to effect this. One woman actually had to take her child three times before she could catch a train.

Then the London parents had also their conditions to make; a few considered it a great favour to allow their children to go at all, although assured that they would not have to pay for their board and lodging. One man hinted that if as a great favour he allowed his children to go, the least that could be expected of the clergyman was that he should travel down all the way with the little holiday-seekers. Mr. Atkinson says that he specially wished to give this pleasant change to one poor little sickly girl, whose growth had been stunted by over-work for a drunken mother. He proposed the plan to the father, and this was the answer he received when the parents had held counsel together—

"Well! me and the wife has talked it over, and we thinks that if Annie could go without any trouble to us, it would do no harm."

There are others, and these not the poorest, who are eager to take all possible advantage from the scheme, and who consider that if their child goes to church or to school it has a right to the holiday. Some made it a sort of pretext to obtain clothing for a whole family, and others were terribly disturbed because their children were declared too dirty to go with the rest; but finally the whole scheme was arranged, and the first batch was sent off in June.

It must have been touching to see those pale-faced, large-eyed children, many of them with shrunken bodies and limbs, each with a label tied round his or her neck with the name, time of starting, and destination of each clearly written thereon, setting forth on this their first journey, for the children selected were always from the large class who have no friends in the country. One would like to know what passed through some of those small minds, and what they thought of the fair meadows and grand trees they saw on their journey. We hear that only one little girl tried to escape from the donkey-cart which was waiting at the station to take her to her country home; it is cheering to hear that the same child at the end of the three weeks' holiday almost refused to go back to London, and cried bitterly at leaving, she had been so happy with her new friends.

The country is evidently a fairy tale to some of these little dwellers in dingy courts and alleys. One child thought that everything came from the cow; even when some one gave her a biscuit she asked if the cow made it! and another expected to find wild beasts roaming about. Some of them were kindly taken in at an orphanage in Wiltshire. The lady superintendent writes, "I found the children most tractable, and they got on well with my own children. One pleasure we were able to give was the sight of a 'grand rainbow.' Some of the children had never seen one, and were both amazed and delighted; they thought it was only in the Bible, and its teaching they explained beautifully."

The little waifs and strays seem to have been thoroughly popular, and there are many requests from their country entertainers to have the little London folk again this year. In several cases the children were asked to stay on as visitors in these rural homes, when the time paid for had expired. Of course all was not *couleur de rose*. One boy, a certain Joey, happened to be placed with a tidy, rigid woman who did not understand boy-nature; but very soon Joey righted the matter himself; at the other end of the village he found a home where he seems to have got on comfortably for the rest of his visit. Between June and October one hundred and seventy children were sent out for country holidays. "On the whole," another of their kind entertainers says, "they were excellent children, and seem to me far easier to influence than country ones. They are so much sharper and understand."

Taking the enterprise as a whole its success was marvellous, for, as Mr. Atkinson says, "it was a serious undertaking, to scatter one hundred and seventy East-end children broadcast over the country in all sorts of villages and homes over which we had no control and with which we had no personal connection." That it turned out such a success he attributes "to the readiness of resource, the exertions and the tact of those who so heartily responded to the appeal, and who helped so effectually." The effect on the children has been excellent both as regards health and conduct; one little pale-faced girl grew so plump and rosy that her own mother turned from her when she went to claim her at the station, she did not know her little bright-eyed child. They are cleaner too in their habits since their return, and they have caught some of the peaceful, whole-some country ways, such as making them-selves extra clean and tidy for Sundays. Though, alas! a little girl who had been placed in one of the bettermost families gave a sad shock to the nerves of her hosts. On the Saturday, when they were all seated at dinner, the little plaintive voice said, "Please, will my Sunday clothes be took out of pawn?"

One can fancy the electrifying effect on these quiet, leisurely souls, who had gone on living this same thrifty life in the same house for generations, knowing nothing of the shifts and excitements or feverish hurry of over-work and improvidence. The country chil-dren seem to have enjoyed the fellowship of these visitors, sharper-witted and doubtless more amusing than themselves; and one country rector says that the common interest taken in the little Londoners helped him to friendly talks with some of his own people who had before held aloof from him, so true is it that no tie draws hearts closer than

"Thoughts of good together done."

One of the London children wrote home to her parents, "I ride all over the country in a carriage;" on inquiry, it was found that she had been placed in the house of the village butcher, who by way of amusing his little visitor took her out every day in his cart when he went his rounds. One of the boys took special interest in the roads, he thought them so superior to the London streets, and was incredulous when told that some country children wished to live in London. I was much amused in talking to some of the children who had the holiday last year. The universal delight of the boys was in hay carts, and the one among them who had been allowed to ride home atop of the hay was evidently looked on with reverence; "Please, I sat in a cart all day," and "I lied in a field all day," were called out as special claims on my admiration. The girls' talk ran on buttercups and daisies, and kit-tens and dogs, and about chickens; "little tiny ones," said a pretty pale child, with big brown eyes full of eagerness, "an' two days before I comed away I saw two little mites just out of a hegg." The row of girls beside her looked up at me as much as to say, "Beat that if you can!" Also some of them had been asked out to tea every night; and this was evidently a great achievement, some-thing to talk of for months to come.

The home-coming was a great excitement. Every child brought home presents, and one of these was sure to be a plant of some kind; one boy actually carried home four pot-flowers. "One broked," he said; "but the others was beautiful, there was a geranium and a blue beany (verbena), and a flower with a lot of like bells hanging down," which turned out to be a fuchsia. The fields had been an especial delight, and the children are never tired of telling about "what we do in the country." Doubtless the dingy close room at home looked still dingier at the end of the brief holiday, and no doubt there was temporary grumb-ling and discontent; but it is hoped that the very discontent thus occasioned may prove useful; it may rouse some of the chil-dren, and the parents too, from the inertness with which they have tolerated dirt and un-tidiness, as a kind of necessity; in time this very discontent may develop into aspirations after a more decent life, and may bear out-ward fruit in cleaner, better-ordered ways at home. It may be, too, that the parents of some of the poor children who were rejected last year may produce them in a less ragged and dirty condition when the holiday season comes round. I hope that funds may flow in so largely that other poor little ones besides those of St. Jude's, Whitechapel, little ones who have never in their lives heard a bird sing in the hedges or taken a run in a green field, may enjoy the blessed sight of fair hedge-rows and daisy-filled meadows, and hear the lark as he sings at heaven's gate in 1880.

Any communications on the subject of the children's holiday should be addressed to Reverend Miles Atkinson, 48, New Road, Whitechapel, E.

A RACE FOR LIFE.

A Study in Black and White by E. Rischgitz.

THE TRUMPET-MAJOR.

By THOMAS HARDY, Author of "Far from the Madding Crowd," etc.

CHAPTER XXII.—THE TWO HOUSEHOLDS UNITED.

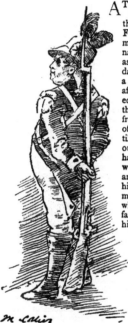

A T this particular moment the object of Festus Derriman's fulmination was assuredly not dangerous as a rival. Bob, after abstractedly watching the soldiers from the front of the house till they were out of sight, had gone within doors and seated himself in the mill - parlour, where his father found him, his elbows resting on the table and his forehead on his hands, his eyes being fixed upon a document that lay open before him.

"What art perusing, Bob, with such a long face?"

Bob sighed, and then Mrs. Loveday and Anne entered. "'Tis only a state-paper that I fondly thought I should have a use for," he said gloomily. And, looking down as before, he cleared his voice, as if moved inwardly to go on, and began to read in feeling tones from what proved to be his nullified marriage licence :—

"'Timothy Titus Philemon, by permission Bishop of Bristol : To our well-beloved Robert Loveday, of the parish of Overcombe, Bachelor ; and Matilda Johnson, of the same parish, Spinster. Greeting.'"

Here Anne sighed, but contrived to keep down her sigh to a mere nothing.

XXI—31

"Beautiful language, isn't it," said Bob. "I was never greeted like that before !"

"Yes, I have often thought it very excellent language myself," said Mrs. Loveday.

"Come to that, the old gentleman will greet thee like it again any day for a couple of guineas," said the miller.

"That's not the point, father ! You never could see the real meaning of these things. . . . . Well, then he goes on : 'Whereas ye are, as it is alleged, determined to enter into the estate of matrimony——' But why should I read on ? It all means nothing now—nothing, and the splendid words are all wasted upon air. It seems as if I had been hailed by some venerable hoary prophet, and had turned away, put the helm hard up, and wouldn't hear."

Nobody replied, feeling probably that sympathy could not meet the case, and Bob went on reading the rest of it to himself, occasionally heaving a breath like the wind in a ship's shrouds.

"I wouldn't set my mind so much upon her, if I was thee," said his father at last.

"Why not ?"

"Well, folk might call thee a fool, and say thy brains were turning to water."

Bob was apparently much struck by this thought, and, instead of continuing the discourse further, he carefully folded up the licence, rose and went out, and walked up and down the garden. It was startlingly apt what his father had said ; and, worse than that, what people would call him might be true, and the liquefaction of his brains turn out to be no fable. By degrees he became much concerned, and the more he examined himself by this new light the more clearly did he perceive that he was in a very bad way.

On reflection he remembered that since Miss Johnson's departure his appetite had decreased amazingly. He had eaten in meat no more than fourteen or fifteen ounces a day, but one-third of a quartern pudding on an average, in vegetables only a small heap of potatoes and half a York cabbage, and no gravy whatever ; which, considering the usual appetite of a seaman for fresh food at the end of a long voyage, was no small index of the depression of his mind. Then he had awaked once every night, and on one occasion twice. While dressing each morning since the gloomy day he had not whistled more than seven bars of a hornpipe without stopping and falling into thought of a most painful kind; and he had told none but absolutely true stories of foreign parts to the neighbouring villagers when they saluted and clustered about him, as usual, for anything he chose to pour forth—except that story of the whale whose eye was about as large as the round pond in Derriman's ewe-lease—which was like tempting fate to set a seal for ever upon his tongue as a traveller. All this enervation, mental and physical, had been produced by Matilda's departure. .

He also considered what he had lost of the rational amusements of manhood during these unfortunate days. He might have gone to Weymouth every afternoon, stood before Gloucester Lodge till the king and queen came out, held his hat in his hand, and enjoyed their Majesties' smiles at his homage all for nothing—watched the picket-mounting, heard the different bands strike up, observe the staff; and, above all, have seen the pretty Weymouth girls go trip-trip-trip along the Esplanade, deliberately fixing their innocent eyes on the distant sea, the grey cliffs, and the sky, and accidentally on the soldiers and himself.

"I'll raze out her image," he said. "She shall make a fool of me no more." And his resolve resulted in conduct which had elements of real greatness.

He went back to his father, whom he found in the mill-loft. "'Tis true, father, what you say," he observed: "my brains will turn to bilge-water if I think of her much longer. By the oath of a—navigator, I wish I could sigh less and laugh more. She's gone—why can't I let her go, and be happy? But how begin?"

"Take it careless, my son," said the miller, "and lay yourself out to enjoy snacks and cordials."

"Ah—that's a thought!" said Bob.

"Baccy is good for't."

"Baccy—I'd almost forgot it!" said Captain Loveday.

He went to his room, hastily untied the package of tobacco that he had brought home, and began to make use of it in his own way, calling to David for a bottle of the old household mead that had lain in the cellar these eleven years. He was discovered by his father three-quarters of an hour later as a half-invisible object behind a cloud of smoke.

The miller drew a breath of relief. "Why, Bob," he said, "I thought the house was a-fire!"

"I'm smoking rather fast to drown my reflections, father. 'Tis no use to chaw."

To tempt his attenuated appetite the unhappy mate made David cook an omelet and bake a seed cake, the latter so richly compounded that it opened to the knife like a freckled buttercup. With the same object he stuck night-lines into the banks of the mill-pond, and drew up next morning a family of fat eels, some of which were skinned and prepared for his breakfast. They were his favourite fish, but such had been his condition that, until the moment of making this effort, he had quite forgotten their existence at his father's back-door.

In a few days Bob Loveday had considerably improved in tone and vigour. One other obvious remedy for his dejection was to indulge in the society of Miss Garland, love being so much more effectually got rid of by displacement than by attempted annihilation. But Loveday was of so simple a nature that the belief that he had offended her beyond forgiveness, and his ever-present sense of her as a woman who by education and antecedents was fitted to adorn a higher sphere than his own, effectually kept him from going near her for a long time, notwithstanding that they were inmates of one house. The reserve was, however, in some degree broken by the appearance one morning, some time later in the season, of the point of a saw through the partition which divided Anne's room from the Loveday half of the house. Though she dined and supped with her mother and the Loveday family, Miss Garland had still continued to occupy her old apartments, because she found it more convenient there to pursue her hobbies of wool-work and of copying her father's old pictures. The division wall had not as yet been broken down.

As the saw worked its way downwards under her astonished gaze Anne jumped up from her drawing; and presently the temporary canvasing and papering which had sealed up the old door of communication was cut completely through. The door burst open, and Bob stood revealed on the other side, with the saw in his hand.

"I beg your ladyship's pardon," he said, taking off the hat he had been working in, as his handsome face expanded into a smile. "I didn't know this door opened into your private room."

"Indeed, Captain Loveday."

"I am pulling down the division on principle, as we are now one family. But I really thought the door opened into your passage,"

"It don't matter; I can get another room."

"Not at all. Father wouldn't let me turn you out. I'll close it up again."

But Anne was so interested in the novelty of a new doorway that she walked through it, and found herself in a dark low passage which she had never seen before.

"It leads to the mill," said Bob. "Would you like to go in and see it at work? But perhaps you have already."

"Only into the ground floor."

"Come all over it. I am practising as grinder, you know, to help my father."

She followed him along the dark passage, in the side of which he opened a little trap, when she saw a great slimy cavern, where the long arms of the mill-wheel flung themselves slowly and distractedly round, and splashing water drops caught the little light that strayed into the gloomy place, turning it into stars and flashes. A cold mist-laden puff of air came into their faces, and the roar from within made it necessary for Anne to shout as she said, "It is dismal! let us go on."

Bob shut the trap, the roar ceased, and they went on to the inner part of the mill, where the air was warm and nutty, and pervaded by a fog of flour. Then they ascended the stairs, and saw the stones lumbering round and round, and the yellow corn running down through the hopper. They climbed yet farther to the top stage, where the wheat lay in bins, and where long rays like yellow feelers stretched in from the sun through the little window, got nearly lost among cobwebs and beams, and completed its course by marking the opposite wall with a glowing patch of gold.

In his earnestness as an exhibitor Bob opened the bolter, which was spinning rapidly round, the result being that a dense cloud of flour rolled out in their faces, reminding Anne that her complexion was probably much paler by this time than when she had entered the mill. She thanked her companion for his trouble, and said she would now go down. He followed her with the same deference as hitherto, and with a sudden and increasing sense that of all cures for his former unhappy passion this would have been the nicest, the easiest, and the most effectual, if he had only been fortunate enough to keep her upon easy terms. But Miss Garland showed no disposition to go farther than accept his services as a guide; she descended to the open air, shook the flour from her like a bird, and went on into the garden amid the September sunshine, whose rays lay like yellow warp-threads across the blue haze which the earth gave forth. The gnats were dancing up and down in airy companies, all of one mind, the nasturtium flowers shone out in groups from the dark hedge over which they climbed, and the mellow smell of the decline of summer was exhaled by everything. Bob followed her as far as the gate, looked after her, thought of her as the same girl who had half encouraged him years ago, when she seemed so superior to him; though now they were almost equal she apparently thought him beneath her. It was with a new sense of pleasure that his mind flew to the fact that she was now an inmate of his father's house.

His obsequious bearing was continued during the next week. In the busy hours of the day they seldom met, but they regularly encountered each other at meals, and these cheerful occasions began to have an interest for him quite irrespective of dishes and cups. When Anne entered and took her seat she was always loudly hailed by Miller Loveday as he whetted his knife; but from Bob she condescended to accept no such familiar greeting, and they often sat down together as if each had a blind eye in the direction of the other. Bob sometimes told serious and correct stories about sea-captains, pilots, boatswains, mates, able seamen, and other curious creatures of the marine world; but these were directly addressed to his father and Mrs. Loveday, Anne being included at the clinching-point by a mere glance only. He sometimes opened bottles of sweet cider for her, and then she thanked him; but even this did not lead to her encouraging his chat.

One day when Anne was paring an apple she was left at table with the young man. "I have made something for you," he said.

She looked all over the table; nothing was there save the ordinary remnants.

"Oh, I don't mean that it is here; it is out by the bridge at the mill-head."

He arose, and Anne followed with curiosity in her eyes, and with her firm little mouth pouted up to a puzzled shape. On reaching the mossy mill-head she found that he had fixed in the keen damp draught which always prevailed over the wheel an Æolian harp of large size. At present the strings were partly covered with a cloth. He lifted it, and the wires began to emit a weird harmony which mingled curiously with the plashing of the wheel.

"I made it on purpose for you, Miss Garland," he said.

She thanked him very warmly, for she had never seen anything like such an instrument before, and it interested her. "It was very thoughtful of you to make it," she added. "How came you to think of such a thing?"

"Oh! I don't know exactly," he replied, as if he did not care to be questioned on the point. "I have never made one in my life till now."

Every night after this, during the mournful gales of autumn, the strange mixed music of water, wind, and strings met her ear, swelling and sinking with an almost supernatural cadence. The character of the instrument was far enough removed from anything she had hitherto seen of Bob's hobbies; so that she marvelled pleasantly at the new depths of poetry this contrivance revealed as existent in that young seaman's nature, and allowed her emotions to flow out yet a little farther in the old direction, notwithstanding her late severe resolve to bar them back.

One breezy night, when the mill was kept going into the small hours, and the wind was exactly in the direction of the water-current, the music so mingled with her dreams as to wake her: it seemed to rhythmically set itself to the words, "Remember me! think of me!" She was much impressed; the sounds were almost too touching; and she spoke to Bob the next morning on the subject.

"How strange it is that you should have thought of fixing that harp where the water gushes," she gently observed. "It affects me almost painfully at night. You are poetical, Captain Bob. But it is too—too sad!"

"I will take it away," said Captain Bob promptly. "It certainly is too sad; I thought so myself. I myself was kept awake by it one night."

"How came you to think of making such a peculiar thing?"

"Well," said Bob, "it is hardly worth saying why. It is not a good place for such a queer noisy machine; and I'll take it away."

"On second thoughts," said Anne, "I should like it to remain a little longer, because it sets me thinking."

"Of me?" he asked, with earnest frankness.

Anne's colour rose fast.

"Well, yes," she said, trying to infuse much plain matter-of-fact into her voice. "Of course I am led to think of the person who invented it."

Bob seemed unaccountably embarrassed, and the subject was not pursued. About half an hour later he came to her again, with something of an uneasy look.

"There was a little matter I didn't tell you just now, Miss Garland," he said. "About that harp thing, I mean. I did make it, certainly, but it was my brother John who asked me to do it, just before he went away. John is very musical, as you know, and he said it would interest you; but as he didn't ask me to tell, I did not. Perhaps I ought to have, and not have taken the credit to myself."

"Oh, it is nothing!" said Anne quickly. "It is a very incomplete instrument after all, and it will be just as well for you to take it away as you first proposed."

He said that he would, but he forgot to do it that day; and the following night there was a high wind, and the harp cried and moaned so movingly that Anne, whose window was quite near, could hardly bear the sound with its new associations. John Loveday was present to her mind all·night as an ill-used man; and yet she could not own that she had ill-used him.

The harp was removed next day. Bob, feeling that his credit for originality was damaged in her eyes, by way of recovering it set himself to paint the summer-house which Anne frequented, and when she came out he assured her that it was quite his own idea.

"It wanted doing, certainly," she said in a neutral tone.

"It is just about troublesome."

"Yes; you can't quite reach up. That's because you are not very tall; is it not, Captain Loveday?"

"You never used to say things like that."

"Oh, I don't mean that you are much less than tall. Shall I hold the paint for you, to save your stepping down?"

"Thank you, if you would."

She took the paint-pot, and stood looking at the brush as it moved up and down in his hand.

"I hope I shall not sprinkle your fingers," he observed as he dipped.

"Oh, that would not matter! You do it very well."

"I am glad to hear that you think so."

"But perhaps not quite so much art is demanded to paint a summer-house as to paint a picture?"

Thinking that, as a painter's daughter, and a person of education superior to his own, she spoke with a flavour of sarcasm, he felt humbled and said—

"You did not use to talk like that to me."

"I was perhaps too young then to take any pleasure in giving pain," she observed daringly.

"Does it give you pleasure?"

Anne nodded.

"I like to give pain to people who have given pain to me," she said smartly, without removing her eyes from the green liquid in her hand.

"I ask your pardon for that."

"I didn't say I meant you—though I did mean you."

Bob looked and looked at her side face till he was bewitched into putting down the brush.

"It was that stupid forgetting of ye for a time!" he exclaimed. "Well, I hadn't seen you for so very long—consider how many years! Oh, dear Anne!" he said, advancing to take her hand, "how well we knew one another when we were children! You was a queen to me then; and so you are now, and always."

Possibly Anne was thrilled pleasantly enough at having brought the truant village-lad to her feet again; but he was not to find the situation so easy as he imagined, and her hand was not to be taken yet.

"Very pretty!" she said, laughing. "And only six weeks since Miss Johnson left."

"Zounds, don't say anything about that!" implored Bob. "I swear that I never—never deliberately loved her—for a long time together, that is; it was a sudden sort of thing, you know. But towards you—I have more or less honoured and respectfully loved you, off and on, all my life. There, that's true."

Anne retorted quickly—

"I am willing, off and on, to believe you, Captain Robert. But I don't see any good in your making these solemn declarations."

"Give me leave to explain, dear Miss Garland. It is to get you to be pleased to renew an old promise—made years ago—that you'll think o' me."

"Not a word of any promise will I repeat."

"Well, well, I won't urge ye to-day. Only let me beg of you to get over the quite wrong notion you have of me; and it shall be my whole endeavour to fetch your gracious favour."

Anne turned away from him and entered the house, whither in the course of a quarter of an hour he followed her, knocking at her door and asking to be let in. She said she was busy; whereupon he went away, to come back again in a short time and receive the same answer.

"I have finished painting the summer-house for you," he said through the door.

"I cannot come to see it. I shall be engaged till supper-time."

She heard him breathe a heavy sigh and withdraw, murmuring something about his bad luck in being cut away from the starn like this. But it was not over yet. When supper-time came and they sat down together, she took upon herself to reprove him for what he had said to her in the garden.

Bob made his forehead express despair.

"Now, I beg you this one thing," he said. "Just let me know your whole mind. Then I shall have a chance to confess my faults and mend them, or clear my conduct to your satisfaction."

She answered with quickness, but not loud enough to be heard by the old people at the other end of the table—"Then, Captain Loveday, I will tell you one thing, one fault, that perhaps would have been more proper to my character than to yours. You are too easily impressed by new faces, and that gives me a *bad opinion* of you—yes, *bad opinion*."

"Oh, that's it," said Bob slowly, looking at her with the intense respect of a pupil for a master, her words being spoken in a manner so precisely between jest and earnest that he was in some doubt how they were to be received. "Impressed by new faces. It is wrong, certainly, of me."

The popping of a cork, and the pouring out of strong beer by the miller with a view to giving it a head, were apparently distractions sufficient to excuse her in not attending further to him; and during the remainder of the sitting her gentle chiding seemed to be sinking seriously into his mind. Perhaps her own heart ached to see how silent he was; but she had always meant to punish him. Day after day for two or three weeks she preserved the same demeanour, with a self-control which did justice to her character. And, on his part, considering what he had to put up with, how she eluded him, snapped him off, refused to come out when he called her, refused to see him when he wanted to enter the little parlour which she had now appropriated to her private use, his patience testified strongly to his good-humour.

CHAPTER XXIII.—MILITARY PREPARATIONS ON AN EXTENDED SCALE.

CHRISTMAS had passed. Dreary winter with dark evenings had given place to more dreary winter with light evenings. Rapid thaws had ended in rain, rain in wind, wind in dust. Showery days had come—the season of pink dawns and white sunsets; and people hoped that the March weather was over.

The chief incident that concerned the household at the mill was that the miller, following the example of all his neighbours, had become a volunteer, and duly appeared twice a week in a red, long-tailed military coat, pipe-clayed breeches, black cloth gaiters, a heel-balled helmet-hat, with a tuft of green

wool, and epaulets of the same colour and material. Bob still remained neutral. Not being able to decide whether to enrol himself as a sea-fencible, a local militia-man, or a volunteer, he simply went on dancing attendance upon Anne. Mrs. Loveday had become awake to the fact that the pair of young people stood in a curious attitude towards each other; but as they were never seen with their heads together, and scarcely ever sat even in the same room, she could not be sure what their movements meant.

Strangely enough (or perhaps naturally enough), since entering the Loveday family herself, she had gradually grown to think less favourably of Anne doing the same thing than she had thought when neither of them was a member, and reverted to her original idea of encouraging Festus; this more particularly because he had of late shown such admirable perseverance in haunting the precincts of the mill, presumably with the intention of lighting upon the young girl. But the weather had kept her mostly indoors.

One afternoon it was raining in torrents. Such leaves as there were on trees at this time of year—those of the laurel and other evergreens—staggered beneath the hard blows of the drops which fell upon them, and afterwards could be seen trickling down the stems beneath and silently entering the ground. The surface of the mill-pond leapt up in a thousand spirts under the same downfall, and clucked like a hen in the rat-holes along the banks as it undulated under the wind. The only dry spot visible from the front windows of the mill-house was the inside of a small shed, on the opposite side of the courtyard. While Mrs. Loveday was noticing the threads of rain descending across its interior shade, Festus Derriman walked up and entered it for shelter, which, owing to the lumber within, it but scantily afforded.

It was an excellent opportunity for helping on her scheme. Anne was in the back room, and by asking him in till the rain was over she would bring him face to face with her daughter, whom, as the days went on, she increasingly wished to marry other than a Loveday, now that the romance of her own alliance with the miller had in some respect worn off. She was better provided for than before; she was not unhappy; but the plain fact was that she had married beneath her. She beckoned to Festus through the window-pane; he instantly complied with her signal, having in fact placed himself there on purpose to be noticed; for he knew that Miss Garland would not be out-of-doors on such a day.

"Good afternoon, Mrs. Loveday," said Festus on entering. "There now—if I didn't think that's how it would be!" His voice had suddenly warmed to anger, for he had seen a door close in the back part of the room, a lithe figure having previously slipped through.

Mrs. Loveday turned, observed that Anne was gone, and said, "What is it?" as if she did not know.

"Oh, nothing, nothing!" said Festus crossly. "You know well enough what it is, ma'am; only you make pretence otherwise. But I'll bring her to book yet. You shall drop your haughty airs, my charmer! She little thinks I have kept an account of 'em all."

"But you must treat her politely, sir," said Mrs. Loveday, secretly pleased at these signs of uncontrollable affection.

"Don't tell me of politeness or generosity, ma'am! She is more than a match for me. She regularly gets over me. I have passed by this house five-and-fifty times since last Martinmas and this is all I get at last!"

"But you will stay till the rain is over, sir?"

"No. I don't mind rain. I'm off again. She's got somebody else in her eye!" And the yeoman went out, slamming the door.

Meanwhile the slippery object of his hopes had gone along the dark passage, passed the trap which opened on the wheel, and through the door into the mill, where she was met by Bob in the hoary character of a miller, who looked up from the flour shoot inquiringly and said, "You want me, Miss Garland?"

"Oh no," said she. "I only want to be allowed to stand here a few minutes."

He looked at her to know if she meant it, and finding that she did, returned to his post. When the mill had rumbled on a little longer he came back.

"Bob," she said when she saw him move, "remember that you are at work, and have no time to stand close to me."

He bowed and went to his original post again, Anne watching from the window till Festus should leave. The mill rumbled on as before, and at last Bob came to her for the third time. "Now, Bob——" she began.

"On my honour, 'tis only to ask a question. Will you walk with me to church next Sunday afternoon?"

"Perhaps I will," she said. But at this moment the yeoman left the house, and Anne, to escape further parley, returned to the dwelling by the way she had come.

Sunday afternoon arrived, and the family was standing at the door waiting for the church bells to begin. From that side of the house they could see southward across a paddock to the rising ground farther ahead, where there grew a large elm-tree, beneath whose boughs footpaths crossed in different directions, like meridians at the pole. The tree was old, and in summer the grass beneath it was quite trodden away by the feet of the many trysters and idlers who haunted the spot. The tree formed a conspicuous object in the surrounding landscape.

While they looked, a foot soldier in red uniform and white breeches came along one of the paths, and, stopping beneath the elm, drew from his pocket a paper, which he proceeded to nail up by the four corners to the trunk. He drew back, looked at it, and went on his way. Bob got his glass from indoors and levelled it at the placard, but after looking for a long time he could make out nothing but a lion and a unicorn at the top. Anne, who was ready for church, moved away from the door, though it was yet early, and showed her intention of going by way of the elm. The paper had been so impressively nailed up that she was curious to read it even at this theological time. Bob took the opportunity of following, and reminded her of her promise.

"Then walk behind me—not at all close," she said.

"Yes," he replied, immediately dropping behind.

The ludicrous humility of his manner led her to add playfully over her shoulder, "It serves you right, you know."

"I deserve anything. But I must take the liberty to say that I hope my behaviour about Matil——, in forgetting you awhile, will not make ye wish to keep me *always* behind?"

She replied confidentially, "Why I am so earnest not to be seen with you is that I may appear to people to be independent of you. Knowing what I do of your weaknesses I can do no otherwise. You must be schooled into——"

"Oh, Anne," sighed Bob, "you hit me hard—too hard. If ever I do win you I am sure I shall have fairly earned you."

"You are not what you once seemed to be," she returned softly. "I don't quite like to let myself love you." The last words were not very audible, and as Bob was behind he caught nothing of them, nor did he see how sentimental she had become all of a sudden. They walked the rest of the way in silence, and coming to the tree read as follows:—

ADDRESS TO ALL RANKS AND DESCRIPTIONS OF ENGLISHMEN.

FRIENDS AND COUNTRYMEN:

The French are now assembling the largest force that ever was prepared to invade this Kingdom, with the professed purpose of effecting our complete Ruin and Destruction. They do not disguise their intentions, as they have often done to other Countries ; but openly boast that they will come over in such Numbers as cannot be resisted.

Wherever the French have lately appeared they have spared neither Rich nor Poor, Old nor Young; but like a Destructive Pestilence have laid waste and destroyed every Thing that before was fair and flourishing.

On this occasion no man's service is compelled, but you are invited voluntarily to come forward in defence of every thing that is dear to you, by entering your Names on the Lists which are sent to the Tything-man of every Parish, and engaging to act either as *Associated Volunteers bearing Arms, as Pioneers and Labourers,* or as *Drivers of Waggons.*

As Associated Volunteers you will be called out only once a week, unless the actual Landing of the Enemy should render your further Services necessary.

As Pioneers or Labourers you will be employed in Breaking up Roads to hinder the Enemy's advance.

Those who have Pickaxes, Spades, Shovels, Billhooks, or other Working Implements, are desired to mention them to the Constable or Tything-man of their Parish, in order that they may be entered on the Lists opposite their Homes, to be used if necessary. . . .

It is thought desirable to give you this Explanation, that you may not be ignorant of the Duties to which you may be called. But if the Love of true Liberty and honest Fame has not ceased to animate the Hearts of Englishmen, Pay, though necessary, will be the least Part of your Reward. You will find your best Recompense in having done your Duty to your King and Country by driving back or destroying your old and implacable Enemy, envious of your Freedom and Happiness, and therefore seeking to destroy them ; in having protected your Wives and Children from Death, or worse than Death, which will follow the Success of such Inveterate Foes.

ROUSE, therefore, and unite as one man in the best of Causes ! United we may defy the World to conquer us; but Victory will never belong to those who are slothful and unprepared.

"I must go and join at once !" said Bob, slapping his thigh.

Anne turned to him, all the playfulness gone from her face. She looked him over, but did not speak.

"But nothing will happen," he added, divining her thought. "They are not come yet. It will be time enough to get frightened when Boney's here. But I must enrol myself at once—it must be in the sea fencibles, I suppose."

"I wish we lived in the north of England, Bob, so as to be farther away from where he'll land," she murmured uneasily.

"Where we are would be Paradise to me, if you would only make it so."

"It is not right to talk so lightly at such a serious time," she thoughtfully returned, going on towards the church.

On drawing near, they saw through the boughs of a clump of intervening trees, still leafless, but bursting into buds of amber hue, a glittering which seemed to be reflected from points of steel. In a few moments they heard above the tender chiming of the church bells the loud voice of a man giving words of command, at which all the metallic points suddenly shifted like the bristles of a porcupine and glistened anew.

"'Tis the drilling," said Loveday. "They drill now between the services, you know, because they can't get the men together so readily in the week.* It makes me feel that I ought to be doing more than I am."

When they had passed round the belt of trees the company of recruits became visible, consisting of the able-bodied inhabitants of the hamlets thereabout, more or less known to Bob and Anne. They were assembled on the green plot outside the churchyard-gate, dressed in their common clothes, and the sergeant who was putting them through their drill was the man who had nailed up the proclamation.

"Men, I dismissed ye too soon—parade, parade again, I say," he cried. "My watch is fast, I find. There's another twenty minutes afore the worship of God commences. Now all of you that ha'n't got fawlocks, fall in at the lower end. Eyes right and dress!"

As every man was anxious to see how the rest stood, those at the end of the line pressed forward for that purpose, till the line assumed the form of a horseshoe.

"Look at ye now! Why, you are all a crooking in. Dress, dress !"

They dressed forthwith ; but impelled by the same motive they soon resumed their former figure, and so they were despairingly permitted to remain.

"Now, I hope you'll have a little patience," said the sergeant, as he stood in the centre of the arc, "and pay particular attention to the word of command, just exactly as I give it out to ye; and if I should go wrong, I shall be much obliged to any gentleman who'll put me right again, for I have only been in the army three weeks myself, and we are all liable to mistakes."

"So we be, so we be," said the line heartily.

"'Tention, the whole, then. Poise fawlocks! Very well done!"

"Please, what must we do that haven't got no firelocks?" said the lower end of the line in a helpless voice.

"Now, was ever such a question! Why,

* Historically true.

Page 444.

you must do nothing at all, but think *how* you'd poise 'em *if* you had 'em. You middle men, that are armed with hurdle-sticks and cabbage-stalks just to make believe, must of course use 'em as if they were the real thing. Now then, cock fawlocks! Present! Fire! (Not shoot in earnest, you know; only make pretence to.) Very good—very good indeed; except that some of you were a *little* too soon, and the rest a *little* too late."

"Please, sergeant, can I fall out, as I am master-player in the choir, and my bass-viol strings won't stand at this time o' year, unless they be screwed up a little before the passon comes in?"

"How can you think of such trifles as churchgoing at such a time as this, when your own native country is on the point of invasion?" said the sergeant sternly. "And, as you know, the drill ends three minutes afore church begins, and that's the law, and

it wants a quarter of an hour yet. Now, at the word *Prime*, shake the powder (supposing you've got it) into the priming-pan, three last fingers behind the rammer; then shut your pans, drawing your right arm nimbly towards your body. I ought to have told ye before this, that at *Hand your katridge*, seize it and bring it with a quick motion to your mouth, bite the top well off, and don't swaller so much of the powder as to make ye hawk and spet instead of attending to your drill. What's that man a-saying of in the rear rank?"

"Please, sir, 'tis Anthony Cripplestraw, wanting to know how he's to bite off his katridge, when he haven't a tooth left in 's head?"

"Man alive! Why, what's your genius for war? Hold it up to your right-hand man's mouth, to be sure, and let him nip it off for ye. Well, what have you to say,

Private Tremlett? Don't ye understand English?"

"Ask yer pardon, sergeant; but what must we infantry of the awkward squad do if Boney comes afore we get our firelocks?"

"Take a pike, like the rest of the incapables. You'll find a store of them ready in the corner of the church tower. Now then—Shoulder—p——r——"

"There, they be tinging in the passon!" exclaimed David, Miller Loveday's man, who also formed one of the company, as the bells changed from chiming all three together to a quick beating of one. The whole line drew a breath of relief, threw down their arms, and began running off.

"Well, then, I must dismiss ye," said the sergeant. "Next drill is Tuesday afternoon at four. And, mind, if your masters won't let ye leave work soon enough, tell me, and I'll write a line to Gover'ment. Now, just form up a minute; here's every man's money for his attendance." The sergeant drew out a large canvas bag, plunged his hand into a family of shillings, and handed them round as the men stood in something like line again. "'Tention! To the right—left wheel; I mean —no, no—right wheel.' Mar—r—r—rch!"

Some wheeled to the right and some to the left, and some obliging men, including Cripplestraw, tried to wheel both ways.

"Stop, stop; try again. Gentlemen, unfortunately when I'm in a hurry I can never remember my right hand from my left, and never could as a boy. You must excuse me, please. Practice makes perfect, as the saying is; and, much as I've learnt since I 'listed, we always find something new. Now then, right wheel! march! halt! Stand at ease! dismiss! I think that's the order o't, but I'll look in the Gover'ment book afore Tuesday."

Many of the company who had been drilled preferred to go off and spend their shillings instead of entering the church; but Anne and Captain Bob passed in. Even the interior of the sacred edifice was affected by the agitation of the times. The religion of the country had, in fact, changed from love of God to hatred of Napoleon Buonaparte; and, as if to remind the devout of this alteration, the pikes for the pikemen (all those accepted men who were not otherwise armed) were kept in the church of each parish. There, against the wall they always stood—a whole sheaf of them, formed of new ash stems, with a spike driven in at one end, the stick being preserved from splitting by a ferrule. And there they remained, year after year, in the corner of the aisle, till they were removed and placed under the gallery stairs, and thence ultimately to the belfry, where they grew black, rusty, and worm-eaten, and were gradually stolen and carried off by sextons, parish-clerks, whitewashers, window-menders, and other church-servants, for use at home as rake stems, benefit-club staves, and pick-handles, in which degraded situations they may still occasionally be found.

But in their new and shining state they had a terror for Anne, whose eyes were involuntarily drawn towards them as she sat at Bob's side during the service, filling her with bloody visions of their possible use not far from the very spot on which they were now assembled. The sermon, too, was on the subject of patriotism; so that when they came out she began to harp uneasily upon the probability of their all being driven from their homes.

Bob assured her that with the sixty thousand regulars, the militia reserve of a hundred and twenty thousand, and the three hundred thousand volunteers, there was not much to fear.

"But I sometimes have a fear that poor John will be killed," he continued after a pause. "He is sure to be among the first that will have to face the invaders, and the trumpeters get picked off."

"There is the same chance for him as for the others," said Anne.

"Yes . . . yes . . . the same chance, such as it is. . . You have never liked John since that affair of Matilda Johnson, have you?"

"Why?" she quickly asked.

"Well," said Bob timidly, "as it is a ticklish time for him, would it not be worth while to make up any differences before the crash comes?"

"I have nothing to make up," said Anne, with some distress, her feelings towards the trumpet-major being of a complicated kind. She still fully believed him to have smuggled away Miss Johnson because of his own interest in that lady, which must have made his professions to herself a mere pastime; but that very conduct had in it the curious advantage to herself of setting Bob free.

"Since John has been gone," continued her companion, "I have found out more of his meaning, and of what he really had to do with that woman's flight. Did you know he had anything to do with it?"

"Yes."

"That he got her to go away?"

She looked at Bob with surprise. He was not exasperated with John, and yet he knew so much as this.

: "Yes," she said ; "what did it mean?"
: He did not explain to her then; but the possibility of John's death, which had been newly brought home to him by the military events of the day, determined him to get poor John's character cleared. Reproaching himself for letting her remain so long with a mistaken idea of him, Bob went to his father as soon as they got home, and begged him to get Mrs. Loveday to tell Anne the true reason of John's objection to Miss Johnson as a sister-in-law.

. "She thinks it is because they were old lovers new met, and that he wants to marry her," he exclaimed to his father in conclusion.

"Then *that's* the meaning of the split between Miss Nancy and Jack," said the miller.

"What, were they any more than common friends?" asked Bob uneasily.

. "Not on her side, perhaps."

. "Well, we must do it," replied Bob, painfully conscious that common justice to John might bring them into hazardous rivalry, yet determined to be fair. "Tell it all to Mrs. Loveday, and get her to tell Anne."

CHAPTER XXIV.—A LETTER, A VISITOR, AND A TIN BOX.

THE result of the explanation upon Anne was bitter self-reproach. She was so sorry at having wronged the kindly soldier, that next morning she went by herself to the down, and stood exactly where his tent had covered the sod whereon he had lain so many nights, thinking what sadness he must have suffered because of her at the time of packing up and going away. After that she wiped from her eyes the tears of pity which had come there, descended to the house, and wrote an impulsive letter to him, in which occurred the following passages, indiscreet enough under the circumstances :—

· "I find all justice, all rectitude, on your side, John; and all impertinence, all inconsiderateness, on mine. I am so much convinced of your honour in the whole transaction, that I shall for the future mistrust myself in everything. And if it be possible, whenever I differ from you on any point, I shall take an hour's time for consideration before I say that I differ. If I have lost your friendship, I have only myself to thank for it; but I sincerely hope that you can forgive."

After writing this she went to the garden, where Bob was shearing the spring grass from the paths. "What is John's direc-

tion?" she said, holding the sealed letter in her hand.

"Exeter Barracks," Bob faltered, his countenance sinking.

She thanked him and went indoors. When he came in, later in the day, he passed the door of her empty sitting-room and saw the letter on the mantelpiece. He disliked the sight of it. Hearing voices in the other room, he entered and found Anne and her mother there, talking to Cripplestraw, who had just come in with a message from Squire Derriman, requesting Miss Garland, as she valued the peace of mind of an old and troubled man, to go at once and see him.

"I cannot go," she said, not liking the risk that such a visit involved.

An hour later Cripplestraw shambled again into the passage, on the same errand.

"Maister's very poorly, and he hopes that you'll come, Missess Anne. He wants to see ye very particular about the French."

Anne would have gone in a moment, but for the fear that some one besides the farmer might encounter her, and she answered as before.

Another hour passed, and the wheels of a vehicle were heard. Cripplestraw had come for the third time, with a horse and gig; he was dressed in his best clothes, and brought with him on this occasion a basket containing raisins, almonds, oranges, and sweet cakes. Offering them to her as a gift from the old farmer, he repeated his request for her to accompany him, the gig and best mare having been sent as an additional inducement.

"I believe the old gentleman is in love with you, Anne," said her mother.

"Why couldn't he drive down himself to see me?" Anne inquired of Cripplestraw.

"He wants you at the house, please."

"Is Mr. Festus with him?"

"No; he's away at Weymouth."

"I'll go," said she.

"And I may come and meet you?" said Bob.

"There's my letter—what shall I do about that?" she said, instead of answering him. "Take my letter to the post-office, and you may come," she added.

He said Yes and went out, Cripplestraw retreating to the door till she should be ready.

"What letter is it?" said her mother.

"Only one to John," said Anne. "I have asked him to forgive my suspicions. I could do no less."

"Do you want to marry *him?*" asked Mrs. Loveday bluntly.

"Mother!"

"Well, he will take that letter as an encouragement. Can't you see that he will, you foolish girl?"

Anne did see instantly. "Of course!" she said. "Tell Robert that he need not go."

She went to her room to secure the letter. It was gone from the mantelpiece, and on inquiry it was found that the miller, seeing it there, had sent David with it to Weymouth hours ago. Anne said nothing, and set out for Overcombe Hall with Cripplestraw.

"William," said Mrs. Loveday to the miller when Anne was gone and Bob had resumed his work in the garden, "did you get that letter sent off on purpose?"

"Well, I did. I wanted to make sure of it. John likes her, and now 'twill be made up; and why shouldn't he marry her? I'll start him in business, if so be she'll have him."

"But she is likely to marry Festus Derriman."

"I don't want her to marry anybody but John," said the miller doggedly.

"Not if she is in love with Bob, and has been for years, and he with her?" asked his wife triumphantly.

"In love with Bob, and he with her?" repeated Loveday.

"Certainly," said she, going off and leaving him to his reflections.

When Anne reached the hall she found old Mr. Derriman in his customary chair. His complexion was more ashen, but his movement in rising at her entrance, putting a chair and shutting the door behind her, were much the same as usual.

"Thank God you've come, my dear girl," he said earnestly. "Ah, you don't trip across to read to me now! Why did ye cost me so much to fetch you? Fie! A horse and gig, and a man's time in going three times. And what I sent ye cost a good deal in Weymouth market, now everything is so dear there, and 'twould have cost more if I hadn't bought the raisins and oranges some months ago, when they were cheaper. I tell you this because we are old friends, and I have nobody else to tell my troubles to. But I don't begrudge anything to ye, since you've come."

"I am not much pleased to come, even now," said she. "What can make you so seriously anxious to see me?"

"Well, you be a good girl and true; and I've been thinking that of all people of the next generation that I can trust, you are the best. 'Tis my bond and my title-deeds, such as they be, and the leases, you know, and a few guineas in packets, and more than these, my will, that I have to speak about. Now do ye come this way."

"Oh, such things as those!" she returned with surprise. "I don't understand those things at all."

"There's nothing to understand. 'Tis just this. The French will be here within two months; that's certain. I have it on the best authority that the army at Boulogne is ready, the boats equipped, the plans laid, and the First Consul only waits for a tide. Heaven knows what will become o' the men o' these parts! But most likely the women will be spared. Now I'll show ye."

He led her across the hall to a stone staircase of semicircular plan, which conducted to the cellars.

"Down here?" she said.

"Yes; I must trouble ye to come down here. I have thought and thought who is the woman that can best keep a secret for six months, and I say, 'Anne Garland.' You won't be married before then?"

"Oh no!" murmured the young woman.

"I wouldn't expect ye to keep a close tongue after such a thing as that. But it will not be necessary."

When they reached the bottom of the steps he struck a light from a tinder-box, and unlocked the middle one of three doors which appeared in the whitewashed wall opposite. The rays of the candle fell upon the vault and sides of a long low cellar, littered with decayed woodwork from other parts of the hall, among the rest stair-balusters, carved finials, tracery panels, and wainscoting. But what most attracted her eye was a small flag-stone turned up in the middle of the floor, a heap of earth beside it, and a measuring-tape. Derriman went to the corner of the cellar, and pulled out a clamped box from under the straw. "You be rather heavy, my dear, eh?" he said, affectionately addressing the box as he lifted it. "But you are going to be put in a safe place, you know, or that rascal will get hold of ye, and carry ye off and ruin me." He then with some difficulty lowered the box into the hole, raked in the earth upon it, and lowered the flag-stone, which he was a long time in fixing to his satisfaction. Miss Garland, who was romantically interested, helped him to brush away the fragments of loose earth; and when he had scattered over the floor a little of the straw that lay about, they again ascended to upper air.

"Is this all, sir?" said Anne.

"Just a moment longer, honey. Will you come into the great parlour?"

She followed him thither.

"If anything happens to me while the fighting is going on—it may be on these very fields—you will know what to do," he resumed. "But first please sit down again, there's a dear, whilst I write what's in my head. See, there's the best paper, and a new quill that I've afforded myself for't."

"What a strange business! I don't think I much like it, Mr. Derriman," she said, seating herself.

He had by this time begun to write, and murmured as he wrote—

"'Twenty-three and half from N.W. Sixteen and three-quarters from N.E.'—There, that's all. Now I seal it up and give it to you to keep safe till I ask ye for it, or you hear of my being trampled down by the enemy."

"What does it mean?" she asked as she received the paper.

"Clk! Ha ha! Why, that's the distance of the box from the two corners of the cellar. I measured it before you came. And, my honey, to make all sure, if the French soldiery are after ye, tell your mother the meaning on't, or any other friend, in case they should put ye to death, and the secret be lost. But that I am sure I hope they won't do, though your pretty face will be a sad bait to the soldiers. I often have wished you was my daughter, honey; and yet in these times the less cares a man has the better, so I am glad you bain't. Shall my man drive you home?"

"No, no," she said, much depressed by the words he had uttered. "I can find my way. You need not trouble to come down."

"Then take care of the paper. And if you outlive me, you'll find I have not forgot you."

PLAIN-SPEAKING.

BY THE AUTHOR OF "JOHN HALIFAX, GENTLEMAN."

II.—VICTIMS AND VICTIMISERS.

THE "noble army of martyrs" sounds very fine; and how many people are, or believe they are, of that goodly company! Whether a large proportion might not wholesomely be deposed thence, and relegated to the uninteresting ranks of mere victims, feeble and cowardly, I should not like to say. But the pride of martyrdom consoles them so much in their sufferings that it would be almost a pity to deprive them thereof, or to suggest that the true martyr carefully covers his hair-shirt with a velvet gown, and presents a placid and ever-cheerful countenance to all beholders, in spite of the vulture gnawing at his heart.

It is for the benefit of these vultures, and with the hope of strangling some of them, that this paper is written.

In the first place, how much ought we poor mortals to allow ourselves to suffer? I mean, not the inevitable sufferings sent, or permitted, by God, but those inflicted on us by our fellow-mortals, which are by far the most numerous and the hardest to bear.

Christianity bases a great deal of its theology on the doctrine of non-resistance. "If a man smite thee on the one cheek, offer him the other; if he take away thy cloak, let him have thy coat also." A great mystery—so great that I cannot help believing translators must be at fault somehow, or (if it be not heresy to say this) that Christ's disciples in repeating their Master's words somewhat misconstrued them. Or else that the command "Resist not evil" is only meant for an age when evil was so rampant that it could not be resisted at all, except by the Divine teaching of self-sacrifice, which was so startlingly opposite to anything the heathen world had ever known. Still, the malediction, "Offences must come, but woe be to them through whom the offence cometh," is sufficiently strong to warrant us in offering a word or two on this other side, the side of the victims against the victimisers.

Most "aggravating," to use no higher term, is it sometimes to notice how the good of this world are oppressed by the bad, the cheerful and amiable by the sour-tempered, the unselfish by the selfish, the careful by the careless or prodigal, and so on. Not a week, not a day passes that the more generous of us do not long to rescue some of these poor victims out of the hands of their tormentors, acting St. George and the Dragon over again, or becoming a modern Perseus for a new Andromeda. Only, alas! the sufferers are seldom young and attractive, and the persecutors often are.

Take, for instance, the case of nervous invalids. These are not seldom the most pathetically fascinating of women, whom, for a time at least, all the men are delighted to serve; who frequently win excellent and devoted husbands—and make slaves and martyrs of them for life.   For the subtle charm of helplessness dominates most strongly over the largest and most generous of natures.   The truly noble man unconsciously protects, and loves that which he protects.   The extent to which such an one is victimised by a weak, selfish, egotistical invalid, or quasi-invalid—for the real invalids are sometimes the most patient, unselfish, and unexacting of human beings—is all but incredible, and wholly pitiable.   More so, I think, than when the case is reversed, because it seems to be woman's natural *métier* to be somebody's "slave" all her life.   But with men, who have, and ought to have, a wider horizon, a larger duty, including not only the family but the world, it is, even granting all the tenderness due from the strong to the weak, rather hard to be tied to the triumphant chariot wheels, *i.e.* the Bath-chair, of a charming, interesting, *exigeante* valetudinarian, to whom the one golden rule for invalids, "Suffer as silently, and make others suffer as little as you can," is a dead letter.

Perhaps these victimisers, being also sufferers, should be handled more gently than another sort who have no excuse at all.

Most families possess some member, near or remote, who is a perpetual "root of bitterness springing up to trouble them." Not necessarily a wicked, but a decidedly "unpleasant" person; weak in many points, but excellent at fault-finding and mischief-making; always getting into hot water and dragging other people after; in disposition touchy, exacting, or morose.   In short, the sort of individual whom all would gladly escape from, but being unfortunately "one of the family," they, the family, are bound to put up with, and do so with a patience that is almost miraculous.   Outsiders, too, for their sakes, imitate them, treating the obnoxious party with preternatural politeness, "making love to the devil," as I have heard it put, and propitiating him or her with much greater care than would be necessary towards the more agreeable relatives.   For peace' sake, all sorts of inconveniences are borne, all manner of lies—white lies—told, until life becomes, when not an actual endurance, a long hypocrisy.

Now, is that right?   Would it not be much more right for the victims to take up arms against the victimiser, and say plainly, "You are an intolerable nuisance.   It is not fair that the many should suffer for the one.   The family—a whole family—shall not be made miserable by you any longer.   You must either mend your ways, or you must be got rid of somehow."

Ay, and this should be done; in the kindest and most prudent way, of course, but decidedly done.   If all the "roots of bitterness" we know of were safely planted out, what a blessing it would be!   For many people, intolerable at home, are quite pleasant and charming abroad, being forced then to exercise with strangers the self-control that they do not care to use in the bosom of their family.   Can no new philanthropist invent asylums for the ill-tempered, or *maisons de santé* for the malicious and egotistical?—since egotism is always a kind of madness, and often the forerunner of it.   At any rate, individual effort might be made, if once we could convince tender-conscienced folk—apt to be ridden over rough-shod by those who have no conscience at all—that the incurable evils of life being so great, to sit down and tamely endure a curable evil is worse than foolish—wrong.

I do not include among these "intolerables" the merely bad-tempered, because, anomaly as it sounds, many bad-tempered people are exceedingly good.   Their besetting sin is often a purely physical thing, arising from nervous irritability or other unhappy physical causes, producing a general *malaise* which causes them to suffer in themselves quite as much as they make others suffer.   If they have the sense to see this and rule themselves accordingly, they deserve sympathy, even in midst of condemnation.   But if they say, "I can't help it.   It's me, and you must put up with it!" or, still worse, if, like drunkards and madmen, who are always accusing other people of being mad or drunk, they imagine everybody is in league against them, and accuse cheerful, innocent hearts of being haunted by the ugly black shadows that so often cloud their own, then let us waste on them no pity—they merit none.   We cannot cure them, we must endure them; but let us at least escape from them, and help others to escape, in every possible way.

It is a hard thing to say, but some of the cruellest victimisers are the people who are supposed to be devotedly attached to their victims; as perhaps they are, but not in a right way.   Instead of a safe and tender embrace, they clutch at these unfortunates with the terrific clasp of an octopus, fancying they love them, when in fact they only love themselves. Many people like *to be loved;* they enjoy the power and glory of showing to the world that they are loved. But of love itself, and of loving—I give the word its widest interpretation—they are absolutely incapable. That deep, faithful, reverent passion, which can project itself out of itself and devote its whole powers, silently or openly, to the service of another—of this they have not the remotest idea. Jealous, exacting, demanding sacrifices and making none; for ever thinking, not "Do I love you?" but "Do you love me?" and always suspecting that love to be less than they deserve—such "lovers," be they men or women—and I must confess that they are oftenest women—are the greatest nuisances that their luckless "objects of attachment" can be plagued with. Often they force their victims to wish ardently that instead of loving they would take to hating, or at any rate to wholesome indifference.

People write of the torments of unrequited love; but a far greater torment is it to be pursued by the egotistical affection of some one—whether friend or relative—who worries your life out with fussy anxiety over your health, who, under colour of aiding you, meddles fatally in all your affairs, and, while calling himself (or herself) your dearest friend, tries to separate you from every other friend you have. Surely no amount of pity, or even gratitude for unasked favours, ought to prevent such victims from resolutely throwing off the victimisers and escaping from their affectionate clutches by every means that Christian charity allows. There are a number of women, old and young, who go about the world bestowing their unoccupied hearts upon their own sex or the other, rushing into vehement sentimental friendships or loves which are as trying to one side as ridiculous on the other. We constantly see some kindly, respectable Sindbad staggering on under the enforced embrace of a devoted friend or attached relative, a veritable Old Man of the Sea, unto whom we long to say, "Throw him off, and let him find his own feet and manage his own affairs!" as in nine cases out of ten he really would, only it is so much easier to be carried.

Besides the regular victims, it is sad to see what a number of well-meaning folk tacitly, and quite unnecessarily, victimise themselves. These are the people who are always afraid of offending somebody, always imagining that somebody will "expect" something—an invitation, a visit, a letter—and be much "annoyed" at not getting it, when perhaps the individual in question never once thought about the matter, and it was only the uneasy egotism of the other individual which supposed he did.

For the dread of giving offence, like the habit of taking it, springs quite as often from self-esteem as from sensitiveness. Vain, self-engrossed people are apt to exaggerate the importance they are to other people, and so to have a nervous terror of "vexing" them; whereas a man of single mind, who does not trouble himself much about himself, never takes offence, and is therefore not apt to imagine he has given any. He goes straight on, neither turning to the right or the left, does the best thing, so far as he sees it, and the kindly thing, whenever it lies in his power; but beyond this he does not afflict himself much as to what people think of him or expect of him. If they expect what they had no right to expect, exact more than they are justified in requiring, above all, take offence where he had no intention of giving any, then he altogether refuses to be victimised. He may make no great stir and present no obnoxious front—indeed, probably he considers the matter too small to fight about—but the victimisers can make nothing of him. He calmly goes on his way, "worrying" neither himself nor his neighbour on the matter. Life is too short for tempests in tea-pots, or indeed for any other unnecessary storms: we must just do our duty, and let it alone.

But in this great question of doing one's duty, I think we cannot too sharply draw the line between what really is our duty and what other people choose to suppose it is, probably each person having a different opinion on the subject. We are apt to start in life with a grand idea of self-sacrifice and a heroic sense of the joy of it—ay, and there is a joy, deeper than the selfish can ever understand, a delight keener than the pleasure-loving can ever know, in spending and being spent for our best-beloved, or even in the mere abstract help of the good and defence of the miserable—that "enthusiasm of humanity," as a great writer once called it, which is at the heart of all religion, the love of man springing from the love of God.

Yet, alas! ere long we come to learn that there are sacrifices which turn out to be sheer mistakes, ruining ourselves and profiting nobody; that unselfishness, carried to an extreme, only makes other people selfish; that "the fear of man bringeth a snare;" and to make one's whole life miserable through a weak dread of offending this person, who has no right to be offended, or of not doing one's duty to that person, who has the very smallest claim to any duty at all, is—well! I will not call it wrong, because it is a failing that leans to virtue's side—but it is simply silly.

To withstand evil is quite as necessary as to do good. And if we withstand it for others, why not for ourselves? Every time that we weakly suffer a needless wrong, we abet and encourage the inflicter in perpetrating it. By becoming passive and uncomplaining victims, we tacitly injure the victimisers. They can but kill our bodies, as they do sometimes by most amiable and unconscious murder, slow and sure—but we may kill their souls, by allowing them, unresisted, to go on in some course of conduct which must result in their gradual deterioration and moral death. It may be a theory startling enough to some people, but warranted by a good long observation of life, if I say that I believe one-half of the self-sacrifices of this world—the endless instances we see in which the good are immolated to the bad, the weak to the strong, the self-forgetting to the exacting and tyrannical — spring not from heroism but cowardice.

We have not too many angels in this world, and we know little enough of the angelic host above: but the angel who always most attracted my youthful imagination, and has attracted many another, was Michael, the strong, the warlike, the wrestler with the powers of evil. That we should so wrestle, even to our last breath, is as necessary as that we should worship good. And, lovely as Mercy may be, there is another, a blindfold Woman with balance and scales, still more] beautiful, and a great deal more difficult to find, at least in this world.

She, I think, would say to these victims—hopeless victims many, for they are not only too weak to struggle against, but they actually love, their victimisers: Pause and consider whether there is not something beyond and above either love or hatred, egoism or altruism. And what is it? It is that sense of right and wrong which, when not corrupted or turned aside, is inherent in every human soul. Fear God and have no other fear. Serve God, and every other service will sink into its right proportions. "For one is your Master, even Christ, and all ye are brethren."

And if we are brethren, why should there exist among us either victims or victimisers?

SOME NOXIOUS INSECTS.

PART II.

NEXT, let us take the Coccus insects which produce the wax, the lac, and the cochineal. These insects feed upon the cactus, a plant exceedingly valuable to mankind, and are closely allied to the "scale" insect which infests our hothouses and greenhouses, and the "mealy-bug," or American blight, which inflicts such injuries on our fruit-trees.

In these few instances the counterbalancing qualities are so directly beneficial to civilised man as to be obvious even to the most unobservant among us. Semi-civilised man finds similar direct benefits in various insects. For example, in many countries the social wasps are almost as valuable as the social bees, the grubs of both being a highly-prized article of food.

In Mexico there are most remarkable ants, popularly called Hormigas miéleras, and scientifically known as *Myrmecocystus Mexicanus*. These ants are most wonderful beings, for they not only collect honey, but store it for future use in vessels so strange that their existence would almost be thought impossible.

The Honey Ant makes its store vessels from the bodies of the workers.

Honey Ant.

First, it bites the end of the abdomen, thereby setting up an inflammation, which closes the apertures of the body. Then it feeds the maimed creature with honey, pouring it into the mouth of the living honey-pot just as the bee pours honey into its crop. This process is continually repeated until the body of the store ant is distended to an astonishing size with honey, the skin being stretched to such an extent that it is sufficiently transparent to show the honey within.

It cannot escape, for its body is so heavy that the limbs are insufficient to carry it, and so it remains in the nest until the honey is wanted. In Mexico these ants are so plentiful that they form regular articles of commerce, being sold by measure in the markets, and used for the purpose of making mead. Specimens may be seen in the British Museum.

Were it not for this property the Honey Ant would be one of the many insects which are called noxious. But its counterbalancing qualities are such that, in its own country, it almost equals the honey bee in its value to man.

Even in Europe the ants are not without their direct use to man. Every one knows the common Wood Ant (*Formica rufa*), some-

Nest of Wood Ant.

times called the Horse Ant, which heaps up fragments of dried grass, broken twigs, dead leaves, and similar objects, into large hills. If one of these hills be opened a curiously pungent odour will be perceived, not unlike that of green wood when heated in the fire. If the face or even the hand be held in the hollow of the nest a sharp, pricking sensation will be felt, as if the skin were pricked with thousands of tiny needles.

This is caused by a peculiar secretion of the ant, called "formic acid," from its origin.

I have seen a dog, who had inadvertently scratched a hole in one of these nests, suffer terribly from his indiscretion. He was half mad with pain and terror, and half blinded by the formic acid which had found its way

XXI—32

into his eyes, besides irritating his nostrils, as if pepper had been thrown into them.

In England, I believe, the use of this acid is not recognised, and the ants are considered simply as noxious insects on account of the pain which they can cause when they attack human beings. In Norway and Sweden, however, the Wood Ants are highly valued, as a peculiar vinegar, flavoured with the formic acid, is prepared from them. A jar of ant vinegar often forms part of a present to a bride on her wedding-day.

As to the clothes moths, it is easy to see that they can do no harm to the naked savage, but not so easy to comprehend that they can be of any benefit to civilised man. Yet the whole tribe of clothes moths are of inestimable service to mankind, whether naked savage or broadcloth-wearing Europeans.

In the first place, let it be remembered that so long as woollen clothes are in use the moth never touches them; but if stored away in treasuries and not put to use by man, the moth comes and uses them. Man does his best—or worst—to waste the gifts of God, but He who made both the recipient and the gift abhors waste, and fixes limits to man's power of wasting.

Where is all the wool that sheep have furnished since sheep were created? Every year it is removed from the sheep, either artificially by man or in the ordinary course of nature, just as birds moult their plumage. Now hair is all but imperishable, as may be seen in the Egyptian wig in the British Museum. Three thousand years have passed since it was shorn, and yet it is as bright and glossy as when it left the hands of the maker. If the wool had been suffered to remain untouched, it would have remained until the present day and choked up the face of the habitable earth. But whether used by man or not, it has still been used, and has returned to the earth whence it came.

Even in our own country it is interesting to trace the return of the wool to its parent earth.

The greater part is used by man as clothing. If he cease to use it, the clothes moths, museum beetles, and their kin attack it, and before long have devoured it, so that it again returns to earth.

Some of it is torn off by brambles and left hanging to the prickles; but it is not wasted. The little birds carry it off and use it for their nests as long as it is capable of acting as a warm, soft bed for the eggs and young. Afterwards, when the birds have left it, the moths and beetles come to it and devour it, just as they devour woollen clothes. If they did not do so the branches of every tree would be so clogged with nests that the leaves could not grow and the tree would perish. Strange, indeed, are the analogies of Nature!

In this country we are but little plagued with the wood-eating insects. Their numbers are few and their size insignificant. Within doors we suffer but little from them, and even at the worst, old furniture can only become "worm-eaten." The little holes with which we are so familiar in old chairs and chests are the openings of tiny galleries which perforate the wood, and by which the insect that has caused them has escaped after passing through its stages of egg, grub, and pupa.

Several insects—all being beetles—make these tunnels, and the principal of them is called *Anobium tesselatum*. Popularly it is known as the "Death-watch," because, in common with several other insects, the male calls to its mate by knocking its head against the wood, and producing a sound bearing some resemblance to the ticking of a watch.

Now the insect is clearly out of place in our houses, where we want to preserve such old woodwork, and nothing is easier than to eject it, and at the same time to render the wood impervious to the attacks of every boring insect.

Make a solution of corrosive sublimate (bichloride of mercury) in spirits of wine. Methylated spirit will answer perfectly well, and the strength should be about a heaped teaspoonful of sublimate to a wine pint of spirit. It will be better to procure the sublimate finely powdered, as it dissolves very slowly. And, as it is very heavy, being a salt of mercury, it has a tendency to sink to the bottom of the bottle, which must be well shaken before the solution is used.

Now take a glass tube, drawn out at one end into a point, so as to leave a very tiny aperture. Put the tube into the solution and suck up the liquid until it reaches within three or four inches of the lips. Rapidly put the thumb over the mouth of the tube, and then, when it is removed from the lips, none of the spirit can escape.

You can now introduce the point of the tube into one of the uppermost worm-holes, and by slightly raising the thumb can allow the liquid to trickle very slowly down the hole. It will be as well to blow out the dust from the holes with a pair of bellows, so as to allow free entrance for the liquid. Very probably the whole of the contents of the tube will be exhausted in the first hole. Fill it again and repeat the operation at another hole, a few inches from the former, and so on in proportion to the number of holes.

The result is almost ludicrous. At first no effect at all seems to have been produced, but all at once tiny beetles will come tumbling out of the holes, often followed by little white grubs. Frequently fresh holes show themselves, the enclosed beetles forcing their way out so as to escape from the poisonous spirit. The result of this very simple operation is twofold. In the first place it kills every insect within the wood, even destroying the eggs; and in the next place the poisoned spirit makes its way by degrees among the fibres of the wood, and prevents any wood-boring creature from attacking it.

By employing this process I have saved many a valuable piece of woodwork from utter destruction.

Out of doors there are but few wood-eating insects, and with one or two exceptions they are not supposed to do much harm in this country.

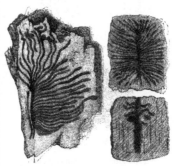

Scolytus destructor tunnels.

One of these exceptions is the *Scolytus destructor*, an insect which, like the sea-serpent and the limits of human life, has the faculty of producing periodical discussions in the newspapers.

Nearly every one knows how the Scolytus infests trees, especially the elm, and how it makes multitudinous tunnels between the wood and the bark, often separating the latter from the tree and causing it to fall in large sheets to the ground. The tree, as a matter of course, dies, and, equally as a matter of course, the Scolytus is looked upon as its destroyer.

Entomologists of the present day, however, are scarcely disposed to take this view of the case, and consider that the Scolytus does not attack sound and healthy trees, but only those which are dying.

Besides the Scolytus, there are very few other wood-devouring beetles sufficiently known to possess popular names. The

. Musk Beetle.

Musk Beetle, conspicuous as it is for size of body, splendour of colour, and sweetness of scent, is curiously little known ; while, except to entomologists, the *Ptilinus*, the *Sinodendron*, the *Clytus*, and *Rhagium*, are not known at all.

The larva of the Stag Beetle feeds upon the roots of trees, and those which are attacked by it may mostly be known by the

Rhagium Beetle. Cocoon.

dead branches at the top. But it is probable that the tree had begun to die before it was attacked, and that the presence of the beetle larva was the consequence and not the cause of the tree's death.

Then there is the caterpillar of the Goat Moth, which feeds chiefly on old willow-trees, and riddles them with its burrows, which in some places are large enough to admit a man's finger. Here again, however, the tree is probably in a dying state before it is attacked by the moth.

In the hotter parts of the world, however, the wood-devouring insects are more than mere annoyances in houses, the most dreaded of them all being the Termites or White Ants. They will devour every piece of woodwork in the house. They find their way into beams, and eat the whole of the wood, with the exception of a shell scarcely thicker than the paper on which this narrative is printed.

They will attack a table, eating their way through the floor into the legs, and hollowing it so that on leaning upon the table, apparently sound as it is, it breaks down and crumbles into a heap of dusty fragments. They have even been known to get into a garden and hollow out the peasticks, so that the first wind blew them down, together with their burden. If they find their way into boxes in which papers are kept, they

Goat-Moth Caterpillar.

will devour almost the whole of every bundle, leaving nothing but the uppermost sheet and the edges of the others.

So in the dwellings of civilised man they are an unmitigated pest. But it must be remembered that house-beams, furniture, and documents are not the normal food of the Termites, which existed for ages before man built houses, made furniture, or penned documents.

Remove man from the scene, and how will the Termites be affected ? Not at all ; for they are found to be flourishing in places where man has never intruded himself. Their chief object is to co-operate with other creatures in preserving the balance of creation, of restoring to earth that which sprang from it, and so to enable earth to reproduce new forms of life.

Remove the Termites and the wood-destroying creatures from the scene, and there would not be a forest left in the world.

Annihilate them all, and see what would happen. When a tree died, it would be blown down, fall, and lie there as long as the world lasts. It would cumber the ground so that no new tree could take its place, and so, in the course of a couple of thousand years or so, instead of a forest, there would be a tangled mass of dead, dry trunks and branches, through which no new growths could force their way.

Then the abolition of the foliage would alter the climate, and produce a perpetual drought, so that even if grass and herbage tried to grow, they would be withered up for want of water. It would be a pathless wilderness—a Sahara of wood instead of sand.

But see what happens when the wood-eating insects come into operation.

As long as a tree is healthy and vigorous they do not touch it; but in the course of nature its term of existence is fulfilled, and it dies. Simultaneously it is attacked by hosts of wood-eating insects, which bore their way into it, lay their eggs, and so establish within it a series of rapidly increasing colonies which weaken its substance. At the first tempest down it comes. Then comes the rain, and penetrates into the wood through the tunnels made by the insects. Fungi now are formed, and still further weaken the wood, making it soft and fit for the food of another set of devourers.

Waterton, in his "Wanderings," details most graphically this portion of insect work : —"Step a few paces aside, and cast thine eye on that remnant of a Mora. Best part of its branches, once so high and ornamental, now lie on the ground in sad confusion, one upon the other, all shattered and fungus-grown, and a prey to millions of insects, which are employed in destroying them.

" Put thy foot on that large trunk thou seest to the left. It seems entire amid the surrounding fragments. Mere outward appearance, delusive phantom of what it once was ! Tread on it, and, like the fuss-ball, it will break into dust."

What happens next is evident enough. It sinks into the ground and is incorporated with it, thus making room for a new tree to spring up in its stead, and supplying to the ground the elements necessary for the nutriment of the fresh growth. Thus it is that, were it not for the Noxious Insects, man would long have ceased to maintain his place in the world.

J. G. WOOD.

THE INFLUENCE OF ART IN DAILY LIFE.

By J. BEAVINGTON ATKINSON.

III.—FURNISHING THE HOUSE.

AN elegant, well-furnished house, in good taste, comfortable to live in and inviting to guests, is a style of thing many persons might desire to realise did they but know how. At the outset a difficulty lies in the way, inasmuch as furniture has long been the chosen sphere for bad taste. Certain preliminary measures which may safely be taken have been indicated in the preceding papers. What is to be desired is that the form and physiognomy of the house, its anatomies and clothings, shall conduce to physical ease and mental gratification, and for this end the furniture and dressings must be agreeable to gentle manners and gentle folks, the final product being repose, a harmony without discord, a beauty without ugliness.

The modern world differs from the old world, and even so does modern furniture depart from the olden models. The conditions under which household furniture is now manufactured are changed; the increase of wealth, the growth in population, and the introduction of machinery have turned out of the market the village carpenter, and in place of a small calling has sprung up a large trade. Three classes or factors are commonly concerned : the designer, who is or should be an artist ; the manufacturer, who is a tradesman ; and lastly the purchaser, who, belonging, it may be, to the new and vulgar rich, is often endowed with more money than taste. The tradesman has seldom any other motive than to supply what will sell, and the adorning of our houses has become too much of a shop transaction. The making of furniture grows as mechanical as the manufacture of pins or nails, and what happens under the infinite subdivision of labour is that the designer and artisan serve as little else than the tools. In olden times, on the contrary, the personality of the artist was felt, he was identified with his workmanship and was brought into contact and sympathetic relationship with the citizen or the squire. And though the social changes have been great, yet signs are not wanting of an approach to former reciprocities ; and assuredly if the artist who creates and the public that consumes could in fellowship join hands, we might expect to find within our English homes, in place of furniture supplied from a store and suited equally to the whole parish or county, articles bespeaking the taste and character of the inmates. Certainly the personal position of the artist was never better assured : he has become a recognised force in the social machinery, he mingles freely by privilege of his calling among all classes and animates by finer spirit the dense masses of the community. And though the shrewd remark is true that the artist, while fit for the best society, should keep out of it, yet if the society be chosen for sympathy and not for show, if the birds of a feather that flock together be not of gay plumage but of accordant note, then the artist may have something to gain as well as benefits to dispense. I have known close friendships spring up between artists and well-to-do people of the world, with the best possible results. It is not to be expected that a man immersed in business should have more than smatterings and aspirations; but the artist, the friend of the family, supplies the lacking knowledge ; he is versed in historic styles and schools, and having at his fingers' ends divers decorative systems, he will readily with pencil and paper in hand sketch out ideas which a clever carpenter can at little cost cast into shape. Thus a man of modest means and unsophisticated instincts would be saved from the rapacity of trade and the emptiness of fashion, and might find the way to gather around him household belongings possibly a little out of the common, because born of a love and animated by a motive.

If the furnishing of a house were altogether easy, the failures were less egregious. The faults committed arise from a complication of causes, such as superfluity of money coupled with lack of taste, the desire for ostentation, with the consequent impatience of mere honest comfort and quietude. Sometimes errors are run into simply from thoughtlessness or haste, from furor for a favourite fad, or from misplaced faith in an infatuated friend or an infallible clique. As a possible safeguard against such mishaps it may be well to give a little consideration to elementary principles such as the following. Furniture must be useful before it aspires to be ornamental ; utility must underlie beauty, construction must sustain and justify ornament. A chair, however attractive to the eye, becomes a snare if it break down under the weight of the sitter ; and a bed, however regal in its adornings, is a delusion if it mar a night's rest. In other words, furniture must be framed for strength, capacity, mobility ; the design must be adapted to the use, to the proportions of the human figure and to the material employed, whether wood, metal or textile fabric; it ought, moreover, to be appropriate to its intended position, and should be in keeping with the decorative surroundings. A table or couch should not appear in a room as an unbidden guest or as an intruder. Furniture in its proportions, and in the relation of the component parts to the whole, must be in balance and symmetry, and preserve, in the midst of detail, breadth and simplicity. As in architecture, the composition will usually prove best in harmony when the constituent parts hold some geometric ratio with each other. Furthermore, furniture as to its construction must be honest and confessed, solid, not sham; in other words, the material and workmanship must appear what they really are without disguise or make-believe. As to the ornament, it must not overcharge or falsify the construction, but repose quietly on the surface, and enrichments, such as carved foliage or flowers, when projecting, must be so arranged as to guard against inconvenience or injury from the dresses of ladies or the dusters of domestics. In fine, in ornamenting the construction care should be taken to preserve the general design and to keep the decoration duly subservient by low relief or otherwise. And the ornament should be so arranged as to assist the constructive strength and enhance by its lines the symmetry and beauty of the sustaining form.

Furniture has sometimes been termed " a sort of toy architecture ; " indeed, the readiest way to understand the art aspects of household furniture is to use architecture as an explanatory key. Designs first constructed and carved in stone were afterwards simulated in wood. The wooden bench took the place of the stone seat; indeed columns, capitals, canopies, cornices, and friezes are often all but identical in either material, while in the nature of things panellings, chests, and seats correspond with the lines and mouldings of doors and windows. The old woodwork in cathedrals, colleges, municipal buildings, and private dwellings illustrate this close relationship. And when furniture is attached bodily to the freehold and ranks amongst the fixtures, the reason is self-evident why wainscots, mantelpieces, and even sideboards and bookcases, accord with the structure of the house and the decoration of the walls. Hence furniture by virtue of its origin assumes definite historic styles, such as the Classic, the Italian, the French Renaissance, the Gothic, and the domestic English. Accordingly Thomas Chippendale, in "The Cabinet-Maker's Director," published in 1754, insists that "architecture ought to be carefully studied by every one who would excel in design, since it is the very soul and basis of the cabinet-maker's art." In like sense Sir Samuel Meyrick, in his introduction to Shaw's "Specimens of Ancient Furniture," shows "that domestic fittings and decorations have invariably consorted with the contemporary architecture— that tables, chairs, and chests have in style been in closest correspondence with the edifices they help to furnish—that, moreover, the character of the furniture serves always as a criterion to the date, the purity, or decadence of the architecture." Hence a revival in the one and a resuscitation in the other have usually gone hand in hand, as seen in the rage for Gothic furniture in our time. But at the present moment the marked phenomenon in' every art, that of furniture included, is the breaking down of old boundary lines and strict historic precedents, and the setting up of an accommodating eclecticism which seeks to unite under one growth what is vital and enduring in all styles.

The old forms of furniture, in fact, need a new birth, so as to meet modern requirements. It will not do to copy ancient designs rigidly. Archaic models are austere, and of Spartan simplicity; archæological furniture is harsh and angular, and must be modified and mollified so as to work smoothly in the midst of our highly polished civilisation. The late Sir Gilbert Scott testifies that "he had long thought the vernacular styles of the present day worn out, and that it is needful to strike out something a little novel. He had," he said, "for some time been endeavouring to do so on the foundation of the Gothic, and should be very glad to see attempts to originate new styles on other bases." In fact, growth is in art, as in nature, the condition of life; without growth death comes. Change and transformation, when not for the sake of mere novelty, bring new development and onward progression. Art has of late years widened its circuit and intensified its activity. She finds the means of meeting our subtle and varied wants; she calls to her aid manifold appliances and processes; she takes as her handmaids sculpture and painting; she is by turns constructive and decorative, and she works with equal zest and impartiality in stone, wood, metal, silk, or cotton. Our

modern artist deems it part of his duty to supervise the minutest detail; he looks to the design of the scraper at the door, of the weathercock on the chimney, of the mantelpiece, fender, or scuttle at the fire. And furniture, sharing in the common movement, forms part of the comprehensive whole. Something may be lost, but much has been gained. The old work of the joiner was rude; the modern cabinet-maker is required to turn to good account his superior advantages; he has at command—often at small cost—fine woods, rich fabrics, efficient tools, so that it is scarcely too much to expect that our every-day furniture shall be, both in material and manipulation, a delectable art product. Thus domestic goods and chattels fall agreeably into the concerted æsthetic system which satisfies the wants of a highly wrought civilisation. Furniture, indeed, has a wide significance, and passes, like certain words in the language, into metaphorical meanings. We speak not only of a house well furnished with couches, curtains, and mirrors, but of a room or a table well furnished with guests, and no less do we commend the mind that is richly furnished with ideas. It may be added that while an unfurnished house is a solitude, a well-furnished house serves as society.

The good is often recognised more clearly by contrast with the bad, and no art yields such egregious examples of false taste as furniture. Instances are quoted of cabinets in mock miniature of Roman temples, and sideboards have been constructed in semblance of sarcophagi or Grecian stone altars. Also deservedly held up to ridicule is a certain notorious buffet, whereon are assembled apostles, philosophers; and doctors, the central position being reserved for Voltaire, with winged genii among clouds above! Censure with equal justice falls on a "jardinière treated as a ruined château, the flowers displayed as growing out of its dilapidated roof;" a chiffonier is also fitly condemned for like misplaced naturalism — the composition comprises rustic scenes with an overgrowth of vines and clustering grapes, birds sheltering among the leaves and building their nests in the branches! The voice of warning is the more called for, because such mistaken efforts have a peculiar fascination for half-educated minds, besides much labour is worse than thrown away, and at half the outlay better results can be got. Monstrosities in art are also censurable as the illicit offspring of debased states of mind; grotesque forms and outrages on the beautiful, like plague spots, fester within the fancy, as do low jokes and false wit. Addison in the *Spectator* turns into ridicule certain literary conceits, such as the rebus, the acrostic, the anagram, the enigma, the quibble, the pun, and other verbal tricks and plays upon words. True wit, like correct art, lies in the resemblance and congruity of ideas; while false wit, which may be termed the false furniture of the mind, and is comparable to tasteless ornament in art, Addison satirises in allegory as follows: "Methought," he writes, "I was transported into a country that was filled with prodigies governed by the goddess Falsehood, and entitled the Region of False Wit. There was nothing in the fields, the woods, and the rivers that appeared natural. Several of the trees blossomed in leaf-gold, some of them produced bone-lace, and some of them precious stones. The fountains bubbled in an opera tune; the birds had many of them golden beaks and human voices; the flowers perfumed the air with smells of incense, and grew up in pieces of embroidery. And I discovered in the centre of a very dark grove a monstrous fabric built after the Gothic manner, and covered with innumerable devices in that barbarous kind of sculpture. I immediately went up to it, and found it to be a kind of heathen temple consecrated to the god of Dulness." Bad art is worse than dull or stupid, it is offensive and evil.

In mediæval days the allowance of domestic furniture was scant, and old woodwork is now so scarce that in some outlying districts the most ancient relic is the village stocks. And, indeed, certain Gothic revivals in furniture might have been almost suggested by such instruments of durance vile; the form is so austerely archaic, the construction so rude, the angles are so harshly abrupt, that the human frame, in vain seeking rest, is stretched as on a rack. Certain ultra-revivalists have, in fact, invested Gothic furniture in unplaned planks, gaping at the joints, knocked together with savage nails, and bound with ragged clasps and rough hinges —the whole construction being worthy to stand among the rushes in "the marsh" of the olden hall, rather than upon a Brussels carpet in a modern drawing-room. The gable end of a house may be made as severe and acute as the most infatuated Gothicist can desire, but like angularities in couches and elbow-chairs subject weary mortals to torture. Gothic times were straitened, frugal, self-immolating; Renaissance epochs, on the contrary, became exuberant, luxurious, and

pleasure-seeking. And it is the unfortunate fatality of fashion to run always into extremes, and so furniture, instead of abiding by the happy mean of moderation, and taking each style in its inherent truth and beauty, has by turns exaggerated the excesses and eccentricities of Gothic, Italian, and French originals. Gothic art, like the checkered life of man upon earth, is beset with contradictions and imperfections, and as if beauty were not an all-sufficing end, ugliness, the visible semblance of sin, is courted and made much of. The dread may be that placid beauty lacks spirit and vigour, but the observation has been shrewdly made in cookery that one grain of garlic suffices to save a dish from insipidity; and so in the arts a little deformity and queerness go a great way. Grotesqueness or character pushed to caricature has been the bane of certain Gothicists; and art, when thus deformed, instead of being, as among the Greeks, a goddess, is transmuted into a gargoyle. Such art, not giving speech to sermons in stones, presents the ungainly image of "laughter holding both her sides."

But Gothic furniture when treated with taste and judgment becomes verily a welcome inmate within our homes. The Englishman who has built himself a cottage in the country under the shadow of trees or near to the parish church, may come upon rustic couches or garden seats, which perchance the local carpenter makes out of woods grown on the spot. I have sometimes been interested to see in the houses of a cathedral close the Gothic style in full possession; the means at disposal are usually moderate, but the good man of the house gathers round him treasures that money cannot buy, and all his little belongings are encompassed by local associations and overgrown with personal habits. Pugin's revivals of domestic Gothic, exquisite in design and detail, the chairs, bookcases, cabinets, and sideboards sometimes decorated with geometric tracery, foliated piercings, or floral carvings, are rare achievements within the reach of the rich only. To my mind such masterpieces are surpassingly beautiful, yet expense need be no object. But frugality has ever been the cry of Gothic pioneers, and accordingly furniture made of deal or other wood, uncostly and easily worked, has been kindly provided for those who desire that their scanty worldly goods shall be impressed by strict mediæval aspiration. The designs, studiously simple, are often piquant in character, and attract attention by a personality and motive

which mere shop goods seldom can show.
Young men making a start in life, their
intellects more richly stocked than their
purses, accustomed to readings in English
history and studies among the early British
poets, have of late addicted themselves to
furnishing after an original fashion. They
may not be wholly exempt from whims and
conceits, but at least they have ideas of their
own which they truthfully seek to carry out
free from conventional trammels. And often
in Bohemian quarters may be found an
honest, out-spoken, and inventive art which
vainly we shall search for throughout Bel-
gravia. Sometimes I have known a brotherhood spring up among artists and amateurs,
a kind of mutual aid society for decorating
and furnishing each other's dwellings. Draw-
ing-rooms and studios have been thus painted
by friendly hands, and cabinets constructed
cunningly, one artist painting a panel, another designing a frieze, a third contriving the
hinges, lock, and other metal fastenings.
Pianos have been particularly favoured. I
remember an instrument carved almost as a
cameo and coloured by inlays of natural
woods as a picture; the panels were painted
with figures of Miriam, King David, and St.
Cecilia. And Mr. Marks, R.A., indulging in
a serio-comic strain, has impressed the Muses
into the same melodious service. I also
recollect cherubs' heads designed by Mr.
Burne Jones for a like destination; and while
these lines are passing through the press a
leading pianoforte manufactory has issued
invitations for the private view of an instrument decorated inside and out by the same
artist, with designs of Orpheus and Eurydice,
of Beatrice inspiring Dante, and, conspicuously, of an undraped female figure personat-
ing fruitful nature, surrounded by Cupid-like
genii. It may be permitted to add that the
value of this unique creation is estimated at
a thousand guineas. There seems an essential fitness in such decorations, a proverbial
semblance subsisting among the harmonies
of sound, form, and colour. And Gothic
growths when grafted on the old stocks
of truth and beauty prove ever rhythmical,
and accord with the gentle cadence of sweet
sounds.

Furniture in its modern forms presents
distinctive nationalities. French furniture is
fantastic, often florid. The designs are
usually borrowed from the Gallic Renaissance, a style proverbial for corruption, yet
bringing into bewitching play the blandishments of the sister arts of architecture, sculpture, and painting. I have sometimes been

struck with amazement before modern French
cabinets, perfect in architectonic proportion,
in symmetry, and beauty; the modelling and
carving truly sculpturesque, and showing
command of the human figure used decoratively, the colouring, light, and shade dependent on rare woods and rich materials tenderly balanced, yet tersely accentuated and
studiously pictorial. Such compositions challenge criticism as consummate works of art;
the masses are preserved in simple breadth,
the details are evenly distributed, so that no
part of the surface is bald, none overcrowded;
as for the workmanship, it is of unsurpassed
excellence. In short, French furniture-makers
of the nineteenth century are perhaps the
only worthy descendants of the great masters
of the Italian Cinque-cento.

But our English cabinet-makers have for
long been striving to vie with their brilliant
rivals across the Channel, and their painstaking revivals are commendable for art-
design, economy of manufacture, and domestic utility. French furniture is in keeping
with the ostentation of the grand palaces of
Louis Quatorze, while English furniture in its
comparative simplicity possesses a fitness for
our British homes. In family life we still
love concords and seek to preserve pro-
prieties; less daring in design and less florid
in ornament than our neighbours, we are content to be more consistent and sober, and
prefer solid truth to surface show. But after
all, in art, as in the science of engineering,
everything can be done if money be no
object. English artisans have economy
thrust upon them, but when lavish expenditure is permitted simplicity can easily give
place to costly elaboration and enrichment;
and I think, all things considered, from a
feeling of patriotism, for the sake of our industrial people, and in the cause of our
struggling and aspiring native art, it behoves
the English householder to show some preference for our home-made produce. It is
well to feel how much may lie in the power
of each one of us to help on the good cause.

English furniture, good in design, sound
in construction, utilitarian, yet in ornament
tasteful, is now made to meet the requirements of all places, peoples, and pockets.
Furniture for the dining-room, as distinguished
from that for the drawing-room, should be
substantial, massive, and handsome, and in
colour somewhat sombre rather than gay.
Drawing-room furniture courts companionship with ladies, and will do well to be
elegant, cheerful, and even festive. In this
brilliant sphere the French are supposed to

shine, yet the English of late have gained a fantasy and delicacy responsive to the lightsome dance, the gleeful song, and sparkling prattle. I have looked with delight on cabinets rich in the resources of the best Renaissance, symmetric compositions forced up to a climax in the cornice, the panels ornate with cameo Wedgwood-ware, and the whole façade rich with inlays of rose and satin-wood, ivory, lapis lazuli, and precious stones, forced up by a system of polychromy to the semblance of a picture. This highwrought furniture is commendable while kept by quiet restraint in chastened beauty, and when worked out in true materials honestly constructed. Such elaborate compositions, if too costly, can be pared down and simplified. Elaboration always represents labour, and labour means money. A complex piece of furniture can, like any other product, be reduced to its constituent elements, which are usually few, obvious, and economic. Balance in proportion, symmetric relation of parts to the whole, artistic mouldings, with some few decorative enrichments, well chosen and rightly placed, will always insure a pleasing effect at slight outlay.

Draperies are to a house what clothes are to the human body; indeed, it were scarcely going too far to compare an undraped house to the nude figure. And drapery, whether applied to walls, to furniture, or to the human frame, has for its end clothing, warmth, and adornment. The appropriateness of all draperies is contingent greatly on climate, locality, and conditions of life, and such fitness usually brings about effects correct in taste. The simplest arrangements, if only harmonious, insure more or less satisfactory results. Draperies, such as curtains, portières, coverlets, may rely for artistic effect merely on pleasing concord of colours. But rather to be preferred, I think, are compositions of a little more complexity, wherein a pattern beautiful in form adds charm to agreeable colour. A surface destitute of design is as a blank sheet of paper—a tabula rasa, which seems to need some idea or design from the artist's hand. The works of nature are never left blank or void; nature is so generously prodigal that she decorates even the surfaces which are hid away from sight, and so art does well to be equally profuse in adorning the under garment of a figure or the inner lining of a tapestry or coverlet. The general principles already propounded for the decoration of walls and floors will, with allowance for change of material, hold good as to draperies. And

the advice to be given for furnishing generally is, eschew fashion, which generally allures but for a moment, and then when it fleets, leaves the stigma of being "out of fashion," and choose in preference forms of art which, founded on immutable truth and beauty, can never grow old, obsolete, or unpleasing. Above all shun show and extravagant outlay, remembering that as Providence clothes the lily, and bestows the life-giving elements of air, light, and heat freely, so art, having regard for the lowly, filleth the hungry with good things, while the rich she sends empty away.

The arrangement of rooms needs to be carefully considered. The fact that articles of furniture are for the most part unfixed, that they are what the French call "meubles," or movables, allows all the greater freedom in disposition or location. Tables and chairs, sofas and footstools, are indeed nearly as itinerant as the persons who use them, and may, in the general artistic composition, be treated almost as figures. And to carry the analogy one step further, some movables may be accounted "occasional," and stand in relation to the more permanent and fixed furniture as casual visitors. And while, perhaps, it may be expected of the members of the family—the abiding tenants —that they shall in dress and general get up more or less accord with the wall-hangings and carpets, the utmost that can be looked for from the visitors is that they shall comport themselves as well-dressed ladies and gentlemen. And so occasional furniture, like the person of "the walking gentleman" on the stage, has little more to do than to fill the allotted part agreeably. And while in the furnishing of a room the guiding rule is "unity," yet at the same time it is well to remember that "variety is charming," and that "unity in variety," when attained throughout the house, leaves nothing to be desired. "Unity in variety" makes a picture pleasing, and a room can scarcely be wrong if arranged as a picture. As to diversity, there can be but little doubt that the Romans introduced Egyptian furniture into their dwellings, and in our days a Gothic chair, provided it be graceful, need never feel awkward in the presence of an Italian cabinet. Yet, not for one moment must be tolerated within a dwelling confusion or uproar; nothing can be worse than the indiscriminate crowding together of heterogeneous objects, as in a curiosity shop; the home, a quiet shelter from the turmoil of the outer world, must not be turned into a museum, menagerie, or Babel. Rather let the furniture associate in cozy coterie as forming a happy home. "A nice and subtle happiness I see thou to thyself proposest," were the approving words addressed to Adam when he craved a companion in his solitude. "A nice and subtle happiness" makes a home. A well-appointed house may perchance bear some comparison to a thoughtful literary composition—one motive presides from preface to finis, and episodes, when thrown in for diversity, conform to the common scheme and blend in the collective whole. And the divers kinds of furniture admissible within a room may be further indicated by the variety of authors allowed a place on the book-shelves. Some volumes may be practical and utilitarian, others poetical and orna-mental; yet all should propose as a com-mon end to improve the mind and add to the enjoyment of life. And, as in a well-stored library, varied volumes ranged in order due satisfy the mental cravings, so in a well-provided household, furniture disposed methodically should minister to the sensuous and supersensuous wants of body and of mind. But above all these things, it is im-perative that every work admitted within the house shall be beautiful; and then seldom will be found intruding serious discord, for all creations in nature and in art possessed of beauty agree well together. And men and women, when thus brought into living fellowship with beauty, are known to grow into like fashion of mind and even of body, while the penalty hangs over those who dwell with ugliness, that day by day they themselves become more ugly.

THE CHURCH, A FELLOW-WORKER WITH GOD IN THE CONVERSION OF THE HEATHEN.

Preached before the Church Missionary Society at St. Bride's, Fleet Street, May 3, 1880.*

BY THE RIGHT REV. THE LORD BISHOP OF ROCHESTER.

"Jesus said, Take ye away the stone."—JOHN xi. 39.

IN a village street under the "purple brow" of Olivet an agitated group had gathered round a tomb. It was a cave, and a stone lay upon it. Some of them had come from afar, for they bore marks of fatigue and travel; while others were from the city on the other side of the hill.

But on one foremost figure all eyes were gazing; for His dignity was only matched by His sweetness; and while His cheeks were wet with recent tears, His frame shook with such strong emotion, that on reaching the grave all He could say was, "Take ye away the stone." In a moment of intelligible sensitiveness a relative reminded Him that her brother had lain there four days. But the delay was only for a moment; the irre-sistible summons was pronounced, "Lazarus, come forth!" and "when he that was dead came forth bound hand and foot with grave-clothes, Jesus saith unto them, Loose him, and let him go."

You may have already felt how this great miracle is also a parable of the co-operation of human effort with Divine grace in the con-version of the world. Lazarus lay dead in his tomb, and the mass of mankind is "dead" —"in trespasses and in sins." The stone be-fore the sepulchre which closed in the decay and shut out the sunlight, means the blind superstition, and subtle mysticism, and stub-born prejudice, and abominable idolatry that hide God from the heathen; and He, who with the same words that wakened the dead could also, had it pleased Him, have rolled away the stone and unswathed the limbs of His friend, and did not, because He desired to stir faith and reward effort, makes us fellow-workers with Himself in His Redeeming Purpose; and giving us the gospel, nay, being Himself the gospel, bids us proclaim Him to the world.

Men, brethren, and fathers—one in the joy of our common salvation and in the hope of the appearing of Christ our King—what words can I find adequate to express the grandeur of the subject on which I this day address you; or the conviction of my heart, that this beloved and honoured Society, in the principles she represents and the doctrines she declares, and the methods she adopts, and

* Though the preacher felt himself unable, under the peculiar circumstances of the moment, to introduce into his sermon the expression of his sympathy with the kindred labours of other missionary societies, it was not from lack of interest, but of opportunity. The names of Moffat and Living-stone, Carey and John Williams, and Duff, and Arthur and Norman Macleod are dear to all who hold Christ dear. True soldiers of the Cross cannot help being brethren; and their only rivalry is how least to please self, and most to honour Him.

the support she conciliates, is not only foremost among the spiritual forces promoting Christ's kingdom among men, but is also one of the most vital and potent institutions of our dear English Church? For this work is so essentially noble, even from the lowest point of view. If truth is the most precious inheritance of man, then the wider the surface it covers, the deeper the problems it solves, the darker the sorrows it heals, the loftier the hopes it inspires, the more beautiful and magnanimous is the task of proclaiming it. The entire world would execrate the selfishness that deliberately concealed an effectual cure for some cruel and infectious disease. And ours is a faith which, in its ideal of a perfect life, in its story of an atoning sacrifice, in its bond of a human brotherhood, in its hope of union with God, at once meets, absorbs, surpasses, and glorifies whatever is to be found in other faiths that have satisfied or attempted to satisfy the religious instincts of men; and if we did not do our utmost to tell our fellows of it, and to press it on their acceptance, the cavil would be unanswerable, either that we secretly doubt its integrity, or greedily monopolize its joy.

Oh, sheep of Christ, whom He has bought with His blood—other sheep He has, which He must find and bring that they may be one flock with you; and you must search them out and bring them to His feet. They are very dear to Him. He has never forgotten them, never forsaken them. Some rays of His glory glimmer on their souls; and in a passionate hunger for truth, which some of us might do well to imitate, many of them bear untold anguish to catch a glimpse of His face. Send them the gospel of His love. Do it *quickly*, for the time is short; *boldly*, for you must not be ashamed of His testimony; *trustfully*, for it is the "power of God unto salvation;" *wisely*, for He does not want our mistakes. Be *patient*, for "long sleeps the summer in the seed." Be *gentle*, for the Cross makes wounds enough without our adding to them. Be *hopeful*, for all He has is ours; be *humble*, for if they have much to learn, they may have something to teach.

Manifest Christ's life of love in your own joyful and steady sacrifices; and in resembling Him you will show them the nature of God.

There is the Grave, the Stone, and the Command.

In the Grave we are to see Heathendom. If the angel of the Apocalypse, flying in the midst of heaven with the everlasting gospel,

should strike the globe in the middle of the Pacific, and then turn westward about 40° north of the Equator, first he would come to Japan, that imitative and keen-witted race, where, ten years ago, our one English missionary saw this notice : " The evil sect called Christian is strictly prohibited ;" and now our own Society alone has 9 missionaries there, and 5,000 persons confess Jesus Christ.

On west, to the mighty Empire of China, with its many zones of climate, its teeming millions, its indefatigable industry, its good-humoured materialism, the nation which, if it knew its strength and could find its Tamerlane, might soon overrun the world. Here we have 100 new out-stations during the last 9 years; 24 missionaries against 20; 8 native clergy against 2; 180 native teachers against 53; 4,054 native Christians against 853.

On over the steppes of Thibet to the crest of the Himâlaya, at whose feet nestles the jewel of the East, sunny and fertile Hindostan, with its manifold races, ancient civilisation; also with its ineffable wickedness and its history red with blood. Here we have 109 native clergy against 57 nine years ago; 1,700 native teachers against 1,370; 90,000 Christian adherents against 64,000; 1,109 schools against 787; 41,000 scholars against 32,000.

The tide of life is rising, though it be far from its flood.

On over Egypt, the eyebrow of Africa, into the heart of that vast continent where, if there is blackness of darkness, dawn is breaking. In all parts of that enormous territory Satan's power is being attacked. On the east coast this Society has 8 missionaries against 1 seven years ago. The banner of the Cross floats over the fountains of the Nile. In the south the great sister society holds an entrenched position. In the west, Sierra Leone recalls our distant and grateful memories. We have also the Yoruba and Niger missions, with 23 native clergy against 11; 96 native lay agents against 41; 7,500 Christians against 2,300.

Crossing the Atlantic towards the Pole, we reach the spacious plains and mighty rivers of the North-West; where, among the roots of the Rocky Mountains, Duncan has given an heroic example of energy and skill in evangelizing almost the lowest races that the gospel can reach; where, moreover, in the basin of the Saskatchewan, the Nelson, and the Mackenzie, in a land that some imagine to be a frozen morass shut in by impenetrable pine-forests, we have 14 missionaries against 10; 12 native clergy against 8; 62 teachers against 19; 11,600 native Christians against 4,200; and it seems to me a sagacity, with no slight statesmanship in it (and reminding those who knew him of the vigorous intelligence of Henry Venn), thus to be occupying a territory which, in the time of our grandchildren, may rival the greatest of our dependencies for resources, population, and enterprise.

Christian brethren, I am not at all apprehensive of wearying you with these facts. I should much more dread fatiguing you with tumid or rhetorical emotion. Yet there is very much more land to be possessed; and while we ought to be unspeakably grateful for what has already been done, and should be on our guard against a feeble dastardliness about this enormous enterprise, the work we are now doing can only be adequately figured by a handful of pioneers, cutting at the Andes with penknives; and the one conviction of all others I would press on you is this, that you will never carry the strongholds of heathenism with a rush. Some of you will remember Edward Irving's grand though eccentric sermon on "Missionaries after the Apostolical School," where he observes that "to be a missionary is the highest preferment in the kingdom of God," and that "the four principal things in the propagation of the gospel are wisdom to address the worthiest people, entire dependence upon God, exemplification of the doctrine, and constant debate with the children of men." But I may also remind you of a sentence of one of the ablest Christian thinkers of our time, who writes:*—"It does appear that among the gifts of our countrymen the rarest is knowing and doing justice to the religious beliefs of other nations."

We talk of heathenism, but are we at the pains to reflect that between the fetichism of the savage of the Niger and the serene mysticism of the Brahmin there is a chasm as wide as the Mississippi? Under any circumstances it is hard, and ought to be hard, to change the religion, whether of an individual or a race. It is hard, because it is so noble. I suppose if anything under the sun should be dear to an honest man it is his religion. It colours his life, shapes his principles, points his motives, consecrates his actions. It is inherited from his parents; it twines round the roots of his childhood; it smiles on his bridal; it softens the shadows of his grave. And when the religion you propose to substitute is a religion with a cross in it,

with no material prosperity for its reward, and a world to come as its distant recompense, is it wonderful that one who asks what the exchange will bring to him, and is told "the reproach of Christ," is slow in giving his reply? Glance at this in detail, and it may become even plainer.

The Karen, the Bedouin of the Jordan Valley, the negro of the Zambesi or the Congo, may present types of a mental and moral quality not indispensably claiming for their suitable handling gifts or culture of an exceptional kind. Though, indeed, it should never be forgotten that savage races are not necessarily deficient in mental force or quickness, and that it needs practised skill, vivid fancy, solid patience, rare sense instinctively to divine what needs instant killing, and what may be left to perish of itself.

But approach the Mussulman—proud heir of a line of conquerors—who looks on the rest of the world as still existing by his clemency, whose missionary zeal at this moment is so fierce and energetic that in Africa his competition may run us very hard, and who simply disdains other faiths as not worth reasoning about; tell him about the Incarnation, and his answer, if he gives you one, will make you shudder for years. This I am sure of, that if you had ever talked with Pfander, as I once did at Constantinople, on this matter, you might not indeed despair, for God is with us; but certainly you would not go with tripping gait and a too complacent cheerfulness to try a fall with Islam.

Or go to the Brahmin. He cherishes a faith which has flourished for three thousand years. His language is the root-tongue of all the dialects of Europe. His sacred books date from seven hundred years before Christ was born. He boasts of a hundred and eighty-five millions of fellow-worshippers. God he considers solely as an Intelligence. His castes* have been regarded as efforts of separation, whereby the best may be ultimately selected for serving Him. What some call the multitudinous idolatry of three thousand gods, others ingeniously explain to be only an indefatigable attempt to find what God is, and where, with the one desire of being finally absorbed in His Essence. Is it quite so easy to win these dreamy but subtle thinkers into a newer and simpler faith?

Once more go to the Buddhist, and there are four hundred and ninety millions of Buddhists, if you include the disciples of Confucius. Their founder lived six hundred

* "Word, Work, and Will," p. 294.

* See "The Religions of the World in their Relation to Christianity," p. 40.

years before Christ. The ·Buddhist is far more catholic and democratic than the Brahmin. The poorest and vilest may become one with Boodha, and when his faith is perfected he is swallowed up in God. The one infallible diagnostic of Buddhism is "a belief in the infinite capacity of the human intellect." Well, is it not plain what skilful and thorough intellectual treatment such a man needs, and is it not desirable to try to give it him? No man has a better claim to be heard on this subject than Professor Monier Williams. But he thus writes in "Indian Wisdom": *—"It appears to me high time that all thoughtful Christians should reconsider their position, and readjust themselves to their altered environments. The sacred books of the three great systems opposed to Christianity are now becoming accessible, and Christians can no longer neglect the duty of studying their contents."

You here to-night, who know the joy of knowledge and the passionate force of a new and lofty idea, I ask, is it not true what Pascal said, that man's dignity consists in his faculty of thinking, and that, though he is miserable, he knows it, and there is his greatness? These thinkers of the East—and, remember, it is truth that ultimately rules the world—they cannot, indeed, cover the earth with iron bars, or talk by wires, or span the ocean with steam; such is *our* greatness. But often they are far deeper and subtler thinkers than we are; and when we go to them, as it is our duty to go, and ask them to listen to us, as it is our privilege to ask, let us beware how we blandly invite them to exchange their faith for ours, unless meeting them on their own ground, and contending with weapons which they can appreciate, we suitably propose to them a life that they can venerate, and a Person whom they can adore. Otherwise they will hardly take the trouble of laughing at us, much less of answering us; and quietly dismissing us with an urbane silence, they will wrap themselves in the mantle of their pride, and rejoice that at least Thought is free.

But Jesus said, "Take ye away the stone."

It may be roughly observed that there are three stages in mission work, with usually a logical order of their own. Though, of course, when it pleases Him, God confounds this order, by cutting across it, or anticipating it, thereby manifesting His sovereignty, and doing all His work Himself.

There is the work of *preparation* by civil-

isation and education, in which the stone is rolled away for light and air to come in.

There is the work of *evangelization*, by which the Word of God is spoken straight into the spirit—"Awake thou that sleepest, and arise from the dead."

There is the final work of watering, and watching, and maturing the young life just born by pastoral care and superintendence. "Loose him, and let him go."

To my own mind nothing is more conspicuous or admirable in the operations of this Society than the patient, resolute courage with which, even at the risk of misconstruction from unreasonable friends and coarse sarcasm from enemies, they have planted schools and cultivated the arts of life. No doubt it is possible to put civilisation in the place of Christ, and you cannot regenerate man by refining him. Yet it must not be forgotten that in some heathen races both conscience and intelligence have in a certain degree to be created before there is a capacity either for morality or faith. Physical habits have to be formed, methods of life to be learned, not only for material comfort, but for moral education. Industry everywhere is the best safeguard against viciousness, and the arts of peace are the surest protection against war. In some tribes a language has to be framed; in almost all the vocabulary must be enlarged before the terms of our religion can be imparted or understood. To give a human being self-respect is a help to the cultivation of conscience. Unless he learns to observe, to reason, to compare, to remember, how can he be an intelligent hearer of the Word of life? But all this means prodigious labour, unwearied patience, and much sympathy. Past efforts in New Zealand, present efforts in Frere Town and Uganda have deserved, and ought to deserve, the gratitude of practical men. Taking our fellow-creatures as we find them, we feel it our duty to make the best of them, and to help them to live for both worlds.

So too with education. Possibly a few may still be of opinion that the sole function of a missionary society is to preach to adults. Yet what in that case would become of the young? In India, no doubt, a certain provision is made by the State, but the teaching is entirely secular, and the Redeemer of the world is only offered a place in the Pantheon of universal benefactors. If this Church Missionary Society did nothing outside its schools, it might claim to be approaching the heathen at the most impressionable period of life. In India alone it expends £10,000 a year on education; and in addition to about 1,000 primary schools for boys and girls it controls 12 institutions for the training of native pastors, evangelists, and teachers; 50 institutions where the youth of both sexes are boarded and lodged; 70 institutions for higher general education, whether high-schools, middle-class, or Anglo-vernacular schools. A sub-committee has recently reported especially on the higher education now given in them, that even as an evangelizing agency it has done, and is capable of doing, much good; and they give instances of native Christians now mission-aries, or occupying influential positions in many parts of India, who owe their conver-sion to the Society's schools for higher educa-tion, and who in all human probability would, but for these schools, never have come into contact with Divine truth at all. And if I might add a word here on two departments of secular knowledge especially useful in taking away the stone from the sepulchre, I should name *history* and *science*. *History*, as Bishop Caldwell has strikingly put it; since how without history is it possible to trace the providential government of the world, or to elucidate one of the most remarkable evi-dences of our religion in fulfilled prophecy? *Science*—for the study of God's laws in the methodical and exact observation of His works is both the readiest and surest way of exploding the monstrous legends of a pol-luted mythology. When to the contempla-tion of God in His works the Church adds the revelation of God in His Word, she com-pletes the system of full-orbed knowledge. Science is then seen to be only a stair lead-ing to God; not the entire account of Him: we approach to observe, and we remain to adore.

Then when the stone is rolled away, and the voice can penetrate the tomb, the vital sum-mons is delivered—" Lazarus, come forth." This is the central, the normal, the essential function of the missionary—to preach Christ as the wisdom of God and the power of God. There are three kinds of power at work in the world, each in a sphere of its own—force over the senses, truth over the intellect, love over the will. As to the first Christ says, " My kingdom is not of this world;" and what is analogous to that in our case—I mean State patronage—would be only a fatal embarrassment to us. All we ask is to be left alone, with hands and lips free. But truth and love we know, for we have tried them; and they are essentially contained, completely revealed, and harmoniously united

in the Incarnate Son. The Person of Christ is the Gospel of our Salvation. In His life He is the Pattern of Righteousness; in His death He is the Propitiation for Sin; in His Resurrection He is the Conqueror of Death; in His Ascension He is Priest upon His Throne. Here, too, lie concealed the cha-racteristic dogmas of our religion in their humbling and unpalatable account of sin and helplessness, as well as in their lofty and exalting revelation of God's purpose for us, and our own vast possibilities. And it is only by the unflinching exposition of man's depravity and weakness, with the elevating exposition of the mystery of regeneration and the glory of redeeming love, that the conscience of the heathen can be reached and wounded, and his mind and spirit ex-alted with the vision of God. Sin the curse of the world, and death its wages; salvation, both from its deserts and dominion, the free and present gift of God to all who repent and believe; the Holy Ghost the author of regeneration and holiness; Scripture our rule of faith; Baptism and the Lord's Supper effectual signs of grace to believers; the Church at once the body and handmaid of Christ: here is our message, to be preached. indeed, with tenderness and wisdom (not as you would fire live shells into an enemy's camp), still unreservedly and continually, at the risk of misconstruction and contempt; also (as the apostles have taught us to do), didactically rather than emotionally, aiming at the understanding as the fittest passage chamber to the soul, with a sagacious sym-pathy that approaches them on the side where they are most vulnerable, and with the honest recognition of truths which they hold in com-mon with us, and which we desire to use as paths into the territory beyond.

Then when the dead comes forth living, yet hampered with grave-clothes, it is the pastor's office to loose him and let him go. It cannot need a lengthened argument to en-force the necessity of a careful, and patient, and systematic supervision of baptized con-verts for months and years afterwards. The Acts tell us that; also that this can ultimately be most effectually done by a native pastorate a moment's reflection may show. Of course, if the Churches in the East are to be kept steady in their hold of catholic truth and fellowship, generations may pass before they can safely dispense with the guidance of their European fathers. Yet the sympathy of common blood, of national history, of local association, of early training is vital and last-ing; and if the Church is to spread widely and deeply—if she is to attract to herself the masses of the people, and to build the Church of Asia on the one foundation of Jesus Christ, there must be ample elasticity both in local arrangement and external machinery; and the Church will grow only as she is wide and free. And, my brethren, shall she grow? These "fields white unto the harvest," shall *our* hands reap them for the Lord; or shall He come and find us sleeping, and so hire others into our places? No words can exaggerate the solemn responsibility which rests with those I see before me to-day, and to whom my heart goes out in the sympathy of one who, for the ' best years of his life, joined with them in their hallowed activities, hopes to be considered their brother still. It is not too much to say that on the provincial clergy of England the progress of missions must depend; for in the great towns, London most of all, the clergy are like men buried up to their waist in a great earth pit of conflicting duties, only half free for work outside. Definite, complete, vigilant parochial organization is the vital element under God of our Society's success; and I am sometimes tempted to tremble when I see how great a power is in the hands of the clergy, for which some of them do not seem to care. May I quote here the unimpeachable testimony of an impartial and incorruptible witness? In a letter written just fifty years ago to the Resident Masters of the University of Oxford, after noticing certain presumed irregularities in the practice of the Society—all of which, be it observed, have since been eagerly and successfully imitated by other Church societies—John Henry Newman then proceeds: "In the case of this Society the authority of our ecclesiastical rules is acknowledged by its very name, which its regulations so well bear out, that you may search in vain through them all for any principle of a sectarian tendency;" and he adds, with the object of gaining for it the support and steadying influence of the entire Church, "It is only necessary for the clergy of each diocese and archdeaconry to take up the management of the association in their own neighbourhood."* And, brethren, that we may do this, and with both hands, earnestly, what shall we ask of God?

Is it faith? Well, we do want faith, and our prayer must ever be, "Lord, increase our faith." For surely it is true, that if there is faith on the earth when the Lord comes back, it will be greatly due to Christian missions. They are the protest of vital

* "Via Media," vol. ii. p. 9.

godliness against a formal and languid religionism. They are the direct challenge of those who tell us that Jesus never rose; they are the emphatic antidote to that sickly and feeble creed, which, with courage neither to believe nor to deny, begins by telling us that life is a journey between two nights, and ends with the consolation that "at intervals a paternal smile traverses Nature." It is the resolute courage that looks right into the tomb with its fetid air and ghastly decay, because He bids us do it, who whispers while we do it, "Said I not unto thee, that if thou wouldest believe, thou shouldest see the glory of God?"

Yet we *do* believe a little, or why are we here to-day? We believe in the redeeming purpose of God, and that it is His will presently to gather together in one all things in Christ; and though He seems to be waiting, He knows why He is waiting; be sure, that when all things are made plain at break of day, there will be no flaw in His perfect righteousness, no speck or stain on the mercy of His heart. And we believe in the Intercession of the Son; that, as He said to His disciples about Lazarus, "This sickness is not unto death, but for the glory of God"— though Lazarus did die—so in some mystery of His love, this condition of the heathen may have a compensating side to it; and that as He looks down on the dark places of the earth, and speaks to us about them, He says, " Obey me, yet trust me."

And, indeed, we believe in the Holy Ghost, the Author and Giver of life, with every fibre and pulse of our being. Perhaps the most consoling feature about these latter days, not too full of consolation, is that the Church's faith seems stirred and invigorated about the work of the Spirit; that this Purpose of the Father, not spent at Pentecost, is being fulfilled to us who believe.

Yet it must be "faith working by love," for, indeed, it seems to me that our great lack is of love; and that because there is so little love—and therefore so little sacrifice—the reproach of a living preacher is so true, " The great vice of human nature is slackness about good;" and so this great daughter of the Church has her checks, and delays, and disappointments in her onward march with the message of salvation; not because Christ stints His grace, but because His people grudge their offering. For, if money is the test of character, slender gifts are the language of lukewarm love.

Also, I think that if ever Christ deserved to be honoured, and His goodness conspicuously recognised, it is to-day. A year of almost unexampled depression has, nevertheless, terminated with a heavy inherited embarrassment entirely swept away, and with what might be almost called the insignificant accident of £3,000 on the debit side.

Moreover, twelve months ago, a shadow on the horizon had gathered into a black mist; and the mist might mean a storm. That, too, has disappeared by God's great blessing on sagacious, kindly counsel; yes, and let me add, on the conscience of a young bishop, about whom none, however seriously they felt compelled to differ from his convictions, ever seriously doubted his love to Christ. Surely all here this evening will ask for him, what he bids us ask for in his own touching language, that he may resume his blessed work with "humility and wisdom, and a deeper spirit of prayer." Therefore I say let us bless God for His goodness. While we ask Him to help us to love Him, we shall show that we love Him by our gifts; and pray Him not only now, but to-morrow and continually,

to bestow on us more of a holy, and serious, and steady, and yet passionate devotion;— a love which is not so much a sentiment as a force in our nature; a love which grows from continual communion with Christ, and adoring contemplation of Him, so that if the fancy sleeps the will is true.

O Jesus of Nazareth, Who from Thy Throne above the stars lookest down in compassion on the heathen that have not known Thee, and on the people that have not called on Thy name; so steep us in the spirit of Thy Atoning Passion—so persuade us of the loss of those who miss Thee, and of the peril of those who forget Thee, that this very night, as did our fathers of old, we may make Thee an offering in some way worthy of Thy unspeakable goodness, and our own indebtedness; and thus, made mighty in the power of Thy Resurrection, and consecrated with the fellowship of Thy Sufferings, we shall ever rejoice to remove this stone from the Sepulchre, and to push the Triumph of Thy Cross.

THE VOICES OF THE FLOWERS.

IF you lie with your ear to the soft green earth,
　When the rain and the sunshine fall,
You can hear the flowers in their gay glad mirth
　To each other whisper and call.

For hush'd, like an infant in sleep, they lie
　In their moist cool cells below,
Aweary of hearing the wind's bleak sigh,
　And the falling of the snow.

But when spring comes down to the earth, and her feet
　Sends a thrill through woodland and plain,
And the clouds weep tears that are soft and sweet,
　But which we miscall the rain,

Then they waken up with a light in their look,
　And in low sweet whispers they cry—
"Sisters, a murmur is heard in the brook,
　And sunshine is seen in the sky.

"It is time we should burst through the young green earth,
　As the stars through the heavens by night,
That the young and the old may rejoice in our birth,
　And we in the calm sweet light."

Then one said, "Sisters, where shall we grow?
I shall grow by the side of the stream,
And all day long I will blossom and blow,
　Till the dews fold me up in a dream."

"And I," said another, "will bloom by the way
　Where the children go in a band;
They will stop for a moment their gladsome play,
　And touch my lips with their hand."

"I will peep from the long rich grass," said one,
　"When the meadows bow to the wind,
And will catch like dewdrops the fairy tone
　Of the music it leaves behind."

"And I," said one, "in some garden rare,
　Where my fairer sisters abide;
And it may be that I may be twined in the hair
　Of the maid as she blooms into bride."

Then a sweeter voice held the rest in thrall—
　"O sisters, what things ye have said!
I shall grow in the sweetest spot of all—
　On the graves of the calm pure dead.

"They will know that I blossom above their dust,
　And will yearn, in their silent abode,
For the grand Resurrection to crown their trust
　In the love and the promise of God."

Thus the flowers whisper, and if you lie
　When the rain and the sunshine fall,
You will hear them question and make reply
　If your heart is at one with all.
ALEXANDER ANDERSON.

" And she, comfortably perched on a large flower-pot turned upside down, was looking at him."

SARAH DE BERENGER.

By JEAN INGELOW.

CHAPTER XVIII.

IT was two years after the lecture before Amias again appeared at the door of his brother's parsonage, two years of growth, expansion, and improvement for him, both mentally, morally, and physically. He was a fine young man now, tall, brown, and broad-shouldered, and with a deep, manly voice.

Felix, in the meanwhile, had been almost stationary. He had, it seemed, reached the limit of his mental growth, and he had come to consider the parish as his world, and the care of it as his life.

Amias, in his mind and thought, lived with that brother, in that parsonage, close to that church; they were the scenery in which he acted out his speculations, and Felix was his audience. They were as familiar to him as his own thumbs and fingers, and yet, the moment he saw them, he was, notwithstanding, aware of a change. The furniture struck him with a sense of surprise; it was so simple, so sparsely distributed about the rooms. And yet he remembered that it had not been changed. And Felix!—dear old Felix wore his newest coat when he came to London, but now he looked what he was, a country clergyman with narrow means.

But then there were the two little girls and Dick to be seen. Let us take the former first, as having been the cause of every real change

XXI—33

about the place. They were most beautiful creatures, their voices soft as the cooing of doves. They were growing tall, but they ran about the garden after Felix as if they had been tame fawns.

Ann Thimbleby and her sister were gone— they had found a vegetarian family to teach —and a widow lady had come to the village who acted as daily governess to the little " Miss de Berengers." Old Sir Samuel came frequently to see them. He was treated almost with uncivil silence and coldness by Mrs. Snaith. Sir Samuel loved them and they loved him; he thought they grew more like his son John. The fact was, that he had imparted a something pathetic to his son's face, out of the pathos in his own thoughts of him, as one whom he loved and who was dead, and that something he now and then beheld in these children's eyes. He liked them to come to him and sit on his knee, and insist on his kissing their dolls; it pleased him that they stroked their soft hands over his beard, and took liberties with his own particular pencil-case. Amabel once begged a silk pocket-handkerchief of him to make a counterpane for her best doll. He gave it, and was exceedingly snappish to Mrs. Snaith, when she brought it in, the next time he called, washed and ironed, and begged to apologize for " Miss Amabel, who had taken a liberty, bless her."

Felix had not the least thought of ever

parting with Amabel and Delia, probably as he took for granted that they must *somehow* be John's children; he thought that was the reason. And yet, if the whole truth had been confided to him, he would, perhaps, have kept them; they were dear to him, as amusing as kittens; they gave him no trouble, and their love was demonstrative and fervent, without being at all exacting.

When he was tired of them he could always say, "There, go to Mrs. Snaith," and, of course, Mrs. Snaith took good care that he should have as little trouble with them as possible. It caused her, some years before, many a jealous pang to see how they would go and peep in at his study window, and stand there awhile for the mere pleasure of looking at him. She never told them not to do it, though the end of it generally was that he would open the window and give each of them a kiss, that they might go away and play contentedly. They always wore lockets that Sir Samuel had given them. Felix thought he knew and they knew what was in them; but once, when he asked Amabel, she shook her head and whispered to him that she was not to tell. He supposed it to be John's hair.

Sir Samuel had decided to leave a younger son's portion between them in his will, but not to allow Felix anything for them in the present. He had been told what they possessed, and knew it was sufficient. It was best to let well alone. But he was improving, and, as his nephew had said, developing a conscience. He showed this in a very convenient way; for when Dick was of a proper age, he came to see Felix, and reverting to his old grievance, that he could do nothing for Amias, he proposed, entirely at his own charge, to put Dick to school.

Felix, who had fully perceived that Amias, with his views, ought not to accept any of the old man's money, was yet far from any such extreme notion as that he himself was shut out from deriving benefit from property which, but for an informal will, would part of it have become his own. He therefore accepted the proposal. Sir Samuel sent the boy to a public school, and paid all his bills also. This, he felt, could establish no claim on him when school days were over; and the result was that the benefit came to his own family, though all the time he felt convinced that he was rewarding the more remote relative for goodness shown to those nearer to him, his grandchildren, who, if he once began openly to provide for them, might in the future put forth a claim—expect perhaps,

when they grew up, to come and live with him.

Though he was such an old man, he always supposed himself to be living when they grew up; he fancied himself at last investigating matters, and of course discovering that they were his son John's offspring. He went through imaginary interviews with their future suitors, in which these gentlemen, requesting to be told his intentions towards his granddaughters, were made to settle handsome sums on the young ladies, and content themselves for the most part with future prospects.

In the meanwhile, the poor invalid, his eldest son, died at last at Mentone, and his second son, Tom, already the father of three little girls, sent them home to England. It seemed a perversity of nature, certainly, that he should have so many children of the wrong sort, but he fondly hoped soon to add a boy.

These children—pale, fair little creatures—were established with their maternal grandmother when they came over from Burmah. Sir Samuel went to the north of the county to see them. They had the delicate complexions and reddish hair of his family, but he saw nothing interesting in *their* likeness to their father. He loved Amabel and Delia best.

The children of a drunken shoemaker, who was a convict! It seems unfair that they should have been the cherished visitors of an old man's dreams; but there is often a strange and curious balance in these matters. He gave where there was no claim; but then he had, with all his might, prevented and thought scorn of the marriage which would, in all likelihood, have caused such a claim.

He loved these little aliens to his blood, but at least they loved him in return, and just in the kind and degree that he did. They loved with the drawings of personal approval and quite unreasonable preference. He was nice; what he did was right. He was not called grandfather, of course, but he had a nickname that he liked just as well.

The simple fact of this equality of affection would have made it sweet and worth having, even if the truth had been discovered. There would not have been that pathos in it which hangs about most friendship bestowed beyond the limits of the family. In general, affection is not equal; one bestows with fervour and cannot help it, the other receives and rewards as well as he or she can.

Amabel was now twelve years old, and Dick was a fine boy, much grown and improved. During his holidays the three children were constant companions. They were all young for their years. Amias rather liked to have them at his heels, as he strolled about the garden with his cigar. His gentleness with them endeared him to Sir Samuel, who, with the usual perversity of human liking, continued to find many good qualities in him, and to regret his contumelious withdrawal, mainly because he had withdrawn, but partly because he had shown, especially of late, an excellent capacity for getting on alone.

Mrs. Snaith, during those years, had greatly improved; she had been drinking in deep draughts of peace. Her voluntary descent had been rewarded with the obscurity she needed. Her renunciation of her two children, also, was only in name; she possessed their hearts, and, excepting when Sarah interfered, their confidence also.

Sarah disparaged her sometimes. "Such a dear kind nurse, my pets, but no occasion to tell *that* to her; ask Cousin Sarah. Little girls are not to be too intimate with servants."

The children listened, tried to obey, and for the moment gave themselves airs; but nature was too strong for them, and they stole away, when Cousin Sarah was not looking, to "help" Mamsey when she was working; or, tall as they were growing, to delight themselves with her caresses, or get her to sit on the rocking-chair and take them both at once on her knees.

Whenever there was anything the matter with them, they were wholly her own. They divided their smiles with others, but all their tears were shed in her arms. Sometimes she wept with them; the child for its passing grief, the mother for her infinite misfortune—the lost and outraged love of her youth, the disgraced life, the self-renunciation. But, after all, when they had wept together, the child, perfectly consoled, would fall asleep on her bosom, and the mother, with impassioned love, would admit to herself, as all keen affection must, that if she could not have both, she grudged their joys far less to others than their tears.

Amias, who had hitherto taken his aunt Sarah for granted, just as she was, felt surprised to find her remarkably foolish; for long absence, without destroying memory, enabled him to look at customary things as if they were fresh. He was surprised no less to remark the complacent affection with which Felix regarded her. She was more slender, more sprightly, and more gaily dressed than ever, and she was obviously most welcome to do and say in his house whatever she pleased.

Sometimes, when he was strolling about the garden, cogitating on some political or literary matter of real importance, he would come upon a scene which for the moment would fling him back with almost painful suddenness into the past, and make the latter years of his life look all unreal and distant to him.

"Yes," Sarah was observing one day, when he came upon them thus, "it is a subject, my dear Felix, which frequently engages my attention. Certainly, as you say, it does not do to generalise too confidently on it, and yet my experience is by no means small."

Felix, with the shadowy smile in his eyes, through which a little harmless malice shone, was calmly digging his plot, and she, comfortably perched on a large flower-pot turned upside down, was looking at him with her head on one side.

"What do you think?" she inquired; "and what does Amias think?"

"About what?" Amias not unnaturally inquired.

Sarah was too deep in thought to give him a direct answer.

She said, "I've got a new gardener, called David—yes. Now, we can hardly suppose that Providence interferes, when a child is named David, to change the colour of his hair if it was going to be black; but it is a remarkable fact, that you will find a man of the name of David always has sandy hair, or, at any rate, light hair."

"So he has," said Felix calmly. "It cannot be denied. But don't you think it may be because David is almost always a Scotchman? They almost always have light hair."

"No," said Sarah. "But I think, as you said, that one can hardly dogmatize about it; it's a mysterious subject."

"He is always a Scotchman," persisted Felix; "and if he isn't, he ought to be."

"But that," continued Sarah, "is only one out of hundreds of names. Does it result from the eternal fitness of things, that a woman named Fanny (always in a book, and generally in real life) is frivolous? Did you ever meet with a ponderous, or a managing, or a learned Fanny? All literature shows what Fanny is! In fact, I believe it is the observation of this which causes people not to use the name half so much as they used to do. Then, again, some names are quite gone out, because it has been observed that the girls who had them always became old maids—Miss Grizzle, for instance. Griselda was once a favourite name—Miss Penelope, Miss Rebecca, Miss Tabitha."

Felix made no reply, good or bad, to this speech, though he seemed to derive a certain satisfaction from it.

"I wouldn't call a son Lionel on any account," she continued, "unless I wished him to go into the army; nor Robert, if I objected to his taking holy orders; nor Godfrey, unless I knew beforehand that he would be fat, and nothing I could do could prevent it; nor Gilbert, if I wished him to pay his debts."

"I don't think there is so much in it as you suppose," said Amias, as gravely as Felix might have done.

"But that," answered Sarah, "is because you have not sufficiently gone into the matter. Yes—we cannot expect to understand everything in this world, nor how things act upon one another."

"I can understand," said Amias, "that a man's name, if he connected a certain character with it, would act upon him; but I cannot understand that he would act upon his name."

"But human knowledge is making great strides," observed Sarah. "Look at the things they have discovered in the microscope. It takes some of these four generations to come round again to themselves! And yet they are atoms so small that if garden worms were as much magnified in proportion, they would reach from here to London. I think, therefore—yes—that we ought not to despair about finding out and understanding anything, though at the same time, as I have just said, we are not exactly to expect it."

Amias found them at peace in the rectory, and he left them at peace. There was a certain air of leisure about them all. When Jolliffe picked the peas, she took her time over them, and strolled up to the bean bed, before she went in, to ascertain if the beans were coming on, which they did, also at their leisure; while, perhaps, Felix, at his leisure, was proceeding into the church, to be ready for some rustic bridal.

Amias spent three weeks with his brother, "partook of his victuals," and also of this leisure, which he found extremely sweet. When he departed, he thought he would come again very soon, and so felt a very bearable pang at parting.

But he did not come soon; it fell in his way to write some articles in a magazine, which brought him into sudden notice.

The youth who had with such extreme difficulty paid his tailor's bill, and eked out his means of living by the sale of an old necklace, began to find himself in easy circumstances. He was *somebody*, and he had the unusual good fortune to be very soon "looked up" by another *somebody*, and offered an appointment which kept his powers almost always on the stretch and his mind always improving; for, besides research, it demanded of him a great deal of travelling.

In the meantime Dick did well at school, Sir Samuel mellowed and improved, Felix almost stood still, and Amabel and Delia grew to be prettier than ever; but Mrs. Snaith, just as the former reached the age of sixteen, fell sick, and was all at once in low spirits without apparent cause. She had a startled and nervous way that surprised all about her; did not like to go out of doors, and, when alone, was often found shedding tears.

"What is it, Mrs. Snaith, darling?" asked Delia when, one day coming into the room still called the nursery, she found Mrs. Snaith standing there, and hastily folding a newspaper and putting it in her pocket. "What is that rubbishing *Suffolk Chronicle* to you?"

"Who told you it was the *Suffolk Chronicle*, Miss Delia, dear?"

Sarah had long ago hinted to Mrs. Snaith that she would do well to add the "Miss" to Delia's name. She had always called Amabel "missy" from her birth.

"Why, I saw it, Mamsey."

Delia was fourteen. Both the girls took after their mother in height, though the poor cobbler had given them his beautiful face.

Delia approached Mrs. Snaith with her arms wide open, and calmly wrapped them completely around her.

"I do think they grow longer every day," she observed of the said arms.

Mrs. Snaith was trembling; Delia's cheek was laid against hers, with a certain moderation of unimpassioned tenderness.

The mother stood perfectly still, but a few heart-sick tears fell down her face; she was consoled by the quiet closeness of Delia's embrace, and in a minute or two she released one hand, and, wiping them away, said, "But I must finish the ironing now, my beauty bright, else your frills and laces won't be ready for Sunday."

Delia kissed her, and, withdrawing a little, looked at her. "You don't get enough air," she said—"always moping in this room. When we were little, you used to iron sometimes out of doors, under the walnut-trees. Oh, Mamsey, do it now!"

"I fare to think it would fatigue me to carry out the things now."

"Dick shall carry them," exclaimed Delia, and she ran out of the room.

She was unusually tall for her age, nearly of the average height already. Her face was dimpled, her hands were dimpled; the whole young growing creature was supple and soft. She had a mischievous delight in teasing Dick and reigning over him, but no one living was so fond of him. Sometimes when with Dick she tried to remember that she was "getting quite old," but with Felix she was still as playful as a kitten.

"What time does Mr. Amias come?" asked Mrs. Snaith, when, with more commotion than was needed, Dick and Delia had brought out the ironing-table, and covered it with a blanket and a white cloth. They set it and some chairs under the great spreading walnut-trees, in the little yard paved with coggle-stones, which was divided from the garden by a long, low rockery.

"What time?" repeated Amabel. "Well, there is no train till five, and Coz is going to wait at the station for him till he comes. Coz is gone to the ruri-diaconal meeting."

"I suppose we must make ourselves fit to be seen," said Delia. "No doubt he thinks he is a great gentleman now."

"Fit to be seen!" exclaimed Dick. "Why, these are the most stunning frocks you ever had."

The girls were dressed in white, and had some blue ribbons about them; but Delia's frock was crumpled. She looked like a tall, overgrown child; her long locks were carelessly tied back with a blue ribbon, and her delicate cheeks were slightly flushed with exercise. Amabel, on the other hand, looked fair and quiet in the lovely shade of afternoon; her ribbons were fresh, her frock clean. Excepting when she talked or smiled, she had still the wistful look of her childhood. Delia had it even at this moment. She and Dick had brought out each an iron. Mamsey was telling them where these were to be placed, and while Dick obeyed, Delia slowly approached hers close to Dick's ear. He naturally started back, and she, as if she had only been making a quiet experiment necessary for the occasion, set it down and ran off for something more, he after her.

But Mamsey, for whom all these preparations had been made, had hardly begun her work, when she became so tired and faint that she was obliged to sit down, and so it came to pass that Amabel and Delia insisted on setting up as ironers on their own account,

and there ensued a great sprinkling of lace and muslin. Dick got a sprinkling also, to make him grow, and was sent continually backward and forward to the kitchen to bring the irons, to bring tea for the girls and for Mrs. Snaith, and to bring more chairs.

"None of them will ever be happier," thought the poor mother, as she gazed at her two young queens, trying their fair hands at the ironing-board, clapping the lace between their palms as they had seen her do, and making Dick feel the Italian-iron with his great brown hand, lest it should be too hot for them when they pinched up the frills and set them daintily upon it.

In the golden shade of afternoon their light-hearted sweetness consoled and soothed her. She was weary of thinking on one only subject, and repeating over certain words, which at first reading them had almost crushed her; but now she escaped to a little welcome rest, while Amabel ironed and laughed, and Delia flitted about, offering a great deal of advice and not doing much, though Dick contrived to give himself the air of one diligently helping her.

CHAPTER XIX.

AND so it fell out, in the very crisis of the ironing, at a quarter before five of the clock, just as Amabel held up delicately a long piece of lace, which, to the deep interest of Dick and Delia, she had managed to finish without either crumpling or scorching, two gentlemen came round from the front of the house—Felix and another.

It was a still, hot afternoon, but the ironing-table was well within the golden shade of the walnut-trees. Mrs. Snaith, in her black alpaca gown, made a due foil in the picture for two fair creatures, busy and important. So did Dick, for, fine boy as he was, he had in some small degree that awkwardness, that nearly loutishness, which often afflicts the youthful man when his legs and arms have grown almost out of his own knowledge, and when, having become suddenly somewhat ponderous, he frequently finds his movements making more noise than he intended.

Dick was inclined to be shy and shamefaced about himself when the girls teased him. It seemed a shame that he should grow so big, when Amabel would ask him for one of his gloves to carry aloft on a stick, as a sufficient parasol; or when Delia would remark that his shoes, when he had grown out of them, should be presented to the little seaside place often mentioned here, that a grateful country, sinking them in the sand, might use them as dry docks for the fishing smacks.

And yet the joy and glory of being with these two girls was already enough to draw him away from the football and cricket, the rowing and running, which, when at school, he delighted in.

So Amabel was holding up the lace when Amias, coming round a corner, first saw with his eyes that there were two young ladies in the garden, and then perceived with his intelligence that they must be Amabel and Delia.

He looked at Felix with a flash of surprise. Amabel was such a fair young creature, and Felix had all these years, in his letters, or during his visits to London, never said or written anything about her which appeared to show that he knew she was beautiful, or even that he was aware she was fast growing up.

The brothers advanced. Mrs. Snaith rose and stood in her place. Delia ran forward and kissed Felix, and Amabel, serene, not surprised, moved only a step or two towards them.

Felix had been away two nights. She also kissed him, as an accustomed and not, as it seemed, specially interesting ceremony to either party.

Amias was absolutely startled, so that a fine red hue showed itself through the brown of his cheek. How would she greet *him?*

In a manner that quite satisfied him. He raised his hat; and she quietly, as though she took a certain number of moments that could be counted to do it in, looked at him with sweet and modest interest, as if she might have been thinking about him beforehand, and then she held out her pretty hand and smiled.

Amias felt for the moment almost as shy as Dick, who, called by Felix, now came blundering up; and the brothers, laughing and each surprised at the appearance of the other, shook hands with hearty pleasure; one thinking, "I did not know he was a swell," and the other, "This fellow will be six feet high before he has done growing."

"We did not think you would be so early," said Amabel.

"We could not have been," answered Felix, "if we had stopped at this station. We met two stations off, and there Amias hired a fly. He wanted to see the country and drive through the park."

"You might have met Uncle Sam," said Dick; "he has been here to give Amabel her riding lesson."

"Coz," said Delia, pouting, "isn't it unfair that he never asks me? I can never ride."

"There's the donkey," answered Felix, smiling and gently lifting Delia's face by putting his hand under her chin. She was manifestly the favourite.

"But he won't go!" exclaimed Delia, throwing such tragic tones into her voice, and such needless pathos into her face as seemed to show that she had nothing more important to use up her feelings for. "Oh, Coz, you did say that some day you would hire a pony, and that I should go out riding with you."

"We'll see about it," said Felix, basely putting off this desired event to some perfectly indefinite date.

Delia sighed, and Mrs. Snaith now beginning to put the ironed lace, &c., into two light baskets, each of the girls took one and went in with it, she and Dick following with the chairs.

Amias stood a moment surprised, and yet he had known the girls were still with his brother. What could he have expected? He roused himself, went into the church with Felix, and was shown a lectern that "old Sam" had given. Sir Samuel appeared to play a much larger part than formerly in the life of the rectory. Then he went into the garden and all over the premises. He asked no questions about the girls, but he thought the position of Felix as their guardian began to be decidedly curious.

He did not see them again that night; they had dined early, and they did not appear till the next morning, about half an hour before service time. To say that they looked fairer, fresher, and more graceful than ever, would not half explain the complicated impressions they made on him. They also both appeared more childlike than before, though Amabel, as befitted her age, was mindful of the presence of an almost strange gentleman; while Delia, regarding him as the brother of Felix (who was quite an elderly man), made no difference in her usual style of talk because of him.

"I want my sermon-case," said Felix.

"Then Delia shall fetch it. Do, Delia," began Amabel persuasively.

Felix was seated on the sofa, already in his cassock. Delia, beside him, had put her arm through his. He was reading his sermon over, and took no notice of the girls.

Amabel was moving across the middle of the room putting on her gloves. As she buttoned one, she turned her head slightly over her shoulder. She was manifestly observing how her train followed her, and how her sash floated after.

Felix, having finished his reading, looked up, and, as if supposing that he had not been heard, told Delia again that he wanted his case.

"But Amabel will get my place if I fetch it," said Delia; "and it really is my turn to walk with you to church."

"You walked with Coz on Wednesday," answered Amabel.

"But that," said the unreasonable child, "was a saint's day, and I don't consider that it counts."

"Fetch the case, goosey," answered Felix. "I remember that it is your turn."

All this time Amias, standing on the rug, amused himself with looking on, and none of them took any particular notice of him.

Delia, now satisfied, started up with a laugh of loving malice at Amabel, and presently brought in the sermon-case; then turning her head, much as Amabel had done, "Look at our new frocks, Coz," she exclaimed—"our frocks that Cousin Sarah gave us; don't they look sweet?"

"Your new frocks?" repeated Felix, turning with no particular intelligence in his glance. "Oh—ah—new, are they? Well, they seem to fit well enough, as far as I can see;" then he added, like a good parson as he was, "But I wish, when you have new habiliments, that they were not always put on first on a Sunday; they take your minds off from attending to the service."

Then he began to talk to Amias, but at the first pause, "Shall we change them, Coz?" asked Amabel, with obedient sweetness.

"No, no," he answered; "no occasion for that."

That such a celestial vision should be desirous of pleasing the "old man," appeared quite ridiculous.

"And she gave us our new hats too," observed Delia. "Look, Coz. She never gave us such a handsome present before."

These hats were white, and, as Amias remarked, semi-transparent. Feathers drooped over one side. Amias, as he looked, felt quite abashed. How could milliners have the conscience to concoct such beautiful things for creatures more than distracting enough already?

"She brought them from London," said Delia.

It was manifest that it was their array, and not themselves, that the two girls were admiring. One of them was almost a child,

and the other almost a woman, but Amias hardly knew yet which he liked best, and he supposed that the new hats must be the cause of their attractiveness. He found Amabel so lovely as hardly to be able to look at her, and yet he admitted to himself that her beauty was not in her features so much as in the pure fairness of her complexion, in the dark lashes that half shaded her pensive blue eyes, and in the slow sweetness of the smile which would adorn her face with such bewitching dimples. It was her hat, it was her feathers, which gave that distinguished air to her head. So he thought; for he could not escape from thinking of her, being the slave for the moment of every pretty girl. Good young men generally are.

So they all went to church, family and servants, excepting Mrs. Snaith, who was left to take care of the house and attend to the early dinner. She had little to do but to prepare some vegetables. The large joint was cold; the custards and the fruit tarts were already made. She got on pretty well at first, in the clean sunny kitchen. Her lips never trembled so long as there was anything to be done, but when she had also laid the cloth in the dining-room and was returning to the nursery, a sudden pang overtook her, and she stood still as she had done the previous day, and wept.

She stood a few minutes, sobbing and shedding heart-sick tears, before she could rouse herself; then she went into the nursery, unlocked a drawer in her old-fashioned bureau, which had been saved from the fire, and took out the *Suffolk Chronicle*, to read for the fiftieth time the miserable news it had conveyed to her.

"To her that have been looking out for tidings from me this fourteen years and two months and six days. I am that vexed to be a misery to you, that are the niece of an honest man and my good friend, that, if I dared, I would leave this thing to take care of itself; but 'tis best to write for your sake. And, first, you will understand that, if he that has a right to trouble you had behaved himself better, you would have had this news full four years ago; but for several years he behaved very bad, and so was kept in to the last moment that the law allowed.

"And came up to where I am, and demanded his wife and children and the property; and I told him the children had died, as I was very sorry indeed to hear was the case soon after we parted. And he pretended to be vexed, and said he were a reformed character, and had the impudence to offer to pray with me, along of my not being in a good frame of mind, for I had the gout in my hand, and was that put out with him, that I was not particular in my language. The end of it is, I am vexed to say, that he went to Bristol, the last place, as he understood, where you were heard of. And so no more, but God keep you, wherever you be, from a canting hypocrite.—G."

Mamsey sat down in the rocking-chair, and thought over, as she had so often done lately, the terms of this letter. Bristol was north-west of the place where she dwelt, and it was not on the same line of railway. But oh, what a little place England is! and how could she be sure that no one whatever knew of her whereabouts?

The Christian names of her children were so uncommon that, in spite of her wretched husband's belief that they were dead, he would not hear them again, if he came near her, without suspicion. What should she do —what should she do? It seemed to her unbearable misery to leave her darlings, but it would be cruel indeed to expose them to any risk. Her husband was at Bristol. Should she fly to London and bury herself there?

She was yet thinking on this subject when the family and Jolliffe came home from church, and something to attend to brought her a little welcome relief.

At the early dinner she waited at table, and Amias noticed a kind of sweet and sad dignity in her manner. When she spoke she used the homely English of her native town, Ipswich; but her movements had a grace that he could not fail to acknowledge.

Not hurried, not inattentive, she yet appeared to be dwelling in some inner world while she went about her duties; and he saw that, when she stood a few moments at the sideboard, her eyes were examining the two girls and Felix, almost as if she was learning by heart their features and air. A singular thing this, since she was so familiar with them. And a singular thing, too, that a guest should occupy himself so much with the servant: but he perfectly observed that he was not alone in being so occupied.

There is no dignity so touching and so telling as that of those who have renounced all. They expect nothing of any man, that they should excite themselves in order to please him. They cannot be patronized, for no one has anything to give that they care to take. Mrs. Snaith was doing her best, and the words "Here we have no continuing city" were present to her thoughts; but she had wept her last tear over the news, and there had come over her mind a great calm. She had never looked better.

She had no sooner withdrawn after dinner, having set fruit and wine on the table, than Felix said to Amabel, "Mamsey looks a little better to-day."

"She said she had slept better, Coz," answered Amabel; "and Mr. Brown says there is nothing the matter with her, if she could but think so." Poor unconscious daughter! Mr. Brown was the doctor.

"Yes," observed Delia, "I heard him tell her that she really must rouse herself. He said he had never met with a person more free from all disease, or one with a finer frame."

"Nothing could be more opportune than our going to the sea just now," said Felix. "I dare say the change will bring her round. We all want a change now and then."

"And Cousin Amias says he will take us out fishing," said Delia.

Dick was immediately devoured with jealousy.

Amias listened to all this with something like jealousy also. Here was Felix, his nearest relation, far more important to him than any other person living. And this parsonage, rather bare, rather shabby, and quite out of the world, was still his home; but of what importance was he in it? Felix was more interested in these two girls, who were always with him, than in his brother. Why, even a servant who made his life comfortable was probably more interesting!

Was this inevitable? Perhaps it was; and if so, he would not grumble at Felix, but he would come more frequently to see them all; he would make himself of more consequence to Felix.

Felix had a great respect for this half-educated woman; her sweet humility touched him. He never asked her any questions, but her evident love for Amabel and Delia made him feel sure that her unhappy marriage had brought her children and she had lost them. As years had gone on he had more and more left her and Jolliffe to arrange all household matters as they pleased. No man could well be less master of his house and his belongings, but all was so well done for him that he scarcely knew it. And now Mrs. Snaith was ill—at least she appeared to think so, for she had asked to see a doctor, and for some little time had been very nervous and sometimes faint. This had changed the manner of Felix. He had felt and expressed some anxiety about her.

"She was bringing in a bunch of blush roses to set on the breakfast table, and she was holding up a very large rhubarb leaf by way of parasol."

Page 473.

After studiously preserving a certain style of speech and bearing towards her, he had unconsciously changed it, and if any one about him had been observant excepting Amias (which was not the case), it would have been as evident to all as it was to him. Felix felt that hers was probably a sickness of the heart, and that it had to do with the convict husband; but he asked her no questions, though he frequently felt what a gap she would make in his household if she withdrew, and how impossible it would be to supply her place.

CHAPTER XX.

As Felix and his party left the church on Sunday morning, Sir Samuel de Berenger had accosted them. His manner to Amias had been extremely cordial, but though Felix noticed this, Amias did not; he had become in some measure accustomed to cordiality, and the ancient fracas between him and his old great-uncle was of no consequence to him now. He had an income which was sufficient for his very simple style of living; he liked his work, and found time, when it was over, for a good deal of public speaking, at religious, philanthropical, and also political meetings.

Amias was a good deal altered; he was no longer afraid as to what people would think of him.

He had lived through his self-scorn, and the scorn of other people, in the notion that

"And here was the donkey."

he must be a fanatic; had said things that he had smarted for afterwards, as suspecting that they were ridiculous—and now, behold, the very people in his little world who had made most game of him, were quoting them as familiarly true. They had only been a nine-days' wonder, and while he was blushing still for them on the tenth, they were adopted by most of those who had not forgotten them. As related to, his religious profession, an almost opposite course had not the less brought him forward to the open confession that he was a sincere Christian.

All Sunday Amias held to his notion that his two child-beauties were lovely by reason of their array. On Monday morning he saw cause to change his opinion; for, before breakfast, he met Amabel in the garden in a morning dress, made of some sort of pale blue cambric. She was bringing in a bunch of blush roses to set on the breakfast table, and she was holding up a very large rhubarb leaf by way of parasol.

She looked prettier than ever. Amias was alternately attracted and repelled. The first feeling drew him to her side; all nature seemed to smile so on her sweetness. She reminded him, in that secluded spot, of a fair lily shaded by its own green leaf. And then the second feeling came like a smart box on the car. He did not like to be so suddenly overcome ; it was not in his plans ; and he knew that, if he did not look out, a very inconvenient sense of incompleteness would soon lay hold upon him, and when he left her, his heart would be torn in two and the best half left behind him.

Now, what was the part of a wise man in such a case? Why, to decide that he *would* look out. So Amias felt, so he did, decide ; and, in pursuit of this resolution, he went on and made the circuit of the garden. But that caused no difference, of course. Amabel, not being present, was only the more there. She was everywhere. The young growing things about him were lovely, for they were like her. The old steadfast trees were interesting, as in contrast to her. And here was the donkey! The very donkey was interesting, because she often tried in vain to make him go. Amias, having thought even this, burst out laughing at himself, and felt that he, too, was an ass.

Then he went in, and Delia was there. He saw the girls meet, and wish each other good morning with a kiss. After that came family prayers, and then, during breakfast, a long discussion between Dick and Delia about the delights of going to the sea. They talked a great deal of nonsense in the prospect of this treat, and then Amabel struck in, and she, too, had a childish joy in the prospect. They argued with Felix as to which of them must go inside and which might go outside the coach that was to take them part of the way. They were almost petulant over his decision. Amias listened, and felt as if he was now safe. She was a child :—who falls in love with a child?

What packing there was that day!—what condoling with the donkey, with the young ducks, the dog, and even the cat, because they were to be left behind! "Though our cat is such a cold-hearted person," said Delia, "that even if she knew she would never see us again, she would not leave off mousing for a single day." And then what rapture they got out of their anticipations of the boating and the bathing! It was worth while, Amias thought, living in a country parsonage for years to find such joy at last in a simple change.

So the next morning they all set forth, and even Mrs. Snaith was in good spirits. She was refreshed by bustle, and glad to feel that every throb of the engine took her farther from Bristol. She had suffered much, and now counted the miles with exultation till the party stopped at a station where the coach met them, and she was made, nothing loth, to take one of the despised inside places, which assured her the shade and seclusion that she loved.

She was manifestly better. She did not now wait at table, and the two brothers seldom saw her excepting when she attended the girls to the shops or to the shore.

Tom de Berenger's three little girls were established near at hand with their grandmother and their governess. They were tall for their years, very fair, and as playful as Delia. No one but old Sir Samuel observed any particular likeness between the two families. He had several times pointed it out, and had been pleased to see how familiarly the three younger girls depended on the two elder, and how they met with the tolerant, easy affection of relatives.

Felix and Amias were treated (much to the vexation of the latter) more as uncles and general dispensers of favours than ever. But at the end of about a fortnight Amias managed to effect a change. Amabel ceased to carry home buckets of forlorn sea anemones, left off grubbing in the cliffs for fossil shells, and sometimes even wore her best hat on week-days. On such occasions Amias was always in attendance, and the three little girls would . be sent off to some desirable place for finding cornelian and amber, while Dick and Delia, who considered it very dull work to saunter along looking at the yachts and keeping their feet dry, would soon fall back, the latter on pretence of emptying the sand from her shoes. After this they generally joined the little girls, leading their revels and enjoying their much more lively society.

Amias got on a great deal better when they were gone. He taught Amabel various things, some by word of mouth, some with his eyes. She took a good deal of teaching, but she mastered the lesson at last.

Amabel was not "wasteful ;" she did not "cheapen paradise." When Amias had taught her to blush, which she could do now most beautifully, she seldom looked him in the face while he talked, and so she blushed the seldomer. But her wakening life and keener thought sometimes caused her almost unbearable pain.

For Amias had twice gone away and spoken at certain meetings some miles off. He was sufficiently far from his old uncle's neighbourhood to do this without violence to his sense of propriety. England was large enough for his speeches and for all the good influence he could hope to exert, though he did keep his distance from the old man's door. He had a decided affection for him, and Amabel increased it by the loving way in which she would speak of him. In fact, Sir Samuel showed himself at his best when he was in the company of his so-called grand-daughters. His natural courtesy was never more agreeably shown than towards the young ladies of his own family. He taught Amabel to ride, himself holding the leading-rein as she rode beside him ; and once, when Delia had been found by him in the school-room "with fair blubbered face," left at home by herself because of the outrageous badness of her French exercise, he set to work with the dictionary, and puzzled his old head, together with her young one, till the others came home from their picnic, and the exer-cise could be "shown up" perfectly right.

Amabel had often heard of the opinions that Amias took such pains to make known. Sometimes she had read reports of his speeches in the newspapers, read them aloud to Sarah de Berenger, and heard that lady's indignant comments upon them.

But these had caused her no pain. She thought in her heart that Amias was right, but she was never asked for her opinion, and Amias was nothing to her. As for Sir Samuel, it almost seemed to her imagination as if he had never heard of such a thing as a tempe-rance lecture. Such things did not belong to his world. This world, her world, and that of Amias, had not hitherto come together—each had been kept remote from the other—and now she began to perceive that they were all one and the same world after all.

And now—now that she knew Sir Samuel was coming in a few days to see his grand-daughters and stay close by—now that some of the local tradespeople had congratulated "Coz," in her hearing, on his brother's elo-quence and zeal—now, in short, that Amias had singled her out as the object of his admiration, and had made her feel that a man of his age was not so very old after all—now she felt a keen sense of discomfort, when, having asked him what he had said at these lectures, he would answer and astonish her with the easy calm of his conviction, when he would tell her how he had tried to impress his audience with the misery of the drunkard and the sin of the drunkard-maker.

"But all these people who keep the gin-palaces that you consider so shocking, I do not think you ought to call them drunkard-makers," she observed once, when he had been talking thus. "They make a mistake, no doubt."

"What is the mistake?"

"It may be that they think more such places are needed than is really the case."

Amias had a more fervid nature than his brother, and he seldom thought of things in the abstract, but of the persons who had to do with them.

"But if it takes about thirty thousand drunkards," he answered, "to build up the fortune of a great spirit-distiller, and give a comfortable livelihood to the landlords and families of all the gin-palaces and public-houses where the liquor is sold, ought that fortune to be built up, ought those men who sell to live on the misery of those who buy?".

"Thirty thousand drunkards!" exclaimed Amabel—"thirty thousand! But they are not obliged to drink unless they like. No-body makes them drink."

"Yes, they are virtually made to drink by constant temptation. The liquor is sold out in such small doses, in such convenient places, and for such trifling sums, that those poor creatures who are inclined to drunken-ness are solicited to their ruin every time they go out of doors. This does not give them a fair chance. It ought not to be any man's interest that they should get drunk."

"But it is perfectly lawful to distil spirits," said Amabel, "and perfectly lawful to keep those places for selling it in. If you—if you could persuade all who do either to give it up, others would instantly start forward in their room, and why are these more than other people to be above the law?"

Something almost piteous in the tone of her voice appeared to give it a penetrative quality. Amias was startled, and felt anew what a different thing it was to hold certain opinions in mere theory, and to hold them as against the wishes or feelings of one beloved.

Disturbed almost to the point of wretched-ness, he walked awhile in silence beside her. For a few unworthy moments it hardly seemed worth while to live and not be in harmony with her wishes. Love, and even affection, is so extravagant, that there can be no fanatic or even enthusiast living who has not gone through this phase of misery.

Amias said at last, "People are seldom able to soar very high above what is expected of them. It is a fatal thing, therefore, not to be able to believe of any man, of any body of men, that they are incapable of living above the laws. I am quite certain that there are thousands of men in our own country at the present time, who, if once convinced that they were doing wrong in that matter or any other, would give up everything rather than continue the wrong."

"Give up everything !" exclaimed Amabel, passing over the main point, and, girl-like, commenting on one small point in it. "Surely you do not think people ought never to have any strong drink at all ?"

"No, we must have some."

"And how much do you think would be enough ?"

"Well," said Amias, laughing, "since you ask me, I will say, at a guess, about a fiftieth part of what is now consumed."

Amabel was silent for a moment ; then, not answering his last speech, she remarked, "And it always makes me uncomfortable to hear you talk of the 'liquor traffic.' I do not like names that sound vulgar."

"It makes her uncomfortable," thought Amias, "to hear *me* express myself in a way she calls vulgar !" He paused, and allowed himself silently to enjoy the pleasure this admission gave him. He was so happy, so lifted into the world of dreams, that for at least five minutes he took no notice of his fair companion—never looked her way.

Then they came to the point where they generally turned homeward. They both turned now, and it was towards each other. Her face was very slightly flushed, and a tear had half stolen down her cheek. "Amabel," he said, and unconsciously held out his hand. She put hers into it ; but when she tried to withdraw it, having wiped away the stealing tear with her handkerchief, he still held it, and she saw him leaning towards her with eyes of yearning tenderness.

"What is the matter? What do you want to say?" she exclaimed, with evident discomfiture and her sweetest blush.

He answered, releasing her hand, "I only wanted—I only meant to thank you."

Amabel wondered what for, and was very glad when they met the remainder of their party, and the discourse turned on a soldier-crab that they had chased and captured, and were now carrying home, tied up in a blue veil.

CHAPTER XXI.

"FELIX," exclaimed Miss de Berenger the next morning, "the girls have been talking to me about a rural entertainment to be given on the race-course. Do you really mean to take them to it?"

"Oh yes, aunt; why not? It will be a kind of picnic for people like us—only the poor will be feasted. I shall like the girls to hear Amias speak."

"I suppose it will have something to do with temperance, then," said Sarah, in some disgust. "I hardly know how it is that there should always seem to be something so second-rate in that subject. One cannot be its advocate without making one's self ridiculous."

"But on this occasion," said Felix, "there will be several other ways open to your choice, if you want to make yourself ridiculous, aunt—jumping in sacks, for instance, donkey races, athletic sports, etc."

"A person of my age is never athletic enough to take part in such things," said Sarah, in all good faith. "I consider that it would be very unbecoming in me to attempt to please the lower classes thus, and to pretend that I like their amusements."

Felix, well as he knew his aunt, was surprised into silence by this speech, and she presently continued—

"You had better mind what you are about, and not tamper with temperance too much. Amabel is not at all happy. My dear uncle will think it very hard if her mind is poisoned in any way. Yes. She tells me Amias said yesterday that unless each one of the great brewers could be sure of having thirty thousand men always perfectly drunk for him—at their own expense—it would not be worth his while to brew at all."

"That sounds rather a wild statement," observed Felix dryly. "I always distrust round numbers."

"I am sure she said so."

"I should have thought forty thousand was nearer the mark. But I don't wish to be captious."

"Should you really?" said Sarah. "Well, I have no doubt, if you could, you would like to do what the Royal Society wished to do to one of their comets (those scientific things are so curious and interesting). I read myself the other day in a lecture, that though a comet is often several hundred thousand miles long, yet such is its tenuity, that you could easily double up the whole substance of it and squeeze it into a pint pot—if you could only get hold of it. But science, you know, has never been able to get beyond the confines of this world on account of there being no atmosphere up there to breathe. So they can't do it."

"It would be better to say a quart pot," observed Felix; "a pint seems so very small."

"Well," said Sarah, "I am not sure about

the exact size of the pot, but the principle is the same. And I have no doubt that you—and you too, Amias, though you seem to think this a mere joke (Amias had just entered the room)—you too would be quite happy if all the spirits in England could be concentrated over and over again till it could be got into such a pot, and could then be solemnly sunk into the depths of the channel."

"That would be a very bad place, if you mean the *Irish* Channel," observed Amias, "because Ireland would certainly fish the pot up again."

"You take things too literally," said Sarah. "It is a great pity, Amias, to turn all the most philanthropic aspirations into mere jokes."

Perhaps Amias felt the truth of this observation, for he made no rejoinder, even when she had added—

"You would, of course, wish in such a case that the sister island should agree to fill a sister pot, and that the two should roll together, in peace and love, at the bottom of the ocean for evermore. Not that I speak as a sympathizer, but my heart and mind, I am thankful to say, are large enough,—yes—to show me what I should wish if I were one."

"You will go, aunt, of course?" said Felix.

"No, I shall not; it would be very inconsistent in me to fly in the face of my own people."

How little the joyous party setting forth to the race-course supposed that the trifling events of this drive were to be hoarded up in memory ever after!

At length they were close to the side of the grand stand, which was draped and bedizened with banners brought from the great house whose owners were the chief givers of the fête.

Then Mrs. Snaith understood that several gentlemen were going to speak; but she only saw the one who stood forward, Amias, and the moment he began, her motherly heart felt that Amabel, sitting beside her, was agitated, was blushing and in utter discomfiture.

It was so obvious that she actually trembled lest some one who knew her darling should perceive it. Oh, could it be that her chief treasure had already taken leave of the peace of childhood, and was entering on the restless, useless self-scrutinies of an unrequited affection? Mrs. Snaith thought of Amias as rather a great gentleman, quite out of her

darling's reach, and when the lovely face drooped a little in spite of its listening attitude, and the fair cheek covered itself with a soft carnation, the tender mother felt so keenly and painfully for the child's shy sensitiveness, that she could hardly look up herself. And yet she did, and just at the right moment; as people generally do when some one whom they know well is passing near.

A gentleman on horseback was coming up very leisurely towards the back of the grand stand. Mrs. Snaith's heart seemed for a moment to stand still as she saw him. Sir Samuel de Berenger! He was moving carefully and quietly among the closing groups of people. He was close; he passed right in front of Mrs. Snaith and her charge, but he did not appear to see them. He reined up his horse only a few feet in advance, among a group of farmers also on horseback, and only just far enough back to be unseen by Amias. Amabel had evidently been listening for him as well as for herself. Her mother saw it, and it only added to her discomfiture to be sure that he had his part also in that complicated state of feeling that made her look so abashed; it was for his sake as well as for her own that she had blushed. She had seen his approach, and what was he now listening to?

"And as for you," were the first words that reached his ears—"for there must be some such here—as for you who know the bitterness of a thraldom that you cannot escape, though it be ruining you body and soul—as for you whom the law has left, and leaves still, to the mercy of the lawless, the tender mercy of those who reach their greatness through your debasement, and build their houses out of your despair—you whose misery is the heaviest of all needless sorrows that weigh down the heart of the world—do not think you are come here to listen to any reproof. The movements of a pity that can dare to spend itself, sinking at the feet of your misfortune, is far too deep for words; but during your intervals of reprieve, when you think with ruth on the children whom you love, and the wife whom, with them, you are dragging down, consider—and relieve your hearts a little so—consider whether you have nothing in your power that will aid to keep them out of the slough into which your feet have slipped. Have you nothing? Oh yes; you all have a certain influence, and some of you have—a vote.

"I have known many of the most unfortunate among your ranks who have used this influence well. I have heard miserable fathers entreat their children to abstain, and point to their own deplored example to give force to their words; but I seldom hear them go to the root of the matter, as I want to do now, when I say to you, never vote a brewer into parliament, however high his character may stand; never vote a brewer's son into parliament, however great his talents may be; never, whatever may be his politics, vote in any man who has the least interest in keeping up the profits of that hateful liquor traffic, which is the ruin of these two fairest islands of the world. Never give them your influence by so much even as silence—never, never. What can they give *you* that shall console for what they take? They stand between you and comfort, they stand between you and duty, they stand between you and honour, they stand between you and God.

"And we must be helpless, we shall be helpless, there can be no good legislature—nothing can ever be done to chain this monster, intemperance—so long as such a body of our legislators draw their revenues from it, and spend their strength in keeping it free."

Dick was sitting beside Delia, and so far from sharing Amabel's shyness and discomfort, these two were both highly amused in watching Sir Samuel, who, with a half-smile and an air of wonder, sat listening and keeping just out of sight of Amias. "Why doesn't he get a little forwarder?" whispered Dick. "I wish he would; and I wish I might see Amias start. But nothing worth mentioning ever does happen in this world. There's nothing for a fellow to see."

"And nothing to hear," echoed Delia. "Dick, I do hate temperance."

Still the fair face drooped, and the old great-uncle, on his horse, sat still and appeared to listen. Now and again he cast a furtive glance about him, and was pleased to find no one in his field of vision that he knew; but now it was evident that Amias had finished his short speech, and that it was only an introductory one for what was to follow.

"There, there he is a-coming forward!" exclaimed a man close at hand; "that's the 'inspired cobbler.' Give him a cheer, boys; give him a cheer."

Some one was moving out as the other horsemen pressed a little forwarder, and Sir Samuel de Berenger, not betraying by his countenance either anger or discomfiture, passed just in front of his so-called grand-daughters, lifted his hat as he did so, and smiled. At the same instant a fresh speaker came forward, and, clear over the heads of the people, rang the voice of Amias—

"Mr. Uzziah Dill will now address the assembly."

Yes, Mr. Uzziah Dill. Hannah Dill lifted up her eyes, and saw her husband. She looked on, and in that instant, during which her daunted heart held itself back from beating, she heard the never-to-be-forgotten sound of his foot as the lame man came slowly to the front. She saw the beautiful, pensive face turned with its side toward her, then a long ringing cheer of welcome broke forth all around her, and she heard a sharp cry close at hand: "Mrs. Snaith—Mamsey dear! Oh, don't! don't!"

What was the meaning of this?

She knew she was falling forward; her face seemed almost on her knees, and her children were powerless to hold her up. She could not lift herself, and her husband's voice, even at that pass, had power over her. She heard its high, sweet tones, and despaired; then came a suffocating sense of breathlessness, and then oblivion.

People generally wake again from a dead faint in a state of repose. Mrs. Snaith was no exception to this rule. She opened her eyes, felt very cold, heard a certain unintelligible buzzing of voices about her, then regained her full senses. Everything settled down into its place, and here were Amabel and Delia kneeling, one on each side of her. She was lying on the grass under a tent; Amabel was putting water on her forehead, and Delia was fanning her.

Several kindly women were about her. They told the girls not to look frightened; they spoke to her encouragingly. She could not at first answer, but she heard them telling her that a fainting fit was by no means an uncommon thing. It was the hot weather, they declared, which had overcome her—nothing more.

She was quite herself now—able to think. She was so close to the back of the grand stand that her poor husband's voice was faintly audible through the canvas folds of the tent. She seemed, during the next few minutes, to be more alive than she had ever been in her life before, and, under the pressure of imminent peril, to be able to make swift and thoughtful decisions. She presently sat up and asked for her bonnet.

"How do you feel, ma'am?" inquired a sympathizer.

"I fare almost as well as usual," she replied; "and that's a good thing, for it was agreed that I should go home to my master's rectory by the next train, to get ready for the family, that is to return the day after to-morrow." She was anxious that the strangers present should know that what she wanted to do was to carry out no new, but a pre-arranged plan.

"You are not well enough yet, Mrs. Snaith, dear," said Amabel. ."You shall not go till you have had something to eat. And look! here is the luncheon-basket. The kind people next to us brought it in."

Something like despair clutched at the heart of the poor woman, but she knew she must yield. The strangers about her left the tent, and she and the girls took some luncheon. She felt better for it; but when Amabel said, "There's another train at night, Mrs. Snaith, dear; why not wait for that?—you still look very pale," she answered, "No, miss, I can't stay here; and I ought to leave by the half-past four train, if it's not gone, else I shall not be in till midnight. Only," she added, looking at Amabel and Delia with yearning love, "when Mr. de Berenger went away among the temperance gentlemen, he told me not to leave you."

Dick, as might have been expected, had taken himself off.

"We shall go with you to the station, then," said Amabel, "and stay in the waiting-room."

This is what Mrs. Snaith wanted; and Amabel longed to get away from the speeches. Mrs. Snaith rose. It was a very short distance to the station. She walked between the two girls with a certain urgency, but when they reached the line the train was gone. It had come in during her fainting fit.

The station was the last place that she meant to stay in. She took the girls to a little wayside inn, the only house near at hand. They were shown into a parlour up-stairs, which overlooked the course, and there the poor mother spent an hour in gazing out. Her pallor, and the strange eagerness in her dark eyes, struck the girls; they felt that she was still unwell, and were the more inclined to stay with her and watch over her; and the "bands of hope," moving about with ban-ners, the freemasons with their ornaments, and the different schools seated in distinct groups, having tea and cake under the auspices of their teachers, sufficiently amused them. "There's the lame man speechifying to those unlucky drum and fife boys," ex-claimed Delia. "How tired they must be of it all! just when the cans of tea and the great trays of cake are ready. How I should hate that man if I were one of them!"

The mother shivered when she heard this. "How horrible that Delia should speak thus of her own father! and oh, what a hypocrite that father must be!" She could hide herself from him, but it was not perfectly impossible that he might come up with Mr. de Berenger and Amias, and hear the girls' names. She almost hated him herself when she thought of such a possibility, and yet she felt that, if only that happened, there was nothing in it. But she should have three days of dreadful anxiety, for she should hear nothing till her darlings came back to the rectory. She should be hidden herself in the inn till he was gone. She was to start at eight, and she bent all her attention towards doing the best for that one evening, and thought she would leave the future to take care of itself.

The girls now, by her suggestion, ordered some tea. "Something," she said, "must be done for the good of the house." When it came up, she asked for a placard setting forth what were to be the entertainments of the day. She had passed several of these on park palings and on the grand stand, and had not cared to look at them.

The placard set forth that Mr. Dill, some-times called the "inspired cobbler," was in that neighbourhood, and had kindly pro-mised to turn aside and deliver one of his thrilling addresses on the race-course; that it was hoped a good collection would be made, to pay his expenses on this gratifying occasion, when the *élite* of the neighbour-hood would be present, to countenance their innocent pleasures, as well as to provide good cheer for some of their poorer friends. The inspired cobbler, as the placard in-formed those whom it might concern, was on his way to Southampton; any contribu-tions intended for his benefit might be for-warded by stamps or post-office order to an address which was carefully given, and the donors might rely on their being thankfully received and duly acknowledged.

"If I can only keep my darlings up here till he is gone, poor man," thought the wife, "there is the best of hope that we shall all clean escape him."

"Ah, here comes the excursion train!" exclaimed Delia. "Look, Amabel! What a crowd of people running up! What bunches of heather! What baskets of flowers! How hot they all look! There are the drum and fife bands, and the lame man."

Mrs. Snaith sat absolutely still and listened. She was far enough from the window not to be seen from below.

"How those boys screech at their fifes!"

"With a start of irrepressible terror, she turned round and faced him."

said Amabel. "It almost splits my ears. There's Coz and the lame man helping them in. What a cram! Now the lame man gets in too."

"Gets in, miss?" exclaimed Mrs. Snaith. "Are you sure?"

"Yes. And now they are off, and there is our carriage."

Mrs. Snaith rose then, drew a long breath, and looked at Amabel.

"It's time for you to go down," she said. "Mr. de Berenger will be wondering what has become of you."

"Mamsey, how earnestly you look at me!" exclaimed Amabel.

"Well, we none of us know what may happen," said the poor mother. "Will you give me a kiss, my—dear."

Amabel kissed her almost carelessly. They were to meet in two days; why should she think anything of such a parting?

Mrs. Snaith preferred the same request to Delia, who hung about her neck with a certain wistfulness which could hardly be called presentiment, but yet that enabled her easily to recall this kiss ever after, and the look in her old nurse's eyes, and the beating of her heart as Delia leaned against her.

And then the two girls went down to join Mr. de Berenger and Amias. Mrs. Snaith sending a message down, "Her duty, and

she would stay there till the right train came up, for it was much cooler in the public-house than in the station." And then she drew close to the window, and saw her darlings put into the open carriage, saw it set off, saw them wave their hands to her, and saw them disappear among the trees and leave her.

"He's gone," she then thought; "he's away, poor man; and I did ought to feel easy, for I've escaped, and my dears have escaped. He's on his way to Southampton, as sure as can be. What is it, then, that make me so full of fears?"

She trembled and sat still on the bedside, holding her throbbing temples between her hands; but gradually as the evening drew on, and the low lights gave even the little shrubs of heather their lengthy shadows, she grew stronger, and some time after sundown, when all was peace in the deserted little station, she came down and sat on the bench outside it to wait for the train.

"Oh for the train!" she murmured—"oh to set forth, and have this over!"

It was very soon over. One man only was waiting in the bare little room behind; the window was open within a foot of her head, and he was leaning out. He coughed, and, with a start of irrepressible terror, she turned round and faced him. All was lost. Uzziah Dill recognised his wife, and Hannah Dill her husband.

SUNDAYS IN MANY LANDS.

By JAMES CAMERON LEES, D.D.

III.—IN SWEDEN.

THE remembrance which the traveller has of Sweden is to a considerable extent of a morose character. As I sit by the fire and recall the days I wandered through that northern land, there rise before me, in a vague way, apparently endless miles of white rocky ground, and forests of dark pine-trees, varied only by great sheets of water—a fourth part of Sweden, be it observed, is under water. It is the most sombre portion of Scandinavia, wanting the grand mountain ranges of Norway and the open green fields of Denmark. But there are two things which stand out in recollection as bright and cheerful. The happy, lively peasantry, and beautiful Stockholm. The people are vivacious and pleasure-loving like the French. If they wore blue blouses and cut their hair short as a scrubbing brush, and drank red wine, they might pass for children of fair Provence. As it is, their locks are long, their dress rough home-spun, and their drink is of the strongest. But they are a joyous, kindly, courteous folk, fond of social gatherings, a dance round a May-pole, a marriage, or a market. They are hospitable to the stranger withal, and when he crosses the threshold of farm or cottage he is a stranger no longer ; a people full of hilarity and good-humour whom it is pleasant to remember.

But it is worth while going all the way to that far-off corner of Europe just to see Stockholm, as one looks at it for the first time from the Baltic ; worth all the tossing on the terrible North Sea, and the days pent up on shipboard in poky cabins, or on land in musty, fusty hotels. When the little asthmatic steamer that has carried you from Gottenborg through long canals and across broad lakes, and by narrow tortuous channels among wooded islands, turns a point, Stockholm comes suddenly into view : a bright, chaste, beautiful city, "kissed," to quote a rapturous guide book, "on one cheek by the ripples of a lake, on the other saluted by the billows of the sea." The lake being the Malär Lake and the sea the Baltic. Indeed, I don't know that any capital of Europe is more picturesque than this of Sweden : not "the grey metropolis of the North," nor Constantinople on the Golden Horn, nor Berne with her girdle of snow-clad mountains. Stockholm rises from the water embosomed in woods of pine and ash and birch, with a background of grey hills. She sits on her seven islands like a queen.

Ding ! dong ! cling ! clang ! go the bells of the city as we stand this fine summer morning looking out on the blue water, and the little skiffs that skim like sea birds along it, and the steamers that puff about like animated onions, for they resemble in shape that excellent esculent. "Going to church, sir?" says a broad-browed, fair-haired Swede, whose acquaintance we had made in the Gottenborg boat. "There is plenty of room in the churches here for strangers ; you can get a pew for your stick, and another for your hat, and another for yourself. People never go to church in this town except when there is a great preacher to hold forth. There is a smart man to-day in the Storkyrka. I'm going there, and will be glad to show you the way." Our friend was a Swede who had been for some time in America. Many of his countrymen cross the Atlantic, and from their skill in forestry make capital backwoodsmen ; but when they make a little money, back they come to settle in their native land. Various cute specimens of the American Swede are met by the traveller in Scandinavia—not always to the advantage of the latter. Our friend, however, was a right good, sound-hearted fellow.

The Storkyrka to which he conducted us is the cathedral church of Stockholm. It is a huge, ungraceful building, on which much whitewash has been spent, when a great deal less would have done. It has a vast interior, and the walls are decorated with large pictures by Ehrenstal. The Swedes are very proud of this artist, though his work does not seem to a foreigner in any way worthy of special commendation. He appears, however, to have had a grim humour of his own. In one of his pictures, representing the Last Judgment, the faces of the actors in the dread scene are those of the courtiers of his time, and the position of some of them in the great assize is by no means enviable. "I guess," says our Swede, "they wouldn't give him many dimes for putting them up there !" This is not the only touch of the grotesque in this old church. To the right of the altar is a huge brazen candelabrum, around the column of which is entwined an eel, with the legend underneath, "The eel is a strong fish, with the bare hand you can

XXI—34

catch him for sure. He who would keep him must spare neither sack nor coffin." The moral of this allegory, if allegory. there be, we are unable to point. The suggestion that it is a hit at the clergy, sleek, slippery, able to elude the grasp of the strongest hand, we reject at once with indignation !

These little jocosities took place while the congregation were gathering themselves together. It was a high festival day, and the Stockholmites mustered strongly to what they term "High Mass." The service, though it bears this name, was Lutheran, for the Swedes are intensely Protestant and have little sympathy with Rome, though they retain many of the rites of the old faith. The clergyman was arrayed in vestments of a very pronounced Roman type: a white "mass shirt," a red velvet cope, a gold cross on his broad back, and deep lace trimmings sufficient plenteously to adorn a bride. This was a high day and his raiment was gorgeous ; on ordinary days his garb is unostentatious as that of a Scotch preacher and very similar—large white bands and a black gown.

The Swedish Church has a liturgy of its own, and a very beautiful and impressive one it is. We made acquaintance with it afterwards through the medium of a translation. The ordinary Sunday service begins with a solemn invocation, then follows a confession of sin, a psalm, the Epistle for the day, and the Apostles' Creed. After this the minister ascends the pulpit, gives out his text from the Gospel, says the Lord's Prayer, reads the Gospel (all standing while this is done), and preaches his sermon. This is followed by an intercessory prayer and a psalm. The minister then descends to the altar and pronounces the blessing of Moses, "The Lord bless thee and keep thee," &c. After which a psalm is sung and the people disperse. The priest attitudinised a good deal, and occasionally turned his back to the congregation, when his dorsal decoration was very effective. None of the Scriptures are read in the ordinary service except the Gospel and Epistle. The people, it seemed to me, did not take much interest in the prayers, and joined in a slow, dawdling way in the psalms, but they appeared to hitch themselves up when the sermon began, and continued wide-awake all through, at least so I was told afterwards. It was a long, long sermon. My eyes wandered from the altar-piece of marble and gold, and from one of Ehrenstal's courtiers to another. Then a most curious thing happened. The great picture seemed to expand like one of the lakes we had crossed

a few days before ; the courtiers bobbed up and down in the water ; saints and angels, sheep and goats, came together in a promiscuous and highly irregular manner, and finally —I fell asleep ! Our Swede had great respect for the sermon and the preacher. A good man and a good sermon ! He *was* long, and had several good chances to stop in his discourse, which he ought not to have let pass, but it was very eloquent. Then followed a story of a minister who made a call once on a friend of his, and seemed never likely to cease his conversation, when the dreadful child of the friend aforesaid stepped up to her father and whispered, quite loud enough to be heard by the visitor, " Papa, didn't the gentleman bring his 'Amen' with him to-day?" Sermons in Sweden are perhaps longer than in any part of Europe, not even excepting Scotland, where the interval between the text and the "Amen" is often considerable.

We lean over the parapet of a bridge that leads to the Riddarsholm or Knights' Island and talk of good things, especially of the creed, and ritual, and government of the Church at whose services we have just assisted. It is a curious Church in some respects this of Sweden, being probably the most thoroughgoing establishment in the world. Here Church and State are one. There is no dissent to speak of. All Swedes belong to the Church ; they are baptized, confirmed, married, and buried by it ; and though there is now toleration for other religions, the place is made pretty hot for them. All education is superintended by the clergy. All young people have to be confirmed by the parish priest after special instruction and examination, and no person can be married or get any civil appointment until they have been confirmed and taken the communion. If any criminal is found on his conviction to have been neglected as regards religious instruction the authorities are down at once upon the parson of his parish for an explanation. The clergy visit regularly all their parishioners, and catechize them to their hearts' content. The government of the Church seems a mixture of Episcopacy, Presbyterianism, and Congregationalism. There is an archbishop and there are eleven bishops, but there is also a great synod or Church parliament (Kyrkmote), and each parish has a local government of its own (Socken Stammer). There are thirteen hundred beneficed clergy. The Church is moderately well endowed. The archbishop has £1,200 a year, and the incomes of the clergy vary from £100 to £300. Their income is derived chiefly from tithes. "They have a quiet, contented appearance," said our friend ; " not like the parsons out West where I was, who have to work for their living, poor boys ! and beg for it afterwards, and a mighty hard time many of them have of it, I can tell you." All the clergy are University men, educated at either of the two national universities of Upsala or Lund, and they must take their degree before they can be ordained. They are elected by the congregations over whom they are placed. Three candidates are appointed to preach by what is called the Consistory, and the one chosen is generally presented by the Crown. The clergy elect their bishop, or rather they send in three names to the King, who nominates one of them. The priests have to officiate for some years as curates, and must be each thirty years of age before they can take a living. Formerly the clergy formed one of the estates of Parliament, but now (as our friend put it) they have a "talking place" of their own. The doctrine of the Church is Lutheran.

All this and much more to the same purpose we were told regarding the National Church of Sweden, but so far as we could learn this great organization does not produce all the effect upon the morality of the people that might be expected. Not that there is no earnest spiritual life within the Church, but religion is looked upon by the people too much as a formality, and too little as a sacred obligation. A Swede graduates as a Christian by taking out his *schein* or confirmation certificate, and does not feel as if very much more is required of him. Notwithstanding the National Establishment, and the marvellously complete system of education, the state of the people is morally deplorable. Drunkenness is everywhere prevalent. The love of finkel, fahlun, and other strong drinks of a vitriolic character is very marked. Nearly half the births in Stockholm are illegitimate, and the state of country parishes is often not much better. Yet it was shown not long ago from undoubted statistics that one in every hundred and twenty-six of the population lives by teaching the Swedes their moral and religious duties. The outcome of all their endeavours is far from satisfactory.

One other church we visited that Sunday, where the sermon is preached in a language which every one can understand, and always from the same text. This is the Riddarholm Kyrkan, used as a Mausoleum for the kings and mighty men of Sweden. It is the Westminster Abbey of Scandinavia. There is little noteworthy about the church itself. It is a long brick building with chapels on either side. The pavement from the great entrance to the altar is covered with the heraldic bearings of the nobles and men of valour who lie beneath. On the pillars are all sorts of hatchments and banners fast turning to dust. In the chapel on the right side of the altar is the sarcophagus of Gustavus Adolphus, the Lion of the North, the hero of Dugald Dalgetty. His body lies in a vault below, and looking through a grating we get a glimpse of the end of his coffin and some of its shining ornaments. All round his chapel are hung the keys of the cities that he captured, the tattered banners, and the drums that he took in battle, and the blood-stained clothes which he wore on the fatal field of Lutzen. The whole arrangement looked like a pawnbroker's shop. Opposite this chapel is that of Charles XII., a hero well known to the schoolboy learning French. A cloak belonging to this sovereign hangs on the wall, also a hat with a bullet hole through it. The bullet also went, we are told, through his brain. There is another chapel dedicated to Bernadotte, the brave French marshal who founded the present royal dynasty of Sweden. He has a great sarcophagus of porphyry, than which it is impossible to conceive anything of the kind more hideous. There are other royal coffins in vaults beneath, would Herr Engliskman like to see them? Never mind, old man, royal dust is like other dust, we believe ! Didn't one of the mightiest of the Cæsars sum up the result of his life in the words, "I have been everything, and it has profited nothing"? And wasn't it the Empress Theodora that said, "The throne is a glorious sepulchre"? And didn't Abdalrahman the Magnificent close his career with the words, "O man, place not thy confidence in the present world"? And has it not been sung that

"Death lays his icy hand on kings;
　　Sceptre and crown
　　Must tumble down,
　And in the dust be equal made
　With the poor crooked scythe and spade"?

"Vanitas vanitatum, omnia vanitas !" Most excellent observations, "most true indeed." Yes, old man, we have had an admirable sermon, a very good sermon, a sound orthodox sermon indeed, no doubt about it whatever. "Wouldn't Herr Engliskman like to see?" No, thank you, old man, not to-day—let us into the sunshine ; the air of defunct royalty is not good. We give our ancient friend the mite our poverty allowed us to bestow, and as he shut the door of the royal sepulchre with a clang he looked as if he could have done with more.

In the evening we made a pilgrimage to the house where the great mystic Emanuel Swedenborg used to live, and in our walk had abundant opportunity of observing how free and untrammelled from Sabbatic restrictions the Swedes are in their observance of Sunday. Crowds were pouring onward to the great pleasure gardens of the suburbs. The theatre was open, and a considerable amount of loudly-expressed jollity everywhere present. As we return the streets are thronged; the boats flash about from island to island; the great palace is lighted up, and there is the reflection of many lamps on the water. The people are gay as the Parisians. We did not find much to remind us of the seer in his old home. Its surroundings are of a very prosaic character. We were shown a kiosk where he had his visions—a shabby wooden shed, painted yellow and green, in a back yard, with a scrubby tree or two in the foreground. They tell, however, rather a good story of him here. He was once being ferried across the Malar Lake by two country girls; instead of giving them any of his conversation, he kept talking, so he told them, to spirits who were with him. "How many have you on board?" they asked. "Twelve," he replied angrily. On reaching the shore he offered coin in payment. "Thirteen marks, if you please, sir, not a stiver less." "And why, pray?" remonstrated he. "Did you not say, sir, you had twelve spirits on board? Are we poor girls to pull them over the lake for nothing?" The visionary, who feared neither ghost nor devil, paid down the fare demanded rather than encounter the clatter of two women's tongues.* Sweden-

* Marryatt, "A Year in Sweden."

borg, like some other great prophets, has not many followers in his own country. Any form of religious earnestness outside the national church is generally found in connection with the Laasare, or "readers," who occupy, in relation to the Establishment, much the same position as the Methodists in England in the time of Wesley. They expound the Bible in common colloquial language, and their preachers are full of fervour. They receive, as a rule, very little encouragement from the clergy; and until lately suffered a good deal of persecution.

Our friendly Swede meets us on one of the bridges, and escorts us to the hotel. He has had a "good time" in the Deer Park, a great garden with many cafés and restaurants, where the citizens love to congregate. He has been discussing politics with a Russian Finlander. "Sweden lost her chance when she remained neutral during the Crimean War. She should have joined the Allies, and annexed Finland, which was hers once, and should be hers again. The Russian bear is a beast that gobbles up everything, but he will have his claws cut yet, and Sweden will have her own again." He continues his conversation over a liquor called "Poonch Svenska," which is on many grounds worthy of approval; and though he had been in the United States, in Canada, in England, Scotland, and Ireland, there are no people so free, so brave, so honest, so well educated, so religious, as his countrymen. So he asserts; and, making every allowance for prejudice, we may admit there is some little truth in his statement, notwithstanding its seeming extravagance. But when he proceeded to depreciate Niagara as nothing compared with the waterfalls of Dalecarlia we considered it time to go to bed. And it was.

FATHERLESS.

A VACANT chair;
No loving smile to greet me sitting there,
No deep expressive eyes,
My image I could trace in their clear gaze,
No sympathizing breast to lean my head :
All these surroundings echo, "Father's dead."

An aching heart,
Bursting with grief, no one to heal the smart,
No loving hands to press
My fingers in a tight and fond caress;
My life is crushed, the link that bound it fled :
These feelings tell me that my father's dead.

A tear-filled eye,
No father's hand to wipe those tears away ;
Ah, no ! that hand is cold,
And powerless those arms that did enfold ;
My streaming tears, red eyes, and heavy lid
Tell me too plainly that my father's dead.

A smother'd sigh
I try to stifle ere it should betray—
So sensitive the heart,
It cannot brook the cold world's cruel sport—
I hide away, betrayal is my dread;
No one will sympathize now father's dead.

An empty space,
A void in my rent heart my feelings trace,
A yearning sympathy.
Oh, Father God, fill Thou this void for me ;
With Thy pure love fill me, Thou living Bread,
Be Father, God, my all, now father's dead.

ELLEN MILLER.

"DIANA SMITH."

PART I.

CHARLES EDWARD SMITH, the subject of this memoir, was a member of the medical profession; but the deeds of heroism which he performed were only partly connected with medicine. He was born at Coggeshall, in Essex, in the year 1837 (October 24th). His family are well known in that district, and belong to the denomination styled Friends, but more commonly known as Quakers. He inherited, as a consequence thereof, the splendid physique common to that body, and all the passive endurance of his sect; which was to stand him in such good stead in after years. He was a bright, quick-witted boy, and at a very early age he manifested a strong love for natural history, especially ornithology; and numerous are the beautiful, rare birds shot by his own gun, and then stuffed carefully by himself, to be found in the houses of his friends. His powers of original observation were conspicuous when a mere child. At nine he wrote "Natural History of Birds, Beasts, and Fishes;" and before he was twelve years of age he noted that the martins only worked at the building of their nests in the mornings, leaving their work to dry in the afternoons; while they spent that portion of the day in search of food. His statement being challenged, the little fellow spent the next morning in watchful observation; and when the time came that the martins left off building and started hunting for food, he ran home with breathless haste to assure his father of the correctness of his observation. He knew all the fauna of his county, and many of its flora. Further he wrote poetry, of a childish character true, at six; a power which remained with him into adult life, and many are his poetical creations remaining in the hands of his old friends. His early efforts manifest the sweet disposition of the child, and also his early industry. In course of time he went to the famous Friends' school at Ackworth, in Yorkshire, where he was afterwards apprenticed as a teacher. Here, when only a boy of fourteen, he delivered a lecture on "Insects," manifesting much shrewd observation as well as extensive reading on the subject. It is a quaint-looking little MS., illustrated on the front page by pen sketches of "The finished dwelling of the termites," of "The crane-fly laying its eggs," and "The larva in the earth eating the roots of grass," &c. He rebukes the cruelty practised towards the cockchafer, and is deeply interested in the ants of South Africa, and the slave-catching marauds of the red ants upon the black ants; the manner in which wasps acquire the material for their paper nests, and other matters; concluding with very devout wishes.

But teaching was not to his mind, so he became a student at King's College Hospital, and afterwards pursued his studies at the University of Edinburgh. He was a fair-haired youth at this time, not much given to study; full of fun and frolic, light-hearted and genial. His mirth-inspiring capacities were generally recognised, and "Charlie" was a great favourite with his fellow-students. His natural amiability was furthered by his capacity to write verses; while his keen powers of observation enabled him to take off the salient points in the professors and their foibles in happy rhymes. As is common enough in youths brought up in austere religious families, there was a slight soupçon of irreverence in his effusions. This was set off more conspicuously by his speech, which consisted much of scriptural phraseology, as does the language of the people of New England. This, though it suggests profanity to others, is not so in people thus brought up. A keen sense of humour made Charlie a great acquisition to a class, but rather from the student's than the professor's point of view. He would pounce instantly on any sentence which would admit of a double interpretation, and a merry ring of laughter, of the most contagious character, would tell the professor of his unfortunate mistake. With several of the professors consequently young Smith was classed among the "black sheep." Not that he was dissipated, as was only too common among the men of his time, but he was careless and negligent. If any one wanted to make a walking tour in the Highlands, Smith was at once ready to accompany him. For him to watch the flight of the falcon, the hover of the hawk, or the dive of the kingfisher, was far more congenial occupation than to attend an anatomical demonstration, or to hear Professor J. Hughes Bennet lecture on the functions of the nervous system. The knowledge that he was risking his certificate for class attendance for the session by so doing, sat lightly on his consciousness, and even on his conscience. If any practitioner near Edinburgh was ill or hard pressed with work, Smith would forsake his proper studies and go to his aid; his kindly bearing making up to the patients for his limited professional knowledge. His power of self-sacrifice was a conspicuous element in his character; and once when a fellow-student could not command the amount of money to enable him to go in for an examination, Smith lent him his month's money, which enabled him to go in. He passed, and became a surgeon in Her Majesty's service; for which he ever held himself indebted to Smith's self-denial. For, too proud to appeal to his father, Smith balanced his accounts by an abstinence from all meat for two months. This was a severe trial for a young man endowed with an excellent appetite, as Smith most undoubtedly was; and it seems especially hard upon him that starvation was his bane in life, and ultimately killed him. His last shilling was at any one's disposal, without inquiry as to what would be its destiny, or the purpose for which the loan was sought. Light-hearted and free from care about the future, as happy when his money was gone as when pay-day arrived, Smith was loved by all who knew him.

His command of English was quite unusual, and his playful verses and off-hand compositions earned for him a distinct reputation among his fellow-students. During this time he was neither a model of propriety nor conspicuously vicious. He liked a glass of beer, and was always welcome among his fellow-students, for his conversation was ever brilliant with flashes of wit or humour, from happily turned sentences, and quick and apt repartee. His power with his pencil led to many a clever caricature, provoking mirth and eliciting fun. He was respected, too, among his companions, for his reputation bore no stain of mean or discreditable action, and was free from imputation of malice or uncharitableness. At this time few, if any, suspected that under this light and gay demeanour there lay those grand sterling qualities which in a short time Smith was to exhibit in so remarkable a degree. It is needless to say that his progress as a student was leisurely, to say the least of it. He liked the dispensary work of seeing poor persons at their homes, for which his kindly disposition fitted him well. His affection for animals was manifested by his one day bringing home a poor little kitten, which he rescued from a premature death. A little dirty, half-singed, unlovely-looking creature it was; but it soon picked up under his guardianship. Another time he was possessed of a disreputable-look-

ing dog acquired under the same circumstances, namely, in the hovel of some dispensary patient whom he attended, where it was perishing from starvation and neglect.

For many years it had been a common practice among Edinburgh students to go on a whaling voyage when they had failed to pass their examinations, or often, rather, when they had not tried to pass them, and their friends were growing angry.

Not wishing to apply further to his father for funds, Smith determined to do something for himself, and would go "whaling." Whaling vessels required a surgeon, but not necessarily a qualified one. The time was most convenient, as the engagement commenced just at the end of the winter session, and terminated in time for the next session. If the vessel was at all fortunate the surgeon drew enough money to pay for his classes and keep him going most of the ensuing winter; during which time usually he and his friends got on good terms again. So Smith decided to go whaling, little dreaming of the momentous issues involved in the decision. These whalers first go in the spring to Greenland, seal-fishing, returning with their capture, and then when the ice farther north has become cleared, they set off on their true whale-fishing in the Arctic seas. The vessel to which he became surgeon was the *Diana*, of Hull, commanded by Captain John Gravill, a man of great experience in Arctic voyaging. Under the heading of "A Good Friday in the Greenland seas (somewhere about lat. 72°, long. 9°)," Smith gives some account of this Greenland voyage. They were anticipating a successful voyage and a speedy return to Hull for a few days, whilst discharging cargo and taking in coals and water in readiness for the whaling voyage to Davis's Straits. "Little did we anticipate how near and terrible a fate was even then threatening us." The vessel was fixed in the ice motionless though a strong breeze was blowing. On Good Friday, March 30, 1866, at 2 A.M., the breeze became a violent gale, the ice, to which the ship had previously been fast, was breaking up; the ship was surrounded by immense masses of ice in violent motion. Each man prepared for the worst, as at any moment they might have to leave the ship and take to the ice. Then for the first time Smith realised what religious convictions were. He writes, "I had never, in the course of my life, felt the reality of these things as of moment to myself." He and the Captain communed gravely face to face with death, and then it was that he first saw his past life from a new and serious point of view; the expressions which he used showing how vividly he realised its unfitness. Having made every preparation in case the ship should go down and they had to take to the ice, Smith went to help the crew to work the "fenders" (masses of knotted rope), so as to break the blow of the masses of ice, "as jagged and hard as rocks." His analysis of his thoughts at this time, when death was imminent, deserves to be preserved. There was no fear of death. "It was only a few minutes in the water." At first his mind was crowded with reminiscences of the most mingled kind. Student life, school life, child life, all came thrusting themselves upon his consciousness. Thus was his mind occupied whilst his body was actively engaged fighting each mass of ice, as in turn it was driven against the ship's side. Daylight enabled them to carry on the struggle successfully, hour after hour. At 2 P.M., after twelve hours of fearful exertion, all hands that could be spared went down to the cabin, where the old captain addressed them, and then prayed fervently—his voice all but drowned by the noise of the storm. This seems to have calmed Smith's mind, and after it, while working away, scraps of hymns and fragments of the Psalms were repeated over and over again. He writes, "And thus the afternoon wore slowly on, my mind intently on the stretch, and occupied at times with serious thought." The faint hopes of escape they entertained were centered in their getting out of the ice before night fell. At 5 P.M. "the welcome news spread rapidly through the ship that the barometer was rising, then gradually the ice grew smaller in size and less numerous, then we passed through streams of young and broken ice (which betokened our approaching the edge of the pack), then crossed patches of open water." Next day the storm raged more furiously than ever, but they were free from the danger of being stove in by ice masses. "The swell was fearful, and being unrestrained by the young ice, broke over our bows and windward quarter, and swept our decks in heavy seas. The cold was intense; everything, spars, rigging, boats, oars, covered with ice, our faces and beards hung with icicles, the decks one sheet of ice, the seas freezing as they came on board, the lee scuppers frozen up with ice, our drenched clothes frozen stiff upon us, the ship's hull coated with solid ice from stem to stern of a thickness of two feet, the yards and rigging marked with ice; everything about us showed the terrible ordeal through which we had passed. There lay our three poor bags of biscuit, there the axes for cutting away the masts, there the oars all frozen together, beside the boats which were to have borne us from the sinking ship to a still more awful, but none the less certain, death upon the ice." The conviction of all was that they had been providentially rescued, nothing else could have saved them. Then he goes on —"Sunday: a most gloriously beautiful day, not a breath of air stirring, the ocean calm and tranquil as a mill-pond; the ship laid to whilst the crew were engaged in ridding her decks, hull, and rigging of the ice. The Island of Jan Mayen in sight at some forty miles north of us. We had drifted down past it in safety. A very numerously attended service in the cabin." The captain never encountered the like of that storm in his fifty years' experience. The mate had been wrecked several times, but he could not recall such a storm. When they got into Lerwick harbour on April 30th, they found that the other ships of the fleet had also been in the storm: he writes—"The terrible nature of the storm is fully corroborated by the officers and crews of all the whaling vessels; there is but one opinion expressed, which is, that such a storm and such a swell amongst heavy ice was never encountered before."

On May the 9th the *Diana* left Lerwick on the true whaling voyage to encounter still more terrible adventures. It turned out, indeed, to be one of the most eventful and painfully interesting of Arctic voyages; the story of which has never been published in full—probably never will. An ordinary looking quarto is that log-book of the *Diana*, but it tells a wonderful story of privation, of suffering, and of endurance. The crew consisted of fifty-one men, of which about thirty were Shetland men. They proceeded to the north in pursuit of whales. The surgeon had apparently very little to do, so he kept a diary. He writes a preface in which, in strange contradiction to what did actually occur, stands the passage: "God grant the retrospect of the voyage may be a pleasant one." When he wrote this he little thought of what was in store for them. He complains of the bad light given by his oil-lamp, and the difficulties under which he will labour in keeping this diary; yet all through there is the same bold, strong handwriting, as clearly written and as straight across the page as if written in a luxurious study. It tells of bird shooting, mainly, up to a certain point; and is illustrated by some very good pen-and-ink sketches of birds, seals, Esquimaux, the ship amidst ice, a map, and many other objects, testifying to his command over his pencil as an artist. They were often in danger, but Smith seems to have become so inured to this that it elicits little remark from him. When his book was full, he continued his diary on some quarto sheets, and ultimately on ordinary note paper. And what a tale of suffering and endurance this diary tells of!

On August 22nd, Captain Gravill was in great doubt about the possibility of getting out through the ice, and had almost decided to make for the Government depôts of provisions on Beechy Island, and winter in Lancaster Sound; and on the 26th they had all ready to leave the ship, and take their chance on the ice—and a poor chance they regarded it. On August 31st, Captain Deuchars, of the *Intrepid*, came on board, and he and Captain Gravill agreed that "the two ships will remain in company for mutual assistance, and if necessary for mutual preservation, as long as possible."

On Saturday, September 1st, he writes:

Charles Edward Smith.

"About 11.30 the *Intrepid* got up steam, and while our boilers were heating, all hands were employed warping the ship along the edge of the floe towards the opening where we were foiled yesterday, and where the ice was beginning to slack off. Got up steam soon after 1 o'clock, but the ice began to run together again, so returned to our old quarters. In a short time the ice slacked once more, and again we attempted to force a passage, but without success. A third time we returned to the charge, but were compelled to desist from the ice closing rapidly, and therefore returned to the edge of the land floe and made fast, shifting afterwards to our old berth in a small bight. The gallant and generous captain of the *Intrepid* was more fortunate, having forced his way through the loose floes and evidently got into clear water, for he was seen from the mast-head to steam away to the south with great rapidity, and by tea-time only his topsail yards could be distinguished with the long glass. Our last chance of succour or of safety was gone, and we had nothing left to depend upon but the merciful providence of God."

Here follow some strong expressions of opinion as to the heartless character of the desertion; for the *Intrepid* had twice the horse-power of the *Diana* and had plenty of coals. Some six or seven miles of ice lay betwixt them, and open water to the southward. Once through this and all was easy; on the other side of it was the gloomy prospect of a winter in the ice far away from any other human being, of cold, starvation, and death, in all human probability. The ice closed upon them the next day, "heaps upon heaps, heaps upon heaps." He writes, "You may depend upon it many an earnest prayer ascended from that helpless and despairing ship's company." He gives a little sketch of the ice to convey some idea of the thickness of it. On the 3rd, the captain called all hands aft, and asked the men to bring in any bread they might have saved; this was done, and all the provisions put under lock and key, the key being given to the head harpooner. The officers to fare like the men. "All this ominous and discouraging, yet very necessary, business passed off satisfactorily."

A dead whale was seen, and a party sent off to bring back as much of the skin as they could, as addition to the small stock of provisions. They failed, and were nearly drowned in getting back to the ship from the newly-formed ice melting. He thought at night of his escape, and wrote, "I don't think I ever felt myself so anxious, uneasy, and so entirely dependent on the mercy of God as I do this night." Next day they caught a few Fulmar petrels, "and are carefully preserving them for food; but ere long every bird, and beast, and living thing in the country will go south ere the winter overtakes them." They alone were to remain! On the 7th they saw, in the far distance, a ship sailing in open water. This was the last sight of anything human, but themselves, till next March.

The ship was fast in the ice, and they were face to face with hunger and cold. Week after week, without hope almost, they lived on; Smith working hard at his diary, apparently from want of anything to do. On the 1st of December the ship received a severe nip, and at midnight all hands took to the ice, on which a tent was rigged. The old captain slept in it one night, and then went back to the ship; it was so terribly cold that he could not stand it. He got gradually worse with dropsy, and the account of his last illness is told very affectively. On Christmas-day they were in terrible danger, and the poor old captain was dressed, as they might have to take to the ice at any moment. The nip was so severe that the very cabin floor was bending under their feet. Next day the captain died, and his loss was keenly felt by all; many of them had served under him for years.

J. MILNER FOTHERGILL.

MUSIC.

BY THE AUTHOR OF "MUSIC AND MORALS."

PART I.

TO discuss music without the aid of instruments, notes, or diagrams, is not an easy and would be an impossible thing, were I mainly dealing with its science, history, or performance. But it is with the general philosophy and *rationale* of the art that I am now concerned. Music has come in for its full share of science, history, and criticism; but how few have dived into its essence, and instead of seeking for the inevitable "how," asked after the eternal "why"!

I have always thought that music should be discussed and written about just like any other art. The musical criticisms of the day deal chiefly in technicality and personality, and it is unfortunate that the few writers who occasionally venture out into the deep, and discourse on music *per se*, are deficient in the one thing needful—"musical perception;" in that ocean they cannot swim, and the sooner some of them get to shore the better. Music has its morals, its right and its wrong, its high and its low, like any other art; and until people can be got to understand how this can be, and why it must be, music will never assert its dignity among the arts and receive its dues. Before Mr. Ruskin wrote people thought that there was no right or wrong about painting, sculpture, and architecture, and musical criticism has been in the same Slough of Despond. And what is the consequence? Painting and sculpture rank above music, yet music, not painting, not sculpture, is *the* modern art. Yet no one has been found to do for the new art of music what Mr. Ruskin has done for painting and architecture—to create for it a moral philosophy as well as a *rationale.* I need not say that in " Music and Morals " I have tried to show why this ought to be, and how it might be done for the art of music, and I repeated those opinions in the *Quarterly Review,* vol. 131, No. xxxvi., and I have been much gratified to observe that writers who are apt to treat my opinions as common, when not wrong, and as wrong when not common, have not always been deterred from the not uncommon practice of appropriating them without reference.

I now glance briefly : I. At the development of music out of the rough elements of sound.

II. At its place amongst the sister arts and its peculiar functions.

III. At the obvious nature of its influence. Music, its origin, function, and influence—that is my subject.

I.—THE DEVELOPMENT OF MUSIC OUT OF SOUND.

We now enter at once into the world of mystery and imagination : of mystery because, though you know how a sound can be produced, you do not know why it produces its effect on you; of imagination, since I must ask you to recall as you read, by way of illustration, the most beautiful sounds you have ever heard. But sounds of less agreeable nature have first to be realised. Before we enter the temple of music or penetrate its inner shrine, we find ourselves distracted with the rough elements of sound, the rabble of noise outside—how out of such elements shall we ever collect the " choirs that chime after the chiming of the eternal spheres " ?

We have sound in the world around us of every conceivable kind. Listen to the distant roar of a great populous city. Its cry goes up by day and night. Myriad voices ascend from sea and land. If you notice the waves as they drag down the shingles on the beach, in their retiring scream they give forth a series of semitones ; and there is a rough and elemental sort of musical sound in the moaning of the wind, which has supplied poets with allusions more sentimental than accurate ; still the wind's harp does go up and down, like the mooing of a cow. And doubtless the rough inflexions of the human voice existed long before music became an art. As the voice rises and falls you have a scale of emotional inflexion which gives it full force ; for it is the sound quite as much as the words used which gives the impression of what is passing in your mind. But even here we have not arrived at musical sound, we have only touched some materials of it. How shall we get at musical sound ? Or, in other words, what is the difference between a noise and a musical note ? A noise is only understood when the nature of a musical note is understood. Roughly speaking, a musical note means a " clang," to use Helmholtz's word, in which there is one fundamental tone, and along with it the third, fifth, and octave as buried tones. When the fundamental is strong, and the hidden tones, the third, fifth, and octave, &c., very faint, you get the impression of one musical note which is invariably the fundamental tone. There are many hidden mysteries in a fundamental tone, a greater or less variety of overtones. I had occasion to dwell more scientifically upon this in my article on " Bells " in GOOD WORDS.

Now, what makes noise is just this. You get the third, fifth, and the octave, or some other overtones, louder than the fundamental note. To illustrate this summarily, we might compare the notes of a violin or a fine bell with a Chinese gong, or you may strike a coal-scuttle or a warming-pan, and produce an equally satisfactory result. A gong is, however, perhaps the best type of noise—not those smooth Japanese metal plates, or bars, which often give one or more very sweet tones, but those horrible gongs, dented all over, that you thump with a drum-stick, beginning *pp.* and ending with a purgatorial crescendo in *ff.* This, I say, is noise, and most of the sounds which fall upon the ear are noise, especially what we hear " whene'er we take our walks abroad " in the streets of London.

When, then, we have found a clear fundamental tone, with its accompanying fainter overtones, we have found a musical note. Now analyze this musical note. It can vary in three ways, and in three ways only. When you know how it so varies you know all that can be known about it. A musical note, then, can vary in pitch, in intensity, and in quality or *timbre.*

1. What makes the pitch of a note ? It depends upon the rapidity of the vibrations. Supposing you take as an illustration the sound given by a note of an harmonium, which is caused by the vibration of a metal tongue. When this tongue vibrates slowly, or only a few times backwards and forwards in a second, you get a note of a deep pitch ;

but when it vibrates at the rate of 67,000 vibrations to the note, the pitch is so shrill that although some cats may hear it no human beings can. The ear of the cat is finer than ours. Cats and some birds are microphones compared to man ; they see sights we cannot see, they smell smells we very fortunately cannot smell, and they hear sounds which we cannot hear. A note is high or low in pitch according as the number of vibrations which produce it are in a given time few or many, fast or slow.

2. What makes its intensity ? It is the length of the vibration waves that determines their loudness or intensity. If the wave or the extent of " excursion " of vibrating molecules be large, the shape of the wave being the same, the sound is loud ; if the reverse, the shape being the same, the sound is faint.

3. What determines the quality ? The quality depends on the *mode* of vibration. It is, as Helmholtz has shown, the number, order, and intensity of the vibrations of the overtones in a " clang " which determines timbre or quality, and which makes the differences between the same note sounded on a violin, piano, harp, flute, &c.

But even now we have only arrived at the composition of musical notes, not at the composition of music. How then did music arise ? Of course the human ear has always been open to sweet and disagreeable sounds, and has gradually been led to choose between them. I do not want to quarrel with the mythical notion that some pristine man or woman, wandering on the sea-shore, may have found a shell with seaweed stretched like strings across it, out of which the wind was making an Æolian harp, and so the first idea of the harp may have arisen. This may have happened for aught we know. The creating of artificial notes for mere pleasure seems to have been a custom from time immemorial.

Bones of extinct mammals have been found made into flutes. At least M. Lartêt says so. What he found looked like a flute to him, and far be it from me to bring art into collision with science by saying it does not look like a flute. I think on the whole it does ; and if so, this may be another proof that primitive man delighted in sweet sounds. But we are still far from the art of music. Here are witnesses to an ancient impulse in the direction of an art, but not the art itself.

We may as well skip Egypt and Assyria, and assume that the musical survival of the fittest remained, after the extinction of these empires, with Greece. However, we need not pause long even in Greece, for although the Greeks had many modes or scales, as they never discovered the natural advantages of the octave completed by the eighth note, their musical art could not progress.

It is useless for philosophers to prose about the emotional advantages and special musical character of the Dorian, Lydian, or Phrygian modes—as if we had lost, or could lose, anything by adopting our system of fixed tonality ; for once get that and you can obviously write in any mode and give your key any special character you like ; and the proof of this is that Berlioz has used the proud Hypodorian mode in the second part of " Christ's Infancy." · Saint Saens opens the " Noces de Prométhée " with it. Gounod uses it in *Faust* for the " Roi de Thule." The Hypophrygian mode colours the close of *William Tell*, act ii. (Rossini) ; and we might multiply instances—but the Greeks could never have written *Faust* or *William Tell*, as will presently appear.

The fact is, that in Greece musical sound was auxiliary to the exercise of the dance, the ceremony of the feast, the discipline of the arena, or the voice of the orator ; it accompanied chanting, and most people are agreed that harmony, in our sense of the word, was unknown. The Greek system, like some others in the realms of theology, philosophy, and science, was elaborate but sterile, and so Greece handed her traditions on to Rome, and still no progress was made, because music, like all other arts, had to bide her time. Her Muse is essentially the dear possession of the modern world ; she lives and moves and finds free development and expansion in our atmosphere alone ; and this is what makes her so absorbing and fascinating, and *entitles* her, now that she has reached her glorious maturity, to rank above the other arts. I say that music is essentially the modern art, although her mystic treasures lay buried for centuries in the womb of Time.

So all things have their supreme moment; so electricity slept in the amber, and was known to the Greek six hundred years before Christ, but was only wedded to applied science in the laboratory of the nineteenth century. Every ancient who boiled a kettle must have observed the rush of steam from its spout, but it remained for Watt and Stephenson to adapt it to commerce, manufacture, and transport. And all arts have fared the same. Like spirits in the vasty deep they wait for their special call. That call is always the same. *It is the deep need of an Age.*

What need has human life of art? What is art? Art is, like sensation, one and indivisible in its essence ; but, like sensation, it is manifold in its channels of expression. It captures in different forms and runs through the five senses. Expression is the imperative mood of our nature : without it we wither and pine ; with it we grow, we develop, we soar. Man is essentially a dramatic animal : he is ever seeking to make known what is in him ; he aspires to the true possession of himself. Life becomes more rich when it passes into word and action. Every moment in proportion as we are truly alive we are longing to manifest ourselves as we can. We are not satisfied till some one else enjoys what we enjoy, knows what we know, feels what we feel, and the great burden-lifters of humanity are those who have told us the things we knew already, but which we could not express for ourselves. These are " the souls that have made our souls wiser." These are the prophets and the poets and the artists, dear kindred, world-embracing spirits that give humanity back to itself, and make it doubly worth having by bestowing upon it those memorable and entrancing gifts of expression that hang like suns in the firmament of Time.

And do you not feel this as you stand before any great work of art—the " Madonna di San Sisto " at Dresden, the "Transfiguration" at Rome ? Do you not feel—" Here is one who has painted my inexpressible thoughts — here before me are the Divine figures I have seen in my dreams ? " When you hear the *Elijah* do you not stand in the cleft of the rock with the prophet, and veil your face as the whirlwind sweeps by, and amid the crash of the thunder and rending of the rocks, you perceive that the Lord is not in the tempest, nor in the earthquake, nor in the fire, but at last in the still small voice ? Yes, you are shaken, you are lifted up in this elemental catastrophe, purified in this majestic outer expression, and you feel how the storm has passed from your own heart, as the last wild and nearly distracted cry dies away, and there comes very softly one of those magic changes in which the whole of the emotional atmosphere shifts. The cry of the spirit is going to be answered with a gentleness and a power above all that it could ask or think. The melody flows on in the clear and silvery key of E major; it passes like the sweeping of a soft, balmy wind. " And in that still voice onward came the Lord, never rising, never pausing, but gentle and strong and pulseless, coming we know not whence, and passing, with ' the tides of music's golden sea, into eternity ! '" (*vide* " Music and Morals "). And upon you has not this had a great and hallowing effect ? Has not music taken your own turbulent emotions, and expressed them for you in the storm, leaving you sublimely elevated and yet sublimely calm at the close ? Such will indeed appear to be the special function of musical art.

But I must not anticipate.

THE AFTERMATH.

THE glamour of the after-light
   Lay clear and fair along the sky,
And made the pathway eerie-bright
   As home we wandered—thou and I.

The meadow-mists were lying low ;
   A shadow held the riverside ;
The water took the western glow,
   And peace, grey peace, spread far and wide.

A sober-heartedness was ours—
   So still the earth, the sky so strange ;
And we had given in sunny hours
   Our youthful hearts their widest range.

We lingered in the meadow-path
   Touched by the twilight's silent spell,
While from the sun's fleet aftermath
   A subtle glory rose and fell.

Dim, wistful thoughts within us grew,
   Forebodings of the life to be,
Till with a sudden thrill we knew
   Time's touch of immortality.

For all the wonder and the awe,
   Far-widening within the west,
Seemed with a mystic power to draw
   Our hearts into its kindly rest.

Yet still it faded, faded fast,
   And night crept up the eastern slope ;
But o'er our lives a strength had passed,
   And left us with a larger hope.

So home we wandered—thou and I—
   That night, sweet wife, so long ago,
And still we watch the western sky
   And strengthen in its mystic glow.
               JAMES HENDRY.

At a Street Corner.

FROM MOGADOR TO MOROCCO.

By RALLI STENNING.

PART II.

WE turn out for the city. How shall we convey our impression? Long stretches of parallel crumbling walls, crooked and fissured from top to bottom, in which are various-sized holes for doors; long covered passages, whose sudden darkness blinds you; alleys two feet wide; entrance to yards; open spaces, heaped up with rubbish, and littered with feathers, decaying flesh and rags; a putrid dog; a fountain with crumbling mosaic; an Arabesque door; a rickety Moorish window, propped up near the wall-top; all mixed and tumbled together—confusion and decay. Now and then we jam against the wall, that a laden camel may pass. How camels pass camels in the six-foot streets of Morocco remains a mystery, unless, like Luther's goats on the narrow bridge, the more obliging lies down while the less obliging passes over.

We stare into shops which are mere holes in the walls leading into dismal dens. A broad bench runs in front of the opening; articles spread on this and suspended on strings tied across the interior make the showman's show. The shoe customer sits down in the road to try on. Every trade has its street, the whole of them form a warren of blind and open alleys shaded by extemporised roofs of mats, skins, and branches of palm-trees. Our passage through them is more than usually difficult; we are Christian, and Christian means all evil. The very name is a scare and a bugbear. There are certain strange and terrible figures at every turn—men, old women, and big boys, who seem charged with the duty of representing this feeling, which they do most cordially by curse, fist, and face. Our guards clear the way with a stick, and we hurry on, and at length emerge into an open space used for a market. The effect is striking—indeed, charming: a square on a gala day—a managery! a gathering of nations! floating in the sunlight. Merchants obsequious, lithe, and majestic, in snow-white *caic* of wool, of silk, of muslin, falling in severe and graceful simplicity, with drawers of crimson damask, slippers of embroidered gold, and ample airy turbans—lounging statuesques of barbaric splendour; simple householders with their white mantles floating in the wind;

farmers from the provinces in strange and grotesque costumes; savage and turbulent warriors from the famous Rif, armed with long guns, whose red case is twisted round the head as a careless turban, with firm fearful faces, rendered horrible by yellow devices; negroes with splendid naked limbs, betraying their owner's pride and care; saints, emaciated and naked as born, grasping a curious staff, preaching with wildest gesture, before whom even the savage warrior of the Rif uncovers and seems reverent; heaps of living rags asleep in the sun, propped against the wall and flattened on the ground; caravans of camels, herds of goats and oxen, troops of beautiful horses and gaily

caparisoned mules. It is the cattle market.

A High-class Moor.

In the market-places the picturesque is triumphant: in the bright sunlight, dress of every tribe, rank, and colour, surmounted by almost every hue of black, brown, brick, brass, and bronze-coloured faces, set in every shade from curly jet to flowing silver hair; in all the personal, tribal, and social caprice of costume; muleteers, camel-drivers, goat-herders, couriers, mendicants, anchorites, Moors, Arabs, Berbers, negroes, mulattoes, Jews. Morocco boasts a market for merchandise and for woven fabrics, one for dry goods (sugar, tea, and spices), one for slaves and butchers; bootmakers, blacksmiths, carpenters, and other trades have each separate streets, as we have said. Cattle are sold in spaces both within the city and outside its walls.

We are attracting attention, so turn into the nearest street through a gateway, and at the other end we pass out by still another gateway. At length it strikes us that every street in Morocco has its defence. The town has evidently to be defended against itself. Inquiry confirms our explanation. Stormy and factious, safety is secured by gates at each end of every street, short and long alike — not mere garden gates, but solid wood-work set in massive archways. At sunset the outer gates of the walls of the city are closed, and when danger threatens, all the street gates are closed too, and strongly

A Bandit.

guarded. The people of each street are thus made prisoners on the spot, with no chance of communicating with those of their neighbouring street. By another labyrinth—along which we pass women who draw their veils more closely at the sight of us, and children who give us timid glances and then disappear—we reach the finest building of the city, the El-Koutoubia, or Mosque of the Bookseller. The mental effect is startling. Morocco's chief church dedicated to the bookseller! Where is enlightenment to match the Moors'? But there is another explanation. Perhaps the pious founder believed, as some one else is said to have done, that all other books were rendered superfluous by the one book, the Koran, and thus its principal church might be fairly known as the bookseller's substitute. Be this as it may, there are no booksellers in Morocco. The very name of the mosque must be satire. Little more can be said of the structure than that its tower is square, of stone, the same width to the top, which is two hundred and twenty feet from its base. It is divided into seven stories, and ascended by inclined planes, not stairs. The body of the spa-

cious building is of brick, and, like everything else we see, in an advanced stage of decay. Our profane eyes may not look upon its sacred interior, so we are left to imagine the effect of " its marble pillars from Spain," and its " curiously wrought roof." Its basement contains a vast bath for religious ablutions. Like some other spacious churches nearer home, El-Koutoubia seems little used. There are three other principal mosques, amongst which the first is Ben Youssef, with its lofty tower—some of the archways are of true Moorish beauty, said to have been brought from Granada and Algesiras. From the lantern of the Koutoubia tower, the eye takes in the position and proportions of the city. It appears somewhat pear-shaped, the point being towards the north. Ten thousand white flat roofs intersected by—as from this distance such six-foot streets must appear—narrow gutters, and dotted everywhere with small squares, through which is thrust up the tops of olives, figs, and diminutive palms, scarcely broken by dome or turret. Near the walls, and completely encircling them, as they encircle the town, is a wide band of enclosed gardens ; and, beyond this, again another band of gigantic date-palms, and still farther away to the north-west lies undulating grounds, and illimitable plains, on which nothing can be distinguished ; and to the south and east, wooded country rising gently towards the vast Atlas wall of the great desert of Sahara.

Near to one of these churches we pass the door of a prison ; there are three in the city, and this is the largest. At the entrance gates sits the vice-governor of the city, a spare,

A Shlub Woman.

tall, fine old man, trying causes. He sits on the bare ground, with his back to the wall, plaintiff, defendant, and witnesses crouching around him and looking pleadingly into his face. Imprisonment is here a serious affair. Moors even call their prisons horrible and foul; yet we cannot conceive anything more horrible and foul than many of their own streets after rain. It seems as though all the utterly abominable parts of Oriental cities had been collected here, surrounded with a wall, and called Morocco.

What, then, must be this criminal-house, filthy to a Moor? A pit, excavated from the earth to the depth of seven or eight feet, arched over with a roof supported on pillars, affording little light, less air, no food. Fetters are rivetted on every leg, iron collars and chains fixed on every neck. No fastidious distinctions are made between criminals great and small. Death from pestilence or hunger is the natural course of things. While we stand by, a dry, mummy-like form is carried out on a stretcher, partly covered with a sheet, on its way to burial, said to be a dead prisoner. Friends may provide food, but the unwhole-

By the Market Wall.

someness of the place kills even men inured to stench. Friends, too, may redeem; for at every stage of justice money answereth all things. But before release, many capricious demands have to be satisfied, from the powerful caid down to the poor policemen; and if the demands leave money behind, released may be imprisoned again until avarice is satisfied. A demand is made for even loan of the fetter, collar, and chain. The city's four thousand prisoners are, for the most, defaulters in taxes. Such criminals are doggedly hunted, while the murderers may escape.

We make our way to one of the gates to take a turn in the gardens outside the walls — a privilege, by permission. We enter the garden, or plunge into what realises our idea of a jungle of olives, palms, figs, oranges, lemons, in wildest freedom, bound together and tangled with climbing ivy, weeds, and grape-vines. We push our way with difficulty through the narrow overgrown paths which here and there intersect the grounds. This wild, rank luxuriance is the Moor's idea of a first-class garden, for it is the garden of a governor,

Morocco Children at play.

caid, or sultan. There is cultivation, after a fashion. We hear the pleasant splash of the waters as they flow along wooden troughs and irrigating ditches; but as weeds and wild growths are up to one's shoulders, we see neither ditch nor well-house. Amongst this wild, splendid vegetation, we have a new sense of nature's productive powers. In fruitful years, the waste of fruit is enormous; oranges are utilised by Morocco boys, as English boys utilise snow, as balls for pelting, notably the unhappy Jews. So seriously inconvenient does orange-balling at times become that the authorities interfere.

Passing along the road, back towards the city, we overtake the ever-poetical camel with an immense load of hides, led by a man riding on an ass; and we are children again. We follow and admire, turning up a court not far beyond the gate, which proves to be an institution standing for our inn, known as a public *fondouk*. These places are houses and yards after the general types of Moorish dwellings, where the countryman, for a halfpenny a day, finds quarters for his beast, and for a penny a day a hovel for himself. The miserable place is full of imaginative interest. Hither come men from the markets of Timbuctoo and the forest of the Soudan, from the snowy heights of the Atlas and the sandy plains of the Sahara; men who have sacked and burned negro villages, captured their youth and slain their age; ostrich and lion hunters, necromancers, astrologers, anchorites; bandits, and men who know no law but the gun, rebels against all authority; men, too, who have crossed the Great Desert, seen its mirages and sand-pillars, lain down under the lee of the camel before the simoon; to whom scenes which in books fired our childhood's imaginings to their highest pitch of wonder are actual events. While gazing down this gateway, life seems an illusion and a dream.

The average male Moor is well-made, and has the appearance of uncultivated ability; as women are seldom seen abroad—their exercises being confined to the house-tops and gardens of their harem—it is difficult to judge of them; but if the few seen flitting by us were specimens of the rest, they are not devoid of beauty, alike of figure and feature. Some of the female peasantry are especially fine; amongst these, the *Shluh* engages in war with ferocious courage—advanced pioneers of women's equal rights! Berber women, well-knit and active, are proverbial for love of their own home and children, and hatred of strangers. This shows itself curiously in their popular curse, " May God burn your father ! " All Moors consider it the greatest insult to an enemy to speak ill of his parents. " Your father died in his bed " is the last charge of cowardice.

Leaving the lower and more populated parts of the town, turning along a main street about nine feet wide, to the south-east, and passing through one of the seven city gates, we reach the locality of the Sultan's palace. Though outside the city it is within walls, high and thick as the city walls, in which are gates guarded by wild-looking native soldiers, one of whom wrapped in his mantle seems fast asleep. It is erected around two courts, and contains, besides the dwelling and harem of the Sultan, courts of audience, offices for ministers of State, and quarters for the Sultan's guard.

The Sultan's empire is composed of a most heterogeneous population, but all are warlike, ignorant, fanatical, cruel, lazy, restless—every class fearing and hating every other, and all the world. Sheiks oppress tribes; caids, territories and cities; pashas, provinces; and the Sultan, all. Agriculture, manufacture, wealth, freedom, life, are at the caprice of his personal will. Their end is his enjoyment. His person is the sea; national interests are the rivers to run into it, yet it is never full. One power, however, is *his* master—Mussulman fanaticism and its inflexible madness. While Christian peoples rise in the rank of being, that goads its victims to ruin.

But we are at the Sultan's palace. Its towers afford splendid views over country well wooded with date-palms, bounded by the Atlas range, lifting lustrous snow summits 10,000 feet into a deep-blue cloudless sky. From the magnificent prospect we turn to the city, to seek out its " Kat Ben Aid, Zaonia-el-Hadar," &c., where the houses of the wealthy are. We enter these "West-ends" by a narrow street of little shops and blank walls. The houses,

At an Inner-court Fountain.

however, with their bald cross-shaped loop-holes and gateways, show few signs of their owners' wealth. No gardens, no windows, no balconies, no porches. Their "front" is within; there groves of oranges and lemons, tiled pathways, and fountains form courts, in which is frequently to be found a tame gazelle. Kitchens, reception rooms, accommodation for wives and children, sleeping apartments, and occasionally a stable, divide the ground floor. From somewhere near the gateway entering the court, a narrow staircase leads to the first floor, where are the rooms in which the owner lives and receives his friends. The sleeping rooms, generally long, narrow, and lofty, contain low beds, hung commonly with striped red and yellow drapery, with coverlets of the same, bordered by thick carpets, pegs for wardrobe, and mirrors for toilet. The dining-rooms are furnished with carpets and hangings, chandeliers standing on the floor, cushion, pillow, and mattress of silk, velvet, and woollen, striped and starred with silver and gold, in all the colours of the rainbow, spread against the walls. Tables, chairs, and other necessaries of European furniture, in the city of Morocco there are none. Fountains flow here and there in the streets, which fairly lay claim to quaintness, occasionally to beauty. From these all the inhabitants fetch their drinking water, a well within the court generally supplying water for ordinary household use.

It is not uncommon to find a rough representation of a hand painted on the doors, or carved in the stucco over it, as a safeguard against witchcraft. All Moors believe in witchcraft; and, by the way, the wealthiest and the poorest wear charms as protection against disease and injury.

Breakfast, tea, and dinner, all of which are frequently taken on beautiful mats and carpets spread in the garden, form the meals of the "upper ten."

Breakfast consists of *cus-cus-su*—a cake of baked granules deftly made of flour, which eats crisp and sweet—milk, butter, omelets, pigeons cooked in oil, sweet potatoes, force-meats, and sweet tarts of honey, butter, and eggs. Tea, which is quite a "course" meal, is taken seated cross-legged on soft carpets spread on the floor, around a handsome and costly tray with dwarf feet raising it a few inches from the floor, furnished with drinking-glasses in place of china cups; the formidable meal—which is served by an upper man-servant—excites the European visitors' wonder and dismay. First, the tea-pot—or kettle, if named after its shape—is filled with green tea, sugar, and water, in such proportions as to make a thick sweet syrup, which is drunk without milk or cream. Then follows an infusion of tea and spear mint. Yet another of tea and wormwood. Yet another of tea and lemon verbena. And yet another, of tea with citron. On great occasions, a sixth is added of tea and ambergris. Nothing is eaten. The "weed" usually follows; but the Moor, though a smoker, is not "an inveterate." Dinner consists of various dishes of mutton, fish, and fowl, ingeniously and artistically served in mixtures of pomades, soaps, spices, and cosmetics; so, at least, Englishmen declare who have had in courtesy to swallow the preparations. Knives, forks, and spoons are dispensed with, perhaps despised. Around a central dish gathers the company, as usual cross-legged on the floor. At "In the name of God," which is the brief grace pronounced by the master of the house, the slave removes the cover from the bowl; lifted hands are thrust into the smoking dish, and morsels of its contents, deftly rolled into convenient forms, are tossed, dripping, into the mouth with a neatness and precision truly wonderful. Exact portions are picked from fowl and fish and mutton bone without delay or effort. Sharp nails are said to act as knives. After the course, water and napkins are brought round. The wash over, another dish, and another plunging of the paws into the savoury mess. Incense is often burnt during dinner, which fills the apartment with delicate aroma. When a meal is served in the open court, the ladies of the house are permitted to gaze on their lords from the balcony which usually surrounds it.

With a sense of relief we take a turn in the Jews' quarters. In Morocco the Jew endures hatred, degradation, persecution, and untold insults, worries, and woes for a pecuniary consideration, which the city seems able and willing to give. So valuable is his monetary capacity, that he cannot get permission to go outside the walls without his wife and family remaining as the pledge of his return.

One of the most pleasing memories of the house in Morocco is the little friendly bird, not unlike our own house-sparrow, which stands on no ceremony, awaits no invitation to dinner, and soon learns to eat out of your hand. Amid such strangely uncongenial surroundings, an acquaintance like this is both human and Divine. Our civilised hearts find it more near to them than mankind, and still more suggestive of the largeness and care of the Father who is over all.

SIR JAMES OUTRAM.

THERE are certain men whose names stand for great qualities. When these names are mentioned we think almost more readily of the quality than of the person. Sir James Outram is of this class. He is pre-eminently the modern knight; and Outram stands for chivalry. The tales of mediæval romance seem possible when we hear of his daring exploits, of his unselfish surrender and indifference to worldly profit. To read of them even in outline must be exhilarating and helpful, especially if we try to trace the process by which his character was formed and his great fame slowly grew. This we are now enabled to do here through the favour of Messrs. Smith, Elder & Co., of early sheets of the admirable memoir by Major-General Sir F. Goldsmid.

James Outram was born at Butterley Hall, Derbyshire, on January 29, 1803. He came of a race which had given honourable names to literature and to the Church of England; but his father, who showed a distinct genius for mechanical pursuits, and has the honour of having been associated with Stephenson and other early railway magnates, was a civil engineer—so active, practical, and persevering that his Christian name of "Benjamin Franklin" did no discredit to the sponsorship implied by it. Some have even traced to the last syllable of his surname the word "Tram," now in common use. Just when he was securing a high rank in his profession he abandoned it to found the Butterley Iron Works Company, in which he was chief partner. His enterprise, tact, and determination would no doubt have fully justified the step had he not died at a comparatively early age, before he was able to realise his projects, leaving his affairs in such a position that a very inadequate result remained for his family. His wife, the daughter of a Scottish gentleman, was a woman of great independence, energy, reticence, and firmness, and at once, on being made aware of the circumstances in which she had been left, resolved, so far as she could, to help herself. Her father had done some service to Lord Melville and to the country, and had incurred loss by it; and her characteristic and independent appeal to his lordship for justice, and her frank statement of the circumstances in which she was placed, brought a small pension from Government. With this and the remnant saved from the wreck of her husband's estate, she devoted herself to the rearing of her five young children, of whom the eldest was Francis, who became an officer in the Indian service, like his more celebrated brother James.

After a few years' residence at Worksop, and then at Barnby Moor (where for the sake of low rent Mrs. Outram bravely occupied a house that was popularly said to be haunted), she removed to Aberdeen. Her own early training and education, we are told, had been very incomplete, and this step was dictated in great part by the resolution that in this respect her children should not suffer. Living and schooling were cheap in Aberdeen; and it exhibits her foresight in the fairest light that she should have faced all the inconvenience and difficulty of removal—far greater at that time than now—for a prospective benefit for her children. At first she lived in a small cottage in the outskirts. When her daughters grew older we learn that she moved to an "upper flat" in Castle Street, that the best tuition available might be within their reach. She herself lost no opportunity of improvement, and when later in life she was free to travel abroad no one would have detected a trace of the early defects in her training. She was "exceedingly accurate and punctual." She boasted, and, it is believed, with accuracy, that she had never of her own fault kept a person waiting five minutes in her life. She was ready to admire excellence in many walks of life. She abhorred meanness; could express herself well, and even wrote verses. She abhorred debt; to avoid it and every form of dependence was her daily thought.

"Her intimate friends," says Miss Catherine Sinclair, who knew her well, "knowing that her income was straitened, made frequent offers of assistance, but all in vain. Her independent Scottish spirit recoiled from receiving an obligation, and she struggled successfully on through every difficulty or privation. Mrs. Outram was formed by nature to be the mother of a hero, and those among her friends who knew the gallant and chivalrous son might see that he had inherited his mother's generous sentiments, his bright talents, his inflexible integrity, and his indomitable energy from a parent of the old Scottish stamp, who has since her recent decease left few equals behind her."

For a short period Outram went to school at Udney, where he showed more skill in draughtsmanship than in grammar, and in manly exercises and field-sports than in Latin and Greek, and was more inclined to defend the little boys against the big bullies than to ingratiate himself with his superiors. "He had the courage and fortitude of a giant," says his sister, "with the body of a pigmy, being very small for his age." His firmness and decision were extraordinary. Once on the seashore, when his hand had been caught by a crab, "he calmly held it up, the blood streaming down on the creature, which thus hung until of its own accord it relaxed its hold and fell to the ground. Not a cry had been heard from the sufferer, not even a wry face made. He wrapped his handkerchief round the wounded finger, coolly saying, 'I thought he'd get tired at last.'" He was so skilful in carving that his mother would have made him a sculptor could she have found a place for him. After four years at Udney School he was removed to that of the Rev. W. Esson, then thought to be the best in Aberdeen; and here he was prepared for Marischal College, which he entered for mathematics and natural philosophy in the Session 1818-19, making very satisfactory progress in these studies. While his mother was anxiously casting about among her friends for advice and aid as to starting him in a profession, James had quietly made up his mind about a career. When it was proposed that, through the patronage of his relative, Archdeacon Outram, he might make his way into the English Church, he said to his sister, "They mean to make me a parson. You see that window; rather than be a parson I'm out of it, and I'll 'list for a common soldier." That necessity was averted through Captain Gordon, member for Aberdeenshire, a friend of his mother's, who procured for him a military cadetship in India. His mother accompanied him to London and saw all the due preparations made; and he sailed in the good ship *York* on the 2nd May, 1819, being then only in his seventeenth year, but with more of stern manhood than most who undertake the same voyage, notwithstanding his puny height—five feet one inch—over which he is said to have mourned. Years afterwards he was described by his brother as the "smallest staff-officer in the army." Bombay was reached on the 16th August, and soon thereafter he was posted as Lieutenant of the First Grenadier Native Infantry, and speedily joined the 2nd battalion. India was then at peace, and it was natural enough that a lad with unbounded energy and high spirits should seek a sphere for the exercise of his energies in field-sports, which he did at the various points at which he was first stationed—Rajkot, and other places. Lieutenant Outram was soon known as an

expert pig-sticker, tiger, and lion-hunter. He ignored difficulties, and had no sense of danger. Many records of his daring doings in this department survive, and suffice to illustrate his character on this side; though, perhaps, that which best bespeaks the man is the resolution with which he hunted down and slew the tiger that had made an end of his much-loved Bheel chief and trusted companion—Khundoo.

His exploits in hunting were, however, wholly thrown into the shade very soon by performances in another and higher field. His indomitable character and his fine sympathy with his men speedily made his influence felt, and before long he was advanced to the post of adjutant, having been in the meantime transferred to another regiment. He was a strict disciplinarian, but mixed humanity with it. His biographer says:—

"His love of field-sports, in which he was ready to join those under him, so far from leading them to be lax in their duties, made every man try to do his best. Duty was always a labour of love with those under him, for he inspired all who were capable of any elevation of feeling with some portion of his own ardour, and made all such willing assistants rather than mere perfunctory subordinates. Thus early did he show that wonderful tact of commanding men which few have possessed in such a high degree."

At this time he was only twenty-one years of age, and his advancement was particularly welcomed, inasmuch as it enabled him to gratify his filial feelings, always strong, in joining his brother in remitting regularly sums to his mother in Scotland.

His physique was much tried by the climate; but he had made up his mind to fight it out with the climate or die. And he did fight it out; for, strange to say, illness after illness did not leave him worse permanently, but appeared only to have strengthened his constitution, till it seemed to be of iron. He was given up in cholera more than once, and experienced fevers and other diseases or complaints, which, humanly speaking, would have killed most men; but excitement and work soon became, and long remained, his best restoratives and tonics. The first opportunity presented to him for really distinguishing himself was in repressing the rising in Kittur, brought about by the death of the Deshai, or native hereditary governor, and a conspiracy to palm off a pretended successor. James Outram was then in Bombay on sick leave. He volunteered for the service, and bore himself so well as to have received special mention. A more important service, and one which was to have more permanent results, was ready for him soon after his return to Bombay. An outbreak occurred in Western Khandesh, in the Malair district, and Outram was sent to quell it. This he did with such decision and dispatch, as well as soldierly craft, that the insurgents were surprised and scattered before the main body of the troops sent forward for the work had reached the scene of action. This marked him out for superior work, and, as the able man is always in his place, Outram was not found wanting when, still a young man of twenty-three, he was relieved from regimental duty and sent forward on the arduous enterprise of raising a Bheel corps in that province for police duty. The Bheels were very unlikely material for this end. Held to be a wholly distinct people from those surrounding them, they stood, to the number of some fifty-five thousand, as hopeless irreconcilables, Indian Ishmaels, their hands against every man. They have been called the Rob Roys of India. Roving, restless, keen for plunder, and quick to find an advantage against those of more settled modes of life, they levied a heavy tax upon all within their reach. Skilful, indomitable, inured by ages to strife and foray, it seemed well-nigh a hopeless task to tame them to servitude and good citizenship. Outram set about the work in a decided way, though he fully appreciated the milder policy of conciliation favoured by the famous Montstuart Elphinstone. First of all he directed his force upon the main centres, persuaded that so long as the spirit of rebellion was fostered by the belief that our troops could not attack the evil at its source, by penetrating to the mountain retreats, nothing effective could be done. With immense difficulty he made his way, with thirty bayonets, to the almost inaccessible mountain head-centre, and surprised the rebels. The suddenness, the confusion, above all the sound of musketry, caused them to scatter in various directions. By a well-concerted plan, which had been entered into with his companions engaged in the work, the soldiers, who were soon reinforced, separated into small parties in pursuit. All the Bheel haunts and strongholds were speedily occupied, and many were taken prisoners. No sooner was their power broken than Outram set himself to conciliation and reconstruction. He urged on the Bheels with whom he came into contact the advantages that would arise to them from accepting regular service in the army, and enlistment forthwith began.

"It is not hard to understand," says his biographer, "the objection of the Bheels to enter on a new line of life on the representation of comparative strangers. They had had ample cause to mistrust authority under native governments, and insufficient experience of the British rule to accept it in a thoroughly trusting spirit. The fears of the men at some supposed lurking mischief were among the main obstacles to enlistment, and three or four of the first comers were frightened away by a report that they had been enticed with a view to eventual transportation beyond seas. At length five of the bolder, and it may be the more intelligent, of the number were persuaded to take the shilling in earnest, and on July 1 Outram had as many as twenty-five recruits. In August the number had increased to sixty-two, and a little later to ninety-two."

His constant endeavour was to remove their fears by free intercourse with them, by talking of the cruelties done to them under the Peishwa's government with marks of detestation and without reserve, by listening to their complaints and redressing real grievances, and by displaying a perfect confidence in them. This policy was highly successful. When some rumours arose of contemplated foul play on the part of the English, scaring the Bheels, he says: "I ordered the Bheels to assemble, and was promptly obeyed. I explained to them how much disappointed I had reason to be in men who, notwithstanding the confidence I placed in them, sleeping under their swords every night (having none but a Bheel guard at my residence), still continued to harbour suspicions of me. The feeling with which they answered me was so gratifying that I do not regret the cause which brought it forth. Others have given early proof of their fidelity." He begs for more latitude in dealing with the Bheels than would be allowed in less exceptional circumstances, and goes on: "Placing early trust in them will naturally be regarded as imprudent, and as placing temptation in their way—yet I am persuaded that this is the only way to make them trustworthy."

And he thus excuses himself to his mother and his friends for his temerity:—

"If I have been carried away by enthusiasm occasionally to expose myself unnecessarily, believe me I shall bear your advice and admonition in mind, and abstain for the future. In my situation a little daring was necessary to obtain the requisite influence over the minds of the raw, irregular people I command; and if ever you hear of any act of temerity I may hitherto have been guilty of, do not condemn me as unmindful of what I owe to you and our family, but attribute it to having been a part of my peculiar duty."

And well he knew his men. All outbreak, marauding, and disobedience were summarily and sternly dealt with; Outram would tolerate no license; he so arranged the pay of the Bheels as to induce temperance and economy, and soon he founded schools both for adults and children. In 1828, the Collector reported that, for the first time in more than twenty years, the country had enjoyed six months of uninterrupted repose. The keen interest and exceeding delight he took in the school for the Bheel children was such as to soften somewhat the blow which at this time fell upon him from the painful and untimely death of his brother Francis.

The complete success of his dealings with the Bheels of the north-east, suggested that the same thing might be done for the Bheels of the Dang, a tract of tangled forest on the west of Khandesh. Outram perceived how Bheels could be used to tame other Bheels. He undertook to march a body of troops into the heart of the fortresses of Dang; and did it with such success that within a fortnight after the commencement of proceedings the desired end was accomplished; the force returned, "with the principal chief our prisoner, and all the others in alliance, after having subdued and surveyed the whole country,"—which, be it remembered, had been hitherto unexplored, and had been deemed wholly impracticable; and all this, by virtue of skill and decision, was attained with the loss of only one life on our side. The thanks of the Bombay Government were sent to Outram for the "highly meritorious service of the detachment on the Dang. . . . Nothing could exceed the indefatigable efforts made by yourself and the officers and troops under your command, bringing this most harassing duty to a conclusion . . . . which has now been most happily effected through the unyielding perseverance maintained, and the judicious measures you have pursued throughout."

But the real secret of his success lay in great insight into character and great firmness, combined with unselfish concern for the good of those he sought to subdue.

"He spared no pains to establish over his out-lawed friends the power which springs from tested sympathy—not that inspired by awe alone. They found not only that he surpassed them in all they most admired, in all that was most manly, but that he thoroughly understood their ways—that he loved them—that he could and did enter thoroughly into their fears and difficulties, their joys and sorrows. . . No wonder that we hear of his memory still lingering in Khandesh, shrouded by a semi-divine halo. We are told that a few years ago some of his old sepoys happened to light upon an ugly little image. Tracing in it a fancied resemblance to their old commandant, they forthwith set it up and worshipped it as 'Outram Sahib.'"

So he continued till 1835 among the Bheels, doing at several other points much the same work as we have noted in Khandesh and Dang; but, not unnaturally, a desire for a wider field uprose in his mind. After a time he was sent on a special mission to arrange some differences in the Mahi Kanta —a distant portion of Guzerat, far above the Khandesh and the Narbada, of which the Kolees form the most numerous inhabitants—a people nearly allied to the Bheels, and like them warlike and rebellious, though less tall and muscular. The Government proposed to survey the tract, and to conciliate the wild inhabitants in the same manner as had been done in Khandesh.

Outram went to Bombay, where he was married to his cousin, Miss Anderson, attended conferences, and was by-and-by appointed to this work. Sir Robert Grant's excessive desire for peace and conciliatory measures somewhat hampered him; for he knew well that with such people a stern front must be shown first; and we find him asking, in a very characteristic manner, how, after having pardoned and taken under protection the chiefs who shall submit to us, he was to deal with those whom they might have injured. "It will, I presume, be necessary to satisfy all well-founded claims against them, both in justice and to prevent retaliation"—a sentence which indicates not only Outram's political sagacity, but his full sense of justice and rectitude.

These circumstances of restraint on the side of mildness threatened to have led to some difficulty respecting the outlawry and treatment by Outram of one of the Kolee chiefs; but his conduct throughout the difficult work had been so conspicuously masterly that, in spite of the apparent departure from the governor's principles implied in this action, the outlawry of Suraj Mall was not only condoned, but admitted to have been successful in the result. In the same way he acted against Kolee disturbers of local authority at many points, putting them down, bringing harmony and order out of confusion and lawlessness; and there can be no doubt that his intrepidity and resolution did much to prevent a general rising, which there is ample proof was at one time threatened. It is very odd to read the mixed strain of protest and of admiration which runs through the dispatches to him as agent in this province, the one sometimes obtaining ascendancy, sometimes the other; but the worst that could be said was that the sphere was too limited for the worthy display of such remarkable military talents, and his justifications of his policy, as being really the mildest, are as skilfully formed as were his military plans.

"Had any negotiations," he says in one dispatch, "with the Bharwatti been attempted, as suggested, I am convinced that the Thakeer would have continued 'out,' in the hope of ultimately gaining his ends; and had any modification in the terms finally decided on and publicly promulgated by Government have been allowed, it would have encouraged a continuance of the system of the Bharwittaism, which I am convinced it is in our power, as it is our duty, I conceive, to put an end to."

It scarcely needs to be said, however, that in view of the success attained, his sensitive mind chafed at the tone of reprimand which too often showed itself in Government orders. In 1838 he was removed from this post, and attached to the staff of Sir John Keane, at Sinde, as an extra aide-de-camp. Added to his cares in the midst of such a change, he had domestic trials: his wife was in ill-health, and had been compelled to leave India. He was solitary and depressed; he worked harder than ever, however—to such an extent as to forego all but enforced exercise. On the first hint of the Afghan war he was ready with his suggestions, remarking on the weakness of the cavalry in the army destined for Afghanistan, and proposing the enrolment of certain classes of natives, under English officers, for this work. Into the peculiar position of Sinde at this time, and the circumstances that led to the Afghan war, it is impossible for us here to enter; but it must be said that Captain Outram and Lieutenant Eastwick were associated in a mission to the Court of Hyderabad in order to bring the Ameer to a clear understanding with reference to these among various other matters: the necessity of a British military cantonment at Thatta; the part payment by the Ameer of our troops quartered in Sinde. On their way through the town, Outram's eyes were busy taking note of its military capabilities; and whilst he was engaged in a survey of the town he was presented with only too marked proofs that the cordiality of the princes in durbar was not shared by the people or by the Belooch soldiery. Demands for explanation were not met by satisfactory replies, and Outram and Eastwick had to embark without a second interview. Their small detachment of sixty-nine men would have been attacked had it not been that all were kept on the alert. War in this case also was only averted by decisive military demonstrations, by which most the Ameers were brought to a better mind. On returning to Jerak, he found that matters were coming to a crisis in Afghanistan, and he was dispatched on a mission to Macnaghten, then in the camp of Shah Shooja.

To Eastwick he wrote what seems to have some practical application even now :—

"Every day's experience confirms me in the opinion that we should have contented ourselves with securing the line of the Indus alone, without shackling ourselves with the support of an unpopular Emperor of Afghanistan, whom to maintain will cost us at least thirty lakhs annually, besides embroiling us hereafter with all the rude states beyond, which it must perpetually do. We have now stretched out our feelers too far to pull them back, however, and must and will carry our objects, for the *present*, triumphantly; but I cannot blind myself to the embarrassment we are storing up for the future."

And again, to Major Felix, about the same time :—

"For our own safety I think it better we should pass peaceably through Afghanistan and fulfil our mission without hostilities; because once involved in warfare, we should have to continue it under lamentable disadvantages in this country. A blow once struck by us at the Afghans will oblige us to become principals on every occasion hereafter, much to our cost and little to our credit. . . . . You will be surprised that *I* should display so little desire for actual war; but I hope you will give me credit for some discretion, which is as necessary as bravery to a good soldier, and do me the justice to believe that I would weigh well the consequences before plunging into war when hostilities can honourably be avoided. I have well considered every side of this question, and am now satisfied that British bayonets need never be pushed beyond the Hala Mountains for the defence of India; that British armies of any strength could not be supplied or supported for a length of time on this, the Afghan, side of these mountains, and that the natural and impregnable boundary of our empire is the Indus."

But the business of the true soldier is to act and not to argue. When war was entered on Outram was a tower of strength. His conduct at the siege of Ghuznee was heroic; he knew no fear; he faced death as if it had no terror. On the day of arrival before Ghuznee, he more than once conveyed his chief's orders to the troops engaged with, or threatened by, the enemy, after the fire had been opened on both sides. Under Sir J. Keane's instructions he placed guns at a point to the western face of the fortress, with the view to check the escape of the garrison; and he afterwards rode to the eastern wall to make arrangements to intercept the fugitives in that direction. And he led in a masterly manner that expedition through Haji Guk[*] and the Kalu Pass in pursuit of Dost Mahommed, which, though it failed by reason of the duplicity of native guides, was one of the most admirable achievements of the campaign.　　　ALEX. H. JAPP.

* A pass 12,000 feet above the ocean, whence they saw the snow 1,500 feet below them.

(*To be concluded in next part.*)

THE TRUMPET-MAJOR.

By THOMAS HARDY, Author of "Far from the Madding Crowd," etc.

CHAPTER XXV.—FESTUS SHOWS HIS LOVE.

FESTUS DERRIMAN had remained in Weymouth all that day, his horse being sick at stables; but, wishing to coax or bully from his uncle a re-mount for the coming summer, he set off on foot for Overcombe early in the evening. When he drew near to the village, or rather to the Hall, which was a mile from the village, he overtook a slim, quick-eyed woman, sauntering along at a leisurely pace. She was fashionably dressed in a green spencer, with "Mameluke" sleeves, and wore a velvet Spanish hat and feather.

"Good afternoon t'ye, ma'am," said Festus, throwing a sword-and-pistol air into his greeting. "You are out for a walk?"

"I am out for a walk, captain," said the lady, who had criticized him from the crevice of her eye, without seeming to do much more than continue her demure look forward, and gave the title as a sop to his apparent character.

"From Weymouth?—I'd swear it, ma'am; 'pon my honour I would!"

"Yes, I am from Weymouth, sir," said she.

"Ah, you are a visitor! I know every one of the regular inhabitants; we soldiers are in and out there continually. Festus

Derriman, Yeomanry Cavalry, you know. The fact is, the town is under our charge; the folks will be quite dependent upon us for their deliverance in the coming struggle. We hold our lives in our hands, and theirs, I may say, in our pockets. What made you come here, ma'am, at such a critical time?"

"I don't see that it is such a critical time."

"But it is, though; and so you'd say if you was as much mixed up with the military affairs of the nation as some of us."

The lady smiled. "The King is coming this year, anyhow," said she.

"Never!" said Festus firmly. "Ah, you are one of the attendants at court perhaps, come on ahead to get the King's chambers ready, in case Boney should not land?"

"No," she said; "I am connected with the theatre, though not just at the present moment. I have been out of luck for the last year or two; but I have fetched up again. I join the company when they arrive for the season."

Festus surveyed her with interest. "Faith! and is it so? Well, ma'am, what part do you play?"

"I am mostly the leading lady—the heroine," she said, drawing herself up with dignity.

"I'll come and have a look at ye, if all's well, and the landing is put off—hang me if I don't!—Hullo, hullo, what do I see?"

His eyes were stretched towards a distant field, which Anne Garland was at that moment hastily crossing, on her way from the Hall to the village.

"I must be off. Good-day to ye, dear creature!" he exclaimed, hurrying forward.

The lady said, "Oh, you droll monster!" as she smiled and watched him stride ahead.

Festus bounded on over the hedge, across the intervening patch of green, and into the field which Anne was still crossing. In a moment or two she looked back, and seeing who followed felt rather alarmed, though she determined to show no difference in her outward carriage. But to maintain her natural gait was beyond her powers. She spasmodically quickened her pace; fruitlessly, however, for he gained upon her, and when within a few strides of her exclaimed, "Well, my darling!" Anne started off at a run.

Festus was already out of breath, and soon

xXI—36

found that he was not likely to overtake her. On she went, without turning her head, till an unusual noise behind compelled her to look round. His face was in the act of falling back ; he swerved on one side, and dropped, like a log upon a convenient hedgerow-bank which bordered the path. There he lay quite still.

Anne was somewhat alarmed; and after standing at gaze for two or three minutes, drew nearer to him, a step and a half at a time, wondering and doubting, as a meek ewe draws near to some strolling vagabond who flings himself on the grass near the flock.

"He is in a swoon!" she murmured.

Her heart beat quickly, and she looked around. Nobody was in sight; she advanced a step nearer still and observed him again. Apparently his face was turning to a livid hue, and his breathing had become obstructed.

"'Tis not a swoon; 'tis apoplexy!" she said, in deep distress. "I ought to untie his neck." But she was afraid to do this, and only drew a little closer still.

Miss Garland was now within three feet of him, whereupon the senseless man, who could hold his breath no longer, sprang to his feet and darted at her, saying, "Ha ha ! a scheme for a kiss !"

She felt his arm slipping round her neck ; but, twirling about on her own axis with amazing dexterity, she wriggled from his embrace and ran away along the field. The force with which she had extricated herself was sufficient to throw Festus upon the grass, and by the time that he got upon his legs again she was many yards off. Uttering a word which was not a blessing, he immediately gave chase; and thus they ran till Anne entered a meadow divided down the middle by a brook about six feet wide. A narrow plank was thrown loosely across at the point where the path traversed this stream, and when Anne reached it she at once scampered over. At the other side she turned her head to gather the probabilities of the situation; which were that Festus Derriman would overtake her even now. By a sudden forethought she stooped, seized the end of the plank, and endeavoured to drag it away from the opposite bank. But the weight was too great for her to do more than slightly move it, and with a desperate sigh she ran on again, having lost many valuable seconds.

But her attempt, though ineffectual in dragging it down, had been enough to unsettle the little bridge ; and when Derriman

reached the middle, which he did half a minute later, the plank turned over on its edge, tilting him bodily into the river. The water was not remarkably deep, but as the yeoman fell flat on his stomach he was completely immersed; and it was some time before he could drag himself out. When he arose, dripping on the bank, and looked round, Anne had vanished from the mead. Then Festus's eyes glowed like carbuncles and he gave voice to fearful imprecations, shaking his fist in the soft summer air towards Anne, in a way that was terrible for any maiden to behold. Wading back through the stream, he walked along its bank with a heavy tread, the water running from his coat-tails, wrists, and the tips of his ears, in silvery dribbles, that sparkled pleasantly in the sun. Thus he hastened away, and went round by a by-path to the Hall.

Meanwhile the author of his troubles was rapidly drawing nearer to the mill, and soon, to her inexpressible delight, she saw Bob coming to meet her. She had heard the flounce, and feeling more secure from her pursuer, had dropped her pace to a quick walk. No sooner did she reach Bob than, overcome by the excitement of the moment, she flung herself into his arms. Bob instantly enclosed her in an embrace so very thorough that there was no possible danger of her falling, whatever degree of exhaustion might have given rise to her somewhat unexpected action ; and in this attitude they silently remained, till it was borne in upon Anne that the present was the first time in her life that she had ever been in such a position. Her face then burnt like a sunset, and she did not know how to look up at him. Feeling at length quite safe, she suddenly resolved not to give way to her first impulse to tell him the whole of what had happened, lest there should be a dreadful quarrel and fight between Bob and the yeoman, and great difficulties caused in the Loveday family on her account, the miller having important wheat transactions with the Derrimans.

"You seem frightened, dearest Anne," said Bob tenderly.

"Yes," she replied. "I saw a man I did not like the look of, and he was inclined to follow me. But, worse than that, I am troubled about the French. O Bob ! I am afraid you will be killed, and my mother, and John, and your father, and all of us hunted down !"

"Now I have told you, dear little heart, that it cannot be. We shall drive 'em into the sea after a battle or two, even if they land,

"With a desperate rush she ran on again."

Page 301.

which I don't believe they will. We've got ninety sail of the line, and though it is rather unfortunate that we should have declared war against Spain at this ticklish time, there's enough for all." And Bob went into elaborate statistics of the navy, army, militia, and volunteers, to prolong the time of holding her. When he had done speaking he drew rather a heavy sigh.

"What's the matter, Bob?"

"I haven't been yet to offer myself as a sea-fencible, and I ought to have done it long ago!"

"You are only one. Surely they can do without you?"

Bob shook his head. She arose from her restful position, her eye catching his with a shamefaced expression of having given way at last. Loveday drew from his pocket a paper,' and said, as they slowly walked on, "Here's something to make us brave and patriotic.. I bought it in Weymouth. Is it not a stirring picture?"

It was a hieroglyphic profile of Napoleon. The hat represented a maimed French eagle; the face was ingeniously made up of human carcasses, knotted and writhing together in such directions as to form a physiognomy; a band, or stock, shaped to resemble the English Channel, encircled his throat, and seemed to choke him; his epaulette was a hand tearing a cobweb that represented the treaty of peace with England; and his ear was a woman crouching over a dying child.

"It is dreadful!" said Anne. "I don't like to see it."

She had recovered from her emotion, and walked along beside him with a grave, subdued face. Bob did not like to assume the privileges of an accepted lover and draw her hand through his arm; for, conscious that she naturally belonged to a politer grade than his own, he feared lest her exhibition of tenderness were an impulse which cooler moments might regret. A perfect Paul-and-Virginia life had not absolutely set in for him as yet, and it was not to be hastened by force. When they had passed over the bridge into the mill-front they saw the miller standing at the door with a face of concern.

"Since you have been gone," he said, "a Government man has been here, and to all the houses, taking down the numbers of the women and children, and their ages, and the number of horses and waggons that can be mustered, in case they have to retreat inland, out of the way of the invading army."

The little family gathered themselves together, all feeling the crisis more seriously'

than they liked to express. Mrs. Loveday thought how ridiculous a thing social ambition was in such a conjuncture as this, and vowed that she would leave Anne to love where she would. Anne, too, forgot the little peculiarities of speech and manner in Bob and his father, which sometimes jarred for a moment upon her more refined sense, and was thankful for their love and protection in this looming trouble.

On going up-stairs she remembered the paper which Farmer Derriman had given her, and searched in her bosom for it. She could not find it there. "I must have left it on the table," she said to herself. It did not matter; she remembered every word. She took a pen and wrote a duplicate, which she put safely away.

But it turned out that Anne was wrong in her supposition. She had, after all, placed the paper where she supposed, and there it ought to have been. But in escaping from Festus, when he feigned apoplexy, it had fallen out upon the grass. Five minutes after that event, when pursuer and pursued were two or three fields ahead, the gaily dressed woman whom the yeoman had overtaken peeped cautiously through the stile into the corner of the field which had been the scene of the scramble; and seeing the paper she climbed over, secured it, loosened the wafer without tearing the sheet, and read the memorandum within. Being unable to make anything of its meaning, the saunterer put it in her pocket, and, dismissing the matter from her mind, went on by the by-path which led to the back of the mill. Here, behind the hedge, she stood and surveyed the old building for some time, after which she meditatively turned and retraced her steps towards Weymouth.

CHAPTER XXVI.—THE ALARM.

WE pass on to a historic and memorable May night in this year 1805, when Mrs. Loveday was awakened by the boom of a distant gun. She told the miller, and they listened awhile. The sound was not repeated, but such was the state of their feelings that Mr. Loveday went to Bob's room and asked if he had heard it. Bob was wide awake, looking out of the window; he had heard the ominous sound, and was inclined to investigate the matter. While the father and son were dressing they fancied that a glare seemed to be rising in the sky in the direction of the beacon hill. Not wishing to alarm Anne and her mother, the miller assured them that Bob and himself were merely going out of doors to inquire into the cause of the report, after which they plunged into the gloom together. A few steps' progress opened up more of the sky, which, as they had thought, was indeed irradiated by a lurid light; but whether it came from the beacon or from a more distant point they were unable to clearly tell. They pushed on rapidly towards higher ground.

Their excitement was merely of a piece with that of all men at this critical juncture. Everywhere expectation was at fever heat. For the last year or two only five-and-twenty miles of shallow water had divided quiet English homesteads from an enemy's army of a hundred and fifty thousand men. We had taken the matter lightly enough, eating and drinking as in the days of Noe, and singing satires without end. We punned on Buonaparte and his gunboats, chalked his effigy on stage-coaches, and published the same in prints. Still, between these bursts of hilarity, it was sometimes recollected that England was the only European country which had not succumbed to the mighty little man who was less than human in feeling, and more than human in will; that our spirit for resistance was greater than our strength; and that the Channel was often calm. Boats built of wood which was greenly growing in its native forest three days before it was bent as wales to their sides, were ridiculous enough; but they might be, after all, sufficient for a single trip between two visible shores.

The English watched Buonaparte in these preparations, and Buonaparte watched the English. At the distance of Boulogne details were lost, but we were impressed on fine days by the novel sight of a huge army moving and twinkling like a school of mackerel under the rays of the sun. The regular way of passing an afternoon in the coast towns was to stroll up to the signal posts and chat with the lieutenant on duty there about the latest inimical object seen at sea. About once a week there appeared in the newspapers either a paragraph concerning some adventurous English gentleman who had sailed out in a pleasure-boat till he lay near enough to Boulogne to see Buonaparte standing on the heights among his marshals; or else some lines about a mysterious stranger with a foreign accent, who, after collecting a vast deal of information on our resources, had hired a boat at a southern port, and vanished with it towards France before his intention could be divined.

In forecasting his grand venture, Buona-parte postulated the help of Providence to a remarkable degree. Just at the hour when his troops were on board the flat-bottomed boats and ready to sail, there was to be a great fog, that should spread a vast obscurity over the length and breadth of the Channel, and keep the English blind to events on the other side. The fog was to last twenty-four hours, after which it might clear away. A dead calm was to prevail simultaneously with the fog, with the twofold object of affording the boats easy transit and dooming our ships to lie motionless. Thirdly, there was to be a spring tide, which should combine its manœuvres with those of the fog and calm.

Among the many thousands of minor Englishmen whose lives were affected by these tremendous designs may be numbered our old acquaintance Corporal Tullidge, who sported the crushed arm, and poor old Simon Burden, the dazed veteran who had fought at Minden. Instead of sitting comfortably in the settle of The Duke of York, at Overcombe, they were obliged to keep watch on the hill. They made themselves as comfortable as was possible under the circumstances, dwelling in a hut of clods and turf, with a brick chimney for cooking. Here they observed the nightly progress of the moon and stars, grew familiar with the heaving of moles, the dancing of rabbits on the hillocks, the distant hoot of owls, the bark of foxes from woods farther inland; but saw not a sign of the enemy. As, night after night, they walked round the two ricks which it was their duty to fire at a signal—one being of furze for a quick flame, the other of turf, for a long, slow radiance—they thought and talked of old times, and drank patriotically from a large wood flagon that was filled every day.

Bob and his father soon became aware that the light was from the beacon. By the time that they reached the top it was one mass of towering flame, from which the sparks fell on the green herbage like a fiery dew; the forms of the two old men being seen passing and repassing in the midst of it. The Lovedays, who came up on the smoky side, regarded the scene for a moment, and then emerged into the light.

"Who goes there?" said Corporal Tullidge, shouldering a pike with his sound arm. "Oh, 'tis neighbour Loveday!"

"Did you get your signal to fire it from the east?" said the miller hastily.

"No; from Abbotsbury Beach."

"But you are not to go by a coast signal!"

"Chok' it all, wasn't the Lord Lieutenant's

direction, whenever you see Reignbarrows Beacon burn to the nor'east'ard, or Eggerdon to the nor'west'ard, or the actual presence of the enemy on the shore?"

"But is he here?"

"No doubt o't! The beach light is only just gone down, and Simon heard the guns even better than I."

"Hark, hark! I hear 'em!" said Bob.

They listened with parted lips, the night wind blowing through Simon Burden's few teeth as through the ruins of Stonehenge. From far down on the lower levels came the noise of wheels and the tramp of horses upon the turnpike road.

"Well, there must be something in it," said Miller Loveday gravely. "Bob, we'll go home and make the women-folk safe, and then I'll don my soldier's clothes and be off. God knows where our company will assemble."

They hastened down the hill, and on getting into the road waited and listened again. Travellers began to come up and pass them in vehicles of all descriptions. It was difficult to attract their attention in the dim light, but by standing on the top of a wall which fenced the road Bob was at last seen.

"What's the matter?" he cried to a butcher who was flying past in his cart, his wife sitting behind him without a bonnet.

"The French have landed," said the man, without drawing rein.

"Where?" shouted Bob.

"In West Bay; and all Weymouth is in uproar," replied the voice, now faint in the distance.

Bob and his father hastened on till they reached their own house. As they had expected, Anne and her mother, in common with most of the people, were both dressed, and stood at the door bonneted and shawled, listening to the traffic on the neighbouring highway, Mrs. Loveday having secured what money and small valuables they possessed in a huge pocket which extended all round her waist, and added considerably to her weight and diameter.

"'Tis true enough," said the miller: "he's come. You and Anne and the maid must be off to Cousin Jim's at Bere, and when you get there you must do as they do. I must assemble with the company."

"And I?" said Bob.

"Thou'st better run to the church, and take a pike before they be all gone."

The horse was put into the gig, and Mrs. Loveday, Anne, and the servant-maid were hastily packed into the vehicle, the latter taking the reins; David's duties as a fighting-man forbidding all thought of his domestic offices now. Then the silver tankard, tea-pot, pair of candlesticks like Ionic columns, and other articles too large to be pocketed were thrown into a basket and put up behind. Then came the leave-taking, which was as sad as it was hurried. Bob kissed Anne, and there was no affectation in her receiving that mark of affection as she said through her tears, "God bless you." At last they moved off in the dim light of dawn, neither of the three women knowing which road they were to take, but trusting to chance to find it.

As soon as they were out of sight Bob went off for a pike, and his father, first new-flinting his firelock, proceeded to don his uniform, pipe-claying his breeches with such cursory haste as to bespatter his black-gaiters with the same ornamental compound. Finding when he was ready that no bugle had as yet sounded, he went with David to the cart-house, dragged out the waggon, and put therein some of the most useful and easily-handled goods, in case there might be an opportunity for conveying them away. By the time this was done and the waggon pushed back and locked, Bob had returned with his weapon, somewhat mortified at being doomed to this low form of defence. The miller gave his son a parting grasp of the hand, and arranged to meet him at Bere at the first opportunity if the news were true; if happily false, here at their own house.

"Bother it all!" he exclaimed, looking at his stock of flints.

"What?" said Bob.

"I have got no ammunition: not a round!"

"Then what's the use of going?" asked his son.

The miller paused. "Oh, I'll go," he said. "Perhaps somebody will lend me a little if I get into a hot corner."

The bugle had been blown ere this, and Loveday the father disappeared towards the place of assembly, his empty cartridge-box behind him. Bob seized a brace of loaded pistols which he had brought home from the ship, and, armed with these and the pike, he locked the door and sallied out again towards the turnpike road.

By this time the yeomanry of the district were also on the move, and among them Festus Derriman, who was sleeping at his uncle's, and had been awakened by Cripple-straw. About the time when Bob and his father were descending from the beacon the stalwart yeoman was standing in the stable-yard adjusting his straps, while Cripplestraw saddled the horse. Festus clanked up and down, looked gloomily at the beacon, heard the retreating carts and carriages, and called Cripplestraw to him, who came from the stable leading the horse at the same moment that Uncle Benjy peeped unobserved from an oriel window above their heads, the light of the beacon fire touching up his features to the complexion of an old brass clock-face.

"I think that before I start, Cripplestraw," said Festus, whose lurid visage was undergoing a bleaching process curious to look upon, "you shall go on to Weymouth, and make a bold inquiry whether the cowardly enemy is on shore as yet, or only looming in the bay."

"I'd go in a moment, sir," said the other, "if I hadn't my bad leg again. I should have joined my company afore this; but they said at last drill that I was too old. So I shall wait up in the hay-loft for tidings as soon as I have packed you off, poor gentleman!"

"Do such alarms as these, Cripplestraw, ever happen without foundation? Buonaparte is a wretch, a miserable wretch, and this may only be a false alarm to disappoint such as me."

"Oh no, sir; oh no."

"But sometimes there are false alarms."

"Well, sir, yes. There was a pretended sally of gun-boats last year."

"And was there nothing else pretended—something more like this, for instance?"

Cripplestraw shook his head. "I notice yer modesty, Mr. Festus, in making light of things. But there never was, sir. You may depend upon it he's come. Thank God, my duty as a Local don't require me to go to the front, but only the valiant men like my master. Ah, if Boney could only see ye now, sir, he'd know too well that there is nothing to be got from such a determined, skilful officer but blows and musket-balls."

"Yes, yes—— Cripplestraw, if I ride off to Weymouth and meet 'em, all my training will be lost. No skill is required as a forlorn hope."

"True; that's a point, sir. You would outshine 'em all, and be picked off at the very beginning as a too-dangerous brave man."

"But if I stay here and urge on the fainthearted ones, or get up into the turret-stair by that gateway, and pop at the invaders through the loophole, I shouldn't be so completely wasted, should I?"

"You would not, Mr. Derriman. But, as you were going to say next, the fire in yer veins won't let ye do that. You are valiant; very good: you don't want to husband yer valiance at home. The thing is plain."

"If my birth had been more obscure," murmured the yeoman, "and I had only been in the militia, for instance, or among the humble pikemen, so much wouldn't have been expected of me—of my fiery nature—— Cripplestraw, is there a drop of brandy to be got at in the house? I don't feel very well."

"Dear nephew," said the old gentleman from above, whom neither of the others had as yet noticed, "I haven't any spirits opened—so unfortunate! But there's a beautiful barrel of crab-apple cider in draught; and there's some cold tea from last night."

"What, is he listening?" said Festus, staring up. "Now I warrant how glad he is to see me forced to go—called out of bed without breakfast, and he quite safe, and sure to escape because he's an old man!—— Cripplestraw, I like being in the yeomanry cavalry; but I wish I hadn't been in the ranks; I wish I had been only the surgeon, to stay in the rear while the bodies are brought back to him—I mean, I should have thrown my heart at such a time as this more into the labour of restoring wounded men and joining their shattered limbs together—u-u-ugh!—more than I can into causing the wounds—— I am too humane, Cripplestraw, for the ranks!"

"Yes, yes," said his companion, depressing his spirits to a kindred level. "And yet, such is fate, that, instead of joining men's limbs together, you'll have to get your own joined—poor young soldier!—all through having such a warlike soul."

"Yes," murmured Festus, and paused. "You can't think how strange I feel here. Cripplestraw," he continued, laying his hand upon the centre buttons of his waistcoat. "How I do wish I was only the surgeon!"

He slowly mounted, and Uncle Benjy, in the meantime, sang to himself as he looked on, "Twenty-three and half from N.W. Sixteen and three-quarters from N.E."

"What's that old mummy singing?" said Festus savagely.

"Only a hymn for preservation from our enemies, dear nephew," meekly replied the farmer, who had heard the remark. "Twenty-three and half from N.W."

Festus allowed his horse to move on a few paces, and then turned again, as if struck by a happy invention. "Cripplestraw," he began, with an artificial laugh, "I am obliged to confess, after all—I must see her! 'Tisn't nature that makes me draw back—'tis love. I must go and look for her."

"A woman, sir?"

"I didn't want to confess it; but 'tis a woman. Strange that I should be drawn so entirely against my natural wish to rush at 'em!"

Cripplestraw, seeing which way the wind blew, found it advisable to blow in harmony. "Ah, now at last I see, sir! Spite that few men live that be worthy to command ye; spite that you could rush on, marshal the troops to victory, as I may say; but then—what of it?—there's the unhappy fate of being smit with the eyes of a woman, and you are unmanned—— Maister Derriman, who is himself when he's got a woman round his neck like a millstone?"

"It is something like that."

"I feel the case. Be you valiant?—I know, of course, the words being a matter of form — be you valiant, I ask? Yes, of course. Then don't you waste it in the open field. Hoard it up, I say, sir, for a higher class of war—the defence of yer adorable lady. Think what you owe her at this terrible time! Now, Maister Derriman, once more I ask ye to cast off that first haughty wish to rush to Weymouth, and to go where your mis'ess is defenceless and alone."

"I will, Cripplestraw, now you put it like that!"

"Thank ye, thank ye heartily, Maister Derriman. Go now, and hide with her."

"But can I? Now, hang flattery!—can a man hide without a stain? Of course I would not hide in any mean sense; no, not I!"

"If you be in love, 'tis plain you may, since it is not your own life, but another's, that you are concerned for, and you only save your own because it can't be helped."

"'Tis true, Cripplestraw, in a sense. But will it be understood that way? Will they see it as a brave hiding?"

"Now, sir, if you had not been in love I own to ye that hiding would look queer, but being to save the tears, groans, fits, swowndings, and perhaps death of a comely young woman, yer principle is good; you honourably retreat because you be too gallant to advance. This sounds strange, ye may say, sir; but it is plain enough to less fiery minds."

Festus did for a moment try to uncover his teeth in a natural smile, but it died away. "Cripplestraw, you flatter me; or do you mean it? Well, there's truth in it. I am more gallant in going to her than in march-

ing to the shore. But we cannot be too careful about our good names, we soldiers. I must not be seen. I'm off."

Cripplestraw opened the hurdle which closed the arch under the portico gateway, and Festus passed under, Uncle Benjamin singing, *Twen-ty-three and a half from N.W.* with a sort of sublime ecstasy, feeling, as Festus had observed, that his money was safe, and that the French would not personally molest an old man in such a ragged, mildewed coat as that he wore, which he had taken the precaution to borrow from a scarecrow in one of his fields for the purpose.

Festus rode on full of his intention to seek out Anne, and under cover of protecting her retreat accompany her to Bere, where he knew the Lovedays had relatives. In the lane he met Granny Seamore, who, having packed up all her possessions in a small basket, was placidly retreating to the mountains till all should be over.

"Well, Granny, have ye seen the French?" asked Festus.

"No," she said, looking up at him through her brazen spectacles. "If I had I shouldn't ha' seed thee!"

"Faugh!" replied the yeoman, and rode on. Just as he reached the old road, which he had intended merely to cross and avoid, his countenance fell. Some troops of regulars, who appeared to be dragoons, were rattling along the road. Festus hastened towards an opposite gate, so as to get within the field before they should see him; but, as ill-luck would have it, as soon as he got inside, a party of six or seven of his own yeomanry troop were straggling across the same field and making for the spot where he was. The dragoons passed without seeing him; but when he turned out into the road again it was impossible to retreat towards Overcombe village because of the yeomen. So he rode straight on, and heard them coming at his heels. There was no other gate, and the highway soon became as straight as a bow-string. Unable thus to turn without meeting them, and caught like an eel in a water-pipe, Festus drew nearer and nearer to the fateful shore. But he did not relinquish hope. Just ahead there were cross-roads, and he might have a chance of slipping down one of them without being seen. On reaching this spot he found that he was not alone. A horseman had come up the right-hand lane and drawn rein. It was an officer of the German legion, and seeing Festus he held up his hand. Festus rode up to him and saluted.

"It ist false report!" said the officer.

Festus was a man again. He felt that nothing was too much for him. The officer, after some explanation of the cause of alarm, said that he was going across to the road which led by Lodmoor, to stop the troops and volunteers converging from that direction, upon which Festus offered to give information along the Broadway road. The German crossed over, and was soon out of sight in the lane, while Festus turned back upon the way by which he had come. The party of yeomanry cavalry was rapidly drawing near, and he soon recognised among them the excited voices of Stubb of Duddle Hole, Noakes of Muckleford, and other comrades of his orgies at the Hall. It was a magnificent opportunity, and Festus drew his sword. When they were within speaking distance he reined round his charger's head to Weymouth and shouted, " On, comrades, on ! I am waiting for you. You have been a long time getting up with me, seeing the glorious nature of our deeds to-day."

" Well said, Derriman, well said," replied the foremost of the riders. " Have you heard anything new ? "

" Only that he's here with his tens of thousands, and that we are to ride to meet him sword in hand as soon as we have assembled in Weymouth."

" O Lord ! " said Noakes, with a slight falling of the lower jaw.

" The man who quails now is unworthy of the name of yeoman," said Festus, still keeping ahead of the other troopers and holding up his sword to the sun. " Oh, Noakes, fye, fye ! You begin to look pale, man."

" Faith, perhaps you'd look pale," said Noakes with an envious glance upon Festus's daring manner, " if you had a wife and family depending upon ye."

" I'll take three frog-eating Frenchmen single-handed ! " rejoined Derriman, still flourishing his sword.

" They have as good swords as you ; as you will soon find," said another of the yeomen.

" If they were three times armed," said Festus—" ay, thrice three times — I would attempt 'em three to one. How do you feel now, my old friend Stubb ? " (turning to another of the warriors). " Oh, friend Stubb ! no bouncing healths to our lady-loves in Overcombe Hall this summer as last. Eh, Brownjohn ? "

" I am afraid not," said Brownjohn gloomily.

" No rattling dinners at Stacie's Hotel,

and the King below with his staff. No wrenching off door-knockers and sending 'em to the bakehouse in a pie that nobody calls for. Weeks of cut-and-thrust work rather ! "

" I suppose so."

" Fight how we may we shan't get rid of the cursed tyrant before autumn, and many thousand brave men will lie low before it's done," remarked a young yeoman with a calm face, who meant to do his duty without much talking.

" No grinning matches at Maiden Castle this summer," Festus resumed ; " no thread-the-needle at Greenhill Fair, and going into shows and driving the showman crazy with cock-a-doodle-doo ! "

" I suppose not."

" Does it make you seem just a trifle uncomfortable, Noakes ? Keep up your spirits, old comrade. Come, forward ! we are only ambling on like so many donkey-women. We have to get into Weymouth, join the rest of the troop, and then march Abbotsbury way, as I imagine. At this rate we shan't be well into the thick of battle before twelve o'clock. Spur on, comrades. No dancing on the green, Lockham, this year in the moonlight ! You was tender upon that girl ; gad, what will become o' her in the struggle ? "

" Come, come, Derriman," expostulated Lockham — " this is all very well, but I don't care for 't. I am as ready to fight as any man, but——"

" Perhaps when you get into battle, Derriman, and see what it's like, your courage will cool down a little," added Noakes on the same side, but with secret admiration of Festus's reckless bravery.

" I shall be bayoneted first," said Festus. " Now let's rally, and on."

Since Festus was determined to spur on wildly, the rest of the yeomen did not like to seem behindhand, and they rapidly approached the town. Had they been calm enough to reflect, they might have observed that for the last half hour no carts or carriages had met them on the way, as they had done farther back. It was not till the troopers reached the turnpike that they learnt what Festus had known a quarter of an hour before. At the intelligence Derriman sheathed his sword with a sigh ; and the party soon fell in with comrades who had arrived there before them, whereupon the source and details of the alarm were boisterously discussed.

" What, didn't you know of the mistake

"Ha, young madam! Now you are caught!"

till now?" asked one of these of the new-comers. "Why, when I was dropping over the hill by the cross-roads I looked back and saw that man talking to the messenger, and he must have told him the truth." The speaker pointed to Festus. They turned their indignant eyes full upon him. That he had sported with their deepest feelings, while knowing the rumour to be baseless, was soon apparent to all.

"Beat him black and blue with the flat of our blades!" shouted two or three, turning their horses' heads to drop back upon Derriman, in which move they were followed by most of the party.

But Festus, foreseeing danger from the un-expected revelation, had already judiciously placed a few intervening yards between him-self and his fellow yeomen, and now, clap-ping spurs to his horse, rattled like thunder and lightning up the road homeward. His ready flight added hotness to their pursuit, and as he rode and looked fearfully over his shoulder he could see them following with enraged faces and drawn swords, a position which they kept up for a distance of more than a mile. Then he had the satisfaction of seeing them drop off one by one, and soon he and his panting charger remained alone on the highway.

CHAPTER XXVII.—DANGER TO ANNE.

HE stopped and reflected how to turn this rebuff to advantage. Baulked in his project of entering Weymouth and enjoying congratulations upon his patriotic bearing during the advance, he sulkily considered that he might be able to make some use of his enforced retirement by riding to Overcombe and glorifying himself in the eyes of Miss Garland before the truth should have reached that hamlet. Having thus decided he spurred on in a better mood.

By this time the volunteers were on the march, and as Derriman ascended the road he met the Overcombe company, in which trudged Miller Loveday shoulder to shoulder with the other substantial householders of the place and its neighbourhood, duly equipped with pouches, cross-belts, firelocks, flint-boxes, pickers, worms, magazines, priming-horns, heel-ball, and pomatum. There was nothing to be gained by further suppression of the truth, and briefly informing them that the danger was not so immediate as had been supposed, Festus galloped on. At the end of another mile he met a large number of pikemen, including Bob Loveday, whom the yeoman resolved to sound upon the whereabouts of Anne. The circumstances were such as to lead Bob to speak more frankly than he might have done on reflection, and he told Festus the direction in which the women had been sent. Then Festus informed the group that the report of invasion was false, upon which they all turned to go homeward with greatly relieved spirits.

Bob walked beside Derriman's horse for some distance. Loveday had instantly made up his mind to go and look for the women, and ease their anxiety by letting them know the good news as soon as possible. But he said nothing of this to Festus during their return together; nor did Festus tell Bob that he also had resolved to seek them out, and by anticipating every one else in that enterprise, make of it a glorious opportunity for bringing Miss Garland to her senses about him. He still resented the ducking that he had received at her hands, and was not disposed to let that insult pass without obtaining some sort of sweet revenge.

As soon as they had parted Festus cantered on over the hill, meeting on his way the Puddletown volunteers, sixty rank and file, under Captain Cunningham; the Dorchester company, ninety strong (known as the "Consideration Company" in those days), under Captain Strickland; and others—all with anxious faces and covered with dust. Just passing the word to them and leaving them at halt, he proceeded rapidly onward in the direction of Bere. Nobody appeared on the road for some time, till after a ride of several miles he met a stray corporal of volunteers, who told Festus in answer to his inquiry that he had certainly passed no gig full of women of the kind described. Believing that he had missed them by following the highway, Derriman turned back into a lane along which they might have chosen to journey for privacy's sake, notwithstanding the badness and uncertainty of its track. Arriving again within five miles of Overcombe, he at length heard tidings of the wandering vehicle and, its precious burden, which, like the ark when sent away from the country of the Philistines, had apparently been left to the instincts of the beast that drew it. A labouring man, just at daybreak, had seen the helpless party going slowly up a distant drive, which he pointed out.

No sooner had Festus parted from this informant than he beheld Bob approaching, mounted on the miller's second and heavier horse. Bob looked rather surprised, and Festus felt his coming glory in danger.

"They went down that lane," he said, signifying precisely the opposite direction to the true one. "I, too, have been on the look out for missing friends."

As Festus was riding back there was no reason to doubt his information, and Loveday rode on as misdirected. Immediately that he was out of sight Festus reversed his course, and followed the track which Anne and her companions were last seen to pursue.

This road had been ascended by the gig in question nearly two hours before the present moment. Molly, the servant, held the reins, Mrs. Loveday sat beside her, and Anne behind. Their progress was but slow, owing partly to Molly's want of skill, and partly to the steepness of the road, which here passed over downs of some extent, and was rarely or never mended. It was an anxious morning for them all, and the beauties of the early summer day fell upon unheeding eyes. They were too anxious even for conjecture, and each sat thinking her own thoughts, occasionally glancing westward, or stopping the horse to listen to sounds from more frequented roads along which other parties were retreating. Once, while they listened and gazed thus, they saw a glittering in the distance, and heard the tramp of many horses. It was a large body of cavalry going in the direction of Weymouth, the same regiment of dragoons, in fact, which Festus had seen farther on in its course. The women in the gig had no doubt that these men were marching at once to engage the enemy. By way of varying the monotony of the journey, Molly occasionally burst into tears of horror, believing Buonaparte to be in countenance and habits precisely what the caricatures represented him. Mrs. Loveday endeavoured to establish cheerfulness by assuring her companions of the natural civility of the French nation, with whom unprotected women were safe from injury, unless through the casual excesses of soldiery beyond control. This was poor consolation to Anne, whose mind was more occupied with Bob than with herself, and a miserable fear that she would never again see him alive so paled her face and saddened her gaze forward, that at last her mother said, "Who was you thinking of, my dear?" Anne's only reply was a look at her mother, with which a tear mingled.

Molly whipped the horse, by which she quickened his pace for five yards, when he again fell into the perverse slowness that showed how fully conscious he was of being the master-mind and head individual of the four. Whenever there was a pool of water by the road he turned aside to drink a mouthful, and remained there his own time in spite of Molly's tug at the reins and futile fly-flapping on his buttocks. They were now in the chalk district, where there were no hedges, and a rough attempt at mending the way had been made by throwing down huge lumps of that glaring material in heaps, without troubling to spread it or break them abroad. The jolting here was most distressing, and seemed about to snap the springs.

"How that wheel do waddle," said Molly at last. She had scarcely spoken when the wheel came off, and all three were precipitated over it into the road.

Fortunately the horse stood still, and they began to gather themselves up. The only one of the three who had suffered in the least from the fall was Anne, and she was only conscious of a severe shaking which had half stupefied her for the time. The wheel lay flat in the road, so that there was no possibility of driving farther in their present plight. They looked around for help. The only friendly object near was a lonely cottage, from its situation evidently the home of a shepherd.

The horse was unharnessed and tied to the back of the gig, and the three women went across to the house. On getting close they found that the shutters of all the lower windows were closed, but on trying the door it opened to the hand. Nobody was within; the house appeared to have been abandoned in some confusion, and the probability was that the shepherd had fled on hearing the alarm. Anne now said that she felt the effects of her fall too severely to be able to go any farther just then, and it was agreed that she should be left there while Mrs. Loveday and Molly went on for assistance, the elder lady deeming Molly too young and vacant-minded to be trusted to go alone. Molly suggested taking the horse, as the distance might be great, each of them sitting alternately on his back while the other led him by the head. This they did, Anne watching them vanish down the white and lumpy road.

She then looked round the room, as well as she could do so by the light from the open door. It was plain, from the shutters being closed, that the shepherd had left his house before daylight, the candle and extinguisher on the table pointing to the same conclusion. Here she remained, her eyes occasionally sweeping the bare, sunny expanse of down, that was only relieved from absolute emptiness by the overturned gig hard by. The sheep seemed to have gone away, and scarcely a bird flew across to disturb the solitude. Anne had risen early that morning, and leaning back in the withy chair, which she had placed by the door, she soon fell into an uneasy doze, from which she was awakened by the distant tramp of a horse. Feeling much recovered from the effects of the overturn, she eagerly rose and looked out. The horse was not Miller Loveday's, but a powerful bay, bearing a man in full yeomanry uniform.

Anne did not wait to recognise further; instantly re-entering the house, she shut the door and bolted it. In the dark she sat and listened: not a sound. At the end of ten minutes, thinking that the rider if he were not Festus had carelessly passed by, or that if he were Festus he had not seen her, she crept softly up-stairs and peeped out of the window. Excepting the spot of shade, formed by the gig as before, the down was quite bare. She then opened the casement and stretched out her neck.

"Ha, young madam! There you are! I knew ye! Now you are caught!" came like a clap of thunder from a point three or four feet beneath her, and turning down her frightened eyes she beheld Festus Derriman lurking close to the wall. His attention had first been attracted by her shutting the door of the cottage; then by the overturned gig; and after making sure, by examining the vehicle, that he was not mistaken in her identity, he had dismounted, led his horse round to the side, and crept up to entrap her.

Anne started back into the room, and remained still as a stone. Festus went on—"Come, you must trust to me. The French have landed. I have been trying to meet with you every hour since that confounded trick you played me. You threw me into the water. Faith, it was well for you I didn't catch ye then! I should have taken a revenge in a better way than I shall now. I mean to have that kiss only. Come, Miss Nancy; do you hear?—'Tis no use for you to lurk inside there. You'll have to turn out as soon as Boney comes over the hill.—Are you going to open the door, I say, and speak to me in a civil way? What do you think I am, then, that you should barricade yourself against me as if I was a wild beast or Frenchman? Open the door, or put out your head, or do something; or 'pon my soul I'll break in the door!"

It occurred to Anne at this point of the tirade that the best policy would be to temporise till somebody should return, and she put out her head and face, now grown somewhat pale.

"That's better," said Festus. "Now I can talk to you. Come, my dear, will you open the door? Why should you be afraid of me?"

"I am not altogether afraid of you; I am safe from the French here," said Anne, not very truthfully, and anxiously casting her eyes over the vacant down.

"Then let me tell you that the alarm is false, and that no landing has been attempted. Now will you open the door and let me in? I am tired. I have been on horseback ever since daylight, and have come to bring you the good tidings."

Anne looked as if she doubted the news.

"Come," said Festus.

"No, I cannot let you in," she murmured after a pause.

"Dash my wig, then," he cried, his face flaming up, "I'll find a way to get in! Now, don't you provoke me! You don't know what I am capable of. I ask you again, will you open the door?"

"Why do you wish it," she said faintly.

"I have told you I want to sit down; and I want to ask you a question."

"You can ask me from where you are."

"I cannot ask you properly. It is about a serious matter: whether you will accept my heart and hand. I am not going to throw myself at your feet; but I ask you to do your duty as a woman, namely, give your solemn word to take my name as soon as the war is over and I have time to attend to you. I scorn to ask it of a haughty hussy who will only speak to me through a window; however, I put it to you for the last time, madam."

There was no sign on the down of anybody's return, and she said, "I'll think of it, sir."

"You have thought of it long enough; I want to know. Will you or won't you?"

"Very well; I think I will." And then she felt that she might be buying personal safety too dearly by shuffling thus, since he would spread the report that she had accepted him, and cause endless complication. "No," she said, "I have changed my mind. I cannot accept you, Mr. Derriman."

"That's how you play with me!" he exclaimed, stamping. "'Yes,' one moment; 'No,' the next. Come, you don't know what you refuse. That old Hall is my uncle's own, and he has nobody else to leave it to. As soon as he's dead I shall throw up farming and start as a squire. And now," he added with a bitter sneer, "what a fool you are to hang back from such a chance!"

"Thank you, I don't value it," said Anne.

"Because you hate him who would make it yours?"

"It may not lie in your power to do that."

"What—has the old fellow been telling you his affairs?"

"No."

"Then why do you mistrust me? Now, after this will you open the door, and show that you treat me as a friend if you won't accept me as a lover? I only want to sit and talk to you."

Anne thought she would trust him: it seemed almost impossible that he could harm her. She retired from the window and went down-stairs. When her hand was upon the bolt of the door her mind misgave her. Instead of withdrawing it she remained in silence where she was. and he began again—

" Are you going to unfasten it ? "

Anne did not speak.

" Now, dash my wig, I will get at you ! You've tried me beyond endurance. One kiss would have been enough that day in the mead; now I'll have it, whether you will or no, if only to humiliate you, and show that I won't be thwarted !"

He flung himself against the door ; but as it was bolted, and had in addition a great wooden bar across it, this produced no effect. He was silent for a moment, and then the terrified girl heard him attempt the shuttered window. She ran up-stairs and again scanned the down. The yellow gig still lay in the blazing sunshine, and the horse of Festus stood by the corner of the garden nothing else was to be seen. At this moment there came to her ear the noise of a sword drawn from its scabbard ; and, peeping over the window-sill, she saw her tormentor drive his sword between the joints of the shutters, in an attempt to rip them open. The sword snapped off in his hand. With an imprecation he pulled out the piece, and returned the two halves to the scabbard.

" Ha ha ! " he cried, catching sight of the top of her head. " 'Tis only a joke, you know.; but I'll get in all the same. All for a kiss ! But never mind, we'll do it yet ! " He spoke in an affectedly light tone, as if ashamed of his previous resentful temper ; but she could see by the livid back of his neck that he was brimful of suppressed passion. "Only a jest, you know," he went on. " How are we going to do it now ? Why, in this way. I go and get a ladder, and enter at the upper window where my love is. And there's the ladder lying under that corn-rick in the first enclosed field. Back in two minutes, dear ! "

He ran off, and was lost to her view.

A MAIDEN'S MESSAGE.

O WIND, that wanderest o'er hill, and vale, and sea,
  Blow round the home where he sleeps peacefully,
And breathe upon his brow a loving kiss from me.

O golden " maiden moon," so calm and pure and bright,
Shed round and o'er him thy soft, tender streams of light;
Tell him how well I love him—tell him so to-night.

O stars all silvery-bright, set on that deep, still blue—
Stars that are watching o'er us both the long night through,
Tell him my love for him is pure like you—and true.

O great, grand, snow-white clouds—slow drifting o'er the sky—
Bear to his heart a message as ye pass him by,
Tell him my love would teach me how to do—or die.

O great, wide sea, on which the night-winds blow
Sing in his ears thy music calm and slow,
Sing to his heart I love him—sing it soft and low.

O tiny, laughing ripples, dancing on the shore—
O mighty ocean waves, thundering your ceaseless roar—
Tell him I love so well, I could not love him more !

O moon and stars—O clouds and deep, blue, sunny sea,
And restless, wandering winds, bear him these words from me,
" My own dear love, I love thee well—and constantly."

                            L. G. M

A TRIP TO CYPRUS.

By LIEUT.-COLONEL W. F. BUTLER, C.B.

ON board H.M.S. *Chimborazo*, in Portsmouth harbour, there is much apparent confusion and disorder. Men in all stages of uniform are busily engaged in operations which have for their ultimate object the preparation of the ship for sea. Boxes of cartridges, bundles of carrots, personal luggage of every description, four horses in boxes, eight dogs in collars and chains, a large cat in a basket, a rocking-horse and a child's wheelbarrow, a semi-grand piano, a tax-cart, many gun-cases, various kinds of deck chairs, square boxes bearing in large letters the names of well-known London tea-sellers, provisions in tins, in bags, in boxes, live stock and poultry, and many other articles and things impossible to mention, are put on board by slings and gangways. Some are passed from hand to hand, others carried in on heads and shoulders, and others again hoisted on board by steam winches and donkey engines, whose fizz and whistle and whirl, amid all the other sounds of toil and turmoil, are loud and ceaseless.

But, amid all this apparent confusion, there is much method and system. One peculiarity is especially observable: the various units of toil are all going straight to their peculiar labour without paying much heed to their neighbours. The human ants are carrying their burdens into separate cells in this great floating ant-nest; they are passing and repassing to different destinations, sorting out as they go all this vast collection of complicated human requirements from the seemingly hopeless confusion in which it lies piled upon the wharf.

At length, everything being on board, the *Chimborazo* surges out from the wharf and steams slowly on her way. It is a mid-winter morning. A watery sun glints from amid clouds that give but faint hope of fair weather outside, and, as the good ship bends her course by Sandown Bay, and plies along the villa-encrusted shore of Ventnor, there loom out to Channel dull patches of drifting fog, between whose rifts the chop of a short tumbling sea is visible, and above which grey leaden clouds are vaguely piled.

We go below, and, descending to the saloon, stoop to look at the barometer; it stands below 29°. That terrible weather-man in America, who is certainly a prophet in England, in whatever estimation he may be held

in his own country, has foretold a succession of storms along the British coasts. For three days we have fondly hoped that the fellow would be wrong; but barometer, fog, sea, and sky all proclaim him right.

And now the *Chimborazo*, holding steadily through mist and fog, steams on down Channel, and in due time rounds out into the Bay of Biscay. At any period of the year a nasty bit of water is this Bay of Biscay. Turbulent even in midsummer, sometimes given to strange moods of placidity, but ever waking up and working back into its almost chronic state of tempest howl and billow roll, intent on having a game of pitch and toss with every ship that sails its bosom. But if the Bay can show its rough ways when the sun hangs high in the summer heavens, what can it not also do in mid-winter's darkest hour!

Let us see if we can put even a faint glimpse of it before the reader.

It is the last day of the old year. Wild and rough the south-west wind has swept for three days and nights against us, knocking us down into hollows between waves, hitting us again and again as we come staggering up the slopes of high running seas, and spitting rain and spray at us as we reel over the trembling waters.

It has been three days and nights of such misery of brain and body, sense and soul, as only the sea-sick can ever know; and now the last night of the old year has come, and foodless and unrested, sleepless and weary, we stagger up on deck out of sheer weariness of cabin misery. How unutterably wretched it all is! The *Chimborazo* is a mighty machine to look at as she lies alongside a wharf or in a quiet harbour; but here she is the veriest shuttlecock of wind and sea. How easily these great waves roll her about! How she trembles as they hit her! How small her size in this black waste of waters! How feeble all her strength of crank and piston, shaft and boiler, to face the fury of this great wind king! Hold on by the rigging and look out on the Bay. Huge shaggy seas go roaring past into the void of the night; great gulfs tumble along in their wake; and between sea and sky there is nothing but grey, cold gloom. Ever and anon a huge sea breaks over the bows and splashes far down along the slippery decks. We have put one more misery to the catalogue already told. We had thought the cup had been full; but to all the previous pangs of sickness there are added wet and cold. And yet, to-morrow or the day after it will be smooth sea and blue sky, and all the long list of wretchedness will be most mercifully forgotten.

MANSHIP THE MARINE.

He was called a Marine, and had doubtless been duly classed and registered as such, and " borne on the strength," as it is called, of the Marine force ; but for all that he was no more a Marine than you are. If you ask me, then, what he was, I should say he was almost everything else in the board-ship line except a Marine.

He cleaned your boots, got your bath, made your bed, brushed you, dressed you, waited upon you at dinner, brought you physic from the " sick bay," told you what the wind and the sea were doing outside, sympathized with you in the misery they were inflicting upon you inside, and generally played the part of servant, valet, nurse, guide, philosopher, and friend to a very large number of more or less helpless human units.

When Manship first volunteered his services as attendant during the voyage there were circumstances connected with his mode of utterance and general appearance that had induced me to respond guardedly to his overtures. Sorry indeed would I be to aver that Manship was drunk on that occasion. Drunkenness is evinced by staggering or unsteady gait, whereas Manship walked with undeviating precision. On the other hand, his articulation was peculiar. He was not a man of many words, as I afterwards learned —action was much more in his line; but as he presented himself in my cabin, on the night before we put to sea, he appeared to labour under such difficulty, that I might indeed say such a total inability to make his meaning evident to me, that I deemed it better for all parties concerned to postpone any further communication or arrangement until the following morning. But as I proposed this course to Manship, I became struck by a singular coincidence in our respective cases. While my words were couched in the simplest examples of pure Saxon English that could convey to a man my wish to put off our conversation to the next morning, I was nevertheless aware that not one particle of my meaning had been taken up by Manship's mental consciousness, and that so far from betraying the smallest evidence of understanding my proposal, he continued to regard me with an expression of eye such as a Bongo or a Nyam-Nyam might have regarded the enterprising author of the " Heart of Africa," had that traveller thought fit to address these interesting peoples upon the subject of German *Kulturkrauft* in the Greek language. Nay, no sooner had I finished my attempt at suggesting a postponement to the morning than he again began to place his services at my disposal with the same inarticulate manner of speech that had before alarmed me.

Bringing a light now to bear upon his countenance, I detected a vacuity of stare, added to a general tenacity of expression about the forehead, that made postponement more than ever desirable. I therefore put a summary end to the interview by ordering his immediate and unconditional withdrawal.

The following morning found Manship duly installed as my attendant during the voyage, inquiries as to his capabilities having resulted in satisfactory testimonials from many quarters. He at once entered upon his duties with a silent alacrity that showed a thorough knowledge of his profession. Boots became his speciality. In the grey light of the earliest dawn, my unrested eye, gazing vacuously out of the uneasy berth, would catch sight of a figure groping amid the wreck and ruin of the troubled night on the cabin floor. It was Manship seeking out the boots. When the four first terrible days had passed, and I had leisure to watch more closely the method of life pursued by Manship, I perceived daily some new trait in his character. It became possible to watch him at odd moments as he stood by pantry doors or at the foot of cabin stairs, or in those little nooks and corners where for a moment eddy together the momentarily unemployed working waifs of board-ship life.

In outward appearance Manship possessed few of the attributes supposed to be characteristic of the Marine. His face was never dirty, yet it would have been impossible to say when it had been washed. His hair showed no sign of brush or comb, yet to say that it was unbrushed or uncombed was to state more than appearance actually justified. He did not vary one whit in his general appearance as the day wore on. He did not become more soiled-looking as he cleaned the different articles that came in his way; nor did he grow more clean-looking when the hour of rest had come and he did his little bit of loafing around the pantry or bar-room doors. I believe that had he been followed into the recesses of his sleeping place he would have been found in costume, cap, and semblance always and at all hours the same.

As I watched him day by day I found that he was the servant of many masters. The navigating lieutenant, the chaplain, the doctor, and two or three others—all were ministered to by him in the matter of boots, baths, and brushing; yet I could not detect that any delay or inconvenience had been experienced by any of his masters. His name Manship was a curious one, and I indulged in many speculations as to its origin, but, of course, none of them were more than conjectural. When he first told me his name on the occasion of our first memorable interview, I thought to myself, " Ah, I will easily recollect that name. It is so intimately connected with nautical life generally, that it will be impossible to forget it." In this, however, I was mistaken; for but only the next morning I found myself addressing him as Mainsail, Mainmast, Maintop, Maindeck, and many other terms more or less connected with the central portion of a ship.

It was a remarkable fact that you never could look long at any portion of the deck, saloon, or cabin, without seeing Manship. He came out of doors and up hatchways quite unexpectedly, and he always carried a supply of boots, buckets, or brushes prominently displayed ; indeed, there is now a widely accepted anecdote in the ship which had reference to a visit of inspection made to the Mediterranean by the Lords of the Admiralty, the War Minister, and several other important functionaries. The *Chimborazo* had been specially selected for their lordships. It was said that on more than one occasion the solemnity of a very important " function " had been completely marred by the sudden appearance of Manship, pail in hand, in the midst of a press of ministers, secretaries, and heads of departments. It was also averred that on these high and mighty occasions Manship, although bundled aside in a most summary manner, when once out of the ministerial zone displayed a most unconcerned demeanour. Those, however, who were best acquainted with him were wont to declare that the evenings of such state receptions as we have mentioned were singularly coincident with the inarticulate phase of his speech which we have already alluded to—a circumstance which might lead to the supposition that Manship had been somewhat overcome by finding himself all at once face to face with the collective dignity of the two Services.

But some days had to elapse ere I became cognisant of a curious "roster," or succession list which Manship kept. One evening I was standing in a group in the indistinct light of the quarter-deck, when I felt my sleeve pulled to attract attention. I turned to find Manship standing near. Stepping aside to ask what he wanted, I was met by a piece of blue paper and a short bit of lead pencil which he handed to me. I approached a lamp, and holding the paper near it I saw that it was the ordinary form upon which all orders for wine, spirits, or malt liquors had to be written. Opposite the printed word "Porter" I saw that some one had written, in a hand of surpassing illegibility, " One bottle," while higher up on the paper appeared, in the same writing, the words " Plese give barer "—no signature was appended.

I looked at Manship. Complete vacuity of countenance, coupled with evident inability to shut his mouth, told me that questions were useless. I have said that the paper was unsigned ; to remedy that want had been the object of Manship's visit. I wrote my signature in the proper place, and, handing back the paper and pencil to him, watched his further movements. He disappeared down the stairs, but through an open skylight I was still able to trace his course. I saw him present his order and receive his bottle, and then I saw two tumblers filled, and while Manship took one of them another man, who had not previously appeared in the transaction, held the second. I noticed that there were not many words passing between them at the time. Both seemed to be deeply impressed with some mysterious solemnity connected with the occasion. Perhaps it was commemorating some great victory gained by the Marines, or drinking to the memory of some bygone naval hero. I could not tell, but I noticed that when Manship had finished the tumbler, which he did without any doubt or hesitation, he drew a long deep sigh, and laying down his glass disappeared into remote recesses of the ship.

This incident had been well-nigh forgotten, when, one evening about five days later, the same circumstances of paper, pencil, and petition were again exactly repeated. I then found that my position was fifth on the " roster," or list for porter, and that every five days I might expect to be called upon to sign my name.

But my second turn did not arrive until some time had elapsed, and to the wild grey seas of Biscay and the Atlantic had succeeded the moonlit ripple of the blue Mediterranean.

"Another hour and the Rock looms before us."

XXI—37

And now, all the storm, and sea roar, and whistle of wind through rigging have died away, and over the mountains of Morocco a glorious sunrise is flashing light upon the waveless waters that wash the rugged shores of the gate of the Mediterranean. Another hour and the Rock looms up before us; then the white houses of San Roque are seen above the blue bay of Gibraltar; and then, with Algesiras, the wide sweep of coast and the hills of Andalusia and the felucca-covered sea all come in sight, until, beneath the black muzzles of Gibraltar's thousand guns, the *Chimborazo* drops her anchor and is at rest.

And then there came two days on shore, with rambles in the long, cool, rock-hewn galleries, and drives to Spanish Lines, and along bastions and batteries, and glimpses, caught from port-hole and embrasure, of blue sea, and far-away Spanish hill-top, and piles of shot and shell and long sixty-eights and thirty-twos and short carronades, and huge mortars and "Woolwich infants," all spread from sea-edge to rock-summit; so thick, that a single combined discharge of all this mighty ordnance might well blow the whole of Spain forward into the Bay of Biscay, or send the Rock itself backward into the Mediterranean.

Relics of the great siege, too, are plenty. These old giants, how close they came to each other in those days, spluttering away at one another with smooth bores and blunder-busses! You could have told the colour of the man's beard who was blazing at you if you had been inquisitive on the point. No wonder their accounts have been graphic ones. They could see as much of the enemy's side as of their own. No wonder that that grim old fire-eater, Drinkwater (singularly inappropriate name), should have told us all about it so clearly and so vividly.

Half-way up the steep rock wall of the North Fort there opens from the dark gallery a dizzy ledge, from whose sunlit platform the eye marks, at one sweep, the neutral ground, the two seas, and the far-off sheen of snow upon the Sierra Nevadas. Right below, in the midst of the level "lines," is the cemetery; around it stretches a circle marked by posts and rails. It is the race-course. Grim satire! the "finish" is along the graveyard wall. The distance-post of the race of life and the winning-post of the "Rock Stakes" stand cheek by jowl; and as the members of the Gibraltar Ring lay the odds and book their wagers, over the fence, half a stone's throw distant, Death on his pale horse has been busy for a century laying evenly the odds and ends of many a life-race.

But meantime the *Chimborazo* has taken in all her coal, and is ready again to put to sea. This time, however, it is all sunshine and calm waters, and at daybreak on the fourth morning after quitting Gibraltar we are in sight of Malta.

The English traveller, or tourist of to-day, as he climbs the feet-worn stairs of Valetta, is face to face with one of history's strangest perversions, yet how little does he think about it!

Ricasoli, St. Elmo, St. Antonio, Florian —all these vast forts and bastions, all these lines, lunettes, ditches and ramparts, were drawn, traced, hewn, built, and fashioned with one sole aim and object—to resist the Turk. For this end Europe sent its most skilful engineers, spent its money, shed its blood.

Here, when Constantinople was gone, when Cyprus, Candia, and Rhodes had fallen, Civilisation planted the mailed foot of its choicest knighthood, and cried to the advancing tide of Tartar savagery, "No farther!"

How well that last challenge was understood by the Turk the epitaph over the grave of a great sultan best testifies: "He meant to take Malta and conquer Italy."

The armies of the Sultan had touched Moscow on the one hand and reached Tunis on the other. From Athens to Astrachan, from Pesth to the Persian Gulf, the Crescent knew no rival. Into a Christendom rent by the Reformation, shattered by schism, the Asian hordes moved from victory to victory. This rock, these stones, and the knights who sleep beneath yonder dome, then saved all Europe.

Let us go up the long, hot street stairs and look around.

How grand is all this work of the old knights! How nobly the Latin cross — a sword and a cross together—has graved its mark upon church and palace, auberge and council hall—Provence, Castile, Arragon, France, Italy, Bavaria, and Germany. Alas! no England here; for the Eighth Harry was too intent upon playing the part of Sultan Blue Beard in Greenwich to think of resisting his brothers Selim or Solyman in the Mediterranean.

Of all that long list of knights—French, Spanish, Italian, and German—who redeemed with their lives the vows they had sworn, falling in the great siege of Malta, there is not a single English name. Not that English chivalry was then extinct. English knights and English lords were dying fast enough in the cause of duty on

English soil. Thomas More and John Fisher, mitred abbot and sandalled friar, and many a noble Englishman, were freely yielding life on Tower Hill and at Smithfield, in resistance to a Sultan not so brave and quite as savage as Selim or Solyman.

Pass by the grand palace of Castile, whose arched ceilings once rung to the mailed footsteps of the chivalry of old Spain; go out on the terrace of the Barraca, and look down upon that wondrous scene—forts, guns, ships, munitions of war, strength and power; listen to the hum that floats up from these huge ironclads lying so motionless beneath; mark the innumerable muzzles that lie looking grimly out of dark recesses to the harbour mouth; and then carry your minds a thousand miles away to where, along the shores of the Golden Horn, the great queen city of the East sits crownless and defiled. How long is her shame to continue? So long as these ships, forts, arsenals, and guns are here as the advanced post of Mohammedanism in Europe. Here is the Turks' real rampart, here his strongest bulwark against the Cross. Above the Union Jack an unseen Crescent floats over St. Elmo; and all this mighty array, which confederated Christianity planted here as its rampart against the Moslem, is to-day a loaded gun primed and pointed at the throat of him who would tear the crescent from St. Sophia's long-desecrated shrine.

Of course this is sentiment. Perhaps it must be called that name to-day, and nowhere more than in Malta. Still, somehow, the truth that is in a thing, be it sentiment or not, does in the long run manage to prevail; and although to-day the auberge of Castile is a barrack, and that of Provence echoes with the brandy and soda and sherry and bitters criticism of certain worthy graduates of Sandhurst and the *Britannia* training-ship, nevertheless, even the history which is made at their hands will ultimately bear right.

Five miles from Valetta, and a short distance to the right of the road which leads to Citta Vecchia, a large dome of yellowish white colour attracts the eye. It is the dome of Mousta church. We will go to it. As we approach we become conscious that it is very large. A friend who is acquainted with statistics informs us that it is either the second largest or the third largest dome in the world, he is not sure which. "But it is unknown to the outer world," we reply. "Mousta, Mousta! who ever heard of Mousta?" Very few, probably; but that does not matter, it is a big dome all the same.

It is Sunday afternoon, and many people are thronging the piazza in front of the church. Three great doors lead from a portico of columns into the interior. We go in. The first step across the threshold is enough to tell us that this dome is indeed a large one. It is something more; it is magnificent! The church is, in fact, one vast circle, 440 feet in circumference, above whose marble pavement a colossal dome is sole and solid roof, all built by peasant labour, freely given "for the love of God." Architect, mason, stone-cutters, common labourers reared this glorious temple, painted, carved, and gilded it, and charged no man anything for the value of one hour's work.

These be freemasons indeed!

Ah! you poor, aproned, gauntletted, pinchbeck-jewelled humbugs, who go about destroying your digestive organs and spending a pound in tomfoolery for every shilling you spend in charity, here is something for you to copy. Go to Mousta and look at this church, "built for the love of God." Look up at its vast height. Mark these massive walls slowly closing in ever so far above. No wood here, all solid stone. Walk round it, measure it, and then come into the centre and go down on your knees, if you are able, and pray that you may be permitted to give up your folly, to become a "freemason" such as these builders, and to do something in the world "for the love of God."

When this grand temple was slowly lifting up its head over the roofs of Mousta, an eminent English engineer came to see it. He had built a great railway bridge over a river, or an arm of the sea, at a cost of only a couple of millions sterling. "Poor people!" he said, looking with pity at the toiling peasants, "they never can put the roof on that span; it is too large. It is impossible." The eminent man had done many things in his life, but there was one thing he had not done, and that was attempting the apparently impossible for the love of God. For the love of man and for the love of fame he had doubtless achieved great things and reached the margin of the possible; but so far as the idea of giving his time or his genius "for the love of God" was beneath, above him, or incomprehensible to him, just so far was the possibility of the impossible beyond him too.

And now the *Chimborazo*, having embarked a regiment of infantry for a far-off Chinese station, has hoisted her blue peter at the fore, and it is time to go on board her crowded decks and settle down again into the dreary routine of sea-life for a few days longer. So once more we sail away, men in forts cheering, bands playing on deck, and all the poor Hong Kong lads doing their best to look jolly.

Two days pass, and then at the sunset hour Crete is in sight. No lower shore-line visible, but, white and lofty, Olympus thrusts aside the envious clouds, and " takes the salute" of the sunset ere the day is done.

Next morning the *Chimborazo* is steaming through a lonely sea, and when a second sunrise has come we are again in sight of land—white chalky hills that glare at one even from beneath the canopy of clouds that to-day hangs over their summits. A wide curve of shore-line lies in front. Glasses and telescopes are levelled upon the land. It looks dry, desolate, and barren. A few tall, dark trees are seen at long intervals. Wherever the glass rests on a bit of ground we see that the colour of the soil is that of sun-baked brick.

We are looking at Cyprus.

YESTERDAY.

IT only seems like yesterday :
   Why beats this heart? 'tis over now ;
And those bright dreams of love and hope
   Are in the far-off long ago ;
Yet time hath wrought no change in me,
My love is linked to yesterday.

It only seems but yesterday :
   How happily those days sped by !
At evening I was sure to meet
   A sunset smile and starlit eye ;
All those sweet smiles died out from me,
With that sweet far-off yesterday.

I sometimes meet a smiling face,
   A kindly word of sympathy ;
But what are they to my crushed heart?
   They only chain my memory
To those fond smiles that cheered my way
In that sweet far-off yesterday.

I wander back to those bright days,
   When all was one untroubled sea—
My life a happy golden dream,
   No mazes of perplexity :
Those golden dreams have died away,
With that sweet far-off yesterday.

Ah, well ! the past is over now ;
   And what there is in store for me
I do not, dare not wish to know,
   Nor penetrate futurity.
I know that all things work for good
To those who put their trust in God ;
And when I reach yon star-paved sky,
The yesterday will be to-day.

           ELLEN MILLER.

SOCIAL PLAGUES.

II.—NOISE. *Section 1.*

"GIVE me health and a day," cries Mr. Emerson, "and I will make the pomp of emperors ridiculous." It is well for you, philosopher, in your sheltered haven, with portals opening on a vista of old trees and garden sloping downward to the glade where the Assabeth, most taciturn of streams, joins the Muskataquid to creep towards the sea—it is well for you, in that temple and palace of rest, to make your mind a kingdom to itself, where your thoughts range serenely from Zoroaster to Thoreau, and from "Oman's dark water" to the cañons of the Rocky Hills, polishing your stanzas and letting your sentences ripen like your apples. But take my sunniest and least dyspeptic day in this suburb of Ironstoneville or Mammonopolis, and you will echo my demand for a third requisite—a moderate amount of Quietude. This has been called a critical age, a democratic age, a philanthropic age, a lyrical age, a ranting age, a canting age, an age of association, of examination, of expedition, over-worked, over-heated, over-mobbed, an age of steam and telegram, of science and incredulity. Above all, it is an age of hubbub and sound and fury, at enmity with quiet, if not with joy, when it seems as if nothing that does not roar can be regarded or permitted to exist. In civilised communities it is at least nominally forbidden to pollute the air with lethal smoke or pestilential gases. Why should the paternal protection of the State be confined to our lungs and noses? Has not an ear nerves, has not an ear susceptibilities? If you enchant it, will it not respond? If you pierce it, will it not wince? Is not the ear the nearest avenue to the brain? Is it not capable of touches of sweet harmony? May it not be driven distracted by harsh and crabbed sounds?

Let our poets leave off inditing their ditties to red-haired damsels and betake themselves to composing odes to Peace; let our reformers abandon their hoarse platforms for the organization of silent clubs. An obscure sufferer and analyst, I confine myself to a few hints towards an anatomy of noise, to me the chief cause of melancholy, black-bile, incapacity for work, and concord with all honest misanthropes—with Timon or Apemantus, with Marius among the tombs of Carthage, or Swift in his Irish hole. The noises that, rushing over the earth daily and hourly, assail the calm of heaven, may be variously classified—as into the better and worse, the evitable and inevitable, the continuous and intermittent, &c., &c. I find it most in accord with Cartesian method to arrange them in the main according to their sources. They fall under three great heads:—

A. Noises of Nature.
B. Noises of Animals.
C. Noises of Instruments, Machines, or Implements.

A. Discerning readers will anticipate the remark that the sounds under the first head are, for the most part, either pleasant or endurable : in this they are like the regular cadences of steady human work. The elements, when not angry, are on the whole gracious to our ears. The rushing of great rivers, the fall of waters—from Niagara to our own mill-dam—soothes us, if not to sleep, at least to restfulness. The wind—save the malignant east—makes melody among the pines, and is only a disturber when it rages at night, and whistles, whines, roars, howls, and groans like a host of perturbed spirits. A brave heart with a good conscience, or a Byron with more of the one than of the other, may set strophes to peals of thunder; though it would be hard to do the same for a hailstorm. The sea is an inspirer or consoler ; unless, about to make a personal trial of the Bay of Biscay, we are a prey to horrible imaginings while—

"Es wallet, und siedet, und brauset, und sischt."

Of this class comparatively few are plagues, and none can properly be called social ; they may, therefore, be dismissed.

B. The etymological paradox, *lucus a non lucendo*, is capped by the familiar phrase, "the dumb animals." Would nine-tenths of them were dumb ! This globe would be comparatively pacific, and "Oh, the difference to me!" Of the vibrations for which they are directly responsible, some are of a collective or congregational character. These are akin to the elemental sounds, and the same remark may be made of both. At the "doves in immemorial elms," at the "innumerable bees," I neither moan nor murmur. I exempt from censure, nay, almost welcome, the cawing of rooks when they are, as Mr. Lowell politically remarks, "settlin' things in windy congresses;" though on some great question of foreign policy the debate threatens to grow keen, there is generally more purpose in it than, for instance, in the baa-ing of sheep. This, too, is inoffensive, except where it is painfully accentuated during the weaning of the lambs. Bird-voices are tuneable, unless they are pent in cages, even when they most violently disagree "in their little nests." But I have been kept awake half the night by an incessant jug-jug-jug till I could exclaim with Mrs. Browning's Bianca, "The nightingales, the nightingales." The exuberance of a canary may be in excess, but we feel for the inevitable fate that sooner or later waits him from the claws of a cat. A parrot, however, is a fatal thing, his shriek being worse than that of an enraged lunatic, and his remarks in perpetual danger of betraying your domestic secrets. He brings us to our second subdivision under this head, that of sounds which are comparatively isolated, that rend and tear the atmosphere instead of merely setting it in motion. It is these that are the bugbears of a country life. If you are a Quietist, in a more sublunary sense than that of Fénelon or Madame Guyon, do not be seduced by the advertisement of "a quiet farm," by its visions of curds and cream and pastoral repose. First, and inevitably, it has a poultry yard, and you will be roused from the sweet sleep of morn by the defiance of a triumphant and active cock. I believe the noise of this animal to be deliberately malignant. He crows over the restless misery which he creates, lapsing into silence with a profligate pretence of lassitude, and breaking out again with all the energy of a retired statesman returning to power. I can imagine a cock at the entrance not of the celestial but of the other gate uttering his exultant cry at each new arrival. France in particular is becoming almost uninhabitable by reason of cocks, who seem perpetually, like Gambetta during the war, refusing to surrender one barley-corn of their yards. All the hens' flesh and eggs in Christendom are insufficient amends for the irrepressible insolence of this *miles gloriosus.* Chaucer is of course, as Campbell, long before Tennyson, told us, "our morning star of song;" but his praises of Chaunticleer must have cost him a spell of purgatory; while Beattie has earned a right to sit in the Muses' shrine by his sympathetic stanza :—

"O to thy cursed scream, discordant still,
ot harmony aye shut her gentle ear;
Thy boastful mirth let jealous rivals spill,
Insult thy crest, and glossy pinions tear,
And ever in thy dreams the ruthless fox appear."

"O Reynard, Reynard, O mon roy," I have often exclaimed in the neighbourhood of "a quiet farm." In the intervals of the egotism of the "grand monarque," you will be distracted by the idiotic chuckling of his silly wives, the cackling of preposterous geese, the gabbling of pompous turkeys, more rarely by the inhuman shrieks of a delirious peacock, the bellowing of a blatant bull that you cannot take by the horns, the mooing of an impatient cow which you cannot milk, or the yelping of curs whose self-assertion is in inverse proportion to their size. The last are the most constant and inevitable pests of town and country in both continents ; nor street, nor lane, nor lawn, nor cot, nor castle is free from them. Feline duets are disconcerting, but it is possible to take a humorous view of the wild vehemence of pussy's agitated heart. Cats make night hideous, but spare the poor day-labourer. The heehaw of an excited ass is the most hideous of uproars, but it is a rare agony ; four-footed donkeys are not found at every corner, and they are generally oppressed and long-suffering. When a mastiff next door obstinately howls at the moon and all remonstrance fails, you may take down your gun and stand the consequences : the provocation, however, must be extreme, for a great hound, with all his faults, is a great cre ature. But bastard spaniels, poodles, pugs, King Charles's balls of wool, spoilt mongrels, terriers, and other rat-like mockeries of the true canine race, loved of misses, hated of "honourable men," are in

"England, France, Germany, Italy, and Spain"

our constant neighbours, and will not permit us to call an hour our own. In season and out of season, at everything and at nothing, they snarl and shriek and brag and skirl. "Darling Dizzy's" yelp insults my best couplet, Flossy's squeal upsets my profoundest problem, and "pretty little Zulu's" howl dislocates a period of which Ruskin might have been jealous. "Love me, love my dog; he won't bite !" "If you love me, you will hang your dog. I have in vain endeavoured to provoke the cowardly wretch to an assault which would in the eyes of the law justify my calling in the aid of the druggist," would be an appropriate fragment of a dialogue between a typical modern Juliet and an honest Romeo. Let us relieve India and pay the expenses of the Afghan war by an enormous tax on puppies. With sacrilegious impropriety they make most merry when families go to church and leave their curs free to run and revel in chorus. The Sundays of all the year round are pre-eminently the dog-days.

Confined to the summer months, but doing much to make us wish for winter back again, is the "infinite torment of flies." How marvellously little has human ingenuity done to suppress our animal scourges. These often mainly affect the sense of touch, but the misery is magnified when they also scarify the ear. I would not grudge even the mosquito his little drop of my blood if he would not make such a fuss about it. His approaches, the dull, incessant threat, making sleep impossible and contemplation a mockery, his trumpet drawing nearer, nearer, shriller than before, and his final yell of malice, convince us, more than the severity of his bite, that his body is inhabited by the spirit of a theological controversialist. In the insect world there is infinite variety of character, indicated as frequently by voice and demeanour as by outward form. The bumble-bee, which gets into our rooms in August, is distinctly a gentleman; his hum may be monotonous, he may make mistakes, but he means well; we may show him out, but would not hurt a hair of his head. The blue-bottle fly, on the other hand, is an insufferable cad. His vulgar buzz and bloated body are those of an offensive costermonger or fraudulent bank director or blustering railway Bounderby. Blue-bottles are the master-pests of every season of fine weather. Morning on morning they swarm on our panes, and there is no prospect of peace or possibility of a sentence till the last of their clamours has been hushed in the death which is their due, the accomplishment of which is generally my first hour's work. The cry is, Still they come; troops of reinforcements are squatted like toads on the sill, waiting to rush in with the breath of air to which you hardly dare to treat yourself. The state of mind of a man who will let one of those creatures escape him is incomprehensible. The proper feeling towards them is not vague annoyance but personal hatred; the pleasure of killing them is a partial but inadequate recompense for the disgust they inspire. The brute whom Uncle Toby, with hare-brained sentimentality, dismissed, certainly on the first chance returned with seven others worse than himself. Specifics for toothache are well, but when all fails there is the *ultima ratio* of the dentist. A panacea for blue-bottles is more urgent, for we cannot cut off our ears, and the man who supplies it will have a claim on his race equal to that of Watt or Stephenson. But how few of the inventions of the century have made life happier; how many of them, adding

to its noise and hurry and struggle for existence, merely multiply our chances of going rapidly mad!

Of the noises made by the human animal, those of the infant come under somewhat the same category as those of the pet dog; in both cases you are expected to admire and belaud your aversion. But the nuisance, "mewling and puking in the nurse's arms," is less frequently in the open air, and you can choose your indoor company. Persecuted by idolaters, your only course is the bold one: say you "hate babies and do not share the prejudice against Swift's proposal," or that they always scream when you touch them, or that you let them fall and break them. The next stage of torment is represented by "girls and boys gone out to play." I don't care how much they whine or how unwillingly they creep to school, and only wish they were never out of it, for a playground is a Pandemonium. No one objects to their exercising their limbs in Spartan silence, but there seems no rhyme nor reason in their incoherent shrieks. In this regard girls are the worst, and by the law of cross-purposes they select the portions of the lawn opposite my study window for their *palæstra*. I drive them away for the benefit of my neighbours, and, such is the baseness of human ingratitude, the parents complain!

Full-grown human animals are in this country, for the most part, only clamorous under conditions of excitement or in the way of business. We need not attend mass meetings, and other riots may, with the aid of the police, be suppressed; but when the world is half civilised *street cries* will be penal offences. Many of them are scarcely human, and cannot be put on paper—as "China to mend;" "Co, co, coal;" "Fresh strawberries," in London—except with notes indicating discord that only Wagner could supply. Under this head we must record a censure on the bad, often profane, language that carters address to their horses. It must hurt the feelings of the superior beings, and should be brought before the Anti-Cruelty and Anti-Vivisection Societies.

Street singers profess to use their voices as instruments of pleasure. These I reserve, as also my memories of a Pyreneean market, where every yell, howl, jabber, and peal of which lungs are capable is combined with a chaos of horns and hounds, over the price of a few beans. Meanwhile here is a milk cart; I must bow to my readers and "silence that dreadful bell."

W. ROSS BROWNE.

SIR JAMES OUTRAM.

PART II.

ON his return from the Kalu Pass, Outram was dispatched to tranquillise the disturbed Ghilzai tribes, between Kabul and Kandahar, which, in face of the greatest difficulties, he accomplished, by a series of the most original and best-planned surprises; surrounding and capturing the chiefs of the tribes, who, if they had escaped to their stronghold, might have "held out successfully against all the material with which the Bombay Division is provided."

No sooner was Shah Shuja on the Afghan throne than Outram was dispatched to Kelat as a volunteer; soon, however, finding a regular position under General Willshire, who knew his value. The same tale in main essentials has to be retold. Outram's bravery at the siege was thus recognised by the general in his dispatch: "From Captain Outram, who volunteered his services on my personal staff, I received the utmost assistance, and to him I feel greatly indebted for the zeal and ability with which he has performed the various duties that I have required of him." And Outram himself was the bearer of this dispatch, deputed to survey the direct route from Kelat by Sonmiani Bandar, and to report its practicability or otherwise as a passage for troops, which the general considered an object of the first importance. The fulfilment of this duty led Outram into passages of adventure that read like a romance.

The step to major, which he ought to have had for Ghuznee, he now received for Kelat, which should have brought a colonelcy and C.B. The Court of Directors in London actually thought that he had attained the two steps, and he was congratulated by Lord Auckland on the supposed well-won promotion. Hostile influences must have been at work. "No explanation has ever been given why this particular promotion, officially announced to Lieut.-Colonel Outram by the Governor of Bombay, did not have effect; but no remonstrance on the subject was ever submitted by the officer concerned, who considered that 'honours *sought* are not to be esteemed.'"

" He also received the thanks of both the Bombay and supreme Governments for the ' very interesting and valuable documents ' relating to the Kalát-Son-miána route. The perusal of these had afforded the Governor-General ' much satisfaction.' Prior to this, moreover, the envoy and minister with Shah Shuja had conveyed his Majesty's bestowal of the second class order of the Durráni Empire, in ' acknowledgment of the zeal, gallantry, and judgment' which he had displayed in several instances during the past year, whilst employed on the king's immediate behalf. Three of the instances in which his ' merit and exertions' were ' particularly conspicuous,' are specially cited :—

" First, on the occasion of his gallantly placing himself ' at the head of His Majesty's troops engaged in dispersing a large body of rebels, who had taken up a threatening position immediately above His Majesty's encampment on the day previous to the storm of Ghazni.'

" Secondly, on the occasion of his ' commanding the party sent in pursuit of Dost Mahomed Khan,' when his ' zealous exertions would in all probability have been crowned with success, but for the treachery' of his Afghan associates.

" Thirdly, for ' the series of able and successful operations' conducted under his superintendence, ' which ended in the subjection or dispersion of certain rebel Ghilzai and other tribes, and which have had the effect of tranquillising the whole line of country between Kabul and Kandahar, where plunder and anarchy had before prevailed.' "

He was well received at the Presidency, and was offered the appointment of Political Agent in Lower Sinde. Scarcely, however, had he settled down to work in Sinde when war in the North-West again began to threaten. At once he put himself at the disposal of the Government, writing thus to Mr. Macnaghten in the course of a long letter :—

" Most gladly shall I obey the summons ; for in addition to zeal for the public service, I have now the impulse of personal gratitude to the Governor-General, to you, and to the Shah. Pray remember also that I require no pecuniary advantage, and would accept of none ; for the moiety of my salary in Sinde, which I would still receive while absent on duty, is most handsome and far above my deserts. I look upon it not only to more than compensate for any services I may have to perform in that country, but also as the purchase in advance of all that I could ever do hereafter in the public service. My wife will arrive in Bombay about May, but I would not wait on that account. As a soldier's wife, she knows and will admit my first duty to be to the public, to which all private and personal considerations should be sacrificed. . . . . Please order me when and where to go and what to do ; you will find me punctual to tryste, and ready to perform whatever is expected of me in any quarter. At the same time pray write for the Governor-General's sanction to my temporary absence from Sinde, the duties of which could, I hope, be fulfilled for the present by my assistants, as no great steps for the improvement of our relations in that quarter can be entered upon until everything has been effectually settled in the North-West."

He had, however, in the meantime, to abide at his political post. The work in Lower Sinde was hard, but more locally important than generally interesting ; the two main features of the first period , were the reduction of taxes on inland produce brought to Kurachee and the relief of the Indian traffic from tolls, and the transfer of Shikarpur to the British Government. By-and-by, through changes that had been long contemplated, he was placed in charge of Upper Sinde as well as Lower. This additional work had its disadvantages as well as advantages. For one thing it practically broke up the domestic life which had just been taken up afresh with the arrival. of Mrs. Outram from England. In spite of all this he intimated himself ready to assume a third charge still more remote in the event of the death of Mr. Rose Bell, who was in seriously bad health. With such responsibilities, he remodelled completely the administration of Lower and Upper Sinde, and in such a manner as made him loved and trusted both by the people and the native princes.

When that old Ameer died, he took farewell of Outram as of a brother—a scene which Outram has thus affectingly described :

" The Ameer, evidently feeling that we could not meet again, embraced me most fervently, and spoke distinctly to the following purport, in the presence of Dr. Owen and the other Ameers : ' You are to me as my brother Nusseer Khan, and the grief of this sickness is equally felt by you and Nusseer Khan; from the days of Adam no one has known so great truth and friendship as I have found in you.' I replied, ' Your Highness has proved your friendship to my Government and myself by your daily acts. You have considered me as a brother, and as a brother I feel for your Highness, and night and day I grieve for your sickness.' To which he added, ' My friendship for the British is known to God. My conscience is clear before God.' The Ameer still retained me in his feeble embrace for a few moments, and, after taking some medicine from my hand, again embraced me as if with the conviction that we could not meet again."

In view of the reversed policy which, in opposition to all the wishes and feelings of Outram, came to be pursued towards Sinde shortly afterwards, there is something touching as well as slightly humorous in his apology to the Governor-General for the premature enthusiasm of Ameer and people, to which his lordship thus replies :—

" You need not have made any apology for the salute which was prematurely fired by the Ameer of Sinde upon the rumour of your promotion. I must feel that goodwill exhibited . . . whilst it is an evidence of kind personal feeling towards you, is an exhibition also of goodwill towards the Government which you represent, and I readily therefore admit of such a compliment being paid you."

Whilst he was thus busy, and moving rapidly from one point of his large territory to another, negotiating new treaties and revising taxation, disastrous tidings from Afghanistan called him to fresh interests. The envoy and his people were shut up in Kabul. His one aim was to prepare support for Kandahar, from whence, he felt, we must look for the retrieval of affairs should we be driven to extremities at Kabul. The line of forts by the Khybur were more complete than by either of the other routes. There was suspense for a time, and then came the worst of news! Outram at once set his whole mind and energies to the task of retrieving the honour of his country, and it should never be forgotten how nobly and eloquently he protested against the suggestion of retiring from Kabul, leaving the prisoners in the hands of the Afghans. He was as nobly consistent in this as he had been in his protests against the war at first, and he did not rest till all that human skill and bravery could do had been done to retrieve that humiliation, supplying the most practical aid and ministering counsel and heartening everywhere by word or by letter; while he sped from place to place and kept in good order the discontented and unruly tribes on the border of his own territory, who might at any moment have risen and caused a new disaster. It is painful to read that his plain and outspoken expression on all these matters only had the effect of bringing on him the displeasure of the higher authorities.

His life indeed became now so thickly sown with incidents, that it is impossible even to outline them. After all his labours for Sinde, and the place he had made for himself in the hearts of princes and people, it was hard to be subordinated and relegated to subaltern duty. He had resolved, however, to do the work as faithfully for General Nott as though he were acting wholly on his own responsibility; and to make his way through Cutchee to Quetta at the most trying time of year and at great risks. He had written to one of his friends, Mr. Willoughby—

"Unless the Court of Directors are pleased to order that on the termination of h stilities in Afghanistan General Notts' political powers over me are withdrawn, I must assuredly most respectfully resign the line in which I have so long endeavoured to serve them and join my regiment, a poorer man than when I left it nearly twenty years ago. It is in no bitter spirit that I write this; these are simply the words of an honourable man willing to do his duty as long as he can do so without dishonour, but not grovelling enough to submit to the least degree of disgrace."

Immediately Outram proceeded by the frontier posts of Khangarh, Chatar, and Sibi, which he subjected to minute inspection, then on by Dadar, through the Bolan Pass to Quetta. Every step was at the risk of his life; but he attained his end of conveying all needful stores to the general, and by the exercise of his usual energy and decision, he contributed materially to the final settlement of the Afghan problem. He was thanked by the Governor-General, and a promise was actually made that in a scheme of the settlement of the Lower Indus being effected, he should be named Envoy; "His lordship being perfectly satisfied with the zeal and ability you manifest in the discharge of your duty." But the promise was not fulfilled. Outram now went to the Residency of Sukkur, from which he put forth many valuable schemes. Unfortunately very shortly a difference arose with regard to some circumstances in the transference to Kelat of the districts of Shawl and Sibi, which had been promised by Lord Auckland as good policy so soon as the difficulties in Afghanistan were brought to a close. This Outram felt was due the more that the young Khan had throughout acted so loyally; but remarks were made at head-quarters which deeply wounded Outram—an error, if error it were, being by the Governor-General substantially spoken of as a fiction in political transactions to which it was not justifiable to resort. Outram on this subject wrote to a friend—

"From the above you will observe that I have incurred his lordship's displeasure, and that I have been ill. The first was caused by my taking on myself to restore the province of Shawl to Kelat, after in vain seeking instructions for two months (having stated that its immediate restoration was essential to preserve the Brahoes faithful)—*which restoration had previously been pledged by Lord Auckland!* Notwithstanding which, and our treaty with the Khan of Kelat, Lord Ellenborough was for leaving him and the Afghans to scramble for what we ourselves had robbed Kelat of in the first instance! My having taken this . . . on my own responsibility caused the extreme wrath of his lordship. . . . . . So much for my own affairs. Oh, by-the-bye, I forgot the allusion to my late illness. It was a serious bout of brain fever, of which I thought little and the doctors thought serious. Now to turn to the satisfactory fact that our troops *are* on the march (though at the eleventh hour, and doing what ought to have been done two months ago) to Ghazni and Kabul."

Receiving but the most formal recognition for great and unwearied services at the greatest personal risks in effecting means of transport to Afghanistan in a country where transport is the chief difficulty in military movements, Outram, after a short time, returned to Bombay, where he was worthily entertained and his work recognised for what it was. Sir Charles Napier had been appointed commander of the troops in Sinde, with entire control over the political agents and civil officers. Outram determined to aid Sir Charles in every way, and a meeting at Sukkur showed the utmost harmony between the two. It certainly surprised Outram and his friends, when very shortly after this, and in face of Sir Charles Napier's reiterated expression of the value to him of Outram's advice and aid, Outram was remanded to his regiment. The reason, as assigned by Outram himself, was his advocacy of the cause of a fellow-officer, Captain Hammersley, against the decision of head-quarters. It was on the occasion of Outram now leaving Sinde that Sir Charles Napier, at a public dinner given to him, used the now famous phrase, "the Bayard of India,"—which becomes charged with a certain irony in the light of some of the later relations of these two great and distinguished men.

To the surprise of all, and most of all, perhaps, to the surprise of Outram, while he was in Bombay, preparing to sail for England, he was directed by the Governor-General to hold himself in readiness for Sir Charles Napier's order to be a commissioner for the arrangement of a revised treaty to the Ameers of Sinde. The order was summary and even peremptory, but Outram wrote:—

"The principle which has ever guided me through-out my career of service—implicit obedience to the orders of Government (and when, as in this case, orders were conveyed, and no option was left to me) —I had no hesitation in following on this occasion, and accordingly replied as follows:—'Sir,—I have the honour to acknowledge the receipt of your letter dated 24th ultimo, and to forward, for the information of the Right Honourable the Governor-General of India, the copy of a letter I addressed in consequence to the Political Secretary to the Government of Bombay, with that gentleman's reply, and of my letter to the Adjutant-General of the Bombay army, in accordance with which I purpose embarking in a steamer which proceeds to Sinde to-morrow. I expect to arrive at Sukkur about the 30th instant. Dated Bombay, December 13.'"

Great work might these two men have done in Sinde, for Outram's devotion to Sir Charles Napier was great; but they differed widely in their views with respect to political changes necessary, and on points regarding which Outram had thought much, and had cherished convictions. Napier wished to overturn the patriarchal system of Government in Sinde, and Outram was opposed to that. These differences so grew that it became difficult for them to work together. Very soon, as every one knows, Sir Charles Napier, by persistence in his policy, had so

far alienated the Sinde princes that they were compelled to regard themselves as likely to meet force, and to prepare for it. It is almost demonstrable that Sir Charles allowed himself to become the tool of a wily Asiatic, Ali Morad, who was plotting to deprive his relative of the turban in order to place it upon his own head. Outram had to become the supporter of such a policy as made him rejoice that "he was only a subaltern." He exhausted all his resources in trying to preserve peace, warning the princes to wait patiently; but without success. When the appeal to arms at last was made against all his representations, he fought, as of old, for his country, but he never ceased to feel friendly to the Ameer and princes.

The attack on the Residency was repelled after a very skilful defence—and with but slight loss, that of two men, due chiefly to Outram's being forearmed. This accomplished, he retired to join Sir Charles Napier at Matári, a town some sixteen miles north of Hyderabad, and from that point a successful effort was made to dislodge the enemy from Miani, where they had concentrated all their available force. The result placed at the disposal of the British Government the country on both sides of the Indus from Sukkur to the sea. It is pathetically told that when the Ameers saw the battle going against them they tried by their spy-glasses to detect Major Outram, that they might surrender to a personal friend. He had procured Sir Charles Napier's leave to embark for Bombay, and left at such a time as to render impossible a personal leave-taking of the princes, which must have been painful; but he wrote to his friend, Lieutenant Brown, to whose custody they were intrusted—

"As you are the custodian of the captive princes, let me entreat of you, as a kindness to myself, to pay every regard to their comfort and dignity. I do assure you my heart bleeds for them, and it was in the fear that I might betray my feelings that I declined the last interview they yesterday sought of me. Pray say how sorry I was I could not call upon them before leaving; that, could I have done them any good, I would not have grudged . . . any expenditure of time or labour on their behalf; but that, alas! they have placed it out of my power to do aught, by acting contrary to my advice, and having recourse to the fatal step of appeal to arms against the British Power."

Though he had parted from Sir Charles Napier with the feeling that it was most improbable they could act together well, yet, hearing that Sir Charles expressed regret at his loss, he offered to return should this be deemed desirable. Fortunately, perhaps, it was not, and he returned to England, where he was active in representing the case of the Sinde princes — a self-imposed duty which led him to be so seriously misunderstood by Sir Charles Napier that interruption of their friendship was the consequence: a sorrowful circumstance to Outram.

He returned to India as Lieutenant-Colonel Outram, C.B., somewhat suddenly, prompted by the hope of finding active service on the outbreak of the Sikh war. There was still too much opposition to him in high quarters, and he was disappointed. He made for Sir Hugh Gough's head-quarters, to be depressed by the tone that obtained there, particularly at the indifference expressed by so many of his brother officers on the annexation of Sinde—a proceeding which he looked upon in the light of usurpation. It appeared somewhat like an insult when he was offered the inferior post of political revenue officer of Nimar, an appendage to Indore, yielding less than he had had ten years before, and annulling practically his services in Mahi Kanta and in Sinde; but he had the good sense to accept the post, and patiently and ably discharged its duties, though he admitted himself dispirited and depressed. On Lord Ellenborough's recall in May he resigned, and after six months occupancy returned to Bombay. He intended to proceed to England, but before he had taken ship war broke out in the Maratta country, for which he volunteered, and in which he rendered such service as called forth the special praise and thanks of the general. This led to his appointment of joint-commissioner of the Maratta country, which he held till another appointment was made. His defence of the policy of Mr. Reeve and himself did not serve to regain him favour at head-quarters. Then he was offered the post of political agent in the South Maratta country. This he declined. He had some service to do, however, in the storming of the forts of Páwangarh and Panala, before taking leave, being among the foremost who entered the latter fort. Then he was employed in quelling the uprising in Sawant-Wari, a country to the south of that he had just quitted, where he had a very narrow escape, and afterwards in the proceedings against Goa.

It was during a short period now spent as Resident at Sattara that he so significantly showed what manner of man he was in his disposal of that "prize money of Sinde." His portion amounted to some £3,000. At first he intended to intimate to Government that he did not wish to receive it, and would

not receive it, but, under good advice, he finally concluded at once to turn it over to philanthropic institutions—one of Dr. Duff's schools and Lady Lawrence's Hill Asylum receiving the larger share. His biographer has followed his own example; and we hear more of this "blood-money" and its disposal in other memoirs than in that of Sir James Outram. Dr. George Smith has a good deal to say of it in his "Life of Dr. Duff;" for Outram, on consenting to receive the money, at once consulted Dr. Duff respecting its disposal, to find that the great Free Church Missionary was then casting about anxiously for means to found and to build a new boys' school, which was much needed, and which has done in every respect a great work. This and Lady Lawrence's Asylum exhausted the bulk of it; and surely seldom has money so obtained been better or more fitly disposed of—one good result, at least, that may be said to have flowed from Sir Charles Napier's Sinde wars. One can hardly help thinking here of Wordsworth's lines in "The Happy Warrior,"—

"Who, doomed to go in company with pain,
And fear, and bloodshed—miserable train—
Turns his necessity to glorious gain."

But the matter did not end here, as it ought to have done for the credit of all parties. Some little time afterwards the Pay Department made a grand discovery—almost worthy of a genius like that of Swift; and it applied the knowledge in a manner that would probably have put Machiavelli to the blush. We may well assume that the Pay Department, because of Outram's principle of doing his good works in secret, did not know how the prize money had been bestowed. At any rate, a claim was made on Outram to refund it, on the ground that he had only held a civil appointment when certain actions were fought; which certainly adds a touch of irony to the whole affair, notwithstanding that this tantalising procedure of the Pay Office was stopped by a hint from higher quarters. It is depressing to learn that after twenty-six years of service Outram held only the regimental grade of captain.

From Sattara he passed to Baroda, and his stay there was made memorable by his efforts against what was called *khutput*, or bribery, by which a premium was put upon bad government; in fact, the corruption that existed, if we may credit good authorities, penetrated into every department. We can easily imagine how such a state of things would affect a mind like that of Outram. He was kept in an attitude of constant protest, and the worry, more than the work, brought on ill-health.

In 1849 he was compelled to leave Baroda and go on sick-leave to Egypt. This was not wholly to rest, however. Mr. Stuart Poole, who saw much of him then, tells us that he fancied Colonel Outram lost mental strength from the power that an *idée fixe* had over him ; the wrongs of the Ameers of Sinde and Baroda bribery being constantly on his mind. When in 1850 he returned to his post, he was ceaseless in his efforts to make an end of this and of other evils. At length he was asked to report, and he did so in a manner so efficient and plainspoken that he received the frowns of Government instead of its encouragement. He was actually told to resign. Writing to his family, he says : "Do not fancy that I am at all cast down by this. I fully expected it, and am not sorry to get away from this 'sink of iniquity;' though, of course, I should have preferred a more honourable retreat." But *khutput* and Outram's report did not end here. It was not possible to shelve either the one or the other in this way. The Court of Directors at Leadenhall Street at last took up the affair, sifted it to the bottom, and demanded Outram's restoration to the very office from which he had been dismissed. Outram, the Court of Directors declared, had done a great and difficult service in a masterly manner.

His final stay at Baroda, however, was not prolonged. From it he went to Aden as Commissioner, and after that he became Chief Commissioner in Oude. He who had in Sinde so upheld the native princes had now to condemn those in Oude as effete and helpless. It was to the interests of the people that he looked, and native princes were to be respected only as far as they held the respect and affection of the people, and ruled for their benefit. On the whole he recommended annexation in Oude, because "in upholding the sovereign power of this effete and incapable dynasty, we do so at the cost of five millions of people."

Outram liked this appointment, and did heroic work in it. Those who knew Oude best wondered at the reformations so quietly and thoroughly effected. Ill health compelled a visit to England in 1856. On Outram's return to India, he took the command of the Persian Expedition, which did the most brilliant service. For this he was thanked by the Government, the approval of the authorities being intimated in unqualified terms, and her Majesty conferred upon him the Grand Cross of the Bath.

Outram was still at Bushire when the following message was addressed by Lord Canning to Lord Elphinstone, and speedily redispatched to its destination : "Write to Sir James Outram that I wish him to return to India immediately. . . . . We want all our best men here." Outram at once posted to Calcutta, and thence to Benares by river. It was a crisis that brooked no delay. Before he had reached Benares, the mutiny had spread through Oude. Sir Henry Lawrence had been killed at Lucknow. Outram was appointed to the post which he had surrendered to Sir Henry's hands eighteen months before, and with this was joined the military control. He chose his staff with rare insight, Robert Napier, now Lord Napier of Magdala, being his military secretary and chief of the Adjutant-General's department. The masterly dispatch of his forced marches from Benares to Allahabad, and then from Allahabad to Lucknow, in spite of sickness and exhaustion among the troops, as well as the bravery and decisive sagacity which he exhibited in the actual relief operations, are known to every one ; but it may not be so clearly remembered how he could not support the idea of superseding Havelock before the great work was done, at last resolving, as he told Colonel Napier, to go "in my political capacity." He had accordingly written thus to Havelock, in a tone which proves the true Bayard : "I shall join you with the reinforcements, but to you shall be left the glory of relieving Lucknow, for which you have already so nobly struggled. I shall accompany you only in my civil capacity as Commissioner, placing my military services at your disposal, should you please to make use of me, serving under you as a volunteer." The account of the seven troublous weeks during which Outram skilfully maintained the position taken up both within and without the still besieged Residency is one of the most exciting, and yet one of the most perfectly satisfying on record, while the plan and execution of the evacuation of the Residency ranks among the most complete and successful of modern military achievements. He died on the 11th March, 1863.

His indomitable courage never faltered ; to his fine sense of justice and of honour he was ever faithful. His duty to the Government he served was brought into harmony with his duty to himself, through many sacrifices ; and at length his nobility υ nature convinced even those whose plans and prospects he seemed to have hindered, that he had been wisest. ALEX. H. JAPP.

THE HEBREW MAID AND NAAMAN'S WIFE.

By JOHN S. HOWSON, D.D., Dean of Chester.

MANY sermons are preached every year concerning Naaman; but comparatively few, I imagine, concerning the Hebrew maid, to whom in truth he owed the cure of his leprosy. Yet for two reasons it is well worth while to attend to this subordinate part (if so we choose to call it) of the narrative, and to take under our notice this little servant-maid—for the sake of quickening our sympathy with the class which, more or less accurately, she represents; and secondly, for the example which she furnishes to all of that class, and in fact to all of every class.

In one respect, indeed, her lot was very different from anything of which we have experience in the social life of modern times. She was a slave, absolutely taken away from her own old home, and absolutely at the disposal of her new master and mistress, with no power of leaving them if she chose, and no remedy against ill-treatment.

It happened that, during the war which then prevailed between the Syrians and Israel, "the Syrians had gone out by companies," had crossed the border, and had brought away captive out of the land of Israel "a little maid," and she became the slave of the wife of Naaman, who was "captain of the host of the king of Syria." There is no proof that she was ill-treated. Still she was a slave, and this is what I meant by saying that her lot was a hard one.

But though in one respect her position could find no counterpart amongst us at present, in another respect she may be taken as a representative of a very large class, and a class to whom we are under great obligations. She was removed from her own natural home, and planted in another which might be termed an artificial home; and on this mere statement hang some considerations of great moment in reference to part of our own social arrangements.

We sometimes forget that our servants are taken from their own homes and placed in ours, and that on this ground (to mention nothing else) they have a strong claim to sympathy, consideration, and forbearance. From this circumstance alone they are liable to certain faults, to which otherwise they might not be tempted. Thus we are sometimes, for instance, surprised that servants in a large household quarrel with one another. Now certainly they ought not to quarrel. With proper religious feeling towards Him which "maketh men to be of one mind in a house," they would be withheld from this fault. Still it must be recollected that they are brought away from very different households to live together in one household. They are brothers and sisters living together under their own father and mother. Even brothers and sisters are not always harmonious. We ought not to wonder, human nature being what it is, that there shall sometimes be want of concord among strangers whom the force of circumstances brings into close relations with each other under one roof.

But if any member of this aggrieved class has special claim to sympathy, consideration, or forbearance, it is the young servant-girl in a small household. Young men go out into the world, and battle in the conflict of life; and in this very conflict they often find a safeguard against temptation. But in the other case, unless great kindness is shown (and great kindness is by no means always shown), there is peculiar isolation, with many risks. Such a case presents the nearest resemblance which modern society furnishes to that of the Hebrew captive girl in the family of Naaman. She was solitary in a home which was not her own. There is no reason, as I have said, to believe that she was treated with any special cruelty. The history, indeed, would rather give us a contrary impression; and perhaps this kindness that had been shown to her cheered and encouraged her in her attempt to do good service to her master. At all events this is certain, that in such instances as those to which I refer among ourselves, kind treatment brings many good qualities to view, opens the heart, breaks down reserve, and trains those who might otherwise go far astray, so as to become very useful and helpful members of society.

To turn now from the duties suggested by the hard condition of this young Israelitish captive, to the suggestions which her example supplies, we appear to see very clearly that, though surrounded by idolaters, she retained her own religious feelings and convictions. It is the Lord's prophet of whom she speaks to her mistress. "She had learnt in her youth to know the God whose eye, though specially over Israel, was still over all the nations;" and thus it was that the great benefit came to Naaman. If we call to remembrance also a certain passage, wherein this history is referred to in the New Testament, we seem to gain a further insight into this girl's religious character. Our Lord said on one occasion to the Jews: "Many lepers were in Israel in the time of Eliseus the prophet: and none of them was cleansed, saving Naaman the Syrian." Thus this Hebrew girl had never known a case of leprosy cured by Elisha; but she knew that he had been enabled to work other miracles; and she inferred that the same Divine power and goodness, acting through the prophet, could deal with this calamity also. It is an instance of the correct reasoning of a simple and devout heart: while it is a proof of the strong hold which her early religious training kept upon her mind.

And does not this remind us, brethren, of the importance of the early religious instruction of the young, and of the blessing which we may expect to follow such instructions? And here comes out into distinct view the great usefulness of our Sunday Schools, and the high reward which may be expected by those who work in such schools lovingly and faithfully.

There must be many Sunday School Teachers among those who read these words. Certainly there are many who ought to be Sunday School Teachers. The recollection of what this captive Hebrew girl did in the court of Naaman should lead the thoughts of all such persons to dwell on the happiness of preparing children now within reach, for duties which they may discharge afterwards elsewhere. In our country more especially such thoughts ought to be natural. When we look upon the young people around us, we feel that a large number of them may in a few years be dispersed all over this world. The circumstances of our commerce, the spirit of enterprise, the shifting of our population, are like the Syrians that "went out by companies," and are continually taking away the young out of the land of their fathers. How essential it is that these inexperienced travellers, these youthful emigrants, shall take with them a good knowledge of true religion, and firm resolutions for the resistance of temptation; and hearts made more ready through Christ and His Grace for the using of the new opportunities that may be put within their reach.

And now, to turn to another point. We observe that this "little maid," who was taken "captive" out of the land of Israel, while true to her religious convictions, was faithful to her new master, and did her best to render him useful service. She did not

suppose that because Naaman belonged to an alien country—no, nor because he was the enemy of her own country—that therefore she had no duties to perform on his behalf. She did not suppose that, because her lot was hard, and caused her, no doubt, to shed many a tear, when she thought of her own home in the land of Israel, that therefore God's providence had given her no opportunities to use. She saw that her master, in the midst of all his greatness, was afflicted with a distressing and humiliating disease—she knew where the best hope of recovery was to be found—and the good, kind-hearted girl obeyed the impulse of her heart. She adopted, too, the wisest and the most sensible course. "She spoke to her mistress." And the result completes the argument derivable from this history to servants, for the discharge of their duties in an affectionate, generous, and faithful spirit. The deliverance of Naaman from that illness which made him a miserable object to all who saw him—every hour of health and comfort which he enjoyed afterwards, as resulting from that recovery—was due to the religious principle, kind feeling, and good sense of this Hebrew maid.

There could not be a better illustration, to those who are engaged in domestic service, of the great principle which ought to guide them in their discharge of duty towards their masters and mistresses. The great principle is this: that they ought to make common cause with those under whom they are placed, and consider their interest to be in fact their own. The way of the world is to adopt a totally different principle, and to assume that interests are conflicting. Thus it comes to pass that servants, instead of saving the money of their masters and mistresses, too often waste it; instead of using time diligently, they trifle; instead of being orderly, they cause confusion. There are many precepts in the New Testament which bear upon this point. Even if masters and mistresses are not what they should be (and all masters and mistresses are not what they ought to be), the duty is the same, though it is not so pleasant. Servants are to be subject "not only to the good and gentle, but also to the froward." All is to be done by them, "in singleness of heart, as unto Christ; not with eye-service, as men-pleasers; but as the servants of Christ, doing the will of God from the heart; with good will doing service as to the Lord, and not to men." And these precepts were given, we must remember, not to servants in the modern sense, but to slaves ; and this circumstance infinitely increases their force. It is partly because this little Hebrew maid was a " captive " and a slave that her example tells upon us with so much weight.

As we part from her now, let us think of her, and of such as her, with sympathy. Her lot was a very hard one. She was taken away by force from her own home. She was among people whose customs were different from her customs, and their religion different from her religion ; and she was very young. There is a most pathetic African proverb which says that " every slave had once a mother." What an infinite blessing it is to this country that slavery is unknown to us ! Let such thoughtful and sympathetic thoughts quicken our desires to study and to profit by this modest example. This young captive maid is most truly a pattern to us all. We are sure to be placed in circumstances when we shall be tested, whether we can be true to our religious convictions among those who deny God. We are almost sure, more or less, to be cut off from old habits and old associations ; and then it will be seen whether we can carry on with us into the new period of life what we have learnt in the old. Opportunities will certainly be given us for doing good ; and our heavenly Father will put us to the test, whether we use these opportunities, while we have them, or let them pass away ; and if we say that such chances of being useful will, in our case, be very scanty and that we ourselves feel very insignificant, we cannot be of less importance than that young Hebrew servant. It was not much that she could do ; but her praise was precisely that of which we read in the Gospels : " She did what she could."

FANCIES.

BY THE AUTHOR OF " MRS. JERNINGHAM'S JOURNAL."

I.—EILY.

WHEN the stars sing lullabies,
　　Eily may lie down to rest ;
Not more innocent the skies,
　　Than the heart within her breast.

Balmy breeze and dropping dew
　　Are not fresher than is she ;
All the earth, and heaven too,
　　Are not dearer unto me.

Slumber is death's counterfeit :
　　When the spell is o'er her laid,
Looks she so divinely sweet,
　　That of death I am afraid.

If she dies, I'll bury her
　　Where the whitest blossoms grow ;
Or, perchance, she would prefer
　　For her grave, a mound of snow.

Waiting for a solemn hush,
　　Bursting into sudden song,
I will tame the sweetest thrush
　　Singing for her, loud and long.

But the bird will only sing
　　Over a deserted mound,
And my flowers I shall fling
　　Only on an empty ground.

For my Eily will have flown
　　To the land I cannot see,
And the heart that is mine own
　　Will be beating there for me.

If she dies, a dull despair
　　Will eclipse the green and blue ;
But for me, I shall not care—
　　If she dies, I shall die too !

II.—AWAKE.

The sun gets up in the morning
And lifts his stately head ;
Open your eyes, my sleepy skies,
The sun is out of bed !
The moon is very timid,
She dare not meet the sun,
With a heigh-ho ! the stars must go,
And hide themselves one by one.

The sun gets up in the morning,
The world is all alight ;
Every tree is full of glee,
Every blossom bright ;
Every bird is singing
A welcome to his King,
With a Well done, beautiful sun !
You glorify every thing.

The sun gets up in the morning,
And so must children too ;
How dare you keep fast asleep,
The sun is calling you !
Mid all the birds and blossoms
Your merry voices raise :
With a Hurrah ! How glad we are
We have got a sun to praise !

THE STOCKING-KNITTER.

A SKETCH.

BY BRENDA N. MELLADEW.

SARAH DE BERENGER.

By JEAN INGELOW.

CHAPTER XXII.

THE husband and wife gazed at one another for a moment without speaking; both seemed to be subdued into stillness by wonder, and one added terror to this feeling.

As Uzziah did not speak, his poor wife felt the slender ghost of a hope that her husband might not be certain of her identity, and she turned as quietly as she could, and had risen and moved towards the station door, when he cried out after her sharply and loudly, "Hannah!"

She still advanced, taking no notice of him. She did not dare to make haste, but with a certain calmness of manner she passed out and walked slowly upon the grass, and went behind a bank among the heather. She was thinking whether she could throw herself down with any hope of hiding, when the fatal sound of the lame foot was behind her, and with a feeling of desolation indescribable she walked on and on, just keeping out of Uzziah's reach, but only just. She knew not what to do, and all her senses were sharpened. It seemed that they had come to her aid; but she questioned them, and it was only to find that nothing could be done—nothing. A great white moon had just heaved itself up. She was keeping the lurid orange sunset well behind her, lest its light should show her face, but now the light was purer in front, and she turned down a little decline and still walked slowly on.

Oh the bitterness of that hour! She still walked on, and the lame man toiled after her, and said not a word. She had come into a desolate cart track which was grassy, between the heath-covered banks that rose high on either side. What good to go on any more? All was lost. He had power over her to prevent her escape. She had felt that it was no use to run wildly away, for she knew that in such a case he had but to call and cry out after her, and she must, she should, return. She gave up hope and sat down on the bank, dropped her hands on her knees, and awaited him without looking up.

The low moon was full on her face; the west had faded, and all was cool and dim. When Uzziah saw her sit down he stood still for a moment, as if not wishing to startle her; then he slowly advanced, wiping his forehead, for the exertion of the walk had been great to him, though she had been little more than two miles.

The place was perfectly desolate and still —a good way from that portion of the great common which had been set apart as a race-course, and far from any road or field or farm.

If Hannah Dill had meant to deny her identity to her husband (but it did not appear that she had), her act in retreating thus

XXI—38

must have made denial useless Uzziah Dill did not appear to intend entering on that question. He came near and sat down on the grassy bank, about two feet from her. Her silence, her evident despair, awed him, and he let her alone, as if he meant to wait till she should speak. And yet his whole soul was shaken by surprise. That if they met she would claim him, hang about him, and sorely interfere with what he called his evangelistic work, had been his fear ever since he had found himself at liberty. She had loved him deeply and faithfully; it had not entered into his calculations that such a state of things could cease.

He took out his handkerchief and again wiped his brow; then the urgent thought found utterance. "I'm afraid, my poor wife, you've acted very bad by me, else you wouldn't be so fearful of seeing my face."

She had taken the money, and concealed his children; she felt for the moment that this was "acting bad" by him. She did not repent, of course, but she had nothing to say for herself.

"If you've not been true to me——" he exclaimed almost passionately, and then seemed to give himself a sudden check.

"True to you!" she answered, turning slowly towards him and quietly looking at him from head to foot. "I never gave it a thought once; all these years, that I had to be true to *you*, but I thank my God He has always helped me to be true to myself."

The astonishment with which Uzziah Dill heard these words came not merely to contradict every recollection he had of his wife, but to produce some few reflections on his own past conduct; yet he presently put these back, and in a characteristic fashion still pressed his point.

"We're all on us poor, vile sinners, and have nothing to boast of."

"Yes," she answered, "I see what you are at. Through the blessing of God it is that I'm able to hold up my head with the best of good wives, that are happy, as I have never been. I have no goodness of my own before God, but I look to be respected by men, because it's my due; and I don't answer like this because you were my husband, but because, let him be high or low, I should answer so to any man."

And then she broke down and burst into heart-sick tears—remembered how she had seen her darlings drive away, and wrung her hands and sobbed. It was not from any sense of consolation in his words, but rather from revulsion of feeling, that she checked herself when he said, "Hannah, this is a very quiet hour, and I feel solemn and nearer to our heavenly Father for it. If I was to relate my experience to you, and how God has dealt with me, it might be blessed to you, my poor wife, as it has been to some others; for though I may say with the Apostle Paul, 'With me it is a very small thing that I should be judged of you or of man's judgment——'"

"Mercy on us!" exclaimed the poor wife, interrupting him vehemently, and shuddering with repulsion. "You're never going to compare yourself, Uzziah, to the Apostle Paul?"

"Why not?" he answered humbly, but without hesitation. "I bless the Lord that I am a sinner-saved by grace, and what else was St. Paul?"

She was so shocked at this speech that she broke forth into tears again, with "Oh, I'm a miserable creature! I can't bear it! This is worse—worse than the loss of my dears!"

"Hannah," he answered kindly, and with something like authority in his manner, "I know you've had misfortunes, and that I've been the cause of some. I know I've many times drank myself mad, and then abused you shameful, and I know (and for all you may think I did not care to hear it, I did care) I was truly sorry when Mr. Gordon told me you had lost your babes. I wish to speak like a Christian man, that I could not call up such love for them as a father ought to feel, but I was sorry for you. I know right well that, when you buried them, it was a very bitter parting to you. Now, don't read yourself so with sobbing; let the past be, and, with the blessing of God, let us live together in a better union for the future; and," he added, like a man who had never known any keen affection all his life, "it's a sad thing you should lament over them still. Forget them—they're well off; and they were but little ones." He took off his hat when he said "they're well off," and looked up reverently.

Though his speech had been so cold, it was an advance on the past. Hannah Dill acknowledged its moderation, saw some contrition in it, and felt its truth; but the real parting had been so recent, and so different from what he supposed, that its bitterness overcame her again, and the tears ran down her cheeks. "Oh, my children, my dears, my only ones!" she sobbed out, "what is there for your mother to remember but you?"

And he thought they were dead. This was eventually to prove a great help to her, but at the moment it gave her a strange dread for them, an almost superstitious fear; as if, indeed, they *were* dead.

Her husband at this moment drew himself a little nearer to her as he sat on the bank, and she started away with instinctive repulsion, whereupon, with a slightly offended air, he retreated to his former position, while she slowly, and without making any effort one way or the other, exhausted her emotion; and the moon, now dimmed by slightly veiling clouds, showed her black figure to her husband as she sat at the top of the bank, looking out over the wide expanse of blossoming heather, and sometimes clasping her hands as if she was in prayer. He also sat perfectly still, and in absolute silence. The balmy air that had been so sultry was now cool and refreshing, a few stars were out, owls were skimming the tops of the heather, and some rabbits dancing and darting about on a dry green knoll. It was long before he spoke, and then it was with suddenness and decision.

"Well, Hannah, it's past eleven o'clock. We had better go to the inn, my dear."

An unwonted termination this "my dear."

"Do as you please," she answered. "But, Uzziah, we are not going together."

"Not together?" he exclaimed. "You've lost that money over the shoe business, and you've hid yourself from me, and never wrote to me once for years; and I've met you and not said one word; and if you'd have come back and done your duty by me, I never would have done, the Lord helping me,—I never would have reproached you at all, but taken you back and made the best of you, as I believe is right; and now, Hannah——"

"Yes, and now," she repeated, "I tell *you* that I forgive the past. And this is true, and so I'll say it, that if I chose this moment to set off and get clean away from you, I could, as you know well; and if you won't give me time to think out my miserable duty, and consider whether I may not truly have the blessed lot of leaving you, or whether I must stay because God wills it, I'll take the thing into my own hands. I'll get away from you this night, and risk the repenting of it afterwards."

He sat silent for several minutes; then he answered, almost with gentleness, "Your words cut me very sharp, Hannah; but I don't see what I have to answer before either God or you, but that I forgive them."

Hannah Dill here felt an instinctive consciousness of a change. When she moved a very little farther off, it was not from any fear lest he should strike her. And she did not strive to hide her feeling of repulsion towards him when she replied, "I fare to think you cannot know, Uzziah, that I had the reading of that letter you sent through Jacob from your prison to Rosa Stock."

"Rosa Stock?" he repeated faintly. "That was a long time ago."

"Not so long but what I have got a copy of the letter."

"I loved that woman," he exclaimed passionately. "I had been her ruin, but she never seemed to think of that; and she had been my ruin, but that did not seem to make it right I should leave her without any comfort from me." Then his voice sank, and he went on, "Oh, I have been a miserable sinner!"

"Ay," answered his wife, with pitiless coldness; "but there's many a miserable sinner that's no hypocrite. It's because you're such a hypocrite that I fare to shiver so while you're near me. I got your letter to me after I had the money, and you'd heard of it, and I've got every word of it cut deep into my heart. You never asked whether *my* child was born, nor how *I* had fared after you turned me out of doors; but you wrote to say (God forgive you!) that you was a reformed character, and you wanted me to keep myself right for your sake."

"Ay, I was a hypocrite," he answered—"I was." He flung up his hands as he spoke, and she shrank hastily from him; but he clasped them upon his forehead and groaned. "Did you think I would *strike* you, Hannah?" he exclaimed, as if such a thought on her part was a most unnatural and cruel one.

She was silent.

"You have no cause to be afraid of me," he continued. "And now I see how it is that I cannot make the sweet offers of the Gospel to you as I can to others. It's because I have been so bad to you. My poor wife, I humbly ask your pardon!"

"No; it's because you make such high talk of religion," she replied, "that I feel as if I could not bear with you. It fared to shock me so, to see you standing up—you that used to get so drunk—and preach to better folks that they were not to drink at all. It fares to turn my blood cold to hear you talk now of doing folks good with your religious experience, and how the blessed God deals with you, when the last I knew of you showed that, if you dealt with aught out of this world, it must have been with the evil one."

"Hannah, do you ever read the Bible?"

"Yes, I read it every day, and pray to God that I may understand it, and live by it."

"There's a thief you read of there that mocked at our Lord while he hung a-dying. He got forgiveness, didn't he?"

"Ay, but he died, Uzziah."

"But, if he had lived, do you think he would have gone back to his wickedness?"

"No, I don't."

"But you think there's no forgiveness for a wretched thief now—you think God cannot forgive a miserable drunkard now?"

"No, I don't think that, my poor husband; God forbid!"

"You think it possible that the blessed God might forgive—even me?"

"Yes, I do."

"But what if He did, Hannah? How should I order myself, if my sins were forgiven?"

"I expect you'd be very humble and very broken-hearted, and quiet about it."

"And not tell other poor wretches that were in the same misery and bondage that there was forgiveness for them too; that Jesus Christ could save them too, and would save them, if they would have Him?"

It was past midnight now, and this last appeal, which had been meant to be so comforting and so convincing, was too much for poor Hannah Dill. "O God, forgive me if I want to do amiss!" she cried, and gave way to an agony of tears. "It does seem as if I couldn't stop with you—I couldn't—I couldn't."

"Well, then," he answered, and rose and took off his hat, "let us pray."

She looked at him and trembled; but she sat still, and the lame man knelt down. His wife could but just make out his figure, for a small dark cloud had come over the moon. She saw that he lifted up his hand, and then she, trembling yet, listened, and he began to pray, beginning with the beautiful and pathetic collect—

"O God, who knowest us to be set in the midst of so many and great dangers, that by reason of the frailty of our nature we cannot always stand upright, grant to us such strength and protection as may support us in all dangers, and carry us through all temptations; through Jesus Christ our Lord. Amen."

And then, after a pause, he went on—the sometime drunken cobbler, the hypocritical convict, and bigamist, went on, with all

reverence and solemnity—"It is a strange thing, good Lord, that we have to say to thee. We are a miserable wife and husband that did not wish to meet—neither of us—and that was, maybe, wrong in thy sight. I did try to find her at first, good Lord, and when I could not, I thought thou hadst answered me, and I might serve thee as a man free from her. I could live on so little, and her money I willingly gave up. And how could she follow me, often in hardship and hunger, when I go to speak well of thee and of thy loving-kindness?

"And she, good Lord, she has lost that love she had for me, and that I did not care for, and she would fain go her ways. Shall I let her go, Lord—may I let her go in peace?—for thou seest it is left to thee. We met by thy will, and we durstn't part without thy blessing. Oh, give us that, and give it now!

"So many times thou hast answered me; but since the day when my sins were forgiven, I have never been in such a strait as I am now, and I want to talk with thee of her side of this matter. Look on her. How hard it seems to come back! Ay, it would be a vast sight harder still, if she could know all. Thou knowest all; I poured it out to thee. It was a base thing to put into words. Maybe it went nigh to break thy heart when thou wert here, that men should have such deeds to confess. Maybe thou knowest what it is to rue, even in thy Father's bosom, the ways and the wants of us that are to thee so near of kin. O Lord Christ Jesus, that we thy brothers may be no more a disgrace to thee, pray to thy Father to make us pure, for thy sake.

"I beseech thee, be content to have the guiding of us, for we cannot guide ourselves. We have great searchings of heart, but come thou and sit between us in this desolate place. Thou knowest what we want, thy blessing on our parting in peace. But if we may not part thus, thy blessing that we may live together in peace. Give it, O most pitiful Master! and give it by the dawning of the day."

When he had got thus far, the lame man arose and went a little farther, and again knelt down, holding up his hands and still praying aloud, but far enough off to plead with God inaudibly, as far as his one human listener was concerned; and Hannah Dill felt then a little comfort in her misery: he was not praying for effect, and that she might hear him—at least, he was not a hypocrite here.

The moon came out—she was near her southing—and as she went down, Hannah Dill saw her husband's face, and knew that it was changed. A soft waft of summer air came about her now and again, dropping as if from the stars; her husband's voice came upon it, and died as it fell, and that was changed; no such tones in it had reached her ears of old. It went on and on, and still it went on. At first it had been almost a cry, a low, pleading cry; but afterwards, as she recalled the beginning, she wondered at its gradual change. No words to reach her, but yet now it was calm, and almost satisfied. This long prayer was more awful to her, in the solemn night, than any of his speeches had been.

It frightened and subdued her, but she would not speak, for while he was so occupied she was left to herself. She leaned her elbows on her knees and propped her face on her hands—her poor face, stained with tears, and pale with long distress—but just as her lulled emotion and fatigue between them had brought her such quietness as might have been succeeded by a doze, the distant voice stopped, and she, missing its monotonous murmur, started and was distressfully awake again. It might be about three o'clock, she thought; the moon was gone, and though two or three stars were quivering in the sky, the restfulness of night was almost over. The hills, she thought, had taken rather a clearer outline towards the east, and there was more air stirring over the heads of the heather.

She saw her husband rise, and a thrill of joy ran through her veins when she observed that he did not mean to approach her. She made out, in the dimness that comes just before dawn, that he went slowly to a little rise where the heather was thickest, and that he laid himself down in it. She knew he was a heavy sleeper, and that in a few minutes he would sleep. Was she not alone? Could she not now steal away from him? No. Before the thought was fully formed, she knew she could not. The sleeping man's prayer had power over her; it seemed to wake yet while he slept. And now that she could feel herself retired from all human eyes, she also arose and kneeled down, and spread out her hands as if she would lay her case before the Lord.

Not a word to say, not one word; but a thought in her mind like this: "It is not because I cannot make my statement clear, that God does not see and pity my case. Let my God look upon me and decide; for whatever it is to be, I consent." A long time silent thus, even till the grass turned green about her, and the birds began to wake—even till the first streak of gold was lying along the brink of the hill, and till the utter peacefulness of the new dawn seemed to make her aware that in her own mind was also dawning a resignation that was almost like peace. If all joy was gone, and all comfort given up, at least they had been stolen away gently, and, as it were, almost with her own consent. "Thou knowest that I cannot bear it," she said quietly. "Oh, bear it for me; take my burden on thyself!"

And almost as she spoke, she felt aware that she had been helped—that all should be right, and was right. Then she too rose from her knees, and heard the lame man approaching; she sat down on the bank, and he sat beside her.

All the east was taking on its waxing flush. She and her husband looked at it together as they sat side by side. She sighed twice; its solemn splendour was so great, and her heart had sunk so low, she could hardly bear to look at it; but at last he spoke.

"Well, Hannah," he said, "there's words to be spoke now; and, my poor wife, it's right you should begin."

"Ay," she answered, faltering, and faint from long emotion and want of rest, "I've a right to say that you must tell me what has become of Rosa and her babe."

"Rosa Stock?" he replied solemnly. "She's dead, Hannah,—dead this seven years; and her babe's dead too."

Naturally this information made a difference. The poor wife sighed again. "But I cannot live with him," she thought, "if I'm to be always living a lie.—You said to God in the night," she went on, "that I didn't know all."

"It's true, Hannah," he replied.

"And no more can you know all," she replied. "What's done, was done for the best. As for me, I want to know no more. I'll ask no questions about anything, nor never reproach you; and these words are my vow and bond that I won't. But in return, you're never to ask me—never—how I came to lose the money, and——"

She paused so long, that he at last said, "If it's clean gone, and nothing I could do could by possibility get it back, promise I do."

"And my children," she began, melting again into heart-sick tears. "If I go along with you, you must promise me, on your solemn word before God this hour, that you'll never, never mention them to me—never, never let their names pass your lips to me more."

He turned to her with a look of surprise. She was quietly wiping away her tears. He would have liked to comfort her; he even began to reason with her. "I should have thought it might be a comfort to you to talk about their pretty ways, and their deaths likewise."

"It is not," she answered. "I fare to believe that it's my duty to stay with you, if you'll consider over this one thing that I demand so solemnly, and promise it with all your heart; but if you won't do that, then let me go my ways."

After a short pause he answered, "Hannah, I promise." And then she gave him her hand, and he helped her to rise. And they walked together in the early sunshine, to get the refreshment they sorely needed at the little inn. Not a word or a look passed between them; one went with silent exultation, and the other with silent tears.

CHAPTER XXIII.

UZZIAH DILL and his wife were both sorely fatigued when, in the rosy flush of a summer morning, they reached the little inn. Its windows were not yet opened, and they sat on a bench outside, under a thickly branched maple-tree. Uzziah Dill was able to observe and reflect. He noticed the neatness and cleanliness of his wife's array. She was one of those women who are far more attractive in early middle life than in youth. The lanky, gaunt figure had a fuller and more gracious outline now; the sometime thin features and great, hungering eyes were softer. It was a long time since any man had struck her, or insulted her, or scowled at her, and even after that night of misery, her expression of countenance bore witness to this fact. She was languid, very weary, and very full of sorrow, but her fear of him, as he had sense to see, was no fear of a blow.

He thought she would soon "come round." She had loved him when he had ill-treated her; surely her very jealousy was a proof that, whatever she might say, she had not utterly ceased to love him even now. And he meant to be so good to her, so—yes, even so loving to her. He had not wished to meet with her—very far from it—but here she was, and he found himself exulting.

There was a pump close at hand, and some sparkling, clear water lying under it, in a wooden trough. Hannah Dill went to it, and, taking off her bonnet, bathed her aching eyes and brow. He watched her; approved in his very heart the semi-methodistic plainness of her dress; saw her twist up her long hair with interest, put on her bonnet and shawl again, and come slowly back.

He thought she would say something encouraging and affectionate to her. He would let her know that she had happiness before her, and not misery; but when she came and sat down near him again, her gentle patience, her hopeless eyes, that did not look at him, seemed to steal his words out of his mouth.

"Hannah," was all he managed to say, "they are astir in the inn now; I'd better go in and tell them to get us some breakfast."

He seemed to wait her reply, and she said listlessly, "As you will."

It had pleased God already to discipline his base nature; he had endured great fear, had found himself to be vile. It had seemed to himself, as he lay once in the prison in solitary confinement, on account of his bad language and coarse insubordination—it had seemed all on a sudden as if some evil spirit drew near him in the dark and took his sins by armsful and heaped them over him, and he saw them as if they had bodily substance, and there were so many that they crushed him down. His first sensation was more astonishment than even fear. All these hateful things, excepting one or two that always haunted him, had seemed to be dead and gone, and now they were alive—not put away, but his, swarming about him, part of himself. He struggled, he trembled, he cried out. Then he thought he would act a more manful part; he tried to fling them off, he would not be so cowed. What could he do by way of occupation? He would recall all the songs he had been used to sing, and sing them now. So he wiped his forehead and began. But lo! it was a quavering, craven voice that sang; it moaned over the wicked words, it sank and choked over the impure ones. There was no comfort here. But something he must and would do, or this stifling weight on his soul would kill him. It was not that he repented, it was hardly remorse that he felt; it was the mere presence always over and about him of this load of wickedness, that he knew to be his own wickedness, that daunted him and made him so wretched. Well, he would say over so many of his school lessons as he could remember, he would set himself sums in his own mind, he would go over the multiplication table.

The chaplain found him one day at this weary work, trying to find some occupation and some thoughts to stand between him and his crimes. His sleep had departed, his mind was clouded, he was willing for once to speak, and seemed to think that no man had ever suffered so before. "I can't get them away!" he exclaimed, tearing at his breast. "How should I?—they are myself. I shall die if they press me down so."

The chaplain had always felt a sort of horror of him, he had been such a hypocrite, he had done so much to corrupt some of the other prisoners. He looked at him attentively, supposing that this was only some new piece of hypocrisy.

"The Almighty has been hard upon me," he continued; "I am cast into hell before my death."

"No," answered the chaplain. "The Almighty has been merciful to you, and given you still your life to repent in."

"I have tried to repent, and I cannot. How should I get to repent?" he answered.

"God, and God only, can give true repentance. You must humbly ask Him to give it to you." And then he looked doubtfully at the prisoner, who seemed so restless and so defiant, and so enraged. "Like a wild bull in a net," he thought within himself.

"I've tried as hard as ever I can to do what you call repent," continued the prisoner. "But even if I could be sorry all my days, here they are, these sins; I could not get away from them."

"No," answered the chaplain; "but you have leave to take them and lay them at the foot of the cross, the cross of Christ."

The prisoner answered, but not irreverently, only with the dulness of despair, "He would have nothing to do with such as I am. And why should He?"

"Why, indeed!" answered the chaplain; "that is more than we know. But if you can believe that God gave Him, and that He was willing to be given, to take away the sins of the world, you know enough."

"Well, I've heard say so all my life," said the prisoner, "but that don't seem to bring me any help. I'm down, that's what I am —sunk in the pit—and I don't see any hope, nor ease, nor daylight, nor way of getting out."

"And I cannot say so much as 'God help you,'" answered the chaplain; "for God offers you help only in that one way, and if you will not have it, there is no help for you in heaven or earth."

"I've done a good many black deeds," reasoned the prisoner, "as the good Lord knows better than you do. If I could only get them down and trample them under my feet, I would kneel then and cry for mercy."

"I tell you that trying to trample down your crimes is of no use. Your character is a part of yourself; you cannot get away from it, nor do away with them; but the Saviour of mankind, if you will go to Him, will not only forgive, but will release you and relieve you of them, and take them on Himself."

"Then let Him," cried the prisoner, flinging himself on the ground—"let Him!" he cried with vehemence, and almost with rage. "Let the good Lord have mercy on my miserable soul! I'm spent with misery, I can do nothing in the world; but if He did die to save such black sinners, and if He can bear with those that cannot even bear with themselves, and can get them free of their sins, and make men of them again, He never had a better chance than He has now. I say it humbly to him, let the good Lord try His hand on me."

In the choking accents both of rage and despair, Uzziah Dill cried out thus as he lay grovelling on the ground, and the young chaplain, starting up, looked at him with something like fear. The coarse nature and the ungoverned passions of the man had been taken hold of by a power too strong for him to cope with, but his own words rang in his ears now, and he lay on the floor silently, as if a great awe was upon him.

The chaplain had nothing to say. A great many convicts had professed repentance, and most of them on release had fallen away. He was about to kneel and offer prayer, when the convict sat up, and said in a scared voice, as if for the first time conscious of that great Presence in which we always dwell, "Those I shouted up were impudent words. I had no call to shout at all," he continued, looking round. "But I say again, the Lord, for Christ's sake, have mercy on my sinful soul!" Then—strange comment indeed on his own prayer—"Now," he continued, still with that look of awe, "now I've played my last card."

The chaplain, feeling shocked both at the wicked fellow's prayer and the violent way in which he had acted, was soon out of his cell. Uzziah Dill was asleep the next time he came to visit him, and the second time was so peaceful and quiet, as to appear more than ever a hypocrite to those about him; but he used no bad language, and was never insubordinate any more.

So, it had pleased God already to discipline his coarse nature. He had been cast into prison for his crimes, and there they had been shown to him as if pointed at by a finger from above; and then they had fallen from him, had been sunk, as it were, in the depths of the sea. And after that had come the discipline of contempt and long suspicion. These lasted almost till the time of his release—during all those years when he had been earnestly trying to improve himself, his intellect and all his powers becoming stronger through long protection from the constant tempting to drink, which had been too much for his feeble nature and weak constitution.

And now another discipline was preparing for him, woven out of circumstances, and from one of the commonest contradictions that prevailed in this contrary world.

He was not so obtuse that he did not perceive his wife's misery, her almost loathing of him. The love she had borne him and which he had never cared for, and long forgotten, flashed back on his remembrance now. He seemed to have a right to it NOW, and every half-hour assured him that to be a good and loving husband to her would be an easy task NOW. And he could not have it.

If God had forgiven him, why could not she? He longed to assure her how different he now was, but his tongue was tied; she would not believe him. He remembered with a pang the many good women that had kindly and even proudly entertained him after his temperance lectures, "for his works' sake;" but the deep humility of dawning love made him all too certain that they did not know him as his wife did, they did not know his past.

They ate and they drank together almost in silence; then, to the astonishment of Hannah Dill, her husband talked humbly and most piously to the landlady while she cleared away. It was very early; and if she and her family were not in the usual habit of having family prayers, he would be very glad to conduct them, for, with apologetic gentleness, "it was indeed so bright and early, that no interruption of business was likely."

The landlady took the proposal well. The poor wife felt that she could hardly bear to hear him "show off" before her; but when Uzziah Dill was told that the inn kitchen was ready for him, and that, beside the household, two carriers, "very quiet men," would be glad to join, he said, so as not to be overheard, "Hannah, I seem to feel as you would

liefer stay here; and I've nothing to say against it."

"No, Uzziah," she answered, instantly changing her mind, "I fare to think I had er go in;" and she sighed and followed him.

The poor ex-convict had a ready tongue, and he already knew his one Book well. He read a psalm, and made a few devout comments on it. His wife, in spite of herself, thought his remarks almost as scholarly and fine as Mr. de Berenger's; and when he began to pray, and faltered a good deal for all his earnestness, she knew as well as if she had been told that it was her presence which took away his self-possession. He desired her approval; he wondered what she would think.

So, when they were alone in the little parlour—for the parliamentary train was not to pass till noon—she said to him, "Uzziah, it is but right I should tell you I'll never breathe to any soul your having been in prison. I'll not interfere with your speeches in that way."

"Thank you heartily," he answered; "but, Hannah, where I think it will do good to tell it, I often have told it myself."

"Do good?" she exclaimed. "How should it do good? Who is to listen if you tell such a thing as that?"

"Many a drunkard will listen," he answered, "if he finds that, through the drink, I have been in a worse case than he has. It's all the drink, Hannah, that does for us. I never wished to do a thing against the law till I was under the temptation of it. When I had once done wrong, I sneaked and was wishful to do better and keep right till I was half drunk again; then the old wicked daring came, and made a wild beast of me. It gave me courage, and cunning too. I saw how to do the bad thing, when my pulse was all alive with that stimulus. But it was my natural way, before I was a converted man, to be a hypocrite. So I must watch most against that sin, and not make out that I've always had a good character."

"Then how do you get a living? Who employs you?" she inquired.

"Well, first place, I'm never called an impostor, for I acknowledge that I'm low down. In general, after I've spoke, there's a little collection made for me; and I have my tools, so if a brother or sister has any shoes to mend, I mend them. Though I say it, they're well done, and through that I often get more custom. Or, so long as I seem to be doing any good in a town, I take

"It was spanned by a wooden bridge."

a little journeyman's work, and so, what with one thing and another, I bless the Lord I have not wanted yet."

If there was anything ludicrous in this speech, that was not the quality in it which most struck his wife.

"You live from hand to mouth, then?" she observed.

"I did 'ought to do," he answered; "but I went to Mr. Gordon to look after you, and he told me there was fifteen pound in hand, and that I was to have thirty pound a year so soon as I could claim it."

"Yes," she replied; "it were but right."

"Well, I took the fifteen, and it seemed as if I was distrusting the Lord, and I could not spend it, Hannah; let alone your uncle never meant his earnings to come into my grip. I have given three pound of it away to some of the Lord's poor, and to a man that I got to take the pledge, and here is the rest in my pocket. We shall go about so cheap, Hannah—sometimes in a smack, and sometimes in an excursion train or a carrier's cart. That thirty pound a year will keep you, with what little extra I can earn."

We? Then he expected to have her always with him!

"But why should you feel any call to go moving about?" she repeated.

"Because I'm a temperance lecturer. But I have not the impudence to offer myself to be paid by any society—none of them would employ a man that had not a good character. I do not preach. I seem to think you'll be glad to hear that."

"You're not a dissenter, Uzziah?"

"No; so I don't interfere with the work of the ministry. But I make the offer of the gospel wherever I can privately, and I go and see poor folks in prisons and work-houses, when I can get leave." He paused, then added, with a sigh, "It cuts me very deep, Hannah, to see you look so miserable, and hardly seem to care about anything. If you knew more about this temperance question, and how drink is the one cause of the ruin of nineteen out of twenty that go to the bad——"

She interrupted. "I know all about temperance—all," she said listlessly.

He looked surprised, then, as if her weary indifference goaded him into making a complaint, he continued—"And if you knew how pleased I am to find you again, and how it cuts me to see that—well, I mean, you used to be fond of me, Hannah."

"Yes."

"And if I'd been so blessed as to have found salvation then, and taken to sober ways, you'd have been a happy woman."

"Yes."

She sighed bitterly, as she uttered that one syllable of reply; she evidently could not rouse herself to care what he thought of her. He went to the window and looked out, trying to find something to say that would please her. The time was getting on, and he had certainly made no way at present. When he looked round, she had slipped out of the room. She had resolved to ask for the bill and pay it herself, that, if any allusion was made to her having been there the evening before with young ladies, she might be the only person to hear it.

"I have no luggage, Uzziah," she said,

when she returned; "and if you ask me why, I cannot tell you, nor which of the four towns I came from, that met here yesterday. But I have paid the reckoning, and I've money in my hand that will buy me clothes for a good while to come." She had, in fact, been paid her quarter's wages a few days previously.

Uzziah Dill seemed to understand that he was to ask no questions, or perhaps he perceived that it would only be a waste of words if he did; so he proceeded to show, as he thought, a great proof of confidence. He laid about two pounds on the table, in silver and copper, and took out a small parcel done up in brown paper. "That's the twelve pound, Hannah," he said, "and there's what money I have. You had better take charge of it, and I can ask you for what I want; I never spend a penny now that I need be ashamed you should know of. I've kept out enough to pay our two tickets."

She shrank from this mark of his trust in her. "I'm not used to carry so much about with me," she said faintly. "You'd better by half put it back again." So he did, looking almost as spiritless as herself; and they walked slowly to the station.

And now began a new and very strange life for Hannah Dill. The third-class carriage was full of people, and her husband, with a kind of uncouth attempt at politeness, began to offer them temperance tracts. Some took them, others argued with him and made game of him. He showed what, to his wife, seemed an unnatural and distressing humility. It seemed not in the least to signify what they said of him or to him, if they would only take his tracts and promise to read them.

It was a very slow train, and Hannah Dill, in spite of herself, dozed; but her sleep was far from refreshing, and she started with a low cry of terror when her husband touched her and said they were to get out.

It was about four miles to the next station, and to that they were to walk and wait till late in the afternoon, when another train would come up and take them on. Uzziah Dill bought some food, and they went on together, he carrying it, and she holding an umbrella over her head, for the day was sultry. There was plenty of time before them, and the walk might have been delightful to a happier woman. They went through newly cut hay-fields and among bean-fields; they came to a little river, full of floating water-lilies—it was spanned by a wooden bridge. Close to it was a small empty cart-shed, and in its shade they sat down to make their noonday meal. After that the ex-convict, not able to repress his joy at his wife's presence, and his thankfulness for God's goodness, proposed to sing a hymn, and forthwith broke out into a well-known strain, full of exultation, joy, and praise.

Thunder had been muttering for some time. And with more than common suddenness a cloud, coming over, burst in torrents of rain; while, just as the last verse was in course of conclusion, two young men dashed across the wooden bridge from the opposite field, and took shelter also in the shed.

"By Jove!" exclaimed one of them, taking off his hat and sprinkling the dust with drops from its brim. "They *are* going it."

He meant the elements. And just then a great green flash seemed to run all over them and among them, and such a rattling, crashing peal of thunder with it, that the water in the little river shook with its vibrations.

"By Jove!" repeated the same young man, in an admiring and more respectful tone, as if he could not think of withholding his tribute to these elements, when they were so much in earnest about their business.

Then the usual thing followed. Uzziah Dill, with humble civility, almost ludicrous, rose, and making his bow to the young men on the other side of the cart, received two nods in reply, while he said, "The gods of the heathen, gentlemen, are no good to swear by in a danger like this. I'll take leave to address a prayer to the true God, for we seem to be in the very midst of the muddle; and I have my dear wife with me, whose safety it's natural I should think of." Thereupon, pulling off his hat again, he held it before his face, and, turning away, murmured into it an inaudible prayer.

The two young men looked at each other, and Mrs. Dill could not forbear to glance at them. She was ashamed of her husband and for him, and yet ashamed of herself for being ashamed.

One of the young men was very tall and dark; he leaned on one of the cart-wheels and smiled, while he looked at the man praying. The other young man was small and fair; he sat on the shaft, and remained perfectly grave; he had a little mouth, which he slightly screwed up with an air of observant intelligence that made him look especially foolish.

When a baby looks thus at a candle, we think the little face has an air of wisdom; but if a young man looks thus at an ordinary hay-cart, we are sure he must be an ass.

Uzziah Dill now turned round, and, after another tremendous clap of thunder, produced a bundle of leaflets, and was just about to make a civil offer of some to the gentlemen, when the tall young man—Lord Robert, in fact—burst into a good-natured laugh. "Why, Peep," he exclaimed, "this is out of the frying-pan into the fire! Put them up, my good man—put them up. This gentleman's pockets," indicating his companion, "are full of them already. They are temperance leaflets, I see."

Uzziah Dill, finding his incipient temperance lecture taken out of his mouth, looked foolish for a moment; but when little Peep said kindly, "Ye-es, I am much interested in the temperance cause," his countenance glowed with joy.

"Indeed, sir," he said respectfully. "Then, sir, I make bold to wish you God-speed with it. I'm only a poor cobbler," he continued, after giving little Peep an unreasonable time to reply in, if he had been so minded, "but I count it a great honour to be able to help such a blessed cause, if it's ever so little."

"Ye-es," said little Peep, and slowly added, taking time to cogitate between every two or three words, "I wish—there was no—strong drink."

Thereupon Lord Bob, taking no notice at all of the cobbler, gave little Peep a dig in the ribs. "No strong drink? You are a pretty fellow," he exclaimed. "Call yourself a Briton, and talk of getting into Parliament, and yet cry out, 'No strong drink!' How's the Government to go on without the revenue from it? Where will you get the money to pay your soldiers and sailors with?"

"I don't—know," said little Peep, looking as much perplexed as if he felt seriously concerned to produce the wherewithal then and there.

CHAPTER XXIV.

How could there be a better opening for a palaver? It was pouring now with steady rain. Little Peep, seated on the shaft, looked much perplexed; Uzziah Dill sat on the shabby carpet-bag that held his tools; and Lord Bob, facing them both, leaned on the wheel of the cart, and, being very tall, looked right over it into little Peep's eyes. "There's patriotism!" he exclaimed. "Do you want the country to go to wrack? Don't you know, and don't you too, cobbler—I beg your pardon——"

"No offence, sir; that's my trade," Uzziah broke in. "Pray go on, sir."

"Well, don't you know, then, that our soldiers and sailors are almost entirely paid out of the revenue that comes from the excise duties?"

"Well, sir," Uzziah presently said, after giving little Peep time to reply, if he chose, "if I am to answer, I'll say that drink costs the country very nigh as much as it pays it. Look at all our criminal courts, what they cost—our judges, our prisons, with all their officers and servants, and the chaplains, and the feeding of the prisoners, and their clothes. Then look at our police force—their wages, and clothes, and all the rest of it, sir. And then consider that, nineteen-twentieths of all the crime being caused by drink, that proportion of the expense would be saved if we were sober."

Even little Peep was startled here. "Ye-es," he said, with what for him was wonderful promptitude; "but nineteen-twentieths is such—a—such a jolly lot to write off."

"Off the crimes, sir, did you mean, or the money?"

"Why, it's the money we want, *and are trying to—scrape together*."

"Well, sir," cried the cobbler, "I'm sure I'm willing to meet you half-way. "We'll say nine-tenths of the expense is saved; we have nineteen-twentieths less crime, and the country saves nine-tenths of the expense, which you have towards the army and navy."

"That's fair," said little Peep.

"And my nineteen-twentieths, sir, includes not only the convictions for crimes done when a man is in drink, but those committed by habitual drunkards, even though they be then sober; men, in short, that have got their wills made weak by drink, and their consciences clouded."

"You have got up the subject, cobbler, I see," observed Lord Robert.

"Yes, sir."

"Well, but granting all you say (for the sake of argument, merely), the sum saved would not half pay."

"I was afraid it wouldn't," said little Peep, screwing up his mouth and shaking his head.

"No, sir; but then, if we had no drunkards, we should have hardly any paupers. Only think what they cost the country. We should save a sight of money there."

"You take a good deal for granted."

"But not too much, sir. I take for granted that, thank God, people have their feelings. There are thousands of poor old folks in the workhouses that have children who'd scorn to leave them there, but that they're almost beggars themselves, along with their families, because they are such slaves to the drink. There are thousands upon thousands of children there as well, because they've lost father, and often mother too, through the drink."

Little Peep here began to look a trifle happier. He glanced at Lord Robert, as if the matter was in his hands, and on his fiat depended the payment of her Majesty's forces. He was in the habit of taking things very much to heart; besides, he had a nasty cough. He must not leave the cart-shed, therefore, while it rained, and while he stayed he would, of course, talk to the cobbler. For these reasons, therefore, and not because he cared about the matter in hand, Lord Bob gave himself an air of conviction, and looked cheerful.

"Come," he said, "I think we're getting on. Besides, you may remember that, with all our sobriety, we shall still derive some revenue—suppose we say one-twentieth—from the excise on strong drink. You can add that."

"And what about the duties on tobacco? Many people sa-ay you're not to smoke," said little Peep.

"It can only be the most hardened villains who say that. Drinking and smoking have nothing really to do with one another. In fact, some of the most sober nations smoke most," said Lord Robert, laughing.

"My doctor always tells me to smoke—in moderation," said little Peep.

"And if you drink toast and water with your pipe, or drink nothing at all, sir, where is the harm of it?" said Uzziah. "Anyhow," he continued, in a burst of generosity, "I should wish the Government to keep that branch of the revenue. We have no call to interfere with it; for ours is the temperance cause, and nothing else."

"Then, if I'm to have all that," said little Peep, cogitating, "won't it be almost enough? or shall we all have to be taxed much more than—than we are now, you know?"

"Even if we are, sir, think how much richer we shall be. We shall hardly feel it. We shall be richer by nineteen-twentieths of all those millions that we are now paying for drink, and by what we earn in regular wages, and by most of the paupers being at home with their parents and with their children. Some taxes will be taken off, and others will be put on."

"And so you think we shall do?"

"I pray God for a chance of trying, sir."

"So do I," answered little Peep.

"I take my leave of you, gentlemen," then said the cobbler. "And if you'll put up your umbrella, my dear, it's about time we stepped over to the station."

Mrs. Dill rose, and, to her great shame, saw each of the gentlemen drop money into Uzziah's hand, and saw him receive it and put it in his pocket. They knew him better than she did, it appeared.

"Thank you, gentlemen," he said. "To give this to me is about the same thing as to give it to the cause; for I live for the cause, in my humble way."

He had not gone many yards, following closely on his wife's heels, when Lord Bob came striding after him. "I say, cobbler," he cried, "you're no fool—I can see that."

"You're very good, sir," answered Uzziah. "Such headpiece as I have is not fuddled with drink, anyhow. I am a sober man now, through the goodness of the Lord."

"Well, look here: there was a little flaw in those fine calculations of yours, which I did not wish my poor friend to see. You make out that, if all the people became sober, they would save—how many millions a year is it? Well, I forget; but suppose it saved, whose pockets is it in?"

"Why, in the people's pockets, sir."

"Exactly so, and not in the pocket of the Government. How do you propose to conjure it there?"

Now Lord Bob being very tall, and the rain pouring down, dropped a good deal from the brim of his hat and splashed on Uzziah's nose as he looked up to answer.

"It seems to me, sir," he said, both men walking on at a smart pace, "that there may be a flaw in your calculations. When God puts it into the minds of a good many people that a certain thing they've been in the habit of doing—as I may say with a clear conscience—is a wrong thing to do, that is a kind of prophecy that the thing, sooner or later, is going to be done away with by them; just as the slave trade was, you know, sir, and then slavery. We that think about it have got, so to speak, such a prophecy, and that you should not leave out of your calculation. This great drink traffic is certain sure going to be done away with; we don't know when, and we don't know how."

"Going to be given up!" exclaimed Lord Robert, laughing.

"Yes, sir. There has been a great deal of talk this forty years about what a sad thing it was to drink, but not half enough about what a sad thing it was to distil the drink, and sell out the drink. A vast many folks have found out this lately. I heard a gentleman lecture on it only yesterday. His name was Mr. Amias de Berenger."

Lord Robert heard this name with great amusement; but it did not suit him to let the cobbler know that he was intimate with Mr. Amias de Berenger. He smiled. "And so this Mr. de Berenger and you temperance folks generally have got a kind of supernatural instinct in you (which you call a prophecy), and it tells you that every man concerned in the liquor traffic is going to be ruined?" Then, after a short pause, his native gentlemanhood coming to his aid, he added, "And all the drunkards reclaimed, while at the same time we may leave Providence to look after the revenue?"

"I don't exactly know about that, sir," answered Uzziah, who felt himself rather at fault there.

"It seems to me that Parliament will have enough to do," continued Lord Robert, half bantering him. "It has first to stop the liquor traffic; secondly, to compensate the whole body of publicans; and, thirdly, to find money for the payment of the forces."

"Well, sir, Parliament had enough to do —and did it—when it had to make folks believe that slavery was not to be borne with, and then to compensate the slave-owners. But then the world has got on since that, and it may be through that. And how do you know that the heads of the liquor traffic will not be the first to show how this thing is to be done?"

"I am no prophet, cobbler; but I think I know better than that."

"Well, sir, and I am no prophet; but if you are sure Parliament will pass no bills to stop the traffic, and no other way can be thought of, why, we have no call to consider how the forces are to be paid. But I have noticed," continued the cobbler, "a strange way there is with people, as if they thought human creatures, when they were added together,,were not as good as every one of the same lot is when he stands by himself. Now, why are you and five hundred other gentlemen not to be willing to do what you yourself are willing to do, sir, for your fellow-creatures?"

Then, as Lord Robert strode beside the limping cobbler, he fell into a short cogita-tion, keeping an amused expression of surprise on his pleasant face, and not in the least attending to Uzziah Dill, who was carefully attempting to explain that, in using the word "good," he did not impute to men any works that had merit in themselves.

Lord Robert heard not a single word of this theological dissertation, but the cobbler was gratified by his silence, and surprised when he suddenly exclaimed, "How do you know that I myself am willing to do anything at all for the benefit of my fellow-creatures? Better ascertain that before you talk of the other five hundred."

"I leave it entirely to you, sir," said Uzziah, with a smile. "You know best; but I am not afraid."

"And you stick to it, that this thing is going to be done?"

"Oh yes, sir. I believe every man will soon have a good chance of being sober; that everything will soon be in favour of his keeping sober, instead of in favour of his getting drunk."

"In spite of the immense interests that stand in the way, and in spite of the determination of the people to have drink?"

"Yes, sir; but how it's to be done I know nothing about. It seems most likely that God will put it into the hearts of the people more and more to band together, to encourage one another, and help one another themselves to give drink up."

"Well, cobbler, I must go, and I will say this——"

"Sir?"

"You are the most downright, thorough-going, unreasonable, incorrigible fanatic I ever met with!"

So saying, and with a good-natured laugh and another half-crown, Lord Robert strode back to the cart-shed as fast as his long legs would carry him. "Well," he said, arguing with himself as he went on, and smiling furtively, "of course there must be a grain of sense in the schemes and dreams of every fanatic, or how could his fanaticism spread? Does this, or does it not, seem more Utopian than the putting away of slavery did in its day? Should I, or should I not, have thought the man such a fool if I had met with him before I was engaged to (well, she's a sweet creature, and I am a lucky dog)— engaged to Fanny? I shall have her fortune down; therefore, cobbler, you are right. I *have* a great willingness in my mind to do something for my fellow-creatures, if I can without inconvenience. No! Come! I am hard upon myself. I cancel those last words. The brewer's sweet little daughter deserves something more of me, considering the pains she takes to make a better fellow of me. Yes, he promised me her fortune down. What a philanthropic old boy he is!—his hand always in his pocket to help the poor. How would it look if, the next time he gave Fanny a good round sum for charity, I got her to spend it in erecting a temperance hall right in front of his distillery gates? Well, not filial, I'm afraid. What fun we had, De Berenger and I, a few years ago, with those ridiculous temperance lectures! We never did the slightest good, that I know of, but we taught ourselves to speak by means of them. They were all on the other tack. What a fool, and what a madman, and what a sinner the drunkard was! and no hint that anybody else was at all to blame. And so drunkenness is going to be done away with, is it, cobbler? Time will show, but not my time, I think. Well, Peep, old fellow, how are you getting on?"

Little Peep replied that he had coughed a good deal, but that it had refreshed him to think of his talk with the cobbler.

"Ah, yes! you temperance fellows all talk of 'the cause,' as if it was the only cause worth living for. What a fool that cobbler is!"

Little Peep here repeated a text to the effect that God made use of the foolish wherewith to confound the wise.

"Yes, when you take to quoting Scripture, I'm always stumped," said Lord Robert. "It's my belief that every temperance man you meet with you write his name in your note-book, and say a prayer for him at night when you go to bed."

Lord Robert did not intend to be profane, but he felt that he had described something ridiculous—suitable for little Peep, but not for a manly character.

"Ye-es," said little Peep, with that pathetic air of wisdom which looked so foolish, "I always pray for them. I think we all pray for one another, and that's why——"

"Why, what?"

"Why we are getting on—so fast."

"Oh!"

"But I say, Bob?"

"Well? However, I know what you mean, so you need not say it."

"What do I mean?"

"Why, that, considering what a promising young fellow I was, a temperance lecturer, and all that sort of thing, it is odd that I should be turning out no better than my neighbours, and almost wicked enough to make fun of 'the cause.' But what is at the bottom of nineteen-twentieths of all the crime in the country, Peep—mine as well as other men's? You ought to know." Here he imitated the countrified twang of the cobbler. "It's all the drink, sir—the drink as has done it."

"The drink, Bob? You're joking."

"Not at all. The drink is going to pay my debts and give me a large fortune, with a pretty wife. Therefore, as Hamlet said, 'I can't make you a sound answer; my wit's diseased'—so I say. I can't cant any more against the drink; my tongue's tied."

"It wasn't cant, Bob."

"No; but look here, Peep. I don't want you to think me any worse than I am. De Berenger took up the subject in good earnest. I helped him for fun. It never was one that I should have chosen of my own accord. Long before I met with Fanny I gave up lecturing."

"Ye-es," said little Peep; "and you and De Berenger gave me a lot of the lectures. I got"—here he considered a moment—"I got four hundred pledges—in all."

"Then you've done all that more for the world than I have done. I never got any."

"I liked lecturing."

"Yes, you good little fool," thought Lord Robert. "With what joy and pride you stood forth with another man's lecture before you! How you got them up beforehand, with that Scotch minister to coach you!"

"I often think—I shall never lecture—any more, Bob." He looked inquiringly at Lord Robert as he spoke.

"Nonsense, nonsense!" exclaimed Lord Robert, in reply. "What do you mean, man? You'll be all right when that cough of yours gets well;" then, knowing that it was unfeeling to make light of what was so serious, he added, "We shall be in town in a week or so, and then you can have more advice about it."

"And it's such a little cough," said the poor young fellow. "But sometimes I feel so weak, Bob, I don't know what to do. I feel —almost as if I was going—to cry."

"Why, there's my brother, in his dog-cart," exclaimed Lord Robert, suddenly turning his back and speaking hurriedly. "Look! he's coming through the lodge gates. I'll meet him. He'll take you up; he can easily drive over the clover, and it has done raining."

"Poor Peep!" was his comment on the conversation as he strode on. "I like that fellow, and felt almost, when he said that, as if I could have cried too."

Some hours after that time there was great surprise and much regret, as well as discomfort, in Hannah Dill's late home, for the three Mr. de Berengers, with their aunt Sarah, and also Amabel and Delia, drove up, luggage and all, in two flys, and the door was opened to them by Jolliffe, who informed them that Mrs. Snaith had not returned home at the appointed time, but that a telegram had been received from her. "And what it means, sir, and what Mrs. Snaith can be thinking of to act so by you, and when there's so much extra work too, I that know her so well, can no more. tell," said Mrs. Jolliffe, "than I can fly. The telegram is on your study table, sir."

Thither the party proceeded.

The telegram was dated from some little junction that none of the party had ever heard of. Mrs. Dill had found opportunity to send it off while Uzziah bought the food which had been eaten under the cart-shed. After the due direction, to "Mrs. Jolliffe, at the Rev. Felix de Berenger's," etc., it ran as follows:—

"DEAR FRIEND,
"I am that hurried that you must excuse mistakes. I could not come home last night. I never do expect to see you again, nor get back to my place. Give my dear love to the precious young ladies."

"She must have paid two shillings for this," exclaimed Sarah.

Tears were rolling down Amabel's cheeks. "Mamsey gone—Mamsey," she almost whispered. "Shall I never see Mamsey any more?"

"I don't believe it!" exclaimed Delia indignantly. "She never would be so unkind." Then Delia began to sob and cry, and came to kiss Felix and lean on his shoulder, and beg him to say he was sure that Mamsey would soon come back again.

"My dears, my dear girls!" cried Sarah. "Mrs. Snaith was certainly a most kind and attentive nurse to you; but really, to cry about her suddenly leaving you is too much. Perhaps——"

"Well, what 'perhaps,' Cousin Sarah?" sobbed Delia. "Do you mean, perhaps she'll come back again?"

Dick all this time was devoured with jealousy, and Amias wished devoutly that Amabel would come and lean so on his shoulder.

"And I was cross to her the day before yesterday," sobbed the repentant Delia. "I said she hadn't ironed my flounce nicely. O Coz! do say you're sure she's coming back again!"

Here Amabel melted into tears anew, and both the girls, as by one impulse, darted out of the study and rushed up-stairs to their own bedroom to cry together.

Poor bereaved mother! Those were the only tears her children ever shed for her, and she never knew even of them.

Amabel and Delia came down to supper looking so sad, that the subject of Mrs. Snaith's sudden withdrawal was avoided as by one consent; but whether Sarah could have refrained from it if she had not already exhausted her vocabulary of blame on the poor absentee, may well be doubted.

"Yes!" she exclaimed, as the two poor children, clinging together, went away the moment they had finished their meal. "Yes, this ought to show you, Amias, how wrong it is to excite the feeling of the lower classes about temperance, or any other of your modern inventions."

Amias looked amazed, and Sarah, finding herself in possession of the house, continued—

"Yes, the girls told me when they came home that the speech Amias made agitated Mrs. Snaith to that degree, that she actually fainted—fainted dead away—and before they could get her to revive, she moaned most distressingly. And there was a horrid little lame man, all the time she was insensible, who told the most terrible anecdotes about drunken men killing their wives. Delia says he quite frightened her, and she was thankful when Mrs. Snaith was able to rise and come away. So now Felix has lost a most excellent domestic; and very likely she has gone off, under a mistaken impression that it's her duty to turn temperance lecturer herself, as those American women did."

"It's not in her," said Felix; "she is not that kind of woman."

But Sarah was not to be repressed. "There is nothing so unlike themselves," she continued, "that people will not do it under a fanatical impulse. I myself felt strongly inclined to lay my pearl necklace in the plate once, when that bishop (you know his name, Felix; I forget it)—that bishop preached about money for the Indian famine."

"But you didn't do it, aunt, did you?"
asked Dick.

"No. Now, Dick, I have several times
pointed out to you that you should never
have jokes and laugh at them apart, in the
presence of others. Yes: you looked at
Amias in such a way just now, that, if it
had not chanced that I was talking on a
serious subject, I should certainly have
thought you had some joke about me."

"Those were the only tears her children ever shed for her."

IN THE FOURTH WATCH OF THE NIGHT.

St. Matthew xiv. 32—33.

LO, in the moonless night,
    In the rough wind's despite,
        They ply the oar.
Keen gusts smite in their teeth;
The hoarse waves chafe beneath
        With muffled roar.

Numb fingers, failing force,
Scarce serve to hold the course
        Hard-won half-way,
When o'er the tossing tide,
Pallid and heavy-eyed,
        Scowls the dim day.

And now in the wan light,
Walking the waters white,
        A shape draws near.
Each soul, in troubled wise,
Staring with starting eyes,
        Cries out for fear.

Each grasps his neighbour tight,
In helpless huddled fright
        Shaken and swayed.

And lo! the Master nigh
Speaks softly, "It is I;
        Be not afraid."

E'en so to us that strain
Over life's moaning main
        Thou drawest near,
And, knowing not Thy guise,
We gaze with troubled eyes,
        And cry for fear.

A strange voice whispers low,
"This joy must thou forego,
        Thy first and best."
A shrouded phantom stands
Crossing the best-loved hands
        For churchyard rest.

Then, soft as is the fall
Of that white gleaming pall
        By snowflakes made,
Stilling each startled cry,
Thou speakest, "It is I;
        Be not afraid."

FREDERICK LANGBRIDGE.

"DIANA SMITH."

By J. MILNER FOTHERGILL, M.D.

PART II.

NOW came a further strain on the surgeon. He had no longer the captain to converse with; he was the only man of education in the ship, and as such was practically in command of her. Responsibility had been thus thrust upon him; fortunately he could bear the strain. Their difficulties were increased by a new trouble, and on January 15th scurvy first showed itself in two of the Shetland men. Hitherto they had been spared that, anyhow. Then there was the necessity of working at the pumps; extra work to do, when the allowance of food was again diminished. Only one cask of beef now remained. An oil lamp was kept burning to melt snow for water.

On January 16th, he writes, "I am sorry to have to add that signs of scurvy are now pretty general amongst us." On the 18th it was found that one of the bread-casks had been robbed by some of the famished crew, which led to the diminution of the allowance by half a pound a week—a very serious matter when there was so much cold and so little food. On the 21st the thieves were discovered. The surgeon says, "I am sorry for these poor lads—three are growing fellows who require more nourishment than bearded men arrived at their full stature and development, and they find it very hard to subsist upon such a pitiful allowance. Indeed, they generally contrived to finish their 3 lbs. of bread by the Friday night, and had to get on as best they could till the following Monday, when their hunger was so ungovernable that they were unable to resist the impulse to make such a heavy inroad upon the biscuits as left them destitute of food again before the return of 'bread-day.' How they will get on on their reduced quantities I know not." (They were reduced ¼ lb. per week, that is to 2¼ lbs., till their theft was worked off.) The grim sternness of the Anglo-Saxon character showed itself in their determination not to throw away their chance, remote as it was, of escape by consuming their provisions. Hungry as they were, they held on unfalteringly. The difficulties of the cook with his diminishing stock of wood are told almost humorously. Their oil lamp was kept going :—" Everything and everybody is covered with soot from the oil lamps—lives in an atmosphere of soot—sleeps amongst soot—breathes soot—is begrimed and smothered with soot; in fact, chimney-sweeps would look respectable beside some of us." On the 26th the daily grog allowance is stopped, and only served out three times a week.

Smith says—"For my part I rarely meddle with it, knowing that alcohol in such a climate is worse than useless; but 'tis waste of breath—in fact, not worth my while—to attempt preaching such a doctrine to the men." It now was again dreadfully cold; the ship's pumps were frozen. He writes—" It may serve to show you in how terribly low a temperature we are making shift to live, when I tell you that Mr. George Clarke's boots, when he pulled them off at night-time, were sheeted inside with glittering ice, the moisture of his feet freezing upon the leather, whilst his horse-hair lining was frozen to the sole." On the 31st he writes, "Intensely cold again last night; this is dreadful work; it is murdering us—we cannot endure it much longer in our starving, exhausted condition." On February 1st he writes, "Thank God, the 1st of February has at last arrived! How wearily and anxiously we have watched and counted its coming! What new hopes, and heart, and life, the advent of a fresh month gives to us! Last month has been remarkably quiet; the ship laid still, and free from pressure, nips, &c.; but to me it has been a month of the greatest anxiety, seeing that the long-dreaded scurvy has made its appearance amongst us." During all this time the cold continued. "A raven flew close past the ship, its neck surrounded by a white glittering ring of hoar frost, the moisture in its breath congealing instantly on its plumage." On the 3rd it became milder; but this caused them more work with the pumps. So they laboured away; and the scurvy spread.

He writes :—" I am surgeon to the ship, but, God help me! what can I do for those poor fellows?" On the 15th the first man died of scurvy. Then it blew a terrible gale. "If the ship goes to-night, i.e. if the ice is brought up by the land, or the berg, or forced down upon us, and the ship stove in, there is no hope of our lives; four-and-twenty hours on the ice in such weather as this would in-

XXI—19

evitably finish off every man and boy of us—not one of us could stand it; 'twould be impossible to rig a tent with such a fearful gale raging. We should have no protection, no shelter, no hope, nothing but sure and certain death." On the 22nd they saw a "mallie," which was a sign that water was not far off. One of their great troubles was the freezing of the pumps, and the necessity for thawing them, which also consumed their fuel. It was terribly hard work for the poor fellows—weak, and wasted, and scurvy-stricken. On the 2nd of March he writes, "Matters are beginning at last to look very bright and cheering." And to estimate this correctly we must bear in mind how almost utterly hopeless their prospects were. Even in the ice the ship leaked so that the pumps were kept going incessantly. What would be requisite when they got into the open sea they so craved for, their provisions dwindling away, while scurvy was spreading?

On the 5th it was decided to raise the allowance of bread to 4 lbs. per week, as the men were so exhausted. On the 6th the loose ice on the port-side opened into a lane of water. They were now well opposite the opening of Hudson's Straits, and drifting in a satisfactory direction. At this time, out of a total of 47 men, 7 only were free from scurvy, and 10 but slightly affected, so that the ship was very short-handed. One poor fellow's bed was wet through with the ice melting in his bunk, the weather being now somewhat milder. On the 9th the ice was noticed to be moving. "Watch employed in the afternoon cutting up stunsail yards for firewood." 11th.—"Last night about 11 o'clock P.M. a swell in, from what quarter uncertain, and the heavy ice in which we have been so long laid hard and fast began to break up." Next day they were at last off the Labrador coast, so long the object of their hopes and wishes. On the 12th, after a broken night's rest from the ice grinding against the ship's side, he found a decided thaw, the ice dropping off the yards, and the men shovelling the ice and snow off the deck; while the engineer cleared the ice from the engine room. "The cabin clock was once more ticking cheerfully, unaffected in its work by internal cold; the linnet and canary singing as if their little throats would burst, no doubt delighted, like ourselves, with the genial sunny weather." They now shipped the rudder and got some canvas on the ship; the breeze fortunately blowing right for them, and the ship made way through the ice. They were now again in terrible, immediate

danger of being stove in by heavy ice. Diarrhoea, too, was prevalent, as the men, with their swollen gums, had to soak their biscuit before they could eat it. On the 14th they got out the mainsail, "working with the energy of men who had long well-nigh despaired of life, but who now, at last, were escaping from a horrible prison-house to life and liberty, and homes and friends." They were now come to the last of nearly everything, the last cask for firewood, the last cask of coals; and the mate remarked, "'Tis a great mercy we are not eating our last biscuit." The master came down from the crow's nest with the cheery news that he could see the outside of the pack plainly. On the 17th the ship was out of the ice, "rising and falling." A strong north wind got up, and an extra pound of bread was served out. At this time the diary is kept several times a day, so intense is the excitement.

Smith looked after his patients, hauled at the ropes, and took a turn at the pump, and then went to his diary alternately. Now comes March the 17th, the last day of the diary. "Ship making good progress; 11.30 ran below to scribble these remarks. As you may suppose, I am as anxious and excited as possible." Whether the ship would swim or not in open water was a question soon to be solved. At "1.45 P.M. Are now well out of the pack!" "Glory be to God that we are at last out of the ice." They were still in imminent danger. "Happily we were bows on to the swell; but I assure you that much and sorely as the old ship has been tried during this fearful winter, she never experienced such a severe hammering as she did whilst running through the last opposing barrier of ice. Meanwhile the night drew on apace; the ship dashed through the innumerable dangers which surrounded her on all sides—sometimes shaving close past some immense mass of ice, hard and dangerous as a rock, whilst we stood looking on with bated breath and trembling, anxious hearts; again driving stem on upon some heavy fragment with a shock that made both us and her stagger again; then recovering her way, on she went towards the dark inky horizon ahead of us, where the blessed open water lay in sight from the mast-head. Terribly exciting work this, gentlemen, running the gauntlet for dear life, with every chance of our ship being stove in, and not the faintest hope of saving your life if accident befell her. Hour succeeded hour; the night fell cold and dreary; the wind increased to half a gale; there seemed no limit to the interminable ice. Such hours as these, I do assure you, seem the longest you have ever lived; such hours of agonizing anxiety are never to be forgotten. However, to cut a long story short and save paper and ink, about 9 o'clock we could see the veritable and unmistakable outside edge; by 9.30 we were past all heavy ice, and running amongst streams of light ice and pancakes. The long rolling Atlantic swell became heavier and heavier, the ship pitched and rolled more and more, and at 10 o'clock the mate came down from the crow's nest and informed us that there was no more ice ahead, that we were at last well out of the pack, and running with all possible sail set on a S.E. by S. course, on our passage home." So ends this remarkable diary.

It was certainly not for want of paper this diary is not continued, but the surgeon had something else to do now. There was the Atlantic to be crossed with a leaky ship and a scurvy-stricken crew, mumbling their biscuits with their loosening teeth and their swollen, bleeding gums. Men were dying, the survivors getting weaker.; the surgeon had his sick to attend to, and took his turn at the watch and at the pumps as well.

"He was one in a thousand, and we should have perished without him," said one of the survivors. He animated them by his example; he cheered them by his undaunted courage; he shared their work as well as their danger. They fortunately had fair winds for "their race with death," as starvation—inevitable death—was behind them. Even at the last, when the land was sighted, the ship was nearly lost in a gale, because they had not men enough to handle her properly. On the 2nd of April they ran into Ronas Voe, in the Shetland Isles. By this time there were nine corpses lying on the deck, and another man died as they entered the harbour. Of the whole crew but four men could stand. Four more of the men died there. It was a terribly narrow escape at last!

Long and anxiously had the people at home waited and waited for news of "the lost whaling-vessel." It was known that she was caught in the ice, and her utterly unprepared condition to meet such accident was equally well known. The *Intrepid*—scarcely a happy name under the circumstances—had carried home word that the *Diana* was left behind. "Men were praying and women weeping for us at home," as Smith wrote in his diary. Now that the lost ship had arrived the joy of all was excessive. A fresh

crew was put into the old *Diana*, while Smith attended his patients till Hull was reached. They and he had been too long together to part. Neither he nor they could bear the idea that they should be in fresh hands. Thousands of persons assembled to see the lost *Diana* enter the port of Hull.

At last their voyage was over. It would be impossible by extracts, however numerous, to convey to the reader an idea of the mental condition of Smith and his companions during this long, long time that they were face to face with death. They never despaired; at least he did not. He saw a providential interference in their numerous escapes from what seemed certain death. When he had to shoot his little dog because they could no longer feed him, he fastened the collar round his arm; so that it might help to identify his corpse when it drifted on to the coast of Labrador—the sole hope and consolation almost that remained to him. Once only his fortitude gave way, and he threw himself on the ice and wished to die. Death was near at hand; it would not be long before the cold hand of death would have chilled the little left of life out of him! But there rushed upon him the thought—"What will these poor fellows do without me?" He got up and went back to the ship. Shortly after this the blacksmith, the finest man in the ship, despaired, and would not take his daily walk on a path cut out of the ice round the foremast. Smith threatened to have him swung from the yard-arm and pushed round. It was no use; the blacksmith declared he would never see his wife and children any more. Smith's own recent experience flashed upon him, and he exclaimed, "I will take you back to your wife, yet!" "Will you, doctor?" He took his word; the blacksmith's breast was once more inspired with hope. Smith kept his word; and the blacksmith at length was restored to his wife and family. No wonder the crew adored Smith! One more anecdote of the ship's crew. Precious few were the biscuits left in the ship when she reached Shetland. One of the crew kept a biscuit, bored a hole in it, and hung it up in his house. Some time afterwards, when Smith went to see him, the seaman pointed to this biscuit and said, "Whenever I feel inclined to quarrel with the Missus about my grub, I just look at that biscuit, and think how precious glad and thankful we were, doctor, for the chance of one of them when up in the ice with the old *Diana*."

The portrait given at p. 488 is from a

photograph taken in Hull just after the arrival of the *Diana*.

The value of Smith's services and the heroism displayed by him met with ready recognition. The doctors of Hull gave him a public dinner, and a silver inkstand to keep it in remembrance. The Board of Trade presented him with a set of surgical instruments, the most complete I have ever seen; together with a testimonial signed by the President, in which his services to the crew are described as having been "generous, humane, and unwearied." The townspeople of Hull and the underwriters of Lloyds presented him with a testimonial and a sum of over one hundred guineas.

The measure of the strain put upon an individual is the length of time it takes for the system to regain its normal condition; and long months of illness and exhaustion followed the strain put upon Smith during those terribly long months of protracted mental tension. Even after this he could not study properly when he returned to Edinburgh, where he was received with enthusiasm. Professors and students were alike proud of the genial, pleasant youth, whose experiences had been so terrible, and who had borne himself so heroically. Nothing, however, could overcome his repugnance to any perusal of his diary with a view to publication; indeed, he seemed almost to regard it with horror. Leaving Edinburgh he went to reside with Dr. Moffat, of Dalston, where he largely regained his old gaiety of character. At this time Sir Roderick Murchison induced him to join Mr. Lamont in a polar expedition; for the Arctic regions seem to possess a fascination, all their own, for those who have once visited them. Few who knew Smith will forget his descriptions of the scenery of Spitzbergen; and the contrast he drew betwixt the conditions of the first *Diana*, and that of the second one with all its comforts. Still his mind had not quite recovered from the remembrance of the horrors he had endured; and on a visit to me in Westmoreland, in 1868, when apparently unobserved, his mind would wander back to the old *Diana*, and he would talk to his old companions. He often spoke of Captain Gravill, to whom he seemed to have been much attached. After a year or two of comparative rest he resumed his medical studies in Glasgow, where "Diana" Smith won a reputation for earnest application. He passed his examinations with much credit, and became house-physician to the Royal Infirmary in that city, where his clinical reports are described as "models of correct English and careful observation." His experiences among rough characters led him at one time to take charge of the navvies engaged in the construction of the Settle and Carlisle section of the Midland Railway; and after that to take a practice in Durham among the colliers. But he could not settle down quietly, so he took charge of the ship *Dunedin*, conveying emigrants to New Zealand. The life of the new country attracted him, and he settled in practice at Otepopo, where he soon became a general favourite, especially with the Maories. He was made a magistrate, so great was the respect felt for him. The life he led was just to his mind; and his extensive practice furnished him with many a rough ride, with surgical emergencies to be encountered at the end of them, which were congenial to his character. He married, and all seemed well with him, when his self-sacrifice once more led him into trouble. Overwork had undermined his health and sapped his naturally robust constitution, when a man was drowned in the harbour; and Smith, who was a strong swimmer, dived for the body, and after repeated efforts succeeded in recovering it. A severe ulcer of the stomach followed this exposure, and he had to give up his practice and return to his native land. No improvement followed, and his last visit to his Essex home was made in an invalid-carriage. It was a beautiful July afternoon, recent rain had made all look fresh and bright, while a gentle wind caused the foliage to flash gloriously in the sunlight. But nothing could lighten up that far-away-looking eye; and he gazed listlessly upon familiar scenes which he well knew he must never see again. Placed on a truck at the tail of the train, the carriage swayed uncomfortably for the invalid, and the look out as we went through some cuttings on the line, which would once have attracted his keen admiration, passed unnoticed. The last time he entered his father's door he was borne on the stretcher of the carriage from it to his bed, which he never left while the remaining sands of life ran out. Worn, wan, wasted, waxen—he met death composedly, as he had looked it in the face many a time and oft before. The playful humour had entirely disappeared, and deep religious feelings took its place. He never in all his experiences of peril and danger had any fear of death, and when it was impending and inevitable, and escape was absolutely impossible, he almost seemed to court it. Quietly, in his Essex home, the wanderer went to his rest in peace on September 6th, 1879. After all his peril in the most distant parts of the world, alike in the Arctic seas and under the Southern Cross, "Diana Smith" died in his bed under his father's roof-tree; leaving the sorrow-stricken old man to furnish what comfort he could to the girlish widow with her fatherless boy. To this boy he left the manuscript diary of that terrible winter in the Arctic seas; and consequently its publication must be deferred till there are but few left who will feel an interest in it. By the kindness of his family it has been lent me for the writing of this memoir, in which but imperfect justice has been done to one who, though he wore no uniform and belonged to the people called Friends, was beyond all question a hero.

LITTLE BIRDS.

By the Rev. J. G. WOOD, M.A.

DID the reader ever see or hear of "Dicky-laggers?" Would he know a "Jowler," a "Duddey," or a "Charbob," if he met one? Would he consider it a mark of the degeneracy of the times that Jowlers have ceased to frequent Piccadilly? Scarcely a year ago, I was as ignorant of these subjects as any of my readers can be, but was enlightened by an omniscient friend who had made a personal study of Dicky-laggers, and obtained his information in their special haunts.

Dicky-lagging, it seems, is a slang term for bird-catching. Lagging being a euphuistic word for denoting capture by the police and subsequent transportation or penal servitude, dicky-lagging becomes a metaphorical phrase for the capture and caging of birds.

"Jowlers" are sparrows; and a dicky-lagger who gave my friend much curious information, lamented the absence of the sparrows from the London streets. Some years ago they used to be so plentiful, that the bird-catchers could spread their nets in Piccadilly. But in these days, the street-cleaning brigade of boys has done its work so effectually, that the sparrows, which used to hop about among the feet of horses and the wheels of vehicles, find no food, and are forced to go elsewhere for a living. The proverbial expression, "Plentiful as sparrows in London streets," has lost its meaning.

Why the men should feel obliged to call a redpole a duddey, and a chaffinch a charbob, is among the many mysteries of their strange mode of existence.

The numbers of these men seem to increase yearly, especially in the outskirts of London and other great centres of population. The first hour of daylight on fine Sunday mornings has seldom passed before the country roads are desecrated by these evil-looking, foul-mouthed, slouching, scowling pests, who not only offend every sense, but are inflicting great and increasing harm upon the country. Their business is simply the capture of birds for the purpose of selling them; some to be caged, but the greater number to be killed in shooting matches at sporting taverns. Were it only for the abominable cruelty perpetrated by these men, their occupation ought to be abolished by the law of the land; but when we remember that they are inflicting a national injury on the country, there is a double reason for interference.

A little knowledge of facts, and a little power of reasoning upon them, are all that is needed to appreciate the importance of the question. As a rule, people seem to think that, with the exception of the hawk and owl and swallow tribes, the birds feed habitually upon seeds, fruit, and other vegetable substances, thereby depriving man of them. Now, as I shall presently show, if we take the whole of the British birds, we shall find that some ninety-five per cent. of their food is of an animal nature, and that eighty per cent. consists of insects, slugs, snails, and similar creatures.

The amount of animal food required for these birds, especially in the nesting season, is almost incredible, and no one could believe it but for the united testimony of facts and figures.

Some years ago, M. Florent-Paradol committed a series of bird murders, for which the bird world ought to feel grateful. Desirous of ascertaining what was the real nature of a bird's food throughout the year, he selected a number of the ordinary species, taking care to include among them those birds which are commonly killed as destroyers of game, fruit, seeds, and young plants.

Among the three commonest Owls, he found that not one of them had eaten game of any kind. From January to April the

Long-eared Owl had fed exclusively on mice. During April and May cockchafers were found in the birds, and occasionally a rat or a squirrel. In June, the cockchafers having disappeared, the birds fell back on mice, meal-worms (so destructive in flour-stores), and various beetles.

The Short-eared Owl, being a less powerful bird, had not even killed squirrels, but had lived almost exclusively on different species of mice, shrews, and the larger insects. The food of the Barn Owl, or White Owl, consisted wholly of mice and shrews. (I have examined the "castings," or "pellets," of many Barn Owl nests, but always found the wings, cases, legs, and other indigestible portions of night-flying insects.) During May, the cockchafer, which is, perhaps, the most destructive of all our British insects, seemed to have formed at least half the owl's food. Waterton's observations exonerate all the owls from the charge of destroying game.

The food of the Rook was almost entirely of an animal nature. In January it had fed on field-mice and cockchafer grubs, adding earth-worms to them in February, when the ground became soft enough for them to approach the surface. From March to May, caterpillars, beetle-grubs, especially those of the wire-worm, chrysalides, slugs and snails, and a variety of similar creatures, had been eaten. From June to August it still fed chiefly on insects, but supplemented them with various birds' eggs and a few young birds.

From August to October it varied its diet with young rabbits, mice, &c., and some barley. From November to the end of the year, its diet was much the same, except that some fruit kernels were found among its food; and when the severe winter frosts set in, it was obliged to eat anything that it could get. In point of fact it mostly goes off to the sea or estuaries, where it can find shrimps, molluscs, small fishes, and carrion.

It will be seen, therefore, that throughout the year its food is almost invariably of an animal character, and mostly consists of insects, snails, and slugs, the greater part of which lie underground, and are unearthed by the strong beak of the bird.

So far from paying boys for driving away rooks from the fields, the farmers ought to employ them for protecting and encouraging the birds.

Then, there are the Starlings. No doubt, in summer and autumn, they do take a small amount of fruit. But, considering the vast hosts of starlings in proportion to the few that eat our fruit, and the services which they have rendered in destroying the grubs, caterpillars, &c., we may consider the modicum of fruit which they take as wages due to them for the work which they have done.

Supposing a boy were paid for handpicking the insects, he could not, in a day's hard work, find and destroy as many as are taken by a single pair of starlings during the breeding season. And if we set the value of the boy's wages against the fruit that will be consumed by that pair of starlings, we should find that the birds had earned their pay ten times over.

No one can deny that the starlings will swarm in newly sown fields, apparently for the purpose of eating the seed. But appearances are always deceptive, and never more so than in cases where we cannot approach closely enough to examine details. A letter which recently appeared in *Land and Water* shows the danger of judging by appearances.

A gentleman had sown a three-acre field with grass seed, and on the next day found hundreds of starlings on the ground picking away with all their might, and apparently engaged in devouring the newly sown seed. He shot two of them, and found that there was nothing in their crops except insects.

Yet these most useful birds enjoy no protection from law, and suffer persecution on all sides. Birdcatchers take them for sale, mostly, as already mentioned, to be used in shooting matches, and they are ruthlessly destroyed by farmers and gardeners under the mistaken idea that they are injurious to the crops. The late Charles Waterton knew better, and did all he could to encourage the starlings to build in his demesne. He seemed as if he could never have enough starlings in his grounds, so great was his faith in the services which they rendered to agriculture. Blackbirds and thrushes, again, both equally useful with the starling, are equally without protection, the law having been ingeniously constructed so as to exclude the very birds which a practical naturalist would have placed first on the roll. The chaffinch is excluded, and so are the rook and crow, in common with all their tribe. Yet we have seen what is the nature of a rook's food, and how it saves us from the ravages of the cockchafer, an insect which passes more than two years underground, devouring the roots of wheat and other plants, and the rest of its time in eating the leaves above ground. What the wire-worm can do in the destruction of corn every farmer knows to his cost. And yet he kills or drives away the very birds which feed on the cockchafer grub and wire-worm, and, if let alone, would rid the fields of these insect pests.

So it is with the Blackbird and Thrush, as deadly enemies to slugs and snails as the rook to cockchafers and wire-worms. A letter from "A Country Parson," which lately appeared in the *Standard*, puts the point forcibly and yet temperately.

"What would you think of a nurseryman who boasted to a friend of mine that he had destroyed *twelve thousand thrushes' and blackbirds' eggs* in one season? Perhaps he did not count them, so call it ten thousand eggs, *i.e.* two thousand nests.

"Now, I have watched a pair of starlings during the breeding season, and found that on an average they brought a grub or fly to their young ones once in three minutes. This for ten hours a day for twenty days gives four thousand grubs to one pair of starlings.

"A pair of sparrows has been seen to come and go from the nest for food four hundred times a day, and this will give eight thousand grubs or caterpillars to one sparrow's nest during twenty days. Thrushes and blackbirds are quite as busy among insects, slugs, and snails in the early spring, so that the wanton destruction of two thousand nests of these sweet songsters saved the lives of some nine millions six hundred thousand slugs, snails, grubs, and caterpillars, which, I sincerely hope, did justice to their benefactor by eating buds and blossom on his fruit-trees."

These calculations may seem at first sight to be exaggerated, but I am of opinion that they are rather within than beyond the limits of truth.

Take, for example, the Redbreast. M. Florent-Paradol found that in all the specimens he killed throughout the year, not one had vegetable food in its crop. Insects, worms, grubs, spiders, insect eggs (found in the winter months), chrysalides, woodlice, &c., formed the whole of its food.

Some years ago, a letter appeared in the *Field* newspaper, stating that the writer had reared a young brood of redbreasts, carefully weighing their food so as to discover how much nutriment was required to keep the birds in health. He found that to keep a redbreast up to its normal weight, fourteen feet of earth-worms, or a proportionate amount of other animal food, were required in twenty-four hours.

On reading the account of these investigations, I could not but wonder how much food a man of average size would consume within the same time, if he were to eat as much in proportion as the redbreast. Taking a German sausage, nine inches in circumference, as analogous to the worm, I weighed a piece of it and then began the calculations.

Arithmetic was never a strong point with me, and the figures assumed such startling proportions that I abandoned the task so far as I was concerned. But, not being desirous of allowing the subject to drop, I asked Mr. J. Heaton, the well-known arithmetician, to make the calculations for me. He kindly did so, and the result showed that I had good reason for being alarmed at the figures.

There is no need of giving the whole of the calculations, but the result was, that in order to consume proportionately as much food as the redbreast, a man would have to eat in every twenty-four hours rather more than sixty-eight feet of German-sausage, nine inches in circumference. In order to put the point in a more striking manner, Mr. Heaton remarked that if the man in question were to lie on his back in the nave of the Crystal palace, and put one end of the sausage in his mouth, the other end would reach considerably above the uppermost gallery!

The Chaffinch cannot be held entirely guiltless of eating seeds, berries, and fruit. That it eats the buds of fruit-trees there can be no doubt. But, taking the average of the food throughout the year, the quantity of animal nourishment is far in excess of vegetable food, and most practical naturalists are of opinion that even the buds are seldom, if ever, eaten unless they be tenanted by the larvæ of some insect, so that the fruit could not have been developed.

This theory is confirmed by the fact that when gooseberry-bushes have been infested with the singularly repulsive larvæ of the gooseberry saw-fly (*Nematus grossulariæ*), a thousand of them have been picked off a single gooseberry-bush. Now chaffinches happen to be particularly fond of these insects, and would be only too glad to eat them, if they were permitted to do so. In one case, when the proprietor of the ground controverted the gardener and allowed the birds to do as they liked, the chaffinches flocked among the gooseberry-bushes, and in two or three days had completely cleared them of the grubs.

Neither do I deny that in the autumn the blackbird revels in fruit, especially gooseberries.

There is an old Scottish metaphor to the effect that when any
one eagerly accepted an offer, he
" lap at it like a cock at grosels."
I never could understand this
saying for a long while. I knew
that "lap" meant leaped, and
that "grosels" meant gooseberries, but why a
cock should leap
at gooseberries, I
could not compre-
hend.

One day, how-
ever, the mystery
was solved.

On a fine autumn
morning, I went to pay
a visit to a friend in
the coun-
try, and
was told on

my arrival that the host had been called away and could not be back for an hour or two. So I went into the garden, and amused myself with watching the various forms of animal life that frequented it, and occasionally taking a little fruit, of which there was an abundant crop.

Seeing something moving in a very strange way under a gooseberry-bush, I stopped to ascertain what it could be. At first it looked like a piece of black rag flapping about in the wind, but the opera-glass showed that it was a male black-bird jumping up and down, and flapping its wings at each hop. With the aid of a little caution, I managed to come quite close to the bird, and then saw that he was jumping at the gooseberries which were out of his reach when standing on the ground. He judiciously selected the ripest fruit, and he and his comrades had emptied almost every ripe goose-berry on the under surface of the bush, leaving nothing but the stalks and ragged fragments of skin.

Suddenly it struck me that the cock which leaped at the gooseberries was Shakespeare's—

"Ouzel-cock so black of
hue,
With orange-tawny
bill,"

Sparrows.

and that the obscure passage had become perfectly clear. The bird, however, seemed to restrict itself to the fruit on the under surface of the bush, and, as long as I noticed it, never attempted to perch among the branches. Whether the birds were deterred by the thorns I cannot venture to say.

There is no necessity for going into the history of the little birds, but the few which have been mentioned as specimens serve to show that several of those which are perse-cuted with the greatest severity, and deprived of protection by the Wild Birds' Preservation Act as injurious to the crops and harvests, never eat vegetable food at all; that those who do so make it only a small portion of their diet; and that, in any case, the services which they render throughout the year in preserving the balance of nature infinitely outweigh the amount of grain or fruit which they consume during a short period of it.

France ought to be a warning to us. In England, we do restrict the title of "game" to a very small number of birds and beasts, even excluding the rabbit from that category. Consequently, when an English sportsman goes out with his gun, he never dreams of shooting anything but game, as he understands the word, and the ordinary wild birds may fly in safety through the fields as far as he is concerned.

But in France, some years ago, any bird, no matter what its species, was considered in the light of game, and a sportsman would be inordinately proud of his success if he brought back half-a-dozen robins, as many sparrows, a couple of black-birds, and a thrush in his gorgeously embroidered and betasselled game-bag.

I well remember, when I was living in France, taking my first country walk. The weather was perfect, the landscape beautiful, but something was wanting. It was the song or twitter of birds. Not a bird was to be seen for mile after mile, the "sportsmen" having shot every one that dared to show itself.

The natural result followed. Rooks and starlings being destroyed, the insects had everything their own way, the trees being stripped bare by cockchafers and the corn blasted by the wire-worms. After a time France discovered her error, and is now wisely doing all in her power to bring back her banished allies. But it is always easier to destroy than to restore, and years must yet pass before disturbed nature can regain her equilibrium.

Although we have not wrought such wholesale destruction as France did, we have a very strong tendency in that direction. Man invariably tries to employ destruction when endeavouring to find a remedy for any evil, be it real or fancied. See what would happen if every one could have his destructive will.

The farmer, who chafes at the ravages made by landlord's hares, rabbits, and pheasants on his crops, would like nothing better than to shoot them all. The gamekeeper, who thinks that every creature which is not game is destructive to game, does his best to exterminate every living creature that might interfere with his " head of game," and I would not be too sure that the thrice sacred fox might not accidentally eat something which disagreed with him, if he took to robbing the pheasant and partridge nests.

Then, the agriculturists generally, whether on a large or small scale, believe that all the predacious birds, owls included, eat their poultry, and that all the non-predacious birds devour their grain and fruit. So they indiscriminately kill every bird that comes within their reach. Only a few days before these lines were written, I read an account of a farmer who found that his men were " frozen out," and so set them to work at killing the finches. The men sometimes brought in as many as seventy dozen in a single day, and both they and their employer thought that they were doing the best for the land.

Still more lately I was reading a leading article in an evening paper. It treated of insects, and the writer summed up the subject by saying that the world would get on much better without them, and that we might cheerfully spare the bee and the silkworm, if by so doing we could be rid of the insects that bit and stung us, or spoiled our clothing, or ate our food. The depths of ignorance and presumption in this suggestion are simply appalling, and I cannot trust myself to do more than mention it.

That we are awaking to a partial sense of our mistake in employing destruction as an aid to agriculture is shown by the passing of

the " Act for the Preservation of Wild Birds." But the wording of the Act shows such astounding ignorance on the part of the legislature which passed it, that it can only be contemplated with bewildered amazement.

The time chosen for the close season is perfectly right, but the principle of selection is an inscrutable mystery. Why are the goldfinch and the hawfinch (which is not a finch at all) protected by the Act, while all the other " finches of the grove" may be destroyed without hindrance, except the siskin, which the framers of the Act do not place among the finches? Why is the goldcrest protected and the fire-crest omitted from the Act? What harm has the skylark done that it should be deprived of protection, while the woodlark is placed under the care of the law?

Then, some of the terms are so vague that no one can understand them. " Warbler" is given as if it were some single species, whereas there are more than a dozen British warblers, including the nightingale and blackcap, both of which have a separate mention. What the dun*bird* may be I do not know. I do know what a dun*lin* is, though why it should enjoy a threefold protection under the names of dunlin, oxbird, and purre I have no idea. Neither can I tell why the curlew and whaup should be mentioned as two distinct birds.

In fact, it looks very much as if the names of the British birds that any one might happen to remember were written down, shaken up in a lucky-bag, and a given number dipped out at random.

Not that the names matter much, for the Act is so framed that any number of coaches and six can be driven through it. In the first place the penalty is much too small, and the present maximum fine ought to be made the minimum.*

But how the Act is to be enforced is a mystery. Suppose that you meet half-a-dozen dickey-laggers, as I do every Sunday morning, with all their apparatus of nets, call-birds, &c., you are powerless. You may know well enough that they are going to catch nightingales and other protected birds, but you cannot prove it ; and unless you happen to be accompanied by a policeman they will not

* Extract from a letter from Mr. J. Colam.　1880. " I have received the inclosed proof of your article by the kind favour of a friend. If the article is intended for early publication, you will thank me for informing you that a bill is now before Parliament for the extension of the close season to *all* birds. It was prepared by this society on the recommendation of the Select Committee of the House of Commons in 1873, which has never been carried into effect, and introduced for us by Mr. L. L. Dillwyn, M.P., Sir John Lubbock, M.P., and Mr. James Howard, M.P."

answer at all, except by foul abuse. It is true they are liable to a forty-shilling fine if they refuse to give their name and address even to the police, but if a man chooses to give his name as John Smith and his address as a lodger at 147, Little Baker Street, Whitechapel, and says that he is only going to catch chaffinches and sparrows, nothing more is to be done.

You can certainly follow them about, and drive the birds away from their nets and lime-twigs, but your time is too valuable to be taken up in this way, and the men know it. An energetic lady of my acquaintance did this. When starting for church on a Sunday morning, she saw what she thought to be a wounded bird fluttering about on the ground, and ran to rescue it. I need hardly say that it was the decoy-bird tied to a stick, and jerked continually, in order to attract other birds.

Not seeing the net, she caught her feet in it and rolled over. The men were infuriated and demanded payment of damages. This she refused to give, and the whole party went off to the nearest police-office. Such was the force of habit that the men walked straight into the dock. The end of the matter was, that the lady left the case in charge of the police and went home, having lost the morning service, but spoiled the day for the dickey-laggers.

These pests seldom venture to any great distance from the town which they honour with their presence, but in the depth of the country there are the bird-nesting boys, who always choose Sunday mornings, knowing that those who are not at their place of worship are probably in bed, or otherwise enjoying themselves at home.

They know nothing about the Act, and if they did, would care nothing about it. They not only pry into every bush, tree, or hedge, but they sneak into private grounds, carefully setting spies to give notice in case of any one approaching the spot. They not only take the eggs, but they pull the nests to pieces and kill the young birds, seldom killing them outright, but slowly torturing them to death in ways which I decline to specify.

How to deal with these boys is a most difficult problem. Parents encourage them because bird-nesting "keeps them out of mischief." The Act as it at present stands is powerless. The Society for the Prevention of Cruelty cannot have its agents everywhere; but that something must be done, and done as soon as possible, is a pressing necessity. As it is, complaints are already made from all parts of the country that birds are rapidly becoming scarce. In one place the dicky-laggers have so effectually swept the birds from the district that the voice of the nightingale is unknown, and 'chaffinches are "as scarce as eagles," to borrow the forcible language of an Essex correspondent.

When a new Act is made, as it must be made, three points must be essential.

1. All birds, without exception, should be entitled to the protection of the law.

2. The penalty for infraction of the law should be severe enough to be an effectual deterrent.

3. The enforcement of the law should be brought within the reach of all those who wish to protect the birds.

POOR JONES.

By T. MARCHANT WILLIAMS, B.A.

I HAVE before me a barrister's brief from which I gather most of the earlier facts in the following narrative :—

On the afternoon of the 21st April, 1873, William Jones and a fellow-workman left their homes at Aberdare to enjoy a half-holiday, that had fallen to their lot, at the small outlying village of Hirwaen. Jones had only very recently returned to his native country from the United States, whither he had accompanied his parents a few years before, and whither it was again his intention to go in company with his wife and children. He carried with him, on the day I have above referred to, a loaded six-barrelled revolver, which he had bought of a friend in New York for ten dollars, but which he had not yet used. In fact, he was totally inexperienced in the handling of fire-arms, and had he not fully intended returning to the Western States of America after a short stay amid his native hills in Wales, he certainly would not have purchased this revolver. However, now that it was in his possession, he very naturally thought he might derive some enjoyment from testing its powers on the wide and somewhat desolate moor that separates Hirwaen from Aberdare ; and it was with this purpose that he and his friend were actuated when they quitted their respective homes for the former place, to spend in its immediate neighbourhood their half-holiday.

It appears though that, owing to some circumstance or other, the two men whiled away their time, not on the moor testing the revolver, but in one of the village inns smoking clay pipes and drinking strong beer. Jones's companion left the inn in time to catch the last train for Aberdare, whereas he himself, seeing that if he went home by rail there would be a distance of a mile and a half to walk from the railway station to his own house, resolved to return as he had come, that is, on foot. His friend remonstrated with him, but to no purpose; he readily admitted that the road across the common or moor was notoriously dangerous, inasmuch as it was infested with beggars and tramps; but had he not a loaded revolver in his pocket, which was guaranteed to carry two hundred paces, and which therefore would enable him to defend himself against any villainous vagabond that might be tempted to molest him?

It was ten o'clock when he left the inn; the night was dark and dismal. As he approached the most lonesome part of his course, he thought he heard persons speaking a little in front. He stood still a moment, slightly alarmed, it would seem, though by this time he held his revolver in his trembling hand, and perhaps was endeavouring to persuade himself that he was ready for any emergency. A stone next came whizzing past his head, and almost at the same instant he heard somebody shout, "Strike him! strike him!" Thereupon Jones himself spoke with all the determination and defiance he could command, and declared he would blow out the brains of the first man that might dare to hurt or even to touch him. He could, by this time, distinguish faintly in the darkness the forms of three persons, who were advancing towards him, and who speedily surrounded him. One of them seized the revolver; which, however, Jones managed to fire twice into the air (as he thought); but the second shot, it appears, penetrated the fleshy part of his assailant's thumb. The three men now fell back, and Jones, literally trembling with fear, continued his course. After he had proceeded a few paces, with the view of warding off pursuit and imparting to himself a feeling of confidence, he fired two more shots, one into the ground and the other upwards into the air. The rest of his journey was performed without any further adventure.

The following morning he went to his work as usual, and with characteristic innocence, and wholly regardless of the sad consequences his adventure of the previous night was thereafter to lead to, he related it in all its details to his comrades, most of whom felt sorely disappointed he was not able to assure them that he had, to say the least, temporarily disabled all of his cowardly antagonists. At that time he was not aware that he had wounded even one of them.

The following Tuesday a neighbour informed him that one of the men had been slightly wounded by him. The news surprised him, but the only reply he could make to his informant was to the purport that the man had received what he well deserved, by a mere accident. On the 29th April, that is, eight days after the event, two police-officers called at Jones's house, when the following conversation, in the Welsh language, took place:—

"Is this William Jones's house?"
"Yes."
"Are you William Jones?"
"Yes."
"Were you returning from Hirwaen to Aberdare along the road across the common on the 21st inst.?"
"Yes."
"Did you meet anybody on your way?"
"Yes; I was attacked by three men."
"Did you know them?"
"No."
"Did they hurt you?"
"Not in the least."
"Did you hurt them?"
"I have been told that one of the shots I fired, in order to frighten them away, slightly wounded one of them."
"You carried a revolver with you then?"
"Yes."
"Where is it?"

Jones hereupon handed to the officer the revolver, two of whose chambers were still loaded. He was then bidden to accompany the officers to the police-station. He did so readily, but not exactly with a light heart, for it at once occurred to him that his detention even for a very brief period might grievously affect the health of his poor wife, who had never been very strong, and who was now weeping bitterly, and seemed altogether inconsolable. In wishing her good-bye he kissed her, and endeavoured to reassure her by predicting his speedy return. He little dreamt that he was bidding her a long, long farewell.

He was not readily identified by his prosecutor; in fact, the latter was, at first, by no means sure that Jones was the man that had wounded him, although he thought he could trace in Jones a strong resemblance to the man. But the whole mystery was solved by the free confession which the former made; he declared with simple candour that he *was* the man that was sought. Why should the prosecutor then hesitate to identify him?

The next morning he was brought before the magistrates at Aberdare, who referred the case to the stipendiary at Merthyr Tydvil, by whom he was committed for trial at the Cardiff summer assizes. He was now conveyed to the Swansea gaol, where he spent ten weeks picking oakum like the meanest felon.

On July 12th the case came on for hearing before Justice Grove at the Cardiff Assize Court. I have little doubt that the counsel for the prisoner performed his task to the best of his ability, such as it was; but I have every reason to believe that the case was, somehow or other (mainly, perhaps, owing to the prisoner's ignorance of English, and his lack of presence of' mind), grossly mismanaged; and the reader will doubtless agree with me when I state that the punishment awarded to the prisoner seems to me to have been scandalously excessive. Why, the poor man was actually condemned to serve ten years in penal servitude! Unfortunately, he had no witnesses to prove that he acted simply in self-defence; nor was he able to prove to the satisfaction of the judge that the prosecutor was wounded by a mere accident. On the other hand, there were three men who swore he was the aggressor, one of whom averred that only two shots were fired, another that the number was three, whilst a third witness, a woman living not very far from the scene of the conflict, declared that she distinctly heard *four* shots. This latter statement, it will be perceived, coincides with Jones's version, who, as has been already stated, fired a third and a fourth shot for the purpose of warding off pursuit. The prosecutor's version was, that he was sitting down by the road-side awaiting his friends, when the prisoner came up to him, and after making use of some savage imprecations, fired at him and wounded him in the thumb. The judge, it would seem, held that this statement was not disproved; although I presume it did not escape him that it was highly improbable that one man should have ventured, in a bleak, solitary spot, and at dead of night, to attack, single-handed, three others (for the prosecutor's friends were admittedly at hand),

without the least provocation, but merely for the "love of the thing." Nay, further, even granting that there may occasionally be encountered a bruté whose innate love of devilry and mischief would lead him to court rather than avoid a murderous scrimmage, surely any one possessing the slightest insight into character would instantly perceive that Jones would be the last man in the world that might be assumed to be of such a type, for a meeker, gentler, more inoffensive and simple-minded little man it would be difficult to find. And. he was but slightly under the influence of drink on this memorable night, for it was clearly proved that he and his friend had consumed throughout the afternoon and evening they spent together at the inn but four pints of beer. I abstain from insinuating what might have been proved at the trial respecting the state of mind in which his antagonists were, and the degree of responsibility that ought to have been attached to their actions. It seems that the prisoner was perfectly dazed at the trial; he could hardly speak, had not the heart even to contradict the prosecutor and his friends when they were stating what was wholly inconsistent with what he himself held to be the truth. The long weary drudgery at Swansea, accompanied as it was by a feverish longing for home, had verily stupefied him. There he stood in the dock, apparently a wreck—poor, friendless, and utterly downcast, both in body and mind; and when the heavy, cruel sentence was pronounced, he practically lost all consciousness for a time. The judge observed that a severe punishment was necessary to serve as a warning to any other person that might thereafter be disposed to introduce into this country the dangerous customs of the Western States of North America. It was not only unnecessary, he added, for civilians to carry fire-arms in England for self-protection, but the practice was very reprehensible and was to be rigorously suppressed.

On August 5th, he was conveyed in the charge of two warders from Cardiff to Pentonville, where he arrived early in the afternoon of the same day. He was at once ordered to the bath, and subsequently was attired in the customary prison costume and shown into his cell, in which the only prominent articles of furniture were a low stool and a slanting board which was to serve as a bed.

His first night in this uninviting chamber was, one may well believe, entirely sleepless, as were also numberless other nights. The thought of his own cruel fate, of his poor struggling (perhaps, starving) wife and children at home, and of his aged parents across the Atlantic, made him weep almost incessantly; and so completely unhinged were his faculties, that for two years he was unable to recall the names of his little children. Throughout the period he spent at Pentonville he was so depressed and humiliated that he spoke not a word to any of his fellow-prisoners, although frequent opportunities for indulging in a short conversation with them presented themselves to him at chapel and elsewhere. He prayed, he told me, daily and many times a day, and his leisure time he devoted to the reading of the Bible, an English copy of which had been given him soon after his arrival. He entreated the prison authorities to give him also a Welsh Bible, but this they declined to do, save on the condition that he would surrender the English copy, which he did not feel prepared to do, inasmuch as then he would not be able to follow the lessons at chapel. Besides, he could not read English well, and he felt therefore that, if he parted with his English Bible, he would thereby be throwing away his only opportunity of perfecting his knowledge of the language. Eventually, however, the chaplain presented him with a Welsh version of the Scriptures, which he read, during his stay at Pentonville and Chatham, from the beginning to the end, five times; the English Bible he read three times. He was unable to commit to memory the simplest passages from either, for his retentive faculty seemed to have temporarily deserted him; and though he admits that he found few parts of the Scriptures which were not deeply interesting to him, still if he had a preference for any part of the Bible rather than another, it was for the Psalms and the Gospels; if he lingered longer and more fondly over any verses than others, those were, generally speaking, in the Psalms or were the words of our Saviour. His life in prison was spent with grief; his years with sighing; his drink was mingled with weeping; and yet, he frequently felt that the "helper of the fatherless" had heard the voice of his weeping; he trusted in Him and was helped.

The work at Pentonville was by no means very hard, most of his time being spent in coir-picking. He discovered, after some time, that owing to his ignorance of prison-life and habits he was working much harder than was necessary. This, however, he never ceased to do, for it served to keep his mind partially free from sad longings and gloomy thoughts. The diet there was better than at either Swansea or Cardiff. The morning meal consisted of one pint of gruel and eight ounces of bread; for dinner on Mondays, Wednesdays, and Saturdays, there were served four ounces of meat, three-quarters of a pound of potatoes, and four ounces of bread; cheese was substituted for the meat and potatoes on Sundays, a pint of stew on Tuesdays and Fridays, and one pound of suet pudding on Thursdays; the last meal in the day consisted of three-quarters of a pint of cocoa and eight ounces of bread.

Eventually he was removed from Pentonville to Chatham, where he was, for a brief period, engaged in filling trucks at the dockyard. This he found a very laborious and trying task, and the diet being (in his opinion) insufficient both in quantity and quality, he soon became haggard and ill. The superintendent, Mr. M——, a very big, powerful man, was excessively stern and severe. He had charge of the new comers and the "incorrigibles." He treated Jones and the other well-behaved and tractable prisoners very kindly, but the insubordinate and impertinent men he handled roughly — would occasionally strike them with his fist. It was the London pickpockets that were most harshly treated; most of these were old offenders, knew the prison ways, and lost no opportunity of shirking their work and annoying their officers. Some would even go so far as to strike their officers, for which offence they would be deservedly flogged. They seemed to be the lowest type of men, indulged in the commonest and vilest expressions, and were ever on the alert for mischief. Jones was practically forced to converse with them at times, on Sundays especially, on parade. He could not enter into their feelings or ways of thinking, and, in fact, he held it to be his greatest punishment that he was driven into the continued company of such a pestiferous herd. The scheme for the classification of prisoners, which is described in the Report of the Commissioners of Prisons for the current year, and which is being adopted at the present moment in some localities, will not meet such a case as this I am now dealing with; and it is not a case of so exceptional a character, that it does not merit the special attention of the Commissioners. Their classification scheme is a good one, so far as it goes, and will, I feel convinced, effect good results; but one of the most serious blots on our prison system will not be removed until this scheme is supplemented with another, which will have for its chief aim the preclusion of free intercourse between prisoners of various types or characters. It is really shocking to think tnat this simple-hearted, God-fearing man should have been forcibly made the constant associate of artful thieves and fierce cutthroats, whose whole delight was to shock his susceptibilities and endeavour to initiate him into the intricacies of their nefarious designs. Repeatedly did they try to teach him burglarious tricks and the art of pocket-picking; but he was an inapt and unwilling scholar, and, singularly enough, he has by this time quite forgotten nearly all the clever hints that were gratuitously given him. The following are some of the details relating to the exploits of a few of his prison mates he is able to recall:—

B—— (A.), a short, dark man, about thirty-five years of age, was a Birmingham footpad. He tripped up a man with a wooden leg, dexterously robbed him of his gold watch, and by quickly diving into a crowd close by, contrived to elude his pursuers. He sold the watch for seven pounds. He was subsequently caught house-breaking, and his single letter A signifies not only the first conviction, but also that he arrived at Chatham in 1874. B would mean 1875; Z, 1873, &c.

W—— G——, a tall man wearing two letters, was serving his time for burglary at Leeds or Sheffield. He was one of three who had planned to break into a suburban house; his companions were to watch outside, whilst he was engaged in entering the house and packing up the booty. By some mishap or other, just as he was leaving the premises, he was suddenly pounced upon by a policeman, whom it was impossible to resist successfully owing to the unexpectedness of the onslaught. His companions escaped. G—— was a thief among thieves—would steal even from his mates anything that might come in his way.

There was another prisoner from Birmingham, a friend of B——. His name was J—— J——, alias B—— (V.D.). He had robbed a butcher in the market—had, in fact, deftly cut away his apron, in which he found a considerable sum of money. He was afterwards caught in his own house. In the prison he worked as a shoemaker.

This last man was not quite so communicative as were some of the men, but, in common with all the burglars and pickpockets, he often pronounced it to be his intention to ply his old trade immediately he obtained his discharge. All of them likewise regarded as a great hero the old sailor who, not very long ago, worked his way through

the floor of his cell into a storeroom underneath; then broke through a cast-iron grating into the prison-yard; next flung his rope, which was made of strips of sheeting knotted together and having attached to it at one end an old gas-bracket bent into the shape of a hook, over the wall, ascended and descended by it; and, after breaking into the house of an official in close proximity to the walls and appropriating to himself a decent suit of clothes and about five pounds in money, made his escape and has never since been heard of.

Jones's uniformly good behaviour, and exceptionally quiet and respectful demeanour, endeared him to his superiors, and one of his earliest rewards was his transfer from the dockyard to the smithy, where he remained as a "striker" during the remainder of his term. The work in the smithy was less irksome than in the dockyard, and it was considered a great privilege and, virtually, a promotion to be permitted to undertake it; for the open air duties were not only heavier and more trying, but they had the additional disadvantage of having to be performed in rain as well as in sunshine, during the hot summer months as well as in the bleak winter, when the snow lay deep on the ground and biting winds swept through the place.

Further promotion fell to his lot in due course; from the third class he was advanced into the second, and had the distinction of a yellow band on his collar. At the end of the third year he was promoted into the first class, with the customary privilege of having blue braid on his dress. Also, he now enjoyed the luxury of having tea substituted for gruel, and roast meat for boiled; he had, too, a double allowance of bread, three walks on parade instead of one, and the favour of writing and receiving a letter once a quarter. When he was in the second class he could receive or write only three letters a year, and only two when in the third class.

From his wife he learnt that unsuccessful efforts had been made, several times, by his friends to induce the Home Secretary to commute his sentence. The present writer waited upon an ex-Home Secretary, laid the case fully before him, and entreated him to intercede with Mr. Cross in behalf of the prisoner. The reply I received was to the effect that it was absolutely useless at that "time of day" to appeal to Mr. Cross for a commutation of the sentence. Why was not an appeal made immediately after the trial? All I could say was that I presumed that the prisoner, being but a poor working man, had no influential friends, and could not command the active sympathy of any others than those in his own station in life; and those, again, were not conversant with the ways in which protests are framed and petitions preferred. Nothing was done, seemingly, until the time for action, according to the ex-Home Secretary, had passed away.

It afforded the prisoner a measure of relief to learn that his friends and former neighbours at Aberdare never ceased to extend kindness and sympathy to his wife and children. She had her house rent free; and, further, her landlady, together with many others, frequently supplied her with articles of clothing and home-made delicacies. But in spite of the kindness shown her, and notwithstanding the considerate assistance she received, her trials were almost too many for her. Her health threatened to break down, for the struggle for existence was a very bitter one. It was her ambition to give her children the best education within her reach, to keep them clean, well-clad, and well-fed; to train them in habits of neatness and industry, and to set them an example of perfect uprightness in thought and action. She nobly succeeded. Her little children attended school regularly and punctually until within a few months of her husband's release, when her health became so feeble, that the eldest daughter was occasionally detained at home to attend to some of the household duties. The children were perfect pictures of health and happiness; and in respect of dress were a pattern of neatness and cleanliness. It is really marvellous that she was able to do so much with so little.

I am now entering upon a part of my narrative which wears the appearance of improbability. The subjoined facts may be safely relied upon. I leave the reader to judge whether the inference deduced from them be legitimate or not.

The result of the appeal to the ex-Home Secretary soon reached the ears of a neighbour of Mrs. Jones, who, being of an ardent and enterprising temperament, induced her son, a collier, by the way, to write a letter in behalf of the poor convict, there and then, direct to her Majesty the Queen! About a month or so subsequently to the date of this letter, Jones obtained his discharge, that is, one year and eleven months in advance of the time he was entitled to it according to the prison rules! Now, the inference generally drawn is, that the Queen with characteristic thoughtfulness promptly forwarded the missive to the Home Secretary, Mr. Cross,

who immediately put himself in communication with the governor of the Chatham establishment, and finding that Jones bore an excellent character there, and that therefore there were strong reasons for believing the unadorned statements of the illiterate collier to be well-founded, suggested that the unfortunate prisoner should be set free.

The news came upon Jones very unexpectedly. He was sent for by the clerk of the governor, by whom he was informed that the Home Secretary had been applied to in his behalf, who had ordered him to be set at liberty that very day. The clerk was good enough to add that not one in a thousand had given the prison authorities so little trouble as he had, and throughout the time he was at Chatham he had lost but *one* mark! The rules were read out to him, and the next day, after having been weighed, and when his marks had been duly counted, his likeness taken, and his prison dress changed for a less distinctive costume, he was permitted to step outside the prison walls and breathe the air of freedom once more. His railway-fare to Aberdare was paid for him, and a few shillings as pocket-money were given him. For a considerable time he hardly knew what to do: he felt as if he had been stunned by a heavy and sudden blow. His fellow-passengers exchanged greetings with him. Some of them questioned him narrowly, and were evidently amused when he confessed, with his usual candour and simplicity, that he was returning home from Chatham, where he had been residing for more than five years. After this admission they were considerate enough to abstain from pressing upon him any further questions.

His wife was not aware of what was in store for her. He had not had time to write and inform her or his friends that his freedom had been given him. It was about seven o'clock in the evening when his train arrived at Aberdare. He hurried out of the carriage, walked quickly through the crowd of people on the platform, not one of whom luckily recognised him; then along the principal street of the town, still unrecognised, with rapid step and throbbing heart. When he reached his house, he found the front door wide open; his wife and a neighbour were busying themselves at the tap, which, apparently, was out of repair. "Is this Jane Jones's house?" asked he, in a slightly faltering voice, for, as he was about to speak he had caught a glimpse of his wife's face, and had seen there the unmistakable traces of the cares and sorrows of many years. She looked very pale, but spoke and moved about as briskly and cheerfully as in days of old. She did not recognise her husband's voice, and therefore replied coolly and pleasantly enough—

"Yes; step in, please, and take a seat. I shall be disengaged presently."

"Are you quite well?"

"Yes, thank you, quite well."

There was now a short interval of silence. Jones was sitting near the fire, gazing wistfully at his wife and with difficulty repressing his tears and checking his desire to reveal himself to her. What was to be done? He was hesitating to speak again lest he should seriously frighten her; and yet, reasoned he, sooner or later he must make himself known to her. At last he ventured a third time to address her. "You are all *quite* well then?"

"What!" she exclaimed, quickly and eagerly looking at him, and evidently recalling the old familiar voice——.

My narrative ends here. Jones has forgiven all his enemies, if he ever had any; and even his prosecutor he has long since pardoned. He now works as in days gone by in a coal-pit, and is greatly respected by both masters and men; and were it not that the state of his wife's health causes him at times a little uneasiness, a happier man than he it would be difficult to find.

HEALTH AT HOME.

By B. W. RICHARDSON, M.D., F.R.S.

PART V.

AT the close of my last paper I described the new mode of using permanganate as a deodorizing fluid. This leads me to explain another method of purification for the air of the closet, and, indeed, for that of any room which may require deodorization and purification.

PURIFICATION BY IODINE.

This plan is inexpensive and extremely simple. It consists in the application of iodine in the pure state, that is to say, the solid shining metalloid itself, not the tincture or spirituous solution of the element. For this employment of iodine first get a common chip ointment box, which can be bought of any chemist; a box of an inch and a half in diameter is sufficiently large. Take the lid off this box and remove the top from the lid so that the ring part of the lid alone remains; then into the body of the box put two drachms weight of the pure iodine, stretch a piece of muslin gauze over the top of the box, and over the muslin press down the ring of the lid so as to make the muslin taut over the top of the box. Lastly cut away the loose muslin around the ring, and complete, and ready for use, is an iodine deodorizing box which will last in action for six weeks or two months, even in hot weather. To bring this box into practical application it is merely necessary to place it in the closet on a shelf or on any resting-place. The iodine will volatilize slowly into the air through the muslin gauze, will diffuse through the air,

XXI—40

will deodorize, and after a time will communicate an odour like that of fresh sea air.

There is no means of deodorizing the air of the close closet equal to this. It is ready, permanent, and effective. In cases where an instant effect is required the iodine may be volatilized in a more rapid manner. A little iodine may be placed on a plate, and the plate may be held over a spirit lamp, within the closet, for a minute or two. The iodine diffused by the heat will pass off as a violet-coloured vapour, and as it passes through the air it will create a rapid purifying action. The iodine so diffused will condense, as it cools, on the walls, and there will maintain its effect of purification.

SPRAY PURIFICATION.

At the annual meeting of the British Medical Association in 1865, I introduced a method of purifying rooms by the process of diffusing deodorizing and disinfecting substances into the air in the form of fine spray. The fluid I used in this method was made by adding iodine to a solution of the peroxide of hydrogen of ten volumes strength. The water was also charged with two and a half per cent. of sea salt, and was set aside until it was saturated with the iodine. When the saturation was complete the fluid was filtered and was quite ready for use. The solution was placed in a steam or hand spray apparatus, and, when required, was diffused in the finest state of distribution at the rate of two fluid ounces in a quarter of an hour. In an ordinary bed-room or sitting-room one ounce of the fluid was found sufficient to render the air active enough to discolour Moffat's ozone test papers to the highest degree of the scale, and that in the course of ien or twelve minutes.

The apparatus for this purpose was constructed for me by Messrs. Krohne & Sesemann, of Duke Street, Manchester Square, and was so simple in action that any nurse could put it into action at once, and could deodorize a room hour by hour on the direction of the medical attendant. In fact, there was produced a sea atmosphere in the room.

If sea water were brought in quantity to London it might, by a most simple method, be diffused at pleasure as fine spray in all houses and in close courts and alleys, so as to impart a cool sea air throughout the whole of the metropolis, an influence which would be as agreeable as it would be salubrious. I was ready to give evidence on this point before the Lords' Committee, which had to report on the introduction of sea water to London during the past session; and I do not think a more important factor in favour of such an introduction could well be advanced.

While these different means of purifying the air are put forward as of immediate service, it should always be remembered that they are temporary measures, nothing more. I mean by this that they are not intended to take the place of thorough and efficient ventilation. In fact, in the presence of perfect ventilation of good natural air, they are not required at all; and when they are called for, the necessity of better ventilation as the permanent remedy is at once proclaimed.

THE CISTERN-CLOSET AND WATER-TANK.

In our modern houses, in towns where there is no constant water supply, where one supply of water in the course of the twenty-four hours is allowed, and where the water has to be stored in large cisterns, we find the landing-place of the house the common situation in which the closet for holding the water tank or cistern is placed. For the purposes of supply, mechanically, no position probably could be better, but unfortunately the little amount of room in the town house suggests the temptation to make the cistern-closet a depôt for all sorts of improper commodities. On the top of the cistern is laid, frequently, various household implements for cleaning, and other articles which are stowed away to be out of sight and,

practically, out of mind. On one occasion I found, on making an inspection of a water-cistern in a large house, a bundle of long, thick bristles, evidently from a brush that was used for scrubbing, in the tank. On inquiry it actually turned out that they came from a round brush which was used for cleansing the adjoining water-closet. The brush, when it had served its purpose, was placed by the housemaid carefully away above the water cistern, and through a wide joint of the lid the broken bristles or rods of the brush fell through into the water below. This water, so seriously and thoughtlessly contaminated, supplied all the bedrooms with water, and also supplied part of the lower part of the house with drinking water. I name here one of the impurities that may steal into the water of the cistern, but this does not include all. Sometimes accidents happen in the cistern-closet which are unexpected, and which do not declare themselves until a fault is disclosed by the water after it is drawn from the tap. I recently had a proof of this in a curious way. Some water drawn from an upper cistern in a large house presented a muddy or filmy appearance, and soon afterwards gave a taste of lime. On inquiry it was discovered that a leakage in the roof of the house had caused water to run down the wall at the back of or over the cistern, and to carry into the cistern lime-wash from the wall, which, floating in part on the water, and adhering in part to the sides of the tank at the water-line, had become coated with fungus vegetation, so as to render the water not only disagreeable, but actually hurtful.

The cistern sometimes becomes a source of impurity from another cause, which is more offensive still. Into the cistern there is occasionally cast, either thoughtlessly or intentionally, dead matter, and so an abominable contamination is produced. A medical friend from a northern city, who was staying at one of our large hotels a few years ago, asked me to luncheon with him at the hotel; and knowing me to be a water-drinker, apologized for the water, which, said he, as he quaffed his glass of ale, "I wouldn't touch, but would rather be poisoned with beer in the long, than with water in the short run." The water truly was offensive, even to the sense of smell. Detecting this so distinctly, I sent for one in authority and explained that such water could only come from a cistern actually polluted with dead animal matter. The evidence was too certain to admit of dispute, and an inquiry was at once instituted. On opening the cistern the odour was poisonous, and the cause for it, fully exposed, was found to be the remains of a dead cat, which lay decomposing at the bottom of the tank. The animal probably had fallen in, and, unable to regain a footing, the water being low, had got drowned, and remained unnoticed until the products of decomposition made known the circumstance.

The closet holding the cistern is usually supplied with a sink, down which the slops from the bedrooms are too commonly poured. The closet is dark, the sink is emptied of water slowly, the sink is kept clean with the utmost difficulty, and from it there arises, unless scrupulous cleanliness be insisted on and daily seen to, the most disagreeable odour. The closet is not ventilated, as a rule, and so soon as the door of it is closed securely the small space has its contained air quickly turned into foul air. That foul air easily diffuses through the open chinks into the cistern itself, and in this manner the water comes into contact with the gases of decomposition, by which another source of impurity is added. From the same emanations, again, the air in the rooms adjoining the cistern-closet is apt to become contaminated.

It will be seen, now, how necessary it is in every household to pay special attention to the closet that contains the water-tank. This closet, first of all, should never be allowed to contain any household implement, or vessel that is not perfectly clean. It should be so free that the lid of the cistern can be opened without a moment's hesitation. Its walls should be washed or distempered frequently. It should have a ventilating tube carried from its ceiling through the roof or into a chimney. It should, if possible, be lighted by a window, even if the window be into the staircase. The sink should have the freest opening for the flow of water that may escape from the tap, and the sink should never be used for the purpose of receiving the slops from the pails that are used in the bedrooms. Lastly, the sink should be specially cleansed, so that there is in it no accumulation of dust or dirt of any kind.

For the cistern, slate is, I think, the best material, after that galvanized iron, and next to that lead. The worst form of cistern is the wooden one lined with zinc. Every cistern should hold a carbon filter, which should often be changed, and the cistern should be frequently inspected to see that it is quite clean, and contains no deposit. It is excellent policy, once a week or so, to allow the cistern entirely to empty of water. I need hardly add that the slop pails should never be allowed to remain in the cistern closet, but, as they are often left there, the advice is necessary.

The consideration of all these facts in relation to the storage of water in cisterns within private houses brings us to a decisive instruction;—to wit, that no effort should be left undone, in towns where these dangers exist, until they are removed by the stored water being replaced by a continuous supply of pure water from a common and pure source. The storage or tank system has been the cause of endless mischiefs in houses from mere overflow and injury done to walls and ceilings and furniture. But these, obvious and costly mischiefs as they are, are trifling when compared with the insidious dangers to health which the system engenders. Damp, dirt, and disease are the first fruits of the system; damage to property is but of secondary consideration, though by appealing to the pocket it often seems to be of first importance.

THE HOUSEMAID'S CLOSET.

The housemaid's closet, as it is usually called, is the third receptacle on the staircase-landing that requires particular attention. This closet is often the *omnium gatherum* of the upper part of the house. Here is likely to be found the bag or basket containing the unwashed linen; here are often brushes and dusters, and various other paraphernalia for the cleaning processes. It is not to be supposed that so important a place as the housemaid's cupboard can be dispensed with, but it should never be neglected or treated as an out-of-the-way nook into which anything may be thrust that has to be put out of sight, and which may or may not be cleaned and purified. Because it is the depôt of so many articles which are used for cleaning, or are waiting to be cleaned, it ought to be the more carefully protected against uncleanliness. It should therefore always, when it is possible to have the light, be lighted by daylight; it should have ventilation of the best kind that is procurable; it should be repeatedly emptied of all its contents and thoroughly washed out; and its walls should be distempered twice a year, whether they seem to require the process or not. In a properly ordered house the housemaid's cupboard should be emptied of its contents once a week as a regular system, and all the things that are stowed away in it should have their proper place. If there be no open window into it from the staircase an opening ought to be made into it above the door, and at the lower part of the door, for the free circulation of air.

THE DRESSING-ROOM AND BATH-ROOM.

The possession of a dressing-room and bath-room on the bedroom floor is rather more than a luxury, and if half the money that is frittered away on empty display in the drawing-room were spent on the bath arrangements, great benefit to health would often be the result to the whole of a family. I do not, however, for my part recommend any very elaborate system of baths for common use. Healthy daily ablution of the most perfect kind can be had at a very small cost, and at very small trouble. I hear it said constantly by people of moderate means that they would like to have a daily bath, and that they know how important it is to have one, but that they have not the convenience of a bath-room in their house, and are troubled because the cost of setting up a bath is so great. I hear rich men say that they have gone into large expenditure in the setting up of the appliances of the bath and bath-room. They have laid on hot and cold water; they have had a shower apparatus placed overhead; they have had the bath itself glazed or enamelled; and, in taking the bath, they have been immersed, douched, cold douched, shampooed, and dried. There can be little objection to all this parade; it is something to talk about or think about, if it be nothing better, and I believe I have known it to be a relief to the minds of some who have little or nothing with which to burthen their minds. But after all the proceeding is very much like a search for a needle in a bundle of hay, and the needle may always be found without any such elaborate cost and trouble.

To wash the body from head to foot every day is the one thing needful in respect to ablution for the pure sake of health. To become so accustomed to this habit that the body feels uncomfortable if the process be not duly performed is the one habit of body, the one craving that is wanted, the one habit that needs to be duly acquired in the matter of body-cleansing. The process may be carried out as speedily as possible. Moreover, it may be carried out as cheaply as possible, and all the hygienic advantages may be the same as if great expense had been incurred. A formal bath is actually not necessary. A shallow tub, or shallow metal bath in which the bather can stand in front of his wash-hand basin; a good large sponge, a piece of plain soap, a large soft Turkish towel, and two gallons of water are quite sufficient for all purposes of health. In the North of England there is often to be met with in the bedrooms of hotels, and sometimes in those of private houses, the most cheap and convenient of these small and useful baths. The centre or well of the bath is about twelve inches in diameter, and about nine inches deep. This centre is surrounded by a broad rim, a rim from eight to ten inches wide, which slopes towards the centre all round. In this bath the ablutionist can stand, and from as much water as would fill an ordinary ewer, he can wash himself from head to foot completely without wetting the floor, since the broad sloping margin of the bath catches the water. To stand in such a bath as this, and from the water of the wash-hand basin to sponge the body rapidly over, and afterwards to dry quickly and thoroughly, is everything that is wanted if the process be carried out daily; and this, after a little practice, may be so easily done, that it becomes no more trouble than the washing of the face, neck, and hands, which so many people are content to accept as a perfected daily ablution. In winter the water should be tepid, in summer cold; or what is a better rule still, the water should always be within a few degrees of the same temperature. If in the summer months the water be at 60° F.; in the spring and autumn at 65°; and in the winter at 70°, a very safe rule is being followed; nor is it at all difficult to learn to follow this rule from the readings, occasionally carried out, of a thermometer which in these days may be obtained for a few shillings, and which it is always convenient and useful to keep on the wall of the bed-room or dressing-room. Once a week it is a good practice to dissolve in the water used for ablution common washing soda, in the proportion of one quarter of a pound to two gallons of water. This alkaline soda frees the skin of acids, is an excellent cleanser of the body, and is specially serviceable to persons of a rheumatical tendency who are often troubled with free acid perspirations.

It is a question often asked in reference to the arrangements of the bath-room, whether the plan should be adopted of taking the bath at night, or in the morning, before going to bed or on rising from bed? The answer to this is simple enough when time is not an important object of those who make the inquiry. It is much better to make complete ablution of the body from head to foot both on going to bed and on rising also, whenever that can be carried out; and indeed so rapid is the process when the habit of it is acquired, there are few persons who could not get into the habit of it as they do into the habit of taking meals at stated times. But if for any reason it be impossible to carry out complete ablution twice a day, then no doubt the general ablution is best just before going to bed. There is no practice more objectionable than to go to bed closely wrapped up in the dust and dirt that accumulate on the surface of the body during the day; nor is there anything I know so conducive to sound sleep as a tepid douche just before getting into bed. I have many times known bad sleepers become the best of sleepers from the adoption of this simple rule. If the body be well sponged over before going to bed, the morning ablution—though it is still better to carry it out—need not, of necessity, be so general. The face, neck, chest, arms, and hands may be merely well sponged and washed at the morning ablution.

I can do no harm, nor shall I uselessly take up space, if in this place I digress for a moment to enforce still more earnestly the importance of making this matter of cleansing the body a habit of life from the first of life. I would impress on mothers and fathers, and on all who have the command of youth, that this practice should not only be commenced at the earliest period, from the first infancy, but should be steadily maintained so that the subject of it shall attain the desire for it, and feel the necessity. I notice it to be a common plan for mothers of the best sort, who feel it almost a crime to omit washing a baby morning and evening, to begin to omit the same process so soon as the child learns to run about and to become to a certain degree self-dependent. It is no doubt an irksome daily task for the mother of a large family to see that every little boy and girl is washed from head to foot every morning and evening. Still the result is worth every penny of the labour. In the industrial schools at Annerley the waifs and strays of puerile society, the worst-born specimens in the matter of health, are so quickly brought in conditions of good health, that, as Dr. Alfred Carpenter once remarked to me when we stood in the midst of the children, "they seem to teach us that not even a generation of change is required to wipe out a generation of defects, when personal health is well looked after." There is all the richness of truth in this wise observation, and I am fully justified in saying that amongst the many agencies by which the able managers of these industrial schools do so much for the health of the children, there is not one agency more telling than the persistent and regular, but at the same time, perfectly simple method of ablution which is practised in the establishment. Practically the system is that which I have described for the household. There are no cumbersome baths, but a series of taps at which the children can cleanse themselves from the crowns of their heads to the soles of their feet as quickly as they can wash their hands and faces in the lavatories of many other institutions in which children and youths are received. These children at Annerley grow up in the habit of ablution, and when they leave the school they are, by the habit, made fifty per cent. more cleanly than the majority of children who are brought up in better circumstances, or even in luxury.

While the easiest, readiest, and cheapest of baths have thus been carefully considered, in order that the pretence or excuse of difficulty in getting a bath may be removed, I have no intention of passing over in silence the bath-room of the comfortable house. Whoever can afford a bath-room should have one, and many a house which is richly and expensively endowed in other respects is deprived, unjustly for health's sake, of its bath-room. Let us therefore study the bath-room with a little care. The bath-room is best located on the third floor in four-storied houses, that is to say on a level with the chief bed-rooms and below the attics. A good bath-room ought to be ten feet wide, ten feet high, and twelve feet long. The floor should be of oak or pine-wood, smooth and well laid. No carpet is required for the floor, but one or two perforated india-rubber mats are of advantage; the walls of the bath-room should be painted in hard paint that can be washed and thoroughly dried, or it should be fitted with tile-work, which is at once clean and effective. The bath, which need not be large, should always be constructed of earthenware, and it should be quite flat at the bottom, so that it is easy to stand upright in it while taking a douche. The well-constructed bath is supplied with hot and cold water; the temperature of the water should be regulated by the rule already supplied, 60° F. in summer, 65° F. in spring and autumn, 70° F. in winter.

The bath-room should be thoroughly well-ventilated and warmed. I know nothing that answers better for warming it than the calorigen stove, of which a description has been given in a previous paper on *Health at Home*. To those who wish for the further luxury of a hot-air or Roman bath in their houses, it is a comparatively easy matter to arrange the ordinary bath-room so as to make it, when required, a hot-air bath. This can be done in the simplest way by introducing into the room a stove heated with coal and constructed, in a large size, after the manner precisely of the calorigen. The air in this case is let into the room from the outside by a three-inch pipe, and is allowed to escape from the stove after it has been heated by a pipe of a similar diameter. With a good ordinary-sized fire in the closed grate of the stove, the air in the room may be brought up to the temperature of 140° Fahr. in a period of from twenty minutes to half an hour, provided that the space to be warmed does not exceed twelve hundred cubic feet, that the door be well closed, and that the escape for the heated air at the upper part of the room be so arranged that it can, at pleasure, be reduced until it is not above twice the size of the opening for the entrance of the air from the stove. For a sick person to whom I thought the use of a hot-air bath would be very useful, I once turned an ordinary bath-room into a hot-air bath in this way with great readiness, and with the best effect, and since, the time when that was done I have repeated the same with results as satisfactory. It is true that the temperature is limited in range in this form of hot-air bath, but for most purposes it can be raised to a sufficient degree, and as the hot air can be shut off at once and the ventilator enlarged at pleasure, it is easy to cool the room rapidly down during the after process of the douche or the water-bath.

For those who have means and who are building a new house to be replete with all modern contrivances, the properly constructed Roman bath should be always introduced in connection with the ordinary bath-room. The Romans, who once inhabited these islands, set us a splendid example in this respect in their habitations. With them, the hot-air bath seems to have been as much of a household necessity as the kitchen; and it is right to admit that by this care they expressed practically a degree of sanitary knowledge which bears imitation to the present hour. In this cold, and damp, and variable climate, the Roman bath in the house is of more importance than it would be in warmer and more equable climes, for here it is less of a luxury and more of a necessity. If, in our heavily fogged London atmosphere, the tired Londoner after a day of oppression could return home, and for an hour before dinner indulge in the light and genial and clarified air of a Roman bath, he would do more to relieve his congested and enfeebled internal organs than by any other process that is obtainable. As it is, he is led too often to seek a false and partial relief from his oppression by resorting to a stimulant drink, which first elates and then paralyzes and injures, or kills outright. In a word, he smothers his afflictions, while in the Roman bath he would disperse them. This is a correct and true definition.

In saying so much in favour of the Roman bath, I am, I know, offering some slight correction of what I spoke on the same subject twenty years ago, when the hot-air bath was being enthusiastically introduced into this country by some of its over-earnest advocates. To me it seemed at that time as if the advocates of the bath were claiming it as a panacea for all maladies, and were fain to declare that to its efficacy fresh air and bodily exercise might well be sacrificed, and a slothful luxury take the place of a hardy, healthful existence. It is but just to state that some of these advocates did go even to this length, and that I and others, thereupon, went perhaps too far the other way in our criticism of them, and so to some extent checked a useful measure while it was new, and before it had taken root. If I ever did wrong in that way I recall it now. Holding as firmly as ever the view that the hot-air bath should never take the place of healthy exercise of body nor of active out-door life in good and wholesome air, I am satisfied from a larger and longer experience that the Roman bath is an addition to the English house which should never be ignored when circumstances admit of its introduction. Last winter, in the treatment of a number of persons who were under my medical care, I would have given anything for the advantage of being able to remove them, under their own roofs, into a well-constructed hot-air bath.

From the multitude of the readers of these Health at Home papers in GOOD WORDS, I am naturally led to receive a considerable number of letters containing questions, suggestions, and information. To the majority of these letters it is utterly impossible to give a special acknowledgment, but as they come in I classify them under different heads, and I hope in a forthcoming number to make a general reply or comment on certain of the more important and practical.

THE SOUL'S ORATORIO.

By RICHARD SINCLAIR BROOKE, D.D.

Psalm ciii. 1.

"AND all that is within me"—greater far
  Than what's outlying in the world within,
Where life and death still wage relentless war,
    The strife of grace and sin ;

'Tis the unbounded kingdom of the soul—
  Thoughts' trackless realm with plan and purpose rife,
And myriad memories, like waves, that roll
    Up the grey strands of life ;

The far yet ever-present hills of hope,
  Whence gush the streams exhaling as they run,
Green slopes where climbs the heart, and from the top
    Just sees its sun go down ;

And far-down regions, where in lonely graves
  Youth's dreams lie buried, once too fair—too brief—
What time the fond heart, dove-like, skimmed the waves,
    And brought home—but a "leaf ; "

The workings of the heart which cannot die—
  The outshoots of the brain—like lightning's glare
Some flash to earth, while others, streaming high,
    Like north-lights shine in air.

O boundless clime ! shut up in straitest cell,
  Concentred realm, so great, and yet so small,
Where time and thought, both infinite, do dwell,
    And earth and heaven and all.

Descend, O God, to animate—inspire—
  Warm with Thy breath of love this sentient frame,
Till "all that is within me," touched by fire,
    Shall wake to praise Thy name.

Spirit, come down—as on a high-strung lyre,
  Strike with Thy hand of power—breathe wide, abroad,
Till from the depths of life each trembling wire
    Shall vibrate up to God.

Give *Grief* her mournful harp, that she may string
  Its chords to sound her sense of errors past ;
Give *Joy* its clashing bells, and let them swing
    Their sweetness on the blast.

Give *Faith* a lark-like song, still warbling higher,
    Up-soaring from her sod through fields of day;
And *Love*, a tenderer note, with strength to inspire
        Each struggler on his way.

Let *Memory's* flute, with its rich dying fall,
    Bring back angelic visits long gone by;
And give to *Hope* its thrilling bugle call,
        Up-echoing to the sky.

Let *Patience* have her lute, for wandering still
    In search of rest, with retrospective eye
She loves to climb the steeps of Calvary's hill,
        And watch her Saviour die.

Seize on our *Fancy*, make it all Thine own,
    Till like some organ pealing high and wide,
Each sounding stop, and swell, and dulcet tone,
        To Thee be sanctified.

On earth's dark suffering pour Thy healing balm,
    May the heart sing, albeit the flesh may groan,
Taking the Master's Prayer for its sweet psalm—
        " Father, Thy will be done."

E'en as Thy saints of old, what time they lay
    In midnight dungeon, sang in spite of scorn,
So may our souls behind these walls of clay
        Sing on through night till morn.

Till then this brain inspire, this breast inflame,
    Touch these cold lips with Thine own altar coal—
Now " all that is within me " bless Thy name—
        Bless, " bless the Lord, my soul."

Dublin.

THE TRUMPET-MAJOR.

By THOMAS HARDY, Author of "Far from the Madding Crowd," etc.

CHAPTER XXVIII.—ANNE JOINS THE YEOMANRY CAVALRY.

ANNE fearfully surveyed her position. The upper windows of the cottage were of flimsiest lead-work, and to keep him out would be hopeless. She felt that not a moment was to be lost in getting away. Running down-stairs she opened the door, and then it occurred to her terrified understanding that there would be no chance of escaping him by flight afoot across such an extensive down, since he might mount his horse and easily ride after her. The animal still remained tethered at the corner of the garden; if she could release him and frighten him away before Festus returned, there would not be quite such odds against her. She accordingly unhooked the horse by reaching over the bank, and then, pulling off her muslin neckerchief, flapped it in his eyes to startle him. But the gallant steed did not move or flinch; she tried again, and he seemed rather pleased than otherwise. At this moment she heard a cry from the cottage, and, turning, beheld her adversary approaching round the corner of the building.

"I thought I should tole out the mouse by that trick!" cried Festus exultingly. Instead of going for a ladder he had simply hid himself at the back to tempt her down.

Poor Anne was now desperate. The bank on which she stood was level with the horse's back, and the creature seemed quiet as a lamb. With a determination of which she was capable in emergencies, she seized the rein, flung herself upon the sheepskin, and held on by the mane. The amazed charger lifted his head, sniffed, wrenched his ears hither and thither, and started off at a frightful speed across the down.

"Oh, my heart and limbs!" said Festus under his breath, as, thoroughly alarmed, he gazed after her. "She on Champion! She'll break her neck, and I shall be tried for manslaughter, and disgrace will be brought upon the name of Derriman!"

Champion continued to go at a stretch-gallop, but he did nothing more. Had he plunged or reared, Derriman's fears might have been verified, and Anne have come with deadly force to the ground. But the course was good, and in the horse's speed lay a comparative security. She was scarcely shaken in her precarious half-horizontal position, though she was awed to see the grass, loose stones, and other objects pass her eyes like strokes whenever she opened them, which was only just for a second at intervals of half a minute; and how wildly the stirrups swung! and that which struck her knee was the bucket of the carbine, and that was a pistol-holster which hurt her arm.

They quickly cleared the down, and Anne became conscious that the course of the horse was homeward. As soon as the ground began to rise towards the outer belt of upland which lay between her and the coast, Champion, now panting and reeking with moisture, lessened his speed in sheer weariness, and proceeded at a rapid jolting trot. Anne felt that she could not hold on half so well; the gallop had been child's play compared with this. They were in a lane, ascending to a ridge, and she made up her mind for a fall. Over the ridge rose an animated spot, higher and higher; it turned out to be the upper part of a man, and the man to be a soldier. Such was Anne's attitude that she only got an occasional glimpse of him; and, though she feared that he might be a Frenchman, she feared the horse more than the enemy, as she had feared Festus more than the horse. Anne had energy enough left to cry "Stop him! stop him!" as the soldier drew near.

He, astonished at the sight of a military horse with a bundle of drapery thrown across his back, had already placed himself in the middle of the lane, and he now held out his arms till his figure assumed the form of a Latin cross planted in the roadway. Champion drew near, swerved, and stood still almost suddenly, a check sufficient to send Anne slipping down his flank to the ground. The timely friend stepped forward and helped her to her feet, when she saw that he was John Loveday.

"Are you hurt?" he said hastily, having turned quite pale at seeing her fall.

"Oh no, not a bit," said Anne, gathering herself up with forced briskness, to make light of the misadventure.

"But how did you get in such a place?"

"There, he's gone!" she exclaimed, instead of replying, as Champion swept round John Loveday and cantered off triumphantly in the direction of Overcombe, a performance which she followed with her eyes.

"But how did you come upon his back, and whose horse is it?"

XXI—41

"I will tell you."

"Well?"

"I—cannot tell you."

John looked steadily at her, saying nothing.

"How did you come here?" she asked. "Is it true that the French have not landed at all?"

"Quite true; the alarm was groundless. I'll tell you all about it. You look very tired; you had better sit down a few minutes. Let us sit on this bank."

He helped her to the slope indicated, and continued, still as if his thoughts were more occupied with the mystery of her recent situation than with what he was saying: "We arrived at Radipole Barracks this morning, and are to lie there all the summer. I could not write to tell father we were coming. It was not because of any rumour of the French, for we knew nothing of that till we met the people on the road, and the colonel said in a moment the news was false. Buonaparte is not even at Boulogne just now. I was anxious to know how you had borne the fright, so I hastened to Overcombe at once, as soon as I could get out of barracks."

Anne, who had not been at all responsive to his discourse, now swayed heavily against him, and looking quickly down he found that she had silently fainted. To support her in his arms was of course the impulse of a moment. There was no water to be had, and he could think of nothing else but to hold her tenderly till she came round again. Certainly he desired nothing more.

Again he asked himself, what did it all mean?

He waited, looking down upon her tired eyelids, and at the row of lashes lying upon each cheek, whose natural roundness showed itself in singular perfection now that the customary pink had given place to a pale luminousness caught from the surrounding atmosphere. The dumpy ringlets about her forehead and behind her poll, which were usually as tight as springs, had been partially uncoiled by the wildness of her ride, and hung in split locks over her forehead and neck. John, who, during the long months of his absence, had lived only to meet her again, was in a state of ecstatic reverence, and bending down he gently kissed her.

Anne was just becoming conscious.

"Oh, Mr. Derriman, never, never!" she murmured, sweeping her face with her hand.

"I thought he was at the bottom of it," said John.

Anne opened her eyes and started back from him. "What is it?" she said wildly.

"You are ill, my dear Miss Garland," replied John in trembling anxiety, and taking her hand.

"I am not ill, I am wearied out," she said. "Can't we walk on? How far are we from Overcombe?"

"About a mile. But tell me: somebody has been hurting you—frightening you. I know who it was; it was Derriman, and that was his horse. Now do you tell me all."

Anne reflected. "Then if I tell you," she said, "will you discuss with me what I had better do, and not for the present let my mother and your father know? I don't want to alarm them, and I must not let my affairs interrupt the business connection between the mill and the Hall that has gone on for so many years."

The trumpet-major promised, and Anne told the adventure. His brow reddened as she went on, and when she had done she said, "Now you are angry. Don't do anything dreadful, will you? Remember that this Festus will most likely succeed his uncle at Overcombe, in spite of present appearances, and if Bob succeeds at the mill there should be no enmity between them."

"That's true. I won't tell Bob. Leave him to me. Where is Derriman now? On his way home, I suppose. When I have seen you into the house I will deal with him—quite quietly, so that he shall say nothing about it."

"Yes, appeal to him—do! Perhaps he will be better then."

They walked on together, Loveday seeming to experience much quiet bliss.

"I came to look for you," he said, "because of that dear, sweet letter you wrote."

"Yes, I did write you a letter," she admitted, with misgiving, now beginning to see his mistake. "It was because I was sorry I had blamed you."

"I am almost glad you did blame me," said John cheerfully, "since, if you had not, the letter would not have come. I have read it fifty times a day."

This put Anne into an unhappy mood, and they proceeded without much further talk till the mill chimneys were visible below them. John then said that he would leave her to go in by herself.

"Ah, you are going back to get into some danger on my account."

"I can't get into much danger with such a fellow as he, can I?" said John, smiling.

"Well, no," she answered, with a sudden

carelessness of tone. It was indispensable that he should be undeceived, and to begin the process by taking an affectedly light view of his personal risks was perhaps as good a way to do it as any. Where friendliness was translated as love, an assumed indifference was the necessary expression for friendliness.

So she let him go; and, bidding him hasten back as soon as he could, went down the hill, while John's feet retraced the upland.

The trumpet-major spent the whole afternoon and evening in that long and difficult search for Festus Derriman. Crossing the down at the end of the second hour he met Molly and Mrs. Loveday. The gig had been repaired, they had learnt the groundlessness of the alarm, and they would have been proceeding happily enough but for their anxiety about Anne. John told them shortly that she had got a lift home, and proceeded on his way.

The worthy object of his search had in the meantime been plodding homeward on foot, sulky at the loss of his charger, encumbered with his sword, belts, high boots, and uniform, and in his own discomfiture careless whether Anne Garland's life had been endangered or not.

At length Derriman reached a place where the road ran between high banks, one of which he mounted and paced along as a change from the hard trackway. Ahead of him he saw an old man sitting down, with eyes fixed on the dust of the road, as if resting and meditating at one and the same time. Being pretty sure that he recognised his uncle in that venerable figure, Festus came forward stealthily, till he was immediately above the old man's back. The latter was clothed in faded nankeen breeches, speckled stockings, a drab hat, and a coat which had once been light blue, but from exposure as a scarecrow had assumed the complexion and fibre of a dried pudding-cloth. The farmer was, in fact, returning to the Hall, which he had left in the morning some time later than his nephew, to seek an asylum in a hollow tree about two miles off. The tree was so situated as to command a view of the building, and Uncle Benjy had managed to clamber up inside this natural fortification high enough to watch his residence through a hole in the bark, till, gathering from the words of occasional passers-by that the alarm was at least premature, he had ventured into daylight again.

He was now engaged in abstractedly tracing a diagram in the dust with his walking-stick, and muttered words to himself aloud. Pre-

sently he arose and went on his way without turning round. Festus was curious enough to descend and look at the marks. They represented an oblong, with two semi-diagonals, and a little square in the middle. Upon the diagonals were the figures 20 and 17, and on each side of the parallelogram stood a letter signifying the point of the compass.

"What crazy thing is running in his head now?" said Festus to himself with supercilious pity, recollecting that the farmer had been singing those very numbers earlier in the morning. Being able to make nothing of it, he lengthened his strides, and treading on tiptoe overtook his relative, saluting him by scratching his back like a hen. The startled old farmer danced round like a top, and gasping, said, as he perceived his nephew, "What, Festy! not thrown from your horse and killed, then, after all!"

"No, nunc. What made ye think that?"

"Champion passed me about an hour ago, when I was in hiding—poor timid soul of me, for I had nothing to lose by the French coming—and he looked awful with the stirrups dangling and the saddle empty. 'Tis a gloomy sight, Festy, to see a horse cantering without a rider, and I thought you had been—feared you had been thrown off and killed as dead as a nit."

"Bless your dear old heart for being so anxious! And what pretty picture were you drawing just now with your walking-stick?"

"Oh, that! That is only a way I have of amusing myself. It showed how the French might have advanced to the attack, you know. Such trifles fill the head of a weak old man like me."

"Or the place where something is hid away—money, for instance?"

"Festy," said the farmer reproachfully, "you always know I use the old glove in the bedroom cupboard for any guinea or two I possess."

"Of course I do," said Festus ironically.

They had now reached a lonely inn about a mile and a half from the Hall, and, the farmer not responding to his nephew's kind invitation to come in and treat him, Festus entered alone. He was dusty, draggled, and weary, and he remained at the tavern long. The trumpet-major, in the meantime, having searched the roads in vain, heard in the course of the evening of the yeoman's arrival at this place, and that he would probably be found there still. He accordingly approached the door, reaching it just as the dusk of evening changed to darkness.

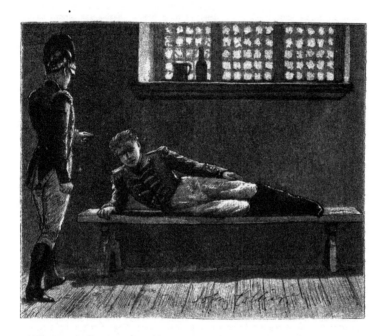

There was no light in the passage, but John pushed on at hazard, inquired for Derriman, and was told that he would be found in the back parlour alone. When Loveday first entered the apartment he was unable to see anything, but following the guidance of a vigorous snoring, he came to the settle upon which Festus lay asleep, his position being faintly signified by the shine of his buttons and other parts of his uniform. John laid his hand upon the reclining figure and shook him, and by degrees Derriman stopped his snore and sat up.

"Who are you?" he said, in the accents of a man who has been drinking hard. "Is it you, dear Anne? Let me kiss you; yes, I will."

"Shut your mouth, you pitiful blockhead; I'll teach you genteeler manners than to persecute a young woman in that way!" and taking Festus by the ear, he gave it a good pull. Festus broke out with an oath, and struck a vague blow in the air with his fist;

whereupon the trumpet-major dealt him a box on the right ear, and a similar one on the left, to artistically balance the first. Festus jumped up and used his fists wildly, but without any definite result.

"Want to fight, do ye, eh?" said John. "Nonsense! you can't fight, you great baby, and never could. You are only fit to be smacked!" and he dealt Festus a specimen of the same on the cheek with the palm of his hand.

"No, sir, no! Oh, you are Loveday, the young man she's going to be married to, I suppose? Dash me, I didn't want to hurt her, sir."

"Yes, my name is Loveday; and you'll know where to find me, since we can't finish this to-night. Pistols or swords, whichever you like, my boy. Take that, and that, so that you may not forget to call upon me!" and again he smacked the yeoman's ears and cheeks. "Do you know what it is for, eh?"

"No, Mr. Loveday, sir—yes, I mean, I do."

"What is it for, then? I shall keep smacking until you tell me. Gad! if you weren't drunk, I'd half kill you here to-night."

"It is because I served her badly. Blowed if I care! I'll do it again, and be hanged to ye. Where's my horse Champion? tell me that," and he hit at the trumpet-major.

John parried this attack, and, taking him firmly by the collar, pushed him down into the seat, saying, "Here I hold ye till you beg pardon for your doings to-day. Do you want any more of it, do you?" And he shook the yeoman to a sort of jelly.

"I do beg pardon—no, I don't. I say this, that you shall not take such liberties with old Squire Derriman's nephew, you dirty miller's son, you flour-worm, you smut in the corn! I'll call you out to-morrow morning, and have my revenge."

"Of course you will; that's what I came for;" and, pushing him back into the corner of the settle, Loveday went out of the house, feeling considerable satisfaction at having got himself into the beginning of as nice a quarrel about Anne Garland as the most jealous lover could desire.

But of one feature in this curious adventure he had not the least notion—that Festus Derriman, misled by the darkness, the fumes of his potations, and the constant sight of Anne and Bob together, never once supposed his assailant to be any other man than Bob, believing the trumpet-major miles away.

There was a moon during the early part of John's walk home, but when he had arrived within a mile of Overcombe the sky clouded over, and rain suddenly began to fall with some violence. Near him was a wooden granary on tall stone staddles, and, perceiving that the rain was only a thunderstorm which would soon pass away, he ascended the steps and entered the doorway, where he stood watching the half-obscured moon through the streaming rain. Presently, to his surprise, he beheld a female figure running forward with great rapidity, not towards the granary for shelter, but towards open ground. What could she be running for in that direction? The answer came in the appearance of his brother Bob from that quarter, seated on the back of his father's heavy horse. As soon as the woman met him, Bob dismounted and caught her in his arms.

The trumpet-major fell back inside the granary, and threw himself on a heap of empty sacks which lay in the corner : he had recognised the woman to be Anne. Here he reclined in a stupor till he was aroused by the sound of voices under him, the voices of Anne and his brother, who, having at last discovered that they were getting wet, had taken shelter under the granary floor.

"I have been home," said she. "Mother and Molly have both got back long ago. We were all anxious about you, and I came out to look for you. Oh, Bob, I am so glad to see you again!"

John might have heard every word of the conversation, which was continued in the same strain for a long time, but he stopped his ears and would not. Still they remained, and still was he determined that they should not see him. With the conserved hope of more than half a year dashed away in a moment, he could yet feel that the cruelty of a protest would be even greater than its inutility. It was absolutely by his own contrivance that the situation had been shaped. Bob, left to himself, would long ere this have been the husband of another woman.

The rain decreased and the lovers went on. John looked after them as they strolled, aqua-tinted by the weak moon and mist. Bob had thrust one of his arms through the rein of the horse, and the other was round Anne's waist. When they were lost behind the declivity the trumpet-major came out and walked homeward even more slowly than they. As he went on, his face put off its complexion of despair for one of serene resolve. For the first time in his dealings with friends he entered upon a course of counterfeiting, set his features to conceal his thought, and instructed his tongue to do likewise. He threw fictitiousness into his very gait even now, when there was nobody to see him, and struck at stems of wild parsley with his regimental switch, as he had used to do when soldiering was new to him and life in general a charming experience.

Thus cloaking his sickly thought, he descended to the mill as the others had done before him, occasionally looking down upon the wet road to notice how close Anne's little tracks were to Bob's all the way along, and how precisely a curve in his course was followed by a curve in hers. But after this he erected his head and walked so smartly up to the front door that his spurs rang through the court.

They had all reached home, but before any of them could speak he cried gaily, "Ah, Bob, I have been thinking of you! How are you, my boy? No French cut-throats after all, you see. Here we are, well and happy together again."

"A good Providence has watched over us," said Mrs. Loveday cheerfully. "Yes, in all times and places we are in God's hand."

"So we be, so we be!" said the miller, who still shone in all the fierceness of uniform. "Well, now we'll ha'e a drop o' drink."

"There's none," said David, coming forward with a drawn face.

"What!" said the miller.

"Afore I went to church for a pike to defend my country from Boney, I pulled out the spigots of all the barrels, maister; for, thinks I—hang him!—since we can't drink it ourselves, he shan't have it, nor none of his men."

"But you shouldn't have done it till you was sure he'd come," said the miller aghast.

"Chok' it all, I was sure!" said David. "I'd sooner see churches fall than good drink wasted; but how was I to know better?"

"Well, well; what with one thing and another this day will cost me a pretty penny," said Loveday, bustling off to the cellar, which he found to be several inches deep in stagnant liquor. "John, how can I welcome ye?" he continued, hopelessly, on his return to the room. "Only go and see what he's done!"

"I've ladled up a drap wi'a spoon, trumpet-major," said David. "'Tisn't bad drinking, though it do taste a little of the floor, that's true."

John said that he did not require anything at all; and then they all sat down to supper, and were very temperately gay with a drop of mild elder-wine which Mrs. Loveday found in a bottle. The trumpet-major, adhering to the part he meant to play, gave humorous accounts of his adventures since he had last sat there. He told them that the season was to be a very lively one—that the royal family was coming, as usual, and many other interesting things; so that when he left them to return to Radipole few would have supposed the British army to contain a lighter-hearted man.

Anne was the only one who doubted the reality of this behaviour. When she had gone up to her bedroom she stood for some time looking at the wick of the candle as if it were a painful object, the expression of her face being shaped by the conviction that John's afternoon words when he helped her out of the way of Champion were not in accordance with his words to-night, and that the dimly-realised kiss during her faintness was no imaginary one. But in the blissful circumstances of having Bob at hand again she took optimist views, and persuaded herself that John would soon begin to see her in the light of a sister.

CHAPTER XXIX.—A DISSEMBLER.

To cursory view, John Loveday seemed to accomplish this with amazing ease. Whenever he came from barracks to Overcombe, which was once or twice a week, he related news of all sorts to her and Bob with infinite zest, and made the time as happy a one as had ever been known at the mill, save for himself alone. He said nothing of Festus, except so far as to inform Anne that he had expected to see him and been disappointed. On the evening after the King's arrival at Weymouth John appeared again, staying to supper and describing the royal entry, the many tasteful illuminations and transparencies which had been exhibited, the quantities of tallow candles burnt for that purpose, and the swarms of aristocracy who had followed the King thither.

When supper was over Bob went outside the house to shut the shutters, which had, as was often the case, been left open some time after lights were kindled within. John still sat at the table when his brother approached the window, though the others had risen and retired, and Bob was at once struck by seeing how his face had changed. Throughout the supper-time he had been talking to Anne in the gay tone habitual with him now, which gave greater strangeness to the gloom of his present appearance. He remained in thought for a moment, took a letter from his breast-pocket, opened it, and, with a tender smile at his weakness, kissed the writing before restoring it to its place. The letter was one that Anne had written to him at Exeter.

Bob stood perplexed; and then a suspicion crossed his mind that John, from brotherly goodness, might be feigning a satisfaction with recent events which he did not feel. Bob now made a noise with the shutters, at which the trumpet-major rose and went out, Bob at once following him.

"Jack," said the sailor ingenuously, "I'm terribly sorry that I've done wrong."

"How?" asked his brother.

"In courting our little Anne. Well, you see, John, she was in the same house with me, and somehow or other I made myself her beau. But I have been thinking that perhaps you had the first claim on her, and if so, Jack, I'll make way for ye. I—I don't care for her much, you know—not so very much, and can give her up very well. It is nothing serious between us at all. Yes, John, you try to get her; I can look elsewhere." Bob never knew how much he loved Anne till he found himself making this speech of renunciation.

"Oh, Bob, you are mistaken!" said the trumpet-major, who was not deceived. "When I first saw her I admired her, and I admire her now, and like her. I like her so well that I shall be glad to see you marry her."

"But," replied Bob with hesitation, "I thought I saw you looking very sad, as if you were in love; I saw you take out a letter, in short. That's what it was disturbed me and made me come to you."

"Oh, I see your mistake!" said John, laughing forcedly.

At this minute Mrs. Loveday and the miller, who were taking a twilight walk in the garden, strolled round near to where the brothers stood. She talked volubly on events in Weymouth, as most people did at this time. "And they tell me that the theatre has been painted up afresh," she was saying, "and that the actors have come for the season, with the most lovely actresses that ever were seen."

When they had passed by John continued, "I am in love, Bob; but — not with Anne."

"Ah! who is it then?" said the mate hopefully.

"One of the actresses at the theatre," John replied with a concoctive look at the vanishing forms of Mr. and Mrs. Loveday. "She is a very lovely woman, you know. But we won't say anything more about it—it dashes a man so."

"Oh, one of the actresses!" said Bob, with open mouth.

"But don't you say anything about it," continued the trumpet-major heartily. "I don't want it known."

"No, no—I won't, of course. May I not know her name?"

"No, not now, Bob. I cannot tell ye," John answered; and with truth, for Loveday did not know the name of any one actress in the world.

When his brother had gone Captain Bob hastened off in a state of great animation to Anne, whom he found on the top of a neighbouring hillock which the daylight had scarcely as yet deserted.

"You have been a long time coming, sir," said she in sprightly tones of reproach.

"Yes, dearest; and you'll be glad to hear why. I've found out the whole mystery—yes —why he's queer, and everything."

Anne looked startled.

"He's up to the gunnel in love! We must try to help him on in it, or I fear he'll go melancholy-mad like."

"We help him?" she asked faintly.

"He's lost his heart to one of the play-actresses at Weymouth, and I think she slights him."

"Oh, I am so glad!" she exclaimed.

"Glad that his venture don't prosper?"

"Oh, no; glad he's so sensible. How long is it since that alarm of the French?"

"Six weeks, honey. Why do you ask?"

"Men can forget in six weeks, can't they, Bob?"

The impression that John had really kissed her still remained.

"Well, some men might," observed Bob judicially. "I couldn't. Perhaps John might. I couldn't forget you in twenty times as long. Do you know, Anne, I half thought it was you John cared about; and it was a weight on my heart when he said he didn't."

"Did he say he didn't?"

"Yes. He assured me himself that the only person in the hold of his heart was this lovely play-actress, and nobody else."

"How I should like to see her!"

"Yes. So should I."

"I would rather it had been one of our own neighbours' girls, whose birth and breeding we know of; but still, if that is his taste, I hope it will end well for him. How very quick he has been! I certainly wish we could see her."

"I don't know so much as her name. He is very close, and wouldn't tell a thing about her."

"Couldn't we get him to go to the theatre with us? and then we could watch him, and easily find out the right one. Then we would learn if she is a good young woman; and if she is, could we not ask her here, and so make it smoother for him? He has been very gay lately—that means budding love; and sometimes between his gaieties he has had melancholy moments—that means there's difficulty."

Bob thought her plan a good one, and resolved to put it in practice on the first available evening. Anne was very curious as to whether John did really cherish a new passion, the story having quite surprised her. Possibly it was true; six weeks had passed since John had shown a single symptom of the old attachment, and what could not that space of time effect in the heart of a soldier whose very profession it was to leave girls behind him?

After this John Loveday did not come to see them for nearly a month, a neglect which was set down by Bob as an additional proof that his brother's affections were no longer exclusively centered in his old home. When at last he did arrive, and the theatre-going was mentioned to him, the flush of consciousness which Anne expected to see upon his face was unaccountably absent.

"Yes, Bob; I should very well like to go to the theatre," he replied heartily. "Who is going besides?"

"Only Anne," Bob told him, and then it seemed to occur to the trumpet-major that something had been expected of him. He rose and said privately to Bob with some confusion, "Oh yes, of course we'll go. As I am connected with one of the—— in short, I can get you in for nothing, you know. At least let me manage everything."

"Yes, yes. I wonder you didn't propose to take us before, Jack, and let us have a good look at her."

"I ought to have. You shall go on a King's night. You won't want me to point her out, Bob; I have my reasons at present for asking it."

"We'll be content with guessing," said his brother.

When the gallant John was gone Anne observed, "Bob, how he is changed! I watched him. He showed no feeling, even when you burst upon him suddenly with the subject nearest his heart."

"It must be because his suit don't fay," said Captain Bob.

CHAPTER XXX.—AT THE THEATRE ROYAL.

IN two or three days a message arrived asking them to attend at the theatre on the coming evening, with the added request that they would dress in their gayest clothes, to do justice to the places taken. Accordingly, in the course of the afternoon they drove off, Bob having clothed himself in a splendid suit, recently purchased as an attempt to bring himself nearer to Anne's style when they appeared in public together. As finished off by this dashing and really fashionable attire, he was the perfection of a beau in the dog-days: pantaloons and boots of the newest make; yards and yards of muslin wound round his neck, forming a sort of asylum for the lower part of his face; two fancy waist-coats, and coat-buttons like circular shaving-glasses. The absurd extreme of female fashion, which was to wear muslin dresses in January, was at this time equalled by that of the men, who wore clothes enough in August to melt them. Nobody would have guessed from Bob's presentation now that he had ever been aloft on a dark night in the Atlantic, or knew the hundred ingenuities that could be performed with a rope's end and a marling-spike as well as his mother tongue.

It was a day of days. Anne wore her celebrated celestial blue pelisse, her Leghorn hat, and her muslin dress with the waist under the arms; the latter being decorated with excellent Honiton lace bought of the woman who travelled from that place to Overcombe and its neighbourhood with a basketful of her own manufacture, and a cushion on which she worked by the way-side. John met them at the Radipole Inn, and after stabling the horse they entered the town together, the trumpet-major informing 'hem that Weymouth had never been so full before, that the Court, the Prince of Wales, and everybody of consequence was there, and that an attic could scarcely be got for money. The King had gone for a cruise in his yacht, and they would be in time to see him land.

Then drums and fifes were heard, and in a minute or two they saw Sergeant Stanner advancing along the street with a firm countenance, fiery poll, and rigid staring eyes, in front of his recruiting-party. The sergeant's sword was drawn, and at intervals of two or three inches along its shining blade were impaled fluttering one-pound notes, to express the lavish bounty that was offered. He gave a stern, suppressed nod of friendship to our people, and passed by. Next they came up to a waggon bowered over with leaves and flowers, so that the men inside could hardly be seen.

"Come to see the King—hip, hip, hurrah!" cried a voice within, and turning they saw through the leaves the nose and face of Crip-plestraw. The waggon contained all Derriman's workpeople.

"Is your master here?" said John.

"No, trumpet-major, sir. But young maister is coming to fetch us at nine o'clock, in case we should be too blind to drive home."

"Oh! where is he now?"

"Never mind," said Anne impatiently, at which the trumpet-major obediently moved on.

By the time they reached the pier it was six o'clock; the royal yacht was returning—a fact announced by the ships in the harbour firing a salute. The King came ashore with his hat in his hand, and returned the saluta-tions of the well-dressed crowd in his old indiscriminate fashion. While this cheering and waving of handkerchiefs was going on Anne stood between the two brothers, who protectingly joined their hands behind her back, as if she were a delicate piece of statuary that a push might damage. Soon the King had passed, and receiving the military salutes of the picket, joined the Queen and Princesses at Gloucester Lodge, the homely house of red brick in which he unostentatiously resided.

As there was yet some little time before the theatre would open, they strayed upon the velvet sands and listened to the songs of the sailors, one of whom extemporised for the occasion:

"Portland Road, the King aboard, the King aboard!
Portland Road, the King aboard,
We weighed and sailed from Portland Road!"

When they had looked on awhile at the combats at single-stick which were in progress hard by, and seen the sum of five guineas handed over to the modest gentleman who had broken most heads, they returned to Gloucester Lodge, whence the King and other members of his family now reappeared, and drove at a slow trot round to the theatre, in carriages drawn by the Hanoverian white horses that were so well known in Weymouth at this date.

When Anne and Bob entered the theatre they found that John had taken excellent places, and concluded that he had got them for nothing through the influence of the lady of his choice. As a matter of fact he had paid full prices for those two seats, like any other outsider, and even then had a difficulty in getting them, it being a King's night. When they were settled he himself retired to an obscure part of the pit, from which the stage was scarcely visible.

"We can see beautifully," said Bob, in an aristocratic voice, as he took a delicate pinch of snuff, and drew out the magnificent pocket-handkerchief brought home from the East for such occasions. "But I am afraid poor John can't see at all."

"But we can see him," replied Anne, "and notice by his face which of them it is he is so charmed with. The light of that corner candle falls right upon his cheek."

By this time the King had appeared in his place, which was overhung by a canopy of crimson satin fringed with gold. About twenty places were occupied by the royal family and suite; and beyond them was a crowd of powdered and glittering personages

"Two forms crossed this line at a startling nearness to her."

of fashion, completely filling the centre of the little building—though the King so frequently patronised the local stage during these years that the crush was not inconvenient.

The curtain rose and the play began. To-night it was one of Colman's, who at this time enjoyed great popularity, and Mr. Bannister supported the leading character. Anne, with her hand privately clasped in Bob's, and looking as if she did not know it, partly watched the piece and partly the face of the impressionable John, who had so soon transferred his affections elsewhere. She had not long to wait. When a certain one of the subordinate ladies of the comedy entered on the stage, the trumpet-major in his corner not only looked conscious, but started and gazed with parted lips.

"This must be the one," whispered Anne quickly. "See, he is agitated!"

She turned to Bob, but at the same moment his hand convulsively closed upon hers as he, too, strangely fixed his eyes upon the newly entered lady.

"What is it?"

Anne looked from one to the other without regarding the stage at all. Her answer came in the voice of the actress, who now spoke for the first time. The accents were those of Miss Matilda Johnson.

One thought rushed into both their minds on the instant, and Bob was the first to utter it—

"What! is she the woman of his choice after all?"

"If so, it is a dreadful thing!" murmured Anne.

But, as may be imagined, the unfortunate John was as much surprised by this rencounter as the other two. Until this moment he had been in utter ignorance of the theatrical company and all that pertained to it. Moreover, much as he knew of Miss Johnson, he was not aware that she had ever been trained in her youth as an actress, and that, after lapsing into straits and difficulties for a couple of years, she had been so fortunate as to again procure an engagement here.

The trumpet-major, though not prominently seated, had been seen by Matilda already, who had observed still more plainly her old betrothed and Anne in the other part of the house. John was not concerned on his own account at being face to face with her, but at the extraordinary suspicion that this conjuncture must revive in the minds of his best-beloved friends. After some moments of pained reflection he tapped his knee.

"No, I won't explain; it shall go as it is!" he said. "Let them think her mine. Better that than the truth, after all."

Had personal prominence in the scene been at this moment proportioned to intentness of feeling, the whole audience, regal and otherwise, would have faded into an indistinct mist of background, leaving as the sole emergent and telling figures Bob and Anne at one point, the trumpet-major on the left hand, and Matilda at the opposite corner of the stage. But fortunately the dead-lock of awkward suspense into which all four had fallen was terminated by an accident. A messenger entered the King's box with dispatches. There was an instant pause in the performance. The dispatch-box being opened, the King read for a few moments with great interest, the eyes of the whole house, including those of Anne Garland, being anxiously fixed upon his face; for terrible events fell as unexpectedly as thunderbolts at this critical time of our history. The King at length

beckoned to Lord ——, who was immediately behind him, the play was again stopped, and the contents of the dispatch were publicly communicated to the audience.

Sir Robert Calder, cruising off Finisterre, had come in sight of Villeneuve, and made the signal for action, which, though checked by the weather, had resulted in the capture of two Spanish line-of-battle ships, and the retreat of Villeneuve into Ferrol.

The news was received with truly national feeling, if noise might be taken as an index of patriotism. "Rule Britannia" was called for and sung by the whole house. But the importance of the event was far from being recognised at this time; and Bob Loveday, as he sat there and heard it, had very little conception how it would bear upon his destiny.

This parenthetic excitement diverted for a few minutes the eyes of Bob and Anne from the trumpet-major; and when the play proceeded and they looked back to his corner, he was gone.

"He's just slipped round to talk to her behind the scenes," said Bob knowingly. "Shall we go too, and tease him for a sly dog?"

"No, I would rather not."

"Shall we go home, then?"

"Not unless her presence is too much for you?"

"Oh, not at all. We'll stay here. Ah, there she is again."

They sat on and listened to Matilda's speeches, which she delivered with such delightful coolness that they soon began to considerably interest one of the party.

"Well, what a nerve the young woman has!" he said at last in tones of admiration, and gazing at Miss Johnson with all his might. "After all, Jack's taste is not so bad. She's really deuced clever."

"Bob, I'll go home if you wish to," said Anne quickly.

"Oh no—let us see how she fleets herself off that bit of a scrape she's playing at now. Well, what a hand she is at it, to be sure!"

Anne said no more, but waited on, supremely uncomfortable, and almost tearful. She began to feel that she did not like life particularly well; it was too complicated: she saw nothing of the scene, and only longed to get away, and to get Bob away with her. At last the curtain fell on the final act, and then began the farce of *No Song no Supper*. Matilda did not appear in this piece, and Anne again inquired if they should go home. This time Bob agreed, and, taking her under his care with redoubled affection, to make up for the species of coma which had seized upon his heart for a time, he quietly accompanied her out of the house.

When they emerged upon the esplanade, the August moon was shining across the sea from the direction of St. Alban's Head. Bob unconsciously loitered, and turned towards the pier. Reaching the end of the promenade they surveyed the quivering waters in silence for some time, until a long dark line shot from behind the promontory of the Nothe, and swept forward into the harbour.

"What boat is that?" said Anne.

"It seems to be from some frigate lying in the Roads," said Bob carelessly, as he brought Anne round with a gentle pressure of his arm and bent his steps towards the homeward end of the town.

Meanwhile Miss Johnson, having finished her duties for that evening, rapidly changed her dress and went out likewise. The prominent position which Anne and Captain Bob had occupied side by side in the theatre, left her no alternative but to suppose that the situation was arranged by Bob as a species of defiance to herself; and her heart, such as it was, became proportionately more embittered against him. In spite of the rise in her fortunes, Miss Johnson still remembered—and always would remember—her humiliating departure from Overcombe; and it had been to her even a more grievous thing that Bob had acquiesced in his brother's ruling than that John had determined it. At the time of setting out she was sustained by a firm faith that Bob would follow her and nullify his brother's scheme; but though she waited, Bob never came.

She passed along by the houses facing the sea, and scanned the shore, the footway, and the open road close to her, which, illuminated by the slanting moon to a great brightness, sparkled with minute facets of crystallized salt from the water sprinkled there during the day. The promenaders at the farther edge appeared in dark profiles; and beyond them was the grey sea, parted into two masses by the tapering braid of moonlight across the waves.

Two forms crossed this line at a startling nearness to her; she marked them at once as Anne and Bob Loveday. They were walking slowly, and in the earnestness of their discourse were oblivious of the presence of any human beings save themselves. Matilda stood motionless till they had passed.

"How I love them!" she said, treading the initial step of her walk onwards with a vehemence that walking did not demand.

"So do I—especially one," said a voice at her elbow; and a man wheeled round her and looked in her face, which had been fully exposed to the moon.

"You?—who are you?" she asked.

"Don't you remember, ma'am? We walked some way together towards Overcombe earlier in the summer." Matilda looked more closely, and perceived that the speaker was Derriman, in plain clothes. He continued, "You are one of the ladies of the theatre, I know. May I ask why you said in such a queer way that you loved that couple?"

"In a queer way?"

"Well, as if you hated them."

"I don't mind your knowing that I have good reason to hate them. You do too, it seems?"

"That man," said Festus savagely, "came to me one night about that very woman; insulted me before I could put myself on my guard, and ran away before I could come up with him and avenge myself. The woman tricks me at every turn. I want to part them."

"Then why don't you? There's a splendid opportunity. Do you see that soldier walking along? He's a marine; he looks into the gallery of the theatre every night; and he's in connection with the press-gang that came ashore just now from the frigate lying in Portland Roads. They are often here for men."

"Yes. Our boatmen dread them."

"Well, we have only to tell him that Loveday is a seaman to be clear of him this very night."

"Done!" said Festus. "Take my arm and come this way." They walked across to the footway. "Fine night, sergeant."

"It is, sir."

"Looking for hands, I suppose?"

"It is not to be known, sir. We don't begin till half-past ten."

"It is a pity you don't begin now. I could show ye excellent game."

"What, that little nest of fellows at the Three Tuns? I have just heard of 'em."

"No—come here." Festus, with Miss Johnson on his arm, led the sergeant quickly along the parade, and by the time they reached the Narrows the lovers, who walked but slowly, were visible in front of them. "There's your man," he said.

"That buck in pantaloons and half-boots, a-looking like a squire?"

"Twelve months ago he was mate of the brig *Pewit;* but his father has made money and keeps him at home."

"Faith, now you tell of it, there's a hint of sea-legs about him. What's his name?"

"Don't tell!" whispered Matilda, impulsively clutching Festus's arm.

But Festus had already said, "Robert Loveday, son of the miller at Overcombe. You may find several likely fellows in that neighbourhood."

The marine said that he would bear it in mind, and they left him.

"I wish you had not told," said Matilda. "She's the worst."

"Dash my eyes now, listen to that! Why, you chicken-hearted old stager, you was as well agreed as I. Come now, hasn't he used you badly?"

Matilda's acrimony returned. "I was down on my luck, or he wouldn't have had the chance," she said.

"Well, then, let things be."

ANDREW HISLOP, THE MARTYR.

[About a mile to the north of the parish church in Eskdalemuir, and not far from the river, a solitary tombstone on the grassy hillside bears the following inscription:—"Andrew Hislop, Martyr, shot dead upon this place by Sir James Johnston, of Westerhall, and John Graham, of Claverhouse, May 12th, 1685." The death of Hislop was attended by some circumstances of even unusual atrocity on the part of Claverhouse.]

ANDREW HISLOP! shepherd lad,
   "Martyr" graven on your tomb;
Here you met the brutal Clavers,
   Here you bore his murderous doom!

Coming from the hill that morn,
   Doing humble duty well;
Free in step, your honest look,
   Born of sunlight on the fell.

Here the Eskdale mountains round you,
   In your ear the murmuring stream;
Here, 'tis May, the bleating lambs;
   Life but seems a peaceful dream.

With no weapon but the crook
   Your soft helpless flock to guide;
Here they shot you, shepherd lad,
   Here you poured your warm heart tide!

"Ere I pass into the Presence,
   May I make a prayer to God?"
"Not one word," said brutal Clavers,
   "We've no time, you wretched clod!

"Draw your bonnet o'er your eyes,
   That is boon enough for thee."
"I pass to God with open face,
   Whom you will hardly dare to see!"

Westerhall and Claverhouse,
   Turn now since the deed is done!
What care ye for rebel corpse?
   Let it bleach beneath the sun!

So they left you, martyr brave,
   Left you on the reddened sod;
But no raven touched your face;
   On it lay the peace of God!

On the moor, the widow-mother
Bows to lot of dule and pine;
And Westerhall and Claverhouse
Have merrily rode back to dine!

J. VEITCH.

"IN ARDEN."

"They say, he is already in the Forest of Arden, and a many merry men with him; and there they live like the old Robin Hood of England: . . . . and fleet the time carelessly, as they did in the Golden World."—*As You Like It.*

HEN the illustrious Micawber of never-to-be-forgotten memory thought of turning his attention to coals, "he," says his wife, "very properly said the first step to be taken clearly was to come and see the Medway."

I suppose that, in like manner, because we were bent on visiting the Forest of Arden (in the Belgian Ardennes), part of which is now called "La Chasse de Saint Hubert," the first step seemed to be to go and see the town of St. Hubert, though there is actually nothing to see there, except the huge church which commemorates the saintly legend.

We had planned this journey for many years past. We had turned a deaf ear to the suggestion that "a Forest of Arden exists in Warwickshire, and was doubtless the scene of *As You Like It.*" We knew that the country called the Ardennes was still a huge forest, cleared here and there for cities and villages among its lofty hills, while charming rivers wind through the wooded valleys, and we knew that this vast forest reaches from Liége southwards to the French frontier, but we also knew that between Marche and La Roche lies a special extent of unbroken forest land, which is said to be the veritable forest of *As You Like It.*

For years, then, we had dreamed of this journey, and now we came by way of Dinant to take our long-planned excursion through the Forest of Arden. We had come by railway omnibus from Poix to St. Hubert, a pleasant drive of an hour or so. The road out of Poix is picturesque, bordered by high rocks jutting out roughly here and there; but this soon ended, and we came to open country, our way shaded by an avenue of ash-trees and sycamores, with the little river Lomme murmuring through a flowered meadow on the right, while all around us lay the forest. The sparkling river dashes and foams over grey stones that lie in its winding course, till at one point it gets so pent in and angry that it rushes madly over some rocks in a little waterfall.

Very soon we see the houses of St. Hubert among the poplar-trees ahead of us. "Voila l'abbaye," said our driver; and, rising above the trees on the right, we see the square black-capped towers of the abbey church.

As we clattered up the hill to the Place in front of the church we were quite surprised to see so grand a building in such an out-of-the-way little town. Pilgrimages are made to St. Hubert, and miraculous cures are believed to be worked by the stole of the saint, especially in cases of hydrophobia. But we were very hungry and tired, and the inn looked invitingly clean and pleasant, so we determined to dine before we visited the shrine of St. Hubert.

It was amusing to see in the entrance of the hotel hat-pegs made in imitation of a deer's foot; the handle of the bell-rope was also a deer's foot, and antlers abounded. It would be in keeping if the inn had a supply of venison steaks for the benefit of hungry travellers. However, we got an excellent dinner, ending with *jambon des Ardennes,* doubtless made from a wild boar killed in our Forest of Arden; at least, we told each other this, and found the flavour of the ham excellent. While we digested our meal we turned to our books for information respecting La Chasse de St. Hubert.

In the time of the famous saint the forest stretched away westward as far as the Meuse, St. Hubert seems to have been a rich noble of the court of King Pepin, so greatly addicted to hunting that he neglected all besides. It happened that he was hunting one Good Friday in the forest, when all at once he saw a fine stag bearing between its horns a golden crucifix. For an instant Hubert paused, struck with wonder at the strange vision, then, believing it to be some delusion, he urged his horse towards the stag; but, instead of turning to fly, the animal stood confronting him with mild, imploring eyes, and a voice sounded in the huntsman's ears, "Hubert, Hubert! how long will this idle passion for the chase tempt you to forget your salvation?"

Conscience-stricken, Hubert dismounted, and, falling on his face, he cried out, "Lord, what shall I do?—I am ready." The voice answered, "Go to Maestricht to seek out St. Lambert. He will tell you what to do." And then the stag disappeared as suddenly as it had come.

Hubert seems to have made his profession in the Monastery of Stavelot, and some years after he went to Rome. St. Lambert had suffered martyrdom, and the Pope appointed Hubert his successor as Bishop of Liége instead of Tongres. It was during his consecration that an angel is said to have brought to Hubert the famous stole, which is reported not only to cure hydrophobia, but to have the power of rendering the bite of a mad dog harmless to those who had touched the relic.

A church had been founded in the forest as early as the year 102, on the site of the present Abbey of St. Hubert; a fortress was built near it called Ombra. However, Attila the Destroyer passed that way, and the place once more became a thorny wilderness.

It happened that towards the end of the seventh century, a few years after Hubert's conversion, Plectruda, the wife of King Pepin, was journeying through the forest of the Ardennes, perhaps on her way to see the hermit of Celles St. Hadelin, when she and her cavalcade stopped to rest in a marshy, lonely region. After taking some refreshments her attendants all fell asleep, while Plectruda, who seems to have been a "notable" princess, looked after the horses and prevented them from straying. Looking about her, she saw among the reeds in the marsh a fragment of old wall, the remains of the church destroyed by Attila. Plectruda had never heard of this church, and she sat

down wondering whence these stones came. All at once, says the legend, there fell at her feet a tablet, on which was written, in letters of gold, "This place is chosen by God for the saving of many souls; it is holy ground worthy of Him, honoured and predestined as the hermitage of the servants of God. It will increase and have powerful protection, but it will also suffer many tribulations. May he who shall trouble this place wither at his root, so that his branches yield no fruit, or may he suffer the pains of Divine vengeance." Plectruda on her return informed her husband of the miraculous event. The king caused a monastery to be built next year on the spot, and, placing it under the care of St. Berengius, he called it Andaye, from the number of springs found there.

St. Hubert had been a friend of St. Berengius while they were both at the court, and he often visited him in his Monastery of Andaye.

When St. Hubert died after a thirty-years' episcopate he was buried at Liége, but the monks at Andaye had no peace till they had obtained permission to transport his body to their monastery. The reigning emperor, Louis le Débonair, accompanied the procession that bore the saint's body as far as the Meuse, and the name of the monastery from that period was changed from Andaye to St. Hubert.

The bell was ringing for vespers as we crossed the Place between the inn and the church. At the top of the great building, between the two towers, is a large figure of St. Hubert kneeling before the miraculous stag. A woman and a girl at a stall in front of the flight of steps leading up to the church were selling rosaries, medals, and the usual accessories of a celebrated saint.

"Monsieur," the woman said as we stopped beside her stall, "monsieur and madame will surely buy some medals. They have but to wait in church till the end of the office, and then the priest will bless them, and then monsieur and madame will be for ever secure from the bite of a mad dog."

We bought some pretty little medals representing the legend of St. Hubert, and then we went into the church. It is a grand but uninteresting building in late Gothic. However, the music was beautiful—better than in any of the cathedrals we had visited—the voices were good, and the whole service was reverent, though the church looked much too large for its congregation. When the service ended we went to look at the shrine of St. Hubert, a splendid monument by Geefs, erected by the late King Leopold; the carved stone work is marvellously fine. While we were admiring it a tall, dignified-looking priest, who we fancied had been keeping an eye on us during the service, came up and asked if we had any medals or anything we wished to be blessed. We thanked him, but we did not show him our medals. There is absolutely nothing to see in the hilly little town of St. Hubert; but the memory of the saint is kept green after a lapse of one thousand two hundred years by innumerable articles suggestive of the miraculous stag, which appear in the shop-windows.

The carriage we had ordered to take us through the forest looked comfortable when it appeared at the hotel door, and the horse, a stout little Ardennais, seemed in good condition; the driver was an Ardennais also, brown-faced and full of talk; and we started off at a good pace; but our speed only lasted for a short time. Then, as we went slowly up what our driver evidently considered a steep hill, the little horse shied, and bolted across the road, as if he meant to turn back to St. Hubert. Our driver jumped off his seat at this, pulled the animal into the middle of the road, gave him the whip, and turned round to us with a grin on his broad, brown face.

"See now, madame," he said, "you must, if you please, excuse the behaviour of my little horse; he is so accustomed to make journeys with *messieurs les commis-voyageurs* that he has fallen into their bad habits; he insists upon stopping at every pothouse he sees. Ah! but he is an original beast. I forced him but now to pass a pothouse, as you see; and he makes a grimace to pass the pothouse; it is not good behaviour to a lady, *mais enfin* "—and he grinned again, and shrugged his shoulders.

"Pothouses" seem to abound near St. Hubert. As we went slowly up-hill the horse stopped quite half-a-dozen times, and our driver not only dismounted at every stoppage, but, doubtless in order to soothe the animal's feelings, he drank a glass of beer at every stoppage, and grew more and more cheerfully communicative.

"Ah!" he said, "my horse is well known in this country; every one knows him. His name is Rocquet, and when we reach La Roche you will see the people come out of their houses, and they will say, 'Good day, Rocquet; how is it with you, Rocquet?'"

While he talked we have been looking ahead; in the distance the forest is appearing on all sides.

"Yonder, madame," says our driver, pointing to the left, "is the Chasse St. Hubert."

We are now driving over a sort of wild— "the skirts of the wild wood"—covered with broom and bracken. On one side is a far-reaching extent of firs and copsewood, while before us, on the other side, rises a mass of seemingly boundless forest, which our driver tells us "covers four thousand one hundred and ten hectares of land." It stretches away on the left to the Forest of Bande, where the scenery is wilder and more romantic. "Much game," he says, "is killed in the Chasse St. Hubert, besides stags, wild boars, and wolves, but the season has not yet begun; we are still in August."

We asked if wild boars were plentiful in the forest; the question seemed to excite him. He turned round eagerly, and left Rocquet to follow his devices.

"I should think they are, madame; and it is easy enough to get permission to hunt them at any time. Only a fortnight ago my brother killed two in the forest there"—he pointed with his whip towards the trees on our left—"and one of them, madame, was as big as Rocquet."

We asked him about wolves.

"Wolves, *mon Dieu!* they are hard to find except in winter, when they sometimes come into the town at nightfall, when the weather is very severe. As to the boars, that is quite another affair; they increase so fast that we are thankful to get them killed."

Now we cross a small road, and enter the forest itself, "famous Ardeyna," as Spenser calls it in "Astrophel." "Well," says Rosalind, "this is the Forest of Arden," and the fool answers her with a groan of fatigue, "Ay, now am I in Arden." On our right we hear the murmur of a tiny stream overhung with brambles—"the briars of this working-day world"—and ferns, and rushes. On each side of us tall beeches rise up from the grassy edge of the road, their satin-like trunks doubtless far more slender than of yore, relieved by the dreamy green light of glades reaching far into the depths of the forest. Before us is a long interminable stretch of white road, now rising, now falling, but ever going on straight between its borders of lofty trees. The murmuring little brook that runs beside us recalls Celia's directions to Oliver—

"Down in the neighbour bottom:
. The rank of osiers, by the murmuring stream."

Was it beside such a brook that the melancholy Jaques reposed watching the stag, "augmenting it with tears."

"Do osiers grow in the forest?" I ask our driver. He turns round and looks at me hard. He could understand that we felt an interest in *la chasse*, but this curiosity about osiers evidently puzzles him.

"Yes, madame," he says carelessly, "oh, yes, there are osiers. The basketmakers come to supply themselves in the forest, but the osiers are far away from here in the marshes yonder"—he points among the trees on the left of the road—"the trees are larger before you come to the marshes."

Still we doubted whether, as in Shakespeare's time, any "old oak, whose boughs were mossed with age and high top bald with dry antiquity," stood in the very depths of this forest of to-day. Of necessity the forest has greatly changed since the time of St. Hubert, and many a noble tree has fallen before the woodman's axe.

When Shakespeare wrote there were probably only a few cottages near the Abbey of St. Hubert, and the peasants would not have come so far afield to cut wood as they do now.

Soon we came to a whitewashed cottage beside the road; too near the road for Rosalind's home in the wood. There is a shed on one side and a barn on the other; opposite it still runs the tiny brook, completely overhung with brake and bramble, but there are no "olive-trees," and we saw neither sheep nor "sheep-cote." The forest is very dense hereabouts; the green glades here afford no space for the sylvan banquet of the Duke and his friends, so roughly broken in upon by Orlando, just before Jaques delivers his sermon on the seven ages of man.

We now left the carriage, and strolled into the deep, olive-green glades. As we advance we find that the trees are larger. The evening sunlight comes through the lower branches, making sometimes golden, sometimes crimson patches on the leaves and trunks, and on the thickly-matted beech-mast that hides the tree roots. We wander on into the forest, denser and more tangled as we advance, and we see it is already getting dark in the depths before us. We wonder if the wild boars are rousing in their lairs. We had brought *As You Like It* with us, and we read snatches now and then of the wondrous idyl. It seems to us that, as we wander farther and farther among the trees, we are in the very spot created for the loves of Orlando and Rosalind.

Presently we come to a group of larger trees with spaces of green light around them, where fairies may hold their court on the brown-red ground, or where the foresters of the banished Duke may have sung glees under the greenwood tree, and Amiens helped Jaques "to suck melancholy out of a song." Doubtless it was in such a spot as this, reposing on the ground strewn with brown acorn-cups, that the Duke, musing upon life, found "tongues in trees, books in the running brook, sermons in stones, and good in everything." But we saw no trace of Jaques's friends, the poor "dappled fools, the native burghers of this desert city." There was not even a rabbit or a squirrel. I confess the stories of the wild boars told by Rocquet's master had made me afraid to wander very deeply into the forest, delightful as it was, for if some terrible denizen of the place should all at once rise snorting from his feast of beech-mast and acorns in the long grass, we had no "boar-spear in our hand" like Rosalind.

As we linger the light lessens, the tender green has changed to olive, and the pale beech-stems show like phantoms in the gloom. Unwillingly we turn upon our steps, and linger lovingly as we go.

"Monsieur, madame," our driver cries from the road, "we must hasten if we will not be benighted before we get to La Roche."

So, though we long to dream a while longer in Arden, we stumble back through the trees—and once more life turns to prose. But nothing can take from us the sweet memory that we have been "in Arden."

After all, we felt it was fitting that the Duke, his daughter, and niece, and the rest should go back to the world. Those still, sombre glades were fitter haunts for the peevish Phœbe and her humble, devoted lover, who knew nought of the world, or for my lord Jaques and old Adam, who had had enough of it, than for clever-tongued Rosalind, for the inimitable Touchstone, or for the gay company of courtiers.

Our driver was impatient to talk again. He told us the wild boars are hunted at night from the marshes, where they sleep. "The dogs drive them out towards the hunters," he said. "Ah! it is good sport; it is very exciting, but it is necessary too. Only a few days ago some of these animals destroyed a field of wheat and another of potatoes with their cursed snouts. They will destroy everything."

Presently we came to a deserted-looking farm-house.

"Do you see that?" said our driver. "Close by is the spot where one thousand two hun-

"IN ARDEN."

See page 592.

dred years ago St. Hubert hunted one Good Friday, and was converted by the miraculous vision. It is called La Converserie."

But he said this as a matter of course, or rather of history, without any of the reverence a Breton would have shown in relating such an incident.

We were now about half way on our journey to La Roche, when the road, which had been hitherto almost straight, emerged into a high-road running right and left, where there was a small refreshment house. We stopped for a short time at the little inn to get some milk, and for Rocquet to have some black bread and some water.

When we start again we follow a road on the left; it is less wild, and is bordered by a close avenue of mountain ash-trees, now bright with large clusters of berries, some scarlet, some orange. When our driver saw that we admired them he made frantic efforts to cut off a bunch with his whip, slashing at them furiously as we drove along fast to La Roche. There was still light enough to show that the road became more and more beautiful and varied, with lofty, dark hills on one side, and a deep, chasm-like valley on the other, whence we could hear the murmuring of the Ourthe. The road descends rapidly as it circles round and round these lofty hills.

There is more light here than there was in the forest; and now, at a rapid turn, we come in sight of a meeting of hills and valleys, some of the hills turning abruptly, as if they shouldered one another; others with a gap between, where delicate mist wreaths, repeated till they melt in indistinctness among the distant hills, hint at many wild gorges in this mountainous region. There is a lovely light over all, for, except in the deep valleys, the sun seems to be lingering till we reach La Roche.

"You are close to her all this time," our driver says, "but you cannot see her; she lies in a hole."

All at once we turn the corner of a hill, and there is the swift Ourthe winding round, and then curving out again, with the houses of La Roche built beside it, and the dark, ruined castle, black as night, rising from the rock on which it stands, in the middle of the town, frowning down, as it has done for centuries, over this meeting of valleys, in the centre of which stands the little town, the Heart of the Ardennes.

KATHARINE S. MACQUOID.

FOUNDERS OF NEW ENGLAND.

II.—JOHN WINTHROP.

THE establishment of the Pilgrim Fathers at New Plymouth was but the first stage in the Puritan settlement of New England. It was, however, the most important among the many attempts to colonise that part of the North American continent. Other persons had gone thither to make money by trading with Indians or catching fish, whose main end, in the opinion of Winthrop, "was carnal and not religious." Captain John Smith, who was an energetic advocate of the colonisation of a region which he was the first Englishman to explore and describe, depicted it as a place where riches could be rapidly and certainly acquired. When the Pilgrim Fathers crossed the ocean, five years after these words were published, they did not prove by their conduct that Captain John Smith had misjudged the motives which would influence his countrymen. These men had not enjoyed either ease or honours; the life which they led in Holland being so much the reverse of luxurious that it was a fitting preparation for bearing hardships in America.

While the sturdy band in which William Bradford was then a leading spirit sacrificed little which was well worth retaining, and gained much which they highly valued, by emigrating to New England, the complete colonisation of the country by Englishmen might never have been effected had the example of these Puritans been unavailing. Ten years after landing at New Plymouth the colony numbered three hundred only. If left unsupported it might have remained as isolated and exceptional a body of men as the Pitcairn Islanders. But the necessary support and countenance were not lacking. Moreover, an absolute disproof was afforded of the dictum of Captain Smith when, in 1630, a large band of Puritans under the leadership of John Winthrop landed in New England and founded the Commonwealth of Massachusetts Bay.

John Winthrop was born on the 22nd of January, 1588, at Edwardston, a village in Suffolk. This place is not far distant from his family estate of Groton Manor. Three generations of his family had been noteworthy for piety and attachment to the Protestant faith. Nothing more is known about Winthrop's education than that he was entered at Trinity College, Cambridge, at the early age of fourteen. Later in life he wrote that in his youth he "was very lewdly disposed, inclining unto and attempting (so far as my heart enabled me) all sorts of wickedness, except swearing and scorning religion, which I had no temptation unto in regard of my education." At Cambridge he "fell into a lingering fever," and then he became anxious about religion and diligent in prayer. He left the University without taking a degree. When he was seventeen years, three months, and four days old, as his father carefully records, Winthrop married Mary Forth, the daughter and heiress of John Forth, of Stambridge, in Essex. He obtained "a large portion of outward estate" by his marriage with Mary Forth, who was his senior by four years. He also became a more serious Christian. The result of this alteration in himself can be best set forth in his own words: "Now I came to have some peace and comfort in God and in his ways; my chief delight was therein. I loved a Christian and the very ground he went upon. I honoured a faithful minister in my heart, and could have kissed his feet. Now I grew full of zeal (which outran my knowledge, and carried me sometimes beyond my calling), and very liberal to any good work. I had an insatiable thirst after the word of God; and could not miss a good sermon, though many miles off, especially of such as did search deep into the conscience." These last words are significant, and they afford an indication not merely of Winthrop's frame of mind, but also of the prevailing sentiment among his fellow Puritans. They had an abiding consciousness of sin, and they were ready to search their consciences, or to submit to this being done for them, in order that their inherent and exceeding sinfulness should be made manifest. They had a morbid desire to magnify their own wickedness. When living what seemed to be blameless and exemplary lives, they confessed in their diaries that they were altogether vile. The few memoranda by Winthrop which have been preserved abound in self-accusations. At one time he writes how, being at church in Groton, he suffered the thought of visiting his wife and her relations in Essex to enter his mind during the sermon, whereupon he delighted in the prospect, and "was led into one sin after another." He misses the obvious explanation that the sermon did not absorb his attention, and that he might be less to blame than the preacher. On another occasion he describes how, after examining himself, his conscience upbraided him with remissness as a magistrate in detecting and punishing sin, with spending his days idly and unprofitably, and with giving too much time to sleep and recreations. - He notes "in all his exercises of conscience" that, when he was most impressed with the "guiltiness of sin" his inattention to sermons was most frequent and deplorable. Again, he is convinced that chief among his sins stands that of unbelief. Among the enumeration of his backslidings there is a passage resembling one in which Benjamin Franklin tried to show that self-denial was not only the most reasonable, but the most pleasant thing in the world. Franklin argued that self-denial was merely refusing to do something for which one had a strong desire, on the ground that it would prove injurious, or, in other words, "because it would cost more than it was worth." This business-like test is thus applied by Winthrop to his own conduct: "After the committing of such sins as have promised most contentment and commodity, I would ever gladly have wanted the benefit, that I might have been rid of the sin. Whereupon I conclude that the profit of sin can never countervail the damage of it, for there is no sin so sweet in the committing, but it proves more bitter in the repenting for it." In common with other godly men of his age, Winthrop was a self-tormenter. Much of his time was occupied either in wrestling with Satan or in devising measures to frustrate his wiles. He found "by often and evident experience" that a temperate diet contributed to the frame of mind which he desired to maintain, but he also admitted that "the great variety of meals" led him to eat more than was good for him; hence, in limiting his diet, he was providing for the common advantage of mind and body. He was concerned for the welfare of others also, and especially of those belonging to his own household. Among a series of resolutions which he set down for his guidance, there is one to the effect that, while liberal with his bounty, he "must ever be careful that it begins at home," and another that he will banish profaneness from his family. He also resolved to forbid card-playing in his house. Indeed, he appears to have been scrupulous in shunning evil-doing himself and discountenancing it in others; to have had a tender conscience and a strong will; to have been diligent in seeking after the truth, and resolute in upholding what he believed to be right.

There is a lack of information respecting Winthrop's daily existence after his marriage. It is said that he was made a justice of the peace when he was eighteen; he practised the law, as his father and grandfather had done before him. Later in life he became an attorney in the Court of Wards and Liveries, and then he had to make many journeys to London on professional business. That court, which was instituted in the reign of Henry VIII. and abolished in the reign of Charles II., examined into and determined the tenures of land held of the Crown, and, on the death of a Crown tenant, the court inquired into the circumstances in order to learn the extent of the estate, the age of the heir, and other facts whereby the sovereign might receive certain payments and exercise certain privileges. In 1615 he lost his wife, who had borne him six children, three sons and three daughters. He pronounced her to have "proved a right godly woman," after he had persuaded her to adopt his religious views. Six months after her death he married again, his second wife being Thomasine Clopton, the daughter of a neighbouring landowner. A year afterwards he buried her and an infant daughter. He wrote a narrative of her last illness, which is as curious, owing to its minuteness of detail, as it is interesting as a picture of his own mind. The following character, which he wrote of his wife, is as beautiful a tribute as was ever paid to any woman's memory: "She was a woman wise, modest, loving, and patient of injuries; but her innocent and harmless life was of most observation. She was truly religious, and industrious therein; plain-hearted, and free from guile, and very humble-minded; never so addicted to any outward things (to my judgment) but that she could bring her affections to stoop to God's will in them. She was sparing in outward show of zeal, &c., but her constant love to good Christians and the best things, with her reverent and careful attendance of God's ordinances, both public and private, with her care for avoiding of evil herself, and reproving it in others, did plainly show that truth and the love of God did lie at the heart. Her loving and tender regard of my children was such as might well become a natural mother: for her carriage towards myself, it was amiable and observant as I am not able to express; it had this only inconvenience, that it made me to delight too much in her to enjoy her long."

Winthrop had a strong liking for the married state. The records of his private thoughts contain frequent lamentations over his sinfulness during the short intervals in his life when he was a widower. Sixteen months after the death of his second wife, he became the husband of Margaret Tyndal, who belonged to the family with which Tyndal, the reformer and the translator of the Bible, was connected, and whose religious views were in entire accordance with his own. Two of his love-letters to her are preserved. They are extraordinary productions, being quite as long as a sermon, and cast in the same mould. In one of them he devotes much space to warn her against wearing fine clothes. He says that he was too bashful to mention this orally; certainly he did not hesitate to express his mind with great fulness and plainness in writing, and also to intimate no mean opinion of himself, as is shown in the opening sentence, where he wishes his future wife "a large and prosperous addition of whatsoever happiness the sweet estate of holy wedlock, in the kindest society of a loving husband, may afford." The marriage did not give satisfaction to the bride's family, her brothers being strongly opposed to it. However, they were reconciled to it, after their opposition proved futile, and they soon became good friends with Winthrop. One of them accompanied him to New England.

From the date of his third marriage to that of his departure for New England, there are but few facts of general interest in Winthrop's career. He had additions to his family, and he had an increase of business. His eldest son was sent to finish his education at Trinity College, Dublin, and he was admitted to the Inner Temple in February, 1624. Winthrop's father died at the ripe age of seventy-five in 1623. In announcing this in a letter to his son, Winthrop does so in the following graceful and tender phrases : "He hath finished his course, and is gathered to his people in peace, as the ripe corn into the barn. He thought long for the day of his dissolution, and welcomed it most gladly. Thus is he gone before; and we must go after, in our time. This advantage he hath of us—he shall not see the evil which we may meet with ere we go hence. Happy those who stand in good terms with God and their own conscience : they shall not fear evil tidings ; and in all changes they shall be the same." The concluding part of the foregoing passage indicates that Winthrop was disquieted in his mind about public affairs. Two months before, he had added a postscript to a letter to his son at Dublin : "Send me word in your next how Mr. Olm-

sted and that plantation prospers. I wish oft God would open a way to settle me in Ireland, if it might be for his glory." It was, doubtless, the attempts which were made to substitute Protestant for Roman Catholic communities in Ireland which raised his desire to settle there. His dissatisfaction with the state of things in England, towards the end of the reign of James I., was increased when Charles I. ascended the throne, and gave evidence of his purpose as a ruler. The following phrase, with which he ends a letter to his eldest son at the close of 1626, supplies a proof of this : "The good Lord guide us all wisely and faithfully in the midst of the dangers and discouragements of these declining times." In 1629, writing from London to his wife, he says : "My dear wife, I am verily persuaded God will bring some heavy affliction upon this land, and that speedily." These remarks denote the current of his thoughts, and they help to explain why he resolved to leave the country.

In the year 1628 he was smitten, when in London, with a "hot malignant fever," from which he recovered with difficulty. He notes in his diary that his illness was sanctified to him, and also that "among other benefits I reaped by it, this was one: deliverance from the bondage whereinto I was fallen by the immoderate use and love of tobacco, so as I gave it clean over." There are several references to tobacco in such of his letters as have been preserved. Two years before this illness he informed his eldest son in London that he wanted "some leaf tobacco and pipes." Next year he again wrote from Groton, "We want a little tobacco. I had very good for seven shillings a pound, at a grocer's by Holborn Bridge. There be two shops together. It was at that which was the farthest from the bridge, towards the Conduit. If you tell him it was for him that bought half a pound of Verina and a pound of Virginia of him last term, he will use you well. Send me half a pound of Virginia." The consumption of tobacco at Groton Manor must have been considerable. Nor was Winthrop the only smoker. His wife, writing to him when in London, says, "My good mother commends her love to you all, and thanks you for her tobacco." Winthrop's renunciation of the use of tobacco, after his serious illness, does not seem to have been absolute. In a letter written to his wife at Boston nine years later, he asks her to send him some wearing apparel, and adds, "I pray thee also send me six or seven leaves of tobacco dried and powdered." Many of his fellow Puritans regarded the practice of smoking with an aversion equal to that of James I., believing it to be a subtle device of Satan to ruin mankind. Yet the example of such a man as Winthrop proved to them that piety was not inconsistent with smoking, while his experience made him feel that "the immoderate use and love of tobacco" was the snare to be deprecated and avoided. Many persons will admire him none the less when they learn that, in common with his great contemporary, John Milton, he thoroughly enjoyed a pipe of tobacco.

In the spring of 1629 Winthrop remarked, in a letter to his wife, that they ought to be thankful for enjoying "so much comfort and peace in these so evil and declining times, and when the increasing of our sins gives us so great cause to look for some heavy scourge and judgment to be coming upon us." One of the occurrences which afflicted him was the triumph of Richelieu over the Huguenots at Rochelle. He feared that the Protestant Church in England was in danger, and he considered it imperative to carry the gospel to New England, and there "raise a bulwark against the kingdom of anti-Christ which the Jesuits labour to rear in those parts." Furthermore, he was disposed to leave England because the land was so overpeopled that the poor found their children to be great burdens instead of the chiefest of blessings. In addition to the superabundance of people, there was such an excess of competition in all trades that the honest man found it hard to get a living. These drawbacks existed at home, while a whole continent, both fruitful and fitted for man's use, lay waste across the ocean. That continent had a few native-born inhabitants who, as they neither enclosed the land nor had tame cattle and a settled habitation, were held by Winthrop to possess only "a natural right to those countries." He arrived at the conclusion, which was more convenient to him than to the natives, and which less scrupulous men after him have reached without elaborate argument, "If we leave them sufficient for their use, we may lawfully take the rest, there being more than enough for them and us." He communicated his plans and his reasons for adopting them to several friends, among them to Robert Ryece, who was "an accomplished gentleman and a great preserver of the antiquities of Suffolk." The latter, though agreeing with Winthrop in the main, advised him to stay at home, urging the following weighty consideration :—

"The Church and Commonwealth here at home hath more need of your best ability in these dangerous times than any remote plantation." Had other patriots of that day, such as Pym, Hampden, Cromwell, Haslerig, Holles, and Strode, left the country also, the course of English history might have taken a different direction. A fable originated by Cotton Mather, and included as an authentic fact in many carelessly compiled histories, is current to the effect that three of the men just named were turned back by force when about to embark for New England. Winthrop was unshackled by any obstacle in carrying out his design to leave his native country, and begin life anew in a strange land, where he might have no cause to dread the tyranny of Charles I. in civil affairs, or the Romanizing innovations of Laud in the doctrine and discipline of the Church. When contemplating emigration he naturally turned his thoughts toward America. Many colonies had been founded there, and the suitability of the land for colonisation had been demonstrated. In 1628 a Puritan colony had been established at Salem, in Massachusetts, with Endecott as the governor. The company which sent forth this colony did so under the security of a patent obtained from the Council for New England. Desiring to enlarge the scope of the enterprise, the company applied for a royal charter, and obtained one empowering "The Governor and Company of the Massachusetts Bay in New England," to make laws and govern the territory on certain conditions, and to resist by force of arms all attacks made upon themselves and their property, whether on land or water. Charles I. signed this document on the 21st of March, 1629; a few days afterwards he intimated his intention of governing the country without a parliament. It may be surmised that the king looked upon a Puritan emigration as most desirable, insomuch as it lessened the number of his adversaries. The writings of Laud supply evidence in support of such a conclusion. In a report made to the king in 1636, Laud remarked that a lecturer at Yarmouth having gone to New England there was peace in the town, and that Mr. Bridge, a Puritan clergyman, had departed from Norwich to Holland. After reading this Charles wrote on the margin, "Let him go; we are well rid of him." Indeed, so far from showing any desire to detain the Puritan leaders in England, the king was resigned to their departure and was prepared to exclaim out of the fulness of a thankful heart, "We are well rid of them."

Twelve gentlemen met at Cambridge in August, 1629, and resolved that, if the charter could be legally transferred to America, they would embark for the plantation of Massachusetts Bay by the first day of the following March, with the view " to inhabit and continue in New England," and that they would take their wives and families, if the latter would consent to accompany them. They likewise agreed that any one who failed through his own default in keeping this agreement, should forfeit £3 for every day that he was unprepared to start. Winthrop was present at the meeting and assented to the resolutions. Two days later, a general court of the Company was held in London, when it was resolved that the government should be transferred to the plantation itself. At the same meeting, John Winthrop was elected governor of the Company. In April, 1630, he set sail in the *Arbella* for the Western continent. Sir Simonds D'Ewes, writing four years later, thus describes how this expedition was viewed by contemporaries. Previous emigrants to New England had " chiefly aimed at trade and gain, till about the year 1630, in the spring, when John Winthrop, Esq., a Suffolk man, and many other godly and well-disposed Christians, with the main of their estates, and many of them with their entire families, to avoid the burdens and snares which were here laid upon their consciences, departed thither." Nathaniel Morton, who was at New Plymouth when the Puritans sailed from England, writes in his " New England's Memorial," " This year, 1630, it pleased God of His rich grace to transport over into the Bay of Massachusetts divers honourable personages and many worthy Christians. . . . Among the rest, a chief one amongst them was that famous pattern of piety and justice, Mr. John Winthrop, the first governor of the jurisdiction, accompanied with divers other precious sons of Zion, which might be compared to the most fine gold." Before sailing, Winthrop issued a farewell address to his brethren in the Church, wherein he said for his associates and himself that " we esteem it an honour to call the Church of England, from whence we rise, our dear mother, and cannot part from our native country, where she specially resideth, without much sadness of heart, and many tears in our eyes."

Winthrop had taken a personal farewell of his friends and associates at a dinner before embarking. When about to drink their healths his feelings overpowered him, and the company wept in concert at the thought of never seeing each other's faces any more.

But it was a still greater trial to part from his wife, who, expecting an addition to her family, could not accompany him. She was a devoted wife and mother. When her husband's departure had been determined on and while he was making the final preparations in London, she wrote a beautiful letter from Groton, in which she thus expresses her feelings and her hopes : " My request now shall be to the Lord to prosper thee in thy voyage, and enable thee and fit thee for it, and give all graces and gifts for such employments as he shall call thee to. I trust God will bring us together before you go, that we may see each other with gladness, and take solemn leave, till we, through the goodness of our God, shall meet in New England, which will be a joyful day to us." His answer is contained in a post-script to another letter which he had written before receiving hers : " Being now ready to send away my letters, I received thine ; the reading of it *has dissolved* my head into tears. I can write no more. If I live I *will see thee* ere I go. I shall part from thee with sorrow enough ; be comfortable, my most sweet wife, our God will be with thee." These touching words came straight from his heart ; those printed in Italics are almost illegible in the manuscript from the tears which watered the paper. The sacrifice which Winthrop made in leaving his native land has seldom been equalled by any self-exiled Englishman. He left a fine estate, where he lived as a county gentleman in the receipt of an ample income and enjoying the esteem of his neighbours. The best society of the age was open to him. He had everything, in short, which constitutes human happiness, and it proves the strength of his religious sentiments, that he parted with his property, withdrew from all the attractions of society, and separated himself from a dearly beloved wife, in order that he might help to establish what he considered to be a pure Church and commonwealth on the North American Continent.

He arrived at Salem on the 12th of June, 1631, after a voyage of two months' duration. The sea was often very rough, but, as Winthrop records, however the tempest might blow and the waves rage, it was the exception for Sunday not to be duly kept, and two sermons be preached. Every Tuesday and Wednesday the passengers were catechized. On board ship Winthrop composed, and probably delivered, a discourse entitled " Christian Charity." In the course of it he set forth the objects of their society, which was composed of persons professing to be fellow-members of Christ, who were "seeking out a place of cohabitation and consortship under a due form of government both civil and ecclesiastical," whose end was the improvement of their lives, and who hoped to attain it by bringing "into familiar and constant practice" what most of the Churches in England "maintained as truth in profession only." It was essential, to prevent shipwreck of their plans, for them to be knit together as one man: "We must entertain each other in brotherly affection. We must be willing to abridge ourselves of our superfluities, for the supply of others' necessities. We must uphold a familiar commune together in all meekness, gentleness, patience, and liberality. We must delight in each other; make others' conditions our own; rejoice together, mourn together, labour and suffer together, always having before our eyes our commission and community in the work, as members of the same body." He urged, moreover, that if they succeeded, the desire of other persons would be to copy their example, while failure would cause their principles to be ridiculed; that they would be as a city set up on a hill, the cynosure of all eyes. On the sixtieth day after sailing land was seen; "There came a smell off the shore, like the smell of a garden." Four days later Winthrop was able to record that he and others went on shore, where they supped on "a good venison pasty and good beer," and that some of the passengers "gathered store of fine strawberries at Cape Ann."

The settlers at Salem numbered three hun-·dred when Winthrop arrived. About a thousand persons were transported in the ships which sailed with him or followed after. The cost of the enterprise was reckoned at £192,000. The vessels were laden with provisions to feed the settlers, wood and iron wherewith to build houses, and sheep, pigs, cattle, and horses wherewith to stock the land. Most of the goats and horses died at sea, and only half of the cows survived. This was not the worst. The settlers were in great straits for food, and stood in need of the assistance which the newcomers expected from them. Fever broke out, and carried off two hundred before Winthrop had been six months in the country. At least a hundred returned to England, both because they were in dread of famine, and also because they objected to the strictness of the discipline which prevailed. Deputy-Governor Dudley, when informing the Countess of Lincoln, by letter, what had occurred, states that those persons who thought of joining them for worldly ends had better stay at home, but that, if influenced by spiritual motives, they would find in New England what would satisfy them; that is, "materials to build, fuel to burn, ground to plant, seas and rivers to fish in, a pure air to breathe in, good water to drink till wine and beer can be made, which, together with the cows, hogs, and goats brought hither already, may suffice for food. As for fowl and venison, they are dainties here as well as in England. For clothes and bedding, they must bring them with them till time and industry produce them here. In a word, we yet enjoy little to be envied, but endure much to be pitied in the sickness and mortality of our people."

Winthrop had more to bear than many of his associates. His second son, Henry, who had missed getting on board the *Arbella* before she sailed from the Isle of Wight, and who followed in another ship, was drowned the day after reaching Salem. His third son, Forth, whom he left behind at Cambridge, who was destined for the ministry, and who was to embark for New England as soon as his studies were finished, died after a short illness. His infant daughter, Anne, died at sea shortly after his wife had sailed to rejoin him. The reunion of husband and wife took place in November, 1631. The arrival of Margaret Winthrop and her children was the subject of rejoicing among the people, who were unfeignedly glad that their governor's happiness was increased. Winthrop was greatly impressed with the demonstration, remarking that "the like joy and manifestation of love had never been seen in New England." His eldest son, John, came also, bringing a wife with him. He had completed the sale of Groton Manor, though at a price far below what his father desired, the sum obtained being £4,200, and the valuation being £5,760. William Bradford, the Governor of New Plymouth, made a journey in order to congratulate "his much honoured and beloved friend," the Governor of Massachusetts Bay, on being surrounded by his family in his new home.

The story of Winthrop's life during the nineteen years passed in New England is virtually the history of the rise and progress of the Company of Massachusetts Bay. As some of the principal incidents in his career will be narrated hereafter in connection with the lives of other founders of New England, I shall merely indicate now the main incidents in it. It was owing to him that the peninsula then called Shawmut, upon which Boston now stands, was selected as suitable for settlement, an excellent spring of water being the chief attraction. The Rev. William Blackstone, who claimed the right of ownership, was paid a small sum for permitting houses to be erected on Shawmut, and he left the spot when he found that he was to be under subjection to stricter Puritans than himself. He was a clergyman of the Church of England who had emigrated to America in the hope of being unmolested there on account of his religious principles. He assigned as the reason for leaving Shawmut that, having quitted England to escape from the tyranny of the Lord Bishops, he was not disposed to submit in America to the tyranny of the Lord Brethren. For the first three and the last three years of Winthrop's life in New England he was annually chosen governor; he was deputy-governor for three years. His chief fault, in the opinion of his associates, was that he was too tolerant. His excuse was that he thought it right, in the infancy of a plantation, not to be very rigid in administering the law, seeing that the people were more ignorant of their duties than they would be in an older and more settled State; however, the ministers having enjoined greater severity, he deferred to their judgment.

An epidemic, which raged in the summer of 1647, carried off Margaret Winthrop. Her husband records the fact in these concise and happy terms : "In this sickness the Governor's wife, daughter of Sir John Tyndal, left this world for a better, being about fifty-six years of age ; a woman of singular virtue, prudence, modesty, and piety, and especially beloved and honoured by all the country." Four years previously, he had noted that he felt age and infirmities coming upon him, and that he thought the time of his departure out of the world was not far off. Yet he was no more reconciled to remain a widower at the age of sixty than he was thirty years earlier. Accordingly, before his third wife had been six months buried, he married Martha Coytmore, a widow, and within a year after his marriage he became a father for the sixteenth time. No other Governor of Massachusetts has been more frequently married or more largely blessed with offspring. His death took place not long after the birth of this child. On the 26th of March, 1649, he passed away at the age of sixty-one. His loss was generally lamented, and he was buried " with great solemnity and honour."

Winthrop was singularly well qualified for his position. He was not a man of large information, nor of brilliant intellectual capacity. A list of the books taken from his own library and presented to Harvard College supplies a clue to his literary preferences. Out of the thirty-nine volumes two only relate to profane subjects, Livy's " History of Rome," and Polydore Virgil's " History of England," the others being either sermons or dissertations on theological topics ; there is but one biography, and that, strange to say, is the " Life of the Virgin Mary." He excelled in the art of ruling men, doing this in such a way as to gain their affections. His puritanism was genuine and profound, yet it was devoid of bitterness. Unlike Dudley, Endecott, and other colleagues, he never thought it consistent with the profession of Christianity to hate such of his fellows as differed from him in opinion. He was a proficient in the happy art of giving the soft answer which turneth away wrath. He was moderate in all things, and, while ready to sacrifice much for conscience' sake, he was loath to compel others to sacrifice anything. Many illustrations of his good-nature and thoughtfulness are extant. He was in the habit of sending his servants to pay calls on his poorer neighbours at meal-times, in order that he might learn which of them required assistance. During a very severe winter an officious person informed him that a needy neighbour stole wood from his pile. Winthrop undertook to cure him of stealing in the future. When the offender was brought before him, he said, " Friend, it is a severe winter, and I doubt you are but meanly provided with wood; wherefore I would have you supply yourself at my wood pile till this cold season be over." And he then merrily asked his friends " whether he had not effectually stopped this man of stealing his wood ? "

One of Winthrop's failings was to be even more superstitious than his associates. He saw " special providences " in events which had no supernatural character. This was his weak side ; his strength lay in the common-sense view which he took of all affairs, and the conciliatory spirit which he displayed on all vexed questions. When he left England in 1630 he had a good estate ; he died penniless in Massachusetts nineteen years afterwards. He left children behind him who inherited and perpetuated his virtues as well as his name. His descendants in the sixth generation are among the honoured citizens of the Commonwealth of Massachusetts.

W. FRASER RAE.

THE SLOW STREAM.

AH me! I said, the stream is slow,
  My spirit chides delay;
How languidly its waters flow
  Throughout the summer day!
It creeps along with sleepy song,
  And loiters on the way.

Beneath the ivied arch it seems
  To pause in dusky rest,
As if it wearied of the beams
  Of sunlight on its breast,
And loved to sleep in shadows deep,
  By willow-boughs caressed.

It dallies with the golden flowers
  In meadows cool and green,
And murmurs under feudal towers
  Of glories that have been;
Too long it stays in woodland ways
  Among the ferns, I ween.

There waits an eager heart for me
  Far on the shining main;
It is the sea, the open sea,
  My soul is sick to gain.
To moss and stone in dreamy tone
  The river mocks my pain.

"Oh, peace," my guardian angel sighed
  (His voice was sweet and low),
"Love, work, and pray, and day by day
  The stream will faster flow;
It rests with thee, if Time shall be
  A river swift or slow."

              SARAH DOUDNEY.

THE SPIRIT OF PROPHECY.

By R. HERBERT STORY, D.D.

WE read, in the Book of Isaiah, of a time when the armies of the King of Assyria encompassed Jerusalem, and the borders of the land were all overrun by the invader, when the people were in sore dismay and terror, and when the king, shut up in the city, was sitting in the House of the Lord, covered with sackcloth, and crying, "This is a day of trouble, and rebuke, and of blasphemy." Then, as at many another time of distress and anguish, the presence of the prophet was the one centre of light and hope, the voice of the prophet the only note of peace. In a striking passage of a famous history the historian relates how, during one of the most horrible massacres which the world's annals record, high above the heads of the struggling throng in the streets of a great city, there sounded every half-quarter of every hour from the belfry of the cathedral the "tender and melodious chimes." So, above all the calamities and fear and confusion that befell the disobedient children of the Covenant, the voice of God's prophet, God's remembrancer and interpreter, ever rose, calm and unshaken, testifying to the eternal truth and the Divine righteousness, mingling with the rebuke and admonition of the sinner words of cheering and good hope for the faithful and godly. And thus, when the king was hidden from his people's sight, a humble and awe-stricken suppliant before the altar, his royal robes rent, wearing sackcloth instead of purple and fine linen, and with ashes on his head, discrowned and low—when Judea was devastated by the Assyrian spoiler, encroached upon and hemmed in on every side, the prophet was able to look beyond the present extremity and disaster, and to see the coming time when Hezekiah should be again upon his throne in all the pomp and splendour of his rank and power, when the borders of the land should be rid of the defiling presence of the heathen; and he sang, "Thine eyes shall see the king in his beauty: they shall behold the land that is very far off;" or rather—as the Hebrew words strictly mean—"the land of far distances," the king's land, as it seems truest to interpret it—no longer limited and overrun, but with its borders stretched to their utmost bound, far beyond that within which the enemy had pent them now.

This seems the real and original meaning of the passage to which we have referred; and yet for many a generation this special promise has been believed to hold far wider meanings. And those to whom its hopeful and beautiful words have been familiar and dear, may feel as though these were robbed of their full significance when thus brought down to their simple bearing on the time and place and circumstance, in connection with which they were spoken at the first. They may feel as though we had no right to restrict to any local or temporary application words which have been found comforting and helpful by so many generations of Christians; whose promise has brightened many a closing eye from whose vision the world was fading, and cheered many a lonely heart that was ready to fail, because of the greatness and the solitude of the untrodden way; words in which Calvin read the name of a greater king than Hezekiah, for, "I pursue here," he says, "no allegories, for these I do not love; but because in Christ alone is found the stability of that frail kingdom of his, the likeness which Hezekiah bore leads us to Christ, as it were, by the hand;" words in which Keble discovered the assurance of that day of the restitution of all things, which shall make good the losses, the frailties, the failures of this mortal life, that day in which he says—

> "These eyes that, dazzled now and weak,
> At glancing motes in sunshine wink,
> Shall see the King's full glory break.
> Nor from the blissful vision shrink.
> Though scarcely now their laggard glance
> Reach to an arrow's flight, that day
> They shall behold, and not in trance,
> The region very far away."

But is this feeling justified? Have we any right to feel as if robbed of something that we were entitled to, if we are told that the text can be interpreted only as speaking of a Jewish king and his little Judæan kingdom? I do not think we have. We value the promises of God—if we understand them rightly—not just because of the exact thing they seem to promise, but because of that which they reveal to us of God. The promise in itself, in its letter, in its outward form, is often little else than an illusion. God, for instance, promised to give Abraham the land of Canaan, that he and his children might dwell there. The promise never was fulfilled.

The only portion of the Holy Land that Abraham ever possessed was the field, with the cave in it, that he bought from the stranger, that there he might bury his dead. So with Isaac, so with Jacob, the promise was but a vision and a dream. When, long afterwards, their children did settle in the promised land, the region that they had hoped to find "flowing with milk and honey" was one full of heathen enemies and turmoil and labour and war. And yet these patriarchs made no complaint. They did not think they had been deceived. We are told, "They all died in faith, not having received the promises." The promise that eluded their grasp did not unloose the bands of their strong faith, because they knew that

> "'Twas not the grapes of Canaan that repay,
> But the long faith that fails not by the way."

They knew that the promise was, so to speak, but the signal from the Father's hand to lead them on, and show them He was *there*. And so the promise is ever most precious to us when we perceive that it is revealing Him, and know what it is that it reveals. It is a little matter to us that in the day of Jewish distress and shame, Isaiah, the son of Amos, had such confidence in his country's destiny as to foretell that the Assyrians should yet be overthrown, and the King of Judæa be reseated in his palace, and all his borders be purged of the heathen invasion; but it is much to us to know that in that cloudy and dark day, when men's hearts were failing them for fear, and when their faith was well-nigh shaken from its rest, the Lord God of their fathers had compassion on His forlorn people, and through His prophet's courageous words sent them a message that should lift up their hearts and strengthen their hands; that He saw their trouble and knew their need, and sent them help from His holy habitation. We feel that the ancient promise renews itself for us, because it reveals to us the character of the same God in whose name it was spoken then. It encourages us to trust to the same mercy—to believe in the same fatherly good-will—to endure in the time of distress, because sure of the support of the same arm that is now, as it was then, "mighty to save." It teaches us to understand that, amidst all our sins and unworthiness, it is "of His mercy that we are not consumed, and because His compassions fail not."

But are we therefore to think of any of the promises of God as having no substantial reality behind them, as only vague, general indications of His character and will?

We have but slender ground to go on in arriving at an answer. We read the promises, and we know that again and again we fail to find the fulfilment. Christ promised His disciples that that generation should not pass away, till all the things He had spoken of were accomplished. Some of them are not accomplished yet. The early Church was taught by the Apostles to look for and to hold fast the blessed hope of the return of the Lord, in their own day. And now in this nineteenth century there are still those who cling to the letter of that early expectation, and believe that ere this generation has fallen asleep, the reign of the Lord and of His saints shall have begun. But still after more than eighteen hundred years the time "is not yet." No such promise would seem to be absolute. Its realisation hinges more or less on the state and the qualification of those to whom it is made. Their faith, their righteousness, their ability to receive the fulness of the promise, become conditions which have a share in determining how, or when, or to what extent, it shall be fulfilled. "The Lord is not slack concerning His promise as some men count slackness;" but the time and the manner of its fulfilment rest with Him. Not one word that He has spoken shall ever fail; but it may be fulfilled otherwise than we have expected, because we have not understood the inner meaning, the true secret, the spirit of that which was spoken, and which is fulfilled to those that walk not after the flesh but after the spirit. The fulfilment is part of that "secret of the Lord" which is with them that fear Him, and into which, as into the promised land of old, there are always multitudes who cannot enter "because of unbelief."

Now, there is a special sense in which ancient prophecy and promise have grown dear to Christ's people, and which this principle of the spiritual fulfilment rather than of the literal fulfilment of prophecy and promise may be said to justify. They have been accustomed to read in the words which spoke of God's early kingdom, of its laws, its kings, its judges, its heroes, meanings which point to the eternal kingdom of which Christ is king, and to find in all that was true and sacred and beautiful in the elder dispensation foreshadowings of Him. St. Paul himself seems to warrant this use of the old as the forerunner of the new, when he says that the ordinances of the Mosaic law were "a shadow" of things to come; but "the body," he says, the reality, the substance, "is of Christ." He is the "first-born of every creature," the "beginning of the creation of God," the original type and reality, that is to say, of all that is true and beautiful and good. And so all that is excellent in the old time before Him is understood in its full excellence only after He has manifested the high ideal, of which that was but the partial anticipation. And the heroes, and prophets, and kings of the Old Testament become to the Church types of Christ, her head, not because of mere coincidence here and there between points in their history and events in His, but because they were, each in their several degree of attainment, promises of the coming of the Perfect Man. And the purity of Joseph, the governance of Moses, the courage of Joshua, the strength of Samson, the faith of David, the wisdom of Solomon, the righteousness of Josiah, were regarded as bearing witness to Him who was the perfectly pure and wise, and strong, and mighty, and righteous, the Captain of our salvation, the author and finisher of the faith. And so too, since He has come, all human goodness, all beauty of true art, all righteousness of character, all loftiness of ennobling influence, all that testifies to us, in any way or degree, for a life that is higher than our own, that is not of the earth earthly, but is of heaven and from above, is likewise to us a witness for Christ, a remembrancer of Him, a reflection of His light, a step in "the world's great altar-stairs that slope through darkness up to God," that helps us to come up higher. All these, to the mind that is full of God, that seeks in His light to see light, are not screens coming between it and Him tending to hide Him, because making us content with something lower than the highest, and meaner than the best, but are aids to our infirmity, and helpers to our faith; as it were friendly voices, kindly hands, that reach us through the twilight and amid the perplexities of our way, and bid us strive and hope. Whatever is true, whatever is beautiful, whatever is pure, whatever is noble in human thought or deed, whatever is best that the mind of man has imagined or his hand portrayed, is but the minister of "the man Christ Jesus."

> "The shadows of the beauty of all time,
> Carven and sung, are only shapes of Thee."

It seems, then, not wrong, not a mere idle play of the devout imagination, as it is certainly not unnatural, that Christian people reading these words of ancient promise about the Jewish king and the Judæan kingdom should bring out of them more than he who spoke them first could understand, but not more than the spirit of God, uttering God's message of mercy and hope through him, will warrant us in discovering there.

Those promises of the earlier dispensation, in which we of the later find new life and fulness, remind one of the old device of the Spanish monarch who engraved upon his coins the image of the "Pillars of Hercules," the farthest gateway of the world, according to the primitive belief, and took for his motto "No more beyond;" but when Columbus had discovered the new world in the West, and added it to that monarch's dominions, the two graven pillars looking out upon the sea were still retained upon the shield, but a word was struck out of the motto, and so it was changed into "More beyond." The confine of the old world had become the open threshold of the new. So the prophecy, the vision, the promise, which to the Jewish eye and ear unfolded only some blessing of the ancient covenant, to us who have known the Father and Him in whom He is revealed, acquire a vaster scope—

> "There is no speech nor language
> Where their voice is not heard."

There is no limit to their horizon; they stretch beyond the farthest bounds of the everlasting hills, where "gleams that untravelled world whose margin fades, forever and forever, when we move."

And if then to us, who are citizens of the city of God, there should sometimes befall the day of trouble and rebuke, when the enemy presses on us from without, and the heart is faint and downcast within; when some adversity or scandal or error of the Church distresses us, and we are apt to feel as though the very ark of God were taken ; when our Lord and King seems, as it were, driven from His throne and is lost sight of amidst the bitter strifes of those who wrangle and contend for what they call His truth and His rights, but which are often in reality only their own conceits, then there may come to us out of the words of the old promise, in a larger meaning than the prophet deemed, a note of encouragement and hope—"These poor conflicts and jealousies will pass away. The true life of the Church will not be holden of them. The Christ whose sacred presence they obscure will yet be manifested in His people, 'the hope of glory.'"

Or, if sometimes that hope of glory seems to us to burn but low and dim, by reason of the sins that darken and the failures that impair the lives of which it ought to be the life ; if our faith even in the Divine original is almost strained to breaking by the dull imperfection of the human reflections of it; if we find deformity where we had looked for beauty, insincerity where we had expected truth, carnality where we had believed there was purity of soul, baseness where we had trusted there was some vision of the high ideal; then, too, amidst the disappointment, the weariness and disgust of heart, the inner ear may detect the voice of ancient comfort, "These are but the failures, the unworthinesses, the fallings short of men. The blemishes of earth cannot stain the white purity of heaven. There is One who is perfect, and who will draw all of those who have not yet attained to His likeness, but who desire to attain to it, towards His own perfection. Oh, thou afflicted and tempest-tossed! thine eyes shall yet behold His beauty."

Or if, again, it may be our lot to feel, and to suffer in feeling, how far short the Church of Christ, at her best, falls of her great mission and work in the world; to feel our love chilled by her lack of unity, our faith straitened by her want of faith, our devotion hampered and restrained by her imperfect offices, our vision of the eternal city with its many entrances, its ample walls, its unfading light, over-clouded by the very smoke that rises from our earthly altars; if it is borne in on us that it is hard to realise how great God's kingdom is, because of the jealousy and narrowness and poverty of man's conceptions of it; then, too, we are saved from despondency and distrust when His word reminds us, though it be but in a figure, that although His City may for a time be beset with foes, it is *His* City still; that although the life within its walls may be enclosed and burdened, yet it *lives;* that though the land may seem to be hemmed in and narrowed, His people will one day possess it wholly, and shall find that it is vaster than their need, and that the boundaries of the kingdom of God are wider than they deem.

And so amid all human trial, and change, and want, considering that He who gave of old the temporal blessing, the release from cruel siege and shameful overthrow, will not withhold the spiritual gift, will not deny to Christian faith and hope any good thing, we may seek help to do and to endure in the words, of which we make bold to believe that Christ is Himself the "Substance," and which say to us, "Be not dismayed, be not overcome, be not daunted and restrained in the hopefulness of your effort, in the freedom and fulness of your life. Suffer not yourself to sink to the world's low level, to take your pattern even from the best of what you see around you here, to receive for doctrines of Christ the commandments of men, to call any man master upon earth, to rest in, or be satisfied with, anything, how good soever it may be, which, because your king is hidden from you for a time, might seem to represent to you His blessed and glorious presence. Hold fast your faith in Himself, and in the eternal kingdom of which He is King. Believe that somewhere in God's wide universe that kingdom's everlasting bounds are set, and wait to receive all His faithful ones whose lives have been true and upward, who have walked by faith and not by sight, to receive these into rest and peace, and into the perfect vision of the King. The time may be protracted and weary, the night may be long of breaking, but yet the dawn shall come, when you shall see Him, not as now under the veil of earthly things and through a glass darkly, but as He is; when you shall no longer need the aid of symbol or ministry to help you to discern His aspect, but shall behold Him openly; when sin, and folly, and sorrow, and ignorance shall no more contract His dominion within narrow and sordid bounds, but when you shall see it stretch far beyond your utmost view. Yet awhile, if you live as strangers and pilgrims on the earth, not content with aught that it can offer, still amidst all its resting-places seeking the city which hath foundations, amid all its loveliness desiring that uncreated beauty which no type can embody or fully shadow forth; still amid all its disciplines holding fast the confidence that these are but the earnests of the life to come; then, at the end, when all worldly vision is fading from your sight, when all worldly possession is dwindling down to the few feet of earth that shall cover your decay, then your eye shall be opened to the glory to be revealed within the veil—to see the King in His beauty and the land of wide expanse."

SOCIAL PLAGUES.

II.—NOISE. *Section 2.*

MR. FREDERICK HARRISON, passionately, and Mr. Matthew Arnold, sweetly and lightly, uphold the Latin races against Mr. Edward Freeman and Teutomaniacs to whom the word "Charlemagne" is the unpardonable sin. Mr. Harrison failed to lead our armies on a march to Berlin ; but Mr. Arnold's imperturbable assurance has yet to be convinced of fallibility. When, however, Jacques Bonhomme—with his good-humour, frugality, industry, and Malthusianism —is held before us as the sole hope of the future, some defects of detail are still apt to suggest themselves. It can, for instance, scarcely be controverted that the modern Gaul is obstinately given to chatter and perversely given to lie, less from conscious vice than from a morbid, almost a contemptible, love of approbation, intensified, when occasion offers, by the desire to turn a doubtfully honest franc. Put a question ; he asks himself what answer it will most gratify you to receive : the truth is a matter of no consequence. When you are not called on to act on your misinformation, this foible may be regarded as a mere curiosity ; when you are, it is often disconcerting. There are quiet spots even now in the "plaisant pays de France ;" but I shall not blab their character away. Tourists should keep their counsel, or we shall ere long pursue repose as vainly as the mass of men pursue pleasure. The Pyrenees, for example, are no more as they used to be, "Consule Planco." The great Biscay waves are no longer broken on solitary rocks at Biarritz, nor do they roll up silent sands near Arcachon. The grandeur of the Cirque de Gavarnie—Nature's triumphant copy of the Colosseum (to accept the splendid anachronism of a friend with whom I gazed at both)—is ineffaceable ; but you approach the precipices, crowned with snow and sunsmit with morning and evening fire, through a storm of donkeys, and the voices that upraise them.

Quite recently I revisited a haunt of twenty years ago in search of retreat from the hubbub and strife of elections, presbyteries, councils, and conclaves of various verbosity, and entered a lodging on an upland slope as a likely hermitage. For the nonce, quiet reigned, and to every interrogation and appeal, searching, or pathetic, or severe, the well-bred dame who was my doom had one unvarying response, "Monsieur, la tranquillité est ad-

mirable ;" till I yielded to her winning ways, engaged her seductive rooms, and imported my baggage and my books. "Ah, who the melodies of morn can tell !" I had pitched my tent on the very "bank and shoal" of discord. On one side of the house the foundations of a new building were being laid, the earth and stones being slowly carted by solemn-eyed bullocks goaded by Gascons, who seemed alternately transported with rage and convulsed by garrulity. A remaining strip of the same plot was hired out for carpets brought at an atrocious hour by asses incessantly braying for their breakfasts. On the other side there were—a carpenter's shed in which the saw seldom ceased, a playground, a dog kennel, an omnibus station, a recognised stand for itinerant minstrels, and three poultry yards, in each as many cocks, with hens to match. Within this eligible mansion for a nervous patient or poetaster, the landlady was, in her sixtieth year, beginning to take lessons in music, which she touchingly declared to be her passion. We came presently to an arrangement and separation ; but my next adventure was equally disastrous. Over-persuaded to settle in the attractive and reputedly quiet hotel of a watering-place hopefully out of season, I found that the fascinating hostess had concealed the fact that my "appartement" was edged between the "Place" and the market. In the former there were the daily rattle of voitures with their bells, and the inevitable "hoops !" of the voituriers ; and, weekly, in the latter a scene indescribable, almost unearthly. The French, unlike Ariel, cannot do either their "spiriting," or their work, or their bargaining gently. They rise abominably soon, and from 4 A.M. bibble-babble, jabber, and shriek till vespers. Later on they gather in squads on the squares, and intermittently break into such explosions of mutual abuse that one rushes to the window, fearing to be the spectator of some murderous violence ; it is but a matter of the price of a bunch of cherries, or the hire of a vehicle, and gesticulations like those of a maddened Roscius end in beer and laughter. The turmoil of a Pyreneean mart surpasses all preconceptions of the storming of the Bastille ; it is a thing never to be forgotten nor again endured.

These uproars are of course augmented by the instruments of aural agony which in all countries profess to give pleasure. Among ourselves, Mr. Babbage and Mr. Leitch have been their most eminent and notorious martyrs; but countless deaths and blasted careers, due to the same cause, have had no sacred bard to sing them. Of indoor torments of this kind, the most constant is piano-practising. The man who suffers it under his own roof is a simpleton whom "it were base flattery to call a coward;" but what is to be done with your immediate neighbours, whose strophes and antistrophes up and down the scales threaten to strum you out of your five senses? There should, in every considerable community, be statutory buildings, far withdrawn, and with walls as thick as those of Parkhurst, to which practising novices should be compelled to resort.

Outdoor musicians—organ-grinders, German bands, blind fiddlers, street-singers, Italian or Irish improvisatori in rags, Scotch bagpipers in kilts, and others of the tribe who make day hideous, with Christmas waits and evening buglers, should be driven to move on, and ever on, like the Red Indian before the advance of civilisation. While the complicated atrocities accompanying dancing-bears, performing-dogs, and pitiful monkeys are permitted to exist "this great lubber the world" must be reckoned in his infancy.

Plainly, in addition to our magnified tax on curs, there ought, in this prancing age, to be an almost prohibitive duty on vocal or instrumental advertisements, nor should they be tolerated at all, save under strict conditions. The street-crier in any well-regulated state would have to "pass" in the grammar and elocution of his native tongue, or, failing, carry a dumb placard, with this advantage to the public that his lies—as "*ripe* fruit," "*fresh* herring," "*best* coals," "*caller* oo"—being on written record, might be proved against him. Under no circumstances should drums, beaten with the fury of a Turk at Plevna, be endured; still less the miscreated dinner-bells in the hands of irresponsible brats, swinging as if they would never grow old, to announce the advent of endless carts of milk and water. While these born imps are suffered to shatter the noon with a clangour,

"Horrible, hateful, monstrous, not to be told,"

there must be increase of headache, fever, insanity, and every kind of sorrow. In London and other semi-civilised places they are already ostracised, but, in the city of the "dura ilia" and the ears of adamant, the air is . saturated with them as a sponge with water, and thronged as a glen with midges. Unless we except the cannon-firing near

barracks as an *advertisement* of the willingness of the defenders of their country to die for her, the most prominent of the other intimations of this kind are under shallow pretexts alleged to be *warnings*. It never seems to occur to those who institute them that to many minds the cure may be worse than the disease, and that the certainty of cacophonous life is more to be shunned than the remoter and generally avoidable risk of a short one.

The ringing or shrieking of ships in a fog must perhaps be endured, but when a river runs through districts populous with man it is intolerable that every tug or ferry-boat should start a horn—to which the appropriate name of "American devil" has been applied—not only to intimate its presence, but for miles round to make every being who is not an outer barbarian long for it to be swamped. The ordinary admonition to move slow is protection sufficient for all who deserve to live. The application of the screech-horn—to which the screech-owl is as Mozart to a tom-tom—to the call of men to labour in the dim hours of a winter morning is an assault on the innocent sleep—"sleep that knits up the ravelled sleeve of care"—undreamt of in southern latitudes, and only tolerated in the commercial capital of long-suffering, dimly conjecturing, omnivorously believing, orator-behumbugged Hyperborea.

Sounds of labour are among the least offensive, because they are continuous, and do not take the ear by surprise, and partly because the sense of their utility doth add to them a reasonableness that breeds content. They are the throbs of the world's great heart, and seldom intrude on our hours or resorts of privacy. The chipping of stones for masonry is a natural accompaniment to the reading of Ruskin; to the cutting of wood, if it be not for political purposes, and a few yards off, we can be habituated or reconciled; the hammering of a dock suggests the flag that "braves the battle and the breeze;" "Week in, week out" you can hear the smith's bellows blow with patience, as long as it is with measured beat; so on Sundays we condone or approve the sexton according to the quality of the village bell.

Noises of removal, on the other hand, are irregular, suggestive of change of government, and vexatious. The rumbling of vans, as of trains, might be indifferent were it not for the shouting in the one case and the whistling in the other. But the limit to our endurance of cabs and omnibuses is over-stepped in the experience of some Paris streets and Liverpool squares, where vehicle after vehicle rattles with steed after steed—

> "His four feet making the clatter of six,
> Like a devil's tattoo played with iron sticks,
> And kettle-drum of granite."

The master nuisance of household affairs is the unhallowed practice of *carpet-beating*, which in late April, early May, and November makes the suburbs of half our cities wholly untenable. The one advertisement exempt from all tax should be, "*Don't beat your carpets, send them to be cleaned.*" Otherwise they should be conveyed like convicts to some far corner among the hills. To fling men, and women too, with the fury of soldiers leading a forlorn hope, on your filthy rag, to flaunt your brow-beaters in front of your neighbour's house, to cannonade his slumbers and thunder through his day, is an outrage on human nature that links us to the chimpanzee and makes pale the wildest dreams of Bulgarian atrocity.

Finally, there is no sphere or phase of life in which there is so clamant a call for a Bismarckian rule as in that of heedless, ruthless noise. If the noblest of our senses is to be the source of "pleasure and exaltation," instead of distraction and despair; if we are to be rescued from the creed of "Ecclesiasticus" and "Candide," of Schopenhauer and Hartmann; if our aspirations are to exceed the everlasting rest of Nirvana, these perpetual and growing assaults on our most sacred rights must be brought to a close. The lacerated ear of the world, despite the shade of Cobden and the body of Bright, demands PROTECTION.

W. ROSS BROWNE.

SANDOWN BAY.

OH, the summer sunshine
    Flooding Sandown Bay,
Making gladness gladder
    While the children play !
Building mimic mountains,
    Digging mimic lakes,
Leaving great things dearer
    For the small things' sakes !

Loud waves, grey and curling,
    Foam in freshening spray,
God's mysterious music
    Mingling with the play.
All the broad sea's glory
    Dimly stretched away,
Like that unknown story
    Children know some day.

Rippling baby chatter !
    Sunny baby smiles !
What can greatly matter
    While you keep your wiles ?
Does God hear this music
    Mingling with the sea's ?
Does He love the laughter
    Sounding on the breeze ?

F. M. OWEN.

"Here he stood, staring at the beehives."

SARAH DE BERENGER.

By JEAN INGELOW.

CHAPTER XXV.

AMIAS rose early the next morning and went into the dewy garden. It was looking its best. Red lilies and white ones stood side by side scenting the air; a thick bush of climbing clematis leaned towards him from a tall cherry-tree. Towering hollyhocks in a long row went straight across the garden, and directed the eye to the old yew-tree hedge, which looked almost black in its shady station.

"I must leave it and leave *her*," thought the lover, and turned to look at the white-curtained windows, behind which he supposed Amabel to be sleeping. Felix was seen advancing, and forthwith Amias began with diligence to examine the beehives, before which he had been standing.

A certain something, of which he had hitherto been scarcely aware, now made itself manifest to him. It was this: that he had begun to think Felix was a man to be

much considered, that it was natural to respect him.

Felix had been pleasant and brotherly, of course, but his manner now and then had been changed a little, just for the moment. Amias had been sensitive to this change—had shown a certain deference towards Felix, which it now occurred to him that the latter had taken advantage of. Had he accepted it as his right? Amias could not help thinking that he had, and he chose to pretend to himself, as Felix approached, that there could be no reason for this, and that it had better be done away with.

Well, then, he would do away with it, and address Felix exactly as he should have done in the old days, without thinking of what he was going to say. Ridiculous! The idea of considering how he should address his own brother, on occasion of their first meeting in the morning! But here he stood, staring at the beehives, and knowing that he *was* desirous to please Felix, and undecided what to say, knowing now that Felix, standing beside him, felt no answering embarrassment.

"I feel exactly as I might if he was her father," thought the poor victim; and now the whole thing was confessed to himself. And still he watched the bees coming out, and still Felix did not speak.

"What a strong smell of clary there is!" he said at last.

"Yes," said Felix indifferently; "so many bees settling on it and fluttering about it, cause it to give forth that strong odour."

Amias, while he said this, had time to remember that the last thing the girls had done before they went to the seaside had been to pull the clary blossoms and spread them on sheets of paper in a spare attic, to be dried for making wine, and that the scent of clary was so strong on their gowns and capes when they came in that they had been obliged to change these habiliments. Mrs. Snaith had hung them in the air on a clothesline. How interesting they had looked—especially one of them.

"Fool that I am; he is thinking of the same thing," thought Amias. "What could possess me to mention the clary, for——"

"That reminds me——" said Felix calmly, and paused.

"I knew it would," thought Amias, and he interrupted: "I always think the emanations from that plant must have substance. Surely, with a magnifying glass, one could detect the particles floating over the flowers?"

"I think not," said Felix, who, not being himself embarrassed, could easily get on without returning to his first opening. "I think not. But, Amias, I'm glad you rose so early, for I particularly wanted to speak to you."

"To speak to me, old fellow? Oh—well, let us sit down, then." He moved on with a pretence of calmness, possessed himself of a stick as he went, and acknowledged to himself that he was quite sure what the talk was going to be about. "How beautiful and how dewy everything looks!" he said, as they sat down on a rustic bench.

"Yes," said Felix again.

Amias took out his knife and began to whittle the stick, because he had an unwonted consciousness of his hands; they seemed to be in his way.

"I wanted," said Felix, "to speak to you about Amabel."

'Amias could not say a word.

"Have you considered that she is not yet out of the schoolroom?"

Amias said nothing, and Felix quietly went on.

"I should like to know whether you are aware how extremely young she is?"

Then he felt obliged to answer. "Yes, Felix, I am; I know she was sixteen on the twelfth of last month."

"I think you have been taking some pains to please her."

"I don't know that I have any cause to suppose that you would dislike the notion of my having succeeded."

"Have you succeeded?"

"I don't know."

"You must not make any more efforts in that line—at any rate, for the present."

Here the worm felt as if he was going to turn. But he did not; he remained silent.

"I think I have a right to say that you are not to pay her any more of these half-playful attentions," continued Felix, "or we shall get nothing more done in the schoolroom; and also that I cannot allow her, at her tender age, to receive any letters."

"Playful attentions—playful!" repeated Amias, with a burning sense of wrong. "Do you mean to say that you think I am not in earnest?"

"No, my dear fellow," said Felix, with perfect gentleness; "I had no idea of saying anything to annoy you. But perhaps I may say now, that she certainly is not old enough to know her own mind, and therefore, for your own sake as well as for hers——"

"My own sake!" exclaimed Amias with scorn. "Pray leave me to take care of my own feelings; speak only for her sake, and of hers."

"I take for granted that she is old Sam's grand-daughter," continued Felix, "and that he has ascertained the fact, because, though he has never been at the pains to let me know it, he continues to treat the girls with constantly growing affection. If, therefore, you think he has a better right over her future, or think that the general facts of the situation throw her more naturally upon his care than on mine, you may go and speak to him if you wish it."

"I think nothing of the kind, Felix. I beg your pardon for my heat. If she had been a brother's child instead of a cousin's, you could not possibly have done more—only——"

"Only what?"

"It hurts me deeply that you should disapprove in this general way. If you have any particular fault to find with me——"

"I have certainly a particular fault to find with you, and no other. It is that you have made love to a good little girl, who was very happy, obedient, and childlike. I notice a difference in her; you have robbed her of a full year of childhood."

"Have I?" said Amias in a choking voice.

But he hardly knew whether the accusation was most bitter or most sweet. He thought he would rather have died than have made this sweet creature restless and unhappy. But, then her unrest, if she felt it, was on *his* account!

"If she was a year or two older, then? if I was willing to wait?" he began; but, oh, what a long time even one year seemed! He paused to consider it.

"Yes," observed Felix; "if she was two years older—that is, if you like to wait two years and then come—you may say what you please to her with my approval, provided nothing whatever is said now, and nothing written."

"I meant to say something decisive before I went," said Amias, under a deep conviction that some other fellow would seize upon his jewel, if she was left free for such a long time. He expressed this alarm to his brother at great length.

Felix was not in the least impressed. "Amabel is not the only young girl in the world, that every man must needs fall in love with her," he remarked.

Amias thereupon, at equal length, argued that she was, as it were, *almost* the only young girl in the world—so much more charming, desirable, sweet, &c., &c. He rather hinted this than said it. Felix would not have found any raptures bearable; and, besides, his raptures were far too deep to be spread forth to the light.

For all reply to this Felix said, "But she never sees anybody."

"Never?" cried Amias.

"Excepting a curate now and then."

Amias admitted to himself that he was not afraid of the curates.

"But in the shooting season, and at Easter, Uncle Sam has a houseful of fellows."

"And she will see them at church," answered Felix. "Yes, she will. Well, you must run that risk." He spoke of the risk with a contempt which Amias thought not warranted.

"And they will see *her*," he continued.

"And ask Sir Samuel who she is," observed Felix. "I should much like to know what answer he will make to that question when it shall be so asked that he must answer."

"And *you* see her," Amias was about to add; but he paused, and yet the flash that came into his eyes, and his sudden checking of himself, were so manifest that Felix noticed them.

"Well?" he inquired.

"It was nothing—at least, nothing that I care to utter."

"Then it must have been what I suspected." He laughed, and his dark cheek mustered colour. "Why, you ridiculous young fellow!" he exclaimed, laying his hand on his brother's shoulder, "are you preposterous enough to be jealous of—*me!*"

"No, I am not; but any other man might be!"

Felix looked at him.

"How can you possibly suppose I could fall in love with one of these dear little girls?" he said, in a tone of strong remonstrance. "I stand almost in the relation of a father to them."

"I should say, on the contrary, that your position toward them makes it quite inevitable that you should fall in love with one of them, unless you already love some one else."

"Besides," said Felix, not directly answering this last thrust, "I should not care to be more nearly allied to John—poor fellow!—if John's they are. And if they are not, I certainly should not care to be allied to nobody knows whom."

Amias winced a little on hearing this, but Felix had not done with him.

"However, it is not impossible that you may be right," he continued, not without a touch of bitterness. "It may make you feel more at ease to learn that I have been *these many years* attached to some one else."

No more jealousy was possible now, but also no more rebellion. Felix was master of the situation.

"And so," he said, as he rose, "if you wish this time two years to see Amabel, you will come here again; and in the meantime I consider you are bound in honour to leave her absolutely alone, and not make her an offer till she is eighteen."

He looked at Amias, who had to answer, "I consent."

And just as he said it, Amabel and Delia came down the garden, as if on purpose to show him how hard this newly vowed consent was to be. He did not say a word, but his eyes dwelt on Amabel's face. There was a tender sadness on it—a certain, almost forlorn expression. We understand people so well when we love them. Amias felt that this fair young creature had been so waited on, so attended to, so watched and loved by her nurse, that, this tendance and this fencing in from loneness withdrawn, she was looking about her, as if she felt herself pushed out into some colder world, and knew not how to order herself in it. He remembered the flattery of observance with which "Mamsey's" eyes had dwelt on her young lady. Sometimes he had thought that his eyes, waiting on her, had not been unmarked either. But she was not thinking of him now.

"Is there any letter, Coz, from Mrs. Snaith?" she asked.

"No, my dear—none."

"What do you think she means, Coz? It cannot be that she is ill?"

"No, my dear; I feel confident that she is not ill."

"But have you any idea what it all means?"

A certain something passed over the face of Felix then, which Amias noticed as well as Amabel.

"You have, Coz?" she said.

"I have no *definite* idea," answered Felix. "Even if I had, I could not tell it to you."

Amias noticed that he pitied the two girls in this withdrawal of their faithful maid and old nurse, far more than he did himself in the loss of an excellent domestic.

All this time the girls had been standing before the two brothers, who were seated; but now Delia made herself room beside Felix, and Amias, starting up, moved to Amabel to take his place; so now Felix was sitting between the two girls, and Amias was looking at the group. That Felix remembered just then what had so lately passed between him and his brother was evident, for as the two girls seemed to lean towards him for comfort and support, his dark face again took on a hint of colour, his eyes flashed as if with involuntary amusement, and he even looked a little embarrassed.

Foolish Amias! how could he have put such a thought into his brother's head?.

But here was Aunt Sarah coming also, her carrot-coloured curls flying, and her pink morning wrapper jauntily fastened up with a silver clasp.

It was rather a narrow gravel walk that led to the house, and the girls went in to breakfast down it, pressing their skirts to them lest the dewy bending flowers should wet them. Sarah followed next, then Felix, and lastly Amias, which arrangement he naturally felt to be very disagreeable.

"Should he read to them that morning?"

he inquired of the girls after breakfast, in the presence of Felix.

"No, they had no time, thanks; they were going to be extremely busy."

Amias sighed, and after breakfast disconsolately wandered about indoors, or read the various newspapers that he always had sent to him wherever he was. At last, about eleven o'clock, he saw the two girls sitting together under the walnut trees, shelling peas for the early dinner. He joined them. Jolliffe was very busy, they said, and they had asked her what they could do to help, now dear Mamsey was gone. So she had asked them to gather some fruit and the peas, and then to shell them.

"You might have let me help!" exclaimed Amias.

"Coz never helps at that kind of thing," said Delia, as if this was an exhaustive answer.

"Fancy Coz shelling peas!" said Amabel.

Dick was gone; he had departed the previous evening to stay two days with a boy-friend.

"Dick will be back to-morrow," observed Delia, "and then we can make him help." There was no emphasis on the word "make;" it only expressed a familiar truth in simple language.

"Dick is a lucky dog," said Amias, forgetting himself: "he will have another three weeks here before he goes back to school." He spoke with such bitter regret in his voice that the girls both looked at him.

"Don't you like going away?" asked Delia composedly.

Here he remembered his promise. "Not particularly," he said.

"Then why don't you stay?" she inquired. "I'm sure Coz would be very glad—and so should we," she added, and stooped to seize another handful of pods with her dimpled fingers. Amabel had a more slender hand; she held it out just then, half full of peas, and as they ran out into the dish he noticed a handsome pearl ring. He had observed it before, with certain misgivings. How could he possibly go away with any doubt as to the meaning or history of that ring? There had been neither assent nor dissent in her face when Delia had said "so should we;" she had not looked up at him.

His thought was urgent for utterance, but it would have been contrary to his promise to ask such a question as he would have liked to do. He said, "That ring runs a risk of being stained with the peas."

"Does it?" exclaimed Amabel hastily; and she drew it off, colouring with anxiety, as he thought, while she looked at it.

"And pearls, you know, will not bear soap and water," he continued.

"It's all right," said Delia; "I saw you," she continued, in a rallying tone, to her sister. "I saw you take off your glove in the ribbon-shop the other day, and let your hand hang out over the ribbon-box—pretending to choose; I saw you stick your finger out, fastening your cuff, the other day on the pier, that those two lieutenants might see it. Dear creature! And she promised to give me one too," continued Delia, with a sigh.

"*She* promised!" exclaimed Amias, with involuntary delight. "Oh, it was a lady who gave it, then?"

"It was dear Mamsey," said Amabel, taking up the ring and putting it gently to her cheek, and then to her lips. "She saved out of her wages for three years and bought me this. It has some of her hair in it. And I asked her to let her name be engraved on the inside, and she had it done; but only her Christian name, you see."

She let Amias receive the ring in his hand. He wished he might have kissed it too, but he only looked at it and saw the name, "Hannah."

Amabel was beautifully shy now. She blushed, because she felt that Amias would know she had been glad to explain to him about this gift of a ring; but just as he, finding no pretext for holding it longer, was stretching out his hand to return it, Aunt Sarah came out again, meddling old woman! He thought she looked inquisitive, and perhaps Amabel thought so too, for she shelled the peas with great diligence for a few minutes more, and then the task was finished. One of the girls carried in the peas, the other the basket of pods, and Sarah and Amias were left alone together.

Amias did not see Amabel again till the early dinner, and very soon after that Sir Samuel appeared. He had brought two ponies, and proposed to take both the girls out for a ride.

Circumstances were helping Amias to keep his promise. The girls considered it a great treat to go out riding with Sir Samuel.

While they were gone up-stairs to put on their habits, Mrs. Snaith's departure was mentioned by Sarah. She wished very much to know what she might have confided to the old man; whether it was through her, or through John himself before his death, that these girls were known by him to be his grand-daughters. That he did know it she had no doubt, else why was he so fond of them?

"Not gone for long, I suppose?" he said coolly.

"Yes, gone for good," she replied.

"Where is she gone, then?" he inquired sharply.

"That we cannot tell, uncle. You can see the telegram."

Sir Samuel turned the telegram about, read it with earnestness, and almost, as it seemed to Sarah, with consternation.

"It does not signify, of course?" said Sarah, in a questioning tone.

"What does not signify?" he replied. Having scrutinised the telegram thoroughly, he was now folding it up, and presently he put it in his purse, and stood for some minutes so lost in thought, that when the girls came in ready for their ride he did not notice them.

"Well, good-bye, my dear," he said at last to his niece Sarah. "I cannot have you to luncheon to-morrow, though I said I would. I am going out."

CHAPTER XXVI.

AMIAS was exceedingly vexed when, about two hours after this, Sir Samuel rode up to the rectory door alone.

He had been pacing about on the lawn, and cogitating over his chance of lifting Amabel down from her pony.

Sir Samuel laughed when he saw him. It was a good-natured laugh, but not altogether devoid of a little harmless malice. Amias had come up to him to ask what he had done with the girls, but this laugh awoke in him an uneasy suspicion that the "grandfather" might have observed his devotion, might have other views for Amabel—might not approve.

"Ah, Mr. Lecturer," said Sir Samuel, and laughed again. "You were not aware, I suppose, that I was among your auditors the other day when you were holding forth on the common?"

Amias felt rather foolish; wondered whether he had been extravagant in any of his assertions. He was relieved to find what the laugh meant, but he longed for some opening for asking about Amabel.

"I did not mind it," continued the old man, naturally feeling that Amias would rather he had not heard that particular speech. "You are a born orator, my lad.

Tom—Tom always used to stutter so when he tried to speak. I shall never make anything of Tom. I should like very well to see you in the House, where you would have matters worth mention to spend your eloquence on. Should you like it? Eh?"

"Very much, uncle; but there is no chance of such a thing for a long time to come."

"You had no notion that your old uncle was present, had you?"

"Of course not," exclaimed Amias, quite shocked.

"And if I am not mistaken, there was no personal feeling in your invectives—none of them were directed specially against me?"

He touched the young man's shoulder with his riding-whip so gently, that it was almost like a caress; he spoke as kindly as a father might have done.

"How should I have any personal feeling against you, uncle?" exclaimed Amias. "I always think of you as the kindest person I know. What do you take me for?"

"You young fanatic," said Sir Samuel, laughing, "do you really think it your duty to keep out of my way?"

"No!" exclaimed Amias, with genuine astonishment.

"Then why do you never come near me when I am in London?"

Amias here felt extremely ashamed of himself, for the whole conversation was such a confession of liking on the part of the old man, and he felt that on his part nothing had signified but that he should know why Amabel did not appear. It was hard on the old uncle. It was a shame!

That last question really made him able to think of the matter under discussion, and at the same moment came a flash of recollection that this was *her* grandfather who was so kindly disposed towards him.

"You quite astonish me, uncle," he said. "If you invited me to come to your house in London, I should be truly pleased, but——" Here he paused.

"'But you never do,' was what you were going to add, wasn't it?" said Sir Samuel. "That is true. Well, I thought, if I did, you might be afraid I should tempt you to join me again."

"I never could have had such an idea," exclaimed Amias, very much surprised.

"Well then, come and see me whenever you have nothing better to do."

"I will, uncle," said Amias, with cordial earnestness.

"For," continued the old man, "I feel sometimes a great wish to have some of my own people about me." ("He never shows any care to have Felix about him," thought Amias.) "Tom has been away so long."

"He'll be home soon for his long leave," observed Amias consolingly.

"But he'll go to his wife's people," said the old man. "I shall see very little of him. His wife's people are everything to him. And since I lost John—— You don't remember John very well, do you?"

"I was almost a child when he went abroad," said Amias, faltering a little over those last words. He remembered no good of John, of course. "I can recall his face sometimes," he added.

"Ah! he was a fine fellow—a dear fellow. He would have come home long before this and been my companion," said the father. "Tom's a good fellow too, only he's taken up with other things. He has been very long away, and you know the proverb says, 'Better is a neighbour that is near, than a brother afar off.' That son John of mine—he is very far off, though always in my thoughts."

"Why, what a strange quotation, and what a confused speech!" thought Amias; "but he never can bear to speak of John." Then, intending to console, he said, "But I am more than a mere neighbour, uncle, you know. I am a blood relation, and of course I cannot help feeling an affection for you—*and for Amabel's grandfather*," was the addition in his mind. It gave a natural and pleasant earnestness to his tone, which was as cordial as his feeling.

Sir Samuel smiled, and was manifestly pleased. "The young," he said, "never return the affection of the old, but they give them what they can, my boy. God bless them! they give them what they can."

Amias could not be so base as to pretend for a moment that he had any such degree of regard toward Sir Samuel as the old man had made evident toward himself; he felt at that moment that he had always been aware there was, according to the proverb, a "good deal of love lost" between them, and that now he must cultivate some return. Amabel would make this easy, and now he ventured to say, "Where's Amabel, uncle, and where's Delia?"

"I left them at the Hall.—Oh! here you are, nephew parson. I came to find you and your aunt Sarah. I left the girls at the Hall; they are going to dine with me, and I'll send them home at night in the carriage, unless you can spare them for a few days. In fact, I have been thinking that you might be glad, as Mrs. Snaith is gone, if I took them in."

Amias was desperately disappointed, but not a word could be said by him, and Sarah arranged the matter, and sent off her maid in charge of the various things that they would want.

"Come and dine with me to-morrow, Amias," said Sir Samuel as he rode off; and this, at least, was a consolation.

"I wonder whether it would make any difference to his liking for me," thought Amias, "if he knew that I loved his favourite grand-daughter?" He revolved this in his mind till the evening, when Dick came home, and was extremely sulky when he found that the girls were out; very angry with them, too, for accepting the invitation, and much inclined to be uncivil to his aunt Sarah, when she enlarged on the convenience of the plan.

"It's a disgusting sell!" quoth Dick. "What is a fellow to do loafing about the place by himself?"

"In my opinion," said Aunt Sarah—"yes! in my opinion—a 'fellow' could not do better than get some cow-parsley to feed the rabbits."

"I shall feed Delia's rabbits," replied the schoolboy; "but as to Amabel's, she should not have left them. She is old enough to know better."

"Well, you may leave Amabel's to me, then," said Amias, with what was meant to be a gracious air, but which had far too much eagerness, and too much the manner of one seeking for a privilege.

And what a privilege it was! What interesting rabbits those were! All the information that Dick volunteered about them was so delightful: "Delia 'swapped' that old doe with Amabel for two bullfinches; the bullfinches fought and killed one another, and then Delia said she ought to have the doe back again, but Amabel wouldn't give it to her."

"And very right too," exclaimed Amias.

"But Amabel generally gets the worst of it in all her bargains with Delia," observed Dick. "Delia's such a shrewd little puss, she can take anybody in."

"Gets the better of Amabel, does she?"

"Yes; Amabel's rather *soft*. However, they both cried like anything when a third of the bullfinches picked his brother's eyes out. That's the only thing I don't like

about girls—they're so tender-hearted. Felix took the blind bullfinch away, and did for him out of their sight."

Amias inspected all the pets and helped to feed them, waiting on chance for a word about Amabel; then he went and found his brother Felix.

Felix was up in the church-tower. The parish clock was unconscionably slow. Felix was having it put right, and agreeing with the man who had regulated it to let a good many of the cottagers know of the change. He never had any alterations made during working hours, or either the farmers or the labourers would have felt themselves aggrieved.

Amias looked out upon the chimneys of the rectory house, and at the long white road in the park that led up to the Hall. Then the two brothers got on to a convenient little platform on the roof and enjoyed the cool air, for it was a hot evening.

"I have been thinking, old fellow," said Amias, "about some of the things you said this morning of Uncle Sam."

Felix had actually forgotten for the moment the sentence that he was alluding to.

"The fact is," continued Amias, "I always knew that he liked me."

"Of course," said Felix; "he never sees me without asking after you. I believe he likes you almost as well as he does Tom."

"Well, and I like him well enough."

"So I suppose. If I had to drive bargains with him, I should not like him; as it is, we get on excellently well. I should think he will take the girls away when they are grown up."

"I have been thinking, Felix, if it really would not annoy you at all, I should like to do as you said this morning. I was either to abide by your wishes, you know"—he said this half reproachfully, for Felix did not seem quite to understand him—"or you said I might consult him about Amabel. I think I chose amiss. I wish you would consider that the matter has yet to be decided."

"Well?" said Felix.

"Of course I shall always feel that you have been everything to the girls. If I ever win Amabel, I shall feel deeply grateful to you; in fact, I do now."

"And you want to lay the matter before old Sam instead?"

"Yes."

"You are bold."

"Am I, Felix? Well, I shall ask for nothing but his consent. He hates laying money down. In my case he will know, for

I shall tell him, that I expect none, and in fact——"

"In what should have been the sequel to those last words lies the gist of the matter; and if he is to give his beautiful grandchild nothing, she ought not to marry a man of very moderate means."

"Very true, Felix; but I tell you I love her, and the more doubt there is as to his consent, the more I feel urged to speak. Besides, he has asked me to come and see him in London, and expressed great regard for me. I must not go and see him and make myself as agreeable as I can, and all the time feel that I am doing it not for his sake but for hers."

"You are aware that I know nothing about her parentage?"

"Know nothing?" repeated Amias.

"I conjecture a good deal, but I *know* nothing. As I said this morning, I take for granted that these are John's children, and that is all."

"Yes, Felix, I am aware of the fact. It makes no difference to me."

"If old Sam knows anything more, it sometimes occurs to me that it cannot be agreeable, or why should he keep it to himself?"

"I am not such a fool as to dislike the notion of the Dissenting minister's daughter."

"Of course not. Who is?"

"I have always known that there was some sort of doubt as to their parentage."

"Some sort of doubt. That exactly expresses the matter; and occasionally it occurs to me that this doubt is less a disadvantage to them than the truth would be. Therefore I never probe it; I ask Uncle Sam no questions."

"I am astonished that the girls never ask any."

. "They are good and pure-minded little girls, and know little of disgrace and nothing of sorrow. No one, by talking of either parents, has excited any imaginary love or fancied regrets. They do not forbear to question, but simply no questions occur to them."

"Old Sam always treats Amabel as his grand-daughter."

"And such I am persuaded she is. But that does not prove that she has a right to his name."

. "She shall have a right to it, though," cried Amias, "if she will only take it. But you used always to feel sure that John had married Fanny. What has made you doubtful?"

"Nothing but time. In course of time I feel that this almost must have come out. What motive could her family have for concealing it?"

"She might have run away with him."

"Yes, poor little fool, she might," said Felix with a sigh, "and have concealed herself from them; but her marriage certificate in such a case could assuredly have been found, if old Sam had set to work to do it."

"Why, you seem to have almost taken for granted now that everything was as I most wish it might not have been."

"No; it would have cost a good deal of money to investigate the matter. I believe he also had his doubts—chose to take the children as they were, and also to save his money, hoping for the best."

"Or John might have married somebody else?"

"Even so."

"Mrs. Snaith gave over their little fortunes to you, did she not?"

"Yes, and told me nothing."

"I am very sorry she is gone."

While Felix and Amias, as evening drew on, sat looking over the harvest fields, and across to the somewhat over-wooded park, and the long, quiet mere or pool where Amias had chased the white owl and her chicken, Sir Samuel watched the two girls as he sat over his claret and they flitted about in the flower-garden, and his regret was the very echo of his nephews'. He thought bitterly of Mrs. Snaith. "I am sorry she is gone," he also repeated; revolved in his mind how to find her, and regretted the whole course of his own conduct for the last twelve years.

Felix had done him no wrong: it was mainly because he grudged the expense, that he had made no investigations. The love of money almost always increases with age, and it has no relation whatever to the uses its possessor may be supposed to intend it for.

Money accumulated with Sir Samuel every year. His eldest son was dead. His son John was dead also. His son Tom was as saving as himself. He had more sense for his only remaining son than for himself. He sent a very handsome sum to his daughter-in-law, and proposed that Tom should buy her some jewels, as they were in the part of the world where these are finest; also a costly Indian shawl or so. Tom persuaded her, who was nothing loath, to save this also. Sir Samuel began to feel disturbed; he himself always kept a handsome

fashion? I shall
now have to bribe
her to appear, and buy
the information she pos-
sesses at whatever sum she
chooses to ask for it. I am
sorry. I would do differently
if my time came over again."

CHAPTER XXVII.

SIR SAMUEL went for a long drive
the next morning, and did not take
Amabel and Delia with him. He went
to a hotel in a town about twelve miles off,
and there met a man from a " private inquiry
office,"—a man whom he had sent for from
London.

He wanted to have a certain woman
found for him. He would give a handsome
sum to those who could put her in communication with him; and they might offer
any sum that was necessary to induce her
to appear.

He began, of course, by giving her a wrong
name.

Her name was Hannah Snaith ; she was
a widow. She was a nurse when first he
met with her, and after that she had lived
nearly twelve years as an upper servant in
the family of his nephew, the Rev. Felix de
Berenger. She left clandestinely, and tele-

table, a proper stable, a due staff of servants, &c. He loved money, but he was
not a miser, and he began to fear that Tom
was.

"And I am saving all this for him, and
neglecting the claims of my dear John's
children. Ah, he was no miser," thought
the old man. " But then, as long as that
woman stayed, what was the good of setting
expensive investigations on foot, which would
have ended in my having to make the darlings a handsome allowance ?"

Sir Samuel never admitted the least doubt
on that head. " I could not have let Felix
keep them for so small a sum, when once
I had *proved* that they were my dear John's
daughters. But I am sorry. How could I
guess that woman would run off in such

graphed to the family many hours after her departure, to say that they need not expect to see her again.

"Did she leave her place through any fault?"

He did not think so.

"Had she left anything behind her—books, clothes, letters?"

That he did not know.

"Well, Sir Samuel, if you should hear that a *friend* of Mrs. Snaith's is making inquiries about her in the village and at the rectory, you will not be uneasy. Anything that I gather up you will learn of me by letter from a distance, and nobody hereabouts will know that you had anything to do with my inquiries."

Sir Samuel then had his luncheon and drove home again; but before he reached his gates, a man, travelling by railroad, walked down the village and called at the back-door of the rectory.

Mrs. Jolliffe opened it, and he asked for Mrs. Snaith's address.

Mrs. Jolliffe was sorry she could not give it. "Was he a friend of Mrs. Snaith's?"

"Yes, he was very much her friend. He wanted to tell her of something to her advantage. In fact, if he was not mistaken, an advertisement would come out in the *Daily Telegraph* the next day, setting forth that if Hannah Snaith, lately in the service of the Rev. F. de Berenger, would apply to ——, and certain friends named in the advertisement, she would hear of something to her advantage."

Mrs. Jolliffe was deeply interested. "If you'd put it in an Ipswich paper, now," she observed, "instead of a London one, 'twould be more likely to meet her eye."

"You think so?"

"Yes, because she always took an Ipswich paper."

Here was a valuable clue. Mrs. Jolliffe would by no means have given it, if she had known that this man wanted to find Mrs. Snaith, whether she would or not.

The man felt his way. "Ah, true, it would have been better. An Ipswich paper? Which was it, I wonder? There are mostly two, one on each side." He seemed to be questioning more with himself than with Mrs. Jolliffe. "When there's a nice little sum of money lying ready for her, it seems hard she should miss it, just for the sake of not knowing."

Mrs. Jolliffe asked him in; and out of a drawer in the adjoining room forthwith produced several copies of the *Suffolk Chronicle*.

"She was a widow?"

Mrs. Jolliffe's manner became cold and rather stiff. "She was very respectable; I should judge she was a widow. But if you are an old friend, I should judge you should know."

"Did she leave anything behind her—clothes, letters, books, or what not?"

"Yes, everything she had."

"Could you let me see them?"

"Certainly not, sir, unless Mr. de Berenger knew of it."

"Oh, I wouldn't think of putting you to the inconvenience of asking him."

"You can keep the old newspapers, sir, if you like. Do you think the money is coming to her from Australia?"

"Why should it?"

"Well, to be sure, she never said she had friends out there; but, then, she was a close woman—wonderfully close."

"Well,"—taking out a pencil—"I shall advertise for her in the Ipswich papers, as you think she came from those parts."

"I never said a word of the sort, sir."

"But if her letters chiefly came from there?"

"If you'll believe me, sir," said Mrs. Jolliffe, "she never had a letter from year's end to year's end."

"It's usual to put in the maiden name as well, in an advertisement of that sort. Let me see—how did she spell it?"

"I thought you said you was an old friend," said Mrs. Jolliffe; "and you seem to know less about her than I do. Well, I don't rightly remember how she spelt it."

The man looked angry. "I shouldn't have thought you would have stood in the light of your friend," he said; but he did not like to ask what the name was.

Now, Mrs. Jolliffe was not very great at her spelling, but, feeling herself reproved, she found a way out of her difficulty. "I have no call that I see to go over every letter of it to you," she observed; "if I just tell you it was Goodrich, you may write it down yourself and make the best you can of it."

Having said this, she immediately felt angry with herself, remembering afresh that it was odd this "old friend" should not know more concerning Mrs. Snaith.

"Then you think you cannot help me any further?" said the man blandly, but by no means intending to go.

"I don't see but what you can find any woman by as much as I have told," said Mrs. Jolliffe, "if she wants to be found."

"And why should she not want to be found?"

"How should I know? I never heard a word breathed to her disadvantage," said Mrs. Jolliffe shortly. "I suppose you'll say next that I told you she wanted to hide herself."

After this nothing prospered with the visitor. He soon put Mrs. Jolliffe into a good temper again, and induced her to talk of Mrs. Snaith, but she either could not or would not say any one thing that was of the least use to him.

He went away, knowing, through Mrs. Jolliffe, no more than this of Mrs. Snaith: that her maiden name was Goodrich, that she had no correspondence even with her nearest relatives, and that she took in a newspaper called the *Suffolk Chronicle.*

The copies of this paper which had been presented to him, had all arrived during the time that Mrs. Snaith had been at the seaside. After anxious scrutiny the man decided that there was nothing in them that could help him, and he left the neighbourhood for the present.

Sarah de Berenger was to dine with the old baronet that evening, as well as Amias. She entertained him as they drove over with remarks on the sums of money that Felix gave away in his parish. "I suppose he will never leave off while I live."

Amias smiled.

"Of course I shall *tie it up,*" she continued.

"Tie what up, aunt?" said Amias, purposely not understanding her.

"Why, the property, of course. Felix is no man of business. Yes! dear fellow, he must let my house; and I shall take care to leave all proper directions for his guidance in my will."

"Do, when you *make* it, aunt! I don't believe you ever have made one yet," said Amias, smiling.

"What!" exclaimed Sarah. "Never? What can you be thinking of?"

"You best know whether what I thought was correct," answered Amias. "And it is no business of mine."

"I cannot imagine what put such an idea in your head—yes!"

"Oh, I always think so when people talk often of their wills," said Amias. "Why, there are the two girls walking in the park, when it's just dinner-time."

"And why not?" answered Sarah. "There is a dinner party to-night, and of course they cannot be present; they are not *out.*"

So this was the occasion that he had pictured to himself in such glowing colours. A family party of five. Sir Samuel drawing out the two girls and delighting in their girlish talk—in Delia's little affectionate audacities, and Amabel's sweet modesty. He should sit and look on, and then afterwards, when they retired in his aunt Sarah's wake, would come the great opportunity. He should be left alone with Amabel's grandfather, and should ask leave to make himself agreeable to this fairest creature. And she was not *out*—not to sit at the dinner-table. Oh, what should he do? How ridiculous his request would appear!

Sarah was placed at the head of the table, and a good many guests were present, all of whom seemed to Amias to be more or less stupid.

He was not to see Amabel, and nothing that Felix had said produced such an effect on him as this proof of what the world thought concerning his sweet little school-girl. But she would be in the drawing-room after dinner. Yes, there she was, she and Delia, in white muslin frocks and blue sashes; she certainly did look rather young, among the young lady guests.

She and Delia were told to play a duet, and she was decidedly shy about it.

"Poor Sir Samuel!" murmured one stately dame to another.

The answer floated back to her so softly that Amias wondered it could reach him, though he alone of the guests was standing near. "Lovely creatures! I think he has made up his mind. He *will* introduce them, you'll see."

Amias heard this, and understood all that it implied, with an almost unbearable pang. The deep disadvantage so slightly hinted at weighed his spirits down. Did every one take it for granted, then? He had thought, when he thought about it, that their retired bringing up had kept them out of all unkindly observation; he was bitterly angry with their grandfather for the moment. Here they were for the first time, and two women of rank, belonging to the chief families in the county, were familiarly hinting at their supposed position, as if everybody knew all about it.

For the first time in his life a kind of faintness and giddiness oppressed Amias, that made him long for air. He stood perfectly still for two or three minutes, gathering strength and steadiness to move; then, just as he observed that his old uncle's attention was attracted to him, he turned toward the nearest window and got out into the flower-garden. He walked quickly through it, amazed to find that he was denouncing his uncle, and those ladies, and John de Berenger, and his aunt Sarah aloud; that his passion was quite beyond his own control, and yet that he was trembling all over, even to the lips, so that the angry words, that came thick and fast, were so confused that he hardly knew them, any more than he did the husky voice, for his own.

He got over that stage of feeling as he walked vehemently on. This had been a stunning blow. And yet what was it more than Felix had hinted at the previous evening? Oh, it was this more—that then they had seemed to have the subject all to themselves, as if it was or might have been sacred from all other observation, and at least more likely than not to yield comfort on investigation.

And now this painful thing had met with him in a drawing-room, so gently, so dispassionately uttered, that it seemed to admit of no denial.

Whether truth or fiction, it was a familiar opinion. Lady Lucy did not doubt that Lady Ann would understand her allusion. Lady Ann saw nothing dubious in the situation. As Sir Samuel was silent, was it not manifest that there was nothing to say? Not that she thought so just then; the neighbourhood had settled the matter years ago.

So much for letting things drift. He almost put himself in a passion again as he thought this over, and urged his way along the straightest drive in the park, walking at the top of his speed as if to get away from it. And how should he get away? He could not bear to think she should ever know what was said. He would emigrate with his darling; he would expatriate himself, that no disadvantage might ever attach to her or to their children. But what if she should find it out, and the thought should distress and sully her maiden heart?

How powerless he was! What should he do? He had walked beyond the confines of the park before he came to himself. His passionate emotion was over. He wondered at them all, at their inconceivable inertness and obtuseness. Nothing had been said, as was evident, and no awkward questions were ever asked; but these circumstances ought alone to have been enough to show what was felt.

His heart bled. It would be better for him to give up all hope. Sir Samuel was no fool; he did know, and know the worst.

He got back to the same open window that he had left, just as the last carriage full of guests drove off in the mild summer moonlight. Sir Samuel met him, seemed to have been waiting for him.

Servants were in the room, putting out the lights in the chandeliers. One preceded them into Sir Samuel's own study, carrying a lamp. Amias sank into a chair, and the moment they were alone, "What, in the name of Heaven, is the matter, Amias? You staggered out of the room!" exclaimed Sir Samuel. "A walk at this time of night, and such a walk—and now you look—— What is it, my dear fellow?"

There was alarm and there was wonder in the voice.

"You are ill; you want some wine."

"No, I don't," said Amias. "Let me alone, uncle."

There was a knock at the door, and Sarah de Berenger came in. Both she and Amias were to sleep that night at the Hall. Sarah said she wanted some letter-paper; the note-paper in her bed-room was not large enough for her purpose. Amias was sitting listlessly, with hands in his pockets, pale, and his great brown eyes wider open than usual; but the shaded lamp made these circumstances less evident, or Sarah's mind was full of other things, for she scarcely noticed his presence. She took a few sheets of paper and withdrew to her own room, and then and there she made her will for the first and only time.

Amias put his hand to his throat; his lips were dry and parched.

"What is the matter?" asked the old man, with sympathetic gentleness.

"Matter!" repeated Amias. "Matter, uncle! You have let me love Amabel and never told me."

Sir Samuel gazed at him.

"How could you be so cruel!" he continued, in a husky voice. "Not that it makes any difference. I would, I must have loved her just the same, but you might have given me warning; I should have been prepared." He spread out his hands before him, as if to express his helplessness.

Sir Samuel thought of his own morning interview at the hotel with confused alarm. Could the man possibly have come back and told Amias anything?

He brought his nephew a glass of water from a carafe which was standing on the table, and gave it to him with a trembling hand. "What have you heard?" he muttered.

Amias mastered himself and told it.

Then Sir Samuel put himself into just such a passion as Amias had done, and reddened to the roots of his white hair. He too denounced everybody he could think of, but it seemed to Amias mere bluster; the conviction had so thoroughly forced itself on him during his walk, that his uncle must have investigated everything.

"Only tell me what I have to hear at once," he said, and was amazed at himself when he heard a sound of sobbing, which he scarcely knew to be his own, till he felt the hot tears splashing on his hands.

"I have nothing certain to tell, Amias, my boy," said the old uncle, almost piteously.

"What, all your investigations have been fruitless?"

"No, Amias—no; but till this morning (there seemed no occasion) I never made any."

"Then it was true what Felix said!" exclaimed Amias, with scathing scorn. "You sat down in presence of this doubt, and grudged the money to be spent on giving a name to your own grand-daughter." He was choked here with both emotion and passion, but astonishment enabled him to subdue the one and swallow the other, when the old man took out his handkerchief and wept quietly, sitting opposite to him, and finding for some moments not a word of answer.

"It's true, Amias," he said at last, humbly and despondingly. "I don't understand how it was, but I did let things drift; only you must remember I might have solved the doubt the wrong way. I might——"

This seemed to Amias now so more than likely, that it brought him to reason again.

"Uncle, I beg your pardon," he sighed out, for it distressed him to see the old man so utterly subdued. "I had no right to be so violent. The wrong you have done is not against me, but against them, and against yourself. How could you know—sweet creature!—that I loved her?"

"And it will be a great blow to my dear little girl if she hears this opinion. She is a very modest girl, and very religious."

"Yes, I know."

"She will be greatly shocked if she hears that her mother was a disgrace to her. But I hope for the best. She is almost a child. There is ample time for the uttermost to be done that can be done, Amias, before you can come forward; and though you have confided your love to me, I hold you to nothing, considering the circumstances."

"I meant to ask you for her," said Amias; "and hoped to show you that, though she was somewhat above me, I had reasonable hope of being able to maintain her in comfort by the time she was old enough to bless me with her hand. But if she is a poor little waif, that a man may take and thank no father, but only God, for her, I desire no more of you than that you take her and her sister quite away from this neighbourhood, and put them to a good school, so that all knowledge that would be bitterness to them is kept far away. In the meantime, I shall try to get something to do abroad, in Canada, or—well, I hardly know where I can go that ill news may not reach her. She may boast of her family, and bring out the truth, but I'll do my best."

"It's not the time to say that I should be well pleased, if all proves right, to give her to you——" began Sir Samuel.

"Yes, it is, uncle," interrupted Amias. "I feel more glad of the regard that I know you feel for me, than I ever did before. I know very well that you are the only human being that can truly sympathize with me now."

"And if there's anything in reason, or not in reason, that I can settle on her, to make it up to you——" and then he paused, suddenly remembering the affair of the necklace.

"I don't want anything," said Amias pointedly. "Spend her fortune in finding me a good mother for her."

Extraordinary as it may seem, this speech actually raised the old man's spirits. Though he knew that some of his descendants must have his money, having to settle anything, even on his favourite Amabel, during his lifetime, he could not contemplate without a pang. He would have done it; but to be told it was not needed, was balm.

Amias sat a few minutes, getting the mastery over himself and recovering his manhood; but the side issue raised about the money had a strange attraction for the poor old man.

"She has a trifle of her own already," he said; "and people are never the worse for beginning on small means."

"And she has never been accustomed to luxury. Then you have begun some investigations? What are they?" asked Amias.

Sir Samuel told him. But Amias wanted a mother, not a nurse. He wanted an unimpeachable marriage register, and proposed that such a sum should be offered as would have set every parish clerk in the three kingdoms searching or forging; then he wearily gave it up, remembering that, if it brought nothing else, it would bring the most undesired publicity.

It was very late when the old great-uncle and Amias went, each his way, to his own apartment. Sir Samuel spent a miserable night, reviewing his own past conduct, wondering at himself, and not at all aware that the instinct of avoiding all outlay of money was so strong in him, that if parallel circumstances should occur, he would do the like thing again, in spite of this warning. Amias had exhausted himself, as much by exertion as by expression, and he slept profoundly.

He was just about to go down to breakfast the next morning, when his aunt's maid knocked at his door, and said Miss de Berenger begged that he would go first to a little morning-room that she always had the use of when she was at the Hall.

He found his aunt there, and Sir Samuel.

"Yes," said Sarah, looking very much flustered, and not a little important, "I wanted you to witness the signature of this document for me, Amias — in short, my will."

Sarah's will was such a joke in the family, that, in spite of their discussion the night before, Sir Samuel and Amias exchanged amused glances on hearing this.

She tossed back her curls. "Yes, and Peach "—Peach was her old maid—" Peach shall be the other witness."

So then, with as many flourishes and as much fuss as could be got out of the occasion, the document was duly signed and witnessed.

"I deliver this," said Sarah, with awful emphasis, "as my act and deed."

Peach, as nobody else spoke, murmured, "Very well, ma'am."

Then the document was sealed up in a large envelope by Sir Samuel, who carried it down-stairs. Sarah, Amias, and Peach followed. The latter seemed to think that she had not done with it yet. Sir Samuel opened an iron safe, and put in the document. Peach looked on, and when she saw it lying in state among several other documents, on a little iron shelf, she appeared satisfied, and, curtseying, withdrew.

Sarah followed, to tell her on no account to mention what had happened.

"This time," said Sir Samuel, "she can have left nothing to you, Amias, my boy. I am sorry. How many wills does this make, I wonder?"

"One," answered Amias decidedly. "And I think she has left her property to Felix;

she intimated to me yesterday that she should."

"Well, so long as she leaves it to one of you, I do not care; but, last week, she talked of building a fine new spire for D—— minster."

CHAPTER XXVIII.

AFTER breakfast that morning the two girls were sent out for a ride, under charge of an old coachman, and Sarah was fetched into Sir Samuel's own peculiar den, which he called his study, that she might tell him, in the presence of Amias, all she could remember as to her first finding of Amabel and Delia. To describe her delight when she found that there was a love-story going on under her very eyes, and to describe the trouble she gave, both to the old man and the young man, would be needlessly to try the patience of any other man, or woman either. She yielded up her testimony with so much besides, she doubled back on what she had told with so many confusing comments, she took so much for granted, and she was so positive in all her conclusions, that it was not till Amias took a large sheet of paper, and, sifting out the bare facts, wrote them down, that even Sir Samuel knew on what a slender foundation he had taken for granted that Amabel and Delia were his grand-daughters. But Sarah, though to the last degree romantic and unpractical, had an accurate memory, and was not untruthful. She was vexed, even to the point of shedding tears, when Amias, having done questioning her, asked Sir Samuel if he would stand an examination also; and she could not help seeing that Amias was yet more anxious to prove that the children were no relation at all to her, than she had ever been to show the contrary.

Sir Samuel was very direct and straightforward.

Amias read over his own selections from the evidence, and his countenance cleared.

"The matter seems to stand thus," he said. "Aunt Sarah saw two little girls at the seaside, forty miles from her home. Their name was De Berenger. She asked if they were John's children; their nurse declared that they were not—that they were no relation whatever to our family. The nurse took them away. Two years after this Aunt Sarah saw them again, with the same nurse, who told the same story. Aunt Sarah after this wrote and urged the nurse to bring them here. The nurse did so; but she told Jolliffe she came in order to get away from scarlet-fever, which was in a village where she had been living with them. She always said she had the sole charge of them.. Aunt Sarah told Uncle Samuel of them, and he went to see them. The nurse declared to him also that they were not related to him, and that he owed them no kindness at all. She professed not to have heard of such a person as Mr. John de Berenger; but during the same interview she proposed to get a letter forwarded to him, and did it. Three years after this she gave over to Felix the money that had been intrusted to her for their maintenance, and he became their guardian. The nurse declared that the children were born in wedlock, and that she could easily prove it if she pleased.—" Now," said Amias, after reading aloud, "have you, uncle, or have you, aunt, anything to add to this?"

Sir Samuel said "No." Miss de Berenger added a good many opinions and sentiments, and also some reproaches to Amias.

"But have you any fact to add?" he persisted.

"Yes, the fact that Felix believes they are John's children."

"But you made him think so, aunt. And why are these sweet and lovely creatures to have their status in society taken from them, and their honest descent called in question, that you may indulge a romantic fancy, after dragging them here that their little fortunes might help to educate Dick, and eke out our housekeeping?"

"That is a very cruel way of putting it, Amias," said Sarah, wiping her eyes, "as well as depriving my dear uncle of his grandchildren."

"If they are the grandchildren of this house," said Amias, "let the grandfather prove it; but, till then, all justice and mercy make it incumbent on us not to give them the benefit of the doubt, but of the positive and repeated assertions of this woman that they are not related to us at all."

"How could she get a letter sent to John if she knew nothing about him?"

"I have known for years that my cousin John had communication with people here. He wanted sometimes to hear about his father, and one or two other people."

"Who told you that?" asked Sir Samuel, pleased to think that his much-loved son should have cared to hear of him, and not thinking much about those "other people."

"Jolliffe knew it, uncle. I have heard her hint over and over again, that such-and-

such things would be known to Mr. John very shortly."

"And you never told me," cried Sir Samuel.

"I was a mere child, uncle, and I cannot say I had any distinct idea that you did not know his address; besides, children seldom or ever do tell things that they suppose to be matters of secrecy."

"There was always known to be a mystery about those children," Sarah now said. "Yes, you must admit that there was great secrecy, Amias. They know nothing whatever about their parents, and the nurse told nothing excepting—yes, she told that she brought them from London. She told it to the woman whose lodgings I first saw her in."

"Why should they not have been the children of some petty London tradesman, then—a baker, a greengrocer?" observed Amias.

"Why should they?" cried Sarah, very indignant at such a supposition.

"Let him alone, Sarah," exclaimed Sir Samuel; "he has as much right to his suppositions as we had to ours, and they are much kinder."

Amias turned to the old man. "Well, I thought it might be so, because the sum left for maintaining them is so small. The woman, dragged by you, Aunt Sarah, among people of superior class, may have felt that to have their antecedents known would be a disadvantage to the children. This trumpery motive may alone have kept her silent. The mother might have been a dressmaker, and the father a cobbler, for anything we know."

"Precious creatures!" cried Sarah; "and here they come. They look like a petty tradesman's daughters, don't they?" And she rose and bustled out of the room to receive the girls. To do her justice, she had a keen and tender affection for them; they were the only young things that had ever fallen at all under her dominion, and besides, they were so pretty.

Sir Samuel looked at them. Delia's dimpled face was rosy with exercise, Amabel had her usual sweet pensiveness of expression. It seemed so suitable a look for the circumstances under discussion, if she had but known them. There was a portrait of John over the chimney-piece. Sir Samuel turned, and, leaning on the back of his chair, looked up at it. His deep and enduring affection for this favourite son had been one main reason for the interest he had taken in Amabel and Delia. He had pleased himself with the thought that they resembled

John. Amias also looked up; remembered what a bad fellow John had been, acknowledged a certain likeness in hue and in delicacy of appearance, but not in beauty, expression, or grace. The portrait-painter had done his best, but only the bereaved and unsatisfied affection of the father could have imparted anything noble and lovable to the commonplace face.

We all try to be merciful to the delusions that come of love. Amias felt a pang of pity when he said, "Uncle, I hope you have not thought me unkind?"

"No, Amias, no. You must think of yourself, and of them. I promised you they should go to school, and they must."

"And in the meantime we must make long investigations; then, if we are so happy as to bring them home as your granddaughters, with a full and proved right to your name, you will not be more deeply thankful than I shall."

"He found his aunt there, and Sir Samuel."

"The girls may know something about themselves that they never told us," observed Sir Samuel. "Who knows what the nurse may have said to them before she went away; or, indeed, what recollections they may have of their infancy?"

"Aunt Sarah is not the proper person to question them, and Felix would make a sad bungle of it; but, of course, it should be done."

"A very delicate matter to manage. Do you want me to undertake it?"

"If you will."

But it did not prove half so difficult as might have been expected.

Soon after luncheon Amias drove his Aunt Sarah back to the rectory. All prudence and propriety now made him feel that to say anything decisive to Amabel was out of the question. She was to go to school. He must go to school too—a much harder one. That she did not take leave of him without a fluctuating blush, and a good deal of agitation, he might well be pardoned for

" They all, as by one consent, went into Sir Samuel's study."

perceiving; for her feeling, whether it was disappointment, or maiden shyness, or presentiment of some deeper affection, was not successfully concealed.

They all, as by one consent, went into Sir Samuel's study, for there Sarah's pony-carriage could be seen, and Sarah, with her nodding feathers, and Amias. Then, when they were out of sight and there was nothing to do, Delia asked if they might stay, and Amabel wanted to mend the pens; Coz had taught her how to do them.

"Ah, and so you saw Coz this morning?"

"Yes, because we wanted to hear whether there was any letter from Mrs. Snaith."

"And was there, my little girl?"

"No."

"Had she ever led you to expect that she should go and leave you?"

"When she was unwell, just before she went to the sea, she once or twice said things to Delia. She often said things to Delia."

"Ah, indeed! I wonder what they were?"

Delia was seated beside Sir Samuel, on a sofa; he had always petted her a good deal. She was now smoothing the top of his velvet sleeve with her little dimpled hand; pleased with its softness, she next laid her cheek against it. Sir Samuel looked down at her childlike, untroubled face, as she lifted it up. "I don't love anybody so much as you," she said; and she leaned her cheek against his coat again, with a certain fondness by no means devoid of reverence. "But Mamsey *always* said, 'The baronet is very kind to you, Miss Delia; but he has no call to be, unless he chooses.'"

The old story.

"Did she, my pet? And what answer did you make to that?"

"I said I should love you as much as I pleased; so did Amabel."

"And what was it that she said when she was ill?"

"She said she had had a vast deal of trouble in life, and sometimes she could hardly bear to think of it; we should be surprised if we could know what she had gone through. But if she ever had to leave us, we were to be sure she loved us all the same, and she hoped we never should forget her."

"And we never shall," Amabel put in; "but still, we did not suppose she would really go."

Sir Samuel was not at all interested either in the nurse's misfortunes or her affection. He brought the conversation round again, and said, in a cheerful voice, but with a pang at his old heart, "And so she said I had 'no

XXI—44

call' to love you. Did she never tell you anything more?"

Delia's face took on a more tender expression, and Amabel said, "She told us once— a long time ago—something more. I was a little girl then, and I was ill. It was in the night, and I cried and said I wanted a mamma too, like other little girls, that she might pet me; and then Mamsey cried."

"Well, tell me what else took place."

"Delia woke, and got into my bed to comfort me; and Mrs. Snaith cried a long time, and said she took it unkind that we should fret after a mother, when she had always been so kind to us. Then she said that our mother was not such a mamma as I had wished for. And she told us that our mother was not a lady."

Sir Samuel started, in spite of himself. Surely this was bad news. He knew not how to ask any further question, but Amabel presently continued—

"But she said it would be very shocking and very ungrateful to God if we were ever ashamed of her, of our poor mother (who had never done any wrong to us or to any one). And she should pray for us that we never might be."

"Did she tell you when your mother died?" asked Sir Samuel.

"No; but it must have been when we were almost babies, for neither of us remember her. Mrs. Snaith said, 'Your poor mother was a most unhappy wife; your father was not kind to her.'"

"Is that all?"

"Yes, that is the very whole."

"Excepting about the picture," observed Amabel, in correction, and she looked up at the portrait over the chimney-piece. "When you were in London we came here once with Mrs. Snaith, and she saw *it*."

"Well? Speak, my dear."

"You should not have told that," said Delia, her face covered with blushes.

"I wish particularly to know what Mrs. Snaith said."

"It was rude, though."

"No matter."

"She said he was a shabby-looking little man, and had sloping shoulders."

Sir Samuel was wroth and reddened.

"Well, what next?" he inquired.

"Delia whispered to her, 'Mamsey, did you ever see our father?'"

"Well, my dear little girl, go on."

"She said she had seen him, and he had a handsome face—a beautiful face—and a brown moustache." When Delia had said this she burst into tears, and when she had wiped them away, she pressed her cheek again against Sir Samuel's sleeve, and said, "But I wish we could be something to you *somehow*."

The brown moustache had plunged Sir Samuel afresh into his delusion. "John wore one," he thought, "some years after that portrait was taken, and when he was a more personable and finer man."

"Now listen to me, my dear little girls," he said cheerfully. "Are you quite certain that Mrs. Snaith never happened to mention to you what church or what town your mother and father were married in?"

"No, she never did."

"Did you never ask her any questions, my dears?"

"Yes, when Aunt Sarah told us."

"And what did she say?"

"Sometimes she would say, 'I am not half such a foolish woman as Miss de Berenger takes me for.'"

"Here the mystery crops up again," thought Sir Samuel. "What could that woman's motive be?"

"And so the main thing Mrs. Snaith told you was, that your mother was a good woman, but not in the same rank of life as your father."

He did not intend to misrepresent matters when he said this, and Delia answered, in all simplicity, "She used sometimes to make use of strange phrases, and she said——"

"Well, she did?"

"She said a true church parson put on your mother's ring, and you have no call to think about your father at all."

Sir Samuel here lifted Delia's sweet face and kissed it; then he kissed Amabel. "Unless I find out something more, and can prove that these dear children are mine, as they should be, or as they should not be, I have 'no call,' as that woman said, to give them anything." This was his thought. How little he knew when he said this, that every morning, when "that woman" prayed, she besought of God that he never might so mistake matters as to leave her children anything that ought not to come to them!

Her prayer was answered at that moment. Sir Samuel had received affection, and given it. He had received pleasure, and given it; so far all was fair. He had taken no trouble, and he was to give none. The only time he was ever to interfere in their concerns was to be for good.

And what about those investigations?

At first he paid money to make them, and they always failed. Where he heard that there were people of his own name, he looked them up; but as time went on he tried more and more to do this cheaply, and at last he first forbore them, and then justified it. For Amias was at work himself. Sir Samuel knew this, and why should the same thing be paid for twice over?

Amias left his brother the next morning without having said anything to him on this subject; he seemed to be in such low spirits, that Felix took for granted there had been some objection made cheaply by the old man to the proposed engagement. There might be another cause, and that Felix took care not to investigate.

Amias went away, and a few days after the two girls were brought home by Sir Samuel, who afterwards privately, to the great astonishment of Felix, said that he and Amias wished them now to spend a couple of years at school. He produced a cheque for so much more than Felix could have thought needful, and gave it with so much composure, that for a few minutes astonishment at the proposal was lost in astonishment at this unwonted conduct.

"I am not sure that I shall wish them to go," he said, after examining the cheque with deep but perfectly unconscious scrutiny. He had taken the children into his charge through the management of Sarah, he had gradually got used to them, then become fond of them, and now they were almost his sole amusement and delight.

He expressed this to Sir Samuel, who in return, and not without putting himself into a passion over the story of what his two guests had said, related all that had passed.

"Seven hundred pounds is a great deal to spend upon two years at school," said Felix, who was a good deal nettled at being thus set at nought, and expected to do exactly as other people chose—other people who had taken no trouble about the girls, and incurred no responsibility.

But the matter was soon so set before him, that he himself saw the wisdom of the step. The thing must be done, and in less than a month it was done. The most ample inquiries were made, the most excellent references required; a handsome outfit, with every little luxury and comfort, was bought for the girls; and Felix, after taking them to the lady who was to have the charge of them, found himself at home again, "monarch of all he surveyed," walking about his solitary garden, called in to his solitary meals, and wondering what to do with himself.

THE NEWPORT MARKET REFUGE.

MY first visit to this really charitable institution was on a cold, wet evening in the month of December, 1879. In fact, so unfavourable was the weather that had it not been for a promise given to one of the honorary secretaries who had kindly offered to meet me at the Refuge, and explain to me the working of the institution, it is more than probable that my courage might have succumbed before reaching it; and so I kept manfully on my road, and it is only common justice to say that in the end I was well rewarded for my perseverance.

On entering the building I was received by my friend, and he kindly offered to conduct me over the whole of the establishment, with the exception of the industrial school, which he proposed to show me on the following day. "My reason for the delay," he continued, "is that we shall presently take in the night applicants for relief, and the greater portion of these are generally much fatigued, and after their suppers are anxious to get to bed. Now one of the points we are particularly proud of in our school is the efficiency of our military band, which I should like you to hear somewhat at length, but by now doing so we should greatly disturb the sleepers, for which they would not be thankful." I readily admitted the excuse, and we then commenced our tour of inspection.

We first visited the kitchen, and examined its management and appointments somewhat minutely. The result was that although I could find nothing whatever to object to, I found much not only to approve, but to admire. The quality of the food which was then in process of cooking for the expected guests appeared excellent in quality, while that already cooked, and which awaited them, might have been partaken of with pleasure even by the most fastidious; and an air of strict cleanliness pervaded the whole kitchen which could not have been surpassed in the home of any respectable private family. I may further state that the same air of cleanliness was to be remarked in the whole of the building, and which was the more praiseworthy when the quality and habits of many of the poor who apply to the Refuge for relief are taken into consideration.

The time had now arrived for the admission of the applicants, who had already assembled in considerable numbers; but I did not see them as they then were, as they would all have to pass singly before me before they were taken in. I was now shown into a small office, where I and my friend seated ourselves behind the superintendent, who had to examine the applicants in rotation. It would occupy too much time to go at any length into a description of these poor creatures, who all, by the way, wore an aspect of great poverty; one or two examples must suffice. The first who particularly attracted my attention was a tall, care-worn, elderly man. His name, age, and two or three other necessary inquiries having been answered, he was asked what had brought him to the destitute condition he was in.

"Want of work, sir," was the man's reply.

"What are you?"

"Well, sir, I was formerly in a small way of business, and managed by it to keep my wife and family off the rates. We had no easy matter to do it, however, but we had nothing much to complain of till an opposition shop in the same line—we were in the general way, I suppose you would call it a chandler's shop—with more money than we had started against us, and then things began to go wrong. My wife was taken ill too and died, and then that completely upset me. I still, however, struggled on, and then my eldest boy, about fourteen, went wrong and got into trouble. Then things went on worse than ever, till at last I was sold up. I then tried to get a place as light porter, and succeeded; but that did not answer. I was not strong enough for the work—or rather the hours were too long, and then there was no one to look after my little girls, one ten and the other six. Well, the elder was then struck down by fever, and then I lost my place, the wife of my employer thinking that I might bring the disease into her family. I removed my poor girl into the fever hospital, where she died—fortunate for her perhaps, though it almost killed me. And then the little one gradually sank, though there did not seem to be any disease about her, at least so far as I could make out. I took her to the hospital, however, and they examined her, and they said that I must take her back again, as medicine was of no use to her. What I must do was to feed her up. It was very easy for the doctor to say 'feed her up,' but not so easy to do it. And then when I had got almost to my last shilling of ready-money she died. As I could not bear the idea of her being buried by the parish, I sold off every stick of furniture I had, and, that gone, I had not one penny to put upon another. I was also so shabby it was no use my looking for employment in any shape, and at last I was near starving. I then asked a sandwich-board man how he became one. He told me, and I determined to try it, and by it I contrived to keep body and soul together for more than a month. And then this rainy weather came on, and I could get no work. During the last three days I have not been able to earn a farthing, and I have nothing worth pawning—and that's my case, sir, and a true one too. If you could give me a night's lodging and a meal I should be most thankful to you; if not, I must wander about the streets till to-morrow morning, for I won't apply to the workhouse for relief. I have never done so yet, and it's hardly worth while to begin now."

The poor fellow was of course admitted, and then another applicant presented himself —a young man not more than twenty-five years of age. He was dressed in a well-made suit of clothes, which, however, were threadbare and thoroughly wet through, and his coat was tightly buttoned up to his throat, evidently more with the intention of concealing the absence of a shirt than from dread of the weather. His boots were also in a most dilapidated condition, the soles with difficulty keeping their hold of the upper leathers. His face was deadly pallid, his eyes deep sunk in his head, and altogether there was an expression of wildness on his features which was particularly distressing.

"Have I not seen you before?" said the superintendent who was seated at the table.

"Yes, sir; last year."

"Did we not do something for you then?"

"Yes, you were very kind to me, and I should be ungrateful indeed if I ever forgot it."

"Let us hear what you have been doing since," said the superintendent.

"Well, sir, after I left you last year I went as you advised me to Woolwich to try to get admitted as a recruit into the Artillery, and I applied to a recruiting-sergeant, and told him I wanted to enlist. After looking at me for a moment he told me he thought I should do, and he the next day took me to the doctor, but he would not pass me."

"I remember you now quite well," said the superintendent. "You came back to us, and we got you employment in a shop in the country. Why did you leave your situation?"

The applicant made no reply to the question, although he certainly heard and understood it. He gazed wildly over the head of the superintendent for some moments, and then, evidently without object, nervously round the room.

"Why do you not answer me?"

For an instant the applicant's gaze was fixed on the superintendent's face, and he then said in an undertone, but very distinctly—

"Drink; there's no use denying it."

"But yours, then, is a case we cannot entertain," said the superintendent. "Our aim is to help the deserving and unfortunate, not the incorrigible. We have already done what we could for you, and in return you have proved to us that you are no object for commiseration. Your case is one for the casual ward, not for us."

"For God's sake don't say so," said the applicant, "or you'll drive me mad—and I am more than half-way there already. If you'll only take me in to-night, I promise faithfully I will never trouble you again." Then noticing an expression of doubt on the features of the superintendent, he continued, "Oh, you may believe what I say, sir. If drink has been the cause of my going wrong, I am sober enough now, at any rate. Not a drop of anything nor a scrap of food has passed my lips for the last twenty-four hours. I am so weak I can barely stand upright, and my brain seems hardly my own."

Then the applicant's voice faltered, and his eyes filled with tears. The superintendent evidently felt for the poor fellow, and he turned round to my friend and two other members of the managing committee who had joined us, but placed in such a position that they could not be seen, to ascertain their views as to the admission of the applicant, and an affirmative sign having been made to him, the poor fellow was taken in.

Judging from the description I have given of the latter case, the reader might imagine that the society was open to a charge which in one instance was somewhat recklessly made against them—that of encouraging vagrancy, by indiscriminate assistance being rendered alike both to the deserving and undeserving, those really objects of legitimate sympathy and the habitual idler and vagabond. Such a conclusion, however, would be a most erroneous one, for, as a rule, the greatest caution is taken by the officials of the Refuge in separating those worthy of sympathy from those who are not. No better or more convincing proof of the truth of this statement could be given than the following figures, quoted from the sixteenth report of the operations of the Refuge. In the first three months of 1877, out of 1,133 applicants, men and women, only 488 were admitted; yet only on three nights during the whole time were the wards entirely full, those rejected being left to apply for shelter to the workhouse casual wards, they not being considered fit objects for private charitable relief. Again, in the winter three months of 1878, this judicious caution was carried out in a still more marked manner; the number of cases admitted being 486, the number rejected being 729; yet during the time the men's wards were only completely filled on seven nights. "The figures," the report continues, "will show to what proportion of these men we are able to point out as having been permanently saved through our agency from sinking into the ranks of pauperism." It should also be mentioned that the men are received for seven days only, unless there is special reason for a longer delay. Charity Organization Society's cases are kept on as long as the committee may request, for months in some cases—in one case for as long as six months.

Of the many male applicants I saw admitted into the Refuge, perhaps the former of the two cases I mentioned would offer the ordinary type. And the reader could not form a better idea of this class than by watching attentively for a few moments a string or line of what are called "Sandwich-board" men. Any experienced medical man could give evidence to the fact that out of ten of these poor creatures not more than one is capable of doing an average day's hard work—if, indeed, one such could be found among them. It is almost impossible to select one among them who, from physical disability alone, has not an indisputable title to be admitted into the workhouse and be maintained for the remainder of his life at the cost of the ratepayers, and where he would be far better housed, fed, and clothed than he possibly could be on his miserable earnings, even if there were not wet days in the year to keep him inactive—not idle, though willing to labour. These poor creatures, rather than suffer the degradation of pauperism, will endure a daily ten hours' slow march through the street-gutters, with the incessant risk of being crushed or run over by an omnibus or cart, and be thankful to providence should the day be sufficiently fine to allow them to undergo their task, so as to escape from the degradation of poor-law relief. And yet

there are some rigid (so-called) philanthropists who consider such men as these are debased by receiving some temporary assistance from the really benevolent, such, in fact, as those who take an interest in charitable institutions similar to the one I am describing.

I had no opportunity of being present at the reception of the female applicants, which took place in another part of the building, that duty being performed by Sister Zillah, whose name is now a household word in the locality, and always mentioned with affection and respect. I regret my absence the more (though I believe it is against the rules for any male visitor to be present on these occasions, and if so, the rule is worthy of commendation), for certainly the scene would have been a most interesting one, at least judging from the list of ordinary applicants which had been given me. Among the 3,326 nights' lodging given to female applicants in the course of six months were to be found all sorts and conditions of womanhood. Among them were dressmakers, book-folders, charwomen, embroideresses, governesses and school-teachers, laundresses in great numbers, nurses, flower-makers, bookbinders, and even actresses and artists; in fact, there appeared no class of female occupation which was not represented. Although the secrets of Sister Zillah's confessional ought to be respected, the thought struck me how interesting some of the confidences made to her must have been, and still more what had been the effect of the advice she had given in return. Though destitute of all powers of absolution she is certainly endowed with another scarcely less to be respected. If she cannot release souls from purgatory, she has snatched many from the brink of perdition and assisted them to remain honourable women. If she cannot forgive sins, she has kept hundreds from sinning, who were being driven to it by those terrible adversaries, hunger and destitution.

When the admission of the male applicants was completed I rose to leave the Refuge, accompanied by my friend, the honorary secretary. After quitting the office some further conversation passed between us relative to the amount of good performed by him and his fellow-workers, and in what manner the funds were obtained to cover the working expenses. His replies fully confirmed me in a conclusion I had already arrived at, and that was—of the many admirable philanthropic institutions I had visited, there was not one in which that most ex-

· cellent gift of charity could be found more pure and undefiled, or more thoroughly un-ostentatious, than within the walls of the Newport Market Refuge, of course including the excellent Industrial School which I shall presently mention. The care and attention given by those who have the management of the funds is worthy of all praise. Nor are these charitable efforts confined merely to their contributions and personal superinten-dence, they carry them far beyond the walls · of the building. By the report of their pro-ceedings for the year 1879 alone I found that more than 9,000 nights' lodgings had been given to destitute men and women, as well as nearly 20,000 breakfasts, dinners, and suppers to poor creatures, many of whom, when they applied for relief, were so narrowly removed from starvation that another day's total privation might have ter-minated their earthly existence. And many of these when they left the refuge were not sent forth without further assistance, should it be found that they absolutely required it. From the same report I found that no fewer than 179 men, and, still better, 135 women, had been provided with respectable employ-ment or homes. The value of this last act of charity it would be impossible to rate too highly, especially in the case of women. All who have had any experience in such matters will admit the lamentable effects of destitu-tion on the temporal and spiritual welfare of women, and how noble is that act of charity which provides them with the means of earn-ing a respectable livelihood after removing from a terrible temptation.

But another beautiful result may be noticed in the administration of the charitable funds placed at the disposal of the managing com-mittees of the Newport Market Refuge and other kindred institutions, and one which traces an ineffaceable line between them and poor-law relief, and that is—gratitude. No-thing is more· common than for an applicant who enters the Refuge with a marked feeling of latent anger against all others in better circumstances than himself, to leave it the next morning not only in a better frame of mind, expressing himself, and evidently truthfully, as thankful for the kindness he has received; but who ever heard of a grateful pauper? And yet the amount expended on the latter, including house-rent, was perhaps double that of the inmate of the Refuge. This feeling of gratitude is particularly noticeable among women. Nor is the lesson which has been taught them altogether lost, even after a considerable time may have elapsed

since they learnt it, and they frequently prove it in the' most gratifying manner. Nothing is more common than for a woman who has received hospitality and shelter in a charit-able Refuge, when in better circumstances to bestow it again on some poor woman or girl requiring it, not only sharing her room and her bed with her, but her food as well, and without estimating the while the compara-tively more liberal act of beneficence she was performing, one which, if rightly considered, fully equalled the beautiful lesson taught by the widow's mite. Lessons such as these are frequently learnt by women who have them-selves been recipients of acts of charity; but who ever heard of a charitable feeling en-grafted on the mind of a casual in any poor-law establishment, notwithstanding the con-siderate treatment they as a rule really re-ceive from the officials, notwithstanding the stereotyped abuse it is customary to heap on them? But after all it is doubtful whether the poor are to be blamed for the want of gratitude they exhibit for the relief afforded them by the poor-law. The poor them-selves, proportionate means being taken into consideration, are the heaviest ratepayers. The needlewoman who pays two shillings a week for a back top-room in a Peabody dwelling has included in her year's rent the sum of £1 10s. for municipal taxation, the heaviest item in it being for the poor's rate; and yet when in distress herself she shrinks with aversion from applying to it for assist-ance, while she will receive not only without shame, but with positive gratitude, any pecu-niary or other assistance which may be afforded her from kind-hearted individuals or charitable sources.

On the following afternoon I again visited the Refuge for the purpose of inspecting the Industrial Schools, and on my arrival found Mr. Charles Ramsden, who for more than ten years has ably performed the duties of general superintendent, waiting to receive me, and he at once conducted me to that portion of the building set apart for the boys. He first took me into a very large and lofty room fitted up as a gymnasium as well as a play room, with every appliance in it cal-culated to develop the muscular power of the pupils. They were at the moment going through a variety of exercises under the direc-tion of a teacher, and certainly they showed great address and agility. One thing parti-cularly struck me, and that was the healthy condition, as well as the strength of the poor lads, totally different from what I had ex-pected to find them, the majority, as I understood, having been before their admission in a sickly, half-starved state, the result of long-protracted privation. On mentioning this fact to Mr. Ramsden, he replied:—"I can assure you that the description you have heard of their condition when first admitted into the school was by no means exaggerated, but of that I will give you an opportunity of judging for yourself." So saying, he led me into a small side room, calling by name to two young boys to come with us.

"Take off your jackets and shirts, my lads," said Mr. Ramsden. His order was immediately obeyed, and two more emaciated creatures than these poor children it would be difficult to imagine. The boys then dressed themselves, and two others were called for. "The two lads you have just seen were admitted in the course of last week," said Mr. Ramsden. "These have been with us for about six months, and were in the same condition as the others when they entered." The new arrivals now took off their shirts, and the contrast they presented to the others in muscular development was very great. They were not only well fed, but the hardness of their flesh on the arms and shoulders proved it to be healthy.

Mr. Ramsden also showed me the boys' copy-books, and other proofs of the good education bestowed on them, all of which were fully on a par with that of a first-class elementary school. On my inquiry as to the state of their education before being admitted, he informed me that fully a third had been unable to read and write, and the others but very imperfectly.

I was now conducted into a large room on the first floor, where I found, standing in three ranks, some twenty-five or thirty boys with military musical instruments in their hands, and their bandmaster (Mr. Dust, late of the Royal Artillery band) at their head. At my request they played three somewhat difficult pieces with great precision—in fact, little less so than an average military band. On making the remark to Mr. Dust he told me that he hoped the greater portion of them would soon be able to occupy positions of the kind—in fact, he was training them for that purpose. I suggested that he might have some difficulty in carrying out his wishes. "I am very hopeful, from the success I have hitherto had," he replied, "that will not be the case." Mr. Ramsden then informed me that already no fewer than 21 pupils from that school had been admitted into the bands of the different regiments of the Guards, 12 into

the 93rd Highlanders, 13 into the 97th Foot, 21 into the 99th Foot, and no fewer than 64 more into the bands of other regiments, all of whom had given satisfaction.

Before quitting the building I asked a few more questions of Mr. Ramsden, and among them were the following, and his answers to them:—

"What was the average cost, all expenses included, of each boy in the school?" and I found it to be about 30 per cent. less than the cost of a child in one of the metropolitan district schools.

"Have you any difficulty in finding respectable employment for these boys?"

"None whatever," was his reply. "We can get them out as fast as we please. Out of every 100 boys for whom we have found employment only 4 have turned out unsatisfactorily."

"To what class do the majority of their parents belong?" I inquired.

"The poor working classes generally," he said. "Out of the 60 boys at present in the school no fewer than 44 are the children of widows, principally needle-women, laundresses, and charwomen, who have still 193 more children to support out of their miserable earnings."

I cannot conclude this short article better than by quoting *verbatim* the termination of a description of the Newport Market Refuge which appeared in the *Daily Telegraph* in the autumn of 1877, and which is perfectly applicable to the present time:—

"Now that the weather is fine and the trees can shelter there are not so many taps at the Refuge door, not so many pitiful appeals for admittance. But the summer will soon be over and the icy winter will be at hand; the leaves will fall from the plane-trees in the park, and London will be once more desolate. It is then that the good work will begin again, and then that the treasurer of this excellent institution will look despondingly at the diminishing contributions, and probably regret the absence of a fixed income, however small. True it is that the Refuge has baffled the storm for more than thirteen years, thanks to the energy of good friends; but the end may come sooner than any one expects. It cannot be that 'the cry of the children,' the anguish of the men, or the whisper of the women will be neglected when there is so great a reward contained in the motto of this beautiful charity, 'I was an hungred, and ye gave me meat; I was a stranger, and ye took me in.'"

WM. GILBERT

Larnaca.

A TRIP TO CYPRUS.

By LIEUT.-COLONEL W. F. BUTLER, C.B.

PART II.

SIX months had scarcely gone since Cyprus had been a word of interest to every English ear. Daily journals, weekly reviews, monthly magazines, all made it a topic of animated discussion. Forgotten history was searched to find episodes of early English dominion in the island. Political parties made its acquisition matter of grave parliamentary debate, and even popular preachers drew pulpit parallels between the record in Holy Writ of Saul and Barnabas sailing for Salamis, and British civilisation in the shape of a brigade of regular infantry and a division of Sepoys landing at Larnaca.

Nor was it to be greatly wondered at that the mind of the British nation should have eagerly fastened upon the new possession with a considerable amount of popular enthusiasm. It had come after long months of doubt and manifold anxieties, the sole solid bit of "boot," in the exchange which gave us "peace with honour" for armed expectancy and distrust. It possessed associations connected with the earlier ages of our recorded history which rendered it a familiar name to every school-boy. It was to be another link in the chain of ocean fortresses which bound us to our vast Eastern possessions. Its occupation by us was accompanied by many incidents that cast around it more the éclat of warlike conquest than the less demonstrative acquisition of peace

or purchase. The popular mind once excited, becomes capable of strange enthusiasms. Cyprus grew in imagination into an earthly paradise; "Paphos of the hundred streams," the snow-fed rivulets that flowed from Olympus, all the pictures woven of sensuous fancy of the Greek and Roman poets were reproduced, with the morning muffin, to swell the chorus of delight that greeted our acquisition of this once-famed isle.

Maps soon appeared showing zones of cultivation, the very titles of which were sufficient to cause English readers intense anticipations of pleasure: the zone of the olive, of the orange, of the fig, of the grape and of the pine, were like so many terraces of ·delight, gradually ascending from a lower world of cotton and tobacco—where the Zapteah, the Mudir, and the Kaimakhan (we are wont sometimes to confuse Eastern titles) fulfilled the natural destiny of the black or coloured races by unremitting toil— to one where, under the pines of Olympus, the Anglo-Saxon proprietor sipped his cup, cooled by the snows of Troados, or lay lazily lulled by the murmur of the wind through the pines of triple-peaked Adelphi.

And there were other persons of less æsthetic tastes who regarded the new island with more practical outlook. It was to produce an excellent outlet for the talents and the energies of the younger son. We required such an opening, and Cyprus gave it to us. The professions had all become immensely overcrowded. Competitive examinations had sadly interfered with the efficiency of the services civil and military. The colonies had developed, under representative institutions, a tendency to bestow their little gifts of place and emolument upon their own younger sons instead of upon ours; but here, in Cyprus, no such unjust prejudices were likely to prevail, and any little difficulties of education resulting from too close an attention on the part of our younger sons to Ruff's Guide and the Racing Calendar would be of small moment in a

Cathedral at Nicosia.

country where the official language was Turkish, and where the people were either black or olive-coloured. Thus wagged the little tongues of that great Babel called public opinion, and ere a week had passed from the date of the announcement of our Cypriote acquisition, a picture had arisen of our new possession as utterly false to the reality as though some German, deeply read in the Roman History of Britain, had become the purchaser of a property in Sussex, and expected to find existing in full sway upon his estate the manners and customs of Boadicea.

The Cypriote canticle had in fact been pitched in too high a key, and a collapse was inevitable ere that song had reached its second part.

The men who sailed for Cyprus, and who

had been likened by the popular preacher to Saul and Barnabas landing at Salamis, were for the most part persons not disposed to be hypercritical in matters of heat, glare, and barrenness; they came from Malta in July, and in July Malta fulfils as many conditions of heat, glare, and sterility as can be found on this side of the Sahara. But to the eyes and the senses of these men Cyprus was a place of almost intolerable heat and blinding glare; compared to it Malta was a land of verdure, of running streams, of spring-like coolness, and the worst day of sun and sirroc that had ever blistered or stewed the denizens of Valetta was as nothing compared to the fierce heat and blinding dust-storm that burned and swept the camp at Chefflick Pasha.

But when a question of fact becomes a matter of political discussion it loses a great deal of the force it usually possesses, and is not at all the stubborn thing it is credited with being. One might have supposed that the salubrity or unhealthiness of the island, the question of whether Englishmen were well or ill there, was easy of solution; but nothing proved more difficult.

Fever or no fever became not a common every-day matter of fact, but assumed the much graver and more important bearing of a great parliamentary and political question. The papers took sides upon it, hon. members made motions upon it, people wrote to the leading journals upon it, and even a vote of censure was openly hinted at by some of the most extreme leaders of opinion.

But on the other hand the Government stoutly averred that the whole thing was a delusion from beginning to end. They were in receipt, it was said, of most conclusive testimony to the excellent sanitary state of the troops in Cyprus. The few cases of fever that had prevailed after the arrival of the troops had been of the febricular type, which, it was explained, was fatal only in the event of its being complicated with symptoms of a hepatic character. This was reassuring, so far as it went; but an hon. member pointed out that in the actual operations of war a man sick was almost as bad as a man dead. This point was not made a question of discussion, and, to use the phrase of the morning papers, the subject dropped.

But while thus theories took the place of facts the army of occupation began to sicken rapidly, and stray waifs of fever were wafted to the English shore. Clubland soon became enlightened upon the real nature of a summer in Cyprus. "I would not for the world say it to every one," said the veteran Puffin in the morning room of the Inseparable Noodles; "I am too good a Conservative to let it be known; but I will tell you in confidence that there is not such another cursed hole on earth." As this confidential communication was made to at least seventy members of the Inseparable Club seven times, and as these seventy had retailed it without loss of time to at least an equal number of their friends and acquaintances—of course always in the very strictest confidence—the opinion gained a widespread notoriety in a few hours. The tide of public opinion began quickly to turn, serious doubts were thrown in more than one quarter upon the projected cultivation of the olive and the grape by the ordinary English agriculturist in a temperature of 165° Fahrenheit in the sun.

The theory of zones also underwent amplification which was not at all satisfactory. A medical journal published a map of Cyprus showing, in colours, the zones of disease—there was the malarious fever zone occupying the low coast-lands; there was the enteric fever zone, mostly confined to the towns; there was a zone of aguish fever, where the limestone formation touched upon the disintegrated granite; and finally, there was a dysenteric zone, the limits of which had not yet been traced with any degree of certainty by medical investigations beyond 4,000 feet above sea-level. But amid all this revulsion of feeling and collapse of brilliant expectation one theory remained intact: it was the younger son theory. It might almost have been said to have gained strength from the fact that fever was found to be a calculated factor in the programme of his emigration. This was, however, in the circle of his family; for himself he showed a singular amount of obstinacy in the matter, and although, during a brief sojourn in a Cypriote sea-port, he had succeeded in establishing a race meeting, and had inculcated the Greek population into the mysteries of "handicapping," "laying off," and "hedging," and also proved to them that it was by no means necessary that the best horse should win, he nevertheless, on his return to the bosom of his inconsolable family with the proceeds of a "Consolation Stakes" and the seeds of a malarious fever, steadily refused to again tempt the goddess of Fortune in the Island of the Goddess of Love. Indeed, at the sherry and bitter table of the "Waif and Stray" Club, he set his opinion upon record. "The place isn't fit for a gentleman," he said. "It will take a dozen years before they're civilised enough to lay you more than two to one on anything, and no fellow who hasn't something to leave in a will should attempt to go there."

* * * *

A lonely sea washes the shores of Cyprus. Commerce seems almost to have completely fled the nest in which it first had life. The wanderer who now from the thistle-covered site of Salamis looks eastward to the sunrise, or he who casts his glance from the shapeless mounds of Paphos, beholds waves almost as destitute of sail-life as though his standpoint had been taken upon some unmapped island in the South Pacific.

To the north and south this characteristic of loneliness is but little changed. Across the bluest blue waters of the Karamanian Gulf the icy summits of many mountains rise above a shipless horizon, and the beauty of the long indented north shore of Cyprus, from Kyrenia to far-away Cape Andreas, is saddened by the absence of that sense of human existence and of movement which the white speck of canvas bears upon its glistening wing. To the south commerce is not wholly dead. Between the wide arms of Capes de Gat and Chitti ships and coasting craft are seen at intervals, and the sky-line is sometimes streaked by the long trail of steamer smoke from some vessel standing in or out of the open roadstead of Larnaca; but even here, although the great highway of the world's commerce is but a day and a half's sail away to the south, man's life upon the waters is scant and transient. But the traveller who stands upon the shores of Cyprus will soon cease to marvel at the absence of life upon the waters outspread before him; the aspect of the land around him, the stones that lie in shapeless heaps at his feet, the bare brown ground upon whose withered bosom sere and rustling thistles alone recall the memory of vegetation —all tell plainly enough the endless story of decay; and, as he turns inwards from a sea which at least has hidden all vestiges of wreck beneath its changeless surface, he sees around him a mouldering tomb which but half conceals the skeleton of two thousand years of time.

Stepping out upon the crazy wooden stage that does duty for a jetty at Larnaca, the traveller from the West becomes suddenly conscious of a new sensation; he has reached the abode of ruin. And yet it is not the scant and dreary look of all things which heretofore, to his mind, had carried in their outward forms the impression of progress. It is not the actual ruin, the absence of

settlement, or the mean appearance of everything he looks at, that forces suddenly upon him the consciousness of having reached here in Cyprus a place lying completely outside the pale of European civilisation; it is more the utter degradation of all things—the unwritten story here told of three hundred years of crime; told by filthy house, by rutted pavement and squalid street; spoken by the sea as it sobs through the sewaged shingle, and echoed back from the sun-baked hills and dull, brown, leafless landscape that holds watch over Larnaca.

And yet they tell us that it is all improved —that the streets have been swept, the houses cleaned, the Marina no longer allowed to be a target for rubbish. The men who tell us this are truthful, honourable men, and we are bound to believe them; but the statement is only more hopelessly convincing of unalterable desolation than had Larnaca stood before us in the full midnight of its misery.

As the day draws on towards evening we are taken out to visit the scene of the encampment of troops at Chefflick Pasha when the island was first occupied. We are in the hands of one of the chief regenerators of the island — Civil Commissioner is the official title: and we are mounted on the back of an animal which enjoys the distinction of having made himself almost as uncomfortable to the First Lord of the Admiralty, during a recent official visit to the island, as though that Cabinet Minister had been on the deck of the Admiralty yacht in a gale off the Land's End.

But if the spirit of ruin had been visible in Larnaca, the ride to Chefflick Pasha revealed the full depth of the desolation that brooded over the land—the bare brown land with its patchwork shreds of faded thistles over which grey owls flitted as the twilight deepened into darkness. As we rode along through this scene, my friend, the assistant regenerator, appeared to regard the whole thing as superlatively hopeful—the earth was to bloom again. What a soil it was for cotton, for tobacco, for vines, for oranges, citrons, olives! Energy was to do it all—energy and Turkish law. He had been studying Turkish law, he said, for seven weeks, and he was convinced that there was no better law on earth. We thought that the East generally had been studying the same law, or codes similar to it, for seven hundred years, and had come to a different conclusion regarding its excellence. "What Cyprus had been in the past it would be again in the future. It only wanted British administration of Turkish law over the island to set everything right. Man had done the harm; man could undo the harm." And so on, as we rode back through the lessening light into Larnaca.

Was it really as our friend had said? Could man thus easily undo what man had done? All evidence answered "No."

For every year of ruin wrought by the Turk another year will not suffice to efface. The absence of good government may mar a people's progress. The presence of good government can only make a nation when, beneath, the foundation rests upon the solid freedom of the heart of the people. The heart of Cyprus is dead and buried. It was dying ere ever a Turkish galley crossed the Karamanian Gulf, and now it lies entombed beneath three hundred years of crime, no more to be called to life by the spasmodic efforts of half-a-dozen English officials than the glories of the Knights of Malta could be again enacted by the harmless people who to-day dub themselves Knights of St. John, and date the record of their chapters from a lodging-house in the Strand.

The mail-cart running between Larnaca and Nicosia usually left the former place at five A.M.; but as the English mail-steamer had arrived from Alexandria at midnight, the hour of the post-cart's departure had been changed to half-past three A.M. A few minutes before that time we had presented ourselves at the point of departure, only to find office, stable, and stable-yard sunk in that profound slumber which usually characterize the world at that early hour. A glow of ruddy light falling across the street from a large open door suggested some one astir, and we bent our steps in its direction. The red light came from a blacksmith's forge. At the anvil beat and blew a swarthy smith, and yet a courteous son of Vulcan too, for he stopped his beating and his blowing as we came up, and put a candle-end in a bottle, and put the bottle on a bench and placed a rough seat beside it for our service. He hails from Toulon, he says. Simple services all of them, but of great value when it is borne in mind that ten minutes previously we had called at the post-office and received from the wearied official in charge a packet of English letters and papers just sorted from the mail; so, as the blacksmith beat we read, waiting in the small hours for the mail-cart to Nicosia.

Suddenly there was a clatter of horses and a rush of wheels along the street. The mail-cart had started! We rushed wildly into the still dark street. It was too true, the cart was off! With a roar that ought to have roused Larnaca, we gave chase. The roar failed to arouse the sleeping city, but, doing still better, it halted the flying mail-cart. Ten seconds more and we were beside the vehicle, and beside ourselves with breathless rage. A Greek held the reins, another Greek sat on the back seat. When the driver found that the roar had only proceeded from a passenger who had been left behind, he was about to resume his onward way; but it could not be allowed. A short altercation ensued. The Greek driver, reinforced by the proprietor of the cart, a Frenchman, gesticulated, swore, and threatened the combined penalties of Turkish and English law. We calmly replied that, acting under the direction of the French proprietor, we had presented ourselves at the mail office at half-past three A.M., that for two mortal hours we had waited for the cart, and that now the cart must wait until our bag, still at the forge, could be brought up and placed beside us. The Frenchman declared, "It was impossible; the delay of a minute would be his ruin. The mules must proceed."

"No; not until the bag was brought up."

"Forward!" roared the proprietor. The driver shook his reins and shouted to the mules. There was nothing for it but to seize the reins and stop further progress. The mules, four in number, instantly declared themselves on our side of the controversy; they stopped dead short, and the imprecations of their owner and driver being alike powerless to move them, the bag was brought up, the imprecations ceased, and we jolted out of Larnaca. Day was breaking.

Softly came the dawn over the face of the weary land. Over hill-tops, over swamps, and shore and sea, touching miserable minaret and wretched mosque and squalid building with all the wondrous beauty that light has shed upon this old earth of ours since two million mornings ago it first kissed its twin children, sea and sky, on the horizon of the creation.

And now, as the sun came flashing up over the eastern hills, Cyprus lay around us, bare, brown, and arid. Water-courses without one drop of water; the surface of the earth the colour of a brown-paper bag; the telegraph poles topped by a small grey owl; a hawk hovering over the thistle-strewn ground; a village, Turkish or Greek, just distinguishable from the plain or the hill by the lighter hue of its mud walls and flat mud roofs— east, west, or north, on each side and in front, such was the prospect.

The owls on the telegraph-posts seemed typical of Turkish dominion. The Ottoman throned on the Bosphorus was about as great an anomaly as the blinking night-bird capping the electric wire.

Twenty-five miles from Larnaca the road ascends a slight rise. As the crest is gained the eye rests upon a cluster of minarets—houses thrown together in masses within the angles and behind the lines of a fortification, and one grand dark mass of Gothic architecture towering over house and rampart. Around lies a vast colourless plain. To the north a broken range of rugged mountains lift their highest peaks three thousand feet above the plain. Away to the south-west higher mountains rise blue and distant.

The houses, ramparts, and minarets are Nicosia, and the Gothic pile, still lofty amid the lowly, still grand amid the little, stands a lonely rock of Crusaders' faith, rising above the waves of ruin.

If the Turk had marked upon Larnaca the measure of his misrule, upon Nicosia he had stamped his presence in even sharper lines of misery and of filth. People are often in the habit of saying that no words could fitly express the appearance of some scene of wretchedness. It is simply an easy formula for begging the question.

The state of wretchedness in which Nicosia lies is easy enough to express in words—in these matters the Turk is thorough. There is nothing subtle in his power to degrade; there is no refinement in his ruin. The most casual tourist that ever relied on Murray for history, and Cook for food and transport, could mark and digest the havoc of the Ottoman.

The Goth might ravage Italy, but the Goth came forth purified from the flames which he himself had kindled. The Saxon swept Britain, but the music of the Celtic heart softened his rough nature, and wooed him into less churlish habit. Visigoth and Frank, Heruli and Vandal, blotted out their ferocity in the very light of the civilisation they had striven to extinguish. Even the Hun, wildest Tartar from the Scythian waste, was touched and softened in his wicker encampment amid Pannonian plains; but the Turk—wherever his scimitar reached—degraded, defiled, and defamed; blasting into eternal decay Greek, Roman, and Latin civilisation, until, when all had gone, he sat down, satiated with savagery, to doze for two hundred years into hopeless decrepitude.

The streets of Nicosia, narrow and tortuous, are just wide enough to allow a man to ride along each side of the gutter which occupies the centre. No view can anywhere be obtained beyond the immediate space in front, and so many blank walls, by-lanes, low doorways, and ruined buildings lie around without any reference to design or any connection with traffic, that the mind of the stranger soon becomes hopelessly confused in the attempt at exploration, until wandering at random he finds himself suddenly brought up against the rampart that surrounds the city.

It is then that ascending this rampart, and pursuing his way along it, he beholds something of the inner life of Nicosia. The houses abut upon the fortifications, and the wanderer looks down into courtyards or garden plots where mud walls are broken, unpainted lattices are fringed by many an orange-tree thick-clustered with golden fruit.

In the ditch on the outer side lie, broken and destroyed, some grand old Venetian cannon, flung there by the Turk previous to his final departure. His genius for destruction still "strong in death," he would not give them to us, or sell them, so he defaced and flung them down.

We wander on along the northern face. Looking in upon the city all is the same, mud and wattle in ruin, oranges, narrow streets, brown stone walls, minarets, filth, and the towering mass of the desecrated cathedral.

But as the sunset hour draws nigh, and the wanderer turns his gaze outwards over the plain, he beholds a glorious prospect. It is the sunset-glow upon the northern range.

Beyond the waste that surrounds the ramparts—beyond the wretched cemeteries and the brown mounds, and the weary plain, the rugged range rises in purple and gold. What colours they are!

Pinnacled upon the topmost crags, the gigantic ruins of the Venetian castles of Buffavento and St. Hilarion salute the sunset last of all, and then the cold hand of night blots out plain, mountain, mound, and ruin; the bull-frogs begin to croak from the cemeteries, and night covers with its vast pall the wreck of Time and of Turk.

THE INFLUENCE OF ART IN DAILY LIFE.

By J. BEAVINGTON ATKINSON.

IV.—BEAUTY.

"There's beauty all around our paths,
  If but our watchful eyes
Can trace it 'mid familiar things
  And through their lowly guise."

IN the preceding papers it has appeared incidentally how beauty enters in many ways into our daily life—how in the building, decorating, and furnishing of our homes beautiful objects and arrangements minister to refined enjoyment. And the assumption was made, perhaps somewhat gratuitously, not only that beauty has a bodily existence, but that it can be readily distinguished, taken possession of, and applied; and yet its positive entity is by some called in question, and people in general are content with the vaguest impressions, and know or care so little that they can look even upon ugliness with impartiality and indifference. Nevertheless truly is it written that "Beauty has been appointed by the Deity to be one of the elements by which the human soul is continually sustained." And it appears to me that in the present time we have special need for this high service. Just in proportion as the pressure of life, the heat and the burden of the day, become hard to bear; just in measure as the practical details of business and the hurry and worry of the world wear wearily on body and mind, is the need felt for such calming and healing beauty as nature and art can give. And it furthermore would seem that if beauty be a want we shall do well to discriminate between the true and the false, so that we may not be taking poison for food. And it is to be feared that in these matters the mind is peculiarly prone to deception, and that even when intent on being guided aright it clings by some unaccountable perversity to the thousand and one forms of the unbeautiful that crowd and disfigure the world. I think, then, some practical good may be gained by a few simple suggestions, which while eschewing metaphysical subtleties shall serve to show what beauty—the life and soul of art—really is, and how it may be distinguished from its contraries.

How can beauty be discerned—what are her outward signs? In the first place, I would premise that we are here not within the sphere of certainty, or of positive science. There are no axioms or definitions by which beauty can be precisely or dogmatically designated. Yet she can be described, pre-sented by examples, and approached by way of probabilities. As to description or illustration, a classic capital, an Etruscan vase, a Gothic window tracery are all beautiful, and yet the reason why, it is not easy to say.

Accordingly all authorities, however otherwise they diverge, agree that the sign, if indeed not the very essence of beauty, is the pleasure it incites. The mind is made for beauty just as the eye is framed for light. A thing of beauty leads from joy to joy, bringing sunshine within the soul, and lighting up faculty after faculty till every chamber of consciousness glows with warmth and colour. The mind greets with rapture the approach of beauty, and garnishes a dwelling for her; the affections grow kindly, and the currents of life flow evenly and gently; unruly passions are laid to rest, and discords soften into harmonies. Beauty, too, like Spring garlanded with flowers, is jocund and health-giving. Thus Addison of such states of delectation writes, "Delightful scenes, whether in nature, painting, or poetry, have a kindly influence on the body as well as the mind, and not only serve to clear and brighten the imagination, but are able to disperse grief and melancholy, and to set the animal spirits in pleasing and agreeable motion. For this reason, Lord Bacon, in his essay upon Health, has not thought it improper to prescribe to his readers a poem or a prospect." In fine the proof and the purpose of beauty is the pleasure it brings, the intent being to adorn life and add to the sum of human happiness.

I have sometimes felt it derogatory to the arts to hold that beauty, their vital breath, is chiefly if not exclusively pleasure-giving. But a sufficient reply seems to be that the pleasures of the mind become high or low according to the faculties called into play. There are not only the pleasures of the senses, but the poets sing of "the pleasures of hope" and "the pleasures of the imagination." Beauty has many phases or modes of manifestation; there is physical beauty as seen in a Greek athlete, æsthetic beauty as sometimes found in highly wrought and artistic types of girlhood and womanhood, intellectual beauty as portrayed by the poet

Shelley, moral and religious beauty as displayed by martyrs and saints and depicted in sacred art. And these divers forms of beauty corresponding with cognate states of mind evoke varying pleasures. The beauty is of a base order that appeals to passion, but beauty becomes soul-moving when it inspires to worship. And the dignity of the arts may in like manner be appraised by the worth of the ideas delineated and of the emotions evoked. The doctrine has often been propounded, and is not destitute of reason, that there subsists an underlying union between beauty, truth, and goodness; beauty answering to the æsthetic sense, truth to the intellect, and goodness to the conscience, each and all being essential to a perfect work either of nature or of art. Beauty thus indissoluble from truth and goodness becomes ideal—it is without blemish, it stands the attribute of high minds, the source of pure and noble pleasure. The belief that mind alone inspires beauty finds expression in the following oft-quoted lines; the first are by Akenside, the second from Michael Angelo:—

" Mind, mind alone, bear witness earth and heaven,
The living fountain in itself contains
Of beauteous and sublime."

" Deep in that source whence our existence flows,
Beauty's transcendent forms are all combined
Beyond all other attributes of mind."

And when once we have learnt to think worthily of beauty, we may next consider its distribution and favourite habitats. These are primarily in nature and derivatively in art. And here I wish to guard against the notion that beauty is a boon " too bright and good for human nature's daily food." We are taught by the poet of nature that "the lowly have the birthright of the skies," that "heaven lies about us in our infancy," that "the meanest flower that blows can give thoughts that do often lie too deep for tears;" and so is it with beauty, she is near and dear to the simple and true-hearted.

Perhaps it may be of some use to point out how we may distinguish beauty in nature and what the artist can do for us. In the world beauty is scattered, unequally distributed, and often sorely defaced. To this her marred and mutilated estate may be applied Milton's famous simile concerning truth: " Her lovely form is hewn into a thousand pieces and scattered to the four winds," and artists and others "imitating the careful search that Isis made for the mangled body of Osiris, have gone up and down gathering limb by limb as they could be found;" yet all the scattered fragments have not been found, but still the search goes on, hoping that every joint and member may at length be moulded " into an immortal feature of loveliness and perfection." Now the function and mission of the artist has ever been to collect the dispersed beauties of nature into a consistent composition and a concentrated whole. And these the finer essences of created things, sculptors, painters, and art-workmen help to infuse into our daily life, mitigating its severity and ruggedness, and rarefying its denseness and grossness.

Let us recur for a moment to the practical question of how the beauties of nature may be assimilated. The main difficulty is that the majority of persons are not rightly attuned. The mind nowadays hankers after novelty and excitement, it becomes dissipated and distracted by vain shows, life is discoloured and taste tortured by frivolous fashion, wild invention, and caprice, till at length the modesty, the law, and the order beloved by nature are ignored by society. A wholesome mode of escape from " the busy dance of things that pass away " may be found in an excursion to the country with a volume of Wordsworth in hand. " The presences of nature in the sky and on the earth, the visions of the hills, and souls of lonely places " bring healing to the fevered pulse. Still better restorative is sketching among silent woods or babbling streams, for their beauty speaks as it were personally to the mind, and seems to enter at pencil-point and permeate through nerve and fibre till the artist or amateur grows into the life of nature.

When thus the mind, " by interchange of peace and excitation, finds in nature its best and purest friend," the thoughts become attuned to beauty, and intuition is a sure guide. The perfections of nature find, so to say, replicas within the mind, and a thrill of delight announces the sense of the beautiful. But this rarer essence in created things is not left to the testimony of intuition only, nature usually affixes some stamp as a visible sign. It will be found that the most highly-developed forms, the perfected types, are usually beautiful, while ugliness attaches as a stigma to what is physically sickly or abortive. The observance of nature's laws tends to the perfecting of animal and vegetative structures, in other words to the embodiment of beauty. And nature appears in perpetual struggle to cast aside and obliterate what is faulty or unsound, and to strengthen and mature the higher germs of life, and so through successive stages to insure a progressive beauty.

It would seem for us a profitable pastime in our daily walks to seek out diligently the latent beauties in the landscape and its living tenantry, so as to observe and inwardly muse over whatever is lovely in the forms and colours of animated nature, birds of the air, foreground flowers, mountain distances, and sunset skies. The memory well stored with such images becomes a perpetual feast.

Beauty as placed in the world is not free from perplexities. Lord Bacon, with his usual breadth of vision, writes in view of these anomalies: "That is the best part of beauty, which a picture cannot express; no, nor the first sight of the life. There is no excellent beauty that hath not some strangeness in the proportion." The fact is such strangeness perpetually crops up owing to the presence of ugliness, which, as tares among wheat, grows up in the fields of beauty. It is not very easy to tell why all things were not created beautiful; it is not, for example, quite evident why some few women should be made ugly. But as we have the best authority for suffering the foolish gladly, so we shall not be far wrong in receiving the ugly with resignation. And nature certainly makes kindly effort to recompense for occasional shortcomings; accordingly it is proverbial that she endows persons lacking in beauty with compensating goodness. Thus much it seems necessary to say, otherwise the objection might hold that the picture here drawn of beauty is wanting in truthful shadow and relief. And I think the contrast which nature and even art obtains in a certain small percentage of ugliness is not without a lesson. Beauty is apt to cloy; furthermore it may enervate; therefore the sweet is spiced with the bitter.

Beauty has received varying treatment from art. Unhappily some painters, such as Brauwer and Jan Steen, instead of striving to express "the best part of beauty," have grovelled in the mire, while others have glossed art with tinsel show, riband, star, and belted rank. But the painter who works as nature works will cast aside whatever in man is ignoble, and, seeking to carry out the general scheme of development, will improve upon the actual model and by felicity of invention push onwards to the perfect type. And thus beauty in art as in nature becomes progressive—a beauty which rises in the scale of existence according to the worth of the idea it embodies.

Yet Sir Joshua Reynolds deplores that the artist must be content to suffer the sublime distress which a great mind alone can feel,

"that having dedicated his life to the attainment of an ideal beauty, he will die at last without having reached it." And Hogarth, in a more comic strain, relates how a certain "dancing-master once declared that after much study and successive improvements, he still despaired of being able during the rest of his life to do complete justice to, or to bring out fully the capabilities of, his favourite dance." Whatever be a man's calling, singleness of devotion cannot fail of reward, and though to the end of life ideal beauty may still be beyond our reach, yet year by year it can be approached more nearly. The resolve is itself sufficient reward.

In our search after beauty much may be learnt from the practice of the greatest artists in divers countries over long periods of time, and under diversified civilisations. The painter and sculptor are perpetually on the look-out for pleasing and perfect aspects in nature and in life, and thus the works that have been handed down may be said to serve as historic shrines or emporiums of beauty. And as good society is the best teacher of polished manners, and the reading of select authors one of the surest means of forming a good literary style, so the study of the master works of art is the most direct way of cultivating the taste and rectifying the sense of the beautiful. It will not be amiss therefore to enumerate a few examples in art which may be accepted as standards. Let us place in the front rank Grecian temples and Gothic cathedrals; some excel others, but all are more or less beautiful. Then consummate after their kind are Greek and Etruscan vases and tazze, and Classic and Italian cameos and intaglios; also marble reliefs, of which the Elgin are nearly faultless. In the same category come ornamental compositions of foliage, flowers, and figures in Classic, Italian, and French styles. Of course it will not be right to accept any work blindly; each component part must be examined critically, the chaff will have to be sifted from the wheat, and the essential beauty when found should be analyzed, and the effects referred to their causes. Nothing short of this is educational.

As types of the ideal, and as analytical exercises to bring out prominently the principles and properties of beauty, we cannot do better than to take a few of the best-known pieces of sculpture, such as the Fates of Phidias, the Faun and Cupid by Praxiteles, the Venus of Milos, the Apollo Belvedere, the Lizard Slayer, and the Antinous and the Genius of the Vatican. These and other figures are now happily made familiar to students and the public at large by casts in the class-rooms of art schools throughout the country. They are rightly used as models of truth and beauty, and being raised above common nature, and freed from the accidents and flaws of individual humanity, they reach the generic and the immutable. Deformity, like error, dies out; while beauty, like truth, lives on. The student will do well to distinguish one species of beauty from another. In Greek and the best Roman sculpture the subtle essence is concentrated and sublimated; it dwells apart as in serene heights undisturbed by the tumult of lower spheres.

A new and inspired spirit of beauty dawned with the advent of Christian art. There would seem good reason to believe that the inward graces of faith, hope, and charity were by the old painters translated into form, and transferred to panel and canvas, so that the beauties of the soul, though in themselves invisible, became the objects of sense. And the foundation for this belief grows more assured from the well-accredited narrative that Fra Angelico went direct from prayer to his easel to paint the vision received from heaven, not daring to alter a line because all was given by God. Endless examples might be adduced of how many early, and a few late Italian masters—Fra Angelico, Benozzo Gozzoli, Francia, Fra Bartolommeo, Da Vinci, and others—created and made eternal a world of beauty, and the revelation inspired a love and a worship. And in these modern times, when beauty has become less spiritual and more carnal, it is no slight benefit that the masterpieces of early Italian art have been brought by the publications of sundry societies within the reach of rich and poor alike. Such supersensuous beauty, touching sometimes the confines of the supernatural, thrown into the quiet pauses of daily life, raises the mind above the level of common things. The subjects may pall somewhat by sameness, yet besides such lovely and oft-repeated creations as Madonnas and Holy Families, a world of beauty opens on the sight in angels, and heavenly choirs, and winged creatures flocking the sky or visiting the lower earth. In such pictorial compositions the lines and movements seem attuned to heavenly music. But again and again changes come over the spirit of the dream, and beauty as conceived by Raphael grows supremely symmetric and even geometric, thus "Sibyls" and the figures in the "Poesia," perfect in equipoise, become wholly rhythmical, mind and body blending harmoniously without jar or dissonance. And

XXI—45

so the austere and self-immolating beauty of primitive epochs little by little relaxes till we come in the Venetian school to such rapturous and passionate scenes as Titian's "Bacchus and Ariadne," "Venice enthroned," by Veronese, "Mercury and the Graces," and "Ariadne and Venus," by Tintoret. I wish to indicate how Italian painting unfolds not a narrow or exclusive, but a wide and representative beauty. And it becomes instructive to spell out and read the old pictures as if they were historic records of the conditions of churches and commonwealths, or as if they were books or so many pages transcribed from the life. The beauty which ever varied with the life and the faith of a highly sensitive people ministers all the more sympathetically with the pulsations of our own highly wrought existence.

The vital principle that has endowed with immortality the masterpieces of painting, sculpture, and architecture, inspires, though perchance in less degree, subsidiary and decorative handicrafts. The living spark of beauty which shines in the lowly flower animates the humblest work of art; and it is interesting to observe with what care and devotion smallest objects have been preserved and handed down through centuries, provided only they are impressed with beauty. The world hitherto has not been enamoured by ugliness, nor has it as a rule sought to perpetuate deformity. But lovely objects, a jewel or a casket, or a piece of iron or brass, such, for example, as the treasures of metalwork in Westminster Abbey, are deemed priceless, for if destroyed the void felt could not be filled. Ugly forms are allowed to pass out of mind into oblivion, but the many illustrated volumes on decorative sculpture, on ivory or wood carving, on metal-work, tapestry, and textile fabrics, prove with how great solicitude designs of beauty are preserved, recorded, and handed down. Thus by means of drawings, engravings, and reproductions, poetry of form and colour are woven into the tissue and texture of our lives. And if I may adduce my own experience I would speak of the advantage of treasuring within the memory representative examples of the beautiful—some typical vase, some rare cameo or jewel, some choice form in glass or porcelain, some faultless arrangement in wall decoration, wood-work, or drapery. Such models of excellence serve as standards whereby to measure the departure from correct taste in ordinary and average households. In the present day there can be no excuse when the furniture and decoration of a dwelling, when wall-hangings, mantelpieces, chairs, couches, curtains, table-cloths, lamps, candlesticks, inkstands, paper-knives, &c., show themselves unsightly, because all things ugly in our surroundings stand reproved by a host of historic testimonies. And judging from the experience of the past, it becomes positively sure that whatever works are malformed and hideous will gravitate downwards, will pass from higher to lower grades in social life, from the palace to the cabin, till at last they are swept away and lost, while all things of beauty live on, and the older they grow the more they are revered.

Beauty has received loving regard from philosophers, poets, and painters alike. Lord Bacon takes an impartial but not wholly favourable view in the closing words to his essay, as follows : " Beauty is as summer fruits, which are easy to corrupt and cannot last ; and for the most part it makes a dissolute youth and an age a little out of countenance ; but yet certainly again, if beauty light well, it maketh virtues shine and vices blush." The poets toy with beauty, the term becomes clothed in metaphorical meanings ; a landscape and a lady, a mountain and a monument, a piece of music, a poem and a picture, being esteemed indiscriminately beautiful. Instruction and delight come from the perusal of many metrical musings on beauty, and the mind does well ever and anon to pass from the literature of the subject to the visible embodiments in art. Some poets, such as Spenser and Shelley, pen hymns to intellectual and heavenly beauty, and, like Michael Angelo, drink deeply of the philosophy of Plato. Spenser writes :—

" Therefore it comes that the fair souls which have
The most resemblance to the heavenly light
Frame to themselves most beautiful and brave
Their fleshly bower, most fit for their delight."

" For of the soul the body form doth take ;
For soul is form, and doth the body make."

Passing from poets to metaphysicians, we find that Sir William Hamilton has most nearly arrived at the abstract theory of beauty. His doctrine may be briefly stated as follows : " Beauty brings into action both the imagination and the understanding. Imagination has its delights in the variety of parts, while the understanding finds pleasure in combining the multifarious parts into a whole ; the greater the number of parts given by the imagination, and the more complete the unity wrought by the understanding, the greater will be the pleasure excited, and the more perfect the beauty attained." Number-

less are the passages bearing out this view, and certain artists, among whom stands conspicuous Hogarth, taking side glances at metaphysics, have dashed off specious theories. Hogarth, in his " Analysis of Beauty," written with " a view of fixing the fluctuating ideas of taste," believed he had discovered the whereabouts of beauty in variety, multiplicity, uniformity, regularity, symmetry, simplicity and fitness. And this theory—if so it may be called—which fits loosely within Hamilton's definition, Hogarth was good enough to illustrate by diagrams. Thus he sketched on a painter's pallet a serpentine line, and wrote beneath, " The Line of Beauty ; " and furthermore, on the title-page of the " Analysis " he delineated a pyramid, and within its three sides drew a serpent, and then wrote below, the word " Variety." And so we arrive at yet another manifestation of the ever-recurring maxim, " unity in variety." Again, I repeat, these ingenious speculations stand at dubious distance from practical results, and yet, I think, like the tentative outlines and first sketches which have come down to us from the old masters, they shadow forth permanent truths, and may be used as stepping-stones in the temple of beauty.

The ideas comprised within this short essay might with greater ease have been expanded into a volume. However, in settling the scheme of these papers, I deemed that beauty should find a prominent place, because I hold faith in its high function in life. An inevitable curtness in treatment may possibly have entailed confusion, or indeed incomprehensibility. I can only ask the reader patiently to consider what has been imperfectly expressed ; and to aid him in forming some definite conclusions, I beg to submit, as the issue of the preceding argument, the following propositions.

Forms accounted beautiful come with the greater sanction when they have been accepted over long periods of time, or over wide areas of space, or when they have been identified with high states of civilisation. Such manifestations acquire a historic stability, and are more trustworthy than the phantoms of fashion or the devices of individual or momentary caprice.

Beauty usually accords with geometric proportions or numeric ratios ; thus, in outline and composition it often falls within such figures as the circle, ellipse, or pyramid, and arranges itself according to numbers, such as 2, 3, 5, 7, &c. This numeric theory is supposed to have originated with Pythagoras, and in recent days it found a fanatic advo-cate in Mr. Hay, of Edinburgh. The con-jecture has been that such ratios rest on the undulatory theory, and determine alike beauty of form, colour, and sound ; in other words, that the beauty of the human figure, of the prismatic rainbow, and of a Beethoven sonata obey like fundamental laws.

Forms of beauty, whether elementary or complex, are primarily found in nature, but the creative idea is often marred, dross de-basing the pure gold. Yet nature strives to purge away impurities, to cast out deformi-ties, and to preserve and develop the normal type ; whenever nature reaches her standard of perfection she is beautiful.

Beauty constitutes the ideal, and the true ideal in art corresponds to the perfected real in nature.

Outward and visible beauty is announced and determined by the response and approval of the mind, the mind being made for beauty as the eye is constructed for light : the in-ward intuitions planted in man pulsate, as chords of a lyre, to the vibrations or im-pressions from without.

Beauty obtains a twofold sanction when it exists as the perfection of outward nature, and when it obtains the approving response of the best minds.

Beauty stands in some undefined relation with truth and goodness. Partial and in-completed beauty often contains an admix-ture of error and badness, but perfect beauty is without alloy, and lies in continuity with truth and goodness; the three conjoined making an unbroken circuit, each fortifying the other.

All beauty becomes the more confirmed when it has been sanctioned and made mani-fest by the great artists of the world, and when it is embodied in the masterworks of the foremost architects, sculptors, or painters. Beauty resides within every true and good work of art, just as the soul dwells within the human body,—it is there to a certainty,—we have only to find it out.

And forms of beauty appear with over-whelming evidence when they obtain, as just indicated, a threefold warranty : when they possess the impress of the Creator in nature ; when they have gained the approval of the artist by a place in universal art ; and lastly when they have awakened within humanity an allegiance and a love.

And these manifold phases of beauty declare what they are by the pleasure they impart : beauty always pleases, and what dis-pleases is unbeautiful ; it is her privilege to lead from joy to joy. The worth of any beauty is measured by the dignity of the emotions awakened ; the use of beauty is to elevate, adorn, and add to the enjoyment of life.

MAXIMILIAN HORNBLOWER'S EVENING IN VENICE.

By Lieut.-Col. L. W. M. LOCKHART.

TABLEAU I.

I HAD made an Herculean effort, and failed. The picture that was to have shown the world that a new era in painting had begun arrived too late—the doors of Burlington House were closed. I repre-sented to the hanging committee the fatal mistake they made in refusing it entrance. But in vain; they would none of it.

Disappointed and disgusted I cast over in my mind what I should do. The feverish toil of months was telling on me mentally and bodily, and I felt I could handle a brush no longer. A craving for a new life and fresh scenes came over me. In another country, in a different atmosphere, my under-mined constitution would revive. The thought acted like a tonic, and roused me to action. To Venice! I exclaimed, there to muse on men and manners, and with such light *hors d'œuvres* as the jottings of my pen on art and poetry, to please and titillate the public palate until I can feed the world with my true *pièce de ré-sistance.*

Yes, I said to myself at last, the voices of the people should not be silent. Genius should not cramp itself into a single groove. Utterance denied at one point should be sought at another. Even the fugitive thoughts of a certain kind of man are valuable, either intrinsically or from their suggestiveness. I fancy I am of that kind. The lives of com-monplace men only are commonplace. Em-phatically I am not of that class. Romantic and dramatic incidents cluster habitually round the path of genius. The clear-seeing mind's eye has microscopic properties. The eagle beholds a world of life and movement in that which is blurred, black, and chaotic to the owl and the bat. I am an eagle. My vision is microscopic as well as telescopic. Scanning the book of human nature by the light of humoristic sympathy, I see in what is often an empty page to the mere eye endless revelations of the beautiful, the pathetic, the heroic, the comic, and the farcical.

To think is with me to act. From philosophic musing I can pass with energy to the business of every-day life. My arrangements were soon made, and the scheme carried into effect.

The evening of my arrival in Venice, tempted forth by the beauty of the moonlight, I stood, not on the Bridge of Sighs, but in front of St. Mark's, contemplating it with an admiration which can be understood. Fair was the scene indeed, and exquisite the night. Not a breath stirred the calm air where I stood; but, up above in the clear heavens, some light current carried now and then a gauzy cloud across the full moon's disc, so that her beams played fitfully on all that elaborate wealth of intricate, wondrous sculpture which enriches the goodly frontal of St. Mark's. And thus was lent a simulated motion to alabaster flower and marble leaf, and stem and branch of porphyry and jasper; and the birds set among them by the sculptor's hand seemèd quivering with life, and weird movements of expression came to pass upon the solemn graven faces—faces that seem to regard each other as if in mystic commune touching the destinies of the venerable fane. Venice! the heart of Venice! it was hither that Hope and Freedom and nascent Civilisation had fled desperate, when hunted to the death. It was here, in the embrace of the Adriatic—within the loving circle of her outstretched arms—that they had found a refuge and a strength. It was here that, amid sterile foam and solitary marsh, sprang up—strange as the fabled town which rose to the magic of mysterious strains—a state, a city, and a life, the glory and exemplar of the world!

And so I mused, now swelling into rhapsody uttered aloud, now groping my way through the recondite labyrinth of some metaphysical subtlety. Venice! the heart of Venice! "Come!" I cried, "let me gaze." I did so. And gradually the long perspective grew peopled with shadowy spectres; and gradually the spectral shadows became substantial forms, and I knew them and called them by their names. Divided by no Dantean circles they moved about, and

scanned each other with strange inquiring glances, that changed to looks sometimes of reverence, and sometimes of horror and of hate. These were the doges, the councillors, the grand seignors, the illustrious in arts, in arms, in commerce—a great and goodly company!

Haughty miens, reverent courtiers, waving plumes, burnished armour! Rustling silk, flowing velvet, the sheen of silver and of gold, the flash of every gem the world knows —a goodly sight, a lordly company!

Ha, Paolo Anafesto! I greet thee first, as first of all the dukes. And here comes noble Ziani—hailed as a conqueror. Pass on, noble Doge; right lovingly I greet thee! But who is this without a head? Ha, ha! without a head! groping, with wrinkled hands, his way among the crowd that shrinks to let him by! Marino Faliero! Thou? Headless even here! Ill use thou madest of thy subtle brain on earth; so shalt thou be headless in the land of shadows. Pass on, old man, and headless; 'tis better so. Ha, ha! And ye would limn the hoary traitor, ye three that, with crayons and with tablets and with backward glances, pass in front of him? Ha, great and gentle Titian! excellent Tintoret! bright-eyed Giorgione! I greet ye well!

Noble was thy life, Andrea Dandolo, and thy memory is green, for thou hast left memorials of Venice and thine own virtue. Thy grave is with us to this day—a worthy tomb!

Pass on, right honourable Andrew, remembered and beloved! Francis Foscari! Henry Dandolo! mighty men of valour, I greet ye well; but pass and make way, and let me behold. For who is this with dusky gaberdine, with scales and knife in hand? A Jew! Dog! what dost thou in such worshipful company? What sayest thou, greybeard? Ne'er wast thou in the flesh, yet more than all these doges hast thou been for men a living man! Thy name is Shylock. It is sooth! Sadly it is sooth. Away then, Shylock! get thee to the Bridge of Sighs, and weep and mourn for Jessica and all thy kin, and for thyself, and drop some tears on my account, and heave a sigh or so for me. And Shylock disappeared.

Finding myself in good thinking trim, I lit a cigar and took another look at St. Mark's, to strike, as it were, the key-note of a new train of thought, and, finding it, was off at once. From looking at the splendid idiosyncrasies and gorgeous confusions which characterize the architecture of St. Mark's, from observing here the predominance of the Gothic, and there (to speak generally) of the Oriental, I began to think of it, on the whole, as probably a fair and progressive expression of Venetian thought and life and feeling, as they were during the progress of its creation, and to perceive, on reflection, that this was really the case. *Eureka*, I have it! The Temple of——

The brusque intrusion of sharp antithesis from the outer and lower world is what all contemplative men of genius have constantly to suffer. No sooner had I pronounced the magic word "*Eureka*," than a person emerged from the shadow, approached and addressed me. He was a little Englishman of dapper appearance, and with a manner lacking that slavish deference which, I confess, I like in the first approaches of a stranger, showing as it does that he recognises my— my *je-ne-sais-quoi*, and saving the trouble of explanation. I am bound to say, however, that the man was civil.

"Beg pardon, sir," he said; "but I think, in case you are not aware of it, I ought to let you know that you have been making and —raising, I should say, your voice to a very remarkable height. I heard you at the other end of the Piazza, and I believe the police here don't like noise in the streets at night, and—in short, perhaps you had better be a little quieter. You'll forgive the intrusion?"

"Certainly, sir," I replied; "and even with thanks. Like all great thinkers, I have a *mauvaise habitude* of thinking aloud; and when I get far away into the vast empyrean of thought, I am told that I sometimes shout as though alone in the unpeopled desert. I thank you for your considerate *interruption*."

I made a ceremonious bow, and emphasised the last word to indicate that, though condoned, an interruption had taken place, and might now terminate. He missed my meaning, however, and remained beside me, presently offering his snuff-box. Now, I abominate snuff; but when proffered by the Frank, it has something of the significance of the Bedouin's bread and salt; so I took a pinch.

"*Viva!* ha! ha!—too pungent for you," exclaimed my new acquaintance as I slightly sneezed.

"We won't blame the snuff, sir," I said good-humouredly. "I have a delicate membrane; my whole organism is delicate and tense. We won't blame the snuff."

"Well, it would be difficult to say a word against that snuff. It's the very best 'Blackguard'; but, for some noses, a dash of 'Taddy' or 'Lundyfoot' might improve it. That's what you would say now, I dare say?"

"On the contrary, sir, I have no opinion to offer on the subject."

"Well, I've always stuck to the 'Blackguard.' Many's the dispute I have with my uncle about it. My uncle has tried everything, from the 'Regent' to the 'Blackguard,' and every sort of mixture: but for many years past he has used nothing but 'Lundyfoot,' nothing. He says in his waggish way—for he is a bit of a wag, my uncle—'"Lundyfoot" is my only joy.'"

I could feel no possible interest in his uncle's habits, so I remained silent.

"And my uncle," he went on, "is about right, for he is a very heavy snuffer. I have known him to empty his box—an ounce box —in an evening. The doctor says that by this time his canals and ducts must be coated with 'Lundyfoot'—when I say 'coated,' I mean thickly encrusted—and that there will be a complete block some day. His post-mortem examination, the doctor says, will be something to make you open your eyes and sneeze."

I continued silent. In death as in life, his uncle was nothing to me. My silence was also intended as a rebuke. I felt this introduction of his uncle to be an impertinent intrusion. Nothing, indeed, short of his uncle's agonising death from the total obstruction of all his canals and ducts by "Lundyfoot" could have justified it; and, even then, propriety and good breeding would have suggested some such form as this:—"A man I knew (in fact, an uncle of mine), whose canals and ducts had become encrusted with 'Lundyfoot' tobacco-snuff, died," &c., &c.; or, "The subject of the autopsy had died from inordinate use of 'Lundyfoot,' his canals and ducts being," &c. "He stood to me, by the way, in the relation of uncle."

But "*my uncle*" implied that his uncle was not only a well-known public character, but known also in his relation to my interlocutor, and so universally as to convey to me at once the idea of an individuality with which I was bound to be acquainted. Napoleon III. might have spoken of "my uncle" without impropriety, but no one else I know of. It was intolerable.

I am not, however, vindictive or churlish, so I thought I might properly address a few civil words to him before we separated.

Waving my hand, therefore, in the direction of St. Mark's, I said, "All this is very noble and suggestive."

"Which?" said the little man.

"All this," I replied, with a wider sweep of my arm, to include many other celebrated buildings.

"Well, that's not much in my line, you know; but I dare say you're right."

"I think, sir, that the *nil admirari* and *poco-curante* spirit might hesitate to assert itself here, even in a whisper."

"Perhaps it does," said the man, looking a little puzzled.

"Yet, apparently, it does *not.*"

"Doesn't it, indeed?"

"I should say that *you* were able to speak with perfect precision on that point."

"Well, no; the fact is, it ain't much in my line; but how do you find Venice, sir— as to the life of the place? I find it as dull as ditchwater—flat and sodden as a yesterday's pancake."

"Venice, sir, is in a state of transition. We must not be too hard upon her. One perhaps might expect to find here that the *genius loci* would have a quickening effect upon the inhabitants, but——"

"You'd be disappointed if you did. They're in the slows here, and no mistake."

"I think the expectation would be unphilosophical. Use blunts everything—from a saw to a sentiment. You don't find inquiry alive or noble speculation common among the Alps; and, on much the same principle, you will find that under the shadow of the Vatican and here in Venice inquiry and speculation are at a standstill."

"Right you are, sir. I have no correspondent here; but I took a cast round to-day, and there seems to be no inquiry in any line. As for speculation—Powf! How are they to do it?"

"Well, they are in a state of transition: give them time."

"That's what all bankrupts cry for; but I don't seem to see it."

"Englishmen are apt to be a little impatient."

"Not when they see their way; but no Englishman would see his way here."

"I see you are not sanguine."

"Perhaps not; I know I don't like long dates."

"Long dates, sir?"

"Yes, long dates. I like six better than nine, and three better than six."

"Your metaphor is a little fantastic and remote, sir; but perhaps I grasp your meaning, and I may——"

"And then 'renewals' are always doubtful. I put no faith in them."

"Still, we have had some great instances of renewals. I can't share your feelings about them. I protest I have every faith in renewals—Renaissances, that is."

"I don't know how Renaissances manage their affairs, and every man to his taste, and of course you know your own system best; but, in my experience, the fattest men are not the renewal men; and I dare say you would be a fatter man to-day yourself if you agreed with me."

"I protest, sir, I entirely fail to comprehend you," I said stiffly.

"There are none so deaf as those who won't hear; none so blind as those who won't see."

"I lose myself in your metaphors. Perhaps" (sarcastically) "you are a poet?"

"Well, yes, I am—that is, I was; it's queer that you guessed it. Yes, I was on the poetry lay for a bit—well thought of, too. I could repeat yards of mine; but I didn't seem to fatten, and dropped it. Then I took to the travelling line. I have a roving turn, and never could abide steady routine and desk-work. Am I right?"

"I confess to a certain sympathy with you there. The roving element is essentially one of the factors of the poetic temperament. If a man desires to live in a world of beautiful illusions he must change his *venue* frequently; without locomotion you have stagnation. Realism is the child of stagnation; stagnation too often leads a man to *realise*——"

"It's a bad job when it comes to that; but, of course, if stagnation is obstinate many a poor soul is driven to realise everything, and at a ruinous loss too."

"Well, the loss is, in some sense, ruinous, though your utilitarians would tell you differently."

"I don't care who tells me differently. The man who does so is a donkey—D-O-N-K-E-Y!" And the little man snapped his fingers rapidly to the spelling.

"Well, I don't object to your enthusiasm at all," I said with a good-humoured smile; "for my part, I sympathize with it."

"If you don't you're a D-O-N— No, I don't mean that; but you'd be wrong. It's a matter of common sense and plain figuring."

"Well, well, sir, to return to Venice. I have found it a place eminently favourable to speculation. If the inhabitants are, as you say, dead-alive, the traveller, at least, may reap and carry off a noble harvest."

"Well now, that's exactly what I've been saying he can't do. I took a cast round to-day, as I tell you, and there was nothing to be done. No inquiry."

"I was speaking of myself, sir," I said haughtily.

"What!" cried the little man, "are you a traveller?"

"I am, sir. Is there anything to wonder at in that?"

"Well, yes; I wouldn't have guessed by your cut that you were one of us."

"I can't say that the admission does credit to your perceptive powers. But, be that as it may, I have this very night come to a most remarkable conclusion on a speculation which may have the most stupendous results."

"You don't tell me so!" cried the fellow with unwonted interest.

"I do, sir."

"What, here?—in Venice?"

"On this very spot."

"Well, I'm blowed! Was it on your own account?"

"I protest, sir, I don't see on whose account such a process could be carried on, except on my own," I said with a laugh; the man's questions and remarks were occasionally so inconsequent.

"Well, then," said he, "your principals have nothing to do with it?"

"The remark seems irrelevant. I am not aware that I have mentioned any special principles as directing my speculations. All such processes are necessarily more or less dependent on the laws of association."

"Oh, I see! it's a 'limited' concern."

"When I ask your opinion on the subject you will, perhaps, kindly favour me with it," I said loftily.

"No offence, sir—no intrusion; it's not my line. I won't ask another question, if you don't like it. I know how to respect trade secrets and trade susceptibilities, as the Mounseers say. Mum-m! is the word."

"Trade secrets, sir?"

"Yes, sir. A man who don't respect trade secrets won't respect domestic dittos. Am I right?"

"Well, of course; but what on earth——"

"'Glue' is my Christian name, sir, and 'Wax' the name of my family in both departments."

"Now, sir——"

"Now, sir, I'm not going to spy or to pry into your 'undertaking,' but I'll give you a bit of friendly advice. I heard you talking to yourself, you know—don't be alarmed—I only heard you mention 'Ford's Eureka.'"

"I may have unconsciously pronounced the word 'Eureka,' but——"

"Well, it's an old cry."

"It has been on the lips of the arch discoverer in all ages."

"Ah! well, very likely; but you take my advice, and drop it. Ford used it up *completely.*"

"Ford, sir?"

"Yes, Ford—F-O-R-D. Why, bless you, where were your eyes? Some twelve or fourteen years ago it was all over London and the provinces. I gave it a lift myself—I did. The best poetry I ever did was on the 'Eureka.' I had a lot of copies struck from the advertisement. I kind of fancied them; and I've got some in my pocket-book at this moment. Here, I'll give you one."

He took out his pocket-book, and gave me from it what appeared to be a newspaper slip, and went on with great volubility—

"But, bother it all, leave old Ford his word. Don't go pirating it. I've got a kind of a personal feeling about the 'Eureka.' Besides, it wouldn't pay. If you want a catchword it *must* be original, particularly if what you're bringing out is in the same line. I ask no questions."

"Pray, sir," I said, "have you taken leave of your senses?"

"Come, I say, needn't be so proud. And, after all, what do *you* travel in?"

I was puzzled with the fellow's strange talk, and peevish with him; so, answering the fool according to his folly, I replied—

"If you can't see that I am in broadcloth and tweed, sir, I must attribute your eccentricities to the effects of liquor."

"Well, I should like to know how I was to tell. You might just as well have been in coals, or in wine; in fact you've got rather a coaly, or even winey air about you; and to a man who turns out to be only in cloth, I take it that's rather a compliment. And, by my wig! if you're in cloth, you needn't turn up your nose at Ford's shirt. Cotton and calico's as good as broadcloth and tweed. Better even. Don't you go turning up your nose at the old Eureka shirt. It ain't professional. It ain't gentleman-like."

"Donner und Blitz! who and what do you take me for? Who and what are you?"

"Why, you've just been telling me who you are. As to who I am—no objection in the world to explain. Haven't got a card, but I'm Tom Spankie; commonly called 'Hankie Spankie,' travelling for Fogo, Roker, and Shunt—with a share. Fogo's my uncle. We're in seed; and we're to some extent in cotton—not much now. We work for Oomraurettee and Dhollerah exclusively, but inquiry has been languid since '66, so we've let cotton run loose a good deal. Then we sometimes dabble a bit in coffee, and rice, and shellac—even in tallow. Bless you! we're pretty general, but seeds is our staple. My uncle, who is a bit of a wag, says, 'The seed is the *root* of the business.' Twig?— ha! ha! I keep them up to the general line—part of my roving character—eh?—ha! ha! Well, they didn't do badly when they made me their traveller. My uncle said at the time, 'Tom is a bad salesman, but he may travel well. Try him.' Our Mr. Roker shook his head, but it's a different tune now. Tom is growing warm, sir—warm!—a very much warmer bird than he was when he soared aloft on the wings of song for Hyam, Mechi, Doudney, Mappin, and many city cheap-jacks."

"It comes to this, then," I gasped when I could collect my senses, which had collapsed under the shock; "it comes to this, that I have been all this time conversing with a Bagman!"

"Bagman, yourself!"

"Have a care, sir! have a care!—this rattan——"

"Now, come, don't be so rusty, governor. If I travel in seeds, you travel in cloth; one's at least as good's t'other. I've no pride: 'bagman,' if you please—it ain't a word liked in the profession—what of that? Still, what's sauce for the goose kitchens the gander; and if I'm a bagman, you're a bagman: come now!"

"You must be stark-staring mad, sir! You *actually* suppose me to be a commercial traveller?"

"Rather! Didn't you tell me so yourself? Are you mad? Didn't you tell me you were a traveller? Didn't you say you found no spirit of speculation here? Didn't you say there was no inquiry for any sort of commodity in Venice? Didn't you say you didn't mind taking Venice people's paper at long dates? Didn't you say you went in for giving them time and renewing their bills? Didn't you tell me you had fixed up a speculation to-night? Didn't you say you were working for a 'Limited Company'? Haven't you just said you are in cloth? Well, bother it all! a firm's as good as a 'Limited Company'; and a traveller for a 'Limited Company' is as much a bagman as a traveller for a firm. Come now, put your pride in your pocket, and confess. Come now, be candid!"

"This is too horrible! I wish you a good night, sir. Not another word, I beg—I can't

bear it. Go, sir, go! I feel I may offer you a personal violence if you remain. Go, sir, for your own sake!"

The little man went off in high dudgeon, pretty hurriedly at first, but slackened his pace, when at a safe distance, to assert and reiterate that a "Limited Company" is no better than a firm—that it takes nine tailors to make a man; so that (logically), if my cloth company was not composed of, at least, twenty-seven shareholders, he (Tom Spankie) had, even numerically, a more important constituency in Fogo, Roker, and Shunt than I in the said blessed "Limited Liability Company." These and other sarcasms he kept bawling out as he retreated, till, at last, the Bocca di Piazza swallowed him up, and I saw him no more.

"Strange egotism!" I cried when I had to some extent recovered my composure; "how strange is the egotism of the viler classes! To think that this groundling should have been interpreting my philosophic diction, my philosophic thoughts, as the loathsome cant, as the guttery ideas of commercial life! Faugh! How it clouds even the *oculus externus*, distorting even the outward and visible symbols of heroism and culture into those of a miry, money-grubbing proletarianism. True, I had accepted him and placed him on the footing of a philosophical conversationalist; but we who live in the upper empyrean of thought overlook the pismire in gazing upon the mountain; and we are so rapt in the contemplation of our own ideas that the *nuances* of thought and style belonging to the mere men with whom we converse are naturally lost upon us. We think nothing of them, but conversation is practically a monologue, and it is well it is so."

After walking about for some time thus reflecting, I, half mechanically, fell to reading, by the light of the moon (profaned by looking on such garbage), the verses which the miscreant had given me. Although a man of some considerable stamina I felt so weak and sick after perusing them, that I sank down upon a step in a sort of stupor, only conscious of intense moral and physical nausea. How long I continued in this condition I know not. Gradually I seemed to be awaking from some hideous dream, and at last the cool, bland air and sympathetic moonbeams restored me to myself; and, to give an idea of my recuperative power, I was able in a short time to go at some length, and with sufficient spirit, into the theory that "curvature" is essential to the beautiful in form.

THE TRUMPET-MAJOR.

BY THOMAS HARDY, AUTHOR OF " FAR FROM THE MADDING CROWD," ETC.

CHAPTER XXXI.—MIDNIGHT VISITORS.

MISS GARLAND and Loveday walked leisurely to the inn and called for horse-and-gig. While the hostler was bringing it round the landlord, who knew Bob and his family well, spoke to him quietly in the passage.

"Is this then because you want to throw dust in the eyes of the *Black Diamond* chaps?" (with an admiring glance at Bob's costume).

"The *Black Diamond*?" said Bob; and Anne turned pale.

"She hove in sight just at dark, and at nine o'clock a boat having more than a dozen marines on board, with cloaks on, rowed into harbour."

Bob reflected. "Then there'll be a press to-night; depend upon it," he said.

"They won't know you, will they Bob?" said Anne anxiously.

"They certainly won't know him for a seaman now," remarked the landlord laughing, and again surveying Bob up and down. "But if I was you two, I should drive home along straight and quiet; and be very busy in the mill all to-morrow, Mr. Loveday."

They drove away; and when they had got onward out of the town, Anne strained her eyes wistfully towards Portland. Its dark contour, lying like a whale on the sea, was just perceptible in the gloom as the background to half-a-dozen ships' lights nearer at hand.

"They can't make you go, now you are a gentleman tradesman, can they?" she asked.

"If they want me they can have me, dearest. I have often said I ought to volunteer."

"And not care about me at all?"

"It is just that that keeps me at home. I won't leave you if I can help it."

"It cannot make such a vast difference to the country whether one man goes or stays! But if you want to go you had better, and not mind us at all!"

Bob put a period to her speech by a mark of affection to which history affords many parallels in every age. She said no more about the *Black Diamond*; but whenever they ascended a hill she turned her head to look at the lights in Portland Roads, and the grey expanse of intervening sea.

Though Captain Bob had stated that he did not wish to volunteer, and would not leave her if he could help it, the remark required some qualification. That Anne was charming and loving enough to chain him anywhere was true; but he had begun to find the mill-work terribly irksome at times. Often during the last month, when standing among the rumbling cogs in his new miller's suit, which ill became him, he had yawned, thought wistfully of the old pea-jacket, and the waters of the deep blue sea. His dread of displeasing his father by showing anything of this change of sentiment was great; yet he might have braved it but for knowing that his marriage with Anne, which he hoped might take place the next year, was dependent entirely upon his adherence to the mill business. Even were his father indifferent, Mrs. Loveday would never intrust her only daughter to the hands of a husband who would be away from home five-sixths of his time.

But though, apart from Anne, he was not averse to seafaring in itself, to be smuggled thither by the machinery of a press-gang was intolerable; and the process of seizing, stunning, pinioning, and carrying off unwilling hands was one which Bob as a man had always determined to hold out against to the utmost of his power. Hence, as they went towards home, he frequently listened for sounds behind him, but hearing none he assured his sweetheart that they were safe for that night at least. The mill was still going when they arrived, though old Mr Loveday was not to be seen; he had retired as soon as he heard the horse's hoofs in the lane, leaving Bob to watch the grinding till three o'clock; when the elder would rise, and Bob withdraw to bed—a frequent arrangement between them since Bob had taken the place of grinder.

Having reached the privacy of her own room, Anne threw open the window, for she had not the slightest intention of going to bed just yet. The tale of the *Black Diamond* had disturbed her by a slow, insidious process that was worse than sudden fright. Her window looked into the court before the house, now wrapped in the shadow of the trees and the hill; and she leaned upon its sill listening intently. She could have heard any strange sound distinctly enough in one direction; but in the other all low noises were absorbed in the patter of the mill, and the rush of water down the race.

However, what she heard came from the hitherto silent side, and was intelligible in a moment as being the footsteps of men. She tried to think they were some late stragglers from Weymouth. Alas! no; the tramp was too regular for that of villagers. She hastily turned, extinguished the candle, and listened again. As they were on the main road there was, after all, every probability that the party would pass the bridge which gave access to the mill court without turning in upon it, or even noticing that such an entrance existed. In this again she was disappointed: they crossed into the front without a pause. The pulsations of her heart became a turmoil now, for why should these men, if they were the press-gang, and strangers to the locality, have supposed that a sailor was to be found here, the younger of the two millers Loveday being never seen now in any garb which could suggest that he was other than a miller pure, like his father. One of the men spoke.

"I am not sure that we are in the right place," he said.

"This is a mill, anyhow," said another.

"There's lots about here."

"Then come this way a moment with your light."

Two of the group went towards the cart-house on the opposite side of the yard, and when they reached it a dark lantern was opened, the rays being directed upon the front of the miller's waggon.

"'Loveday and Son, Overcombe Mill.'" continued the man, reading from the waggon. "'Son,' you see, is lately painted in. That's our man."

He moved to turn off the light, but before he had done so it flashed over the forms of the speakers, and revealed a sergeant, a naval officer, and a file of marines.

Anne waited to see no more. When Bob stayed up to grind, as he was doing to-night, he often sat in his room instead of remaining all the time in the mill; and this room was an isolated chamber over the bakehouse, which could not be reached without going down-stairs and ascending the step-ladder that served for his staircase. Anne descended in the dark, clambered up the ladder, and saw that light strayed through the chink below the door. His window faced towards the garden, and hence the light could not as yet have been seen by the press-gang.

"Bob, dear Bob!" she said through the keyhole. "Put out your light, and run out of the back-door!"

"Why?" said Bob, leisurely knocking the ashes from the pipe he had been smoking.

"The press-gang!"

"They have come? Who can have blown upon me? All right, dearest. I'm game."

Anne, scarcely knowing what she did, descended the ladder and ran to the back-door, hastily unbolting it to save Bob's time, and gently opening it in readiness for him. She had no sooner done this than she felt hands laid upon her shoulder from without, and a voice exclaiming, "That's how we doos it—quite an obleeging young man!"

Though the hands held her rather roughly, Anne did not mind for herself, and turning she cried desperately, in tones intended to reach Bob's ears: "They are at the back-door; try the front!"

But inexperienced Miss Garland little knew the shrewd habits of the gentlemen she had to deal with, who, well-used to this sort of pastime, had already posted themselves at every outlet from the premises.

"Bring the lantern," shouted the fellow who held her. "Why—'tis a girl! I half thought so. Here is a way in," he continued to his comrades, hastening to the foot of the ladder which led to Bob's room.

"What d'ye want?" said Bob, quietly opening the door, and showing himself still radiant in the full dress that he had worn with such effect at Weymouth, which he had been about to change for his mill suit when Anne gave the alarm.

"This gentleman can't be the right one," observed a marine, rather impressed by Bob's appearance.

"Yes, yes; that's the man," said the sergeant. "Now take it quietly, my young cock-o'-wax. You look as if you meant to, and 'tis wise of ye."

"Where are you going to take me?" said Bob.

"Only aboard the *Black Diamond*. If you choose to take the bounty and come voluntary you'll be allowed to go ashore whenever your ship's in port. If you don't, and we've got to pinion ye, you will not have your liberty at all. As you must come, willy-nilly, you'll do the first if you've any brains at all."

Bob's temper began to rise. "Don't you talk so large, about your pinioning, my man. When I've settled—— "

"Now or never, young blow-hard," interrupted his informant.

"Come, what jabber is this going on?" said the lieutenant stepping forward. "Bring your man."

One of the marines set foot on the ladder, but at the same moment a shoe from Bob's hand hit the lantern with well-aimed directness, knocking it clean out of the grasp of the man who held it. In spite of the darkness they began to scramble up the ladder. Bob thereupon shut the door, which being but of slight construction, was as he knew only a momentary defence. But it gained him time enough to open the window, gather up his legs upon the sill, and spring across into the apple-tree growing without. He alighted without much hurt beyond a few scratches from the boughs, a shower of falling apples testifying to the force of his leap.

"Here he is!" shouted several below who had seen Bob's figure flying like a raven's across the sky.

There was stillness for a moment in the tree. Then the fugitive made haste to climb out upon a low-hanging branch towards the garden, at which the men beneath all rushed in that direction to catch him as he dropped, saying, "You may as well come down, old boy. 'Twas a spry jump, and we give ye credit for 't."

The latter movement of Loveday had been a mere feint. Partly hidden by the leaves he glided back to the other part of the tree, from whence it was easy to jump upon a thatch-covered out-house. This latter movement they did not appear to see, which gave him the opportunity of sliding down the slope and entering the back-door of the mill.

"He's here, he's here!" the men exclaimed, running back from the tree.

By this time they had obtained another light, and pursued him closely along the back quarters of the mill. Bob had entered the lower room, seized hold of the chain by which the flour-sacks were hoisted from story to story by connection with the mill-wheel, and pulled the rope that hung alongside for the purpose of throwing it into gear. The foremost pursuers arrived just in time to see Captain Bob's legs and shoe-buckles vanishing through the trap-door in the joists overhead, his person having been whirled up by the machinery like any bag of flour, and the trap falling to behind him.

"He's gone up by the hoist!" said the sergeant, running up the ladder in the corner to the next floor, and elevating the light just in time to see Bob's suspended figure ascending in the same way through the same sort of trap into the second floor. The second trap also fell together behind him, and he was lost to view as before.

It was more difficult to follow now; there was only a flimsy little ladder, and the man ascended cautiously. When they stepped out upon the loft it was empty.

"He must ha' let go here," said one of the marines who knew more about mills than the others. "If he had held fast a moment longer he would have been dashed against that beam."

They looked up. The hook by which Bob had held on had ascended to the roof, and was winding round the cylinder. Nothing was visible elsewhere but boarded divisions like the stalls of a stable, on each side of the stage they stood upon, these compartments being more or less heaped up with wheat and barley in the grain.

"Perhaps he's buried himself in the corn."

The whole crew jumped into the corn-bins, and stirred about their yellow contents; but neither arm, leg, nor coat-tail was uncovered. They removed sacks, peeped among the rafters of the roof, but to no purpose. The lieutenant began to fume at the loss of time.

"What cursed fools to let the man go! Why, look here, what's this?" He had opened the door by which sacks were taken in from waggons without, and dangling from the cat-head projecting above it was the rope used in lifting them. "There's the way he went down," the officer continued. "The man's gone."

Amidst mumblings and curses the gang descended the pair of ladders and came into the open air; but Captain Bob was nowhere to be seen. When they reached the front door of the house the miller was standing on the threshold, half dressed.

"Your son is a clever fellow, miller," said the lieutenant; "but it would have been much better for him if he had come quiet."

"That's a matter of opinion," said Loveday.

"I have no doubt that he's in the house."

"He may be; and he may not."

"Do you know where he is?"

"I do not; and if I did I shouldn't tell."

"Naturally."

"I heard steps beating up the road, sir," said the sergeant.

They turned from the door, and leaving four of the marines to keep watch round the house, the remainder of the party marched into the lane as far as where the other road branched off. While they were pausing to decide which course to take one of the soldiers held up the light. A black object was discernible upon the ground before them, and they found it to be a hat—the hat of Bob Loveday.

"We are on the track," cried the sergeant, deciding for this direction.

They tore on rapidly, and the footsteps previously heard became audible again, increasing in clearness, which told that they gained upon the fugitive, who in another five minutes stopped and turned. The rays of the candle fell upon Anne.

"What do you want?" she said, showing her frightened face.

They made no reply, but wheeled round and left her. She sank down on the bank to rest, having done all she could. It was she who had taken down Bob's hat from a nail, and dropped it at the turning with the view of misleading them till he should have got clear off.

CHAPTER XXXII.—DELIVERANCE.

But Anne Garland was too anxious to remain long away from the centre of operations. When she got back she found that the press-gang were standing in the court discussing their next move.

"Waste no more time here," the lieutenant said. "Two more villages to visit to-night, and the nearest three miles off. There's nobody else in this place, and we can't come back again."

When they were moving away one of the private marines, who had kept his eye on Anne and noticed her distress, contrived to say in a whisper as he passed her, "We are coming back again as soon as it begins to get light; that's only said to deceive ye. Keep your young man out of the way."

They went as they had come; and the little household then met together, Mrs. Loveday having by this time dressed herself and come down. A long and anxious discussion followed.

"Somebody must have told upon the chap," Loveday remarked. "How should they have found him out else, now he's been home from sea this twelvemonth?"

Anne then mentioned what the friendly marine had told her; and fearing lest Bob was in the house, and would be discovered there when daylight came, they searched and called for him everywhere.

"What clothes has he got on?" said the miller.

"His lovely new suit," said his wife. "I warrant it is quite spoiled!"

"He's got no hat," said Anne.

"Well," said Loveday, "you two go and lie down now and I'll bide up; and as soon as he comes in, which he'll do most likely in the course of the night, I'll let him know that they are coming again."

Anne and Mrs. Loveday went to their bedrooms, and the miller entered the mill as if he were simply staying up to grind. But he continually left the flour-shoot to go outside and walk round; each time he could see no living being near the spot. Anne meanwhile had lain down dressed upon her bed, the window still open, her ears intent upon the sound of footsteps, and dreading the reappearance of daylight and the gang's return. Three or four times during the night she descended to the mill to inquire of her stepfather if Bob had shown himself, but the answer was always in the negative.

At length the curtains of her bed began to reveal their pattern, the brass handles of the drawers gleamed forth, and day dawned. While the light was yet no more than a suf-

"They proceeded with their burden at a slow pace to the lower garden gate."

fusion of pallor, she rose, put on her hat, and determined to explore the surrounding premises before the men arrived. Emerging into the raw loneliness of the day-break, she went upon the bridge and looked up and down the road. It was as she had left it, empty, and the solitude was rendered yet more insistent by the silence of the mill-wheel, which was now stopped, the miller having given up expecting Bob and retired to bed about three o'clock. The footprints of the marines still remained in the dust on the bridge, all the heel-marks towards the house, showing that the party had not as yet returned.

While she lingered she heard a slight noise in the other direction, and, turning, saw a woman approaching. The woman came up quickly, and, to her amazement, Anne recognised Matilda. Her walk was convulsive, face pale, almost haggard, and the cold light of the morning invested it with all the ghostliness of death. She had plainly walked all the way from Weymouth, for her shoes were covered with dust.

"Has the press-gang been here?" she gasped. "If not they are coming!"

"They have been."

"And got him?—I am too late!"

"No; they are coming back again. Why did you——"

"I came to try to save him. Can we save him? Where is he?"

Anne looked at the woman in the face, and it was impossible to doubt that she was in earnest.

"I don't know," she answered. "I am trying to find him before they come."

"Will you not let me help you?" cried the repentant Matilda.

Without either objecting or assenting Anne turned and led the way to the back part of the homestead.

Matilda, too, had suffered that night. From the moment of parting with Festus Derriman a sentiment of revulsion from the act to which she had been a party set in and increased, till at length it reached an intensity of remorse which she could not passively bear. She had risen before day and hastened thitherward to know the worst, and if possible hinder consequences that she had been the first to set in train.

After going hither and thither in the adjoining field, Anne entered the garden. The walks were bathed in grey dew, and as she passed observantly along them it appeared as if they had been brushed by some foot at a much earlier hour. At the end of the garden,

bushes of broom, laurel, and yew formed a constantly encroaching shrubbery, that had come there almost by chance, and was never trimmed. Behind these bushes was a garden-seat, and upon it lay Bob sound asleep.

The ends of his hair were clotted with damp, and there was a foggy film upon the mirror-like buttons of his coat, and upon the buckles of his shoes. His bunch of new gold seals was dimmed by the same insidious dampness; his shirt-frill and muslin neck-cloth were limp as seaweed. It was plain that he had been there a long time. Anne shook him, but he did not awake, his breathing being slow and stertorous.

"Bob, wake; 'tis your own Anne!" she said, with innocent earnestness; and then, fearfully turning her head, she saw that Matilda was close behind her.

"You needn't mind me," said Matilda bitterly. "I am on your side now. Shake him again."

Anne shook him again, but he slept on. Then she noticed that his forehead bore the mark of a heavy wound.

"I fancy I hear something!" said her companion, starting forward and endeavouring to wake Bob herself. "He is stunned, or drugged!" she said; "there is no rousing him."

Anne raised her head and listened. From the direction of the eastern road came the sound of a steady tramp. "They are coming back!" she said, clasping her hands. "They will take him, ill as he is! He won't open his eyes—no, it is no use! Oh, what shall we do?"

Matilda did not reply, but running to the end of the seat on which Bob lay, tried its weight in her arms.

"It is not too heavy," she said. "You take that end, and I'll take this. We'll carry him away to some place of hiding."

Anne instantly seized the other end, and they proceeded with their burden at a slow pace to the lower garden-gate, which they reached as the tread of the press-gang resounded over the bridge that gave access to the mill court, now hidden from view by the hedge and the trees of the garden.

"We will go down inside this field," said Anne faintly.

"No!" said the other; "they will see our foot-tracks in the dew. We must go into the road."

"It is the very road they will come down when they leave the mill."

"It cannot be helped; it is neck or nothing with us now."

So they emerged upon the road, and staggered along without speaking, occasionally resting for a moment to ease their arms; then shaking him to arouse him, and finding it useless, seizing the seat again. When they had gone about two hundred yards Matilda betrayed signs of exhaustion, and she asked, " Is there no shelter near ? "

" When we get to that little field of corn," said Anne.

" It is so very far. Surely there is some place near ? "

She pointed to a few scrubby bushes overhanging a little stream, which passed under the road near this point.

" They are not thick enough," said Anne.

" Let us take him under the bridge," said Matilda. " I can go no farther."

Entering the opening by which cattle descended to drink, they waded into the weedy water, which here rose a few inches above their ankles. To ascend the stream, stoop under the arch, and reach the centre of the roadway, was the work of a few minutes.

" If they look under the arch we are lost," murmured Anne.

" There is no parapet to the bridge, and they may pass over without thinking."

They waited, their heads almost in contact with the reeking arch, and their feet encircled by the stream, which was at its summer lowness now. For some minutes they could hear nothing but the babble of the water over their ankles, and round the legs of the seat on which Bob slumbered, the sounds being reflected in a musical tinkle from the hollow sides of the arch. Anne's anxiety now was lest he should not continue sleeping till the search was over, but start up with his habitual imprudence, and scorning such means of safety, rush out into their arms.

A quarter of an hour dragged by, and then indications reached their ears that the re-examination of the mill had begun and ended. The well-known tramp drew nearer, and reverberated through the ground over their heads, where its volume signified to the listeners that the party had been largely augmented by pressed men since the night preceding. The gang passed the arch, and the noise regularly diminished, as if no man among them had thought of looking aside for a moment.

Matilda broke the silence. " I wonder if they have left a watch behind ? " she said doubtfully.

" I will go and see," said Anne. " Wait till I return."

" No; I can do no more. When you come back I shall be gone. I ask one thing of you. If all goes well with you and him, and he marries you—don't be alarmed ; my plans lie elsewhere—when you are his wife tell him who helped to carry him away. But don't mention my name to the rest of your family, either now or at any time."

Anne regarded the speaker for a moment, and promised ; after which she waded out from the archway.

Matilda stood looking at Bob for a moment, as if preparing to go, till moved by some impulse she bent and lightly kissed him once.

" How can you ! " cried Anne reproachfully. When leaving the mouth of the arch she had bent back and seen the act.

Matilda flushed. " You jealous baby ! " she said scornfully.

Anne hesitated for a moment, then went out from the water, and hastened towards the mill.

She entered by the garden, and, seeing no one, advanced and peeped in at the window. Her mother and Mr. Loveday were sitting within as usual.

" Are they all gone ? " said Anne softly.

" Yes. They did not trouble us much, beyond going into every room, and searching about the garden, where they saw steps. They have been lucky to-night; they have caught fifteen or twenty men at places farther on ; so the loss of Bob was no hurt to their feelings. I wonder where in the world the poor fellow is ! "

" I will show you," said Anne. And explaining in a few words what had happened, she was promptly followed by David and Loveday along the road. She lifted her dress and entered the arch with some anxiety on account of Matilda ; but the actress was gone, and Bob lay on the seat as she had left him.

Bob was brought out, and water thrown upon his face; but though he moved he did not rouse himself until some time after he had been borne into the house. Here he opened his eyes and saw them standing round, and gathered a little consciousness.

" You are all right, my boy ! " said his father. " What hev happened to ye? Where did ye get that terrible blow ? "

" Ah—I can mind now," murmured Bob with a stupefied gaze around. " I fell in slipping down the topsail halyard—the rope, that is, was too short—and I fell upon my head. And then I went away. When I came back I thought I wouldn't disturb ye ;

so I lay down out there, to sleep out the watch; but the pain in my head was so great that I couldn't get to sleep. I had no baccy, that's how it was; so I picked some of the poppy-flowers in the border, which I once heard was a good thing for sending folks to sleep when they are in pain. So I munched up all I could find and dropped off quite nicely."

"I wondered who had picked 'em!" said Molly. "I noticed they were gone."

"Why, you might never have woke again!" said Mrs. Loveday, holding up her hands. "How is your head now?"

"I hardly know," replied the young man, putting his hand to his forehead and beginning to doze again. "Where be those fellows that boarded us? With this—smooth water and—fine breeze we ought to get away from 'em. Haul in—the larboard braces, and —bring her to the wind."

"You are at home, dear Bob," said Anne, bending over him, "and the men are gone."

"Come along up-stairs; th' beest hardly awake now," said his father; and Bob was assisted to bed.

CHAPTER XXXIII.—A DISCOVERY TURNS THE SCALE.

In four-and-twenty hours Bob had recovered. But though physically himself again, he was not at all sure of his position as a patriot. He had that practical knowledge of seamanship of which the country stood much in need, and it was humiliating to find that impressment seemed to be necessary to teach him to use it for her advantage. Many neighbouring young men, less fortunate than himself, had been pressed and taken; and their absence seemed a reproach to him. He went away by himself into the mill-roof, and, surrounded by the corn-heaps, gave vent to self-reproach.

"Certainly, I am no man to lie here so long for the pleasure of sighting that young girl forty times a day, and letting her sight me—bless her eyes!—till I must needs want a press-gang to teach me what I've forgot. And is it then all over with me as a British sailor? We'll see."

When he was thrown under the influence of Anne's eyes again, which were more tantalizingly beautiful than ever just now (so it seemed to him), his intention of offering his services to the Government would wax weaker, and he would put off his final decision till the next day. Anne saw these fluctuations of his mind between love and patriotism, and being terrified by what she had heard of sea-fights, used

the utmost art of which she was capable to seduce him from his forming purpose. She came to him in the mill, wearing the very prettiest of her morning jackets — the one that only just passed the waist, and was laced so tastefully round the collar and bosom. Then she would appear in her new hat, with a bouquet of primroses on one side; and on the following Sunday she walked before him in lemon-coloured boots, so that her feet looked like a pair of yellow-hammers flitting under her dress.

But dress was the least of the means she adopted for chaining him down. She talked more tenderly than ever; asked him to begin small undertakings in the garden on her account; she sang about the house, that the place might seem cheerful when he came in. This singing for a purpose required great effort on her part, leaving her afterwards very sad. When Bob asked her what was the matter, she would say, "Nothing; only I am thinking how you will grieve your father and cross his purposes if you carry out your unkind notion of going to sea, and forsaking your place in the mill."

"Yes," Bob would say uneasily. "It will trouble him, I know."

Being also quite aware how it would trouble her, he would again postpone, and thus another week passed away.

All this time John had not come once to the mill. It appeared as if Miss Johnson absorbed all his time and thoughts. Bob was often seen chuckling over the circumstance. "A sly rascal!" he said. "Pretending on the day she came to be married that she was not good enough for me, when it was only that he wanted her for himself. How he could have persuaded her to go away is beyond me to say."

Anne could not contest this belief of her lover's, and remained silent; but there had more than once occurred to her mind a doubt of its probability. Yet she had only abandoned her opinion that John had schemed for Matilda to embrace the opposite error— that, finding he had wronged the young lady, he had pitied and grown to love her.

"And yet Jack when he was a boy was the simplest fellow alive," resumed Bob. "By George, though, I should have been hot against him for such a trick, if in losing her I hadn't found a better! But she'll never come down to him in the world; she has high notions now. I am afraid he's doomed to sigh in vain!"

Though Bob regretted this possibility, the feeling was not reciprocated by Anne. It

was true that she knew nothing of Matilda's
temporary treachery, and that she disbelieved
the story of her lack of virtue; but she did not
like the woman. "Perhaps it will not matter
if he is doomed to sigh in vain," she said.
"But I owe him no ill-will. I have profited
by his doings, incomprehensible as they are."
And she bent her fair eyes on Bob and
smiled.

Bob looked dubious. "He thinks he has
affronted me now I have seen through him,
and that I shall be against meeting him. But,
of course, I am not so touchy. I can stand
a practicul joke, as can any man who has
been afloat. I'll call and see him, and tell
him so."

Before he started, Bob bethought him of
something which would still further prove to
the misapprehending John that he was entirely forgiven. He went to his room, and
took from his chest a packet containing a
lock of Miss Johnson's hair, which she had
given him during their brief acquaintance,
and which till now he had quite forgotten.
When, at starting, he wished Anne good-bye,
it was accompanied by such a beaming face,
that she knew he was full of an idea, and
asked what it might be that pleased him so.

"Why, this," he said, smacking his breast-
pocket. "A lock of hair that Matilda gave
me."

Anne sank back with parted lips.

"I am going to give it to Jack—he'll jump
for joy to get it! And it will show him how
willing I am to give her up to him, fine piece
as she is."

"Will you see her to-day, Bob?" Anne
asked with an uncertain smile.

"Oh, no—unless it is by accident."

On reaching Radipole he went straight to
the barracks, and was lucky enough to find
John in his room, at the left-hand corner of
the quadrangle. John was glad to see him;
but to Bob's surprise he showed no immediate contrition, and thus afforded no room
for the brotherly speech of forgiveness which
Bob had been going to deliver. As the
trumpet-major did not open the subject, Bob
felt it desirable to begin himself.

"I have brought ye something that you
will value, Jack," he said, as they sat at the
window, overlooking the large square barrack-
yard. "I have got no further use for it, and
you should have had it before if it had
entered my head."

"Thank you, Bob; what is it?" said John,
looking absently at an awkward squad of
young men who were drilling in the enclosure.

"'Tis a young woman's lock of hair."

"Ah!" said John, quite recovering from
his abstraction, and slightly flushing. Could
Bob and Anne have quarrelled? Bob drew
the paper from his pocket and opened it.

"Black!" said John.

"Yes—black enough."

"Whose?"

"Why, Matilda's."

"Oh, Matilda's!"

"Whose did you think then?"

Instead of replying, the trumpet-major's
face became as red as sunset, and he turned
to the window to hide his confusion.

Bob was silent, and then he, too, looked
into the court. At length he arose, walked
over to his brother, laid his hand upon his
shoulder. "Jack," he said in an altered
voice, "you are a good fellow. Now I see
it all."

"Oh, no—that's nothing," said John
hastily.

"You've been pretending that you care for
this woman that I mightn't blame myself
for heaving you out from the other—which
is what I've done without knowing it."

"What does it matter?"

"But it does matter! I've been making
you unhappy all these weeks and weeks
through my thoughtlessness. They seemed
to think at home, you know, John, that you
had grown not to care for her; or I wouldn't
have done it for all the world!"

"You stick to her, Bob, and never mind
me. She belongs to you. She loves you.
I have no claim upon her, and she thinks nothing about me."

"She likes you, John, thoroughly well; so
does everybody; and if I hadn't come home,
putting my foot in it—— That coming home
of mine has been a regular blight upon the
family! I ought never to have stayed. The
sea is my home, and why couldn't I bide
there?"

The trumpet-major drew Bob's discourse
off the subject as soon as he could, and Bob,
after some unconsidered replies and remarks,
seemed willing to avoid it for the present.
He did not ask John to accompany him
home, as he had intended; and on leaving
the barracks turned southward and entered
the town to wander about till he could decide
what to do.

It was the 3rd of September, but Weymouth still retained its summer aspect.
The King's bathing-machine had been
drawn out just as Bob reached Gloucester
Buildings, and he waited a minute, in the
lack of other distraction, to look on. Immediately that the King's machine had entered

"There is no parapet to the bridge."—P. 654.

the water a group of florid men with fiddles, violoncellos, a trombone, and a drum, came forward, packed themselves into another machine that was in waiting, and were drawn out into the waves in the King's rear. All that was to be heard for a few minutes were the slow pulsations of the sea ; and then a deafening noise burst from the interior of the second machine with power enough to split the boards asunder ; it was the condensed mass of musicians inside, striking up the strains of "God save the King," as his Majesty ascended from the water. Bob took off his hat and waited till the end of the performance, which, intended as a pleasant surprise to his Majesty by the loyal burghers, he probably tolerated rather than desired. Loveday then passed on to the harbour, where he remained awhile, looking at the busy scene of loading and unloading craft, swabbing the decks of yachts, at the boats and barges rubbing against the quay wall, and at the green-shuttered houses of the Weymouth merchants, with their heavy wooden bow-windows which appeared as if about to drop into the harbour by their own weight. All these things he gazed upon, and thought of one thing—that he had caused great misery to his brother John.

The town clock struck, and Bob retraced his steps till he again approached the Esplanade and Gloucester Lodge, where the morning sun blazed in upon the house fronts, and not a spot of shade seemed to be attainable. A huzzaing attracted his attention, and he observed that a number of people had gathered before the King's residence, where a brown curricle had stopped, out of which stepped a hale man in the prime of life, wearing a blue uniform, gilt epaulettes, cocked hat, and sword, who crossed the pavement and went in. Bob went up and joined the group. "What's going on ? " he said.

"Captain Hardy," replied a bystander.

"What of him ? "

"Just gone in—waiting to see the King."

"But he's in the West Indies ? "

"No. The fleet is come home ; they can't find the French anywhere."

"Will they go and look for them again ? " asked Bob.

"Oh, yes. Nelson is determined to find

'em. As soon as he's refitted he'll put to sea again. Ah, here's the King coming in."

Bob was so interested in what he had just heard that he scarcely noticed the cavalcade in which rode the King, the Dukes of York, Cumberland, and Cambridge, and a body of attendant gentlemen. He went on thinking of his new knowledge: Captain Hardy was come. He was doubtless staying with his family at Portisham, a few miles from Overcombe, where he usually spent the intervals between his different cruizes.

Loveday returned to the mill without further delay; and shortly explaining that John was very well, and would come soon, went on to talk of the arrival of Nelson's captain.

"And is he come at last?" said the miller, throwing his thoughts years backward. "Well can I mind when he first left home to go on board the *Helena* as midshipman!"

"That's not much to remember. I can remember it too," said Mrs. Loveday.

"'Tis more than twenty years ago anyhow. And more than that, I can mind when he was born; I was a lad, serving my 'prenticeship at the time. He has been in this house often and often when 'a was young. When he came home after his first voyage he stayed about here a long time, and used to look in at the mill whenever he went past. 'What will you be next, sir?' said mother to him one day as he stood with his back to the doorpost. 'A lieutenant, Dame Loveday,' says he. 'And what next?' says she. 'A commander.' 'And next?' 'Next, post-captain.' I'd warrant that he'd mind it to this very day if you were to ask him."

Bob heard all this with a manner of pre-occupation, and soon retired to the mill. Thence he went to his room by the back passage, and taking his old seafaring garments from a dark closet in the wall conveyed them to the loft at the top of the mill, where he occupied the remaining spare moments of the day in brushing the mildew from their folds, and hanging each article by the window to get aired. In the evening he returned to the loft, and dressing himself in the old salt suit, went out of the house unobserved by anybody, and ascended the road towards Portisham.

The bare downs were now brown with the droughts of the passing summer, and few living things met his view, the natural rotundity of the elevation being only occasionally disturbed by the presence of a barrow, a thorn-bush, or a piece of dry wall which re-

mained from some attempted enclosure. By the time that he reached the village it was dark, and the larger stars had begun to shine when he walked up to the door of the old-fashioned house which was the family residence of the Hardys.

"Will the Captain allow me to wait on him to-night?" inquired Loveday, explaining who and what he was.

The servant went away for a few minutes, and then told Bob that he might see the Captain in the morning.

"If that's the case, I'll come again," replied Bob, quite cheerful that failure was not absolute.

He had left the door but a few steps when he was called back and asked if he had walked all the way from Overcombe Mill on purpose.

Loveday replied modestly that he had done so.

"Then will you come in?" He followed the speaker into a small study or office, and in a minute or two Captain Hardy entered.

The Captain at this time was a bachelor of thirty-five, rather stout in build, with light eyes, bushy eyebrows, a square broad face, plenty of chin, and a mouth whose corners played between humour and grimness. He surveyed Loveday from top to toe.

"Robert Loveday, Captain, son of the miller at Overcombe," said Bob, making a low bow.

"Ah! I remember your father, Loveday," the gallant seaman replied. "Well, what do you want to say to me?" Seeing that Bob found it rather difficult to begin, he leant leisurely against the mantelpiece, and went on, "Is your father well and hearty? I have not seen him for many, many years."

"Quite well, Captain, thank ye."

"You used to have a brother in the army, I think? What was his name—John? A very fine fellow, if I recollect."

"Yes; he's there still."

"And you are in the merchant-service?"

"Late first mate of the brig *Pewit.*"

"How is it you're not on board a man-of-war?"

"Ay, Captain, that's the thing I've come about," said Bob, recovering confidence. "I should have been, but I've waited and waited on at home because of a young woman—lady, I might have said, for she's sprung from a higher class of society than I. Her father was a landscape painter—maybe you've heard of him, Captain? The name is Garland."

"He painted that view of Portisham," said

Captain Hardy, looking towards a dark little picture in the corner of the room.

Bob looked and went on, as if to the picture, "Well, Captain, I have found that—— However, the press-gang came a week or two ago, and didn't get hold of me. I didn't care to go aboard as a pressed man."

"There has been a severe impressment. It is of course a disagreeable necessity, but it can't be helped."

"Since then, sir, something has happened that makes me wish they had found me, and I have come to-night to ask if I could enter on board your ship the *Victory*."

The Captain shook his head severely, and presently went on: "I am glad to find that you think of entering the service, Loveday; smart men are badly wanted. But it will not be in your power to choose your ship."

"Well, well, sir; then I must take my chance elsewhere," said Bob, his face indicating the disappointment he would not fully express. "'Twas only that I felt I would much rather serve under you than anybody else, my father and all of us being known to ye, Captain, and our families belonging to the same parts."

Captain Hardy took Bob's altitude more carefully. "Are you a good practical seaman?" he asked musingly.

"Ay, sir; I believe I am."

"Active? Fond of skylarking?"

"Well, I don't know about the last. I think I can say I am active enough. I could walk the yard-arm, if required, cross from mast to mast by the stays, and do what most fellows do who call themselves spry."

The Captain then put some questions about the details of navigation, which Loveday, having luckily been used to square rigs, answered satisfactorily. "As to reefing topsails," he added, "if I don't do it like a flash of lightning, I can do it so that they will stand blowing weather. The *Pewit* was not a dull vessel, and when we were convoyed home from Lisbon, she could keep well in sight of the frigate scudding at a distance by putting on full sail. We had enough hands aboard to reef topsails man-o'-war fashion, which is a rare thing in these days, sir, now that able seamen are so scarce on trading craft. And I hear that men from square-rigged vessels are liked much the best in the navy, as being more ready for use. So that I shouldn't be altogether so raw," said Bob earnestly, "if I could enter on your ship, sir. Still, if I can't, I can't."

"I might ask for you, Loveday," said the Captain thoughtfully, "and so get you there that way. In short, I think I may say I will ask for you, so consider it settled."

"My thanks to you, sir," said Loveday.

"You are aware that the *Victory* is a smart ship, and that cleanliness and order are, of necessity, more strictly insisted upon there than in some others?"

"Captain, I quite see it."

"Well, I hope you will do your duty as well on a line-of-battle ship as you did when mate of the brig, for it is a duty that may be serious."

Bob replied that it should be his one endeavour; and receiving a few instructions for getting on board the guard-ship, and being conveyed to Portsmouth, he turned to go away.

"You'll have a stiff walk before you fetch Overcombe Mill this dark night, Loveday," concluded the Captain. "I'll send you in a glass of grog to help ye on your way."

The Captain then left Bob to himself, and when he had drunk the grog that was brought in he started homeward, with a heart not exactly light, but large with a patriotic cheerfulness, which had not diminished when, after walking so fast in his excitement as to be beaded with perspiration, he entered his father's door.

They were all sitting up for him, and at his approach anxiously raised their sleepy eyes, for it was nearly eleven o'clock.

"There; I knew he'd not be much longer!" cried Anne, jumping up and laughing in her relief. "They have been thinking you were very strange and silent to-day, Bob; you were not, were you?"

"What's the matter, Bob?" said the miller, for Bob's countenance was sublimed by his recent interview, like that of a priest just come from the *penetralia* of the temple.

"He's in his mate's clothes, just as when he came home," observed Mrs. Loveday.

They all saw now that he had something to tell. "I am going away," he said when he had sat down. "I am going to enter on board a man-of-war, and perhaps it will be the *Victory*."

"Going?" said Anne faintly.

"Now, don't you mind it, there's a dear," he went on solemnly, taking her hand in his own. "And you, father, don't you begin to take it to heart" (the miller was looking grave). "The press-gang has been here, and though I showed them that I was a free man, I am going to show everybody that I can do my duty."

Neither of the other three answered, Anne and the miller having their eyes bent upon the ground, and the former trying to repress her tears.

"Now don't you grieve, either of you," he continued, "nor vex yourselves that this has happened. Please not to be angry with me, father, for deserting you and the mill, where you want me, for I *must go.* For these three years we and the rest of the country have been in fear of the enemy; trade has been hindered; poor folk made hungry; and many rich folk made poor. There must be a deliverance, and it must be done by sea. I have seen Captain Hardy, and I shall serve under him if so be I can."

"Captain Hardy?"

"Yes. I have been to Portisham, walked there and back, and I wouldn't have missed it for fifty guineas. I hardly thought he would see me; but he did see me. And he hasn't forgot you."

Bob then opened his tale in order, relating graphically the conversation to which he had been a party, and they listened with breathless attention.

"Well, if you must go, you must," said the miller with emotion; "but I think it somewhat hard that of my two sons neither one of 'em can be got to stay and help me in my business as I get old."

"Don't trouble and vex about it," said Mrs. Loveday soothingly. "They are both instruments in the hands of Providence, chosen to chastise that Corsican ogre, and do what they can for the country in these trying years."

"That's just the shape of it, Mrs. Loveday," said Bob.

"And he'll come back soon," she continued, turning to Anne. "And then he'll tell us all he has seen, and the glory that he's won, and how he has helped to sweep that scourge Buonaparty off the earth."

"When be you going, Bob?" his father inquired.

"To-morrow, if I can. I shall call at the barracks and tell John as I go by. When I get to Portsmouth——"

A burst of sobs in quick succession interrupted his words; they came from Anne, who till that moment had been sitting as before with her hand in that of Bob, and apparently quite calm. Mrs. Loveday jumped up, but before she could say anything to soothe the agitated girl she had calmed herself with the same singular suddenness that had marked her giving way. "I don't mind Bob's going," she said. "I think he ought to go. Don't suppose, Bob, that I want you to stay!"

After this she left the apartment, and went into the little side room where she and her mother usually worked. In a few moments Bob followed her. When he came back he was in a very sad and emotional mood. Anybody could see that there had been a parting of profound anguish to both.

"She is not coming back to-night," he said.

"You will see her to-morrow before you go?" said her mother.

"I may or I may not," he replied. "Father and Mrs. Loveday, do you go to bed now. I have got to look over my things and get ready; and it will take me some little time. If you should hear noises you will know it is only myself moving about."

When Bob was left alone he suddenly became brisk, and set himself to overhaul his clothes and other possessions in a businesslike manner. By the time that his chest was packed, such things as he meant to leave at home folded into cupboards, and what was useless destroyed, it was past two o'clock. Then he went to bed, so softly that only the creak of one weak stair revealed his passage upward. At the moment that he passed Anne's chamber-door her mother was bending over her as she lay in bed, and saying to her, "Won't you see him in the morning?"

"No, no," said Anne. "I would rather not see him. I have said that I may. But I shall not. I cannot see him again."

When the family got up next day Bob had vanished. It was his way to disappear like this, to avoid affecting scenes at parting. By the time that they had sat down to a gloomy breakfast Bob was in the boat of a Weymouth waterman, who pulled him alongside the guard-ship in the roads, where he laid hold of the man-rope, mounted, and disappeared from external view. In the course of the day the ship moved off, set her royals, and made sail for Portsmouth, with five hundred new hands for the service on board, consisting partly of pressed men and partly of volunteers, among the latter being Robert Loveday.

CHAPTER XXXIV.—A SPECK ON THE SEA.

IN parting from John, who accompanied him to the quay, Bob had said: "Now, Jack, these be my last words to you: I give her up. I go away on purpose, and I shall be away a long time. If in that time she should list over towards ye ever so little, mind you take her. You have more right to her than I. You chose her when my mind was elsewhere, and you best deserve her; for I have never known you forget one woman, while I've forgot a dozen. Take her then, if she will come, and God bless both of ye."

Another person besides John saw Bob go. That was Derriman, who was standing by a bollard a little farther up the quay. He did not repress his satisfaction at the sight. John looked towards him with an open gaze of contempt; for the cuffs administered to the yeoman at the inn had not, so far as the trumpet-major was aware, produced any desire to avenge that insult, John being, of course, quite ignorant that Festus had erroneously retaliated upon Bob, in his peculiar though scarcely soldierly way. Finding that he did not even now approach him, John went on his way, and thought over his intention of preserving intact the love between Anne and his brother.

He was surprised when he next went to the mill to find how glad they all were to see him. From the moment of Bob's return to the bosom of the deep Anne had had no existence on land; people might have looked at her human body and said she had flitted thence. The sea and all that belonged to the sea was her daily thought and her nightly dream. She had the whole two-and-thirty winds under her eye, each passing gale that ushered in returning autumn being mentally registered; and she acquired a precise knowledge of the direction in which Portsmouth, Brest, Ferrol, Cadiz, and other such likely places lay. Instead of saying her own familiar prayers at night she substituted with some confusion of thought the Forms of Prayer to be used at sea. John at once noticed her lorn, abstracted looks, pitied her, —how much he pitied her!—and asked when they were alone if there was anything he could do.

"There are two things," she said with almost childish eagerness in her tired eyes.

"They shall be done."

The first is to find out if Captain Hardy has gone back to his ship; and the other is —oh, if you will do it, John!—to get me newspapers whenever possible."

After this dialogue John was absent for a space of three hours, and they thought he had gone back to barracks. He entered, however, at the end of that time, took off his forage cap, and wiped his forehead.

"You look tired, John," said his father.

"Oh, no!" He went through the house till he had found Anne Garland.

"I have only done one of the things," he said to her.

"What, already? I didn't hope for or mean to-day."

"Captain Hardy is gone from Portisham. He left some days ago. We shall soon hear that the fleet has sailed."

"You have been all the way to Portisham on purpose. How good of you!"

"Well, I was anxious to know myself when Bob is likely to leave. I expect now that we shall soon hear from him."

Two days later he came again. He brought a newspaper, and, what was better, a letter for Anne, franked by the first lieutenant of the *Victory*.

"Then he's aboard her," said Anne, as she eagerly took the letter.

It was short, but as much as she could expect in the circumstances, and informed them that the captain had been as good as his word, and had gratified Bob's earnest wish to serve under him. The ship, with Admiral Lord Nelson on board, and accompanied by the frigate *Euryalus*, was to sail in two days for Plymouth, where they would be joined by others, and thence proceed to the coast of Spain.

Anne lay awake that night thinking of the *Victory* and of those who floated in her. To the best of Anne's calculation that ship of war would, during the next twenty-four hours, pass within a few miles of where she herself then lay. Next to seeing Bob, the thing that would give her more pleasure than any other in the world was to see the vessel that contained him—his floating city, his sole dependence in battle and storm—upon whose safety from winds and enemies hung all her hope.

The next day was Weymouth market, and in this she saw her opportunity. A carrier went from Overcombe at six o'clock, and having to do a little shopping for herself in Weymouth, she gave it as a reason for her intended day's absence, and took a place in the van. When she reached the town it was still early morning, but the borough was already in the zenith of its daily bustle and show. The King was always out-of-doors by six o'clock, and such cock-crow hours at Gloucester Lodge produced an equally forward stir among the population. She alighted, and passed down the esplanade, as fully thronged by persons of fashion at this time of mist and level sunlight as a watering-place in the present day is at four in the afternoon. Dashing bucks and beaux in cocked hats, black feathers, ruffles, and frills, stared at her as she hurried along; the beach was swarming with bathing-women, wearing waistbands that bore the national refrain, "God save the King" in gilt letters; the shops were all open, and Serjeant Stanner, with his sword-stuck bank-notes and heroic gaze, was beating up at two guineas and a crown, the crown to drink his Majesty's health.

She soon finished her shopping, and then, crossing over into the old town, pursued her way along the coast-road to Portland. At the end of an hour she had been rowed across the Fleet (which then lacked the convenience of a bridge), and reached the base of Portland Hill. The steep incline before her was dotted with houses, showing the pleasant peculiarity of one man's doorstep being behind his neighbour's chimney, and slabs of stone as the common material for walls, roof, floor, pig-stye, stable-manger, door-scraper, and garden-gate. Anne gained the summit, and followed along the central track over the huge lump of freestone which forms the peninsula, the wide sea prospect extending as she went on. Weary with her journey, she approached the extreme southerly peak of rock, and gazed from the cliff at Portland Bill.

THE CHILDREN'S MUSIC.

WE asked where the magic came from,
   That made her so wondrous fair,
As she stood with the sunlight touching
   Her gloss of golden hair,
And her blue eyes looked towards heaven
   As though they could see God there?
"Hush!" said the child, "can't you hear it,
   The music that's everywhere?"

God help us! we could not hear it,
   Our hearts were heavy with pain;
We heard men toiling and wrangling,
   We heard the whole world complain;
And the sound of a mocking laughter
   We heard again and again,
But we lost all faith in the music:
   We had listened so long in vain.

"Can't you hear it?" the young child whispered,
   And sadly we answered, "No.
We might have fancied we heard it
   In the days of long ago;
But the music is all a delusion,
   Our reason has told us so,
And you will forget that you heard it
   When you know the sound of woe."

Then one spoke out from among us
   Who had nothing left to fear;
Who had given his life for others,
   And been repaid with a sneer.
And his face was lit with a glory,
   And his voice was calm and clear
As he said, " I can hear the music
   Which the little children hear."

F. M. OWEN.

ON KANGAROOS.

THE visitor to our zoological collections naturally pauses awhile before the kangaroo sheds to remark the curious aspect of these animals, or even to gaze without remark at beings to whose history attaches much that is strange and interesting. The mere look of a kangaroo is, to say the least of it, ungainly and awkward in the extreme. The animal somewhat resembles the frog in the extreme development of the hind-limbs as compared with the front members, and when at rest sits in much the same position as the latter, only differing from the frog or cat in that its fore limbs are completely free from the ground. Resting in its cage, the kangaroo sits on a kind of tripod (Fig. 1), the two hind limbs and the strong tail forming the three legs of its support. Moving about in its den, the animal progresses in awkward fashion, hopping on two hind limbs, and occasionally assisting its movements by tilting itself over for support upon its short fore limbs, but invariably coming to rest upon the tripod once again. The non-zoological visitor to the kangaroos is, as a rule, perfectly conversant with the fact that they come from Australia—that curious continent which gives us the *Ornithorhynchus*, or " duck-billed water-mole," and other curious creatures. The animal just mentioned, indeed, is a near neighbour of the kangaroo, and presents a strange appearance, in that it possesses a duck-like bill and webbed toes. So curious was its outward aspect that when first brought to England, about the close of last century, it was regarded as a manufactured monstrosity; but more exact examination of the animal served to dissipate the erroneous impression, and to establish its position as one of the lowest quadrupeds. With the opossums—which, by the way, are limited in their range to the New World—the kangaroos also possess near relationship; and the wombats, koalas, Tasmanian devil, and like beings, hail them as near kith and kin. We may learn much, not merely respecting quadrupeds at large, but the manner in which the existing population of this world has been distributed and arranged, from a simple study in zoology, such as that we now propose to undertake. Let us, therefore, try firstly to gain some ideas regarding the broad structure of these animals, and concerning the relations of the kangaroos to their own kith and kin, and to the world which they may especially call their own.

That the kangaroo is a quadruped or mammal, and that it therefore belongs to the same great class which includes man as its head, are facts known to every one. But such information, whilst leading us to expect that between the highest animals and the kangaroos there should exist certain broad likenesses of structure and function, also prepares us conversely to expect to find marked differences between the kangaroos and most other quadrupeds. It may be said that man and the kangaroo agree in the broad structure of their bodies. Their bodies, along with those of all other quadrupeds, conform to a general type or plan, which may be said to run through the whole class of mammals. Apart from this broad likeness, however, there are many and important differences to be discerned upon even a very short acquaintanceship with the lower forms; and to some of these differences and characteristic belongings of the kangaroo tribe we may now direct attention.

All kangaroos—and of the race there are various genera and many species—agree very closely indeed in their general structure and appearance. It would require no scientific training to enable an observer to parcel out the kangaroos from all other quadrupeds. True there are the " kangaroo rats," belonging to the kangaroo family, which are, perhaps, strictly speaking, not true kangaroos; and there are the tree kangaroos of New Guinea, in which fore and hind limbs are nearly of the same size, and which possess scaly tails, not used as supports after the fashion of the common species. But even these animals might justifiably enough be called kangaroos, and the naturalist places them in the kangaroo family, to which he gives the name *Macropodidæ*. The representative family (or generic) name of the kangaroo is *Macropus* — a term meaning "long-footed," and the derivation of which we shall presently note. The members of the family derive their special names from some peculiarity of colour, size, or structure. Thus we speak of one kangaroo as *Macropus major*, of another as *Macropus rufus*, and of a third as *Macropus Brunii*. This is saying much the same thing as if we were dealing with a race of Smiths, calling one group the London Smiths, another the Edinburgh Smiths, and a third the Dublin Smiths. When we come to the tree kangaroos we speak of them as *Dendrolagus*, and such a variation of name implies the difference which we might regard existing between our friends the Smiths and the Smythes. They really spring from the same family-tree, but the variations in personal features and structural history have necessitated the separation of the tree kangaroos into a distinct genus or group of the kangaroo family. And similarly with the kangaroo rats and with the rock kangaroos and other branches of the family—we recognise their relationship to the kangaroos with which we are so familiar, but we also note their differences, and make allowance accordingly for their removal to a little distance from the familiar heads of the house. The only animals existing outside the kangaroo order which so closely resemble the kangaroos that they might be mistaken at first sight for our "long-footed" friends, are the little creatures named "Jerboas," which occur chiefly in Northern Africa, and which are also represented in North America. These are little animals, allied to the rats and mice, and included in the group of the *Rodents* or "gnawers." When the kangaroos were first seen, indeed, their likeness to the little jerboas—which likewise sit upon their long hind legs and leap like the kangaroos—was duly remarked. But the naturalist would point to many and important differences between jerboas and kangaroos; these differences including variations in bones, teeth,

Fig. 1—Kangaroos.

brain, and many other points. Hence the resemblance in question is at the best but superficial, as also is that between the kangaroos and those curious little creatures, the elephant shrews of Africa, which are really little shrew-mice, but which also possess a miniature proboscis or elongated nose, and resemble our Australian animals in having long hind legs.

So much for the family resemblances of the kangaroos. A word or two concerning their discovery may not prove uninteresting, if only by way of accounting for the origin of the name. In 1770 Captain Cook visited Botany Bay in the *Endeavour*, which had been dispatched in 1768 on a scientific mission. In the course of the voyage, and when anchored in Endeavour River, an exploring and foraging party returned to the ship with the news that they had seen a new and curious animal, of a mouse colour, and about as large as a greyhound, which moved with surprising dexterity and swiftness. This animal was seen next day, on which occasion also one of the seamen brought the surprising intelligence that he had seen the devil!— this information relating to an animal which he said had horns and wings. The animal proved to be minus the horns (which were, no doubt, its ears), but to possess wings, and appeared in the shape of a large fruit-eating bat. The new animal of the mouse colour and of the size of a greyhound was duly seen by Captain Cook himself, who remarked its long tail, and also that it leapt like a hare or deer. On Saturday, July 14th, a Mr. Gore shot one of the new animals, which was ascertained to be called "kanguroo" by the natives, and which was likewise proved to be remarkably good eating at the voyagers' dinner of Sunday, July 15th, 1770. Such was the description given by Captain Cook of the now well-known kangaroo. Antiquarian researches in zoology, however, inform us that De Bruins, a Dutch traveller, saw a kangaroo as early as 1711. This animal was kept domesticated at Batavia, and was named "Filander," and appears to be the species now called *Macropus Brunii*, after its discoverer.

The kangaroos' personal characters are both easy and interesting to study. The great length of the hind limbs as compared with the fore limbs has already been remarked, and the resemblance between the human arm and the kangaroo's fore limb is very close, inasmuch as both possess five fingers. The hind limb, however, is provided with a different number and a varied arrangement of its toes. The name "longfooted" applied to the animal is fully deserved, since the bones of the instep are exceedingly long, and upon this lengthened part of the foot the animal chiefly rests. But more noticeable are the toes. These number four in all (Fig. 2. A), but only two of the four toes (4, 5) appear to compose the really useful part of the foot. Of these two big toes the inner one (4) is by far the larger, and is provided with a large claw or nail. On the inner side of this large toe in turn we find two other and

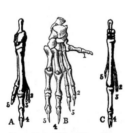

Fig. 2.—Feet of different Marsupials.

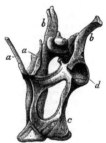

Fig. 3.—Haunch Bones of Kangaroo.

extremely small toes (2, 3), which are bound together in one fold of skin, and which clearly represent the second and third toes in man's foot. So that a kangaroo possesses all the toes we see in man with the exception of the first or great toe, which is completely absent. This foot the animal uses as a means of defence, frequently killing dogs with a single blow. One of the most remarkable features regarding the kangaroos and their neighbours consists in this disposition of their toes. It is somewhat surprising, when we think of it, that in the foot of a kangaroo used for leaping (Fig. 2, A), in that of its neighbour the koala used for climbing, and in that of the ground-living bandicoot and in other Marsupials (such as the Phalanger (B) and *Chœropus* (C)) we should find essentially the same composition of foot. This resemblance and conformity to one type, beneath varied uses and ways of life, can only be reasonably explained by the theory that these varied beings are descended from a common ancestor, and this theory, as we shall see, is supported by other facts of kangaroo existence.

Not the least interesting part of kangaroo history is included in the details which relate to the early life of these animals. Born in a weakly state, the young, as every one knows, are carried and protected within the pouch or *marsupium* of the mother for a considerable period after birth. We know that the young of a kangaroo, which stands over six feet high when full grown, are each about an inch long at birth, and hence we see the necessity for their protection until they are of an age to shift for themselves. The young are transferred to the pouch, and are there duly protected and fed by means of the milk secretion of the parent. Even the throat of the young is so constructed that in

XXI—47

its early and feeble condition it can obtain its nourishment without incurring any danger of suffocation; and we may perceive in this latter fact an evidence of that complete adaptation to a singular manner of life which is so frequently demonstrated by the studies of the naturalist. The "pouch" in which the young are protected is supported upon a couple of bones (Fig. 3 *a, a*), which may be said to be peculiar to the kangaroos and their neighbours. These bones arise from the brim of the haunch-bones, and in their nature they may be regarded as essentially differing from the true skeleton. They represent parts which in other animals exist as the tendons or sinews of certain of the muscles in front of the body. The observation that the bones of the pouch are merely altered sinews again presents to our notice the consideration that nature has adapted these animals for their peculiar life, not by the development of new structures and parts, but by the modification of parts which are common to all animals. It is noteworthy that an adaptation somewhat similar to that seen in the pouch of the kangaroos and their neighbours is seen in those curious little fishes common in our aquaria, and known as *Hippocampi*, or "sea-horses." The males of these fishes possess a pouch in which the eggs are not merely contained, but in which the young are also thereafter protected. The most curious feature of this latter relationship betwixt parent and young, however, consists in the fact that it is the male fishes which tend and nurse the progeny, thus reversing the common rule of animal existence.

The internal anatomy of the kangaroo presents many points of extreme interest to the zoologist and anatomist, but which may be but lightly touched upon, if mentioned at all, within the limits of a popular article. Thus the lower jaw of the kangaroo and its neighbours is bent inwards, or "inflected," as the technical term runs, at its lower and hinder portion; such a peculiarity being of high importance as a character of the group. The kangaroo is well provided in the matter of teeth, and these organs are adapted in turn for their work of cropping and bruising the grasses and other vegetable matters upon which the animals feed. There are six front or cutting teeth above and two cutting teeth below, the latter pointing straight forwards. No "eye-teeth" exist in the kangaroos, but five grinders are seen in each half of the upper jaw, and the same number exists in the lower jaw behind. Thus these animals are provided with twenty-eight teeth,

being only four less than man. The true or American opossums—not to be confounded with the "opossums" of the Australian colonist, which latter are merely species of Phalangers (the foot being figured at B Fig. 2)—possess, on the other hand, almost double the number of teeth found in our kangaroos. In some of the opossums fifty teeth are found; and they are perhaps most notable as possessing a larger number of cutting or front teeth than any other animals. In some of the latter animals, it may be likewise mentioned, the pouch is represented by a mere fold of skin, useless for protecting the young, whilst the bones of the pouch, however, are well developed. In such a case, however, the opossum's habits fully compensate for the want of her portable nursery, in that the young are carried on the mother's back, and obtain a secure lodgment thereon by twisting their tails around hers.

Concluding thus the personal history of the kangaroo, we may briefly glance at the characters of the "order" of animals to which it belongs, by way of introduction to the past history of the kangaroo race. These animals agree with the opossums of America, and with the bandicoots, koalas, and other Australian animals, in possessing the pouch, or at least its characteristic bones, and likewise in the possession of the inflected jaw just alluded to, as one of their principal characters. Accordingly, the naturalist classifies all of these animals to form a single "order" called the *Marsupialia*, or that of the pouched quadrupeds, which has Australia as its head-quarters, and which possesses but one single family outside the boundaries of that island-continent, namely, the opossums (*Didelphidæ*) of America. Now, it may be fairly enough asked, have we any record in zoological or other history to show how Australia came to be the home of marsupial quadrupeds? how the opossums came to settle down in America, and far apart from their only kith and kin in Australia? and how marsupials are absent from all other parts of this world's surface? Without presuming to overrate the importance of our present study, we may safely say that the answers to such questions deal with some of the most important phenomena in the past history of our globe, and bring us, through a simple study such as ours, within the grasp of a deep philosophy. Let us once again briefly consider the problem before us. We are dealing with the case of a peculiar order of quadrupeds, named "Marsupials" from their possessing a pouch; we find these to be confined to Australia, with the exception of a single family, the opossums, which occur in America. On what theory may we explain satisfactorily these two facts: firstly, the limitation of the kangaroos and their neighbours to Australia; and, secondly, the exceptional nature of the home of their opossum friends in the New World?

To answer these important queries, we must pass, firstly, to the province of geology and the history of fossils. The naturalist takes leave of us for the present by reminding us that the marsupials are quadrupeds of lower structure than our cows, horses, dogs, cats, and ordinary mammals; and he also begs to remind us that when Australia was first colonised, no other or higher quadrupeds—save, perhaps, a recently introduced rodent and a bat or two—were found there. The sheep, cattle, horses, dogs, and other familiar animals now found abundantly in Australia, are all importations, and not native products. So that we begin by esteeming our kangaroos and their neighbours as mammals of a low type, in truth, but which nevertheless represent, in their way, the original quadruped population of Australia. Geology now takes up the thread of the story. Australia, it tells us, was as practically distinct in its animals at a far-back period in this world's history as it is to-day. A little channel called the Straits of Lombok, fifteen miles wide, but a channel of deep water nevertheless divides the Indian region, as we term it (consisting of so much of the Malay archipelago, with its monkeys, its rhinoceroses, its tigers, &c.), from the Australian region, in which, as we have seen, monkeys are unknown and higher quadrupeds totally wanting as native animals. The geologist continues his tale, and shows us that the lowest quadrupeds are older than the higher ones, and that the marsupial animals occur as fossils in rocks of a period long before our familiar quadrupeds were in existence. The marsupials and their neighbours were, in fact, the first quadrupeds to appear on the earth's surface; the higher animals being the children of a later growth and of succeeding ages.

Next in order, the geologist tells us that the first traces of marsupial life—and necessarily of the first quadrupeds at large—appear as fossils in those rocks which are called the Trias, and which are much older than the far-back Chalk rocks themselves. Arranging these rocks in the order of their formation, we place them in a column, thuswise—

Recent,	Last formed rocks lying nearest the surface.
Tertiary,	
Chalk,	
Oolite,	Mesozoic Rocks, or middle-life Period.
Trias,	
Permian,	Upper rocks of the oldest series.
Coal, or Carboniferous,	

In the Triassic rocks of Europe as well as in the Trias of North America mammalian jawbones appear as the oldest traces of quadruped life, these fossils being unquestionably those of marsupial animals. Indeed, in the Stonesfield slates lying above the Trias, we find the remains of a marsupial which must have been remarkably like the little "banded ant-eater" alive in Australia to-day. All important, therefore, is the information which thus comes to hand, namely, that *we find the fossils of marsupials in Europe and America, thus proving that in the Triassic and succeeding period they had, if not a world-wide distribution, at least a very extensive range over the earth's surface as it then existed.* In the words we have emphasized lies the key to the mysteries and curiosities of marsupial distribution to-day. In Australia we do not find the fossil remains of any other quadrupeds save marsupials, thus proving that no other mammals, save those allied to its existing population, have ever been tenants therein. We do find in Australia, however, the fossil remains of kangaroos and like animals, differing from their living neighbours in their immense size. Think of a kangaroo whose head alone was about three feet long, and one may conceive of the race of marsupial giants which inhabited Australia in *geologically* "recent" times, and of which our kangaroos and their neighbours are the pigmy descendants.

In the Triassic period, then, and in the Oolite and succeeding epochs, it is certain that marsupials and their allies were the only quadrupeds developed on the face of the earth. That they overran the world's surface and represented in their day and generation the varied quadrupeds of to-day, leaving here and there the fossil relics from which the "coming race" of mankind would construct their history, are likewise plain facts of geology. We see Australia — then joined to what we now name the Asiatic continent — obtaining its marsupial population from the Triassic stock like the rest of the world. Next we perceive Australia to become detached from Asia, its marsupials being thus cut off from all subsequent communication with their neighbours elsewhere. Soon the higher quadrupeds begin to appear, however, and the marsupials, which had hitherto held undisputed sway of the world's surface, come off defeated in the "struggle for existence." The higher and stronger quadrupeds thus came to possess the earth; and the worsted marsupials, killed off in all parts of the world save Australia, at length died out entirely—with the exception of the nimble opossums, which, existing in Europe even in Tertiary times, ultimately found a safe home and haven in the New World. There they have lived and flourished since the close of the Miocene period, when their reign in Europe came to an end. To the question, then, why kangaroos are only found alive in Australia? we reply, because, on account of the early severance of Australia from other lands, they have there been free from the inroads of higher and stronger animals. To the query, Why are the opossums, of all marsupials, found in America alone? we answer, because they represent the later and surviving remnant of that marsupial population which, beginning to exist in the Trias, once overspread the whole earth, which died out in Europe at the beginning of the Tertiary period, but which now flourishes (as the opossum family) in America, since the "struggle for existence" has in the New World not been too hard for the welfare of their race. The opossums do not appear to have formed part of the original stock from which our kangaroos and their allies are derived. Their fossil remains do not occur in Australia; this fact proving that the opossums never resided within the bounds of that island-continent. They probably, therefore, represent a later development and a highly modified race of the marsupial group.

Thus, when we next look at our marsupials, we may in our mind's eye once again see the world peopled by that curious race of quadrupeds and their neighbours; once again we may see the conifers, tree-ferns, and cycads growing around us, as in the days of the Triassic and Oolitic worlds; and once again we behold the spine-bearing fishes and the Port Jackson sharks of Australian coasts in our seas. Thus, in field and forest, lake and sea, the scientific imagination pictures for us series after series of strange forms succeeding each other in "the files of time," filling our earth with the curious array of quadruped life, at the head of which stands the last creation, man, and at the base of which dwell our friends the kangaroos and their neighbours of Australia, together with the opossums, now of the other side of the world, but originally tenants of the Eastern Hemisphere itself.

ANDREW WILSON.

THE EDEL-WEISS.[*]

To the Memory of William Howitt.

I WAS born in my little shroud,
　　All woolly warm, and white,
I live in the mist and the cloud,
　　I live for my own delight;

I see far beneath me crowd
　　The Alpine roses red
　　And the gentian blue, sun fed,
That makes the valleys bright;

I bloom for the eagle's eye,
　　I bloom for the daring hand,
I live but for God, and I die
　　Unto Him, and at His command!

DORA GREENWELL.

London, February 20th, 1878.[†]

[*] The edel-weiss (noble or princely white) grows at the height of 7,000 feet above sea-level: it is worn by the chamois hunters in their caps.
[†] "The hoary head is a crown of glory, if it be found in the way of righteousness." This poem was sent by me, in the autumn of 1878, by the hand of the late Mr. James McDonell, to William and Mary Howitt, then living in the Tyrol, and was received by them with pleasure.

A VISIT TO THE ANCIENT SEE OF ST. AUGUSTINE.

TELEGRAPH work sometimes leads its followers into odd corners of the earth's surface, far out of the beaten track of ordinary travel; and so it happened that I found myself, in the summer of 1875, at the Algerian town of Bona, once the site of the Roman Hippo, and now famous through all Christendom as the ancient see of St. Augustine. As I left Charing Cross on July 10 for Marseilles, the smoky crown of St. Paul's Cathedral was being gilded by the evening sun.

It was harvest time in the valley of the Rhone as our train rushed south towards the Mediterranean, past the old walled towns, the castles, the lonely hermitages and wayside shrines, the smiling vineyards, and rich gardens of Provence. Under that cloudless clime the teeming plains were green with mulberry-trees, or olive groves tossing off sheets of glittering light; the fields were standing yellow with corn, and in shady nooks among the poplars by the river's brim the kine herded, fetlock-deep in meadow grass. On the warm slopes the grapes were beginning to blush in the sunshine, and great baskets of ripe apricots, cherries, and purple figs stood piled among the orchards of this peasant's paradise, where "dance and Provençal song and sun-burnt mirth" seem still to close the Arcadian day. After traversing the vast alluvial plain of the Camargue, whose blank expanse of whity-brown soil was the stage of a fine mirage, where Italian villas appeared to mirror themselves in a vaporous lake, we penetrated the luxuriant suburban gardens of olive and fig which lie behind Marseilles, and after catching a glimpse of the deep blue Mediterranean, with its grey limestone shores clad in sombre pinewoods, and the castellated island of Château d'If, we arrived at that city as the setting sun gleamed on the golden spire of Notre Dame de la Garde.

The Messagerie steamer *Bastia*, in which I left Marseilles for Bona, called on her way at the town of Ajaccio, in the island of Corsica. The entrance to Ajaccio is grand and beautiful, the rugged granite mountains of the interior being dappled with patches of blue heath; the tall, yellow Italian houses of the town with their flat red-tiled roofs, and here and there a brown belfry, crowd up the hillside from the bay.

We go ashore, guided by that mysterious cherub who looks after the stranger and manages to show him all the most interesting sights of the places he may chance to visit. Now the one "lion" of Ajaccio is the great Napoleon, who was born and bred there, and one cannot go far in Ajaccio without coming upon memorials of the fact. We go up a wide acacia-lined boulevard, and pass a fine marble statue of him, supported on four granite lions, hewn from the native rock. This leads us to an open square, where another equestrian bronze statue of the great soldier, surrounded by his four brethren on foot, looks out over the violet haze of the Mediterranean. Close by, in the Place Letitia, is the original home of the Buonapartes. It is a plain, white, three-story building, a middle-class house of considerable size and pretension for the times a century ago. A marble tablet over the doorway bears the brief legend—

"Napoleon—né dans cette maison, 15 Août, 1769."

Opposite the house is a little flower garden, containing a date-palm, an old olive-tree, and vine-covered arbour surmounted by an eagle. It is the garden in which Napoleon played. A stair leads from the front door up to the first flat, that inhabited by the Buonapartes. We pass in first through the drawing-room, with its chairs and sofas of faded yellow satin, its large mural mirrors and rich cabinets; then cross a small oblong court, ornamented with lilies and geraniums in pots, which is now open to the air, but was once roofed with a vine trellis, of which only one vine remained. From this we enter the room in which Napoleon was born, a small room furnished in white. There is a gilt mirror over the white marble chimney-piece, and on one side of it hangs a picture of the hero's mother, a pleasant, clever-looking woman, with red cheeks and dark hair, while on the other hangs a print of his grandfather. On the mantel itself stands a small bust of the Prince Imperial as a boy. Opposite the fireplace is the bedstead on which Napoleon first saw the light, a slender framework of carved wood, painted grey, and in simple contrast to the splendid mausoleum which now enshrines his dust.

Many of the streets of Ajaccio have been named after members of the Napoleonic family and the leading events of their history. The old ones are narrow and steep, and lined with stores full of a rude merchandise, chiefly onions, twine, and glazed pottery. The people are half French, half Italian—a mongrel population without the virtues of either of the parent races, and with all their vices. The streets are full of dirty, hirsute vagabonds, eminently suggestive of the *vendetta* and the assassin's dagger; gangs of ragged urchins, old female beggars, and vulgar priests.

"Voila l'Afrique!" exclaimed a Parisian fellow-passenger as the *Bastia* heaved in sight of the Algerian coast on the following afternoon. Before it neared the land the sun had dropped like a golden disk behind the liquid edge of the wave, suffusing the soft haze with orange light, which deepened every moment, and stole round the rim of the sky, then burned a hectic red. The arid hills of Africa loomed darkling against the luminous after-glow; the rosy twilight bow faded out, and soon the brilliant planets irradiated the night sky above, and matched the phosphorescent turmoil of the sea below; while, to complete the eastern night, the full moon ascended upon the scene and hung in the air like a golden lamp. By-and-by, amid the rattle of chains and shouted orders, the *Bastia* came to rest alongside one of the new wharves of Bona. It was nearly midnight, but on the pier there was congregated a motley crowd of spectral Arabs in their long white bornouses, Jews in the slippered costume of Ali Baba, swarthy Maltese, and Europeans.

The seaport of Bona, or Bône, or in Arabic Beled-el-A'neb (the city of the jujube trees), is situated on a bay of the same name at the mouth of a small river, the Seybouse, which runs down from the spurs of the Atlas Mountains behind. It is surrounded by a modern rampart erected outside the old Saracenic wall and citadel, which is still standing. The modern part is well laid out in the French style, with cafés, hotels (of which the chief is the Hôtel d'Orient), shops, and squares. Here the Franks and wealthier Jews and Arabs reside and do business. In the old quarter of the town, the poorer classes of Moors, Arabs, Soudan Negroes, Turks, and Jews live, and the thrifty Maltese immigrants who flock to the town to make their modest fortunes by hand labour, which the Arab is too proud or lazy to do, live in an intermediate class of shabby tenements. There are barracks for the French Chasseurs and Zouaves and for the native Spahis, schools of all kinds, reading-rooms, hospitals, Roman Catholic chapels, Mahommedan mosques, Jewish synagogues, a Protestant church, and a cathedral dedicated to St. Augustine, the patron saint of the town. Bona is the chief seat of the Mediterranean coral fishery. It exports iron ore from the mines of Mokta-el-Hadid in the vicinity, marble, cork, grain, hemp, olive oil, tobacco, cattle, native garments, such as tunics, slippers, and sashes, leather, and skins of the leopard and lion, hunted in the cork woods on the summit of the Atlas.

Bona is the ancient Aphrodisium, the port of Hippo Regius, or Ubbo, in the ancient Numidia, the ruins of which are to be seen on a conical hill about a mile and a half west of the town, near the Seybouse River. Hippo, the famed bishopric of St. Augustine, was burnt by the Arian Vandals in 430, partially restored by Belisarius, and sacked by the Arabs in the seventh century. These latter conquerors built the town of Bona, or Annaba, which has since passed through many vicissitudes, having been held in turn by the Italians, the Spaniards, and in the sixteenth century by Charles V. The French *Compagnie d'Afrique* then established themselves in the country, and traded with Bona. Finally it was captured by the French in 1832.

The population of Bona numbers over twenty thousand, and is principally composed of French merchants, Jews, Arabs, and Maltese. With respect to the Frenchmen, it is a proverb that every honest one amongst them went there by land. They mostly amass considerable fortunes, and spend an idle, sensuous existence, drinking at cafés with officers from the garrison, or attending the *bains de mer* east of the town. The Jews, who wear their national costumes, are mostly shopkeepers and traders, and are often very rich. The Arab, who dislikes the Jew even more than he does the Frank, is a good-for-nothing idler.

The Arab women, who often tatoo their faces red and blue till they resemble the painted figure-head of a ship, are little better than slaves. The Maltese, though partially of Arab race, and speaking a tongue evidently Arabic, are respectable, industrious folk, who work hard as tradesmen and dock labourers, and live chiefly on bread and vegetables, in order to save a competence and retire to their beloved Malta.

The old town of Bona is built of rectangular whitewashed buildings, with blank exteriors and tesselated inner courts, adorned with rich arabesques and Moorish tracery. The wynds are steep, stony, and narrow, and here the European rarely penetrates. The children playing about are little Moorish children, some of them pretty, with tawny skins, and eyebrows united with a brown curve of henna. On glancing into the open courts one sees only groups of voluptuous Jewish women in their long coloured robes, reclining at rest, or working some primitive mill with their long bare arms. Veiled Arab females move to and fro along the streets, dirty Arabs squat round the native coffee houses, and play at cards or listen to some story-teller. In the shops, which are often mere recesses from the street, a tailor may be seen embroidering a jacket with gold, or a shoemaker cobbling a pair of yellow morocco slippers; here a cook is busy over his charcoal fire and earthen fleshpots; there a public notary is plying his trade on small wooden tablets.

The day breaks in Bona with a lemon-coloured dawn suffusing the cloudless eastern sky; the mueddins utter their call to prayer from the minarets of the mosque; the storks on the flat housetops wake up and preen their wings, while the swallows gambol high in air. Then the hot scorching African day begins; the cafés are opened, and the Arabs commence to move stealthily about. At sunset an orange glow illumines the west like an effluence from the darkling hills, and the starry eastern night sets in. Then the sightseer may wander up any of the narrow wynds of the native quarter with perfect safety, and without even an ill-bred look or remark from the motley population who have turned out to enjoy the evening coolness. Here and there an oil lamp lights up the whitewashed walls and deepens the shadows. White-stoled Arabs are moving stealthily along in the gloom, but otherwise a perfect quiet reigns. Now and again a hideous Soudan negress flits past, her black face being sufficiently veiled by the darkness in which it is harmoniously merged; or a pair of shy young Jewesses in the sacred costume of Rebecca, with all their riches strung in festoons of gold coins across their foreheads, come forth and squat on the threshold of their home.

The most interesting excursion that can be made at Bona is a visit to the remains of Ancient Hippo, the home of St. Augustine during the prolific part of his busy life. We leave Bona by the western gate, and strike south-east across the arid but fruitful plain, with its sullen green foliage and hazy distance. We pass by Arab douahs, or villages of wattle and daub huts, nestling behind great hedges of the Barbary fig or prickly pear, and brick farmhouses surrounded by groves of olive and fig, and fields of vines, melon, rice, and millet. Poplars, oleanders, and eucalyptus trees fringe the beds of the irrigation channels and

the roads. Here and there the eye rests on sunny copses of wild olive-trees overhung with vines and brambles, and laced like a Surrey hedgerow with the starry flowers of the sweet briony. Tall thistles and wild thyme luxuriate in the shade of these olive bowers, and lazy Arabs make their noonday couch under them. As we ride along we encounter perhaps a troop of Kabyles driving their flocks of sheep and cattle before them,.the women riding on mules. These Kabyles are the children of the ancient Berbers, the aborigines of the country; but occasionally one sees among them one of those fiery chevelures sacred to English art as the national complexion of the Scot. These red-haired Algerians are probably descendants of the early Gothic invaders. We pass, too, a cavalcade of Spahis, or Arab troops, marching out of town, mounted on their fine horses and high-backed saddles. Everywhere dotted about the country are little square white structures surmounted by round domes. These are the tombs or shrines of marabouts, or holy men; and usually at the wooden entrance door one sees an Arab kneeling barefooted and muttering his prayers.

The ruins of Hippo stand on a conical olive-clad hill about a mile and a half west of Bona. The soil of the whole hill is interspersed with fragments of pottery and stone, the rubbish of the ancient city. At the foot of it, by the roadside, there is a gigantic arch which is supposed to be the only remaining portion of a great aqueduct, and near this arch there is a stone quarry, in the upper strata of which many square cavities are exposed in which the quarrymen found human bones. Ascending the grassy slopes of the hill we reach a vast pile of ruined buildings among the olive-trees, the lofty arches of underground halls, whose series, so connected and so massive, were evidently designed to bear a stupendous load or superstructure. The masonry is many feet in thickness, and the thickset grit stones in the interior are crumbling to dust, although the cement still keeps entire. In the junctions of the massy arches forming these darksome vaults and halls, are square apertures for ventilation. There are three of these halls, one of which is so large as to be quite an amphitheatre. At one end of it there is a stone staircase leading to a gallery which extends across the entire width of the apartment. This gallery appears to have been an official seat or spectacular throne, and the hall was perhaps a public court, perhaps a theatre. Some writers have, however, set this building down as being once a cistern. To us it appeared rather to have been a palace.

Here, in a corner of this spacious hall, there is an Arab altar, the shrine at which many poor fowls have been slaughtered, for the ground is ankle-deep in feathers. The altar, a stone in the foundation-wall of the ruin, is scrolled with Arabic symbols and dyed with blood. Here, on Fridays, come Arab women to dance and slay their offerings.

As we walk through these sombre vaults, a species of awe comes over us in spite of the brilliant sunshine which bursts down through the olive-trees and broken arches into their silent depths. The mind in a single moment flies from the days of Hippo's pride, when the stately Roman trod her streets and the echoes of St. Augustine's voice resounded from her temples, back to the present, when a descendant of the savage Briton strays among her ruins, from whose mouldering walls the wild fig and the cactus spring, and over whose rended marble floors the bramble creeps and the jackal seeks his lair.

The hill all about these ruins is strewn with blocks of marble, potsherds, and fragments of mosaic pavement, and a deserted Arab blockhouse crowns the summit. On the eastern slope, overlooking the garden plain, with its grey olive groves fronting the white pile of rectangular buildings constituting the town of Bona, and the deep blue expanse of the Mediterranean, there stands a bronze figure of St. Augustine. It is railed round, but the stones of the base are carved with many names from all the nations in Christendom. It is said to commemorate the spot where one of his leg bones is buried, the only relic of him that remains on the scene of his busy apostolic life and of his sublime Christian death, while the Arian Vandals were thundering at the gates of Hippo. J. MUNRO.

VERSES FOR LITTLE ONES.

I.—THE DAISY.

PRETTY is it, as we pass,
  To see the daisy in the grass ;
Day's-eye, as named of old,
For closing from the nightly cold.

You can see them, if you look,
In the mead, or by the brook,
Shrunk into a half their size
When the twilight veils the skies.

Pretty daisy, silver-fair,
I would fain thy meekness share—
Seek to win such honest praise
As poets give thee all the days.

I, like thee, would turn away
From all that is not of the day ;
I would shrink from strife and ill,
And ope my heart to goodness still.

II.—MAY.

The lilac is out, and the thrush on the spray
Is telling the story of beautiful May ;
The hawthorn sheds its sweet scent on the
  breeze,
And the wind is embracing the tall poplar-
  trees.

The birds in sweet chorus are singing a glee :
Wild-rose like a garden the hedge makes to be;
The convolvulus trails its sweet wreaths over
  all,
While the sparrows are busy at each other's
  call.

The wren on the roadside is active and glad ;
The stock-dove is telling the joy that it had
To its mate, when at morning it hurried to find
The food that was most to her ladyship's mind.

The lizard is waking on hillside, in glade,
To lie in the sun where a path has been made
By the footsteps of rovers; it loveth the sand
When the sunshine glows warm all over the
land.

The Maytime has come with its gladness and
flowers;
The hollies and ferns are making them bowers;
The lilac is out, and the thrush on the spray
Is telling the story of beautiful May.

III.—A SUMMER MORNING.

Get up, and see the
sun rise!
The happy lambs at
play
Would gladden all the
children's eyes
And cheer the
longest day.

The sun shines on the
meadow;
And, sparkling in the sun,

Then leaping into shadow,
The chattering brook doth run.

The birds are singing snatches,
The bees go droning by,
The swallows making matches,
And the flower-like butterfly

Is fluttering o'er the roses,
And the honeysuckle too;
The gard'ner's boy makes posies,
And all the sky is blue.

IV.—PRETTY RABBIT.

Pretty rabbit in the fern,
You can scamper rarely;
Tufted ears so softly furred,
Nibbling late and early.

You keep house in burrow deep;
I could wish to join you
When you sit with wife and child,
But I would not pain you.

Mrs. Rabbit I can see
At the head of table;
Master Rabbit, full of glee,
Eating all he's able.

Very serious you are
If others come to see you.

From all your troubles out and in
Would that I could free you.

A very pretty life is yours
In your sandy burrow,
Winding round and round about,
Nor thinking of to-morrow.

V.—DARLING DOLLY.

Darling Dolly's house shall be
High as lofty apple-tree;
It shall have a floor inlaid,
Of the sweetest light and shade.

It shall have for pictures fair
Fancies that are rich and rare;
It shall have a golden roof,
And tapestry with stars for woof.

And it shall have a dome of blue
With the moonlight stealing through ;
And stately pillars straight as firs,
Bending to each wind that stirs.

And her drink shall be of dew,
Bubbling up from fountains new
In the house, through golden sand,
Whereon Dolly's feet shall stand.

Darling Dolly's friends shall come
With music of the wild-bee's hum,
The swallow's twitter, linnet's song—
A music that shall make her strong.

And her talk they all shall know,
And at her bidding come and go
She shall be a Queen of Hearts,
To know the secret of such arts.

And she shall never fear to see
The creatures that make children flee.
She shall have a fair command,
And rule, with gladness o'er the land.

Darling Dolly's house shall be
High as lofty apple-tree ;
It shall have a floor inlaid,
Of the sweetest light and shade.

                                A. H. J.

MAXIMILIAN HORNBLOWER'S EVENING IN VENICE.

By Lieut.-Col. L. W. M. LOCKHART.

TABLEAU II.

THE finest processes of thought are circumscribed by conditions of time, like everything else in this sublunary sphere ; and the noblest thinker has a gastric system which demands a grosser aliment than ambrosial reflection. Thus it suddenly occurred to me that I was strangely hungry, so I struck the metaphysical flag, and bore down upon the French restaurant for supper.

On entering the saloon of the restaurant I at first saw no one. Perfect silence reigned, the lights were burning rather low, and apparently it was empty. Moving up the room, however, I discovered a waiter reposing himself upon a sofa. He was asleep, and his head hung back over the arm of the seat in a painful attitude ; his long black hair drooping perpendicularly like the water of a cascade.

The man was young, and though his features were somewhat pale and haggard, they were exquisitely chiselled, and stamped with a romantic high-souled sort of beauty, which one often sees ludicrously associated among his countrymen with the *métier* of the cook or the waiter.

"This fellow," I said aloud, "might have awakened the Divine rage of Italy's greatest sculptors and painters. Transferred to their marble or their canvas, he might have bloomed in the ambrosial glory of a god, or a hero ; and here he sleeps the sleep of an exhausted trencher-bearer. I wonder what these old masters would have made of him. Not an Antinous—scarcely an Apollo—too sad, too worn for that. Before George ! though, he would make a first-class Lucifer. He would indeed—the lines—— Come, come, though, I must sup ; so we'll vote the poor wretch 'Lucifer,' *nem. con.,* and wake him up to fetch the *vivers*."

"Nothing of the sort, sir ! The merest tyro could see that he is ' Greece, but living Greece no more!' Have the goodness to get out of the light ; you interrupt my study, and whatever you do, don't awaken him."

These words, uttered in a harsh whisper, caused me to turn round, and I saw the hitherto unobserved speaker seated in a recess, half concealed by the hangings of a window. He appeared to be short and stout. His face was fat, flabby, pale, and without any shade in it—a defect not corrected by his hair, which was close-cropped, and of the colour of hay. His shirt collar, turned over and very wide open, revealed a fat bulgy neck, and half his body was draped in a loose cloak suggestive of the transpontine melodrama. His elbow rested on a small table ; his head, surmounted by a tall Calabrian hat, rested on his hand ; and his large green eyes, which seemed to have lost the power of winking, were fixed in a wide-open stare—a little blank in consequence of my body having interpolated itself between them and the object of their contemplation.

Startled by his sudden address, I continued gazing silently at the man till he spoke again.

"Move, sir ! move, I say, to the right or left. Do you not see in your egotism that you come between me and a subject of artistic study? Who knows what the consequences to art may be, if that man is awakened? *Sh! sh! sh!*" and he inculcated silence by three solemn wags of his fore-finger towards me.

"Sir," I said, dropping my voice, however, to a whisper, with instinctive courtesy, "Sir, this is all very well, but do you not see in your egotism, that you would come between me and the means of obtaining necessary sustenance? Who knows what may be the consequences to my gastric system, if Lucifer is *not* awakened?" I was a little nettled, not only by his general manner, but by the cavalier way in which he dismissed the Lucifer theory. So I took the opportunity of insisting upon it.

"Lucifer!" he exclaimed. "Now what a folly is there! Show me a single trait in that face suggestive of the character, of the conception of Lucifer? There is not a line, sir, that can bear an interpretation so absurd. All is calm there—not even the calm of conscious power, or even of desperation; it is the calm of exhaustion—of apathy. There is much beauty in that face, but it is not passion-beauty; there is no latent tempest splendour there; the storm-glory has passed from it for ever. Do you see any menace in that lip? Any potential, haughty resolve in that unquivering nostril? The thunder-cloud has discharged itself; the crater is cold. *Emphatically* he is 'Greece, but living Greece no more.' Just look at his chin——"

"Confound his chin, sir!" I exclaimed out of all patience; "I have been wandering for some hours in the field of abstract speculation, and, frankly, I have had enough of it for the time. Therefore in common fairness to the gastric juices that man must be awakened, and at once."

"Ah!" whispered the stranger, in a gentler tone, "remember! remember! *Ars longa, vita brevis.*"

"Your art, sir, or, at least, your *quasi* artistic rhodomontade, would certainly contribute to the abbreviation of my life. So I shall take the freedom of cutting it short."

"Sir, you are a Philistine!"

"Sir, you are inexact. I am, by blood as by habit, cosmopolitan. On the assumption that the Philistines were of the Kokasian stock, it is possible that, among many others, that strain may be represented in my veins; but in my composition no nationality has a decided preponderance, so that in predicating of me that I am a Philistine, you are, as I say, altogether inexact. You may as well say that I am a Hittite, or a Hivite, a Connemara Kelt, a Kentucky loafer, a Jebusite, a Shunamite, or a Paisley 'body,' in fact——"

"You quibble, sir," interrupted the man; "you are a Philistine in an Arnoldian sense."

"I protest to you that I hear of Arnoldian sense for the first time."

"Tush! quibbler. What's your æsthetic bias—Aryan or Semitic?"

Now, all this time the fellow never looked at me, but kept his eyes fixed hungrily upon the waiter; so, seeing that he was merely attempting to gain time to continue his artistic contemplation by stratagem, I rose and said, "A truce to balderdash! I am going to rouse the man."

"No, no, no!" he said in great excitement, also rising; "it would be the merest act of Vandalism."

"Upon my life, sir! your coolness has long enough overcome my common-sense and my self-respect. I never waited for any one before, and I won't—yes, I will; I will give you exactly two minutes and a half by my watch, and at the expiration of that period I shall call for my supper, whatever may be the consequences to art; and whether this man be Lucifer, or the Apollo Belvedere, or the Colossus of Rhodes, he shall bring it me, or I shall know the reason why." I took out my watch, planted myself firmly against a pillar, and added, "Now, sir, you shall have one hundred and fifty seconds. Stare away as hard as you can; for it is my ultimatum. Are you ready?"

"Now! now! now! I beseech you to reflect. I beseech you to reconsider. By the finger of Phidias! by the eye of Apelles! by the soul of Praxiteles! I beseech you to——"

"Are you ready?"

"No! Is your watch by Benson?"

"Never mind, sir; are you ready? One!"

The fellow continued to stare, making now and then an effort to draw me into conversation, which I checked by simply waving my hand; and when the time had expired, I moved towards the waiter, but instantly he threw himself upon me, pinioned both my arms, and poured into my ear impassioned prayers and adjurations—"By the beauty of the Beardless One," "by the foam-flecked flank of Cytherea," &c., &c., &c. My patience was quite exhausted, however, and I shouted at the full pitch of my voice *Waiter! Kellner! Cameriere! Garçon!*

"*Excellenza!*" The spell was dissolved; the slumberer was awakened and standing in front of me, confused and apologetic, demanding my pleasure.

"Supper," I said; "some maccaroni, a lobster, and a flask of Lachrymæ Christi—*subito !*"

The waiter was off like an arrow, and the contemplative one sank down on the vacant sofa and groaned out, "Miserable man ! you have slain an idea; you have stabbed art; you have robbed posterity; and shut the portal of Fame's Temple against one who is honest in his cultus of the Beautiful and the True ; all for a trumpery lobster, a few strings of maccaroni, and a bottle of vile wine ! *Eheu ! Eheu !*"

As I had now carried my point, I was not indisposed to indulge the humour of this strange person, so I said, "I am sorry to have inconvenienced you ; but—pardon me —may I ask how I have been guilty of all these crimes ? and with what purpose you scrutinised the features of this waiter so intensely ? "

"Sir, that waiter is my model. It is now some weeks since I first detected him in that attitude from which you have just roused him. By a lightning inspiration I saw in his features, in his expression, in his pose, all the materials for a great art triumph. I studied him then, but my opportunity was short ; and night after night have I come here and waited, on the pretext of trifling with some slight refection, till the closing of the premises, in the hope—growing fainter and fainter—of surprising him in a similar con-, dition. This night for the first time he again slept ; and with breathless interest I saw stealing over his features the precise phenomena which had at first attracted me, and inspired the thought that carried to my canvas or my marble, and spiritualised by the magic of genius, these features, these phenomena would evolve a true and glorious conception of ' Dead Greece.' Something seemed to whisper to me, At last the stars are propitious ! At last behold the key that, even in this age, shall unlock Fame's port for thee ! Gaze, then ! gaze and draw into thy soul, through thine eyes, *Germs* which shall spring and fructify beneath the sunbeams of that genius which the gods have given thee ! I had just addressed myself to the task when you— but you know the rest. Dead Sea fruit ! Dead Sea fruit ! Eheu ! Eheu ! "

"May I ask, sir, if you are a painter or a sculptor ? "

"You may, sir ; and I answer unhesitatingly that, despite the dicta of the Royal Academy, I am both, and in the highest sense. As Wagner's music awaits the appreciation of a higher civilisation, so do Fitkin's paintings and Fitkin's sculpture, and Fitkin's fame, buried at present beneath entombing ignorance, envy, spite, scepticism, and depravity in art, await a glorious resurrection and a martyr's crown in a riper age."

"You, sir, then are Fitkin ? "

"I, sir, am Fitkin."

We stared at each other gravely for a few seconds, and I went on.

"Does it not occur to you to purchase the service of the waiter as a model ? Were he removed to your studio when his daily duties were over, and supplied with a sofa, it appears to me that fatigue would soon do the rest."

"Impossible, sir ! It is the old, old story —chill penury and noble rage ; genius and hunger. Eheu ! Eheu ! "

"Are you hungry at this moment, sir ? "

"The hunger of the wolf is proverbial, but I should say it falls short of what I now experience. Every *lira* I can scrape together goes first to the purchase of artistic materials; secondly, to the payment of rent for my poor atelier ; and, lastly, to the support of my body and the bodies of two good souls— worshippers of genius—who frequent my society as disciples hanging upon my words, but whose spiritual cravings do not represent all their needs. There is little left for these last purposes, I assure you ; and the hiring of models is out of the question. Therefore it behoves me to be in earnest when chance casts a subject like this waiter in my way. And now you know my story, so I shall say good night. I will try to forgive you the wrong you have done me ; but it will take time—it will take time."

He drew his melodramatic cloak around him, doffed his Calabrian hat, making me a solemn reverence, and would have withdrawn, but I cried out—

"Stay, Signior Fitkin ! never shall it be said that a brother artist carried the hunger of the wolf from the table of Maximilian Hornblower. Stay, and partake with me, I beseech you."

"Sir, I will accept your hospitality as the payment, the part payment, of a debt. On that understanding I will seat myself, but on that alone."

"Pray be seated, sir, on that understanding. Another lobster, waiter ; more maccaroni ; more Lachrymæ Christi. Away with you ! "

"You spoke of yourself as a brother in

art," said Fitkin as he seated himself; "your name is——?"

"A well-known name, sir; Hornblower—Maximilian Hornblower."

"It is unknown to me."

The man's manner had passed through many phases, from the imperious and bullying to the supplicatory, the pathetic, almost the dignified; now it changed again it was *brusque*, and even at times brutal.

"The name, sir, is entirely unknown to me," he repeated firmly, "either as an artist or anything else."

"Then, sir," I replied, "I am not surprised that until five minutes ago I had never heard the name of Fitkin."

"Tut! tut! that partakes of the nature of a childish *tu quoque;* and, after all, why be petulant? Why fret at obscurity? It may well be, though I cannot think it likely, that the remark applies to your case—it well may be that the noblest artists are unknown to men. Oppose yourself to the pedantries of art, and the art pedants, who are the successful men—your R.A.'s, and so forth—will stamp you out if they can. This has been my case; they have *tried* to stamp me out. Ha! ha! as well hope to stamp out the prairie fire with an infant's feet; but they *have* tried it, and they *have* put me under a temporary eclipse. It will pass. And whence this enmity? Simply because I said, 'I will have none of your lecturings and your slavish copyings, your cramping formulas, your childish rules. I will read nothing; I will copy nothing. I will turn a deaf ear to the voice of the modern. Nature shall teach me everything, with now and then a hint from old-world art.' That was my heresy; and nature has taught me everything. I am against schools in all departments. Their lessons are crude and misleading. The unspoken comments of a *genius loci* are worth all the prelections of philosophers and divines. Well it was for me that in my golden youth, from the Pincian, from Pentelicus, from Parnassus, from Olivet, I gazed over lovely lands and beheld beneath me the cradles of FAITHS and PHILOSOPHIES; for there and then, informed by the helpful air, I unriddled those imperious problems which, left unsolved, confuse men's lives and make them sterile. And well for me that in my homage I rescued myself from the *banalities* of art schools, declining to sit at the feet of the pedagogue, declining to seek inspiration in the platitudes of vapid pages. The old-world of art has contributed *something* towards the perfection of my æsthetic intuitions; but I owe almost everything to ALMA NATURA. From Niagara's watery avalanche, from the roaring river-birth in the Himalayan glacier, from the fiery sunsets of the Sahara, and from solemn Arctic dawns, I have formed my conceptions of the SUBLIME; and for the BEAUTIFUL, my instructors have been the murmuring lips of the Ægean waves, the summer whispers of Achæan breezes, uttering among glimmering groves and ruined temples, the Eternal Liturgy of Pan! Take, then, the wings of the morning——"

"On the contrary, sir, I propose to take a claw of this lobster, and to offer you another."

The man had risen and delivered himself of the above tirade with the greatest volubility and with much gesticulation, swaying himself from one foot on to another, and alternately elevating and depressing his arms; and as it was obvious that he was "boiling up," so to speak, for a lengthy flight, I thought it expedient to stop him effectually—and nothing does put such an effectual stopper upon "high faluten" as the shock of a sudden appeal to very homely material considerations. On this occasion nothing could have been more successful. He stopped as if he had been shot, and dropped into his chair.

"Take a claw," I said.

"Certainly, a claw."

When furnished with this food, I am bound to say that my guest displayed as much concentration with regard to it as he had bestowed upon his slumbering model, never removing his eyes from his plate or pausing to say a word, but eating, I may say, ravenously. By-and-by the length of the silence became awkward, and I felt it might be painful for a guest to contribute nothing to the entertainment—silent, perhaps, under the impression that we had no subjects in common. So I hazarded a remark in his own province.

"I was thinking, Mr. Fitkin, a good deal about Rembrandt this morning, and I got rather adrift. I would like to have your view of him. How say you now? is he among the number of the most illustrious?"

"Rembrandt, sir," replied Fitkin, stopping with the same abruptness in his meal, "was a monster; his style was degraded and degrading. He was a monster."

"A monster? Strong words! strong words! Pray, how do you get over the 'Night Watch'?"

"I don't get over it; it is a monstrosity, simply."

"Come, come, sir, be just; let us say that

his manner is eccentric, but let us admit that 'monstrosity' is too strong a word."

"It is not half strong enough."

"You will admit, I presume, that he is great in *chiaroscuro* ? "

"I will do nothing of the sort; and if you think he is, either you don't know what *chiaroscuro* is, which is more than probable, or you never saw a 'Rembrandt,' which is very likely."

The fellow's impudence astounded me; but the laws of hospitality are sacred, and I commanded myself to reply.

"We need not, I think, sir, lose sight of courtesy in a discussion of this sort."

"Courtesy I there is an eternal and universal antagonism between Courtesy and Truth. But in art there is no *via media* between Truth and Falsehood; and in discussions upon art any idea of such a *via media* must be excluded. A spade must be called a spade, and a lie a lie, in all such discussions. Courtesy I Rubbish I"

"At Rome," I said with a slight laugh, "as Romans do, and in Bohemia, I suppose, as the Bohemians; and on that understanding I will resume the conversation. Now, may I ask you if you think it likely that Rembrandt's manner was affected by the circumstance that his first studio was his father's mill, and that the peculiarity of the lighting of the mill——"

"He never painted in his father's mill."

"Why ?"

"His father never *had* a mill I"

"It is an accepted tradition."

"It is a false one I"

"His father was a miller."

"It is a lie; he was a tanner I "

"That is a lie."

"It is not a lie I"

"I say it is an abominable LIE I "

I had become greatly excited, and rose as I shouted this; but the artist remained perfectly calm, and merely remarked, "Vulgar intensification and savage redundancy are errors in language as they are crimes in art."

I recovered myself at once, and said, "I spoke in a Bohemian sense, sir; but I admit that my language was too strong."

"No offence; I merely say it was a vulgar lie—that it is a lie that Rembrandt's father did not keep a mill, and was a tanner."

"To my ear, sir, the word ' lie ' is so offensive, even when used in a sort of technical sense, that I will not pursue the discussion. Let us change the subject."

"By all means. I could eat some more."

"You shall;" and I gave the order for

another lobster, remarking, on the appearance of a very fine one, "A good subject there for a Flemish artist."

"A fit subject for a grovelling school."

"What—you have no sympathy with Flemish art ? "

"Don't talk to me of Flemish art, sir, here in Venice. It is a profanation."

"Hoity I toity I toity I Think, my good sir, of Rubens."

"I say of him as Hamlet says of Yorick's skull, ' Pah I how he smells of earth I ' "

"Ho I ho I Well, Wouvermann's——"

"A moss-trooper painting with a spur dipped in blood and wine could have done as well."

"Ha I ha I Gerard Dow——"

"A trickster."

"He I he I Albert Dürer——"

"Without a soul."

"Oh I oh I Cuyp——"

"He snores on canvas."

"Come, then, Paul Potter ? "

"A clever sign-painter."

"And yet I should say truth was a very special characteristic of all these men."

"That is a lie. These men were true to Nature, not to Art; and Truth to Nature, and Truth in and to Art, are very different things, as the veriest booby knows."

"I cannot stand the reiteration of the word lie, sir. I must beg that you will conclude your supper as soon as convenient, and let us part, since reasonable conversation seems impossible between us."

"I take exception to the term; reasonable, like all other kinds of conversation, requires two or more participants, and you have said nothing reasonable as yet. Perhaps if you could advance anything of the sort we might agree better."

"Address yourself to your lobster, sir, not to me," I said haughtily.

No shade of discomposure came over his stolid features, and he continued to eat and drink silently, without ever looking at me. At last, finding the bottle empty, he struck it two or three times significantly with his knife, but this receiving no attention, he said, "If we were on speaking terms I would ask for more wine. The wrong and annoyance to which you have subjected me, and of which this supper is, in part, the compensation, have developed in me an abnormal thirst."

I called to the waiter to supply his want, without saying a word to my guest, who went on eating and drinking, while I remained standing with my back turned to him, as a hint that the elements of haste and readiness for the road must not be lost sight of for an instant.

Matters continued in this sort of dead-lock for a considerable time, only disturbed by requests on the part of Mr. Fitkin for Parmesan cheese and various condiments, which were acceded to without comment on my part; but at length I was thoroughly aroused by being struck on the back of the head by the shell of a lobster, and turned fiercely round upon my guest.

"Take no notice of it," he said quietly; "it was an irresistible impulse; something seemed to say, 'there is Patience on a monument. Does he smile?' and I was irresistibly impelled to solve the problem. Hence the lobster—*hinc illæ lachrymæ* (not those of the bottle, for they are, alas! absorbed)—and now I see you do *not* smile: frankly, why?"

"Frankly, sir, because I am irresistibly impelled to treat you to your merits, and trounce you heartily as an impertinent, blackguardly, outrageous humbug."

I advanced towards him with my rattan uplifted, but the fellow neither flinched nor moved, and simply said, raising his forefinger,

"What did we agree about 'intensification'? and how about the laws of hospitality? Is not the one anathema? are not the others sacred?"

This made me hesitate. "Sir," I said, "intensification may be the logical result of a morbid state of things, and the laws of hospitality may be violated by either party brought into the relation which they contemplate. Your conduct logically justifies intensity of speech and action, for you have violated the laws of hospitality, and with singular grossness, for your *corpus delicti* is actually constructed by the body of my lobster, which I have hospitably permitted you to use."

"Ha, ha! *Negatur.* I only threw the *shell*, which is not the *body* — that is the *corpus*; but a *corpus delicti* implies a *corpus*—without a *corpus* there can be no *corpus delicti*, and without a *corpus delicti* no indictment—therefore, logically, no offence. *Q. E. D.* Or, similarly, the *corpus* of the lobster, on which you rely as a *corpus delicti*, is at present trying conclusions with the gastric forces *within my corpus*, and therefore it cannot possibly be playing the part of a *corpus delicti without my corpus*; but without a *corpus* there can be no *corpus delicti*, and, without a *corpus delicti*, no indictment, and, logically, no offence. *Q. E. D.* Any fool can see that.

From your own premises a conclusion falls logically dead against you."

"Logic or no logic, sir, a blow has been struck which cannot be overlooked. As a compromise, however, if you apologise and leave the place I may be induced to withhold the chastisement. Otherwise—" I paused and twirled my rattan.

"Now, now," cried Mr. Fitkin, "I forgive you. Your *pose* there was really fine, and that pause—what rhetorical figure is it?—quite admirable, too! There *is* a dash of art about you, after all. I begin to like you a little better; I do indeed. Sit down, then, and let us discuss the whole affair in a friendly spirit. If you had stood upon the word 'shell' everything would have been different; but you chose to lean your case upon the word *body*, or *corpus*, and sacrificed a fairly tenable position to a foolish pun. You are out of court; you are non-suited; but I am above petty feelings of triumph. A 'shell,' you observe——"

"Stay, sir! no more about the detestable shell. This matter is not to be trifled over with buffooning casuistry. The question before me is whether to chastise you or not; the question before you is whether to apologise and retire or not. As my course, in some sort, depends upon yours, I will suspend my decision for exactly two minutes."

I took out my watch.

"What! our friend Benson again?" cried Fitkin.

"Never mind, sir, the period I have granted has commenced. Silence!"

"I declare I would like to paint you!"

"Hush."

"Or sculpt you. I think I can see you as Achilles sulking in his tent about Briseis; and, if you please, posterity shall see it."

"Don't try to cajole me, sir; the time will soon expire."

"But tell me the precise conditions; I forget them."

"To apologise and retire, or be whipped."

"Supposing I retire without apologising?"

"That will not do."

"Supposing I apologise without retiring?"

"That is different, but you shall cease to be my guest."

"But I shall cease to be your guest in any case; if I apologise and retire, if I apologise without retiring, if I retire without apologising. Your real position, I take it, is 'apologise or be whipped.'"

"Exactly."

"Then why this savage redundancy? Fie, fie!"

"Come, sir; the time has all but elapsed, and be assured that I shall act at once."

"Stripes are not for the free; and as for an apology, you have made that impossible by your stupid crotchet about the crab's body. Logic forbids it—for logically there has been no offence, and without an offence there can be no apology. On the whole, as it is now late, I think I will retire, without, of course, apologising. I may add that if you attempt to impede me I shall take away your life, regretting that no more artistic instrument than this supper-knife" (he took one from the table) "is available for the purpose. Salaam Aleikoum!"

He rose and began to move warily to the door, but I shouted "Stop!" in a voice of thunder, and was rushing forward to assault him (he facing round on the defensive with his supper-knife), when an unlooked-for interruption took place.

"Ulloa, guv'nor, 'ere you are! My stars! Jim, 'ere he be at last!"

The words were spoken at the threshold, and were immediately followed by the entrance of two men of somewhat shaggy appearance, and with that air and contour of garment which one associates with bailiffs, soldier-servants, detectives, and professional cricketers.

"Now then, guv'nor," exclaimed the first to enter, "'ere we've bin a-'untin', and a-prowlink, and a-drorrin of every crib in this 'ere blessed place! It is too bad; a sight too bad!"

"After your promidge, Mr. Fitkin, after your promidge!" ejaculated Number Two, reproachfully.

"Your anxiety, my friends," said Mr. Fitkin, falling into an easy attitude, and furtively pocketing the supper-knife, "is flattering, but a little embarrassing. Now let me introduce to you my friend—a-hem! a distinguished Russian officer, a field-marshal, who knew me in better days."

He winked portentously at me, and by many facial contortions implored me to play the Muscovite.

"And these are the worthy fellows, Marshal," he went on, "of whom I spoke, willing to abandon the safe routine of a mechanical existence, and become acolytes in the temple of the Beautiful; deeming themselves happy to sit at my feet, as at the feet of a Socrates or Gamaliel in art."

"Now then, sink that!" growled Number One.

"Their names are Crickles and Rook—not euphonious, but serving, perhaps, the purposes of identification as well as more highly sounding cognomina."

"Stow it, will you? Stow it!" muttered Crickles between his teeth, and settling himself in his garments as if for some physical exertion.

"You see here, Marshal, an instance of intensification which is not vulgar, because it is the natural outcome of an intense, and if I may be allowed the expression, an untrammelled nature. Crickles has prodigious intensity; but I confess that his ebullitions have for me something of the ferocious grandeur and fitness which we admire in the noisy crash of the avalanche, hurtling from its parent Alp. Calm yourself, however, Thomas; allez doucement, mon brave!"

Crickles, however, declined to calm himself, and seizing Mr. Fitkin firmly by the arm, began to draw him from the saloon. observing—"We've 'ad enough of this 'ere blessed Greek and necromancy; and we'll finish it when you're snug. Come now, trot!"

"Well, Marshal," said Mr. Fitkin, smiling back at me, in the pose of Garrick between the Comic and the Tragic Muse, "well, Marshal, you see it is sometimes a sort of servitude to be too well befriended. What can I say to these neophytes? How allay, but by compliance, this craving for the immortal guest of Hippocrene." But Crickles at this juncture hustled the artist out of the place, who cried back to me in perfect good-humour, "Logical to the last! I retire without apologising. Io triumphe! but it would have been, Væ victis! if I had caught you. Cock-a-doodle-doo!"

"What," I said to Rook, who lingered behind, "what is the meaning of this? How am I understand it?"

"Somethink in the noospapers about a landskip done it."

"Done what?"

"Done 'im. He was tooken at Verona, and we kem out for him."

"Taken?"

"Tooken cranky. Bless my 'art, don'; you see he's a lunick?"

"A lunick?"

"Yes; 'omicidal too, now and agin."

"You mean that he is a lunatic with homicidal tendencies?"

"That's his fit, sir, to the inch."

"Bless my heart! it had not occurred to me."

"Then sir, skews freedom, but you're bound to be as big a lunick as the guv'nor. Night, sir."

And he was off.

SARAH DE BERENGER.

By JEAN INGELOW.

CHAPTER XXIX.

AMABEL and Delia were extremely happy with their girl companions; they made very fair progress under the masters provided for them. Amabel grew more beautiful, and Delia taller and more graceful, and, as is the way with youth, they both lived a good deal in the present. They ceased to want Mrs. Snaith, and they did very well without Coz. Of course the rectory was still home, and Coz was in their thoughts, and what he would think when they were reproved for any little acts of idleness or inattention, but Sir Samuel, now they neither heard of him nor from him, receded into the background of their minds. So did not Amias or Dick.

They did not come home for Christmas, and would have been greatly surprised if they could have known the long discussions there were between Sir Samuel, Sarah, and Felix, as to where their midsummer holidays should be spent.

Nothing concerning their parentage had been discovered. Mrs. Snaith could not be found, and there was a great wish that they should not return till something certain was known about them.

Tom de Berenger came home soon after Christmas, with his wife and another infant daughter. He had all his father's kindly, pleasant manner, and far more than his father's love of money. He was almost a miser, and one of his first conversations with Felix was a remonstrance.

How could Felix have allowed such a lavish house to be kept at the Hall? Such servants, such waste; and never, as a clergyman, have lifted up his voice against it!

Mrs. Tom de Berenger had so completely adopted her husband's views, that she never spent a shilling where sixpence could be made to do, and all her discourse was on prudence, moderation, and economy.

Nothing in his long life had taken such effect on him as the behaviour and discourse of his son and his daughter-in-law took on Sir Samuel. He saw himself caricatured; he was exceedingly ashamed, both for himself and for them. For Tom could discuss even at table, with all earnestness, the wasteful way in which windfall apples and pears were left under the trees, and he did not hesitate to say that "there were a great many more vegetable marrows grown than could be used in the household."

Sir Samuel, though a hot-tempered man, had great self-control, and each of his sons, one after the other, had kept that virtue in full exercise. He would redden sometimes, when his daughter-in-law would strike in after Tom, and agree with melancholy emphasis; but he generally managed either to hold his tongue or to master his temper, and rally his son with tolerable equanimity. But Tom de Berenger was one of those provoking people who are almost always serious; he would try to argue the most minute points of economy with his father, not perceiving that, whether he was right or wrong, his noticing such things at all was mortifying and ridiculous. Then, when the old man was secretly fretted almost past bearing by such discussions before his servants and his guests, Tom would make him break out at last by some finishing touch, that left it hard for other auditors to keep their countenances.

There was nothing in the nature of expenditure that was not important and interesting to him—from the fires in the saddle-rooms to the wasted ends of wax-candles.

He was a good deal out of health, and that circumstance helped his father to be forbearing. He bore a great deal. John had never led him such a life as Tom did, and Tom was not half so bad as Tom's wife.

There were three nice little girls, to be sure—good, obedient children; and there was the baby, also a girl. Sometimes Sir Samuel would say something kind to their father about them. "You'll have one of the *right sort* by-and-by, my lad." "Yes," the poor fellow would answer, with a sigh, "a man had need exercise all due economy who has such a family—four daughters already—and most likely four sons coming, or four more daughters."

They had naturally, and by Sir Samuel's own desire, taken up their abode at the Hall with him, and were all supposed to find their family reunion a great blessing and comfort, but when Parliament met, Sir Samuel went to town with a certain alacrity, though Tom was to remain in the country, London smoke not suiting his delicate chest.

Amias often dined with Sir Samuel in London. His reticence as to Tom's peculiarities could not be exceeded. He had got his only child home again; come what might, he was determined to make the best of him. Tom had no debts; he was, excepting one little foible, everything that a father could desire. How much better that he should be such as he was, than a gambler or a spendthrift! He was a family man, a model father and husband. "If I only see a grandson, I shall have all that a man can wish for in this world," Sir Samuel would often say to himself. And Amias, knowing all about his troubles when in the country, cautiously forbore to ask any awkward questions; Felix having let him know that the heir went round every day to the greenhouses and forcing-houses, to see that the gardeners did not use too much coal and coke. He was said to have poked a lump out here and there that he thought superfluous; and everybody heard this anecdote concerning him, excepting his father.

After the Easter recess, Sir Samuel came to town again, looking rather worried. He had gone through a good deal, and was very glad to find that Tom and his wife meant to go to Clifton for a few weeks. Tom had a nasty cough; his wife wanted him to try the air there, and stay with her mother.

This was all that Amias heard about the matter. He knew his uncle was in town, and meant to go and see him, but he was busy, and had not accomplished the visit, when one morning, just as he had finished his breakfast—Felix, who had come up to town for a few days, being with him—a telegram was brought in from the old uncle's head servant.

"Will you please, sir, come and see Sir Samuel? We have lost Mr. de Berenger. He died at midnight."

"Lost Mr. de Berenger!"

How terrible it seemed, when, not two

minutes previously, they had been making merry over his peculiarities! Felix, so far as the title was concerned, and the very
small portion of the property that was entailed, was the heir.
Neither of them forgot that.

"I had better not see the poor old man," said Felix.

"But I shall be glad if you will come with me to the
house," said Amias. "He may prefer to give directions to
you."

"He never will," said Felix.

When they reached the house, Sarah and some
weeping women-servants met them in the hall. They
asked how the calamity had happened. "He broke a
blood-vessel," she whispered, "and only lived a few
hours. They fetched his father from the House to
hear this awful news."

Amias felt his heart and courage sink as
he turned the lock of the library door and
entered it alone.

Sir Samuel was seated on a sofa,
with his hands clasping his knees and
his head down. One small
leaf of the shutter behind him
had been folded back, and a
narrow beam of sunshine
streamed down from the aperture; otherwise nothing had
been changed since the previous night, and a lamp was
still burning on the table.

Amias sat down and had
not a word to say. He felt
perfectly powerless to find any
consolation for such a calamity
as this.

The old uncle appeared to
notice his presence, for in two
or three minutes he slowly
lifted his head, and looking at
him with a puzzled and half-
stupefied air, said, "I thought
you would come." Then he
added, in a low, inward voice,
"It was one o'clock when

"And a beam of sunshine streamed down from the aperture."

they fetched me home; but"—spreading his
hands about—"it was no use,—I had no son
to send my answer to."

Amias was distressed for him to the point
of shedding two or three compassionate tears,
and they did more for the desolate old man
than any words could have accomplished.
At the sight of human emotion and pity he
seemed to wake up from the stupor that was
killing him, and, as if by imitation of another,
to thaw, and be no more a statue, but a
man.

He was able to weep for his lost son—his
last child: but the suddenness of the blow
had almost prostrated him; his mind was
confused and his speech was thick.

"Is there anything I can do for you?
Are there any arrangements that you would
wish me to make?—or shall Felix make
them?" asked Amias, afterwards.

"Felix may go to Clifton, and do—whatever he pleases. You must stay with me."

"You will not see Felix?"

"Certainly not. I have enough to bear
without seeing him."

"He will not like to act without some instructions."

"Then I leave you two to arrange matters
between you. *You* know that I shall be
satisfied."

So the two cousins of this poor miser,
having leave to do what they thought fitting

for the only son and heir of the now desolate father, had his body brought home to Sir Samuel's country house, invited a number of guests, and had him buried with even more state and pomp than is usual. Considering that one of them was, in part, his heir, and that the other had been almost his rival in the old man's affections, this seemed to them to be the proper thing to do.

Amias brought the father down to attend the funeral, and Felix read the service.

"It was a grand burying," said one of the admiring crowd. "But, dear sakes! how he would have grudged the expense, poor gentleman, if he had known!"

Sir Samuel went back to his desolate home. His son's widow and her four children soon joined him, and the former made him as miserable by her jealousy of the two nephews as she had done previously by her parsimony.

"She never lets me have a quiet hour," he said to Felix; "she's always hinting that her poor children are nothing to me, compared with Amias and you."

"You might at least tell her that she has no cause for jealousy so far as I am concerned," replied Felix, in his most dispassionate manner. "But as to Amias—I think I should be jealous of Amias, if I were in her place."

"She ought not to grudge me what little comfort I have left in this world."

"Then you should not leave her in any doubt, uncle, but tell her plainly what splendid provision there is for her and her children."

"I want Amias to live in my house always when I am in London."

Then, when Felix was silent, he went on.

"You don't suppose his temperance notions would annoy *me?* Besides, I have told you before that I mean to retire if I can get a good offer for the concern. Why should I keep it up any longer—that is, if I can sell it advantageously?"

Felix being still silent, he said, with irritation, "But you understand nothing of business, nephew parson."

"I can fully understand that, at your age, and with your considerable wealth, it must be best for you to retire."

He then inquired about Amabel and Delia. Felix confessed that he could not decide where to take them for their midsummer holidays, but that he did not mean to be parted from them during that time.

Sir Samuel replied that Mrs. de Berenger wanted to take her children to the sea; and as his affliction had been so recent there would be no visitors at his house; therefore the whole party, including Amias and Dick, had better come and stay with him.

If Mrs. de Berenger was to be absent, Felix felt that the girls would be safe from risk of hearing anything that he wished to shield them from. She was the only person likely to speak. But he did not care to leave his own home, though he promised to bring the girls frequently to see—"to see their kind old friend," he concluded, after a pause.

In the meantime the poor mother of these loved and admired creatures tried hard to bear her life without them. It was strange, she thought, that she should have so deeply loved her husband when he was unkind, debased, and unworthy, and yet that she could not love him now, when he was trying so strenuously to do well, when he loved her, was proud of her, and wished nothing more than to work for her and make her comfortable. She tried, with tolerable success, to hide her dislike. She never said a bitter thing, and would sit for hours patiently sewing, and never once asking him to leave off singing those hymns that she knew were intended for her pleasure and edification. She cooked his meals punctually, she kept his clothing clean and whole, but when he went out on his temperance errands she would drop her work on her knees and think, and the tears would steal down her cheeks unaware. And her conscience sometimes disturbed her; her sense of duty sometimes appeared to pull her two different ways. Had she truly been kind to her darlings? What if, after all, they should discover what she had done? Oh, how far more bitter it would be for them, than it could have been to have grown up aware of their father's disgrace! And yet what happy, peaceful lives she had bought for them, and paid for these with the best years of her own—with the effacement of her own prospects. She had lost them for herself, but won them to such a far better lot that they could well dispense with her. She had procured for them such good teaching that she was for ever their inferior. She had robbed herself of their love, but she would rather rue the loss of it than that they should want for anything.

It was Uzziah's reformation that turned all her axioms into doubt; he never said any bad words now. If she had kept her daughters in their own rank of life they might have come back to him, and learned no evil in their humble home. And he would have been pleased with them; he must have loved them. Yes, but she felt that this need not trouble her. He did well enough without them; never had seen one, nor cared for the other. She need not think of him. The children were hers, and she humbly prayed every day that she might be forgiven for the concealment she had practised, in giving up everything for their sake.

Uzziah was not very observant. He was satisfied when she would talk, and did not notice how she always drew him away from personal matters—from his expressions of pleasure at her presence, pride in her appearance, or love for her person; and was willing to hear him enlarge on his speeches of all the "temperance gentlemen" who patronized him, and the good he hoped he was doing.

Sometimes the sudden utterance of a familiar name would make her turn white to the lips.

"He's a rare one," Uzziah exclaimed one night, speaking of Amias; "he does know how to lay about him!"

She trembled on hearing this, but dared say no more than, "Oh, he do? Well, I've heard you say so before."

"Now, his brother," continued Uzziah, "I don't know what to make of him. I really don't."

"Why not?"

"Why not? Well, he doesn't seem to know how to hit the right nail on the head. Mr. Amias is all downright and straightforward. He's against the publicans and against the brewers, and more than all against the distillers. But his brother—what's his name, again? Not Stephen, I know, but something like it. His brother's notion seems to be to hit out pretty generally all round. He seems to think we're all to blame. My word, he made me feel, though I am temperance lecturing, as if he said to me, 'Thou art the man.'"

"He can't well make out that you encourage folks to drink, nor to sell drink, nor to make drink," observed Mrs. Dill, who was willing to hear anything Uzziah might have to say about her children's guardian.

"Well, my dear, in a manner of speaking, he does. A good many of the chief sympathizers were aggravated with him for that, as I could see last night. 'What's the good of our denying ourselves everything for this cause,' says one of them to me, 'if we're to be treated like this?' I took particular notice of what Mr. de Berenger said, because I thought, so far as there seemed to be anything in the argument, I would use it. But it was nothing of an argument at all. He

says the world is ruled by opinion, and that so long as folks—a good many of them—are ashamed of their opinions, then their opinions cannot spread as they should do. He says it is the Spirit of God under whom the conscience of the world grows, and it is often those who conceit themselves that they have the most light that are most full of doubt, and so keep that great conscience back from its expansion. 'If you pretend to be candid,' said he, 'and if you say that the vast body of men who get their living by this traffic can never be expected to give it up—you, too, who believe yourselves to be on God's side —you are in an awful case; you are fighting against Him. How dare you think,' says he, 'that such and such improvements are not to be expected? Who taught you that they were needed? Their guilt is small, whose covetousness urges them on to sell this poison, compared with yours, who are ashamed to believe and confess that the Spirit of God is moving yet on the dark face of the waters.'"

"Then," said Mrs. Dill—for he paused here, and she wanted to continue talking of her late master—"I expect, if we are to prepare for the time when no more spirits at all to speak of are to be drunk, there must be hobs made to every grate, for keeping the teapots warm."

"Not so," replied Uzziah; "for, my dear, if you'll believe me, the doctors want to take a good part of our tea from us too."

"No!" exclaimed Mrs. Dill. "Well, I wonder what next?"

"Well, they say that tea—so much as many of us drink—makes folks to have shaking hands; they say there's no nourishment in it worth naming, and we ought to drink either pure water, or cocoa, or good milk."

"The land that grows barley and hops won't be enough, then," she remarked, "to lay down in grass for the cows that are to yield the milk."

"Not it. I said so to Mr. de Berenger, after the meeting."

"I expect you had him there," observed the wife.

"No. What do you think he made for answer? Why, that water was one of the most nourishing drinks a man could take, and very fattening too!"

"My word!" exclaimed Mrs. Dill, quite surprised, and looking up with a soft colour in her cheeks, which had been brought there by the pleasant excitement of this talk concerning one who was so near to her darlings.

"He did indeed, my dear, and Mr. Amias

backed him. But if it ain't a liberty to say it, I think for once he was mighty glad to step down from the platform when our lecture was over; for if ever there were two pretty young ladies in this world, Mr. de Berenger brought those two with him, and set them down beside an old lady with long curls, right in front of the platform. And I think one of those two made the temperance cause seem to Mr. Amias as if he wished it was further."

"Oh, my beauties, my dears!" thought the mother. "How near I was to going with your poor father to that lecture; and to think now that I should thank God I kept away and did not see you!"

CHAPTER XXX.

"WHEN God gives," said Uzziah, "He gives with both hands. He has given me pardon for my crimes, He has given me back my wife (ten times better than she was before), and now this child."

Uzziah took up the baby as he spoke, and the little fellow opened his dark eyes and spread out his two-days'-old hands.

The doctor left the chamber, but not without an involuntary elevation of the eyebrows, and a scrutinising glance at this man.

"My dear," said Hannah Dill, as the door was quietly shut, "you have no call to use that word. It worry me more than I can tell to hear you do it."

"What's for ever in a man's mind must come out now and then," he answered.

Her white lips trembled slightly; and, a different husband altogether from his former self, he immediately apologized. He promised to use more circumspection. Then, mindful of her late danger, he began to employ some of the kindly flattery that a new-made mother loves best to hear, admiring the infant.

"Did anybody ever see such big dark eyes?—for all the world like yours, my dear. I hope, please God, he will be like you. A very pretty boy, to be sure; and what a weight on my arm already!"

"Yes," said the feeble mother, turning her head on her pillow, "he is a very fine babe to look to."

"I shall be as proud as ever was of the little chap," continued Uzziah, laying him down beside her with a smile of real affection; "it's what I've been wanting this long time, though I scarce knew it—a child of my own. Ever since I had you again I felt I could not be easy; as if it hurt me to see you in the house all alone."

"Did you feel to want those that are gone?" asked the mother, with a certain pang. She was beginning to do more than tolerate her poor husband, and the notion of his having yearned for the children she had taken from him gave her keen pain.

"Well, I did; but there are things you know as we agreed never to speak on."

"Ay," answered the wife, "but you may say what you have in your mind this once." She thought this addition to her punishment for having made them happy at her own expense, was a bitterness that she must not shrink from as regarded these lost treasures, and she listened when he said—

"My dear, you would have been all the mother to them. I should like to have seen it. And there ain't a doubt but what they'd have been great blessings to us, and I should soon have got very fond of them."

She looked at him with pity, almost with fear.

"Only," he continued, "they would have known."

"They must ha' known," she answered, sighing.

"Ay."

"Don't you think, then, Uzziah, 'tis best as it is?"

"'Tis best as God willed it," he answered seriously.

"Ay; but that's not what I meant," she cried piteously. "The only time we spoke on these, you said, 'They're well off.'"

"We know they are, Hannah."

She assented with hysterical tears. "Ay, I know my blessings, my dears are better off than ever they could be with me. Let me hear you say that you do not wish we had them again."

"I could not exactly say that, my dear; for since I knew this little fellow was coming, I have many times dreamed that I was in quod again, and that I saw that other little one with flaxen hair—a pretty creature!—trotting about on the floor. Considering what a bad father I made her, you'll think that was strange. Little Ammy—why, she would have been very nigh seventeen year old by this time." Seeing that she was unable to restrain her tears, he added, "Don't fret, my dear; we have talked about her again for once and for all, for you see it has been once too often."

"Ay, it's more than I can bear. God forgive me!" replied the mother.

Uzziah, mistaking her meaning, continued, "So now let them sleep in the bosom of the Son of God; you shall have them again.

And meanwhile get well so fast as you may, for the sake of this new blessing."

He presently went out, and Hannah Dill turned her head, and looked with yearning pity and love at her new-born child. An inheritance of shame was his. He was to know from the first that his poor father had been a disgrace to him. But yet in his case there could be nothing to conceal; he would sit upon the knee of this man, his poor father, and get used to him—would like to drink out of his cup, and be carried on his shoulder. He would not shrink then from him. No; but perhaps he would be not the less dragged down, but the more, for that. What would a father mean in his mind? Why, somebody who was good now, but had been wicked. A father was an ex-convict, the kindest man he knew; the only one, perhaps, who was fond of him.

Must he, then, be told so young? Yes; or else it must be concealed from him till accident or necessity made him aware of it, and then he must stand the shock as best he could.

"You're not to play at getting drunk," said a poor mother to her little five-year-old boy.

"Father used to drink."

"Ay; but poor father never drinks now. He never rolls about, he never strikes Dicky now. Father's kind, father's good."

"And Dicky means to be good," said the child; "but Dicky must get drunk first, and have larks too, just as father did."

Dicky was far too young to be reasoned with, and he had something more than knowledge already. He had experience; limited certainly, but disastrous, for it showed him that a man was a creature who ought to be good in the end, but must be expected to play with evil first—go down into the mire, in fact, and there remain, until he had sufficiently disported himself.

Hannah Dill, though her husband had loved her and trusted her, and found in her his whole delight and comfort since he had got her back, was by no means at peace; she knew that the burglary he had been tried for was not the only crime he had on his conscience. She had got used to fear on his account; every unexpected knock at her humble door startled her. He had himself from time to time fits of depression, when something, she knew not what, but guessed to be the memory of a crime, would seem to fall on him like a blight; and then, whatever he was doing, he would rise and go to shut himself up in a little empty attic that they

rented, and there she would hear his inarticulate crying to God, and sometimes his groans and sighs. She would sometimes steal upstairs after him and listen, but she was too much awed to call to him. Though he had risen into an atmosphere in which she could not breathe, it had been from a deep that she had not sounded.

One evening, however, when the child was about four months old, an incident, small in itself, added greatly to her feeling of insecurity. She was nursing him, in the presence of his father, when a sudden noise seemed to startle the infant, and he turned his dark eyes with an evident expression of apprehension.

"Bless the babe!" she exclaimed; "how intelligent he do look now and then!"

"He is the very moral of you," replied Uzziah, "when he looks round in that sort of way."

"Do I have a startled, frightened look, then?" she answered, and immediately repented her words, for Uzziah became extremely pale; and, looking down at her babe, she seemed to see in his little face something like an inherited expression. As she had beheld the reflection of their father's yearning wistfulness in the faces of his sisters, she thought now she could trace the thought of her own heart in the eyes of this child.

She continued to look down on the little head, for she could not meet her husband's eyes. She heard him sob, and then he fell on his knees. "O God, it was a sin—it was a sin!" he muttered. "O God, forgive me —I took her back!"

"You did not wish to take me back!" she replied, still without looking at him. "You know we both of us wished we might part that night when we prayed as we knelt asunder on the common."

"Ay, but the next morning, and while the storm went on, and when I knew how miserable you were along of coming back to me, I seemed to be urged many times to let you go. And it was too hard."

She answered with quiet moderation, "But you cannot help but know that now I have this babe at my breast, I cannot wish what I might have done if God had not sent him.— He will never be a disgrace to us, Uzziah," she presently added, in a still kinder tone. "I have heard you pray nights for him, so deep and so hearty, as people cannot pray, I am certain, unless God has answered already in heaven. No, the poor lamb, God bless him! will never be a disgrace to any one."

"But I shall be a disgrace to him," cried

" She thought she could trace the thought of her heart in the eyes of the child."

the father, almost grovelling on the floor. " I shall enter in ; but, oh ! it will be through a bitter death, for I shall die as—as I should do."

" Who told you so ?" she answered, white to the lips ; and then she added more faintly, " And what death do you mean ?" But she knew.

He lifted himself slightly till he could lay his arms on the seat of the wooden chair, then with his face resting upon them, " Who told me so ?" he repeated. " The same voice in my soul that told me of my pardon. I am always told so. The Gospel saves, I thank my God, but the law must take its course— and it will."

" Oh ! I fare very faint," cried the poor woman, and a strange fluttering in her heart and in her throat appeared almost to suffocate her ; but when she fell back in her chair, and he, starting up, brought her some water and seemed as if he would take the child from her, she cried out, though faintly, " No, no; let him be. I shall not drop him. No."

" I'm not to touch him ? " asked Uzziah.

" No."

She struggled with herself and sat upright, though still deadly pale. The poor man was sitting opposite to her, looking more haggard and melancholy than usual.

" Uzziah," she said, " I wish to say something to you, as soon as I fare able to get out my words."

He waited some minutes, while she wiped away a few heart-sick tears, and gathered her child again to her breast.

"I wished to say," she sighed at last, "as I've noticed something in you lately that's much in your favour."

Her manner was cold, though perfectly gentle. He made no reply.

"I've noticed that you're much more humble lately—more abased before God, and quiet. I believe God have forgiven you. But this babe"—then she paused, as if irresolute; and suddenly, with passionate anguish, went on—"if God does indeed hear your prayers, I, that am his mother, beg you—I that almost died to give him birth, and that love him more than any mortal thing—I beg you to pray God to take him from me, and to leave me desolate—soon. Pray that he may be taken soon."

"You must not talk like that," answered Uzziah, with frightened eyes.

"Yes, I will. O Jesus, take him!"

"Listen to me, Hannah. I don't know how it was I came to speak so plainly, but, whatever it may cost me, if you will, I'll now let you go your ways, and take him with you."

"No. Whatever happens, I must be nigh, that I may know it. It would seem to come to pass every day if I was from you."

"There have been times, Hannah, when I've thought it might be my duty to confess it."

She shuddered.

"Oh, I don't mean to _you_, my poor wife."

"It could never be your duty," she answered, almost calmly, "unless somebody else was suspected—that he had done the deed, and not you."

"That is what I have come to think."

"Reach me down my bonnet, Uzziah. I shall suffocate unless I get out into the air."

"You cannot carry the babe, Hannah," said her husband, when her bonnet was on, and she was drawing her woollen shawl over her shoulders and the infant's head.

"Yes, I can."

"It's ten o'clock at night."

"I know it is."

"Hannah, if you mean to go for good, you'll give me a kiss first—won't you, Hannah?"

She turned and looked at him as she stood in the doorway. Her intentions came like a flash, and changed so roughly that they seemed to tear her heart to pieces—as a

stormy sea tears the trembling strand; her intention had come, and it was gone—for how could she kiss him?

She stood with her white face intent on his white face, and she stared into his eyes. "I am coming back," she said huskily. "Only let me go out, if only for a moment."

"I shall not follow you, Hannah. And you may be sure that I believe you are coming back."

"Why?"

"Because, if I thought the other thing, it would be I that should go out. Would I leave my wife and babe to flee away at this time o' night? Hannah, sit you down in the rocking-chair, and I'll go, and never come near you but once a week, just to bring you what money I've earned. I'll go now. Only say you forgive me, and let me have a kiss of you and the child."

"Forgive you for what?"

"For taking you back."

"I thought at the time it were right I should come back, and I cannot think now ——"

Then she looked at him again—at his face, and at his hands—and knew she could not give the desired kiss; so she repeated, "And I mean to come back."

He opened the door. The night was still and dark; but quite clear. She longed for light, and wanted to see movement. The little tenement she and her husband rented was a lean-to against some warehouses belonging to a great Manchester manufacturer; the alley, of which it formed one whole side, being faced by another warehouse, was perfectly silent and deserted at that time of night.

She went out down the alley, and soon found herself in a well-lighted street, full of shops, and as she walked, was suddenly startled out of her deep reverie by finding herself near a great concert-room, in which a temperance lecture had lately been held, and which she had attended. There had been a concert in it that night, which was just over; the people were streaming out, and calling for their carriages. She shrank back again, and passed from among some women, who were admiring the ladies' dresses and commenting on their appearance. There was some mistake, as there so often is. Some of the people were waiting by one door, while their carriages were at another. The shutters of a shop close to her were put up, and she leaned against them for support, while the noise made by the footmen and cabmen served in some sort to distract her from her importunate sense of misery and suffering and fear. Then, striking full on her ears, and rousing her at once to keen attention, came a name that she knew.

"Sir Samuel de Berenger's carriage stops the way." And there it was. She knew the footman, she knew the coachman, and she turned her faded eyes to mark who would enter. But no, the intended occupants did not appear, and when it had stood for ten short moments allotted to it, the police made it pass on and give way to another.

"It's a chance missed," she murmured faintly. "I'd rather have seen even Sir Samuel than nobody that belonged to *them* at all ; " and as she turned, and there were more carriages, and there was more shouting —"Come on, come on ! " cried a voice close at her elbow; "I see the carriage. Keep it in view, and I'll bring out the girls, or we may wait here till midnight."

Dick de Berenger!—and the person to whom he had spoken was Amias. She stood as if fascinated, till some one brushed her elbow—a lady, who wore the hood of her opera cloak over her head. She was dressed in white, and before the poor woman could take her dazzled eyes off her, and notice that Felix had her on his arm, another lady passed on the other side, and a little laugh assured her that it was her Delia.

"Hold your shawl well over you," cried Dick; "you'll not catch cold."

The mother followed, irresistibly drawn on. "Oh, no!" answered Delia. "As if I ever caught cold ! "

"Amabel touched my babe's head," murmured the mother, "and my shoulder." She looked down. Yes, there was proof of it : two or three petals from an overblown rose in Amabel's bouquet had fallen on her shawl and were resting on the head of the child.

The mother felt a strange sense of warmth and joy as she pressed on. She could still see the carriage, and the two white figures were being quickly conducted after it. She did not dare to come very near, but she saw them both enter, and heard them both speak while gathering up the fallen leaves from her shawl, as if they had been drifts from paradise.

Dick and Amias followed them in, and the carriage proceeded.

"He often talks of a particular providence," she murmured, as she lost sight [of it, and mused on the little scene. They had rather enjoyed their pursuit of the carriage. They had white shoes on their pretty feet. Delia was holding up her gown with a little un-gloved hand. Their mother soothed her anguish with thinking how lovely and bloom-ing they had appeared, and how easy and careless. Three gentlemen to take care of them !

"It's a particular providence," she murmured. "The Lord thought upon my trouble, and has sent me a sweet drop of comfort this night."

She turned. A man was standing so close behind her that they could not but look one another in the face, and a glance of keen surprise darted into his. It was Mr. de Berenger.

For an instant his astonishment daunted her, but her homely dignity came to her aid. "I hope I see you well, sir," she said quietly. Then, glancing down at her babe, "Many things have taken place since I left your service." She manifestly meant to call his attention to her child.

"It is Mrs. Snaith, I see," he answered. "We meet very unexpectedly."

"Yes, sir. I once told you something of how I was circumstanced. My poor husband——"

"I remember," exclaimed Felix, suddenly losing his air of disturbed astonishment.

"Yes, sir, it was all at once my duty to join him—nearly a year ago, sir, you know." Then, when he was silent, she added, "I did not come here with any thought of seeing the young ladies."

Tears dazzled her eyes and dropped on her cheeks ; she knew not what more to say, and he said nothing. She was about to move away, when he stopped her, putting out his hand.

"I need not ask whether you have suffered," he said, "your countenance shows it too plainly. My poor friend ! "

"I have, sir," she answered.

"Is the man good to you ? "

"Oh, yes, sir ! It is not that."

"And you seem to have a fine healthy child," he remarked, as if he would find somewhat on which to say a few comforting words.

She looked down on the little fellow, who, now awake, was lying on her arm, staring at the gas-lamp with clear, contented eyes. "Ay, sir," she answered ; "but I pray the Lord to take him from me. Bless him ! " she continued, looking at him with all a mother's love. "His mother would pray him into heaven this night if she could, and not grudge the breaking of her own heart, to save him what he will find out if he lives long enough."

She began to move on, and Felix walked beside her, apparently too much shocked to answer; but when she turned from the great thoroughfare he stopped her again.

"Listen to me, Mrs. Snaith," he said. "You have often thought of the time when you lived with me, of course?"

"Yes, sir; it's all the joy I have, to think on it."

"Do you believe that I would do anything for you that I could?"

"Yes. I don't know another such gentleman."

"Well, then, tell me. Is there anything?"

"Yes, sir, there is," she murmured, after a pause; "but it's not what you might expect."

"I don't understand you."

"It's almost strange, considering all things, that I have never met you nor Mr. Amias when I have been along with my poor, wretched husband. You might do me—oh, the greatest favour and kindness a poor creature could ask—if ever you should——"

"If ever I should see you with him?" asked Felix, stopped by his surprise, as she was by her earnestness.

"Yes, sir."

"Why, what is it, Mrs. Snaith?" he exclaimed, gazing at her in more astonishment than ever.

"To make as if you knew nothing about me, and had never seen me in your life before."

"Are you so much afraid of him?"

She made no answer.

"Give me a moment to think."

She walked before him, silent.

He repeated her words aloud to himself. "'To make as though I knew nothing about her, and had never seen her in my life before.'" Then, after another pause, "Well, Mrs. Snaith, you can only be asking me this as a protection to yourself. I promise you."

"Thank you, sir. And Mr. Amias—I should be very deeply obliged to you if you would tell all this to him."

"How should we ever see you with the man?" exclaimed Felix.

"But if you do, sir?"

"Yes—well, I will do it. Mr. Amias shall know. But is there nothing else, that seems more reasonable, that I can help you in?"

"No, sir, thank you kindly. I do not want for money. Sir, will you let me wish you good-night? I am later than I meant to be."

"But, my friend," said Felix, "you left us in a hurry, and my uncle, Sir Samuel, would now gladly give you a handsome sum for information as to the parentage of the two girls."

"Sir, I always say alike. They have no claim on him whatever. I trust you'll let me go."

"No claim?"

"No, sir, none."

Felix put out his hand. "God bless you, my poor friend, and comfort you!" he said. Then he turned back the same way they had come, that she might see he had no thought of finding out whither she was going.

CHAPTER XXXI.

It was nearly midnight when Hannah Dill came up the alley toward her humble home, and noticed with alarm a small group of people standing outside the window, and apparently glancing into it. She could see, as she advanced, that a candle was burning inside, and she was struck by the silence of the people, till, just as she joined them, one man whispered to the other, "To think of it!" "Well, I'll always believe there's real saints in the world from this time forrard," answered his fellow; and making way for her as she came straight up to the window, they all quietly passed on. Uzziah was kneeling on the floor, with his hands clasped and his eyes upraised. She could only see the side of his face, but, remembering how they two had parted, she was astonished both at the utterly absorbed expression and the depth of its calm.

"He is not crying to God now," she murmured, half aloud; "he is thinking on Him. I have seen him do that before. Art a murderer, my poor wretched husband, or art a saint? Can a man be both one and the other? It's past my knowledge to give an answer to that. But the Lord have mercy on thee and on me, and take our innocent child to Himself!"

She tapped lightly at the door, and Uzziah, with perfect calmness, rose and opened it to her. He looked at her fixedly, as if he expected her to say something decisive, something important to him; but her strength was spent, and her spirits had fallen again. She went forward, sat down on the rocking-chair, and laying her babe down on her knees, looked at him and said, "Have you done as I told you? Have you prayed for the death of the child?"

"I seemed to have no power to do it. My prayer had no wings; it would not ascend."

She sat many minutes silent. Then she said, "Aren't you afraid you're making yourself too conspicuous—more easy to find — lecturing and spreading your name about as you do?"

"I have left all that to my patient Judge. I must work now while it is day; when the bitter call comes I must kiss the rod, and be ready."

"I have thought sometimes, since I've been out, that I may have made a blessed mistake, and the thing was not so black as I feared. Don't name it to me, but if it was not the darkest deed a man can do, say so."

"It was, in the eyes of the law."

"What do you mean by that?"

"They made me drunk first, Hannah. I was three-parts drunk when — when I did it——"

"You cannot say, then, what I wanted to hear you say?"

"No."

"You had better take the poor babe, then."

Her arms dropped at her side, and her head sank. Uzziah was only just in time to save the child, when she fell forward, and all his efforts could not save her from a fall and a heavy blow.

Some very bitter and anxious weeks followed. Hannah Dill, lying on her bed, took little notice of

her husband, or even of her child. She scarcely seemed to care what became of her. She had no heart to recover herself, and her wasted features, faded eyes, and feeble pulse showed how much she suffered.

"The wages of sin." She was linked with the sinner, and those wages had been paid out also to her. She felt more than the fear that he suffered, for he had gone forth to meet the Avenger—had lain at his feet, and craved his pardon; but the more fully he was able to believe that pardon had been granted, the surer he always felt that in this world his sin was to find him out.

But now the despair of this woman, whom he deeply loved, was too much for him. She dreaded him; she could not bear him to touch her or her child. He knew this, and knew how she tried to hide it. She perfectly acknowledged to herself that he was a changed character; but though she could command her countenance as to expression, she could not as to hue, and when he approached, or when he accosted her, she would often turn white, even to the lips.

Uzziah felt as if he had not known suffering, or even remorse, before. It was only for a short time that such a man as he could taste of love and joy and domestic peace; they were all gone. He saw himself, as it were, with his wife's eyes, and knew how vile he was. He perceived that the opinion of his fellow-creatures was more to him than that of the just and holy God.

It was past midnight, about six weeks after Hannah Dill's brief sight of her children, when, coming home once from a dinner party, Amias de Berenger let himself into his own chambers with a latch key. The fire, in a comfortable room very much cumbered with books, had been made up for him, and a reading-lamp was burning near it on a small table.

There were book-cases ranged about his walls, and there were red curtains let down before the windows. The sound of passing vehicles was heard, as well as the general murmur made by the multitudinous noises of London. But as Amias sat, with his feet on the fender, a slight tap roused his attention, and it was repeated several times. He threw up the window and looked out. A man at the same moment had withdrawn from the door and was looking up. He shrank back when the light fell on his face, but Amias saw that it was his "inspired cobbler," his favourite temperance lecturer, and, wondering what the man could want

at that time of night, he went down and let him in.

"You want to speak to me?" he asked, as he shut the door of his sitting-room, and moved to Uzziah to sit down.

The "inspired cobbler" made no answer. His face was pale; he looked inexpressibly forlorn. In his best black clothes, Amias had always seen him looking the picture of neatness, as if he had the ambition to hope that he might be taken for a third-rate dissenting minister. Now his hair was wild, his dress disordered, his face pale. He shivered, and as he spread out his hands to the fire, Amias noticed that they were blue with cold, and that his breath came with a series of involuntary sighs.

"Well," exclaimed Amias, when he did not speak, "what is it, man?"

"Sir, I can't speak at your lecture to-morrow."

"You should have let me know before, Mr. Dill. And why cannot you?"

"There's two reasons," answered Uzziah, uttering the words with difficulty, his sighs almost suffocated him; "and they're both of them as bad as they well can be."

"Indeed! I fear you mean more than you say."

"I mean, first, that I've got down into the slough again. I did not think it could be; but I've fallen. God forgive me! I presumed; I was too sure of myself; and the drink (I was very miserable)—and the drink (I'd been a long way, and had nothing, and was faint)—and the drink was at every street-corner. I passed fifty public-houses, and counted them aloud to keep myself out, but at the fifty-first I went in; and I reeled home, sir, as drunk as ever."

"I am truly sorry for you," was all Amias said.

"Oh, sir, and it took so little to overcome me. I went home to my poor wife, and now the thirst and the longing for it are upon me, and I shall do it again."

"No," answered Amias; "this will go off; you must not despond. But how came you to be so imprudent as to walk till you were faint? And what misfortune has made you miserable?" he continued, calling Uzziah's words to mind.

"Oh, I am a miserable man!" was all the reply his "inspired cobbler" made; and he sank upon his knees before the fire, and covered his face with his hands.

"I am truly sorry for you, Dill," repeated Amias, very much shocked. "But the worst thing you can do is to talk in this despairing way. Pluck up courage; be a man. Come, I'll give you something to eat at once; and I'll see you safe into your own home. But I am afraid—yes, I am afraid you cannot speak any more at these meetings,—at least, for a time."

"I cannot eat," answered Uzziah; "but you are good, sir, to say you'll walk home with me. I'm in such mortal fear that I shall be drawn into those mantraps again; they catch body and soul. My head never would stand the half of what another man can take," he moaned. "Oh, why did I do it!—But I know: I longed for it; I kept muttering to myself as I came to you this night, 'Oh for one drop—oh that I could have one drop!' I longed for it more than for the air I breathe."

"Did this come upon you all on a sudden?" asked Amias.

"It came on same time as all the rest of the misery."

"What misery?" asked Amias.

Uzziah started up, seeming to recollect himself; he sat down again, and looked at Amias as if he was trying to collect his thoughts.

"It would not be safe to tell you," he said; and instantly seemed to feel that to have said even that was far too much.

Amias drew his chair slightly farther off.

"Yes, sir," said the cobbler, as if answering his thought; "I'm no worse than I always have been since long before the day you first saw me. But you have no call to demean yourself to sit so near. It's more than my wife will do. I thought God, that knew all, had forgiven me; but now it's all dark.—O God, Thou hast taken me up and cast me down."

"You must not despair of the goodness of God. He knows the great temptation the constant sight and smell of drink is to such as you. You will recover yourself soon, I hope, and even, perhaps, may be allowed to speak again in public."

Amias said this because he knew what joy and honour it always seemed to the cobbler to stand forth and utter his testimony. He had a ready flow of words, many anecdotes at his command, and took a simple and harmless pride in his own popularity.

Uzziah shook his head. "My wife says no to that," he answered, sighing; "she says it would be tempting providence."

Amias again offered him food, and when he would not take it, renewed the offer of walking home with him; and the two men set forth together, Amias feeling sufficient

distrust and dislike of his companion to keep him very silent. But what was his astonishment when, having conducted the poor man to his own door, he knocked, determining to see him enter it before he left him, and it was opened by his brother's old servant, Mrs. Snaith—yes, Mrs. Snaith—evidently the mistress of that humble home, and she had a baby in her arms.

He was on the point of addressing her, when he remembered his brother's account of the interview he had lately had with her, and how she had begged that, if either of them met her with her husband, he would not recognise her.

She looked aghast, but almost instantly recovered herself. He checked himself just in time, and as Uzziah passed in, said, as if to a stranger, "Your poor husband has been with me to-night, Mrs. Dill, and I have walked home with him. I am very sorry for him, but I am full of hope that this will soon pass off."

"Will you come in, sir?" answered Mrs. Dill, with entreating eyes.

Amias entered, and Uzziah Dill went straight up-stairs, shutting the staircase door behind him.

Mrs. Dill, who had not moved nor spoken again, was standing with the candle in her hand listening, and her head slightly raised. She now set it down on the small deal table. "He will not come down any more, poor man," she said, almost in a whisper; "he has shut himself in for the night, but whether to pray or to sleep I cannot say. He never seems to have a moment's ease of mind now."

"It is a piteous sight to see his repentance," Amias answered; "but, Mrs. Snaith——"

"Mrs. Dill, sir."

"Yes—Mrs. Dill. You must not let him get morbid; I mean that you should encourage him. He ought not to think that such a fault is past reprieve."

"What fault, sir?" asked Mrs. Dill, with a certain air of fluttered distress. "Oh yes, sir—yes, sir; he was overcome by temptation, and he fell." She trembled now, and looked so faint and frightened, that Amias could not answer at once, he was too much surprised; but when she repeated, "Overcome by temptation, and he fell—that was what you meant," he at once perceived that both husband and wife had more on their minds than a mere drunken fit, and he again experienced the strange revulsion against this man which had impelled him to draw away his chair. He did not like to hear his footsteps overhead.

"Mrs. Dill," he said, leaning towards her as he sat, and speaking in a whisper, "I have thought of that poor man, your husband——"

"Yes, sir; my husband."

"Well, I have thought of him as a saint."

"And so have I, Mr. Amias."

"But you are very much in fear of him?"

"I believe he is a saint, sir."

"I think you ought to answer me. Are you in bodily fear of him?"

"No, sir, I am not. He is perfectly gentle, and a pious Christian, poor creature, when he is sober, and I trust in the mercy of God that he will not drink again. He and I have kneeled down together, and begged and prayed the Lord that he never might so fall again; and I do believe, sir, that we are heard."

"And yet, Mrs. Dill, when you opened the door, if ever I saw a woman's face express mortal fear, yours was that face."

Mrs. Dill said nothing.

"It is only a few days, is it, since this took place—since he got drunk?"

"Only a few days."

Amias pondered, and at last said, "I do not like to leave a person whom I have long known and respected in any danger, or in such a state of terror as I found you."

"I was afraid, sir, when I heard the knock, for how should I know that it was you?"

Amias looked at her; the words "You are afraid *for* him, then, not *of* him?" were almost on his lips, but he spared her.

"I don't fare to regard a few pangs of fright, more or less," she presently added, "my life, sir, is so full of misery; but when I saw Mr. de Berenger, and now that I see you, I know what a wide gulf there is betwixt me and that happy life I led, when I went in and out without fear, and lived so quiet and respectable, all comforts about me, and answered the door without any alarm, and—and waited on my dear young ladies."

She could not possibly forbear to speak of her children, so sore was her longing to hear of their welfare. Amias, who took her mention of them chiefly as a proof, among others, of her regrets for her old occupation and the old place, felt as if desire to talk of them was all his own. A glow came into his dark cheek and a flash into his eyes. It became evident to him that he ought to indulge himself—their old nurse naturally wished to hear about them—and almost with reverence the lover allowed himself the delightful privilege of uttering Amabel's name.

He was fully occupied now with his own feelings, or he could not have failed to notice how the waxen pallor of the nurse's face gave way to rose colour, and how her expression became first peaceful, then almost rapturous. She turned her eyes away from him, and scarcely asked a question, and she also was too full of her own feelings to notice his.

She tried to keep her gladness moderate, and to hear of their welfare, improvement, and beauty with as much seeming calm as he tried to give to his words in telling of them. If a third person had been present this attempt would, on both sides, have been equally vain. Amias ended with, "And I often hear them speak of their dear old nurse, and wish they had her again."

Then the nurse lifted up her hand and looked up. "Bless their sweet hearts!" she said, with impassioned tenderness. "I love them, but I pray the Lord in His great mercy to keep them and me always apart."

Amias was very much struck by this speech, and by her earnestness. "I was almost thinking, Mrs. Snaith, that I could, perhaps, bring them to see you," he exclaimed.

"This is no place for them to come to," she interrupted.

"And you do not wish to see your young ladies?"

"No, sir; I pray you to keep them away."

The clock of a neighbouring church struck one. Amias rose.

"Some things you say make me very uneasy," he began.

"Sir, you have no call to be afraid for me," she repeated, interrupting him again.

"Do you know my address?"

"Yes, sir."

"If ever you should want help, come, or write to me."

"I will, and I am truly thankful for your kindness; but I want nothing so much as this, that, if we meet, you should make as if you did not know me."

"I shall remember."

"And I would fain, if I might, send my love to my dear young ladies."

Her love, which she was so desirous not to reveal, so as to excite his suspicions, and his love, which, unless he kept it hidden, got the mastery over his calm, made them both so self-conscious and restrained, that again neither could notice the other, and Amabel's mother and her lover parted strangers, in spite of what might have been so mighty a link between them.

Hannah Dill had at last recovered her health, and begun to take in hand her husband's affairs. He had lost energy and hope since he had again fallen under the influence of drink, but after he had seemed to become like himself, and had begun to eat and to work again, he was a second time drawn into a gin-palace, and then, when the next day he was lying in despair on his bed, racked with headache, and almost beside himself with remorse, she came up to him and deliberately

proposed that she should lock him up—lock him in to that little whitewashed garret, bring him his food and his work, supply him with coal and candle, and not let him out till she thought he was safe.

He accepted her proposal thankfully, and it spoke well for his sincerity that he armed her against himself, his own probable entreaties or commands, by giving her a paper, desiring her to use her best judgment, and show no false mercy by letting him out till she was satisfied of his cure. He signed it, and she kept him locked in for three weeks. But he was used to confinement—that did

him no harm; he was accustomed to the companionship of accusing thoughts and wretched memories. She took these things into account, and did not let them influence her; but there was one thing she did not take into account, and this was his strong, absorbing love for herself.

She brought him his meals, she swept out his room, she took care that he had candle light, and all such comforts as their slender means would permit; but when she had done all such obvious tasks she did not sit with him, or linger to chat, or bring the child and lay it on its father's bed while she worked. No, nothing of this kind: when she had waited on him she went down again.

Uzziah felt this, and he found nothing to say. Every day he thought he must and would open a conversation with her, if it was only to ask a few harmless, commonplace questions, such as, "Have you been to the shop, Hannah? Well, sit you down and tell me about it." "Got the baby a new hat, did you? Bring up the little chap and let me see him in it." He rehearsed many such questions and remarks with himself when alone; but when he heard his wife's step on the stair, and heard her turn the key, he never could utter them. She always found him silent, and every morning she made him the same apology, "Wishing you better, my poor husband, and feeling it hard I should have to take away your liberty."

"I don't feel as much better as I could wish," was often the answer. "I'm parched with thirst and long for liquor;" but he could not add, "and I long for your company."

And she was only able to talk with him on the matter in hand—what he thought it might be best for him to eat and what to drink. When she had done and said all, she would turn away very quietly, almost slowly, and close and lock the door again; but then he used to hear her run down-stairs, as if it was a deep relief to get away from him.

And so it was.

At last one day he said, "Hannah, I've

no longing at all upon me now for liquor, and I bless the Lord for that."

" Well, and I bless the Lord for it too," she answered, almost cordially.

She observed that he had put on his best clothes and brushed his hair.

" I feel as if I might go out," he said. " Only, what do you think, my poor wife? Am I fit to go alone?"

" I'll go with you," she answered; and his whole appearance changed. She could not but feel a pang of pity for him, for his face was so like what her heart had felt when she had last seen her lovely children. Her proposing of her own accord to go out with him was such a cordial, and yet he knew it was only as a guardian that she was to go. She would be near to help him out of mischief and temptation—as a duty, and not a pleasure.

" And where do you want to go?" she inquired.

" Well, Hannah, first I must look for

work; for what I used to earn by my efforts for the temperance cause I have lost now."

" Too true," she replied.

" And, second, I must go to Mr. de Berenger. He will wonder what has become of me all this time. I want to say to him what you have to hear first."

He saw then the sudden pallor which often distressed him in his wife's face, and did not know that her fear of meeting with Amias was what had brought it on, not of what he might have to say.

" If you're agreeable to it, my dear, I feel as if I had better go away from London. I might find a country place—I seem to know of several—where there are not any public-houses tempting one at every turn. I could not keep us quite as well as I have done, but I would do my best."

He paused and looked at her earnestly, and she answered what she knew was in his mind.

" Yes, Uzziah, I would go with you."

PLAIN-SPEAKING.

BY THE AUTHOR OF "JOHN HALIFAX, GENTLEMAN."

III.—"ODD" PEOPLE.

" For ye suffer fools gladly."

YES, because we recognise them as fools; and there is in our human nature a certain Pharisaical element which hugs itself in the thought that we are not "as other men are." Therefore we regard them and their folly with a self-contented and not unkindly pity. We understand them and put up with them, and it soothes our vanity to feel how very much we are above them.

But these others, the "odd" people, are somewhat different. We do not understand them; they keep us always in an uneasy uncertainty as to whether we ought to respect or despise them; whether they are inferior or superior to ourselves. Consequently we are to them often unjust, and always untender. They puzzle us, these people whom we designate as "unlike other people" (that is, unlike ourselves and our charming and highly respectable neighbours); whose motives we do not comprehend and whose actions we can never quite calculate upon; who are apparently a law unto themselves, quite independent of us; who do not look up to us, nay, we rather suspect look down upon us, or are at least calmly indifferent to us, and

consequently more irritating a thousand times than the obvious and confessed fools.

An "odd" person. How often one hears the word, and generally in a tone of depreciation, as if it implied a misfortune or a disgrace, or both. Which it does, when the oddity or eccentricity is not natural but artificially assumed, as is frequently the case. Of all forms of egotism, that of being intentionally peculiar is the most pitiful. The man who is always putting himself in an attitude, physical or moral, in order that the world may stare at him; striving to make himself different from other folks under the delusion that difference constitutes superiority — such a man merits, and generally gets, only contempt. He who, not from conscientiousness but conceit, sets himself against the tide of public opinion, deserves to be swept away by it, as most commonly he is, in a whirl of just derision. Quite different is the case of one who is neither a fool nor an egotist, but merely "odd," born such, or made such by inevitable, and often rather sad, circumstances and habits of life.

It is for these, worthy sometimes of much sympathy, respect, and tenderness, never certainly of contempt, that I wish to say a word.

I once knew a family who, having pos-

XXI—49

sessed a tolerable amount of brains in itself for more than one generation, had an overweening admiration for the same, and got into a habit of calling all commonplace, ordinary people "chuckie-stanes"—every Scotch school boy knows the word. It describes exactly those people exactly like everybody else whom one is constantly meeting in society, and without whom society could not get on at all, for they make a sort of background to the other people, who are not like everybody else.

But in all surface judgments and unkindly criticisms there is some injustice. No one is really a "chuckie-stane." Every human being has his own individuality, small or large, his salient and interesting points, quite distinct from his neighbours, if only his neighbours will take the trouble to find them out. One often hears the remark, especially from the young, that such a person is "a bore," and such a house is "the dullest house possible." For myself, I can only say I wonder where the "dull houses" are and where the "bores" go to, for I never succeed in finding either. Only once I remember a feeling of despair in having the companionship for two mortal hours of a not brilliant young farmer; but I plunged him at once into sheep and turnips, when he became so enthusiastic and intelligent that I gained from him information which will last me to the end of my days on agricultural subjects.

Very few people are absolutely uninteresting except those that are unreal. A fool is bearable, a humbug never.

Now "odd" people, whatever they are, are certainly not humbugs. Nor are they necessarily bad people—quite the contrary. Society, much as it dislikes them, is forced to allow this. Many men and women whom others stigmatise as "so very peculiar," are, the latter often confess, not worse, but much better, than themselves; capable of acts of heroism which they know they would shrink from, and of endurances which they would much rather admire than imitate. But then they are such odd people !

How? In what does their oddity consist?

Generally, their detractors cannot exactly say. It mostly resolves itself into small things, certain peculiarities of manner or quaintnesses of dress, or an original way of looking at things, and a fearless fashion of judging them; independence of or indifference to the innumerable small nothings which make the sum of what the world considers everything worth living, worth dying for, but

which these odd people do not consider of so much importance after all. Therefore the world is offended with them, and condemns them with a severity scarcely commensurate to their deserts.

Especially in things most apparent outside—their manners and their clothing.

Now, far be it from me to aver that either of these is of no consequence. Dress especially, as the "outward and visible sign of an inward and spiritual grace," is of the utmost consequence. They who, by neglecting it, make themselves singular in the eyes of strangers, or unpleasant in those of friends, are strongly to blame.

But not less so are the people who wear out their own lives, and those of others, by fidgeting over trifles — bemoaning a misfitting coat or an unbecoming bonnet, and behaving as if the world had come to an end on account of a speck on a boot or a small rent in a gown. There is a proportion in things. Those who worry themselves to death, and others too, over minute wrongs and errors, commit a still greater wrong and overlook a much more serious error. How many of us would prefer to dine upon potatoes and salt, and dress in a sack with sleeve-holes, rather than be ceaselessly tormented, with the best of intentions, about what we eat, drink, and put on ! "Is not the life more than meat, and the body than raiment?"

Yes; but society must have its meat and also its raiment, and that in the best and most decorous form which the general consensus of its members considers is decorous. To set one's self rampantly against this is, when not wrong, simply foolish. The obnoxious plebeian who insisted in vindicating that "a man's a man for a' that," by presenting himself at a patrician dinner in rough morning garb, the conceited young artist who appeared so picturesque and snobbish at a full-dress assembly in his velvet painting-coat, were certainly odd people ; but their oddity was pure silliness—neither grand nor heroic in the least. Nor, I must say, can I consider much wiser the ladies, young and old, whom I see yearly at private views, dressed not like the ordinary gentlewomen of the day, but just as if they had "stepped out of a picture," only the pictures they choose to step out of are not always the most beautiful—often the most bizarre of their kind.

As a general rule, any style of dress, whether an exaggeration of the fashion of the time or a divergence from it, which is so different from other people as to make them turn round and look at it, is a mistake. This sort of eccentricity I do not defend. But I do defend the right of every man and woman to dress himself and herself in their own way ; that is, the way which they find most comfortable, suitable, and tasteful, provided it is not glaringly obnoxious to the community at large.

A gentleman who, hating the much-abused but still-endured chimney-pot hat, persists in going through life with his noble brows shaded by a wide-awake ; a lady who has manfully resisted deformity in the shape of tight stays and high-heeled boots, has held out successfully against hoop-petticoats and dresses tied up like umbrellas, who declined equally to smother her fresh young face under a coal-scuttle bonnet, or to bare her poor old cheeks to sun and wind and critical observation by a small string-less hat, good neither for use nor ornament—such people may be set down as "odd ;" but they are neither culpable nor contemptible. They do what they consider right and best for themselves ; and what possible harm do they do to other people?

Besides—though this is no excuse for all oddities, but it is for some—the chances are that they are people no longer young, who have learnt the true value of life and the true proportions of things much better than their accusers or criticizers. Possibly, too, they are busy people, who have many other things to think of than themselves and their clothes. It is the young, the idle, the small-minded, who are most prone to vex themselves about small things and outside things. As years advance and interests widen we see with larger eyes, and refuse to let minute evils destroy in us, and in those dear to us, that equal mind which—accepting life as a whole, in all its earnestness and reality, its beauty and sadness combined—weighs calmly and strikes bravely the balance of good and ill.

Perfection even in the humblest and commonest details is to be striven after, but not to the sacrifice of higher and better things. I have known a young lady sulk through half a ball because her dress was not quite as tight-fitting as the mode exacted ; and an elderly gentleman make a happy family party miserable for a whole dinner-time because there chanced to be too much salt in the soup. Such exactingly "even" folk as these drive one to appreciate those that are "odd."

The world still contains many who persist in tithing "mint, anise, and cummin," and neglecting "wisdom, justice, and the weightier matters of the law." It is they who are hardest upon the odd people. Their minds, absorbed in the mint, anise, and cummin of existence, cannot take in the condition, intellectual and moral, of a person upon whom those "weightier matters" weigh so heavily that he is prone to overlook lesser matters, and objects to be tied and bound by certain narrow social laws, which, indeed, being of no real importance, he refuses to consider laws at all. Therefore he is set down as a law-breaker,| laughed at as eccentric, or abused as conceited, when probably there is in him not an atom of either conceit or egotism, and his only eccentricity consists in the fact that his own large nature cannot comprehend the exceeding smallness of other people's. He gives Tom, Dick, and Harry credit for the same quick sympathies, high aims, and earnest purposes that he has himself, and is altogether puzzled to find in them nothing of the kind. They can no more understand him than if he spoke to them in Chinese. They only think him "a rather odd sort of person"—smile at him and turn away. So he "shuts up"—to use a phrase out of that elegant slang which they are far more adepts at than he—and Tom, Dick, and Harry hate him for evermore, with the relentless animosity of small souls towards another soul, into whose depths they cannot in the least penetrate, but sometimes suspect it to be a little deeper and larger than their own.

And occasionally, rather to their annoyance, the fact is discovered, even by the purblind world.

Take, for instance, that very "odd" person Don Quixote, whom successive generations have laughed at as a mere fool ; but this generation begins to see in the poor old knight a pathetic type of that ideal Christian chivalry which spends itself in succouring the weak and oppressed, which believes the best of every human being, and is only led astray by its expectation of finding in others purity, truthfulness, honour, and unselfishness which are to itself as natural as the air it breathes. But they are not the natural atmosphere of half the world, which accordingly sets down those who practise these virtues—who have a high ideal of life, and strive through endless difficulties and deficiencies to carry it out—as "Quixotic," or, at best, rather "odd" people. Yet these are the people who mostly influence the world. It is they who do daring acts of generosity or heroism, while others are only thinking about it ; and perpetrate philanthropic follies with such success, that society, which would utterly have scouted them had they failed, now praises them as possessing the utmost wisdom and most admirable common sense.

Again, many are odd simply because they are independent. That weak gregariousness which is content to "follow the multitude to do evil" (or good, as it happens, and often the chances are pretty equal both ways) is not possible to them. They must think, speak, and act for themselves. And there is something in their natures which makes them a law unto themselves, without breaking any other rational laws. The bondage of conventionality—a stronghold and safeguard to feebler folk—is to them unnecessary and irksome. They mean to do the right, and do it, but they cannot submit to the trammels of mere convenience or expediency. Being quite clear of their own minds, and quite strong enough to carry out their own purposes, they prefer to do so, without troubling themselves very much about what others think of them. Having a much larger bump of self-esteem, or self-respect, than of love of approbation, outside opinion does not weigh with them as it does with weaker people, and they go calmly upon their way without knowing or asking what are their neighbours' feelings towards them.

Therefore their neighbours, seeing actions but not motives, and being as ignorant of results as they are of causes, often pronounce upon them the rashest judgments, denouncing the quiet indifference of true greatness as petty vanity, and the simplicity of a pure heart and single mind as mere affectation. For to the worldly unworldliness is so incredible, to the bad goodness is so impossible, that they will believe anything sooner than believe in either. Any one whose ideal of life is above the ordinary standard, and who persists in carrying it out after a fashion incomprehensible to society in general, is sure to be denounced by society as "singular," or worse.

It always was so, and always will be. That excellent Italian gentleman—I forget his name—who felt it necessary to apologise for Michel Angelo's manners, doubtlessly considered the old sculptor as an exceedingly "odd" person. Odder still he must have been thought by many an elegant Florentine, when, for some mere crotchet about the abolition of the republic, he abruptly quitted Florence and all his advantages there; nor ever returned, even though leaving unfinished those works which still remain unfinished in the Mausoleum of the Medici—monuments of the obstinacy, or conscientiousness, or

whatever you like to call it, of a poor artist, who set his individual opinion and will in opposition to the highest power in the land.

Poor old fellow, with his grim, saturnine face and broken nose! How very "peculiar" he must have appeared to his contemporaries! One wonders if any one, even Vittoria Colonna, had the sense to see into the deep heart of him, with all its greatness, sadness, and tenderness. There is a Pietà of his at Genoa, and another in St. Peter's, in which the Virgin Mother's gaze upon her dead Son lying across her lap, seems to express all the motherhood and all the grief for the dead since the foundation of the world. And yet the sculptor might have been rough enough, and eccentric enough, outside; and his friend might have been quite excusable in craving pardon for his "manners."

There are cases in which eccentricity requires more than an apology—a rebuke. Those peculiarities which cause people to become a nuisance or an injury to other people, such as unpunctuality as to time, neglect or inaccuracy in business matters, and all those minor necessities or courtesies of life which make it smooth and sweet— these failings, from whatever cause they spring, ought, even if forgiven, not to be pardoned without protest. They are wrong in themselves, and no argument or apology will make them right. The man who breaks his appointments, forgets his social engagements, leaves his letters unanswered and his promises unfulfilled, is not merely an "odd," but a very erring, individual; and if he shelters himself for this breach of every-day duties and courtesies by the notion that he is superior to them, deserves instead of excuses sharp condemnation.

But the peculiarities which harm nobody, and are not culpable in themselves, though they may seem so to the "chuckie-stanes" of society, who are afraid of anything which differs from their own smooth roundness— these are often more worthy of respectful tenderness than of blame or contempt. For who can tell the causes from which they sprang? What human being knows so entirely his fellow-creature's inner and outer life that he dare pronounce upon many things, crotchety habits, peculiar manners or dress, eccentric ways of life or mode of thought, which may have resulted from the unrecorded but never obliterated history of years? For it is mostly the old who are "odd," and when the young laugh at them, how do they know that they are not laughing at what may be their own fate one day? Many an oddity may have sprung from some warped nobility of nature, many an eccentricity may have originated in the silent tragedy of a life-time.

Of necessity, these "odd" people are rather solitary people. They may dwell in a crowd, and do their duty in a large family, but neither the crowd nor the family entirely understands, or has much sympathy with them; and they know it. They do not always feel it—that is, to the extent of keen suffering, for their very "oddity" makes them sufficient to themselves, and they have ceased to expect what they know they cannot get. Still, at one time probably they did expect it. That "pernickity" old maid, whom her nieces devoutly hope they may never resemble, may have been the "odd" one—but the thoughtful and earnest one—in a tribe of light-minded sisters, who danced and dressed, flirted and married, while she —who herself might possibly have wished to marry once upon a time—never did, but has lived her solitary, self-contained life from then till now, and will live it to the end. That man, who was once a gay young bachelor, and is now a grim old bachelor— not positively disagreeable, but very peculiar, with all sorts of queer notions of his own, may have been, though the world little guesses it, a thoroughly disappointed man; beginning life with a grand ideal of ambition or philanthropy, striving hard to make himself, or to mend the world, or both, and finding that the task is something

> 'Like one who strives in little boat
> To tug to him the ship afloat."

And so, though he has escaped being swamped, he at last gives up the vain struggle, folds his arms, and lets himself float mournfully on with the ebbing tide.

For the tide of life is almost sure to be at its ebb with those whom we call "odd" people. Therefore we ask for them, not exactly compassion—they seldom need it, and would scorn to ask it for themselves— but that tenderness which is allied to reverence, and shows itself as such. Young people have, in a sense, no right to be odd. They have plenty of years before them, and will meet plenty of attrition in the world, so as to rub down their angles, and make them polished and pleasant to all beholders. Early singularities are generally mere affectations. But when time has brought to most of us the sad "too late," which in many things more or less we all must find, the case is a little different. Then, it becomes the generation still advancing to show to that which is just passing away, tenderness, considera-

tion and respect, even in spite of many harmless weaknesses.

For they know themselves as none other can ever know them except God. Others see their failures; but He saw how they struggled, and conquered sometimes. Others count their gains and triumphs; they have to sit night and day face to face with their perpetual losses. The world distinguishes, shrewdly enough, all they have done, or not done; they themselves only know what they meant to do and how far they have succeeded. If they are "odd," that is, if having strong individualities, they are not afraid or ashamed to show them, to speak fearlessly, to act independently, or possibly, plunging into the other extreme, to sink into morbid silence and neither look nor speak at all— what marvel? Better that, perhaps, than be exactly like everybody else, and go through life as evenly and as uselessly as a chuckiestane.

For undoubtedly odd people have their consolations.

In the first place they are quite sure not to be weak people. Every one with a marked individuality has always this one great blessing—he can stand alone. In his pleasures and his pains he is sufficient to himself, and if he does not get sympathy he can generally do without it. Also, "peculiar" people, though not attractive to the many, by the few who do love them are sure to be loved very deeply, as we are apt to love those who have strong salient points, and in whom there is a good deal to get over. And, even if unloved, they have generally great capacity of loving; a higher and, it may be, a safer thing. For affection that rests on another's love often leans on a broken reed; love which rests on itself is founded on a rock, and cannot move. The waves may lash, the winds may rave around it; but there it is, and there it will abide.

The loneliness of which I have spoken is also something like that of a rock in the great sea; which flows about it, around it, and over it, but cannot affect it, save in the merest outward way. This solitude, the possible lot of many, is to these few a lot absolutely inevitable. No use to murmur at it, or grieve over it, or shrink from it. It is in the very nature of things, and it must be borne.

They whose standard of right is not moveable, but fixed, not dictated to them from the outside, but drawn from something within; whose ideal is nothing in themselves or what they have around them, but something above and beyond both; whose motives are often totally misapprehended, because they belong not to the seen, but the unseen; and whose actions are alike misjudged, from their fearlessness of and indifference to either praise or blame—such people will always seem "odd" in the eyes of the world;—which knows its own, and loves them, so far as it can.

But these it never does love, though it is sometimes a little afraid of them. Now and then it runs after them for awhile, and then, being disappointed, runs back and leaves them stranded in that solitude which sooner or later they are sure to find. Yet this solitude, increasing more and more as years advance, has in it glimpses of Divine beauty, an atmosphere of satisfied peace, which outsiders can seldom comprehend. Therefore they had better leave it, and the "odd" people who dwell in it, with deep reverence, but without needless pity, in the hands of the Great Consoler.

A TRIP TO CYPRUS.

By Lieut.-Colonel W. F. Butler, C.B.

PART III.

TEN miles north of Nicosia a road or track crosses the north range of hills through a depression about 1,200 feet above the sea level. A mile or two beyond the foot of the range on the north or farther side from Nicosia, Cyprus, unlike her great goddess, sinks into what she rose from—the sea. Here, in this narrow strip between hill and water, it would seem as though nature strove to show to man a remnant of what the island once had been. The green of young corn overspreads the ground; the shade of the karoub-tree is seen; myrtle clothes the hill-sides, and the dark grey olive-tree is everywhere visible over the landscape.

Looking down from the summit of the pass one sees Kyrenia clustered by the shore, whose gentle indentations can be traced many a long mile away towards Karpos to the east, washed by a blue waveless sea.

But our goal is Kyrenia.

Our companion has been over the ground many times already, and we are late upon our road. As we descend the ridge the north face of the range opens out to the right and left behind us. It is green with foliage. We have left aridity behind us beyond the mountains. A couple of miles away to the right a huge mass of masonry can be seen rising from groves of olives. Towers, turrets, and battlements lift themselves high above the loftiest cypress-tree; but no minaret is visible. It is the Venetian monastery of Bellapays. We will have a nearer view of it later on.

Kyrenia was the head-quarters of another assistant regenerator—a practical man, who seemed to have already realised the fact that the collection of taxes was by far the most important part of the administration of Turkish laws.

A couple of hours before sunset found us climbing the steep paths that led to Bellapays. Everywhere around spread olive-trees of immense age. Their gnarled trunks, clasped round with great arms and full of boles and cavities, still held aloft a growth as fresh as when Venice ruled the land. The fig-tree and the orange grew amid gardens that had long run wild. Here and there a colossal cypress-tree lifted its dark tapering head high above all other foliage. The path, winding amid dells of myrtle, led right beneath the massive walls of the monastery, where a spring gushing out from a fern-leaved cave formed a dripping fountain of pure cold water.

From the rock above the spring towered the great front of the building; in mass and architecture not unlike the Papal palace at Avignon. Within the walls ruin had scarcely touched. The cloisters had suffered, but the great hall of the building was intact; one hundred feet in length, with high vaulted roof and Gothic windows that looked out over green groves and long lines of shore and longer stretch of sea, from whose blue waters rose the snow-clad peaks of distant Karamania.

Beautiful Bellapays! while thy great walls rise over the fruit-clad land the loveliness of Cyprus will not be wholly a name. How perfect must thou have been in the olden time, when the winged lions flew over yonder fortress of Kyrenia! Well have they named thee beautiful, whose beauty has outlived the ruin of three hundred years, and defied the Turk in his fury and in his dotage!

Behind the monastery, and nearer to the mountain, a Greek village stood deep in orange gardens. In this village dwelt one of the representative Greeks of the island.

We found Hadgi at the door of his courtyard ready to welcome us to his house. A steep wooden stair led to the upper story. In a large corridor open at both ends, and with apartments at either side, we were made comfortable with many cushions spread upon a large wooden bench. Here a repast was soon served. First, coffee in tiny cups was handed round; then a rich preserve of fruits with cold spring water; then oranges of immense size, peeled and sliced into quarters, were produced, together with Commanderia wine, in which the fruit was steeped. A small glass of mastic closed the feast. Many children, servants, and women stood around, and the host did the honours with that natural politeness and ease which characterize the peasant of every land save the "free born" Briton's. Hadgi's experience went far back in Cyprus. His love for the Turk was not strong, nor was it to be wondered at. He could remember one year when thirty thousand of his countrymen fell beneath the bullet, the rope, or the yataghan. And yet he was not an old man. Hadgi saw us into our saddles, and we rode back towards Kyrenia as the sunset shades were gathering over sea and land. We followed a more direct path than the one by which we had come. On both sides the ground in many places was thickly covered with square stones, showing that buildings had once been there. Probably from Kyrenia to Bellapays one long street had once existed. Next to the Turk ranks the goat as a destroyer, in Cyprus. As we drew near Kyrenia a large herd was being driven in for the evening. Each goat was making the most of a lessening opportunity. Here and there one could be seen in the gnarled fork of some old olive-tree stretching forth his head to grasp a leaf. The lower branches of the trees had all been cropt off long ago; but goats were standing on their hind legs vainly trying to reach some pendent branch. One in particular, a little longer than his comrades, did succeed in catching between his teeth the lowermost twigs of a bough. Long experience had doubtless taught him that if he attempted to pull down his prize all would be lost; his efforts were, therefore, directed towards maintaining a balance upon two legs and holding on by the bough until assistance came to him. This it quickly did: in an instant twenty goats were ready to lend a

helping foot. Out of these some half-dozen succeeded in getting their teeth into a twig, then all lent their weight together to the pull and down came the olive bough to the ground, to be instantly devoured by the rush of animals which settled upon it.

The advantages of pillage upon co-operative principles were here plainly apparent. Had the goat learned them from the Turk, or was the goat the tutor to the Turk?

Leaving Kyrenia on the morning of January 20th, we held our way between the mountains and the coast towards the east. About six miles from Kyrenia we passed out of cultivated land, and began gradually to ascend the north range.

The country became wild and broken. Great glens, covered with dark-green myrtle, led from the range to the sea. The path wound along the edges of these valleys, passing many nasty places where the sure-footed ponies had all their work to do to keep their footing, and where the stones and gravel, loosened by the hoof, rolled many a yard ere the bottom was gained. There had been a heavy fall of rain during the previous night, making the clayey places even more treacherous than the gravel, and causing the ponies to slide in their thin Turkish shoes as though they must go over. But somehow they never did go over, and when a couple of hours riding had carried us to the mountains, the track, though rough, became safe. Passing the summit of the depression in the range, where Pentahaclyon lifts his five crags directly over the path to the left, we began to descend the stony and now arid south side. Below us the great plain of Morphu, and that which lies between Nicosia and Famagusta, spread out under clouds that come drifting up from the Olympian range.

Suddenly, a turn in the path brought us in sight of the strangest natural sight to be seen to-day in Cyprus. It was the spring of Kytherea. Out of the sun-baked mountain gushes a stream of pure cold water—"no stinted draught, no scanty tide," but a rush that seems to come from an inexhaustible subterranean source, that no neighbouring indication can possibly account for. Above and around nothing can be seen save bare brown hills utterly destitute of water; below the spring a long line of foliage and cultivation runs down the mountain-side and spreads out into the plain beneath. Thickly cluster the houses along this life-giving stream. To right and left rills of water are led off along the descending slopes, and the baked and barren hill-sides are made to bloom in many

On the Road to Kyrenia.

shades of green; for corn and vine, olive and fig, orange and citron, are all springing in luxuriant life around these packed houses, and children's faces peep out of leaf-covered courtyards, and the blacksmith's anvil, and the carpenter's bench, and the weaver's shuttle, are busy, all called into life, and sustained, by that single spring of clear, cold water, whose source, in these arid hills, no man can tell.

Perhaps in the old days Cyprus possessed a score of such springs. If they or others can again be made to flow, then may the island see her golden age revived, and count her million souls, and her "hundred-streamed cities."

At the lower end of Kytherea, where the lessened stream runs faint, we stopped to rest and lunch in a large Greek house, occupied by two officers of the Royal Engineers, who were employed in the trigonometrical survey of the island.

Then away across the level plain towards Nicosia. A Zaptieh guide, who had accompanied us from Kyrenia, appeared to think that the moment had now arrived when he could execute to the fullest advantage a cavalry charge after the manner of a Bashi-bazouk. During the earlier part of the journey, while we were yet at the north side of the mountains, he had developed this instinct in a strong degree. Without any visible cause whatever, he would suddenly start off at full gallop straight ahead along the pathway. His headlong impulse to scatter mud on all sides was apparently only controlled by the duration of his turban in shape around his head. While his turban lasted he was a Bashi-bazouk, when it fell off

he became an ordinary Ottoman. One of these headlong flights, however, terminated more disastrously. He was going along at a tremendous pace, stirrups clattering, a bag of coppers jingling at his belt, when his pony, pitching heavily forward, rolled its rider to the earth. The turban flew one way, the bag of brass *caimes* rolled another; never was the spirit of Bashi-bazouk taken more completely out of a hero. During the remainder of the ride to Kytherea he kept a crestfallen position in the rear; but now, on this Nicosian plain the spirit again revived, and he began to gallop furiously, at intervals, along the track.

As there were no women, or children, or fugitives, he did not pursue his wild career beyond certain limits, and as there was no enemy whatever, he did not retire when his charge had spent itself at the same pace as he had gone.

Darkness had fallen when we reached the walls of Nicosia. Skirting the city by its eastern ramparts, we ascended the ridge of old tombs upon which stands the new Government House, the lights from whose wooden halls formed the only visible objects in the wide circle of surrounding gloom.

At a place called Mathiati, some fifteen miles south of Nicosia, a regiment of infantry was in camp. After many sites had been tried, all more or less unhealthy, this place,

Mathiati, had been selected ; and huts, sent out from England, had been erected on a level space surrounded by hills. A few olive-trees, a small Greek mud village, and, farther off, the blue ridges of Mount Adelphi, made a prospect not wanting in beauty, but utterly destitute of any other feature that could give an interest to the existence of an English regiment ; sport, society, the coming and going of human beings—all were wanting, and except to the tomb hunter or to the student, Mathiati could vie, in absence of life, with any station in the wide circle of British garrisons round the earth.

The regiment now in camp at Mathiati had only lately arrived from Nova Scotia ; and the contrast between the cradle of a new-born civilisation which they had quitted, and the grave of the old world's decay in which they found themselves, was vividly put before them. As may be supposed, their views of the latter were not hopeful. They spoke of Cyprus as a place of exile, dashed with a kind of humour learned, perhaps, in the New World.

"The medical fellows never knew the use of the spleen until we got to Cyprus," said one of the garrison—"but they've found it now."

"What is it?".

"Two months' sick leave out of this infernal hole," replied the first speaker. "The spleen has been what they call a dormant organ of the human body until we took pos-session of the Island, now its use is clearly understood."

As day broke over Nicosia plain, on the 23rd of January, a small party of horsemen crossed the dry bed of the river channel that lies ,at the base of the rocky ledge on which stands the Government House, holding their way westward towards Peristeromo. They were bound for Mount Olympus, in search of a site for a summer encampment. The experience of the past summer had been sufficient to show that men could not live in health in the plains, or along the shore, during the summer months.

Before the sun had again entered the Northern tropic a camp in the mountains must be found.

At the same hour and at the same instant of time (for the line of sunlight through Cyprus and through Zululand are one) that this small party of horsemen rode out to the west from the hill of tombs near Nicosia, a few horsemen, the last of a weary and spent British column, were moving off from a ridge, leaving a thousand dead comrades, lying tombless, to the vultures that watched on the rock ledges of Isandlana Hill.

High up above the ledges one great frontlet of rock frowned over the ghastly scene— the "Lion's Head," some early traveller had named it. If sermons are spoken by stones and lion ever speaks to lion, surely this stone lion could have spoken that day a curious homily

Venetian Monastery of Bellapays.

to his brother on the mound at Waterloo. What that homily would be we may not write now; nor would the dawn at Isandlana and the dawn at Nicosia on the 23rd of January meet in these pages, if that day's work at the first-named place had not been destined to turn, in the future, the footsteps of the four men here bound for Mount Olympus towards Zululand.

We reached Peristeromo, fourteen miles, in two hours. Here mules were waiting to carry us farther into the hills. The Greek priest had come out to the river (at last it was a river and not a dry channel) to welcome us into the village. Arrived at his house there was the usual hand-shaking and coffee-sipping, and then the saddles were changed from the ponies to the mules, and all made ready for the onward journey.

Three of the four mules were animals in fair condition, the fourth was, it would be wrong to say skin and bones, for so much of his skin had vanished under the abrasions of pack-saddles and uncouth harness gear that the bones in many places were alone represented. Poor beast, he was a dreadful sight! When the saddles were placed on the mules outside, somehow or other the skinless mule fell to the lot of the writer of these pages. That it was most unconscionable cruelty to ride the beast there can be no doubt; but what was to be done? The halting-place for the evening lay twenty miles distant, high amid the hills. The only alternative was to abandon the expedition. There was nothing for it but to accept the inevitable and mount the lacerated back. Then came fifteen miles of gradually ascending pathway, amid hills scantily covered with small pine-trees. As the track wound along the ridges the air became crisp and fresh, the sound of rushing water arose from deep valleys, and the bright blue vault above rested on the clear cut edges of the hill-tops. How pleasant would it have been to jog along those narrow paths upon an animal of sound skin; but now there was an ever-present sense of pain inflicted to mar the whole scene, and to cause each step of the ascent to be mentally as painful to the rider as it was bodily so to the poor mule.

For many miles of the track a stray raven kept hovering aloft in the blue heaven—was he scenting his prey? At last we reached the mountain-village of Litheronda, which was to be our halting-place for the night. It stood on the southern slope of the hills, at an elevation of about 4,000 feet above the sea. The air was keen and frosty, for the sun had gone down behind Olympus, whose white ridge could be seen to the west. The village houses were all of the lowest kind; they projected from the hill-side, out of which they had been dug, so that the slope of the hill and the roof of the houses formed one continuous line. Thus a person could walk down the hill on to the roof, until reaching the edge of the front wall, he looked down six or seven feet upon the door-step. A few of the rudest and most antiquated implements of husbandry lay on the paved space around the door-step; a lean pig, or a leaner dog, grunted or barked at the intruder. The mule had long ago given out; but it was infinitely more pleasant to follow the track on foot, driving the wretched animal in front. The rest of the party had gone on out of sight, and by the time the mule and his driver drew near Litheronda, camp had already been made on the farther side of the village. As we descended the path, a Greek riding a fine young horse suddenly appeared coming towards us from the village. With many vehement signs he signified that he had been sent to meet us; the horse was for our especial use; the mule might be trusted to find its own way to the camp. So, mounting the Turkish saddle and accommodating feet to the slipper stirrups and legs to the short leathers as best we could, we trotted on towards the camp. It stood under some large walnut-trees, now leafless, and by the side of a small stream. A huge fire of dry logs blazed before the tents, at another fire, farther off, dinner was being prepared. A few villagers stood gaping at the Englishmen—the first without doubt who had penetrated to their remote nook. How they must have speculated upon the reason of the visit. Did it mean fresh taxation, new law of grape gathering, relief from some of their many loads? The village headman, an old Greek, stood, the nearest figure towards the fire, at the farther side—the blaze of the pine logs fell full upon his strongly marked face. He wore the usual thin dress of blue cotton, the long boots to the knees, the loose jacket and the swathed waist. He was poor, dirty, and picturesque; his appearance afforded cause for biblical parallels in the mind of one of the English bystanders. "Now, that old fellow at the other side of the fire," said one of them, "is neither better nor worse in looks than one of the apostles. Peter and Paul were probably quite as dirty-looking."

"Yes, quite as dirty-looking," said another; "but after all, in that case dirt did more than ever cleanliness will be able to do.

Just think that a dozen old men like that one yonder have done more on the earth than all the soldiers who have ever lived. I'll give you Cæsar, Alexander, Bonaparte, Tamerlane, and Charlemagne, all the great generals the world has ever seen, on one side, and I'll take that dozen seedy, dirty old men on the other, and with all the sword and soap you like into the bargain, yet you'll be nowhere in the race."

Is there not too marked an inclination in this modern world of ours to shun controversy of this kind ? to avoid meeting the every-day thrusts of a commonplace criticism with the weapons lying close to our hands ?

No need to search through Scriptural verse or theologian's canon for the "counter" to the cut, or the parry to the thrust, of nine-tenths of the criticism that is to-day aired on Christ and Christianity. Take up the gauntlet as it is thrown down. Meet the attack on the ground on which it is made ; meet it with common-sense if it be made with common-sense, and common-nonsense if it be made in idle jest, and you will be a poor layman if you cannot double up your assailant with any of his own weapons or upon any ground he may choose for his attack.

One poor carpenter and a dozen men—fishermen, tanners, publicans—able, even in the material aspect of their work, to beat all the conquerors, pyramid builders, statesmen, law - makers, philosophers, kings, swash-bucklers, and big-wigs that this planet of ours has ever known.

Great doctors of the body have, in modern times, given up much of the old jargon of medicine, and come back to the common rules of food and air and water for the cure and care of human bodies. Might not our soul-doctors, too, sometimes take a leaf from this old tree of Christian common-sense, if necessary cut a cudgel from it, and do more in ten minutes to demolish the shallow scepticism of the modern anti-Christian critic than could be done by a month of quotation from the theologians of five hundred years?

Of the features of English character brought to light by the spread of British dominion in Asia, there is nothing more observable than the contrast between the religious bias of Eastern thought and the innate absence of religion in the Anglo-Saxon mind. Turk and Greek, Buddhist and Armenian, Copt and Parsee, all manifest in a hundred ways of daily life the great fact of their belief in a God. In their vices as well as in their virtues the recognition of deity is dominant.

With the Western, on the contrary, the outward form of practising belief in a God is a thing to be half-ashamed of, something to hide. A procession of priests in the Strada Reale would probably cause an average Briton to regard it with less tolerant eye than he would cast upon a Juggernaut festival in Orissa ; but to each alike would he display the same iconoclasm of creed, the same idea, not the less fixed because it is seldom expressed in words, "You pray ; therefore I do not think much of you." But there is a deeper difference between East and West lying beneath this "incompatibility of temper" on the part of modern Englishmen to accept the religious habit of thought in the East. All Eastern peoples possess this habit of thought. It is the one tie which links together their widely-differing races. Let us give an illustration of our meaning. On an Austrian Lloyd's steamboat in the Levant a traveller from Beyrout will frequently see strange groups of men crowded together on the quarter-deck. In the morning the missal books of the Greek Church will be laid along the bulwarks of the ship, and a couple of Russian priests, coming from Jerusalem, will be busy muttering mass. A yard to right or left a Turkish pilgrim, returning from Mecca, sits a respectful observer of the scene. It is prayer, and therefore it is holy in his sight. So, too, when the evening hour has come, and the Turk spreads out his strip of carpet for the sunset prayer and obeisance towards Mecca, the Greek looks on in silence, without trace of scorn in his face, for it is again the worship of the Creator by the created. They are both fulfilling the *first* law of the East—prayer to God—and whether the shrine be Jerusalem, Mecca, or Lhassa, the sanctity of worship surrounds the votary and protects the pilgrim.

Into this life comes the Englishman, frequently destitute of one touch of sympathy with the prayers of any people, or the faith of any creed ; hence our rule in the East has ever rested, and will ever rest, upon the bayonet. We have never yet got beyond the stage of conquest, never assimilated a people to our ways, never even civilised a single tribe around the wide dominion of our empire. It is curious how frequently a well-meaning Briton will speak of a foreign church or temple as though it had presented itself to his mind in the same light in which the City of London appeared to Blucher—as something to loot. That other idea, that a priest was a person to hang, is one which is also often observable in the British brain. On one occasion, when we were endeavouring to enlighten our minds upon the Greek question, as it had presented itself to a naval officer whose vessel had been stationed in Greek and Adriatic waters during our occupation of Corfu and the other Ionian Isles, we could only elucidate from our informant the fact that one morning, before breakfast, he had hanged seventeen priests. From the tone and manner in which he thus summed up the Greek question, there appeared to be little doubt that he was fully prepared to repeat his performance upon any number of priests, at any hour, or before any meal—indeed, from the manner in which he marked the event as having preceded his breakfast, it might almost have been surmised that his digestive organs had experienced the want of similar stimulants ever since that occasion.

Meantime, however, while thus we stand before the camp fire at Litheronda, the snow begins to fall through the leafless walnut-trees, and the night wind blows cold over the white shoulder of Mount Olympus. At daybreak next day it blows colder still; the ridge, across which our onward track lies, is white with snow, which holds its own even as the sun climbs higher into the eastern sky; and the guides, who are to lead us across the shoulder of Olympus to Pasha Leva, assert that the route will be impracticable for some days to come; so, striking camp, we held our way for nine miles along a rocky glen that led to the village of Manikito, and then turning westward, and crossing some very rough and broken ground, we reached at three o'clock in the afternoon the hill village of Platris, on the south slope of Olympus.

Behind Platris, to the north, the mountain rose steep and pine-clad; below Platris, to the south, many valleys led the eye downwards to the sea, where the coast beyond Limasol, and the ruins that mark the site of the monastery of the Knights of St. John, built when Acre had fallen to the Saracen, lay, twenty miles distant in reality, but seemingly close at hand, seen through the blue and golden light that filled the whole vast vault, far out beyond the land, into the shipless sea. To-morrow our line would lead us down to that shore, but now—to-day—ere the sun, already far into the west, should reach the sky-line beyond Paphos, we had a chance of scaling the lofty ridge that rose behind the village, and of planting a footprint in the snow of Olympus.

Away on fresh mules up the mountain.

There is no time to lose, and anxiously we watch the aneroid to note our upward progress, and the sun to mark the time that yet remains to us. At a point about five thousand five hundred feet above the sea-level the snow becomes too deep for the mules, so we dismount and tie them to pine-trees; then, while two of the party turn off to the right to select a site for the summer encampment, we strike up the hill, alone, to make a race, for Olympus, with the sunset. The ridge is very steep, but the snow holds a firm crust, and the air is keen and bracing. The aneroid soon shows another five hundred feet gained, and a hill, which seems to be the summit, appears close at hand. It is won, but at its farther side the ground sinks abruptly only to rise again out of a deep valley into the real Mount Olympus. Better had we kept more to the right and avoided this deep glen that now lies across our line to the summit. There is nothing for it but to retrace our steps to the right, and then take the crest of the curving ridge which runs round almost at our present level to the foot of Troados. But every second is precious. Away we go at topmost speed along the crest, which, though level when looked at from a distance, is broken into many hills and valleys when seen nearer. All is silent around save the quick crunching of the snow beneath rapid footsteps. Lofty pine-trees rise on every side.

We are now under the shadow of Olympus, whose white head, bare of pine-trees, has hidden the low-sunk sun. Through the pines to the north the eye catches glimpses of the low country, the north range, and the far-away sheen of snow on the mountains of Asia Minor; but there is no time to note anything save the lessening light and the bare summit that rises above the dark pines. We pass out from the shadows of the trees, and stop a moment to take breath for the last ascent. Looking across the valley, around three sides of which we have just circled, the sunlight is seen still bright upon the crest we started from, but the rays fall level; and already around us, in the shadow of Olympus, the blue light of evening has fallen upon the snow. Nothing but the croak of a solitary raven, from a withered pine-branch close at hand, breaks the intense silence of the scene. Another four minutes' hard pull and we stand upon the bald crest of Troados. The sun has not yet set. Far out, resting on a ring of immeasurable sky-line, he seems to pause a moment ere he sinks into the sea. There is a faint crescent moon in the western heaven.

A vast circle spreads around, and within this huge horizon all Cyprus lies islanded beneath the light of sunset.

There is sea beyond the north range, and beyond the sea there is sun on a long line of snow set far above the gathered shades of evening. There is sea in the wide curve of Salamis, and beyond the ruined ramparts of Famagusta; sea where Paphos sinks into a golden haze of sunset in the west; sea where Karpos stretches his long arm into the arch which the earth's shadow has cast upon the eastern sky, for all Cyprus, below this lonely Troados, lies in twilight, and the great circle of the sea is sunless, save where, on the western rim, the blood-red disc sinks slowly from a sky whose lustre pales in lessening hues, from horizon to half-zenith. And now the last speck of sun has gone beneath the waves. Olympus is cold and blue, like many a lesser ridge around him; the crescent moon grows clearer cut against the heaven; grey and cold, the sky rim narrows, and the wide bays and long-stretching promontories of the island lie in misty outline upon the darkening sea; far away to the north Karamania still holds aloft one last gleam of sunlight upon his frozen forehead.

We will stay until this "light of Asia" is blotted out. Another moment and the Karamanian range is cold; and then, fading into the night, Cyprus lies in the gloaming —a vague but mighty shadow, from whose forgotten tombs and shattered temples the night wind comes to moan its myriad memories amid the pines of Olympus.

"POST TENEBRAS LUX."

By the Rev. Canon VAUGHAN, M.A., of Leicester.

IT has been well said,[*] "One of the best known modes of progress in knowledge is that which has received the name of the *reductio ad absurdum*, or *correction of the premiss :* that is, the fundamental thought, which is taken as the starting-point in any given case, being imperfect, false conclusions are rendered necessary ; and by the casting aside of these conclusions a truer fundamental thought is brought in." And again: "By means of the false conclusions the premiss is rendered more complete ; for by them men are driven to seek a truer thought. On how grand a scale this method of learning has been carried out, it needs but slight acquaintance with science to perceive. All the ancient astronomy, before the discovery of the earth's motion, was one magnificent demonstration in this form. Ignorance of that one fact compelled it to be so."

And the same writer adds very justly and forcibly, " If we overlook this law, we turn our efforts into a false direction. The true use of the results that are gained by our very best efforts, on a starting-point that is incomplete, consists not in their being held, but in their being given up in the right way. To discover that right way of giving up even the very best results we could attain, is man's true task—the task that perpetually comes to

him, and must come to him again and again, so long as his knowledge remains incomplete, and his powers of perceiving limited. Our true end is to banish the ignorance within, and attain a true starting-point; and if we do not thoroughly accept this true end, we divide into hostile camps the powers which nature gave us for mutual aid, and waste in fruitless fighting energies which, if we perceived our task aright, would be found to be each other's complements."

The progress of thought—of distinctively *religious,* as well as of what may be considered purely *secular,* thought — seems to have brought us in these days, in more than one field of mental activity, just to such a point as our writer describes in the words which I have quoted ; a point at which we find ourselves compelled, in consequence of the conclusion which we have arrived at, to go back to our premiss—our fundamental thought and starting-point—reconsider it, and correct it. And this, as our author has shown us, involves *giving up something ;* and this giving up has to be done *in the right way.* Now this is very hard—harder, often, than words can express.

It will be best to clear our ground at once by an illustration, which should remove all ambiguities and bring into distinct view the line of thought which it is my purpose to pursue. When our Lord Jesus Christ came on earth, and began his public ministry amongst his Jewish fellow-countrymen, He

* See "The Place of the Physician: being the Introductory Lecture at Guy's Hospital, October, 1873, with other Essays," by James Hinton, Aural Surgeon to the Hospital, pp. 33, 35, 46.

found their minds entirely pre-occupied and taken up with a radically false notion of what the promised Christ, or Messiah, must *be* and *do*. This premiss—their fundamental thought or starting-point—was utterly wrong. And yet they had not the smallest suspicion that it was wrong, but went on, in perfect good faith, feeding their minds with the prospect of a Messiah who should prove a magnificent King and Conqueror, should break the Roman yoke, set their nation at the head of all the nations, and make Jerusalem the metropolis of the whole world. And for this false notion of theirs there was a great deal to be said. They could easily quote passages from their own Holy Scriptures in support of it. And yet, for all *that*, it was absolutely and utterly false; and, on the strength of this false notion, they rejected and crucified their true Messiah, Jesus. It is not for us to judge them. They had to do just what in such matters it is so hard to do: they had to go back to their premiss, and correct it. Even the disciples of Jesus themselves found it impossible to do this, or at least to do it with any real thoroughness, until their adored Master had been taken from them by death and restored to them by the Resurrection. Then it is recorded of them, "He opened their understanding, that they might understand the Scriptures, and said unto them, Thus it is written, and thus it behoved the Christ to suffer, and to rise from the dead the third day."

St. Paul began his life with the same false premiss; and, on the strength of it, he persecuted the Christians. It was his conversion that first put him upon suspecting the soundness of his premiss, and compelled him to reconsider it, and ultimately to revise, or even reverse it. It was indeed time for him to think of revising his premiss, when he found himself asking, "Who art thou, *Lord ?*" and received for reply, "I am *Jesus*, whom thou persecutest;" and then had to say again, "*Lord*, what wilt thou have me to do?" And thenceforth, whenever, as a missionary of the gospel, he came in contact with Jews, he always made it his first business to persuade them to do what he had himself been compelled to do, namely, go back to the false premiss—this false fundamental thought and starting-point of the whole nation—and *correct* it; *giving up something* which had been very dear to them, and giving up *in the right way*. Thus, for example, we read of him at Thessalonica, where there was a large and important colony of Jews, that, "*As his manner was*, he went in unto them, and

three Sabbath days reasoned with them out of the Scriptures, opening and alleging," or. as we should say, "explaining and proving." "that the Christ, the Messiah, must needs have suffered, and risen again from the dead; and that this Jesus, whom I preach unto you. is the Christ."

Let us not fail to thoroughly understand how difficult it was for those unhappy Jews. who crucified Jesus, to correct their false premiss. St. Paul was a very able, a very intelligent, and a very learned man, a *well-educated* man in every sense of the word, a master of Greek literature and philosophy, as well as of Rabbinical lore; yet he was so possessed with this false notion of the Christ, that nothing but his conversion could drive it out of him. He and his fellow-countrymen had sucked this notion in with their mothers' milk, as it were. It was part and parcel of the intellectual and religious atmosphere which they breathed as they grew up. All the past glories, and all the present miseries. of their nation combined to make this faith of theirs in a grand conquering Messiah almost a *necessity* with them, a conviction which it seemed death to part with. And then it had so much to say for itself. The language of Holy Scripture seemed to lend it so much countenance; such language as this, for example, which every Jew of that day would at once interpret as referring to the Messiah, "He shall smite the earth with the rod of his mouth; and with the breath of his lips shall he slay the wicked;" or this, "The day of vengeance is in mine heart, and the year of my redeemed is come; and I looked, and there was none to help; and I wondered that there was none to uphold; therefore mine own arm brought salvation unto me; and my fury, it upheld me."

Having cleared our ground and defined the general lines of our subject by this illustration, we may go on to ask whether there is anything in our own position which answers or is analogous to the condition of things which the preceding illustration reveals to view. It seems to me that, in more directions than one, we may trace its counterpart; the same need of correcting a false premiss, the same immense difficulty in doing so, the same need of *giving up something*, the same immense difficulty of *giving up in the right way*. I might instance at once that dogma of the infallibility of the Bible, which the men of my own generation received by tradition from our fathers as an axiom, a self-evident truth, which admitted of no discussion. Every one knows how widely that dogma has been shaken during the last twenty years, how impossible it is to maintain it in its old rigidity, how essential and inevitable it is that, in this direction at least, we should go back to our premiss and faithfully correct it, giving up what must be given up, and yet taking all care to give up in the right way.

And this is really the process in which, consciously or unconsciously, all thoughtful minds are, and for long have been, engaged; and this not without heat and strife and bitterness—how could it be? the process being what it is, at once so immensely difficult and so unspeakably important. But we may rest assured that the end will be peace. We may accept without reserve, and apply without hesitation to the process in which we find ourselves willingly or unwillingly engaged, the language of the writer from whom I have already quoted—"There is an infinite joy again in this, that, though the *working out* of the correction of a premiss is a process of darkness, a very mystery of evil, compelling strife, and making peace impossible in spite of all desire; yet, when once its meaning is understood, all is changed: a new light breaks over the past; a new spirit descends into the present. The strife ceases; a meaning and end become visible in every part; an assured victory is made manifest in each defeat."

Into this particular instance, however, of that general law of human life which is under our consideration now, I do not propose to inquire further. It is too obvious to need investigation. More difficult, it seems to me, in some respects, and scarcely, if at all, less important, is the inquiry into another illustration of the same law, which, to a great extent, runs parallel with this, and at many points runs up into it and twines itself with it. Closely connected with the dogma of the infallibility of the Bible is that view of *faith*, which regards it as equivalent to *holding correct religious opinions*. The same progress of thought which has resulted in discrediting that dogma has also had the effect of throwing suspicion upon this view of the nature of faith. Here, too, it would seem to be incumbent upon us to return upon our steps,

and correct our premiss. And if this is to be done wisely and well, the thing which above all things will have to be considered is the teaching of our Master Himself upon this great subject; a teaching from which it is only too likely that we may have drifted far away. A slight contribution to this inquiry is all that I can offer; and I know of no passage in the Gospels from which such an inquiry can so well set out as from *this* one: "Jesus said [unto him, If thou canst believe, all things are possible to him that believeth. And straightway the father of the child cried out, and said with tears, Lord, I believe; help thou mine unbelief." (Mark ix. 23, 24.)

The first thing, I presume, that will strike us here, will be the large, the literally boundless promise which Jesus makes to faith— "All things are possible to him that believeth." And this is no exceptional or unusual style of speaking on His part. Again and again He speaks in the same strain, and makes the same large promises to faith. Thus the same Evangelist who records these words records also the following, spoken within a few days of the end: "Jesus answering saith unto them, Have faith in God. For verily I say unto you, that whosoever shall say unto this mountain"—this solid Mount of Olives, upon which the feet of his disciples were then treading—"Be thou removed, and be thou cast into the sea; and shall not doubt in his heart, but shall believe that those things which he saith shall come to pass; he shall have whatsoever he saith. Therefore I say unto you, Whatsoever things ye desire, when ye pray, believe that ye receive them, and ye shall have them." And this saying of his laid such hold on the minds and memories of his disciples, that it passed quite into a proverb among them. Therefore St. Paul, in his famous description of charity, writes, "Though I have all faith, so that I could remove mountains." And the phrase is a household phrase amongst us to this day: We still speak of faith, in its highest and strongest form, as a faith that can remove mountains; meaning, that it can triumph over difficulties and obstacles that to an ordinary observer seem quite insuperable and beyond all remedy.

(To be concluded in next number.)

LUCREZIA.

By Mrs. COMYNS CARR.

PART I.

LUCREZIA had no parents. She had been heard to say laughingly herself that she had never had any parents, and there were people in the village who said the same thing, and could even have explained the matter in a way she herself little dreamed of. For when she said that she had never had any parents she merely meant that she did not remember them, and that it was enough for her to be the niece of Pietro, the farmer, and of Teresa, the best linen-weaver in the whole country-side. Lucrezia was a young woman who could have held her own anywhere, but it certainly was a good beginning to be the niece of such a strong character as Teresa.

Lucrezia lived at Santa Caterina, on the sundown side of the Lago Maggiore, where chestnuts grow densest, and mountains rise rocky from out green and foamless water. She was decreed by many to be the village belle, though some gave the palm to tall Marrina, whose dark head towered a foot above the other's light-brown curls.

Santa Caterina is a fishing hamlet. The cottages hem the edge of the rocks, and are shaded by tall walnut and spreading chestnut trees. Fishermen's dwellings stand near the water's level lower down on the path; farmers' cottages higher up on the cliff's crest. Lucrezia lived on the cliff, for old Pietro was a farmer. The village is a very peaceful village. The path that leads up to it is too steep for pleasure-seekers to climb; strangers never visit it, nor has a fair been seen in its vicinity. It is a little dull. There would be no chance of amusement at all, indeed, were it not that good Catholics must always hear mass of a holy day, and that, when their own chapel is closed, the villagers must seek a ritual elsewhere. Lucrezia was a good Catholic. She went across the water to Stresa of a Sunday or saint's day, and heard mass and saw the world a bit. She had always been a trouble to guardians and confessors, and some said it was not amiss she should go so often to church. But some had a different tale. Anyhow, it is certain that Lucrezia was, what the aunt herself used to call "a real torment," though she would never have allowed others to use the expression. The old folks were proud, in their gruff and silent way, of this only bit of youth which had been left to grace their life's waning. They had had a son of their own once, but he was dead. The aunt was glad when people said that Lucrezia was a lady-like wench, such as sculptors love to model and painters to paint. After that what did it matter, even though some in the village should decree that tall Marrina was the handsomer damsel? And, indeed, every one had a kindly smile, if it came to that, for the merry little maid with her smooth, sallow face and wistful, bright, brown eyes, even though ofttimes she had but saucy words and sharp country sarcasms wherewith to reward her admirers. She was a pert little peasant, for all her winsomeness; but, though matter-of-fact and unimaginative on the surface, she had a quick, tender little heart and a poetic temperament that could soon be laid bare by the simplest emotion. She was of those who can toil and rest, and sleep and sport, with never a thought of weariness. Her tears were quickly chased away by smiles, and whether she plaited her glossy brown hair or scrubbed her copper saucepans it was with a wholesome pride of success that far outweighed all self-consciousness. Lucrezia could take a jest and give it back again. But she knew nothing about love. Her day was yet to come.

Lucrezia was small. She consoled herself with the thought that the proverb says, "While the tall one stoops the little one has run her day." Indeed, before the "hours" chimed at midday across the lake she often had the pot on the fire in a well-swept kitchen, and had plucked the fruit that the uncle sold at Stresa, after cleaning the stable and turning the cattle out to grass. She was a very thrifty maid; and to-day—one day towards September's end—when the chestnuts were near to falling, she stood, her morning work done, with neatly plaited hair and pretty costume, waiting for an escort across the water. Her clothes were pretty clothes, and suited her well. She wore a dark-blue homespun gown with quiet apron and amber kerchief; her gold ornaments were heavy and strangely wrought, and her little feet were hidden beneath clumsy leather shoes that beat an angry rhythm on the stone pavement as she sat waiting for one who came not. She complained loudly to the aunt within for this crossing of her will.

"No, I tell thee he does it on purpose!"

"The village children, a ragged gang, thronged the porch."

she was reiterating in reply to some soothing remark from the old *contadina*. "But I'll make him pay for it! Oh, that will I!"

"Lucrezia, child, calm thyself," remonstrated the voice from within. "Surely, if thou let him see an ugly temper before thou art married to him he might have a mind to let thee be! And what should I do? It would be a scandal in the country. Come, now, for the love of Heaven be reasonable!"

"A scandal, indeed!" laughed the girl, tossing her head. "So a wench is to marry a man who does not please her because of what the country may say! I promise you I am not afraid of the neighbours. Santa Caterina is but a dull place, and it will amuse them to have something that will make their eyes open wider."

"See now what a life she leads me!" moaned the aunt, standing on the threshold and uplifting withered hands to Heaven, as though taking the saints to witness of her woes. She had been a tall, massive woman

XXI—50

in the days of her youth, and even with a back prematurely bowed by the carrying of weights, and shoulders rounded, Teresa stood up a powerful figure still, and had some dignity even in her ugliness; for it was not an ugliness of the mind that lay upon her shrivelled features, it was but the wear and tear of a hard life in the natural pursuit of natural duties; it was but the end to which even the pretty girl before her, living such a life as she had led, must come some day; it seemed to be in the just order of things. "A man who does not please her!" she exclaimed, still apostrophizing the unseen, lifting up her eyebrows beneath the red kerchief that bound her forehead, and bringing her hands down again upon her hips. "When I myself wanted her to take the rich miller down at Pallanza, and she told me she would rather be the Lord's own bride in a convent and have done with it! Dear heart alive, what dost thou want? No one can say thou takest Paolo for his riches—as poor a lad as you could find in Lombardy! But

I said, if his presence pleases the girl, let be! It shall never be whispered we forced her to marry a man for his money—and indeed, the miller *would* have been better suited to one of my own age—but then he would soon have died. That's what I said to thine uncle. And now thou maintainest that Paolo pleases thee not!"

"Well, well, whether he pleases me or pleases me not, I tell you I will teach him a lesson, *zia mia!* What, he thinks he can do as he likes, and that, for love of his brown face, I will always forgive? Oh, he shall see he is mistaken! He shall see how little his poor presence matters to me! Do you know how proud he is? Last week at the dance, because I did not choose to be always with my betrothed like an old maid who is afraid to lose him, because I bade him behave himself, he must needs go away and leave me!"

"He thought to please thee."

"You would have me believe that! No—I know better. He has the proud spirit, and that must not be. A proud husband? Never for me!"

"Wouldst thou have a man be a milksop? Thou dost not like such, nevertheless."

"A milksop of a gallant, no! Paolo is even too much so. But a milksop of a husband—that is a good thing! Do not I know what a husband should be? Go to!"

"Well—I suppose thou wilt go thine own way! But have a care!"

"You think I fear to remain a maiden? I promise you I should know how to set the example of being a matchless one all my life! Yes, and perhaps even without going into a convent!" The girl planted her feet stiffly against the wall and looked up defiantly.

"*Lucrezia mia*, for the Virgin's love be quiet, or the Saints might take thee at thy word!"

"The Saints do not mix themselves in such matters! Paolo must please me or I let him be, I tell thee! Even though every lad in the land should swear afterwards so bad a temper was not worth a pale face!"

"What ails thee thus at Paolo?"

"He does as he likes, even now that we are not married!"

"It seems to me, however, that he studies much to please thee!"

"Studies! Yes, that does he! But a man should know how to please a wench without *study!* He presses me by the arm when the neighbours are round, and yet, if I tell him to behave, he goes a mile off! There is study! And when I pretend I do

not like a thing he takes me at my word! And when I have a new kerchief he knows no more of it than a fish, but stares ever at my face! He is a *contadino* of a lover. I could put up with that perhaps; but to be proud too, and to make me wait half an hour, as now! No, that does not suit me. And who knows if one day I do not show thee that a girl can snap her fingers at the men, after all!"

"Heaven forbid!"

"Go to thy spinning again, aunt. I will wait alone for Paolo beneath the vine."

"See now, she will never be patient with the fellow!" deplored old Teresa to the heavens again. "And, at times, these men they will have fire in the veins!" But nevertheless she went within doors and the distaff began to move.

The piazzetta without old Pietro's cottage was stone-paved, and large loose stones had once been placed roughly around it, after the fashion of a wall. That was a long time ago, for Pietro and Teresa were no longer young folks, and the cottage had belonged to them all their lives: the roof had been new-thatched many a time, though it was brown and moss-grown now. Two sunken stone steps led from the house-door on to the terrace, and some still more uneven ones went from the terrace down into the luxuriantly ragged bit of garden, where golden gourd blossoms trailed their tendrils along the ground, and red tomatoes stood, with sunflowers and Michaelmas daisies in a row. All the stones were sunk, and moss grew up between them, even between the flags on the piazzetta, which was vine-hung. Sitting on the wall of it you could see straight across the lake, above the chestnut-trees that fringed the cliff's edge, and between the branches of walnuts close by. Stresa lay opposite—a row of white dwellings on the water's edge, Baveno a little farther down, Pallanza to the right at the head of a bay—the three islands between the two shores. The water on which they lay was dancing now in the sunlight, for it was scarce ten o'clock and the sky was blue. Black boats crossed the green lake here and there; the plash of their oars could almost be heard up on the terrace, so still was the air this warm autumn morning. Chestnut boughs and late summer flowers scarcely stirred in it.

Lucrezia leaped on to the wall of the piazzetta, whence she could see if the boat were coming along on this side the lake. Paolo did sometimes come that way, and it was late. He was not there, but, as she had

"She sat hanging her feet on the wall and looked across at Stresa."

Page 715.

jumped, one of the big shoes had come untied from the foot to which it was strange and that it fitted so ill. She sat down to settle it again. Shoes must be worn, however uncomfortable, for they were genteel, and Lucrezia was always a little proud of having been once called genteel. Engrossed with the business of making fast her latchet, she did not hear a step come slowly up the stair.

"Lucrezia," said a voice at her ear, and a sudden arm was flung around her. It held her fast, though she had sprung up fiercely and would have pushed the intruder aside.

It was Paolo, to be sure, but that was not the way he should have come. Lucrezia had prepared a whole scene of reproaches on her part, and of excuses on the part of her lover, and this cool beginning did not fall in with her views. "Leave me alone!" cried she, tartly; her white face was a-flame, and her brown eyes moved with a restlessness as of anger. "Who gave you leave to take such liberties with me? I do not require your attentions. Take them elsewhere! Do you call those good manners?"

"There, there, she does not mean it," said Teresa, hastily coming to the threshold. "Come within doors for a couple of minutes, there's a good lad!"

Paolo did as he was requested, but his cheek had blanched with annoyance, though he whistled an air from the *Trovatore* with as good a grace as he could.

"Recollect yourself, child," whispered the aunt to the pouting girl, and then hastened to assuage the feelings of the insulted swain with as interesting a conversation as she could devise. They talked of wheat, and beans, and potatoes, and then of the Stresa news. But the words rang in Paolo's ears—"Take your attentions elsewhere!" Did Lucrezia mean them? No doubt *she* could find other attentions quickly enough. Already his breast swelled with jealousy, though the aunt tried to smooth matters by hinting that Lucrezia was so very genteel that she liked no peasant ways of lovemaking, even though her heart would have been with them.

"Nevertheless, I am a *contadino*," answered Paolo, half dejected and half proudly, and then they went back to speak of the crops again, while Lucrezia stood alone on the terrace choking down her tears and smoothed the best garments, which had been displaced by that untoward embrace. Yes, her yellow kerchief was certainly awry, and her apron crumpled. How did her hair look? She would dearly have loved a peep in the broken fragment of mirror that lay upon the window

sill in her attic bedroom; but she would not have passed through the kitchen for worlds, and have Paolo know she was going to look at herself in the glass! She sat, hanging her feet on the wall, and looked across at Stresa while she listened to scraps of the conversation from the kitchen; it was about the chestnuts, the vintage, and everything excepting herself. Was that the way in which a lover should behave? Lucrezia put on all the dignity of which she was capable, but Paolo did not come out, so at last she was obliged to walk sulkily to the door and make the first move herself.

"Do not trouble to pick the rice, aunt," she said. "I go to take off my dress, and then I will see to it!"

"There, there, what a wench it is," deplored the elder woman, "when she has thought of nothing all yesterday but this *festa!*"

"*Festa!*" grumbled Lucrezia. "It is little of a *festa* to me. And now it is too late to go."

"The ceremony only begins at the half hour," said Paolo quietly, "and I wait to hear the Stresa clock strike eleven."

Paolo had not even been late.

"Come, then, all is well!" put in Teresa cheeringly, trying to cement this step towards peace. "Thou wilt have thy comfits after all, though thou scarce deservest them, wayward wench that thou art!"

"Will you go, Lucrezia?" asks Paolo anxiously, coming closer to her, while the old woman moved away into the back-yard.

He ought not to have done this. He ought to have gone on being firm and proud. Perhaps Lucrezia would have liked him the better for it; perhaps she would have been glad that she had found her master; perhaps —but wherefore surmise? Paolo was not domineering, nor was Lucrezia reasonable.

"Oh, yes," answered she, laughing—at sight of his eager face—that pretty laugh which had cost him his heart. "Since you wish it so much, I do not mind going. Though, to be sure, you almost took away the very desire I had for a little recreation. Will you promise not to molest me any more by your country manners?"

"I always thought girls liked being wooed," sighed the poor gallant.

"Well—well, and if they do, why should they say so? Don't you see that these things should understand themselves? That is how it is with the educated people."

"We are not educated, Lucrezia, you and I. We are only *contadini*. Why should we not conduct ourselves as God has put it into our hearts to do? I am not disagreeable to you, since you will marry me. Why, then, must I hold aloof from you?"

"Listen to the man!" smiled the little tormentor. "I suppose, now, you think it is always for love of a lad's brown face that a girl marries! What a peasant you are!"

"Yes, I am that," said Paolo with some pride; "a peasant, and an honest one, thank God! That is why I believed you liked me, since you said you would marry me, even though I am no fine townsman!" Then softening quickly, as was his wont towards Lucrezia, he added tenderly, "But you *do* like me, do you not, dear heart?" The aunt looked another way, and Paolo took a little brown hand in his. Alas! Lucrezia was not so easily sobered. She only laughed, and snatching away her hand called out gaily: "I declare we shall be late for the wedding, after all!" The thwarted lover could but make answer with a sigh, for she was gathering up her skirts, and with a hasty good-bye to the old woman, and as hasty a promise to be back at mid-day, she jumped down the steps into the orchard. To make love to her in such a mood was but waste trouble; but as he strode beside her Paolo could not but remember the pretty smiles she used to bestow on him *before* they were betrothed; smiles that, alas! she sometimes bestowed on others even now. He looked eagerly for one gentle touch of the brown fingers in passing; but even when they came to the rugged bit of way, over which he had often helped her, Lucrezia would have none of his strong arm this morning. "I have a couple of words to say to Caterina, the lame one," said she, hurrying forward, and when they reached the foot of the hill—under the pretence of a weighty commission—she had her kerchief settled and took a glance in the mirror, which did more to restore her good-humour than poor Paolo's efforts could have done in an hour. Alas! what a vain girl was Lucrezia!

They took seat in the boat. Paolo began to feel more at ease as he grasped the friendly oars, but he was sorely perplexed still. He had been taught to believe that the humouring of a woman is an evil thing. Yet he loved Lucrezia so dearly that he scarcely dared be cross with her, lest so wayward a damsel should give him the slip altogether! Again he said to himself, "Patience!" but he felt no patience. By nature he was of a hot temper and swift to retort. Many wondered at seeing the fisher youth so changed, as he

used to be when he was beside old Pietro's niece.

"Shall I send thee a basket of the good pears from my mother's house tree?" said he at last, by way of an attempt, adopting once more the friendly "thou."

"Yes, if you like," answered she, scorning the familiar pronoun.

Paolo moved the stretcher at his feet and took out grease to ease the rough rowlocks for his oars. He fidgeted uneasily. Had he remarked her pretty blue frock or noted the amber kerchief on her bosom, or even said that the *spadillas* in her hair were deftly put in, he might have had better success. But he was only a poor, illiterate fisherman, as Lucrezia was wont so often to tell him! He knew that she was pretty, that the sight of her in any costume—perhaps most in her homely farm dress—made his heart glow and his eyes kindle proudly, but he certainly could not have described in what garb she was habited. Whereas this was just what Lucrezia would most have wished him to notice. She was not a little vain of being more refined and of dressing more quietly than the peasant girls about. But Paolo did not care for her to be refined; he was only a peasant-born fisherman; he only wanted a peasant wife. It vexed him sorely that his betrothed should insist so much on gentility of manner, for there was a tale whispered around which made him ashamed, if Lucrezia was noticed as being different from the country girls. She had never guessed at the rumour herself—no one dared repeat it in her presence; but this was it:—She was not Teresa's niece, folks said. She was not a born *contadina*. She had been placed out to nurse—as children of the nobility often are—and there she had been forsaken, in Pietro's house, brought up with Pietro's own boy. Of course there was no proof of this, for Teresa was a terrible woman when she chose, and she had chosen not to open her mouth, to Paolo or any one else, on the subject of Lucrezia's birth. Nevertheless, the village gossips had no doubt of the truth of their surmise. Lucrezia was "gentle-born," and, if "gentle-born," why forsaken—unless for some grave reason? Well, well, Teresa had been a good foster-mother to the wench, and that was fortunate, since she was surely never to know a mother of her own. Only, the girl must not give herself airs! When she did so, it was luckless Paolo who suffered for it at the neighbours' hands.

Lucrezia little guessed, when she scoffed at her lover for his lack of dignity, that *he* was often scoffed at for his choice of her!

But Paolo could be a passionate lover, peasant as he was; the girl had bewitched him, and if she would but love him and be true to him folk might say what they liked, he could turn a deaf ear to all tales, and be as loyal in defence of her as any knight errant of chivalrous times. Lucrezia had a peasant's notion of honour, whatever her birth—that he would swear to, in spite of all her wayward speeches; she could do peasant's work as a peasant's wife should; what more did he want? Paolo was not afraid of his venture, only it annoyed him—as it was annoying him now—that the girl should be proud of the very thing which he most feared to see in her.

He pulled silently at the oars; just a shade of gloom spread itself over his handsome face, that was usually so good-natured. He could never tell her his thought, and yet sometimes his thought troubled him.

He looked across at the pretty face. One note of gentle womanliness—such as she knew well enough how to give—would have soothed the trouble; but, alas! Lucrezia, untutored peasant lass as I remember you, what a coquette you could be when you chose!

Paolo was vexed at her coolness. He was foolish; he should be still more vexed; she would show him her power. It was so sweet to cultivate dignity, and though the process was a little dull for a holiday pastime, Paolo would sue for her favour presently—would court and admire, and praise her, and then she would be graciously condescending. That was how a lover should behave, and Paolo was so devoted that in time she could surely teach him how to woo as a very gentleman! So she spread her skirts around her, and a gay kerchief to shield her head from the mid-day sun, and for a while sat calmly in the stern of the boat, gazing at Paolo till he was fairly out of countenance. It was but a poor amusement, and Lucrezia was a foolish girl. Even she herself thought so at last. A haughty silence generally overpowered Paolo into respectful rhapsodies to her taste, but to-day he was obdurate. Perhaps she was silly. Here was a handsome man ready to court her—for Paolo *was* handsome, tall, and strong, lithe in his movements, and with keen bright eyes that shone from beneath black eyebrows, and a bush of curly black hair. He had put on his soldier's cap to-day to please her—Lucrezia liked a soldier's cap. Yes—she certainly was silly—

the conviction brought a blush to her cheek. Would it not be well for her to make the most of her gallant when she arrived at the town? Every one knew she was but seventeen and had no dowry, and would not the Stresa girls be envious when they saw her with such a good-looking lover? But for that she must smooth his annoyance, for a cross-looking gallant was a credit to no girl.

"Paolo, did you catch good fish this morning?" she began graciously.

"I did not go out."

"The lazy man!"

"I might have been late home, and I would not have kept you waiting."

Paolo was innocent of intention to wound with this shaft, which might have been dealt by Lucrezia herself.

"Hast put on the gold I gave thee?" asked he presently.

"Does a well-behaved girl go about with a man without wearing the gold he has given her?" answered Lucrezia. "I should be mistaken for a servant-wench!"

Paolo stood reproved. He had seen the gold chain on her bosom, and had only asked the question by way of conversation.

Fortunately, the magic sound of bells across the water had permanently established Lucrezia's temper, and there was no pretence now in her good-humour. She had the proverbial Italian light heart that nothing can quench when a sight is to be seen, the merry rush of life to be heard. The shady shores of Isola Madre had been left behind, and the boat was skirting the magnolia groves of Isola Bella when first the bells began to ring, but Lucrezia left Paolo no rest till their keel had grazed the shingle of the main land, and all the remainder of the journey she kept repeating—

"Ah, Paolo, Paolo, make haste, or we shall be late," to which Paolo made the comforting reply, that a Sindaco's daughter would surely have the bells rung for her wedding full half an hour before.

Lucrezia used the time in speculating what the bride was about now, and who was bid to the festivities; but every time the big bass hurled itself in chastisement after the cadences of merry little bells, every time the triplets, after a lame ending, began again cheerfully at the top of the scale, Lucrezia looked reproachfully at Paolo, and folded up her gay kerchief afresh, as though to emphasize the fact that she was impatient. Fortunately the brawny arms could pull a long swift stroke; but the poor lad was but scantily rewarded for his pains, for when they reached the shore Lucrezia would scarce wait, in her excitement, while he moored the boat. But he forgave her the want of courtesy for the sake of her restored good-humour, and was even so pleased at the sight of her gay spirits as to hurry up the road after her, and venture upon offering his arm. She drew her little person up to its full height and gave him a look which was meant to freeze the very marrow in his bones. •

"Hast forgotten that in company one never does such things?" said she. "That is for peasant folk. Make haste, or we shall lose a place for the sight!"

They went up to the church. It stood on a little hill, a trifle above the town. Many people were gathered together, for the wedding of a Sindaco's daughter does not happen every day; and she was to have a silk dress, and more rings than had ever been seen on a bride's fingers before. The village children, a ragged gang, thronged the porch in hopes of a shower of comfits when the benediction should be over.

The last trace of Lucrezia's ill-temper had disappeared in the genial atmosphere of gay colours and a crowd; but she was determined to reach the centre of the manœuvres, and pushed her way valiantly, nodding a hasty greeting now and then to right or left. Standing-room was gained near to the broad flight of steps up which the bride must pass, and Lucrezia was satisfied so long as no one ventured to press before her, in which event her small stature would prevent her from seeing. She looked eagerly for the wedding party. But though the noisy bells seemed to have been ringing a long time now, the Sindaco's daughter still tarried. Lucrezia began to weary; the sun was very hot. Paolo's arm presently stole around her waist. She did not notice it. "What a long while the bride's toilette takes!" sighed she, and in the heat she looked white and languid. Paolo's gaze rested proudly upon her. He was no "man of education," as Lucrezia used to say, but, as he looked at her the words of a popular Lombard song came into his head, "Thou seemest on the hedge a jessamine." Peasant comrades used to tell Paolo that his Lucrezia was too frail and too sallow, but these were they who only admired "much presence" in a woman. They looked at her, whatever they said. No one could help looking at the pale, pretty, oval face, with its dewy brown eyes and its frame of loosely waving chestnut hair; nor at the supple firm-knit little figure, so slender and yet so strong.

But though Paolo did not like folk to cry down his betrothed, he did not like them to admire her too much either. That sculptor last year who had told her that the nightingale's song dwelt in her sweet and swelling throat, the sound of the sea in her little shell-like ears, was a fool! Paolo would have been angry again had he noticed some one who was even now admiring Lucrezia too much—would have been all the more angry as the pair of eyes fixed on his betrothed belonged to no peasant, but to a "man of education," a signore. He was not handsome, as Paolo was; his face was worn and aged before its time, his mouth was thin-lipped and somewhat cynical, and, for all his fine clothes, he was less refined than the fisher-lad. But he wore a diamond ring, he lounged easily, and not as the shop lads; and had Lucrezia, wonderful to tell, not been innocent as yet of an admiring pair of male eyes, I fear her heart would surely have swelled with pride, and Paolo would have had reason to be angry.

There was an old cherry-tree wedged up into the corner of the wall. The new admirer leaned up against it and smiled as he watched the changing face before him. "What a pretty picture the *contadinella* would make!" he said to a comrade at his side.

A greater shouting of the crowd at last announced the arrival of the bride. Stronger bodies forced themselves before Lucrezia.

"Paolo, Paolo," she complained, "tell them to move. I see nothing!"

Paolo laughed. "They also wish to see," said he. "But, come, I will lift thee in mine arms."

To this, however, the girl only pouted. It was not to be done. How was she to see the sight? They looked round the piazza. "I will climb on the wall by that cherry-tree!" she exclaimed, and hastened to push her way through the crowd. "She will be gone before I get up," moaned the child-woman.

Paolo cleared a passage as fast as he could, and some one besides Paolo made a little space on the wall. Both were too much engrossed to notice who it was.

"Thou art right," whispered the young Signore's companion to him; "she is a pretty girl!" And the other stood so near to Lucrezia that he could note the curve of her neck and the swell of her shoulders.

"Look, look, Paolo!" she cried. "There is the bride's silk dress! Is it not beautiful? There is nothing I should like so well as a silk dress; I would give *anything* for it! Surely thou mightest give me such a dress when we are married in Carnival."

"I like thee best in thy working-frock, dear heart."

"Thou mockest me!"

"No, indeed. And well thou knowest a poor fisherman has no money to buy silk dresses with."

"I suppose not," sighed she. "See her rings! She has nine on one finger! How many wilt thou give me?"

"It remains to be seen how much I can earn before the Carnival. What I can will I give thee; of that rest assured. Have I not bought gold for thee, as much as thou canst wear?" And he touched the rude ornaments in ears and hair.

"As much as I can wear?" ejaculated she. "No, indeed! Well, let us speak no more of it. We poor folk must have patience, I suppose."

"Would it not be a real pleasure to give the child a silk dress, eh, Mario?" whispered the signore to his comrade, while he still looked at Lucrezia.

Bride and bridegroom, with many attendant relatives, swept into the church. Those of the throng who could not find room within the building waited, eagerly conversing, without. Paolo and Lucrezia sat on the stone wall, and presently Lucrezia had time to notice the strange eyes whose glances fell so admiringly on herself. She dropped her own bright ones coquettishly, and blushed with pleasure. She did not tell Paolo that there was a well-dressed man standing hard by who sought a look from her. Paolo could see him if he chose. And presently Paolo did see him; but he only said, "There is one of those gentlefolks who come for the water cure. They think a little fresh air will cure all their evils."

"Paolo, you should not speak so," said Lucrezia. "He is a great gentleman, if I mistake not."

"A great one, indeed," sneered the fisher swain, looking with contempt at the spare form of his unsuspected rival. "And if *I* mistake not, his greatness will but last him a short time to play the fool with."

"You frighten me, Paolo!" cried the girl, aghast. "How can you say such things? I will not listen to you."

"Well, well, we must all die some day," added Paolo cheerfully. "And I meant nothing. How do I know about the man? At all events, we won't let the sight of any puny-limbed aristocrat make *us* sad. We are strong and hearty. Nothing is going to happen to us, and we are going to be merry."

"Yes," sighed Lucrezia, who hated every thought of sadness, "we are going to be merry."

The bridal party came out of church, comfits were scattered, sweetmeats and comments passed freely around. Village children scrambled for the former; village gossips hastened to supply the latter. Some said the bride's gown was of finest fabric, some said the silk was mixed with cotton, and the embroidery of the petticoats nothing but machine-work. And Lucrezia listened to all this; but she listened half sadly. The day was not very far distant when she should play such a part, but, alas! Paolo was but a poor fisherman, and could provide no such state as this stiff and starched finery. Lucrezia knew she was pretty, and this bride was not pretty; but then the gold of her dowry was all displayed to view on her person, and there was much of it, and she was grand—yes, almost as grand as a lady! Lucrezia sighed, for dearly indeed she would have loved to outshine the Sindaco's daughter. Her heart was filled with envy as she watched the bridal party wend its way to the scene of coming festivities. And the Count, leaning against the cherry-tree, seemed to understand it all. But the pop-guns were being let off at the close of the ceremony, and Paolo was saying to his betrothed, "Come, dear heart, the aunt will want thee at home, and thou must eat a mouthful with me at the tavern before we go." And the Count heard it all, and saw Lucrezia pout; for she had no mind to go home yet. Why did Paolo always remind her of passing holidays and coming duties, and disagreeable things in general? Alas, poor fellow! he always had the misfortune to say the wrong thing. He soon saw that he had said it now, for she tossed her head and turned away from him disdainfully.

"Who knows if I have not business in Stresa during the afternoon?" said she.

"Didst thou not even promise thine aunt to be back to cook the dinner?"

"And is one always to reflect how one can perform when one makes a promise? Why, the meal is cooked by this time, and it takes an hour to row across the lake. Thou art wool-gathering!"

"Oh, my Lucrezia," laughed Paolo, good-humouredly, "thou art hard to please, in truth! Oh, but do as thou wilt. If thou hast business in Stresa, thou canst see to it while I walk round to Baveno to speak with

Maso about the new boat. Anyhow, now we will go to the *trattoria.*"

This met with Lucrezia's approval. She jumped down from the wall. In doing so she dropped one of her heavy ear-drops. Neither she nor Paolo saw it fall, but the man whom Paolo had stigmatised as a ne'er-do-weel picked it up after Lucrezia had left the piazza.

The tavern to which Paolo took his companion stood on the quay. There was a little bit of vine-trellised *pergola* in front of it, beneath which marble tables invited passers-by to partake of ices and coffee. A row of pollard acacias stood across the way, and between the acacias and the *pergola* the carriages drove past, going to Baveno and Pallanza. It was gay, and Lucrezia liked anything gay. She talked fast and laughed merrily. The *polenta* tasted much better off this marble table than it did at home; and she had a glass of sour Monferrato, which did not fall to her lot every day. She allowed to herself that Paolo had behaved very well, for he had studied her tastes, and had not brought her to any low eating-house for the sake of saving a few *soldi.* Here they were quite in the fashionable part of the town, and with Monferrato to drink, which must have cost at least eight *soldi* the bottle. Yes, Lucrezia allowed to herself that she was proud of her betrothed—proud that folks should see her made much of—proud to be promised to a man before she was seventeen, and she without a morsel of dowry. She forgot the envy with which she had regarded the grand bride—forgot the polished young Count, whose admiring glances she had been so pleased to note. Both of them forgot that they had ever quarrelled.

Paolo leaned back in his chair when the simple meal was over, looking with satisfaction at the pretty face beside him, and jingling in his pocket the copper change out of paying the score.

"Well, hast thou renounced the idea of doing business in Stresa?" laughed he, emboldened by her happy countenance.

It was a luckless speech. The happy half-hour at the tavern had only made Lucrezia the more anxious to prolong her holiday. She wanted to walk up and down outside, and show off her gallant. "Why should I renounce it?" said she. "Thou hast said that thou too hast affairs to attend to."

"My affairs can wait," replied Paolo. "Believe me, thou dost well to return now."

Alas! even gratitude, even the conviction that she was going to defeat her own aim, could not quell Lucrezia's obstinacy. Even did she no longer desire it, with her to have determined on a thing was to do it.

"If thy affairs can wait mine cannot," said she curtly, and rising from her seat.

Paolo sighed as he followed her out of the tavern. He knew that it was of no use objecting further now.

"Shall I come with thee, or go to Baveno?" asked he resignedly.

Now, as we have said, Lucrezia would have liked to parade awhile up and down attended by Paolo, but she was not going to hint at such a thing if he was not sharp enough to divine it. So she only said coldly, "Please thyself."

"I will go to Maso's, then," sighed Paolo. He did not guess that a girl might be proud of him. She might be going to see some female friend, and he would be in the way. "Shall I call for thee at thy cousin Maddalena's house?" asked he presently, as Lucrezia made no remark.

"No; I do not go to the cousin's. She does nothing but exclaim every time, 'Oh, how small thou art, Lucrezia! How pale thou art grown!' as though she had never seen me before. She wearies me. When I have done that which I have to do, I will sit and wait for thee on the shore."

"That will not be amusing."

"Yes, yes; it pleases me," she protested, though in reality she was disappointed at this result of her obstinacy. "Go, now, and hasten back, for then we will go home."

"In an hour I shall be back, or shall I remain longer?"

"No, no; an hour will do. You will find me just here on this bench," said she, for they had left the scanty shade of the pollarded acacias, and stood in the best avenue now, where the summer visitors walk and drive. The "Bagni" stood opposite. There would be no mistaking the spot.

"Good-bye, Lucrezia," said Paolo sadly. He said it as though it were for a long time instead of only for a short hour! And even Lucrezia—foolish girl—though she had made the parting, was sorry now! But she said a curt word as usual in leave-taking. It was only when Paolo's back was turned, so that he could not see her, when he was walking away along the dusty high road, that she chose to show her feelings. Then she gazed after him tenderly as long as he was in sight.

FALLS OF THE DOCHART, PERTHSHIRE.
A Study in Black and White.
By E. Jennings.

THE TRUMPET-MAJOR.

BY THOMAS HARDY, AUTHOR OF "FAR FROM THE MADDING CROWD," ETC.

CHAPTER XXXIV.—(*Continued.*)

THE wild, herbless, weather-worn promontory was quite a solitude, and, saving the one old lighthouse about fifty yards up the slope, scarce a mark was visible to show that humanity had ever been near the spot. Anne found herself a seat on a stone, and swept with her eyes the tremulous expanse of water around her, that seemed to utter a ceaseless unintelligible incantation. Out of the three hundred and sixty degrees of her complete horizon two hundred and fifty were covered by waves, the *coup d'œil* including the area of troubled waters known as the Race, where two seas met to effect the destruction of such vessels as could not be mastered by one. She counted the craft within her view: there were five; no, there were only four; no, there were seven, some of the specks having resolved themselves into two. They were all small coasters, and kept well within sight of land.

Anne sank into a reverie. Then she heard a slight noise on her left-hand, and turning beheld an old sailor, who had approached with a glass. He was levelling it over the sea in a direction to the south-east, and somewhat removed from that in which her own eyes had been wandering. Anne moved a few steps thitherward, so as to unclose to her view a deeper sweep on that side, and by this discovered a ship of far larger size than any which had yet dotted the main before her. Its sails were for the most part new and clean, and in comparison with its rapid progress before the wind the small brigs and ketches seemed standing still. Upon this striking object the old man's glass was bent.

"What do you see, sailor?" she asked.

"Almost nothing," he answered. "My sight is so gone off lately that things, one and all, be but a November mist to me. And yet I fain would see to-day. I am looking for the *Victory.*"

"Why?" she said quickly.

"I have a son aboard her. He's one of three from these parts. There's the captain, there's my son Ned, and there's young Loveday of Overcombe—he that lately joined."

"Shall I look for you?" said Anne after a pause.

"Certainly, mis'ess, if so be you please."

Anne took the glass, and he supported it by his arm. "It is a large ship," she said, "with three masts, three rows of guns along the side, and all her sails set."

"I guessed as much."

"There is a little flag in front—over her bowsprit."

"The jack."

"And there's a large one flying at her stern."

"The ensign."

"And one on her topmast."

"That's the admiral's flag, the flag of my Lord Nelson. What is her figure-head, my dear?"

"A coat-of-arms, supported on this side by a sailor."

Her companion nodded with satisfaction. "On the other side of that figure-head is a marine."

"She is twisting round in a curious way, and her sails sink in like old cheeks, and she shivers like a leaf upon a tree."

"She is in stays, for the larboard tack. I can see what she's been doing. She's been re'ching close in to avoid the flood tide, as the wind is to the sou'-west, and she's bound down; but as soon as the ebb made, d'ye see, they made sail to the west'ard. Captain Hardy may be depended upon for that; he knows every current about here, being a native."

"And now I can see the other side; it is a soldier where a sailor was before. You are *sure* it is the *Victory?*"

"I am sure."

After this a frigate came into view—the *Euryalus*— sailing in the same direction. Anne sat down, and her eyes never left the ships. "Tell me more about the *Victory,*" she said.

"She is the best sailor in the service, and she carries a hundred guns. The heaviest be on the lower deck, the next size on the middle deck, the next on the main and upper decks. My son Ned's place is on the lower deck, because he's short, and they put the short men below."

Bob, though not tall, was not likely to be specially selected for shortness. She pictured him on the upper deck, in his snow-white trousers and jacket of navy blue, looking perhaps towards the very point of land where she then was.

The great silent ship, with her population of blue jackets, marines, officers, captain, and the admiral who was not to return alive,

XXI—51

passed like a phantom the meridian of the Bill. Sometimes her aspect was that of a large white bat, sometimes that of a grey one. In the course of time the watching girl saw that the ship had passed her nearest point; the breadth of her sails diminished by fore-shortening, till she assumed the form of an egg on end. After this something seemed to twinkle, and Anne, who had previously with-drawn from the old sailor, went back to him, and looked again through the glass. The twinkling was the light falling upon the cabin windows of the ship's stern. She explained it to the old man.

"Then we see now what the enemy have seen but once. That was in seventy-nine, when she sighted the French and Spanish fleet off Scilly, and she retreated because she feared a landing. Well, 'tis a brave ship, and she carries brave men !"

Anne's tender bosom heaved, but she said nothing, and again became absorbed in con-templation.

The *Victory* was fast dropping away. She was on the horizon, and soon appeared hull down. That seemed to be like the beginning of a greater end than her present vanishing. Anne Garland could not stay by the sailor any longer, and went about a stone's throw off, where she was hidden by the inequality of the cliff from his view. The vessel was now exactly end on, and stood out in the direction of the Start, her width having con-tracted to the proportion of a feather. She sat down again, and mechanically took out some biscuits that she had brought, foreseeing that her waiting might be long. But she could not eat one of them; eating seemed to jar with the mental tenseness of the mo-ment; and her undeviating gaze continued to follow the lessened ship with the fidelity of a balanced needle to a magnetic stone, all else in her being motionless.

The courses of the *Victory* were absorbed into the main, then her topsails went, and then her top-gallants. She was now no more than a dead fly's wing on a sheet of spider's web; and even this fragment diminished. Anne could hardly bear to see the end, and yet she resolved not to flinch. The admiral's flag sank behind the watery line, and in a minute the very truck of the last topmast stole away. The *Victory* was gone.

Anne's lip quivered as she murmured with-out removing her wet eyes from the vacant and solemn horizon, "'They that go down to the sea in ships, that do business in great waters——'"

"'These see the works of the Lord, and

His wonders in the deep,'" was returned by a man's voice from behind her.

Looking round quickly, she saw a soldier standing there; and the grave eyes of John Loveday bent on her.

"'Tis what I was thinking," she said, try-ing to be composed.

"You were saying it," he answered gently.

"Was I?—I did not know it. . . . How came you here?" she presently added.

"I have been behind you a good while; but you never turned round."

"I was deeply occupied," she said in an undertone.

"Yes—I too came to see him pass. I heard this morning that Lord Nelson had embarked, and I knew at once that they would sail immediately. The *Victory* and *Euryalus* are to join the rest of the fleet at Plymouth. There was a great crowd of people assembled to see the admiral off; they cheered him and the ship as she dropped down. He took his coffin on board with him, they say."

"His coffin?" said Anne, turning deadly pale. "Something terrible, then, is meant by that! Oh, why *would* Bob go in that ship?—doomed to destruction from the very beginning like this !"

"It was his determination to sail under Captain Hardy, and under no one else," said John. "There may be hot work; but we must hope for the best." And observing how wretched she looked, he added, "But won't you let me help you back? If you can walk as far as Church-Hope Cove it will be enough. A lerret is going from there to Weymouth har-bour in the course of an hour; it belongs to a man I know, and they can take one pas-senger, I am sure."

She turned her back upon the Channel, and by his help soon reached the place indi-cated. The boat was lying there as he had said. She found it to belong to the old man who had been with her at the Bill, and was in charge of his two younger sons. The trumpet-major helped her into it over the slippery blocks of stone, one of the young men spread his jacket for her to sit on, and as soon as they pulled from shore John climbed up the blue-grey cliff, and disap-peared over the top, to return to Weymouth by the Chesil Road.

Anne was in the town by three o'clock. The trip in the stern of the lerret had quite re-freshed her, with the help of the biscuits, which she had at last been able to eat. The van from Weymouth to Overcombe did not start till four o'clock, and feeling no further interest in the gaieties of the place, she strolled on through Radipole, her mind settling down again upon the possibly sad fate of the *Victory* when she found herself alone. She did not hurry on; and finding that even now there wanted another half-hour to the carrier's time, she turned into a little lane to escape the inspection of the numerous passers-by. Here all was quite lonely and still, and she sat down under a willow-tree, absently regarding the landscape, which had now begun to put on the rich tones of declining summer, but which to her was as hollow and faded as a theatre by day. She could hold out no longer; burying her face in her hands, she wept without restraint.

Some yards behind her was a little spring of water, having a stone margin round it to prevent the cattle from treading in the sides and filling it up with dirt. While she wept two elderly gentlemen entered unperceived upon the scene, and walked on to the spring's brink. Here they paused and looked in, afterwards moving round it, and then stooping as if to smell or taste its waters. The spring was, in fact, a sulphurous one, then recently discovered by a physician who lived in the neighbourhood; and it was beginning to attract some attention, having by common report contributed to effect such wonderful cures as almost passed belief. After a considerable discussion, apparently on how the pool might be improved for better use, one of the two elderly gentlemen turned away, leaving the other still probing the spring with his cane. The first stranger, who wore a blue coat with gilt buttons, came on in the direction of Anne Garland, and seeing her sad posture went quickly up to her, and said abruptly, "What is the matter?"

Anne, who in her grief had observed nothing of the gentlemen's presence, withdrew her handkerchief from her eyes and started to her feet. She instantly recognised her interrogator as the King.

"What, crying?" his Majesty inquired kindly. "How is this?"

"I—have seen a dear friend go away, sir," she faltered with downcast eyes.

"Ah!—partings are sad—very sad—for us all. You must hope your friend will return soon. Where is he or she gone?"

"I don't know, your Majesty."

"Don't know—how is that?"

"He is a sailor on board the *Victory*."

"Then he has reason to be proud," said the King with interest. "He is your brother?"

Anne tried to explain what he was, but could not, and blushed with painful heat.

"Well, well, well; what is his name?"

In spite of Anne's confusion and low spirits, her natural woman's shrewdness told her at once that no harm could be done by revealing Bob's name; and she answered, "His name is Robert Loveday, sir."

"Loveday—a good name. I shall not forget it. Now dry your cheeks, and don't cry any more. Loveday—Robert Loveday."

Anne curtseyed, the King smiled good-humouredly, and turned to rejoin his companion, who was afterwards heard to be Dr. ——, the physician in attendance at Gloucester Lodge. This gentleman had in the meantime filled a small phial with the medicinal water, which he carefully placed in his pocket; and on the King coming up they retired together and disappeared. Thereupon Anne, now thoroughly aroused, followed the same way with a gingerly tread, just in time to see them get into a carriage which was in waiting at the turning of the lane.

She quite forgot the carrier, and everything else in connection with riding home. Flying along the road rapidly and unconsciously, when she awoke to a sense of her whereabouts she was so near to Overcombe as to make the carrier not worth waiting for. She had been borne up in this hasty spurt at the end of a weary day by visions of Bob promoted to the rank of admiral, or something equally wonderful, by the King's special command, the chief result of the promotion being, in her arrangement of the piece, that he would stay at home and go to sea no more. But she was not a girl who indulged in extravagant fancies long, and before she reached home she thought that the King had probably forgotten her by that time, and her troubles, and her lover's name.

CHAPTER XXXV.—A SAILOR ENTERS.

THE remaining fortnight of the month of September passed away, with a general decline from the summer's excitements. The Royal family left Weymouth the first week in October, the German Legion with their artillery about the same time. The dragoons still remained at Radipole barracks, and John Loveday brought to Anne every newspaper that he could lay hands on, especially such as contained any fragment of shipping news. This threw them much together; and at these times John was often awkward and confused, on account of the unwonted stress of concealing his great love for her.

Her interests had grandly developed from the limits of Overcombe and Weymouth life to an extensiveness truly European.

During the whole month of October, however, not a single grain of information reached
her, or anybody else, concerning Nelson and
his blockading squadron off Cadiz. There
were the customary bad jokes about Buonaparte, especially when it was found that the
whole French army had turned its back upon
Boulogne and set out for the Rhine. Then
came accounts of his march through Germany
and into Austria; but not a word about the
Victory.

At the beginning of autumn John brought
news which fearfully depressed her. The
Austrian General Mack had capitulated with
his whole army. Then were revived the
old misgivings as to invasion. "Instead of
having to cope with him weary with waiting,
we shall have to encounter This Man fresh
from the fields of victory," ran the newspaper
article.

But the week which had led off with such
a dreary piping was to end in another key.
On the very day when Mack's army was
piling arms at the feet of its conqueror, a
blow had been struck by Bob Loveday and
his comrades which eternally shattered the
enemy's force by sea. Four days after the
receipt of the Austrian news Corporal Tullidge ran into the miller's house to inform
him that on the previous Monday, at eleven
in the morning, the *Pickle* schooner, Lieutenant Lapenotiere, had arrived at Falmouth
with dispatches from the fleet; that the
stage-coaches on the highway from Exeter to
London were chalked with the words "Great
Victory!" "Glorious Triumph!" and so on;
and that all the country people were wild to
know particulars.

On Friday afternoon John arrived with
authentic news of the battle off Cape Trafalgar, and the death of Nelson. Captain
Hardy was alive; he had escaped with the
loss of his shoe-buckle. But it was feared
that the *Victory* had been the scene of the
heaviest slaughter among all the ships engaged, though as yet no returns of killed
and wounded had been issued, beyond a
rough list of the numbers in some of the
ships.

The suspense of the little household in
Overcombe Mill was great in the extreme.
John came thither daily for more than a week;
but no further particulars reached England
till the end of that time, and then only the
meagre intelligence that there had been a gale
immediately after the battle, and that many
of the prizes had been lost. Anne said
little to all these things, and preserved a
superstratum of calmness on her countenance;

but some inner voice seemed to whisper to
her that Bob was no more. Miller Loveday
drove to Portisham several times, to learn
if the Captain's sisters had received any more
definite tidings than these flying reports; but
that family had heard nothing which could
in any way relieve the miller's anxiety.
When at last, at the end of November, there
appeared a final and revised list of killed
and wounded as issued by Admiral Colling-
wood, it was a useless sheet to the Lovedays. To their great pain it contained no
names but those of officers, the friends of
ordinary seamen and marines being on that
occasion left to discover their losses as best
they might.

Anne's conviction of her loss increased
with the darkening of the early winter days.
Bob was not a cautious man who would
avoid needless exposure, and a hundred and
fifty of the *Victory's* crew had been disabled
or slain. Anybody who had looked into her
room at this time would have seen that her
favourite reading was the office for the burial
of the dead at sea, beginning, "We therefore
commit his body to the deep." In these first
days of December several of the victorious
fleet came into port; but not the *Victory*.
Many supposed that that noble ship, disabled by the battle, had gone to the bottom
in the subsequent tempestuous weather; and
the belief was persevered in till it was told
in Weymouth that she had been seen passing
up the Channel. Two days later the *Victory*
arrived at Portsmouth.

Then letters from survivors began to
appear in the public prints which John so
regularly brought to Anne; but though he
watched the mails with unceasing vigilance,
there was never a letter from Bob. It sometimes crossed John's mind that his brother
might still be alive and well, and that in his
wish to abide by his expressed intention of
giving up Anne and home life he was deliberately lax in writing. If so, Bob was carrying out the idea too thoughtlessly by half, as
could be seen by watching the effects of suspense upon the fair face of the victim, and
the anxiety of the rest of the family.

It was a clear day in December. The
first slight snow of the season had been sifted
over the earth, and one side of the apple-
tree branches in the miller's garden was
touched with white, though a few leaves were
still lingering on the tops of the younger
trees. A short sailor of the royal navy, who
was not Bob, or anything like him, crossed
the mill court and came to the door. The
miller hastened out and brought him into

the room, where John, Mrs. Loveday, and Anne Garland were all present.

"I'm from aboard the *Victory*," said the sailor. "My name's Jim Cornick. And your lad is alive and well."

They breathed rather than spoke their thankfulness and relief, the miller's eyes being moist as he turned aside to calm himself; while Anne, having first jumped up wildly from her seat, sank back again under the almost insupportable joy that trembled through her limbs to her utmost finger.

"I've come from Spithead to Portisham," the sailor continued, "and now I am going on to father at Weymouth."

"Ah—I know your father," cried the trumpet-major, "old James Cornick."

It was the man who had brought Anne in his lerret from Portland Bill.

"And Bob hasn't got a scratch?" said the miller.

"Not a scratch," said Cornick.

Loveday than bustled off to draw the visitor something to drink. Anne Garland, with a glowing blush on her face at she said not what, had gone to the back part of the room, where she was the very embodiment of sweet content as she slightly swayed herself without speaking. A little tide of happiness seemed to ebb and flow through her in listening to the sailor's words, moving her figure with it. The seaman and John went on conversing.

"Bob had a good deal to do with barricading the hawse-holes afore we were in action, and the adm'l and cap'n both were very much pleased at how 'twas done. When the adm'l went up the quarter-deck ladder Cap'n Hardy said a word or two to Bob, but what it was I don't know, for I was quartered at a gun some ways off. However, Bob saw the adm'l stagger when 'a was wownded, and was one of the men who carried him to the cockpit. After that he and some other lads jumped aboard the French ship, and I believe they was in her when she struck her flag. What 'a did next I can't say, for the wind had dropped, and the smoke was like a cloud. But 'a got a good deal talked about; and they say there's promotion in store for'n."

At this point in the story Jim Cornick stopped to drink, and a low unconscious humming came from Anne in her distant corner; the faint melody continued more or less when the conversation between the sailor and the Lovedays was renewed.

"We heard afore that the *Victory* was near knocked to pieces," said the miller.

"Knocked to pieces? You'd say so if so be you could see her. Gad, her sides be battered like an old penny piece; the shot be still sticking in her wales, and her sails be like so many clap-nets : we have run all the way home under jury top-masts; and as for her decks, you may swab wi' hot water, and you may swab wi' cold; but there's the blood-stains, and there they'll bide. . . . The cap'n had a narrow escape, like many o' the rest—a shot shaved his ancle like a razor. You should have seen that man's face in the het o' battle, his features were as if they'd been cast in steel."

"We rather expected a letter from Bob before this."

"Well," said Jim Cornick, with a smile of toleration, "you must make allowances. The truth o't is, he's engaged just now at Portsmouth, like a good many of the rest from our ship. . . . 'Tis a very nice young woman that he's a-courting of, and I make no doubt that she'll be an excellent wife for him."

"Ah!" said Mrs. Loveday in a warning tone.

"Courting—wife?" said the miller.

They instinctively looked towards Anne. Anne had started as if shaken by an invisible hand, and a thick mist of doubt seemed to obscure the intelligence of her eyes. This was but for two or three moments. Very pale, she arose and went right up to the seaman. John gently tried to intercept her, but she passed him by.

"Do you speak of Robert Loveday as courting a wife?" she asked, without the least betrayal of emotion.

"I didn't see you, miss," replied Cornick, turning. "Yes, your brother hev' his eye on a wife, and he deserves one. I hope you don't mind."

"Not in the least," she said with a stage laugh. "I am interested, naturally. And what is she?"

"A very nice young master-tailor's daughter, honey. A very wise choice of the young man's."

"Is she fair or dark?"

"Her hair is rather light."

"I like light hair; and her name?"

"Her name is Caroline. But can it be that my story hurts ye? If so——"

"Yes, yes," said John, interposing anxiously. "We don't care for more just at this moment."

"We *do* care for more," said Anne vehemently. "Tell it all, sailor. That is a very pretty name, Caroline. When are they going to be married?"

"I don't know as how the day is settled,"

answered Jim, even now scarcely conscious of the devastation he was causing in one fair breast. "But from the rate the courting is scudding along at, I should say it won't be long first."

"If you see him when you go back give him my best wishes," she lightly said as she moved away. "And," she added with solemn bitterness, "say that I am glad to hear he is making such good use of the first days of his escape from the Valley of the shadow of Death!" She went away, expressing indifference by audibly singing in the distance—

" Shall we go dance the round, the round, the round,
Shall we go dance the round?"

"Your sister is lively at the news," observed Jim Cornick.

"Yes," murmured John gloomily, as he gnawed his lower lip and kept his eyes fixed on the fire.

"Well," continued the man from the *Victory*, "I won't say that your brother's intended ha'n't got some ballast, which is very luckily for'n, as he might have picked up with a girl without a single copper nail. To be sure there was a time we had when we got into port! It was open house for us all!" And after mentally regarding the scene for a few seconds Jim emptied his cup and rose to go.

The miller was saying some last words to him outside the house, Anne's voice had hardly ceased singing up-stairs, John was standing by the fireplace, and Mrs. Loveday was crossing the room to join her daughter, whose manner had given her some uneasiness, when a noise came from above the ceiling, as of some heavy body falling. Mrs. Loveday rushed to the staircase, saying, "Ah, I feared something!" and she was followed by John.

When they entered Anne's room, which they both did almost at one moment, they found her lying insensible upon the floor. The trumpet-major, his lips tightly closed, lifted her in his arms and laid her upon the bed; after which he went back to the door to give room to her mother, who was bending over the girl with some hartshorn.

Presently Mrs. Loveday looked up and said to him, "She is only in a faint, John, and her colour is coming back. Now leave her to me; I will be down-stairs in a few minutes, and tell you how she is."

John left the room. When he gained the lower apartment his father was standing by the chimney-piece, the sailor having gone. The trumpet-major went up to the fire, and,

grasping the edge of the high chimney-shelf, stood silent.

"Did I hear a noise when I went out?" asked the elder in a tone of misgiving.

"Yes, you did," said John. "It was she; but her mother says she is better now. Father," he added impetuously, "Bob is a worthless blockhead! If there had been any good in him he would have been drowned years ago!"

"John, John—not too fast," said the miller. "That's a hard thing to say of your brother, and you ought to be ashamed of it."

"Well, he tries me more than I can bear. Good heaven! what can a man be made of to go on as he does? Why didn't he come home; or if he couldn't get leave, why didn't he write? 'Tis scandalous of him to serve a woman like that."

"Gently, gently. The chap hev done his duty as a sailor; and though there might have been something between him and Anne, her mother, in talking it over with me, has said many times that she couldn't think of their marrying till Bob had settled down in business with me. Folks that gain victories must have a little liberty allowed 'em. Look at the admiral himself, for that matter."

John continued looking at the red coals, till hearing Mrs. Loveday's foot on the staircase, he went to meet her.

"She is better," said Mrs. Loveday; "but she won't come down again to-day."

Could John have heard what the poor girl was moaning to herself at that moment as she lay writhing on the bed, he would have doubted her mother's assurance: "If he had been dead I could have borne it, but this I cannot bear!"

CHAPTER XXXVI.—DERRIMAN SEES CHANCES.

MEANWHILE Sailor Cornick had gone on his way as far as the forking roads, where he met Festus Derriman on foot. The latter, attracted by the seaman's dress, and by seeing him come from the mill, at once accosted him. Jim, with the greatest readiness, fell into conversation, and told the same story as that he had related at the mill.

"Bob Loveday going to be married?" repeated Festus.

"You all seem struck of a heap wi' that."

"No; I never heard news that pleased me more."

When Cornick was gone Festus, instead of passing straight on, halted on the little bridge and meditated. Bob, being now interested elsewhere, would probably not resent the siege of Anne's heart by another; there could, at any rate, be no further possibility of that looming duel which had troubled the yeoman's mind ever since his horse-play on Anne at the house on the down. To march into the mill and propose to Mrs. Loveday for Anne before John's interest could revive in her was, to this hero's thinking, excellent discretion.

The day had already begun to darken when he entered, and the cheerful fire shone red upon the floor and walls. Mrs. Loveday received him alone, and asked him to take a seat by the chimney-corner, a little of the old hankering for him as a son-in-law having permanently remained with her.

"Your servant, Mrs. Loveday," he said, "and I will tell you at once what I come for. You will say that I take time by the forelock when I inform you that it is to push on my long-wished-for alliance wi' your daughter, as I believe she is now a free woman again."

"Thank you, Mr. Derriman," said the mother placably. "But she is ill at present. I'll mention it to her when she is better."

"Ask her to alter her cruel, cruel resolves against me, on the score of—of my consuming passion for her. In short," continued Festus, dropping his parlour language in his warmth, "I'll tell thee what, Dame Loveday, I want the maid, and must have her."

Mrs. Loveday replied that that was very plain speaking.

"Well, 'tis. But Bob has given her up. He never meant to marry her. I'll tell you, Mrs. Loveday, what I have never told a soul before. I was standing upon Weymouth Quay on that very day in last September that Bob set sail, and I heard him say to his brother John that he gave your daughter up."

"Then it was very unmannerly of him to trifle with her so," said Mrs. Loveday warmly. "Who did he give her up to?"

Festus replied with hesitation, "He gave her up to John."

"To John? How could he give her up to a man already over head and ears in love with that actress woman?"

"Oh! You surprise me. Which actress is it?"

"That Miss Johnson! Anne tells me that he loves her hopelessly."

Festus arose. Miss Johnson seemed suddenly to acquire high value as a sweetheart at this announcement. He had himself felt a nameless attractiveness in her, and John had done likewise. John crossed his path in all possible ways.

Before the yeoman had replied somebody opened the door, and the firelight shone upon the uniform of the person they discussed. Festus nodded on recognising him, wished Mrs. Loveday good evening, and went out precipitately.

"So Bob told you he meant to break off with my Anne when he went away?" Mrs. Loveday remarked to the trumpet-major. "I wish I had known of it before."

John appeared disturbed at the sudden charge. He murmured that he could not deny it, and then hastily turned from her and followed Derriman, whom he saw before him on the bridge.

"Derriman!" he shouted.

Festus started and looked round. "Well, trumpet-major," he said blandly.

"When will you have sense enough to mind your own business, and not come here telling things you have heard by sneaking behind people's backs?" demanded John hotly. "If you can't learn in any other way, I shall have to pull your ears again, as I did the other day!"

"You pull my ears? How can you tell that lie, when you know 'twas somebody else pulled 'em?"

"Oh no, no. I pulled your ears, and thrashed you in a mild way."

"You'll swear to it? Surely 'twas another man?"

"It was in the parlour at the public-house; you were almost in the dark." And John added a few details as to the particular blows, which amounted to proof itself.

"Then I heartily ask your pardon for saying 'twas a lie!" cried Festus, advancing with extended hand and a genial smile. "Sure, if I had known 'twas you, I wouldn't have insulted you by denying it."

"That was why you didn't challenge me, then?"

"That was it! I wouldn't for the world have hurt your nice sense of honour by letting ye go unchallenged, if I had known! And now, you see, unfortunately I can't mend the mistake. So long a time has passed since it happened that the heat of my temper is gone off. I couldn't oblige ye, try how I might, for I am not a man, trumpet-major, that can butcher in cold blood—no, not I, nor you neither, from what I know of ye. So, willy-nilly, we must fain let it pass, eh?"

"We must, I suppose," said John, smiling grimly. "Who did you think I was, then, that night when I boxed you all round?"

"No, don't press me," replied the yeoman.

"I can't reveal; it would be disgracing myself to show how very wide of the truth the mockery of wine was able to lead my senses. We will let it be buried in eternal mixens of forgetfulness."

"As you wish," said the trumpet-major loftily. "But if you ever *should* think you knew it was me, why, you know where to find me." And Loveday walked away.

The instant that he was gone Festus shook his fist at the evening star, which happened

The *Victory.*

to lie in the same direction as that taken by the dragoon.

"Now for my revenge! Duels? Lifelong disgrace to me if ever I fight with a man of blood below my own! There are other remedies for upper-class souls! . . . Matilda—that's my way."

Festus strode along till he reached the Hall, where Cripplestraw appeared gazing at him from under the arch of the porter's lodge. Derriman dashed open the entrance-

hurdle with such violence that the whole row of them fell flat in the mud.

"Mercy, Maister Festus!" said Cripplestraw. "'Surely,' I says to myself when I see ye a-coming, 'surely Maister Festus is fuming like that because there's no chance of the enemy coming this year, after all.'"

"Cr-r-ripplestraw! I have been wounded to the heart," replied Derriman with a lurid brow.

"And the man yet lives, and you wants yer horse-pistols instantly. Certainly, Maister F——"

"No, Cripplestraw, not my pistols, but my new-cut clothes, my heavy gold seals, my silver-topped cane, and my buckles that cost more money than he ever saw. Yes, I must tell somebody, and I'll tell you, because there's no other fool near. He loves her heart and soul. He's poor; she's tip-top genteel, and not rich. I am rich, by comparison. I'll court the pretty play-actress, and win her before his eyes."

"Play-actress, Maister Derriman?"

"Yes. I saw her this very day, met her by accident, and spoke to her. She's still in Weymouth —perhaps because of him. I can meet her at any hour of the day—— But I don't mean to marry her—not I. I will court her for my pastime, and to annoy him. It will be all the more death to him that I don't want her. Then perhaps he will say to me, 'You have taken my one ewe lamb'—meaning that I am the king, and he's the poor man, as in the church verse; and he'll beg for mercy when 'tis too late—unless, meanwhile, I shall have tired of my new toy. Saddle the horse, Cripplestraw, to-morrow at ten."

Full of this resolve to scourge John Loveday to the quick through his passion for Miss Johnson, Festus came out booted and spurred at the time appointed, and set off on his morning ride.

Miss Johnson's theatrical engagement having long ago terminated, she would have left Weymouth with the rest of the visitors had not matrimonial hopes detained her there. These had nothing whatever to do with John Loveday, as may be imagined, but with a stout, staid boat-builder on the Old Quay, who had shown much interest in her impersonations. Unfortunately this substan- tial man had not been quite so attentive since the end of the season as his previous manner led her to expect; and it was a great pleasure to the lady to see Mr. Derriman leaning over the harbour bridge with his eyes fixed upon her as she came towards it after a stroll past her elderly wooer's house.

"Od take it, ma'am, you didn't tell me when I saw you last that the tooting man

"Anne swept with her eyes the tremulous expanse of waters around her."

with the blue jacket and lace was yours devoted?" began Festus.

"Who do you mean?" In Matilda's ever-changing emotional interests, John Love- day was a stale and unprofitable personality.

"Why, that trumpet-major man."

"Oh! What of him?"

"Come; he loves you, and you know it, ma'am."

She knew, at any rate, how to take the current when it served. So she glanced at Festus, folded her lips meaningly, and nodded.

"I've come to cut him out."

She shook her head, it being unsafe to speak till she knew a little more of the sub- ject.

"What!" said Festus, reddening, "do you mean to say that you think of him seriously—you, who might look so much higher?"

"Constant dropping will wear away a

stone; and you should only hear his pleading! His handsome face is impressive, and his manners are—oh, so genteel! I am not rich; I am, in short, a poor lady of decayed family, who has nothing to boast of but my blood and ancestors, and they won't find a body in food and clothing—— I hold the world but as the world, Derrimanio—a stage where every man must play a part, and mine a sad one!" She dropped her eyes thoughtfully and sighed.

"We will talk of this," said Festus, much affected. "Let us walk to the Look-out."

She made no objection, and said, as they turned that way, "Mr. Derriman, a long time ago I found something belonging to you; but I have never yet remembered to return it." And she drew from her bosom the paper which Anne had dropped in the meadow when eluding the grasp of Festus on that summer day.

"Zounds, I smell fresh meat!" cried Festus when he had looked it over. "'Tis in my uncle's writing, and 'tis what I heard him singing on the day the French didn't come, and afterwards saw him marking in the road. 'Tis something he's got hid away. Give me the paper, there's a dear; 'tis worth sterling gold!"

"Halves, then?" said Matilda tenderly.

"Yes—anything," replied Festus, blazing into a smile, for she had looked up in her best new manner at the possibility that he might be worth the winning. They went up the steps to the summit of the cliff, and dwindled over it against the sky.

CHAPTER XXXVII.—REACTION.

THERE was no letter from Bob, though December had passed, and the new year was two weeks old. His movements were, however, pretty accurately registered in the papers, which John still brought, but which Anne no longer read. During the second week in December the *Victory* sailed for Sheerness, and on the 9th of the following January the public funeral of Lord Nelson took place in St. Paul's.

Then there came a meagre line addressed to the family in general. Bob's new Portsmouth attachment was not mentioned, but he told them that he had been one of the eight-and-forty seamen who walked two-and-two in the funeral procession, and that Captain Hardy had borne the banner of emblems on the same occasion. The crew was soon to be paid off at Chatham, when he thought of returning to Portsmouth for a few days to see a valued friend. After that he should come home.

But the spring advanced without bringing him, and John watched Anne Garland's desolation with augmenting desire to do something towards consoling her. The old feelings, so religiously held in check, were stimulated to rebelliousness, though they did not show themselves in any direct manner as yet.

The miller, in the meantime, who seldom interfered in such matters, was observed to look meaningly at Anne and the trumpet-major from day to day; and by-and-by he spoke privately to John.

His words were short and to the point: Anne was very melancholy; she had thought too much of Bob. Now 'twas plain that they had lost him for many years to come. Well; he had always felt that of the two he would rather John married her. Now John might settle down there, and succeed where Bob had failed. "So if you could get her, my sonny, to think less of him and more of thyself, it would be a good thing for all."

An inward excitement had risen in John; but he suppressed it and said firmly—

"Fairness to Bob before everything!"

"He hev forgot her, and there's an end on't."

"She's not forgot him."

"Well, well; think it over."

This discourse was the cause of his penning a letter to his brother. He begged for a distinct statement whether, as John at first supposed, Bob's verbal renunciation of Anne on the quay had been only a momentary ebullition of friendship, which it would be cruel to take literally; or whether, as seemed now, it had passed from a hasty resolve to a standing purpose, persevered in for his own pleasure, with not a care for the result on poor Anne.

John waited anxiously for the answer, but no answer came; and the silence seemed even more significant than a letter of assurance could have been of his absolution from further support to a claim which Bob himself had so clearly renounced. Thus it happened that paternal pressure, brotherly indifference, and his own released impulse operated in one delightful direction, and the trumpet-major once more approached Anne as in the old time.

But it was not till she had been left to herself for a full five months, and the blue-bells and ragged-robins of eighteen hundred and six were again making themselves common to the rambling eye, that he directly addressed her. She was tying up a group of tall flowering plants in the garden: she knew that he was behind her, but she did not turn. She had subsided into a placid dignity which enabled her when watched to perform any little action with seeming composure—very different from the flutter of her inexperienced days.

"Are you never going to turn round?" he at length asked good-humouredly.

She then did turn, and looked at him for a moment without speaking; a certain suspicion looming in her eyes, as if suggested by his perceptible want of ease.

"How like summer it is getting to feel, is it not?" she said.

John admitted that it was getting to feel like summer; and, bending his gaze upon her with an earnestness which no longer left any doubt of his subject, went on to ask, "Have you ever in these last weeks thought of how it used to be between us?"

She replied quickly, "Oh, John, you shouldn't begin that again. I am almost another woman now!"

"Well, that's all the more reason why I should, isn't it?"

Anne looked thoughtfully to the other end of the garden, faintly shaking her head; "I don't quite see it like that," she returned.

"You feel yourself quite free, don't you?"

"*Quite* free!" she said instantly, and with proud distinctness; her eyes fell, and she repeated more slowly, "Quite free." Then her thoughts seemed to fly from herself to him. "But you are not?"

"I am not?"

"Miss Johnson!"

"Oh—that woman! You know as well as I that was all make up, and that I never for a moment thought of her."

"I had an idea you were acting; but I wasn't sure."

"Well, that's nothing now. Anne, I want to relieve your life; to cheer you in some way; to make some amends for my brother's bad conduct. If you cannot love me, liking will be well enough. I have thought over every side of it so many times—for months have I been thinking it over—and I am at last sure that I do right to put it to you in this way. That I don't wrong Bob I am quite convinced. As far as he is concerned we be both free. Had I not been sure of that I would never have spoken. Father wants me to take on the mill, and it will please him if you can give me one little hope; it will make the house go on altogether better if you can think o' me."

"You are generous and good, John," she said, as a big round tear bowled helter-skelter down her face and hat-strings.

"I am not that; I fear I am quite the opposite," he said, without looking at her. "It would be all gain to me—— But you have not answered my question."

She lifted her eyes. "John, I cannot!" she said, with a cheerless smile. "Positively I cannot. Will you make me a promise?"

"What is it?"

"I want you to promise first—— Yes, it is dreadfully unreasonable," she added, in a mild distress. "But do promise!"

John by this time seemed to have a feeling that it was all up with him for the present. "I promise," he said listlessly.

"It is that you won't speak to me about this for *ever* so long," she returned, with emphatic kindliness.

"Very good," he replied; "very good. Dear Anne, you don't think I have been unmanly or unfair in starting this anew?"

Anne looked into his face without a smile. "You have been perfectly natural," she murmured. "And so I think have I."

John, mournfully: "You will not avoid me for this, or be afraid of me? I will not break my word. I will not worry you any more."

"Thank you, John. You need not have said worry; it isn't that."

"Well, I am very blind and stupid. I have been hurting your heart all the time without knowing it. It is my fate, I suppose. Men who love women the very best always blunder and give more pain than those who love them less."

Anne laid one of her hands in the other as she softly replied, looking down at them, "No one loves me as well as you, John; nobody in the world is so worthy to be loved; and yet I cannot anyhow love you rightly." And lifting her eyes, "But I do so feel for you that I will try as hard as I can to think about you."

"Well, that is something," he said, smiling. "You say I must not speak about it again for ever so long; how long?"

"Now that's not fair," Anne retorted, going down the garden, and leaving him alone.

About a week passed. Then one afternoon the miller walked up to Anne indoors, a weighty topic being expressed in his tread.

"I was so glad, my honey," he began, with a knowing smile, "to see that from the mill-window last week." He flung a nod in the direction of the garden.

Anne innocently inquired what it could be.

"Jack and you in the garden together," he continued, laying his hand gently on her shoulder and stroking it. "It would so please me, my dear little girl, if you could get to like him better than that weathercock, Master Bob."

Annè shook her head; not in forcible negation, but to imply a kind of neutrality.

"Can't you? Come now," said the miller.

She threw back her head with a little laugh of grievance. "How you all beset me!" she expostulated. "It makes me feel very wicked in not obeying you, and being faithful —faithful to——" But she could not trust that side of the subject to words. "Why would it please you so much?" she asked.

"John is as steady and staunch a fellow as ever blowed a trumpet. I've always thought

"Are you never going to turn round?"

you might do better with him than with Bob. Now I've a plan for taking him into the mill, and letting him have a comfortable time o't after his long knocking about; but so much depends upon you that I must bide a bit till I see what your pleasure is about the poor fellow. Mind, my dear, I don't want to force ye; I only just ask ye."

Anne meditatively regarded the miller from under her shady eyelids, the fingers of one hand playing a silent tattoo on her bosom. "I don't know what to say to you," she answered brusquely, and went away.

But these discourses were not without their effect upon the extremely conscientious mind of Anne. They were, moreover, much helped by an incident which took place one evening in the autumn of this year, when John came to tea. Anne was sitting on a low stool in front of the fire, her hands clasped across her knee. John Loveday had just seated himself on a chair close behind her, and Mrs. Loveday was in the act of filling the teapot from the kettle which hung in the chimney exactly above Anne. The kettle slipped forward suddenly; whereupon John jumped from the chair and put his own two hands over Anne's just in time to shield them, and the precious knee she clasped, from the jet of scalding water which had directed itself upon that point. The accidental overflow was instantly checked by Mrs. Loveday; but what had come was received by the devoted trumpet-major on the backs of his hands.

Anne, who had hardly been aware that he was behind her, started up like a person awakened from a trance. "What have you done to yourself, poor John, to keep it off me!" she cried, looking at his hands.

John reddened emotionally at her words. "It is a bit of a scald, that's all," he replied, drawing a finger across the back of one hand, and bringing off the skin by the touch.

"You are scalded painfully, and I not at all." She gazed into his kind face as she had never gazed there before, and when Mrs. Loveday came back with oil and other liniments for the wound Anne would let nobody dress it but herself. It seemed as if her coyness had all gone, and when she had done all that lay in her power she still sat by him. At his departure she said what she had never said to him in her life before: "Come again soon!"

In short, that impulsive act of devotion, the last of a series of the same tenor, had been the added drop which finally turned the wheel. John's character deeply impressed her. His determined steadfastness to his lode-star won her admiration, the more especially as that star was herself. She began to wonder more and more how she could have so persistently held out against his advances before Bob came home to renew girlish memories which had by that time got considerably weakened. Could she not, after all, please the miller, and try to listen to John? By so doing she would make a worthy man happy, the only sacrifice being at worst that of her unworthy self, whose future was no longer valuable. "As for Bob, the woman is to be pitied who loves him," she reflected indignantly, and persuaded herself that, whoever the woman might be, she was not Anne Garland.

After this there was something of recklessness and something of pleasantry in the young girl's manner of making herself an example of the triumph of pride and common sense over memory and sentiment. Her attitude had been epitomized in her defiant singing at the time she learnt that Bob was not leal and true. John, as was inevitable, came again almost immediately, drawn thither by the sun of her first smile on him, and the words which had accompanied it. And now instead of going off to her little pursuits up-stairs, down-stairs, across the room, in the corner, or to any place except where he happened to be, as had been her custom hitherto, she remained seated near him, returning interesting answers to his general remarks, and at every opportunity letting him know that at last he had found favour in her eyes.

The day was fine, and they went out of doors, where Anne endeavoured to seat herself on the sloping stone of the window-still.

"How good you have become lately," said John, standing over her and smiling in the sunlight which blazed against the wall. "I fancy you have stayed at home this afternoon on my account."

"Perhaps I did," she said gaily:

"'Do whatever we may for him, dame, we cannot do too much,
For he's one that has guarded our land.'

And he has done more than that; he has saved me from a dreadful scalding. The back of your hand will not be well for a long time, John, will it?"

He held out his hand to regard its condition, and the next natural thing was to take hers. There was a glow upon his face when he did it: his star was at last on a fair way towards the zenith after its long and weary declination. The least penetrating eye could have perceived that Anne had resolved to let him woo—possibly, in her temerity, to let him win. Whatever silent sorrow might be locked up in her, it was by this time thrust a long way down from the light.

"I want you to go somewhere with me if you will," he said, still holding her hand.

"Yes? Where is it?"

He pointed to a distant hill-side which, hitherto green, had within the last few days begun to show scratches of white on its face. "Up there," he said.

"I see little figures of men moving about. What are they doing?"

"Cutting out a huge picture of the king on horseback in the earth of the hill. The king's head is to be as big as our mill-pond, and his body as big as this garden; he and the horse will cover more than an acre. When shall we go ?"

"Whenever you please," said she.

"John!" cried Mrs. Loveday from the front door. "Here's a friend come for you."

John went round, and found his trusty lieutenant, Trumpeter Buck, waiting for him. A letter had come to the barracks for John in his absence, and the trumpeter, who was going for a walk, had brought it along with him. Buck then entered the mill to discuss, if possible, a mug of last year's mead with the miller; and John proceeded to read his letter, Anne being still round the corner, where he had left her. When he had read a few words he turned as pale as a sheet, but he did not move, and perused the writing to the end.

Afterwards he laid his elbow against the wall, and put his palm to his head, thinking with painful intentness. Then he took himself vigorously in hand, as it were, and gradually became natural again. When he parted from Anne to go home with Buck she noticed nothing different in him.

In barracks that evening he read the letter again. It was from Bob; and the agitating contents were these :—

"DEAR JOHN,—I have drifted off from writing till the present time because I have not been clear about my feelings ; but I have discovered them at last, and can say beyond doubt that I mean to be faithful to my dearest Anne after all. The fact is, John, I've got into a bit of a scrape, and I've a secret to tell you about it (which must go no further on any account). On landing last autumn I fell in with a young woman, and we got rather warm, as folks do ; in short, we liked one another well enough for a while. But I have got into shoal water with her, and have found her to be a terrible take-in. Nothing in her at all—no sense, no niceness, all tantrums and empty noise, John, though she seemed monstrous clever at first. So my heart comes back to its old anchorage. I hope my return to faithfulness will make no difference to you. But as you showed by your looks at our parting that you should not accept my offer to give her up—made in too much haste, as I have since found—I feel that you won't mind that I have returned to the path of honour. I dare not write to Anne as yet, and please do not let her know a word about the other young woman, or there will be the devil to pay. I shall come home and make all things right, please God. In the meantime I should take it as a kindness, John, if you would keep a brotherly eye upon Anne, and *guide her mind back to me.* I shall die of sorrow if anybody sets her against me, for my hopes are getting bound up in her again quite strong. Hoping you are jovial, as times go, I am,

"Your affectionate brother,

"ROBERT."

When the cold day-light fell upon John's face, as he dressed himself next morning, the incipient yesterday's wrinkle in his forehead had become permanently graven there. He had resolved, for his only brother's sake, to reverse his procedure before it was too late, and guide Anne's mind in the direction required. But having arranged to take her to see the excavated figure of the king, he started for Overcombe during the day, as if nothing had occurred to check the smooth course of his love.

HYMN.

O FOR a heart from self set free,
And doubt, and fret, and care,
Light as a bird, instinct with glee,
That fans the breezy air !

O for a mind whose virtue moulds
All sensuous fair display,
And, like a strong commander, holds
A world of thoughts in sway !

O for an eye that's clear to see,
A hand that waits on Fate,
To pluck the ripe fruit from the tree,
And never comes too late !

O for a life with firm-set root,
And breadth of leafy green,
And flush of blooming wealth, and fruit
That glows with mellow sheen !

O for a death from sharp alarms
And bitter memories free :
A gentle death in God's own arms,
Whose dear Son died for me !

JOHN S. BLACKIE.

No. 1.—Le Bric Castaluzzo from the Bear Inn, La Tour.

AN ADVENTURE IN THE VALLEYS OF THE WALDENSES.

THE valleys of the Waldenses have been heard of by everybody. These obscure and inconsiderable ravines among the spurs of the High Alps of Piedmont, though affording but a few square miles of habitable earth, have nourished a hardy handful of men who have made deeper marks on the history of Europe than countries many times their size and natural importance. They have drawn out the sympathies of all who value lofty heroism, or can admire indomitable pluck. They have enlisted the active, enthusiastic help of statesmen like Oliver Cromwell, and of soldiers and philanthropists like General Beckwith. They have attracted the respectful notice of historians and theologians, and afforded to students of ecclesiastical lore their most primitive models of church life and doctrine. Every rock in those valleys has its legend, every pool its thrilling tragedy, every precipice its story of love and war, and every pass among the mountains that hem them in, gives its witness to the long and weary struggle of truth against falsehood, in which truth has been victorious at last. And the natural charms of the country of the Vaudois are as singular as its historic associations. There are few scenes in the world more lovely than are to be found in the Val Angrogna or the Val Pelice, and few more stern and terrible than the upper portion of the Val Lucerna or Germanasca; while, for wild and untrodden passes amid Alpine snows and icy regions, the Col St. Julian and the Col d'Pis, or the steeps of Monte Viso or Monte Genevre, may take rank with those of the Oberland itself.

Full of romantic anticipations, and primed with the history of this interesting people, I found myself, one autumn, at the Bear Inn, in La Tour Pelice. For a fortnight I gave myself up to the happiness of intercourse with the natives, making pilgrimages to every spot sacred to the memory of heroic actions in the four valleys which are still the patrimony of the Israel of the Alps. During that time I visited every principal village, and every scene of primary interest to which their historians have directed attention, as many other travellers have done before me. But there was one point of high interest, which all the Waldensian writers mentioned, but of which, nevertheless, no one in the valleys could give me definite information, and which no one I met seemed to have ever visited. It was the great Cavern of Castaluzzo. Leger, Muston, Gilly, Beattie, Bramley-Moore, and Worsfold, all tell us much about this celebrated cavern. For centuries, during several successive persecutions, it seems to have formed the chief hiding-place of the long-suffering people of all the towns and villages in the Val Penice. Whenever the inhabitants of La Tour, Villaro, or Bobbio were threatened with massacre—and they were frequently threatened —the women and children were conveyed there. Leger tells us that as many as four hundred persons, young and old, lay at one time, and that for a considerable period, concealed in its recesses. He describes it with some particularity, and it is well worth careful description, for a more marvellous retreat could hardly be conceived, and perhaps a place so admirably adapted to the purpose is not to be found in the world as that which God provided for these tried and persecuted people, in close proximity to their principal centres of population. Dr. Gilly felt its importance in the history of their persecutions to be so great that he made repeated efforts to reach it. His account of the manner in which he ultimately succeeded — by means of a rope-ladder and a band of trusty companions—is to be found in page 509 of his later Waldensian

No. 2.—Monte Viso from the top of Castaluzzo Rock.

Researches. He ascended with infinite difficulty to the top of Castaluzzo, and, with a number of guides, approached the edge of the precipice, which he says, and says truly, was as perpendicular as a wall. He was utterly incredulous of any cave *there*, or, if there were a cave, of any human creature being able to reach it. He "stretched "his body and neck over the precipice in "vain." "Not the slightest hold to a man's "hand or foot was to be seen." His guide "explained that the descent was to be "achieved by stooping over the projecting "crag, on the edge of which he stood, and "catching hold of the rough points of the

"cliff, and so letting yourself down, till you "come to a sort of chimney, by which, one at "a time, it was easy to descend into the "cavern. But," he adds, "how men, women, "and children and aged fugitives were to per-"form this exploit, which we confessed our-"selves utterly afraid to attempt, did not "appear." His guide "supposed there had "been a second entrance, which was now lost, "and most pertinaciously insisted that by the "very means he had described, men he knew "had actually got into the cavern. He di-"rected their attention to immense blocks of "stone at the base of the cliffs, which appeared "as if they "had recently "fallen from "the rocks "above, and "which had "rendered the "descent more "difficult than "formerly." Dr. Gilly and his party then gave up the at-tempt in de-spair, although he heard of two persons, Chamforan and Ricca, who had got into the cave in their youth. Some time af-terwards he made a fresh attempt, pro-vided with a rope-ladder, spade, pickaxe, hatchets, lan-tern, and cords, and this time he was more successful. Making a detour by Borel, he once more reached the point where his guide had conducted him on the 6th of July. "Nothing," says he, "presented itself "to the eye which gave the slightest idea that "the wall of rock down which we looked with "shuddering gaze contained an accessible "hiding-place, large enough to admit four "hundred people. The two notable climbers, "Chamforan and Ricca" (whose services he had secured) "pulled off their shoes and stock-"ings and stripped off their upper garments, "and looked" (says the amiable doctor) "as if they were rallying their courage for

"an exploit. Two young mountaineers be-
"sides, one twenty, the other sixteen, signified
"their intention to follow the elder moun-
"taineers at all risks; and the coolness with
"which they stood over the precipice and
"moved along its dizzy edge satisfied us that
"they had nerve enough for anything. When
"the guides were ready for the descent they
"addressed their countrymen, M. Bonjour
"and M. Revel, and told them that they
"would not dare to go down. 'Then what
"will our
"friends
"do?' said
"they.
"'They are
"English,'
"replied
"Chamfo-
"ran, 'and
"will break
"their necks
"rather
"than turn
"back.'
"Presently
"they dis-
"appeared.
"How they
"sustained
"their foot-
"ing, and to
"what pro-
"jecting
"point they
"clung, I
"could not
"imagine.
"I looked
"down, but
"the cliff
"projected
"so much
"that I
"could not
"distinguish
"the means
"by which

"risk which the men encountered who de-
"scended without the rope-ladder consisted
"in passing from ledge to ledge, where the
"hold was very slight and insecure. What,
"then, must have been the horrible nature of
"the persecutions which compelled women
"and children to trust themselves to the peril
"of such an enterprise? It is probable that
"ropes had been before used to facilitate the
"descent, for I observed several places which
"looked as if they had been indented by the
"friction
"of cord-
"age."

This, then,
was the
place to
which my
inquiries had
been direct-
ed. The crag
in which the
cavern lay
is seen from
all parts of
the valley of
the Pelice.
On going
out on to
the balcony
of the Bear
Inn, early on
the morn-
ing after our
arrival, it
was the first
object which
strikes the
eye. Mount
Vandolin
lies on the
north side
of the valley,
the first of a
vista of emi-
nences
which bound
the view to

No. 3.—From the Cave, looking down on La Tour.

"they descended. Presently a shout from
"below directed us to lower the rope-ladder."
And then with infinite precautions and infinite
congratulations the worthy doctor stepped
down the hempen staircase. He estimated
the distance from the top of the cliff to the
top of the "chiminee" at twenty feet, and
the further distance fifty feet, and then a few
feet more landed him on the floor of the
cavern. His agile companions took care he
should come to no harm, and he adds, "The

the right. On the side of Mount Vandolin,
towering above the villages and vineyards
of the valley, a castellated spur juts out,
and rises in a bold bluff against the sky,
called, from its tower-like appearance, Le
Bric Castaluzzo, and connected with the
masses of the Vandolin by a neck of narrow
upland. In the steep face of this cliff a
mere ledge may be discerned from La Tour
with a glass. This is all that can be seen
from below of the once famous cavern. Nor

XXI—52

is it easy to see that, for amid the seams and ledges which score the face of the precipice, it is difficult to say with certainty which of them it is. This accounts for the vagueness with which old residents in La Tour, whose whole lives had been passed in sight of it, answered my inquiries as to its exact locality. Their replies were conflicting and perplexing. The existence of a secret rock-refuge among the unscaleable precipices of Le Bric Castaluzzo was known by everybody. The way into it was known by none: and even the possibility of finding access to it was stoutly denied. No one could be induced to accompany me in an attempt to reach it, and I had not read Dr. Gilly's account of his visit to it, or I should not have attempted it without the appliances by which he was, as we have seen, at last successful. A dismal story was carefully repeated to me of two young Waldensian students of the college, who had, some years before, made the attempt, and one of them having slipped was dashed to pieces on the rocks, and his companion returned without having accomplished his purpose.

But there it was, staring me defiantly in the face every day, hung aloft, as it were, like the very key to the whole of Waldensian history. So, leaving La Tour at four o'clock in the morning of the 19th of September, I set off alone for Chabriole, one of the villages just at the foot of the mountain. The sun rose in Alpine magnificence as I entered the village. An old Waldensian patriarch, who was stirring early, told me no one in his village had ever been into the cave, and no one could now get down to it, except by a difficult descent from the top of Castaluzzo, down the face of the precipice. He knew a man, however, who would show me the way to the top. This man was brought, and answered to the name of Davy Gardiol. He was a fine, strapping fellow, whose honest face won my instant confidence and regard. So he and I belted up, and set to scale the mountain. Groves of magnificent chestnut-trees shaded us for some time from the rays of the sun. But vines and shady chestnuts too were soon left below, and after a steep climb we reached a cluster of two or three huts, "clitched," as they say on Dartmoor, to the side of the mountain. Davy knew nothing of the secret way into the cave; but he knew a shepherd lad who did, and that boy lived in this hamlet. When inquired for, however, the boy had gone to Paris! At last another shepherd boy was heard of who,

it was thought, would know the way. He was sent for. His name was, as near as I could catch it, Jan Cooen, a lithe young mountaineer of thirteen or fourteen. He led me up round the steep side of Castaluzzo to the narrow col between it and Vandolin, and thence, after a hot and fatiguing climb, to the summit of Castaluzzo itself. There we were well repaid by a view of peerless interest and magnificence. Turin, the Superga, the winding Po, and most of the marquisate of Saluzzo, Cavour, Paesana, Campiglione, Fenile, were all in sight beyond the Vaudois territory; San Giovanni and La Tour lay at our feet, Villaro and Bobbio to the westward, and the torrents of Pelice. Angrogna and Biglione, winding threads of silver, at intervals through their valleys; while, peering over the shady ridges of L'Envers, above Roccabetta, and apparently close opposite to us, the snowy peak of Monte Viso shone like a gigantic pharos of frosted silver. The tableland of the summit where we stood was dotted by patches of rhododendron, scrub, and heather; but most of it was just a seamed and wind-swept rock, sloping down on three sides towards a precipice of vast depth and dizzy steepness. First we wound our way to the crevice, or crack in the rock, to which Dr. Gilly was taken, and which he was told had formerly communicated by an underground passage with the cavern. This place seems exactly in the condition in which he found it, more than half a century ago. We then proceeded, as he did, to the edge of the precipice, and reached the spot, which it would have been impossible to discover without a guide, where, the lad said, we should have to descend. I looked in vain for any sign or semblance of a descent, or any possible means of getting on to the face of the rock, which here sunk down to the base of the cliff with absolute perpendicularity. Jan Cooen would not argue with me, but sat down on the edge and pulled off his shoes. His feet were thrown over the edge, and rested, two or three feet below, on a ledge, a foot or two wide, from which a plumb-line might have been dropped clear for some hundred feet. Suddenly he began to thrust his feet inwards through an unseen "trou," or hole, which seemed to pierce the cliff. Gradually his body disappeared, and I soon heard his voice some distance below calling me to follow. I hesitated for a moment, till assured that there was no other means of discovering the mysterious cave. There was nothing for it but to follow; so, removing my shoes and stockings, I squeezed feet fore-most through the "trou" with some diffi-culty, and found myself on the face of the precipice below it, and just able to get on to a sharp and rapidly descending ridge, on to which I clung, and very slowly and carefully hitched down, face foremost, in the direction in which my agile guide had disappeared. The ridge seemed to get steeper and steeper, and to lead into the air below, after the manner of falling dreams. One foot was hanging over the precipice, and beneath it could be seen villages and fields far below.

No. 4.—From the Cave, looking eastward.

I felt like a fly creeping on a vast wall, but unprovided with that adhesive secretion which emboldens the insect to walk, or those filmy integuments by which, when it can no longer walk, it can fly. I may confess that at this moment the strangeness of the posi-tion and the uncertainty of what unknown difficulties lay below, so impressed my ima-gination, that if I could have turned round and got back again I should have done so, and given up the pursuit. But it was im-possible. The utmost care was needed to avoid being overbalanced by projections of the rock, which jutted inconveniently out-wards, but afforded no holding. I could now and then hear the voice of the lad some distance below, but during all the descent never caught a glimpse of him, or could learn by what peculiar gymnastics he had got down. The thought of however I was to get back obtruded itself uncomfortably; for just then a moment's indecision or loss of nerve must have destroyed me. Gathering myself together I crept down, and rounding a projection which hid the lower part of the descent, I came to the top of all that is now left of what the old Waldenses called the "chiminee." It probably was formerly a shaft through the rock. It is now simply an open cranny, down which the climber must get inch by inch, planting his feet firmly against one smooth and sloping side of it and his back against the other. He must then look sharply for certain thin ledges one or two inches in breadth, to prevent a fatal slip; and at this point he will experience the importance of having removed his socks as well as his shoes. The prehensility of the naked foot was invaluable to me. By the aid of it I reached the bottom of this open chimney in safety, though every limb trembled with the unaccustomed exertion; and soon after, relaxing not a muscle, but gingerly descend-ing from projection to projection, I found myself at last in what is left of the great cavern of the Waldenses. It is now an open horizontal gallery of rock cleavage, deeply indenting the southern face of the precipice. It was so exposed that at first I felt some doubt whether it could be the veritable cavern. But my doubt was instantly re-solved. For there, on the sides of it, stared me in the face, carved on the rock, the names and initials of the very few visitors who have ever managed to get into it. There was the large name of Gilly and of A. Vertu, of Caffa-dou, of Henri, of I. Gott, Meille, and Th. Malan, Rl., for Revel, and a few initials, includ-ing J. D., to which I added my own, with the date of my visit, feeling that I might possibly doubt hereafter whether I had really visited such a place, unless the record of the visit could be appealed to on the spot. It was more than fifty years since Dr. Gilly's visit, and during that time, with a few rare excep-tions, this place had been unvisited, and was now almost unknown.

Calling my young companion to kneel beside me, I offered up a thanksgiving to God for His mercy, and a prayer that we might be worthy inheritors of those great and vital doctrines for which the Waldenses had been so often driven to take refuge in this inaccessible fastness. I then made those sketches which illustrate this paper — one in each direction—and which, imperfect as they are, may serve to convey some idea of this interesting locality. I picked up at the lower end of the gallery a fragment of some iron implement, which I have carefully treasured, as it probably belonged to the refugees in the old time. There was a solemn stillness, full of awe and sweetness, about the place, which my young companion did not seem inclined to break. But he showed me the place where he had been told the Waldensian marksmen picked off their Papist foes, resting their nine-foot-long guns on the outer edge of the rocks. Another place was pointed out where buckets or baskets were let down for those provisions which supported the refugees, and in which, he said, children had been sometimes sent swinging down, to run—at the risk of their lives—with information of the movements of the enemy, and to return with news and provisions. From this lofty aerie the poor Waldenses could have seen distinctly their houses in flames, or heard, on still days, the shouts of their brutal pursuers or the cries of their martyred relatives. From this scene of strange loveliness the persecutors and the persecuted have alike long since passed away to judgment, not without leaving behind them indelible foot-prints upon the sands of history, indicating to all after ages

the principles by which they were respectively animated. But enough. It was time to return, and it required some resolution to face the climb once more. But the ascent was many times less trying than the descent, chiefly because I knew exactly what to expect. There, at the top on the ledge, lay my shoes, socks, and umbrella, and from thence I reached the house of my friend, M. Seeli, after having been absent about seven hours.

It is quite clear that this is the great Cavern of Waldensian history. It is equally clear that it is not in the condition in which it afforded shelter to so large a body of persons. It seems that Dr. Gilly's guide explained the matter when he pointed to the "rocks, crags, and mounds confusedly hurled" at the bottom of the cliff. The face of the rock has fallen, including one of the three sides of the shaft or chimney, and all the outer walling of the cave itself, in which formerly the windows were pierced. Only the inmost parts of it are now left. But its shelter is no longer required. A fresh set of perils, more subtle than the open and bloody persecutions of former times, has now set in. But on to this ground we must not venture. My object will have been attained if I shall have roused interest and curiosity by this narrative of a perilous adventure among the wild rock refuges of Waldensia.

FRANCIS GELL, M.A.

"POST TENEBRAS LUX."

BY THE REV. CANON VAUGHAN, M.A., OF LEICESTER.

PART II.

JESUS was speaking quite in accordance with his usual manner and wont, when He said to this sorrow-stricken father, "If thou canst believe, all things are possible unto him that believeth." We in our ignorance might, perhaps, have expected that He would make the father's faith easy to him by then and there, first and foremost, healing his son. Whereas what He really does, is to require the father's faith as a condition of the son's restoration to health. "If thou canst do anything," says the father to Jesus, "have compassion on us, and help us." To which the answer is with another "If:"—"If thou canst believe, all things are possible to him that believeth." But this, again, is entirely in accordance with the invariable rule and method of Jesus. He always steadily re-

fused to work miracles, when challenged to do so, in proof of his mission—whether to refute opponents or to convince unbelievers. He always demanded faith, or, at least, a predisposition towards faith, as a condition of the exercise of his wonder-working power. "He did not many mighty works there because of their unbelief;" such is St. Matthew's record of what He did, or refrained from doing, in Nazareth; to which St. Mark adds, "Save that He laid his hands upon a few sick folk, and healed them." We, again, in our ignorance, fancy that the natural thing for Him to do would have been to work miracles, on account of their unbelief, and in order to remove their unbelief. He knew better. He knew that unbelief can never be removed by miracles—that faith can never be built upon miracles. He knew what was in man, when He closed his terrible parable of Dives and Lazarus with the weighty, solemn words, "If they hear not Moses and the prophets, neither will they be persuaded, though one rose from the dead."

Not a few of the difficulties of belief in our own day arise out of a total misunderstanding of the position taken up by Jesus with reference to this fundamental question of miracles. We find it exceedingly hard to rid ourselves of the notion—(it is another instance of a much-needed correction of the premiss)—that He appealed constantly to miracles in attestation of his mission, and in proof of his right to speak with authority in the name of God and as the Son of God. And now that miracles have come to be looked upon in some quarters with a certain amount of suspicion, we fancy that a fatal flaw has been discovered in the evidence to which the Christian Church has been all along trusting, and upon which Christ Himself rested his claim. To us, who do not believe in the infallibility of the Christian Church, it is matter of comparatively small account that it should have erred on this point. The error, so far as there has been an error, is not Christ's error, but the error of his Church; an error committed by his Church in spite of repeated warnings on his part. And now that the necessities of the case have compelled us to look carefully into this question and to define to ourselves very clearly the attitude of Jesus in relation to his own miracles, the discovery of what that attitude really was ought to be a very great relief to us, and a very great aid to our faith in Him. It does indeed seem as if, in his foresight of the future, He had distinctly measured and carefully provided against the special intellectual difficulties of an age, perplexed and perplexing, such as ours is. Now, that He should have done this, that He should have been able to see so far in advance and provide against the perils of so remote a future, is of more avail than ten thousand miracles to guarantee his title to our homage and to warrant our confidence in his ultimate triumph. The "desire of all *nations*" is also the desire of all *ages*. There is not the shadow of a sign that his power over the human heart can ever decay or become obsolete. The ancient promise of Holy Writ will yet be realised : " There was given Him dominion and glory, and a kingdom, that all people, nations, and languages should serve Him : his dominion is an everlasting dominion which shall not pass away, and his kingdom that which shall not be destroyed."

As to the suspicion with which in these days miracles are viewed in some quarters, I cannot help regarding it as a transient phase of thought, the shadow of a passing cloud, a needless exaggeration of present difficulties, an intellectual craze which in due time will cease to trouble us. But whether this be so or not, at any rate it is quite certain, that (to say the very least) our Lord Jesus Christ placed his own miracles in a very subordinate position, so far as faith in Himself was concerned. And the question is, How did He think about faith? What did He understand by that faith to which he made such boundless promises? What did He mean, for example, when he said, "If thou canst believe, all things are possible to him that believeth"? And what was the nature of that faith of the father, which made it (if we may say so) possible for Jesus to heal his son, and which expressed itself in the tearful cry, "Lord, I believe : help Thou mine unbelief."

It is a great deal easier to say what faith is not, than to say exactly what it is. For example : The yielding of the mind to evidence is not faith. The feeling which we have, when we have gone through a proposition of Euclid and are satisfied with the result, is not faith; is not faith in Christ's sense of faith, nor, indeed, in any reasonable sense of the word "faith." Faith is not the assent of the mind to demonstration. Now this, obvious as it is, is often, I think, forgotten at the present day; and people are put, in consequence, on a wrong scent in their search after faith. They say, "We want evidence, more and stronger evidence, evidence which shall satisfy our minds, and prove to demonstration, that things are as the Christian advocate affirms them to be." Now such evidence is not forthcoming—cannot, must not, be forthcoming. The Christian advocate can never hope to have the last word. There will be always something to be said on the other side, whoever it may be who has spoken last, whether Christian advocate or unbeliever. The infidel can no more have the last word than the believer can. The controversy, from the very nature of the case, must needs go on *ad infinitum*, in one interminable series; nay, often, as a circulating or recurring decimal, in which you get the same weary round of figures for ever and for ever repeated. But, more than this, even if the series could be cut short by one conclusive demonstration on the side of Christianity, the assent of the understanding to this demonstration — an assent which could not be withheld, if it were demonstration—would not be *faith*.

The yielding of the mind to evidence, then, is not faith. Neither, again, is faith *the receiving certain articles of belief on authority*. Not very long ago a letter appeared in the newspapers, written by a man well known in the English ecclesiastical world, in which the writer explained his reasons for forsaking the Communion of the Church of England and taking refuge in the Church of Rome. "Catholic instinct," he explained, led him on, step by step, until he was made to see that *authority* is the one only basis for faith and practice, and that only the Church of Rome claims this authority. "When I became convinced," so he wrote, "that the right principle of faith and practice in religion was authority; when I saw clearly, that it is of less moment *what* one believes and does than *why* one accepts and practises, then I had no choice as to my course. The only spiritual body which I could realise that actually claimed to teach truth upon authority, and that visibly exercised the authority which she claimed, was the Church of Rome." I hope I do not misunderstand or misrepresent him. I should be very unwilling to do so. To me the letter seemed a very pathetic production, hardly fitted for the rough climate of the columns of the *Times*. It carried my thoughts back to Dr. Newman's famous work, his "Apologia pro vitâ suâ." The writer of the letter was evidently quite in earnest, just as Dr. Newman was. He was following, too, the logic of his convictions, just as Dr. Newman did. "Catholic instinct" landed him inevitably, by an inexorable syllogism, a humble suitor for admission into the fold of the Church of Rome. One would have thought that the conclusion, in which his syllogism landed him, ought to have made him suspect the soundness of the premiss from which he set out. "*Authority, the revealed basis of faith*" (I quote his own words)—let the revelation, which makes authority the basis of faith, be produced. Where is it? Where is it to be found? Not in the words of Jesus, who said, in the most solemn moment of his earthly career, when life and death were trembling in the balance: "To this end was I born, and for this cause came I into the world, that I should bear witness unto the truth; every one that is of the truth heareth my voice." Nor yet in the Epistles of St. Paul, who wrote: "Not for that we have dominion over your faith, but are helpers of your joy." Nor yet in the Epistles of St. John, who wrote: "Ye have an unction from the Holy One, and ye know all things: I have not written unto you because ye know not the truth, but because ye know it." Nor yet in the Epistles of St. Peter, who wrote: "The elders which are among you I exhort, who am also an elder;" that is, an elder along with you, one of yourselves. We shall search the Scriptures in vain for anything which shall give colour to the notion, that faith rests upon authority, and is merely the receiving certain articles of belief, be they many or few, on authority. And if revelation affords no warrant for such a notion, certainly reason does not. It would, indeed, be the suicide of reason to do so.

It is, however, comparatively easy to say what faith *is not*. It is much more difficult to say what faith *is*. We turn for assistance to the words and actions of Jesus. We read that, when he had said, "If thou canst believe, all things are possible to him that believeth," "straightway the father of the child cried out, and said with tears, Lord, I believe; help Thou mine unbelief." And immediately Jesus proceeded to heal the child. Evidently, then, Jesus was satisfied that the father *did* believe in that true sense of the word "believe," which He had Himself intended when He said, "If thou canst believe, all things are possible to him that believeth." In the judgment of Jesus, then, the cry of the father, "Lord, I believe; help Thou mine unbelief," is the cry of faith—of a true and genuine faith, though as yet perhaps weak and wanting in courage. The subsequent action of Jesus, coupled with his own antecedently imposed condition, puts his "imprimatur" upon the father's cry, and endorses it as the language of *faith*. And, as the language of faith, it may well help us to understand, what, in the view of Jesus, faith is. Let us endeavour to analyze it, and see what we find in it.

The man had come to Jesus, bringing with him this afflicted son of his, in the hope that Jesus could do him good. "Master, I have brought unto Thee my son; if Thou canst do anything, have compassion on us, and help us." The fact of his being at the trouble to bring his son to Jesus showed a certain amount of confidence in Jesus, for which, no doubt, he could have assigned reasons. If asked for his reasons, he would probably have said, "I heard that such and such a person had got good for himself—or for some member of his family, as the case might be—by coming to Jesus; and so I resolved that I would at least give the thing a trial for my own poor afflicted son." A certain amount of reason, or of reasoning, went into the father's action, bringing him at last to his

" if : "—" *If* Thou canst do anything." But this, in the view and insight of Jesus, was not enough. Hence *His* " if : "—" *If* thou canst believe." This balancing of the evidence, on the father's part, ending in the " If Thou canst do anything," was not faith. It needed something more to transmute it into faith. And what was *that?*

What it was is very clearly declared by the earnest, tearful cry which followed. The tears showed how thoroughly in earnest the father was. For *men* do not shed tears, except on very rare occasions, and only when they are very strongly and deeply moved. Evidently the man's whole soul and will went into that cry of his, " Lord, I believe ; help Thou mine unbelief." His reasoning powers had carried him to a certain point—to the edge, as it were, of a great resolve. Then the words of Jesus touched his soul and quickened his will ; and he cast himself in conscious weakness upon Him. " Lord, I believe; help Thou mine unbelief :"—as though he would say, " Lord, I would fain believe ; yea, I *do* and *will* believe, in spite of all the unbelief which whispers in my ear, and would pluck me from Thee, and would stay the healing word that can restore my son. Oh, tear this unbelief out of my heart, and enable me, in very truth and deed, to believe ! "

We can never be sufficiently grateful for this wonderful and most pathetic Gospel story, and for the steady light which is thrown by it upon the nature of that faith to which the promises of Jesus are made ; and, particularly in these difficult and dangerous days, these days of darkness and doubt, when so much claims to be faith and passes for faith which is really unbelief ; and so much is stigmatized as unbelief which is really, if not distinctively faith, at least closely akin to faith, and ready to become in a moment, at one touch of the Master's hand, faith. The wider our experience of men's minds and ways of thought, the more tolerant shall we be, and the more leniently shall we judge them, if we must judge them at all, in this matter of faith.

Wherever there is earnest clinging to and moving towards the larger, loftier, holier hope, *there*, it seems to me, there is *faith; faith* such as Christ Himself can own as faith, spite of all its unbeliefs, and dashed and checkered though it be with many a doubt. The father cried out, " Lord, I believe ; help Thou mine unbelief." There was unbelief in his cry, as well as faith. He was perfectly aware of it. Yet, in the judgment of Jesus,

there was more of faith in the cry than of unbelief. It could be recognised by Him as the cry of faith, to which his healing word might respond. The seeming unbelief, which a complacent orthodoxy is ready at once to denounce, may have more of faith in it than that very orthodoxy itself. For the saving, justifying virtue of faith lies more in its *will*-element, than in its *reason*-element; more in its *moral* factor, than in its *rational*. The great question is, Does the will choose firmly, and move steadily towards, the highest—that which is *morally* highest ? Is there fidelity, fealty, loyalty, allegiance of the moral nature to its true liege Lord, "under circumstances and amid the temptations of usurpation, rebellion, and intestine discord ? " I have known those, whose minds seemed to me to be honeycombed with intellectual doubts and denials, who yet, so far as I could judge, had more of " the root of the matter " in them, than many others, whose minds, to all appearance, had never been crossed or shaken by a single misgiving. Into this innermost shrine of the soul, however, only one eye can look and judge—the eye of Christ. Of one thing alone we may rest most positively assured, and it is this : Wherever there is the honest, earnest cry, " Lord, I believe ; help Thou mine unbelief," *there*, there is faith,—a faith which Jesus Himself can justify. Let there be that cry, and let there go along with it a persistent effort to eradicate by degrees the unbelief, which troubles and saddens it ; and all must be well at the last. The vital germ of the faith which saves and justifies, which brings healing and righteousness into the soul, is *there.*

I would most earnestly press this *moral* aspect of faith, as the work of the will, choosing the highest simply because it *is* the highest ; because reason and conscience combine to proclaim that it *is* the highest. In these days of doubt and controversy, I frankly admit that a special strain is put upon the *will*-factor, as contrasted with the *reason*-factor, of faith. We must call into requisition, with all the moral force at our command, the earnest, energetic, "Lord, I believe," of the Gospel story. It will not always be so. The strain upon the will-element, as contrasted with the reason-element, will not always be felt as a strain. It is a peculiarity of our own days, that it should be so. Sooner or later, the reason-factor will come once more into harmonious working with the will-factor. The false premisses will be corrected. The new light will break over the past : the new spirit descend into the present.

TO A DEER IN A PARK.

GRACEFUL, winsome creature,
   So fair of form and feature,
With eyes as soft as sunshine,
And dark as ebony ;
I love to see thee flitting
Athwart the green, or sitting
Beneath the spreading tree.
In every dainty curve and line—
In slender limb and head's decline—
I see the grace of Nature ;
And when thou flittest through the trees,
Amid the sunshine and the breeze,
Art image fair of beauty ;
Or stooping o'er the little lake,

Whereon no ripple comes to break
The perfect shadow given ;
Ah, then, my heart is full of thanks,
That beauty moves through many ranks,
And makes us dream of heaven ;
For thou, sweet creature, meet'st the mood,
O'er which the fairest dreams still brood
Of sylvan bliss and glory
In earliest Grecian story :
Art shy, retiring, thinking not
Of thine own charms ; thy only thought
Is to fulfil thy nature ;
A message good to me hast brought,
Thou graceful, winsome creature.

E. C. G.

PLAIN-SPEAKING.

BY THE AUTHOR OF "JOHN HALIFAX, GENTLEMAN."

IV.—A LITTLE MUSIC.

"WILL you favour us with a little music?"

Such, in my young days, used to be the stereotyped request. And truly the "favour" was small; likewise the gratitude. When the music began the talking began also, louder than ever, and probably only the hostess, standing politely by the piano, was much the wiser for that feeble, florid performance of "La Source," or "Convent Bells," or "Home, sweet Home, with variations"—very varied indeed. Perhaps, afterwards, one or two people condescended to listen to a mild interpretation of "She wore a wreath of roses," or even of "The heart bowed down," and "I dreamt that I dwelt in marble halls." But anyone who remembers what was the standard of drawing-room vocalism a quarter of a century ago will understand how the gentle sentimentalisms of Poet Bunn and Michael Balfe sufficed all our needs. A good many of us young folks sang—some in tune, some out of tune; it did not matter much, nobody listened particularly. And some of us could play our own accompaniments—some could not. These last fared badly enough, falling into the hands of young ladies who "had never been used to play at sight," or being hammered into nothing by some wild pianist who considered the accompaniment everything, the voice nothing. And, our performances over, the listeners or non-listeners said "Thank you!" and went on talking faster than ever. All had done their duty, the evening had been helped on by "a little music"—as little as possible—and everybody was satisfied.

This, I believe most middle-aged people will allow, is a fair picture of what English drawing-room music was like, from five-and-twenty to thirty years ago.

In the concert-room things were not much better. There were—so far as I can call to mind—no educated audiences, and therefore no classical repertoires to suit them. Ballads and bravuras, theatrical overtures, and pots-pourris of operatic airs, a few showy, noisy pianoforte pieces, or arrangements for violin and flute—this was the ordinary food provided for music-lovers. Such a bill of fare as nowadays true musicians revel in, of Saturday afternoons at the Crystal Palace, at the Philharmonic, or the Monday Popular was absolutely unknown. No-body would have cared for it. I myself remember when Mendelssohn's "Lieder Ohne Worte" were first played, here and there, and nobody listened to them particularly, or thought very much of them. And sixteen years ago I heard a large and fashionable audience in a provincial town keep up a steady remorseless monotone of conversation all through one of Charles Hallé's best Recitals.

People do not do that now. Whenever or wherever you go to hear a Beethoven symphony, you have the comfort of hearing it in silence. Nevertheless, to a great many people might still be applied the withering sarcasm which was hurled at myself the other day, on daring to own to an artist that I did not admire all Old Masters. "Madam, there are people who, if you play to them a fugue of Bach's, will answer, 'Yes, very fine!' but in their hearts they prefer 'Pop goes the weasel.'"

It is in the hope of raising the masses from this depth of musical degradation, that I am tempted to use a little plain-speaking.

If we believe, as most of us do, in our own great superiority to our grandfathers and grandmothers, why not hope that our grandchildren may be superior to ourselves? The old ways are not always the best ways, and the weakest argument one can use against a new thing is its being new. With unalloyed pleasure I admit in how many things I have seen the world improve—even in my own time. For instance, last night, I heard a young lady scarcely out of her teens give Handel's "Whene'er you walk," in a thin soprano, certainly, but with perfectly true intonation and correct taste. Her mother accompanied her; and afterwards played a page or two of dear old Corelli, in a way to refresh any musical soul. And I have lately been staying in a peaceful provincial family, where the father and son sang, "The Lord is a man of war," almost as well as I had heard it at the Handel Festival the week before; and where, out of business hours, the whole house was alive with music; one boy playing the violin, another the organ, a third the pianoforte, and all being able to take up a glee or anthem and sing it at sight, without hesitation or reluctance.

Of course, this implies a considerable amount of natural musical faculty, as well as of cultivation. The chief reason of the low standard of what may be called domestic music, in England, where professional music is as good as anywhere in Europe, is not so much the lack of talent as of education. A professional musician of long experience said to me the other day that he believed everybody had a voice and an ear—a fact certainly open to doubt. But, undoubtedly, the number of persons, male and female, who have voices and ears, and could—with some little trouble —be made into musicians, is sufficiently numerous to prove that we have only ourselves to blame if the present state of English drawing-room music is—well! all true musicians and music-lovers know what it is, and how much they have to endure.

I once heard a non-musical friend say of herself and another, after listening to an exquisitely-played trio of Mozart's, "It was eighteen pages, and we bore it well!" To which, of course, a laugh was the only possible answer. But the negative sufferings of unmusical people can be nothing to the positive agonies of those others, blessed, or cursed, with a sense of time and tune, when doomed to be auditors of "a little music." As to the instrumental, one braces one's nerves for what is going to happen; but when it comes to the vocal, one often feels inclined to put one's fingers in one's ears and scream. The torture—I use the word deliberately—that it is to sit and smile at a smiling young lady singing flat, perhaps a quarter of a tone, with the most delightful unconsciousness, or pounding away at a deafening accompaniment, which is sometimes a blessing, as it hides all errors of voice and style! And what patience it takes to say, "Thank you!" to a young man who has perhaps a really fine voice and great love for music, but has never learnt his notes, and sings entirely from ear. Consequently his unhappy accompanyist has to run after him, stopping out a crotchet here, and lengthening a quaver there; abolishing time altogether, and only too glad to be "in at the death" with a few extempore chords. Yet both these young sinners probably consider themselves, and are considered by their friends, as accomplished performers.

There is a delusive tradition that music is an "accomplishment," and those who exercise it must be "performers." Whereas it is an art, or rather a science, as exact a science as mathematics (which perhaps accounts for the fact that many mathematicians have been also musicians), and all who pursue it ought to be careful, conscientious, laborious students. Thoroughness in anything is good and right —thoroughness in music is indispensable. While "the pianoforte and singing" are taught merely as superficial branches of education, with a view to showing off, so as to play a well-taught piece or sing a bravura song, so long will the standard of music remain as low as it now is among our young people. They may be performers, after a fashion, but they will never be artists. For the true artist in any art thinks less of himself than of his art, and the great charm of music, to all educated musicians, is that it is a combination art. That is, the aim of it is not—at least never should be—simply to exhibit one's self, but to be able to take a part in a whole, and so contribute to the general benefit and enjoyment of society. Therefore, a pianoforte player who "hasn't brought her music," a vocalist who "doesn't know that duet—has never learnt it," or a part-singer who is "very sorry, but cannot sing at sight," are a style of musicians much to be deplored, and a little blamed. Until music is so taught from the first, that every one, who pretends to love and practise it, shall be capable of doing this in concert with others, of sitting down to play an accompaniment at sight, or reading a part in a glee as easily as out of a printed book, I fear we cannot be considered a musical nation. And it would be better for us if we were, since of all the arts music is the most social, and sympathy therein the most delightful and the most humanising.

Another superstition of the last generation I should also like to drag to light and annihilate. It was considered right and fitting that young ladies—all young ladies—should learn music, to sing if they could, but at all events to play. Young ladies only. The idea of a boy playing the piano was scouted entirely.

Now, both boys and girls who show any aptitude for music should be taught without hesitation. Nay, for some things, the advantage is greater to boys than to girls. It is a common complaint—how very helpless a man is without his work! Should sickness or other necessity keep him away from it he goes moping about the house, restless and mournful, "as cross as two sticks," a torment to everybody, and above all to himself. Women have always plenty to busy themselves withal —employment for heads and fingers; but men, unless blessed with some special hobby, have almost nothing.

But then, as I said, music must be studied as an art, and not as a mere amusement. Whether or not my clever professor be right, and everybody has a voice and ear, only needing cultivation more or less, still, in many cases, it requires the more and not the less, "Everything that is worth doing at all is worth doing well," and music is one of those things which if not done well is better left undone, for the sake of other folk. A man may hide his feeble sketches in his portfolio, and publish his bad poetry in books which nobody reads, but an incapable violinist, an incorrect pianoforte player, or a singer out of tune, cannot possibly be secluded, but must exhibit his shortcomings for the affliction and aggravation of society.

Therefore, let no child be taught music who has not a natural aptitude for it. Decided musical talent generally shows itself early. Many children sing before they can speak. I have written down, with the date affixed, so that there could be no mistake, more than one actual tune, invented and sung by a small person of three years old. But the negative to these positive instances is less easily ascertained. The musical, like many another faculty, develops more or less rapidly according to the atmosphere it grows in. And there is always a certain period of "grind" so very distasteful that many a child will declare it "hates music," and wish to give it up, when a little perseverance would. make of it an excellent musician. I am no cultivated musician myself—I wish, with all my heart, the hard work of life had allowed me to be! but I feel grateful now for having been compelled, three times over, amidst many tears, to "learn my notes," which was nearly all the instruction destiny ever vouchsafed me.

Nevertheless, I believe I did a good deed the other day. A mother said to me, "My child is thirteen, and has been working at music ever since she was seven. She has no ear and no taste. If she plays a false note, she never knows it. Yet she practises very conscientiously two hours a day. What must I do?" My answer was brief: "Shut the piano, and never let her open it more." The advice was taken, and the girl, who now spends that unhappy two hours upon other things, especially drawing, in which she is very diligent and very clever, would doubtless bless me in her heart if she knew all.

But the love of music, which she had not, often exists without great talent for it. Still in such cases cultivation can do much. Many vocalists, professional and otherwise, have begun by being *vox et præterea nihil*, that is, possessing a fine organ, but no skill in using it. While, on the other hand, many delightful singers, I recall especially Thomas Moore and Sheridan Knowles, have had scarcely any voice at all. The expression, the taste, the reading of a song are as essential and delightful as the voice to sing it with;

and these last long after nature's slow but inevitable decay has taken away what to a singer is always a sore thing to part with, so sore that many are very long—far too long !—in recognising this. Sadder to themselves even than to their listeners is the discovery, that now, when they really know how to sing a song, they have not the physical power of singing it.

But art, cultivation, and a little timely clearsightedness—or clear-hearingness—can prop up many a failing voice. Any one who remembers how Braham sang at seventy-five will acknowledge this. A then young, but now elderly musician, once told me how he remembered having had to accompany the great tenor in the "Bay of Biscay," given with a fire and force almost incredible in a septuagenarian, and received with thunders of encores. "My boy," whispered Braham, "play it half-a-tone lower." Again it was given, and again encored. "Half-a-tone lower still," said the old vocalist; "they'll never find us out." Nor did they. And the applause after the third effort was loudest of all, so completely did art conceal the defects of failing nature. But suppose the singer had not been an artist, or the accompanyist had only understood a little music, and been incapable of transposing the song "half-a-tone"?

If music is studied at all it ought to be studied thoroughly, and from the very first. Parents are apt to think that anybody can teach music to a child, and that any sort of piano is good enough for a child to practise on. No mistake can be more fatal. A child who is fit to be taught at all should be taught by a capable musician with intelligence enough to make the groundwork not merely superficial, but solid ; and not only solid, but interesting. A great deal of the preliminary study of music is not at all interesting, unless the teacher thoroughly understands it, and takes the trouble to make the child understand it—the infinite and complicated beauty of the science of harmony, in opposition to the dulness of mere strumming. Then the little soul, should there be a musical soul, will soon wake up—will comprehend the why and wherefore of the most wearisome of scales and the hardest of exercises, and conceive an ambition not merely to "play a piece," but to become a true musician.

The too early playing of pieces or singing of songs is the most fatal thing possible. It substitutes clap-trap for pure taste, and outside effect for thoroughness of study. It is also very bad for the young performer. Many a nervous child can play well enough alone, but if set to show off before a room full of indifferent people is absolutely paralyzed. And an inferior child who is not nervous is probably made intolerably self-conceited by this showing off, which foolish parents applaud and are delighted with, ignorant that the true aim and end of music is first the delight of the musician himself, and next that he should be able, either singly or as part in a whole, to contribute to the delight of other people. Cultivated people first, but likewise all people; for, in spite of my friend's severe remark about "Pop goes the weasel," I believe that the very highest art is also the simplest, and therefore will always touch the masses; perhaps far more than art a degree lower and more complex. There may be two opinions upon Beethoven's "Mount of Olives," grand as it is; but I think the veriest clown that ever breathed could not listen unmoved to Handel's "Hallelujah Chorus," or to what, after twenty-five years, I remember as the perfect expression of musical art and religious faith—Clara Novello's singing of "I know that my Redeemer liveth."

It is art such as this, and taste cultivated so as to be able to appreciate it, which I would desire to see put in place of that "little music" which, like little learning, is a "dangerous thing." Dangerous, in the first place, because all shallow and superficial acquirements must be so; and secondly, because it inclines to a system of personal display at small cost, which is always the deterioration of true art. Surely it would be none the worse for us in England—it is not in Germany—if, instead of each person being taught to sing or play for himself, more or less badly, the general aim of musical education was that every member of every family should try to be able to take part in a simple family concert—classical chamber music or pleasant after-dinner part-songs and glees.

In the good old times probably it was so. "Pepys's Diary" seemed to imply that in his day everybody could bear a hand, or a voice, in an after-supper catch; and farther back still we have plenty of evidence that the Elizabethan soldiers thought none the worse of themselves for being able, not only to sing, but to compose an Elizabethan madrigal.

But even in my own generation I have seen music advance so much that I have hope in the "good time coming," which often casts its shadow before. It did on me the other day at a garden-party, where one of Mendelssohn's concertos for piano, violin, and violoncello was given by three young people, not professional, in a manner that Mendelssohn himself would have liked to hear. Afterwards a brother and sister played a Handel duet—violin and piano—after a fashion that implied many a pleasant evening of fraternal practising. And in the singing, though one voice was a little past its first youth, and the other owed more to cultivation than nature, and the third, which was exceedingly beautiful—well, the luckless accompanyist had now and then to count five crotchets in a bar in order to keep time—still every vocalist showed taste, feeling, and expression, and every song was well chosen and pleasant to hear. Between whiles people wandered to the simple tea-table under one tree, and the fruit-table under another, but they always came and filled the music-room—filled it, I am glad to say, with an audience that was *perfectly silent*.

And here let me end with one passionate and indignant protest against the habit which ill-conditioned guests indulge in, and timid hosts and hostesses allow, of talking during music, a breach of good-manners and good-feeling which, whenever it is found, either in public or private, should be put a stop to firmly and remorselessly. If people do not like music they need not listen to it; they can go away. But any person who finds himself at a concert, or in a drawing-room where music is going on, and does not pay it the respect of total silence, is severely to be reprehended.

To recapitulate in a few words the aim of this "Plain-Speaking." Let every child, boy or girl, be taught music, or tried to be taught, till found incapable. In that case, abolish music altogether, and turn to more congenial and useful studies. Secondly, let no one pretend to learn music who does not really love it, but let those who do, study it well and thoroughly, so far as the work of life will allow; always remembering that the aim of their studies is not to exhibit themselves, but *the music*—for the best of musicians is only an interpreter of other people's language. There are endless varieties of language to choose from; each reader may have a different taste and different style; nay, I will go so far as to say, that he who plays "Pop goes the weasel" with spirit, force, and accuracy, is not at all to be despised. But one thing is inexorably right and necessary—let every one who does anything in the science of sweet sounds try to do it as well as he possibly can.

Then, haply, we shall gradually cease to be "favoured" with that great abomination to all appreciative souls—"a *little* music!"

COFFEE-ROOMS FOR THE PEOPLE.

By LADY HOPE OF CARRIDEN.

" EYES and no eyes!" was a poem of great popularity among youthful minds when I was a child. It was driven into our memories by repeated study, and recalled to our attention perpetually by the sharp-voiced reproof of some governess or instructress. Notwithstanding the hammer-and-chisel force used to make us see our deficiencies in the observance of the lessons therein inculcated, we liked the little poem, and read it many times. Since I have grown older, circumstances have constantly brought vividly to my mind the simple lines; and I have too often been aware of my own sightlessness, and of that strange phase of the same, which may be called "wilful blindness," amongst my acquaintances.

When we rise in the morning to a comfortable breakfast, and enjoy the bright fire that greets us, the bundle of friendly letters brought by the postman, and the pleasant sitting-room gladdened by the sunlight, and furnished with many a luxury, to know that there is no fear of hunger to-day in our house, no prospect of hard work, no dread of ill-treatment, or likelihood of beholding painful or terrible scenes—do we ever think of the fact that all are not so sheltered from these sorrows as we are? Why have we been given these comforts? Why are we given those riches? Why have we been intrusted with our education? We pass through towns and villages every day in our drives and walks. Do we never think of the hidden sorrows that lie concealed behind many a window-pane, eating away the happiness, and often the very life, of the sin-stricken, or, from other causes, suffering inmates?

We can never think that because, in the afternoon, when our carriage stands beside the door of the shop in which we are making our purchases, all is quiet and orderly, the passers-by clean and respectable, and the opposite cottages bright and pretty, that this millennium state is uninterrupted, and constant in its duration. We could not make a greater mistake. "All is not gold that glitters," and those pretty cottages are by no means what they look. Each one is full of real life—joy and sorrow, passions of love and hatred, careful anxiety alternating with seasons of moderate prosperity. Self-denial, such as we know little of, may be found there, and selfish cruelty, perhaps, beyond our most sensational imagination. The interior of those "romantic little places" (as some one called them the other day) is by no means as smooth as the surface of an unused pillow. And yet, judging by the apathetic way in which hundreds and thousands of such abodes are passed every day by the ladies and gentlemen who live, as we say, "in the lap of luxury" themselves, and know nothing but "a downy pillow," as far as their own outward lot is concerned, we might think that such was their tacit opinion.

"Do you take any interest in the people?" I asked a gentleman as he showed me his garden radiant in the spring bloom of rhododendron and early foliage, pointing out delightedly his exquisite conservatories full of rare flowers, and the bright-coloured foreign birds that inhabited them. We were looking down on the town of which he was a neighbour, and admiring in the half-distance its rustic beauty, which stood out as a background to the nearer loveliness.

"Oh yes," he said, and turned round to me as he spoke, "I go down to it constantly;" and then a very quizzical smile overspread his handsome face, as he said—"when the people do anything *wrong*, that is to say."

My friend was a magistrate, and I soon found that his visits only occurred when any court business had to be attended to. A case of drunkenness, or theft, or improper rioting, he considered his summons to the duty devolving on him, on account of his near neighbourhood to the little town. He was right, no doubt, and kind so far to take an interest in the people. But the punishment of the evil-doer can hardly be the sole application of the Scriptural injunction, so plainly given as the second command, and *like unto the first*, viz., "Thou shalt love thy neighbour as thyself." I acknowledge a state of obedience to the *second* of these must result entirely from a pervasion of the whole being by the *first;* and place their order as you will, the one is impossible without the other. But as there are many amiable and philanthropic men connected with every town, no doubt, in the country, the question is worth considering: Ought our duties, as neighbours, to consist *entirely* in punishing the lawless? This seems hardly Christlike! There is much more, surely, to be done in reform before the man, woman, and child may reach the state of morals which must bring them before the magistrate, or to the prison cell.

If we wait until they pass into the character of confirmed criminals, we tacitly acknowledge, either that for human nature there is no remedy, or that in our hearts there is no love. Did we love our neighbour, it would grieve us that he should drink, and curse, and swear, and every day sink lower (often against his will) into the mire of open crime. From such evils it is ten times more difficult to reclaim him, than from their first beginnings. How many a young man, too, is standing about the street-corners, outside the public-house, in the low dancing-hall, perhaps taking his first essay at such life, merely because he wants some occupation, some source of interest in the long evenings, some friend, in fact, with holy influence and loving tact, who will take him by the hand and show him a better way. He has not learnt yet to care for the degrading sources of amusement that are just opening up before him, but having no very strong principle, or a principle that is beginning to succumb to exceedingly powerful influences on the wrong side, he feels himself slipping down into the career that he dreads. What is he to do? Where is he to go? How is he to escape?

"Stay at home," you answer. This answer is so common a palliative to our consciences when we see the young men of our country by thousands and thousands going astray, that it is worth replying to again. One room, or possibly two, of twelve feet square, is scarcely a tenement that you or I would like to use without an outlet! Cooking, sleeping, dressing, and every other family occupation carried on within those very narrow walls by father, mother, sons, daughters, little children, and often lodgers, who can wonder that from an early age the boys are found in the street during the entire evening? This is their earliest habit, and it grows upon them. Certainly, family customs among both rich and poor are as varied as the leaves on a tree; but, still, we shall find, in a very large proportion of cottage homes, that the parents by no means encourage their own sons to spend all their leisure hours cooped up in the little room. The domestic arrangements are hindered by their presence, the room is too crowded to be pleasant; and for these reasons, even from the better class of mothers, I have constantly heard the expression—"You ain't wanted. Get your cap, and go out." "Mind you don't come in again!" the mother will often add, as the retreating form of the boy is seen. Of course the lodgers are not expected to sit in the small room. They do not pay for this luxury.

Bed alone they pay for; so they must go out. And, too often, as we well know, the father also finds home irksome without books, without resources, without music, without the easy-chair which our gentlemen consider so indispensable after a long day's work. Then he seeks resource outside his house; and what is the result? He is quickly laid hold on by other working men who have learnt to frequent the public-house and dancing saloon. One evening he is amused, and another and another, until his name is added to the list of criminals in the town. Then he is brought before the magistrate, and for the first time in his life a gentleman speaks to him; but it is a condemnatory sentence — "Hard labour," "six months," or whatever it may be. Whereas, a kindly shake of the hand, a friendly word, an open place of positive, not negative, benefit, and an influence exerted for his soul's good, as well as the suggestion of new thoughts to his mind, might easily, by God's blessing, have saved that man. Multiply the *one man* by thousands upon thousands, and who can dare to say we have no responsibilities?

Let us cast those responsibilities upon God, and go forward!

Before discussing this subject amongst ourselves, may I say that whilst so doing, we may handle very freely the working man's lack of economical resource, his restricted space in the tiny home, and the drawbacks he is subjected to in the congregating together of very uncongenial elements in the shape of lodgers, that every possible shilling may be drawn into the vacuum of needs daily created by frost and rain, and many mouths and huge appetites; yet in speaking to himself I would touch upon the subject very differently. I would urge upon him (and I wish we could do this amongst these men in mass meetings!) the *sacredness of his home*, reminding him that if the churchyard is "God's acre," how much more is the place of *life* hallowed by His kept law, and adorned by ties of love—with its burdening responsibilities and its unequalled joys—worthy of such a title! God has created all the earth in families. Family life has been ordained from the earliest ages, and like all God's works, remains the unchanged custom still, as well as the natural fact. Animal, bird, insect, and flower life all testify to this same marvellous arrangement from a Creator's hand for the happiness and well-being of His created world. Unhappy instances we see of the frustration, through man's would-be wisdom, of this blessed law, and instances too, how frequently, of the pollution of these sweet streams by uncontrolled evils.

Let us prove to him, if possible, that these are the evils we desire to remedy, and that in our effort we require his aid. If we can enlist his sympathy, and, better still, his enthusiasm, we have gained something, we have done much, in fact, towards carrying our point. As we all know so well, neither an Englishman nor a Scotchman will be "driven," he must be "drawn." The great thing, therefore, is to get him on our side, *i.e.* on the side of such reform. The difficulty of this is appalling if we look at the whole question at once, and, taking it from our usual stand-point, at a little distance from him. Sitting in our drawing-room arm-chair, newspaper in hand, we feel disposed to shake our head hopelessly, and who can wonder? The police reports and other accounts of crime wherein our evil genius, "the drink," figures so largely, however abbreviated they may be out of regard to polite ears, are quite sufficient to make us feel helpless to stay the torrent or mitigate its force. Unlike the Danish king, we are speechless before the wave.

But these difficulties are not so great if we look at them from a different level. In the first place, taking our stand amongst the working men, rather than above them; and in the second, calling to our aid the Omnipotent Help that is promised and has ever been given to those who in their own insufficiency of resource are ready to rely upon it, we may very confidently make an advance. A hand-to-hand fight offers on the whole, perhaps, the surest prospect of success. Making friends with the mass, man by man, we gradually overcome prejudice, and introduce new thoughts among minds singularly frank and open, and often very susceptible to impression. A kind word, a friendly act, the forming of an individual acquaintance, will often give us the good-will of a whole gang of men who before they knew us were inclined to ignore or to think hardly of the lady or gentleman who could "drive," while they "must walk," and in other ways led what they considered a life of ease.

The great thing is to go among the people. We need not fear moral contamination if we are zealous in doing good. God's truth is our "shield and buckler," and in using our own energies—mental, spiritual, and bodily —we do not succumb, as the onlooker might expect, to the enemy's weapon. Eloquence will do a great deal, but personal love and true personal interest will do a great deal more. Thus we benefit our neighbour and we benefit ourselves too. How many an objectless existence, and therefore a suffering existence, has, on either side, been by this means transformed into a bright and happy one? An empty cup becomes an overflowing one by the mutual imparting and reception of any real benefit. If we share "*His* benefits," we do indeed throw a halo of sunshine around us, and reap an "hundredfold" in return.

In any spot where this subject has been discussed by thoughtful minds a variety of volunteers may generally be found, each of whom has discovered some medium or channel by which he or she may present the *one* all-sufficient remedy to the people. One can speak, another can read, another can sing, another can visit, another can converse, another can adopt the method of the silent, uncouth man, who confessed himself to be "no scholar," but who wrought much for *the kingdom.* "I can put my arm round a fellow's neck and say, 'Come,' and the Lord *brings* him." If we dare not class ourselves amongst the more gifted ones of 1 Corinthians xi., we may at least take rank under that comprehensive though unpretending title, which carries with the rest *His* cross of honour, "*Helps!*" But let none of us be left out from the great throng of workers, however humble be our part.

Old Father Humphrey used to say that a man once complained of a smoky chimney. Immediately a visitation of sympathising neighbours became the penalty that he had to pay for his difficulties. In they flocked. One suggested one cure, and one another, until the unfortunate owner of the misfortune was sadly bewildered. Happily for him he was saved from the dilemma of choosing remedies by the "happy thought" at last suggested by some Solomon of the party that *he should try them all*. If I recollect my story rightly, this last advice was taken, the result being *a cured chimney!* This relation from the pen of one who understood somewhat of the ills of life, must be my apology for introducing at this juncture of my paper an earnest advocacy of the *Coffee-House* scheme.

There are many and varied phases of this useful specific now to be seen and heard of in most quarters of the British Isles, each taking its rise generally from the brain and pocket of the higher educated and more moneyed portions of our community.

To begin with the largest, we find in London, Glasgow, Edinburgh, Liverpool, Manchester, and other cities, one brilliant rival to the gin-shop, repeated many times in the shape of the coffee-palace. Its large, brightly lighted windows, spacious saloons, ample provision for the supply, occupation, and re-creation of mind and body, are generally well supported by the prosperous trade it attracts. Drinks of every description (non-intoxicating) are to be found here; and they are popular. This is an excellent index to the state of public feeling on these points, and proves that when the working man is tired or thirsty he does not frown when you replace the whisky bottle by a cup of coffee, ginger ale, lemonade, or some other beverage. These palaces are no longer charities, but self-supporting institutions. If, therefore, they are carried on from a right basis, and ruled by a sound principle, there is no reason why they should not multiply *ad infinitum*.

Again, we find the working man's club. In the smaller towns some phase of this is very general. It succeeds or fails entire according to the management. The head that takes the lead is the respons: one here, and either concentrates or d perses the various human elements, accord ing to the direction in which his own mer force works. If controlled by some genii earnest, and respected character—with s cial gatherings at the expense of the mes bers, well planned and effectively and bese ficially carried out—they ought to succee: remarkably well for a certain class. To : movement which naturally keeps itself rath select there must always be a large number outsiders. At this we cannot be surprised. the very fact of membership implies sobrie and respectability to some degree at least, anything like irregularity would result natu ally in a downfall.

(*To be concluded in next part.*)

YARROW.

THE simmer day was sweet an' lang,
　　It had nae thocht o' sorrow,
As my true love and I stood on
　　The bonnie banks o' Yarrow.

I took her han' in mine, an' said,
　　"Noo smile, my winsome marrow;
The next time that we come again
　　You'll be my bride on Yarrow."

A tear stood in her sweet blue ee,
　　An' sair she sigh'd in sorrow,
"I dinna like the sugh that rins
　　Alang your bonnie Yarrow.

"It soun's like some auld dirge o' wae,
　　It chills my bosom thorough,
An' it makes me creep close to your side;
　　Oh, I dinna like your Yarrow.

"For aye I think on the wae an' dule
　　That auld, auld sang brings o'er me;
An' aye I see that bluidy fecht,
　　An' the deid, deid men afore me."

I clasp'd my true love in my arms,
　　I kiss'd her sweet lips thorough,
Her breast lay saft against my ain,
　　On the bonnie banks o' Yarrow.

"A tear is in your sweet blue ee,
　　A tear that speaks o' sadness.
Noo what should dim its happy hue,
　　This simmer day o' gladness?

"The Yarrow rins fu' fresh an' sweet,
　　The licht shines bricht an' clearly,
An' why should we sad thocht be ours,
　　We wha lo'e ither dearly?

"The Yarrow rins, an' as it rins
　　Nae sadness can it borrow
Frae that auld sang that's far awa',
　　When I'm wi' thee on Yarrow."

I pu'd a daisy at my feet,
　　A daisy sweet an' bonnie,
I put it in my true love's breast,
　　For she was fair as ony.

But aye she sigh'd, an' aye she said,
　　"I fear me for the morrow.
Oh, tak' awa' your bonnie flower,
　　For see, it grew on Yarrow.

"The bluid still dyes its crimson tips,
　　It speaks o' dule an' sadness,
An' the deid that lay on the gowany brae
　　An' woman's wailing madness."

I took the daisy frae her breast,
　　I flung it into Yarrow,
An' doon the stream wi' heavy heart
　　I cam' wi' my sweet marrow.

O simmer months, hoo swift ye flew,
　　Wi' a' your bloom an' blossom!
O death, hoo waefu' was thy touch
　　That took her to thy bosom!

For my true love, sae sweet an' fair,
　　Lies in her grave sae narrow,
An' in my heart is that eerie moan
　　She heard that day in Yarrow.

ALEXANDER ANDERSON.

SARAH DE BERENGER.

By JEAN INGELOW.

CHAPTER XXXII.

AMIAS was standing on the rug in the room where he had talked with Uzziah Dill. It was a pleasant morning; the red curtains of the windows had been partly drawn, and shafts of sunshine came in between, casting a fine glow upon the figures of an old man and an elderly lady, who sat on two comfortable chairs.

"Yes, my dear uncle is much disappointed," said Sarah. "He thinks the little girls look thin and weakly. Yes! and dear Amabel and my pretty Delia——"

"Why mention them in the same breath with the others?" interrupted Amias. "My uncle, I understood, was come here to talk over his affairs—express some of his wishes as regards his grand-daughters."

"And dear Amabel and my pretty Delia," Sarah went on, as if she had not heard him, "have each had an offer of marriage. Yes, very natural, I am sure, and does the young men no special credit."

The dark cheek of Amias mustered colour, and his eyes flashed. Sir Samuel, in spite of a little depression which showed itself in his air, smiled furtively here.

"No special credit," she went on, "for anybody might see, with half an eye, what charming, desirable girls they are—though, to be sure, the lovers, both in the army, had nothing at all but their pay. However, as they said to me, there's always hope of a scrimmage. War, war—that's what they all look to, what they daily pray for. But it's rather shocking to think of their dropping on their knees—whole rows of them—and deliberately entreating a merciful Providence to send 'battle, and murder, and sudden death,' that they may get their promotion! Yes; but that's what, as I'm informed, they always do."

Sir Samuel sat through this speech in silence, and, as he still said nothing, Sarah spoke again.

"Some girls are far too rich," she observed, "and others far too poor. It would be much better if my dear uncle would have his six grand-daughters as before. Punctilios are quite out of place in family matters; and you are so particular, Amias, about your rubbishing proofs, that now you see the consequences. The property, as my dear uncle has said, must go to those four pale-eyed, sickly girls (not the least like the family), and their fortunes will be so large, that they will be the victims of all the neediest scamps out."

"I am not so sure of that," said Amias, "if Felix is to have the charge of them, and I am to be their guardian."

"Much too rich, poor children! But when my will comes to be investigated, perhaps it may be found that I have been less regardless of the family interests than you have, and have not thrown dear John's children over just because he died before he could come home to claim them—and produce his marriage certificate," she added, after a short pause, "which he had no reason to suppose we should ever think of asking for."

"If you please, sir," said a servant, entering, "Mr. Uzziah Dill wishes to speak with you."

"I will see him in a few minutes," replied Amias. "Now, aunt," he continued, when the door was shut, "you have been giving me rather a long lecture this morning."

"Well, perhaps I have," she answered, looking up at him affectionately, "and I must say you have borne it like a lamb. Yes! but it will have no effect upon you, Amias."

"You accuse me, among other things, of meddling in the affairs of this world, of a strong wish to make it better and happier. Now, there is a poor, weak wretch of a lame cobbler down-stairs——"

"Yes! going to prove that my remarks were so much wasted breath."

Amias turned from his aunt to his uncle. "I say, uncle, that I feel a wish just now to see the world—at least, those few atoms of it which are held together by the body of that lame cobbler—a little better and a little happier."

"Then there's money in the wish," said Sir Samuel, smiling rather grimly. "By how much money is the little demagogue to be made better and happier? I remember him. I heard him rant when you were at the seaside, a year or two ago."

"I think five-and-twenty pounds would satisfy me."

Sir Samuel lifted his eyebrows involuntarily, he was so much astonished at the audacity of Amias in naming so large a sum. "This comes," he thought, "of my having laid myself under an obligation to him by making him my girls' guardian."

XXI—53

"The poor man's case is hard, and I deeply pity him," continued Amias. · "He was a reformed drunkard, and kept himself sober for years ; but in a time of deep distress—an illness of his wife's, I think—he was overcome by temptation, and drank again. Now he almost despairs, and his living is lost, for of course he cannot rant, as you call it, on temperance any more."

Partly in gratitude to Amias, but more in pity for the man, Sir Samuel took out his purse, and, to the surprise of Sarah, gave Amias, in gold and notes, the five-and-twenty pounds.

Amias, thanking him, took the money and went into a little waiting-room, where he found poor Dill and his wife. Uzziah looked the shadow of his former self, and was very desponding.

Amias applauded him for his intention of leaving London, held out no hope that any more temperance lecturing was possible for him, but gave Mrs. Dill the money, and said it was a generous gift from a friend.

Mrs. Dill accepted it with beautiful and homely dignity. "It was a king's ransom to her," she said ; "it would give her husband hope and courage, and that was what he mainly wanted to keep him sober."

She had money, more than this sum, lying in the hands of Mr. Bartlett, but since a certain dreadful fact had come to her knowledge, she feared the very sight of a lawyer, and had made her husband more timid than herself.

"Then I suppose I've got to retire into private life, sir," said poor Uzziah, in a desponding tone.

Amias with difficulty forbore to smile.

"I am sorry for you, Dill," he began.

"It's a sore blow, but a meet punishment," interrupted the poor man.

"We have taken up enough of Mr. de Berenger's time," said the wife, with gentle firmness. Amias shook hands with her, but not with her husband, and when Uzziah saw that he was determined to say no more, he made his bow, and departed.

He and his wife went and sat down on a bench in Kensington Gardens, for Uzziah was too weak to walk all the way home without a rest, and the Gardens were in their way.

The poor man was very wretched, and his wife understood his misery. He wiped his brow as he seated himself, and spoke for the first time.

"He never gave me the least hope,

Hannah ; he never even said I might stand forth again at some future time."

She was silent.

"To think I could do good and help the cause was almost what I lived for. It was not only the applause I got, Hannah ; you must not think it."

"I do not think it."

"I was buoyed up by it. It enabled me to deny myself."

"Ay, my poor husband ; but it made you *forget.*"

Uzziah wiped his forehead again.

"Am I to have nothing to do, then, for God ? "

"Ay, truly ; you've got to get our living by your trade. So far as I can see, that is God's will about you just now, and that it may last His will, I daily pray."

"Then, if I am to go, let it be a long way off. There's plenty of money. Let us go where I may forget."

He spoke weakly and almost peevishly. His wife encouraged him, but from that day she recognised a change. His crime, which it seemed he had almost forgotten, was now ever present to his mind ; he had supposed that in the end he should be discovered as its perpetrator, but because he believed that God had forgiven it, he had felt that he was free of it in the meantime.

He now discovered his mistake. No need to tell him to be distant and humble in his manner to his wife, or meek and silent with others ; he was all this of his own accord. With a touching patience he undertook such work as he could get, and contented himself with such fare as it would procure.

Hannah Dill could find no consoling words for him ; but she forbore from all reproach, and gradually, as he left more and more to her, she took the guidance of him and of their small earnings. In one thing she always yielded. He had sometimes a fit of restlessness, and would long to leave the town or village where they were. Then she would produce Sir Samuel's money, and by some cheap excursion train, and still cheaper steamer, they would go on. It was always in the same direction—always north. At last, after a full year of such wandering, they found themselves at Whitby, and here the change of scene, the cordial manners of the people, and perhaps the fine air of the place, seemed at last to revive the poor man. He settled to his work with more hope, slept better, and would sometimes walk about the shore and into the country, evidently refreshed by the beauty of the scene.

Hannah Dill felt relieved, for she could not but be influenced by the deep depression she always saw in him. Gradually it passed, she scarcely knew when or how. He was very humble, very silent still; many an hour he would spend in prayer, lying on the floor of the little chamber; but at meal-times he would now sometimes converse with her, or he would whistle to the child, now grown a fine, rosy little fellow. Sometimes he would read aloud, and always he would work diligently at his calling.

Hannah Dill calmed herself by degrees, and began to live from day to day. She had been long looking for a catastrophe: it did not come. She now began to feel some refreshment in the present. The constant changes of the sea fed her observant mind. Sometimes the harbour would be full of heavy rolling waves, and the tugs and vessels would rock on them like ducks, while the pier lighthouse would be drenched by the breakers that reared at it, and rushed on, hiding it for the moment, in a great fountain of seething foam.

Every day she took her child on her arm and walked forth, that he might enjoy the bracing air.

And she could again enjoy it. The sweet life of the rectory was remote as Paradise might have been to Eve's imagination when she had left it; but she had another child to love and tend, and she had much ado to make the money cover their small expenses. Then she took in needlework when she could get it, and sometimes did a little clear-starching, so that she had plenty of occupation, and yet not of a sordid kind. They were poor, but there was no grumbling in their home, and though the parents frequently went without meat with their potatoes, there was always a cup of milk for the child.

The year thus spent by Hannah Dill proved a very eventful one for the De Berengers.

Sir Samuel, now eighty years of age, began slightly to lose his memory, and to depend more and more on his niece Sarah and on his two great-nephews. To describe the anguish this caused to his daughter-in-law, Mrs. de Berenger, would be quite impossible. When she heard that Amias had gone to live with the old man, and always attended to his affairs while he was in London, and sat at the head of his table,

she was taken ill from sheer anxiety—so likely, it seemed to her, that Amias would influence him to the prejudice of her four children. She wrote to Sarah frequently, and, expressing the deepest solicitude about the old man's health, begged that she would use her influence to get him into the country. He had already given up his seat in Parliament, and disposed of his business; how much better it would be for him if he would live in the fresh country air. It was such a needless expense, too, as he saw hardly any company, to have two establishments.

Sarah, showing the letter to Amias, who saw its real meaning, the old man was easily persuaded to go into the country; but there matters were no better. Sir Samuel did not want his daughter-in-law, would not invite her and her children to come to him. He wanted Amias—always Amias; and as he could not have this favourite nephew in the country, he got Felix to come about him as much as the parson nephew would consent to do, and at other times, rather than be alone, he would come and stay at the rectory, contenting himself with the quiet life led there, and paying for himself and his old servant a due proportion of its expenses, and no more.

From week to week, though his mental decay was so slight as to be scarcely perceptible, he seemed to become more conscious of a change in himself, and to be more desirous of guidance; more afraid, especially in money matters, of committing some imprudence, more openly dependent on the opinion of one or other of his two great-nephews; while, at the same time, his spirits improved, and his temper grew sweeter, partly from the absence of all business or political worries, partly from the delightful consciousness of how much money he was saving by living so frequently at the rectory.

His presence was never regarded as a trouble there; quite the contrary. Felix, who had been keenly aware of his foibles some years previously, became now very indulgent to them. From mere sociability of temper, he always liked to have his house full. He was never easy when Amabel and Delia were away; his aunt Sarah's presence had always been a pleasure to him; and now Sir Samuel frequently in and out, riding with the girls, going to sleep in his most comfortable chairs, and conforming to the early hours of the rectory, was decidedly agreeable to him.

If anybody had taken the trouble to observe the fact, and place it to its true account,

"Every day she took her child and walked forth."

Felix must have been held to be changed. He was much more particular in his dress; he was altogether brushed up, and looked better and younger: but his temper was not quite so indolently gentle as it had been, and he was sometimes a little unfriendly toward a certain young officer in the army, who frequently rode over to the rectory about this time, and would turn very red, and half choke himself with sighing, whenever Delia condescended to look at him or to speak to him.

Delia thought this young man a great bore, for a certain instinct of propriety made her aware that, as she did not mean to let him get friendly and intimate—as she would not let him help to feed her young ducks, or knock down the sweetest crab-apples for her, or beat the donkey when she indulged in a canter—she must, therefore, take the trouble to smooth her wandering locks for him, and treat him to her best frock. She never gave him a smile, but then she took care that her sash was not awry.

Nothing, however, could repress the gallant soldier's love, and one afternoon, when Delia was out—gone out riding with her sister and old Sir Samuel—he laid his modest prospects before Felix, together with his manly hopes, and begged leave to make his offer in due form.

It was his last hour in the neighbourhood, his leave was up. Felix was perfectly sure that Delia cared nothing at all about him, but he consented to lay the matter before his ward; and when the two girls returned, rosy and beautiful, from their ride, he called her into his study.

Felix was seated on his sofa. He had seldom in his life looked so well. Delia looked at him, and thought so. There was more fire in his dark eyes than usual; there was even a shade of red under the dark cheek. He began quietly to state the soldier's wishes.

"What a goose he is!" said Delia, when the story had been told.

Felix was gratified. He would have liked to rise and set a chair for Delia, but that would have been such an unwonted proceeding that it must have roused her attention, and for the present he did not dare to do that; he wanted to let things drift.

"Was he very droll, Coz?" she next inquired.

"Droll!" exclaimed Felix; "droll, poor fellow! No. Why?"

Delia was standing before him, with her whip in her hand; she was twisting round it a long bine of wild briony that she had gathered in the hedge. "Oh, because you look so—so amused. I don't like you to look pleased."

Felix could not help looking pleased.

"Why?" he inquired, almost faintly.

Delia made no answer for the moment. She seemed to cogitate; then she said, in a pleading tone, "I suppose I'm not obliged to try to like him, Coz, if I don't wish?"

"Certainly not," replied Felix.

Delia came and sat down beside him next, and she blushed, and seemed to look inquiringly at him. So sweet a hope had never dawned in the heart of Felix in all his life, as swelled it in that happy moment, but he said not a word.

Then the unreasonable young creature laughed, and shrugged her shoulders. "If you want me to send an answer to him," she said, "you'd better tell me what to say; for, of course, I don't know."

Felix was so sure she did not care for her lover, that he found no difficulty in doing him justice, and in taking care that his suit was duly presented.

"How can I tell what to say, unless I know what you feel?" he inquired.

"I don't feel anything particular," replied Delia—"excepting when he comes," she added.

"And what then?"

"And then I do so wish he would go."

Felix laughed. He felt that the situation was getting the mastery over him. This child of his adoption was so sweet, so familiarly affectionate in her manner towards him, that he could not but retain his old household ways with her, and yet she did not now give him her good-morning kiss without making him tremble from head to foot. He started up hastily from his seat, and began to pace the room. Delia still occupied her hand with the strand of wild briony, and he looked at her: a beautiful blush went and came on her rounded cheek; it seemed that she could not meet his eyes.

"Delia," he said, stopping opposite to her, and speaking not without some tremblement in his voice, "you must say yourself what I am to repeat to him. You must make a direct answer to his proposal."

"He's so old," said Delia, as if excusing herself for not caring about him.

"Old!" exclaimed Felix, astonished and almost horrified. He felt himself turning chill, and a sudden dimness seemed to becloud all his dearest hopes. "He is only six-and-twenty," he went on, sitting down and sighing.

"He's much older than Dick," said Delia. "Oh—I would much rather—wait—for Dick."

Felix looked at her earnestly while she spoke; a flood of rosy colour covered her fair face and throat. She bent her head a little, and was too much absorbed in her own trouble to notice that Coz was pale.

"Wait for Dick?" exclaimed Felix, in the quietest of tones.

Delia felt something unusual in it; a certain dulness and dimness made it seem far off. She blushed yet more deeply. "I did not think you would mind," she began.

"Dick is a mere boy," said Felix. "Is it possible that he has spoken already?"

"No, he hasn't yet," answered Delia, excusing him; "but he will soon."

"He will soon?" repeated Felix, between astonishment and dismay, and instantly Delia started up and ran to him. He rose to meet her, and, putting her dimpled hand on his shoulder, she sighed out—

"Oh, Coz, don't tell him. I did not mean to say it."

"Never mind, my sweet," he answered, and it seemed as if he was consoling her—"never mind; it cannot be helped."

"But you'll never tell any one?" she entreated, and she laid her cheek for a moment against his.

He answered, "No."

"No, Coz, dearest, don't," she repeated; "and there he is coming." She had caught the sound of Dick's foot outside the door, and, with a mischievous little laugh, she snatched up the train of her habit, and, darting out at the open window, ran to join Sir Samuel, who was sitting under a chestnut-tree on a low bench.

She spent the next quarter of an hour in thinking a good deal about her cheeks, now and then laying her dimpled hand upon them, to ascertain whether they were growing cooler.

Felix spent the same time in his study, sitting perfectly motionless and silent. He had wasted his youth on a long, obstinately cherished attachment; it had melted away quite unaware, and for the last few weeks—only a few weeks—a new one had risen, suddenly as a star. Delia was so young. He knew, of course, that at present she felt only a childlike love for him, but he never supposed that she loved any one else ; and now she herself had told him that she did, and if he could believe that she knew her own mind, his hope was lost, and his day was over.

CHAPTER XXXIII.

LITTLE Peep was dead. Amias wrote a long, affecting account of his last illness to Amabel, how for many alternate nights he and Lord Robert had watched by him, how patient and content he was, and how kind Mr. Tanner had been.

Amabel kissed the letter; it pleased her to think that Amias had such an affectionate heart.

Lord Robert, it seemed, had " broken down " at the funeral. Yes, but Lord Robert had got a fine appointment in one of the colonies; he would sail in a few days with his pretty wife, and soon forget poor little Peep. Amias never would.

Little Peep, in his last will and testament, left several thousand pounds in trust to Amias, to build a temperance public-house, and his portrait was to hang in the bar.

Little Peep was there represented as a young man of average size, and a decidedly intellectual countenance. The temperance lecture that Amias had written appeared in his hand as a folded scroll, and he was coming forward on a platform to read it.

The poor young fellow took much innocent pride in this picture, and the last night of his life, when Lord Robert and Amias were both with him, he told them what he intended to have done with it.

" Some people think it an excellent likeness," he said faintly. " I enjoy public-speaking, and if it had pleased God to prolong my life, I might have made myself a name by it. I might have done something great."

" That you would, dear boy," said Lord Robert ; and soon after this he died.

" He had so many endearing qualities," said Amias, speaking to Lord Robert the night after his funeral—" so many endearing qualities—that it was impossible to despise him, and yet I think, on the whole, he was the greatest fool I ever knew."

" He was not by any means the greatest fool I ever knew," answered Lord Robert, pointedly, and in a tone of good-natured banter.

" Why, what have I done now ? " exclaimed Amias.

" Oh, nothing now; but I do not see why you are to be allowed to go about the country making yourself conspicuous for this temperance cause, without being made to pay for it."

" I have paid," answered Amias. " I paid when I was a boy."

" But I have a fine eye. I observe the march of events. You'll see that poetical justice will be done upon you before long. I don't say that I should not take a certain pleasure in seeing it done."

" What do you mean, Bob ? "

" When you took yourself off from your old uncle, he had three sons. They have all died, one after the other, and every year he became more attached to you. Now, there's a great uncertainty about the ways of this world ; people don't always do in real life what is expected of them. But if you had been a man in a book, Amias, the old uncle about this time would have done poetical justice upon you; he would have let you know—in fact, he would have said in the presence of those friends you most liked (would, perhaps, have convened them on purpose to hear it)—that but for your rebellious, unfilial, and unfeeling conduct to him, he would have (leaving a poor fortune to each of his grand-daughters)—he would have adopted you, and made you his principal heir."

" Verdict, ' Serve me right,' " said Amias.

" The march of events distinctly points to such a catastrophe," continued Lord Robert. " Depend on it, he will say something of the sort before he has done with you."

" Poor old man ! " answered Amias. " No, Bob, he never will ; he will say nothing of the sort."

" But am I to have these noble aspirations after poetical justice for nothing ? "

" Time will show."

" If I had been blessed with such an uncle, would I have so treated him ? Yes, Amias, I repeat it : little Peep was not the greatest fool I ever knew."

A very eventful year followed for the De Berengers, but Hannah Dill, who thought of them unceasingly, never had a hint of anything that concerned them ; her darlings, as she often felt, with an almost unbearable pang, might be dead and buried, while she knew nothing of it. But her little son helped her to endure this uncertainty, as he also helped to fill the empty, aching heart.

Her husband had quite, for the time, got over those paroxysms of craving for stimulus ; he could trust himself alone about the town, but he never proposed to speak at meetings again, and she did not conceal her opinion that this was best.

But now the last of Sir Samuel's money was spent, and though Uzziah worked hard, his poor earnings did not quite keep them. Several of their best articles of clothing had been sold, yet he could not make up his mind to let his wife write to Mr. Bartlett for the money due to her, so much was he afraid now of bringing himself into undesirable notice.

And yet money was sorely wanted—money for the quarter's rent now nearly due—and, after the only discussion they had held since leaving London, Dill consented to write to Mr. Bartlett, authorising him to give the money to his wife, and then consented to her going to London and taking the letter by hand, so as not to betray his whereabout.

With great difficulty, and by the sale of every article that they could possibly spare, they scraped together just enough money to pay for an excursion ticket, and then, some small provision of food tied up in a handkerchief, the husband and wife proceeded to the station, the former carrying his child.

"Keep a good heart," said the wife as she took leave of him; but unaccountable depression weighed down her own heart. She had not an easy moment during the long journey, and she walked to Mr. Bartlett's house full of wretched forebodings.

A pale, faded woman, he scarcely knew her at first, but she soon recalled herself to his mind, and, almost to her own astonishment, she got all the money due to her, with only the little formality of waiting for her husband's signature, which she wrote for and obtained, before she could carry it away.

"And now you have got it," he said to her, with a certain dispassionate curiosity, which was more an interest in the event than in her, the human agent that was to bring it to pass—"now you have got it, Mrs. Hannah Dill, do you mind telling me what you are going to do with it?"

"Why, take it to my poor husband, sir."

"Oh!" was all he answered; but he looked at her in a way that suggested both surprise and incredulity. "I only asked you as a friend," he observed. "Of course it does not matter to me what you do. I am perfectly safe."

"Yes, sir; but what else should you think I would do?"

"Should I think?" he repeated. "Well,

I may have thought you would go on as you began."

"Sir, in the other case I only acted against Dill to save, if I could, his poor children; not to save myself."

"And this poor child?"

"I fare to think he cannot be saved, sir," she answered, melting into tears. "His father sets that store by him that I could not be so cruel as to carry him off."

"Well, well, Mrs. Dill," he answered, "it is no business of mine—none at all."

"I was never treacherous to him," she interrupted. "I never said to him that former time, 'Dill, I am off to get our money. Keep a good heart; I am coming home as soon as I can.'"

"And you did say so this time?"

"Certainly."

"Well, Mrs. Dill, I am truly sorry for you."

His voice was rather kind, but his manner suggested all manner of doubts to her—doubts as to what she really meant to do, and doubts whether, knowing what she meant to do, she was wise; but she had hardly reached her humble lodging before she became calm and assured again. She had promised her poor husband that she would go back to him, and go she would.

But, oh! with what fear she returned; with what crowding unfortunate presentiments! What they meant she could not tell, but she never lost them for a moment till she stopped at Whitby Station, and saw her landlady waiting to meet her, and smiling in cordial, pleasant fashion, as she stepped up to the carriage-door.

"Dill was off to a little hamlet some miles off," she explained, "and would not be back till the next day. A poor man, whom he sometimes went to read to, was near his end, and had just sent to beg that he would sit up with him that night and pray with him."

"And Dill is all right?" asked the wife.

"As right as can be," was the answer.

Where now were all her fears?

She was so wearied and exhausted with what she had gone through, that her knees shook and her head ached. The relief was great of finding her superstition, as she now called it, unjustified by any reasonable cause, yet she could not settle to any work. What she had gone through is by no means a rare experience; it had been a restless sense of conscious danger or of deep need, weighing down the spirit of her husband, and having power to affect her, making her a partaker of his misery, without imparting to her the cause.

She knew she should not be quite at ease till she had seen Uzziah, and she wanted to pass away the time, so as soon as she had taken something to eat, she dressed her boy in his best, and went forth among the visitors to the pier that forms one side of the harbour. She had been so deeply brooding over her own thoughts, that during the journey she had hardly noted anything that passed around her. Now her eyes wandered with conscious refreshment, and her ears were thankful and attentive; all that passed helped to fill her mind with fresh images. Two old fishermen were coiling ropes close to her seat. "Ay, ay," quoth one to the other, speaking with deep pity of the visitors, "there they was, dawdling about, poor souls; nought to do but listen to the pestilent music tootle-tooing, fit to drive 'em distracted. Folks should be piped to their work, and not to their play.'

"Darting out at the open window, ran to join Sir Samuel."—P. 757.

"What's a lugger?" some boy coming up asked the other fisherman.

His companion quietly went on with his business, while he answered, in his broad dialect and soft, persuasive voice, "What's a lugger? Why, that's one; her that has a small mizzen, and lug sail on it."

"Won't her masts come out?" asked a still younger boy.

"Ay, for sure; they have kin' o' steps in the boat for to rest 'em on—yo' can see 'em. They make the foremast rake avast. Now, mebbe yo' doon't see what that's fur."

Neither of the urchins pretended that he did see.

He continued, "It's to give the wind more power, so's to lift the sail—git under it like; and so, if she's heavy laden wi' fish, to lift her at the bows moor out o' t' watter."

This valuable information was given with

conscientious care: in his deep pity for these poor children of the land, the old seaman would neglect no opportunity, but do his manifest duty towards them, which was to put the A B C of shipping life (and what other life is worth the name?) plainly before them.

Mrs. Dill looked at their rosy faces with interest. A great many little boys are brought up by old fishermen to take to the water. A few quaint phrases stick in their minds. The loss of that one life-boat, the Whitby life-boat, has alone caused many youths to risk their lives, for danger that ends in death has a fearful attractiveness; it draws the island children out, quite as strongly as that which is surmounted and comes safe home again.

"Ay, t' harbour dues are high," she next heard on her other side. "What do they come to? Why, nigh upon sixpence a ton!"

"Oh!" said the lady who had inquired. "Then, how much will that ship pay?" indicating a vessel with her finger.

"That collier schooner?" asked the fisherman, with genuine pity in his air. "She's not a ship at all, mem. Well, mebbe eighteen shillings. Folks say t' new dues keep out t' vessels. But I doon't complain; when God shuts one door, He mostly opens another. There's less shipping, but there's moor fish.——Who pays for t' lights? Why, every vessel that passes Whitby lights has to pay a halfpenny."

"All those vessels out there? Why, surely it's not worth while to send out to them for only a halfpenny?"

The old fisherman straightened himself up when he heard this, and looked at his mate, as if he would have him testify that the words had truly been said.

"The vessels pay wheer they start from— say Hull. You've heerd talk of Hull?" he then replied, doubtfully.

"Why, of course!"

"Oh, I wasn't sure. Hull, or Sunderland, or wheer not."

"Your boat's ready now, mem," said the second old man.

"Take extry care on 'em, mate," whispered his fellow, with something like contempt; "for they're real landlubbers, and no mistake. And her, the mother of a family, too, to know nothing more than the babe unborn!"

"Bless you," replied his companion, "what should she know of *dues*, nor what's reasonable? If yo'll me believe, she asked me las' night whither theer were any difference atwixt a roadsted and a harbour!"

Mrs. Dill smiled, so exquisite was the enjoyment of the old fishermen over this ignorance "in the mother of six." She watched the boys and this rosy-faced parent down to their boat. They were going to fish—at least, they thought so; the old fisherman was going to bait the lines, and they were going to hold them.

It was a still, warm day. A great bulging cloud, black and low, was riding slowly up from the south. The cliffs had gone into the brooding darkness of this cloud, which had stooped to take them in. The water was spotted with flights of thistledown, floated from the meadows behind the church, and riding out to sea. Suddenly a hole was blown in the advancing and lowering cloud; the sun glared through it, and all the water where his light fell was green as grass, and the black hulls of the crowded vessels glittered; while under the cliff a long reach of peaked red roofs looked warmer and more homelike than ever, and on the top of them the wide old church seemed to crouch, like a great seabeast at rest, and the ruined abbey, well up on the hill, stood gaunt and pale, like the skeleton ribs and arms of a dead thing in sore need of burial.

So Mrs. Dill thought; but then she was not cultivated enough to love death and decay. She felt the weird gloom of the cloud and the blackness of the nearer water; something of its gloom came over her also; the short respite that change had brought was over. A weight fell down upon her; the peculiar instinct of coming sorrow was upon her again. A step was drawing near rather slowly. She knew it, and a more than common pang of pity shot through her heart; it included her husband and herself, and the child. While seated on her knee, the little fellow held up his arms and babbled, "Daddy, daddy!"

Hannah Dill looked up at her husband, and at the moment was too much struck by his appearance to speak. His eyes were not absolutely looking at her, though, a little wider open than usual, they seemed to take in the whole scene—the lowering cloud, the grass-green sea, the rocking boats, and herself and her child. Was it the arrest of some great surprise that held him motionless? That could not be all. He was lost in thought, and wonder, and perplexity. There was nothing like fear in his face, but no fear could have made it more utterly pale.

"Uzziah!" she exclaimed, with a sharp cry of terror and suspense. Then, as it seemed, he brought his eyes to look at her, and his lips moved; but he uttered no sound. "Whatever is it? Do speak!" she said faintly.

And in a low, mumbling tone, he said slowly, "I went to read with Jonah."

"Well?" she cried. That was no answer to her question.

"He's dead," proceeded Uzziah.

"Well?" she repeated, shuddering; for he looked distraught, and it seemed as if his thoughts were still remote. But as he saw the terror in her face he appeared to note it (yet not till he had examined her well with his eyes), and then to rouse himself with a sudden start, and with a violent effort to regain almost his usual manner and voice.

"It looks like a storm coming up," he said, while his wife,.trembling and sick at heart, wiped away a few tears.

He was folding up a newspaper in his shaking hand; he now put it in his pocket, and when his child slid from the mother's knee and toddled towards him, he retreated, saying—

"No! Maybe you'd liefer lead him yourself, Hannah! And I've nothing to say against it."

She rose then. There was something wrong, and she did not dare to hear it, or ask what it was. He preceded her to the house, and she noticed that, his hand in his pocket, he kept hold of the newspaper all the way. Yet when they got home the strange manner was all but gone: he was less pale, more observant; he could even eat. And she was very thankful for a comfortable meal. She ate and drank almost with urgency, for she thought there must be something terrible for her to hear, and that she would fortify herself for it beforehand. Something, she thought, was impending. But nothing occurred; as soon as he had eaten, he told her he was going out to the shore to pray, and he did not return till ten at night.

"I am not going to bed this night," was all he said, when she, weary with her journey, roused herself up to let him in.

She went up to bed, and while she undressed, heard him as he sighed to God, and afterwards heard the same sighing in her dreams; but she was greatly wearied, and when at last she woke, in full daylight and all the splendour of an August morning, it startled her to find that there was silence below at last.

She stole down-stairs. Her husband, dressed in all his best clothes, had opened the window, and was sitting with his head leaning on the sill, fast asleep. He looked ex-

hausted, and she thought he must be ill. He had not treated himself to a holiday for many months. As he had said nothing, there could, she now thought, be nothing to say; he must and should have a day on the heather, and breathe the air from the hills. She went out quietly, bought some fish for breakfast, made the fire, and dressed the child.

It was not till past eight o'clock that he woke, and she called him to his breakfast, and laid her plan before him. Oh, how gentle and quiet he was! How little was left of the husband of her youth! He was to see what money she had brought. Yes, he would. He was to rouse himself up. He would try. He was to go with her and the child in the railway to a place he had loved the previous summer, and they were to sit together on the hills. Yes—so best. She began to get alarmed again, as she saw how quietly he sat while she made her simple preparations.

And they went. They stopped a few miles out of Whitby, at a station called Gothland, between two great expanses of heather. They climbed the steep, cliff-like hill on the left-hand side, and reached a long expanse, all purple and gold; a lovely, peaceful view spread itself forth in successive descents at their feet. The place was remote from life, and yet it was not lonely, for every valley, as it lay open for inspection, had its own farm-house, and on every space of grass kine were feeding.

What peace appeared to rest as a presence over the purple moor! The child was happy with his flowers; the mother sat quietly looking about her, and feeling thankful for the rest. She thought change might have done her poor husband good. He had eaten, and was wandering hither and thither. She watched him awhile; then her eyes were attracted to a steep declivity, down which a sparkling beck was leaping. In the vale, where it spread itself out into a shallow, lonely pool, a crowd of rooks walked on the moss in companies, and a flock of little finches washed themselves sportively. She was still tired. Her eyes rested on these careless creatures with a dull contentment that was almost pleasure.

She had forgotten her husband for the moment. Where was he? Wandering about in the heather, most likely. Not at hand, for she turned and could not see him. And what was this?. Close where he had been sitting, and almost under her hand, he had spread out his handkerchief, and laid upon it most of the money she had given him in the

"The child was happy with his flowers, the mother thankful for the rest."

Page 760.

morning. It was all in gold. Her heart sank. Why had he done this? She counted it: he had taken with him seven pounds. She looked about her again, and at last there he was, descending the steep path toward the station. He was half a mile off, and before she could decide what to do, a train came up and stopped. The lame man's figure was visible, running hard to reach the little lonely station. He was the only passenger. She stood up in her place; she saw that he was in time, that the train went on, and that he was gone.

Very few trains stopped there.

It was evening when Hannah Dill and her child got home. Her husband was not there; she had scarcely expected it would be so. Where, then, was he gone? She looked about her, and saw her husband's every-day coat hanging behind the door. She took it down with a trembling hand. She was always looking for evil tidings, and however heavy the blow might be that fell on her then, it was not a shock, it was hardly a surprise.

A south-country newspaper was in the pocket. Her eyes ran down the columns.

She felt, before she saw, what it was that concerned her. The assizes were going on. The judge would be at a certain town that was named, on such and such days. There were several important trials, and one—— Hannah Dill cried out, and flung the paper down and wrung her hands. She saw a name that she knew, the name of a murdered man. Some of the details of the crime were given; she remembered them. The murderer was found, it appeared, and was about to be tried.

She quieted herself with difficulty. This could not concern her, then? And yet her terror all concentrated itself upon those assizes. The paper had been read and re-read and wept over; it was still limp with tears. She must go down to this town in the south-west. It was not far from the place where her little Delia had been born. Her husband had been tried there. She should die if she remained in ignorance. Why did she think he had gone there? She could not tell; but she must go, and if her husband did not prove to be there, she was a happier woman than she feared.

A VISIT TO THE PARIS INSTITUTION FOR BLIND YOUTHS.

OF the many material blessings which Christianity has brought us in its train, not the least is the provision made for persons deprived of sight, hearing, and speech. The methods used for their relief in our own land are generally well known. But the system of treatment of these unfortunate ones pursued in France is not so familiar, and a brief account of a visit paid by the writer to the excellent institution for blind youths, in Paris, may not be without interest.

A word about its origin will serve to introduce the subject. A poor weaver of St. Just-en-Chaussée, in Picardy, was the honoured father of two sons of whom France may well be proud: Réné Haüy discovered the law of the formation of natural crystals; the other, Valentin, left even a stronger claim to celebrity, as having inaugurated the first efforts for the relief of the blind. He has himself related the singular circumstance by which his attention was drawn to them. "Passing, on May 18, 1782, over the Place of Louis XV., I observed," he writes, "ten poor blind men in a café, tricked out in a very extraordinary manner. They wore paper caps on their heads, had eye-glasses made of cardboard, without lenses, on their noses, pieces of music were spread out before them, and lighted candles on the table, placed in derision for them to read by, while they played on various instruments in the most discordant fashion. At the door were sold engravings of the atrocious scene, with verses written in mockery of the afflicted men." This inhuman and shameful burlesque deeply roused Haüy's generous indignation, and led him to reflect upon the helpless misery of the blind, which left them exposed to such injurious treatment. His compassion soon bore fruit in action. Beginning with a few friendless ones whom he found amid the slums of Paris, and clothed, fed, and educated, he persevered in his noble work of philanthropy until, as the number of his protégés increased, it became necessary to provide a suitable asylum for them. This he eventually secured, and, in spite of the many difficulties and discouragements incident to such an undertaking, he carried out from step to step this noble purpose on which he had set his heart. Unhappily, however, his work was interrupted by the political changes that followed the first Revolution.

Having incurred the displeasure of the first Napoleon, he became an exile, and retired to Berlin and St. Petersburg, in both of which cities he established similar schools for the blind. On his return to France, after the accession of Louis XVIII., he lived for several years in privacy, and died in 1822. Like many another benefactor of mankind, he was not permitted to see the final success of his enterprise. But it could not be said of Valentin Haüy, as Antony said of Cæsar, that, "the good he did is interred with his bones." This very valuable institution, which claims him as its founder, is his enduring and most honourable monument.

The exterior of the building will not detain us long. Plain, substantial, and unpretending, it in no way rivals the splendid edifices in which Paris, the city of palaces, abounds. It stands on the Boulevard des Invalides. The only objects which strike the eye as we approach it are the façade, on which is carved in stone a representation of Haüy surrounded by a group of blind boys and girls, and his statue, which stands within the railing in front.

My visit was paid during the mid-day hour of recreation. As soon as I entered I saw a number of youths streaming along the wide corridor with all the sportiveness and animation of boys let loose from school. A few less boisterous ones, linked arm in arm, were descending the stairs with more caution. In another moment all were in the playground, a spacious, airy courtyard, planted with trees. I followed them, and was pleased to find that, although they did not engage in any regular games, these poor blind lads seemed as full of life and spirits as others of their age, running fearlessly about, and occasionally trying each other's strength in mild wrestling matches. All appeared quite unconscious of their great misfortune, and played in perfect good-humour. After half an hour the bell sounded through the building, and with equal alacrity they dispersed to their various occupations. The morning classes were over, and most of them assembled in their workrooms. In one of these they were engaged in chair-covering, under the direction of a superintendent. Very neatly did they do their work. Even little fellows, that had just been initiated into the art, showed great dexterity. Chairs were turned out such as would have done credit to experienced mechanics blessed with the vision of both their eyes. In another room they

were employed in making nets for various uses. Some were of a strong, coarse texture, for fishing purposes or gymnasia; others were of a finer quality, intended as receptacles of ladies' hair, or the happily almost antiquated and always obnoxious anti-macassars. One fine lad, lately admitted, seemed very loath to apply his tiny fingers to his task. He had not long left his mother's care, and was unused to anything but play. But no harsh words were spoken, or coercive measures adopted. I was pleased to notice the patient, gentle way in which the motherly woman who presided over the department was endeavouring to interest her tiny pupil in his work, and to overcome his reluctance. The porter, too, who was my guide, put in a kindly word: "Le pauvre enfant a été un peu gâté," was his only comment. Such appeared to be the prevailing tone of the institution. The law of love, carried out by mild yet firm discipline, as far as a visitor could judge, seemed to regulate the many wheels of its machinery so that they worked without much friction.

I next inspected the printing-room, and was not a little surprised and gratified to find that the directors had been adventurous enough to establish one. Very wisely they have not attempted to train the blind to competition with those who can see, in an art to which, above all others, quick sight is of the first importance. For this reason their efforts are exclusively directed to the special purposes of the house. They receive no orders from outside, and are not taught the use of ordinary type, but devote themselves entirely to preparing books in raised characters for their own use. Still, the comparative rapidity and accuracy with which the blind compositor picked out his types was most astonishing. Each box had its own character raised in relief upon it, otherwise, of course, their task would be impossible. Composition was the only branch of the trade which they could practise unassisted. In the use of the press and the other processes, they had the help of boys, whose sparkling and intelligent eyes shone in painful contrast to the lack-lustre countenances of their comrades. But it may be asked, what characters have been adopted in this establishment? It may be well, therefore, to offer here a word of explanation. The system of stenography, which is a leading feature in their treatment of the blind, has been arrived at by slow degrees. At first the founder devised a method of printing in ordinary characters simply abbreviated, and with marks to distinguish doubled or similar letters. But this proved too elaborate, and failed to enable the blind to communicate or read their own writing. In 1821 a French cavalry officer, M. Charles Barbier, being an enthusiastic student of shorthand writing, invented an entirely new system. He put aside all attention to orthography, and directed his thoughts only to the sounds. Having discovered thirty-six sounds to represent every inflection of the voice in the French language, he arranged these in six lines. Each distinct sound he expressed by a certain number of points. Thus the point became the germ from which the present method of blind writing was developed. His scheme was, however, still imperfect. It was in itself too complicated and confusing, and had the further disadvantage of not being adapted to either arithmetical or musical notation—two essential branches of the education of the blind. These serious defects remained for some time without a remedy, and it was left to one who had himself fought through the difficulties of the situation, to add the final improvement, which now appears to satisfy in great measure the wants of the blind. Louis Braille was a former pupil of this institution, and had remained as a professor in it. He was an exceptionally intelligent man. The son of a saddler, he had lost his sight at the early age of three years, while playing with his knife. So distinguished did he become, that his bust now stands in the entrance-hall in memory of the invaluable services rendered by him to his fellow-sufferers. By means of points, disposed horizontally and vertically and in different number and order, he contrived a perfect alphabet, applicable to both figures and musical notes. Those used for the first nine figures are the same as for the first nine letters. The signs are all very simple, the most complicated consisting of three dots above the line and two below.

For writing purposes, to obviate confusion in the lines, he devised a small frame of zinc, bordered with wood, with lines sunk into it, and a movable copper rule of the width of two lines, in which are drilled two lines of rectangular holes, twenty-six in each line. Between the frame and the rule is passed a sheet of thick paper. The marks are made with a sharp pointer, and when the first two lines are full the rule is slipped down to the next, and so on to the end. By this simple but ingenious contrivance the order of the lines is strictly preserved, and the marks never run into each other. It is, moreover, possible to write on both sides of the paper, the writing on the reverse side

being inserted between the lines of that first written. In this way the friends of the pupils soon learn to correspond with them. The dreary chasm, interposed by their infirmity between them and distant friends, is thus bridged over. Nor is this all, for they are enabled, not only to communicate their own thoughts and feelings to others, but to enjoy the unspeakable benefit of converse with the good and great of ancient and modern times, and, greatest blessing of all, to study for themselves that inspired Word of God which giveth light and understanding unto the simple.

At the same time, since, as we have seen, the same signs are employed as musical notes, a source of much innocent enjoyment, evidently intended by a merciful Providence as a compensation to the blind, is opened to them, as well as, in many cases, a valuable means of support provided. The reading of music has by this means been rendered almost as easy to them as to those who can see. They who possess the talent, by a patient exercise of memory, can develop their gift to any extent. These advantages have been fully appreciated by the directors of this institution. The founder, indeed, did not realise all its value. He introduced it into his system merely as a recreation. But in 1815 Dr. Guillié, who was then the director, evinced more practical discernment than those who had gone before him. With the assistance of eminent "artistes" of the day, he developed the musical element in the education of the blind so completely, that we now find, as the result of his plans and exertions, a school of music of the first order existing here. The following is the system pursued:—As soon as a child has learned the notes he is assigned an instrument, for which he has shown the greatest aptitude, and learns to play it under the tuition of a master, himself generally blind. A considerable part of the building is devoted especially to this purpose. The second and third floors are partitioned off into small studies, the door of which is partially glazed, that each pupil may be open to inspection. He is thus left to practise alone. The second floor is assigned to the various wind instruments, the third to pianos. On the first floor is a concert-room, containing a large organ of considerable power, where they occasionally meet for rehearsals and united public performances. As one stands at the end of the corridors leading to these studies, a Babel of sounds, such as may be better imagined than described, almost deafens the listener. Harmony there seems none. Various melodies, discoursed on various instruments, are blended in marvellous confusion.

A considerable number of the pupils were assembled in the common hall below under the direction of two blind professors. It was not, however, in this case the blind leading the blind. The piece selected was a very effective composition, by one of the masters himself. It was also admirably executed. The time was given with two hollow wands, struck against the hands. Generally, as I was informed, they practise classical music. Gluck, Beethoven, and Weber are their favourite composers. They often take three months in learning one of their works, so thorough and painstaking is their manner of teaching. More rapid progress too is not possible, as they meet for united practice only for one hour five times a week. The instruction is principally given to each pupil separately. With a view to elevate their standard of excellence, and to stimulate them to the highest efforts, they are taken to hear some of the best concerts in Paris ; in fact, no attainable means is neglected to cultivate this talent to the utmost. As we might expect, the results fully justify the pains bestowed. Concerts, to which the public are admitted, are given frequently during the season, at which the performances are said to be of a decidedly high character. The success also which has marked the lives of many of the pupils, after they have left the institution, speaks very loudly in its favour. From January 1, 1848, to December 31, 1872, during a period of twenty-four years, out of 514 boys admitted 53 have left capable of gaining a livelihood as either organists or tuners of instruments. Five have even attained considerable eminence in music by winning prizes at the Conservatoire, while eleven have received honourable mention. In fact, it has been the aim of the directors to make the cultivation of music, as a profession, the leading feature and object of their establishment. And so important has this its character appeared to Maxime du Camp, a writer of great repute and influence in social questions, that he has gone so far as to advise that this metropolitan asylum should be exclusively devoted to the promotion of this art. He

would have all the blind who give no promise of excellence in it drafted off to other institutions in the provinces. Whether this would be an act of justice to that large number of those afflicted ones not endowed with this special talent may, perhaps, be questioned. Certainly the successful prominence thus given by our neighbours to the utilisation of a gift, with which a merciful God has especially distinguished the blind, may suggest the inquiry whether more might not be done amongst ourselves in the same direction.

It is gratifying to know that so much is effected both here and in France for the relief of this peculiarly tried class. Most thankful do we feel that the inmates of this valuable school have had their reasoning powers developed, their mental darkness in great measure dispelled by instruction, and their characters formed amidst the softening and elevating influences of moral culture. It is also ground for hearty congratulation that they who must otherwise have been through life helpless burdens to their friends and families, have left the institution happy and useful members of society. Only one serious drawback will be received with deep regret by all who feel the immense importance of a thoroughly Christian education as the only sound basis of morality. It is one which the religious condition of France renders, perhaps, inevitable at present. The Roman Catholic, as the dominant faith of the country, seemed to be alone represented here. The religious teaching appeared to be exclusively Roman. The services of the chapel are of this type, and the only spiritual instruction given in the classes is of the same kind. Some small part of the New Testament has been printed in raised characters, but I did not find a single copy of the Holy Scriptures, or of any part of them, in the hands of the pupils. That truest source of light and consolation which in our own more favoured institutions has contributed so greatly to the elevation and comfort of these poor sufferers, is wanting here. With the exception of this one most serious defect, the highest praise is due to the ingenious philanthropy which devised, and to the judicious energy and untiring charity which maintain, this truly excellent institution.

WILLIAM BURNET.

Bergen and its Harbour.

BERGEN.

By Lieut. GEORGE T. TEMPLE, R.N.

EVEN a Deal boatman would have admitted that it was "well on to fresh" when we left Stavanger, towards the close of a raw, gusty day in the early summer, *en route* for Bergen; and dismal were the sounds of woe that issued from the passengers' cabins throughout the night. The weather improved towards morning, however, the sky cleared, "visages pale and wan" solemnly emerged from gloomy recesses between decks, and a charming panorama of coast scenery was unfolded before us as the steamer threaded her way through the labyrinth of narrow, winding channels which form the inshore route along the west coast of Norway. The company on board consisted of a district judge, who was on a business tour with a subordinate; a couple of Bergen dignitaries, who talked politics and stock-fish; an elderly gentleman, who was going all the way to the North Cape to burn a hole in his hat by the midnight sun; and a Quaker, who said such a long grace before meat that the meat got cold; the sort of company, in fact, that is not specially lively or entertaining. After dinner, however, the captain and I discovered that we were, or ought to be, old shipmates, and strange legends of the sea, partly inspired, no doubt, by the attentive steward, beguiled the time until my new friend announced that there was only one point between us and Bergen. With the point came a heavy shower, which blurred the landscape and sent the passengers below to moralise on the fallaciousness of human hopes, especially when their fulfilment depends on the weather. From an artistic point of view, the situation of Bergen leaves nothing to be desired; but being nearly surrounded by lofty hills, which collect and condense the moisture-laden clouds from the Atlantic, it has a flourishing trade in umbrellas and waterproofs, and an unenviable notoriety in the matter of rain. In this respect, however, the old town is not fairly treated, for though it is true that rain falls frequently, yet it seldom lasts long, and the intervals of fine weather are so lovely that they quite atone for the temporary discomfort of a wet jacket. The yearly rainfall is 71 inches, or 8 inches less than that of the Sönd-fiord and Nord-fiord districts, while it is far exceeded in some parts of our own islands.

The difference between Bergen and all other Norwegian towns is very striking, the representatives of the Hanseatic League who ruled, or rather misruled, it for more than three centuries, having left indelible traces behind them. The people are quick, energetic, and of a somewhat yielding disposition; while their countrymen generally are very deliberate, and possess great firmness of character. More than a hundred years have passed since the power of the Hanseatic merchants was finally destroyed in Bergen; but the massive tower built by Christopher Walkendorf, to awe them into the semblance of decent behaviour, and the long line of counting-houses and warehouses on the north side of the harbour—the so-called "Tydskebrygge," or German wharf—form interesting monuments of the lawless sway of a confederacy which once commanded the respect, and defied the power, of kings.

The Tydskebrygge is still the emporium of the great Nordland fisheries, and when the old-fashioned jægts come streaming in from the north by hundreds at a time, with their great square sails swelling to the breeze, and their cargoes stacked high up the masts behind the lofty prows, we half expect to see portly merchants coming down to the waterside in the quaint costumes of the Middle Ages. But the scene is too busy and animated for the indulgence of day-dreams, and the prosaic clank and whirr of steam-winches and other modern appliances remind us that we are part and parcel of the nineteenth century. From four or five o'clock in the morning to ten or twelve at night the turmoil is unceasing. The atmosphere is impregnated

Fish-Market at Bergen.

with the odour of marine stores, and of some millions of dried and salted fish packed in barrels and bundles, which are swinging from derricks and flying about in all directions. Stevedores rushing to and fro, with wet and dirty ropes trailing after them, seem to be solely bent on tripping up the unwary. Sailors with stentorian voices are exchanging nautical compliments and pungent comments on things in general in half-a-dozen different languages; wheelbarrows and casks, loaded and unloaded, are trundling and tumbling about in the slippery, greasy mud, as if they too shared the general excitement, and had suddenly gone mad; ships' dogs mounted on capstans are barking and howling with frantic energy to a running accompaniment of ships' bells and steamers' whistles; everybody and everything, in short, appears to be inspired by a common ambition to add something to the bewildering din and confusion, which attains its climax when a salute is fired from the guns of the fort, and seems strangely at variance with the respectable, old-world appearance of the town and the stately repose of the surrounding hills. These great maritime fairs, which are called "stævnerne," or "meetings," have been held twice a year for more than six centuries, and while they last a visit to the Tydskebrygge requires a cool head and no little activity. The first "stævne" is in May and June, the second in August and September.

There is yet another famous exhibition peculiar to Bergen, and it is open from six to nine every Wednesday and Saturday morning, when the fish-market is held. On these days no right-minded Bergenser would allow meat to appear on his table; it would indeed be superfluous, for the newly-caught fish are superb, and the Norwegian mode of cooking them is not to be surpassed.

To appreciate the fish-market, however, we ought first to pay a visit to some of the countless islands between Bergen and the sea, which are inhabited by a very peculiar race—a race primitive as to their mode of life, of small intellectual capacity, and un-susceptible of cultivation. It has been suggested that they are not Norwegians at all; but whether they are descendants of the aboriginal people of Norway, or whether their idiosyncrasies are merely the result of circumstances, is a question that must for the present be left to ethnologists. They speak Norwegian, after a fashion of their own, but it is very difficult to understand them, and there is reason to suppose that their idioms have a Samoyede root.[*] These people are known in Norway as "Strils," pronounced "Streels." A distinction is drawn between "Land-Streels" and "Sea-Streels;" but the latter is the more correct designation, as they nearly all live by fishing. They are, in fact, an amphibious race, and it may be truly said that to them—

Bargaining with a Stril.

"The teeming seas supply
The food their niggard plains deny."

Their rude hovels are built on barren, rocky islets, where agriculture is almost entirely confined to a small patch of earth, producing about half a bushel of potatoes. Cows there are, but of a very diminutive breed, and their pasturage is of the most original description, for they too look chiefly to the sea for subsistence, and, like the dogs of Newfoundland, eat fish-heads and offal, eking out their scanty meals with marine plants and anything else that may be cast up by the sea or thrown aside by the fishermen. The milk of these animals is said to have a certain maritime flavour in consequence, somewhat resembling cod-liver oil. The pig lives with the family, and so do the fowls, which show their gratitude by laying all through the winter.

The sea is really the Streel's heritage; the halibut, cod, and herring his best live-stock. His treacherous broad acres swallow up friends and relations, and may crave his own life before the harvest is yielded; but he still ploughs on with unwearied patience, and still regards the sea as his natural element and his home. That it is so in reality no one who has seen the Streel afloat and on shore can possibly doubt. Accustomed from his earliest childhood to handle the oars, his body is out of all proportion to the lower

* V. St. Lerche, a well-known Norwegian artist and author, to whose works I am indebted for several of the ideas in this paper.

limbs, which are undeveloped and weak. Rowing is, therefore, his natural means of locomotion, and his awkward, wavering gait exposes him to many jeers and witticisms, accompanied by snowballs in winter and still more disagreeable missiles in summer, from the street boys of Bergen, whose well-known vivacity is not of the most pleasing kind.

Early on Wednesday and Saturday mornings the Streels may be seen racing for the harbour, each boat pulling two or more pairs of oars. It is the most original regatta that can be imagined, and every man does all he knows to get the best place, for it is a case of first come first served, and the early Streel catches the customer. At the inner end of the harbour, where the fish-market is situated, there is a final desperate struggle, and then an acre or two of boats are firmly wedged together under the wharf in a compact mass, the volleys of abuse with which the competitors have been regaling each other begin to slacken, and the Streel indemnifies himself for the past excitement by assuming an apathy of demeanour which nothing can disturb. The market-place is enlivened by the varied and picturesque costumes of peasants from the surrounding districts, who come to dispose of the produce of their farms and gardens and buy fish; but the chief interest is centered in the boats. The wharf beside which they lie is only a few feet above the water, and, fortunately, a strong iron railing runs along the edge, for it is thronged from end to end with servant girls, all vociferating, clamouring, scolding, and wrangling, in the shrillest treble, quite oblivious of their reputation for amiability. Away from the fish-market these lively handmaidens, with their short sleeves, roguish eyes, and coquettish little caps, are pleasant to look upon. But for the Streel they have no attractions; on him they expend neither smiles or glances, but bending nearly double over the iron railings of the wharf, they belabour his head and shoulders with umbrellas to attract his attention, screaming all the time in shrillest concert, "Streel! Stre-e-e-l! What will you take for the fish?" while one points at a cod, another at a coal-fish, a third at a halibut, a fourth at a lobster, a fifth at a bucketful of herrings, a sixth at a plaice, and all seem bent on excelling each other in superfluity of gesture and expression.

The incessant racket, combined with the treatment to which he is subjected, might well be expected to goad the Streel to reprisals. But not a bit of it. There he stands on a thwart with his hands in his pockets,

serene as a summer's morning, seldom moving except to transfer a huge quid from one cheek to the other. Clearly the Streel is a philosopher! Occasionally, however, he condescends to answer one of the many questions put to him, that is when he is lucky enough to identify the questioner and the object referred to. Whatever his reply may be, he will inevitably be asked if he is mad; about half the sum demanded will be offered, and so the haggling goes on, the fair customer expressing herself in language far more forcible than elegant. Every sentence that falls from the delicate lips contains matter for at least five actions for defamation, but the Streel is calmly indifferent, and does not abate his price. He knows the power of masterly inaction, and simply allows his opponent to scream herself hoarse; then, when voice and adjectives are fairly exhausted, a bargain is struck, and the dispute closes with the transaction.

Still worse fares the Streel who comes too late to get a place near the wharf, for he must struggle through the crowd with his wares, and find room for them amongst carts, barrels, tubs, and stalls, in the market-place itself. Here he is terribly out of his element, and no doubt gets sorely badgered, but he has the one consolation of knowing that he is not so much exposed to the *argumenta ad hominem*, which, with the help of umbrellas, are so freely expended upon his compatriots in the boats.

Many interesting relics of the Hanseatic merchants are still to be seen in St. Mary's, or the German church, which, as the latter name implies, was given up to the occupants of the old German quarter on account of its situation. The interior is very old and curious, much of it in pure Norman style: and there are some interesting remains of the art of the Middle Ages. Amongst the numerous votive pictures is the portrait of a Dr. Johannes Neuhavius, a venerable-looking man with a majestic white beard, whose claims to distinction are summed up in the following laconic epitaph:—"He was the last Catholic and the first Lutheran priest of this church"—a Scandinavian vicar of Bray, in fact. The walls of the chancel are adorned by the portraits of various bishops, and probably owing to want of space, it was found necessary to hang one of them over a small window. One night some thieves broke into the church through this window, and finding the bishop in the way, they simply cut a hole in his back and crept through it. The damage seems to have been irreparable.

for the prelate's waistcoat still bears traces of the sacrilegious treatment to which he was exposed. But perhaps there is nothing quite so unique in the whole church as the font, and a stranger attending a christening for the first time would be not a little astonished. The child cries, the nurse tries to pacify it, the sponsors look at each other, but no font is to be seen. Presently, however, the priest comes out of the vestry, and, "Hast du nicht gesehen!" down comes a life-sized angel from the roof in a cloud of dust, and hovers at a convenient height before the altar. The figure holds out a basin, into which the clerk pours some water, and retires to its former position under the roof when the service is over, there to lie in wait for the arrival of the next " little stranger."

Amongst the other lions of Bergen, the museum and collection of pictures by Scandinavian artists are well worth visiting; and here it may be observed, that the Bergensers have honourably distinguished themselves by their encouragement of science and art. Perhaps, however, they are better known to the majority of English travellers for what is certainly as much to be praised, their genial kindness and hospitality, qualities which are no doubt held in pleasant remembrance by many readers of GOOD WORDS besides myself.

PROPAGATION OF FOOD FISHES.

AT the meeting of the German Fishery Association at Berlin, March, 1877, the President, Herr von Behr, observed, "A disagreeable word demands admission at the gates of Germany, as it does in most of the states of Europe, and this word is *depecoration*.* This word, unfortunately adopted by our language, I call disagreeable, for it means that the number of those quadrupeds whose flesh supplies food for man is decreasing both absolutely and relatively, if compared with the increase of population."

Allowing only fifty pounds of meat annually for each of the forty-two millions of people in the German Empire, the quantity of meat required for the annual increase of population ought, it seems, to be twenty million pounds. Instead of that Germany is being "depecorated." That ugly word denotes the existence of a state of matters to be deplored by all who know how important it is that animal food shall be supplied in such proportions as are needed for maintaining the physical energies of the people. Science has demonstrated that flesh-eating animals are generally stronger than those which are herbivorous, and that no other substance equals animal food in the reparation of the muscular energy expended in labour. A half-starved nation is robbed of half its strength, and criminal statistics demonstrate that public peace and morality have no greater enemy than hunger.

It is comforting to know that though a country may be dolefully "depecorated," it need not be depopulated, or even reduced to scanty fare. Three-fourths of our terra-

* From *de*, privative, and *pecus-oris*, a herd or flock.

queous globe consisting of water, the quantity of alimentary matter derivable from fish is inconceivably great, if communities would only wisely avail themselves of the bounties of Providence. In the ocean by which we are surrounded, in the lakes, rivers, and canals by which the British Islands are intersected, we are provided with alimentary substances of the greatest value, and to an extent which is inexhaustible. But of these bounties we have not wisely availed ourselves. We have done almost all that can be done by ignorance and folly to reduce the productiveness of our fisheries. Of the scarcity of salmon and oysters we need not write. It is very necessary, however, that we should be brought to perceive the disastrous impolicy of a great maritime nation, possessing extensive and valuable fisheries, enfeebled by multitudes of the people living only a few degrees above starvation, because they have not been stimulated to put forth their hands and gather the easily attained food stored up in the bounteous reservoirs of the earth-encircling sea. It is amazing to how small an extent our people are fish-eaters. A ploughman's wife once told us that she thought little of herring, and that she had never tasted fish-pudding or fish-soup, and this in a locality where fish-carts frequently pass her door. The astonishing fact in connection with the penury of certain portions of the British people is this—employment unfailing, and sufficient to supply all their wants, is at hand; but they will not resort to it. The Celtic race seems affected with somewhat of the horror of the sea which characterizes the modern Hindoo. The starving

Irish will not be persuaded to develop the resources of the Irish fisheries, and actually import large quantities of salt fish and herrings. Enterprising foreign craft come to the coast of Ireland and carry off the treasures of the deep before the very eyes of the often famished natives. It is the same in the Hebrides, where the proprietors are so little successful in their encouragement of sea-fishing that they have difficulty in procuring a supply of fish for their own table.

As to Scotland in general, we are not a fish-eating race to anything like the extent that might be expected from our maritime position. We do not eat salmon largely, because they are so dear ; cod and haddock are not habitually eaten, even by the middle classes ; skate, generally undervalued, is scorned by the multitude ; and as to eels, the national antipathy to them is so notorious, that to ask a Scotsman to make a meal of them would be almost as distasteful as to present him with a slice of the sea serpent. It is very puzzling that a people so sagacious should have been so slow to avail themselves of the alimentary resources of the ocean, though these stand first in that venerable book which contains the Divine command, " Have dominion over the fish of the sea."

Owing to the rise in the price of butcher meat we may possibly be unusually predisposed to listen to those who advocate the extension of our fisheries, and recommend the merits of a fish diet. To furnish the means of forming a judgment upon a matter of such importance to the national wealth and to individual comfort is the object of this paper.

Before we can become covetous of more fish as an article of frequent diet we must be satisfied that it is really good as a means of maintaining a household.

That we can demonstrate by pointing to the long experience of a singular fish-eating community—Comacchio, on the shores of the Adriatic, and not far from Ferrara. Its inhabitants, in addition to wine, chestnuts, flour-pudding, and some fruits, live upon fish alone, and, above all, upon eels. "And yet," observes M. Coste, " this diet, far from injuring the public health, maintains it in the most flourishing condition. Those submitted to its permanent influence are robust, and live as long as those who in other countries live on butcher meat. Their elevated stature, the breadth of their chest, the muscularity of their limbs, the elasticity of their bodies, their animated look, their bright complexion, their thick black hair, are proofs of vigour as striking as can be seen in any other part of Italy."

Comacchio is remarkably healthy. Intermittent fever, so common in the neighbouring marshes, is not frequent, and scurvy is of exceptional occurrence. And thus, when the young of the neighbouring district are threatened with consumption, they are sent to the lagoons of Comacchio, to share in the toils and fare of the fishermen. In short, the value of a fish diet is demonstrated by an experiment unique in the history of the world.

The nutritive virtues of fish diet being undeniable, medical writers have investigated its effect upon the public health, and especially upon tubercular consumption, so common among the working classes throughout the kingdom. From the records of the Public Dispensary at Plymouth, as furnished by Dr. Cookworthy, it appears that of six hundred and fifty-four cases of confirmed lung disease only four were of fishermen's families, which is in the ratio of 1 to 163. It appears, then, to be undeniable that the sanatory action of fish fare is remarkable, and that in every respect it is to be desired as an important means of public alimentation.

But, with the price of almost all sorts of fish constantly rising, it may seem chimerical to expect that it may, in this country at least, enter largely into family use. On the contrary, our position highly favours such a possibility. Great Britain and Ireland have a coast line of more than four thousand miles ; and of the more than eight thousand fishes described by naturalists, two hundred and fifty-three inhabit the fresh waters of Britain and the surrounding seas. Our shores abound with those kinds of fish which exist in the largest numbers, and yield an unfailing supply of most grateful food. The noble salmon has, it is true, been extirpated in many of our rivers, and our lakes and streams are too often tenanted by species of fish comparatively worthless. There is a remedy for all this, however, which has already done wonders, and which, if steadily and intelligently prosecuted, will add immensely to our comfort and our wealth. The acclimatisation of animals must be a difficult and costly process, owing to their size and the care required in moving them to a great distance from their original habitat. But the ova of fishes are easily transportable, so that already the eggs of Tay salmon have been transferred to Australia, and those of

California salmon have been safely deposited in many of the streams of New Zealand. And such is their vitality that they bear with impunity long transport by sea and land, and are hatched thousands of miles from their native rivers. As this new application of natural history is interesting and important in no ordinary degree, we shall proceed to make our readers acquainted with the processes of pisciculture, and with the places where it has been most successfully prosecuted. Our intention is to give prominence to the doings of the United States Commission of Fish and Fisheries, as detailed in the last bulky volume published by the Commissioners. We do this because the proceedings of European pisciculturists are on a smaller scale, and better known in this country.

For the happy idea of artificially impregnating the ova of fishes, and placing them in running water till hatched, we are indebted to the German naturalist Jacobi. Observing how flowers are impregnated by the fertilising dust conveyed by winged insects lighting on them, it occurred to him that, in like manner, the prolific seed of one living creature could be artificially transferred to another. In 1758 he artificially impregnated the ova of trout and salmon. Taking the female fish when her ova were mature, he gently pressed them out into a vessel of pure water, into which, in like manner, he immediately introduced the milt of the male. The impregnated ova were deposited in long cases, the bottoms of which were covered with an inch thickness of sand and gravel, on which was a bed of pebbles, of the size of a nut or an acorn. Through this he conducted a streamlet of pure water. The experiment was perfectly successful. The young fishes came forth as well formed as those naturally propagated. It was near Nortelem, in Hanover, that he carried on his interesting researches. They afforded results so important, fishes thus obtained having become a considerable article of commerce, that England awarded him a pension in acknowledgment of his services.

How a process so evidently fitted to add to the national wealth by creating an inexhaustible supply of precious food, should have yielded such slender results until recently, is a great mystery. Two humble French fishermen, Géhin and Rémy, living in the obscure village La Bresse, department of the Vosges, brought it into renewed notice in 1841. In ignorance of Jacobi's proceedings, they were led to precisely the same method of fecundating fishes. In 1844 the Vosges Société d'Emulation bestowed on them a bronze medal and a small sum of money. Being subsequently employed to apply their system to the streams and rivers of the department, they speedily demonstrated its value by stocking these waters with millions of trout. Fortunately for them and for France, Dr. Haxo, Secretary of the Société d'Emulation, brought their proceedings under the notice of the Academy of Sciences at Paris. The Academy at once appreciated their importance, and invited the attention of the Government; which with equal readiness afforded the ingenious fishermen ample field for the application of their system, by employing them to stock with fish certain rivers, and teach the peasantry how elsewhere to carry it out. Pisciculture was soon consigned to the care of a Commission of distinguished men of science, prominent among whom was M. Coste. His reports led to the creation of a great piscicultural establishment at Huningue—a veritable *piscifacture*, to which from all parts of Europe came inquirers anxious to learn the most efficacious modes of propagating fishes. At the instigation of the late Dr. Esdaile the salmon fishing proprietors of the Tay commenced, in 1853, those experiments in salmon rearing at Stormontfield, about five miles above Perth, which have added largely to our knowledge of fishes, and also to the rental of the Tay fisheries.

As many of our readers may desire to know how the fecundating process is conducted at Stormontfield, we shall describe it.

A gravid female salmon and a male having been procured from the neighbouring river, the first thing to be ascertained is whether they be "ripe," that is, whether the roe and the milt readily flow from the fish when gentle pressure is applied. If not "ripe" the fish are placed in "the lying-in hospital," that is, a space in the mill-lade close at hand, shut in by gratings, and where they remain till fit to be spawned. The ova are extracted by gently stroking the belly of the fish, from whose vent they flow as readily as pellets from a shot-belt. They are received into a tub one-fourth full of water, and into this the milt is expressed by similar manipulation, care being taken that the vent, both of male and female, shall be under water. The impregnation is effected by stirring with the hand the contents of the tub. It seems to take place instantaneously, and is followed by a heightening of the salmon colour of the ova. Those which are injured turn white, and are rejected.

The ova of fish are exceedingly hard and tough, and so elastic as to rebound when thrown on the floor—a beautiful provision of nature to prevent them being crushed or injured by the stones among which they are deposited. This elastic toughness facilitates the transport of fish ova for the purpose of pisciculture; and experience has demonstrated that they can be transported hundreds of miles, either by land or water, if carefully packed in layers of moist moss, or of rough sponge the size of a walnut, and well cleaned.

The breeding boxes in which the impregnated ova are placed are inexpensive; the dimensions, inside measurement, being 5 feet 10½ inches long, 1½ feet broad, and 1 foot deep, and are made of 2-inch wood. There are 30 rows, and 12 boxes in each row. The boxes are placed in double rows, with a footpath 18 inches wide between each double row. The water passes through each row of boxes from the canal stretching along the upper end of the pond by gravitation; this canal being copiously fed with water from the filtering bed. This is an essential part of the arrangement, in order to prevent the introduction of trout ova, injurious insects, and plants which are apt to choke up the boxes with fungus growths very pernicious to the ova. Vivification is effected in about 120 days, according to the temperature of the season.

The young salmon has at first an ungainly tadpole-like appearance, owing to the disproportionate size of the head, and to the umbilical appendage attached to its belly. This protuberant bag is a singular provision for supplying it with food for the first five weeks of its existence, during which it takes no external nourishment. When turned into the rearing pond the fry are regularly fed with boiled ox and sheep liver ground small. In 1868 the fry were so unusually plump and large as to suggest inquiry regarding the cause. On examining an aquatic plant growing in the pond it was found to be covered with mollusca of various sizes, ranging from that of a mustard seed to that of a pea. This was ascertained to be *Lymneus peregra.* As the famed Loch Leven trout is believed to owe the flavour and colour of its flesh to the circumstances of its feeding on a small red shell-fish, there is much probability in the surmise as to the nourishing qualities of *Lymneus peregra.*

The fry are about 1½ inches long, and distinctly show the transverse bars characteristic of the parr. Until, in 1836, Mr. Shaw demonstrated this little fish to be the young of the salmon, it was almost universally believed to be a distinct species of fish, of little value, and therefore allowed to be killed by everybody. The Stormontfield experiments made us acquainted with some perplexing anomalies in its history. When the young salmon is a year old the transverse bars on its sides begin to be covered with those silvery scales which characterize it in the smolt stage. Until so covered it shows no desire to migrate to the sea, and dies if placed in salt water. In fifteen months those reared at Stormontfield were decided to be parr on 2nd May; and thus corroboration was given to the theory that two years elapse before salmon fry assume the smolt aspect. But by 17th May so many of the fry were seen to be smolts that the tacksmen of the Tay fisheries insisted that they should be permitted to begin migration into the sea. Their request being granted, it was found that only about half of the fry would migrate, the rest still being destitute of the silvery lamination, without which they will not proceed to sea. And this was followed by something more singular still. While one portion was still in the pond, tiny creatures of about three inches long and little more than an ounce in weight, the other portion which had proceeded to sea were returning to the river, and were being caught as beautiful grilses. That is to say, within six weeks after leaving the pond a smolt weighing a single ounce had developed into a grilse weighing at first three or four pounds, and, as the season advanced, eight or nine pounds. At two years and eight months old it has been known to become a salmon weighing fifteen pounds. After that the rate of growth has not been ascertained; but by the time it becomes thirty pounds in weight it has increased 115,200 times its original weight. A salmon caught in the Tay produced £7 10s. in the London market, and was sold in retail for £13. No creature increases so rapidly in value as a salmon, and this without cost to any one. After fattening himself at sea he insists on returning to his native river, and surmounting innumerable obstacles stupidly thrown in his way. He will infallibly find his way to where we may catch him, unless *en route* he be poisoned by river pollutions, or foully circumvented in some unreasonable way. The salmon, moreover, possesses the power of multiplying itself to such a degree that for each pound of weight the female is roughly estimated to produce a thousand ova. And, stranger still, the male, while still in the parr state, has milt so developed that at Stormontfield it was successfully employed for the impregnation of the ova of full-grown salmon.

When shall we awake to a practical perception of the fact that *aquaculture* yields harvests cheaper and more abundant than those which reward the labours of the agriculturist? He knows what it costs to rear an ox fit for the market. No fish, flesh, or fowl should be so cheap as salmon. Unless we violently interfere with them they import themselves, free of charge, for our consumption. The farmer may have a salmon river at his door, and year after year allow his servants to *leister* gravid fish, and "burn the water," and never ask whether it would be his interest to make them respect the law, and hinder this senseless slaughter of valuable fish.

When the Stormontfield experiments commenced they were spoken of disparagingly by those wiseacres who discourage all innovations. "You may rear salmon fry artificially," they said, "but there is not the millionth part of a chance that they will ever return to reward their early benefactors." The fact is, some of these people, we know, were obliged to eat in their words after having dined on Stormontfield fish, admitted so to be in consequence of their wanting the second dorsal fin, of which they were deprived on their leaving the rearing pond. The Tay fishermen have been very unwilling to aid in determining the proportionate number of the artificially reared fish captured in the river. We suggest an expedient by which every eater of a salmon may be a witness to the place of its birth.

M. Millet has shown that powdered madder mixed with the food of salmon fry colours their bones. yellowish red. Without mutilating the fish, or encumbering them with rings of silver or copper wire or gutta percha, the bones of every artificially reared fish may be made to bear a certificate of the place of its birth; and ladies and gentlemen feasting on its flesh will simultaneously exclaim, "Stormontfield!" If some one will suggest other kinds of colouring matter which can be safely used in feeding the fry of different rivers, more light will be thrown on the migratory habits of salmon. If we can thus indicate by the different colour of their bones the various rivers in which salmon have been reared, we shall no longer be dependent on reluctant and lazy fishermen for information regarding the migrations of salmon; every grilse or salmon eaten at our tables may supply us with new facts in the natural history of fish.

The piscicultural experiments at Stormontfield are most trustworthy. The only thing unsatisfactory is the limited extent to which they have been carried. An annual rearing of some five hundred thousand ova is a trifle as an addition to the number of salmon in a river like the Tay.

Turning to the proceedings of the Commissioners of Fishings in the United States, we find that they are on a scale more proportionate to the magnitude of the work in which they are engaged.

Well may the Americans be proud of their magnificent country, and look with disdain on the small size of British lakes and rivers, in comparison with their own, teeming with a vast variety of valuable fishes. The abundance of salmon of several species in the Columbia River has long excited astonishment, and made it appear extremely improbable that it would be necessary to have recourse to artificial propagation. And yet the decrease in the yield of salmon has been so marked that "the canners" have memorialised Congress to restrict the capture of the fish, and to favour artificial fish culture. The canning industry on the Columbia, though of very recent introduction, now consists of fourteen large establishments, employing nearly two thousand men, turning out twenty million pounds of canned salmon. The process of canning is thus described. A large rack, capable of holding one or two thousand salmon, being filled, the salmon are passed to the cleaning bench, where the heads, tails, fins, and entrails are removed, and the body of the fish thoroughly washed in three different waters. They are then passed on to the cutter, where revolving knives cut the fish into pieces about four inches long. Chinamen, who, it is satisfactory to know, must wash their hands every half hour, cut the fish with meat knives into pieces suitable for canning, and pack them in cans of a pound each. The next set of Chinamen solder the cans, which are then boiled, washed, labelled, packed, and removed to the wharf for shipment.

In some of these establishments the tin alone for the cans costs from fifty to a hundred thousand dollars. The canned salmon if all placed lengthways would reach upwards of five hundred miles.

That such a river as the Columbia should exhibit alarming signs of diminishing supplies of salmon is sure evidence of reckless fishing. To arrest the diminution of so valuable a fish, salmon breeding, on a great scale, has been resorted to on the McCloud River, in Shasta County, California.

Seven years ago the United States paid the Canadians forty dollars a thousand for salmon ova, but now the United States Fish Commission is sending them from California to the British colonies of the Pacific for fifty cents a thousand.

The California salmon, termed *Salmo quinnat*, differs from *Salmo salar* in its ability to endure a temperature of 80 or even 85 degrees Fahrenheit, which quickly proves fatal to *Salmo salar*. This, of course, is an immense advantage when transporting ova. But even with this it is no small exploit to have introduced them abundantly into ten of the rivers of New Zealand.

Strenuous efforts are being made to diffuse "the Shoodic" or "landlocked salmon," which abounds in the State of Maine, and of which a variety is found in numerous waters of Nova Scotia and New Brunswick. Though the idea be discredited by the Commission, this was thought to be really a landlocked sea salmon, a veritable *Salmo salar*, which, for some reason, has remained in the fresh waters instead of repairing to the sea, and by restriction in run has been reduced in size, while containing all the characteristics of its larger relative as to flesh and attractiveness to the angler. As the sea-trout is known to breed when so confined that it cannot follow its instinct of annual migration to the sea, it is probable, we think, that the true salmon may have lost its oceanward tendency, and become the "landlocked" salmon of America, and also of Lake Wenern, in Sweden, where, in 1820, were caught no less than twenty-one thousand eight hundred and seventeen salmon, which could never have been in the sea, their average weight being six or seven pounds. If by artificial feeding, and placing them within certain limits, salmon lose their migratory instinct, we shall be greatly benefited. We have them in places where we can always lay hands on them; we secure them from the attacks of otters, seals, and porpoises; we may in almost every county have lakes abundantly stocked with salmon not *anadromous*, that is, which do not visit the sea. The United States Commissioners of Fishings have the merit of having propagated so valuable a fish. The idea was not new to us. In 1865 we thus wrote: "In Scotland we have about one hundred and eighty miles of canals. Why are they fishless, when they might so easily be stocked with many valuable species of fish? Why do the Water Company, owners of the compensation pond among the Pentland Hills, not try to swell their annual dividend by the introduction

into their capacious reservoirs of the species of salmon so abundant in Lake Wenern? In order to induce a private proprietor to do what a Water Company may not have the spirit to attempt, we suggest a locality admirably suited for the experiment.

"If our readers have ever travelled by rail to Perth *viâ* Fife, they doubtless remember the little Loch of Lindores, two or three miles from Newburgh. Within half an hour's journey from the populous towns of Perth and Dundee, and distant from Edinburgh and Glasgow not more than two and four hours respectively, such a locality has every advantage for carrying out the experiment we suggest." *

It is provoking that we were not listened to, and that thus, instead of being on comfortable terms with ourselves, we are nationally humiliated because our American friends have gone far before us in fish culture. In a speech in defence of the Colonies, which ever since has rung in the ears of every boy born or bred in an American seaport town, the great British orator Burke spoke thus:—

"For some time past has the Old World been fed from the New. The scarcity which you have felt would have been a desolating famine, if this child of your old age, if America, with a true filial piety, with a human charity, had not put the full breast of its youthful exuberance to the mouth of its exhausted parent. Turning from the agricultural resources of the Colonies, consider the wealth which they have drawn from the sea by their fisheries. What in the world is equal to it?" Then follows a glowing eulogium on the energy exhibited in prosecuting the whale fishery. The Americans of to-day deserve the same admiration. Their liberality and ingenuity have not been confined to propagating salmon, but extended to food fishes generally. To new waters they have distributed 4,098,155 ova of California salmon, but 24,263,350 ova of shad have also been distributed by the United States Fish Commission. And as no species of American food fish is superior to the white-fish (*Coregonus albus*), more than twenty-six millions of its ova have been distributed. There has also been an enormous distribution of carp eggs.

Though the flesh of the sturgeon is not particularly tender, it is very nutritive, and is known as "Albany beef." The main object being the production of food for the masses, forty thousand of its ova were placed in a

* "Contributions to Natural History." By a Rural D.D. P. 77.

shad-box in the Hudson, and behold! after three days forty thousand young sturgeons were hatched.

There is another American process especially worthy of being introduced into this country, which will put an end to the deplorable loss of precious food when many tons of fish are destroyed because unfit for use. We allude to freezing fish for winter food.

To equalise the supply of fine fish, several varieties of which are superabundant in summer and scarce in winter, the fish-dealers of New York have erected three large refrigerating houses, in which many tons of frozen fish are stored. When the supply of fish in the market is likely to be in excess of the daily demand, the wholesale fish-dealers select the best and remove them from the vessels to the freezing-houses, where each fish is cleaned and prepared for the refrigerator. When frozen stiff, the fish are taken to the apartment of the special owner, and there laid away in the cold till wanted. Before September the work of refrigeration is usually at its height, and this season it was expected there would be over 250,000 lbs. of frozen fish in the storehouses of New York. The rarest fish will thus be obtainable for the rich man's table in the depth of winter ; and sheep's-head, salmon, blue-fish, Spanish mackerel, and many other kinds, only known to ordinary consumers during summer, can be supplied at rates which may be deemed cheap, considering the labour and cost of preserving the fish.

D. ESDAILE.

THE INFLUENCE OF ART IN DAILY LIFE.

By J. BEAVINGTON ATKINSON.

V.—DRESS.

"At least put off to please me this poor gown,
This silken rag, this beggar woman's weed :
I love that beauty should go beautifully :
For see ye not my gentlewoman here,
How bright, how suited to the house of one
Who loves that beauty should go beautifully."

IN previous papers the decoration of dwellings has fallen under notice, and now will be considered how far the same art principles apply to the adornment of the human body. One point of distinction may be premised, that whereas a dwelling-house is constructed by man, our fleshly tabernacles have been made by God : the body, as taught by some old writers, is a temple, though perchance in ruins. And without pursuing this idea in its consequences, it is an admitted fact that the human frame is the most beautiful form, the most perfect piece of construction and mechanism in creation. And a preliminary lesson should be, that this Divine framework deserves to be treated reverently ; a truth too often forgotten in the caprice, frivolity, and falsity of the world's fashions. And another introductory thought is, that while man is the most complete of created beings, he is the only animal not provided by nature with clothing. We all know how many have been the devices for supplying this need, and, speaking generally, it can be said that the best dress is that which accords most nearly to right reason and good taste, which conforms most closely to the conditions of nature, to the proportions and functions of the body, which enhances its perfections and adds to its beauty without hindrance to its utility. And thus in dress we at once arrived at the axioms already laid down for the decoration and furnishing of a house : utility must underlie ornament, organic form and structure must sustain and justify superincumbent draperies. Moreover, in dress, as in other surface decorations, the bodily construction must be confessed and pronounced ; the design or pattern in scale and line of composition must be in proportion, balance, and symmetry, preserving in the midst of the details breadth and simplicity. In fine, in dress and draperies, nature and art alike teach that grace flows out of law and order, and that beauty finds alone its safe foundation in truth.

The philosophy of fashion may be briefly stated. Fixity, as in the Quakers' costume, is false to nature, and is neither feasible nor desirable ; the mind loves variety, and a monotonous sameness palls on the senses. Finality is found nowhere in creation ; in the animal and vegetable kingdom alike rudimentary beginnings develop into perfected forms ; and so also, notwithstanding disturbing retrogressions, a progress from savage to civilised times is established, by a kind of Darwinian selection, even in dress. And an interesting and not unlooked-for analogy may be pointed out between architecture and the art of dressing, between the structures raised for man's dwelling and the costumes contrived for his clothing. Each art arose equally out of necessity; man coming into the world drapeless and houseless, the readiest expedients were at first resorted to, but little by little appliances grew, till plain utility gave place to ornament and beauty. The house was decorated with a carved or painted frieze, and at the same time bodily garments received the ornament of a border or fringe. Moreover, the house, as it became homish, was furnished and draped; and so, as by natural evolution, the draperies on the walls and the dressings on the backs of the inmates grew in agreement. Thus it may be more easy to understand how, when at length the world had developed into "an art epoch," the house, palace, temple, and church, the internal fittings, the decorations, furniture, draperies, and paintings, and lastly, yet not least, the dress of the living tenants, were found one and all for better or for worse in absolute accord. Hence costume becomes of grave significance, and, therefore, do historians, historians, and ethnologists study dress as an index to civilisation and as part of the physiognomy of races. And the costume of society, as we have seen, is subject to fashion. Yet fashion, writes an accomplished critic in the *Quarterly Review*, to whom the present writer acknowledges indebtedness, has laws and boundaries of her own, deep-seated in the nature of things; she always preserves certain balances and proportions, thus "when the farthingales were large the ruffs were enormous, when the waists were short the foreheads were low, when the sleeves were wide the coiffures were wide also, and, moreover, when the sleeves were tight the heads were small," and so on. "Of course, in the time of transition, when a struggle is taking place between the plumage that is casting off and that which is coming on, some apparent confusion may occur, as all birds are shabby in their moulting season." The once single-minded sect called "the Friends" would seem to be now passing through the "moulting season:" in dress they are divided between the Church and the world. "But the worst discrepancies are occasioned by the class of foolish women, who have not the sense to be off with the old love before they are on with the new, and try to combine the old chrysalis with the new wings."

Persons there are of finer instincts who

still look to the possibility of costumes which shall be artistic and beautiful, and at the same time utilitarian. And painters often show the way by eschewing or evading prevailing fashions, which in their singularity will surely appear monstrous in the eyes of posterity. Sir Joshua Reynolds and other great portrait painters had a mode of generalising costume, which thus served as a kind of everlasting drapery, suited more especially to those mortals who pose themselves for posthumous fame. And Mr. Watts, R.A., in an eloquent paper to a contemporary, throws out ideas which serve to correct prevailing errors. He deplores, "as one of the most striking points of difference between ancient or mediæval and modern life," the present want of "the untiring interest, the pains, the love bestowed formerly upon the perfecting and decorating of almost all the objects of daily use, even when the service required was most material." And, coming to the ordinary modes of attire, he complains that "the human form, the noblest and most interesting study for the artist, is distorted in the case of men's dress by the most monstrous garments, and in the case of women's dress by extravagant arrangements, which mar simple nobility and impede refined grace of movement." And then he urges, that in our public schools the sense of beauty should receive such cultivation that "the educated gentleman would no longer encourage by admiration the vagaries of female fashion." "The eye must appreciate noble form and beautiful colour before the jar consequent on the sight of ugliness is felt, which feeling would, as a rule, prevent its existence. In modern life the cultivation of the eye is sacrificed to all kinds of meaner considerations." The materials out of which paintings are composed, the picturesqueness of costume, the unbought grace of life, no longer exist in society, and hence "daily and social life loses with its former ceremonies almost all dignity and grace, and so art of the highest kind is deprived of its very breath, and must die." "It must be remembered that the artist, no less than the poet, should speak the language of his time; but if the visible language by which alone the artist can make his thoughts intelligible is out of tune with beauty, the painter is forced to invent his language." The sense of beauty is passing away as a natural possession, refinement of taste gives place to habits of mind accounted more robust and healthy, and the ways of relaxation and pleasure are so unlovely and gross that a beauty-

loving art no longer ventures to reflect outward life or the manners and costumes of
either the higher or the lower classes. Hence
the artist in his utterance "is obliged to
return to the extinct forms of speech, if he
would speak as the great ones have spoken."
Dress is itself a language; it tells of the
mental state of the wearer; in all times it
has been the visible sign of the actual civilisation. The artist in our day surely has a
crying grievance; he cannot find in town or
country a man or woman in a condition fit
to be put on canvas or in marble. People,
in wearing an ugly dress, do injustice to
themselves and an injury to others. Let the
question be asked how they will look in a
picture; let them try in their own persons to
be a picture.

A few examples may be given of scenes at
home and abroad rendered wholly unpaint-
able by reason of the absence of beauty of character and personality in costume. A dinner
of the staff of writers on a leading journal
takes place on the banks of the Thames, the
guests number somewhat short of a hundred,
and among the company are men of state,
clergymen, lawyers, doctors of medicine, all
picked men, ample in development of brain,
and marked in intellectual countenance; and
yet the dinner-table could not have been
painted, there was nothing artistic to invite
the eye or the pencil; not only was there no
colour, but all lines of composition were
absent; the most that could be said in favour
of the coats was that they were easy to the
wearers, but instead of expanding at the
chest amply they were contracted by a button,
while the neck was throttled; the hands,
which, for literary men especially, are delicate
and skilled instruments, were negligent; and
the heads, the organs of thought, looked supremely indifferent to the impression made on
the spectator. All this may be very much as it
should be, except for the purposes of a picture.
Titian would have turned away in despair,
and Veronese might have left the banks of
the Thames for the shores of the Adriatic.
How vastly more scenic were the tables at
which Ben Jonson, Shakespeare, Goldsmith,
and Sheridan sat! A few weeks later the
writer happened to be present at an evening
gathering of German artists, their wives,
daughters, and friends at the "Malkasten"
or "Paintbox" Club, most pleasantly located
in the famous Jacoby Gardens, Düsseldorf.
Here, at any rate, something pictorial might
have been looked for, but the idea seemed to
be to drop "the shop;" the figures that walked
the bowery paths beside the babbling brooks

had not assuredly stepped out from pictures,
and certainly the artists ran no risk of being
mistaken for their models. The men, as in
England, appeared to shun the suspicion of
taste or sentiment; they affected deshabille,
and rejoiced in negligent disorder; in their
favour it may be said that they looked as if
they never gave a thought to what they put
on; and yet when the music sounded the
dirty browns of wide-awake hats struck dis-
cordantly against the pure sky of starlight.
An incongruity no less harsh marred a religious procession along the banks of the
Rhine at Stolzenfels: the country lasses were
clad as Manchester factory girls. The scene
changes next to Cologne Cathedral, at high
mass, Sunday morning. The music sounds
divinely, the choir of the church rises as a
canopy of colour, illuminated by frescoes
and tapestries, and jewelled with painted
glass; but the heavenly pageant was brought
down to the grossness of earth by a motley
crowd "black as Erebus." The dress, of
course, had no pretence to Christian grace or
comeliness, and scarcely did it affect Vanity
Fair. The same evening the waters of the
Rhine shone as opal in the mingled light or
sunset and moonrise, and on the bridge of
boats which crosses the river passed in black
shadow the moving panorama of the city population, a sight abhorrent to artistic eye. The
picture was absolutely colourless, and even
as to light and shade, the figures cut as dark
silhouettes against the sky and background.
Costumes, though pictorial, are costly, and
the lower orders make a willing sacrifice of
taste in the cause of utility, convenience, and
economy; and yet what could be less costly
or more comely than wreaths of the oak, the
vine, and the wild convolvulus, as twined by
Rhine peasants round their heads? But in
England and on the Continent, for the most
part, the phases are alike; the lack of money
and education induce cheap show, flash tinsel,
and common imitations machine-made. As
for the men it is well when they care to be
just clean and tidy; and as for the women,
they do wisely in putting decently upon their
shoulders the warm and comfortable fabrics of
modern manufacture; and then as to the girls,
who naturally desire to please and make an
impression, we must try to excuse the tawdri-
ness and vanity, not to say vulgarity, of untutored youth. The fact is that from an
artistic point of view the state of things is as
bad as it well can be, and might seem all but
hopeless. There is no desire to mend it;
there is no consciousness of doing wrong.
The unspoilt peasant, nature's nobility, will

become extinct like the dodo, and artists already are driven to seek costume and native charm among the beauty and grandeur of mountains and valleys inaccessible to civilisation.

Fashions have wandered so widely from essential truths that it may not be unsalutary to revert to some of the fundamental principles to which dress should conform. On the utilitarian side of the question are the proportions of the human figure, health, sex, age, height, size, climate, season of the year, economy, ease, convenience, and decorum. And out of these actual conditions grow the more expressly art elements of beauty of form and harmony of colour. As to the human figure, we unhappily all know in how many ways dress has marred and mutilated its proportions, and at the same time equal outrage has been committed on sanitary laws. Dr. Richardson delivered a lecture on dress with the purpose of showing what reforms are required in the interests of health, and some of his incidental remarks may be here fitly quoted. He appropriately premised that the character of dress stands in such close relations to the character of the person who wears it that it is hard to touch on the one without introducing the other. All kinds of sympathies are evoked by dress; political sympathies are on the most intimate relationship with it, social sympathies are indexed by it, artistic sympathies are a part of it. The lecturer did not deprecate good fashion in dress; on the contrary, he deemed it the duty of every one to cultivate good fashion, and he thought that every woman ought to make herself as becomingly beautiful as she possibly could. Good health and good fashion would always go well together. The errors of fashion in dress arise, as a rule, from the fact that the fashions are dictated and carried out by vain and ignorant persons neither skilled in art nor in the rules of health. What is wanted in the reform of dress is good fashion for both sexes in social intercourse and in every-day life. The lecturer denounced corsets, waistbands, garters, and tight shoes. The dress should be loose, and the weight of it borne by the shoulders. The argument broke down only when the doctor came to the specification of the precise reforms required. "Let the mothers of England," he said, "clothe the girls precisely as they clothe the boys, permitting knickerbockers if they like, but let them add the one distinguishing mark of a light, loose, flowing gown, and the girls will grow into women as vigorous, as healthy, and as well-formed in body as their companions of the sterner sex." But "knickerbockers" for girls surely savours full much of the "Bloomer costume," which years ago was deservedly hooted out of London by the boys in the streets.

As to a distinctive dress for the two sexes, there can be no question as to its propriety and desirableness. We find that when nature clothes with her own hand the nobler animals, she puts some indicative marks upon the sexes. The flowing mane of the lion, the branching antlers of the stag, the bright head gear and wing trappings of many birds, distinguish with intention the male from the female. To merge the traits of sex in costume, as at present attempted, is contrary to the order of creation, to the true instincts of the human mind, and to the practice of all peoples. It is not needful to enlarge; suffice it to add that modesty planted by nature in the heart makes her presence known specially in decorous attire. Let man's dress be manly, and woman's dress womanly.

Conditions of age, good looks or otherwise, demand self-knowledge and discriminating tact and taste. The time comes when angles take the place of curves, and what shows beauty to advantage may not prove the best foil to its contrary. Certainly "a costume expressly adapted for the display of natural charms is hard upon those who never had any to begin with, or who have parted company with them some time ago." "And if all ages are to dance to one tune, it should be a minuet and not a jig; and if there is to be but one standard of garb, we are bound in duty to consider the grandmother first." A lady wise in her generation should decide unmistakably what are her points and paces, and dress accordingly; but instead of cautiously meeting the urgency of the case, she usually acts on the pleasing but hazardous assumption that she is sister of the Graces. One art is appropriate to a Venus, another to a Dutch-built craft; and most will have occasion sometimes to call in aid the art which conceals art or veils nature when not at her best. The present fashion of dressing close to the figure is unwise, to say the least of it; ladies may be seen every day on railway platforms in garbs which almost defy motion, struggling forward to catch a train, and displaying outlines, modellings, and movements the reverse of graceful and lovely. And like mistakes are made by men also: this season might be seen in the Düsseldorf Exhibition a gentleman who dressed in the fond belief that he combined in his own person Apollo and Hercules, and on fine afternoons he showed off his figure accordingly to the satisfaction of himself and his admirers. But others not so highly favoured by nature are prudent to call to their assistance subterfuges and disguises. Colour is often a crucial trial with both sexes, and when the hair passes from auburn into pronounced red, the problem to be solved becomes delicate and difficult. One expedient is to thrust into the midst of the hair a red camellia or a full-blown poppy; and thus the obnoxious colour may be reduced to comparative innocence and neutrality. Other foils will suggest themselves; sometimes ladies have to contend against uncomely complexions; and two sisters, whose hair and skin were suggestive of curry-powder or brick-dust, hit upon the daring device of dressing in hot hues of mustard and cayenne pepper; the combination was fiery and alarming, threatening spectators with ophthalmia. Nature, when she has only beauty to deal with, makes the converse arrangement; the old and new red sandstone formations are draped with green verdure, and in like manner the flower of the red geranium is thrown up by green, its complementary colour. Of course, in dealing with the face and figure, each case will have to be treated according to personal exigencies.

And scarcely of less import than sex and age are the height, size, and general proportions of the figure. Tall and stumpy people cannot with impunity be dressed in one pattern, the stately lady sweeping through marble halls can gracefully carry queenly robes that would crush the pretty little lady dwelling in a cottage. The present inclination is to treat dress as drapery, and to consider the one as simply utilitarian, and the other, as if of necessity, supremely artistic. The points of the figure are used as pegs whereon to hang out decorative fabrics, and possibly Sartor Resartus might stigmatize our living ladies as lay figures, and our intelligent men as stalking clothes-horses. Some dresses are for sitting or standing only, some for walking, while others reduce the free action of the figure to physical endurance. A lady making a morning call was asked to take a seat, but she begged to be excused because having on "a walking costume" she could not sit down. Yet nature in building up the human framework had a more extended scheme, which fashion would do well not so relentlessly to thwart. As to the length of a dress, that will much depend on whether the feet are of a beauty deemed to be worth displaying; if inviting to cast a glimpse on, they will probably be permitted "like little mice to peep in and out," hence some ladies wear "gowns always short when other people's are long, and go about holding them up above the highest water-mark in fine weather." The shoulders, which call for at least as much anxious care as the feet, admit of varied decorations, as with scarf, shawl, mantilla, veil, robe, toga. "A black scarf carries an air of respect, which is in itself protection. A woman thus attired glides on her way like a small close-reefed vessel, light and trim, seeking no encounter but prepared for one. Much, however, depends on the wearer; indeed, no article of dress is such a revealer of the character. Some women will drag it tight up to their shoulders, and stick out their elbows in defiance beneath. Such are of the independent class with strong opinions. Others let it hang loose and listless like an idle sail, losing all the beauty of the outline—both moral and physical. Such ladies have usually no opinions at all, but none the less a very obstinate will of their own." A real lady hits by intuition the happy mean; she does not "put on a turban to drink tea with two people, or an innocent white frock for a party of two hundred;" she does not appear as a milliner popped out of a band-box, or as an artist just stepped from a picture, or as an antiquary kept usually as a curiosity under a glass case; she moves at respectful distance from the extremes of fashion, and though society does not "know what she has on," she is not in danger of being mistaken for either Aspasia or Queen Anne. What she wears, though perchance homely, is always good; not a scrap of tinsel or trumpery appears upon her; "she deals in no gaudy confusion of colours, nor does she affect a studied sobriety; but she either refreshes you with a spirited contrast, or composes you with a judicious harmony." And the secret of her success simply consists in her "knowing the three grand unities of dress—her own station, her own age, and her own points. And no woman can dress well who does not."

Of all the unities in dress, that of colour is the most imperative; and the whole question involves such difficulties and nice distinctions that another occasion must be sought for their solution. Often the colour of the hair, of the eyes, and the complexion will strike the keynote for the dress, especially that of the head, neck, and shoulders. A blonde and brunette obviously call for diverse dispositions. And then, again, conflicts arise between bright positive colours and broken neutral hues; each system has its attendant advantages and disadvantages. A shimmering silk has been likened to a sunny shoaling sea of lovely blue playing into green, spangled with drops of dew. And minds sensitive to half shades and shadows find a fanciful suggestiveness in such transitional and gliding notes, for as "songs without words," so are colours without names. Other tastes take a more sensational turn; and of late a despairing rush has been made at the colours of the rainbow, and little girls may now be seen skipping along red as lobsters, prawns, and pillar letter-boxes. Such alarming garments might serve, like the scarlet cloaks of the old women on the Welsh coast, to frighten away the enemy. Yet unity, however violent, is at least saved from discord, and one note oft repeated seldom fails of attention. Sometimes sisters come to a family agreement as to colour; three perhaps dressing in blue and two in pink; and when all five are seated in their drawing-room of blue and gold, the effect is cheerful yet not irritating. In the Dresden Gallery the eye is caught by a modern picture of three sisters, the daughters of a townsman, all dressed in pink; and as if the artist had not enough of the one colour, he has added to the figures a pink background. When sisters sing a duet or trio, it is a common-place remark, "how charmingly the voices of sisters blend in harmony;" and evidently a like thought led the Dresden artist to play on one key of colour, not caring to accentuate a climax, but content with the repose of a dying cadence. A kindred arrangement, which at any rate has the recommendation of ease and safety, was recently carried out successfully in a large choir at a German festival. Five hundred girls all wore varying tones of blue and turquoise greens, passing into bluish whites as the high lights. Under such a disposition, of course, the harmonies could hardly be broken by discords, and the collective pictorial effect was comparable to a bank of spring or summer flowers, the faces of pearl and rose with the brown and the gold of the hair rising in brilliant relief, as from calyxes or leaves of shadowy green. When the choruses of Mendelssohn's *St. Paul* sounded, fancy might recall the singers and minstrels placed by the Italian painters in the upper sky—so great is the glory of colour and sound in unison.

The revolutions in dress within modern times, which avowedly are momentous, have in some measure corresponded to the changes from hand labour to steam-power, and from stage-coach travelling to railway transit. Man, as the bread-winner, is like a wheel or axle, part of the general social machinery, and in dress shows himself as perfect a piece of unadorned utility as a steam-engine. Yet some of the attendant consequences are not inartistic. Manufacturing firms find the use and the profit of beauty, and in matters of dress they improve fashion by producing at reasonable cost good designs, often adaptations from antique work; and thus, as in cheap literature by means of printing, the best ideas of our ancestors are brought into the possession of the multitude. And the higher classes, who can indulge in costly tastes, have the choice of rich materials, which fall into graceful folds and clothe the figure in lines and masses that compose harmoniously as drapery posed for a sculptor. Never, perhaps, has there been better opportunity for dressing artistically than at the present moment, whether as to quality of material, beauty of design, or variety of colour; and many ladies cultivate the commendable habit of drawing and composing their own costumes, and thus personal guarantee is given that the dress they wear reflects their characters and expresses their ideas of the true, the beautiful, and the good. For the labouring and lower classes the actual state of things is scarcely so favourable. The honest endeavour to make in expenditure the two ends meet, is combined with the ambition to be smart and to dress as the upper classes; and thus recourse is had to cheap and flimsy materials, to base imitations and gaudy colours. And such flash displays are the more to be regretted, because the once quiet and respectable appearance of the lower and middle classes is fast becoming a thing of the past. And in very deed the motley crowds in the streets of our great cities on Bank and other holidays present a melancholy spectacle. And the outward demonstrations are censurable because, with the same or less outlay, by the choice of forms and colours in simple unobtrusive harmony, the peoples of our towns and country might make an appearance befitting allegiance to the laws of nature and of God. On all sides and in all conditions of life do we see abundant signs of how, with taste, it is easy to keep right, while without taste to go wrong is certain.

It were almost impossible to make too much of the reforms which in recent years have arisen from the practice among artists of designing fashions for themselves. And amateurs there are so thoroughgoing that, holding in contempt the anachronisms of former days, which permitted the placing of a classic portico before a Gothic structure, begin at the very beginning by building a house in some approved English style, and then proceed to decorate and furnish the rooms in accord, and as a finishing stroke dress the household to the same pattern. And the question now asked is, not whether a gown will wear and wash, but whether it will paint. All this is much as it should be, and, indeed, always has been, in the best and truest art periods, for dress is but part of a greater whole—a means and a medium whereby man and woman are brought into harmony with the surroundings of life and of nature. Yet it may be feared that matters are being pushed rather far; there has grown up what may be called "pre-Raphaelitism in dress"—a mediævalism which, transmuting forms and colours alike, eschews classic and renaissance harmonies, and affects Gothic angles and scrags. And when the figure happens to be bony or a little ancient the effect is a sight indeed, yet by securing notoriety it may serve to save the wearer from oblivion. In contrast are a few who recline gracefully in long sinuous robes and pose themselves statuesquely. In other cases, draperies having taken the place of dress, they are pitchforked on the back anyhow, and the figure is reduced to a mass of material. At other times, the wish to bring the whole household into harmony induces a lady to appear in the pattern of a wall paper, or to match her dress with the cups and saucers on the tea-table. Others, again, of a more dissipated turn, make a random dash at harlequins, and cut up their persons into patches, each apart to be admired and wondered at for wealth of material. The Bohemian lives of some artists—seldom in the first rank—naturally pass from manners to costumes; "tall talk" finds its replica in "loud dress," and wishing good-bye to the "senatorial dignity" applauded by Reynolds in the portraits by Titian, such circles in a free-and-easy way fall into sloppy, negligent attire—the garb of genius, doubtless, especially when in a garret! The bandits in the landscapes of Salvator Rosa are of the same company. The general impression produced by such æsthetic phases of life is that of a perpetual picnic, or of a continuous fancy ball, or of a ubiquitous sketching party. It is a pity pre-Raphaelites and others cannot take as models for dress the saints as they appear in early Italian pictures.

A gentleman said to a friend, "I like to dress as if I were going to have my portrait painted, or as if I were about to meet the lady who might be my wife." And the requirements of distinguished portrait-painters, such as Holbein, Vandyke, and Reynolds, are no bad criterions of the costumes most becoming. The great artists select, and then improve on, what is best and therefore most enduring in the dress of the period, and by affixing their sign-manual establish patterns and precedents good for all time; while inferior limners, such as Lely and Kneller, pandering to vanity, paint what passes away. Holbein seems to have held that "fifty years and upwards was the only sensible time of a woman's life, and those who had the misfortune to be younger must make the best of it." With Vandyke came in "the airy, ringlety style of coiffure; it did well for faces like trim little villas, which may be overgrown with creepers or overhung with willows; but fine features, like fine mansions, want space around them, and least of all can the smooth expanse of the forehead be spared." The next epoch is adorned by Reynolds, who, "like Holbein and Vandyke, put his stamp upon the times, or, rather, as a true artist and philosopher, took the aggregate impression which the times gave;" and "for the most part we go through a gallery of his portraits with feelings of intense satisfaction that there should have been a race of women who could dress so decorously, so intellectually, and, withal, so becomingly." But one fallacy in dressing in every-day life as for a portrait, is that a lady cannot always command the same curtains and tapestries as a background; and thus, when she next graces an evening assembly, the pink of her perfection may prove wholly out of place.

There is no surer sign of birth and breeding than in the form, movement, and keeping of the hands, and as in life so in art, here is the test of taste and skill. The hands, of course, as the head, need a set-off, and the wrists invite, like the neck, to ornament, such as cuffs or bracelets. Specially demanded is freedom for the turn of wrist, the play of the fingers, and the action of the forearm. The hand is an instrument of expression, and it should be made to speak. The hand must use the same language as the head; the two are in mutual accord and co-operation, and the accessories of dress should but enhance nature's gifts of intellect and beauty.

So dress has to carry out the general design of nature : of character, nature sketches the outline ; it is for art to complete the picture. Beauty of form, concord in composition, harmony in colour, constitute the perfect painting, and a figure will be faultless in draping when brought into like agreement.

Nature loves law and order, lays her foundation in simplicity, and builds in beauty. So dress has to accord with the wa,ss and works of nature, for " behold the lilies of the field how they grow ; they toil not, neither do they spin, and yet Solomon in all his glory was not arrayed as one of these."

LUCREZIA.

By Mrs. COMYNS CARR.

PART II.

THE warm morning sun had grown quite too hot now that it was afternoon ; the sky was white with a dazzling glare, instead of being blue, as it was three hours ago, and the dust rose in clouds around the carriages as they rolled slowly past. Lucrezia wandered up and down awhile upon the pavement where ladies and gentlemen were walking. She had nowhere to go, and she was listless. The gay costumes amused her for a bit, but even these lost their interest when there was no one by with whom to comment upon them. And then—ah, that was worst of all—she fancied that folks stared at sight of a *contadina* in *festa* dress walking unattended. They

pitied her—that was horrible ! She soon left the crowd and went down on to the strip of shingle below, where the lake's waters were lapping idly. She felt that she had punished herself in sending Paolo away ; but Paolo should not have gone. Paolo should have understood that she had no real business at Stresa, but only wanted to make the sport last a little longer for them both. Paolo should not have thought of the new boat when she was by. He should have remembered that a pretty girl is ashamed to be seen without a gallant when she is out for a walk. She could not tell all the folk that she had a betrothed, that she was really going to be married, though she looked so young. And how could they guess it when she wandered about alone?

Lucrezia began to forget that it was she who had dismissed Paolo, and not he who was inconsiderate. She said to herself that perhaps, even now, while she sat alone, he was drinking with comrades in Baveno!

Luckless Paolo, travelling along the white road, with scarce a nod to merry companions, who, at any other time, could easily have pressed him into their ranks, counting the quarters on the harsh village clock, till it was time to return to Lucrezia —that was how he was being judged meanwhile!

Lucrezia sat upon the shingle. Her shoes were off, and she dabbled her feet in the cool waters of the lake. A pout was on her pretty mouth—she was still thinking of her grievance. Thus it was that she failed to hear some one descend the steps close beside her from the promenade. The voice of the strange gentleman whom she had seen at the wedding startled her from her dream. She rose up confused, and remembered that she had taken off her shoes. She was not ashamed of her bare feet—she always went bare-foot at home, but since she did possess these marks of civilisation, it was a mortification to her that in the presence of such a fine gentleman—a gentleman with white hands and a cigar in his mouth—she should be discovered casting, as it were, the appendages of gentility from her.

"Excuse me," said the intruder graciously, holding out a golden ear-ring : "you dropped this on the piazza. I lost sight of you at first, but I am glad to have the opportunity of restoring it."

It was not true that the Count had lost sight of the girl : he had waited till Paolo left her. Lucrezia took the trinket and put it back in her ear. The idea of having nearly lost it was foremost in her mind at present, and filled her with horror.

"A thousand thanks," she said shyly. "What should I have done if I had not recovered it? And I never even perceived the loss!"

"It seems you have been well occupied! Was it that young man who was with you, and has left you here alone, who gave you that gold?"

Lucrezia felt the sting.

"He has work to do, and so have I," said she, mortified. "We are poor folk, we cannot always amuse ourselves like the gentry."

XXI—55

"When one takes a pretty girl out for a holiday, one should have no work to do," answered the Count. "But perhaps I mistake, and he is your brother!"

"Oh, no!" exclaimed Lucrezia, smiling readily enough this time. "We are betrothed, to be sure; we marry in Carnival."

She was flattered at the admiration of a gentleman, but she was proud also to be able to tell him that she had a betrothed.

After that there was a pause, for Lucrezia scarcely knew what to say to this new acquaintance who had suddenly descended from the sphere of her dreams to talk commonplace familiarities with her. Ever since the day when the aunt told her that a sculptor had admired her, Lucrezia had longed to be looked at again by a signore, but now that the moment had come, she was not sure that she liked it. She stooped down to pick up her shoes, and would have gone away had she not feared that it would be rude to a "man of quality." Presently, taking the cigar from between his lips, the "man of quality" began again.

"Thou art young to be married, child," said he.

Lucrezia noticed, with distrust, that he had dropped into the use of the familiar pronoun.

"Yes," replied she gravely. "I am only seventeen ; but Paolo is a good man, and I have no dowry."

"And it is prudent to take the first man who offers, since thou hast no dowry, eh?"

"A girl must marry," murmured Lucrezia, "and it is a bad thing for a woman to be poor."

"That is bad for all," laughed the Count.

And then he paused, and smoked, and looked at her.

"Foolish wench!" he said at last. "Dost thou not know that thy face is thy dowry? What will such a lover give thee in exchange for it? Will he give thee rings and gold, and silk gowns, such as the bride wore just now?"

Did he guess that she had envied that silk gown, thought the guilty conscience? But she answered demurely—

"He will not give me silk gowns, because I am a *contadina*, but he will give me an honest heart and a good name."

"Thou lovest him?"

"Yes, as one should love one's husband!"

"Perhaps thou dost well then; though I do not think thou wouldst need to remain a peasant all thy life if thou didst but wait awhile."

Was it possible she could ever have the

chance of marrying a gentleman? To be sure, she was like a lady. She sighed, but she murmured again—

"Paolo is a good man."

"Does he tell thee that thou art not like a *contadina*?" continued the Count, who had heard something in the village that day of Lucrezia's story, as well as of her little vanities, and knew well enough where to place the magnet. "Does he tell thee that thou hast a face as fine, and a presence as fair, as the Madonna's in church?"

"Oh, no!" smiled she.

Even her own vanity had scarcely aimed at refinement so great as that, and certainly the Count's words were very different from the rough sort of compliments paid by Paolo; who, moreover, always steadily denied her claims to a delicate appearance, and was even annoyed when she was proud of it. Remembering this peculiarity of Paolo's, she somehow began to wish more and more that the Count would go and that Paolo would come back. But Paolo had not been gone nearly an hour, and strangely enough the Count showed no inclination of finishing his cigar anywhere else but on the smooth shingle at her feet.

"So," he continued at his leisure, "thou wilt marry him, and labour all thy life, and grow old before thy time, and he does not even know thou art pretty! It is hard on thee, child! Though I'll wager thou hast seen that face in the mirror till thou dost not require me to tell thee it is fair! And thou canst blush too! Thou dost well, it becomes thee!"

The red flushed redder than ever in Lucrezia's pale cheek; but it was neither with pride nor coyness—she was angry. Paolo—that useless and aggravating Paolo—why had he left her thus unprotected? It would serve him right to see her now. As she thought of her anger, she almost smiled again in the midst of her annoyance, and was tempted to put him to the trial! The spirit of mischief was in Lucrezia. The Count sat languidly watching her till he had finished his cigar. The changing emotions on her sensitive face were amusing to watch. Then as she smiled again, planning her little revenge on Paolo, and almost forgetting the presence of this other admirer, he rose, and throwing away the end of his cigar, said quietly—

"Thou wouldst make a better picture with a smile than with a frown. What is thy name, child, and where dost thou live?"

At the sound of his voice the smile vanished, the blush crept up again in its stead. Lucrezia was sure that she did not like the Count now; but it did not strike her at the moment that to tell him where she lived was not only inviting a visit, but also encouraging his familiarity. To tell him seemed at first sight only the natural reply to a question. So she said moodily—

"They call me Lucrezia, and I live over the water at Santa Caterina."

"I will come and see thee, and bring thee better ear-rings than those thou hast."

The words roused her; there was something amiss.

"The gold which my lover gives me is good enough for me," said she, moving away.

"Well, well, we will say no more of trinkets then," added the Count, following her; "but when I come to see thee over the water at Santa Caterina——"

Lucrezia interrupted him, almost crossly. She saw now what she had done, and must remedy the evil.

"There is no Santa Caterina over the water," she blurted out.

The Count laughed.

"But what if I know the village well?" said he.

"The poor cottage of the uncle is not fit for gentlefolks," pleaded the girl, beginning to be thoroughly frightened.

"Never mind; I like a poor cottage when there is a pretty wench in it."

Lucrezia turned round—her whole little white face trembling.

"Ah, no, signore, you will not come to Santa Caterina after a poor girl like me!" she said. "What will the aunt say, and the villagers—and Paolo?"

"Paolo!—ah, I can't think what Paolo would say," smiled the Count. "We will ask him! Come, come, child—do not be frightened; I will not harm thee."

"It is my hour for confession," faltered she hurriedly. "I will wish your honour the good day."

"Ah, the little madonna is a white liar, but she is a good Catholic!" laughed he once more. "Well, well, that is very pretty." And as Lucrezia made her little salute and advanced hurriedly towards the steps, he added, "We shall meet again—at Santa Caterina, over the water! Good-bye, child."

And then he stood looking after her, and making everybody else look after her, while she ran across the road and up the hill, and into the church. What a shameless man he was! Paolo had been right when he had scoffed at him on the piazza; and he was one of those who laughed at confession, and the priests too! She had been told there were such men, but she had not believed it. Indeed, she had been a foolish girl to be flattered by the admiration of such an one only because he was a gentleman, and had made her fancy she looked something like a lady, when Paolo was a hundred times handsomer, and even better mannered, in spite of his fisherman's dress.

Lucrezia was ashamed of herself; but she told herself that if she had known the gentleman was a bad Catholic, she would not even have listened to him so long. And thereupon she knelt down on the damp flag-stones without the altar rails, and, with intent of invoking the Madonna and her own patron-saint for their pardon, began telling her beads diligently—though, alas! the remembrance of how the Count had said she was like no child of peasant origin kept recurring to her mind with a strange persistency. And as she prayed she vowed she would never have any-thing to say to a signore again, though she would confront Paolo with this incontestable tribute to her gentility of appearance when-ever he was inclined to be proud or perverse.

When her prayer was ended, Lucrezia sat up on the oaken bench dreaming of ladies and brides, and silk dresses and gold orna-ments, till afternoon shadows began to lengthen, and afternoon lights to fall more and more dimly through the high windows of the church, making strange patterns on the old Venetian pavement. She began to be dull at last, and to wonder peevishly why Paolo did not come. She forgot that Paolo had no means of guessing where she was. When she remembered it, she lifted up her hands in silent ejaculation—scolding herself for her own stupidity; but as she ran down the steps again, and approached that place on the shore where they were to have met, she forgot her own fault in the matter, smiling at the thought of that "poor man wan-dering anxiously up and down in expecta-tion!" She said to herself, with satisfaction, that he would indeed be glad to see her, but she was not prepared for the fact that, though Paolo had been on the promenade several times since she had left it, he was not there now, seeing that he had grown weary at her absence, and had gone to the cousin Madda-lena's, and to several other places that she frequented, to look for her. Lucrezia forgot all these possibilities. She was cross at not finding Paolo and, as was usual with her, did not pause to reflect. He had forgotten her; he was drinking at Baveno; he was late; she

had waited five minutes, and he had not come! She tossed her head angrily with the impatient motion that poor Paolo knew so well, and walked quickly along the road. "If this is the way he treats me," she said angrily to herself, "I will get some one else to row me home!"

Where the water washed into a little lip of land, at a bend of the road, an old fisherman whom Lucrezia knew was making ready his nets. The slanting rays of the afternoon sun lay across the lake. The clear green water swayed gently about the old brown boat, a yellow sail rested on its bows ready for use, and more sails, some brown and some brightest orange, stood against the pale sky or against the green background of wooded shores. Behind the fisher's head the trim terraces of Isola Bella rose one above another, with a middle dis-tance of bright water between, and the broken mass of Isola de Pescatori's half-ruined build-ings beyond. It was a peaceful scene, but Lucrezia felt no peace in her heart; it beat with the excitement of many emotions. She looked along the white road that wound round the water's edge, at the foot of hills and in front of houses and churches and villas and gardens. Sometimes a bend in its own length or the overhanging boughs of walnut and chestnut woods hid a piece of it from her sight, but Paolo did not appear from any of the hidden places any more than he was to be seen on the open road. Boats dipped up and down on the lake, that a little breeze was ruffling; some were fishing-smacks pulled by weather-beaten boatmen; some were pleasure-boats rowed by handsome fellows in bright striped shirts, but Paolo was not in any of them. And the sun would be setting in a short hour, for waiting and watch-ing and talking had used the whole day. There was no good in loitering longer. Paolo must be treated as he deserved.

"Good evening, Gian-Battista," said Lu-crezia, as soon as she got within ear-shot of the fisherman. "Since you are putting out will you row me across to Santa Caterina, for I have missed him with whom I should have returned, and I am late?"

"Willingly, my pretty one," replied the old man. "Though it is but sorry work for a comely lass to be driven to ask such a thing! What is thy gallant about?"

"He had business in Baveno," said Lu-crezia curtly, "and we have missed one another."

The old man scratched his head. "Well, now," said he, "most men don't have business when they take a pretty wench out for a holi-

think you can make me angry," laughed she. "You cannot do it, I tell you!" Her cheeks a-blaze belied the words.

Gian-Battista replied with a grin. "Maybe you sent him about his business yourself for a bit." He chuckled, and Lucrezia flushed up more angrily than ever. Had he seen her talking to the Count? Well, and if he had, she was not going to deny it. She had not sought the interview, and was not ashamed.

"I tell you Paolo had affairs to see to," she retorted sharply.

"Yes, yes, and it's poor sport waiting alone for a lover," said the old man, nodding his head.

But Lucrezia stepped quickly into the boat. "Come, have done with your nonsense!" said she. "If your tackle is ready

day. Paolo Ferrari has worse manners than I gave him credit for."

"No worse than most of you, I'll wager!"

you must need to be out as much as I need to be home. Let us go!" She sat down, and Gian-Battista put his nets together.

"You're a foolish wench if you gave Ferrari such a long while to himself," said he, "for he may have found some bonnier fisher-wench down Pallanza way on such a fine day as this! Well, well, perhaps he is not much of a loss, and maybe you think now you can do better for yourself, seeing you're so fond of finery." He jumped out on to the beach and shouted to a group of youths on the road for one to give a hand in pushing off the boat.

"Give me an oar," said Lucrezia, in a loud, hard voice, and, seizing one, she began pushing with a strength that seemed scarcely her own.

"See, see!" cried Gian-Battista, "she wants to show us she can put a boat off for her gallant as well as the fisher-wench could, lads! But you tell her she's better fitted for a fine gentleman!" And the lads standing round on the beach joined in a loud laugh. They did not understand the gist of the matter, but it was enough for them that some one was being made fun of.

Lucrezia, however, had never been one to be trifled with, as those in her own village knew to their cost. She had swallowed her wrath to-day longer than she would have done had she been at home. But the last taunt was too much for her. Her brown eyes darkened and blazed, her full lips were pressed tightly together, the red blood gathered beneath her sallow skin, and she stood up in the stern of the boat with one arm raised above her head. Any one looking at her must have known that she was going to say something that would astonish her hearers. But that something never came. Just as the lads—standing ankle-deep in the water to push off the boat—looked up to see whose was the figure that had suddenly risen between them and the sunset, and saw Lucrezia with the red light shining on her face, and catching the golden kerchief on her shoulders till it was almost like flame—just as the girl herself opened her lips to speak, a shout was heard to the right, and looking round she saw Paolo standing up in a boat as though he had been scanning the shore. The words were frozen on her lips. She did not move.

"So there you are at last!" cried old Gian-Battista. "Well, I wouldn't have left a pretty girl so long out of my sight when I was a young man! But times are changed!"

"Santa Vergine, Lucrezia! where hast thou been?" asked Paolo, pulling his boat up alongside of the one that was just afloat, and disregarding every one else. "I have sought thee everywhere these last two hours. Thou hast frightened me!"

"Well, I waited for you," answered the girl sulkily, though many emotions betrayed themselves by a sound as of tears behind her voice. "I was alone in the church for a weary while. You should not have delayed."

"Delayed!" exclaimed Paolo, vexed outright. "It was scarce I who delayed! How was I to find thee in the church when we agreed to meet on the shore?"

"I did not wish to wait on the shore."

"Lucrezia, thou art purposed to vex me."

"Eh!" muttered the old boatman; "and you'll be more vexed still before you've done with her. 'Didn't wish to wait on the shore,' indeed!—what humbugs women are!—when I saw her myself on the shore full half the afternoon discoursing with that good-for-nothing from Milan, who comes here every year and goes making portraits of the girls around! Portraits, indeed! I'm sorry to vex you, my girl, but if you did not mean to tell him yourself, it was but right I should undeceive the poor man."

"Who told you I did not mean to tell him?" was on Lucrezia's lips to say, but her pride rebelled even at this appearance of self-defence, and she held her peace.

There was a silence while Paolo waited to hear if she could deny the charge. Then he said, with a kind of hoarseness in his voice, "Is this true, Lucrezia?"

She paused a moment. There was a struggle, but, alas! it was again pride that conquered. "True? Yes, it is true," she said coldly. "Dost thou think no better man than thyself cares to discourse with me?"

"Why didst thou not tell me? Thou wast ashamed of it."

"Ashamed! I am not a fool, Signor Paolo, and I know how to conduct myself."

"It seems there are two opinions on that subject," said Gian-Battista, laughing again.

Lucrezia turned disdainfully away. "Peasants fancy that a girl must needs always blush and be foolish because a gentleman speaks to her," sneered she; "but I know better." She would rather have died at that moment than have confessed the truth, that she had been frightened of the Count. She wanted to make the bystanders think that he had talked to her as he would have talked to a lady. She did not know that they were all too familiar with his character to be easily deceived about him. She did not know either that most of them had heard that rumour at which, had she ever guessed, may be she would not have held her head so high.

"Well, even if women are not to be trusted generally," said he, trying to bring the whole affair to a happy close, "I know this wench well enough to be sure *she* wouldn't bandy words with a scamp!"

Alas! he worked the wrong way to establish peace. The words roused Lucrezia's smothered wrath afresh. It was not to be borne that the compliments, out of which—disagreeable as they had been to her—she meant to make capital, should be held up to the ridicule of the very villagers.

"The Count is no scamp," she said; "he only followed me to return me this ear-ring, which he had picked up. He spoke fairer to me than *you* can find words to do!"

She drew herself up proudly and sat down again in the boat. She was not prepared for the roar of laughter with which her speech was received by the listeners. It stung her to desperation. It stung Paolo too, who had been sorely tried that day and whose patience was not exhausted.

"Come, Lucrezia," said he, grasping her wrist roughly across the edge of the boat, "enough of this. We will go home. Dost thou not see," added he in a lower tone, "that this tale will be all over Stresa, and us both a laughing-stock for all?"

Lucrezia *did* see it only too well, and was ashamed of the temper that had led her to forget her genteel demeanour and to betray herself before strangers; but the evil was done. She stood committed to a scene now, and would go on with it to the bitter end rather than allow herself to be subdued. "Who are you to dare touch me thus!" cried she, shaking off Paolo's arm furiously and standing up once more. "Oh! you need not speak below your breath. I have done nothing to be ashamed of! Here is a man who leaves a girl alone for hours and then is astonished because she has spoken to some-one else!" she went on in her fury, addressing the group on the shore, while Paolo drew back aghast. "I will thank you for your opinion, neighbours. Am I to blame?"

There was a moment's silence, for Paolo looked a tall, strong figure, standing up solitary against the sunset, in the boat that had drifted away with the force of Lucrezia's angry movement. She won the day, however. A shout of laughter arose from the beach, quickly followed by a tumult of hasty voci-ferations. "No, no," cried one; "is a pretty girl *ever* to blame?" And another shouted, "Give it him, pretty Lucrezia; you know how, though you *are* half a lady!"

The speaker repented the words almost before they were spoken. Had he been able to see Paolo's face better he would never have uttered them. For though the strong arms had been crossed on the broad chest, ominous glances had shot from the black eyes, and the last taunt would have been too much for greater self-control than this peasant could boast. With a sudden oath, and a bound so swift that it would have sent the boat out into the lake had not Lucrezia instinctively seized it, Paolo sprang from the prow into the midst of the little crowd, and, before any had time to interfere, had planted so firm a blow into the chest of that last and rashest speaker that, without a chance of defence, the lad reeled and fell over on to his back.

"Now you all of you know what to expect if you dare to speak another word," said Paolo with trembling voice and white lips; "and if you had not been an old man, Gian-Battista, you would have had the same lesson before this."

Still panting with his rage, he stood there waiting for who would dare to defy him. For an instant a murmur ran round. Lucrezia stood up eagerly, for dearly would she have loved to see a real fight. But old Gian-Battista, though he muttered a curse below his breath, knew that further to provoke such an antagonist was but to come off worse than he cared to risk; while the lads around, looking at Ferrara's six feet of height and well-knit muscles, were but too well convinced that he had no match among a handful of striplings such as they. Whispering among themselves, they turned aside, and the boy who had been so summarily punished had no solace but in impotent swearing, as he picked himself up and slunk away.

Gian-Battista went about his business, and the little crowd had vanished like smoke. Then, and only then, Paolo got into his boat again, and silently held out his hand for Lucrezia to step across. Her heart beat strangely, and she was quite pale. There was something in Paolo's face that frightened her. She took her seat without a word, and Paolo grasped the oars. This was the end of their day's holiday-making!

The boat made its way silently through the calm water, and the land was fast being left behind. A choking at her heart and a gloomy brow sitting opposite to her—that was the end of all the fun! thought the girl, half aggrieved and half penitent. A growing distrust of her whom he loved, a cruel disappointment, and a heartless deception!—that was the end of all his patience, thought Paolo. And the one sat silent because she was conquered for the moment and a little afraid; the other, because every stroke of his oars was but a new phase in that hardest of all battles—the battle with self. Paolo's hour had come; Lucrezia's lay a little way off yet, and neither her grief nor her repentance were really heavy on her. But he—yes, he was doing a hard battle.

He was not angry any longer. His pent-up fury had found a vent in the sudden blow dealt to not perhaps the most culpable of his offenders. He was not angry; but for his bitter disappointment there was no cure, and that, alas! was the worst pain. He could not beat Lucrezia, even if that would have eased his sorrow. What should he do? He worked sternly at the oars and knit his brow. Could it be that the lightly spoken prognostications of friends and comrades had really more truth in them than he had chosen to allow? "She comes of a bad stock," they used to say to him—"of a depraved race. She is vain as they are vain, and selfish; she will cheat you before you know where you are, for the sake of a little finery and a little admiration. You are a fool to put your trust in a girl without a name." Many such warnings had often been given to him, and others, again, had laughed openly at him for not rather choosing to wed an honest *contadina* of his own class. He had always done his best to make light even of her being a foundling, and, at all events, had stoutly repudiated the very notion of her being a coquette. But was to-day's trouble not almost convincing proof to the contrary? Why had she pretended business in Stresa after seeing that scamp on the piazza? Why, having been cross, did she become amiable when he had so blindly consented to leave her alone? Why, again, had she concealed the meeting with the Count until it was betrayed by another? It was all clear enough. If she had deceived him he could never forgive her, he could never trust her again!

He ground his teeth together, to stifle his wrath; and Lucrezia dragged her little hand through the cold water, trying to attract his attention. She was subdued, but, alas for herself! she was not conquered yet.

Twilight fell around. Where the sunset had just faded, battlements of clouds were sweeping up across the west; they were purple with colour from the afterglow. Upon the hill-tops circlets of mist, still rosy with brightness, floated and sank. The day-time had been burning hot and dazzling, but as the dews fell mists seemed to gather, though even now the breeze that played furtively about smote hot upon the face as it passed, laden with sweet scents. There was something still and secret about this evening air that oppressed even Lucrezia, who was always so merry and matter-of-fact. She sighed impatiently. The crooning chants of returning fishermen, or the wilder songs of contented pleasure parties, floated distantly over the dusky water; but she did not strike a tune on her own account, as was often her wont. She was still a little frightened.

"We shall have rain," she said presently.

"It will be good; we have had too hot a day for September; it is not healthy," answered Paolo: and then, the silence being broken, he asked her, after a pause, if it was the gentleman of the piazza whom she had met afterwards upon the shore.

"Yes," replied she; but she did not volunteer any further information.

She thought a lover ought to trust his betrothed, if he had any opinion of her at all. If he had not seemed to doubt her, she would have told him all; but the pride that was her undoing would not let her take the first step towards a reconciliation.

"I am sorry that you were not frank with me, Lucrezia," continued Paolo severely, and in a voice very remote from his usual round and ringing one. The tone of it annoyed her further, for she had never been used to upbraiding from Paolo. He had spoilt her.

"A girl does not always say everything to a man," she said provokingly, taking her hand out of the water and drying it on her apron; "if I had been to the Cousin Maddalena's, and had talked of stays and embroidery, wouldst thou still have wished to hear all about it?"

"Be serious, Lucrezia. I tell thee, I have no mind to joke now."

"But what if I have? Thou art gloomy enough for two, and I do not like gloom." She trembled a little as she said this, with a smile—for the expression of Paolo's face was not encouraging—but she would not have liked him to guess she was afraid of him.

"I say I have no idea of always being put off with childish nonsense," repeated he doggedly. "I have a question to put to you, as to a sensible woman, and I want an answer given quietly, as a girl should do."

"And *I* say that I will not be preached at, nor called a child either, do you see! And as for being a sensible woman, I see no need for that till I be in the forty years, and have a pack of children to my back—and, at all events, not when I am out for a holiday."

The day was nearer than Lucrezia thought when she was to be made a sensible woman of! When it dawned, she would have given much to have had that other day over again, that she might have chosen to be sensible then.

"I want to know," asked Paolo quietly, disregarding her laughter, "whether you ever met that fine gallant—rascal that he is!—before, or if he is a new acquaintance?"

"What if I have met him before?" answered the girl mischievously, crossing her arms and smiling at the black countenance opposite to her.

"Only that I think we should have to reconsider our relations, Lucrezia."

"Oh, I see; you would not like your wife to have an acquaintance in the gentry! Well, of course you have a right to your opinion. But I cannot promise to give the cold shoulder to one who is polite to me, only to please you. What if the signore should want to make my portrait? They say he makes beautiful portraits; and I can tell you, he finds my face a pretty one, for he told me it was like the Madonna's very own!"

"He did, did he!" muttered Paolo, with a low growl like that of a dog about to spring. "And what didst thou answer to it?"

"That's my affair," laughed she lightly, delighting to teaze him. And to teaze him for his jealousy was surely a very legitimate amusement.

"What dost thou expect of such a one?" said he.

"A few gracious words, which I do not get from every one!"

"Nothing more?"

"Well—— that remains to be seen." She was thinking of the possible portrait that would dearly have flattered her vanity.

The oars cleft the water. The drops stood on Paolo's brow, though he had rowed neither far nor fast.

The truth seemed to stand out all too clearly before him. And should he forfeit the esteem of many who were dear to him, bring the stain of a doubtful birth into his own honest family, of which he was as proud as was any nobleman, all for the sake of one who could treat him thus lightly?

"He seems to please thee better than I do," he muttered at last, below his breath.

"The proud man! Does he expect to be as good as a gentleman born?" laughed Lucrezia softly. But she sent her last shaft with something of a misgiving.

The lights of Santa Caterina began to appear in the near distance. They seemed, in the darkness, as though they were hung up the face of the cliff, and belonged to no human habitation, but, like will-o'-the-wisps or phantoms of the water, dwelt without reason where they would. It struck even Lucrezia, to whom the sight was familiar. "One would think we lived in the trees or on the rock," laughed she; "there is no house to be seen." And she turned round and gazed up at where the village stood above them, hoping that Paolo would respond to this return to familiarity. He, however, only shipped the oars in silence when they reached the shore.

"I am glad to be at home," cried Lucrezia, stepping on to the boat's prow. "We must be very late."

"Take care," was all Paolo's answer, "the boat has run aground," and he sprang out into the shallow water to pull her ashore.

"I can jump," she said, and leapt across on to the dry shingle.

"Brava Lucrezia!" laughed she, in praise of herself, and ran up the steep little path almost half-way before she turned round to call out, with the mischievous merriment that was stronger than usual on her to-night, "Come up to supper when you have finished what you have to do. I don't doubt there'll be enough for four where there's enough for three; and I have two words to say to you."

"No, Lucrezia, not to-night; I shall be occupied," he answered; and when she called out again: "Come, that's a white lie; you have nothing to occupy you," he said nothing but. "Good-bye, Lucrezia," and went on pulling at the boat as though he had not heard. Only as she ran merrily singing up the path —all the more eager because of her bad behaviour that Paolo should find a good supper when he came—then her lover turned a moment and left his work. And so long as the little graceful figure was in sight, springing lightly from boulder to boulder, so long did his eyes strain into the growing darkness watching her greedily. Then he turned back to his labour, and, looking out across the lake, saw that lights were lit in Stresa opposite, and that night was come.

THE TRUMPET-MAJOR.

By THOMAS HARDY, Author of "Far from the Madding Crowd," etc.

CHAPTER XXXVIII.—A DELICATE SITUATION.

"I AM ready to go," said Anne as soon as he arrived.

He paused as if taken aback by her readiness, and replied with much uncertainty, "Would it—wouldn't it be better to put it off till there is less sun?"

The very slightest symptom of surprise arose in her as she rejoined, "But the weather may change; or had we better not go at all?"

"Oh, no!—it was only a thought. We will start at once."

And along the vale they went, John keeping himself about a yard from her right hand. When the third field had been crossed they came upon half-a-dozen little boys at play.

"Why don't he clasp her to his side, like a man?" said the biggest and rudest boy.

"Why don't he clasp her to his side, like a man?" cried all the rude smaller boys in a chorus.

The trumpet-major turned, and, after some running, succeeded in smacking two of them with his switch, returning to Anne breathless. "I am ashamed they should have insulted you so," he said, blushing for her.

"They said no harm, poor boys," she replied reproachfully.

Poor John was dumb with perception. The gentle hint upon which he would have eagerly spoken only one short day ago was now like fire to his wound.

They presently came to some stepping-stones across a brook. John crossed first without turning his head, and Anne, just lifting the skirt of her dress, crossed behind him. When they had reached the other side a village girl and a young shepherd approached the brink to cross. Anne stopped and watched them. The shepherd took a hand of the young girl in each of his own, and walked backward over the stones, facing her, and keeping her upright by his grasp, both of them laughing as they went.

"What are you staying for, Miss Garland?" asked John.

"I was only thinking how happy they are," she said quietly; and withdrawing her eyes from the tender pair, she turned and followed him, not knowing that the seeming sound of a passing bumble-bee was a suppressed groan from John.

When they reached the hill they found forty navvies at work removing the dark sod XXI—56

so as to lay bare the chalk beneath. The equestrian figure that their shovels were forming was unintelligible to John and Anne now they were close, and after pacing from the horse's head down his breast to his hoof, back by way of the king's bridle-arm, past the bridge of his nose, and into his cocked-hat, Anne said that she had had enough of it, and stepped out of the chalk clearing upon the grass. The trumpet-major had remained all the time in a melancholy attitude within the rowel of his Majesty's right spur.

"My shoes are caked with chalk," she said as they walked downwards again; and she drew back her dress to look at them. "How can I get some of it cleared off?"

"If you was to wipe them in the long grass there," said John, pointing to a spot where the blades were rank and dense, "some of it would come off." Having said this, he walked on with religious firmness.

Anne raked her little feet on the right side, on the left side, over the toe, and behind the heel; but the tenacious chalk held its own. Panting with her exertion she gave it up, and at length overtook him.

"I hope it is right now?" he said, looking gingerly over his shoulder.

"No, indeed!" said she. "I wanted some assistance—some one to steady me. It is so hard to stand on one foot and wipe the other without support. I was in danger of toppling over, and so gave it up."

"Merciful stars, what an opportunity!" thought the poor fellow, while she waited for him to offer help. But his lips remained closed, and she went on with a pouting smile—

"You seem in such a hurry. Why are you in such a hurry? After all the fine things you have said about—about caring so much for me, and all that, you won't stop for anything."

It was too much for John. "Upon my heart and life, my dea——" he began. Here Bob's letter crackled warningly in his waistcoat pocket as he laid his hand asseveratingly upon his breast, and he became suddenly sealed up to dumbness and gloom as before.

When they reached home Anne sank upon a stool outside the door, fatigued with her excursion. Her first act was to try to pull off her shoe—it was a difficult matter; but John stood beating with his switch the leaves of the creeper on the wall.

"Mother—David—Molly, or somebody—

do come and help me to pull off these dirty shoes!" she cried aloud at last. "Nobody helps me in anything!"

"I am very sorry," said John, coming towards her with incredible slowness and an air of unutterable depression.

"Oh, I can do without *you*. David is best," she returned, as the old man approached and removed the obnoxious shoes in a trice.

Anne was amazed at this sudden change from devotion to crass indifference. On entering her room she flew to the glass, almost expecting to learn that some extraordinary change had come over her pretty countenance, rendering her intolerable for evermore. But it was, if anything, fresher than usual, on account of the exercise. "Well!" she said retrospectively. For the first time since their acquaintance she had this week encouraged him; and for the first time he had shown that encouragement was useless. "But perhaps he does not clearly understand," she added serenely.

When he next came it was, to her surprise, to bring her newspapers, now for some time discontinued. As soon as she saw them she said, "I do not care for newspapers."

"The shipping news is very full and long to-day, though the print is rather small."

"I take no further interest in the shipping news," she replied with cold dignity.

She was sitting by the window, inside the table, and hence when, in spite of her negations, he deliberately unfolded the paper and began to read about the Royal Navy she could hardly rise and go away. With a stoical mien he read on to the end of the report, bringing out the name of Bob's ship with tremendous force.

"No," she said at last, "I'll hear no more. Let me read to you."

The trumpet-major sat down. Anne turned to the military news, delivering every detail with much apparent enthusiasm. "That's the subject *I* like!" she said fervently.

"But—but Bob is in the navy now, and will most likely rise to be an officer. And then—"

"What is there like the army?" she interrupted. "There is no smartness about sailors. They waddle like ducks, and they only fight stupid battles that no one can form any idea of. There is no science nor stratagem in sea fights—nothing more than what you see when two rams run their heads together in a field to knock each other down. But in military battles there is such art, and such splendour, and the men are so smart, particularly the horse-soldiers. Oh, I shall never forget what gallant men you all seemed when

you came and pitched your tents on the downs! I like the cavalry better than anything I know; and the dragoons the best of the cavalry—and the trumpeters the best of the dragoons!"

"Oh, if it had but come a little sooner!" moaned John within him. He replied as soon as he could regain self-command, "I am glad Bob is in the navy at last—he is so much more fitted for that than the merchant-service —so brave by nature, ready for any daring deed. I have heard ever so much more about his doings on board the *Victory*. Captain Hardy took special notice that when he——"

"I don't want to know anything more about it," said Anne impatiently; "of course sailors fight; there's nothing else to do in a ship, since you can't run away. You may as well fight and be killed as be killed not fighting."

"Still it is his character to be careless of himself where the honour of his country is concerned," John pleaded. "If you had only known him as a boy you would own it. He would always risk his own life to save anybody else's. Once when a cottage was afire up the lane he rushed in for a baby, although he was only a boy himself, and he had the narrowest escape. We have got his hat now with the hole burnt in it. Shall I get it and show it to you?"

"No—I don't wish it. It has nothing to do with me." But as he persisted in his course towards the door, she added, "Ah! you are leaving because I am in your way. You want to be alone while you read the paper—I will go at once. I did not see that I was interrupting you." And she rose as if to retreat.

"No, no! I would rather be interrupted by *you* than . . . . Oh, Miss Garland, excuse me! I'll just speak to father in the mill, now I am here."

It is scarcely necessary to state that Anne (whose unquestionable gentility amid somewhat homely surroundings has been many times insisted on in the course of this history) was usually the reverse of a woman with a coming-on disposition; but, whether from pique at his manner, or from wilful adhe- rence to a course rashly resolved on, or from coquettish maliciousness in reaction from long depression, or from any other thing,—it was that she would not let him go.

"Trumpet-major," she said, recalling him.

"Yes?" he replied timidly.

"The bow of my cap-ribbon has come untied, has it not?" She turned and fixed her bewitching glance upon him.

The bow was just over her forehead, or,

more precisely, at the point where the organ of comparison merges in that of benevolence, according to the phrenological theory of Gall. John, thus brought to, endeavoured to look at the bow in a skimming, duck-and-drake fashion, so as to avoid dipping his own glance as far as to the plane of his interrogator's eyes. " It is untied," he said, drawing back a little.

She came nearer, and asked, " Will you tie it for me, please ? "

As there was no help for it, he nerved himself and assented. As her head only reached to his fourth button she necessarily looked up for his convenience, and John began fumbling at the bow. Try as he would, it was impossible to touch the ribbon without getting his finger-tips mixed with the curls of her forehead.

" Your hand shakes—and you have been walking fast," she said.

" Yes—yes."

" Have you almost done it ? " She inquiringly directed her gaze upward through his fingers.

" No—not yet," he faltered in a warm sweat of emotion, his heart going like a flail.

" Then be quick, please."

" Yes, I will, Miss Garland ! B—B—Bob is a very good fel——".

" Not that man's name to me ! " she interrupted.

John was silent instantly, and nothing was to be heard but the rustling of the ribbon ; till his hands once more blundered among the curls, and then touched her forehead.

With a deep sigh the trumpet-major turned away hastily to the corner-cupboard, and rested his face upon his hand.

" What's the matter, John ? " said she.

" I can't do it ! "

" What ? "

" Tie your cap-ribbon."

" Why not ? "

" Because you are so . . .! because I am clumsy, and never could tie a bow."

" You are clumsy indeed," answered Anne, and went away.

After this she felt injured, for it seemed to show that he rated her happiness as of meaner value than Bob's ; since he had persisted in his idea of giving Bob another chance when she had implied that it was her wish to do otherwise. Could Miss Johnson have anything to do with his firmness ? An opportunity of testing him in this direction occurred some days later. She had been up the village, and met John at the mill-door.

' Have you heard the news ? Matilda Johnson is going to be married to young Derriman."

Anne stood with her back to the sun, and as he faced her his features were searchingly exhibited. There was no change whatever in them, unless it were that a certain light of interest kindled by her question turned to complete and blank indifference. " Well, as times go, it is not a bad match for her," he said, with a phlegm which was hardly that of a lover.

John on his part was beginning to find these temptations almost more than he could bear. But being quartered so near to his father's house it was unnatural not to visit him, especially when at any moment the regiment might be ordered abroad, and a separation of years ensue ; and as long as he went there he could not help seeing her.

The year eighteen-hundred-and-seven changed from green to gold, and from gold to grey, but little change came over the house of Loveday. During the last twelve months Bob had been occasionally heard of as upholding his country's honour in Denmark, the West Indies, Gibraltar, Malta, and other places about the globe, till the family received a short letter stating that he had arrived again at Portsmouth. At Portsmouth Bob seemed disposed to remain, for though some time elapsed without further intelligence, the gallant seaman never appeared at Overcombe. Then on a sudden John learnt that Bob's long-talked-of promotion for signal services rendered was to be an accomplished fact. The trumpet-major at once walked off to Overcombe, and reached the village in the early afternoon. Not one of the family was in the house at the moment, and John strolled onwards over the hill, without much thought of direction till, lifting his eyes, he beheld Anne Garland coming towards him with a little basket upon her arm.

At first John blushed with delight at the sweet vision ; but, recalled by his conscience, the blush of delight was at once mangled and slain by a glacial expression, as he would have scotched and killed a snake. He looked for a means of retreat ; but the field was open, and a soldier was a conspicuous object : there was no escaping her.

" It was kind of you to come," she said with a pretty smile.

" It was quite by accident," he answered with an indifferent laugh. " I thought you was at home."

Anne blushed and said nothing, and they rambled on together. In the middle of the field rose a fragment of stone wall in the form

"Nothing was to be heard but the rustling of the ribbon."

of a gable, known as Faringdon Ruin; and when they had reached it John paused and politely asked her if she were not a little tired with walking so far. No particular reply was returned by the young lady, but they both stopped, and Anne seated herself on a stone which had fallen from the ruin to the ground.

"A church once stood here," observed John in a matter-of-fact tone.

"Yes, I have often shaped it out in my mind," she returned. "Here where I sit must have been the altar."

"True; this standing bit of wall was the chancel end."

Anne had been adding up her little studies of the trumpet-major's character, and was surprised to find how the brightness of that character increased in her eyes with each examination. A kindly and gentle sensation was again aroused in her. Here was a neglected heroic man, who, loving her to distraction, deliberately doomed himself to pensive shade to avoid even the appearance of standing in a brother's way.

"If the altar stood here, hundreds of people have been made man and wife just there, in past times," she said with calm deliberateness, throwing a little stone on a spot about a yard westward.

John annihilated another tender burst and replied, "Yes, this field used to be a village.

My grandfather could call to mind when there were houses here. But the squire pulled 'em down because poor folk were an eyesore to him."

"Do you know, John, what you once asked me to do?" she continued, not accepting the digression, and turning her eyes upon him.

"In what sort of way?"

"In the matter of my future life, and yours."

"I am afraid I don't."

"John Loveday!"

He turned his back upon her for a moment, that she might not see the spasm of woe which shot through his face. "Ah!—I do remember," he said at last, in a dry, small, repressed voice.

"Well—need I say more? Isn't it sufficient?"

"It would be sufficient," answered the unhappy man. "But——"

She looked up with a reproachful smile, and shook her head. "That summer," she went on, "you asked me ten times if you asked me once. I am older now; much more of a woman, you know; and my opinion is changed about some people; especially about one."

"Oh, Anne, Anne!" he burst out as, racked between honour and desire, he snatched up her hand. The next moment it fell heavily to her lap. He had absolutely relinquished it half-way to his lips.

"I have been thinking lately," he said, with preternaturally sudden calmness, "that men of the military profession ought not to—ought to be like St. Paul, I mean."

"Fie, John! pretending religion!" she said sternly. "It isn't that at all. *It's Bob!*"

"Yes!" cried the miserable trumpet-major. "I have had a letter from him to-day." He pulled out a sheet of paper from his breast. "That's it! He's promoted—he's a lieutenant—he'll be a gentleman some day, and worthy of you!"

He threw the letter into her lap, and drew back to the other side of the gable-wall. Anne jumped up from her seat, flung away the letter without looking at it, and went hastily on. John did not attempt to overtake her. Picking up the letter, he followed in her wake at a distance of a hundred yards.

But, though Anne had withdrawn from his presence thus precipitately, she never thought more highly of him in her life than she did five minutes afterwards, when the excitement of the moment had passed. She saw it all quite clearly; and his self-sacrifice impressed her so much that the effect was just the reverse of what he had been aiming to produce. The more he pleaded for Bob the more her perverse generosity pleaded for John. To-day the climax had come—with what results she had not foreseen.

As soon as the trumpet-major reached the nearest pen-and-ink he flung himself into a seat and wrote wildly to Bob:—

"DEAR ROBERT,—I write these few lines to let you know that if you want Anne Garland you must come at once—you must come instantly, and post-haste—*or she will be gone!* Somebody else wants her, and she wants him! It is your last chance, in the opinion of—

"Your faithful brother and well-wisher,
"JOHN.

"P.S.—Glad to hear of your promotion. Tell me the day and I'll meet the coach."

CHAPTER XXXIX.—BOB LOVEDAY STRUTS UP AND DOWN.

ONE night, about a week later, two men were walking in the dark along the turnpike road towards Overcombe, one of them with a bag in his hand.

"Now," said the taller of the two, the squareness of whose shoulders signified that he wore epaulettes, "now you must do the best you can for yourself, Bob. I have done all I can; but th' hast thy work cut out, I can tell thee."

"I wouldn't have run such a risk for the world," said the other in a tone of ingenuous contrition. "But thou'st see, Jack, I didn't think there was any danger, knowing you was taking care of her, and nursing my place for me. I didn't hurry myself, that's true; but, thinks I, if I get this promotion I am promised I shall naturally have leave, and then I'll go and see 'em all. Gad, I shouldn't have been here now but for your letter!"

"You little think what risks you've run," said his brother. "However, try to make up for lost time."

"All right. And whatever you do, Jack, don't say a word about this other girl. Hang the girl!—I was a great fool, I know; still, it is over now, and I am come to my senses. I suppose Anne never caught a capful of wind from that quarter?"

"She knows all about it," said John seriously.

"Knows? By George, then, I'm ruined!"

said Bob, standing stock-still in the road as if he meant to remain there all night.

"That's what I meant by saying it would be a hard battle for ye," returned John, with the same quietness as before.

Bob sighed and moved on. "I don't deserve that woman!" he cried, passionately thumping his three upper ribs with his fist.

"I've thought as much myself," observed John, with a dryness which was almost bitter. "But it depends on how thou 'st behave in future."

"John," said Bob, taking his brother's hand, "I'll be a new man. I solemnly swear by that eternal milestone staring at me there, that I'll never look at another woman with the thought of marrying her whilst that darling is free—no, not if she be a mermaiden of light. . . It's a lucky thing that I'm slipped in on the quarter-deck; it may help me with her—hey?"

"It may with her mother; I don't think it will make much difference with Anne. Still, it is a good thing; and I hope that some day you'll command a big ship."

Bob shook his head. "Officers are scarce; but I'm afraid my luck won't carry me so far as that."

"Did she ever tell you that she mentioned your name to the King?"

The seaman stood still again. "Never!" he said. "How did such a thing as that happen, in Heaven's name?"

John described in detail, and they walked on, lost in conjecture.

As soon as they entered the house the returned officer of the navy was welcomed with acclamation by his father and David, with mild approval by Mrs. Loveday, and by Anne not at all—that discreet maiden having carefully retired to her own room some time earlier in the evening. Bob did not dare to ask for her in any positive manner; he just inquired about her health and that was all.

"Why, what's the matter with thy face, my son?" said the miller, staring. "David, show a light here." And a candle was thrust against Bob's cheek, where there appeared a jagged streak like the geological remains of a lobster.

"Oh—that's where that rascally Frenchman's grenade busted and hit me from the *Redoutable*, you know, as I told ye in my letter."

"Not a word!"

"What, didn't I tell ye? Ah, no; I meant to, but I forgot it."

"And here's a sort of dint in yer forehead too; what do that mean, my dear boy?' said the miller, putting his finger in a chasm in Bob's skull.

"That was done in the Indies. Yes, that was rather a troublesome chop—a cutlass did it. I should have told ye, but I found 'twould make my letter so long that I put it off, and put it off; and at last thought it wasn't worth while."

John soon took his departure.

"It's all up with me and her, you see,' said Bob to him outside the door "She's not even going to see me."

"Wait a little," said the trumpet-major.

It was easy enough on the night of the arrival, in the midst of excitement, when blood was warm, for Anne to be resolute in her avoidance of Bob Loveday. But in the morning determination is apt to grow invertebrate; rules of pugnacity are less easily acted up to, and a feeling of live and let live takes possession of the gentle soul. Anne had not meant even to sit down to the same breakfast-table with Bob; but when the rest were assembled, and had got some way through the substantial repast which was served at this hour in the miller's house, Anne entered. She came silently as a phantom, her eyes cast down, her cheeks pale. It was a good long walk from the door to the table, and Bob made a full inspection of her as she came up to a chair at the remotest corner, in the direct rays of the morning light, where she dumbly sat herself down.

It was altogether different from how she had expected. Here was she who had done nothing, feeling all the embarrassment; and Bob, who had done the wrong, felt apparently quite at ease.

"You'll speak to Bob, won't you, honey?' said the miller after a silence. To meet Bob like this after an absence seemed irregular in his eyes.

"If he wish me to," she replied, so addressing the miller that no part, scrap, or outlying beam whatever of her glance passed near the subject of her remark.

"He's a lieutenant, you know, dear,' said her mother on the same side; "and he's been dreadfully wounded."

"Oh," said Anne, turning a little towards the false one; at which Bob felt it to be time for him to put in a spoke for himself.

"I am glad to see you," he said contritely; "and how do you do?"

"Very well, thank you."

He extended his hand. She allowed him to take hers, but only to the extent of a niggardly inch or so. At the same moment she glanced up at him, when their eyes met, and hers were again withdrawn.

The hitch between the two younger members of the household tended to make the breakfast a dull one. Bob was so depressed by her unforgiving manner that he could not throw that sparkle into his stories which their substance naturally required ; and when the meal was over, and they went about their different businesses, the pair resembled the two Dromios in seldom or never being, thanks to Anne's subtle contrivances, both in the same room at the same time.

This kind of performance repeated itself during several days. At last, after dogging her hither and thither, leaning with a wrinkled forehead against doorposts, taking an oblique view into the room where she happened to be, picking up worsted balls and getting no thanks, placing a splinter from the *Victory*, several bullets from the *Redoutable*, a strip of the flag, and other interesting relics, carefully labelled, upon her table, and hearing no more 'about them than if they had been pebbles from the nearest brook, he hit upon a new plan. To avoid him she frequently sat up-stairs in a window overlooking the garden. Lieutenant Loveday carefully dressed himself in a new uniform, which he had caused to be sent some days before, to dazzle admiring friends, but which he had never as yet put on in public or mentioned to a soul. When arrayed he entered the sunny garden, and there walked slowly up and down as he had seen Nelson and Captain Hardy do on the quarter-deck; but keeping his right shoulder, on which his one epaulette was stuck, as much towards Anne's window as possible.

But she made no sign, though there was not the least question that she saw him. At the end of half an hour he went in, took off his clothes, and gave himself up to doubt, and the best tobacco.

He repeated the programme on the next afternoon, and on the next, never saying a word within doors about his doings or his notice.

Meanwhile the results in Anne's chamber were not uninteresting. She had been looking out on the first day, and was duly amazed to see a naval officer in full uniform promenading in the path. Finding it to be Bob she left the window with a sense that the scene was not for her; then, from mere curiosity, peeped out from behind the curtain. Well, he was a pretty spectacle, she admitted, relieved as his figure was by a

dense mass of sunny, closely trimmed hedge, over which nasturtiums climbed in wild luxuriance; and if she could care for him one bit, which she couldn't, his form would have been a delightful study, surpassing in interest even its splendour on the memorable day of their visit to the Weymouth theatre. She called her mother ; Mrs. Loveday came promptly.

"Oh, it is nothing," said Anne indifferently ; "only that Bob has got his uniform."

Mrs. Loveday peeped out, and raised her hands with delight. "And he has not said a word to us about it! What a lovely epaulette ! I must call his father."

"No, indeed. As I take no interest in him I shall not let people come into my room to admire him."

"Well, you called me," said her mother.

"It was because I thought you liked fine clothes and uniforms and all that. It is what I don't care for."

Notwithstanding this assertion she again looked out at Bob the next afternoon when his footsteps rustled on the gravel, and studied his appearance under all the varying angles of the sunlight as if fine clothes and uniforms were not altogether a matter of indifference. He certainly was a splendid, gentlemanly, and gallant sailor from end to end of him ; but then, what were a dashing presentment, a naval rank, and telling scars, if a man was fickle-hearted ? However, she peeped on till the fourth day, and then she did not peep. The window was open, she looked right out, and Bob knew that he had got a rise to his bait at last. He touched his hat to her, keeping his right shoulder forward, and said, "Good day, Miss Garland," with a smile.

Anne replied, "Good day," with funereal seriousness ; and the acquaintance thus revived led to the interchange of a few words at supper-time, at which Mrs. Loveday nodded with satisfaction. But Anne took especial care that he should never meet her alone, and to insure this her ingenuity was in constant exercise. There were so many nooks and windings on the miller's rambling premises that she could never be sure she would not turn up within a foot of her, particularly as his thin shoes were almost noiseless.

One fine afternoon she accompanied Molly in search of elder berries for making the family wine which was drunk by Mrs. Loveday, Anne, and anybody who could not stand the rougher and stronger liquors provided by the miller. After walking rather a long distance over the down they came to a grassy hollow, where elder bushes in knots of twos and threes rose from an uneven bank and hung their heads towards the south, black and heavy with bunches of fruit. The charm of fruit-gathering to girls is enhanced in the case of elder berries by the inoffensive softness of the leaves, boughs, and bark, which makes getting into them easy and pleasant to the most indifferent climbers. Anne and Molly had soon gathered a basketful, and, sending the servant home with it, Anne remained in the bush picking and throwing down bunch by bunch upon the grass. She was so absorbed in her occupation of pulling the twigs towards her, and the rustling of their leaves so filled her ears, that it was a great surprise when, on turning her head, she perceived a similar movement to her own among the boughs of the adjoining bush.

At first she thought they were disturbed by being partly in contact with the boughs of her bush; but in a moment Bob Loveday's face peered from them, at a distance of about a yard from her own. Anne uttered a little indignant "Well!" recovered herself, and went on plucking. Bob thereupon went on plucking likewise; and they looked at each other from their respective bushes like a Jack and a Jill in the green.

"I am picking elder berries for your mother," he at last said humbly.

"So I see."

"And I happen to have come to the next bush to yours."

"So I see; but not the reason why."

Anne was now in the westernmost branches of the bush, and Bob had leant across into the eastern branches of his. In gathering he swayed towards her, back again, forward again.

"I beg pardon," he said, when a farther swing than usual had taken him almost beside her.

"Then why do you do it?"

"The wind rocks the bough, and the bough rocks me." She expressed by a look her opinion of this statement in the face of the gentlest breeze; and Bob pursued: "I am afraid the berries will stain your pretty hands."

"I wear gloves."

"Ah, that's a plan I should never have thought of. Can I help you?"

"Not at all."

"You are offended: that's what that means."

"No," she said.

"Then will you shake hands?"

Anne hesitated; then slowly stretched out her hand, which he took at once. "That will do," she said, finding that he did not relinquish it immediately. But as he still held it, she pulled, the effect of which was to draw Bob's swaying person, bough and all, towards her, and herself towards him.

"I am afraid to let go your hand," said that officer; "for if I do your spar will fly back, and you will be thrown upon the deck with great violence."

"I wish you to let me go!"

He accordingly did, and she flew back, but did not by any means fall.

"It reminds me of the times when I used to be aloft clinging to a yard not much bigger than this tree-stem, in the mid-Atlantic, and thinking about you. I could see you in my fancy as plain as I see you now."

"Me, or some other woman," retorted Anne haughtily.

"No!" declared Bob, shaking the bush for emphasis, "I'll protest that I did not think of anybody but you all the time we were dropping down channel, all the time we were off Cadiz, all the time through battles and bombardments. I seemed to see you in the smoke, and, thinks I, if I go to Davy's locker, what will she do!"

"You didn't think that when you landed after Trafalgar."

"Well, now," said Lieutenant Loveday in a reasoning tone, "that was a curious thing. You'll hardly believe it, maybe; but when a man is away from the woman he loves best in the world, he can have a sort of temporary feeling for another without disturbing the old one, which flows along under the same as ever."

"I can't believe it, and won't," said Anne firmly.

Molly now appeared with the empty basket, and when it had been filled from the heap on the grass, Anne went home with her, bidding Loveday a frigid adieu.

The same evening, when Bob was absent, the miller proposed that they should all three go to an upper window of the house, to get a distant view of some rockets and illuminations which were to be exhibited in Weymouth at that hour in honour of the King, who had returned this year as usual. They accordingly went up-stairs to an empty attic, placed chairs against the window, and put out the light, Anne sitting in the middle, her mother close by, and the miller behind, smoking. No sign of any pyrotechnic display was visible over Weymouth as yet, and Mrs. Love day passed the time by talking to the miller, who replied in monosyllables. While this was going on Anne fancied that she heard some one approach, and presently felt sure that Bob was drawing near her in the surrounding darkness; but as the other two had noticed nothing she said not a word.

All at once the swarthy expanse of south-ward sky was broken by the blaze of several rockets simultaneously ascending from different ships in the roads. At the very same moment a warm mysterious hand slipped round her own, and gave it a gentle squeeze.

"Oh, dear!" said Anne, with a sudden start away.

"The candle shed its waving light upon John's face and uniform."

"How nervous you are, child, to be startled by fireworks so far off," said Mrs. Loveday.

"I never saw rockets before," murmured Anne, recovering from her surprise.

Mrs. Loveday presently spoke again. "I wonder what has become of Bob?"

Anne did not reply, being much exercised in trying to get her hand away from the one that imprisoned it; and whatever the miller thought he kept to himself, because it disturbed his smoking to speak.

Another batch of rockets went up. "Oh, I never!" said Anne, in a half-suppressed tone, springing in her chair.

"Poor girl, you certainly must have change of scene, at this rate," said Mrs. Loveday.

"I suppose I must," murmured the dutiful daughter.

For some minutes nothing further occurred to disturb Anne's serenity. Then a slow, quiet "a-hem" came from the obscurity of the apartment.

"What, Bob ? How long have you been there ?" inquired Mrs. Loveday.

"Not long," said the lieutenant coolly. "I heard you were all here, and crept up quietly, not to disturb ye."

"Why don't you wear heels to your shoes like Christian people, and not creep about so like a cat ? "

"Well, it keeps your floors clean—to go slipshod."

"That's true."

Meanwhile Anne had been gently but firmly trying to keep her hand disengaged, but finding the struggle a futile one, owing to the invisibility of her antagonist, and her wish to keep its nature secret from the other two, she arose, and saying that she did not care to see any more, felt her way down-stairs. Bob followed, leaving Loveday and his wife to themselves.

"Dear Anne," he began, when he had got down, and saw her in the candlelight of the large room. But she adroitly passed out at the other door, at which he took a candle and followed her to the small room. "Dear Anne, do let me speak," he repeated as soon as the rays revealed her figure. But she passed into the bakehouse before he could say more ; whereupon he perseveringly did the same. Looking round for her here he perceived her at the end of the room, where there were no means of exit whatever.

"Dear Anne," he began again, setting down the candle, "you must try to forgive me ; really you must. I love you the best of anybody in the wide, wide world. Try to forgive me ; come." And he imploringly took her hand.

Anne's bosom began to surge and fall like a small tide, her eyes remaining fixed upon the floor ; till, when Loveday ventured to draw her slightly towards him, she burst out crying. "I don't like you, Bob ; I don't ! " she suddenly exclaimed between her sobs. "I did once, but I don't now—I can't, I can't ; you have been very cruel to me ! " She violently turned away, weeping.

"I have, I have been terribly bad, I know," answered Bob, conscience-stricken by her grief. "But—if you could only forgive me—I promise that I'll never do anything to grieve ye again. Do you forgive me, Anne ? "

Anne's only reply was crying and shaking her head.

"Let's make it up. Come, say we have made it up, dear."

She withdrew her hand, and still keeping her eyes buried in her handkerchief, said. "No."

"Very well, then ! " exclaimed Bob with sudden determination. "Now I know my doom ! And whatever you hear of as happening to me, mind this, you cruel girl, that it is all your causing ! " Saying this he strode with a hasty tread across the room into the passage and out at the door, slamming it loudly behind him.

Anne suddenly looked up from her handkerchief, and stared with round wet eyes and parted lips at the door by which he had gone. Having remained with suspended breath in this attitude for a few seconds she turned round, bent her head upon the table, and burst out weeping anew with thrice the violence of the former time. It really seemed now as if her grief would overwhelm her, all the emotions which had been suppressed, bottled up, and concealed since Bob's return having made themselves a sluice at last.

But such things have their end ; and left to herself in the large, vacant, old apartment, she grew quieter, and at last calm. At length she took the candle and ascended to her bedroom, where she bathed her eyes and looked in the glass to see if she had made herself a dreadful object. It was not so bad as she had expected, and she went down-stairs again.

Nobody was there, and, sitting down, she wondered what Bob had really meant by his words. It was too dreadful to think that he intended to go straight away to sea without seeing her again, and frightened at what she had done, she waited anxiously for his return.

CHAPTER XL.—A CALL ON BUSINESS.

HER suspense was interrupted by a very gentle tapping at the door, and then the rustle of a hand over its surface, as if searching for the latch in the dark. The door opened a few inches, and the alabaster face of Uncle Benjy appeared in the slit.

"Oh, Squire Derriman, you frighten me ! "

"All alone ? " he asked in a whisper.

"My mother and Mr. Loveday are somewhere about the house."

"That will do," he said, coming forward. "I be wherrited out of my life, and I have thought of you again—you yourself, dear

Anne, and not the miller. If you will only take this and lock it up for a few days till I can find another good place for it—if you only would." And he breathlessly deposited the tin box on the table.

"What, obliged to dig it up from the cellar?"

"Ay; my nephew hath a scent of the place—how, I don't know! but he and a young woman he's met with are searching everywhere. I worked like a wire-drawer to get it up and away while they were scraping in the next cellar. Now where could ye put it, dear? 'Tis only my few documents, and my will, and suchlike, you know. Poor soul o' me, I'm worn out with running and fright!"

"I'll put it here till I can think of a better place," said Anne, lifting the box. "Dear me, how heavy it is!"

"Yes, yes," said Uncle Benjy hastily; "the box is iron, you see. However, take care of it, because I am going to make it worth your while. Ah, you are a good girl, Anne. I wish you was mine!"

Anne looked at Uncle Benjy. She had known for some time that she possessed all the affection he had to bestow.

"Why do you wish that?" she said simply.

"Now don't ye argue with me. Where d'ye put the coffer?"

"Here," said Anne, going to the window-seat, which rose as a flap, disclosing a boxed receptacle beneath, as in many old houses.

"'Tis very well for the present," he said dubiously, and they dropped the coffer in, Anne locking down the seat and giving him the key. "Now I don't want ye to be on my side for nothing," he went on. "I never did now, did I? This is for you." He handed her a little packet in paper, which Anne turned over and looked at curiously. "I always meant to do it," continued Uncle Benjy, gazing at the packet as it lay in her hand, and sighing. "Come, open it, my dear; I always meant to do it."

She opened it and found twenty new guineas snugly packed within.

"Yes, they are for you. I always meant to do it!" he said, sighing again.

"But you owe me nothing!" returned Anne, holding them out.

"Don't say it!" cried Uncle Benjy, covering his eyes. "Put 'em away. . . . . Well, if you *don't* want 'em—— But put 'em away, dear Anne; they are for you, because you have kept my counsel. Good night t' ye. Yes, they are for you."

He went a few steps, and turning back

added anxiously, "You won't spend 'em in clothes, or waste 'em in fairings, or ornaments of any kind, my dear girl?"

"I will not," said Anne. "I wish you would have them."

"No, no," said Uncle Benjy, rushing off to escape their shine. But he had got no farther than the passage when he returned again.

"And you won't lend 'em to anybody, or put them into the bank—for no bank is safe in these troublous times. . . . . If I was you I'd keep them *exactly* as they be, and not spend 'em on any account. Shall I lock them into my box for ye?"

"Certainly," said she; and the farmer rapidly unlocked the window-bench, opened the box, and locked them in.

"'Tis much the best plan," he said with great satisfaction as he returned the keys to his pocket. "There they will always be safe, you see, and you won't be exposed to temptation."

When the old man had been gone a few minutes, the miller and his wife came in, quite unconscious of all that had passed. Anne's anxiety about Bob was again uppermost now, and she spoke but meagrely of old Derriman's visit, and nothing of what he had left. She would fain have asked them if they knew where Bob was, but that she did not wish to inform them of the rupture. She was forced to admit to herself that she had somewhat tried his patience, and that impulsive men had been known to do dark things with themselves at such times.

They sat down to supper, the clock ticked rapidly on, and at length the miller said, "Bob is later than usual. Where can he be?"

As they both looked at her, she could no longer keep the secret.

"It is my fault," she cried; "I have driven him away. What shall I do?"

The nature of the quarrel was at once guessed, and her two elders said no more. Anne rose and went to the front door, where she listened for every sound with a palpitating heart. Then she went in; then she went out: and on one occasion she heard the miller say, "I wonder what hath passed between Bob and Anne. I hope the chap will come home."

Just about this time light footsteps were heard without, and Bob bounced into the passage. Anne, who stood back in the dark while he passed, followed him into the room, where her mother and the miller were on the point of retiring to bed, candle in hand.

"I have kept ye up, I fear," began Bob, cheerily, and apparently without the faintest recollection of his tragic exit from the house. "But the truth on 't is, I met with Fess Derriman at the Duke of York as I went from here, and there we have been playing Put ever since, not noticing how the time was going. I haven't had a good chat with the fellow for years and years, and really he is an out and out good comrade—a regular hearty! Poor fellow, he's been very badly used. I never heard the rights of the story till now; but it seems that said uncle of his treats him shamefully. He has been hiding away his money so that poor Fess might not have a farthing, till at last the young man has turned, like any other worm, and is now determined to ferret out what he has done with it. The poor young chap hadn't a farthing of ready money till I lent him a couple of guineas—a thing I never did more willingly in my life. But the man was very honourable. 'No, no,' says he; 'don't let me deprive ye.' He's going to marry; and what may you think he is going to do it for?"

"For love, I hope," said Anne's mother.

"For money, I suppose, since he's so short," said the miller.

"No," said Bob, "for *spite*. He has been badly served—badly served—by a woman. I never heard of a more heartless case in my life. The poor chap wouldn't mention names, but it seems this young woman has trifled with him in all manner of cruel ways—pushed him into the river, tried to steal his horse when he was called out to defend his country—in short, served him rascally. So I gave him the two guineas and said, 'Now let's drink to the hussy's downfall!'"

"Oh!" said Anne, having approached behind him.

Bob turned and saw her, and at the same moment Mr. and Mrs. Loveday discreetly retired by the other door.

"Is it peace?" he asked tenderly.

"Oh yes," she anxiously replied. "I—didn't mean to make you think I had no heart." At this Bob inclined his countenance towards hers. "No," she said, smiling through two incipient tears as she drew back. "You are to show good behaviour for six months, and you must promise not to frighten me again by running off when I—show you how badly you have served me."

"I am yours obedient—in anything," cried Bob. "But I am pardoned?"

"A too easy pardon is apt to make folk repeat the fault. Do you repent?"

It would be superfluous to transcribe Bob's answer.

Footsteps were heard without.

"Oh, I forgot!" said Bob. "He's waiting out there for a light."

"Who?"

"My friend Derriman."

"But, Bob, I have to explain."

But Festus had by this time entered the lobby, and Anne, with a hasty "Get rid of him at once!" vanished up-stairs.

Here she waited and waited, but Festus did not seem inclined to depart; and at last, foreboding some collision of interests from Bob's new friendship for this man, she crept into a storeroom which was over the apartment into which Loveday and Festus had gone. By looking through a knot-hole in the floor it was easy to command a view of the room beneath, this being unceiled, with moulded beams and rafters.

Festus had sat down on the hollow window-bench, and was continuing the statement of his wrongs. "If he only knew what he was sitting upon," she thought apprehensively, "how easily he could tear up the flap, box and all, with his strong arm, and seize upon poor Uncle Benjy's possessions." But he did not appear to know, unless he were acting, which was just possible. After a while he rose, and going to the table lifted the candle to light his pipe. At the moment when the flame began diving into the bowl the door noiselessly opened and a figure slipped across the room to the window-bench, hastily unlocked it, withdrew the box, and beat a retreat. Anne in a moment recognised the ghostly intruder as Festus Derriman's uncle. Before he could get out of the room Festus set down the candle and turned.

"What—Uncle Benjy—haw, haw! Here at this time of night?"

Uncle Benjy's eyes grew paralyzed, and his mouth opened and shut like a frog's in a drought, the action producing no sound.

"What have we got here—a tin box—the box of boxes? Why, I'll carry it for you, uncle! I am going home."

"N—no—no, thanky, Festus: it is n—it—not heavy at all, thanky," gasped the squireen.

"Oh, but I must," said Festus, pulling at the box.

"Don't let him have it, Bob!" screamed the excited Anne through the hole in the floor.

"No, don't let him," cried the uncle. "'Tis a plot—there's a woman at the window waiting to help him!"

Anne's eyes flew to the window, and she saw Matilda's face pressed against the pane.

Bob, though he did not know whence Anne's command proceeded, obeyed with alacrity, pulled the box from the two relatives, and placed it on the table beside him. "Now look here, hearties — what's the meaning o' this?" he said.

"He's trying to rob me of all I possess!" cried the old man. "My heart-strings seem as if they were going to crack, crack, crack!"

At this instant the miller entered the room in his shirt-sleeves, having got thus far in his undressing when he heard the noise. Bob and Festus turned to him to explain; and when the latter had had his say Bob added, "Well, all I know is that this box"—here he stretched out his hand to lay it upon the lid for emphasis; but as nothing but thin air met his fingers where the box had been, he turned and found that the box was gone, Uncle Benjy having vanished also.

Festus, with an imprecation, hastened to the door, but though the night was not dark, Farmer Derriman and his burden were nowhere to be seen. On the bridge Festus joined a shadowy female form, and they went along the road together, followed for some distance by Bob, lest they should meet with and harm the old man. But the precaution was unnecessary: nowhere on the road was there any sign of Farmer Derriman, or of the box that belonged to him. When Bob re-entered the house Anne and Mrs. Loveday had joined the miller down-stairs, and then for the first time he learnt who had been the heroine of Festus's lamentable story, with many other particulars of that yeoman's history which he had never before known. Bob vowed that he would not speak to the traitor again, and the family retired.

The escape of old Mr. Derriman from the annoyances of his nephew not only held good for that night, but for next day, and for ever. Just after dawn on the following morning a labouring man, who was going to his work, saw the old farmer and landowner leaning over a rail in a mead near his house, apparently engaged in contemplating the water of a brook before him. Drawing near the man spoke, but Uncle Benjy did not reply. His head was hanging strangely, his body being supported in its erect position entirely by the rail that passed under each arm. On after examination it was found that Uncle Benjy's poor withered heart had cracked and stopped its beating from damages inflicted on it by the excitements of his life, and of the previous night in particular. The un-

conscious carcass was little more than a light empty husk, dry and fleshless as that of a dead heron found on a moor in January.

But the tin box was not discovered with or near him. It was searched for all the week, and all the month. The mill-pond was dragged, quarries were examined, woods were threaded, rewards were offered; but in vain.

At length one day in the spring, when the mill-house was about to be cleaned throughout, the chimney-board of Anne's bedroom, concealing a yawning fire-place, had to be taken down. In the chasm behind it stood the missing deed-box of Farmer Derriman. Many were the conjectures as to how it had got there. Then Anne remembered that on going to bed, the night after the collision between Festus and his uncle in the room below, she had seen mud on the carpet of her room, and the miller remembered that he had seen footprints on the back staircase. The solution of the mystery seemed to be that the late Uncle Benjy, instead of running off from the house with his box, had doubled on getting out of the front door, entered at the back, deposited his box in Anne's chamber where it was found, and then leisurely pursued his way home at the heels of Festus, intending to tell Anne of his trick the next day —an intention that was for ever frustrated by the stroke of death.

Mr. Derriman's solicitor was a Weymouth man, and Anne placed the box in his hands. Uncle Benjy's will was discovered within; and by this testament Anne's queer old friend appointed her sole executrix of his said will, and, more than that, gave and bequeathed to the same young lady all his real and personal estate, with the solitary exception of five small freehold houses in a back street in Weymouth, which were devised to his nephew, Festus, as a sufficient property to maintain him decently, without affording any margin for extravagances. Overcombe Hall, with its muddy quadrangle, archways, mullioned windows, cracked battlements, and weed-grown garden, passed with the rest into the hands of Anne.

CHAPTER XLI.—FAREWELL.

DURING this exciting time John Loveday seldom or never appeared at the mill. With the recall of Bob, in which he had been sole agent, his mission seemed to be complete.

One mid-day, before Anne had made any change in her manner of living on account of her unexpected acquisitions, Lieutenant Bob came in rather suddenly. He had been to Weymouth, and announced to the arrested senses of the family that the —th Dragoons were ordered to join Sir Arthur Wellesley in the Peninsula.

These tidings produced a great impression in the household. John had been so long in the neighbourhood, either at camp or in barracks, that they had almost forgotten the possibility of his being sent away; and they now began to reflect upon the singular in-frequency of his calls since his brother's return. There was not much time, however, for re-flection, if they wished to make the most of John's farewell visit, which was to be paid the same evening, the departure of the regi-ment being fixed for next day. A hurried valedictory supper was prepared during the afternoon, and shortly afterwards John arrived.

He seemed to be more thoughtful and a trifle paler than of old, but beyond these traces, which might have been due to the natural wear and tear of time, he showed no signs of gloom. On his way through the town that morning a curious little incident had oc-curred to him. He was walking past one of the Weymouth churches when a wedding party came forth, the bride and bridegroom being Matilda and Festus Derriman. At sight of the trumpet-major the yeoman had glared triumphantly; Matilda, on her part, had winked at him slily, as much as to say—— But what she meant heaven knows; the trumpet-major did not trouble himself to think, and passed on without returning the mark of confidence with which she had favoured him.

Soon after John's arrival at the mill several of his friends dropped in for the same pur-pose of bidding adieu. They were mostly the men who had been entertained there on the occasion of the regiment's advent on the down, when Anne and her mother were coaxed in to grace the party by their supe-rior presence, and their well-trained, gallant manners were such as to make them interest-ing visitors now as at all times. For it was a period when romance had not so greatly faded out of military life as it has done in these days of short service, heterogeneous mixing, and transient campaigns, when the *esprit de corps* was strong, and long expe-rience stamped noteworthy professional cha-racteristics even on commonplace rank and file; while the miller's visitors had the addi-tional advantage of being picked men.

They could not stay so long to-night as on that earlier and more cheerful occasion, and the final adieus were spoken at an early hour. It was no mere playing at departure, as when they had gone to Exeter barracks, and there was a warm and prolonged shak-ing of hands all round.

"You'll wish the poor fellows good-bye?" said Bob to Anne, who had not come for-ward for that purpose like the rest. "They are going away, and would like to have your good word."

She then shyly advanced, and every man felt that he must make some pretty speech as he shook her by the hand.

"Good-bye. May you remember us as long as it makes ye happy, and forget us as soon as it makes ye sad," said Sergeant Brett.

"Good night! Health, wealth, and long life to ye!" said Sergeant-major Wills, taking her hand from Brett.

"I trust to meet ye again as the wife of a worthy man," said Trumpeter Buck.

"We'll drink your health throughout the campaign, and so good-bye t' ye," said Saddler-Sergeant Jones, raising her hand to his lips.

Three others followed with similar remarks, to each of which Anne blushingly replied as well as she could, wishing them a prosperous voyage, easy conquest, and a speedy return.

But, alas, for that! Battles and skirmishes, advances and retreats, fevers and fatigues, told hard on Anne's gallant friends in the coming time. Of the seven upon whom these wishes were bestowed, five were dead within the few following years, and their bones left to moulder in the land of their campaigns.

John lingered behind. When the others were outside, expressing a final farewell to his father, Bob, and Mrs. Loveday, he came to Anne, who remained within.

"But I thought you were going to look in again before leaving?" she said.

"No; I find I cannot. Good-bye."

"John," said Anne, holding his right hand in both hers, "I must tell you something. You were wise in not taking me at my word that day. I was greatly mistaken about my-self. Gratitude is not love, though I wanted to make it so for the time. You don't call me thoughtless for what I did?"

"My dear Anne," cried John, with more gaiety than truthfulness, "don't let yourself be troubled. What happens is for the best. Soldiers love here to-day and there to-mor-row. Who knows that you won't hear of my attentions to some Spanish maid before a month is gone by? 'Tis the way of us, you know; a soldier's heart is not worth a week's purchase—ha, ha! Good-bye, good-bye!"

Anne felt the expediency of his manner, received the affectation as real, and smiled her reply, not knowing that the adieu was for ever-more. Then he went out of the door, where he bade adieu to the miller, Mrs. Loveday, and Bob, who said at parting, "It's all right, Jack, my dear fellow. After a coaxing that would have been enough to win three ordinary Englishwomen, five French, and ten Mulotters, she has to-day agreed to bestow her hand upon me at the end of six months. Good-bye, Jack, good-bye!"

The candle held by his father shed its waving light upon John's face and uniform as he turned with a farewell smile on the doorstone, backed by the black night; and in another moment he had plunged into the darkness, the ring of his smart step dying away upon the bridge as he joined his waiting companions-in-arms, and went off to blow his trumpet over the bloody battlefields of Spain.

THE END.

A TRIP TO CYPRUS.

BY LIEUT.-COLONEL W. F. BUTLER, C.B.

PART IV.

Cathedral at Famagusta.

DOWN the snowy side of Troados we ran at topmost speed, ploughing deep into drift and crushing through crust, doing more in a minute of time than had been done in ten minutes of toil upon the upward road. There was not a moment to lose. Never did night gather her shadows more quickly around her than now as we went plunging down into her depths. Scant is the measure darkness gives in the Mediterranean when once the sun has gone below the horizon; but now we lessened that short interval by each rapid stride, for we were literally descending into darkness.

Some fifteen hundred feet lower down the mule had been left picketed beneath a pine-tree. To that tree there was no track, save the footprints of our upward course in the snow. These were, in many places, only to be observed on the closest scrutiny; in others, where the breeze was drifting the light frozen particles, they had become invisible. It was therefore a matter of moment that we should make the most of the afterglow to get out, at least, from the denser pine-trees and deeper snow of the upper mountain, and set our faces straight in the direction of the mule.

As before it had been a race with the sun up mountain, in which we had won, now it was a race with the night, in which we were the losers. Still, enough of light remained to enable us to follow our footprints clear of the broken ground below the summit ridge, and, before darkness had quite fallen, to see that our course was set straight down hill towards the south.

At the edge of the snow there suddenly appeared right in front two large ears projected forward in relief against a faint afterglow that lay along the lower sky from north to south. It was the mule looking wistfully towards the new-comer. His companions had long since been taken away, and the prospect of spending a hungry night on the cold shoulder of Olympus had doubtless convinced the mule that there were worse things in life than his old enemy—a rider. Still, when he realised that he was not to spend the night in cold and hunger, he began at once to manifest his old repugnance to the saddle.

At last the girths were tight, and we began

to descend the steep hill-side. It was now quite dark. We had got into a maze of rocks, pine-trees, and brush-wood. A general goat-track seemed to pervade the entire mountain, upon which the mule appeared to be now quite content to spend the remainder of the night. At last, amid a labyrinth of rocks, he came to a stand-still. Dismounting, we endeavoured to lead him; but he would not be led. Passing the halter behind we now tried to drive him before us; he would thus find the right road, and would lead the way into camp. In the new order of things it will be sufficient to say that he at once entered into that part of the programme which had reference to finding the right road; but there appeared to be a vast difference in his mind between finding the road for himself and showing it to his driver, for no sooner had he set his head straight down-hill than he determined to set his heels in the opposite direction, with the view of dissolving partnership with his master. Out of the darkness in front there suddenly came two vicious and violent kicks; the Turkish shoes just reached us, but not close enough to do serious damage; a couple of inches nearer would have soon ended the matter of the partnership, and left us alone on the shoulder of Olympus. To jump aside amid the rocks and haul vigorously at the halter was only the work of a second, and soon we succeeded in slueing round the animal's head. The saddle was again occupied, not to be quitted under any pretence until mule and man were safely landed in the camp at Platris.

An hour later lights shone below, and we reached the camp, to find a relief party about to start up the mountain to look for us.

Six hours' ride, next day, carried the party to Limasol, from which port the writer of these pages set out to cross the mountains to the monastery of Kiku and the west shore of the island. An interpreter, a muleteer, and three mules; a Zaptieh riding in front; an order, in Greek and Turkish, to the mudirs of the towns *en route* to board and lodge us; small kit of apparel and slender store of commissariat hastily got together, and we leave with little regret the hot streets of Limasol and the low coast-lands of Kolossi. Ruins of temples along the narrow track; at intervals a village, with cultivation and a few orange-trees around it; then upwards in a long ascent by arid hills, from which at every turn the eye looks back at bluest sea and buildings cleaned and freshened by sun and distance.

As on we ride an old negro suddenly issues from a cave from the wayside and invites us to stop a moment and refresh with coffee. His cave is twenty feet deep in the rock, fairly lighted from its large entrance, and with a lean-to hut on one side forming a porch. He is very black and very garrulous. His name is Billali. Many years before a Turk named Seyd brought him from Upper Egypt to Cyprus. He became free, and took to this cave, where now he cultivates the land around. He had sent his wife away. He was born in Kordofan, in the midst of the desert, and there his name had been Tameroo; that was a long while ago—before the time of Mehemet Ali Pasha. He is very happy up on this hill, for he can look down on the sea and on the houses, and till his land as he likes. His wife used to bother him a good deal; but he sent her away, and now he is quite happy. So spake Billali, once Tameroo of Kordofan, as he blew the embers about his little Turkish coffee-pot and prepared the tiny cup of real coffee for us. Then we parted from this poor old black Tameroo, and held our course by Shivellas and Everssa towards Mallia.

We reached the latter place in a downpour of rain at sunset. The mudir had a room ready, the Zaptieh having gone on in front to announce us. Dinner soon followed, and then coffee, cigarettes, and much conversation. Mallia was a purely Turkish village, and all the talk was of the Turk. There were one or two present who had been to Mecca. There were many questions asked about the future of the island, about the discovery of gold—"a mountain of gold," they say, in Midian—and about politics, foreign and domestic. There seemed to be an impression amongst them that if this mountain of gold could only be discovered in Cyprus all would be right. I replied, through the interpreter that there was plenty of gold lying around, but that it was in the wine, the oil, the wheat that came yearly from the ground; that the Egyptian, the Roman, the Venetian, and the Greek had left but little of other treasure remaining, but that each returning summer called again to life the riches of which I spoke.

Meantime there is much bringing of coffee and rolling of cigarettes among the cross-legged circle grouped before the large kitchen fire, and finally it is time to lie down for the night.

The wine at Mallia was good, and with generous hands my Turkish hosts filled my glass, declining to join me themselves; but rumour said that they were not always so shy, and that Mallia knew the flavour of a flagon of Commanderia and the smack of Mastic as well as any wine-bibbing village of Greek or Maronite persuasions.

Early next day we are again on the track. Rough and stony, it leads to Arsos, and through the mass of ruins called Hy Nicolo into the beautiful valley of the Carissos River. As the mules in single file wind down into the valley two eagles come soaring close above our heads. A large stone-pine slants from the hill-side, and beneath his wide-spread branches white Troados is seen ending the upper valley. Then we zig-zag down to the river meadows and halt by the oleander-lined banks for the mid-day rest.

On again across the single-arched bridge of Jellalu, up the farther side of the valley. A very old Greek church stands in ruins on the slope, and near it one solitary pine-tree eleven feet in girth. Then the ascent becomes steep, the zigzags are short and severe, and we see above us the pine-clad crest beyond, which is the monastery of Kiku, our destination.

At last we gain the summit. The track now leads along the crest or sides of narrow ridges. Troados lies to the right, rising in long profile out of a very deep glen; innumerable other deep glens sink around on

The Castle at Famagusta.

every side. The sides of the hills descend so steeply into these valleys that the stones go rolling from the feet of the mules as we jog along; but the sense of the steepness of the declivity is lessened by the pines and arbutus-trees that grow around—the arbutus only on the north faces of the hills.

The atmosphere is intensely clear; we are about four thousand feet above sea-level, and as the sun draws to the west the valley between us and Troados seems shot with varying hues of light, yet all so clear that every pine-tree on the mountain is visible, and the snowy crest looks but a short mile distant. A turn in the path brings the monastery of Kiku in sight; we the road dips a moment along the east side of the crest, which the sun cannot reach, and the ground

is hard bound in frost. As we draw near the monastery a monk comes up the hill-side and joins us. He carries a gun and a bag, but no game. Then we dismount at the great doorway and lead the mules into the courtyard, and presently a portly prior, followed by many Greek monks, come to bid us rest and welcome.

A cell is soon got ready, and the portly prior shows us to it. Three little windows in a very deep wall; low-arched ceiling, from the centre of which swings a brass lamp; a brick floor, with carpet slips laid upon it; a brazier of hot charcoal on one side; a sofa, a few chairs, and a wooden table, and our cell is as comfortable a little den to get into at sunset amid these cold Cypriote hills as traveller could wish to find.

A quaint old place this Kiku, set four thousand feet up in the hills. Long arched corridors and passages run round quiet courtyards. Off the corridors open cells, dormitories, and refectories. A great bell hangs at one corner of the quadrangle; it has come all the way from Moscow—for the fame of Kiku's sanctity goes far over the Greek world. How this bell was ever carried up the mountain must remain a mystery. It is of enormous size and weight, and the path is but a narrow mule track; but there it hangs, all the same, to ring out its deep note in the grey dawn to the misty mountain solitudes, and to wake the moufon on the hills ere the sun has kissed the frozen forehead of Troados. But the glory of Kiku is the church, and the glory of the church is the silver image of the Virgin and Child, given by Alexis in the tenth century, and hidden, so say the monks, from human vision ever since. "As I am not to see it again," said the Greek emperor, when he sent it to Cyprus, "then let no other human eye ever rest upon it." So the head and upper portion of the figures have been veiled from view. All this and more was poured forth by half-a-dozen old monks, in whose care we made the circuit of the monastery. Before we began our inspection sweetmeats and coffee were produced; when the inspection was over our dinner was ready. It was an excellent repast, and, after a long day spent in the keen mountain atmosphere, appetites were not wanting to do it justice. Lest they should be, one priest specially attended to see that the guests lacked nothing. The Commanderia wine was the best we had yet tasted, and the Mastic was old, luscious, and plentiful. As the frost grew harder outside the little cell windows, and boy-attendants brought freshly-fanned charcoal to the brazier, the cell looked indeed a cheerful billet for a mountain traveller.

The portly prior came and sat with us after dinner, and, among other matters, produced a paper that had caused the worthy brotherhood intense astonishment. It was an official document in English, having reference to a return for taxation. The monks could not make much of it, so they had invoked the aid of a passing traveller, versed in Greek and English. Unfortunately he had rendered the English word "pitch," the resin of the pine-forests, into the Greek word "bitch," and the brethren were amazed at finding themselves taxed for ten thousand okes of bitches. We appeased the afflicted and perplexed mind of the prior, and, redo-lent of garlic, he thanked us, bade us good night and retired.

Early morning at Kiku. How very beautiful it is! The sun peeps over Mount Olympus; the tops of the hills are all alight, and the deep valleys are in shadow; far away there are pale glimpses of distant sea; a vast stillness dwells on all things—stillness deepened by distant murmur of mountain stream and the softest whisper of old pine-trees—of that wonderful old forest, now nearly gone—that glorious growth which has given decks to Turkish galleys for three hundred years, that forest for whose destruction Greek and Turk have for once joined hands upon the handle of the felling axe. Burned, hacked, slashed at, barked and wounded, some grand old survivors still stretch forth their gaunt arms, as though they asked for mercy from the destroyer; and still, when the night hides the wreck that man has made, the wind-swept song of their sorrow is wafted in unutterable sadness over the ruined land.

Amid the farewells of the assembled brethren we moved off next morning from Kiku, descending northwards towards Kampo and the Bay of Morphu. It was another day of exquisite views, as, winding down the narrow mule track, we saw below the curve of the Bay of Morphu, the broken north range and the white summits of Karamania far away to the north over the lonely blue sea.

At the village of Kampo we stopped a few minutes. An old Greek woman brought us raisins, and supplemented her offering with an harangue. Its burden was that she expected many things from the English, and she trusted she would not be disappointed. "Tell her," we replied through the interpreter, "that the English expect much from her. When we left England they were full of expectation about this island; all the papers were writing about her and her people." She appeared to be astonished at the information, and we continued down hill towards Levka.

Six hours' ride brought us to Levka. The mudir, engaged at the moment of our arrival in a full court of tax collection, immediately dissolved his court and became our host, adviser, and director. He soon produced a meal of walnuts steeped in honey, of which it will be sufficient to record that for a condiment of singular indigestibility it would be difficult to parallel it in any conglomeration of sugar and fruit known to Western palates. Perhaps we are taking away the character of this condiment, and that, viewed in the capacity of a conserve, it might be approached with comparative safety; but as a *pièce de résistance* to set before a hungry man, after a six hours' ride, walnuts steeped in honey, plentifully administered, would probably solve for ever the "Eastern question" of any Western traveller's farther progress through the land. No wonder the Turk has been the "sick man" of Europe upon such a regimen.

We were afterwards informed that the mudir of Levka had but recently in his own person exemplified the transitory nature of earthly distinction. He had, in fact, undergone incarceration in prison for two months for misappropriation of taxes. He was still, however, administering the laws in Levka, and, so far as we could judge, his misfortune had in no way tended to withdraw from him the confidence of the inhabitants, while it had apparently left unimpaired his reputation as a high-class government official. He was a Turk.

We spent that night at the monastery farm of Xerapotamiss, by the shore of the Bay of Morphu.

After night fell we wandered down to the sea. In a long wave, that rose its crest only to fall upon the shore, the Mediterranean sobbed against the wide curving bay. The moon was over the sea. We wandered along the shore, keeping on a strip of glistening sand close by where the surf broke.

All lonely now this shore, but thick with memories. On this very spot the Turk landed for the conquest of the island. Hither, two thousand four hundred years ago, came the great lawgiver of the Greeks to end his life. In the farmyard of the monastery hard by, but an hour since, our muleteer tied his mules to the acanthus-leaf of a prostrate Corinthian capital. Yonder, in the moonlight, Pendaia's ruins are still dimly visible. Well may the sea sob upon the withered breast of Cyprus, and the pines sigh over her lonely hill-tops!

Two days' ride carried us across the island to the eastern shore, and it was again moonlight when our cavalcade passed the long bridge that crosses the rock-hewn ditch and entered the gate of once famed, now fevered and famished Famagusta.

Within the massive gateway a dead city lay beneath the moonlight. A city so dead and so ruined that even the moonbeams could not hide the wreck or give semblance of life to street or courtyard—and yet, withal, it was modern ruin that lay around. The streets were cleared of stones and rubbish, the massive ramparts were untouched, the roofless houses were not overgrown with creepers. Many of the churches still held portions of roof or window reared aloft against the sky; through lancet window or pointed archway the palm-tree hung motionless against the moonlight. Many owls flitted amid the ruins, and the sole sound was the ring of our hoofs and the roll of the distant surf outside the eastern rampart.

Soon after sunrise next morning we went out to see by clearer light this modern capital of all ruined cities—this skeleton in armour, whose huge ramparts, and deep ditch, and towering cavaliers hid only crumbling streets, squares, churches, and mansions.

We pass out by the grand sea-gate, not a stone of which has been defaced. Above the marble key-stone of the arch the winged lion still holds the open gospel to the deserted wharfs and silent shingle.

The name of the Venetian ruler is still bright in letters that were carved and gilt at the time Columbus was steering his ship to the new world, and when De Gama was about to strike the first blow at Venetian sway by his passage of the Cape of Storms.

A reef of rocks marks the old harbour limits, and the area which it is proposed to dredge into a refuge for iron-clads. "They may dredge out the mud from the sea," says our informant, "but they won't dredge away the fever from the shore."

He tells us the fever is incessant, that every-one gets it, that it is worse than West-African fevers, so far as its sensations are concerned, and that it doesn't matter what one eats or drinks, or where one sleeps—that the fever is bound to come all the same. "There are four of us here," he goes on, "and we were all down together with fever only three weeks ago." Then we go in again into the mournful city, and ramble on through more grass-grown streets and ruins. A plover rises from the waste and calls shrilly as he mounts on rapid wing above the ramparts. We ascend the ramparts. From the cavalier looking north the eye ranges over the mounds that have, for sixteen hundred years, marked the site of Salamis, and farther off the hills of Kanfara dropping into the long peninsula of Karpos.

Along the rampart, two coaches could drive abreast; beneath the rampart are the arched dungeons wherein Venice held her slaves; ruined churches everywhere within the walls—churches with deep doorways traced in curious patterns of stone-carving, with the frescoes still fresh on their walls, and the floors cumbered with overturned tomb effigies and prostrate crosses. Little patches of wheat grow here and there through the ruins. We try to count these churches, but cannot do it. Tradition says there once stood one hundred Christian temples within the walls of Famagusta.

Towering high above all other ruins, the cathedral raises its lofty Gothic towers, the most mournful of all the relics of this saddest of cities. Amid wreck of flying buttress and lancet window of Northern Gothic art, the feathery palms seem strangely out of place.

Older ruins and wreck of time deeper in the bygone can be met on all the shores of the Mediterranean; but nowhere a city like this one of Famagusta, nowhere else a scene which brings us so closely face to face with the grandeur of Venice and the glory of the Norman Crusader, both strangled in the grasp of the Turk, and lying yet unburied by the merciful hand of Time.

We may quit Cyprus—no other scene, within her shores, can grave upon our memory a deeper record of her matchless ruin.

It is evening. We have crossed the ridge that divides Famagusta from Larnaca, and are descending towards the sea for embarkation. The sun is going down behind the steep ridge of Santa Croce, whose white monastery looks like a snow-cap on the summit. The long waves roll in upon a wide-curving shore. Far out to sea, one or two ships are standing to the south, and around us the barren soil spreads a weed-grown waste, with ruins at intervals that stand out wondrously white and clear in the level sunlight. The earth rings hollow under our mule hoofs, for the honey-combed rock beneath has been a tomb for three thousand years. No other word tells of Cyprus so exactly. Tomb of Phœnician, of Egyptian, of Hittite, of Greek, Roman, and Jew; tomb of the exile from Libya, Athens, Pontus; tomb of the rich fugitives that fled before

the armies of the Pharaohs or the hosts of Babylon; tomb of all those countless waifs and strays of conquest, commerce, and commotion, who in the dim dawn of civilisation found in this island a refuge and a grave.

Tomb, too, of Byzantine, of Norman Crusader, of Venetian, and lastly of the Turk, whose grave, scraped shallow amid the ruins of empire, has blurred the record and scattered the ashes of twenty vanished peoples.

*   *   *   *   *

And now what is to be the future of this island? Can it be redeemed from ruin? Yes. By us? No. By its people? Yes. The Turk ruined; the Greek can renew. Let us beware of attempting to lead or to direct a people who, when their first sensation of surprise is past, are bound to hold us in ridicule and in aversion. Already the symptoms of the first are apparent. "What a pity it is," said the people of Limasol as they watched our road-making operations into the mountains—"what a pity it is that God, who has given these English so much money, should not also have bestowed upon them some brains!"

Let us endeavour to develop this island for the Greek peasant, and by the Greek peasant; not for the benefit of the usurer as we have done in India, or for the landlord as we have done in Ireland, or for the benefit of the Manchester man, or the Birmingham man, or the London man, or the outside man generally, as we have done in other parts of the world. My friend the sea-captain, who is still doubtless fully prepared to settle the Greek question after his own fashion, would probably urge the rule of thumb-screw and gallows in dealing with Cyprus; but the world has got beyond that stage now.

If our dominion in Cyprus is to escape the fate of our Ionian experiment, we must try to learn Greek before we attempt to teach English.

THE END.

HUNGRY HEARTS.

BY MRS. FRANCIS G. FAITHFULL.

| "Ich habe genossen das irdische Glück, Ich habe gelebt und geliebet!" | "I have tasted earthly joy, I have lived and loved." |

A MOMENT before, Thekla had been in Max Piccolomini's arms; his eyes had been meeting hers, his fervent parting words had been breathed in her ear; and yet she

counted it her highest happiness not to be loved, but to love.

And she was right. She had found the secret of sure peace and joy. She had a talisman which could never be taken from her, and which, by its magic power, would ease her sharpest pangs.

"It is more blessed to give than to receive," and a love that is worth anything does not barter itself for a return. "Do you think I love you?" a little child was once asked. "I don't know. *I* love *you*," she made answer, going back to her brick-building on the floor with a gay content altogether undisturbed by that hunger for affection which we are sometimes called upon to pity, and—harder task—to satisfy.

Few of us, indeed, lightly prize or willingly forfeit the affection which has fallen to our share, and at first sight it seems natural enough that people should crave for anything which, possessing, they value, and losing, they lament.

Still there is a difference, real though hard to define, between one's sympathy with Enid, as, obeying Geraint's harsh command, she rides before him through the wood, "bearing the sharpness of that pain about her heart," and the compassion excited by Elaine's woeful cry, "In vain, in vain, it cannot be; he will not love me."

Madame Vigée le Brun, gazing as an old woman of eighty upon the fair picture of herself, painted by her own hand sixty years before, might well be pardoned for the tears she shed, whereas the brilliant and gifted Madame de Staël, chafing at the harsh features with which nature had endowed her, becomes almost contemptible.

And we should allow Warren Hastings a sort of right to covet the lost acres of Daylesford, which we should entirely deny to his peasant school-mates.

Yet, whatever lack of dignity there might be in pining for a Sir Launcelot, "who gave no cause, not willingly," and in hankering for the broad lands or the beauty to which one had never any claim, such desires are at least more reasonable than querulous demands for affection and feverish attempts to secure attention.

No one is to blame for being ill-favoured or of mean estate, and the tenderest and truest heart may never find its mate. But it is hardly too much to say that when men and women resent the indifference of their belongings and friends, when they habitually smart under petty injuries or are chilled by neglect, the blame does always lie in some measure with themselves.

Those who are thoughtful and generous, sympathizing and courteous—in other words, loveable and likeable — are cherished not slighted, sought not shunned. And should

we plead that we cannot mend our blunt manner, our fretful temper, our dull wits, then even if it be admitted (and it is a large admission) that the plea is partly valid, there will come as a rejoinder the obvious truth, brought home to us every day of our lives, that we must bear the penalty of our defects no less than of our sins—a hard sentence, perhaps, yet surely not so hard as the privation entailed by poverty or the helplessness often going with deformity.

Happily for the worst of us, we are seldom judged rigidly according to our merits. The strong tie of blood helps to draw together very uncongenial spirits. Common associations in the past, common interests in the present and future form another bond of sympathy; and often grateful memories of former care and service, or the pity for loneliness, feebleness, and pain inherent in fine natures will beget a wonderful forbearance towards the exactions and perversities, not only of infirm and suffering kinsfolk, but of friends, servants, and neighbours.

If, for all that such "extenuating circumstances" can do for us, we still find the world cold and severe, then we are quite powerless. For what we want can neither be bought nor extorted. "Love is a thing as any spirit free." It must come to us unsought, or not at all. Reproaches, sighs, tears never yet kindled or revived affection, though they may awake compunction. And even the vigorous efforts which in many enterprises insure success, here only make failure doubly certain.

Hardly anything more completely destroys the charm even of a pretty face and vivacious manner than the self-consciousness born of a steady determination to attract. Hardly anything is more fatal to happy companionship than the touchiness, or, as the deluded mortals indulging the failing prefer to call it, the "sensitiveness," that commonly goes with an exceeding anxiety to be beloved and highly esteemed.

For they tell both ways—these characteristics. Not only does any suspicion of an underlying design spoil the brightest glance and neatest repartee; not only does it go against the grain to be caressing, or even genial, on compulsion; but also it must be remembered that those bent on producing a favourable impression, or absorbed in watching the impression they produce, are not likely to have so much room left in their hearts and minds for the better simpler emotions, the more worthy interests which could alone make them really admirable or winning. It is scarcely possible for any very keen sympathies, noble ambitions, or "high thinking" to animate people who take umbrage because they have not been formally apprised of some family event or duly consulted in some family difficulty, who stand upon the order of their going down to dinner, manœuvre to monopolise the "star" of the evening, or detect a malevolent meaning in some carelessly worded speech.

Sometimes, indeed, we hear a special appeal made for such as, caring little for distinction or deference, crave only for tokens of love and regard wherewith to satisfy their starved hearts. "Try to content them," say some gentle souls who would almost be "tender over drowning flies." "Try to give them what they so urgently desire."

But if such tokens *could* be given to order, if fond epithets and endearments could be dealt out like a pack of cards, they would do harm rather than good to any so desiring them. They would be like the taste of blood to a man-eating tiger, like brandy to a dram-drinker. A vain woman, an ambitious man—were either ever content while there were more laurels to be won? Why, then, should we expect the passionate pursuit of affection to be more easily abandoned?

Again, it is perhaps urged upon us that if we would teach wayward and unprepossessing children to be more kindly, industrious, or obedient, we must soften them by tenderness, and stimulate them, by every grain of commendation and encouragement that we can in any way honestly administer, to fight against their evil tendencies. And undoubtedly if approbation happens to be in their eyes the highest good, the hope of earning it in larger measure may help them *apparently* to master their indolence, wilfulness, or selfishness, to give up the toy they secretly want for themselves, to show an alacrity about their tasks or a cheerfulness under disappointment which they don't at all feel. But the recompense may become something very like a bribe, and so bribed they may, while learning self-control, learn something else—hypocrisy. What worth can there be in the good-nature or docility that springs from no other motive than a mean desire to be credited with some impulse not really existing?

Moreover, "no man can justly praise but what he doth affect;" and soft sayings uttered of set purpose, be the purpose never so good, will not have the true ring about them, and at their best will be but a poor substitute for the brightening eye, the glad smile, that tell of proud affection, for the tribute of reliance and respect involuntarily paid to all real excellence, and even to those earnest simple-minded struggles against besetting sins which are sometimes profoundly touching. And though where there is a deeply rooted and depressing sense of gracelessness, incapacity, or uncomeliness, a considerate word of approval, a playful compliment may act like a tonic, in those who scheme for it, who expect and claim it, it generally "doth nourish agues."

Surely the spirit we should long to find in ourselves, and in any for whom we have a care, is that inward leaning towards all things lovely, that inward shrinking from all things base which will make right-doing almost instinctive. Such a spirit may only, by slow degrees, grow vigorous and beautiful, and even then it may bend before the force of strong temptation. Still, it is "the native growth of noble mind," and the germ of it may be in many formed of poorer stuff. But the germ will come to nought in any, young or old, who make men's golden opinions their first end and aim; or, even if it develops into feeble life, the blight of double-mindedness will stunt or wither it.

And is there, then, to be no relief for those tormented by this vehement longing for the love, admiration, or esteem they have not been able to inspire? There is sometimes a cure to be found, a service to be done for them. Help them, if possible, to find some vivid outside interests; engage them in some active occupation; light up in them some enthusiasm, which will turn their attention away from that "ego" with which they are so perpetually engrossed to the great world lying round them, with all there is in it to be learnt and loved and hated. There is no fear that they, that we any of us will ever fail to give sufficient thought and care to our personal qualities, concerns, and rights. The fear is all the other way—that we shall care for little else.

But if, as may come to pass through the happy working of good influences, people can be so drawn out of themselves that their hearts begin to throb at any kind of heroism, to burn with indignation at deceit, cruelty, and oppression, and to be pitiful towards misery; if they begin to feel curiosity about the marvels of sea, earth, and sky, and to find keen pleasure in music, books, or painting; then the jealousy, vanity, affectation, and the many kindred forms of excessive self-regard which have disfigured their whole nature will gradually die down and disappear. And in their stead may, perhaps, be seen the fair dealing, gracious bearing, and ready helpfulness which come of quick sympathies with others' claims, feelings, and needs, the ardour excited by close investigations, and the wisdom taught by the study of noble works, until, without knowing it, they will begin to please, without seeking it they will win love.

MUSIC.

By the Rev. H. R. HAWEIS, M.A., Author of "Music and Morals."

II.—The Art-place and Special Functions of Music.

I SAID each art has to bide its time. When a man appears before his time he has to stand down, and another takes up his message later on. And so it is with art. There is affinity between an age and an art ; let music come up before its time another art, sculpture, will elbow it out, and each growth will be rapid in due season, like that of seeds. Sculpture, architecture, painting, music all follow the same law. Look at sculpture in Greece from Agelades and Phidias to Praxiteles and Lysippus, a brief one hundred and fifty years—the art reached its culmination, then dropt, like a flower shedding its petals, throughout the Isles of Greece. It was the same with the Greek drama, with Gothic architecture in the twelfth and thirteenth centuries, with Italian painting in the fourteenth and fifteenth centuries ; and music from Handel to Wagner is following a similar course, for I think the future history of music must be in its combination with the other arts, its adaptation to the ever-restless needs of human emotion.

Now observe the grand fundamental law of art succession. Each art comes as the angelic response to some cry of deep developmental need, and it embodies the ideal tendencies of a whole epoch. Thus, sculpture was the art of the Greeks because they knew nothing higher than the beauty and symmetry of the human body ; that was the climax of their adoring souls, and it came forth in the beautiful, graceful, and sublime forms of Venus, Apollo, and Jove. We pass over Roman art, for that was either done by Greeks in Rome or was simply a pale, too often a mechanical, copy of Greek art. We also pass over the early Christian art, for the early Christians looked askance at art, and yet were subdued by it, for they were forced at last to weave the heathen symbols—legends of Maia and Orpheus—into their sepulchral frescoes. We come later on to the extinction of almost all sensibility in art, through Byzantine forms—in fact, to the year 814, the

time of Charlemagne—a time when the people of Europe were so busily engaged in slaughtering one another that of course there was little to be expected in the way of art, which requires for its development a certain amount of peace and leisure.

But the great human needs are ever silently developing, and by-and-by another art arose, that of Gothic architecture. This became a grand medium for expressing the new thoughts and feelings of the people, the awe, the worship, the grandeur, and above all, the human interests of the new Christianity now spreading rapidly, like some fertile and invincible creeper, over the ruined fragments of the prostrate Roman columns— the foundation-stones of the modern world. Mr. Ruskin has told us how the old monks built their very lives, and along with them the hearts of the people, into those noble cathedrals which are dotted over all Christian lands, and remain the pride and boast of the civilised world. He has made us feel how the recluse must have revelled in his cell as he gazed upon the stone which he was ready to carve, or intrust to the itinerant mason ; how he paced his cloister and dreamed of the execution of those ideas which he had perhaps long cherished, until by degrees his imagination moulded the very life of the period, its activity, its coarseness, its humour, as well as its devotion, into sculptured capital and gargoyle.

The efflorescent and flamboyant wildness of design marked at length the extreme limits of the stone art. To fitful, fanciful impatience or despair succeeded loss of healthy perception, loss of interest, of reason, of law, and Gothic architecture became worse than dead—degraded. But the stone art only fell when its powers as an expressional medium were exhausted.

Art now turned the stonemason's chisel into the painter's brush ; rapidly through the schools of Venice, Florence, and Rome, were the foundations of the art laid, the discovery of perspective, anatomy, and colour. The noble edifice rose from Giotto to Raphael only to exhaust in its turn, and in a comparatively short time, the new, more plastic, more pathetic vehicle of colour, and turn restlessly to seek and to find another medium.

What was that other latest-born minister of expression, eager to seize the torch as it fell from the painter's trembling hands?

It was MUSIC. She offered herself a new emotional medium fitted to express what neither sculpture, architecture, nor painting could express, the mystic and complex emotions of that hidden life made up of self-analysis, sensibility, love, prayer, trance, vision, ecstasy, which Christianity brought into the world, and which gave to the human soul that inner and intense quality of spiritual independence which must · henceforth stamp and qualify all human progress. It is impossible to deny that more secular elements entered into the formation of the modern spirit, although its inwardness was its chief characteristic.

Great geographical discoveries, New Worlds, Australia, America, and the remote East; great commercial activities, great inventions, the printing press, steam navigation, and the electric telegraph; great religious movements, great revolutions, the rise of the English Reformation, the translation of the Bible, many things combined to produce the unparalleled activity of the modern spirit. But amongst all these factors Christianity was paramount; it explored and sifted emotion as it had never been explored and sifted before; it set free the springs of the inner life, and taught men the sublime secret of an independent emotional consciousness, before which the outer world vanished into space, and the changes, the rise and fall, and subtle sequences of mental states became the only realities.

But the hunger of art could not long be evaded. These very states called aloud for expression; they were elaborated in the silence of the cloister, and it was thence that music stepped forth into the world, as the new art medium. Now, as I have elsewhere pointed out at some length, music possesses two qualities *combined* by no other art: first, the quality of velocity—it *moves;* and secondly, the quality of direct appeal—it stirs feelings without having recourse to ideas or images. The drama, indeed, has movement, but it only stirs emotion through ideas; painting stirs us by the ideas presented and the direct emotional impact of colour, but it has no *velocity*, that has to be supplied by imagination. You may ally music with anything you please, but it alone can deal first hand with

emotion, arouse it, control it, direct it, and follow its chameleon life through all its innumerable windings.

This, the secret of music, once stated, is stated for ever; it is revealed in two words, *Directness* and *Velocity*.

And now, having shown the place of music amongst the arts, I should naturally proceed to trace the history of Modern Music through what Mr. Hullah has termed its three periods. We must be satisfied here with but one glimpse.

First period, 370 to 1400, Ambrose (374) selected certain of the Greek modes for chants. Gregory (590) revived the forgotten work of the good Milanese bishop, and added four new scales. Then came Huchbald of Tournay (932), who introduced a sort of harmony which must have resembled the mixture stop of the organ. Guido (1020) of Arezzo, and Franco of Cologne (1200), who between them divide the honours of descant, *cantus mensurabilis*, or division into bars, and flats and sharps, together with the invention of the monochord.

In the second period, 1400 to 1600, we have Josquin des Pres in Belgium, and Palestrina in Italy, and the rise of a true system of tonality; and when we enter the third period, 1600 to 1750, we have reached the true octave, the major and minor scale in which we find the uniform arrangement of semitones and the perfect cadence, ascribed by some to Monte Verde, 1770. When this moment arrived, the basis of a sound musical development was reached, and modern music then first became possible. The science of the cloister had at last stepped forth to wed, to train and discipline the wild, untutored art of the world outside.

Rapid and sudden, like the burst of Greek sculpture or Italian painting, was the rise and progress of modern music, the instant the science of the Church touched the heart of the world.

Carissimi died 1672; he was the type of the transition period. He might have seen Palestrina, and he lived to hear Corelli. In Corelli's lifetime the germ of every style of music since known arose. He witnessed the singing schools of Naples in the south, the rise of the great violin schools in the north, the foundation of the oratorio in Rome, the progress of instrumental music throughout Italy, France, and England. All this took place in the last century, and we are struck with a certain awe when we remember that men are still (1880) alive who may have listened to Mozart (died 1791), and conversed with the venerable Haydn (died 1808).

I return from this by no means irrelevant digression to illustrate the functions by completing the analysis of music, *as the direct language of the emotions.*

Have you ever analyzed your thoughts and feelings? Some say it is an unhealthy practice, but that quite depends; and if it is used for a legitimate purpose, it is interesting to observe what is going on in the realm of emotion. Every moment is occupied by some feeling—good, bad, or indifferent. You are very seldom neutral, and when you are, it is worthy of being noted as a fixed point from which to measure the "excursional" extent of your emotion.

I proceed to analyze first the properties of emotion; then those of sound, as manipulated by music; and we shall find that precisely the same qualities which exist *inwardly* in emotion, exist *outwardly* in sound. And that is the reason why music is fitted to be, and is recognised as, the language of emotion. I pointed this out in "Music and Morals," and when it was pointed out it seemed very simple. Some people said there was nothing in it; others said there was something in it, but they knew it before. "Well," I said to my critics, "all discoveries are simple when they are found out; but if this was so simple, why didn't you state it before?"

Emotion, then, consists first of *elation* and *depression;* that is, it goes up and down like a wavy line. When a lecturer addresses an audience, the interest may go down lower and lower; then, perhaps, he says something which tickles the fancy, and the emotion goes up and up, his hearers' hopes are raised, and they say to themselves, "Oh, it's not going to be so dull, after all." Here, then, is an instance of depression followed by elation.

The next quality is *intensity.* Your emotion varies in intensity. You grow intense and earnest as you listen to a speaker who interests you, until perhaps you are quite, as you say, carried away, or entranced by his eloquence.

Then your emotion has *variety.* We may illustrate this. A man is sitting on a foggy day in his parlour, when a friend suddenly drops in. He is glad to see him, and out of depression he begins to rise into elation. And then comes a story of the hunting field, a well-known wall had to be cleared, and some one was thrown; and as he listens with more and more interest, he finds the climax to be that the narrator himself was the man who was thrown, and that he has come on this depressing day to see him partly on that account. Then other friends drop in, and you ring for cigars and wine. You are informed there are no cigars, and your emotion is now divided by the story, the cigars, the servant, and your friends; you are the subject of a great variety of simultaneous emotions, some not over pleasurable, but at any rate, there is variety.

Then, fourthly, emotion has a *kind of form*—you may give it an arbitrary form; you can represent its direction by lines curved according to elation or depression, thick or thin according to intensity, and you can bracket them together to show that they are simultaneous.

Lastly, emotion possesses *velocity;* it travels, and it is never quite at rest; you may call its velocity *x.*

Now pass to musical sound. The notes in a musical scale go up and down; they have *elation* and *depression*, may vary in loudness from *pp.* to *ff.*, from *crescendo* to *diminuendo*, and so they have *intensities.* Many lines of melody or harmony can be carried on simultaneously, as in a part song or a score of Wagner's; there is then no mistake about *variety.* Then music has *form.* Musical form is as much a recognised musical phrase as "nicely felt colour" is in painting, and it is more to the point, for we have but to cast our eyes over a score of Spohr or Beethoven, and compare it with one of Handel's, to see how widely different is the general form even to the eye. Lastly, from *adagio* to *presto* you have reached in music that crowning property of emotion, *velocity*, for music is never at rest.

Side by side, then, we place, after five-fold analyses, emotion and music, the thing to be expressed and the thing which expresses it. In passing from one to the other we have simply exchanged certain arbitrary lines and an *x* for a set of symbols capable of bringing the various properties of emotion into connection with sound. That set of symbols, so long in arriving, so glorious in its advent, is obviously modern musical notation, and in wedding that to sound we have reached at last the sovereign and direct medium of emotional expression in THE ART OF MODERN MUSIC.

III.—INFLUENCE OF MUSIC.

And now if it be asked, "What is the use of music?" I may ask in return, "What is the use of emotion ?" It colours all life, it inspires all words, it nerves for all action. What would your life be without it? And what is the grandest thought without it? You know you may repeat a grand passage of Shakespeare without emotion. The noblest passages in the Bible are often read aloud without kindling a thrill or quickening a pulse. But apply the heat of noble dramatic action or impassioned religious eloquence, and how changed is the leaden atmosphere! how living and pregnant is the thought! Music expresses no thoughts, stands for no ideas or intellectual conceptions, rouses (except by association) no images; but it stands for independent states of consciousness, it creates the atmosphere in which thoughts are born, it deals with the mystic states in which thought is steeped and coloured.

Without emotion thought would perish, or remain passive and inert. No age, no sentient creature has been quite without a sense of musical sound as the language of emotion. In its rude elements even dumb animals are affected by it. It influences dogs, horses, and cattle generally. Notice how a musical sound, though monotonous, is understood and obeyed, and how the jingle of bells notoriously encourages horses to perform their work. The plough-boy is inspirited by the strains of his own whistling. And do you wonder that the Spartans were enabled to march to victory by the lays of the minstrel Tyrtæus—that our soldiers require the fife and drum? And I have been told that there are people in the North who are very delighted and cheered by that unutterable abomination, the Scotch bagpipe.

I must not trust myself to dwell upon the religious functions of music—active, as in the Lutheran hymn, sung *by* the people; passive, as in the mass or Catholic anthem, sung *for* the people. The songs of the temple have had more attention paid them than the songs of the street; but the time will come when these, too, will be understood as important factors in the life and morality of the people. A great statesman has said, "Let me make the songs of the people, and let who will make their laws." And when we think what might be the influence of music we cannot but regret that the popular songs of England are, in fact, represented by "Tommy, make room for your uncle." The songs of our music halls kindle emotions truly, but of what kind are they? When you employ music, wed it to thought, and thus awaken emotions, you must remember you are playing with two-

edged tools, for the emotions kindled and directed may be such as it is unhealthy and mischievous to cherish. Emotion means fire, and a heap of live coals on your carpet and in your grate subserve very different purposes; for in the one case your house is warmed, and in the other case it is burned down. So it is with music, which kindles and directs emotion. Music under certain conditions elevates, while under certain other conditions it demoralises. Music ought to be used discreetly, advisedly, and soberly. and that is why the particular *kind* of music we adopt, and the words to which music is set, should be very carefully considered.

Music is not intended simply to tickle the ear; music is moral. And here let me remind you that not half enough has been said of the discipline of emotion, a function exercised in the highest degree by music. Upon this very quality of discipline, nobility, and truth of emotional expression, turns the distinction between the modern German and the modern Italian schools, as schools. I say modern Italian, because the old Church schools of Pergolese and Stradella were severe, beautiful, and sublime compared to the modern Italian opera and romance. Yet must we not deny the splendid melodic and even harmonic qualities which are to be found in the essentially false form and spirit of the Italian opera. It has been too much the fashion of the English Wagnerites to decry Italian music; but the German Wagnerite is more liberal and catholic in his appreciation, while Wagner himself is the most liberal and truly catholic musician alive. He can appreciate every kind of music, and so can those who know him and interpret him best.

I remember, when I was at Nuremberg, falling in with Richter (now conducting in London), then conductor of the Beyreuth Festival. We were seated in the parlour of a little old-fashioned German inn, discussing the various schools of music, when I happened to allude to a famous quartet in Verdi's *Rigoletto* as a fine specimen of dramatic part writing, whereupon Richter. the great Wagner disciple—Richter, the conductor of the Beyreuth Festival, the incarnation of the music of the future, sprang up, and lifting high his glass in honour of the great Italian, exclaimed, "Ach, der Verdi—ist ein ganz colossal Kerl!"

To resume. The secret of a good school of music is, that it is a real exponent and a sound discipliner of the emotions. Listening to a symphony or sonata of Beethoven's is not a joke; it is a study, an emotional training. You sit down and listen attentively, and the master leads you through various moods; he elates you and depresses you; your feeling waxes and wanes with various intensities, not spasmodically, but by coherent sequences. You are put through a whole system of feeling, not of your own choosing; you are not allowed to choose, you are to control yourself here and expand there; and at last, after due exercise, you are landed on the composer's own platform, chastened, exercised, refreshed, and elevated. Although urged here and there, the light rein has been upon you, and the master drives you much in the same way that a skilled charioteer drives a spirited steed.

This is the process of all really great music, and the reason why the Italian, as a school, and, indeed, *all* bad music, Italian or otherwise, is injurious is because it deals *unfairly* or untruly with your emotions. It does not give you a balanced, rational, or healthful sequence of feeling. It is like a picture, the effect of which is spoilt by a washy background of raw colour, or like a melodrama such as *The Bells*, which, without any reflection on Mr. Irving's fine acting, we may, however, call a very good melodrama, but of a bad art sort. It is unlike a play of Shakespeare's. If he has horrors to bring before you he prepares you for them; you are not trifled with and exhausted, your emotions are not whipped and spurred until they cease to respond. All bad art trifles with, exhausts, and enervates you, and music most of all, because it deals at first hand with the emotions.

In conclusion, I look for a great popular development of musical art in England. You know very well that "the English are not a musical people." They may cultivate music, they like it and pay for it, but they do not produce anything to be compared with the works of the great masters on the Continent. The national music is about "Champagne Charlie," "Tommy," "Waking the Baby," and "Grandfather's Clock." It is true we have Mr. Sullivan, whose compositions are always welcome; but he studied in Germany, he took the Mendelssohn scholarship at Leipsic, and therefore he may be considered, so far as music is concerned, a German to the backbone; it cannot be said of him that, "in spite of all temptations to belong to other nations, he remained an Englishman."

But in the last forty years the progress of music in England has been very great. Mr. Hullah told me that when he began to examine schools he found children who could not sing two or three consecutive notes in tune, who lacked even the rudiments of a musical ear; but that now, very greatly through Mr. Hullah's own work, this state of things is altered, and he says that if you go through the length and breadth of the land you will find that the national ear has been to a great extent cultivated. But we must not stop here; the national art must be improved, and then the national taste, and above all the education of the nation as a whole, in music.

I should like to see some one who should be responsible for conducting the musical performances of our children. Nothing is more striking in our Board Schools than the admirable management of every other department of instruction, and the muddle, looseness, uncertainty, and general inefficiency of the musical instruction. Sound, popular music, songs, and part singing, at sight as well as by ear, should radiate from the Board Schools. I desire to see cheap sheets of music placed in the hands of the children which they may take to their homes, and so learn the art of singing part songs, as they do in Amsterdam, and, indeed, in Holland generally. Even in Switzerland there is a certain coherent musical part "yodelling," at any rate superior to the "He's a jolly good fellow" style of chorus affected at our own convivial assemblies.

Let the heaven-born art of music spread; let it bless the homes and hearths of the people; let the children sing, and sing together; let the concertina, the violin, or the flute be found in every cottage; let not the only fiddle in the place be hung up in the beer-shop, the only choruses in the village be heard in the choir and at the public-house. And while music refines pleasure, let it stimulate work. Let part songs and sweet melody rise in all our crowded factories above the whirl of wheels and clanking of machinery; thus let the factory girl forget her toil and the artisan his grievance, and music, the civiliser, the recreator, the soother and purifier of the emotions, shall become the music of the future for England.

THE GREAT PROBLEM.

ONE is not tempted to envy either the brain or the heart of the man who has never pored, until the thought has become almost maddening, over the dark difficulties which affront us when we scan, as we are bound to scan, the way of God in the constitution and government of the world. The contrasts and inequalities which meet us, wherever we turn our eyes in this state which we call Christian, might well bewilder us, if we had nothing but the intellect to unravel the perplexities which they unveil. We gain nothing by flinging a cloak over the hard problem which Providence presents to us. We may shut the skeleton away in a closet, but there is an uneasy sense that it is there, which kills all peace and poisons all pleasure. We must bring it out into the sunshine, and look at it in the light of God, or we shall remain its slaves. Perhaps there is nothing in these days that so repels intelligent men from the ministries of the sanctuary, as the easy way in which preachers are wont to dispose of the difficulties which have perplexed the ages, and have strained the reason of the most mighty teachers and leaders of mankind. One has heard preachers in the pulpit explain with a pleasant smile, in five minutes, what the intellect of Christendom has pored over for generations; or else dismiss it as a mere impertinent intrusion on the simplicity of a faith, which is simple only because it leaves nothing but words to be believed. The scheme of the great universe does not lie patent on the surface of things. He tells most with all honest thinkers who shows that he knows where the stress of the difficulty lies, and that he has felt something of the anguish of that doubt through which he is seeking to guide his fellow-men.

We are not God's advocates; we are simply His witnesses. We are too much tempted to speak and act as if we were sent here to advocate His cause, and to make out a good case for Him, no matter what else may fail. All that God asks from us is to bear witness to the truth, and to leave it to advocate itself. However dark and difficult things may seem, to smooth one difficulty or to light up one dark place, otherwise than by showing the truth about it, is in the end to darken God's counsel, and to put a veil of words between Him and human souls. It would be hard to estimate how much essential mischief has been done to the cause of truth, in all ages, by the supposed necessity that its lovers should be its advocates, and should make out a good case for it by smoothing away the difficulties and magnifying the harmonies to the last point which would leave in the advocate any honesty at all. From all temptations to suppress any of the difficult elements of the problem which has to be solved, may the good Spirit keep all his faithful servants free.

There seems to be one great thought running through the vast system of the universe, of which the human body is the supreme expression. Many members, some to the eye honourable and beautiful, some uncomely and unshapely, but tempered together in the unity of the body; and so tempered that what we are tempted to call the meanest and the least comely are the most vital, and of the most essential use. We can trace the working of this law even in the lowest depths of the Creation. Everywhere there are many members in nature. Creatures beautiful and radiant, creatures loathly and obscene appear. But there is unity still; a unity as grand and complete as that of the human frame. The meanest things are on the whole more needful, and higher therefore in the order of use, than the more beautiful. The worm is on the whole probably more needful to the violet than the violet to the worm; and the host of loathsome scavengers in the Creation, are the condition of the pure and lofty unfolding of its life; so that there is no schism in the body of the world. Nature's robe, like her Master's, is seamless; every thread is wrought into the organic texture; and the beauty of the whole is the honour of each filament, even the commonest—nay, chiefly the commonest —of which it is composed.

But it is easy to see how the perplexities deepen as we advance to the contemplation of man, and of the terrible contrasts and inequalities of human society; for in man there is a self-conscious intelligence—reason that " looks before and after; " man can observe, compare, and conclude. He can contrast his poverty, his infirmity, physical or mental, his native propensities, which come to him, perhaps, with contaminated blood from a race of drunkards and roisterers, and all the misery which they make in his lot, with the health, wealth, geniality, beauty, and happiness of his more favoured fellow-men; and he can say to his Maker, and does say to his Maker, " Why hast Thou made me thus?" And there is no real escape for man on the pantheistic principle that God makes good and bad together, as He makes night and day; some of the best sort, some of the neutral sort, and some of the worst sort, thus completing the manifold harmony of the world. If there is one creed more than another in which man finds it blankly impossible to rest, it is the pantheist's. If there is one fact of consciousness which stands out more clearly than another to man in his deepest moments of experience, it is this: There is a will in me which is not God, which is the "I" of my immortal being, for whose decisions I am responsible; and the fruit of whose choice is mine, and must remain mine for ever.

At the same time it is right that we should recognise that, as far as regards essential badness and goodness, and all that is most influential on our eternal destinies, the inequalities are far slighter than appear. Rich and poor, educated and ignorant stand more nearly on a level in this matter than most of us dream. Our estimate of essential evil is not altogether as God's. We confine our strongest reprobations chiefly to the visibly foul and disreputable vices; while the Searcher of hearts sees in the sins which are hidden behind the comely mask or the purple robe more deadly, damning evils, than those which lodge under the beggar's rags or behind the dog-licked sores.

But there is a region, and that the highest, in which the contrast between the privileged few who have enjoyed Christian nurture, and the outcast many who have never heard the Father's name uttered in reverence and love, is dark, dark, indeed. There will be a company of Christians met in a goodly sanctuary, to worship the Father whose name has been familiar to them from their earliest infancy, who are able to explore the deep mystery of His ways by the light of that word which, through early habit of study, yields to them readily its choicest treasures, and lights up with something of heavenly radiance the dark sad passages of life; their ready comfort in every sorrow; their sure guide in every perplexity; their angel to lead them in the way by sure paths through the darkness of the wilderness, and to attend them in the valley of the shadow of death with visions of the glorious home that is beyond. And then there are myriads around them whose very acquaintance with the name of God has been through blasphemous oaths and jests; who have been nursed from their infancy in the belief that all this talk about heavenly things, which lights up a Christian's life with joy, is the babble of fools, or the trade of priests, which a "knowing one" should hold in scorn; who have sucked in the sense that it is a hard world, and that the God who made it is a hard God, from their mothers' breasts; and who have seen nothing to change their faith as they grew up through a struggling, suffering youth to a wretched manhood, in arms against the world around them, avowed enemies of society and of God. And who maketh them to differ? He who answers, God, as if that were the whole clue to the mystery, answers falsely. But it is a part, and a very solemn part, of the answer. The influences of the Christian home, the mother's nurture, the father's faith, the cultivated intellect, the trustful heart, and the hope laid up on high—these are the Father's gifts. "Bless the Lord, O my soul, and forget not all His benefits," should be our song as we lift up our voice to praise. But if that poor brother has none of these gifts it is largely because man's selfishness and tyranny have come between him and the hand that proffered them; it is because the devil has been let in, and that not at all by doors of its own opening, to sow the tares in that young heart. The child born in a vicious home, with tainted blood, with the example of vice and crime before him from his very infancy, was asked about it as little as his fortunate brother, to whom the lines are fallen in pleasant places, and who had all things from the first richly to enjoy.

And yet God is mixed up with it in a very solemn measure. He suffers it. He not only upholds the world in which such things are possible, but He takes it, so to speak, into the scheme of his government, and endures it while He legislates for its cure. And He seems to withhold the agencies under His control by which we think the mischiefs of society might be swiftly and finally remedied. He has ten thousand angels at His right hand whom He might make His evangelists; He could thunder His word so that every human soul must hear. He has terrors which would scare the boldest tyrant; He could arrest by one flashing stroke even a priest of the Inquisition ahunt for blood. But the thunders slumber; the sword rests in its scabbard, or only sweeps rarely in desperate extremities—as it is sweeping over Turkey now, before the eye of a trembling world. "Where is the promise of His coming?" faithful souls are ever moaning, as they contemplate the omnipotent patience. "Awake, O arm of the Lord, awake!" earnest and righteous souls cry out in agony as they gaze on wrongs and miseries which they are help-less to avenge or to cure. And God bears it still. Age after age He watches it from His throne. The foam of this turbid and bloody sea surges up around its pillars; it stains the garments of the immortals; it flecked with blood the brow of His well-beloved Son; but still no stroke, no word. Patience, patience, patience still. And to us this patience, the patience of such a God as we believe in—the God who revealed Himself on Calvary—is pregnant with hope. The fact that He does bear it is the surest of signs that He sees on beyond it, fruits that will justify it to the whole universe and through eternity. But none the less do men who know Him not moan or madden at this patience, and vent their sneers or scoffs at an epicurean or fainéant God.

But does He give no answer to the frenzied appeals of men; no word, no work to help them to believe? Yes, He has one grand answer—the Church. This is its great, solemn, nay, awful ministry, to make plain and justify the ways of God to man. "Ye are my witnesses," saith the Lord; my mes-sengers, my ministers, my almoners, my hus-bandmen, to raise by spiritual pain and toil in the tracks of the great husbandman, out of His seed-field of darkness and sorrow, the golden harvest of eternity.

This life of ours in this mortal state is like the life of the earth in the dark days of winter; how much is damp, cold, bleak, and bare! It is the seed-time; all that is noxious and foul has to be turned and venti-lated, exposed to the air and sunlight, nor less to the winds, the storms, the frosts, the snows. Were the year all seed-time, who could endure the desolation in nature and in life? But the day comes when the seed thus sown in darkness shall wave golden in the sunlight of the new Creation, and the glad reapers shall sheave it and bear it in their strong arms to the garners of the Lord. But this rests largely with us, the Church, on which presses the burden of Christ's ministry to mankind. These vast, these dread differ-ences of advantage and endowment are suffered, we may well believe, that they may give the largest development possible to man's ministry to man. Let that be abund-ant, and all bitterness passes out of the sorrow of the sorrowful; let that be cramped and acrid, and the bitterness engendered in human hearts vents itself not only on man, but on God. Many may be disposed to say, the price is too vast to pay for such a result; ministry is beautiful, and the relations which

spring out of it are beautiful and rich in fruit, but is it worth all this? And the answer is, God only can tell. He seems to see that the development of this ministry of man to man is worth any amount of present pain and strain. Perhaps we shall not learn that it is the most beautiful, the most blessed, the most fruitful thing in this universe, until we see its harvests gathered and garnered in eternity.

And it is worth our while to consider what is the essential bitterness of the suffering which springs out of these dire inequalities of nature, endowment, and condition of life. It is not the pain; man can bear any amount of pain if his heart be at peace. If mere suffering made man's misery, we might find it harder to understand how God endures that there should be so much of it in the world. But it is not the pain. The mere suffering is mixed with moral elements which infuse into it all its bitterness, and these the Christian ministry of which we speak can largely cure. Man can mostly bear any amount of suffering bravely if he be sustained by sympathy and hope. He can be glad even in the midst of it, with a gladness which the world giveth not and taketh not away. In the full consideration of this principle much of the explanation of God's ways will appear. The most blessed men who have ever lived have been the sharpest sufferers. The most blessed One was the Man of Sor-rows. It was when he was in the depths that the joy of David's heart overflowed in song. Paul and Silas, beaten, bleeding, bound, all night long sang praise. Suffering is nothing if it be not in the soul. If the soul is free and glad there will be no more plaints of misery. Sorrow there will be, sobs of pain, but they will be tuned, as they break forth, into songs.

The more one knows of life the more one seems to see that man is made on a very lofty scale, and that an easy life, free from pain, care, and tears, could by no means satisfy his heart. He is made for a wide and deep experience. Anguish and rapture are both within the compass of his scale. Each furnishes a tone which he has to enweave into his harmonies. If we could banish pain and care, the need of struggle, and the fight of faith, we should destroy at a blow the most fruitful factors of man's life. It is well that the young should understand this early. It will put them more in the way of blessing in this life than anything else that they can do. Let the young go forth into life, not afraid to suffer, and not slow to connect the suffering with the hand of their wise and loving God. A man never grows bitter over suffering if the hand of love is touching him tenderly, is making his bed in his sickness, and drawing forth the tale of his woes and wrongs. Sorrows are lightened the moment they are shared. If we can get into the heart of a poor storm-tossed and desperate wayfarer the thought "God cares for me," the night lights up in a moment, and if we wait, it will soon, like the Philippian gaol, be bright with songs.

And the first step towards the conviction that God cares, will often be the thought, man cares. God's children, His disciples, His witnesses care. It is not a matter of indifference to them whether I live a dog's life and die a dog's death or a man's. If I see that their hearts ache for me, I can believe that the Father's heart aches for me; and if it be so, and He still lets me suffer with all His power to help me, I shall see the meaning of it soon. The visits of one truly Christ-like soul in a poor, struggling neighbourhood, where, as far as we can see, the chances are terribly against the growth of all that is best in the being, will assuage, to an extent truly wonderful, the bitterness of the suffering that is there. And why? Man knows in his secret soul that he deserves to suffer, and that it is no impeachment of the goodness of God that he does suffer. He knows, too, that there is a ministry in sorrow altogether heavenly; at least he knows it in his best moments. But there is that in him which tells him that he was not meant to suffer alone. The echoes of the first promise of a helper, a deliverer, are still lingering about the world, and chiefly in the inner chambers of sorrowful hearts. And man longs for sympathy; for the touch of a tender hand, for the tones of a loving voice; for one who can whisper, "I, too, have suffered, am suffering, but I am sustained; I have taken my heartache to the bosom of my Saviour, and there I am at rest."

There is that in the heart of man which expects such ministry as this. How can it be otherwise? God made man for it, and there is a place left void in his nature which it only can fill. These void places in the nature beget its yearnings; they are the stops in the organ of our being which make music to the airs of heaven. Leave the sufferer alone, he broods and becomes bitter; his pain deepens into agony, parent of frenzy and despair. But if his brother seeks him, touches him, makes him feel his oneness with him in his condition of suffering, that

he may become one with him in the condition of blessing, the darkest gloom which envelops the ways of God will be dissipated. The sufferer has passed through the cloud, and if he can look to the Chief Sufferer, he will soon be face to face with the glory. Our ministry, if it be Christ-like, is a witness to Christ's. It makes a man feel how much God feels, and then all falls into a harmony. Let him but see that God stoops to share the burden, and he is man enough to lift it and bear it even joyfully. Who would not follow such a leader; who recks of dangers, sufferings, miseries, with such a Captain and such a prize? This is the way, the only way, to take pure bitterness out of suffering, and to make possible the justification of the ways of God to man.

And what God calls for is a Church which can pour a flood of this loving sympathy, this charity, on the world. The infant Church was full of it, and the people were glad and glorified God when they saw it. There was no lack of the class whose condition we are considering in that Jewish world. The poor they had always with them. And the people were ground to the dust in those days by the rich man's tyranny; and the misery was made doubly bitter by the Pharisee's malignant pride. "This people which knoweth not the law is cursed," was the only benediction which they ever received from the lips of their rulers; "God, I thank thee that I am not as other men are," was the only liturgy which they ever heard. There were bruised hearts and broken spirits enough there in Jerusalem, moaning over the insoluble problem, and questioning whether there were pure gladness for any spirit in any world. But when they saw the brotherhood of the Church they were glad, and in all their penury, in all their pain, they glorified God. The darkness which clouded His ways was lifted. Let heart beat against heart in its pain and fever, and man can endure, and still believe and hope in the loving God. The poor never envy the rich who are gracious; the sad never envy the glad who are genial. But the selfish, careless rich and gay, they regard with an envy which has a touch of bitter hate in it, and which, if pent up, becomes the parent of Revolutions, and of Reigns of Terror too. But let us understand who are the generous. A man may tithe his income twice over, and bestow it in alms, and be before God a miserable niggard still—niggard of that which the poor man wants and values above all the gold. Givers we can get, and enshrine their memories when they are gone in profuse biographies; but the liberal souls, the open-handed, are rare. The open hand is the symbol of the only charity which mates with God's. Let this flow through all the channels of society, and the problem is solved; "Just and true are all thy ways, O thou King of saints!" will then be the joyful testimony of mankind.

The Church has to justify its existence, its high privilege, its boundless blessing, its glorious hope, by holding and using all as God's steward and man's trustee. The sun holds its splendour in trust for the world, the flower its fragrance, the field its corn. All things that live, live to minister, and it is the spring of their gladness. The glad light which plays around the brow of Nature is the outshining of the Creator's joy in making all things blest. And shall that life which lives in a sense of which the life of all other things is but a shadow, and which shall smile and shine in spheres which lie beyond the final fire, arrogate the right to live to itself, and to hug its dear privileges closely to its heart? By the grace of Christ it is what it is; how much of its joy, its power, its blessing, grows out of the gracious dispositions of His hand? That dear old Christian home, the memory of which fills the eyes with tears; that mother's kiss; that father's blessing; let us recall them, and recall all that they have wrought for us in life, and let us pray for—

"Such a heart whose pulse may be
His praise."

Blessed ourselves, let us go forth, like Abraham, to be blessings. Let us taste deeply the sacred, the Divine joy of living to serve mankind. We may have little to give, as men count giving. "Silver and gold have I none," said one to a helpless cripple; "but such as I have give I thee: in the name of Jesus Christ of Nazareth rise up and walk." We can say that to a crippled soul, a crippled company. We can give that gift, the name of Jesus Christ of Nazareth. And there are some still who know how to give it, so that, as of old, "the lame shall leap as an hart, and the tongue of the dumb shall sing." A Church baptized with the spirit of such Divine Charity would make swift progress to the conquest of the world. And there is a joy in it which springs from no other fountain. Man was made to give like God, and only in the life of giving can he be blest. A poorer purse he may have, it may be—though "there is that scattereth and yet increaseth;" but there will be a gladder heart, a brighter home, a nobler name, the name of a living one in Jerusalem; and a treasure waxing daily in that world where the largest claims of the aspiring spirit will be honoured through a long eternity.

J. BALDWIN BROWN.

FAIRY JANE.

(For Music.)

TEASING, pleasing Fairy Jane,
Warbling through the sunny weather,
With a voice like linnet's strain,
With a heart like buoyant feather.

Jane has lips of cherry hue,
Cheeks like peaches, fair and waxen,
Laughing eyes of summer blue,
Rippling ringlets, soft and flaxen.

Pure as light—where'er she treads
All the fragrant air grows sweeter,
Sister flower-buds raise their heads
With a radiant smile to greet her.

Wealth laid down his precious gains,
Hoping in his thrall to bind her;
But she, snapping golden chains,
Cast the shining links behind her.

Wisdom passing, paused to gaze—
Left his lore and followed after,
But she, knowing Wisdom's ways,
Shattered all his plans with laughter.

Then Love came with footsteps coy—
Offered her a slender blossom,
Though she chid the backward boy,
Now she wears it in her bosom.

HENRY JOHNSTON.

"What a goose you are, Delia!"

SARAH DE BERENGER.

BY JEAN INGELOW.

CHAPTER XXXIV.

A FEW days after this, Mrs. Snep, as she stood ironing in her little cottage by the hop-garden, saw a respectable-looking woman standing by her gate. A stout little boy held her by the hand, and was crying lustily.

Mrs. Snep did not recognise her. The young woman was forgotten, but she could not forget. There was the little path, and there were the very clumps of pinks, and the grey bushes of southernwood, and there was

XXI—58

the mistress of the mansion, stouter, and, as she thought, kindlier-looking than before.

Mrs. Snep came out, and as she threw an article of clothing, just ironed, on a bush to air in the morning sun, she cast an observant eye on the stranger, who, coming forward, begged to ask for a seat until the carrier should appear, and if she might have a slice of bread and some milk for her child. She had not been able to give him his usual breakfast, and he was cross, and tired too, for they had been travelling all night.

The stranger expressed her willingness to

pay for what she had, so she was soon made welcome to a seat in the cottage. Some tea was made for her, and while she crumbled bread into a saucer for her boy, and poured milk upon it, a tide of recollections flowed up. She remembered the days before her little Delia was born, and afterwards all that she had suffered. Just so, in that same place, and perhaps in that very chair, her little Amabel had sat beside her, contented with her bread and milk. The click of Mrs. Snep's iron appeared familiar; the hops leaned over the little back window, just as in the former days.

"And so you want to go on by the carrier's cart?" said Mrs. Snep. "It does not pass till noon."

"I know that, ma'am; I have been the journey before."

"Oh, you know these parts, ma'am?"

"I did a good many years ago."

"Well, things don't change here much, that's certain. We've got the same squire, and the same doctor, and the same parson we've had for years."

"The parson's name was Mr. de Berenger," faltered Mrs. Dill, "when I knew these parts."

"Oh, he was the curate. We have no curate now," answered Mrs. Snep.

"Indeed, ma'am."

"He must have been gone these fifteen years."

"And well-nigh forgot by this time, I should judge," sighed Mrs. Dill, for an anguish of desire urged her to speak of him if she could.

"Forgot!" exclaimed Mrs. Snep; "not by any means, I can tell you, ma'am. It's only two years since he came to stay at the vicarage; and I've reason enough to remember that, for my daughter—my second one, that will be three-and-twenty if she lives till Michaelmas—Mary——"

"Yes?" exclaimed Mrs. Dill, with keen interest.

Mrs. Snep paused to take another iron from the fire, then, attacking her narrative at a different point, said, "Miss Sarah de Berenger, and aunt to that Mr. de Berenger, had wrote to our vicar's lady while he was here, and said she wanted a parlour-maid; and she wanted one from a distance, for she could not allow followers. And so our vicar's lady and Mr. de Berenger managed the thing between them. And Mary took the place, worse luck!"

"I know Miss de Berenger quite well, ma'am!" exclaimed Mrs. Dill, a warm flush of joy passing over her face. "I lived in a situation for many years within four miles of her."

"No, you don't say so, ma'am! She was the nearest woman, and the meanest, that ever I had to do with, as you'll judge, when I tell you that I'm ironing my girl's clothes for her next place, and there's not a scrap of black among them."

"Black!" faltered Mrs. Dill. "Why, who's dead?"

"Who should be dead? Why, Miss de Berenger herself. Didn't you know it?"

"Dear me, no. I am come a long way; I've heard nothing. She was in the best of health when last I heard of her."

"And might be now. It was an accident. The old gentleman, that used to be so rich, was driving her out, poor lady, and they got overturned. She never spoke again, my girl says. Ah, there have been many changes in that family; it's as much as there often is in the newspapers to read of them. Perhaps you knew the old gentleman?"

"I've seen him times out of mind, ma'am," faltered the poor mother. She dared not now mention her children. Had those changes affected them?

"They say," proceeded Mrs. Snep, "that of all his fine houses and lands, he have but enough left just to keep him."

"Why, I never heard of such a thing," cried Mrs. Dill. "I did not think rich folks like that could lose their property."

"It was a company he had shares in, my daughter said. All the country rang with it. It arose from what people call unlimited liability. There are two pretty young ladies, that folks do say are his grand-daughters. You've seen them too, mayhap. He likes to ride about what used to be his own park with them, and he's as happy as a king."

The mother sighed for joy; she could not speak. Her children were among the living, then, and they were well.

The operation of sprinkling the clothes occupied Mrs. Snep for a minute or two, and gave Hannah Dill time to recover herself. "Rides about with Miss Amabel and Miss Delia, does he?" she presently found voice enough to say.

"Their very names, ma'am; you have them quite pat."

"But I should have thought to lose his money would break his heart."

"It does not, ma'am. My daughter stayed at the rectory for three months, after Miss de Berenger's death. They wanted extra help, and paid her handsome. They are better off now, of course. She said it was as good as a printed book to see how the old gentleman went on. He is upward of eighty, and has lost his memory. He has no servant left but one old man, that always waits on him, and he has a fat old horse in the rectory stable. He lives with Mr. de Berenger, and does not know that he has lost his money. His notion is that he is making his great fortune greater. Saving up, you know, to leave more behind him."

"He never could bear to spend much money," observed Mrs. Dill. "And so the young ladies ride with him, and are attentive to him?"

"So I hear, ma'am. And what he costs Mr. de Berenger, he has about enough money left to pay for. When he gets tired of the country, my daughter says they put him in the train and telegraph to his other nephew, that lives in London, to meet him. It's not worth while, he says, to have a town house, and that is why he has let it, for he wants to save. He says he must go and see that the people his house is let to are taking care of it. And those folks, knowing the case, always satisfy him, and, as I said, he is as cheerful and as happy as a king."

"Well, I never!" exclaimed Mrs. Dill. She was glowing all over with a warmth and joy that she had hardly ever expected to feel again. They were well, pretty, useful, happy. Oh, there was sunshine yet in this world, and she was basking in it.

"The Mr. de Berengers are better off now, no doubt?" she presently said.

"Not by a shilling," replied Mrs. Snep.

"Well, I always hoped, though Miss de Berenger was so fond of making schemes about her will, that she would do the right thing by her nephews."

"Then she didn't, ma'am."

"Who did her money go to, then?"

"She'd almost doubled it during her life-time, as I heard tell, and they say her house was a sight for the useful things she'd got together—stores of linen, and china, and what not. And she left it all—her farms and her house, and her money—to those two young ladies; everything, down to the very jam-pots on her shelves, and the clothes in her drawers, and the thimbles in her workbox. They say those two young ladies have more than eighteen thousand pounds apiece."

More than eighteen thousand pounds apiece! And the man that had been so good to them—that had brought them up and loved them, and even been proud of them—he had got nothing!

Oh, how sweet it was to hear even this stranger talk of them! But how bitter to hear that the kindness of Felix de Berenger had been so rewarded, and that Sarah, in her wilful mistake about them, should have robbed her own flesh and blood for their sake.

Could any good come of money so in-herited? No; their mother thought it could not. She became cold and pale. It was not till Mrs. Snep mentioned their names again that she roused herself; but it was only to hear what caused her fresh anxiety, and to be shown that a most difficult, a most bitter duty towards her darlings was yet to do.

"One of the two is engaged to be married, as I'm told," said Mrs. Snep.

"It must be the eldest, then," said Mrs. Dill, trembling with excitement.

"Well, now, I should have said not."

"But the other is so very young."

"I know there was a young soldier-officer that made one of them an offer. He went away, and came back lately and offered to her again. I think he is the gentleman, and I think it is the youngest. But they're thoughtless—the young ladies are both thoughtless," continued Mrs. Snep, going off on a part of the subject more interesting to her than Delia's lover. "As I said, Miss de Berenger never left so much as one black gown apiece to her servants, though some of them had lived with her for years. Those young ladies were kind—I will say that; but neither of them had the thought to put the servants into mourning, and my daughter came home without a scrap of black on her."

"Somebody did ought to have told the young ladies what was the custom," said the mother, apologizing for them.

"So I say, ma'am."

"Oh, my Delia!" thought Hannah Dill; "do you love this young gentleman? And must your mother go and tell you that you've no right at all to keep Miss Sarah's money? When will there be an end to my sorrows? Maybe the young man will be off the bargain if you give up the fortune; and if you refuse to do so, your mother 'll never have an easy hour about you any more."

And what was the true state of the case about Delia? This: that the young officer had, indeed, returned at the end of the year, and had again offered her his hand. Urged by Amabel to give him a little time, and not to reject him hastily, Delia had agreed to consider the matter for a few weeks, and to try to like him. She had failed; and that very morning, while her little brother ate his bread and milk, she had, with many flushes and blushes, a great deal of pity for him, and some shame for herself, contrived to tell him so. He was gone, and just as her mother left the house where she had been born, and met the carrier's cart, Delia darted up-stairs to Amabel's room, and stood looking at her sister with blushing discomfiture.

Amabel came up to her and smoothed her cheek gently against hers—a kind of moderate caress that the girls had used from their childhood.

"What a goose you are, Delia !" she said.

"Yes, I know," said Delia ruefully.

"You've sent him away."

"Of course : Coz said I must. I wish— oh, I wish Coz *didn't know !*"

"He'll never tell !" exclaimed Amabel.

"No ; but I know that he knows."

Delia moved to the dressing-table, and in an absent and agitated fashion began to try on some of Amabel's rings. Presently she saw Dick in the garden ; he was apparently deep in thought. Delia drew backward in the room and smiled.

"Coz and Amias have been talking to him all the morning," whispered Amabel. "He says now he should like to go to sea," she continued, nodding towards Dick.

"Does he ?" exclaimed Delia. "Oh no, Dick ; I think you'll find you do *not* wish to go to sea."

"Then you should not have set him against emigrating."

It may have fairly been said of Master Dick at that time, that he did not know his own mind, unless it may have been said more fairly still that he did not know somebody else's mind, any more than he knew how completely that mind had the mastery over his.

Sir Samuel de Berenger had put him to school till he was eighteen years old, and then, when he came home for the holidays, his two brothers had sat in judgment on him and his future ; when it was found that he had done so very well, and stood so very high, that if they let him stay at school another year, he would in all probability get a good exhibition, which would enable him to go to college almost for nothing, and which he would be able to provide for his own living.

And Dick had come home without getting the exhibition. He was now nineteen, a re- markably fine, handsome young fellow, brown all over, taller than either of his two brothers' very engaging, rather inclined to be idle, and quite helpless in the hands of these said brothers, who had, at some inconvenience to

themselves, prolonged his school days for him, and now did not very well know what to do with him.

Dick had only been in the garden a few minutes when he saw Delia sitting in the open window of what had been the nursery. with some "art needlework" in her hand.

"How nice this room looks, with poor Aunt Sarah's things in it !" he said, accost- ing her and sitting on the window-sill. "No one would know it.—I say, Delia !"

"Yes."

"I've had such a wigging this morning."

"Oh ! you should decide, then, what you'll do—what you'll be."

"Well, I said I would go to sea, and they won't let me. Why, Delia, where did you get those rings ?"

"Oh, they belong to Amabel. I'm so fond of rings, and I have not got one."

"Why don't you buy some, then ?" said Dick.

"Amabel never bought one of hers ; rings are supposed to be presents. If I wore rings, and was asked who gave them to me. I shouldn't like to have to say I bought them."

Dick revolved a certain thing in his mind. "Look here," he began ; "if I go to sea for two or three years——"

"It will be so dull," interrupted Delia. "if you go to sea and Amabel's gone."

"Well, but if I do, I could give you a ring for a parting present."

"So you could ; and I could give one to you, with your crest on it."

"If I go to sea." No occasion to wait for that. Dick took himself off in less than five minutes, and in hot haste demanded of Felix a large, old-fashioned gold watch, which had been his father's, and which he had knocked about a good deal at school.

It had plenty of good stuff in it. Felix looked at him almost as if he knew all about it, and gave him the watch in silence and with gravity.

It was four miles to the town, and Dick ran almost all the way. He did not make a bad bargain with the one jeweller that the place afforded, and then the price he was to have for his watch being agreed upon, he set himself to overhaul the whole shop for two pretty rings. It was not till the next morning, about the same hour, that he saw Delia sitting in the same place, all over blushes and dimples. He approached and getting over the low sill, sat down beside her on the couch, and said, "I've got them. Rather jolly ones, I think ; only I'm afraid they are too big for your finger." He looked very shamefaced.

Delia put forth her little finger, the same on which she had worn Amabel's rings. They were manifestly too big for it. Then she put forth her middle finger, and for that they were a little too tight.

"What a pity!" said Delia. "And they're such pretty ones; just the sort I like."

"Well, put them on your third finger, then," rejoined the donor.

"Oh, but I couldn't wear them there," said Delia, blushing till her forehead and throat were all one lovely hue of carnation.

In an instant Dick knew why; but it was his destiny to be a lucky dog. He blushed himself, but he said stoutly, "Why not?"

"Because that's the 'engaged' finger, you know, Dick," she answered.

Dick was holding her hand in one of his, and had the rings in the other.

"Oh," he said, almost with a groan, "what a fool I have been!" And Delia—this exquisite Delia, who all on a sudden had become almost unbearably delightful—Delia was turning away her face from him. "I'm nothing but a schoolboy yet," he said, with deep disgust against himself. "If I had but worked as I ought to have done, it might have been different." But that blush of Delia's was the making of him. "Put them on, if only for a moment," he said, pleadingly. And she let him put them on her "engaged" finger.

"It can only be for a little while," she observed. But how pretty they looked there!

"Even if you won't wear them, you mean to keep them?" he urged.

Delia had closed her dimpled fist, and was looking at them wistfully.

"Suppose you take care of them for me," she said; but she made no movement towards unclosing her hand or taking them off.

"Take care of them till when?"

Delia still looked at them, then her little hand unclosed, and Dick took it in his.

"Coz would be displeased," she whispered.

"You mean that he would, because I've been an idle dog, and because—well, he said it yesterday—because I seem very well content to be loafing about here, doing nothing."

Delia was silent.

"But that's all over now," he added impetuously; "I'm going to Felix directly—

this minute. I intend to settle to something at once—forthwith. And then——"

By this time she had taken off the rings and put them into his hand.

"And then, Delia——" he repeated.

But had not Delia got all she wished for now? Perhaps she thought so. At any rate, Dick's glimpse of Paradise was over. "Oh, then," she said (she had such a mischievous little dimple in her cheek when she laughed) —"oh, then—we shall see."

<h2>CHAPTER XXXV.</h2>

SARAH DE BERENGER was indeed gone; her guiding hand was at last withdrawn.

"I have lost my aunt," Felix would say, and ever after he felt an uneasy want of those fresh and direct expressions of opinion that often showed him what he really thought himself, as well as of her fearless certainties, and her fertile crops of schemes. But he did not know, it never occurred to him to consider, that for many years she had been the doer of everything of the least consequence that had been done in his family. And yet she was a remarkably foolish woman.

Sarah had first, as she believed, discovered an interesting mystery. She had obliged Hannah Dill, contrary to all her wishes, to bring the mystery near; she had, to her own satisfaction, solved it, and she had, for the sake of it, deprived her own nephews of every shilling she possessed. It was all Sarah's doing that Amias was engaged to a little girl who was supposed by all the neighbourhood to have no right to any father's name; but then it was Sarah's doing also that old Sir Samuel, now he had lost his memory, was more happy in the society of the two girls, and received more tender attentions from them, and more real affection, than from any other creatures.

As for Felix, his life for years past had been planned out for him by his aunt Sarah. It is true that he now hopelessly loved this beautiful Delia, but then for many years she and her sister had been his delight, his daily occupation, and his one amusement. He knew that he would not have given up that pleasant, cheerful past, even if by so doing he might have avoided the pain of his present. Perhaps he allowed himself to be more severe on Dick, on her account, than occasion altogether warranted; for Dick was but a youth—a fine, honest, healthy, affectionate youth. Felix considered that Dick was not manly enough; not considering that, but for Delia, he might, perhaps, at his time of life not have been manly at all.

However, Felix changed his mind on one particular morning. Dick had two rings in his pocket. "I will not wear either of them," Delia had said, "till it is decided what you are to be." So Dick had asked to have a conference, a final conference, on this great subject with his two brothers, and then and there he had discussed it—laid down his own views, stated the *pros* and *cons* of all the plans proposed, and expressed his deep desire to work, in a fashion that perfectly astonished them.

Amias was exceedingly amused. Felix sat back in his chair, and looked at him in puzzled bewilderment.

"Why, you young scamp!" exclaimed Amias. "Want to go to London the day after to-morrow!—want to set to work instantly! Well, I'll do my very best for you, as I declared I would the other day, when you didn't seem to care a straw about it. But I cannot think what has come to you."

"The fact is, Delia says——" Dick began.

"Delia says!" exclaimed Amias, in amazement.

"Delia says——" Dick began again, and again stuck fast.

"Well, out with it, my boy,'" said Felix, gravely and kindly.

Dick had a little ring-case now in his hand; he put it down, and the ring rolled out on to the table. Dick picked it up and poised it on the top of one of his great fingers. "Delia says she'll never wear this for a schoolboy. She will not be engaged till I have got some career before me—till I have something to do."

"I—think—she—is—quite—right," said Amias, gazing at the ring, and uttering the sentence as if he required to think between every word. He looked so much surprised, however, that Dick, in spite of his nervousness, burst into a short laugh. Then all on a sudden it flashed upon him that Delia was included in this astonishment. He could not bear that this exquisite creature, so wise, so kind, so loving, should be the subject of any disparaging surprise. He thought his own impetuous presumption was alone to blame. He hastened to declare this. He meant to be worthy of her. Change his mind? Nonsense! How could he change his mind? He had loved her all his life better than any one else in the world. He had always helped her with her lessons. When they played at "houses" as children, she was always his little wife.

Everything he said, while more earnest, became more boyish, till Felix said—

"There, my dear boy, think of improving yourself, not of excusing Delia. The best part of your future is already prepared for you; make the rest suitable for it, and all will be well."

And in the meantime Hannah Dill, with her child, entered the town where she feared to find her husband.

The assizes were indeed going on, but to those who were not directly concerned in them, this gave no air of solemnity; there was little about any whom she accosted which answered to the fear and dread and depression in her own mind. And she found herself unable to ask any questions. She looked about, she wandered about, till she found herself in the market-place, and the buildings about it she felt sure were none of them what she wanted. And what was the building she wanted called? She was not sure whether it was a court-house or a session-house, or a prison, and she could not make up her mind to ask. A forlorn hope that she might get a letter from her husband, sustained her till she reached the post-office; for she had written to Uzziah, at their poor home in Whitby, told him where she had gone, and cautiously hinted at her reason.

Alas! there was no letter at the office, and no telegraphic message for Hannah Dill. Her child, tired and hungry, began to cry for his dinner, and she felt that, when she reached the court, she should not be allowed to enter unless he was perfectly quiet and good. She hastened into an eating-shop, and gave him a comfortable meal, and then, as she glanced out at the window, she saw what she at once perceived to be the place she had looked for; people were hanging about the door, but many more were coming out than going in.

"Why were the people coming away?" she asked. "Were the assizes over?"

"Oh no: but the judges were at lunch; they always had an interval for lunch at this time of day."

"Might one go in and hear the trial?"

"Certainly; a court of justice was always open to the public."

She hardly knew how the next half-hour passed. She was soon standing in the press outside that door. At first all was silence; she seemed to have no chance of getting in. Afterwards there was a little bustle, and voices inside struck upon her frightened ear. Some people were almost as desirous to enter as she was, but her sharpened senses showed her some who were only there for curiosity.

"Five shillings, sir, if I get in," she whispered,

to a stalwart man at her side. Then she turned her pale face, and, selecting another, repeated the same words.

An energetic movement on either side of her soon brought her on. She knew not how it was done, but the money was given, and she was all but inside in a very few minutes. She had not intended to tell her wretched errand, but it was guessed. Her money and these two men were powerful enough to bring her to the front; her face did the rest. She stood within, and, being tall, she could see well over the shoulders and heads of those about her, almost all of whom were women.

There was no trembling, no sinking, now; the people were pressed closely together. The atmosphere was stifling. She had a heavy child in her arms, but she knew no fatigue; all her soul was in her eyes, for at present she could hear nothing.

Oh! now there was a movement; something that pierced her heart with anguish, showed her the judges coming in with all state. These men, who were to doom others to a disgraceful death, were ushered in with honour, with observance. She, poor, wretched woman, felt this with a keenness that had never struck in all her life on her sharpened senses before.

It was right, it must be so; sympathy was all with the law.

In that crowd she felt so utterly alone, as if none of God's creatures could come near enough to know what she even suffered, much less to pity her—the wife of a possible murderer, a possible murderer's child sleeping with his rosy face resting on her shoulder.

Another movement, which it so chanced brought her a little forwarder, and there were the barristers in their wigs, and a name had been called. Some man answering to the call was in the pulpit-like enclosure, which she at once recognised as the witness-box. Then she saw the prisoner, a pale, small man, whose forlorn face looked as if no courage or strength was left in him. As the witness kissed the book almost carelessly, certainly with perfect composure and confidence, he turned his faded eyes upon him. Hannah Dill lifted up hers.

One fear was over. The prisoner being tried was a stranger; but another fear followed closely. Her instinct justified itself by the event. Sitting among the spectators, and a very little way behind the witness, a man leaning forward gazed and hearkened. Not any change that fear or fatigue or shame had wrought had so changed him, that she did not instantly recognise the deeply watchful and utterly colourless face. It was her husband.

A terrible trembling seized her, so that she lost the drift and meaning of the first few questions and answers. All her thought was to know the meaning of Uzziah's expression.

His features were sunk, he was wasted almost to a shadow; his eyes were intent on the witness, and yet there was spread over his face a certain awful peace. Her wretched husband was perfectly calm.

She knew not how long she watched him, but it was till another witness was in the box, and it was because of a great change in Uzziah's face that she turned to look and to listen. It was a confident witness—a witness almost too willing. He was being re-examined by the counsel for the prisoner.

"Remember that you are on your oath."

"I do remember it."

"And you swear that this is the man?"

"I could not forget him."

"But it is seventeen years ago."

"Seventeen years and three months."

"A man changes a good deal in seventeen years and three months."

"Ay, but a club-foot—when one hears it behind one——" Here the witness paused.

"Well?" said the counsel for the prisoner.

"When I heard that man's club-foot, as he was following, I felt as if——"

"You are not to tell the court what you felt."

"Well, I mean I knew that was the very same I heard that fearful time, and I turned myself, and I saw him."

"You saw the prisoner, certainly?"

"Ay; and I knew him at once, and spoke at once. Said I, 'We have met before.'"

"And as another witness has proved, he answered, 'Not to my knowledge.' Now, what had you beside the peculiar sound of the club-foot to go on, when you said to a man whom, by your own showing, you had not seen for seventeen years, 'We have met before'?"

"It was the same man," persisted the witness. "I knew him at once, *and he knew me.*"

"How did you know him? Tell the jury that."

"It was the lock of hair, partly, that hung over his forehead, and, partly, it was the oval shape of his face, as he leaned over poor Cambourne after he'd struck him, that I remembered."

"It's false!" cried a voice that rang through the court—"it's false! You, William Tasker, don't look at the prisoner; look here, look at me!"

Cries of "Turn that man out!" were heard. There was confusion in the place where the sound had proceeded from; a woman fell down in a fainting fit; people rose in their places; but before the officer could reach the man who had spoken, some were helping the woman out, others had started away from him. He was standing alone, leaning on a rail in front.

"You, William Tasker," he repeated, "look at me!"

The terrified witness turned hastily, and gazed at him as if fascinated. The counsel for the prisoner paused. In one terrible instant every eye was upon Uzziah Dill. From the judges downwards all gazed at him—a lame man, with an oval face, and a lock of hair that strayed over his forehead.

He leaned forward, with eyes wide open.

"Delia had closed her dimpled fist, and was looking at them."

He and the witness gazed at one another, and the unfortunate wife gazed also; saw the officers advancing through the crowd to remove Uzziah; heard the witness cry out in a lamentable voice, and beat his breast, "I've sworn against the innocent, and there the guilty stands!" and then heard (not one syllable was spared to her)—heard her husband's answer, as they were about to lead him away, "You've said the truth now, William Tasker; 'twas I that did it. The Lord have mercy on my sinful soul!"

CHAPTER XXXVI.

SOME time after this, Hannah Dill seemed to come back again—she knew not from whence—and she was sitting on some steps in a quiet flagged court. The sun was shining—that was the first thing she noticed; then she observed that she herself was in the shadow; that her child rubbed his cheek against her sleeve, cressing her, and that a tall gentleman was leaning over her, a gentleman whom she had seen before.

"Do you know me, Mrs. Dill?" he asked her kindly.

She thought he might have said that several times before.

"Yes, sir," she answered in a low, dull voice. "It's Mr. Bartlett."

"What can I do for you?"

"I want to go to poor Dill."

"You cannot do that now, my poor friend. He has accused himself; he has given himself up."

"I knew he would," she replied, quite calmly. "That other man's wife is happy now, and I——"

"Your misfortune is very great," said Mr. Bartlett. "I pity you deeply."

"I saw the prisoner's wife get her arms round his neck and hug him, while they led my wretched husband away."

"Have you any place to go to—have you lodgings here?"

"No, sir."

"Well, then, I must arrange for you."

He went quickly from her, and a lady, who seemed to have been standing above her on the steps, came down and addressed her with sympathetic gentleness.

She knew it was Mrs. Bartlett, but the shock she had sustained had been too much for her; her mind was blank and dull. She uttered her passing impressions: "I never thought to see them here; they don't live here?"

"No," said Mrs. Bartlett, glad to foster this momentary lapse from the dread reality. "No; we don't live here, but my father and mother do. This is their house; we are come to stay with them."

After that Hannah Dill knew not at all how many hours or weeks might have passed, when one day, awaking in a decent bed, she found that she was cool; that the furniture, which had long seemed to whirl about her, had settled in its place; that the swarms of passing strangers, who had appeared night and day to approach her bed and gaze at her, were all gone. She slept a good deal that night, and in the morning awoke aware of what had occurred, and able to think.

She had a nurse, as she perceived, but she could not bear to question her. It was not till Mr. Bartlett, hearing she was sensible, came to see her, and brought his wife, that she spoke, sending down the nurse, and gazing at them with hollow, frightened eyes.

"Is he condemned, sir?"

She lay long silent when Mr. Bartlett had told her, by a pitying gesture, that it was so. At last Mrs. Bartlett said, "You must think

of your dear little boy, Mrs. Snaith, and try to get better for his sake. He is very well; I have seen that he was well done by."

"Ma'am, I know you have a mother's heart. Is there no hope for Dill, sir? Must he die that death?"

"He is quite resigned," said Mr. Bartlett, instead of answering her.

"Oh, my God!" cried the poor woman, folding her hands, "have pity on him and on our innocent child!"

"Yes, your innocent child," said Mrs. Bartlett. "In all this bitter misery, Mrs. Snaith, there is one gleam of comfort, and that concerns him. Nobody here knows your husband's name; he has refused to divulge it. He has shown a father's heart in that respect."

"It was his duty. Does he know that I have been so ill?"

"Yes."

"Oh, I must go to him!"

"You cannot yet."

"Oh, I might be too late!"

"There are many days yet. You will not be too late. Your husband has been very ill himself. He has had an epileptic fit."

There are some things that appear quite unendurable; they bear down the soul under such a weight of misery, that life seems impossible. And yet they will not kill; they are not thus to come to their desired end.

When Hannah Dill and her husband met, they both looked the mere shadows of their former selves. They sat hand in hand in the condemned cell, and neither spoke. It seemed a comfort to the wretched prisoner to have his wife by his side, but he never had anything to say. Sometimes he was reading his Bible when she appeared, sometimes he was kneeling in prayer—always deeply humble and generally quite calm, for he was not agitated by any hope; his doom was fixed.

One day, as she was about to leave him, he bared his thin arm, and said, "Oh, Hannah, sometimes I hope——"

"Hope you may die first?" she whispered.

"Ay."

"I spoke to Mr. Bartlett about that," she answered. "My poor husband! he says, for all their suffering, the condemned do not die. And you are at peace. But oh, that it might be!" she broke out, bursting into tears. Then, trying to calm herself, she said, "You are a man forgiven of God, as we both for ever trust; but you have always known that at last you deserved to suffer—and suffer you would."

"Oh, that it was over!—oh, that it was done!" she said, when she got home; and she was so wretchedly ill all that night, that she feared to be laid up again and unable to go to him. But just at sunrise, as she had dropped into an uneasy doze, a flattering dream came to her: she thought she saw her husband standing at the foot of the bed, and that his eyes were full of a rapturous calm.

While she looked, some noise startled her and she woke, mourning over the sweetness of that short respite. How hard that it should have been wrested from her! But there was a noise again; it was under her window. Some one called out her name. She started up. Mr. Bartlett was below. He told her to dress herself and come down to him.

Oh, how beautiful the sunrise was, when she came out—how pure and peaceful!

"Your husband is very ill," he whispered to her; "the chaplain has obtained leave for you to come to him. He had another fit last night."

Her dream had still dominion over her, and she looked at the sunrise; but she hastened to the prison, and was soon in his cell.

Two people were there, the doctor and a warder. They were not sympathetic, not pitiful, merely attentive to what was before them. Her husband was speaking; his voice was perfectly strange to her—a tremulous, piping voice. "Yes, they tempted me; they gave me the drink, sir. I was three-parts drunk when I did it."

The doctor and the warder parted, to let her come to the narrow bed. The signs of his sore struggle during the fit were visible on his face, and on the bruised arms and disordered bed, but he was perfectly calm now; the sunrise was fair upon his wasted features.

He spoke again. "And the mercy of the Most Merciful is over all His works. I trust in Him that I die forgiven." A slight convulsive movement passed over his face, and then there was a deep sigh. She was kneeling beside him now.

"There," said the doctor, coming forward with grave indifference, "I said he would not last more than the twelve hours from the time of the seizure. It's half-past six o'clock."

"Is my poor husband dead, sir?" asked the wife.

"Yes, my good woman—dead."

"May I——"

"You may do nothing at all but leave the prison," interrupted the doctor, with more kindness of manner.

"Not have his poor body to bury it?"

"You may do nothing at all but leave the prison," he repeated; and she rose at once, and Mr. Bartlett took her home again.

A widow, and all that day lying on her bed, unable to lift herself up, and yet lost in a rapture of thankfulness, blessing God for her own and her poor husband's sake.

But the shock of all she had gone through was more than she could bear, and for several weeks she was so utterly prostrate, that to rise, and for an hour or two daily to sit trembling by her fire, was all she could accomplish. She had still money left, and there would be more to come to her in a few weeks, so that she was able to pay for what she wanted. Her kind friends, the Bartletts, were gone.

What still oppressed her was Miss de Berenger's will. As soon as she was able, she must go and seek her children, and, if possible, induce them to give up the bequest. She was too weak to write, too weak to move; it was not till some time in the month of November, some weeks after her husband's death, that, finding how very little of her money was left, she roused herself, and selling all she had that she could possibly spare, set off in the railway with her child. She had an urgent longing upon her to see justice done. Her children could not prosper if they had, however innocently, brought loss upon the family which had cherished them.

And yet how little she could with safety tell them. She pondered over this during the dreary night's journey in the parliamentary train, and almost despaired. There was still nothing but concealment before her. Her daughters would meet her with kindly condescension, though she had gone off from them so suddenly. Yes, and each of them she hoped—she was sure—would give her a kiss. But she had robbed herself of all claim on them; even the bond of faithful service was broken.

CHAPTER XXXVII.

MRS. JOLLIFFE was a woman of consequence—of much more consequence, in some respects, than Mr. de Berenger, though she was generally considered to be a servant, and he a master. On all great occasions Mrs. Jolliffe could make her power felt, and one was approaching.

In fact, the very next day, namely, the eighteenth of November, was to be the most important that for many years had dawned on the De Berenger family. A very large goose pie was at that moment baking in honour of it. Cakes, without end, were ranged on the dressers to be given away in the village. There was great rolling of pastry, stuffing of fowls, clearing of jelly, stoning of plums, roasting of beef. Mrs. Jolliffe was making all her subordinates miserable for fear the oven shouldn't go. It generally went very well; there was no special reason why it should not then. It never had failed since Master came of age. A modest festival had been given on that occasion, and the crust of the pie was burnt.

Nobody in the kitchen had any peace till that goose pie was out of the oven, and was all one clear expanse of gold-coloured crust.

"And quite a credit to you, ma'am," cried the two village matrons who were come to help. Mrs. Jolliffe was pacified for the moment, but now she began to fret about the partridges and the custards, "for, indeed, a wedding is not a thing that takes place every day," she remarked.

"And hadn't need," sighed her weary subordinates.

"There wasn't as much of a spread when Mr. Amias was christened as I could have wished to see," continued Mrs. Jolliffe, who never forgot anything, "and I remember as well as can be, how I said to her that was cook at that time, 'I hope, if the blessed babe lives to eat his wedding breakfast, he'll see finer victuals on the table by half, and more of them.'"

"You might have said you hoped he would make a fine bridegroom," observed one of the attendants.

"But I did not," replied Mrs. Jolliffe, impressively, "and so I tell you truly. But we have all heard that marriages are made in heaven, and so I believe they are—a picked few of them,—this for one. Never was anything like the conveniency of it. Miss Sarah's money going to her own nephew, the right crest on Miss Amabel's share of the plate, and all their things marked 'A. B.' both of them."

"It's very interesting," said the scullery girl; and Mrs. Jolliffe, finding that she had time to pause and be amused when the success of the breakfast hung yet in the balance, severely ordered her into the back kitchen to wash potatoes.

It was long past midnight when Mrs. Jolliffe, satisfied at last, locked up the house and crept up to bed. The servants, all extremely tired, slept heavily and later than usual.

The bridegroom, as perhaps might have been expected, was first awake, and rang for his hot water.

He was in the little room which had been his from a boy. It led out of his brother's room, and commanded a view of the church and the lawn, on which grew two very fine fir-trees.

Amias drew up his blind; rather a thick sprinkling of snow had fallen in the night. It was still snowing. A dark and rather misty morning. The two trees stood like two tall sharp spires, and a tree or shrub of singular shape appeared between them. It did not seem to be so thickly covered with snow as the other shrubs. He looked at it with interest; it was singularly like the figure of a woman crouching down against the fir-tree as if for shelter. A curious freak of the frost, as he thought it. Yes, like even to the minute details; for there, bent down, might be the head, and there, falling into regular creases, was what might be the hood of her cloak!

It *was* a woman!

He called his brother out of his room to look at it. They even thought they saw it move, and both, hurriedly throwing on their clothes, ran down. The shape had already attracted attention below. Felix and Amias had plenty of help, and the helpless creature, not stiff, not insensible, but only powerless to move, was carried into the warm nursery and laid on a couch. Her attitude, as they raised her, was easily explained. She was crouching over a beautiful, rosy child, so as to shield him from the cold. Her cloak folded him to her, and he was warm and sleeping, having leaned against her shoulder.

Hannah Dill! She looked worn and wan; her hair had many streaks of grey in it, and her hollow eyes told of pain and grief and trouble. She made no complaint; her eyes followed her child, and when she saw that they were attending to him, giving him breakfast and warming him, she appeared to sink away into an exhausted sleep.

It was about eight o'clock, and the family were not down. It was not to be expected that at such a time more attention could be devoted to the poor, uninvited visitor than was absolutely needful, especially as she could not talk; but in about an hour she was able to drink some hot tea. Then she seemed to notice that Felix had come in and was standing near her. Mr. Brown, the doctor, was also present.

"And you say she spoke when you first found her under the tree?" he said to Felix.

"Yes; we raised her up, my brother and I, and she stood between us."

Jolliffe took the child and remarked at the

same moment, "She has a widow's cap on."

Then she said faintly, "My poor husband is dead. I trust he went to God."

"She is coming round," said the doctor. "Well, Mrs. Snaith, do you feel better?"

Hannah Dill looked about her. "I had not been there long — there under the tree. It did not seem long," she said, addressing Felix. "I wanted so to see them," she presently added, while the doctor continued to feel her pulse and regard her attentively.

"Her strength must have failed just as she got near the house," he observed, "and she sank down. The cold has done the rest. See how she gazes at the door."

"The young

ladies are not dressed yet, Mrs. Snaith," said Felix, using her old familiar name. "You shall see them shortly. So you were not long under the tree?"

"No; they put me out at four o'clock at the town. I walked on, for my money was all spent, and my boy was hungry."

And this was the wedding morning. Neither of the two brothers liked that Amabel and Delia should begin it with the sight of their old nurse, and the story of what she must have suffered.

Amias came in first with Delia, all in white array as a bridesmaid; her lovely face was sweet and pitiful, but she shrank a little when she saw the hollow-eyed woman stretched on a couch and motionless, except for the turning of her eyes. She came, and, leaning over her, kissed her kindly, and noticing a sort of rapture that came over the poor face, said, "Mamsey dear, you'll be better soon."

Mamsey had hold of a fold of tarlatan. "What does it mean?" she asked, with entreating eyes.

"Why, the wedding, Mamsey—the wedding; that's what it means!"

"You to be married, my beauty bright? You!"

"Oh no," cried Delia, all dimples and blushes; "no. But don't look so frightened, dear."

"Who is it, then?" said Mamsey, very faintly.

"Amabel."

"Then I'm too late," said Mamsey. "I hoped the Lord would let me get here in time. It can't be helped."

What could she mean? She spoke so slowly and seemed so disturbed, that Amias said, "And why should it be helped, Mamsey? Everybody wishes for it."

"Who's the gentleman," she mourned out; "tell me his name."

"Why, his name is the same as mine," answered Amias, smiling down upon her with joy in his dark eyes. "I am the gentleman!"

"You, sir—you?"

"Yes, I—Mr. Amias de Berenger. You remember me, surely."

"Well, then, it's all right," she murmured. "Wonderful goodness of God! I bless His holy Name."

Strangely solemn words; they seemed to have little relation to the circumstances, and she fell away, after saying them, into a kind of faint.

"The bride had better see her before she goes to church," observed the doctor to Felix, who had come in again.

"Why?" asked Felix.

The doctor looked at him. "I think it might be better," he said.

"She changes very much, surely, sir," said Mrs. Jolliffe. "I don't see that she seems to rally."

Hannah Dill recovered from her faint and again gazed towards the door. Delia presently re-entered it, with the rosy little unknown brother in her arms. And after her, floating onwards, lovely and pensive and pitiful, came Amabel, in her bridal gown and floating veil.

"Put it back," she said, "that I may kiss Mamsey."

Amias put the veil back for her, and she looked quietly into his eyes. Then she came on and kissed the prostrate invalid, and sat down beside her. She sat gently and sweetly beside her, but it cannot be supposed that at such a time, within half an hour of her marriage ceremony, she was able to give any very deep attention to her old nurse.

It was Delia who first spoke; she had a sudden idea that human faces seldom could look like Mamsey's long. It must be her own little experience, she thought, that made her feel alarmed, but she yielded to a sudden impulse; she would say the kindest thing in the world, whatever was the event.

"Mamsey dear, look at me—look! I've got the dear, pretty little boy in my arms," she said, in a cheerful and comforting voice. "You will come and live here again, won't you? But if you don't stay, Mamsey—do you understand?—I shall always take care of him."

The dying eyes appeared to thank her; they wandered over the three faces with a wondrous rapture of peace and joy.

"And yet," she presently whispered, "it's not said, and I cannot say it."

"Say what, Mamsey?" asked Delia.

Her eyes fell upon Delia's hand; she saw the rings. "You engaged too, my sweetest sweet?"

For all answer Delia lifted her hand to her lips, and kissed the rings she had so lately begun to wear.

A spasm of anguish passed over the mother's face; all the light and joy in it was gone.

"Do you love him?" she whispered.

Delia murmured, "Oh yes."

"And I've no time to speak," Mamsey repeated. "Miss Sarah's money — Miss Sarah——"

"She's wandering!" exclaimed Amabel.

"Never mind Cousin Sarah's money, dear," said Delia caressingly—her lovely face was all dimples and blushes; her happiness was so new to her—"look at these instead. Don't you want to know who gave them to me?" she whispered. She leaned down till her cheek almost touched her mother's shoulder.

"Who did?" replied Mamsey.

Delia could just hear the words. Mamsey had hold of her ringed hand now. Delia lifted up her face, and answered those beseeching eyes. "Who did? Why—Dick!"

Then the clasp of that cold hand was relaxed, and there came back again a strange rapture of peace. Delia watched it and wondered, till some one came to the door and called the girls away. They gave each a kindly look to their old nurse and passed out of the room, Delia still having the baby-boy in her arms.

They all passed out of that room indeed, at the same moment;—the children to the lot which had been won for them, the mother to her rest.

If it was failure so to live and so to die, having given up all things, even her own children—to live not thanked, and to die not known—yet still it was the failure she had chosen; and there are some who, reflecting on such a life, would say, "If that be failure, let me so fail."

THE END.

WOMEN'S COLLEGIATE LIFE IN AMERICA: WELLESLEY COLLEGE, MASS.

By Mrs. MEREDITH.

A YOUNG country is eminently the place in which women may put forth their best powers. Every member of a community which is only in course of formation, feels eager to bring out all their resources for the good of the common weal. The women of America feel that they have their share of the work of their country to do, and they prepare for it by cultivating their intellect, and so fitting themselves for any post that it may be needful for them to fill. The training they receive gives them that best of qualities in women—adaptability. This very thing prevents their being compelled to settle into grooves that restrict their general usefulness and influence. Physical toil in the home, or the workshop, or brain-work in the professional sphere, are accepted as their duties, whenever circumstances render these incumbent on them; and their employments run so smoothly, that it excites no special remark how they are engaged. Like the perfection of a toilette, their work is done without attracting attention to its details. When we have said this we have said all that can be said about women's work in America. In fact, it is whatever a woman can do, the proof being that she does it, and that she accomplishes good results. What the good results, seen in the social life of the United States, are, it is important to state. An English woman admitted into the homes and families of that country finds a condition of affairs to which she is unaccustomed. Wives know their husband's business, and help him in it. The loss or gain of every day is their affair; and their sympathy is entirely with the labour and the labourer. This leads them to endeavour to understand commercial undertakings. Because the influence of educated mothers, wives, and sisters is beneficial in the domestic circle, men ask their aid in the households of the nation. They are found worthy to be considered on the strength of the army of the State, striving for its progress. Their minds are permitted to be exercised in the political economy of those departments of the public business that fall under the natural cognizance of women. The details in the management of workhouses and prisons that relate to food, clothing, health, &c., are committed to women's care. "Advisory Boards" are formed to secure their co-operation. "Commissions" are organized, in which they are invited to act; and thus their services are utilised in every way, in order to promote the well-being of the country.

What they positively effect to this end is surprising. No English lady can refuse to bear witness to the moral aspect of American society, as compared with England's state at this time. If only one remarkable feature be noticed, which is prominent all over the land, as the influence of woman, it would be enough to crown the fair sex in that country with the greatest earthly honour. They have banished, by their all-powerful effort, the presence of drink from their tables; and, so far, have stigmatized drunkenness as abhorrent to them. Hospitality " without the drink " is the honoured grace of the New World; and this is due to the work of women — not fanatic, superstitious, and unreasonable, but calm, scientific, pious women, resolute in their aim and their action to avoid that which is dangerous to their families, the preservation of which is their special duty.

One remarkable result of the higher education of Christian women in America is the large number who enter the mission field.

The colleges that send forth women of the greatest intellectual culture send out also the largest number of missionaries to preach the gospel of the Kingdom of God, the Holy Spirit thus owning the advantage of education in the work of the ministry. India, Asia, China, Japan, Syria, and many "regions beyond" have received these workers. Their own vast land is a grand theatre for their energy. They move about on the face of it with a devotion and organization that have most extraordinary effects.

In the light of these facts, it becomes very interesting to examine Wellesley College, as one of the training institutions of the Christian women of America. This establishment is the offshoot of a work set on foot by a woman about fifty years ago. The heroine who wrought for female emancipation from the ills and miseries of ignorance, thus addressed her pupils, when she was sending them forth to the battle of life; and when we have quoted this extract we shall have put before our readers Mary Lyon :—

"Now I trust you will be inflexible in regard to *the right.* Do not yield that, even to please kings, but be very careful to distinguish between the right and personal gratification. . . . . Make all you can of your intellectual and moral powers, and of your influence over others. . . . . Do something, have a plan, live for some purpose, be faithful and conscientious and understand what you are to do, but do not expect to make over this world, or to greatly change your condition in it, but seek, rather, to be ready to do and bear what comes in your way. Be willing to do anything anywhere that Providence seems to lay upon you. . . . . Do not expect to be independent because educated. Ladies never can be independent, and those best educated most feel their dependence. They must expect great demands to be made upon their time and strength, and they should meet them in the spirit of Him who came to minister rather than to be ministered unto. You will find no pleasure like the pleasure of active effort. May God give every one of you more and more for your heart and hands to do, and more and more fellowship with Christ in His sufferings. Never be hasty to decide what you cannot do, because you have not physical or mental strength. Never say you have no faith or hope. Always think of God's strength when you feel your weakness, and remember that you can come nearer to Him than to any being in the universe. We

have desired to educate you to go among the rich or the poor, to live in the country or the village, in New England, the West, or in a foreign land. And, wherever you are, remember that God will be with you if you seek to do good to immortal souls."

In 1837 Mary Lyon opened the first of the establishments that now provide American women with colleges in which religion is made of chief concern. Wellesley is the latest and most highly developed of the collegiate institutions that have sprung from the original foundation at Mount Holyoak. We find in it the fully realised ideal of Miss Lyon. She proposed to give women all the advantages that men have for acquiring knowledge. It was her plan that they should be instructed in classics and science, in exactly the same manner as their brothers; not that they should learn a little Latin, and a smattering of mathematics, by some diluted course of study made easy, but that they should thoroughly accomplish all that men do in universities.

Wellesley College is, therefore, not a girls' school called by courtesy "a college." It is a woman's university, and it has all the facilities for them to graduate in every department of knowledge, that any university for the other sex, either in Great Britain or America, has. The system contemplates only the instruction of those who have had elementary instruction of a sound kind. The preliminary schooling must be equal to the best "high school" with which we are acquainted, for the matriculation examination is not beneath the standard of our men's universities.

Until America could produce women capable of organizing, and able to take the professorships of such a college, Wellesley could not have been founded. Now that there are women able to do it, and that the thing is done, there can no more be difficulties in the intellectual cultivation of women. Wellesley College, Massachusetts, is a substantial evidence of power that may be quoted by all English-speaking women, when their prospects are called in question; and it may well be pointed to by Christian people as their victory, given them by God in His mercy, over foolish, ignorant prejudice, which falsely adjudged women's capabilities, and wickedly restrained and restricted their places in the world of letters.

Vassar College, which claims to have attained even a higher intellectual standard than Wellesley, is certainly quite worthy of being regarded in this light too; but, at this time, we mean to deal only with Wellesley, as representing more particularly education in connection with spiritual influence, and as showing the effect of such training on Christian work.

A large capital has been invested in this establishment, which it is to be hoped will return a good interest in money as well as in moral worth. The picture here given of it represents the estate, which comprises some thirty acres of beautiful scenery, in which Nature has bountifully supplied the needs of the students, as to variety of interesting resources. Woodland and fern-ground, hilly walks, pasture and tillage fields, pieces of water for boating and swimming, give plenty of opportunity for exercise and amusement out of doors. The situation of the building is very healthy, as well as very lovely. When the college was planned, every step was considered with a view to promote women's special benefit in student life. The apartments are grouped in suites of three rooms—

General View of Wellesley College and Grounds.

two for sleeping and one for study—accommodating two students in each suite. There are recitation rooms for each class, and demonstration rooms for the practice of the experiments of science; museums; galleries for collections of specimens of all kinds of objects, natural, scientific, instrumental, &c., and a library of large size and copious contents. Beside these are halls for worship, lectures, dining, and receptions; vast corridors, and a domestic department in which all the arts and sciences are utilised to produce the most sanatory and agreeable modes of living. The results are that a charming abode is provided for the students. The collegians do all the household labour of the establishment with their own hands; and thus acquire practical skill in women's work, which they can ever after control, not merely by theoretical assertion, but by actual personal experience. The arrangements whereby they are enabled to do this are such as can be easily carried

Library of Wellesley College.

on wherever they may live and labour, at home and abroad. Wellesley graduates, therefore, propose not only to be distinguished in letters, but in domestic economy ; and to give their households the fruits of their toil, in comforts and enjoyments superior to those yet procurable in ordinary society. A residence of a few days in Wellesley College assured us, that English families would be happier if the ladies of our country understood the operations of cleansing, cooking, and washing, as well as the students there did. It would give them what they now have not — the mastery over their servants ; and cause a sense of independence that, if those troublesome people choose to go off, their absence would not be so great a difficulty as they imagine, but rather a relief, giving an opportunity of putting things straight, that are set astray by the bad methods of ignorant women, who have the rule of our houses too much in their hands. It is needful for us to set forth this

Mary Lyon.

strong defence of the domestic character of American female students, before we enter on the list of their studies, lest our English woman's heart should quail in the presence of its greatness, or, still worse, our English men's feelings be excited against the bluestocking world ; and they be led to exclaim—in fear and dread of their homes being entered by learned Gorgons, instead of lovely girl-graduates, with not only golden locks, but deft fingers, making pies as well as diagrams—"Away with it ! "

All the regular students board in the college, and aid in some of the lighter domestic work of the family. The importance of this will be appreciated by thoughtful parents. This i. not a novel experiment. For many years it has been the rule in some other institutions. While it is not intended to give instruction in the details of domestic work, it is considered desirable that all should understand and take a practical part in systematic housekeeping.

The time thus occupied is one hour daily, and does not interfere with the hours of study. The economy of this course should not be overlooked. It would be easier to hire a much larger number of servants than are employed, and to bear the expense of their wages and board, with the accompanying waste, but it would be necessary, in that case, to make the price for board and tuition nearly double what it now is. This would defeat one great object of the trustees, which is, to give opportunities for a higher education to women of moderate means. The success of this plan in the college leads the trustees to believe that all young women will cheerfully take their share in easy and useful domestic work, when they understand that they are thus helping, in part, at least, to educate themselves. The experience of teachers in the well-known institutions in which this course has been pursued, has proved that the discipline of this domestic work, which unites all in one family as helpers for the common good, is invaluable in its influence upon the moral nature, and its preparation for social life.

A lady physician resides in the college, and gives her personal attention to the supervision of the arrangements connected with the health of the family. She has daily intercourse with the students, and instructs them in the care of their health and the laws of hygiene. They are encouraged to consult with her frequently, and are taught how to establish proper habits of attention and systematic care. No charge is made for medicine, nor for the attention of the resident physician. A hospital, which can be shut off from the rest of the building, in case of contagious disease, is provided for those who need any extra care.

The college grounds give ample opportunities for exercise and recreation. The lake affords a most desirable place for boating in summer, and skating in winter. The exercise of boating is so attractive in itself, and has been found to be so remarkably beneficial to the health of the students, that a large number of safe and convenient boats have been furnished, which they are allowed to use daily. It will be found that everything is done for the health, the comfort, and the happiness of the family in their college home.

A large gymnasium is provided, and the classes are instructed in calisthenics.

There are two departments of instruction, the collegiate and the academic.

The Collegiate Department qualifies for admission to the "freshman" class. Candidates

must be at least sixteen years of age. They must pass satisfactory examinations in the following studies:—*Latin grammar*, including prosody; Cæsar, Gallic War, books 1—4; Cicero, six Orations; Virgil, Æneid, books 1—6; *Arithmetic*, including the metric system of weights and measures; Olney's University Algebra, through involution, evolution, radicals, quadratic equations, ratio, proportion, arithmetical and geometrical progressions, *i.e.* to Part III.; Olney's or Chauvenet's Plane Geometry; modern geography; Guyot's Physical Geography, Parts II. and III.; *English grammar;* English composition. The subjects for 1880 will be selected from Shakespeare's *Tempest*, Scott's Lady of the Lake, or Longfellow's Evangeline, &c., &c.

The Academic Department is wholly disconnected from the Collegiate Department; and has no more influence upon the college classes or courses of study, than it would have if it were a separate institution in another town. The demand for the collegiate education of women is of so recent an origin, that there are as yet no schools exclusively designed to fit girls for college. In some places girls can join the classes of the high schools in which young men are fitted; but these opportunities are comparatively rare. It is therefore necessary to provide for the needs of girls who cannot be prepared for college in their own homes. The academic department is intended to meet this demand.

In order to show the nature of the general course of study, we will extract from the college calendar for 1877-8 the syllabus of the "Freshman year:"—*Latin:* Livy, one book, Tacitus' Germania, Cicero's Letters (selections), Humphrey's Abbott's Latin prose compositions. *Greek*, elective: Iliad and Odyssey (selections), Plato's Apology, Jones's Greek prose composition. *Mathematics:* Olney's Solid Geometry, plane and spherical trigonometry. *German*, elective: Goethe and Schiller, Ballad's Schilen, Jungfrau von Orleans, Wilhelm Tell, Dio Piccolomini, grammar and exercises, essays. *French*, elective: syntaxe française, littérature française contemporaine, dictées et compositions. *Drawing:* Free hand, mathematical, and perspective. *Grecian history:* essay writing; elocution, &c. The "Sophomore" year advances a grade, and there are "junior" and "senior" years, in which a very full course is given; after which honours in classics and science can be obtained by further study.

The scientific course is laid out according to the best scientific and technical schools for men, the scope of instruction differing only as to preparation for professions which are not embraced in the purpose of the ladies' college. Chemistry, mineralogy, lithology, geology, botany, biology, histology, physics, and astronomy comprise the general course in this department.

All the teaching, in every branch, but more especially in the scientific, is done by lectures, aided by text books, &c., with laboratory practice.

In the first year we find them at "qualitative analysis;" and the second solving problems in stoichiometry. Quantitative analysis follows; and in the course optics, acoustics, and electricity find their places. In fact, the curriculum at Wellesley has the widest range of preparation for general knowledge, as well as methods for the special cultivation of any detail, in any department of education. It is very interesting to know that these advantages were made use of by as many as three hundred and twenty-three ladies last year. We passed a few days in the college, and had an opportunity of observing the intense eagerness of the students to excel. It was quite exciting to visit the class-rooms, laboratories, and libraries. There were always young heads in full work; and always pleasant, happy, gratified faces crowding round the professors everywhere. The fact that these professors were ladies did not in the least decrease the respect and attention with which their instructions were received.

All the officers of government and instruction are women; and the order and form of the establishment bears witness to their power. There is a board of trustees which manages the pecuniary department, fifteen of whom are men, and three are women. Ada L. Howard, the president of the faculty, is well able for her arduous post, although she is a gentle, quiet woman, with a prematurely grey head. We could pick out a few of the A.M.'s and A.B.'s, as well as an M.D., who are specially women of power; but we will not do so, as it may imply inequality of capability. It is remarkable that the professors are on a very fair level as to literary standing and power. On the whole the system is in a most healthy state, and affords a very good opportunity for ascertaining what a women's college may become.

It is of great importance to note the effect of collegiate study on young women; and even more so to ascertain the result of collegiate intercourse during collegiate residence. Collegiate intercourse differs from social intercourse, and is different in its effect. Social intercourse has for its object personal purposes;

collegiate intercourse takes a wider scope; and women get by it a glimpse of the field outside and round their home, which gives them a second life besides their domestic one. Nor does it injure the first and chief ideal of feminine existence, but rather strengthens and improves it. The woman learns at college that there are many women as well informed as herself, and with as great and good aims, and she joins a number of other hearts and minds, with them to pursue a common good. Enlightenment and cultivation are esteemed a social benefit, instead of being an isolated and isolating condition. The elevation of one woman here and there above her fellows is a doubtful advantage; but the elevation of all women to a certain standard of education has an influence on society of the most useful kind. It places them in a position, as it regards men, that has much mutual good effect. The permanence of the platform of culture to which both sexes are raised will be found to depend on the height to which women attain. According to this theory, America has a good prospect for her future.

There is a project now being ventilated to found a Mount Holyoak in England, and we cordially wish it success. It is not intended as a rival to Girton College, but as a sister institution, based on a different and distinctly religious foundation. Wellesley College shows how Christian teaching and influence can be combined with the highest intellectual cultivation; and, by God's gracious permission, the latter becomes the implement in the hand of the former.

The library, of which our drawing (p. 841) gives a fair idea, is filled with selected Christian literature. No scientific books, however popular, are admitted there which question the supreme authority of the Divine Word.

Twice every day the whole household meets for prayer and meditation on the Scriptures. There is Divine worship on Sundays, alternately after the manner of Episcopalians and Presbyterians. The teaching of all the ministers who visit is alike Evangelical; nor could any other doctrine be tolerated in the place than "Christ crucified." The leading mind in the institution is that of Mr. Durant. He has, in fact, given Wellesley College to the women of his State. He gave the land, the building, and the furniture; and now he gives his time and energies to the undertaking, in every way that he can, as steward of the establishment, working and living under the heavenly King, his Master and Lord. His functions are very interesting, and much depends on the way in which they are exercised. He uses them for the Saviour, and rejoices in the service. When not busy in the building at Wellesley, he is generally preaching the gospel in other places; and so passes his time bringing sinners to Jesus. The work of grace in the College is extensive. Voluntary meetings of the students for prayer and study of the Bible are numerous and large.

COFFEE-ROOMS FOR THE PEOPLE.

By LADY HOPE OF CARRIDEN.

PART II.

THE coffee-house is another form of the same attempt; sometimes these two are combined. The entrance here is free, beyond the purchase of food or drink at the counter. If the bar be not too small, and the room attractive, the manager liked, and the promoters inclined to visit it in the evenings, and able to exert an influence for good in the town that will secure frequenters, this edition of the temperance scheme ought also to prove a benefit.

The coffee-barrow too supplies a want. By the roadside, in the market-place, on the ice the working man can purchase his penny cup of coffee, and penny or halfpenny bun, ready to his hand. Thus he does not need the dainties of the public-house. Often a fit of craving for stimulant will be warded off by this very efficient remedy, promptly supplied.

Perhaps the most useful of all these, because the most comprehensive, would be a long wooden or brick shed, such as you see in a builder's yard, woollen, leather, or shoe-making factory, purchased for £50 or rented for £10 a year. Another £50 for the purpose of making it absolutely comfortable, that is, air-tight and water-tight, warm and well-lighted, the windows garnished by crimson blinds: £50 or £70 would furnish it throughout with short narrow tables, placed crossways to the walls in rows sided by forms with sloping backs; a long counter, neat and substantial, at one end, with coffee-urns, dishes, cups and saucers, the coffee being heated by spirit lamps or gas, as the case might be, and books on shelves; papers and books on the tables; pictures in glowing tints toned down by a wall of subdued colour; neat, large-printed texts, mottoes, and almanacks; while the remaining £30 would cover the manager's salary for nine months. Long before this, if it were anything like what it would be with good management, this salary and that of an under man might be taken out of the weekly returns. If, there-fore, any ladies or gentlemen were to place in my hands a sum of £300, and say to me, "Will you provide for us (in any town or village) a coffee-room that, by God's blessing, will work out a great reform amongst the masses in our neighbourhood?" I should feel myself *rich* for the purpose with the sum mentioned—£200 for first actual expenses, and £100 as a reserve fund for extras needed. I will venture to say that, under proper auspices, this great coffee-room might be well filled in the evenings. To be a very popular resort it ought, if possible, to hold two, three, or four hundred men. The men would walk miles to attend it. How my heart aches with longing to start such in every place I visit! But barriers inconceivable, only existing in the minds of the rich, present themselves too often. If *one* or *two* places would try this simple plan, they would prove by their success a stimulus to other towns for a similar agency, a qualified delight at the new ideas and thoughts and sensations of rest that are presented to them thereby. Poor fellows! a little brightness, a little relief from carking care, hard work, and sight and sound of evil, these are, indeed, rainbows, sunshine amidst the clouds that too often cover them. A half-crown, or even a shilling toy, will often be worth gold for these reasons to a tired man; and to us for his benefit worth how *much more* than gold, if they should prove successful in leading him out of the pathway of ignorance and sin into scenes of purer delight and more hallowed enjoyments! But far, far higher than this I would carry our aims. I should consider even the result I have suggested a failure did it not lead the working man to think of a Better Home!

In such a Coffee-room you can reach him by many avenues. You sit side by side with him. You can talk with him face to face, reason, persuade, warn, entreat, as the work seems to be given you; and your little mission to that one man, and I will venture to say, very many others like him, may prove more effectual than all the words that flowed over his head out of the high pulpit on the last Sunday that he attended the church. If once you have got a moral and spiritual hold of the man, or men of the town generally, in this way, they will soon begin to flock into the church, that is to say, if they can get comfortable seats, a good welcome, and simple spiritual teaching that will satisfy and strengthen them.

One shelf, within reach of the manager's hand or eye as he stands at the bar, should be stored with games. A difficulty here presents itself as to the choice of such amusements. But it is only theoretical; you would be surprised to know how easily our guests are amused, and for a whole evening too, and every evening, if you have sufficient variety in your lists.

Go into any large toyshop in London, Edinburgh, Glasgow, or Dublin, and you will find hosts of enchanting games. There you discover in endless variety what will present a world of delight to the toil-worn, weary working man, at the end of his day. The difficulty is not where to begin in your choice, but where to end! Nothing delights or puzzles me more than to go into one of these delectable reservoirs of recreation, purse in hand, to chose out for myself, or for a friend who has intrusted me with the charming task, a variety of these pure and simple pleasures, praying the while, how earnestly! that they may prove in skilful hands elements of true *recreation*, spiritual as well as mental. It is an interesting task to introduce the men to these games, and see them understand and take to them as kindly as they do any other specific for true reform that you put immediately within their reach. Only the other day in a coffee-house started really on the right principles, a large quantity of games were laid in, with other stores, for the delectation of the men. But, strange to say, whenever we inquired from those in charge as to their popularity, we were always informed that " the men did not care for the games," "they never played," &c. The coffee-room, excellent though it was in every way, was not yet thoroughly in working order. There were no lady or gentlemen visitors in the evening, and it was plain from the empty rôle during these later hours, that for some reason or other *the men* did not care to come. We made known from the bar during the next few days, that on a certain evening we should be there ourselves, and that some young ladies would sing. As might have

been expected, the large coffee-room was crowded on that evening. Different hymns were sung in parts, and some unitedly, leaflets and books being handed round to the customers. I talked to them a little, in a very free-and-easy way, nothing approaching to a lecture, sermon, or even address, I hope. I did not wish it to be that kind of thing; but we all agreed in wishing the men to know that we cared for them, that we felt an interest in those who came in and out of the coffee-room every day, and that we longed that they should derive from their daily visit a higher benefit than the mere food served at the counter. They earnestly listened, and quite understood and entered into what was said to them. Games were then proposed, and the offer received languidly, except by one or two, who said, " It is a long time since I had a game at anything!" Then a series of confessions followed that did " not know any games." The names of several were mentioned. They " could not play them." However, an offer to teach the use of them was received most gladly, and soon all the occupants of the rooms were busy receiving initiation into the mysteries of chess, draughts, go-bang, fishponds, and other similar amusements. But they required our presence to keep everything up to the mark. Their enjoyment was evident. " We want an umpire!" some said. Others said, " I can't quite hit off these moves. Look here, how does this go?" My pupils, great stalwart working men sometimes, who have been condescending to learn chess from me, have often given me great amusement by their knitted brows, strenuous efforts to learn the game, and remarks made in all innocence, the while. " Just see here, please. This 'ere piece," touching the king, " didn't you say he couldn't move no more than a square at a time?" " Yes!" I have acknowledged the charge. " Well then! it wouldn't hurt to lose him, would it? He ain't much good. Is he?" " Oh, yes!" I have solemnly explained; "you can't lose him. He's the most important person on the board. I told you that you must guard him the whole time, for he must not even be left in check;" and then endeavoured to demonstrate the various ways in which he might be exposed to danger, and ought to be defended. Whereupon after deep thought, and close and penetrating consideration of the board, one of the antagonistic couple has replied, " Well! I do think he is a bother. He can't take care of his self and he wants all the 'tothers to be lookin' arter him. I never! now there's this one, the queen, ain't she! Well! she can run for herself, she can; right across the board, anywhere. *She's* the one I like. It's my go, now. Where's that little crooked thing that goes jumpin' about all over the place. I can't find him. Oh! here he is. Yes! the knight. I remember now. He'll just do here." And thus, slowly but surely, though you would hardly think it, the game has progressed; and when the men do understand it, they are remarkably fond of the "chesses," as they generally call them.

A very large musical box is an excellent thing to have playing on the tables during part of the evening.

But, whatever happens, the room must not be deserted by the friends of the cause. By their presence wonders can be effected. The thought and money lavished on the undertaking at its first start are not sufficient. The ladies and gentlemen, and Christian young tradespeople of the town must come in and out constantly in the evenings, invite the men in, and encourage them by every means in their power. The Bible should be fearlessly read aloud in the middle of the coffee-room, in the course of the evening, whilst it is most crowded. Instead of lessening the numbers in any place, this will increase them. If you don't do it, the people themselves don't see the object of your having taken such trouble for them. If you do it, they see through the whole thing, and respect you for so high a motive, and for having taken so deep an interest in their welfare.

I should like to conduct my readers through the golden few that are doing their duty! My heart rests upon them with comfort and pleasure as my thoughts settle down on the bright little area that is benefited and blessed by them.

I used to drive through a lovely village situated in the midst of beautiful scenery; its rustic cottages trellised over and adorned by a profusion of roses, ivy, and grape vines; but, alas! its moral condition dark, dead, drunken. So I was always told, and I believe it was true. Many a fervent prayer ascended during these enjoyable drives through its precincts. At last some earnest Christian people took the large house close by, and began to devote themselves forthwith to the inhabitants of the cottages. A coffee-house was started. I was asked to find a manager for it. The Lord gave us the man. Never shall I forget my delight when I paid my first visit to the newly-opened coffee-room—its house-warming, con-

sisting of a good hearty prayer-meeting and an address to the people. It was a cheering sight, indeed, to behold such a congregating together of what must have been very nearly the entire mass of adult villagers, their numbers somewhat swelled by visitors from other neighbouring villages. But the coffee-room itself was the acme of comfort. Spacious, and light, it had these all-important first elements of success evidently enough. This was not all, however. The harmony of colour that prevailed everywhere was only an index to the kindly feeling that was prepared to harmonize the various rough elements that had been welcomed into this very novel hostelry. Such, at least, the people seemed to regard it. Their expressions of surprise, as one by one they peeped, and then ventured in, showed how unaccustomed they had hitherto been to such luxuries. I fear my memory is not accurate enough to describe in detail the arrangement; but as far as I can recollect it was something of this description. The walls were whitewashed, or painted a very light colour, and ornamented to a good height by a wainscoting of crimson paper, finished off by a narrow paper. Texts and pictures relieved the upper part, standing out in bold relief, with their frames of crimson paper. These were interspersed with illuminated mottoes, groups of ferns, and suggestive photographs. Steaming coffee-urns poured forth a most appetizing fragrance, and, when tapped, a still more appetizing draught. Clean cups and saucers shone and glistened beneath the glowing lamps that hung from the ceiling and were fastened to the wall. A particularly radiant, genial-looking man stood behind the counter, dispensing smiles as well as tea, coffee, cake, and bread and butter, to all the incomers; his *guests*, he evidently considered them, and he was giving them his best of welcomes. He has a true heart for his fellow working men. He loves them. Yes! positively *loves* them—and so do the gentleman and his wife who with their little children, their servants, and their neighbours, strive to the utmost to impart to their pretty village room the charm of *home*. And no one knows better how to value such an atmosphere, than the man who is too often condemned, by those who are strangers to his inner life, as hard and unfeeling. These he certainly is not. But sometimes these finer virtues must be fostered and drawn out before they will appear. Or the link so tender of home-life, once broken by the intoxicating drink, must be reunited by artificial means—such means as those I have described—the reason of such a necessity being sufficiently palpable. The tie has been severed outside his own hearth, and outside they must be joined again. You cannot find him at home. You must, therefore, meet him away from his home, and bring him by gentle persuasive love, and tidings of forgiveness, back to it again. If a man is fond of home, he is too thankful for the occasional outlet that such a coffee-room affords him. It refreshes and invigorates him for his daily duties, and fosters the love of home, rather than weakens it, for the two lives tally. If both influences are good, truly good, they do not oppose one another. Let our influences lead him a step farther on the heavenward road! that we, as the "compellers" to the royal feast, may bring in a great multitude, "halt, and maimed, and blind," not resting satisfied until, first with the eye of faith, and then more visibly, they have "beheld our King in His beauty," acknowledging with us that He is "altogether lovely;" and "setting to their seal, that God is true," *true* in His invitations—*true* in His promises—*true* in His judgments.

Each one of these means for reaching the people is good, if we can succeed in making it a medium for permanent benefit. From our missionary at Dorking I have a letter only this morning, describing the large coffee-room in the town-hall there as "so packed full last Saturday evening, that fresh comers could hardly make their way up to the counter." That this is not the result of novelty can be proved by the seven-years age of the movement there. But in a short time now, the men will spend their last Saturday night at the town-hall rooms, as, through the generous kindness of a neighbour—this time a *true* neighbour!—a large coffee-house and mission-rooms, very perfectly complete, and, though on the same principles, on a more commodious scale, have been built for their use in the same street. Many touching expressions of gratitude, and countless tokens of their appreciation of the efforts made on their behalf, you would find amongst these honest working men. They acknowledge that their town is a "fortunate one;" that "people who live hereabouts is well off;" and that you don't "find friends like this

everywhere." When any of these men go away to other towns or villages on the various jobs to which at any moment they may be apportioned, they are generally very disconsolate, and "keep on missing the rooms the whole time." Sometimes they "fall," and come back different characters from those under which they were classed when they left us; but as often the recollection of what they have heard, and learnt, and read, beneath the genial influences of the coffee-room, "holds by them," and keeps them "wonderful firm," to the joy and comfort of the poor wife, who will whisper to the presiding lady of the mothers' meeting at the close of the Monday's proceedings—"Bill do go on so beautiful. I'm that glad, I can't keep it to myself." Bill being the "better half" who had previously worn out her poor life with sorrow and poverty. Then when he returns to his manifold friends, and their multiplied greetings and welcomes, each more friendly, smiling, and hearty than another, as he wends his way from the door to the bar, his hand having passed through the process of many long and wringing shakes, he is all aglow, poor fellow (though dreadfully shy!), and how happy if he can answer a nodded "yes" to sundry whispered or looked interrogations. "Have you been all right?" "Keeping yourself easy, Tom?" "Got on first class, haven't you? Heard tell somethink o' that from old George. He went up by your way not so long ago." Then, over a smoking cup of coffee, the lips open, and he confesses, "I'm uncommon glad to get back! I know that. 'Twas a dull place where I been; warn't nothing o' this sort there."

Fresh soil like this is worth breaking up. Yes! and, to continue the farming simile, worth feeding well too! Acres, vast areas of receptive faculty, craving needs, and rare intelligence lie all round us, waiting for the patient, willing labourer, who, "seed basket" in hand, will go forth skilfully to scatter the undying germs of precious truth—truth that will bring forth fruit "an hundredfold" to the well-being of our fellow-man, and to the praise and glory of "Him who is able to do for us, exceeding abundantly above all that we either ask or think."

[NOTE.—In order to make quite clear some references and statements, especially in the latter part of this article, it may be well to add that it was written some months ago, and is published exactly as originally written.—ED. G. W.]

A QUERY.

OH, the wonder of our life,
  Pain and pleasure, rest and strife,
Mystery of mysteries,
Set 'twixt two eternities !

Lo, the moments come and go,
E'en as sparks, and vanish so,
Flash from darkness into light,
Quick as thought are quenched in night.

With an import grand and strange
Are they fraught in ceaseless change
As they post away, each one
Stands eternally alone.

This scene, more fair than words can say,
I gaze upon, and go my way ;
I turn, another glance to claim,
Something is changed, 'tis not the same.

The purple flush on yonder fell,
The tinkle of that cattle-bell,
Came, and have never come before,
Go, and are gone for evermore.

Our life is held as with a vice,
We cannot do the same thing twice ;
Once we may, but not again :
Only memories remain.

What if memories vanish too,
And the past be lost to view ;
Is it all for nought that I
Heard and saw and hurried by ?

Where are childhood's merry hours,
Bright with sunshine, crossed with showers ?
Are they dead, and can they never
Come again to life for ever ?

No—'tis false, I surely trow ;
Though awhile they vanish now, .
Every passion, deed, and thought,
Was not born to come to nought !

Will the past then come again,
Rest and pleasure, strife and pain,
All the heaven and all the hell ?
  . Ah, we know not : God can tell.

E. W. HOWSON.

HEALTH AT HOME.

By B. W. RICHARDSON, M.D., F.R.S.

PART VI.

IN preceding papers in the "Health at Home" series we have studied the healthiness of the bedrooms and the staircase landings. We have considered how these should be lighted, warmed, ventilated, and cleaned. We have passed from these to the water-closets, the housemaid's cupboard, and the closet which contains the water-cistern, and have considered the defects which they commonly present, together with the improvements which are required in them. Lastly, we have moved into the bathroom, and while, on the one hand, we have studied the simplest and cheapest means for rendering daily general ablution easy, we have glanced at what may be called "luxurious household bathing," the plunge-bath, the shower-bath, and, luxury of luxuries, the hot-air or old Roman bath.

We will at this point change our course of study by making a descent into the lower part of the house, and will consider what are the more important improvements in those regions of present domestic insanitation. Before making this descent, however, let me be allowed to add one word of an explanatory kind.

Two classes of readers accost me on the subject of the practical application of the lessons conveyed in these papers. One class expresses that while all that is suggested should and ought to be carried out, the carrying out would be so great an expense that none but those who are blessed with many hundreds a year are able so much as to contemplate any of the proposed improvements. The other class takes quite a different view ; it tells me, as each progressive article appears, that I am not sufficiently radical in suggestion ; that in respect to every detail something more could and ought to be done; that some entirely new system, out and out new and perfect, should be described ; and that to plant new or improved methods upon old foundations is alteration without corresponding improvement. My answer to these friendly critics is, that the aim of this series consists in trying to propose as much as possible in the way of practical improvement on that which at present exists. I know very well that, to insure perfection, our great cities require to be pulled down altogether, and reconstructed on new and better plans. But then, again, I know that this is utterly impossible. The point, therefore, to be arrived at, as it seems to me, is to make the best of what exists, and to implant the necessities in the best manner attainable, even in the midst of current faults and blunderings. By this method necessary reforms will not only be introduced into houses that already exist, but will in time be introduced, *de novo*, into houses that are undergoing construction, and which, from their very foundations, will be laid out with a view to perfection of sanitation. This is a point earnestly to be struggled for at the present time. In this great metropolis houses are springing up in all directions, by the hundred. We go into them during the various stages of progress, and really in not one in a hundred is there any advance at all. The idea of the old class of house is moulded, as it were, in the mind of the builder. If you dare to tell him of an improvement, he replies instantly that it "won't work." If you ask him whether he has ever tried it, he tells you that he "don't want." And resting his argument on these two phrases, as if they were final, he pursues his sullen and ignorant course of wooden wit and unhealthy adaptation.

It appears, therefore, better to begin with improvements in existing houses than to fight a perfectly useless battle in respect to new construction. A man is master of his house when he gets into it, not before, and he may expect half a century to elapse, at least, before improvement *de novo* is the order of the day. Still more to the point is the serious fact that whole cities-full of houses actually exist which cannot be pulled down, and which may remain for ever as they are, unless some new plans be introduced into them as they at present stand. In London itself it is the most difficult thing to find a house that may be demolished and rebuilt. Unless a house be positively "doomed"—that is to say, in plain words, until it is dangerous to those within and those without—it must remain; the most that can be done for it is to transform it, as far as possible and safe, into something better.

To suggest some of these improvements in the existent house is my present purpose, and that is the answer to those who complain of deficiency of suggestion for more radical changes. As to the others who complain of the expense that is necessary to carry out the proposed alterations, all I can say is, that in every particular I have taken the utmost care to reduce the expenditure to the smallest amount. Some expense is necessary, of course; but if those who wish to carry out the various plans that have been put forward will go over them carefully, they will be surprised to find at how small a cost they may all be effected. There is nothing costly in the way of material; there is nothing complicated in the way of reconstruction,—nothing, in short, that an ordinary good workman cannot carry out. And now let me proceed with the next head of my description.

AN AIR-SHAFT THROUGH THE HOUSE.

In arranging a house so as to give to it fair sanitary advantages, it is a most desirable plan to make an air-shaft that shall extend from the top of the house to the basement. There is scarcely any house in which this cannot, with a little trouble and at little expense, be done. The shaft can, as a rule, be cut out of a partition wall, and can run in a straight line from the upper floor down to the passage leading into the area. If it can be cut six inches square, all the better; but a four-inch square is not at all bad. The shaft should be lined with deal all the way it extends, and on the landings the piece of wood that covers it in should be screwed to the wall and made movable, so that it may be easily taken down and replaced.

The value of this shaft is very great in the house. Down through it the water-pipe from the upper cistern can be carried from floor to floor, so that each floor can have a tap for the supply of water, if necessary. Through this shaft, at a small expense, speaking-tubes can also be carried, and speaking communication secured all through the building without the use of the bell, by which arrangement nearly half the waiting-service of the house is saved. Through this shaft the tubes conveying the gas, where gas is used, can be most safely and conveniently carried, instead of being laid, as they now usually are, in every possible dangerous place, under floors of rooms and bedrooms, along cornices, behind book-shelves, and in every conceivable place where it is most difficult to get at them for repair or purification.

In addition to these uses the whole of the remaining space of the shaft can be utilised for the admission of air into the house from the top of the shaft. In the basement the shaft should be closed off, so that the air from that part may not ascend; but at the top the shaft should communicate with the open air, either from an opening under an upper window, or by an opening into and through the roof to the outer air. By side openings from such a shaft as I now describe into the rooms throughout the house air can be freely admitted at all times. When the room is made warm by the fire a current of air streams into it from the upper opening, and a free supply of air is obtained from the best source of supply that is attainable. If between the floors or ceilings of each story there is open communication with the outside air, the air-shaft may be open also in the space between floor and ceiling, by which an additional supply of outside air will be obtained at every floor.

THE BASEMENT.

It is a pity that any one should have to write a word about the basement of a house that is a place of residence for human beings. The existence of a basement, containing a kitchen, a scullery, a housekeeper's room, a store-room, a water-closet, a place for the lower water-cistern, the larder, a butler's pantry, it may be, and even a pretence for a bedroom, is one of the most deplorable of facts in our modern life in large towns. The difficulty, however, stares us in the face everywhere where there is a large and closely packed community. The price of space is so great that the chance of doing away with the basement is the most unlikely of all probabilities and the difficulty, even when the mind is ever so willing, to find a new place for the various offices of the basement, is so great we cannot, I fear, but agree to submit to what at present is a necessary evil.

Happily the basement in most cases need not be so bad as it is. It is very much worse as a general rule than it has occasion to be. It is left too exclusively to the care of servants, who look upon it as their domain, and as a domain which must not be trespassed on; and it is too often treated by the master and mistress in the same spirit. Why should they put themselves to the trouble of going down-stairs? Why should they annoy the servants by troublesome inquiries? What can they do if they go down, unless they go down every day to order what ought to be done, and then pay a subsequent visit to make sure that what has been ordered has been duly attended to and accomplished?

There is felt, without doubt, a certain kind of gloom, causing a dispirited frame of mind, in the basement; so a visit to it is, in truth, rendered very disagreeable. Those who are accustomed to live and work up-stairs find it extremely unpleasant to go down to the dulness in which the servants are obliged to work.' The art of living there must be gained by training, and then it is said to be-

come endurable—nay, some say comfortable. But the very circumstance that these objections are felt; the very fact that the comparative stranger in the best basement feels it cold, dismal, dreary, and unnatural, should lead the conscientious owner and superior to enter the same, and see at regular intervals that the best that can be made out of a bad system is made and kept up, and that all the requisites for securing the very best are faithfully supplied.

The first thing, then, to look after in the basement story is to secure as much sunlight for it as can be admitted into it. Every window, every available point where a window can be placed, should be found and utilised. The windows of the basement should be kept at all times scrupulously clean, and they should be encumbered as little as possible by blinds or by curtains. If from the position of the window direct sunlight cannot be admitted, the difficulty should be at once met by the use of a Chapuis daylight reflector. It is not easy to speak too favourably of these admirable appliances. Kitchens, store-rooms, pantries, nay, cellars that are practically lightless, may often be made quite bright and cheerful by the use of these reflectors. When light is admitted into every room in the basement story it is astonishing how easy it becomes to effect a number of improvements which would otherwise be considered impossible.

THE AREA.

The next point to be thought of after the due lighting of the basement floor is the cleanliness of the area in front and rear of the basement. Too much attention cannot be paid to this matter. It is common for the front area to be the place in which the dust-bin is situated. It is common for the back area to be the place where the larder is situated. We must therefore be very determined to have these parts specially well looked after, for if the dust-bin be neglected there is a constant source of impurity entering the house; and if the area containing the larder be kept unclean there is a constant source of impurity affecting the food which is used in the house. I do not think it a good practice for the front area to be made a constant scene of traffic in and out of the house. There are advantages certainly in letting tradespeople and others come down the area steps to the lower door. At the same time I doubt if the advantages counterbalance the disadvantages. When persons are all day traversing the area; when various articles of food and other household requisites are being brought at different and many times of the day into the area, there is left very soon a dirty condition, which it takes a long time to remove. The area steps get loaded with dirt, which in wet weather washes down upon the stones beneath, and in an incredibly short space of time the well, which the area floor really is, becomes a floor of dirt and refuse, which is rarely, if ever, completely cleansed away. The houses in which the area is not used contrast, consequently, most favourably with those in which the area-gate is at all times open, and through which a constant flux and influx of persons is taking place. The area left free of custom and traffic is easily kept very clean; and if the walls of it be limewashed once or twice a year it is rendered as healthy as such a place can be, one offence in it excepted; I mean the dust-bin.

In London the dust-bin system is one of the worst and most unnecessary of sanitary grievances, in winter unpardonable, in summer intolerable and detestable. In the hot weather the odour of the dust-bin is all but universal in our modern Babylon. We enter the best houses in the best localities to become conscious of it. When we advance to it the sense of smell is oppressed until the stomach also learns the story. The sense of sight gathers up the same. Wherever, in deserts wild, carrion is outlaid, there also will be animals of prey; and in occupied towns and cities where carrion is laid, there also will be animals of prey—not, truly, in the shape of birds, but in the shape of those little winged, ravenous insects which we call flies, which haunt the dust-bin in hosts, and by their presence indicate the putrescence that is near. Or, bring near to the place an ounce or so of strong hydrochloric acid on an open dish, and the dense white fumes of chloride of ammonium which will arise will testify clearly enough as to the decomposition that is in progress under the very doors of the habitation. Into the dust-bin there is too frequently thrown everything that can give rise to this insalubrious air. Every kind of useless organic substance the house can throw out —parings of potatoes, leaves of cabbages, remnants of salads, faded bouquets and other dead flowers, dust from the house, and portions of rags or shoes, together with the only substances which ought under any circumstances to be there, and which alone are innocuous, the cinders and ashes from the grates and stoves. The gases which pass off from the dust-bin under these conditions are all injurious to health. There is carbonic acid; there is sulphuretted hydrogen; there is vapour of water charged with these gases; lastly, there is a series of ammonias, all of which are not merely objectionable to the sense of smell, but injurious to the health of those who inhale them.

The dust-bin nuisance and danger ought to be met in all towns by the local authority, which should provide that every morning, before the streets are occupied by passengers, the dust and refuse of every house should be removed. In some towns this is done. In Scotland, in some places, the old and once filthy system of throwing all the refuse into the gutter is re-modelled into an actually good working method, which consists in the placing at night all the refuse of the house in a closed pail or pan outside the house, and in the collection of it each morning in a dust-cart while the streets are empty. The plan serves a doubly useful purpose; it keeps the houses free of the accumulation of dust and dirt, and it prevents the poisonously large dust-van of London from going in the day-time from house to house on its business of collecting, concentrating the emanations from the refuse of all the houses into the air of the whole of the street, and so out of a series of local nuisances generating a wholesale nuisance.

Until such time arrives as shall see the local authorities everywhere carrying out the sensible plan for removal of the refuse of the house that has been recorded above, it is essential in places where the dust-bin has to be retained to be careful in using it, so that it shall do as little evil as possible. In the exercise of this care it is essential not to have put into the bin anything that decomposes, unless the substance can be completely and fairly buried in the ashes that are thrown in with it. All combustible substances, and those include pretty well everything that is organic and putrescible, should be burned in the kitchen fire day by day, burned as they are made ready to throw away, so not at any time to accumulate into a heap or a store. Cabbage leaves, potato parings, remnants of fruit, remnants of flowers, and all such commodities should be in this manner immediately destroyed. Bones, if they be put into the bin, should be well buried in ashes, and care should be taken at all times to have a good and even layer of ashes over the whole of the contents of the bin, whatever they may be. The bin under all circumstances should be cleaned out once a week, and a good watch should be kept that it is cleaned to the very bottom. Unless it be cleaned so that the stone at the bottom be clean, a dense mass of putrescible matter mixed with damp ashes and dust is sure to accrete on the floor and become a kind of secured floor of decomposing material, which will keep the bin as a nuisance however frequently it may be emptied.

The dust-bin as it is commonly constructed is very indifferently arranged. It is made usually of wood, which soon gets saturated with organic fluid, and so is rendered offensive. The lid is too often left open, or when closed is but an imperfect covering. At the lower part of the bin, in front, is a sliding door, which lifts up that the bin may be emptied of its contents, and which should fit closely down when the emptying is finished, but which in five or six cases out of ten not fitting closely by any means, lets some of the contents of the interior fall out upon the pavement of the area.

To remedy as far as possible these evils connected with the dust-bin I have constructed a new kind of bin which answers uncommonly well, and which I would strongly recommend. It has been made for me and fitted by Messrs. Ewart & Son, of the Zinc Works, Euston Road, from a model which I made for them to copy from. This bin, instead of being one large fixed box, is composed of a series of iron boxes of small size, which stand side by side in a recess in the area, and are all covered by one frame to which is attached as many lids as there are boxes. The boxes, in my area, are five in number, are about eighteen inches high and fifteen square; they stand on a small platform of wood raised three inches from the ground, and they are separated by a three-inch bar of three-quarter inch wood, screwed vertically to the platform. The little bins have each a strong iron drop-handle before and behind. When they are all placed in their proper places they stand in a row against the wall, and are level in height throughout. To a bar in the wall just above them a frame is attached which drops over all the bins at once, covering them all in; but in the frame there are five zinc doors, or flaps, one over each bin, in order that one bin may be open while the others are closed, and each one be, in short, separate from the rest. The mode of use is as follows:—All the bins being empty, and all the lids down, the refuse of the house is cast into the bin farthest from the house until that is rather more than half filled; the lid of this bin is then closed down and the refuse is cast into bin number two,

until that is charged in the same degree, and so on with the rest. Having five bins, it does not often happen that all the bins are fully charged at the same time, but if they are, they are closed in sections, and one section being open does not expose the whole surface to the air. When the dustmen come they have no occasion to bring baskets or to make any dust at all in the area. They have merely to lift up and throw back the frame containing all the lids, when the bins stand before them ready for removal. Each bin is carried up the steps, with the dust in it, to be emptied into the cart, and when all are in this way emptied they are brushed out and replaced. The frame is then let down, the five doors are closed down, and the arrangements are made for a new start. By this means the dust is always removed effectually; nothing remains concealed to infect the air; and, best of all, no bad odour is diffused through the house by the process of emptying the contents of the bin into baskets in the area.

In addition to the dust-bin in the area the cellars and other recesses there require to be frequently tended. The coal-cellar is a common place for the accumulation of refuse, and unless a vigilant attention is paid to the coal-cellar it almost certainly becomes at some time or other a supernumerary dust-bin. Even a coal-cellar calls for an occasional cleansing, and a good coating of lime-wash on the walls and roof is an excellent sanitary provision; it insures the complete cleansing out of the place, and the removal of accumulated organic débris, which is sure to be present in the course of two or three years. These same recommendations apply to all other places in the basement.

Of late years the art of growing creeping and climbing plants in the front areas of London houses has become somewhat fashionable, and we see even in poor neighbourhoods this plan sometimes carried out. I refer to it because it is so very commendable, when it is properly done, and on so many grounds. It is an excellent recreative industry, filling the minds of those who plant the flowers with pure and healthy thoughts and lessons. It is good artistically, the effect on the eyes of passers-by being itself instructive and pleasant, while the cheeriness of effect on those who live in the basement, and are compelled, where there are no flowers or plants, to contemplate day after day nothing but white walls and dark railings, must be an untold blessing. In place of sameness there is introduced to the eye—in small amount, it is true, yet in amount much better than nothing of the kind—some measure of those changes and variations which nature in her splendid fertility offers spontaneously to the more fortunate of her children, and out of which variety much relief of mind must needs be found from the killing monotony of viewing one object and one prospect narrowed to the extremest range, and ever in sight. Lastly, the plan of growing plants, and whenever sunlight can be obtained flowering plants, in the area, is good in a purely sanitary point of view, if the proper care be taken to cultivate what is grown, so as not to defeat the objects that are desired, viz., lessons of re-creation, beauty, and health. The proper care consists, first, in not overdoing the attempt to do. Whenever trailing plants are cultivated from the area, so that they climb the walls and extend over the windows excluding the light, then the thing is overdone. Whenever plants which require much water are too abundantly set about, so that water-vapour charges the air and makes the area wall and front-room damp, too much is done. Whenever plants which require a great deal of soil, so that large barrels or boxes of soil have to be used for them, are introduced too freely, too much is done. Room is in this way unduly taken up; and the soil, from its confinement in a case, gets so wet during wet seasons that it becomes a source of damp and dirt, and is apt to cause the plant itself that is set in it to wither away and die.

For these reasons the number of growing plants placed in the area ought to be limited; nor does the healthy provision in regard to them end entirely with that attention. It must be made a matter of consideration frequently to tend to all the plants; to see that they are in good condition of growth; to keep up the supply; to provide that all round about them is clean, and to remove everything that is dead and useless before it can have a chance of becoming decomposed and offensive.

The great obstacle that lies in the way of cultivating the areas of town houses, so as to carry out the system I am now advocating, in all its wholesome purity, is the instruction of those who have charge of the area, and the tone of their peculiar tastes and dispositions. I have had attendants who have, of their own accord, planted the area and kept it in good taste and condition. I have had others with no taste or desire for anything of the sort, and whom it was vain to instruct. We must not, therefore, I fear, trust to home work for the carrying out of this object. But in every locality there are florists who might undertake such duty regularly at a small cost if they were fairly patronised, and who I am sure for a small rental a year would keep every area beautifully set with the healthiest and most seasonable plants, at all times and seasons. The boon would be incalculable in London, especially in the crowded parts. The plants would purify the air in the worst places, and in winter, spring, summer, and autumn would bring with them a changing gladness, that would fully compensate for all the expense and all the trouble incident to the improvement.

"DREW THE WRONG LEVER!"

THIS was what the pointsman said,
   With both hands at his throbbing head:

" I drew the wrong lever standing here
And the danger signals stood at clear ;

But before I could draw it back again
On came the fast express, and then—

Then came a roar and a crash that shook
This cabin-floor, but I could not look

At the wreck, for I knew the dead would peer
With strange dull eyes at their murderer here."

" Drew the wrong lever?" " Yes, I say !
Go, tell my wife, and—take me away ! "

That was what the pointsman said,
With both hands at his throbbing head.

O ye of this nineteenth-century time,
Who hold low dividends as a crime,

Listen. So long as a twelve-hours' strain
Rests like a load of lead on the brain,

With its ringing of bells and rolling of wheels,
Drawing of levers until one feels

The hands grow numb with a nerveless touch,
And the handles shake and slip in the clutch,

So long will ye have pointsmen to say—
" Drew the wrong lever! take me away!"

ALEXANDER ANDERSON.

LUCREZIA.

By Mrs. COMYNS CARR.

PART III.

THE supper was not cooked, it was not even on the fire. The beans lay ready shredded, and the potatoes pared; but old Teresa stood at the cottage-door, anxiously looking out. The girl was all that was left to her now of past youth and keener interests. She held her all the closer to her heart, that Lucrezia had no mother of her own in whose affection to forget life's little daily disappointments, and she was proud, in simple peasant fashion, of the more than mother's devotion that she bestowed, proud that it had been such as to quench in Lucrezia every suspicion of the real truth. As she stood on the cottage threshold, listening for that light step upon the stones, she thought again of an evening seventeen years ago, when a little swaddled bundle had been left in her charge by a Milanese woman whom she had never seen before. The woman had given her gold, and· had sworn her to silence, saying that the baby was of noble blood, and that its mother wished to put it with her to nurse until such time as she should send for it. The time for its recognition had never come, but Teresa was glad, though there was no more gold sent to her for the infant's maintenance. What was enough for one would do for two, she had always insisted; and when her own boy, Lucrezia's little foster-brother, had been stricken down with cholera at Reggio, and had died, the poor mother's only comfort had been the thought that her foster-daughter was now as her own.

At length Lucrezia returned, and chattered excitedly as she took off her kerchief and folded it up, while Teresa put the pot on the fire, and made preparations. Before long supper was said to be ready; and Lucrezia dished up the soup, and they fell to the task. Pietro declared that the *minestra* was not so good as when she made it—at which insult his wife pretended to grumble. Was it this unsavouriness in the mess that led the girl herself to make so bad a supper, though she had vowed herself hungry enough when first she came in? Or was it because she had an ear listening for a familiar knock at the cottage-door, a well-known tread on the turf without? In spite, however, of a certain abstraction, she talked incessantly of Stresa, and Stresa news, and Stresa girls.

Thus they sat around the square brick hearth on the oaken benches, with the fire-light on their faces; and when the bells across the water struck nine o'clock, they went to bed. And still Paolo had not come.

When Lucrezia got up at four o'clock for the milking, the sky was grey with a greyness that was not only of the dawn, and a cold wind blew instead of the hot breeze which had scarcely stirred the water the evening before. There had been a storm across the mountains: a storm that was only gathering its forces again to roll over the lake district itself.

"Paolo can never have gone a-fishing on such a morning," said Lucrezia to herself, as she sat on the three-legged stool in the dark cow-shed. "Presently he will be up here with his heart in his hand, as usual. Poor fellow! And yet it *is* fun to see him with his mouth full of excuses, when it's I that ought to be ashamed instead!"

She smiled as she planned in her mind the lofty yet gracious bearing that was soon to be condescendingly forgiving to the penitent lover.

When the cows were milked, Lucrezia picked up her pails and stood them in the rough dairy, while she raked out the stable and turned in clean dry leaf. Then she drove the cattle to grass and came back to scour the wooden milk vessels. There would be no time yet awhile to sit thinking of Paolo, and why he never came to supper! For breakfast had to be ready for the farm men in two hours, and there were the saucepans to rub bright to-day, besides the usual job of sprinkling and sweeping the brick floor. When Lucrezia got back to the cottage, she hastened first to fetch water from the well in the great copper cauldron that she poised so cleverly on her head, and then she set busily to cooking and cleaning.

But when she sat down at last with the aunt to pare the potatoes and sort the rice, she had to submit to questions and found leisure to wonder, and even to grow a little anxious. And when the parish bells chimed mid-day, and still that most unaccountable of swains had made no appearance, Lucrezia began to be uneasy in earnest. She pretended that her flax was finished, and asked Uncle to go to the village to get her more from Maria, with hopes that he might hear some news of Paolo. And in spite of thunder and storm Uncle went, to bring back no very cheering news, for Maria did not know till Pietro told her that her son had returned with Lucrezia overnight. So, in spite of a message of raillery from black Marrina, which would have made Lucrezia's cheeks burn and her temper flame on any other day of the year, she was paler and more anxious than ever. To-day she did not pout as usual, nor make fun of Paolo's freak. Even the pinch of garlic could not make the polenta taste right to her.

It was a Friday. The day grew, and with the day grew the storm. Lucrezia had wandered listlessly into the wood on the cliff's edge to pick her chestnuts. She was idle, as was not her wont. When at three o'clock the bells across the lake rang for prayer, she was startled to find that the canvas satchel at her side was but half full. She knelt down to make the sign of the cross, as every good Catholic should at sound of these Friday bells, and then rose up quickly and, taking up her wooden levers, began to open the prickly shells and pick the brown fruit busily. But again she paused—paused to note how angrily clouds were rising in the east to speed with the wind across the sky. Where could Paolo be? Surely not on the lake in such weather! Oh, if she could but know that he was safe—at home in the village below—she thought she would be content even though he did not come to her. If his boat was in the creek he was at home and safe from the storm. She dropped the levers and scrambled down the grassy border where the woodland hems the rock, grasping the birch shrub and the mountain ash to help her perilous way, until she could look right over the margin into the green waves beneath. The boat was not moored there. She knew his well, and it was not anywhere to be seen as far as her gaze could reach over the lake. What was keeping Paolo? Was he staying away to avoid her?

The lake was quite rough. White crests tipped the waves, and the wind caught the water into whirlpools here and there. A grey mist hung around; so thick was it that she could no longer see the opposite shore. She strained her eyes, however, and still stood watching sadly. Something at last did come out dimly from the gloom. It was a boat—and a boat pulling across from Stresa. She leant forward, gazing with all her soul. It rocked upon the treacherous water, but it did not appear to be a pleasure skiff. No, it certainly was not a pleasure skiff. As it came nearer she was sure that it was a big brown boat—a boat that could hold its way even on these waves that swelled so rapidly beneath the breath of the gathering storm—a boat like Paolo's? Yes; the dear old boat in which she had passed so many happy holidays! Surely it must be Paolo at last; who else would venture on that cruel lake with the wind behind the weather as this was? The boat drew near rapidly. There were two people in it. Who could Paolo be bringing with him from Stresa? Now it was close under the very shore. Lucrezia bent over the precipice to see who it could be that was with Paolo. Somebody sat in the prow of the boat doing no work; that could not be Paolo. Then why was the man who was rowing not tall and slim like her betrothed? Why did he pull so

awkwardly ?   Why——?   The truth came home to her slowly, for she was loath to banish the last hope — Paolo was not in the boat!   Lucrezia turned away.   Blindly she clambered up the broken ground again till she stood on the top of the rock.   The tears that had been so nearly coming all the morning flowed unchecked at last.

The boat had drawn to shore —the luckless boat that was not Paolo's — the men had got out, and the one had paid the other in coin that had made him doff his cap obsequiously ; but still the tears lay wet on Lucrezia's cheeks, the choking sobs rose in her throat.   She was sick at heart, and in her sorrow she forgot all about the strange fact that a gentleman should have been rowing over from Stresa on such a day as this, when there was no view to be seen from the c l i ff, a n d w h e n t h e l a k e bid fair to be danger- o u s going h o m e. S i n c e t h e b o a t did not contain h i m w h o m s h e sought it was as no- thing to her. She was all the more startled when a strange voice sounded close behind her, rousing her from the stupor of her grief. "What ails thee, little Madonna?" it said. The tone struck a chill to her soul. She turned slowly, and saw the young Count from the town, he who was the first cause of all her present misery. For a moment she looked at him speechless. She wanted words wherewith to scathe him for the ill that he had wrought her. But her breath still came in gasps, and her eyes were red with weeping. How could she be dignified in such a plight?

She passed her apron hastily over her face and moved away. She had forgotten the Count until that moment, but now that she was forced to remember him it was with anger. And he dared to address her thus unseemly. Was she not a well brought up maiden, and had she no lover of her own that she was thus to be exposed to a fine gentleman's compliments?

"Nothing ails me," she answered pettishly to the repeated question, and keeping her back turned towards the new-comer.

Count Giovanni laughed good-humouredly.

"Nevertheless, thou criest," said he; "and I can tell thee what it is for. It is for thy fisher-gallant of yesterday. What a foolish wench thou art to soil thy pretty face for a block of a man like that!"

Lucrezia turned round. The sobs were scarce yet choked in her throat, her lips trembled still, but her eyes shone. The Count, however, interrupted her speech.

"Dost thou not see what paste he is made of?" laughed he. "This is the second time to my knowledge that he deserts thee. Wilt thou give him a third chance?"

The words froze in the girl's throat, and she stood with her lips parted. Here was the confirmation of her own fears. It was a bad omen.

"Dost thou not see that a man who is but a contadino can scarcely admire thy pale face?" went on her tormentor. "He is tall and strong himself; he needs a strong, bold wench to wife. Such a girl as he might find in Stresa any day, not a white-faced child such as thou."

"I did not make my own face," pouted Lucrezia, mortified in her vanity; "neither did I tell the Creator how He was to make it. No, nor ask Paolo to admire it! That which he said he said of his own free will."

The Count smiled to see that his bait had been taken. "Perhaps he said it for a jest, to pass a holiday noon," suggested he; and Lucrezia remembered that Paolo had been

XXI—60

very often to Stresa of late. "Tell me, now," asked the Count again presently, "do thy parents give thee a handsome dowry for thy wedding? If so Paolo may even yet return."

"I have no parents," answered Lucrezia after a pause, "and my uncle is a poor man; he will not give me a dowry."

The Count knew all this, but he said sympathetically, "Poor child!"

"I never had any parents," added she simply; "but my aunt is a good woman, she would give me a dowry if she could. Though I do not believe Paolo would let me be for sake of a dowry."

"It does a girl no good in the eyes of a contadino that she be dowerless," continued the Count meditatively; "it is as a good name in his eyes, let alone the money's value. And thou hast no parents. Dost thou not remember thy parents?"

"No," answered Lucrezia; "I remember nobody but the Aunt Teresa; she was a mother for me."

"And she often spoke to thee of thine own mother—often told thee of her life and her home, that it should not be said thou didst know nothing of her who gave thee life—is that not so?"

"What need have you to know what the aunt has told me of my mother?" asked Lucrezia, facing her questioner with a face where grief and fear and anger were strangely mingled. "If I have no knowledge at all of my parents, what is that to you?" The neighbours' taunts of yesterday, that she had not noticed at the time, grew up in her memory, and a secret terror took possession of her heart, of which she could scarcely define the shape.

"What is it to me? A great deal, because I have your interest at heart, Lucrezia," said the Count gently, and coming closer to her. "I am sorry for you!"

"I want none of your pity," cried the girl, bridling even amidst her anxiety. "What should I require it for?"

"To be sure," laughed the Count, "for the loss of the man, Paolo, you are but little to be pitied, as I have tried before to show you."

"You cannot annoy me with that as you want to do," answered Lucrezia firmly, though her cheek was as pale as ashes. "You shall see—Paolo will not jilt me! We peasants know better than to treat one another so ill, even though we are not educated as you are."

"Do not class yourself with the peasants,

Lucrezia," said the Count, reaching his point at last. "You are no contadina."

"What do you say?" asked she, turning on him bewildered.

"I say that you are no peasant! No niece of her whom you call Teresa! You are the child of gentle parents, and the woman yonder is but your foster-mother!"

"My foster-mother?" She paused, knitting her brow and pressing her hands together in anxious thought. "To be sure, the grand ladies from town put their children out like that to be nursed in the country. But why," she went on presently, "has nobody ever told me? Why have my parents never come for me? How do you know it?"

The first questions came dropping out dreamily, but she put the last one abruptly.

"It is a fact well known in the village," said the Count.

"Then why have I never been told?" she repeated.

"That I do not know."

"A lady after all!" she murmured, uncertain as yet in her ignorance whether to be pleased or not. "Perhaps Paolo will be glad to know that!"

"I do not think so," answered the Count laconically.

"Why not?" insisted she. "Though I was not born a contadina, I have been brought up as one; I am used to the work, I would make him a good wife. And though I were twenty times a lady, I would choose Paolo sooner than any other."

"But will Paolo choose you? He is not here, he has left you! He is a poor fisherman; why should he take a portionless maiden, when there are rich lasses in Stresa to be had for the asking?"

"Paolo always knew I was poor," faltered she; "and for that matter, if my parents are gentlefolks, they would dower me."

"Do you know who your parents are? do you know where to find them?" asked the Count.

"Teresa will know, Teresa will surely know," moaned the girl. "I will ask her, I will go and ask her now!"

And she moved, putting the man blindly aside as she passed him. The red flushed in her cheeks and crept around her temples. But he grasped her almost rudely by the arm.

"Stay, child!" cried he, "you are but preparing further misery for yourself. Teresa can tell you nothing—she knows nothing of your parents. You do not show your usual good sense. Why deceive yourself further? You are a foundling!"

She started back with a smothered shriek, and lifted up a hand, as though to stave off the knowledge of evil. Her face had grown quite white again. As though in a whirlwind she heard the voice finish: "You have said it a hundred times yourself—you have no parents!" She felt as though her limbs would give way under her. She held on to the bough of the chestnut-tree.

"I will not believe it," she said doggedly. "I will ask Teresa! She must know my parents. They cannot be wicked folk! They will come and fetch me! They——" and here she broke into tears.

"Come, console thyself," whispered the Count again presently. "Believe me, thou wert not meant to be the wife of a contadino!"

"No," said Lucrezia between her sobs. "And now, even if Paolo would still marry me, I can never permit it, knowing what I do. Ah! if I had not played with him, and put him off, we should have been wed by this time, before I had learned what must part us for ever. Ah! why did you come and tell me?" wailed she. "Why must I suffer so hardly for the faults of other people?"

"Thou shalt not suffer, Lucrezia, unless it be through thine own foolishness," continued the Count gently, and still kneeling beside her. "A contadino is proud because he is nobody, but a man who has his own good position can do as he likes. I have seemed to thee cruel, have I not? Forgive me, little Madonna, for now I will show thee that I am not really cruel, and that I have kinder thoughts for thee than thy country lover had."

The Count rose, and took Lucrezia by the arm to help her up; but she shook off his hand and looked up at him, brushing away the hot tears that still dimmed her sight. The changed tone of his last speech had startled her. She struggled to her feet and fastened her eyes steadfastly upon his; but she did not speak, and though somewhat taken aback by her attitude, he continued his say—

"I want such a face as thine to paint in my pictures, Lucrezia," he said; "wilt thou come with me?"

He took her two hands in his, but she withdrew them from his grasp and folded them across her bosom.

"Per Bacco!" she cried, unfolding her hands, planting her arms akimbo, and looking straight at the Count with as defiant an air as though no trouble oppressed her heart.

"Per Bacco! what kind of a girl do you take me for? Do you think I am a fool that cannot understand?"

"Yesterday, you were not so proud," began Count Giovanni; but the girl left him no time for explanation. Her heart was lonely, and sore with mortification, her conscience was tender about the wrongs which, in her thoughtlessness, she had dealt to Paolo; but she was not to be deceived into thinking that a mere blush of vanity could invite such an insult as this! She had no mind to spare the Count.

"You have a wicked insolence and a wicked courage to come here robbing a poor girl of all her happiness only to insult her afterwards!" she cried. "If Paolo has deserted me, it is because *you* brought me into discredit. Is that not enough for you —you cruel man—you coward?"

"Take care, lest I show you a gentleman can be something else besides a coward, in spite of your notions," said the Count between his teeth.

"I am not afraid!" laughed the girl. "There is little harm you can do me but what you have done already! I am not afraid to tell you the truth—that you are bad and cruel, and false, and vain, and that I am glad you have taught me at last it is no honour to be one of you! Yes, vain, I say! For have you not dared to presume that, because you were dressed in fine clothes, a pretty girl would put up with your poor presence? Ah! thank God, if I *am* born of gentle folks, I am a contadina still, and I have our own good taste and our own honesty!"

She raised her arm as she spoke these words, and as she stood there the Count Giovanni felt instinctively that the child was gone and that in her place was a woman with whom he had best not meddle. He turned away.

"You misunderstand me," he said. "Many an honest girl has sat as model in a painter's studio before this. But take your own way!"

"Oh, I am not so foolish as I have seemed!" said Lucrezia, turning back into the wood. "So I will wish your honour a good evening." And, with her own quick, swinging step, she was gone!

The Count looked after her a moment with something like a look of astonishment in his languid eyes. He buttoned his coat around him as he met the keen wind from the water. The fishermen were grouped together on the narrow strip of shingle beneath the rocks, where he turned hastily.

"Where is the boatman who was to wait for me?" cried the Count imperiously above the rush of the elements.

"The lake is rising, your honour, and Gian-Battista would wait no longer," said one of the men.

"If he required to be home for the night he did well," volunteered another, "for surely no mortal can cross the water this evening!"

"Your honour will have to accept the poor shelter that we can offer," said a woman who now joined the group. It was Maria, the village gossip. She who was always at hand when anything or anybody new was to be seen.

The Count muttered something below his breath. Nothing should induce him to remain longer in the village where he had received the rebuff that he had from a mere country maiden; and he offered any one two Napoleons, and then five Napoleons, to row him across. At first no one agreed, but at last a man stepped forward half sheepishly. He had an ailing wife and a parcel of little ones at home, and after all perhaps the gentleman was right, and it was no business of other folks whether he chose to risk his life or no.

When Lucrezia turned into the wood, the black clouds were beginning to shed their first great drops of rain. She picked up her basket of chestnuts on the soft turf, and with her tears quenched for the moment by the anger that boiled within her, began to gather up the fruit feverishly, saying to herself that, rain or no rain, she could not return with so bad a crop. But though she tried very hard to think of her work and not to remember all the revelations and emotions of the last terrible half-hour, nature was stronger than determination, and grief would not be put aside. Almost before she knew it she was crying bitterly at her task, and soon, forgetful of the hastening storm, she sat down beneath the trees and threw her apron over her head that she might mourn alone with the trees and sky. Nobody must guess at her sorrow, and yet, indeed, it was a great one.

The storm had broken now in grim earnest. The wind blew wildly through the trees, the thunder grew louder and the rain poured down in torrents. At any other time Lucrezia would have been frightened, but pride rallied her courage now: she would not go home till her first sorrow was spent and the tears were wiped away. No one, not even Teresa —no longer "the aunt" now—must ask any questions.

The air was cold and dank when at last

she rose to return to the cottage. She turned her skirt over her head to shield her from the driving rain and hurried along the cliff, stilling the sighs at her heart, that no trace of her weeping might be apparent to those at home.

Teresa stood at the cottage-door as she had stood the evening before. " Lucrezia, child," said she as the girl came up the path, "surely thou are purposed to make me uneasy. This is the second time thou de-layest beyond thy wont. Though indeed I am an old fool to trouble myself about thee. Where hast thou been ? "

" I have plucked chestnuts," replied the maiden, flinging down her satchel half pettishly. " The harvest is not good ! "

" How now ? When thine uncle protests, if the rain do but keep off, the fruit is larger than for many past years. But if thou hast been in the wood, then thou hast not heard the news ? "

" No ; what news ? " asked Lucrezia eagerly.

" About the young stranger—the gentle-man who came across from Stresa. What he came for no one can guess, and on such a day as this too ! "

Lucrezia sighed impatiently and turned away her head. " What of him ? I don't doubt he returned quicker than he came."

" In such a storm it would be real mad-ness to return," said Teresa.

But the girl only answered, as if it were a matter of course, " Yes, that is true," and went about her work.

Lucrezia did not waste her time, she got the supper ready as quickly as she did any other evening ; but there was a cloud on her brow and she moved wearily ; there was something amiss ! Yes, something more than the mere fact that Paolo kept strangely away. What had chanced ? Dearly, for once, would Teresa have liked to ask some questions. But she was wise. She said no-thing, she only watched sadly and waited. Perhaps the next day Lucrezia would be herself again.

But when the morrow came things were sadder than ever. The storm had raged all night, and grievous tales of its cruel damage were making their way up to the cottage on the cliff. In spite of damp and gloom Lucrezia had been out at daybreak to the milking, and had wandered out alone after-wards into the wet woods, where the unripe chestnuts lay hurled in prickly masses on the soaking turf amid broken boughs and scat-tered leaves. Sadly in the sad, cold country

she had said her farewell to the summer, and perhaps it was not wonderful that she did not look cheerful when she returned to the cottage.

" Hast thou heard any further news from the village, Lucrezia ? " asked the woman, as the girl went outside to toss the maize in the great flat basket before putting it to dry in the struggling autumn sunbeams.

" Battista's fields are under water," she answered shortly.

" Poor Battista ! the potatoes not yet dug and he with so many children. But Caterina was saying just now there is even worse news than that, for it is feared that the poor gentleman who was over here yesterday has got drowned in returning to Stresa." She looked up furtively as she said this. " That will rouse her," said the woman to herself.

But Lucrezia only said, " The men should have warned him. The water was not fit for a boat last night."

And even when Pietro came up presently with details of the previous evening's scene on the shore, she scarcely left off her work to listen.

Teresa was at her wits' end. How should she thaw this dreadful reserve ? She began by deciding to make an omelette of herbs for dinner. Lucrezia loved an omelette of herbs. She sallied forth into the orchard to pluck parsley and thyme from the plot beside the Michaelmas daisies. When she returned to the kitchen she noticed that the girl, thinking herself unobserved, had stopped her task and was gazing dreamily out across the lake. The elder woman looked fondly out at her over the carnations in the window sill. She had paused, on her way in, to choose a sprig of the marjoram that grew side by side with them. They were the carna-tions that Lucrezia had been wont to give Paolo for his cap on a Sunday.

" I am sadly stiff to-day," said Teresa, speaking loud so that her voice should reach the girl without, and rinsing her herbs as she spoke. " But now, as I stooped to pluck the parsley below, I could have cried aloud with the pain."

" I am sorry," answered Lucrezia.

" When the platters are washed, after dinner, wilt thou go down to Marrina and beg of her two leaves of marsh-mallow ? The decoction always helps my rheumatism."

" I will ask little Tonietta of the neigh-bour's to step down for me," replied the girl. " The loom has lain idle these two days ; and now that I have flax I have a mind to work."

This was not the result which Teresa had hoped from her righteous fraud.

"Ah, let be the loom, child," she cried. "Thou art for ever working. There must be news and to spare in the village to-day—I should like to know more of that poor gentleman's fate, and then to learn who has suffered most from the storm."

At any other time this argument would have proved unanswerable. News, whether good or bad, had always been as meat and drink to Lucrezia. But now she only said half-fretfully—

"Ah! what do I care for news? The uncle will tell thee of the neighbours, and as for the gentleman, he is nothing to us."

The woman within sighed as she whipped the eggs for her omelette with a preoccupied face. The two worked on in silence for a space, and it was nearly dinner-time.

Just as the maccaroni was ready to dish up a sound of bells came from across the water.

Lucrezia stood listening with the wooden ladle in her hand, ready to strain the paste when it was boiled.

Teresa rose and went out on to the piazzetta. After a minute she uttered a low exclamation, and held up her hands as in horror; for the bells were tolling bells—they tolled the knell for a departed soul.

"They are ringing for the poor gentleman who crossed the lake yesterday, Lucrezia," said she, re-entering the cottage. "Holy Virgin! what a sorrow it will be for his parents!"

But still, though her cheek was white, Lucrezia only said quietly—

"We must all die some day," and she went on serving out the mess into the platters with a hand that did not tremble.

"The uncle is late for dinner; he must have been more hungry for news than food," she added, almost bitterly; and she took her own plate out on to the threshold that it might not be observed she could not taste a morsel of its contents.

But even when Pietro came up presently with more comments she would listen to nothing; and when she had washed up the platters she went and knelt by the old wall, gazing out across the Michaelmas daisies and the chestnut-trees to Stresa beyond the lake.

All the afternoon the sound of the bells tolling swept softly and at intervals over the water, and all the afternoon Lucrezia crouched as though spell-bound in that corner of the little court. She had always been afraid of death and burying, and there was no telling whether it was fear or no that fascinated her now.

Presently neighbours began to come up from the village as though with some important news. They looked askance at Lucrezia and did not speak to her. Tall Marrina came, who was her rival for beauty. She came arm in arm with another girl-comrade, and her countenance was eager, as though she bore a great secret. But when her gaze fell on Lucrezia she only delivered some trivial errand and went away. So it was also with others. They had come to see Teresa, they said. And Teresa had gone to milk the cow, her heart failing her to rouse the girl to duties neglected for the first time.

But at last that one came who was never daunted in the telling of a story—Maria, the wife of the miller, the gossip-in-chief. She would wait till Teresa came home, and she waylaid her with the milk-pails just at the foot of the stone steps that lead up to the piazzetta. They stood beside the last of the year's climbing French beans, and almost in the midst of the trailing gourd-tendrils; and Maria, as she talked, plucked withering blossoms of the Michaelmas daisies that had been dashed by the rain.

They spoke in a half whisper, remembering that Lucrezia sat above; but presently, warming with her subject, the neighbour forgot her precautions, and the girl learned in spite of herself what she had not had the courage to ask nor others the courage to tell her. For, after some whispered conversation and sundry ejaculations, she heard old Teresa begin to moan and sob; a thing most unwonted to that strong and busy nature, and she gathered that her foster-mother was refusing comfort for some great and terrible ill.

"We must all have patience, dear heart," Maria declared soothingly, with that placid consolation that comes so easily when the grief is not one's own.

And Teresa replied that she could not have patience; that for herself she could have suffered, for her day was past, but that it was hard if, at seventeen, a life was already to be overshadowed.

"Ah, you fret, as I warned you yesterday, because you fear that no other man will be found to marry the girl, neighbour," added the miller's wife, after a short silence; "but you must not lose heart. Men are queer mortals, and there's no telling what freak they mayn't take up with."

"I don't say," murmured old Teresa, sadly returning to her complaint again, "that a man mightn't be found who wouldn't think overmuch of the wench being a foundling, but I know well enough it won't be easy to get one who would be silent to *her* on the subject; and, dear me, Lucrezia would never take a man she thought knew aught amiss of her. The girl is proud enough for a duchess."

The poor soul took up the corner of her apron again. "Paolo was a good lad that way; he wouldn't have mortified her for a great deal. He *was* fond of her. And to think of his lying there in his shroud before the high altar of Stresa Church as I'm talking, he that was as fine a man as you could see but two days ago!"

Lucrezia, sitting above on the stone wall, knew now why the bells had seemed so sad to her, sounding all the afternoon across the water. Paolo was dead! Yes, dead, and she was not to be married after all! Oh, well, since she was a foundling it was better so, for she could never have married him anyhow, and how could she have told him why? "Alas, for me!" moaned she to herself softly. But she stopped her tears to listen again to what Maria was saying below in her odd, harsh whisper.

"Yes, they found his corpse on the bank just below Baveno," continued the woman. "It was washed up against the high wall, that's half thrown down now by the storm, and the boat was all dashed to pieces, nothing but loose planks of it left. What possessed the man to cross the lake on such a night no one can tell! Some think he must have been right down to Arona and back, for he had not been seen at home for two days. But nobody knew of any business he could have had in Arona. It's a strange tale! Maybe your lass could tell something if she were asked? Perhaps they had a lover's quarrel! They were over at Stresa that day."

"Ah, let the child alone, for mercy's sake!" implored the elder woman. "Hasn't she trouble enough as it is?"

Maria seemed to think she had, for she only murmured, "Well, she's punished herself if it is so. She won't be so wilful to the next as she used to be to him, I should think!" And then she went on telling how they had carried the corpse into Stresa Church, and how the bells had been set a-tolling, and how the waters had been too rough till this afternoon for any one to go over and break the news to the widowed mother. "Gian-Battista, the boat-builder, is there with her now," she said. "But as soon as I had heard what he had to say I thought

to myself, Lucrezia and old Pietro will like to hear this, and up I hurried as fast as my legs would carry me. Ah, there will be a nice funeral in a day or two, for they say the young man had saved not a few *quattrini*," concluded the gossip with unction.

"God rest his soul!" murmured Teresa with a sigh.

"Yes, we must all pray for his soul. Even the girl can do that much for him!" And with this parting comfort the miller's wife suggested that her neighbour would be wanting to go and tell Lucrezia the news, and that it was time she herself went on up the road to carry it elsewhere. "Don't fret for the wench," advised she, picking her way down the slippery path, "for you'll have little ones about you yet before you die!"

Lucrezia, still as in a dream, saw the figure disappear behind a stone wall and come up again on the other side, climbing the grass slope towards a cottage higher up the hill. Then she rose and, choking down her tears, walked into the kitchen, and when Teresa came slowly up the broken stone steps, laboriously carrying the milk-pail on her head, the girl stood quietly waiting within as though nothing had happened.

For a moment the two looked at one another, and Lucrezia's lip trembled. "Give me the pail," said she, almost crossly, and Teresa only answered, "There, go; thou art a good wench," and then she knew that Lucrezia had heard all that Maria had said, and that there was no need for further words.

So the girl cried out her heart in the cowshed, while the new calf laid its nose in her lap, and listened serenely to her wailing; and, beside the kitchen hearth, the old woman prayed silently to her saints for solace to the grief that she might not comfort.

*   *   *   *   *   *

This is the story of Lucrezia, and how she wanted to be thought like a lady.

In the mellow September, when the chestnuts begin to show a streak of brown through their prickly shells, wedding bells have again sounded across the water, but Lucrezia has never cared to go again to see the ceremony, nor been proud to be told of the gentility of her appearance.

Lucrezia is an old woman now, and has served a parish priest as faithful servant these many years past, but she has never seen another autumn so disastrous as the Santi of 1840.

THE END.

PRINTED BY VIRTUE AND CO., LIMITED, CITY ROAD, LONDON.

INDEX.

AMELIE-LES-BAINS. By L. F. Bewley 229
"Arden, In." By K. S. Macquoid 589
Art in Daily Life, The Influence of. By J. Beavington Atkinson
  I. Introductory . . . 356
  II. Interior Decoration of the House 418
  III. Furnishing the House . 452
  IV. Beauty 638
  V. Dress 777
Augustine, St., A Visit to the Ancient See of. By J. Munro . 669

BERGEN. By Lieut. George T. Temple, R.N. . . . 767
Birds, Little. By the Rev. J. G. Wood, M.A. . . . 557
Blind Youths, A Visit to the Paris Institution for. By the Rev. William Burnet, M.A. . 763

CAYENNE, A Visit to the Prisons of. (Note) . . . 72
Children's Creed, The. By A. P. Stanley, D.D., Dean of Westminster 133
Coffee-rooms for the People. By Lady Hope of Carriden . 749, 844
Commandments, The Ten. By A. P. Stanley, D.D. . . 351
Conversion of the Heathen, The Church, A Fellow-worker with God in the. By the Right Rev. the Lord Bishop of Rochester 458
Country Lanes, City Courts and. By K. S. Macquoid . 429
Cyprus, A Trip to. By Lieut.-Col. W. F. Butler, C.B. . 518, 632, 702, 807

"DIANA SMITH." By J. Milner Fothergill, M.D.
  Part I. 485
  Part II. 553

EAR and its Mechanism, The. By Professor J. McKendrick, M.D. 55, 240
Economical, Food for the. By J. Milner Fothergill, M.D.
  I. 18
  II. 123

FAITH and Virtue. By the Bishop of Tasmania . . 170
Firstborn of Every Creature, The. By John Hunt, D.D. . 334
Flags, About. By A. MacGeorge. 194
Food Fishes, The Propagation of. By D. Esdaile, D.D. . 772
French City, An Old. By K. S. Macquoid . . . 344

GOOD, The Final Triumph of. By the Bishop of Tasmania . 265

Gospel, The Mystery of the. By John Hunt, D.D. . . 70
Gothenburg and Sweden. By the Rev. A. Macleod Symington . 317

HAGAR'S Life. By the Rev. Stopford A. Brooke, M.A. . 388
Health at Home. By B. W. Richardson, M.D., F.R.S. . 64, 98, 282, 382, 560, 848
Hearts, Hungry. By Mrs. Faithfull 812
Holland, with Pen and Pencil. By Robert T. Pritchett, F.S.A.
  I. 22
  II. 127
  III. 206
  IV. 373

ICE Hero, An. By Captain A. H. Markham, R.N. . . 88, 169
Insects, Some Noxious. By the Rev. J. G. Wood, M.A. . 414, 448

JOHN THE BAPTIST before Herod. By the Rev. H. R. Haweis, M.A. 92
Jones, Poor. By T. Marchant Williams, B.A. . . 563
Joseph and His Brethren. By the Rev. Stopford A. Brooke, M.A. 212
Joseph and His Life and Death. By the Rev. Stopford A. Brooke, M.A. 235

KANGAROOS, On. By Dr. Andrew Wilson, F.R.S.E. . . 663

LUCREZIA. By Mrs. Comyns Carr. 712, 784, 854

MAN's Judgment. By John Hunt, D.D. 412
Modern Gaelic Bards and Duncan MacIntyre. By Principal Shairp, LL.D. . . 423
Mogador to Morocco, From. By Kalli Stenning . . 311, 493
Music. By the Rev. H. R. Haweis, Author of "Music and Morals" . . . 489, 815

NAAMAN's Wife, The Hebrew Maid and. By John S. Howson, D.D., Dean of Chester . 534
New England, Founders of. By W. Fraser Rae.
  I. William Bradford . . 337
  II. John Winthrop . . 594
Newport Market Refuge, The. By William Gilbert . . 627
New Year's Day, Thoughts for. By the Editor . . . 53

OSPREY, is One of his Highland Haunts, The. By William Jolly, H.M. Inspector of Schools . 261
Outram, Sir James. By Alexander H. Japp, LL.D., F.R.S.E. 500, 528

PLAGUES, Social. By W. Ross Browne.
  I. Advice and Condolence . 103
  II. Noise 525
    (Section II.) . . . 606
Plain-Speaking. By the Author of "John Halifax, Gentleman."
  I. The Tide at the Turn . 244
  II. Victims and Victimisers . 445
  III. "Odd" People . . 697
  IV. A Little Music . . 745
Problem, The Great. By the Rev. J. Baldwin Brown, B.A. . 820
Progress, Educational. By T. Walker 136
Prophecy, The Spirit of. By R. H. Story, D.D. . . 602
Pushing. By James Sully . . 379

REDUCED Circumstances: an Edinburgh Story. By R. D. N. . 14

SA'ID Abu 'Omar Erneb, My Syrian Friend. By the Rev. Professor J. Robertson, M.A. . . 48
Sarah de Berenger. By Jean Ingelow. 33, 73, 177, 217, 280, 393, 465, 537, 609, 681, 753, 825
Scottish Highlands, The Poetry of the. By Principal Shairp, LL.D. 275
Snails and Slugs. By the Rev. J. G. Wood, M.A. . 172, 240
Stanleys of Alderley, The Edward. By R. D. N. . . . 408
Sundays in Many Lands. By J. Cameron Lees, D.D.
  I. In "Holy Russia" . . 27
  II. In Catholic Spain . 165
  III. In Sweden . . . 481

"TENEBRAS LUX, Post." By the Rev. Canon Vaughan, M.A., of Leicester . . . 709, 740
Tight-Lacing, Lung Capacity and. By Joseph Farrar, L.R.C.P., Edin. 202
Trumpet-Major, The. By Thomas Hardy . 1, 105, 145, 249, 321, 361, 433, 505, 577, 649, 721, 793

VENICE, Maximilian Hornblower's Evening in. By Lieut.-Col. L. W. M. Lockhart, Author of "Fair to See."
  Tableau I. 643
  Tableau II. 674

WALDENSES, An Adventure in the Valleys of the. By the Rev. Francis Gell, M.A. . . 735
Will Faith be Lost? By the Right Rev. the Lord Bishop of Rochester 60
Winnipeg via Peace River Pass, Victoria to. By Daniel M. Gordon . . . 116, 158, 305
Woman's Collegiate Life in America, A. By Mrs. Meredith . 838

POETRY.

	PAGE
AFTERMATH, The. By James Hendry	402
"Am Meer." By William Sharp	310
Animals, A Plea for Dumb. By Anna H. Drury	139
Blue Gentian. By the Author of "John Halifax, Gentleman"	81
Border Land, The. By Jane Simpson	350
Boy that Died, My Little. By the Author of "John Halifax, Gentleman"	360
Charity. By E. Conder Gray	97
Children's Music. By F. M. Owen	602
Conflict and Victory. By the Rev. John Glasse	261
Deer in a Park, To a. By E. C. G.	744
Edel-Weiss, The. By Dora Greenwell	350
Fact, A. By William A. Gibbs	200
Fairy Jane. By Henry Johnston	824
Fancies. By the Author of "Mrs. Jerningham's Journal"	536
Fatherless. By Ellen Miller	484
Flowers, The Voices of the. By Alexander Anderson	264
Gethsemane. By Alexander Anderson	281
Good Old Man, A. By Professor J. S. Blackie	70
Haunted Glen, The. By Emily Grace Harding	287
Hislop, Andrew, the Martyr. By Professor John Veitch	588
Hymn. By Professor John S. Blackie	734
Irish Ballad, An. By Alfred Perceval Graves	170
Little Woman, My. By Sarah Doudney	335
Message, A Maiden's. By L. G. M.	517
Novantia. By John Service, D.D.	217
Query, A. By E. W. Howson	846
Rabbit and the Teal, The. (From the French.) By A. H. J.	30
Rest, Seeking. By J. Ashcroft Noble	210
Sandown Bay. By Mrs. Owen	608
Soul's Oratorio, The. By R. Sinclair Brooke, D.D.	575
Stream, The Slow. By Sarah Doudney	601
Torrent, The. By Alison Hughes	387
Verses for Little Ones. By A. H. J.	672
Vigil. By Alison Hughes	135
Watch of the Night, In the Fourth. By the Rev. F. Langbridge, B.A.	552
"Why art thou cast down, O my Soul?" By the Author of "Selina's Story"	423
World as I find it, The. By Frederick Langbridge	372
Yarrow. By Alexander Anderson	752
Yesterday. By Ellen Miller	524
Wrong Lever, Drew the. By Alexander Anderson	853

ILLUSTRATIONS.

		PAGE
The Trumpet-Major	John Collier	5, 8, 11, 105, 106, 112, 148, 153, 156, 256, 258, 324, 329, 332, 361, 368, 433, 436, 437, 441, 505, 506, 513, 580, 585, 652, 657, 724, 729, 732, 796, 801
Sarah de Berenger	W. J. Hennessy	34, 40, 41, 73, 78, 81, 84, 177, 179, 184, 187, 217, 220, 225, 228, 289, 290, 296, 304, 396, 400, 402, 405, 465, 473, 480, 537, 545, 552, 609, 617, 624, 625, 681, 684, 688, 692, 696, 756, 760, 762, 825, 832, 836
Reduced Circumstances	P. Tarrant	17
Holland. Thirty-Five Illustrations	R. T. Pritchett	22, 23, 24, 25, 26, 127, 128, 129, 130, 131, 132, 206, 207, 208, 209, 210, 211, 373, 374, 375, 376, 377, 378
The Rabbit and the Teal	E. Rischgitz	32
El Marhum Sa'id Abu 'Omar Erneb	R. E. Taylor	49
The Ear and its Mechanism. Nine Illustrations		56, 57, 58, 140, 141, 143
Studies in Black and White :—		
Reconciled	T. Davidson	(Frontispiece)
Breton Peasants going to Mass on Christmas-eve	G. Montbard	73
The Haunt of the Ibis on the Euphrates	Irving Montagu	145
A Corner of the Bois de Chaumour, Burgundy	G. Montbard	217
Falls of the Lochy, Perthshire	E. Jennings	320
A Race for Life	E. Rischgitz	433
Falls of the Dochart, Perthshire	E. Jennings	721
An Ice Hero	C. O. Murray, &c.	88, 272
Charity	D. M. Duncan	97
Victoria to Winnipeg via Peace River Pass. Three Illustrations		121, 160, 161
Sundays in Many Lands		168
Snails and Slugs. Four Illustrations		173, 175, 240, 244
About Flags		195
A Fact		201
Lung Capacity and Tight-Lacing. Two Illustrations		204
Amélie-les-Bains. Five Illustrations	Miss Bewley	229, 230, 233, 234
The Osprey in One of his Highland Haunts		264
From Mogador to Morocco. Thirteen Illustrations		321, 312, 313, 314, 315, 316, 493, 494, 495, 496, 497, 498
My Little Woman	Fleming	366
An Old French City. Five Illustrations	T. R. Macquoid	344, 345, 348, 349
The Edward Stanleys of Alderley		409
Some Noxious Insects. Twelve Illustrations		415, 416, 417, 448, 449, 450, 451
"Diana Smith."	Taylor	488
A Trip to Cyprus	R. T. Pritchett, C. L. Seymour, &c.	521, 632, 633, 704, 705, 807, 800
Sir James Outram	T. Scott	528
The Stocking-knitter. A Sketch	Brenda N. Melladew	536
Little Birds. Two Illustrations		560, 561
The Soul's Oratorio		576
Andrew Hislop, the Martyr		588
In Arden. Three Illustrations	T. R. Macquoid	589, 592, 593
The Slow Stream	Fleming	601
On Kangaroos. Three Illustrations		664, 665
Verses for Little Ones. Four Illustrations		672, 673
An Adventure in the Valleys of the Waldenses. Four Illustrations	Quick	735, 736, 737, 739
To a Deer in a Park	Fraser	744
Women's Collegiate Life in America	From Sketches	840, 841
Lucrezia. Five Illustrations	W. J. Hennessy	713, 715, 784, 788, 896

Lightning Source UK Ltd.
Milton Keynes UK
UKHW011429221118
332685UK00011B/2017/P